THE
MANHATTANVILLE
INCIDENT

Other Books by Jason Medina

NO HOPE FOR THE HOPELESS AT KINGS PARK

THE DIARY OF AUDREY MALONE FRAYER

A GHOST IN NEW ORLEANS

GHOSTS AND LEGENDS OF YONKERS

KPPC: A JOURNEY THROUGH HISTORY

A NIGHT AT THE SHANLEY HOTEL (COMING SOON)

THE
MANHATTANVILLE
INCIDENT

An Undead Novel

Jason Medina

To order additional copies of this book, contact:
Xlibris
1-888-795-4274
www.Xlibris.com
Orders@Xlibris.com
704808

Contents

Part III   "Brundlefly"

Brundlefly

Part IV   "Metropolis Of The Undead"

Metropolis of the Undead

Part V   "Patient Zeros"

Patient Zeros

Part VI "Man's End"

FOREWORD

IN THIS COLLECTION of apocalyptic tales we follow the events of a *Biohazard Outbreak*, which begins in a secret bioresearch laboratory in the Manhattanville section of New York City. While working to find a cure for cancer, a scientist inadvertently creates a deadly virus that threatens to wipe out mankind. The virus attacks the bloodstream and quickly spreads throughout the body of the victim eating away every living blood cell and replacing them with a new strain of bacteria that continues to animate the host leaving only the basic survival instincts in control, led by the need to feed.

This virus soon spreads from "Ground Zero" in Manhattan out to the surrounding boroughs, before crossing over into Westchester County, Long Island, New Jersey, and eventually infecting countless victims within the tri-state area.

Although each story stands alone, they are connected to one another and follow a chronological timeline of events. In the first story, we learn how the virus originated. At first, the virus is temporarily contained. However, once it is unleashed, it quickly spreads out of control, as it wreaks havoc on the unsuspecting populace of Manhattan.

This will lead directly into the second story, *Contamination Effect*.

With the infection spreading from victim to victim, at an alarming rate, chaos ensues on the streets of New York City. Soon enough, there are flesh-eating zombies overrunning the city. It will be a long hard fight for the people of New York to escape this nightmare and almost certainly not everyone will make it out alive.

In the next story, *Brundlefly*, we backtrack several hours to catch up with the protagonist of the first story. After barely escaping the ordeal at the laboratory, he returns to his home on Riverside Drive, where he locks himself inside. But now, he is forced to deal with a more personal problem, which could very well mean his end is near.

Metropolis of the Undead is the title of the fourth story, which focuses on what has become the main group of survivors. Through some miracle, they managed to escape Manhattan, but their epic battle to escape a virtual city of the walking dead has only just begun. Will they be able to fight past hordes of zombies and escape a city under quarantine, which now faces a new looming danger, or is it the end of the line?

We are taken back to a moment in the not so distant past for the fifth story, which is a short origin tale called *Patient Zeros*, about the scientist responsible for the virus.

In *Man's End*, the final story, it has been a month since Day One of the Zombie Apocalypse. In that time, the virus has spread throughout the East Coast of the United States and it has, somehow, found its way to other countries beyond its borders. We find ourselves at the end of our saga, as a large group of survivors has gradually dwindled to a handful of post-apocalyptic warriors in this dramatic story about human survival.

Will it come down to a sole survivor being the last man on Earth, or is there still a glimmer of hope for the human race?

ACKNOWLEDGEMENTS

FIRST, I WOULD like to thank my lovely wife, Jo-Ann, my parents, and all of my friends from the 26th Precinct in Harlem, New York, especially my close friend, Andrew Ramnanan, for his creative input. I'd also like to thank my friends and family, who went out of their way to find my book *Ghosts and Legends of Yonkers* at stores, earning them each a part in this story. I doubt I will ever write another story based on so many real people that I know. It was so much fun writing for their characters and capturing their unique personalities, even though some of their names were slightly changed. I hope you will all be able to tell which character represents you. Enjoy your new literary immortality!

In addition, I'd like to thank my wife, Jo-Ann, along with my nephew, Chris Gonzalez, and my uncle, Daniel Medina for being zombies with me in my zombie photo shoot. It was so much fun taking those photos! I'm sorry I did not have more people joining us.

Of course, I must thank the brilliant George A. Romero for his significant role in jumpstarting the zombie craze in the 1960s with his masterpiece, *Night of the Living Dead*. To this day, it remains my all-time favorite zombie film. Thanks to him, many lives were changed, including my own. He has been a great inspiration to so many creative artists, actors, writers, photographers, and filmmakers. I will forever be grateful to Mr. Romero for changing how the world thinks of zombies and introducing us to a whole new genre of horror. Rest in peace.

I would also like to thank Robert Kirkman for inspiring me with his groundbreaking series, *The Walking Dead*. Season after season, it continually keeps me at the edge of my seat with its great stories, fantastic characters, and realistic drama. It was a tremendous inspiration for the last story in this book. I dread the day *The Walking Dead* will come to an end, although I know it is inevitable. This show, as well as its spin-off series, *Fear the Walking Dead*, has had some of the best zombies, or "walkers," ever created. Credit for that must go to the great Greg Nicotero. I must also include Scott M. Gimple, who is the writer and producer of both shows. I bow to you gentlemen for your ingenuity. To be honest, it was because of The Walking Dead that I even considered writing a novel about zombies.

Before really getting into this book, I read a large number of zombie books to use as inspiration. I had to know what stories were out there, so I wouldn't inadvertently write a story that might have already been done. I was also hoping to get some ideas for my book. A few stories I read were pretty good and well written, while others were disappointing. Still, I learned something from every book, so I am thankful to those authors, as well. I might have even used an idea or two, as a way of paying homage to some of those books.

Also, a special thank you to Heliflight Tours in New Jersey and my pilot, Jake, as well as The Intrepid Sea, Air and Space Museum in Manhattan and the Friends of the Croton Aqueduct Tunnel in Ossining.

I hope there are no hard feelings from Columbia University. It was nothing personal. Over the years, I made a few friends, who work or worked at Columbia University. The new building just seemed like the perfect location to start my story. I watched it vigilantly, as it was being constructed and all the while my story was coming to fruition in my mind. The building wasn't even completed when this story was ready for publication.

Last, but not least, thanks to all my readers, supporters, and fans. In the end, this book was written for you because I surely don't make a living as a writer!

DEDICATION

THIS BOOK IS dedicated to one of the greatest masters of horror of all time, George A. Romero. He was an innovator and originator of the way we think of zombies today. His work has inspired hundreds of minds, including my own. I only wish I had the opportunity to meet him before he passed away. I will forever be grateful to him for the years of entertainment he has given me throughout my life. It is mainly because of him this book was even written. If not for his take on zombies, I never would have fallen in love with them.

I also want to dedicate this book to my friend, NYPD Sergeant Paul Tuozzolo of the 43rd Precinct and previously of the 26th Precinct, where we worked together. His life was tragically cut short on November 4, 2016, leaving behind a wife and two children. Rest in peace, my friend.

Last, I would like to dedicate this book to NYPD Sergeant Michael Curtin and Police Officer John Dallara of the NYPD, who both served next door to my precinct at Emergency Service Squad 2. They died bravely in the line of duty on September 11, 2001, while rescuing people from the World Trade Center. I did not know them very well, but I did know them well enough to feel the impact of their deaths. Of all the people that died from that catastrophic day, those two were the ones that brought tears to my eyes. I knew I would never see them, again.

They would never come to my aid anymore, which they had done in the past.

Their sacrifices were not in vain because many lives were saved that day. May they, and all those other victims from the terrorist attacks that day, rest in peace and never be forgotten.

PROLOGUE

"For civilization to survive, the human race has to remain civilized." - Rod
Serling

I T'S A WARM summer night in New
York City. The sky is clear and the
stars are shining down from above, as the moon hangs high and to the
west. It is full and as bright as ever. The streets are a flurry of activity,
despite the late night hour. It isn't a normal summer night. Cars are
blocking intersections, as drivers race to get to safety. The power has
gone out in several sections of the city, making traveling by day or
night unwise, but necessary. Just like a scene from a George A. Romero
film, the infected have overrun the streets, claiming block by block and
leaving a trail of blood and gore in their wake. The unmistakable sound
of screams and gunfire can be heard from all directions, as people fight
for their lives. Fires burn unchecked only adding to the chaos. It is a
nightmare come true, as the city becomes Hell on Earth.

Meanwhile, inside the old Kingsbridge Armory in the Bronx, several
people are hiding in the dark. Together they endeavor to figure out their
next move, hoping no one will learn of their presence.

Built in 1917, this historic landmark was once home to the Eighth
Regiment of the United States Army. That was then. Like many historic

sites, it stood vacant for many years, until plans of redevelopment began to see fruition. Of course, there were delays and it remained in limbo for a while longer. Today, it serves as a makeshift fortification for a group of survivors in what appears to be the end of days.

Only lit by the light of his bright LED flashlight, Charles Foster, an African-American sergeant in the NYPD, addresses the small group.

"New York, the city that never sleeps. They say there are a thousand stories in the naked city. Well, this is one of them," he said solemnly in his deep voice. "It all began on the island of Manhattan. Ever since the 1990s, Columbia University had been buying up real estate on the Upper West Side between Broadway and Twelfth Avenue to expand their assets. Unfortunately, many businesses and residents were displaced, as a result. By the year 2010, it became obvious Columbia University wanted to build a new research facility. That was the real start of it all, if you ask me.

Plans were drawn up and construction began on a new science center that would specialize in medical, brain, and mental health research. It was a noble cause with good intentions. This state of the art facility was intended to be only one part of the new campus.

In the beginning, there were some protests against it, but nothing major. At the time, the people were too caught up with that 'Occupy Wall Street' nonsense. If only they had known then what would happen. They could have focused some of their wasted time on this project, instead. It might have made a difference. Someone smart might have put a stop to it early enough, before it was too late.

Ah, what do I know? I shouldn't blame Columbia University. It's not their fault. How could they have known what would happen?

The blame really belongs to one man, who worked at the new lab. Not that it matters, at this point. Placing blame is just the human way. What's done is done. The lab is finished and now so is life, as we knew it. This craziness all started because of him."

"Hey, Charles," a male voice interrupted, calling out from the shadows of the large dark hangar of the armory. The bulk of the group sat huddled together at its center, while Police Officer Grant Hamilton patrolled the darkness around them using the powerful beam of his own LED flashlight as a guide. "This place is as secure as it can get," he said with a sense of confidence. "We should be able to see anyone who gets close to us from here, *if* anyone manages to get in the building." He paused to scan around them once more, before adding, "I believe we should be okay here for a while. This building is locked up pretty tight. After all, it is an armory!"

"It was anyway," Charles mumbled with regret. "Thanks, Grant. Someone should keep watch," he replied to his friend and co-worker.

Grant was supposed to be his driver for their tour of patrol on Friday night into Saturday morning. The graveyard shift was their normal tour of duty. It was now Saturday night and they still had not changed out of their uniforms, which were wet and filthy, following the intense madness they experienced.

"Already on it," Grant responded. "I got first watch. Marc is up next, then Aramis, and it will be your turn by morning. Three hours each. Sound good?"

"I'll help out, too. I'm not tired," added a young Hispanic woman named Liz, who stood beside Grant, dressed in black and barely visible in the darkened room. There was something about Liz that was admirable. She carried herself in such a way that let you know she was a bad ass and the guys knew it.

"Sounds good," Charles nodded in agreement, before turning his attention back to his listeners. "Okay. Where was I?"

"The beginning," a teenage female voice answered from nearby. Her name was Giselle and she was eighteen years old. Giselle was a tough Hispanic girl, who grew up in the Bronx. She considered herself very street smart, but she did not understand what was going on outside. It was utter chaos to her and her friends.

While they did not really know Charles or the others, they were extremely intent on listening to the story he was telling in hope of comprehending what hell had been unleashed upon the city.

Charles smirked at Giselle and nodded, again, before continuing. In his hands was a black and white composition notebook, which he held open. He still had not begun to read from it, although that was his original intention when he began speaking. First, he felt it was necessary to start with some background information to prepare his listeners for what will probably sound more like it is coming from a scary movie or a survival horror video game.

"It's ironic because the world was actually preparing for this kind of event, as improbable as it seemed. There were task forces being created and strategic contingency plans being put into place, just in case. A few books were written on the subject, but they were mostly attempts at dark humor.

The funny thing is those books could probably serve well as survival guides, right about now. I kind of wish I had one. I suppose we'll just have to make things up as we go.

Of course, there were also numerous films, video games, novels, and comic books about it. Most of us never took it seriously. It was just great entertainment.

Well, most of us didn't. There were a few religious fanatics, gamers and film buffs with big imaginations, and extreme survivalists that were only biding their time, until the apocalypse. I even recall seeing a catalogue that sold zombie rounds of ammo!" He shook his head and smiled at the irony.

"It was make believe, or so we thought. It might have started with special effects, but now the blood and gore is all too real and, to be honest, it scares the hell out of me. They were right. We were wrong. *I was wrong.*" Charles sighed and looked down at the notebook, "I still can't believe it."

An enthusiastic interest began to build up within the others, as they each eyed the notebook in his hands with great fervor.

"You'd think we would have been better prepared. The NYPD is like a small army, but even we couldn't stop it. We sure as hell tried. It just became too overwhelming for us. We were ready for crazy, but not that kind of crazy. It took time before we even realized what was going on. When we did, no one could believe it was actually happening. It seemed too insane to be true. At first, it was chalked up to another Friday night of mayhem in Harlem. After all, crime was up! What else was new?

That's exactly what it was like on what will probably go down in history as Day One of the Zombie Apocalypse.

As I said before, the outbreak originated in the new science center. It was down in some secret underground laboratory. They did a good job of containing it for about an hour. As always, someone got careless. That's when things really went downhill. The hours that followed were a fast paced nightmare for us. Things kept getting worse by the minute. All the cops were tied up trying to maintain control, but it was already lost. Seeing our co-workers and friends die only made it harder and there was nothing we could do to stop it." He paused to regain his composure.

His words also began to hit home with his fellow police officers that had not yet mourned the losses of their fallen co-workers. There simply had not been time for it. They were too busy trying to survive.

Nearby, Grant stared intensely at the floor for a couple of seconds, and then he exhaled and turned away.

Charles sighed and continued, "I suppose you're wondering about this notebook. Well, it isn't an ordinary notebook. It was someone's personal journal and, by chance, it came into my hands. It's still early enough, so I'll read it to you. As I do, please, try not to interrupt with questions or comments. I know there will be many, but if you do, it'll take us all night to get through this book and we'll need to get some sleep. There will be plenty of time for questions in the morning."

And so, Charles began to read from the journal, as everyone in the room listened closely. Grant and Liz kept watch over the group from a safe distance, each looking around every few seconds to make sure no one else was in the room with them. All the while, terror waited beyond the armory's walls and fence that kept them relatively safe... for now.

THE MANHATTANVILLE INCIDENT:
PART ONE

"Biohazard Outbreak"

BIOHAZARD OUTBREAK

Chapter One

"MY NAME IS David Frino..." It was a Monday morning in July, nearly two years ago from today, when David started his first day of work at the new Greene Science Center on Broadway. It was all he could think about, since the day he graduated from Columbia University less than two months earlier.

He had put his name on a waiting list six months earlier. The list was quite long. He spent a large portion of that waiting time interning at Columbia Presbyterian Medical Center. Considering he was number forty on the list, he half expected not to get called at all. Naturally, he was ecstatic when they finally called him in for an interview in mid-June. He had been getting extremely restless, after graduation day.

It was exciting to enter and walk through the new facility for the first time. He could recall being in high school, while it was being built years earlier. He would often look down on the construction site whenever he'd stand on the elevated subway platform at West 125th Street and Broadway to wait for the 1 train. Sometimes, he'd ride his bicycle to the Riverside Drive viaduct, which provided him with another aerial view of the 17-acre site. He always wondered exactly what was being erected.

For a short time, he thought they were building new dormitories for the university's students. By that time, he had already been accepted to the university, so he was already planning how his new dorm room would look. That was before he was able to take over his grandmother's apartment at 244 Riverside Drive. While he was sad that she passed on, he was more than happy to claim her apartment as his home, which fortunately for him was in his father's name. Soon, he forgot all about living in a dorm and, for a while, he forgot about the new facility.

Now, here he was walking through the corridors of the Greene Science Center building on his first day of work. The building was nine-stories tall and four levels deep, as far as he knew. The main entrance and lobby were two-stories in height and surrounded by full-sized windows, which allowed for a brilliant ambience of natural lighting. The many windows were intended to make the facility appear transparent and inviting from the outside, while maximizing the amount of natural light provided by the sun. Along the main corridors, which were painted white to better reflect the sunlight, sleek metallic lamps hung from the high ceiling on long cables that were several feet in length. The large, tan, waxed floor tiles did their part to reflect light, as well.

It seemed everything David walked past was fascinating to him. Every brand new door, the four elevator banks, turnstiles in the lobby, the red and white art deco furniture, and every other piece of decoration simply leapt out at him begging for his attention. There was even a rock-climbing wall! He especially loved that the building was still fairly new. He figured it meant mostly everything within had to be new, too.

Imagine his surprise when he learned the Science Center was largely built using recycled materials. He was impressed, to say the least.

The rest of the campus was also a magnificent sight. It was made up of several buildings that included a new business school for the university, a center for the arts, a building that could act as a forum for events, and fabulous courtyards surrounded by small groves. The new campus even served a great cause. It had been established to take full advantage of creative group efforts among scientists with their main focus being the brain and mental health research. In fact, several mental health programs were offered with a street-level screening facility for neighborhood residents.

As it turned out, David's first day didn't actually consist of any real work. He reported to an office on an upper floor, and then sat in a two-story lounge area, where he waited for about thirty minutes. He passed most of the time enjoying the view from the windows. When someone finally came to retrieve him, he was told to sign several documents and contracts, before being taken to a fancy videoconference room. While there, he had to sit through a boring orientation video, followed by a brief tour of the building and some of the campus. Afterwards, he was sent to lunch and ended up eating at the café on the first floor.

For the first month, he didn't have a high enough security clearance to get the full tour of the Science Center, which included its underground levels, nor did he have full access to any of the research laboratories, yet. During that time he had to sit through several safety seminars, which included CPR and OSHA (Occupational Safety and Health Administration) training. There was also specialized training dealing with numerous laboratory procedures and possible biohazard scenarios. Of course, there was also a drug-screening test, which he passed without a problem.

He preferred to live his life clean and sober, aside from an occasional night out drinking with the boys. He was raised properly, so he never felt the curiosity to try any illegal or addictive drugs. Besides, his father would have ripped him a new asshole, if he did.

Once David got his identification lanyard and security clearance pass, he began working as a bio-safety level-one research assistant giving him access to several state of the art research laboratories. He did this for the first six months and found it rather enjoyable. It gave him a chance to get a feel for the facility and a chance to learn from several brilliant researchers. He also got a lot of exercise running around doing favors for people. Regardless, things were going well for him.

By December he was assigned to work for Professor Herbert Fox in an underground research laboratory, except this laboratory was not on one of the four known underground levels. There was actually a fifth underground level, which was kept secret. It was only accessible to those with the right bio-safety level security clearance. It could either be accessed by using a special key in any one of two particular elevators, known only to those with the proper security clearance, or through a hidden emergency stairwell that led down from the underground loading dock. This clandestine laboratory was not used for conducting brain or mental health research like most of the other laboratories in the building. Instead, infectious diseases and finding cures for them were the main areas of focus.

Dr. Fox, as he preferred to be called, was a middle-aged man with salt and pepper hair and a thick mustache. He wore thick black-framed glasses and had a raspy voice, as if he'd been a cigarette smoker for over twenty years. He handpicked David over several other possible candidates mainly because of David's field of expertise. He was a hematologist, which basically meant that he studied diseases and blood. It was one of several fields, in which, the professor had dedicated his life.

Dr. Fox was an exceedingly prominent scientist having already been the recipient of two Nobel Prizes for medicine and chemistry. He specialized in microbiology and biological, chemical, and genetic research. Many referred to him as a genius. Prior to working at Columbia University he worked at Xavier University in New Orleans, where he first made a name for himself.

As soon as David was assigned to work for the professor, he qualified for a bump up to bio-safety level-three security clearance out of four available levels. Dr. Fox even took the time to train him further regarding laboratory safety procedures. David was moving up fairly quick, despite having to work on a lower level now. He had gone from being a glorified gofer, coffee maker, part-time janitor, and occasional student to assisting with top-secret genetic research experiments. He could finally put his skills to the test. He just hoped he would be able to handle the pressure.

On a sour note, he was disappointed the laboratory was located so far underground. There would be no more bright morning views or warm sunlight because there were no windows, except for the two thick soundproof windows looking out of the main laboratory to the outer hallway and an observation window looking into the smaller biohazard lab, which was separated by a secondary entrance area. For now, he'd have to settle for the dazzling overhead lights, instead.

Biohazard signs adorned the walls and entrances, which did not make for a very comforting environment. Mostly everything was white with a few exceptions. The cabinets, desk drawers, and chairs were all red, and the lockers in the locker room and all closets were a bright orange color. It certainly was not what he expected, but the new position paid much more than what he was getting before.

Still, he found it odd how there were no other employees working with him in this laboratory, aside from the professor. The two of them did most of their own cleaning, so there was no need for anyone from the janitorial staff to access the laboratory. Every day they cleaned and decontaminated their work areas, as required by law, until it became habitual.

There was only one cleaning person, who had access to the hallway outside of the main laboratory. It was an older man, who'd been working for Columbia University most of his life. He was well trusted and highly regarded. He mainly came in to sweep and mop the floor at the end of each workweek, after regular hours, since no one was allowed on the level, while the scientists were working in the labs.

For the most part, it was a lonely place. Dr. Fox did not care much for unnecessary conversation, so it was almost always quiet. On the other hand, it was easier for David to concentrate on his work with minimal distractions. It made him a more productive worker, which the professor greatly appreciated.

After the first month, David grew accustomed to how things worked in their particular laboratory. He enjoyed working for Dr. Fox because every day was a learning experience. In just a short period of time, his knowledge of medicine, biology, microbiology, and chemistry had increased dramatically.

In addition, he had reached bio-safety level-four security clearance, after successfully earning the professor's trust by showing his worth on more than one occasion. David now had access to the small biohazard lab next door, which had previously been off limits to him, although he tried to avoid going in there, as much as possible. He was also able to conduct his own personal experiments, so long as their progress would benefit the Science Center and it did not interfere with his assisting the professor with his experiments. Those were top priority.

There was no doubt David was a hard worker. He normally worked from Monday through Friday, but every other Saturday he could be found at the laboratory working on his experiments, usually on his own time. In this aspect, he was very much like his mentor because, more often than not, the professor could be found right next to him doing the same thing. This dedication certainly placed him on a higher level of standards in the professor's eyes. It didn't hurt that he never complained about having to wear a lab coat and gloves all the time. Sometimes, they even had to use clear plastic face shields.

While the two did not really become the best of friends, they definitely had an understanding that was unparalleled. They worked exceptionally well together. Little words were needed between the two. They seemed to have a system that worked. David knew what Dr. Fox wanted or needed, which kept the professor satisfied. That was normally the extent of his joy. He was not a very emotional man. Nor was he social. It was something David was used to, by this time.

It did not matter. David was not there to socialize. He was there to learn and to work.

In time, the days became weeks and the weeks became months. Before they knew it, the summer was over and autumn had arrived. They had been working together for close to a year when Dr. Fox made a fascinating discovery. He somehow found a way to isolate pathogens in the blood and manipulate them by using stem cell technology to metamorphosize them into antibodies that behave as a virus by attacking antigens eating away at infectious diseases.

Dr. Fox could barely contain his excitement when he called David over to his microscope for a look. David had never seen him like this, so he knew this had to be something big.

"David, you must see this," he called out, sounding very much like someone who was witnessing a UFO sighting. "I believe I have it right this time!"

Dr. Fox had been working on his stem cell research experiment for many years. He only brought David in on it a few months earlier. David was grateful to be a part of the potentially groundbreaking research. He rushed over to the professor's microscope to see what he had to show him.

It was absolute genius, he thought, as the professor walked him through how he managed to transform the pathogens. The exciting part was that if they remained stable after the first transformation, it would mean a cure could be found for numerous diseases. Of course, there would be many tests to run, but that was to be expected.

David looked on with astonishment, but then a thought occurred to him. He furrowed his nose and eyebrows apprehensively and asked, "What if they metamorphosize, again?"

"That is what we shall have to find out," replied Dr. Fox. "Unfortunately, there is no fast way of knowing for certain. It could take us weeks, months, or even *years* before we learn the answer." The thought of waiting years seemed to frustrate him. It was obvious by how he said it, but then he added, "Imagine the possibilities, if you will. This could very well be the scientific and medical breakthrough we've been waiting for. It would certainly mean our work in this laboratory has fulfilled its purpose." He chuckled proudly and took a moment to marvel at his own genius.

David agreed and nodded eagerly, "Yeah, I'd say so. This is amazing, Dr. Fox."

For a moment, they both stared admiringly at the microscope, each lost in his thoughts. This would certainly mean a Nobel Prize and worldwide recognition. Not to mention, the diseases that might be cured and eradicated, once and for all! So many lives could be saved. The impact would be astronomically incredible.

David thought about his grandmother, who died of cancer. She would be so proud to know he assisted in such a profound discovery. Too bad it was a few years too late for her.

Over the next few weeks, they worked together diligently performing a multitude of tests on various living subjects. They moved up the line from plants to insects, and then on to small rodents, mainly rats. The results were positive in mostly every test with a few minor exceptions here and there. However, with each failure, the experimental serum was modified and its ingredients adjusted to compensate with the hope that they would discover the right formula, in due time.

The entire time, they maintained steady observations on all test subjects. Both were anxious to test it out on higher life forms, such as primates, although they could not be hasty. The conditions had to be right for such tests and the serum was not quite there, yet.

Still, the possibility excited them. Apes were the closest thing to humans, so based on any results they acquired from these future tests, they could have a better idea how it would affect a human test subject. Human trials would be the ultimate test. Of course, it would probably be years away. It was going to be difficult waiting that long for something so necessary, but certain rules had to be followed and there were approvals that needed to be gained from the appropriate channels. In short, there was going to be a lot of "red tape" to get through, as they say.

When the holiday season approached David had an important decision to make. Originally, he planned to take his vacation time to visit his parents in Florida. Three years earlier, they bought a house near Orlando in Lake Buenos Vista. While David usually enjoyed a little time away from New York, he was not so sure he wanted to go this time. Florida had been his main destination for his yearly escapes, but due to the recent experiments at work, his mind was preoccupied. He had become obsessed and didn't dare lose his focus by going away, despite the professor's encouragement to go and enjoy some much needed time off. David's mind had been made up. He was staying in New York.

It got to the point where he had trouble sleeping. To compensate he would go to work earlier. He figured why waste the morning in bed trying to sleep? It seemed like a better idea to get a head start on the experiments. He kept his brown hair shaved short, so he wouldn't have to waste time brushing it and he only shaved his face during the weekends.

Each workday he started with a cup of French Vanilla coffee from the nearby Dunkin Donuts on his way to work. Once at the laboratory, he donned his lab coat and gloves, and then checked each test subject for any possible changes. He took notes both on paper and on the computer, at the request of the professor, who hated to rely solely on electronics.

By mid-December the test subjects were showing gradual signs of improvement, which was good. If there were no changes, that was fine, too. The important thing was there were no negative results to report. No more failures. They were doing something right.

One morning, after Dr. Fox got his lab coat and rubber gloves on, David brought him up to speed on the latest test subjects and informed him of the increasingly positive results. He also showed him the meticulous notes he had been taking. The professor was very pleased.

"Good, David. Good," he said with a half smile. "At last, we are showing progress. It appears we are ready to move forward. I am going to make a few calls and see about acquiring us some primates for the next phase of tests. Chimpanzees would especially be perfect, since they so rarely fall ill to cancer. There might be something in their bodies that provides them with a natural immunity. If so, we shall exploit it."

"That would be excellent!" David responded. He was barely able to contain his excitement. He could not believe they had already come so far with their experiments, but the evidence was right there before his eyes. He found himself wondering how well the experiments would work if they used primates, instead, since they were similar to humans. Out of curiosity, he inquired, "How many chimps do you think we can get?"

The professor thought about it momentarily, while he did some quick calculations in his head. When he seemed satisfied with his answer, he replied, "I believe twelve monkeys should serve our purpose well. We shall request both male and females, of course. We can test two at a time, one of each sex, using two different doses."

David chuckled briefly to himself.

The professor gazed at him inquisitively and asked with one eyebrow raised, "May I ask what is so amusing?"

David suddenly felt silly. He replied with a hint of disappointment in his voice, "I take it you've never seen *Twelve Monkeys*? It was a movie from the mid-1990s starring Bruce Willis and Brad Pitt. Bruce went back in time to find out how a virus destroyed the human race. They were in a mental asylum. It was also turned into a television series a few years ago. Not ringing a bell, huh?"

Dr. Fox stared back at him blankly and stated, "Unfortunately, I do not have the time for such trivial forms of entertainment, David. Surely, you must understand. I spend every waking moment working on my experiments." He then shook his head in disappointment, turned around, and went into the restroom. As the door shut behind him, he said, "Excuse me. I must have a moment."

David was left to ponder alone. He shrugged helplessly and sighed.

By the end of the week, he decided maybe he needed a break, after all. He had been working extra hard the past few weeks taking very little time off for himself. He almost reconsidered going to Florida. Almost. The only thing that stopped him was how much the airfare would be, if he were to buy tickets a week away from Christmas. It was too late to get any good travel deals, so staying home would be a wiser financial option.

Besides, he had already sent word to his parents informing them he would not be traveling south for the holidays. They might have already made other plans. It would be a shame if he ruined those plans for them.

Instead, he decided to settle for about seven hours of sleep in his bed.

Before going home, David stopped for a slice of pizza at his favorite pizzeria, Famous Famiglia, on West 111th Street and Broadway. He'd spent many a nights sitting there with his classmates, after a long day of classes. In a way, he missed those times. He didn't miss the studying or the exams, but he did miss his friends. Feeling nostalgic made him realize how lonely he felt.

All of his friends had gone off to pursue professional careers elsewhere. Some had returned to their home states not wanting to remain in New York longer than necessary. The others simply faded into obscurity. He lost touch with them, once he got the job at the Science Center. There was hardly any time for friendships anymore. He was always so busy. He rarely ever spoke to his parents, which was terrible, considering he used to call them once a week. Occasionally, he would spend a few hours with his cousin, Edward, or their friend, Marc Nugent. Of course, they were usually busy with work, too. They were both cops and the NYPD kept them quite busy, especially during the summer months and on weekends. David was mainly free on weekends, so the days he could socialize were limited and he was never really one to frequent bars or dance clubs. He couldn't even recall the last time he went on a date.

He sighed. Was this what his life would be like from now on, he thought? If so, it was going to be depressing and extremely lonely. He hated having no life. There were so many things he wanted to do and dozens of places he longed to visit. Meanwhile, the days were just passing him by.

He sat alone at the back of the pizzeria eating his slice of pizza. Somehow, the magic of the place was gone. It was not the same without his buddies, although much to his amazement Joaquin was still working there. He was the night manager. It seemed like he worked there forever.

Every customer knew and loved Joaquin. He was very friendly and always had a smile on his face to greet the regulars.

In the summertime, Joaquin would often fly down to Mexico to visit his family. During those weeks that he was away David preferred not to eat at Famous Famiglia. It wasn't the same without Joaquin. It was sort of like going to your favorite bar and not being able to speak with your buddy, the bartender, who always listened to your problems and never judged you.

After finishing his pizza, David was ready to leave. He emptied his tray into the garbage and bid farewell to Joaquin. Joaquin could tell something was weighing heavily on David's mind. He did not let him leave without asking what was wrong.

"David, what's wrong? Everything okay?"

David shrugged sadly and replied, "I was just thinking about the old days when I'd come in here with my pals. I miss it. You know? Why does everything good always have to come to an end?" A look of regret came over him.

Joaquin shrugged and replied, "I don't know. Maybe some good things have to end, so new good things can happen."

David looked at him and smiled. "Yeah, I suppose you're right," he said. "I'm glad you still work here. It's always great to see you, pal. Thanks. Stay cool." He waved and turned to leave.

"Goodnight," Joaquin waved back.

The walk home was uneventful. It was only about ten blocks away to the south. It took about a half hour on foot. When David arrived at his building of residence, he took the elevator to the third floor. His apartment was quite spacious, compared to his parents' old apartment on Claremont Avenue.

He removed his shoes, leaving them in the foyer, and crumpled his toes on the living room rug. It felt good to be home. He took off his tie, unbuttoned his shirt, sat down on his favorite sofa chair, and turned on his 3D television. It was one of the earlier models, but it was still pretty good. His father bought it when 3D TV was a new thing. David inherited it when his parents made the big move to Florida.

David switched channels on the remote control several times, before settling on the 1986 remake of *The Fly* starring Jeff Goldblum and Geena Davis.

"Ah, Brundlefly," he mumbled to himself, referring to the main character's metamorphosis at the climax of the story. It was one of his favorite scenes in the film.

David did not realize how exhausted he was, until he sat in front of the television. He was only able to watch the movie for a few minutes, before his eyes ached from using the awkward 3D glasses that came with the set. Wearing them also gave him a headache.

He sighed woefully, "This sucks. I miss regular TV."

Frustrated, he lifted the glasses off his eyes and rested them upon the top of his head. He rubbed his eyes, put his feet up on the coffee table, and yawned. A clutter of different magazines covered the majority of the table. Most of them were over a year old. The table was made of oak and once belonged to his grandmother. It came with the apartment. The magazines were his. The table was quite heavy, so it was never moved from its spot. Most of the magazines were still unread, so they also remained in place. David glanced at them and smirked. He never seemed to have the time to go through them, so he could toss them out. He knew he would probably never read them all, but figured there was no hurry. Besides, it gave him something to put his feet on, keeping the table clean.

Grandma would be pleased.

David closed his eyes. He merely wanted to rest them for a few seconds. He leaned his head back on the comfortable cushion of the chair. It didn't take long before he gradually tuned out the television and felt himself drifting off to sleep. It was such a great feeling. He considered getting up and going to his bed, but that would require standing and he knew he would lose that magical feeling he was experiencing.

Instead, he allowed himself to slip away into unconsciousness.

A short while later, David was dreaming. In his dream it was daytime. He stood outside in the middle of an open field at what looked like Central Park. There were tall buildings beyond the trees and the clouds rushed by overhead at a fast pace, like in a high-speed time-lapse video. When he looked up at the sun, he noticed it was red. Around him, people were running. He wondered where the were going and why they were in a hurry. He almost fell into the lake when someone bumped into him. The rude person had the audacity to call him a moron for standing in the middle of the field.

Was it a man or a woman? David was unsure. It did not matter.

For some reason, he began to cry and covered his eyes with his hands. By the time he looked, again, he was somewhere else.

He was standing at the Harlem Pier at West 125th Street. He looked across the Hudson River toward New Jersey and watched the sunset. It was still red. It looked like it was melting into the horizon causing the sky to turn red, as well. The Hudson River water had also become red like blood.

David stepped to the edge of the metal railing and looked down into the water. It was no longer red. Actually, it was a lot cleaner than normal. He could see his reflection looking back at him clearly, but it was much closer than it should have been. He could reach it, if he wanted to.

Suddenly, his face changed. It became rotten, as if he were dead. His skin was moldy and there were flies buzzing all around him. He did not like what he was seeing, so he punched the water to disturb the reflection. At that moment, the water turned to sand.

He realized he was on the planet Mars, so it was acceptable. He crawled around on his hands and knees, but the sand was too cold. When he stood up it became violently windy, as a sandstorm brewed. It was difficult to see anything. He tried to walk facing downward with his hands stretched out in front of him, as if reaching out for something to grab. More hands appeared around him and did the same. All he could see were these seemingly disembodied arms reaching with their bodies likely hidden by the blowing sandstorm. It was creepy.

He wanted to be alone, so he began running through the storm. He dodged dozens of grasping hands and tried to avoid being touched. He could hear what sounded like a female voice telling him to run toward her.

"Hurry up, David!" She shouted.

As he did, the hands began reaching up from the ground. It became more difficult to avoid them. One grabbed his left ankle and tripped him, causing him to fall forward.

When he hit the ground it splashed like water. It was no longer sand. Instead, he found himself submerged under clear blue water. His eyes were still open. It looked like he was in a swimming pool. He swam up to the surface and emerged from the water of his parents' pool in Florida. The change of scenery didn't seem to faze him. It was a warm sunny day and all seemed well with the world.

He swam toward the ladder and climbed out of the pool. He dried himself with a towel that apparently appeared out of thin air and sat down on a lawn chair, where he relaxed for a few seconds enjoying the warmth of the sun.

Instinctively, he reached out for a glass of homemade iced tea. As it happened, there was a glass within reach on a nearby round metallic mesh table, which had an umbrella sticking up through it providing him with some shade over his face. The glass of iced tea also had a little umbrella in it. The drink was refreshing and iced cold.

Just then, the dream changed, again.

David was no longer a real person. Instead, he was a computerized "Sim" from the popular video game, *The Sims*. Dr. Fox was playing the game and controlling him. After a few moments, the professor grew bored and shut down the game without saving his progress. David knew that meant everything he'd done would be lost due to the professor's incompetence. He yelled out for him to stop, but it was too late. Everything was being deleted around him, as day turned to night and everything went black.

He shouted, "Nooo!"

In that moment, he awoke abruptly from his slumber to the sound of gunshots. He immediately leapt from the sofa and screamed when he saw a zombie reaching for him, but then he realized it was only the television. A zombie film had come on, after the previous movie. He had forgotten the television was still on and his 3D glasses had managed to fall back in place over his eyes making the image appear realistic.

Feeling relieved and slightly amused, he removed the glasses, turned off the television, and went to his bedroom. He wanted to resume his sleep on his bed, although he hoped the crazy dream would not resume.

BIOHAZARD OUTBREAK

Chapter Two

A COUPLE OF weeks had passed and a dozen primates had finally arrived at the lab. *Twelve Monkeys*, David thought, as he smiled to himself.

It was time to begin the next stage of experimentation. There were plenty of new tests to be conducted that would go on for the next few months. David hoped none of the apes would suffer any long-term consequences.

He found it a little strange when Dr. Fox told him to keep quiet about anything that went on in the lab. He stressed the fact that all of their work was confidential. Not to mention, the professor did not want any animal activists showing up outside of the building to disrupt their work. David agreed.

On the day the primates arrived the professor was like a mad man. He ran back and forth in the laboratory trying to multitask. David got a kick out of it. It was amusing to see the professor so excited. Watching him was making David dizzy.

Eventually, David focused on cataloguing the primates. They were already set in place within their cages. All were chimpanzees, half were male and half were female. The cages were placed to one side of the laboratory near the entrance to the biohazard lab. It was the only place where they would not be in the way. Three were set against the wall with another three stacked on top of those. The other six were placed in the same manner across from those, so the apes could watch each other.

As expected, the apes were agitated from being somewhere new. It would take a little while before they got used to their new environment. David gave each a banana to calm them down, so he could focus on his work. It seemed to do the trick. Generally, food was not allowed in the lab, but the apes had to eat. David laughed to himself and wondered if a banana would help calm the professor. "Here you go, Doc," he thought to himself. "Have a banana!"

Each new test subject would need to be checked to make sure they were perfectly healthy, before they could be used for any experiments. Someone would also have to take the time to care for their daily needs. The professor deemed it necessary to bring in a third person to the team. It would also be this person's job to assist with this phase of the experiments in any way necessary. He wanted someone with a particular set of skills, so he chose a veterinarian and biologist named Katherine Hines. She already had a bio-safety level-three security clearance, which made her ideal for the job. She arrived at the lab on the week after the primates, having spent that week being trained in the proper lab procedures.

Katherine was about three years older than David, but she sure didn't look like it. She was slightly shorter than him and looked like she was fresh out of college, but that certainly was not the case. Katherine was a very attractive woman with fair skin, long dark blonde hair tied into a ponytail, grayish colored eyes, and a nicely toned body. She gave the impression she worked out to keep in shape. She knew she looked good and was proud of it.

David immediately had a feeling that having her around was going to be trouble for him. She was definitely going to be a distraction. He figured the professor wouldn't even notice she was a female, so, at least, there would not be any competition. Besides, David knew Dr. Fox did not have time for such trivial forms of entertainment anyway, as he might put it.

On a positive note, Katherine seemed to carry herself very professionally, which was good because it would help David to remain focused on his job. She didn't mind being addressed by her first name either, unlike Dr. Fox. It really bothered David that after working closely with the professor for so long, he still had to address him formally. What happened next bothered him even more.

Katherine asked, "Excuse me, Doctor?"

"Yes, my dear?" He said with a smile. That dirty old devil, thought David.

She continued, "I have a small box of personal belongings. I was just wondering where I could put it. Perhaps, there is a desk drawer, cabinet, or a spare locker I can use?"

"Yes, of course. David, show Ms. Hines to the locker room. There should be six empty ones to choose from. David and I each have two. If you require a second, that would be fine. We are the only ones allowed down here, as you may have noticed by all the secrecy."

David began walking toward the locker room and reached to open the door for her. The door was usually kept unlocked. He felt foolish when he realized he did not offer to help carry her box, although it was not large and she did not seem bothered by it.

She followed him and responded, "Oh? That's interesting. Thank you, Doctor. I think two lockers would be great. By the way, you guys can call me Katherine."

Dr. Fox called out from across the room, "Not a problem," and then he added the icing on the cake, "And please, call me Herbert! Doctor is way too formal. After all, we are all friends down here." He then turned his attention back to his work.

David cringed and gripped the doorknob tightly. He had to fight hard to contain his sarcastic response. He suddenly felt the urge to chastise the professor, but did not want to appear disrespectful. He had always felt slightly annoyed by the professor's stuck up attitude and occasional snide remarks, although it was never enough to make David angry, until now. The nerve of him treating her differently, just because she was a pretty woman with a nice body!

Memories that seemed trivial, at one time, began rushing to him building up into silent rage, which he fought off with some difficulty. His knuckles whitened, as his hand squeezed tighter into a fist around the doorknob. He thought about the professor's usual comments regarding his lack of interest in movies. At first, they didn't really bother him too much. However, the more he thought about it, the more he felt like the professor was somehow putting him down in a subtle way. The audacity!

David recalled another time when he tried to tell the professor a joke during a break to relieve the tension from the constant tests they were conducting. Of course, "Herbert" did not laugh. Instead, he stared blankly and professed his need to take a much-needed shit. Well, he may have worded it differently. It was more like he needed to desperately have a moment of contemplation in the restroom. He didn't return for another fifteen minutes and, when he did, the restroom was pretty much off limits for the rest of the day. David considered moving one of the biohazard signs and placing it on the door.

While the joke he told was not great, it was funny to David.

It went something like this - A blonde and a lawyer sit next to each other on a plane. The lawyer asks her if she'd like to play a game. She agrees. He tells her for every question he asks that she doesn't know the answer to, she would have to pay him five dollars. By the same token, he says every time she asked him a question that he didn't know the answer to, he would pay her fifty dollars.

Again, she agrees, to which the lawyer asked her the first question, "What is the distance between the Earth and the nearest star?"

Without a word the blonde pays the lawyer five dollars. Now, it is her turn. She asks, "What goes up a hill with four legs and comes back down with only three?"

The lawyer thinks about it momentarily, but he's stumped. He eventually gives up and pays her fifty dollars, as promised. When he asked her what the answer was, without a word, the blonde gave him another five dollars.

David laughed, again, just thinking about it. He was so lost in his thoughts, he had forgotten all about Katherine, who was staring at him in amusement. She asked in a loud voice, "Hello? Are you going to block the doorway all morning, or can you please stand aside, so I can find an empty locker?"

"Huh? Oh, man! I'm so sorry. My mind was elsewhere," he explained.

She laughed, "Yeah, I noticed." She then asked sounding genuinely concerned, "What's wrong? You seemed a little upset, but then you just laughed for no reason. Will my being here become problematic for you? Please, tell me you are not one of those guys, who hates working with women."

She caught him by surprise with her inquiries. He immediately responded, "No, of course not!" He added more regretfully, "It's not you. It's me. I was thinking about something. You caught me off guard is all." He felt like such an idiot. He was making one hell of a first impression. She probably thought he had all kinds of issues already. For a moment, he thought about telling her the blonde joke hoping to lighten the mood, but considering the color of her hair, it might not go over well.

She smiled and shot back a witty response. "I see. So, you are already giving me the 'it's not you, it's me' excuse on our first day together. I wonder. What does that say for the future of our relationship?" She pouted playfully.

Once again, David was taken aback. He tried unsuccessfully to clarify what he meant, "No, I wasn't. I mean... I'm not. Wait... relationship? Um, I uh... What I meant to say was that..."

"Jeez! Relax," she interrupted before he choked on his tongue trying to explain. "I'm only teasing. It was a joke. Don't you have a sense of humor? I hate to think it's going to be all work and no play around here."

He stared at her dumbly and a grin slowly formed on his face. She was smiling at him brightly and what a beautiful smile she had. Finally, he said in his defense, "I have a sense of humor."

"Good," she replied with relief. "Maybe you've been working too hard. I think you need a break. How about you take me out to lunch later? I don't really know what there is to eat around here. I've mainly been eating at the café upstairs for the past week. I'm not from this area."

He smiled and replied happily, "Yes!" He caught himself and said more calmly, "I mean, yeah. Sure thing. I can totally do that."

"Totally?" She teased.

He smiled, again. "Yes. Totally," he said feeling embarrassed. "I'm sorry. Sometimes, the professor drives me nuts."

A look of complete understanding washed over her face, as she nodded and said, almost to herself, "I see, so he's one of those."

"Excuse me? One of what?" David asked sounding confused.

She smirked and said matter-of-factly, "A pain in the ass."

They both laughed. At last, he felt a moment of comfort with her. He had a feeling he was going to enjoy working with her. He sincerely hoped that would not cause any future problems for them or with the experiments. He desperately wanted someone around that he could converse with, who had a good sense of humor. She seemed to fit the bill. It didn't hurt that she was absolutely gorgeous.

He asked her almost in a whispered voice, "Do you know what's funny?"

She looked at him curiously and before she could respond, he answered, "In the year I've known him, he never told me to call him by his first name. He's also never referred to me as his friend. In fact, he insists I call him Dr. Fox. Yet, he calls me by my first name all the time."

"What? Get out! That's crazy," she exclaimed in amusement. "Aw, now I feel bad. I'll tell you what," she added. "I won't call him by his first name either, no matter how many times he insists. We will keep it professional, if that's how he prefers."

"Ha! That would be great," David laughed. "Thanks."

Throughout the rest of the morning, he quickly forgot about the professor and directed most of his conversations toward Katherine. They weren't long conversations, mind you. There was much work to be done. It was his job to get her familiar with the workings of the lab, which suited him just fine. They made small talk whenever they could, while checking the health of each primate and preparing them for future experiments. David did not want the professor to deem her a distraction and get rid of her. That would be tragic.

Luckily, Dr. Fox was too preoccupied with formulating new calculations to make the tests suitable for their newest test subjects. He barely noticed David and Katherine, as they slowly created a bond of friendship in those first few hours. In fact, they could have been having wild sex on a laboratory table with the apes cheering them on and he probably would not have noticed. At least, that's what David thought briefly to himself.

When lunchtime came, David became overjoyed, although he kept his excitement in control. The professor usually went up to the café for lunch or skipped it all together, so it was not a problem when David and Katherine left the building at noon. David still had not thought about where they could eat. He was just pleased to be taking Katherine out to lunch. It was almost like a first date, at least, in his mind.

When they stepped out onto Broadway, he offered the available choices to her. There were plenty of options within walking distance. There were fast food spots nearby where they could get fried chicken, fish, or burgers, as well as restaurants that served Chinese food and barbecue. Plus, there was a deli nearby for sandwiches. He left it up to her.

She thought about the locations he listed and finally came up with her pick, "I want pizza!" David stared dumbly at her for a moment. He was relieved when she laughed and said, "Relax, David! I'm only messing with you! I may be blonde, but I am far from dumb."

The joke from earlier came to mind. It was a good thing he did not tell it to her. He smiled at her. She seemed like she was a bit of a clown, which was great. He liked that a lot. It was so refreshing that she had a sense of humor, unlike the "stiff" they worked for.

Katherine turned to him and suggested, "I'll tell you what. Why don't you pick a place, instead? Honestly, I could go for any of the options you mentioned, but I really want to know which one *you* prefer."

David thought it was an interesting thing for her to say. It sounded to him like she was trying to figure him out and learn his likes and dislikes. Was she openly flirting with him? It seemed like she was into him almost as much as he was into her.

It certainly appeared work was going to be much more fascinating with Katherine as part of the team.

David quickly considered what location would impress her most. It was a difficult choice. It wasn't as if any of them were classy restaurants. He also didn't want to waste too much time deciding because they had to be back at the lab by 1 pm, which was already less than an hour away. He wanted to make sure they had time to eat and talk.

Finally, Katherine said, "David, just let your stomach guide you. It's not that hard. What are you in the mood for?"

She undoubtedly had a way of making him realize he was an idiot. She was right. He was thinking about it too hard. He shrugged and asked, "Would you like burgers for lunch and barbecue for dinner?" He wished he could pat himself on the back for the smooth way he made a decision and asked her out on a date in the same sentence.

She smiled and stared at him for a moment, as if sizing him up. Then she replied, "Okay, Slick. If you're buying dinner, then count me in, but we go Dutch on lunch. This isn't a date. Deal?"

"Deal," he responded quickly, followed by, "Does that mean when we have dinner, it *will* be a date?"

She turned away and began walking toward the McDonalds on West 125th Street. She did not bother to look back at him when she answered, "You're pretty smart. I'm sure you'll figure it out when the time comes."

Now, he panicked, although he tried to hide it with a crooked smile. He worried and started to freak out, in his mind. What if he was misreading her? What if she was one of those girls, who does not like to date co-workers? Then again, what if she does like him and he fails to make his move when she leaves the opportunity open, and then loses interest in him believing him to be a clueless moron? Even worse, what if she ended up liking old Herbert more than him and dated him, instead?

NO!

David held back a gag reflex, and then walked faster to catch up to Katherine. Once he did, the two walked quietly side by side toward their destination.

David realized he was being silly. He was getting frustrated over nothing. He had forgotten something very important. He was having a great time with a beautiful woman and had been doing so pretty much since the moment she first spoke to him. Why was he trying to ruin that by worrying about something that did not matter? He needed to focus on the moment. He needed to focus on her.

"Read the signs," he told himself. What was she doing? How was she behaving? She certainly seemed interested enough. She accepted the invitation to dinner. Hell, it was her who asked him out to lunch! Sure, she mentioned lunch wasn't a date, but it was implied that dinner would be, when she insisted he pay.

That was all the logic he needed. He was taking her on a date later, but for now, they'd eat burgers and fries with Chicken McNuggets. The only real question would be sweet and sour or barbecue sauce?

BIOHAZARD OUTBREAK

Chapter Three

IT WAS ALMOST 5 pm, which was when David and Dr. Fox usually shut down all of the experiments for the day. Afterwards, they would usually clean up, put everything away, and lock up. Next, it would be time for them to get cleaned up. Finally, it would be time to leave. Sometimes, the clean up process alone took about an hour.

Now that Katherine was working with them things had changed for the better. She assisted them with the clean up, shutting everything down, and putting everything away into its rightful place. They were able to finish up a lot sooner allowing time for them to discuss the project, which they did briefly. David really did not want to waste too much time talking to Dr. Fox. He was far too anxious for his dinner date with Katherine.

Dr. Fox decided to remain at the laboratory a little longer than usual. He said he wanted to write down a few relevant notes and go over his research, in private, for a while. As for David and Katherine, they left together. They had both been looking forward to the opportunity to get to know each other better.

They walked to the Dinosaur Bar-B-Que restaurant, located on Twelfth Avenue. It was a short walk away. Within minutes they had arrived and were seated rather quickly at a table near three large windows that faced Twelfth Avenue underneath the Riverside Drive viaduct. It was not much of a view, but none of them cared about looking outside. They were too preoccupied with looking at each other, as they secretly studied one another.

A couple of minutes later, they ordered their meals. Both ordered the rack of ribs with potatoes, a corn muffin, and mac and cheese. David had a beer and Katherine had an apple martini. During dinner they made small talk, discussing Katherine's first day at work. All in all, it was a good first day.

After dinner, David paid the bill, as agreed, and they stepped outside. It was just starting to get dark. Katherine looked at the time on her cellphone and, in that instant, David realized the date was in danger of coming to an early end. He needed to get her attention fast.

"You know? Meeting you was the best part of my day," he said, seemingly out of the blue.

Katherine beamed at him with admiration and replied, "Oh, it was? I think that is the sweetest thing anyone has ever said to me. Thank you, David. I'm glad we met." Her eyes twinkled, as she grinned from ear to ear. He definitely chose his words wisely making her forget all about the time. She continued, "You seem like a decent guy." She paused before adding, "You have no idea how hard it is to find a decent guy these days. I am so sick of meeting losers, who only want one thing from me. They never care about what I do for a living and they never give a damn about me. I can see you are genuinely interested in my career and you seem to take yours very seriously."

"Thanks," he replied proudly. "I am and I do."

It was a beautiful night, considering it was January. The sky was clear and the stars were as visible as they could be over Manhattan. The moon was full, too. David looked over to his left and noticed how well lit the Harlem Pier Park looked. It also looked like it had a high potential for romance with a fabulous view of the Hudson River, New Jersey, and the George Washington Bridge.

"Would you like to take a walk by the pier?" He asked her. "The view is exceptionally great. I promise you won't be disappointed."

"Sure," she agreed. "That sounds nice."

They had to walk under the Henry Hudson Parkway overpass to reach the pier and there was very little lighting in that area. David felt a boost of confidence, as he thought of an excuse to touch her in a polite manner. He took a chance and grabbed her by the hand to lead her to the pier.

"Watch your step," he warned. "It's kind of dark underneath the highway. You never know what's waiting to be stepped on around here at night."

She didn't seem to mind him taking her by the hand. She also heeded his warning by looking down, as she walked. The last thing she wanted to do was step on anything that could potentially gross her out.

They walked all the way to the edge of the pier, hand in hand, and leaned against the black metal railing. It was indeed a magnificent view. New Jersey looked peaceful, while the views looking both to the north and south were quite satisfying. A freight ship crawled slowly up the river toward the bridge, which stretched out across the river connecting New York and New Jersey. This vital link served thousands of commuters on a daily basis, never getting a break from traffic. At night, its brightly colored lights acted as beacons for sea vessels and air traffic, burning with a slightly purple hue.

When David and Katherine faced south on the Manhattan side of the river, they could see the historic tomb of former president and Civil War General Ulysses S. Grant, situated at West 122nd Street and Riverside Drive across the street from Riverside Church whose well-lit tower peaked high above it.

It was a view David usually enjoyed when he was alone and wanted to ease his mind. This was the first time he had ever come here with someone else. He hoped she would be impressed enough with the view to allow him the guilty pleasure of a kiss on their first date.

With regards to her way of taking the initiative, he thought it might be wise to let her make the first move or, at least, wait for her to hint that it was okay for him to try. He had a feeling if she wanted him to kiss her, she'd let it be known.

There were a few benches to sit on that were lined up along the concrete boardwalk that were illuminated by a row of tall black streetlamps. A perfect place for them to sit, David thought. The lamps and benches stretched out across the length of the boardwalk. The bright lights from the lamps reflected onto the darkened water of the river, creating the illusion of underwater lights.

The couple silently stared out over the river. Aside from the traffic on the parkway behind them and the waves crashing gently against the pier, there were no other sounds for nearly two minutes. It was a superbly romantic moment and they both knew it. Neither of them dared to ruin it. However, David decided it was up to him to break the silence. Otherwise, he'd miss his opportunity to kiss her. After all, time waits for no man.

"Where were you born?" He inquired, while still staring out across the river.

"Kings Park," she answered.

"Where is that?"

"Smithtown, Long Island," she answered.

"Hmm. Never heard of it," he said shaking his head. "I was born here. Grew up around here. I even went to school around here. The only time I ever leave the tri-state area is when I visit my parents in Florida. They moved down there, after my dad retired a few years ago. He was a teacher at Columbia." There was regret in his voice, as he spoke.

She looked at him and could tell he seemed saddened. She asked, "Do you miss your parents?"

He thought about it briefly and said, "Yeah, but I know they are happier down there. It's just that, sometimes, I feel like my life is going nowhere. I work and go home each week with nothing to show for it, but a nice empty apartment."

She stared at him sympathetically and thought about what he said. She often felt the same. Lonely. She mustered up a smile and asked, "If you had a choice for a dream vacation, where would you like to go?"

He turned to her making eye contact and asked, "Can I pick anyplace I want?"

"It's your dream vacation, so there's no limit," she stated, as she continued to stare directly at him.

He hesitated, turned away, and smiled before admitting, "I wish I could go to Mars."

"Okay, *John Carter*," she laughed sarcastically. "This time pick a place *on Earth*. Pick somewhere that's a real possibility. Be serious, David. I'd really like to know."

He laughed briefly, looked into her waiting eyes, and apologized, "I'm sorry."

"It's fine," she said softly, holding his gaze.

She looked so beautiful, he thought. It made it difficult to think about anything but kissing her. He concentrated and thought of an honest answer to her question. Where would he like to go? How about that nearby bench to make out with her? Be serious, he reminded himself. She wanted to know. There were so many fantastic places he dreamed of visiting. It wasn't easy to choose only one. At last, he responded, "Mexico is kind of nice, but if I have to choose only one place, then I'd say Egypt. I've always wanted to go to Cairo to see the pyramids and the Sphinx."

She watched him intriguingly and commented, "You sure like places with sand, don't you?"

He shrugged modestly, nodded with a smile, and then answered, "Yeah, I suppose I do. I always loved going to the beach as a kid. Maybe that's why I like places with sand. You don't enjoy much sand growing up on Manhattan Island."

"True enough," she agreed with a nod. She hesitated a moment, before asking, "David?"

"Yes?"

It was as if she wanted to say something, but appeared to change her mind. Instead, she said, "I'm really sorry, but I should probably be heading home now. It's getting late and I live in Astoria. I know it isn't super far away, but when you're tired, fifteen miles might as well be fifty and we do have to work tomorrow morning."

"Oh. Right. Sorry," he said with disappointment. "I guess I lost track of the time. Sorry."

He cursed himself silently for not taking advantage of the romantic moment by getting her to the bench and trying to kiss her. He wanted to do so even more now. Her lips looked so inviting.

"It's fine," she said tenderly, "Really. I had a nice time. Thank you for being a perfect gentleman and not trying to make any moves on our first date. I really appreciate it. It shows me you are a respectful man. I really like that in a guy. I'm glad we got a chance to know each other. I had a nice time."

"Me, too," he said. He smiled at her and breathed a sigh of relief. Almost screwed the pooch on that one, he thought. It was a good thing he did not make a move, after all.

She smiled back and asked, "So, which way are you heading?"

He pointed southbound and stated, "I live pretty close by. It's just a few stops on the 1 train. Three, to be exact."

"I can give you a ride, if you'd like," she offered. "My car is in the parking structure back at work."

"No way!" He stated firmly. "You have a longer ride than me. Go home. I'll be home before you even cross the bridge into Queens. I'll see you tomorrow. Thank you, though."

"Well, at least, let me drive you to the train, that way you can walk me to my car. These streets are kind of desolate at night."

He nodded, "You've got a deal, Kate. Oh, I'm sorry. Is it okay if I call you that?"

She grinned like a schoolgirl with a crush, as she wrapped her arms around his arm and said, "Call me Kat. That's what my dad always calls me. I like it better than Kate. My grandmother is Kate."

He smiled at her and replied, "Okay, Kat."

They walked silently to the parking structure. There were only two other cars there. She got into her car, which was a white Honda Accord. David got into the passenger seat, fastened his seatbelt, and they pulled out onto the road.

She drove him to the train station at West 125th Street and Broadway. There was no kiss goodbye. However, she did smile brightly at him, as she gave him her phone number. He grinned happily and made her promise to text him as soon as she got home, so he'd know she was safe. She agreed.

And just like that their date was over.

Moments later, David waited on the elevated platform for about five minutes, before the train arrived. He stared down at the Science Center remembering its early days and how it looked when it was being built. He tried to recall what businesses were there previously. He remembered a gas station, some kind of storage warehouse, a few restaurants, a car wash, and an automotive garage.

He boarded one of the center cars of the train. It was practically empty, so he was able to choose a seat facing west. He liked that view best for the duration of the elevated ride. Before the train reached the next station it entered the subway tunnel at West 122nd Street and would remain underground, until the last stop at the southern end of Manhattan. David would only be riding the train to West 96th Street. That was his stop. The ride went by quickly.

Upon arrival, he stepped off the train and walked upstairs out of the subway station to the street level. He took his time walking toward his building on Riverside Drive. During the walk his mind was on his date with Katherine. He was glad it went well. He took the elevator up to his third floor apartment. It faced the front of the building providing him with a view of Riverside Park, which was across the street. The tall trees blocked part of his view of the Hudson River, but he could see enough to satisfy him.

He looked at the time on his grandmother's old grandfather clock in the hallway. It was a quarter to 11 pm. He checked his phone. Katherine had not sent any messages, yet. He plugged his cellphone to an adapter to charge the battery, changed his clothes, and got ready for bed.

That's when the notification sound on his phone sounded off. He had a new message. It had to be Katherine. When he checked the message he saw that it was written in text shorthand. It read, "Thank u 4 making my 1st day @ work wonderful! Dinner was yummylicious! See u 2morrow ;)"

"Yummylicious?" He muttered to himself. He shook his head in amusement and grinned. He texted her back with a simple, "You're welcome," followed by a "Goodnight."

She responded, "Gnite," followed by a series of emojis of happy faces.

Within minutes, he was in bed ready to sleep. He unplugged his cellphone, so the battery would not overcharge. That's when the notification sounded, again. It was another new message. He checked it and was surprised the message was from Katherine, again.

This time she texted, "Sweet dreams."

Yep, he thought. She's hooked, too.

David placed his cellphone on the nightstand next to his bed, and then rolled over on his side to go to sleep. He normally had trouble falling asleep, unless he was lying on his side. Tonight he would have trouble sleeping for a different reason. All night long, he kept thinking about being with Katherine and imagining that moment when they would share their first kiss. How would her lips taste? How long would it last? He knew it was only a matter of time.

The thought made him happy. It had been so long, since he truly felt happy.

Naturally, he dreamt about her. By the time he awoke, most of the dream was forgotten. All he could recall was walking with her along some beach, while they held hands. She wore a see through white gown and looked amazing. It was such a simple dream, but it was so very perfect.

BIOHAZARD OUTBREAK

Chapter Four

O VER THE NEXT few weeks, Dr. Fox had his team working hard. They conducted numerous experiments on the primates using two test subjects at a time. They would inject each with a different disease and attempt to combat the diseases using the professor's experimental virus-like anti-virus. That was the best description for his serum, which he began calling the Fox Serum.

There wasn't much time for conversation aside from anything that had to do with the experiments, although David and Katherine made time to share a few smiles and small talk whenever possible. In time, their close friendship developed into a romance. They were respectful enough to limit their romantic interludes to their personal time, as opposed to flaunting it at work. They wanted to remain as professional as possible around Dr. Fox.

On the other hand, David began enjoying the weekends much more than in the past. He and Katherine would often spend those days together, since they did not have to work. Gone were the days when he would go to the laboratory on his days off. Instead, the couple went on dates or sometimes stayed over each other's apartment. David liked when Katherine stayed with him because they would take walks through Riverside Park, spend romantic days near the river, or visit historic sites throughout the city. It seemed they both shared a love for history. He also enjoyed going to her apartment in Astoria because it was nice to be somewhere else for a change. It felt as if he were taking mini-vacations when he spent the weekend at her place. It did wonders for lowering his stress level.

By the end of the first month, they had injected four primates with two different non-fatal diseases and apparently removed all traces of each disease. They were all overjoyed. It was cause for celebration.

David suggested, "Hey, how about we all go out and celebrate?"

Katherine agreed with excitement, "That's a great idea! This is a big achievement!"

However, Dr. Fox had to be convinced. "There is still much work to be done, before we should begin celebrating," he said. He wanted to remain at the laboratory alone to update his notes.

David was almost ready to leave him to his work, but he knew that would be thinking selfishly, since he preferred to be alone with Katherine. The truth was it could not be a proper celebration without Dr. Fox, especially since it was his project. After combining their efforts, both David and Katherine were able to convince him to join them for a quick dinner.

The trio agreed to meet up for dinner at Carmine's, an Italian restaurant located on Broadway between West 90th and 91st Streets. Katherine offered to drive everyone there in her car, but Dr. Fox preferred to drive his own car that way he could head home afterward. Of course, David accepted her offer, since he did not own a car.

Owning a car and living in the city usually meant a lot of headaches brought on by the financial problems created by traffic tickets, alternate side of the street cleaning, and other parking burdens. Those were David's main excuses. Anyone who lived in Manhattan tended to agree. Besides, the trains, buses, and taxis took him wherever he needed to go.

Katherine usually had a hard time finding a parking spot where she lived, while Dr. Fox was the lucky one. He owned a home in Westchester County and had his own driveway.

When they arrived at the restaurant they all shared an entree of lasagna served with garlic bread and a bottle of red wine. They drank the wine slowly. David had to drink most of it, since the other two would be driving later. He didn't mind. It was a celebration! As for the meal, one entrée at Carmine's was enough to feed a party of four. They were each full by the end of their meal.

Dr. Fox kept the conversation focused on work throughout dinner. He was absolutely thrilled about the results of the experiments and was eager to speak about them, as well as sharing his plans to advance to the next phase.

"I must admit I am grateful for the opportunity to sit here with you both and discuss how well the experiments are going. We are progressing faster than anticipated. Soon, it will be time to move on to the next phase and I have both of you to thank."

David and Katherine smiled and simultaneously raised their glasses for a toast.

"To our success," said David with a smile.

"To our success," Katherine and Dr. Fox repeated.

For some reason, the professor was very careful not to discuss exactly what the next phase would entail. David and Katherine found it odd, although Dr. Fox was quite insistent on keeping it under wraps. At some point, the couple made eye contact with each other and decided to talk about it later in private.

After dinner, Dr. Fox insisted on picking up the bill. He made the most money and they could not argue with that. Once outside, he quickly walked toward his car and drove away without so much as a goodbye. He made some excuse about forgetting something at the lab that he needed to get in a hurry before security locked down the building for the night.

Katherine offered David a ride home, which he accepted, even though he only lived a few blocks from the restaurant. As they got into her car, David began to speculate.

"I bet he's going back to continue working. That man's got nothing better to do with his time. He's not married, so there is no great need for him to get home, especially not while work is on his mind. We used to do it all the time, staying after hours. I only stopped when you and I started dating. He probably still does it."

"I don't know," Katherine replied with skepticism. She looked at David and asked, "If that's the case, then why the lies and secrets? That's what I don't get."

"I'm not sure. The only thing I can think of is he's doing something he should not be doing," David responded suspiciously.

Katherine still felt doubtful, as she asked, "What makes you say that? I don't understand why you think he would risk everything by breaking the rules. He's too close to a breakthrough that could net him a Nobel. I doubt he'd be that foolish."

"You don't know him like I do, Kat. The man is getting impatient playing with monkeys. He's too eager to move on to humans."

Katherine was shocked by his comment and exclaimed, "David! You know he can't do that! Not yet, at least. Without approval, he could lose everything he's been working so hard to achieve."

David wasn't convinced. He replied, "That's why he's not including us in his plans. He's doing it alone without anyone's knowledge. It's the only way he can get away with it."

Katherine began to look worried. She wondered if David could be right. She turned to him and asked, "What should we do? If he is breaking the rules and the law, we could also get in trouble. Right?"

David looked at her and nodded apprehensively, "That's what I'm afraid of. There's only one thing we can do. Let's go there. Now. We need to catch him in the act. If he's doing something wrong, we'll try to reason with him. Otherwise..." His voice trailed off.

"Otherwise, what? What if we can't reason with him? What if he doesn't listen and threatens to fire us? He barely knows me, so it wouldn't be a great loss to him and you claim he doesn't consider you a friend, so what's to stop him from threatening us with losing our jobs?"

David contemplated what she said. Was keeping their jobs more important than stopping the professor from breaking the rules? The job did pay well and without a job, David would have a hard time keeping his apartment. If both he and Katherine lost their jobs, they would probably be able to sue to get them back. It would surely be the start of a huge scandal. Columbia University definitely would not want that, especially if it involved their new campus. Then again, Dr. Fox didn't have to fire them. He could simply get them kicked out of his lab. That wouldn't be such a big deal, except then no one would be able to keep an eye on him. He'd basically win. Of course, when it came down to it, David didn't want to put the professor on the spot and cause a rift between them unnecessarily. Still, he couldn't just stand by and do nothing. Someone had to find out the truth. It may as well be him, but what if he were wrong?

Finally, he answered, "It's a chance I have to take."

Katherine started the car and reluctantly drove north on Broadway toward the Science Center. She still wasn't sure if going to the laboratory was the best idea, especially after they just finished celebrating.

David tried to reassure her by saying, "Drop me off at the lab. I'll pretend like I forgot my house keys. You can wait in the car. That way, you're clear to make your own decision based on what I find out. If he is up to no good, then I will confront him and take it from there."

She nodded half-heartedly. This was something she did not feel comfortable doing. She preferred not knowing. Worried, she asked, "What will you say to him, if you find out he's doing something wrong?"

David was intense, as he replied. "Like I said, I will cross that path when I get to it. Remember, I'm only going there to search for my lost keys. Here's what I'll need you to do. Call me on the lab's landline in fifteen minutes, after I go in, to let me know you found my keys in your car. It will give me my excuse to leave, if I need one."

"Ooh! I like that idea!" She said enthusiastically. "It sounds like a good plan! Please, be careful, babe. If he is up to no good, he might get desperate and do something drastic," she warned.

"I can handle Dr. Fox," David replied with confidence.

Katherine glanced at him nervously, but then refocused her attention on the road. After a few moments of silence, she said, "Make sure *you* don't do anything drastic."

He realized she was right. He had to be careful how he handled this situation. If it turned out the professor was doing something wrong, things could get ugly and there would be no witnesses, aside from the security cameras. People tend to see what they want when they see video footage and it is not always the whole truth.

Perhaps, it was best to sneak into the laboratory quietly. Then again, if the professor noticed him sneaking in, it would certainly arouse his suspicions. However, if David strolls in leisurely looking for his keys, Dr. Fox might stop whatever he is doing and pretend to be doing his usual research.

There is another way this could turn out. On the off chance that the professor was telling the truth about forgetting something, he might have already found what he was looking for and left. The laboratory could very well be empty. That would be great.

As for the security cameras, they are capable of picking up most of what happens within the main laboratory and some of the biohazard lab. Even the supply closets have cameras watching them. True, there are ways around the cameras, which the professor would know, all too well. Come to think of it, there are four rooms that do not have cameras due to privacy laws. The locker room, restroom, dormitory, and decontamination room are all private locations.

It's highly doubtful the professor would be hiding anything in the restroom, locker room, or decontamination room. Therefore, all David really had to do was check the dorm. It seemed like a simple enough plan.

It did not take long for them to arrive at the Science Center. As Katherine parked in front, she began to get cold feet.

"Maybe we should leave," she suggested. "We could keep a close eye on him during normal work hours. If he's doing something wrong, the guilt will eventually start to show on his face. I'm sure he'll slip up. Maybe he'll even invite us in on whatever he's up to. Who knows?" She shrugged.

David turned to her in surprise and asked, "Is that what you want?"

"No!" She answered quickly. "I just mean, we don't have to do this now. We could leave. We could go back to your place and forget all about old Herbert. I have a better idea of how we could pass the time." She winked her eye at him and forced a smile, causing him to hesitate. She then said in a seductive voice, "Come on, babe. Let's go back to your place. I'm *really* in the mood right now. Wouldn't you much rather be laying on your bed with me?"

The idea was extremely tempting. He licked his lips subconsciously and stared at her body. He swallowed hard and almost changed his mind, but then he shook his head and stepped out of the car. "I really need to do this, Kat," he said apologetically. Before he closed the door, he looked at her, again, and said, "Don't lose the mood. I promise I won't take long." He then turned away and entered the building.

After telling his made up story to the night shift security guard, Ivan, he pressed the call button for the elevator and waited. He pulled out his cellphone and sent Katherine a quick text message letting her know Dr. Fox was definitely down in the lab, according to Ivan.

The elevator arrived and he stepped inside, before she could send a reply. There would be no more text messages, until he left the underground levels, since there was no signal down there.

When he reached the lowest level, where their laboratory was located, he stepped out. All the lights were off, except for the light over the elevator and the one at the end of the hall over the entrance to the emergency stairwell.

Just then, a thought occurred to him. What if the professor was asleep in the dorm? It made perfect sense! Dr. Fox was working day and night, so why not cut out the thirty minute commute to the city from Westchester at the crack of dawn? Not to mention, there were four perfectly comfortable twin size cots in the dormitory.

David inserted his security key card and opened the double doors to the main laboratory. He walked inside and the doors closed behind him, automatically locking. He moved about quietly, trying not to bump into anything. He did not wish to alarm the apes. They were all sleeping peacefully in their cages only a few feet away. It was difficult to see anything because it was practically pitch black. The only light came from the two in the hallway, which were barely visible through the two windows. He pulled out his cellphone and used it as a flashlight.

When he reached the door to the dormitory, he stopped and placed his ear against it to listen. He did not hear any sounds coming from within, although he was unsure if that was because the door was so thick it was probably soundproof or because the room was simply quiet. He did not wish to awaken the professor, if he was asleep inside. He decided not to take a chance by opening the door.

He slowly made his way toward the telephone, so he could answer it quickly when Katherine called. At the same time, he had to perform for the security cameras, in case he brought on any suspicion by entering the lab so late. He looked around the tables and floor to pretend he was searching for his keys. He bent over near the telephone and pretended like he was picking up his keys and placing them back into his pocket. He feigned a smile and waited impatiently for Katherine's call.

"Any minute now," he whispered to himself.

He had never realized how creepy the laboratory could be at night when it was dark. He looked around and could see several shadows lurking nearby. He knew it was only the lab equipment, but his eyes were telling him different.

Suddenly, the phone rang and he nearly leapt out of his skin. Instinctively, he grabbed it and picked it up.

"Shhh!" He said without thinking.

Katherine was confused by this and asked, "Why are you shushing me when I haven't even spoken?"

David realized what he'd done and shook his head. He whispered into the phone, "I meant the phone. It was too loud. Never mind. If he's here, he has to be sleeping in the dorm. All the lights are off. I'm getting out of here. I'll talk to you when I see you."

She only had time to say, "Okay," before he hung up.

He quickly slipped out of the laboratory without drawing any attention from the apes. He took the elevator back up to the ground floor and walked past Ivan.

"Found them," he said, while jingling his keys for Ivan to see.

Ivan smiled and said, "Great! Have a goodnight!"

"Thanks! You, too!"

David walked outside and tried to open the door to Katherine's car, but it was locked. She immediately unlocked the doors and let him back in.

"Sorry," she said, as he sat down beside her.

Confused, he asked, "Why did you lock the door?"

"I always lock the doors when I sit in the car alone, especially at night near the projects. Force of habit," she explained. "Never mind that. What happened?"

David sounded disappointed when he responded, "It was too dark to see anything. I didn't turn on the lights for fear that I might wake the apes. I'm pretty sure he was asleep in the dorm, but I didn't check. I didn't want to wake him unnecessarily. It was really quiet down there. Maybe it was too quite. To tell you the truth, it was kind of creepy."

"But you think he was sleeping in the dorm?" She replied, trying to dismiss David's unwarranted fears. All of a sudden, a look of realization came over her. She practically shouted when she said, "Oh, man! We are so stupid! Here we are creating these silly scenarios in our minds and the poor man is just sleeping at work because he has no life. That's so sad." She pouted.

David eyed her peculiarly and answered, "Yeah, I suppose." He shrugged when he realized she could be right. He admitted with reluctance, "We are pretty dumb. I realized that when I was standing with my ear pressed against the door of the dorm trying to listen. Of course, I didn't hear anything." He paused, and then said, "Let's get out of here. We've wasted enough time."

She turned to him and grinned devilishly, "Well, there is a way you can make it up to me. After all, you did tell me not to lose the mood. Besides, I am way too tired to drive all the way to Astoria alone."

He looked at her and suggested, "You should probably stay over my place. I wouldn't want you to get into an accident."

She smiled and started the car, "Great idea! I'm so glad you suggested it!"

She pulled away from the Science Center and drove toward his home. The ride went by fast. They did not speak. It was as if they were each lost in their own thoughts. She was, no doubt, planning how to spend the next hour or so, having already forgotten about their silly theories regarding Dr. Fox. As for David, his mind was still at the lab. He wondered why the professor chose to keep his sleeping there a secret. The man had no shame, so he couldn't have been embarrassed about it. Perhaps, he felt he drank too much wine and did not want to take a chance driving home?

David could not help thinking there was still something wrong. Maybe it wasn't anything obvious, yet, but he had a bad feeling and could not shake it.

When they arrived at his apartment they wasted no time. The couple enjoyed a night of passion that started in the doorway, worked its way into the living room, and ended in the bedroom. It was a nice way to work off the stress they were building up in their heads earlier.

Afterwards, they laughed about their silly ideas and fell asleep in each other's arms.

BIOHAZARD OUTBREAK

Chapter Five

THE NEXT MORNING when the alarm went off David struggled to open his eyes. He wanted to stay in bed a few more hours, but he had to go to work. He cursed himself for drinking so much wine the night before at the restaurant. At least, he had Kat to look forward to, he thought.

That's when he remembered she was laying right next to him. He watched her momentarily and admired her peaceful beauty. She was sound asleep. He wondered what she was dreaming about because she appeared to be smiling. Perhaps, she was still laughing at their ridiculous ideas from the night before, he thought.

Alas, time was wasting. They'd both have to get out of bed, if they were going to be at work on time. He woke her up by gently saying her name in a low voice, not wanting to startle her.

"Kat, wake up." He nudged her softly and called her name, again, "Kat..."

"Huh? What time is it?" She groaned and before he could reply she popped up into an upright position scaring the living daylights out of him. He jumped back and almost fell out of the bed.

"What the hell?" He shouted. "Why did you do that?"

"Oh, man!" She said, as she rubbed her eyes, "I feel like a butt. Sorry, babe. I had such a crazy dream last night. Dr. Fox had us strapped down on tables and he was experimenting on us. He had on that crazy oxygen mask he wears sometimes in the biohazard lab, so he looked extra freaky."

David laughed and when she realized how funny it sounded, she did, as well. She nodded, "Yeah, I know. Stupid."

"No," David said with a grin, "It's appropriate, after last night. I have a feeling it's probably how we'll be spending our day at work, if we don't start getting ready soon!"

They both laughed, again, and then Katherine climbed out of bed taking the bed sheet with her to the bathroom as a makeshift robe.

David also got out of bed and grabbed some clothes to wear for later, after his shower. For now, he'd have to wait until Katherine came out of the bathroom. There wasn't much time for breakfast with the two of them taking turns to use the bathroom. He hoped she would not take too long. He wanted to kick himself for not resetting the alarm to an earlier time, which would have allowed them both enough time to get ready.

Once both of them were showered and dressed, they rushed down to Katherine's car and headed straight to work. There was no time to stop for coffee, although they were only about five minutes late. They parked in the parking structure, rushed into the lobby, and took the elevator down to the fifth underground level.

It was always a hassle taking the elevator down because they had to make sure no one else was on it with them, since no one could see that there was a hidden level below the fourth. That's one reason why it was beneficial to arrive on time. There were usually less people trying to use the elevators going down. Otherwise, they had to wait until it was empty, before they used their special key. The key worked much like a "fireman's key" and would send the elevator straight down to their level without stopping.

By the time they reached their level, they were fifteen minutes late. David used his key card to unlock the double doors to the main laboratory. Obviously, Dr. Fox was already there. His face was glued to a microscope when they entered. He barely glanced up to acknowledge their presence.

"Sorry we're late, Doc," David said, nonetheless, as he and Katherine went into the locker room to put on their lab coats and gloves.

"No worries," he responded, sounding rather uninterested in them. He was too preoccupied to care about the time. He had been there all night and started work earlier than usual, so he lost track of the time long ago. Instead, he instructed, "Do me a favor and take a look at this specimen."

David approached the microscope and the professor stepped aside to give him space. When he peered through the microscope lens, David could see swirling organisms devouring each other in a rapid manner that seemed rather disturbing.

Dr. Fox stated, "Those are parasites."

Surprised, David asked, "Is this a blood sample from one of the apes?"

Katherine became interested and moved closer.

"Precisely," replied Dr. Fox. "Absolutely fascinating. Is it not?"

Katherine looked on in silence and hoped she might get a chance to look, too, as she stood by impatiently.

The professor went on, "It appears the blood has mutated and created these parasites, as we originally suspected it would. In fact, the process does not seem to stop, once it has begun. They devour everything in their path, until they are left alone. I am intrigued at the possibility of what might occur once the disease has been eradicated from the system. Will they be forced to stop devouring and become docile or will they seek out a new form of sustenance? Curious."

"That would be bad," David said grimly. "These are parasites. We can't expect them to behave like medicine. If you insist we continue to test them, perhaps a decrease in the dosage would be wiser. They are just too unpredictable."

Dr. Fox grasped at his chin and contemplated. "I've considered that already," he said. "On the other hand, I have also considered increasing the dosage."

"Increasing?" David asked, obviously against the idea. He did not wish to oppose the professor's ideas, but it sounded like a huge mistake. His worries were justified. Increasing the dosage would likely lead to disastrous results and almost certainly put the test subject at risk. At once, he offered a suggestion, hoping to talk some sense into his supervisor without sounding disrespectful.

"Do we even have enough apes to spare? Maybe we shouldn't take such drastic chances so early on. At least, not without knowing the possible repercussions to the test subjects. After all, we only have a limited amount and plenty of time to get this right."

"True enough, but how can we properly know the full repercussions without learning them first hand?" Dr. Fox replied, before pausing to give David a chance to respond. He did make a good point.

David tried to think of a clever response, but came up blank.

"Katherine," Dr. Fox turned to her, as he spoke. "We will need two new test subjects to test this on, so we can try both methods. Please, prepare two primates. David, I will need you to inject them both with the same disease. Let's step it up to a level three pathogen. Something we can cure, just to be on the safe side."

David nodded reluctantly, "Sure thing, Doc."

Katherine hesitated and glanced at him, but he was already heading to the storage cabinet to prepare two syringes. She frowned and turned to walk toward the cages.

Dr. Fox called to her, "Oh, Katherine! Be sure one is male and one is female."

"Yes, professor," she responded somberly.

"Herbert," he corrected.

She pretended not to hear him, as she selected two primates for experimentation.

The next few days went by slowly with much of the time spent observing the primates' behavior and checking their blood and vitals for significant changes. It would be a few days before they'd learn if the diseases were in regressive stages. Each day David compared the notes to document any changes, while Katherine monitored their vital signs and watched for changes in their health.

The apes showed some signs of improvement, but the disease was still present in their systems. Things continued in this way for the next couple of weeks.

Dr. Fox decided to try improving his serum, so it would work faster and more efficiently. For weeks, he was completely engulfed by his experimental research and mostly worked in the biohazard lab alone, leaving David and Katherine to focus on the test subjects. In that time, he barely said a word to them unless he needed them to do something for him and it would usually be something that kept them busy for hours. Sometimes, he'd even request David's assistance in the biohazard lab. There was very little time for socializing.

By April Dr. Fox felt ready to inject another two test subjects with a stronger version of his serum that he believed would be a significant improvement over the previous version. The apes were infected with a different non-fatal disease. They were then injected with doses of the improved experimental serum. One was given a small dosage and the other received a rather large dosage, against David's better judgment.

It would be another couple of days before there was any notable progress with these new test subjects, but they did seem to improve significantly. At the end of the week, most of the disease had been eradicated from their systems. By the next week, these two apes were disease free.

The new version of the serum appeared to be a success!

Dr. Fox smiled, as David and Katherine both cheered. "Thank you, thank you," he said. "While this is a great success for us, we will need to begin testing fatal diseases, if we are to call this a victory. In the meantime, we should continue to monitor these primates and make sure there are no side effects."

David and Katherine agreed. At last, they began to feel more hopeful.

By the end of April, the professor felt confident enough to put in a request for a higher budget. He had a lot of plans for the advanced studies of his new serum, but it was going to take more money than their budget allowed and perhaps a larger laboratory with more rooms. They would also require additional test subjects. He knew it was a lot to ask for, but he had a feeling the university would comply.

It did not take long for the President of Facilities to respond to his request. It was only days later. Dr. Fox seemed extremely agitated and stressed out when David and Katherine arrived for work. He paced back and forth near his desk. David asked what was wrong and the professor responded gravely, "My request has been denied. According to the powers that be, we seem to be exceeding the limits of our budget and showing little progress. Humph. 'Little progress,' they said. Would you believe that?"

David was dumbfounded. He couldn't believe what he was hearing. He responded with a hint of anger in his voice, "That's ridiculous! So, Columbia can afford to buy up all of Upper Manhattan, but they can't sanction a groundbreaking experiment that could mean the cure for diseases, such as cancer, at one of their own facilities?"

Dr. Fox nodded, "They seem to believe we have a sufficient amount for our budget to accomplish whatever *high end dreams* we are working on. Apparently, they are not quite convinced that we are onto anything tangible, yet, despite the latest successful experiments."

Katherine frowned, "Wow. I can't believe it. I thought for sure they'd be enthusiastic regarding the latest test results."

Suddenly, Dr. Fox slammed his hands on his desk and yelled, "Those blind imbeciles are not taking me seriously! They have no idea how close we are to finding a cure all for every disease known to man! The president is a stuck up buffoon with no more brains than a vile cockroach! I should have expected as much! They underestimate my skills, but I'll show them. Just wait and see."

Both David and Katherine were startled when he slammed his hands and yelled. They were not expecting such feelings of intense anger from their normally unemotional colleague. It was out of character for him.

David tried to be the voice of reason and spoke more calmly, "Hey, maybe we are looking at this the wrong way. What if they just don't have the money to fund us? We are asking for a lot and I just remembered this site was built using a donation."

"Excuses," mumbled Dr. Fox. "I am sick and tired of excuses."

David knew it was going to be a rough day, so he whispered to Katherine and suggested they keep their distance from the professor unless absolutely necessary. It was best to give him space. They had plenty of work to keep themselves busy. They focused their attention on the latest two primates under experimentation for the rest of the day.

As for the professor, he took it pretty hard and spent the whole day sitting at his desk.

By early May, Dr. Fox was determined to take his experiments a step further. He asked David and Katherine to prepare two more test subjects, so they could test the latest version of his serum. It was time to see if the serum could battle cancer. The two apes were both infected with the same form of cancer, which meant if the serum did not work, they would possibly die.

Katherine did not like it and made her feelings known to David in secret. He reminded her that the apes were not there to act as pets. She wasn't too pleased with his response, but she knew he was right.

Dr. Fox personally injected each of the new test subjects with different doses of the serum, which had been tweaked over the weekend. Not many words were spoken in the laboratory for the next few days. They all waited impatiently to see what would happen. Every day they'd sit and watch the apes. Tests were conducted with minor results.

It took another week for the results they were waiting for to become apparent. The female ape that was given the larger enhanced strain of the serum was in remission. However, the male ape, which was given a smaller dose of the serum, had grown sicker.

Over the next few days, they continued to watch both apes closely. Meanwhile, the previous two apes that were cured of their non-fatal diseases in April were perfectly healthy and doing well. They even seemed happier and more energetic than the other apes, especially the earlier apes that were experimented on. The first four apes seemed tired all the time and had become sicker. Further tests revealed they were each still infected with diseases. Meanwhile, the two apes that had been experimented on in March were no longer diseased, but they seemed depressed and spent most of the time asleep.

David wondered if this was due to unfortunate side effects from the serum. At least, the apes were no longer sick, he thought. It meant they were a step closer to finding a proper cure. Depression could be dealt with in many ways, so long as the disease was cured.

Over the next weekend, the latest experiments hit a wall. The male ape that was sick with cancer died, while the female remained in remission. It was unfortunate to lose an ape, but, on the other hand, it was amazing that the other was still in remission.

Once the dead ape had been removed from the laboratory, David shared his thoughts with Dr. Fox, "It's a shame we lost that one ape, but I can't believe the other one is still in remission. To think her cancer was pushed into remission by your serum is incredible! I think it won't be long before we can, at least, delay the fatal effects caused by cancer, if not cure it completely. It's a start."

Dr. Fox nodded unenthusiastically, "Yes, it is. Still, if we can improve the serum used to place the test subject into remission, a cure might not be far off. I must try my best. We are close. I can feel it."

Katherine cringed and David noticed it. He knew how she hated whenever the professor called the apes test subjects, as if he did not want to acknowledge they were living beings. She knew he could care less about the ape that died. According to him, it was just one of twelve test subjects. Still, his serum did seem to be working on the female ape. Katherine could not ignore those results.

She figured she'd add in her two cents by saying, "Losing that ape was an unfortunate sacrifice, but I think the world is going to owe you big time, professor. Based on what I've seen accomplished in this lab, I am definitely impressed. Even if we never find a cure for cancer, I am confident our research here will help lead to a cure someday."

He replied, "While your confidence and praise is welcoming, my dear. I am far more inclined to believe we will *definitely* find a cure for cancer sooner, rather than later. Now, if you'll excuse me, I have much work to do." And with that he sat at his desk and began going over his notes diligently.

Katherine turned her attention to the female ape that was in remission. She looked at the ape and noticed she seemed sad. Katherine frowned and spoke softly to her, "Aw, you miss your friend. Don't you? I'm so sorry we couldn't save him, but we will save you. I promise."

The ape stared at her with big brown eyes, and then looked over toward the empty cage, where her companion once resided. Her cancer might have been in remission, but her heart was broken. There was no quick cure for that.

David approached Katherine and asked, "What's up?"

She pouted and answered, "Look. She's sad. She misses her buddy. It makes me sad to see her that way."

David sighed, "You know, I keep telling you, it's not a good idea to get attached to the test subjects of a research laboratory. You should know better."

"Oh, hush! You meanie! Stop calling them test subjects. You know I don't like it," she stated. She then turned to him and asked, "Don't you care about these apes?"

He nodded instantly, "Yeah, of course, I care about them, but not as if they were my pets. I wouldn't want to see them abused or senselessly murdered. At the same time, you have to keep in mind there is a chance they could die in the name of science. It's a good cause," he reminded her. "Therefore, I prefer to keep my distance emotionally and I recommend you do the same."

"Fine," she frowned. "I'll try. It's just that I became a vet because I love animals. I won't lie. It's been rough doing these experiments over the past few months. I keep telling myself, it's for a greater good. I know the work we are doing will someday save a lot of lives. That makes a few sacrifices worth it. Right? Still, it's not easy to see them suffer. This was our first loss. We never lost an ape, until now. Don't mind me, though. I'll be fine. I just need a little time to get over it and so does she."

"No problem. I get it. I'm not a 'meanie,' like you think," he said in a caring tone.

Katherine reached out and hugged him, "I know. I love you, Dave."

He immediately looked over at Dr. Fox, who was lost in his notes. He turned back to Katherine and whispered, "I love you, too, but let's take it easy with the hugging around here. Remember?"

She pulled away and apologized, "Oh, sorry. I forgot for a second."

"It's okay, Kat. Just try to focus on something else for now. We still have a bunch of sick apes that need some TLC."

"Very true," she agreed. "I'll check on them now. Thanks."

David smiled at her, as she went to check on the sick apes. He glanced back over at Dr. Fox. He had not noticed their embrace. David was unsure if the professor was aware of their relationship. Either way, he did not want to flaunt it in front of him. They had to remain professional, while at work.

He turned his attention to his own research notes and, soon enough, became just as lost as his mentor.

At the start of the next week, David and Katherine arrived at the laboratory to find Dr. Fox transfixed over a microscope, as he carefully studied what appeared to be his first real breakthrough, since the female ape's cancer went into remission. They put on their lab coats and gloves, before joining him at his side.

After several minutes of silence, he acknowledged their presence, "Yes! At last! I believe I've done it. David, come quickly." He looked around and was startled to see they were standing right beside him. "Oh, ha, ha, you are already near me! Splendid! Come, I want you to see this," he beckoned excitedly.

David moved toward the microscope, as the professor stepped aside.

Katherine looked on curiously. It bothered her that the professor never asked her to look at the slides under the microscope. She wanted to see, too. Of course, he was oblivious to her wants and needs. They did not matter to him.

While David looked into the microscope, Dr. Fox explained, "As you can see, not only are all traces of the cancer gone, but the cells have become like an aggressive army in search of any sign of it that they can devour. They have become replicating mutagens... antibodies, if you will, which are basically designed to attach to the DNA, so they can mutate it."

David responded, without taking his eye off the microscope, "Is this from the same parasites or are you using prions now?"

Dr. Fox hesitated, "Well, as you are aware, we are not dealing with something as simple as infectious proteins that affect the nervous system, as we would, if this were say... mad cow disease. No, these came from the parasites and they target the DNA directly. It's brilliant. Keep in mind this is not an infection. It is a cure and it may very well be *the cure*."

David stepped away from the microscope and asked, "Do you really think this will work? They still seem overly aggressive to me."

Dr. Fox sighed impatiently, "Yes, of course! There's really nothing to worry about. I've done enough tests to know this *will* work. You worry too much. Mark my words, we shall be ready for human trials sooner than expected."

David eyed him skeptically and said, "Doc, you know something like this requires far more time before it can ever be used on a human subject. I mean you basically used parasites to create a virus that will infect a living organism and change it. Am I correct?"

"Yes, in a way," the professor agreed. "However, what I have created is something that will actually help the body, rather than cause harm to it. This is... something new. Something different."

David still looked skeptical. He inspected the slide under the microscope, again, and said, "I hope you're right, Doc. Somehow, I'm not as convinced, as I thought I'd be. We still have several apes. I think we should keep going with the tests for as long as it takes, rather than try to rush through them. Let's wait and see what happens to the apes we tested. What about the female in remission? We could try it on her."

Katherine shot David a sharp look. Although she said nothing, he could feel her glaring eyes burning holes into him. He avoided looking her way and kept his gaze upon the professor.

"Or we could test it on a new pair," he quickly added, trying to save face with her.

Dr. Fox considered the suggestion and replied, "We will indeed test a new pair. Trust me. This will work. You will see. In time, we shall find the ultimate cure for all diseases. My Fox Serum will be sought after by the entire world and we will be well known for our collaborative work here," he said with certainty. "Besides, I have also been working on a possible nucleoside analogue and enzyme inhibitor combination to work as a potential anti-viral serum, just in case. It can act as a DNA substitute, which should stop the mutagens from replicating. It's still in its earliest experimental stage, but I believe it should be ready soon. That should set your mind at ease."

David was relieved to hear that and responded, "That's good to know. I only hope it will work. So, when can we begin testing it?"

The professor did some mental calculations before answering, "Let us conduct a few tests with the newest version of the serum first, before we worry about the anti-serum. Hopefully, we shall never need to implement it. Of course, when the time comes we can add interferons to quell any lingering fears you may have. The addition of these proteins should help trigger a defensive immunity strategy that should kill off any lingering viruses, as well as my serum, considering it contains viral properties."

"Okay, then let's do that," replied David. "The last thing we need to do is create some new kind of unstoppable pathogen."

"You worry too much, David," said Dr. Fox, as he shook his head. "This is one of those times you should be celebrating."

David nodded his head, "I suppose. It is... interesting. I'll give you that," he hesitated only a moment, but it was long enough to get a rise out of Dr. Fox.

"Interesting???" The professor repeated sounding rather agitated. He faced David and asked, "Is that all you can say about what could be the biggest scientific and medical breakthrough in years?"

David immediately apologized, "I'm sorry, Doc. It's just that the bacteria has me worried. It's too aggressive. What if they attack something else in the blood, once the disease is eradicated from the system? What if they don't stop at the disease?"

"Nonsense! Is that all you can think about? I assure you they will only combat diseased cells and once all traces of the disease have been erased, they will continue to act as a defense mechanism ensuring that no other viruses enter the system. In fact, I have already tested it on two of the earliest subjects over the weekend. You will be pleased to know the serum completely eradicated the injected disease and ceased all aggression. So, there you have it. Now, do you realize what this means?"

David was only slightly impressed. He was more surprised to hear that Dr. Fox had already experimented on test subjects, while he was alone in the laboratory. It felt like a betrayal.

However, before he could respond Katherine answered, "The end of all sicknesses?"

Dr. Fox replied with a grin, "Precisely, my dear! Now, we will need to monitor all of the test subjects over the next few days, if we are to move on to the next phase." She nodded, as he continued, "I want you to check specifically for aggressive or irregular behavior. We want to make sure David is not disappointed," he added sarcastically, as he leered at his assistant.

David glared back at him, although he was still thinking about what the professor had mentioned earlier. Why would he conduct tests on subjects without their help? He was going through the apes too fast, knowing that the university already denied the request for additional funding. Furthermore, the new serum was more aggressive and unpredictable than the last versions. Anything could easily go wrong. David was curious exactly how the serum was tweaked this time to make it so intense.

Unable to contain himself any longer, he finally asked, "And what, may I ask, will the next phase consist of?"

Dr. Fox grinned slyly and turned away. He walked toward his desk, as he spoke, "That, my good man, is a topic for another time. I have much work to do." Dr. Fox sat down at his computer and began going through his folders and checking files. For him, the conversation was over. His mind was now focused on his research. David's inquisition would have to wait.

For David, it felt more like a new conversation had just begun. He became frustrated and sneered at the professor. He knew Dr. Fox would not tell him anything further. Not until he was good and ready.

Katherine noticed David's uneasiness and approached him.

He saw her approaching, turned to her, and escorted her into the locker room. Once inside, he asked in a low voice, "Why do I have a feeling he's already started the next phase and it isn't legal?"

She eyed him suspiciously and reminded him, "Let's not jump to conclusions, again. Remember what happened the last time we thought things like that. We both ended up feeling pretty silly."

David grimaced, as he responded, "I just don't like how he answered, or rather, how he avoided my question. I know he's working on something more and he's keeping it a secret from us. He's already proven that he is willing to experiment on test subjects, while we are not around. I won't argue that it's slightly possible he's waiting until he gets positive results first, but I doubt it. Trust me. He's keeping secrets from us and they are not good. I feel it in my gut. Think about it, Kat. He spends most of his time here, after hours, by himself. He has way too much time to advance his experiments and conduct tests, while no one is watching over his shoulders to make sure he follows the rules."

She didn't seem to agree, as she responded, "You don't think he trusts us enough to share his full research with us? We are all he has to confide in. You said it yourself. He has no family, at least, not that we know about. I think you're reading too much into this, babe. He's probably just going over the research thoroughly and making sure everything is copasetic," she explained.

David wasn't convinced. He asked her, "What do *you* think the next phase will consist of?"

She shrugged and took a wild guess. "I don't know. I suppose we'll probably move on to some other intelligent animal and start testing them with the serum, while comparing the results with what we got on the apes."

David rolled his eyes, "Come on, Kat! There is no other intelligent animal to use, after apes. What do you think? He's going to bring dolphins in here? Open your eyes. You heard what he said. He wants to use humans. For all we know, he's already begun. Either that or he plans to start soon."

Katherine stared at David looking extremely doubtful, but then her eyes opened wide with sudden realization and she exclaimed, "David! Are you serious? He wouldn't do that. It's way too soon to move on to humans. He knows that better than we do. There are still so many variables to consider and more tests to run. You are going too far with this. I can't believe you would think that." She shook her head in disbelief and continued, "We work with this man almost every day. No one knows him better than us. I'm pretty sure he's only holding back information, until he's certain, so he won't look like a fool to us. Humans? Really?"

David gave in to her for the time being, "Fine. I've made my opinion clear to you. That's all that matters. Let's say you are right. If that's that case, good. I will gladly admit I was being ridiculous, but in the meantime, I am going to keep a close eye on him. Just keep in mind that we could lose our jobs, if he skips around the rules and injects some poor sap with an unapproved experimental drug."

She shot back, "Well, you keep in mind that no one else is allowed in here without the proper clearance."

David smirked, "Yeah, but it would be real easy for old Herbert to pay some poor homeless guy from the mental health clinic upstairs a few bucks and sneak him down here at night through the emergency stairwell. Either that, or he could bring him down the elevator when that security guard from the nightshift, Ivan, is on duty. Those two are buddies. Ivan would probably hold the door open for them!"

Katherine shook her head, "I don't know about that. I think you're letting your discontent for Dr. Fox get the better of you."

David sneered and replied, "Kat, I don't dislike him. Yes, he drives me nuts, sometimes, and I don't trust him, as far as I can throw him, but I don't dislike the man."

She smirked, "Okay, fine. So, you don't dislike him, but you also don't think much of him."

He shrugged, "Okay, I'll give you that one. It's just too easy for him to bend the rules, which makes it more likely that he'd be willing to do it. It's not as if anyone checks up on him. Like you said, no one else is authorized to come down here, so not many do."

"What about the progress reports he does for the head of the department? Doesn't he, at least, know what's going on down here?"

David scoffed, "I thought so, too, at one time. That is until I noticed that Dr. Fox piles them in his locker and they never go anywhere. No one ever comes looking either. Honestly, sometimes, I think they put him down here to forget about him. I'm starting to think he's not as prestigious as he claims to be." He thought for a second and added, "Well, maybe he sends them via e-mail. I don't know. It doesn't really matter. No one else outside of this lab cares. The bottom line is he's got a secret he's not telling us."

Katherine considered his words carefully and came up with a possible solution. However, she had a feeling David wouldn't like it. She scratched her head and pitched her plan, "There's a simple solution to this dilemma. Why don't we just confront him and ask him to tell us the truth? We can explain why we are so worried. I think he'd understand."

That remark only earned her a look of sarcasm. David wasn't even going to justify it with a verbal response. Her face became sour. Afterwards, both remained silent, as they contemplated how to proceed.

Eventually, Katherine glanced at her cellphone and noticed it was almost quitting time. She decided it was an opportune moment for a change of scenery and a new topic of conversation. She wanted to get David's mind off of work and onto something they could agree on.

"It's almost time to go. Why don't we start cleaning up, so we can get out of here? I seriously doubt he'd even notice if we left. I'm starving and I have a craving for pizza."

David sighed and agreed, "Yeah, sounds good to me. You drive, I'll buy."

"Sounds even better to me," she replied happily.

BIOHAZARD OUTBREAK

Chapter Six

IT WOULD BE about another month later when all would finally be revealed to David and Katherine. It was a warm Friday night in July, the weekend after Independence Day, following a long stressful week at work.

Earlier in the week, Dr. Fox had made an advanced version of his Fox Serum. It would be the final version David and Katherine would have the opportunity to work on with him. It came as a result of the tragic loss of their first four apes, after being injected with the previous version of the serum.

Dr. Fox tried to administer his experimental anti-serum, but it was too late. They were gone and would not be replaced.

This unfortunate setback caused David to become more hesitant than ever. He kept insisting the professor stop altering the serum, until they could properly figure out what was wrong with it. Dr. Fox got upset at David for trying to tell him how to do his job and rudely reminded him that he was *his* assistant and not the other way around.

Afterwards, Katherine had to calm David, so he would not punch the professor in the mouth. She couldn't believe how overheated things had gotten between them. One thing became clear. They definitely needed a break from each other. It was a good thing the weekend was upon them.

The best part of the week was that the female ape with cancer was still in remission, so there was hope she could be cured someday.

In order to recover from their stressful week, Katherine drove David to her apartment in Astoria for a weekend of relaxation. First, the couple stopped at the market to pick up a few groceries. Katherine had an intimate weekend planned for them and wanted to be sure they would have plenty of food to keep them satisfied.

Sometime later, after arriving at her apartment, David sat on the sofa in the living room. He turned on the television at Katherine's insistence, while she prepared dinner. Reluctantly, he flipped through the channels using the remote control and stopped when he came across a rerun episode of *The Walking Dead* on AMC. There was a marathon of episodes being shown over the weekend.

Right around the time when he began getting into the show, Katherine called out to him from the kitchen, "Dave, would you prefer it to be cheesy, meaty, or saucy?"

Her words left him feeling confused because, at that moment, he was watching a zombie, or a "walker," devour someone on the show. He chuckled and asked, "What exactly are we talking about here?"

"The lasagna, you nasty boy!"

"Oh," he laughed when he realized what she meant. He also found it humorous how she thought he meant something sexual by his question. He shouted back to her over the loudness of the television, "I guess you can make it meaty with a good mixture of cheese and lots of sauce!" He snickered and waited for her response.

She peeked out of the kitchen and leered at him.

He grinned back at her and shrugged, "Give me a break! I'm watching blood and gore here! The question threw me off!"

She looked at the television and cringed. Her suspicious expression quickly faded. It was replaced by a loving smile. She rushed over to him and kissed his lips. She then glanced back at the television and commented, "This show is creepy. I don't like seeing people eat other people. The special effects make it look too real for my sake."

"Baby, these are '*walkers*' eating other people," he corrected her. "That makes it okay!"

"You're silly," she snapped back, causing him to smile. She grabbed his face gently and said, "Damn, I love the way you smile!" She then kissed him, again.

He blushed instantly, as she pulled away slowly and skipped happily back to the kitchen to resume cooking, leaving him feeling aroused.

After dinner, David found his thoughts drifting back to Dr. Fox. In fact, he was having a hard time keeping work off his mind. He was still angry about what the professor said to him. Furthermore, his suspicions that Dr. Fox was experimenting in secret without their knowledge was still bothering him. He did not bring it up to Katherine, since he already knew her feelings on the matter. Instead, he dwelled on it in silence, subconsciously allowing it to distract him from time to time.

It was a tremendous relief when Katherine was done washing the dishes. He felt guilty that he was unable to help, but she practically chased him out of the kitchen when he offered. He found it funny how territorial she was when it came to her kitchen.

"Dinner was delicious," he told her. "Thank you."

"You're welcome, babe," she said. "Glad you enjoyed it. Are you ready for dessert?"

"Depends. Are you dessert?"

She walked toward him and sat on his lap. She smiled and wrapped her arms around him, before asking, "Is that what you want, lover boy? And here I thought you wanted Coconut Cream Pie? I guess I could toss that out and we could skip to the fun part of the evening."

He immediately changed his mood at the thought of her throwing out his favorite kind of pie. "Now, wait one second, Ms. Hines! You are flirting with danger! I don't see why I can't have both," he stated, in an attempt to reason with her. Surely, she was off her rocker, if she wanted to throw a perfectly good pie away, he thought.

She kissed him on the cheek casually and stood up, "If you say so. I will cut us a couple of slices, while you turn on the air conditioner in the bedroom. That way the room will be nice and cool by the time we are done with our pie."

"Oh, yeah! I keep forgetting you don't have central air conditioning," he teased.

Katherine called out from the kitchen, "Well, excuse me, Mr. Moneybags. It's not up to me. I didn't make the building this way."

"Yeah, yeah! Excuses, excuses! I'm sick and tired of excuses!" He said mocking Dr. Fox by repeating what he had told them a while back. "Bring me that pie, so I can devour it, and then you!"

She returned with two small plates of pie and responded, "You mean like a zombie?"

He growled back, "No! I mean like a *walker!*" He then pretended to bite her hand and she giggled, while squirming around in his arms.

They sat at the dining room table and ate their slices of pie in a hurry. The whole time, they kept looking at each other hungrily. Katherine licked her lips, which got David pretty excited. She could tell by the way, he gulped down the last bits of pie.

"Easy, tiger. You're going to choke on it," she warned with a laugh.

He laughed, too.

Suddenly, his cellphone vibrated in his pocket. He ignored it, as he finished up his pie. When Katherine took their plates to the kitchen, his phone vibrated, again. He sighed and took it out of his pocket. It was two messages from Dr. Fox.

The first one simply stated, "Call me." The second message read, "David. I am at the lab. Please, call me on the landline."

David thought about whether or not he cared enough to call when Katherine entered the room wearing only her bra and panties.

"Oops," she said playfully. "It seems that my clothes have fallen off in the kitchen." She then strutted past him and went into the bedroom. Before stepping in, she turned to him and asked, "You coming or are you just gonna sit there playing with your phone?"

His mouth gaped open, as he put his phone down on the table and forgot all about it. He stood up and followed her into the bedroom. They closed the door behind them and found their way into each other's arms. The next stop was the bed, where they made love.

It was almost dark by the time the couple emerged from Katherine's bedroom wearing only their underwear. They sat down on the living room sofa and stared out the nearest window, which faced north. In the distance the lights from the Robert F. Kennedy Bridge could be seen, although some stubborn New Yorkers still called it by its old name, the Triboro Bridge. Katherine was one of those people. David often teased her about it to get a rise out of her. It was all in fun.

He liked how they could play around with each other and not argue. That was one of the best things about being with someone who had a good sense of humor. They joked with each other a lot. He had even told her the corny blonde joke he knew and she laughed her ass off. She really was great, he thought. He found himself wondering how he ever got along without her in his life.

There were other girlfriends throughout his life, but he never felt the same about them, as he did with her. She was truly special. "One in a million," as the saying goes. She was the kind of girl you take home to meet the parents. She was marrying material.

True, it was too soon to be thinking about marriage. However, he could not help himself. He had to consider how serious their relationship had become. They had been dating for six months now. It was only natural to think about their future together. He already knew he wanted to spend the rest of his life with her. He just wanted to make sure she felt the same, before he even considered popping the question. The timing and the mood had to be just right. Everything had to be perfect.

Katherine interrupted his thoughts by saying softly, "It's such a lovely night. It's so perfect." She stood up and walked toward the window.

David was surprised by her choice of words. He cursed himself for not being ready. He still had not purchased an engagement ring. He figured it was too soon. He thought, maybe in another few months? Now, he was wondering if she was ready for the next step in their relationship. It sure seemed like it.

Katherine hid behind the curtains, as she peered out the window at the stars. After all, she was practically naked! "The stars are so bright and look, it's a full moon," she pointed. "It's just like the night, after we first met."

David stood up and moved directly behind her. If she moved back an inch, she'd surely bump into his rock hard erection. He tried to control his urges, but then he figured why should he? She wouldn't mind. He moved a bit closer and observed how clear the sky looked. He made note of how brightly visible the stars were, as well.

"Wow. There are so many," he said, as he pressed against her. She leaned against him letting him know she was okay with it. He smiled and gazed at the stars with her. He rarely took the time to truly appreciate their beauty, but whenever he did, it was always magical.

After a few moments, he turned his attention to Katherine. He kissed her gently on her neck and said, trying to sound as romantic as possible, "As beautiful as the stars might be tonight, they could never compare to your beauty."

She turned to face him and her grayish colored eyes lit up like lamps in the darkness. David felt his heart skip a beat at the sight of them. Katherine became overcome with romantic notions and hugged him tightly, as she replied, "Aw, that's so sweet, babe! Thank you! You always know the perfect things to say to me." She gazed at him lovingly and added, "You've made my night. This night cannot be anymore perfect."

At that moment, he really wished he had that ring available, so he could prove her wrong. Instead, he did the next best thing. He told her, "I love you, Katherine Hines." He then wrapped his arms around her waist.

"I love you, too, David Frino" she smiled back at him.

If ever there was a more perfect picture of love, it was the silhouette of this couple standing at the window with the full moon behind them in a star filled sky.

They kissed deeply, completely forgetting they were standing in front of the window in their underwear. It was a good thing Katherine lived on the fifth floor. It was less likely that anyone from the outside would take notice. They held each other close for what seemed like an eternity.

Yet, it was hardly enough time, considering what would happen in the next few hours. Their lives were about to change forever.

After making love, again, the couple remained laying on the living room sofa. Katherine was quite comfortable in David's arms and he was not about to move.

It was around that time when his cellphone began vibrating repeatedly on the dining room table. He sighed when he realized it was a phone call because it would not stop. It went to voice mail, at some point, but then it began vibrating, again. Whoever was calling would not be satisfied, until he answered. He suddenly remembered the messages he received earlier from the professor.

"You should probably answer it," Katherine mumbled in a sleepy voice. Her eyes were still closed when she spoke. "It might be important. Well, it better be, considering the time."

"True," he agreed. He stood up carefully, as she shifted off of him and remained on the sofa with her eyes closed. She looked about ready for bedtime. "I'm sorry," he said to her, and then he walked over to the dining room table to answer the call. He was annoyed to see it was indeed the professor calling from the laboratory phone.

"Hello?"

"David! At last! Thank God! I've been trying to reach you all evening!"

"I was busy. What's the problem, Doc?"

Katherine opened her eyes and sat up, once she realized who was on the phone.

Dr. Fox responded in an anxious voice, "David, you were right! I messed up. Please, you must come to the lab! It's an emergency!" He spoke so loudly that Katherine could hear what he was saying.

"What's he going on about?" She asked.

David shrugged at her and replied, "Are you nuts? I'm not going to the lab, now! I'm in Queens and I don't drive. Whatever it is will have to wait until Monday."

The professor paused, "I see. You are with Katherine. I am sorry, David, but I really need your help." He sounded more desperate, as he tried, again, to convince David to come to his aid, "You do not understand. Something has gone terribly wrong! I... I cannot explain it over the phone. You need to come quickly!"

There was someone yelling in the background. It could have been one of the apes, but it sounded more like a man or maybe it was more than one. It was difficult to tell over the phone.

"What the hell was that? Was that an ape?" David asked. "I'm not going there, until you tell me exactly what you did. What are we dealing with here? Who's there with you?"

"Okay, fine! I'm afraid I have done something I should not have done and, now, they are having a violent reaction. There are too many for me to control on my own. I... I need your help, David! Please!"

At this point, Katherine had moved nearer to David. She wanted to know what was going on, too.

David looked furious when he demanded, "They? What do you mean *they?* Please, tell me you are referring to the chimps."

Dr. Fox answered with regret in his voice, "Actually, no. I mean my human subjects."

"Human??? Are you kidding me???"

Katherine's eyes opened wide. Her heart began pounding rapidly. She wanted to ask what was wrong, but she had a feeling she already knew. David had been correct all along. Still, she kept whispering to him and asking what he heard over the phone, but he did not answer her.

"What's going on, David? What did you hear? Is he...?" She did not finish her question because David had begun speaking, again.

"How many humans, Doc?" His question was met with silence on the other end of the line. Frustrated, he asked, again, "Damn it! How many???"

"Ten," Dr. Fox responded shamefully.

Now, it was David's eyes that opened wide, as he responded in shock, "TEN??? Are you insane?"

Dr. Fox tried to explain, "You must believe me! They all volunteered! They're homeless! Bums with nothing to lose! They each had mental issues and some form of cancer. They were eager to be cured, in exchange for a few measly dollars. I was only trying to help them." He paused momentarily and added coldly, "Besides, I figured, if anything went wrong, no one would miss them. They are already dead, as far as the rest of the world is concerned. Surely, you must understand. I did it in the name of science and medicine!"

David shook his head negatively, even though the professor could not see him, "No, I must not understand! That does not make it any better! They are people, for Christ's sake! What the hell is wrong with you, Doc? Damn it! Don't you realize you're going to get us all fired, or worse? I don't plan on going to jail for your screw ups!"

"Please, David," the professor pleaded. "That's why I need your help! No one must ever know about this. Not even Katherine. You are the only one I can truly trust."

David rolled his eyes angrily and snapped back, "Yeah, well! It's too late for that! Kat is right next to me! She already heard part of the conversation and I don't plan on keeping this a secret from her like you did to both of us! If you want my help, she is going to know everything that I find out or else you are on your own!"

Dr. Fox hesitated for a split second, and then agreed, "Fine, bring her with you, if you must. Please, understand, I was keeping this from you both for your own good. I did not want to involve you."

"Then why the hell are you calling me, now?"

"Because, David. I am frightened," Dr. Fox replied desperately. "I don't know what else to do. I tried to administer the anti-serum, but they attacked me. They have become quite volatile. They keep screaming like mad men! I had to leave the room. Now, I don't know what to do. Please! Help me, David! You are my only hope!"

There was a good *Star Wars* reference wasted there, David thought. He spoke more calmly, when he answered, "Okay. Relax. Take a deep breath. Now, tell me. Where are they, at this very moment?"

Dr. Fox complied and took a deep breath, before answering, "They are in the dormitory."

David sighed and shook his head, "Damn it! I knew it! I knew you were up to something. Oh, man. I cannot believe this shit. Why didn't I just check the dorm when I had the chance?"

Dr. Fox ignored the rhetorical question and pleaded his case, once more, "David, will you help me? I am begging you. Time is running out."

David looked to Katherine, who was standing close and listening. She looked worried, but then nodded adamantly. He sighed heavily and answered with reluctance, "Yeah, sure. What did you do with the anti-serum? Is it still in the dorm with them?"

"Yes," replied the professor. "It was in a syringe, but I accidentally dropped it. I believe it rolled under one of the cots on the right side of the room."

"Damn," David replied. He sighed, again, in annoyance and instructed, "Never mind that. We'll think of something, later. We'll be over, as soon as we can. It may take a while. Stay away from the dorm. Okay? Lock yourself in the biohazard lab's prep room."

Dr. Fox breathed a sigh of relief and replied, "Oh, thank you, David! That is a fine idea. I am sorry I kept this from you. I was wrong to do so. You are a lifesaver. And thank Katherine for me, as well."

"Right. Whatever. Did you hear what I said? Stay away from the dorm," David warned a second time, but Dr. Fox had already hung up.

The Greene Science Center on Broadway

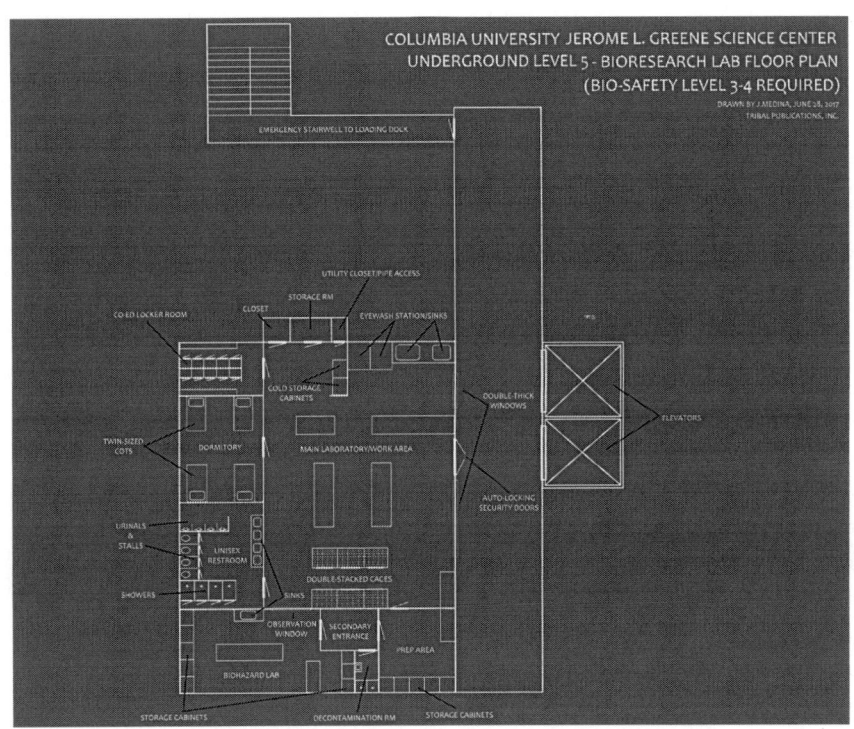

The Science Center's Underground Level 5 Floor Plan.

BIOHAZARD OUTBREAK

Chapter Seven

WITHIN MINUTES, DAVID and Katherine showered and got dressed. They rushed out the door and down to Katherine's car. It was parked around the corner from her building. They promptly got in and she started it up.

"I can't believe this guy," David said, half to himself, while shaking his head in disbelief. "I mean I had a feeling he would do this, but I kept telling myself he had more sense than that. I didn't really want to believe it. You know?"

"I know, babe. You were right," Katherine reassured him. "I should have listened to you. You kept saying it and I didn't believe you. I'm sorry."

David shook his head, "No, don't do that. It's not your fault and it's not mine. It's his. He did this alone. He is such a damn idiot! Let's just get there."

Katherine nodded and her car pulled away from its parking spot. They headed toward the Robert F. Kennedy Bridge, which would take them into Manhattan. On the bridge, they raced around heavy traffic as carefully as possible. There were a lot of cars going toward the city, most likely people heading to the nightclubs and bars. It was Friday night, so it was to be expected.

"Don't get us killed getting there, Kat. He brought this upon himself. We'll get there when we get there," David told her. He was still angry with the professor, but he felt whatever mischief Dr. Fox caused was no reason for them to get into an accident. It could wait for them to arrive safely.

"I'm sorry," she said. "I'll try to be more careful. It's just crazy how there seems to be more traffic heading into the city ever since they removed the toll plazas."

Once in Manhattan, they traveled west along 126th Street, passing by the 26th Police Precinct, where David's cousin, Edward, and his best friend, Marc, worked. He wondered if they were on duty, but then looked at the time and realized it was still too early. They worked the midnight shift and it was only about a quarter to 10 pm.

When they reached the Science Center on Broadway Katherine parked in one of the spaces under the elevated train tracks. It was closer than going to the parking structure. As they entered the building, they did not notice if the security guard was around. They ran straight to the elevator and pressed the button repeatedly.

They looked around nervously, as they waited impatiently for it to arrive. Katherine fidgeted anxiously. David wished he didn't have to bring her, but it was too late to think about that. The elevator could not come fast enough.

When it arrived, they stepped inside and turned to face the doors. David inserted his key, turned it, and the doors closed. He tapped his foot nervously. He wasn't quite sure what to expect when they reached the laboratory. He hoped the professor listened to him and locked himself in the biohazard lab's prep room. The door to that room was extra thick.

Mere seconds later, the elevator doors opened onto a dimly lit hallway. For some reason, the lights in the main laboratory were off. That much was apparent through the two large windows. The whole floor was dark, just like it was on that night when David snuck inside the lab. Only the lights over the elevator and emergency stairwell were lit. It was enough for David and Katherine to feel alarmed. Why would the professor leave the lights off, if he were expecting them? It didn't make sense.

At this point, David did not care about the security cameras anymore. He was not planning to walk around in the dark with his girlfriend, while there were ten potentially dangerous homeless men in the next room. He unlocked and opened the doors to the laboratory and flicked on the lights. Katherine stayed close behind him, as they cautiously stepped inside.

The laboratory appeared relatively peaceful. They walked toward the entrance to the biohazard lab. David opened the door. The lights inside were off, so he turned them on. It was empty. Dr. Fox did not do as he suggested, but why?

Katherine whispered, "Where do you think he could be? Do you think he would be foolish enough to go back into the dorm?"

David whispered back, "I hope not. He said he left those homeless men in there. Maybe he's hiding in one of the closets waiting for us to arrive, or he could be in the locker room or restroom."

Katherine tugged at the back of his shirt to hold him from walking forward and suggested, "Maybe we should wait for him to come to us. He has to notice that we are here by now. He should have heard the doors open and seen that we turned on the lights."

David stopped in his tracks and agreed, "Yeah, you're right. Let's hang back here by the entrance, so we could leave in a hurry, if need be." He then called out, "Dr. Fox?"

They waited for about two minutes and nothing happened. The laboratory was still quiet, aside from one or two apes in their cages making whimpering noises. David and Katherine carefully navigated around the tables on their way across to the other side of the laboratory. They figured if Dr. Fox were there, he had to be hiding in one of the closets on the opposite end. The main laboratory was clearly empty with exception to the apes. Most of them seemed to be asleep, for the time being. The cages were covered with white cloths, so they could not be seen without physically checking under the cloths.

David opened the door to the closet. It was empty. He checked the small supply room next to it and it was also empty. The utility closet was located in a corner of the room, just past the other two doors that he checked. There was no one in there either.

Katherine looked at David and asked, "Well, now what?"

He stared past her toward the locker room, which was now behind her. He pointed, "There. Let's check the locker room. Stay close to me."

"You better believe I will," she assured him, as she turned around to follow him.

The couple moved stealthily toward the locker room door. David put his hand on the doorknob and swallowed hard. He half hoped the room would be empty out of fear. The suspense was becoming too intense for him. His heart was pounding hard. He took a deep breath and turned the doorknob. The door opened. The lights were off inside. He turned them on instantly and prepared to slam the door shut, but the room also appeared to be empty. He sighed a breath of relief.

"It looks empty," he said, before going inside to make sure by checking both sides of the room, which was divided in half by a wall to allow privacy for both sexes. When he was satisfied he whispered, "Come on." He led Katherine into the room and said, "Wait for me here. We are running out of rooms."

She looked at him defiantly, "No! I'm staying with you!"

"Kat, please. Wait for me in here," he insisted. "I'll feel a lot better, if I know you are safe. Get inside and lock the door."

She sighed and did as he said.

With her safely hidden away in the locker room, he felt he could better focus on finding the professor. He deliberately walked past the dormitory and over to the door of the restroom. He had a feeling it would be empty. He opened the door and turned on the light. He was right. No one was inside.

That left only one room to check, the dormitory. He knew there had to be someone within that room. At least, ten people, to be exact. He began to wonder if the professor left the level and went to wait outside and, somehow, they missed him. Maybe he used the stairs? Of course, that was it!

He walked over to the landline, which was on the professor's desk and called his cellphone. At that moment, David could hear a phone ringing behind him on the floor near the entrance to the dormitory. He turned around and knew it had to be the professor's cellphone. It vibrated on the floor, as it rang.

Katherine opened the door to the locker room when she heard the ringing. She peeked out to see why there was a phone ringing, since she knew David's phone was on silent mode. He noticed her peeking and waved at her to go back into the locker room, which she did reluctantly.

He then walked over, bent down, and picked up the professor's cellphone to check it. It barely had a signal, but it was enough for it to ring. The screen was cracked, as if it had fallen on the floor.

"Hmm. That's not good," he muttered quietly to himself.

He faced the door to the dormitory, again. There was only one thing left for him to do. He closed his eyes and took a deep breath. When he opened his eyes, he placed his hand on the doorknob, and turned it slowly. There would be no turning back. The door opened.

David opened his eyes and tried to get his bearings. He realized he was lying on the floor of the main laboratory. His head hurt for some reason. Some of the lights had been broken in the main laboratory leaving the room dimly lit. One light kept blinking erratically. There was a lot of crashing and smashing around him. Some glass from the lights and light bulbs had fallen to the floor around him. It was a good thing that most of the laboratory equipment that would normally be made of glass was made of plastic. Otherwise, there would be broken glass all over the place. As a safety precaution against possible viral outbreaks, laboratories like this one had to use plastic, instead of glass.

Nearby, the apes were going apeshit in their cages. Both men and apes were yelling and screaming. It also sounded like they were fighting.

David wondered what the hell could have happened. Did he somehow black out or was he knocked down? Why wasn't he dead, unless no one noticed him because he was behind the door? He did sort of use it to hide behind when he opened the door. The force of the homeless men pushing it must have knocked him down causing him to hit his head and pass out. Afterwards, they probably started destroying the laboratory.

David tried to stand up, but felt a little dizzy. The screaming sounded uncomfortably close, so he dropped back to the floor and stayed down. He began crawling across the floor and hastily made his way toward the locker room. It sounded as if the homeless men were banging on the cages to get at the apes, which kept most of them preoccupied. It was hard to be sure without looking, but he tried to avoid being seen or heard, as he moved quickly over the floor. He had to reach Katherine. That was all that mattered now.

Just then, a metal beaker support stand fell on the floor in front of him and he panicked. Did someone see him? He froze instantly out of fear. After no one attacked him, he realized he had not been seen, yet. He continued crawling on his hands and knees toward the locker room door, while trying not to crawl over broken glass from the lights. The blinking light nearby affected his vision and made it hard to focus.

"Ouch! Shit!" He whispered, as a shard of broken glass made its way into the palm of his right hand. It was a good thing he was left-handed. He carefully pulled it out and winced from the pain. He was bleeding, but it wasn't too bad.

He began to wonder where the professor could be in this mess. Was he still alive? Was he injured? The answer to those questions would have to wait, until he reached Katherine.

Distracted by his thoughts, he crawled over another piece of glass that stuck him in the knee. He cursed silently at his carelessness. When he was ready, he pulled out his leather wallet from the back pocket of his pants and wiped it across the floor to brush aside any other shards of glass. In doing so, he made some noise and also caught another piece of glass with his elbow. He suddenly wished he were wearing thick gloves and a long sleeve coat.

"Damn it!"

One of the homeless people noticed the noise coming from where David was hiding and headed in that direction. When David saw him approaching, he panicked. He knew he had to move swiftly or he would be an easy target on the floor, which meant no more crawling around. It was time to act fast.

He stood up and raced toward the main entrance of the laboratory. One of the deranged homeless men was closer than he thought. The man grabbed for him, but David was quick. He leapt over a table and knocked a chair down on the floor behind him. The homeless man reached over the table to grab him, but missed. A second homeless man ran around the table, but tripped over the chair on the floor.

David had just enough time to scan the laboratory and see what was going on. It was complete madness. Much of the laboratory equipment was completely destroyed. Boxes of files had been tossed on the floor and their contents scattered. The primates' cages were no longer covered and neatly stacked. They were knocked over on the floor and scattered around that side of the room. Some had been ripped open and there was blood everywhere. One ape was hanging in the corner of the room from the security camera for dear life. The camera was barely connected by cables and looked like it was about to break from the weight of the ape. Three other apes were in a corner beating a homeless man to death. He was already a bloody pulp and likely dead.

The other homeless men all turned their attention toward David. It was as if it were happening in slow motion. All of a sudden, time sped up, as they all screamed and charged at him. He raced for the exit, left the laboratory, and pushed the doors closed behind him. They locked automatically and just in time, as the homeless men rammed into them. They pounded savagely against the doors, although David could not hear them anymore.

He ran to the elevators and pressed the button desperately. He would have to go for help. There was no way he could get to Katherine. Once he reached the ground floor, he could text her and let her know to remain in the locker room and keep quiet at all costs. If they had no idea she was there, they would not try to reach her. She just had to stay hidden.

Before the elevator arrived, he realized there was a small flaw in his plan. There was practically no signal down on this level. She might never get his message.

Suddenly, he could see the locker room door open through one of the windows in the hallway. He shouted in terror, "NO!!!"

Of course, his screams were wasted, since she could not hear him through the thick walls and glass. Katherine barely had time to peek out before being noticed. She screamed and the three closest homeless men rushed toward her. She struggled desperately to pull the door shut, but they were starting to overpower her and force themselves into the room. A few other homeless men began moving in that direction. Within seconds, they would be inside with her.

David moved faster than he ever moved in his life. He grabbed the fire extinguisher from the wall just as the elevator arrived. He opened the double doors to the laboratory and as soon as he did, several of the homeless men charged at him, but he was ready. He unloaded the contents of the fire extinguisher into their faces, as a white cloud temporarily filled the hallway. The crazed men blindly charged forward stumbling clumsily into the elevator.

If David had not been terrified, he might have laughed at the scene. Instead, he carefully reached inside, after them, and pushed the button for the second floor. It was the first button he could get his finger on. The elevator doors immediately closed and took them up and away from the laboratory.

With some of the threat eliminated, David charged bravely into the main laboratory with the empty fire extinguisher in his hand ready to wield it as a weapon. Another homeless man charged at him. David noticed the door to the biohazard lab prep room was still open. He stood in front of the doorway to lure the homeless man in that direction.

When the man got close enough, David sidestepped and swung the fire extinguisher hitting the man in the back of the head. The man went down tumbling into the biohazard lab prep room. David shut the door and locked him inside.

He turned to the locker room and a feeling of dread came over him when he saw the door was wide open. He ran straight for it. As he entered, his heart was racing and practically pounding its way through his chest. He could hear Katherine screaming and struggling just around the dividing wall.

He soon came face to face with one of the homeless men. Without a second thought, David struck him on his head as hard as he could with the fire extinguisher. The man dropped to the floor and began convulsing.

Katherine was on the floor still fighting with one man, who was looming over her. David bashed him across the face with all his might, once again, using the fire extinguisher. That man went reeling back into the lockers and hit the floor.

The fight appeared to be over, for now. David looked at Katherine, who was covered in blood. She was breathing heavily, but seemed okay, for the most part. She had been fighting them off with a broken broomstick handle.

David helped her to her feet and they embraced.

A moment later, he pulled away from her to check her wounds. She appeared to have bite marks and scratches on her arms. Her wounds were bleeding. Concerned, he asked, "How do you feel?"

She trembled frantically with tears in her eyes, "Those psychos were biting me! It's like they were trying to eat me alive!" She looked around behind him and noticed the professor was nowhere to be seen. "Where's Dr. Fox?"

David shook his head negatively, "I don't know." He took a moment to catch his breath. He was obviously exhausted, but he knew there was no time to rest. Not yet. "Come on. Let's get out of this room, in case these guys get up."

"Hit them, again," she cried.

"Kat! That would be murder. These guys are not themselves. I'm sorry. I can't. Let's just get the hell out of here. We'll lock them in here and go for help."

He pulled her by the hand and escorted her out of the locker room, before closing and locking the door behind them. At that moment, he noticed the door to the dormitory was slightly ajar. It was possible Dr. Fox could be inside. If he were injured, he would need their help. They could not simply abandon him.

"Wait. I never got to see if Dr. Fox was in the dorm," he said. "We should check."

She nodded nervously, "Okay."

David cautiously stuck his head into the dormitory. The light was on inside. Ten chairs were crammed into the squared room between the four cots. Some were knocked over. So was a plastic trolley cart. One of the apes was hiding in the corner of the room, behind a cot. It was the female with cancer. She looked absolutely terrified. A body lay on the cot closest to the door covered in blood. It was Dr. Fox!

They both rushed over to his side.

Katherine covered her mouth in horror when she noticed all the bite marks on him, "Oh, my God! Look at his arms and face! There are so many bruises. Are those all bite marks, too? What the hell is wrong with those men? Why were they trying to eat us?"

"Doc! Can you hear me?" David called out, as he tried to shake the professor awake.

Dr. Fox slowly moved his blood covered hands upward and gradually opened his eyes. He looked like he was trying to speak, but nothing was coming out. His hands began making grabbing motions, as if he were desperately clinging to life.

Katherine cried out with hope in her voice, "He's alive!"

David was relieved. He tried to help the professor to his feet, but he felt like dead weight. "Ugh! He's heavier than he looks! Help me with him. We can't leave him here," he told her. She did so and grabbed the professor by his other arm. Together they helped him out of bed and onto his feet.

Without a word, Dr. Fox turned to Katherine and began biting into her cheek hard. She lashed out pushing the professor away and let out such a high-pitched shriek that it almost gave David a heart attack, "Arrggghhhh!!!"

The ape in the corner of the room ran out screaming and hooting into the laboratory.

David instinctively let go of the professor, but Dr. Fox did not fall to the floor, as expected. He remained standing on his own, although rather wobbly. It didn't look normal. He had a strange lifeless look in his eyes and his pupils were severely dilated. Even his skin looked a bit yellow. It was unlike anything David had ever seen, aside from in movies or on television.

Meanwhile, Katherine stood against the wall holding her face and was crying from the pain. "I can't believe he bit me!" She exclaimed in complete shock. "Why the hell is everyone trying to eat me???"

"Kat, slowly move around him and come toward me," David instructed in a calm voice. "We need to get out of here... *now*. Don't make any sudden moves." He wasn't exactly sure what was going on, but he did not wish to agitate Dr. Fox into attacking, again.

Katherine did as David instructed and they both left the dormitory. David shut the door, locking Dr. Fox inside, along with the anti-serum, which he never got a chance to pick up from the floor. He wasn't even sure which cot it would be under. He turned to Katherine and checked her facial wound. It was worse than her other wounds and was bleeding profusely.

He opened a cabinet under one of the tables and pulled out a first aid kit. He picked up the chair he had knocked over earlier and said, "Sit down here." She did so, and then David told her to hold the wound and apply pressure, which she also did. "We need to stop the bleeding. Give me a second," he said, as he looked through the first aid kit.

She cried from the pain and began to look dizzy. She muttered weakly, "It hurts so bad." It looked like she was having a hard time keeping her eyes open.

"Stay with me, Kat," he said firmly, as he shook her abruptly. "If you pass out, it's going to be a lot harder for me to carry you out of here."

"I... I'm trying... Feel so weak. It itches. Why's it... itch so much, allova sudden?"

"Don't scratch it," he advised her. "That will probably make it worse."

"O-kay," she replied almost in a whisper. She blinked her eyes repeatedly and said, "I feel weird. My eyesight's gettin' blurry... and my chest hurts. Actually, my whole body aches. Oh, man. I think I'm gonna hurl."

"Not in my direction, please," he commented with haste. "Hold still. Let me clean your wounds. Take your hand off your face." When she did blood spurted out at his face. He wiped it away unbothered and began cleaning her wounds with alcohol wipes, as best as he could.

"Jeez, David! That burns! What *is* that? Holy water?"

"Sorry, babe. It's an alcohol wipe. See?" He showed her. "You're not possessed, but you do have something in you, an infection of some kind. Hopefully, it's nothing too serious. Regardless, I need to clean your wounds. You're definitely going to need a tetanus shot and stitches," he told her. He knew that would have to wait. He placed some gauze on her cheek and taped it tightly in place. Her arms weren't too bad. He placed a few band-aids on those wounds and asked, "Can you walk?"

She blinked her eyes, again, in an attempt to clear her vision. She rubbed them with her blood-covered hands when that didn't work, smearing blood all over her face.

David rolled his eyes, "Oh, Kat! You just wiped blood all over your face, again. Here, let me wipe it off." He cleaned her face a second time and noticed she was looking very pale. He knew he had to get her to a hospital fast. Whatever she had might be fatal, if not cured in a timely manner. He didn't dare mention that to her, though. "Okay, we need to go. Now," he stated firmly. "Come on, stand up."

She nodded faintly, and then threw up on the floor. She tried not to get any on his shoes, although some splashed on her own.

He expected that to happen, sooner or later. It was for the best. She had to get this infection out of her system. He waited patiently, until she was done and asked, "Did that help?"

She shook her head feebly. "Gimme a minute," she said sounding agitated, "Just need a minute."

"Okay, Kat" he replied. He felt bad for her and hoped she'd be able to recover from whatever this sickness was that had a hold on her. He felt angry that he dragged her into this mess with him. He should have come alone.

While he waited for her to gather her strength, he glanced around to see where the apes had gone. They seemed to be hiding. At least two had been killed in their cages. He became distracted by a banging sound coming from the locker room. The door kept shifting forward from the pressure. One of the homeless men within was yelling incoherently and trying desperately to get out. David wanted to be gone before that happened.

On the other hand, he was relieved the man was still alive. It meant he could be saved later. David did not wish to explain how he needed to murder someone in self-defense.

He wondered what could have gone wrong. How could a serum that was meant to cure them have such a disastrous effect? More importantly, why were they trying to eat their victims? They were behaving like crazed cannibals.

And then David realized it was just as he feared. It was the serum's overly aggressive qualities. It had an insatiable hunger. That had to be the cause. It was the only explanation that made sense.

"Damn you, Herbert," he mumbled to himself.

He tried not to think about it. Katherine motioned to him that she was ready to go. She was all that mattered now. He helped her walk out of the laboratory, allowing the doors to shut and lock on their own. The two stopped in front of the elevator bank.

Before he pressed the call button, he remembered something. "Oh, no," he stated. "I lured a bunch of those men into the elevator to get rid of them. What if they're still inside?"

Katherine turned her head to face him and stared curiously in his direction, but could not really see him anymore. She strained her eyes, which had become bloodshot and watery.

David stared into her once beautiful eyes and felt so helpless. He wanted to help her so badly, but there was nothing he could think to do. She tried to say something, but fainted. As she dropped, he rushed to catch her, preventing her from falling hard. He gently laid her on the floor of the hallway and knelt down beside her. He placed his hand on her forehead to check for fever. As he suspected, she was burning up. He became distraught.

"What did they do to you? Kat! Come on, baby! We need to get out of here and I can't carry you!" He tried to calm himself, so he could focus on getting them outside. "You have to get up, baby," he said tenderly. "I'll help you. Okay?" He gently slapped her healthy cheek to wake her.

She appeared to be coming to.

"Oh, thank God! Kat, can you hear me?"

She nodded weakly and her eyes were still closed. She coughed up some blood, which hit David right in the face. He used his shirt to wipe his face clean. That was the second time she got him.

A thought occurred to him. If he could get the anti-serum, he could inject her and maybe make her better. He only had to worry about getting around Dr. Fox. He could do that with his eyes closed.

He stood up and peered into one of the windows of the laboratory. He had to do this... for her. Before he could unlock the doors, he watched in horror as the locker room door burst open from the inside out. One of the homeless men inside rushed out into the lab. It was the one David sent flying into the lockers when he hit him. He began to think he should have hit him, again, as Katherine suggested.

It was going to be a lot harder to avoid that man and he did not look happy.

The man noticed David staring into the window and ran toward him. The man pounded his hands and face savagely against the thick glass to no avail. Blood splattered all over the place, but there was no way he'd be able to break it with his bare hands, or his head. It was too thick. Fortunately, the lab door was locked, so he wasn't getting out that way either. Of course, it meant David would not be able to get the anti-serum, as planned. The thought frustrated him to no end.

Katherine began moaning behind him, so he turned his attention back to her. All of a sudden, her eyes shot wide open and she began screaming in agony. Her body twisted and jerked around violently on the floor. Startled by her abrupt movement, David jumped back and moved away from her. When he realized she was in pain, he moved closer to her and tried to comfort her.

"What is it? Kat! What's wrong? Talk to me, baby!" He shouted almost in one breath.

For some reason, she did not or could not respond to him. Instead, she only screamed savagely and twisted out of control. She panted heavily, as her body kept jerking from side to side. The cheek, where she was bitten, had become swollen. It looked like the skin under the gauze pad was blackening because the rest of that side of her face was black and blue.

David didn't know what to do, as he looked on frantically. He kept yelling, "Kat! Kat! Kat!" It was no use. He could not get through to her.

Finally, she stopped moving around and her body momentarily became limp. Seconds later, her eyes became wild like a girl possessed by a demon. She sat up unexpectedly, turned her gaze upon David, and glared at him hungrily. Her arms and legs began to twitch.

He was kneeling on the floor no less than two feet from her. His heart began beating fast, as he became terrified. He opened his mouth to speak, but all that came out was her name, "Kat?" His voice trembled with fear.

In that instant, she lunged at him and gripped his right arm tightly. He promptly yanked it away, causing her to scratch him tearing his skin. He grabbed at his arm instinctively and stumbled back, as he tried to stand. She rushed across the floor at him on her knees, until he got too far for her to reach. She then forced herself to her feet angrily and charged at him. He dodged her and shoved her into the doors of the lab. She fell to the floor and screamed in frustration.

David didn't want to hurt her or leave her, but it was either that or she was going to kill him. He turned and ran for the emergency stairwell down the hall, disregarding the elevators. There was no time to wait for them and he still wasn't sure if one, in particular, would be empty or filled with very angry homeless men. He prayed no one would be in the stairwell waiting for him.

Katherine leapt to her feet and chased after him screaming like a banshee.

He raced up the stairs to the loading dock and pushed the door open with such force, he thought he broke something. Katherine was only seconds behind him. She slammed the door open, before it had a chance to close completely.

David fled up the entrance ramp and out onto the street. He ran around the building with his crazed girlfriend right on his heels. She definitely was not herself. It didn't take him long to realize this madness that resulted from the Fox Serum must be contagious. His worst fears were coming true.

The nightshift security guard named Ivan was standing just inside the main entrance when he saw David running past him. He seemed surprised to see Katherine running after him. Curious, he asked, "Hey! What's going on? Is everything all right? What are you guys running from?"

David shouted, as he ran past, "Run, Ivan! Just run! Don't let her get you!"

Ivan's eyes followed David toward West 125th Street. He still had not processed what David shouted. When he turned his attention to Katherine, it was too late. She brutally knocked him backward into the lobby, held him down, and began gnawing on his face.

The fall alone left him hurting, which made it harder to stop Katherine's furious onslaught.

David looked back long enough to see it happen. He cringed when he heard Ivan screaming in terror. His heart broke and tears rolled down his cheeks, as he turned his back on his girlfriend and poor Ivan. He continued forward, until he reached West 125th Street and noticed a yellow taxi stopped at the red light facing eastbound at Broadway.

He yanked opened the back door, got in, and shouted, "Drive! Someone's chasing me and they want to kill me!"

The taxi driver, a born and bred New Yorker, didn't think twice or question David's odd request. He merely activated the meter, turned right at the red light, and began driving south on Broadway.

The taxi driver was an older Caucasian man with light brown hair and a beard. He looked as if he'd been driving taxis for many years. He looked into his rear view mirror and glanced at David, who was sweating and panting heavily. The driver studied his passenger for a short time and said rather calmly in his gruff voice, "It's okay. I can easily pretend I thought it was all right for me to turn right at the red light, even though I know it's not allowed in the city. It's funny how you can turn right on red everywhere else, but not in New York City, huh?" He paused, but David said nothing, so he continued, "So, what's wrong? Who's tryin' to kill you? Your ex-girlfriend's new boyfriend?" Before David could respond, he asked, "Hey, do you want me to drive you to the 26th Precinct? It's not far from here. No offense, buddy, but I'd rather not get dragged into your affairs. I got my own problems. You know?"

"Yeah. Sure. I mean, no!!! DON'T DO THAT! Drive me home, mister. Please, I need time to think. Take me to 244 Riverside Drive."

The driver nodded and complied, "Yeah, okay. You got it. Heh! These summer weekends can be crazy, huh?"

David did not answer. He was still in shock about Katherine. He kept telling himself there was a way to fix everything. He desperately thought of how he could handle this situation, which had gotten way out of control. It really bothered him that he missed his opportunity to save her with the anti-serum. If only he'd thought of it sooner. There was plenty of time to get it. He failed her miserably.

Not to mention, he knew once everything boiled over, he was going to have to answer some serious questions. He needed to think of some believable answers, which wasn't going to be easy, considering the facts.

More importantly, what if there was no way to cure Katherine? The thought left a lump in his throat. What happened to her must have been a side effect caused by the Fox Serum that had been injected into the homeless men. Over the past few months, they had spent so much time experimenting with viruses, diseases, different forms of bacteria, and parasites. Could they have inadvertently created vectors for the serum? It certainly acted more like a virus with the way it was spreading to others, like Katherine and Dr. Fox.

Come to think of it, Dr Fox really looked terrible. His injuries appeared to be far more severe than Katherine's. The homeless men had actually taken large chunks out of his body. They were acting like zombies, despite their very lively appearances. It was the same with Katherine how she chased after him and attacked Ivan.

However, Dr. Fox was different. He moved slower and did not act crazy like the others, although he did bite Katherine on the face. Why didn't he yell and scream like the others? Why was this infection affecting him differently? He moved about as if he were drunk. And that empty look in his eyes... It was too creepy. If anything, he was more like a zombie.

For a split second, David wondered, was he?

No, that's silly, he told himself.

And what of poor Ivan? What would become of him? Would he run around screaming like a mad man, while attacking people, or would he end up more like Dr. Fox? Maybe it depended on the extent of his injuries. One thing was certain. Katherine was not going to stop with him. She was still out there and so were those six other homeless guys that ran into the elevator. They could be lurking in the building or worse. They could be out on the streets causing mayhem like Katherine.

David knew that was his fault. He led her out of the laboratory. If those six homeless men attacked anyone, that was on him, too, for leading them into the elevator. He should have made sure to send them to another underground level. Instead, he pressed the first button he felt. Who knew where they ended up?

Things were getting so far out of control. This thing was definitely contagious and that was a big problem that could not be ignored. A lot more people could become infected before the night was over. This could easily lead to a pandemic. David knew he had to do something about it. He was the only one, who knew the danger being faced by everyone.

There was one card he could play. It was the most logical option. He had to warn his cousin and their buddy, Marc. The police could handle this situation. They had the manpower to do whatever had to be done.

He pulled out his cellphone and sent a text message to Edward and Marc urging them to both call him, as soon as possible. He didn't provide too many details. Maybe if he explained the whole thing to them over the phone, they would be able to walk him through a safe solution. No matter what happened to him later, he would never forgive himself, if he did not warn them.

Just then, he remembered his personal journal. He had been keeping a detailed daily journal, since he first began working at the Science Center two years earlier. In it he documented everything down to the smallest detail, including his suspicions of Dr. Fox. He could update it when he got home and explain the chaotic events of tonight. It would help him to later put it into words that made sense. If he wrote down every detail, he'd have something to show in his defense when the time came.

Katherine's face came to mind, again. Everything happened so fast. He hoped she was not lost to him forever. There had to be a way to cure her with the anti-serum. He did not want to accept that she was incurable. He couldn't give up on her. Hopefully, the police would find her when they rounded everyone up. David could tell them about the anti-serum. They'd have to listen and administer it. It was the only way to cure this thing and set things right.

His phone vibrated. It was Ed responding to his message. He was already at work and in the locker room changing into his uniform. He said he'd call him afterward. Good. David would, at least, be able to explain everything to him.

He thought about what might happen in the meantime when Katherine and those homeless men encounter other people. He hated feeling helpless, but all he could do now was wait. He shook his head in despair and sighed. It was in God's hands for now.

David hadn't realized it, yet, but Day One of the Zombie Apocalypse had begun.

David Frino's text messages sent to his cousin, Edward Frino, and best friend, Marc Nugent:

Message sent by David to Edward and Marc –

"SORRY IF I ABBREVIATE. I NEED TO MAKE THIS FAST. R ANY OF U WORKING TONIGHT? PLEASE CALL ME ASAP!!! SOMETHING CRAZY HAPPENED AT JOB! LITERALLY SCARED SHITLESS! NEED ADVICE! MATTER OF LIFE N DEATH!!! CALL ME PRIOR TO GOING ON PATROL! NO JOKE!!!"

[*Message sent at 2230 hours*]

Reply from Edward –

"Yep, we're both working tonight. I hope everything's ok. I'm sure it's not that serious. No offense, but you worry too much, cuz. I'll call after rollcall. In the locker room now and reception sucks down here! LOL."

[*Message sent at 2235 hours*]

Reply from Marc –

"Dude! Sounds serious with all those caps, but it's gonna have to wait, D. Gonna be late for rollcall. Call you soon."

[*Message sent at 2255 hours*]

Reply to all from David –

"CALL ME!!!"

[*Message sent at 2257 hours*]

NYPD RADIO CODES

10-1 (Call command)
10-2 (Return to base)
10-3 (Call radio dispatcher)
10-4 (Message acknowledged)
10-5 (Repeat last message)
10-6 (Stand by)
10-10 (Other crime)
10-13 (Officer needs assistance)
10-34 (Assault in progress)
10-53 (Vehicle accident)
10-54 (Aided case/Emotionally disturbed person - EDP)
10-84 (Arrived at the scene)
10-98 (Available for jobs)

Note 1: This is not a complete list of radio codes. These are only the codes used in the next story. These codes have been provided for your convenience to help you understand the police radio chatter. Sometimes, the codes are shortened and the "10" is left out.

Note 2: Throughout the next story the radio dispatcher will be in communications with two police precincts on the same radio division in the northern part of Manhattan. They are the 26th and 30th Precincts. At times, you will notice the radio dispatcher shortening the precinct numbers to save time, such as saying "6" or "O" (rather than 0).

THE MANHATTANVILLE INCIDENT:
PART TWO

"Contamination Effect"

CONTAMINATION EFFECT

Chapter One

FRIDAY, EARLY JULY:

THE 26TH POLICE Precinct is located in Harlem, which is on the Upper West Side of Manhattan in New York City. Its boundaries generally stretch from West 110th Street to West 135th Street and from St. Nicholas Avenue to the Hudson River. However, between Amsterdam and St. Nicholas Avenues it extends further north to West 141st Street, due to City College and St. Nicholas Park. Other well-known locations within the precinct's boundaries include the historic Hamilton Grange House, Grant's Tomb, Riverside Church, St. John the Divine, Mount Sinai St. Luke's Hospital, and Columbia University.

For the most part, it is normally a quiet precinct, surrounded by other busier precincts, hence its longtime nickname "The Hole in the

Donut." Tonight, that is about to change. It's Friday night in July, a few days after Independence Day.

Hell on Earth is about to be unleashed.

2240 HRS, 26TH PCT, MALE POLICE OFFICERS' LOCKER RM:

Several police officers have already arrived for the midnight shift. Most prefer to arrive early enough to give themselves time to change into their uniforms. Of course, there are also a few that push their luck and arrive with minutes to spare.

It is still early, so there is time to fool around in the locker room and talk amongst themselves, while they prepare for their shift. An outsider would not expect the kind of conversations that take place in the average police locker room. It is a fun way to pass the time on an otherwise serious job. Sometimes, these conversations can be quite amusing. They are almost always entertaining.

"Hey, guys. If you were a survivor in the zombie apocalypse, who do you think you'd be more like? Rick or Shane?" This wasn't the usual question Police Officer Patrick Larkin would ask someone, but he had just spent the last few hours binge watching a marathon of *The Walking Dead* at home. Suddenly, it seemed like a good conversation starter.

His steady work partner, Steven Blake, didn't really want to answer the silly question, but felt the need to speak up and say something regardless. It was just his way. He began, "First of all, it's 'whom,' not 'who.' Second, when are you going to get it through your red Irish head? There will *never* be a zombie apocalypse. *Never!* Do you know why? It's because zombies are not real. That's why. You watch way too many movies and TV shows and all of them are bad." Suddenly, Steve felt someone bump into him, as that person entered the locker room, "Hey! Watch where you're going, mongrel."

"Sorry, Steve," apologized Robert Jenkins, a very tall African-American officer, who was running later than he preferred. Actually, it was pretty much his usual time to arrive.

Steve watched Robert go into his locker aisle, which was the next row past his own, and decided the "bump" was worth breaking his balls for a few seconds. There was plenty of time to spare before rollcall. Besides, he so loved messing with Robert. The two were great friends, but you wouldn't know it by listening to them go back and forth with each other.

"Did you really have to rub your ashy elbows on me when you passed by, Rob? Those things are atrocious! Who knows when they were cleaned last?"

Robert opened his locker and replied, "What are you talking about, Steve? I clean my elbows every time I take a shower."

Steve smirked and asked, "With what, a dirty sock?"

Robert laughed mockingly, "Ha, ha, very funny, Steve. I use soap and water like most other people, unlike yourself."

Steve responded, "Right. And you think that makes it clean? You might want to try something stronger next time, such as bleach or a brillo pad."

Curious, Robert asked, "What do you use, smart guy?"

"A luffa, of course," Steve replied in a matter of fact way. By this time, he was almost completely dressed in his uniform. He only had his boots and gun belt to put on.

Edward Frino exited the bathroom, which was further into the locker room, just in time to hear the last part of the conversation. He walked to his locker and said, "I'm beginning to think I should have stayed in the bathroom taking a shit. What kind of gay conversation are you guys having this time?"

Steve ignored his snide remark. He then explained, "I was explaining to this mongrel that just because he uses soap and water on his chalky elbows, it doesn't make them clean. It was a perfectly normal conversation. There's nothing gay about it. How do *you* clean your elbows?"

Edward responded from the other end of the locker room, where his locker was located, "I use a washcloth. They're clean, if you feel the need to check." He added with a hint of sarcasm.

Steve did not check, mainly because he would have had to walk all the way to the other end of the locker room to do so, but he did feel the need to ask another question. "Tell me, Ed, do you use the same washcloth to clean your privates?"

A few of the other guys that were in the locker room changing into their uniforms began to laugh at the absurdity of the conversation that went on across the room.

Edward looked confused, as he answered, "Yes, I do! Remind me why we are talking about this, again?"

"Ah, I see," said Steve. "So, do you clean your face before or after?"

"BEFORE," Edward called out.

There were a few more laughs.

Robert still wasn't done with Steve, yet. He asked, "Steve, why do you think my elbows are not clean enough, if I only use soap and water? Soap is clean and sterile. Better than your stupid luffa!"

Steve turned his attention back to Robert, now that he was fully dressed and ready to head upstairs to the muster room. First, he needed to set Robert straight. He walked toward Robert's locker, so he could see his friend and asked, "Rob, do you *really* think soap is sterile?"

"Yes! Why wouldn't it be?"

Steve shook his head and asked, "Do you use the same bar of soap to clean your face and entire body when you shower?"

"Yes," Robert answered, as he strapped on his gun belt.

Steve continued, "And your sons use the same bar of soap, too. Right?"

Robert nodded, "Yeah, of course."

Steve then asked, "Are you trying to tell me that after you and your sons wash your balls and asses with the same bar of soap, you all wash your face with that very same bar of soap the next day, and so on every day after, until the soap is used up?"

Robert leered at Steve and shouted, "Shut up, Steve! You're gonna make me late for rollcall, and then I'm gonna have to kick your ass."

Edward and a few of the other guys in the locker room laughed. Just then, Marc Nugent came running into the locker room. He was only running a little late, so he still had time to change.

"Hurry up, rookie," said Louie Rosaly, a fifteen-year veteran of the force, as he walked past the others and went upstairs to the muster room. Louie was usually one of the first guys ready to go upstairs. He didn't waste as much time fooling around as some of the others.

Patrick Larkin sighed and said, "We should start heading up, too. It's almost time."

Ricky Colon, one of the younger cops, agreed, "Yep. You guys can continue this stupid conversation in the morning when we get ready to go home. It'll help keep us awake."

"Don't you get me started," Steve said to Ricky.

Ricky looked back at Steve and asked in shock, "Started? You mean you haven't even started, yet??? Oh, man! It's going to be a long night."

The guys all laughed, as they walked out of the locker room and up the stairs to the first floor, where the muster room was located. It was almost time for rollcall.

2320 HRS, 26TH PCT, MUSTER RM:

"First platoon! Fall in for rollcall!" Shouted the midnight shift patrol supervisor, Sergeant Charles Foster, as he entered the muster room with the rollcall assignment sheets in his hand. In typical fashion the sheets were stapled together and listed in order by assignment.

All the officers in the muster room lined up in front of the sergeant's wooden podium forming two ranks. Most of them began pulling out their memo books, so they could write down their assignments for the night. One or two did not bother, believing they could either commit their assignment to memory or just ask their partner what they were doing. It was the usual routine.

The sergeant began reading off the names of officers from the sheets, their assigned sectors or posts, and meal periods.

"Carmen Richards and Jasmine Perez," he began, "You're going to have the response auto, Sector Adam/Boy, with a three o'clock meal. Steven Blake and Patrick Larkin, you guys will have Sector Charlie/David with a four o'clock meal. Pay special attention to Grant Houses," he instructed. "They had some trouble with teens hanging out in front on the 4 to 12 shift."

"You got it, Sarge," said Steve.

Sectors Adam, Boy, Charlie, and David covered the lower half of the precinct, below West 125th Street. When there were not enough sector cars, one car would be assigned two sectors to cover. It was the norm at most precincts in the city. There was rarely a separate Sector Boy or David in the 26th Precinct.

The sergeant continued, "Robert Jenkins and Ricky Colon, you've got Sector Eddie/George with a five o'clock meal. David Castillo and Elizabeth Neal, Sector Frank with a six o'clock meal."

David grimaced when he learned he would be in Sector Frank. It was his least favorite sector to work. It covered City College and St.

Nicholas Park, but it also had a high crime rate, more family dispute jobs, and there was little to eat in that area. Most of the good restaurants were south of West 125th Street.

The sergeant turned to the last page and read, "Louie Rosaly and Debbie Calderon will be the Conditions Auto. Take a five-thirty meal. By the way, I hope one of you is looking to collar up tonight. The CO is expecting you to bring in a DWI, so if a 10-53 comes over the radio, pick it up. Considering it's a Friday night, chances are good someone will be intoxicated."

Lou shook his head skeptically and responded, "I don't know, Sarge. It might be hard for us to find a DWI, if we get stuck on a big accident. Those kinds of jobs could take up the whole night."

Steve rolled his eyes and commented, "Are you kidding? Those kinds of jobs usually happen because of a DWI. Besides, like you really want to find a DWI anyway."

Everyone laughed and the sergeant commented like a father speaking to his children, "Play nice. I don't make the rules. I just enforce them. Grant Hamilton, you're driving me."

Grant nodded with a smile. He got along great with the sergeant and enjoyed whenever he got a chance to drive him. They had a lot in common, so their conversations were always entertaining and helped the night to go by fast.

The sergeant read off the last few names, now that all sectors had been accounted for, "Ed Frino, you're going to be on the fixer at 1-2-5 and Amsterdam. I'll have someone relieve you for meal at around four. Marc Nugent, you'll have Skywatch in front of 550 West 1-2-5 with someone from Housing. You two can work out your meals amongst yourselves and Julie is already on the telephone switchboard."

At that moment, Edward felt his cellphone vibrate in his pocket. He did not answer it, yet. It would have to wait, until rollcall was over. He had a feeling he knew who it was already. His younger cousin, David, had sent him a text message earlier, while he was still in the locker room. He had something urgent he wanted to speak about.

The sergeant was almost done with rollcall. He addressed the first platoon one last time before finishing up, "Okay, guys. You know the drill. Robberies are up. Summonses are down, so I won't bother saying it." A few people chuckled, since he said it anyway, and then he added in a more serious tone, "More importantly, be safe out there. I don't want any of you getting hurt. The most important thing is that you always sign out at the end of tour. I'll see you out there. Dismissed."

Rollcall was over. The officers began to leave the muster room, so they could prepare to go out on patrol. They grabbed fresh batteries for their portable two-way radios and car keys, if applicable.

Before the sergeant could leave the muster room on his way back toward the desk area, Jasmine Perez got his attention. She looked hesitant as she asked, "Sarge, if it's a slow night, do you think I'll be able to take lost time at around six?"

"On a *Friday* night? Hmm," he answered doubtfully. "We'll see. If, by some miracle, it's a slow night, then I don't have a problem with it. Of course, we'll have to run it by the lieutenant, first. However, you may have just jinxed us by wishing for a slow night."

Jasmine cringed, "I hope not. Thanks, Sarge. I'll keep my fingers crossed!"

"You may want to cross your toes, too," joked the sergeant, as he stepped behind the large wooden desk that stretched across one side of the main room.

The desk officer was usually stationed behind that desk. Tonight the job belonged to Sergeant Ryan Taylor. He was less senior than Charles Foster and was still learning the ropes as a fairly new sergeant. The platoon commander, Lieutenant Andrews, wanted to keep him inside, so he could teach him how to properly tend to the duties of the desk officer. The beginning of the shift was the busiest time for the desk officer because the logs had to be updated and the property had to be inventoried. Half way into the tour, he could switch assignments with Charles to give him a rest from patrol. That was the plan.

Lieutenant Andrews was a decent guy. Most of the guys liked and respected him because he was fair. No favoritism was his motto. He knew his stuff, too.

The lieutenant called out from behind the desk, "Let's go, midnight sectors! Central is holding jobs in Sector Adam and Sector Frank! Pick up those jobs and get out there, so the 4 to 12s can go home!"

Jasmine crossed all of her fingers and hoped she didn't just jinx the platoon. She really wanted to go home early, if possible, because she had plans for Saturday afternoon.

The officers from the previous shift gradually began entering the station house through the rear handicap entrance ramp, which led in from the driveway. Most officers entered that way, as opposed to using the main entrance, especially after parking their patrol cars. It was the fastest way to get to the door leading down to the locker rooms.

One 4 to 12 officer named Murtaza came in laughing and joking with a few other guys from his shift. Mostly everyone called him Taz, mainly because they could never remember his actual first name. A few of the supervisors referred to him as the "Tasmanian Devil" because he once had a reputation for being a troublemaker, as a former PBA union delegate. However, these days everyone pretty much liked Taz. He had a great personality and loved playing pranks on his fellow officers. He figured he might as well earn his nickname.

"Hey, midnights," he called out in general. "Watch your backs out there! Those people are hungry tonight," he laughed. "Would you believe we had a job of someone who was bitten by some crazy dude, as he was getting into a cab to LaGuardia Airport? You can't make this stuff up."

Grant laughed and responded, "No shit?"

Taz said, "I shit you not, my friend. Have a safe one!" He waved at his midnight friends, before opening the door to the staircase and heading down to the locker room.

"Thanks for the heads up," Grant said. "Goodnight."

Steve scoffed, "It would be just my luck to get bitten by some crackhead tonight and end up with AIDS."

Grant, Patrick, and Ricky laughed.

Grant replied with a smile, "At least, it will be a 'line of duty' injury."

Ricky got a chuckle out of that, too, as the midnight shift officers began heading out the door to the driveway apron.

2330 HRS, 26TH PCT, COURTYARD/DRIVEWAY:

As the midnight tour was getting underway, the officers began placing their equipment into their patrol cars and prepared to head out on patrol. Two cars had already left to pick up the jobs that came over just as the previous shift was ending.

Marc joined the others outside, after a quick stop in the bathroom, "I guess I won't be handing out any 'papers' today, considering I'll be stuck in the *Sky Box*."

Patrick scoffed, "Oh no! You mean, the mail won't get delivered?"

"Yeah," Marc nodded. "No autographs from me tonight."

Patrick laughed.

Steve shook his head disapprovingly, "Stop. Please, just stop. It's not cute when you talk like that."

Marc laughed, "What's the matter, *Steven?* Oh, I forgot you don't like when I refer to summonses as '*papers*.' I can't help it if I like the smell of black ink. You're so testy!"

Steve cringed and responded, "Please, do not call me by my first name, you mental case. We are not friends. I merely tolerate your existence because I have no choice. How did you ever become a cop anyway?"

Both Patrick and Ricky laughed.

Marc answered sarcastically, "Actually, it was quite easy. My high school guidance counselor recommended I find a nice simple job that even a monkey could do. The next step was obvious."

Steve replied sadly, "That is so bad, but so true."

Robert joined the conversation, "Hey, joke all you want, but it's not that easy being a cop. We have to make life and death decisions in the blink of an eye. That's something a lot of people don't seem to understand about our job. Think about that while your sitting at Skywatch, kid."

Marc raised his eyebrows impressed by the words of wisdom from Robert, who was one of the more senior officers on the first platoon. He made a good point.

Ricky didn't like that his partner was beginning to make the conversation sound too serious, so he tried to keep the lighthearted tone going a little longer, "Oh, boy. Here we go. Jenkins is trying to make our job seem important."

Steve responded sarcastically, "Oh, please! The only reason he took this job was because he thought it was a good way to get food on the arm." That was slang for getting free food.

Robert looked honestly shocked by his buddy's comment, "Steve! I resent that remark. That really hurt." His voice cracked a little when he said the last word. Robert was pretty good at playing up the drama. "You cut me to the core, brother," he went on exaggerating his feelings, as he tended to do when he wanted sympathy. "I thought we were friends?"

Again, Patrick and Ricky laughed, pleased that things were back to being humorous.

Steve smirked, as he replied, "Oh, shut up, Rob! You know it's the truth. I've seen you jabbering away with Joaquin at Famous Famiglia pizzeria hoping he'll toss you some left over pizza slices before closing time."

Robert responded honestly in his defense, "I think not, my friend. I'll have you know I always pay for all of my meals. Of course, there are occasional discounts here and there that apply to *all* city workers, which I cannot deny that I enjoy from time to time."

Everyone laughed this time, even Robert.

Steve scoffed, "Ri-i-ight! Buy one and take two free! I get it."

Robert replied with a smirk, "Yeah, keep it up. You've got me all wrong and here I thought you were a good judge of character, Steven."

Steve laughed, "Now, I know you're full of shit!"

At that point, they all had a good laugh.

One of the female officers, Debbie, shook her head in disbelief and laughed, as well. She could not believe the relentless onslaught her co-workers enjoyed putting each other through each night without fail. However, it was one of the things she enjoyed most about working with them. They were always having fun together. She shared her feelings with them, as she got into her patrol car, "You guys are terrible! I love it. Don't ever change."

She loved how these guys made going to work as a cop during the midnight shift in Harlem a lot easier. She always felt safe with them at her side. Despite the distasteful jokes and almost constant fooling around, when the shit hit the fan, these guys put on their game faces and took care of business. They were damn good at what they did, too. It made her proud to work with them, even if they were clowns most of the time.

By this time, Marc still had not gone to his post, which was a face-to-face relief post. That meant the guy from the previous shift could not leave, until he showed up to take his place. Naturally, he was too busy laughing along with the others. When he realized the time, he finally asked, "So, I don't suppose someone can give me a ride to Skywatch?"

Steve was genuinely surprised he was still there when he turned to him said, "It's only a block away! You should have been there by now!"

He then added with heavy sarcasm, "Even a *monkey* could've gotten there without a ride."

Marc nodded in defeat, "Ah. I get it. I have a big mouth. I guess I'll walk it."

Edward, who had been gassing up his car at the precinct pumps, said, "Come on, Marc. I'll give you a lift, but only so the 4 to 12 cop doesn't have to walk back late because of you."

Marc smirked at his supposed buddy, "Gee, thanks. What a pal."

Edward chuckled and replied, "Don't mention it. Besides, I need to get over to my post, too."

Marc answered, "Yeah, but at least, you have a car. I'm gonna be stuck like a Jack in the box."

Steve shook his head in disappointment at their utter lack of responsibility, as he opened the door to his patrol car and got into the passenger seat. He called out through the car window and corrected Marc, "Don't you mean a Jackass in the Box?"

Marc stuck his middle finger up at Steve in response, as they drove away from the precinct. The other cars soon followed them, one by one. With the usual nightly banter over, it was time to start patrol. Sadly, they had no idea it would be their last night on patrol together. Their world was about to change for the worse.

CONTAMINATION EFFECT

Chapter Two

2340 HRS, SKYWATCH POST IN FRONT OF 550 W. 125TH ST:

EDWARD DROVE MARC to the Skywatch post. Essentially, it was a small police booth elevated by a crane several feet off the ground, which in some cases was attached to a police van. In this case, it was not. Skywatch was used to observe crime around the Housing Developments, while also deterring criminal activity. One officer would sit in the booth and observe from above. A second officer usually sat in a car parked below. Two officers were assigned for safety reasons. They usually changed places half way into the tour. This type of deterrent patrol worked well in most areas. It was a program shared by Housing police and the local precincts.

Before arriving at the post, Marc asked Edward, "Hey, did you hear from Dave tonight? I just remembered, he texted me earlier when I came in. I forgot to call him back."

Edward answered, "Yeah, he texted me, too, while I was in the locker room. It sounded urgent. He even tried to call me during rollcall, but I haven't had a chance to call him, yet. If he was trying to contact us both, maybe it is important."

Marc agreed, "Yeah, I'll give him a call, now." He pulled out his cellphone and called his friend, since he still had about a minute before he'd have to get out of the car. They were waiting at a red light, a block from his post. "It's ringing," he said. "Hello? Dave! Hey, buddy... what? Huh? What are you talking about?" Marc became anxious, as he spoke to Dave, which made Edward worry. Marc continued, "Slow down, Dave, you're not making any sense. Yes, what about the Science Center? What do you mean crazy homeless men? Dave, relax, bro. Things have been pretty quiet. No jobs about any homeless men. Me? No can do, pal. I'm stuck at that stupid Sky Prison in front of the projects. Well, I'm sorry, but I can't leave my post. Yeah, as a matter of fact, he's right next to me," Marc looked at Edward, as he responded.

Edward began to look impatient, considering they were already in front of the Skywatch post. He rushed Marc, "Dude, you need to speed it up or continue the call on your post. We're here."

Marc turned to Edward with a look of irritation on his face and replied, "Ed, call your cousin. He's talking crazy talk." He covered the phone, as he said it and got out of the car. The officer he was relieving got inside taking Marc's place in the front passenger seat.

Edward sped back to the precinct and dropped off the officer from the previous shift. Next, he drove quickly to his own post at West 125th Street and Amsterdam. Another police car parked there from the previous shift sped away immediately back to the precinct. Edward had a feeling that officer was not too pleased he arrived late. He noticed the time. It was already 11:50 pm.

"Damn," he cursed, as he parked the car on the northwest corner in front of the Dunkin' Donuts. "I hope I won't hear about being late when I go in for meal later," he worried, as he pulled out his cellphone. He pulled up his cousin's number from the contacts list and called. He prepared for whatever crazy story he was going to hear regarding homeless men. Unfortunately, he was also required to remain at his post. He would not be able to travel to wherever his cousin was requesting Marc to go.

The phone rang a few times before his cousin answered.

"Hey, Dave. Sorry, I took so long to call you back. You know I can't answer the phone when I'm at rollca..." he was interrupted by his cousin and did not finish his sentence. He listened for a moment and replied in shock, "Say what? You're boss did what? Wait a minute! What do you mean he infected ten homeless men?" He listened carefully, as his cousin explained the insane series of events that happened to him earlier in the evening.

At last, he asked, "Hey, are you sure you should be telling me all of this shit? I can't keep this shit secret. You do realize I'm going to have to notify my supervisor, right? Whoa! Take it easy there, cuz! No need to get hostile. I'll see if someone can take a ride over there for me. Why not? Katherine did what???"

Edward could not believe the things he was hearing. If not for the fact that it would be out of character for his cousin, he would swear this was all part of a prank.

"She attacked the night watchman? Are you kidding me? No, no, I believe you! It just sounds crazy. You know? I'm sorry, man. I will keep an eye out for her." He paused and answered another question, "Yes. Well, it's like Marc told you before, there haven't been any jobs on the radio regarding homeless men. Right now, the radio is pretty quiet."

At that moment, the Central Radio Dispatcher came over the radio, which had indeed been fairly quiet, up to that point. Edward's eyes moved to the radio, as he listened intently, "In the 2-6, I'm getting a 10-10, several males running and screaming up and down Broadway near West 125th Street. 2-6 Charlie?"

Edward swallowed hard and suddenly wished he were back home.

2338 HRS, SECTOR C/D, W. 125TH ST:

A few minutes earlier, only a few blocks from Edward's location, 26 Sector Charlie/David coasted slowly across West 125th Street. It went past Twelfth Avenue on its way toward the Hudson River. Patrick Larkin was the operator, so he drove. His senior partner, Steven Blake, hated driving and preferred to be the recorder, which meant he'd be answering the radio and taking all the reports for the night. He didn't mind because he was good at it, even if his handwriting was appalling.

The reports would later be typed into a computer, so his handwriting was irrelevant, as far as he was concerned.

"Hey, Pat," he said in a lazy voice, "Do me a favor? Drive me into the river and end it now. I can't wait another five years to retire. It's torture dealing with you guys."

Patrick glanced at Steve and responded sourly, "Oh, goody. I see you are your regular cheerful self tonight."

"Shut up and die," was Steve's response, as he closed his eyes to rest them.

"O-kay," replied Patrick. "I see how this night is going to go already. Maybe I'll take a ride down the highway. If you're lucky we can crash and burn."

Steve smiled slightly and stated in a calm voice, "That sounds like a great idea. I bet we'll even end up finding a DWI before the Conditions Auto."

Patrick laughed, "Definitely. I wouldn't mind some OT." Both Steve and Patrick enjoyed making arrests and getting plenty of overtime, which most guys referred to as OT.

They entered the Henry Hudson Parkway heading south. Traffic wasn't too bad on the three-lane parkway, considering it was a Friday night. Patrick kept their car in the right lane and maintained a casual speed on his way toward the next exit at West 96th Street. Steve scanned the vehicles on the roadway and kept an eye out for violators. They made small talk along the way.

Steve started, "I can't believe I couldn't get tonight off because of minimum manning with all of the idiots working tonight. This stupid 'no excusals' thing throughout the summer is ridiculous. Do they even bother checking how many cops are working or do they just stamp each rollcall with 'no excusals'?"

Patrick shrugged with indifference and said, "You got me."

"It was a rhetorical question," Steve responded sarcastically.

Patrick rolled his eyes, "Then why ask it? Keep it to yourself."

"Quit complaining. I'm the one who should be complaining. I shouldn't even be here."

Patrick glanced at his partner and replied, "I'm not the one complaining over here."

"Well, you would be complaining, if you had someplace you needed to be and were denied a day off, so that you could be one of five sectors in a precinct, where nothing ever happens... stupid Hole in the Donut. This place shouldn't be called the 'Hole in the Donut.' It should be called the shit at the bottom of my shoe. I'm sick of this place."

"Ha, ha, ha," Patrick laughed. "It is fitting, though."

Steve turned to him and asked, "Which one?"

Patrick laughed, "Both."

Steve shook his head unamused, "I wonder what genius came up with the Hole in the Donut. I can just see some 3-year hairbag, who thinks he has a sense of humor, sitting in an RMP, drinking coffee and eating a donut on Riverside Drive saying, 'Hey, this place is like my donut,'" he said in a mocking voice. "'It's got all kinds of stuff happening around the empty hole, which represents us, a dead precinct, where nothing happens at all, surrounded by busy commands.'" He sighed exaggeratingly and wished he were with his wife at a family event he was missing. "Oh, man. Shoot me now."

Sometimes, Patrick wished he could, if only to have a peaceful night at work.

As they took the exit and went around under the parkway, the Central Radio Dispatcher, who was female on this night, called them for a job over their department radios. "In the 2-6, I'm getting a 10-10, several males running and screaming up and down Broadway near West 125th Street. 2-6 Charlie?"

Steve exhaled and answered, "2-6 Charlie, 10-4. Show us responding."

By this time, their car was already heading back northbound on the parkway. Patrick went a little faster than he did for the ride going south. He took the next exit at West 125th Street and turned right heading east toward Broadway. It was only two blocks away from the exit ramp. They slowed down, as they got closer, and made a left onto Broadway stopping at the northeast corner facing north.

Steve spoke into his radio, "2-6 Charlie is 84."

Central Radio Dispatcher responded, "10-4, Charlie."

Steve looked around and didn't see anything out of the ordinary. He turned to Patrick and asked, "Do you see or hear anything?"

Patrick lowered the driver's side window and listened. He could barely hear someone yelling. It sounded like a man, but it was coming from a few blocks south from their location. He told his partner, "I heard a guy yelling, but it came from behind us. Maybe near Tiemann Place or LaSalle Street. It sounded like a few blocks away."

Steve rolled his eyes, "Of course, it's probably the idiots in front of the projects. The sergeant said they were acting up earlier." Just then, Steve saw someone about a block ahead of them running across the street. He asked, "Hey, did you see that?"

"No," Patrick replied. "What?"

"Someone just ran across Broadway toward the Manhattanville Houses. Take a slow drive toward 131st Street and turn right on Old Broadway," he instructed his partner. "Let's just make sure there's no real crime going on up here, before we waste our time on those noisy numb nuts."

The Central Radio Dispatcher came over with another job, interrupting their stealthy drive up Broadway. This time, she called for another sector in their precinct. "26 Eddie? I'm getting a 10-53, pedestrian struck, in your sector at West 125th Street and Twelfth Avenue."

"26 Conditions Auto to Central," Louie Rosaly's voice came over the radio, before 26 Sector Eddie/George could respond.

The Central Radio Dispatcher answered, "Conditions Auto, go with your message."

Louie told her, "Show us picking up that 53 and have 26 Eddie disregard."

The Central Radio Dispatcher replied, "10-4. Eddie, redirect? You can disregard. Conditions will handle that 10-53 in your sector."

Robert Jenkins, who was in 26 Sector Eddie/George, responded, "10-4. Thanks, Conditions. Show us 98."

A short time later, Louie said, "Conditions Auto is 84."

The Central Radio Dispatcher added, "10-4, Conditions. There should already be a 'bus' at your location. Be advised, I'm also getting a call of a dispute there."

Louie responded casually, "Yeah, we see the ambulance. We will advise if we need anything further." Ambulances were generally referred to as busses over the radio.

Meanwhile, Patrick and Steve had turned onto Old Broadway, but did not see anyone running or anything suspicious. They stopped briefly and looked around, but everything seemed quiet.

Patrick commented, "Hmm. I thought I saw an ambulance back on Twelfth when we came off the highway."

Steve replied, "Yeah, I noticed it, too. I figured we could always go back for it, if this turned out to be nothing." He looked around once more, before he suggested, "Let's drive down through the path toward West 129th Street, just to make sure."

Patrick did not respond, but he complied. He carefully drove their patrol car onto the sidewalk and took a small path that traveled between the Manhattanville Housing buildings. The path went east and west connecting Old Broadway to Amsterdam Avenue, but it also went south to West 129th Street. That was the way Steve wanted to go. It was a much quieter and darker street, so it would be a better place for someone to go, if they wanted to hide. When they emerged from the path, they drove off the sidewalk and onto the street. They looked around, but all seemed quiet.

"Screw it," Steve said. "Let's head over to Grant Houses and tell those morons to keep it down. We could always come back here later and look around some more."

Patrick agreed and drove toward West 125th Street. From there, he turned south onto Broadway. They did not notice anything going on, so they made a U-turn when they reached LaSalle Street. They drove back north on Broadway slowly passing in front of the Housing buildings. The first building at the corner was 3150 Broadway. It seemed quiet enough.

"Viper Base to Central," someone from the Housing Viper Base spoke over the radio. The Viper Base controlled all the security cameras that covered the Grant Houses. There were several cameras all over, watching the entrances, lobbies, elevators, playgrounds, walkways, and parking lots. However, the only thing the officer at the Viper Base could do was describe anything the cameras saw and send a patrol car to that location to check it out. He could not respond because he was an inside post located elsewhere and needed to remain there to monitor the cameras.

The Central Radio Dispatcher responded, "Viper Base, go with your message."

The male officer at the Viper Base said, "Be advised I just picked up something really strange on the camera in front of 3170 Broadway. It just happened a few seconds ago. I was about to call it over. It looked like someone ran up on a group of teens and attacked them. It almost looked like he was biting them. It seemed so out of the ordinary I thought they were messing around, at first, but then everyone ran into the lobby to get away from him. He gave chase and there was a struggle, and then they all ran into the stairwell going up. I don't see anyone in the lobby now. Cameras are clear. Central, could you have the sector check the stairs?"

Steve rolled his eyes, "Oh, great. We have an EDP running around biting people. This is right up your alley, Pat. You and your stupid zombie crap."

Patrick did not say anything. Instead, he drove the car further north to the next building, which was 3170 Broadway. They didn't see anything from the car, so they got out and walked toward the entrance of the building. The door was propped open. Carefully, they entered the lobby. There was a blood trail of droplets on the floor leading toward one of the two stairwells.

Steve went over on the radio with their findings, "26 Charlie to Central. Be advised, there is a trail of blood in the lobby leading to the stairwell."

At that point, the patrol supervisor went over the radio and said, "2-6 Sergeant, show me going over to 3170 Broadway with Charlie. Viper Base, on the air?"

The Viper Base answered, "On the air."

The 26 Patrol Supervisor said, "Let us know if you see anyone exiting the back door or in the elevators."

Viper Base responded, "10-4, Sarge. So far, it looks quiet all around."

0005 HRS, 3170 BROADWAY:

Sergeant Charles Foster had a feeling it was going to be one of those nights, as he stepped out of his vehicle and walked toward 3170 Broadway. His driver, Grant Hamilton, walked along side him. The two had raced out of the precinct to investigate a strange job that one of the sectors was on.

Of course, it would have to be at a Housing location, without originally coming over as a Housing job. If it had come over as a Housing job, in the first place, a Housing unit would have been assigned to handle the job.

When they stepped inside the lobby Steve updated the sergeant on the job. Grant felt his phone vibrating, so he pulled it out of his shirt's breast pocket to check it. He was receiving a call from his fellow officer and friend, Edward Frino, who was parked at the fixed post at West 125th Street and Amsterdam Avenue. Grant noticed Patrick was standing guard looking around, so he figured there was time to speak quickly.

He answered the call in a low voice, "What's up, Ed?"

Edward replied, "Grant, I need to speak with the boss in person. When you guys get a chance, can you swing by my post? It's really important and it might be related to the job you're on."

"Really?" Grant asked. "That's interesting. Are you sure?"

Edward stated somberly, "I have a really bad feeling the guy you're looking for is not the only one out there like that. I hope I'm wrong, but there might be similar incidents coming over the radio soon."

Grant was curious why Edward would say such a thing, so he probed for more information. Almost forgetting he was at a crime scene, he inquired, "Why would you think that?"

Edward sighed heavily and answered, "That's what I need to talk to the Sarge about, but it has to be in person. This is going to sound too crazy over the phone, not that it will sound any better in person. Just trust me. Get here, as soon as you can. Mark my words, we are going to have our hands full tonight." Edward hung up, after making his grim prediction.

Grant frowned, as he pocketed his cellphone. His mind seemed to be elsewhere. More similar incidents, he thought. He then remembered what Taz, from the previous shift, told him about someone getting bitten, while getting into a taxi on his way to the airport. Could the person they were looking for be the same guy who bit that man or was there more than one person going around biting people?

Patrick noticed he looked disturbed. He approached and asked, "What's up? Who was that on the phone? Is everything okay?"

"No, I don't think so," Grant answered with regret. He turned to the sergeant and said, "Sarge, we may have a bigger problem than we think."

Charles looked at Grant and asked, "What do you mean?"

Grant shook his head and replied, "I'm not one hundred percent sure. I was just speaking with Eddie and he believes there's going to be more than one guy running around attacking people in this manner. Taz told us there was a similar incident on the 4 to 12 shift. Eddie wouldn't explain what he knows over the phone, but he sounded worried. He definitely knows something we don't. He wants to talk to you in person, as soon as possible."

Charles appeared to be deep in thought, as he rubbed his chin. Finally, he decided, "Let's do a vertical of the building, first. We'll take the elevator to the top and come down through the stairs, checking each floor as we go. Two of us at each staircase."

There were two staircases in the stairwell on opposite sides from one another. They could both be accessed on each landing of the building, but otherwise were not connected in the stairwell.

Steve acknowledged, "Let's do it."

Patrick asked, "What about the blood? Shouldn't someone watch the crime scene?"

Charles responded, "Yeah, Viper Base can do that through the cameras. Our safety comes first. We'll do this quick."

Grant nodded, "Oh, goody."

The four men walked to the elevator and pressed the call button. Over their radio, they heard a Housing sector car responding to their location. They were all surprised and impressed.

"Housing 92-20. Show me pulling up 84 at 3170 Broadway."

"10-4," responded the dispatcher.

Once the elevator arrived, the others waited in the elevator and held the doors open for the Housing officers to enter, before taking the elevator up. Seconds later, two male Hispanic Housing officers in their mid-thirties entered the lobby. Both were assigned to PSA 6, the nearest Housing station house. They paused at the doorway when they noticed the blood trail in the lobby.

One officer noticed the others waiting in the elevator and asked, "Another fight? I take it we don't have a victim, yet?"

Sergeant Foster shook his head. He quickly brought them up to speed on his plan and asked the Housing officers to keep an eye on the lobby and make sure no one stepped on the blood. They agreed to do as he asked without question.

"You got it, boss," one said.

Before the elevator doors could close, something unexpected happened. Debbie Calderon, who was assigned to the Conditions Auto screamed into the radio, "2-6 CONDITIONS! 10-13 WEST 125TH STREET AND 12TH AVENUE! MY PARTNER IS DEAD!"

The officers in the lobby and elevator all felt chills down their spine. Whenever another officer called a 10-13 over the radio, it was serious business. It meant they needed immediate help. It took priority over mostly every other job. Saying your partner is dead has got to be one of the worst things you can say into the radio.

Charles, Grant, Steve, and Patrick ran out of the elevator instinctively and raced for the exit. For a split second, the sergeant turned and looked back at the Housing officers, who were standing in the lobby unsure what to do. All of a sudden, they all knew what had to be done.

One of the Housing officers waved him on, as he shouted, "Go, we got this!"

Charles did not waste another second standing there.

The 26th Precinct located on West 126 Street.

Police vehicle in front of 3170 Broadway.

CONTAMINATION EFFECT

Chapter Three

0016 HRS, W. 125TH ST. AND 12TH AVE:

GRANT TOOK THE left turn from Broadway onto West 125th Street pretty fast causing the patrol car to fishtail. Patrick followed at the same speed. Both patrol cars raced toward Twelfth Avenue to answer the call for help from their friend and co-worker.

When you are a police officer, the one thing you dread is hearing that one of your own has fallen. If you are on duty, at the time, and it is within your ability to rush to your fallen brother or sister's aid, you don't think twice about it. You drop whatever you are doing and hit the pedal to the metal. Your heart races and you are overwhelmed with adrenaline, as you speed to the location. You hope you are not too late to save a life, but how do you react when you hear a cop screaming into the radio and say that her partner is already dead?

The answer is simple. You go even faster and you prepare to kick some ass.

Both patrol cars screeched to a halt when they reached Twelfth Avenue. An ambulance from Mount Sinai St. Luke's Hospital was parked facing north perpendicular to the Conditions Auto, which faced west. The rear doors of the ambulance were wide open. No one seemed to be in the driver's seats of either vehicle. A civilian silver four-door sedan was stopped at the center of the intersection in mid-turn going north onto Twelfth Avenue from West 125th Street. A body was lying on the ground in front of it.

Three more patrol cars came screeching across West 125th Street to their location with their sirens blaring and lights flashing brightly. It was Sectors Eddie/George and Frank, followed by Edward Frino in his patrol car.

Grant and Charles got out of their car and approached the body on the ground. It looked like a civilian female. She was covered in blood and part of her face was missing. It looked horrible.

Grant grimaced when he noticed her face, "Damn! What the hell happened to her?"

Charles answered, "It came over as a pedestrian struck. It definitely looks like there's more to it. She looks like someone tried to rip her face off."

Grant commented, "Either that or someone fed her to a pack of hungry wolves."

Just as he was about to take a closer look, the other three patrol cars pulled up to the scene and the officers got out.

By this time, Patrick and Steve had already exited their vehicle. They unholstered their weapons and cautiously stepped around the ambulance to the rear doors with guns drawn, just as a precaution. It was better to be safe than sorry. They peered inside and were caught off guard when they saw that one of the Emergency Medical Technicians, or EMTs, was inside covered in blood from head to toe.

Patrick gasped, "Wow. This is really bad. We need to find Debbie fast."

"Yeah, no shit," said Steve.

Robert and Ricky approached them from behind and stood at the side of the ambulance. Robert looked around and asked, "Where are Debbie and Louie?"

Steve turned to him and answered grimly, "We don't know, yet. We just got here. Everything seems too damn quiet."

Robert peeked into the ambulance at the bloody EMT and commented, "Oh, man! That's not good."

Charles looked around the intersection and wondered where his officers were located. He still had not seen any sign of them, aside from their empty vehicle.

David and Elizabeth approached him and David asked, "Where's Debbie?"

Charles shook his head, "We still don't know. Look around for her and stay together. Guns out. We still haven't found Lou either."

Grant took a closer look at the victim on the ground. She appeared to be a Caucasian in her twenties or early thirties. He felt her wrist to check for a pulse. There was no pulse, but her wrist still felt slightly warm. She must have died recently. He shined his flashlight on her face to get a better look at her. The entire right side of her face looked like an animal had eaten it, which made no sense. He moved the light down her body and saw that her chest was also ripped open. At least, two ribs could be seen.

"Shit," he said, "There is no way a car did this."

At around the same time he made his observation, the voice of the Central Radio Dispatcher came over the radio and said, "2-6 Sergeant, your base wants you to 10-1, as soon as you get a chance, in regards to your jobs. I am still showing you on two."

"10-4," Charles replied. "I am 98 from 3170 Broadway. Housing will give back a disposition. I will advise on the 10-13, as soon as I get a chance." He then turned to Grant and asked, "What did you just say?"

Grant stepped closer to Charles and whispered, "She didn't get those wounds because she was hit by a car. Something was eating her. There are teeth marks on her face and around her breast area."

Charles looked unconvinced. He looked around Grant, who was blocking his view, and stared down at the victim. Grant put his flashlight beam on her, so she could be seen more clearly. Charles had not realized she looked that dreadful. His face became stern, as he stated, "We need to find Debbie, now."

"Agreed," said Grant.

Edward walked over to them and looked down at the female on the ground. He swallowed nervously and had a feeling he knew what killed her. He also did not believe it was a car.

Another patrol car from the neighboring precinct came racing to the scene along Twelfth Avenue. It was 30 Sector Frank. Both remained in their vehicle. The driver called out to Charles and asked, "What do you need us to do, Sarge? Do we have a description for a perp, yet?"

Charles shook his head, "Negative. We haven't even found the officer that called, yet. Do me a favor? Take a ride by the pier and let me know if you see anything there and be careful."

"10-4, Sarge," the driver responded, before putting the car in reverse and making a B-line for the Harlem Pier Park, which was a block to the west, past the elevated Henry Hudson Parkway.

Charles turned to Edward and said, "We'll talk, after we find Debbie. I want to know what you know."

Edward nodded silently. He wasn't quite ready to admit what he thought was going on. It sounded too crazy, but what he was seeing, so far, might justify what his cousin told him.

All of a sudden, Ricky called out, "I FOUND LOU!"

Charles, Grant, and Edward followed the sound of Ricky's voice. They found him on the other side of the ambulance, bending over. His gaze was fixed under the ambulance. Charles bent down and got on his knees. He felt his heart skip a beat when he saw Louie Rosaly lying face down under the ambulance. He wasn't moving. Debbie had already said he was dead over the radio. Charles swallowed hard. In his five years as a sergeant, he had never lost an officer. This was a first for him.

At that moment, Louie began to move. Charles had to do a double take.

Ricky asked, "Am I crazy or did he just move?"

"Both," Grant said, as he shined his flashlight on Lou. He called out, "Louie? Can you hear me? We thought you were dead, buddy!" He was relieved to see Louie moving. He asked, "Can you come out of there on your own or do you need a hand?"

Louie moved his head upward and struck it on the under carriage of the ambulance. He moaned and tried to crawl out toward Ricky, who reached down to help him.

"Let me give you a hand there, big guy," he said.

Louie grabbed violently with his blood-covered hands and scratched Ricky on his wrist.

"Ow!" Ricky pulled his hand back instinctively, "What did you do that for? I was only trying to help you out. Fine, get out on your own."

Steve and Patrick stood beside Ricky and stared down at Louie, who was crawling awkwardly under the ambulance, as if he was uncertain how to get himself out from such a position. Grant, Charles, and Edward walked around to the west side of the ambulance and stood next to the other guys. They all watched Louie, who was staring at them wildly. His eyes looked so empty, his neck was covered in blood, and for some reason he kept making biting motions with his mouth.

Edward stepped back two steps. Grant could not help, but notice the reaction.

"What is it?" Grant asked him.

Edward shrugged, "I'm not sure, but it doesn't look right. Lou is not himself."

The others all looked at Edward, and then looked back down at Louie. He was still struggling to get out from under the ambulance. It seemed his gun belt was stuck on something under the ambulance and he could not free himself. It was very odd that he did not speak. Instead, he only stared at them with his unusually empty eyes and made biting motions, as he reached for them.

Ricky asked, "What's wrong with him?"

"No idea," said Steve.

Robert slammed the rear doors of the ambulance getting their attention and scaring the shit out of some of them.

"Damn it, Rob!" Steve commented. "Was that necessary?"

Robert looked frightened and about a shade lighter than usual when he answered, "Yeah, as a matter of fact, I think it was. That EMT in there was dead a minute ago. Right?"

Steve nodded, "Yeah, why?"

Robert swallowed and answered in a shaken voice, "I was afraid of that. He started moving and coming toward the doors, so I figured it might be best to close them."

Patrick's eyes opened wide, "What??? He moved???"

Robert nodded, "Yeah. Trust me, Pat. You don't want to doubt me on this one. Those doors are staying closed." He seemed prepared to fight anyone, who thought differently.

Charles spoke, "Leave the doors closed and step away from Louie. Until we find out what's going on here, we keep our distance. We still have to find Debbie and I need to call the lieutenant."

The guys all nodded in agreement.

0028 HRS, W. 125TH ST. AND 12TH AVE:

It had been a few minutes since the 10-13 was called. One officer was still missing. It was still uncertain what was wrong with the other officer, but it did not look good. The rest of the officers were getting restless, until 30 Sector Frank went over the radio and said, "2-6 Sergeant, on the air?"

Charles felt anxiety, as he spoke into his radio and answered, "On the air." He hoped there was some good news because, so far, things were looking pretty grim.

30 Sector Frank said in a cheerful voice, "We found your officer. She's fine. Bringing her to you shortly."

The officers all felt a swell of relief when they heard the transmission. A few of them smiled and thanked God she was okay.

Robert wiped sweat from his brow in relief and cried out, "Oh, thank God!"

Seconds later, 30 Sector Frank pulled up to the scene with a very shaken Debbie Calderon in the backseat. Charles opened the door for her, so she could get out. He turned to the officers from the 30th Precinct and thanked them.

"Thank you so much, guys. We owe you," he said.

"No problem, Sarge," the driver replied remorsefully. He then asked, "Any word on her partner?"

Charles thought about Louie, who was still snagged on the undercarriage of the ambulance. He might have been acting strange, but at least he wasn't dead. Taking that into account, Charles was able to answer with full sincerity when he said, "I am happy to say we found him and he is alive."

The officer in the driver's seat grinned and replied, "Really? That's great!"

"Yep," agreed Charles.

26 Sector Frank returned to the scene, now that the search for Debbie was over. David and Elizabeth exited their vehicle and approached her. Debbie found herself surrounded by friends and co-workers. They hugged her with relief.

30 Sector Frank was soon called away from the mini-celebration, after a job of a disorderly male came over in their precinct, only a few blocks away at the nightclub on West 133rd Street and Twelfth Avenue.

Charles turned his attention back to Debbie and asked, "Deb, what happened here? Why were you at the pier and why did you say Lou was dead?" Obviously, he had a lot of questions for her. The other officers stood by and waited for her to answer. These were questions on their minds, as well.

She took a deep breath and began with her explanation, "When we initially arrived at the job, the ambulance was already here. The rear doors were wide open, so Louie went to talk to the EMTs. There was a woman lying on the ground in front of that silver car. I was in shock when I saw her condition. She looked terrible! I couldn't believe a car could do that to a person."

Grant and Charles looked at one another.

Debbie continued, "Just thinking about her face makes me think I'm going to have nightmares about this later. Nothing on this job has ever made me, as sick as I felt in that moment. It's embarrassing, but I ran over to the corner and threw up into the sewer grating. When I was done, I went back to our car and used some napkins to clean myself up. Unfortunately, I didn't have any water, so I still have that horrible taste in my mouth."

Grant casually passed her some gum. "Here you go," he said kindly.

"Oh, uh, thank you, Grant," she replied, still bothered by her memories.

"No problem," he said. "Please, continue."

She forced out the next words, "I started wondering what was taking Louie and the EMTs so long to come out of the ambulance. I figured they were talking to the driver of the car. I needed to get the driver's paperwork to fill out the accident report, so I walked to the rear of the ambulance and what I saw almost made me faint." She paused and took a breath. "Instead, I screamed when I saw one of the EMTs in the ambulance eating the other one, while some crazy looking bitch was... she was on top of Louie on the street off to the side." She cried.

"He was lying next to the ambulance and wasn't moving. I thought he was dead. That girl was covered in blood and biting his throat like a savage! She was eating him!"

Patrick gaped at Steve and was reminded of their discussion in the locker room regarding the existence of zombies.

Steve could feel his partner's stare burning a hole into him. He turned to Patrick and whispered, "Do not even go there. The girl was an EDP. Nothing more."

"When I screamed," Debbie uttered, "She looked at me and jumped to her feet. I was about to pull out my gun, but she came running at me like a bull making its charge. I didn't have time to pull out my gun, let alone to take aim, so I ran. That bitch chased me all around here for about five minutes! *Five minutes!*" She emphasized. "I don't know how in the world I had the energy to keep moving. I dropped my radio somewhere under the highway, after I called for help and I lost her near the pier, but only because she ran after a couple that was walking near the water. It's like she forgot all about me. I found a place to hide and stayed there, until I saw the car from the 3-O. I'm sorry, but I needed to catch my breath."

Everyone remained silent, as they took in the morbid story and let it sink in. It was clear Debbie had no idea Louie was still alive. Unfortunately, it also sounded like she would have no idea why he was acting so aggressively. On the other hand, his injuries explained why he could not speak. In addition, there were a few key things Debbie mentioned that stood out. She mentioned there were two EMTs in the back of the ambulance. One was allegedly eating the other. However, now there was only one locked inside and he had previously appeared to be dead. There was also the question of this crazed girl, who attacked Louie. Where was she? Did she ever get that couple walking along the pier? If so, why hasn't it come over as a job on the radio, yet? Was the couple able to escape unscathed?

Charles spoke first, "Debbie, Louie is alive, but something is wrong with him. Come look," he escorted her to the west side of the ambulance and pointed under it. Louie was still on the ground and struggling to break free with little luck. His arms were reaching desperately and his mouth kept making biting motions, just as before. His eyes stared at them with that eerie empty stare. Occasionally, he moaned out of frustration, but otherwise said nothing intelligible.

She gasped, "Oh, my God! Louie???" Confused and angry, she asked, "Why haven't you helped him out from there?"

Ricky spoke up in his defense, "I tried, but he attacked me! Scratched my wrist. He's not himself, Debbie, and we don't know what's wrong with him. Whatever it is, it's not normal."

Patrick kept thinking something no one else wanted to admit. After spending most of the previous day watching zombies on his television at home, he could not help think there were too many similarities. The EMT in the ambulance, who they believed was dead, and Louie, who was acting way too much like a zombie. The only thing that stopped him from saying anything was the fact that if he said it first, he would be looked at as the crazy one for suggesting such a silly thing. Feeling frustrated, he walked around the front of the ambulance and toward the front of the silver car to get a look at the girl on the ground. He had to see her for himself.

Imagine his surprise when she was not there. All that remained in her place was a smeared puddle of blood on the street. He gasped in terror and shouted, "Holy shit! She's gone!"

0037 HRS, W. 125TH ST. AND 12TH AVE:

Everyone stopped what he or she was doing when Patrick cried out and ran around the ambulance to the other side to see what he was shouting about.

He looked around the silver car to see if she had managed to crawl behind it. Maybe she was still alive and he was overreacting. Then again, maybe she was indeed a zombie, he thought. He considered pulling out his gun, but didn't wish to shoot her in a panic, and then later realize she was still alive and only trying to get help. That certainly would not go over well. His thoughts distracted him enough that he did not notice when she approached him from behind and reached out for him.

Just as she was about to attack, in a desperate attempt to warn his partner, Steve shouted, "Pat, she's behind you!"

Patrick turned to face the threat, but she was already too close. She bit him on the left forearm, which he quickly raised up to block his face. He then punched her in the face with his other arm and knocked her down to the ground. She had bitten off a large chunk of flesh in the process. Also, his fist had made contact with the open side of her face and was now covered in her blood. He shook it off and grabbed the bite mark on his other arm.

"Damn! She bit a piece off of me! Holy shit! It hurts like a mother! How the hell did she bite me? She should be dead! Damned zombie!"

She should be dead indeed, but instead, she was standing up, again. This time, Patrick took cover behind the nearby silver car. She turned to Steve, skipping past Ricky, who was the next closest potential victim. She began walking toward Steve with her arms outstretched. She had the same empty look in her eyes that Louie had. Not to mention, she was missing half her face and her chest was torn open around her breasts with her torn blouse drenched in blood and barely hanging from her shoulders.

Steve and Ricky both moved back fast and the other officers did the same. No one wanted to get bitten next. To make matters worse, Louie had managed to free himself from under the ambulance, although no one had noticed, yet. He began crawling out and moving toward Debbie, who screamed, as soon as she saw him, and leapt back about two feet. Charles ran to her side and pushed her behind him to protect her. In that instant, Louie stood up and stumbled forward with his arms outstretched in an attempt to grab either one of them.

Robert tackled Louie down to the ground from behind and Charles immediately moved in to help. With few other options available to detain their friend, they handcuffed him and held him down making sure to keep clear of his biting mouth. Grant put on his thick leather gloves and helped to hold Louie's head flat to the ground, so he could not bite any of them.

Charles went over the radio and called for Emergency Service to respond to their location, "2-6 Sergeant to Central."

The Central Radio Dispatcher answered, "6 Sergeant, go with your message."

"Have ESU respond to West 1-2-5 Street and Twelfth Avenue for a violent EDP." He decided not to mention that it was a member of the service. "We're also going to need another bus," he added.

"10-4, Sergeant," she replied. She then asked, "Is that in regards to the 10-13?"

Charles responded, "Affirmative and be advised all officers are alive and accounted for. We are looking for a female perp in regards, who fled in an unknown direction from the Harlem Pier. She should be easy to find, since she's covered in blood. Advise the units she is extremely dangerous."

"10-4. I have ESU Truck 2 responding," she said, and then repeated his message regarding the female perpetrator, so that the other units on the division would be aware.

Meanwhile, on the other side of the ambulance David had pulled out his 9mm handgun and was taking aim at the bloody woman. She walked slowly in his direction with her empty gaze now locked on him. He warned her to stop, "Police! Don't move! I will shoot you, if you keep coming close!"

Steve tried to stop him by saying, "No, Dave! We can grab her and hold her down. She's small. Just don't let her bite you. If we move together, we can take her down easily. Ricky, get behind her and trip her feet. When she falls, Dave and I will move in and hold her down."

David responded, "Are you nuts? I'm not touching that thing!"

Ricky also looked a little unsure about the hands on plan.

Steve told them, "Stop being babies. She's badly injured, not dead. She's just a person. Put your gloves on. Ricky, trip her and we'll grab her," he repeated.

David reluctantly lowered his gun and put on his leather gloves, while Ricky cautiously crept up behind the woman. He kicked her legs from behind and she fell to the ground.

Steve shouted, "Now!"

He and David rushed in and got on top of her. They each grabbed her arms and pulled them behind her. Together they placed handcuffs on her small wrists.

"Make sure she can't slip out," instructed Steve. "Tighten them, if you need to."

They held her down and figured they could keep her that way, until Emergency Service arrived. She was not strong enough to push them off.

Steve told Elizabeth, "Liz, kindly let the sergeant know we now have two EDPs at this location."

"Okay," she said as she went around the rear of the ambulance to inform the sergeant about the woman they were holding down on the other side.

David avoided looking at the woman's face. He found it absolutely disgusting. Zombie or not, she was gross. He couldn't believe she was still alive, considering her injuries. It was crazy.

Meanwhile, Patrick was cleaning his wound with an alcohol wipe from the trunk of his car. He then wrapped it using a torn piece of his t-shirt from under his uniform shirt. He desperately hoped he was not infected with anything.

Edward stared at the woman Steve and David were holding down. By all accounts, she should be dead, but she was moving. How was that even possible? Also, what was wrong with Louie? To make matters worse, there was another crazed woman out there, somewhere, and a missing EMT. He wondered if the woman could be his cousin's girlfriend, Katherine.

He thought about the job Steve and Patrick were on not too long ago. They found a trail of blood in the hallway of one of the Housing buildings, but no perp. That was another crazy person on the loose. It made him think about what his cousin told him over the phone concerning infected homeless people. Were these jobs all related?

He certainly hoped not. He began to feel overwhelmed with the knowledge he had and how it related to what was going on. He knew he was going to have to explain everything his cousin told him to the sergeant, as soon as possible. If there was a connection, then it was something that was going to need containment procedures of some kind. If there were people running around biting other people and passing along some crazy infection, the sergeant needed to know, especially now that Louie and Patrick had been bitten.

Edward walked over to the sergeant and decided it was time he knew everything. When he realized the sergeant was busy holding Louie down, he knew his information would have to wait a little longer, until the situation was better under control.

In the meantime, he knelt down and held Louie's legs.

CONTAMINATION EFFECT

Chapter Four

0050 HRS, W. 125TH ST. AND 12TH AVE:

THE OFFICERS OF the 26th Precinct had their hands full. The night was starting out to be quite busy. What they did not realize is that it was only the beginning. Things were about to get worse and not just for them, but for the entire city.

The Central Radio Dispatcher broke the brief moment of silence on the radio by giving out a job in the nearby 30th Precinct, "In the 3-O, I'm getting a violent EDP at 3333 Broadway. Multiple calls saying a male, who appears to be homeless, is attacking and biting people in front of location. 3-O Adam?"

30 Precinct Sector Adam answered in a calm voice that generally came from someone with years of experience, "10-4. Show us responding."

30 Precinct Sector Charlie also answered, "Show 'O' Charlie on the back, Central."

"10-4. Thank you, Charlie," she responded. "'O' Sergeant, should I show you going, too?"

"That's a four, Central. Show me pulling up 84," the male 30 Precinct Patrol Supervisor responded.

The Central Radio Dispatcher acknowledged, "10-4. Be advised, I'm also getting a 34 at the same location. It might be one in the same."

30 Precinct Sector Adam said, "10-4, Adam's 84 with the sergeant. We'll advise."

The Central Radio Dispatcher replied, "10-4, Adam. Thank you."

30 Precinct Sector Charlie began to put themselves on the scene when they were surprised by what they were seeing, "3-O Charlie's rolling up 84. Holy..."

Just then, the 30 Precinct Patrol Supervisor went over the radio, "3-O Sergeant to Central!" He sounded a little more excited than he did before. It was obvious whatever was going on was bad, just by the sound of his voice.

"'O' Sergeant, go with your message," she said anxiously.

"We're going to need ESU for a violent non-voluntary EDP, and, at least, three buses to this location. Better make it four buses. I have injuries to numerous civilians, including two children."

The Central Radio Dispatcher responded, "10-4, 'O' Sergeant... I already have FD responding. They want to know the nature of the injuries."

He answered simply and to the point, "Multiple bites and scratches."

Officer Edward Frino was listening intently to his department radio and becoming more anxious by the minute. His stomach felt queasy when he heard the type of injuries the victims had. The building where this job was taking place was not far from his current location and only a few blocks north from where his cousin worked. He knew it had to be one of the homeless men his cousin told him about.

Edward still had not been able to explain to his sergeant what he believed was happening. There simply was no time. First, they responded to a 10-13, and then they had to search for a missing officer, Debbie Calderon. Once they found her, they had a new threat to worry about. One of their own officers had tried attacking them, while a hit and run victim seemed to literally come back from the dead. Plus, there was a previously dead EMT locked in the rear of an ambulance. It was all too much to take.

Edward did not realize Grant was standing beside him. Grant could tell he had a lot on his mind, so he spoke in a low voice that no one else would hear when he reminded him, "Eddie, you know, sooner or later, you're going to have to tell the sergeant what you told me. The sooner the better."

"Yeah, I know," he agreed. "Just waiting for a chance to talk to him in private."

"Hmm," Grant's responded. "The other guys should hear this, too."

Both men stood staring northbound on Twelfth Avenue toward West 133rd Street, where 30 Sector Frank had gone earlier for a job of a disorderly male. They were still on that job.

By this time, officers from the Emergency Service Unit Truck 2 had arrived. They were taken aback by what they were seeing. Emergency Service officers deal with some crazy things in their line of work, but none of these officers were prepared to deal with potential zombies, if that's what they were. It was without doubt the best way to describe them.

More jobs began coming over the radio, so the sergeant did what he had to do. He sent two of his sector cars to handle those jobs. Sector Eddie/George handled an aided case in their sector, while Sector Frank handled a family dispute. On a positive note, they seemed like the typical jobs one would expect to handle. There was no mention of anyone biting anyone. Robert, Ricky, David, and Elizabeth were relieved to be back to normal police work, after what they saw.

A short time later, the 30 Precinct Patrol Supervisor advised the dispatcher they had their EDP in custody and would be escorting an ambulance to the hospital. He sounded out of breath when he did so, "3-O Sergeant to Central, show 3-0 Adam and myself escorting the bus to Harlem Hospital."

"10-4," she responded.

0107 HRS, W. 125TH ST. AND 12TH AVE:

Thanks to the assistance of the two responding officers of Emergency Service Truck 2, the situation at West 125th Street and Twelfth Avenue was finally under control. Three additional ambulances had been dispatched to the scene. Louie, the EMT, and the bloody woman were strapped up tightly and placed on stretchers. Paper masks were placed over their mouths to prevent them from biting anyone. They were sent to Mount Sinai St. Luke's Hospital, which was the nearest hospital, to determine what was wrong with them. It was amazing they were still alive, considering the extent of their injuries.

For the moment, there was not a sector car available to send with them, but Sector Adam/Boy was on another assignment at the hospital. Charles planned on having them watch over the three infected people.

Steve drove his partner, Patrick, back to the 26th Precinct station house. Another ambulance was called to the station house to tend to Patrick's wound.

Upon checking the paperwork in the vehicle from the accident scene, Debbie realized it matched up with the female they had in custody. It made no sense. That would mean she was the driver of the vehicle, not the victim, as originally suspected. So, where was the victim?

Debbie had a feeling it was the vicious woman, who attacked her partner and chased after her. Apparently, she was not injured too badly by the accident. She must have attacked the driver. When EMS arrived, she must have attacked them, as well. Just as when Debbie and Louie arrived, they were attacked.

It was the only thing that made sense.

Debbie shared her theory with the sergeant. Charles figured it was as good an explanation as any, in comparison to all the questions he had.

One thing was certain, finding that woman became a top priority. He told Grant to drive around the area with Debbie to see if they could locate her. Debbie was able to find her lost department radio, but they did not have any luck locating the woman.

As planned, Charles contacted Sector Adam/Boy and told them to meet up with the ambulances in the Emergency Room and watch over Louie, the EMT, and the female driver, since the hospital was in their sector. He felt bad for Officer Jasmine Perez because he knew she wanted to leave work early, if the night turned out to be slow. That definitely was not the case. It was going to be a long night for everyone.

The Emergency Service officers stood by, after the ambulances were gone. They wanted to speak with Charles, now that everything was under control. They had more than a few questions to ask him and he knew it. He didn't blame them. As a matter of fact, he had a few questions to ask Edward.

Edward knew it was time for everything to be revealed and the job fell to him. He explained what he knew to the sergeant and to the ESU officers. He told them everything his cousin, David, told him about strange secret experiments at the Science Center, deranged homeless men on the loose, and his cousin's girlfriend, Katherine. They believed Katherine could be the girl they were searching for. She sure fit the description Debbie gave them.

Debbie commented with excitement, "It has to be her! The Science Center is not far from here. She could easily have ended up here. She probably ran in front of that poor woman's car and when the woman got out to check on her, Katherine attacked her."

Grant found himself thinking about the job Taz mentioned, again. If the man who was bitten took a taxi to the airport, it would potentially mean this infection has spread further than expected.

One of the ESU officers named O'Grady said, "Sarge, we're going to go check out the Science Center. If this Katherine person attacked a security guard, chances are he might have been infected in the same way your officer, the EMT, and the woman driver were. If that's the case, it will be best if we go."

Charles nodded in agreement, "Agreed. Let me know if you see anything out of the ordinary and I'll meet you there."

"10-4," said O'Grady, as he and his partner got into their truck and drove away.

Charles turned to Edward, "Stay here and keep an eye on the crime scene. We'll throw up some crime scene tape and block off most of the intersection. I'll send the Evidence Collection team over, as soon as I can. Debbie, are you okay to keep working?" He asked, as he turned to her.

"Not really," she said, rather shakily, "But I need to do my part. We're shorthanded. What do you need me to do?"

Charles smiled at her proudly and answered, "That's my girl. Help us put up the crime scene tape, and then follow me in your patrol car. We'll go to the Science Center. If what Edward's cousin said is true, we are going to have another crime scene there. I'll need you to keep an eye on it."

"Okay," she said.

Grant pulled out a large roll of yellow crime scene tape from the trunk of the sergeant's patrol car. There were plenty of useful items in the trunk that only the sergeant's car usually had, including a large shield, which could prove useful against Katherine, if she were to return.

They worked together fast to put up a thin barrier of crime scene tape all around the ambulance and the silver car, as well as a large portion of the intersection. The only reason they left open a small part of the intersection was because they lacked the manpower to close it off entirely. More than one patrol car would be required to divert traffic.

Once they were done, Grant got into the sergeant's car and started it up. Before Charles got into the passenger side, he turned back to Edward and said, "If you see the other EMT or Katherine, do not approach them on your own. Call for another car."

"Absolutely," Edward said without hesitation. "I don't have a death wish. Hey, wait. Do you want me to try calling my cousin, so you could speak with him?"

"Yes, please do," he said. Charles then walked over to the driver's side of Edward's patrol car and waited, while Edward made the call.

Edward let the phone ring several times, but there was no answer. He wondered if his cousin had gone to bed. He sometimes liked to shut off his cellphone to conserve power. After two attempts, he said, "No good. He's not answering."

Charles thought for a moment and told him to try, again, as he walked to his patrol car and got into the front passenger seat. Grant began driving toward the Science Center. Debbie's patrol car followed, leaving Edward alone to guard the crime scene on Twelfth Avenue.

As Grant drove, he told the sergeant what was on his mind. "What if this thing has already spread beyond our precinct boundaries? It started before our shift."

Charles sighed heavily and responded, "We can't do much about what happens outside of this precinct, but I will make a call later to someone I know at 1PP," which was the designation for police headquarters. "She might be able to help. We came on the job together. Besides, I still have to notify the Duty Captain. That's going to be fun.

I'll be lucky if I don't wind up getting psyched off the job when he hears what I have to say. For now, let's try to get to the bottom of this mystery."

Grant agreed.

Meanwhile, Edward sat in his patrol car and fidgeted around nervously. His eyes were focused toward West 133rd Street, although he glanced around, occasionally. The car doors were locked and the windows were closed. He was not taking any chances. He kept wondering why the 30th Precinct sector car had not finished up with that relatively routine job at the nightclub. He hoped they were okay. He could see their empty patrol car parked in the distance.

"Come on, guys. Give the job back already and go 98," he muttered to himself.

0125 HRS, GREENE SCIENCE CENTER ON BROADWAY:

Police Officers Mike O'Grady and James Lenno have been assigned to the Emergency Service Unit for less than three years, but in that time they have proven themselves to be worthy and dedicated officers of the unit. Together, they have saved the lives of numerous suicidal jumpers from bridges, drowning victims, and emotionally disturbed individuals, while also coming to the aid of countless police officers for various types of jobs ranging from bats flying around apartments on Riverside Drive to a barricaded felon with a gun in an apartment filled with hostages. No lives have ever been lost on any of their jobs.

Tonight was definitely a first for them, although for a different reason. It was the first time they ever had to deal with anyone that was moving around and fighting them, who should have been dead. It left them feeling utterly baffled. Whatever was going on in the 2-6 was definitely something unlike anything they have ever experienced. They were not sure what to think and, frankly, it caused them both to feel more nervous than ever, as they pulled up to the Science Center on Broadway. They wondered what they would find. Would there be more infected people?

Both were grateful to be wearing heavy body armor over their uniforms. They donned their armor helmets and turned off their truck. The first thing they noticed, as they grabbed their Colt M4 Carbines and stepped out of their vehicle, were the three broken windows of the Science Center facing Broadway. The glass was on the sidewalk, indicating the windows had been broken from the inside out. The lights inside the building were all off, so it was not something easily noticeable to anyone passing by in a car that might have been minding his or her own business.

When the officers reached the doors, they noticed one was unlocked. Cautiously, they stepped inside and found blood on the floor in the lobby. They made sure not to step on it and used flashlights attached to the front ends of their rifles to find their way through the darkened lobby, moving side by side, as they went. They followed the blood trail, which took them west along the main corridor toward the center of the building. Once they reached the center, they put their backs against each other and scanned the area with their flashlights. It appeared to be empty.

Suddenly, a noise could be heard coming from the end of a perpendicular hallway that led out to West 129th Street. It sounded like a grunt.

Both officers immediately pointed their rifles down that hallway simultaneously. As they did, they could see a bald male in a security guard uniform. He stood with his arms hanging loosely at his sides, while half hunched over. He turned to face them and began shuffling toward them at a slow pace.

Lenno shouted, "Stop! Police! Don't move!"

The security guard kept shuffling toward them ignoring his commands.

"I won't tell you, again!" Lenno warned.

O'Grady began to wonder, if maybe the guard was incapable of answering or hearing them due to any possible injuries. He suggested to his partner that they do not make any hasty decisions. He said, almost in a joking manner, "Let's wait until we get a better look at him, before we blow him away. Just to be safe. He looks unarmed."

"Right, okay," Lenno agreed reluctantly.

They kept their weapons and flashlights aimed at the security guard, as he continued to shuffle toward them. It felt like he was taking unbelievably long. As he got closer, he reached out with his arms, which made it slightly difficult to get a good look at his face.

Lenno's finger twitched on the trigger of his Colt M4 Carbine. He was not taking any chances. He didn't want to end up like that officer they strapped to the stretcher and sent to the hospital.

O'Grady decided to step a little further to the right to make it harder for the security guard to attack both of them at the same time. He'd have to choose one of them.

The guard did not even glance at O'Grady. He seemed determined to reach Lenno, no matter how long it took. It only made Lenno's trigger finger twitch that much more.

Once more, he shouted, "Stop or I will shoot you!"

The guard kept coming and he was finally getting closer.

O'Grady knew what had to be done, as he said, "Get ready to take him down."

"Way ahead of you, partner," replied Lenno, as his trigger finger gradually squeezed tighter. A second later, a loud "BLAM" went off in the hallway. The security guard stumbled back and fell to the ground. The single shot had struck him directly in the chest.

Both Lenno and O'Grady moved in closer, while still aiming their weapons at the security guard. He was still moving, so Lenno put down his rifle and pulled out a set of handcuffs. The rifle was still hanging from his shoulder by its strap. Therefore, it would not be difficult to take up arms, again, if need be. He knelt down and placed the guard's right wrist in handcuffs, while O'Grady covered him by aiming his rifle at the guard. As Lenno grabbed at the guard's left wrist to cuff it, the guard sat up and tried to grab his neck. O'Grady put down his rifle and moved closer to help his partner subdue the guard.

Lenno shouted, "Stop resisting!" He had to straddle the guard to hold him down. O'Grady grabbed the guard's loose hand and forced it closer to the other, so he could be handcuffed. In the struggle the guard managed to bite Lenno on his wrist. Once his teeth got a hold of Lenno's wrist they would not let go.

"DAMN IT! GET HIM OFF OF ME!"

O'Grady tried to pull them apart, but the guard was biting in too deep. He tried punching the guard in the face. That wasn't working. Instead, it was only causing Lenno more pain.

He shouted, "SHIT! GET HIM OFF!"

Lenno began punching at the guard himself. It had no effect. In a desperate attempt to release his wrist from the grip of the guard's teeth,

Lenno placed his hand back on his rifle and aimed it at the guard's head. Before taking a shot, he warned, "Get back, Mike!"

BLAM!

At last, the guard's grip loosened enough for Lenno to yank his arm free. The guard's head fell back to the ground and did not move anymore. He was dead.

O'Grady stood over him and asked, "Did he break into your skin with his teeth?"

Lenno could see the blood around the teeth marks that were left behind by the bite. A look of worry came over him and he muttered, "Shit. He did."

Just then Charles, Grant, and Debbie came running into the hallway. O'Grady quickly turned his rifle on them and they stopped in their tracks.

"Whoa! It's only us," Charles exclaimed with his hands up in front of him.

O'Grady lowered his rifle and looked back at his partner, who was still staring down at the wound in his wrist.

"What now?" He asked sounding terrified.

O'Grady answered, "I don't know, buddy. Get away from him, in case he's still alive."

Lenno stared down at the splattered brains that were smeared across the floor. He stood up, while holding his wrist and stated, "I doubt that very much."

The other three kept a safe distance, as they looked on in shock.

Finally, Charles said, "Let's go back to the 2-6. We have some calls to make. We'll get you situated and call an ambulance for you. The faster we act, the better our chances."

Lenno and O'Grady agreed.

Debbie looked at the body of the security guard on the floor. She turned to her sergeant and asked, "What about him?"

Charles had a feeling the guard would not be getting up, again, but considering how the night was going, it was best not to take any chances. He put on his leather gloves and finished the job Lenno started by placing the handcuffs on both wrists.

He then turned to Debbie and said, "Wait outside in your car, but keep a close eye on the entrance. Do not let your guard down for a second. If you see any movement whatsoever coming from in here, call a car to the scene immediately. Do not come back in here alone. Is that understood?"

"If you think I plan to come back in here, you're nuts," she assured him.

"Good," Charles replied. "I'll call the Crime Scene Unit, but keep in mind they usually take a while to respond, since they are coming from the Bronx."

"Okay," she said.

Grant looked at Debbie and felt worried for her. She had already been through a frightening ordeal tonight. He was impressed by her determination to stick it out and stay at the crime scene by herself. "Be safe, Deb," he told her. "Don't let anyone, or anything, sneak up on you. If you need anything at all, call me and I'll come right over."

She nodded with a half smile and said, "Thank you, Grant."

They all left the building and got into their vehicles. The others all went to the 26th Precinct, while Debbie parked her patrol car directly in front of the entrance. She turned on the side alley light atop her vehicle and shined it into the building's entrance, so she could see the hallway better. She also took out her 9mm and placed it beside her, just in case. She locked the doors of her car and waited.

CONTAMINATION EFFECT

Chapter Five

0145 HRS, 26TH PCT, DESK AREA:

WHEN THE SERGEANT'S car and ESU arrived at the 26th Precinct, they noticed an FDNY ambulance was parked outside. Two EMTs were in the precinct checking out Officer Patrick Larkin's bite mark, which had swelled up and turned black and blue. Patrick was also feeling feverish, dizzy, and nauseous, so he was sitting down in one of the cushioned seats of the complaint room, as the EMTs examined him and filled out their paperwork. They were just about ready to transport him to the hospital when the sergeant walked into the building.

Sergeant Charles Foster had a lot of calls to make and even more paperwork to fill out. It had been a crazy night and it wasn't even 2 am, yet! First, he made sure Lieutenant Andrews and the desk officer, Sergeant Ryan Taylor, were both at the desk, so he would not have to explain the situation twice. Charles told them both everything he knew about what had occurred in the past couple of hours at 3170 Broadway, West 125th Street and Twelfth Avenue, and at the Science Center. He informed them how each incident was most likely related and told them about Edward's cousin's story regarding the infected homeless men. He also offered his speculation that he suspected the EDP handled by the 30th Precinct at 3333 Broadway might have also been related. It was surely a lot to take in and not much of it was believable. Not to mention, there was close to no proof to back up the theory about the homeless men, aside from a dead security guard. However, Charles did have more than enough reliable police officers that could verify a large portion of the story, since they were all first-hand witnesses.

Lieutenant Andrews responded first, "Charles, this all sounds so far-fetched. I'm not exactly sure you should document it in those words on a department form. Even if that is exactly what took place, when they read this at the Borough, they're going to send you to Psych Services."

Charles agreed, "You think I haven't already thought about that? That's why I am having ESU fill out witness statements, along with every officer that was at the accident scene. I'm hoping the doctors at the hospital can figure out what's wrong with Louie Rosaly, so they can make him right. Come to think of it, I'm worried about Patrick Larkin and that ESU officer. The people that bit them were likely infected with some kind of unknown virus that might be contagious."

Lieutenant Andrews replied, "If that's the case, we need to keep a close eye on both. Where are they now?"

Ryan answered, "They're in the complaint room. The EMTs are checking them out. Steve said they would be transporting both to Mount Sinai St. Luke's Hospital soon."

Lieutenant Andrews nodded, "Oh, okay. We should send a sector along to keep an eye on them. Who do we have that's available?"

Charles shrugged and replied, "Honestly, we are already down to two sectors, as it is. I have Eddie/George and Frank answering jobs. I had to move the fixer from Amsterdam to watch a crime scene and I left Debbie at another crime scene. In addition, I believe Housing is still on the first crime scene from 3170 Broadway. Sector Adam/Boy was already at the hospital, so I told them to keep an eye on Lou and the others, but I can't ask them to watch two more officers. There's no way they can be in five places at once. Steve is the only extra body we have."

Lieutenant Andrews asked, "What about the second ESU officer? What's the deal with him?"

Charles replied, "Well, he needs to stand by and wait for the Duty Captain. He was involved in a shooting."

"Oh, that's right," recalled Lieutenant Andrews. He thought about his options and answered, "We'll have to send Steven Blake to watch his partner and the ESU officer. I'll make a call to the hospital and explain the situation to them. I will strongly advise they move all these patients to a secluded area for a potential quarantine. Maybe we can free up a sector, in the process. While I do that, Ryan, why don't you give the Duty Captain a call? He is going to want to be apprised of the situation ASAP. Advise him we had a shooting with a DOA on Columbia University property and contact the University's security, as well."

"Oh, boy. You got it, boss," Ryan responded.

Lieutenant Andrews turned to Julie, the telephone switchboard operator, and instructed, "Julie, have sector Eddie/George 10-2. I want them in the complaint room, just in case. At least, until we get these guys to the hospital. We'll also have them escort the ambulance to the hospital."

"Okay, boss," she replied, as she rolled her seat from the telephone to the computer, so she could send the message to Sector Eddie/George directly through the dispatcher.

In the meantime, Grant and Steve stood nearby and spoke about what was going on.

Steve complained, "I still can't believe that woman bit Pat on the arm. And what's the deal with Louie? All this craziness and not one perp is sitting in the cells to answer for it. This night is turning out to be one of the worse nights we ever worked and that's saying a lot, considering how much this place sucks."

Grant added, "It still has the potential to get worse. Think about what Taz said earlier before going down to the locker room. He said someone was bitten on the way to the airport. If that person was bitten by one of these infected people running around out there, we could have a huge problem in this city. As it is, we haven't found that other EMT or that woman who attacked Louie and Debbie. I'm surprised things have been quiet at 3170 Broadway."

Steve remarked, "That's a housing location. It's their problem, now. We have our own mess to clean up and we're running out of cops."

0155 HRS, 26TH PCT, COMPLAINT RM:

The EMTs had finished their initial paperwork. Both officers' wounds were cleaned and wrapped. Now, all that remained was to transport them to the hospital. Sector Eddie/George had been brought in to escort the ambulance to the hospital. Steve would also follow in his patrol car. As per the lieutenant, he'd be staying at the hospital to watch over the officers. He hated going to the hospital, but if his partner had to be there, he knew that's where he needed to be, too.

Patrick said he did not feel well enough to walk, so he was placed onto a stretcher. Just as the EMTs were about to strap him in place, he sat up and curled over.

One EMT asked, "What's wrong?"

Patrick yelled out, "HOLY SHIT! IT HURTS!"

The EMT calmly instructed him, "Lay back and we'll get you out of here, as soon as possible. We just need you to lie down, so we can strap you in place."

Patrick nodded, but then jerked upward, again. He held his stomach and turned to the side, as vomit poured out from his mouth onto the floor. The EMT stepped back instinctively, but the vomit had already splashed onto his shoes. A second later, Patrick fell off the stretcher onto his vomit.

Steve gagged and stepped out of the room. It was more than he could take. Robert also looked away in disgust.

However, Ricky felt slightly amused. The only thing that stopped him from laughing was the seriousness of the situation. He sincerely hoped Patrick would eventually feel better. He just wasn't so sure and that scared him. He secretly glanced down at his wrist, where Louie had scratched him earlier, when he tried to pull him out from under the ambulance. The scratch had been worrying him all night. It itched him. The skin in that area began to darken and swell. He placed a band-aid over it hoping no one would notice. He was able to get one from the EMTs upon his arrival at the station house.

Patrick began rolling on the floor and screaming, which drew the attention of everyone in the precinct. The two civilians that normally took reports in the complaint room had been sitting quietly nearby and looking on curiously. Now, they wanted to leave the room desperately. However, they were trapped because Patrick was on the floor and the EMTs were blocking the way, as they tried to pick him up and place him upon the stretcher. Grant and Robert tried to help. The supervisors all stood outside the room and looked on helplessly. There was not much they could do, if they could not get into the room.

Officer Lenno had already left the room, by this time. He began to worry and wondered if the same fate would soon befall him. The thought caused his heart to beat faster and he began sweating profusely. He kept staring at his wrapped wrist and wanted to scratch it so desperately. It was itching badly.

Patrick screamed more and more, as they tried and failed to get him back onto the stretcher. It took five guys to finally get him strapped in. Grant, Robert, and Ricky assisted the overwhelmed EMTs, but Robert was injured in the process when he fell. He was glad he did not land on the vomit.

Steve could not bring himself to enter the room, as long as it smelled like vomit. Otherwise, he'd be throwing up, too.

It was not long before the stretcher was brought out and rolled across the first floor, past the desk, and out the handicap ramp to the driveway's apron. Grant, Steve, and Ricky walked out with the EMTs. Lenno had already gone out the front door. He was waiting near the ambulance. Charles was watching him from a safe distance to make sure he did not freak out, as well. O'Grady stood beside him.

O'Grady asked him, "Sarge, do you think my partner will behave like that, too?"

Charles nodded, "I believe it's only a matter of time."

O'Grady frowned, "Damn it. I can't believe this is happening. Should I go with him?"

"No," Charles replied. "The Duty Captain is going to want to talk to you."

"Ah, I see," O'Grady nodded.

Meanwhile, back in the complaint room, Robert was sitting on a seat and holding his arm, which he believed might have been sprained, as a result of his fall.

The lieutenant took a quick look at him and asked, "What happened, Rob? Are you okay? Did he bite you?"

"NO!" Robert answered immediately. "I think I sprained my arm when I fell. It hurts when I try to move it. I think I scraped it, too. I'm sorry, boss, but I think I'm going to need to go to the hospital, too."

Lieutenant Andrews sighed in defeat. This night was not going well at all, he thought. He nodded silently and limped back behind the desk. He had to use a cane to walk due to a line of duty injury he acquired several months back when chasing after a robbery suspect. The injury prevented him from going out on patrol, so he was forced to spend each night at work inside. He already had two operations, but none had been successful. He wasn't even sure if he'd ever be able to walk normal, again. Obviously, he was a man with enough problems on his plate.

He stood by the desk for a moment, as he considered how best to handle the increasing madness occurring in his command. He began to feel a sharp pain in his leg, so he sat down to rest his leg. He closed his eyes and tried to fight the pain. There was no time to think about it. Not now. It was so frustrating to constantly battle with this pain, but he managed. He had to, especially tonight.

He looked around for the patrol supervisor, but could not see him. He figured he was probably outside. He picked up his phone and dialed Charles' number. When Charles answered, he said, "Charles, are you outside with the ambulance? Okay, good. Listen. Have Steven Blake and Ricky Colon go out as Sector Eddie/George. Robert is injured and won't be going back out on patrol. He thinks he sprained his arm. Oh, and I called up the hospital. They set up an area for all of these patients. Sector Adam/Boy will have to watch them all on their own. Have Eddie/George escort the ambulance, but once the officers are in the ER, I want them to go 98. I think Central is holding a job."

Lieutenant Andrews hung up and winced from the pain in his leg.

Julie looked at him with concern and asked, "Are you all right? You don't look so good."

"It's just my leg. I'll be fine," he answered.

Ryan, who was also outside, came back into the station house. He returned behind the desk and noticed the lieutenant looked like he was about to cry. Concerned, Ryan asked, "Lieutenant, are you okay? Is it your leg?"

"Yes," he responded. "I'm fine. I just need to rest my leg."

Ryan replied, "Why don't you go upstairs to the locker room and lie down for a while. I'll take care of things down here."

Lieutenant Andrews shook his head and replied, "While it's a nice gesture, I'm afraid I cannot do that. I'll need to speak with the Duty Captain when he arrives."

Ryan frowned and responded, "About that. I called the Borough. The Duty Captain is stuck at Harlem Hospital in regards to a multiple homicide in the 3-2. They have no idea when he will be available, so they are sending the Duty Inspector, instead."

Lieutenant Andrews moaned, "Oh, great. Which inspector has the duty, again?"

"Deputy Inspector Ehrenberg," replied Ryan. "I believe one of the guys mentioned he used to be the Commanding Officer here a while back."

"That is correct," said the lieutenant. "We are going to need another ambulance for Robert Jenkins. He sprained his arm. I think he went downstairs to the locker room. I need to take my pills, but forgot them in my locker. This pain is killing me. I'll be upstairs for a few minutes. Let me know when the inspector arrives, if I am not down in time."

Ryan replied, "Sure thing," as he watched his lieutenant struggle up the stairs to the supervisors' locker room. He felt bad for him. The lieutenant was a good guy. He didn't deserve this grief.

0213 HRS, 26TH PCT, LOCKER RM:

Robert Jenkins stood in the bathroom of the male locker room down in the basement level of the 26th Precinct. He stared at his arm, which he believed was sprained. It sure hurt enough when he moved it. It was only because he could move it that he knew it was not broken. However, something more important bothered him. It was the other wound on his arm, the one that looked like a bite mark.

Several minutes ago, Robert helped the EMTs to lift up his buddy, Patrick, who was on the floor of the complaint room screaming in pain. Together with the help of Ricky and Grant, they were able to place Patrick on the stretcher and strap him down. In the chaos that ensued before that, Robert was knocked to the ground, injuring his arm. In that moment, he recalled feeling something sharp scrape his elbow. He did not think anything of it, at the time. Getting Patrick to the hospital was more important. It must have been Patrick, he thought. Patrick bit him, while they were both on the floor.

Robert stared long and hard at the bite mark. He hoped he was wrong. Perhaps, it was a scrape, as he originally thought. No. There was no question in his mind it was a bite mark. It was already beginning to itch. He instantly knew what that meant. He was infected.

He thought about his three children, who were at home with his mom. He wanted to be with them now more than ever, but that would not be wise, if he really were infected. He needed to be as far from them as possible. His wife came to mind. He missed her so much. He wished she were still around, so he could see her one last time.

He slammed his healthy hand down on the sink and yelled, "Damn it!" Why was life so unfair? First, his wife succumbed to cancer and now he had this crazy infection. Would he die from it? Would he ever be cured? He did not know. All he knew was that in about an hour, he was going to be freaking out like Patrick, and like Louie.

"No," he whispered with tears in his eyes. They began to slide down his cheek. He swallowed hard. He knew he could not put his fellow officers at risk. Too many had already been infected for one night. This madness had to stop. He would not be a part of it. He could not. He didn't want to spread this infection to his partner or to anyone else he knew. These guys have become his second family. He cared about all of them very deeply.

As the tears slid down his cheeks, he knew there was only one real solution. He had it right there in the bathroom with him. He carried it at his side almost every day. He watched in the mirror, while his hand seemed to involuntarily pull his 9mm out of its holster. Tears continued to roll down his cheeks, as he raised the weapon up to the side of his head. His hand trembled with fear. He knew this was wrong.

He took a deep breath and closed his eyes. He saw his dead wife's face in his mind. He tried to focus on her. "I'll be with you soon, baby," he said.

His finger hesitated, as it touched the trigger. He fought what felt like a losing battle against his own will. He knew what had to be done, but kept fighting it. His finger tried to squeeze tightly around the trigger, but part of him didn't want to do it. He wanted to see his two boys and his daughter one last time. He really did. Their faces were stuck in his mind's eye.

He breathed faster to match his heartbeat. He began to choke on his tears. Was his finger moving closer to wipe the tears? No, it had betrayed him. It was moving closer to pulling the trigger, squeezing tighter and tighter, until... NO! He tried to stop, but it was too late.

BLAM!

0210 HRS, 26TH PCT, DESK AREA:

Moments earlier, it was unusually quiet in the precinct. Both sergeants were keeping busy behind the desk. Sergeant Charles Foster was typing up an unusual occurrence report known as a 49. It would basically state everything that has occurred in connection to the insane events of the evening. He was having a hard time finding the right words to use, so no one would think he was off his rocker. Behind him, Sergeant Ryan Taylor was busy making entries in the command log. The lieutenant was still up in the supervisors' locker room.

Nearby, Julie sat at the telephone switchboard playing games on her cellphone. It was how she preferred to pass the time when she had nothing else to do. She was also a police officer, but she was on restricted duty for medical reasons, like the lieutenant. She tried to keep the cellphone hidden, so the sergeants would not notice what she was doing. She had planned to stop, as soon as the Duty Inspector arrived. They were still waiting on him.

A past assault came over the department radio, temporarily breaking the silence. The job was assigned to David and Elizabeth, the officers assigned to 26 Sector Frank, since it was in their sector. It occurred on West 133rd Street and Amsterdam Avenue.

Shortly afterward, a disorderly male came over in transit at West 125th Street and Broadway on the elevated platform. Of course, Transit police were unavailable, so the job was assigned to the only other available car, Sector Eddie/George. They were just leaving the hospital.

Julie shoved her cellphone into the desk drawer in front of her and hopped to her feet shouting, "Attention!" Both sergeants stood up straight away, as a sign of respect. Deputy Inspector John Ehrenberg had just entered the building.

"At ease," he said and Julie sat back down.

Charles shook the Deputy Inspector's hand to greet him and said, "We have a serious situation here, boss It's unlike anything this city has ever seen. I can't make heads or tails of it. I was just finishing up the 49, if you want to read it. Otherwise, I can tell you. Either way, you're not going to believe it."

Deputy Inspector Ehrenberg knew Charles from the past. They were cops together back in the day. So, he knew when Charles was pulling his leg and when he was being dead serious. There was no question about it. Charles was as serious as a heart attack.

He hesitated, and then sat down. "I'll read what you have, first, Charlie," he said.

Charles waited patiently. He had a feeling the inspector would not be reading all of what he wrote without making a comment. Ryan also looked on eagerly.

It took fifteen seconds, before Deputy Inspector Ehrenberg said, "You've got to be kidding." He eyed Charles, who was shaking his head negatively. The inspector turned back to the computer screen and kept reading. "What???"

At last, he turned to Charles and asked, "Is this stuff for real?"

Charles nodded, "Yes, sir. It's not over, yet. We are waiting for the Crime Scene Unit to respond and there is still no word from the hospital on the current condition of the officers or the other victims."

Just then, two FDNY EMTs entered the station house. It was a male and female team. The male, a tall lean Hispanic with a thick mustache, approached the telephone switchboard operator and asked, "Hey, there. You guys call for a bus?"

Before Julie could open her mouth, there was a loud gunshot coming from downstairs.

BLAM!

Charles and Ryan looked at each other and ran for the stairwell. One led up and the other went down. It was hard to tell which way the shot came from. The two civilian employees in the complaint room, Mr. Brown and Ms. Butler, also rushed out to see what the sound was that they heard. At the same time, Grant came inside through the handicap ramp, after putting gas in their car.

"What was that loud bang?" He asked.

Mr. Brown called out from across the room, answering in a southern flamboyant voice, "That sounded like a gunshot!"

Deputy Inspector Ehrenberg stood up and asked, "How many others are in this station house?"

Charles replied, "There should be two more."

When Lieutenant Andrews appeared at the top of the staircase with a look of bewilderment on his face, Charles ran downstairs skipping steps along the way. He threw open the door to the male officers' locker room and raced through the aisles looking left and right. Ryan and Grant entered the locker room only seconds behind him with the inspector not far behind. When Charles reached the restroom he stopped short and almost lost his breath. His eyes welled up with tears, as he looked down upon the body of Police Officer Robert Jenkins.

"No..."

The two had actually known each other long before joining the New York City Police Department. They met many years ago in their early twenties, while delivering packages for the United Parcel Service. It was not how they wanted to spend the rest of their lives. They both had big dreams to change the city and make it safer. It was decided they would take the test together for the NYPD. They both passed and went into the Police Academy together, but after graduating they drifted apart. It would be several years before they'd meet up, again, at the 26th Precinct.

Now, Robert was gone.

Charles closed his eyes and turned away. It was not something he wanted to see. Grant and Ryan gasped when they saw Robert's body on the floor surrounded by blood. Deputy Inspector Ehrenberg did not need to look. He already knew. Instead, he gently escorted his friend, Charles, away from the doorway and sat him down on the nearest bench.

It was becoming a very dark day for the NYPD.

CONTAMINATION EFFECT

Chapter Six

0215 HRS, SECTOR E/G, W. 125TH ST. AND BROADWAY:

O FFICERS STEVEN BLAKE and Ricky Colon were now working together as 26 Sector Eddie/George, since both their partners were unavailable. Steve's mind was on his partner, Patrick. Steve always gave him a hard time, but at the moment he was worried about him. It was still unknown whether or not Patrick would ever recover and be normal, again. It was a scary feeling. As for Ricky, his mind was on his own injury. It was only a scratch, but he kept staring at it, while he drove the patrol car.

They had just left the hospital and were now en route to a job at the train station at West 125th Street and Broadway. It came over as a disorderly person on the platform. It almost seemed criminal to waste time on such a trivial job, considering everything that was going on tonight.

As they pulled up to the stairs leading up, Steve spoke into his radio and said, "26 Eddie is 84."

The Central Radio Dispatcher responded, "10-4, Eddie. I show you 84. Eddie, I am getting another call through 911. Now, the job is coming over as a 34, assault in progress. The caller is stating there is a male on the platform attacking people, as they come off the train. He's biting them.

Steve and Ricky gave each other and a quick look and jumped out of their patrol car. They put on their leather gloves and were about to run toward the staircase when they heard a scream from above. Both officers stopped and looked up. In that instant, a body came flying down from the platform and landed on the street behind their car creating a splat sound.

Both officers froze in place and checked themselves for blood. That body came very close to landing on top of them. Had they continued running, one of them might have been hit. Blood had indeed splattered on their legs and boots.

Steve went over the radio and advised the dispatcher, "26 Eddie to Central. Be advised we have a possible jumper at this location. Notify the sergeant and show us going up into the station. Please, send another unit to this location."

"6 Eddie, I do not have any other units to send, at this time. 2-6 Frank? Are you still out on your job?"

David responded, "Affirmative, Central. Could you please advise the patrol supervisor that my victim here was bitten by an unknown perp, who fled the scene heading north on Amsterdam?"

"10-4, Frank," she said. "2-6 Sergeant? I have two of your sectors that need you. Are you still out at the station house?"

Lieutenant Andrews answered the radio, "2-6 Base to Central. The sergeant is still out here with the Duty Inspector. Can you have Night Watch respond to the 2-6 station house?"

"10-4, 6 Base." She replied, before notifying the overnight detective unit by phone.

Steve and Ricky ran up the stairs and jumped over the turnstiles on their way up to the platform. They headed straight for the uptown side, since that was the side where the person had fallen or jumped from. They pulled out their guns, as they approached the platform.

There were several people on the floor screaming in pain just like Patrick did. About three others appeared to be eating another person, who was on the ground and not moving.

Steve aimed his gun at the group eating the victim that wasn't moving and was about to yell for them to stop, but Ricky grabbed him and whispered, "Don't! Be quiet. Let's get the hell out of here. These people all look infected. They don't even realize we're here. When they do, I have a feeling we are going to have to run for our lives. They are behaving the same as Pat. It's too late for them."

This wasn't how police operate, Steve thought. He looked at Ricky and could see the fear in his eyes. He knew he was right. If these people were all infected, they would all become aggressive soon. The best thing to do was to back away slowly and head back down the stairs, so they did.

When they got back down to the turnstiles, Steve went over to the booth. He told the clerk, "If anyone comes running downstairs, hide. Don't let them see you and do not come out of that booth no matter what. We are going to call Transit and have the trains bypass this station. Don't let anyone else go upstairs either. This station is now closed. Is that clear?"

The clerk asked, "What happened officer?"

Ricky answered, "There is a viral outbreak causing people to attack one another. The platform is overrun with infected. It might be wise for you to leave this station and get to safety."

The clerk looked at Ricky, as if he were crazy and said, "I can't just leave my booth. I'll lose my job. I need to call my supervisor."

Ricky replied, "Fine, suit yourself."

Steve said, "Trust me. Do not leave this booth. You are safer inside. Just don't let them see you in there or they might try to get at you."

The clerk nodded nervously, "Okay, officer. Are you going to leave them up there?"

"For now," Steve nodded. He contacted the dispatcher and informed her to notify Transit and have them bypass the station. He also informed her of the several potentially dangerous people on the platform and asked if there was another car available, yet, who could back them up.

She raised the next sector, "2-6 Adam? Are you still out at the hospital?"

Again, Lieutenant Andrews answered, "2-6 Base to Central. Be advised Adam is going to be at the hospital for the remainder of the tour. In fact, take Adam off the rundown."

Steve complained, "Are you kidding me? We need more sectors. Who else is out there?"

Ricky thought for a moment and answered, "Edward and Debbie, but they are both at crime scenes and probably will be all night."

"Damn it," Steve cursed. "Let's go back down and check on the DOA. We can't just leave a dead body on the street, while we wait up here for these guys to come down."

Ricky shrugged and agreed.

0227 HRS, W. 125TH ST. AND 12TH AVE:

Several blocks away from Sector Eddie/George was Officer Edward Frino. He still sat alone in a parked patrol car at the accident scene. Of course, it wasn't really an accident. There was no pedestrian struck. She was gone and had not been seen since nearly two hours earlier. No one knew where she went. Edward was in no hurry to see her either. He didn't want to end up like Louie Rosaly. He wondered if Lou was all right. Debbie was lucky to get away with her life.

He checked the time on the dashboard clock. It was nearly 2:30 am! The 30th Precinct sector that responded to the nightclub a few blocks north from him was still there. Come to think of it, the patrol supervisor and sector that went to Harlem Hospital were still out on their EDP job, too. There were only two sectors in the 30th Precinct and they had been running around answering jobs all night. Not one has had the time to come down to Twelfth Avenue to check on 30 Sector Frank.

As if she were reading his mind, the Central Radio Dispatcher tried to call them on the radio, "3-O Frank. Are you still out on Twelfth Avenue?" She waited for a response, but there was none. She was used to calling sectors at the nightclub and not getting an immediate response due to the loud music that was normally playing at the establishment. Edward figured that was the reason she was being so casual about them still being on that job. On the weekends, when the nightclub was open a sector car would usually put themselves out at the location for about an hour on a directed patrol. Edward knew that was not the case this time. Central called, again, "3-O Frank? Are you on the air? Are you still out?" There was still no response. "Okay, 0229 hours and no response from 3-O Frank," she said, as a way of documenting that she did her job and tried to contact them, but they failed to respond. She moved on to the next car that had been out for a while. "3-O Adam, are you still out on your EDP?" There was no answer. "3-O Sergeant, on the air? Are you still out?" Nothing.

Edward began to wonder if the 30th Precinct was going through something similar like his precinct. Perhaps, they were just keeping it under wraps.

Suddenly, he thought he heard something. He rolled down the driver's side window slightly, just about four inches. He listened carefully and could hear yelling. It was coming from the nightclub. Was it a fight? He was tempted to drive over and check on 30 Sector Frank. If they were in trouble, he'd never forgive himself for waiting at a crime scene a few blocks away and doing nothing. He had to go.

He put the car into drive and began driving toward West 133rd Street. He stopped the car when he reached West 132nd Street. He could see a lot of people inside and they all seemed to be looking in his direction. In the next instant, they all began screaming. The crowd raced forward and leapt through the windows. Some pushed through the doors, but all were coming toward him, including the two officers that were out on that job all this time. He thought he might have seen Katherine in the mob, as well.

"Holy shit!" He shouted, as he made a fast U-turn and raced back toward West 125th Street. He made a right turn toward Marginal Street and hoped they would all follow. He then made a fast left and another left stopping under the parkway, where they could no longer see him. He wanted to give them all enough time to run to Marginal Street. He had just enough time for a quick radio transmission, "2-6 post on West 1-2-5 Street and Twelfth Ave to Central?"

"Go with your message," she responded over the radio.

"Show me out with a large disorderly group running south from the nightclub at West 133rd Street and Twelfth Avenue. I'm going to need some help here," he said. He really did not want to call over a 10-13 because it would mean cops that had no idea what was going on would come rushing to his aid and to their doom. At the same time, he couldn't just let a crowd of potentially infected people run wild in the streets without saying something.

He sped forward past Twelfth Avenue and headed east along West 125th Street. He swerved his car sideways, screeching the tires, and blocked the street at Broadway, so no cars would drive west toward Twelfth Avenue. It was the only thing he could think to do that might save some lives.

A moment later, Ricky and Steve pulled up beside him in their car facing the opposite way, so that Ricky, who was the driver, was closer to Edward.

Ricky asked, "What's up, Ed? Large crowd at the club?"

Edward replied, "That ain't the half of it! I think they're all infected! We are going to need the big guns out here! This is getting beyond our control! Why hasn't the sergeant come back out, yet?"

Ricky stated, "No idea. We have a similar problem above us on the uptown platform. It looks like there are about ten infected people up there. Plus, we have a DOA on the street. FDNY is with him now, so we figured we'd make sure you were okay."

Edward's eyes opened wide, "Thanks, but did you just say you had about *ten* infected people on the platform? We can't just ignore all of these infected people and hope they go away! We need to do something fast!"

Steve responded, "No shit, Sherlock. We need SRG, at least, and a lot of them. I'm going to call Grant and see what's up with the sergeant. Paperwork can wait, until this craziness is over."

"Good idea," said Edward. He kept looking west toward Twelfth Avenue to make sure the crowd from the nightclub was not coming.

Steve dialed Grant's cellphone and waited, until there was an answer. It rang a few times. When Grant finally answered, Steve said, "Hey, Grant. What's going on in there? We need the sergeant out here and we need SRG to respond. Is he coming out soon?"

Grant only said one thing, "Robert is dead."

Steve felt a cold chill move up his spine and the phone fell out of his hand onto his lap. His best friend was gone.

The infected running south on 12th Avenue from the nightclub.

0235 HRS, 3170 BROADWAY:

By now, Housing PSA 6 car number 9220 had been out at 3170 Broadway for a couple of hours. In that time, they had grown increasingly impatient. It was not a good way to spend a busy Friday night, especially while officers were out there in need of assistance. Still, someone had to watch the crime scene. It did not make them any less frustrated. The first hour was spent awaiting the Evidence Collection Team (ECT), who was notified to photograph the blood in the lobby and to take samples.

Police Officer Winston Fong of the Evidence Collection Team already had a busy night himself. He and his partner had responded to two felony jobs in the first hour and a half of their shift. Winston agreed to go to 3170 Broadway on his own because the Housing officers had already waited long enough and he figured it would be a fast job. It took him a little more than a half hour, but he was finally done.

He packed up his equipment and waited for the Housing officers to come back down to the lobby. They went upstairs to check the building for a possible perpetrator about thirty minutes earlier and still had not returned. He looked at his watch and began to feel impatient.

"Where are these guys? I don't have all day," he complained to himself. "I'll give them five more minutes, and then I am out of here."

After about three minutes, he heard a thunderous sound coming from above. It sounded like it was in the stairwell. He walked closer to the doors of the stairwell and listened closely. The sound grew louder and louder, as it got closer. Someone was running down the stairs. It could be the other officers in pursuit of the perpetrator, he thought.

He put down his equipment toolbox and pulled out his 9mm Sig Sauer handgun and took aim at the doors. There were two near each other. He expected one to open any second. If it were just a bunch of teens, he'd apologize later, but he was not taking any chances. He had been paying close attention to the jobs coming over the radio all night. He wasn't sure if it was because of the full moon, but he could tell this was no ordinary night. He could feel it in his gut and he was ready for anything.

Of course, he would not be ready for what he was about to experience. How could anyone be ready for this madness?

The door on the right swung open and out came two teenage boys. They skidded to a halt and slipped on the blood when they came face to face with Winston's firearm. Both teens looked like they had just seen the Devil himself.

"Police! Don't move!" He shouted, as he was required to do. He waited for the two Housing officers to exit the stairwell, after the teens. That's not what happened, though.

Instead, one man exited the stairwell. It appeared to be a homeless male, covered in blood. His wild bloodshot eyes made eye contact with Winston and, right away, Winston knew that was the man they were searching for all night. The teens scurried hastily to their feet and moved behind Winston.

One shouted, "Yo, what you waitin' on, Jackie Chan! Shoot dat crazy ass bitch! Dat nigga just kilt about five people on the tenth floor, including your peeps!"

The infected homeless man charged at Winston, who fired his weapon twice hitting the male directly in the chest. The homeless man was pushed back by the force and knocked to the ground.

"Yeah, son! Dat's what I'm talkin' about!" Shouted one teenager, as he cheered.

Winston kept his weapon aimed at the man on the floor, as he spoke into his radio and told the dispatcher what was going on, "ECT to Central!"

She responded, "Go with your message, ECT."

He continued, "Shots fired at 3170 Broadway! I have one male perp down in the lobby and two possible officers down on the tenth floor! I'm going to need another unit here, ASAP!"

Right away, Steve and Ricky raced to the scene. They were less than a block away. While they were still shaken up by the news of their friend's death, they knew they had a job to do. Part of that job meant making sure no other cops had to die tonight.

Steve informed the dispatcher, "26 Eddie is rolling up 84, Central."

"10-4, 6 Eddie."

They exited their car and rushed toward the lobby. Seconds later, they heard a gunshot coming from inside. They ran as fast as they could.

Before they could reach the entrance, Winston shouted into the radio, "ECT TO CENTRAL! THE PERP JUST ATTACKED ME! I SHOT HIM THREE TIMES, BUT HE CHASED TWO TEENAGERS OUT THE REAR DOOR!"

Steve and Ricky raced into the lobby, which was a mess, and asked, "Are you okay?"

Winston replied from a seated position on the floor, "Yeah, I think so. That guy must be on some powerful drugs! He came at me, so I shot him, but then he got up and came at me, again, so I shot him, again! He lost interest in me and ran after those teenagers. I got the wind knocked out of me. They ran out the back door," he pointed. "You can still catch them, if you hurry."

Steve asked, "Were you bitten by him?"

Ricky added, "Or scratched?"

"Did he spit at you?" Steve then asked.

Winston shook his head and responded, "No to all. Why?"

Steve replied brusquely, "Long story. Come on, Rick."

Both officers ran out the back door, leaving a dazed and confused Winston to pick up the items from his toolbox, which had fallen out and were spread across the lobby floor, including the evidence he just finished collecting.

"Shit," he groaned quietly.

CONTAMINATION EFFECT

Chapter Seven

0240 HRS, SKYWATCH POST IN FRONT OF 550 W. 125TH ST:

POLICE OFFICER MARC Nugent sat twenty-five feet above the ground in the Skywatch observation tower. The height gave him an advantage over crime around him. He could see all the way down the block in both directions, as well as having a good view of the Housing grounds between 550 West 125th Street and the rear of 3170 Broadway.

Still, Marc had been dying to do some "real" police work all night. He was bored from sitting up in the tower. At last, someone called over a pursuit on the radio and it was within his view. He scanned the area behind 3170 Broadway and saw the two teenagers running from what looked like some deranged looking homeless man, who was covered in blood and filth. His hair was about as wild as the look in his eyes. It made him think about his phone call with his friend, David Frino, near the start of his work tour.

He spoke into his radio to update the other officers, "2-6 Skywatch to Central."

The Central Radio Dispatcher answered, "Skywatch. Go with your message."

Marc said, "I have eyes on the perp from my vantage point. Advise the units he's now chasing after only one teenager. They're heading northbound toward 125th Street. The other teenager got away and ran south toward LaSalle Street. The perp is now passing behind my tower and heading into the street." Marc knew he'd never bring the tower down fast enough to catch him, so he shouted to his Housing partner, Kahn, who sat in a parked patrol car behind the Skywatch," Kahn! Grab that guy!"

Officer Kahn quickly got out of the patrol car, but the homeless man had already stepped into the street. Cars going both east and west skidded and swerved to avoid him. One car that was traveling west crashed head on into another going east pushing it into a spin and causing it to crash through the windows of the Dunkin Donuts on the corner. The homeless man seemed confused by the traffic and did not know which way to run. Kahn tried to stop traffic with hand signals, as he rushed toward the homeless man to grab him. Steve and Ricky came running out of the Housing grounds into the street to assist Kahn.

Steve shouted, "Kahn! Don't grab him! Wait for us! He's infected!"

Kahn turned to Steve looking confused and asked, "Did you say he was *infected*?"

The homeless man noticed Kahn nearby and moved in on him.

Steve shouted, again, "Behind you, Kahn! Don't let him bite you!!!"

Kahn turned back to face the homeless man and was tackled to the ground. The homeless man began biting him in the face. Kahn screamed out in pain and struggled to push his assailant off of him. Steve and Ricky reached him and began yanking the man away by his legs. He let go of his grip with his teeth and tried to reach for Steve and Ricky with his hands to no avail. They dragged him by his legs pulling him away from Kahn. Afterwards, they jumped on top of him and held his face down against the pavement, so he could not bite them.

Steve warned his eager young partner, "Be careful. We don't need anymore of us getting infected tonight."

Ricky was using his elbow to hold down the man's head and press his face into the street. He grunted, as he replied, "Don't worry about me. This son-of-a-bitch isn't getting a chance to bite anyone else tonight. Isn't that right, stinky?"

The homeless man tried unsuccessfully to free himself. However, the two officers on him were not giving him any leeway.

Steve called over to Kahn, who was sitting on the street nearby holding his face, "Kahn? How are you doing over there, buddy? Can you speak?"

Kahn groaned in pain, as blood poured out from his cheek. He seemed to be in shock.

Marc lowered the Skywatch tower and got out of the booth. He ran over to Kahn's side and when he saw the wound, he rushed to the patrol car to grab some napkins from the glove compartment. There was usually a ton jammed into each glove compartment from the meals purchased by the three shifts of officers throughout the day. He rushed back to Kahn with several napkins in his hand.

"Kahn, you need to apply pressure. Use this," he said, while passing him the napkins. "I already called for an ambulance and let Central know about the 53 at Dunkin Donuts."

Steve managed to handcuff the homeless man, while Ricky held him down. Together they were both stronger than him, so it was not too difficult. The key was making sure not to get bitten. Still, Steve found it absolutely disgusting that the man was covered in blood because now his uniform was also covered with infected blood.

"Ugh, gross. 26 Eddie," Steve spoke into his radio. "We have the perp in custody in front of 550 West 1-2-5. He's an EDP, so we're going to need a bus for him. Notify the sergeant."

The Central Radio Dispatcher responded, "10-4, Eddie. 6 Sergeant on the air?"

Charles finally answered from within the station house, "6 Sergeant acknowledged. Show me 98 from the station house and going to West 125th Street."

Just then Edward, who was sitting in his patrol car on Broadway called for help on his radio, "2-6 portable to Central! 10-13 at West 1-2-5 and Broadway! I have a large crowd running in the street toward me from Twelfth Avenue. Advise the sergeant they are all infected!"

It seemed the proverbial shit had hit the fan.

0252 HRS, W. 125TH ST., BETWEEN AMSTERDAM AVE. AND BROADWAY:

Officer Edward Frino knew he could no longer sit in his patrol car and block traffic on Broadway. There was a mob of approximately one hundred people charging toward him on foot from Twelfth Avenue and there was a ninety-nine percent chance they were all infected by an experimental virus. He had no intention of joining their numbers. A short time ago, he took out the three cones from the trunk of his car and set them up in a line across the westbound lanes of West 125th Street on the west side of Broadway. Those cones would have to take his place because he was leaving.

Edward drove toward the Skywatch post to meet up with his fellow officers, just as the sergeant's car pulled up to his intersection. He hit his siren once and waved for them to follow him. On his way, he grabbed the PA microphone from the dashboard and shouted into it, "FDNY! GET IN YOUR TRUCK AND GET THE HELL OUT OF HERE NOW!" His amplified voice echoed loudly over the intersection.

The six firefighters standing around near the dead person, who either fell or jumped from the elevated train platform on the east side of Broadway, just north of West 125th Street, heard the sound of yelling growing louder by the second and decided to heed the advice of the passing officer. If two police cars were driving away, there was no reason for them to stick around.

Richie, who was their lieutenant and operator of the fire truck got into the rig and waited for the rest of his crew from Engine 37 to climb aboard. "Let's go, boys! Forget the body, for now," he shouted out the driver's side window. "There's something coming this way and I don't want to be here when it arrives!"

They all climbed aboard and he began to roll forward. The truck was facing north, so he had to go through West 125th Street. As he began making the right turn from Broadway, he heard the sound of glass breaking followed by a loud thump hitting the truck. Richie looked back and asked, "What the hell was that? It sounded like something fell on the rear!"

Sean, one of the younger guys in the backseat looked and saw a body lying on the rear of the truck. It twitched and jerked around, but it didn't look like it would be standing anytime soon. "Uh oh! I think someone just jumped from the train platform onto the truck," he said with uncertainty.

Richie looked to his left and saw the swarming mob rushing toward him, as they crossed Broadway. "Holy shit! Close your windows and lock the doors! Quick!"

Not a second later, the mob literally rammed into the left side of the truck, as if they could run right through it. The truck rocked back and forth. Some of the infected began trying to climb it and others slammed on the windows with their hands. Half the mob completely disregarded the big candy apple red truck and continued their charge forward toward Amsterdam Avenue, where the cops stood.

Edward stopped his patrol car near his fellow officers in front of 550 West 125th Street and yelled from the driver's side window, "Haul ass, boys! They're coming!"

By this time, the ambulance that was at the station house for Robert followed the sergeant's car out and had arrived at the scene. The Hispanic male EMT was standing over the homeless man that Steve and Ricky grabbed, while his female partner had just started bandaging Kahn's face.

Charles went over the radio and said, "2-6 Sergeant to Central. I am going to need a Level 1 Mobilization. Have the units meet me at West 128th Street between Amsterdam and Convent Avenues. Tell them to come in through Amsterdam. It's a dead end street. I'm going to need SRG at this location ASAP. Advise the Duty Inspector. He should still be at the 26th Precinct station house. We might have an epidemic on our hands. Advise all units responding to avoid getting bitten, at all costs."

"10-4, Sergeant," responded the dispatcher. She then transmitted his mobilization message to the rest of the borough of Manhattan North. It would mean each precinct would be sending a patrol car with two officers. Charles hated the idea of putting the lives of more officers at risk, but he knew this situation was getting beyond his ability to control. He needed all the help he could get.

Deputy Inspector Ehrenberg was the first to respond with his driver, who was an "old timer" that had been waiting in their unmarked car the whole time. As a twenty-four year veteran, he didn't feel the need to go into the station house and follow the inspector around. He usually waited in the car, since their visits were typically no longer than a few minutes. The last thing he wanted to do was respond to a Level 1

Mobilization. He knew there was a strong possibility the inspector could increase the mobilization to a higher level, if he deemed it necessary to bring more police officers to the location. He had a strong feeling this would be one of those days, as they pulled into the dead end street and parked at the far end to wait for the sergeant to arrive.

Meanwhile, Marc helped Kahn into the back of the ambulance, and then jumped into the front seat of Edward's patrol car. Steve and Ricky jumped into the patrol car that was parked behind Skywatch. The keys were still in it and it was running. There was no time to bring the EDP, so they left him on the floor.

The female EMT got into the rear of the ambulance with Kahn and closed the rear doors, while her partner got into the driver's seat and floored the gas pedal. He turned right onto Amsterdam Avenue and sped toward the hospital, which was at West 113th Street.

Three police cars drove toward Amsterdam and stopped there. The sergeant wasn't about to just abandon everyone to the infected. He had a plan. It just wasn't a very good one.

Marc asked Edward, "What is he doing?"

Edward replied, "I don't know, but I am sticking with him. Whatever he does, I'm doing."

Marc groaned, "Oh, that's perfect. I hope he doesn't get us all killed."

Ricky skidded his car into a fishtail and lined up behind Edward's patrol car. He wasn't sure what they were doing either, but he figured it had something to do with General Custer's last stand at Little Big Horn. He glanced at his itchy wrist and took a deep breath. If he had to go, he'd rather go out fighting.

Charles got out of his car and pulled out his gun. Grant did the same. Edward and Marc followed, as did Ricky and Steve.

Marc grinned, "Now this, I like. Let's put an end to this crazy night."

Charles shouted, "Aim for infected only! The fish market was crowded, which means there are a lot of healthy people running for their lives! Do not shoot anyone, if you are unsure! If you can save a life tonight, then you would have done your job well!" At this point, he was not sure they'd make it out of this alive, but he was prepared to die. "It was a pleasure working with you gentlemen! Make me proud!"

BLAM! BLAM! BLAM!

They each took aim and fired their weapons. Not every shot was a direct hit and not every hit took down its target. The sergeant was right. There were a lot of people running around, making it difficult to choose targets and they were not exactly marksmen.

BLAM! BLAM! BLAM!

Shooting the infected might have been a good idea, at the time, but some of the uninfected that were fleeing thought the cops were just shooting everyone randomly. They did not like being sacrificed. Two gangsters, who were carrying illegal firearms, began returning fire at the police forcing them to take cover behind their cars.

It did not take long before there was a full-scale riot on West 125th Street.

0305 HRS, W. 125TH ST., BETWEEN AMSTERDAM AVE. AND BROADWAY:

When Deputy Inspector Ehrenberg heard multiple gunshots coming from West 125th Street, he yelled at his driver and told him to get there, right away.

The Specialized Response Group (SRG) was already on its way. Police sirens could be heard screaming in the distance coming from the East Side across West 125th Street toward Amsterdam Avenue.

Suddenly, Officer Jasmine Perez's voice could be heard shouting into the radio, "2-6 ADAM TO CENTRAL! 10-13 AT ST. LUKE'S HOSPITAL!!! THEY'RE GOING CRAZY IN HERE!!!"

Charles shouted to Steve and Ricky, "Get to the hospital! SRG's coming! We'll be fine!"

Ricky and Steve looked at each other and did as they were told. They got back into the patrol car, made a U-turn, and headed south on Amsterdam toward the hospital.

As if one 10-13 wasn't enough, Officer Winston Fong of the Evidence Collection Team found himself in need of assistance, as well, as he shouted into his radio, "ECT to Central! 10-13 3170 Broadway! I've got several people fighting in the lobby! They came out of the elevator! Two are trying to eat another one! Wait! Hey, back off or I'll shoot! BLAM! Shots fired, Central! I got one, but the other one is on me! I need help! Hey! Come back! I just helped you! Hey! HELP ME!"

Charles never felt more helpless. To hear a cop calling for help and not be able to respond in what may very well be a life and death situation, drove him insane with anger and frustration.

About a minute later, the first of the Specialized Response Group cars had finally arrived. There were five in a row. Cops in special tactical gear exited their vehicles and rallied behind the sergeant.

Another sergeant named Kepster asked, "What the hell's going on here?"

Just as the Deputy Inspector arrived, Charles explained as quickly as he could to the group, "We have a bunch of people running around, who are infected with some kind of contagious virus. It spreads when they bite you, so don't get bitten. Not everyone on this block is infected. The infected attacked the crowd in front of the fish market and everyone started running. We took out a few infected, but some morons began shooting back at us because they thought we were shooting everyone at random. Some infected were sent to the hospital, but now we have a situation there. Another cop just called for help in Housing. No one has been able to go there, yet. And that's only been the past ten minutes."

Sergeant Gregg Kepster nodded and replied, "We'll take it from here, Sarge. Get your men to safety and help that Housing cop." He turned to his team and said, "Grab your shields, boys. Let's take out the infected in wedge formation. Don't let anyone get close enough to bite you."

Charles didn't feel it was necessary to correct him to say it was a cop from Evidence Collection and not from Housing. It didn't make a difference, at the moment. A cop was a cop and he needed help.

Within seconds the Specialized Response Group officers formed a triangle-shaped wedge formation and went into the block between Amsterdam Avenue and Broadway moving forward at a slow and steady pace. They seemed quite confident with their training and abilities, for the time being.

A few people that had been hanging out in front of the fish market managed to fight off the crowd of attackers, get into their cars, and drive away. They all headed through the disorderly crowd toward the Henry Hudson Parkway. One car from New Jersey went straight for the George Washington Bridge. Two others went back to the Bronx, where they came from. It wasn't worth the trouble sticking around, while crazy people were biting them and police were shooting into the crowd. There was way too much action in Harlem tonight and they knew it was time to head home and lick their wounds, so to speak.

At the same time, three police cars from other precincts responded to West 128th Street. Upon their arrival, they saw the action going on at West 125th Street and went there, instead. The Deputy Inspector went over the radio and called for any other responding units to meet him at West 125th Street. He also upgraded the mobilization to a Level 2, which meant vans filled with, at least, eight cops and one supervisor each would be sent, as soon as possible. Also responding would be an Emergency Service Unit vehicle and a helicopter from the Aviation Unit.

Of course, it would not be easy to fill that need with the limited manpower on the midnight shift. This type of mobilization also included a command post vehicle, a "paddy wagon," and a barrier truck, but with the way things were going, it was unlikely those vehicles would make much of a difference.

0310 HRS, EMERGENCY SERVICE UNIT, TRUCK 2 BASE:

A block away at the 26th Precinct, Officer O'Grady ran next door to where Emergency Service Unit Truck 2 turned out and where he was assigned. His regular partner may have been out at the hospital, but there was still one other officer from the unit that could help out, which meant they could respond to the mobilization.

"Iliadis! Suit up!" He shouted, as he entered the building and ran upstairs. "I need you, pal. Lenno is already at the hospital. D.I. Ehrenberg just called a Level 2. We need to respond. All hell is breaking loose on the other side of the block from here."

Detective Iliadis got dressed for patrol quickly, as he asked, "How is Lenno doing? Did someone really bite him?"

"Yeah, man," responded O'Grady. "He doesn't look good. It's some kind of infection going around. A few guys from the 2-6 got it, too. One's really bad. This thing affects the body in a very crazy way. We've been dealing with people that have life-threatening open wounds and they're going around trying to eat people!" He raised his eyebrow curiously and asked, "Dude, were you asleep?"

Detective Iliadis responded, "Hell no. I was taking a shit. I'll be ready soon. You want me to drive Big Bertha?" He asked, referring to their armored truck. That was its nickname.

O'Grady replied, "Yeah, sure. Lenno was the operator. Here are the keys." He passed them to his new partner, who had seniority over him. He hesitated before he added, "By the way, there was also a suicide next door. It's someone you know."

"What???" His heart sank. It was not something you ever wanted to hear someone say to you. "No, man. Don't tell me that. Who?"

"Robert Jenkins."

Detective Iliadis' mouth gaped open and he found himself falling back down to his seat. He'd known Robert for over twenty years. He was the younger brother of his former partner, who was now retired. He'd seen Robert grow from a teenager to a responsible man with a family of his own. He had three kids! It was bad enough when they lost their mother to cancer, but now this? It wasn't fair.

O'Grady felt bad being the bearer of bad news. He said, "I'm sorry, pal. It just happened less than an hour ago. Suicide. In the locker room."

"Suicide? Why would he do that?" He asked confused, as his eyes became watery.

O'Grady replied, "They found a bite mark on his arm. He was infected. He saw what happened to his buddies that were infected. I guess he wanted to go out on his own terms, not like some raving lunatic hungry to infect anyone within biting reach. I think I might have done the same, if I were in his shoes."

"I don't know. I suppose. Who can really say what they would do in that kind of situation without ever being in it?" He exhaled and stood up. He wiped aside his tears and said, "Let's kick some ass."

"For Jenkins and all the other cops, who were infected tonight," O'Grady added.

Detective Iliadis nodded, "Especially for them."

Less than a minute later, the blue garage door opened downstairs revealing a large armored truck inside. It's powerful headlights shot to life and the engine revved up. As it rolled out onto the street the rotating lights on the top began to spin, while strobe lights flashed at a super speed, lighting up the block. Big Bertha pulled away from her abode and the garage door closed behind her.

Detective Iliadis hit the loud air horn one time, glanced over at O'Grady, and said, "For Lenno." He then pulled out a Metallica CD from the glove box and inserted it. *Enter Sandman* began to play.

O'Grady smiled and said, "Let's give 'em hell, brother."

"You know it, junior."

0310 HRS, W. 125TH ST., BETWEEN AMSTERDAM AVE. AND BROADWAY:

Meanwhile, back at West 125th Street, at around the same time, Deputy Inspector Ehrenberg was confident that they could put an end to the situation using good tactics and more manpower. "Charles," he said, "I need you to take that sector with you and go around to Broadway. I want to box these numb nuts in, until more help arrives. Don't let anyone slip out. We need to contain this situation. Shoot, if you need to."

Charles asked, "What about the 10-13 at 3170? I was about to go there. There's an officer from ECT fighting someone who's infected."

Deputy Inspector Ehrenberg frowned and said, "I'm sorry to say this, but if he's fighting someone that's infected, it's probably already too late for him. The streets are bleeding! I need to think about the bigger picture and that's gaining control of this block. I can't send the guys that just responded, until I've had time to brief them on what's going on. Otherwise, I'm going to have more dead officers on my hands. They're not ready, so I need you to go to Broadway and lock down that intersection, forthwith. Okay?"

Charles nodded with reluctance and answered, "You got it, boss." He looked at Edward and Marc. "You heard the man. Let's go to Broadway. We'll take West 126th Street. I want you guys to head south and take LaSalle Street. If you happen to stop at 3170 Broadway in the process, I won't be upset. Just don't take too long. Grant and I can't hold them on Broadway alone."

Edward smiled and nodded, before speeding away. Grant and Charles got into their patrol car, drove to West 126th Street, and raced west toward Broadway, where they made a sharp left turn and went south one block. They were quite surprised to see firefighters battling infected at that location.

Grant smirked with pride, as he noted, "Wow. These guys really are New York's Bravest, but they're being over powered. We need to help them."

Charles nodded, "Right. I'll get Debbie to come down and give us a hand." He went over the radio and called for her to respond. "Debbie, get down to 1-2-5 and Broadway."

Debbie knew it was the sergeant's voice calling her into battle. She had been expecting it. She answered reluctantly, "Okay, Sarge. I'm coming." Her voice was shaky when she spoke. Naturally, she was terrified, but she knew how much worse she'd feel, if she stood by and let her friends die.

Grant and Charles parked their patrol car at the southwest corner, a strategic distance away, and got out. It was time to rock and roll. Grant grabbed the crow bar out of the trunk and Charles eyed him strangely. Grant shrugged and explained, "Just in case. We can't shoot all of them."

They ran across the street to where the firefighters were doing battle against several infected. They were standing on the fire truck, using axes and long poles with hooks on the ends called Shepherd's crooks to hold off the infected that surrounded their truck. An illegally parked car on the bus stop around the corner blocked their way and it didn't seem right to just run over hoards of people, even if they were being extremely disorderly. Not to mention, it isn't legal.

One of the infected had managed to climb onto the fire truck. He rushed toward the fire fighters that had been standing their ground from the top of the truck.

Grant aimed his weapon carefully, took a deep breath, and fired his 9mm handgun shooting the infected male directly in the side of the head. The body fell sideways and dropped off the truck onto the street. Grant sighed with relief. He realized he did not shout the usual warning required of the NYPD prior to firing his weapon. It never even crossed his mind to do so. It wasn't like before when Charles ordered them to shoot into the crowd. In that moment, they thought they were about to die. It was a desperate move. This time was different, or was it? There was something almost exhilarating about it.

Charles shot another infected male in the face and that one also dropped down and did not get back up. As far as Charles was concerned, they had to do what was necessary to survive and they were badly outnumbered. He did not feel the same excitement, as his driver.

Unfortunately, the infected had become well aware of their presence. Half of them turned away from the fire truck and charged at them. Charles and Grant retreated back to the other side of the street. Grant was able to swing the crowbar at one that got too close, knocking him back. Two other infected were mowed down by Debbie's car when she skidded onto the scene and took the attention away from them.

Several infected then surrounded her car and began banging on the windows and hood. She put the car in reverse and hit the gas dragging some of the infected across the intersection, as she did. Most of them lay scattered on the street.

Charles was so proud of her. She saved the day. At the same time, he dreaded the amount of paperwork and explaining that would follow, once this crazy nightmare was finally over. He still had not realized there was no coming back from this mess. He was hopeful they would persevere, no matter how long it took. In the meantime, there was no time to think inside the lines anymore. They had to break some rules, if they were going to survive the night. It was all out war on the infected. No holds barred.

One of the infected ran toward Debbie's car and she instantly recognized her. It was the same female, who attacked Louie on Twelfth Avenue and chased her around earlier. Katherine. Debbie knew she had to get this one.

She revved up her engine and raced toward Katherine at full speed, running over two other infected that were on the street. Just before hitting the Katherine, Debbie gritted her teeth and scowled, "Remember me, bitch?"

However, she was so caught up in aiming for the infected female that she did not realize the large iron support beam for the elevated train behind her. Debbie's patrol car smashed into her target, and then rammed into the beam destroying the front end of her car and causing the airbags to deploy. When they did, the one on the driver's side slapped into her face hard and left her dazed.

"Debbie!" Charles called out and ran to her aid. He shouted over to his driver, "Cover me, Grant!" Charles opened the driver's side door to Debbie's patrol car and asked, "Are you okay?"

She looked at him and smiled, before giving him a thumb's up signal.

He grinned back and said, "Sweet Christmas! You're crazy, girl. Let me get you out of there, before we get overrun." He helped her out and they moved closer to Grant.

Grant turned to Debbie and said, "That was some serious badassery, Deb. I'm impressed. Thanks, for saving our asses!"

She smiled and felt proud of herself. No one had ever called her a "bad ass" before.

Charles reminded them they were still in danger. "We need to find a better place to make a stand. I don't think we can hold this intersection for long. There seem to be more of them than before. It must be the ones that were attacked at the fish market. They all seem to be infected. We need to help out those firefighters, as best we can. They're still surrounded. If we join together, we'll have a better chance.

Grant and Debbie agreed. They all selected targets around the fire truck and began shooting. Two more of the infected were killed.

The firefighters finally got a break and were able to jump down from the truck. Unfortunately, the driver, Richie, was already dead. Three infected had managed to yank him from the truck's cab and devour his face and arms. His half eaten corpse lay on the ground beside the truck, while his companions jumped down from the opposite side facing the sidewalk.

One of the firefighters, a burly-looking old timer, called out to the officers, "Thanks, guys! We owe you, big time!"

Within minutes, Edward, Marc, and Winston came running over to join them. They also began shooting at the infected on the intersection.

Winston saw his old friend, Grant, and said, "Hey, Grant. Long time no see."

Grant smiled at him and replied, "It's good to see you alive, old buddy. With the way you were screaming into the radio for help, I thought you were done for sure."

Winston responded in his defense, "I wasn't screaming. I was just a little... excited."

Charles chimed in, "Yeah, you were screaming." He was also surprised to see Winston with them. He looked him over briefly and asked, "So, were you bitten?"

"Again with the was I bitten questioning?"

Charles explained curtly, "There's a virus going around. Were you bitten or not?"

Winston shook his head and responded jokingly, "No, Sarge, I don't think they like Chinese."

Charles and Grant both managed to chuckle, despite the madness going on around them.

"Good," Charles responded.

Winston hated not knowing the whole story. He felt he had risked enough to know the truth, so he asked the sergeant, "What the heck is going on, Sarge? Please, don't give me the bullshit version. I know this isn't normal. This has gotten way out of control!"

"Tell me about it," Charles agreed. "Remind me to fill you in later. No time now. Do me a favor? Shoot as many of these infected individuals, as you can, and don't miss."

He nodded.

All of a sudden, there was a thunderous rumbling sound. At first, it came from above them, so they thought it might have been the train on the elevated tracks, but then they realized it came from the staircase of the elevated train station, which was right next to them. Charles looked up at the stairs and noticed about a dozen people running down to the sidewalk. He gulped nervously and shouted, "Heads up! We have more company on the right! Ed, Marc, watch our backs!"

When the infected mob got to the bottom of the staircase they turned and charged blindly at the officers. There were simply too many of them. There was no way the officers could shoot them all in time. There was only one thing left to do.

Charles yelled, "RUN!"

The emergency room entrance of Mt. Sinai St. Luke's Hospital.

CONTAMINATION EFFECT

Chapter Eight

0311 HRS, MT. SINAI ST. LUKE'S HOSPITAL:

T HE CENTRAL RADIO Dispatcher called out on the radio, "In addition to the 10-13 in the ER, I am getting multiple calls of an EDP running around the first floor of the hospital and attacking people."

As if on cue, Officer David Castillo came over the radio and yelled, "2-6 Frank to Central, we're going to need more cars at the hospital! There are infected patients attacking everyone! Shots fired!"

Steve spoke into his radio next. He advised, "26 Eddie is 84 at the hospital!"

Ricky skidded their patrol car to a halt outside of Mount Sinai St. Luke's Hospital's Emergency Room entrance on West 113th Street. He and Steve arrived just in time to help one of the EMTs, who only minutes ago transported their friend, Kahn.

The male EMT was fighting with none other than Kahn himself. The EMT was using an oxygen tank to keep Kahn at bay. He kept swinging it and using it to push Kahn away. His female partner was lying in the back of the ambulance and was not moving. She was covered in blood.

Steve knew this meant Kahn was already lost to them. Without a cure there was no way to save him. Taking him into the hospital was no longer an option with things out of control inside. Plus, they still had to go in to help Sectors Adam and Frank.

Steve tried to close the ambulance doors to lock Kahn inside the back, but Kahn stepped out and down to the driveway of the ambulance bay, where the ambulance was parked. At that point, the rear door was the only thing between Kahn's teeth and Steve's face. Suddenly, Ricky grabbed Kahn from behind, spun him around, and tossed him to the ground. It was only a temporary solution, but it was enough for Steve to pull out his weapon and take aim. He fired two shots. One hit Kahn in the face. He immediately fell limp and stopped moving.

Steve grimaced, "I'm sorry, Kahn."

Ricky wiped his brow, "Whew! That was a close call." He looked down at Kahn and frowned. "Poor bastard," he said. "This night is really turning out to be shitty."

"You said a mouthful," Steve agreed. He then turned to the EMT and asked, "Hey, are you okay? Did he bite you?"

The EMT, whose last name was Perez, according to the name tag on his uniform, responded enthusiastically, "Hell no!"

"Lucky for you," Ricky smirked.

Perez frowned, "Yeah, but not for my partner! Your boy attacked her! Shit, let me check if she's still alive!" He rushed to the rear of the ambulance and Steve grabbed him, preventing him from climbing inside to check on his partner.

"Be careful!" Steve warned. "*If* she's alive, she's infected now. You don't want to get too close, if it can be avoided."

Perez swallowed fearfully and asked, "So, there's no cure to this thing?"

Steve shook his head and replied, "No. Not as far as we can tell. We still aren't sure what it is either. We think it's an experimental drug of some kind. It's definitely deadly and very contagious. That's pretty much all I can say, for now. The rest is just speculation."

Perez let out a sigh and stared at his partner's lifeless body lying on the floor in the back of the ambulance. She did not appear to be breathing and there was a lot of blood everywhere. It was hard to tell if the blood was hers or Kahn's. It was most likely a combination of both, which made it hazardous. Perez did not want to risk getting infected. He was pretty sure his partner was dead. There was no need to get close to verify. He closed both doors, sighed heavily, and turned to the officers.

"So, what now?"

"Wait out here," Steve said. "We need to go in and check things out. Someone called for help in the ER."

Before he and Ricky could enter, David and Elizabeth came rushing out.

Steve noticed Elizabeth looked weakened and possibly injured. David was helping her to walk. Steve immediately inquired, "Are you guys okay? Did you get bitten? Where's Sector Adam?"

David rested his weakened partner on the rear metal bumper of the ambulance and took a moment to catch his breath before answering any questions. He was exhausted and his uniform was disheveled. His partner looked too shaken up to speak. She just stared straight ahead with the same look of a deer caught in the headlights.

A moment later, David explained the situation, "Carmen is dead. Pat killed her. He also attacked two nurses and a doctor, before I had to take him down."

Steve looked saddened by the news.

David noticed and added, "Sorry, Steve. I honestly had no choice. We did what we had to do. Jasmine killed Louie, after he bit her. She's not dead, but she is definitely infected. I lost her somewhere inside. It's total chaos. That freak from the accident scene is still in there roaming around, too. Some stupid doctor thought he could handle her and she escaped, after biting into his face. We brought someone in, too, who was bitten. He told us a homeless man attacked him on West 133rd Street and Amsterdam. He was able to fight him off long enough for a car filled with people to pass by and get his attention. The homeless man ran north chasing the car like some stupid dog. I waited around for the sergeant and ended up calling him. He told me some bad news about Robert."

Steve nodded, "We already heard."

"It's crazy," David continued sadly. "I still can't believe he's gone."

They were all quiet for a moment, while they thought about the deaths of their friends.

Finally, David finished his story, "So, that guy we brought in. He freaking went nuts and attacked everyone around him. He was a pretty big guy. One of the hospital security guards, Marko, came to help, but some other patient stabbed him for no reason. He kept shouting some nonsense about the end of days. I had to shoot him. Either that or he would have continued stabbing Marko. The next thing I knew, Liz was getting attacked by that ESU cop, who was with us at the accident scene. That's when she was bitten. I tried to shoot him, but couldn't get a clean shot. He chased after a nurse. I heard screaming and thought about trying to help her, but then I looked at my partner and decided it was best to get her out."

Steve closed his eyes and put his head down. He knew it was only a matter of time before she became aggressive and tried to bite them. He looked at her and she could tell what he was thinking.

She mumbled in a scared voice, "I'm gonna be like them. Aren't I?"

Steve looked up at her in surprise. It was good that she was able to speak, he thought. It was just sad that she was infected. He nodded at her and said, "I'm sorry, Liz."

Ricky shook his head in disbelief and said, "I can't believe our entire tour is being taken out, one by one, all because of some stupid virus. We'll probably all be dead by the time the day tour starts."

"Ricky!" Steve scolded him. He gestured toward Elizabeth, who was starting to cry.

David turned to her and put his arm around her. He tried to console her, even though he knew there was nothing he could say that would fix things. She was infected and she would eventually die. It was a cold hard fact. They all knew it.

Ricky asked David, "Hey, Dave? Did you say there are still aggressive infected people running around in there?" He pointed toward the entrance of the Emergency Room, which was directly behind them. Steve and David looked toward the entrance simultaneously. The doors were metal with rubber edges, which only required a soft push to open. A set of automatic glass sliding doors was the only protection past that.

Right away, Steve said, "We need to block these doors. Perez," He turned to the EMT. "Can you use your ambulance to block these doors?"

Perez hesitated before answering. He wasn't too crazy about giving up his ride. He wasn't about to be stranded without a means to get back to his base at the end of his shift. The wheels began turning fast, as he came up with an alternative solution. Finally, he replied, "Actually, I have another idea. Let's move that vending machine over there in front of the doors. We can lay it down blocking both doors. Then you guys can park one of your *three* patrol cars out here to hold it in place."

Steve smirked at him. He wasn't too pleased with the response, but he understood. No one in his right mind would deliberately give up his means of transportation, especially on a night like this.

"That might work," he said. "Let's try to keep quiet with the vending machine. We don't want to make too much noise or someone will hear us and come out."

The men all grabbed it together and were able to practically lift it. They moved it over a few feet and set it into place. Next, they laid it down gently against the doors.

"Okay," Steve said, as he looked at David. "I don't suppose you got Jasmine's keys before she ran off?"

David grinned and pulled them out from his rear pants pocket. He replied proudly, "As a matter of fact, the lieutenant wanted me to bring their car back to the station house because he took them off the rundown and figured we may need an extra car with the way things were going."

Ricky beamed, "Awesome!"

Steve said, "Perfect. We'll take their car and leave the Housing car we were using here. We can put Kahn's body in the driver's seat. I don't want to leave him on the ground."

David nodded and gave the keys to Steve.

Perez pulled his ambulance out of the ambulance bay and parked in front of the main Emergency Room waiting area entrance. A secured locked door separated the waiting area and triage from the main Emergency Room, so it was unlikely any infected would come out that way. As the ambulance moved out of the way, Ricky backed Kahn's patrol car into the bay and stopped against the vending machine bumping it slightly. There was no way anyone would be able to push the doors open from the inside.

They moved Kahn's body into the vehicle, and then Steve removed Kahn's weapon and ammo clips from his gun belt.

"We can't leave this here," he said.

Someone slammed against the doors from the inside. The doors barely budged against the weight of the vending machine and patrol car. Whoever it was began screaming and pushing at the doors.

Elizabeth shrieked loudly and David grabbed her. He quickly led her away from the doors.

The rest followed rapidly and stood a safe distance away at the edge of the curb near their vehicles.

Steve frowned despairingly, "This hospital is lost to us. That's a huge problem, considering what we are dealing with here.

David agreed, "Yep. So, what's the plan?"

Steve glanced at Elizabeth and replied, "Take her to the station house and put her somewhere safe. We're going back to West 125th Street to help the sergeant."

Ricky added, "And keep an eye on her! You don't want her biting you."

Elizabeth gave Ricky a dirty look, while Steve and David shook their heads in disappointment. Sometimes, Ricky had no tact when he spoke. He often spoke without thinking about the things he said or their consequences.

"What?" He asked, "Am I lying? I'm just telling it like it is. She's a big girl. She can handle it. She knows what's going to happen. It's no secret to any of us." He felt more frustrated because he was really talking about himself. He knew he was infected. It was only a matter of time, before that would make a difference.

David became annoyed, "Enough, Ricky. Yes, we know. Let's just get out of here. Jesus Christ," he shook his head and escorted his partner to their patrol car.

Steve began walking toward Sector Adam's car and said to Ricky, "Let's go, Ricky." He then tossed Ricky the keys, so he could drive.

Perez asked, "What should I do?"

Steve shrugged, "Follow us, if you want. You can be our new mobile hospital, if we need you. Park the ambulance someplace quiet like on Claremont Avenue. Oh, and get rid of your partner's body. You know? To be on the safe side."

Perez had no intention of dumping his partner's body just anywhere, so he ignored the remark. He had been working with her for too long. They were not just partners. They were friends. He did think of something he could do. He said, "I'll notify my dispatcher and let them know not to send anyone else to this hospital. My supervisors can deal with it."

Steve replied, "I'll do the same with my dispatcher. We need to consider this hospital closed. It's a good thing there are other hospitals in Manhattan North."

Perez followed Sector Eddie/George across West 113th Street to Broadway, and then north toward West 125th Street. A few blocks before West 125th Street, they reached LaSalle Street. Perez turned left and went to Claremont Avenue, as Steve suggested. He'd continue north through that avenue and park at the next intersection, which was Tiemann Place. He'd wait there, until he was needed.

When the ambulance came to a stop, he decided to leave it running, in case he had to move fast. From his vantage point, he could look east toward Broadway. He heard several gunshots coming from that direction.

0320 HRS, W. 125TH ST., BETWEEN AMSTERDAM AVE. AND BROADWAY:

As Emergency Service Unit Truck 2's "Big Bertha" turned from Old Broadway onto West 125th Street, Detective Iliadis finally began to appreciate the severity of the situation he was heading into straight on. His eyes opened wide and he cried out, "Holy shit!"

There were nearly one hundred people running around back and forth from one side to the other. Most of them were infected chasing after the last of their victims on that street. Considering it had been a Friday night, there were more people on the streets than the typical weeknight. The fish market had been packed when things began to go bad. There were double-parked cars in front of it, as usual. A bus was stopped at the bus stop near Broadway facing east. Somehow, an infected person must have gotten inside and attacked the passengers and driver because only infected were on the bus now.

The police managed to set up a blockade at Amsterdam Avenue, but they were losing ground. The Specialized Response Group tried marching down the street in a wedge formation, but the infected were not like the typical disorderly crowd. They attacked the police and surrounded them, until the wedge formation had crumbled away and turned into a Roman shield wall. Cops fought for their lives to escape the hungry crowd that now dominated West 125th Street.

Over on Broadway, there was a fire truck blocking the road heading east. One police car was parked across the intersection, while another was crashed against an elevated train support beam. The cops on Broadway were running from a crowd of infected people that came down the stairs of the train station. A few firefighters were beckoning for them to run into a fried chicken restaurant behind the parked bus. There was also a car boxed in between the bus and fire truck that looked empty.

Iliadis turned the truck a hard right toward Broadway, abandoning his original plan to go toward Amsterdam. He stopped Big Bertha next to the fire truck in a way that blocked the rest of the intersection. Now, they had an armored wall to work with, he thought. He turned to his younger partner and said, "Let's get out there and make a difference."

They climbed out of the truck and up onto its roof using a ladder in the rear. We'll hold our ground up here. Shoot anything that looks menacing."

O'Grady began by shooting the infected that were chasing the officers into the restaurant. He aimed his Colt M4 Carbine and fired one shot at a time picking off a target with each round. He wanted to make sure not to miss any shots, so he took his time making sure to breathe slow steady breaths. He figured they were safe on top of the truck, so there was no need to worry about being attacked. There was little or no danger that the infected would shoot back.

Iliadis focused his shots on trying to save the SRG cops, who were dwindling down fast.

The firefighters cheered them on, which was ironic, since FDNY and ESU always seemed to be rivals in the past. This time, they felt like they were on the same side, although they always were.

Meanwhile, Charles and his officers ran into the Lincoln Fried Chicken with the firefighters. The firefighters struggled with the security roll down gate, which was electronic. It had to be closed from the outside. That was going to be a problem with everyone on the inside. One firefighter named Yanko went back out and yanked the gate down using a Shepherd's Crook he was carrying. He was able to pull it all the way to the ground.

Just as he did, two infected people tackled him and began eating his flesh. Like with most of their other victims, the infected devoured his face first because it was the easiest part of the body to bite, since it was uncovered. Yanko screamed in terror, as his friends and the other officers looked on helplessly from within the restaurant. At least, they were safe now because of his sacrifice.

O'Grady could not get a clear shot, so he jumped over to the fire truck and ran along the top, until he had a clear shot. He fired down at both infected attackers and they fell beside their victim. It was too late. Yanko lay still with most of his face missing and covered in blood.

"Damn it," O'Grady cursed.

0323 HRS, 3170 BROADWAY:

Ricky and Steve continued north on Broadway toward West 125th Street. As they did, a job came over their radio.

"In the 2-6, I'm getting a 10-34, assault in progress, at 3170 Broadway on the tenth floor hallway. Be advised, I'm also getting an EDP on the same floor. It might be one in the same. Housing 92-20? Are you still at that location? Can you please pick up these jobs upon completion? I have no available sectors in the 2-6."

Naturally, there was no response, since they were probably already dead.

Ricky remembered their original patrol car was still parked in front of 3170 Broadway. He turned to Steve and said, "Our car is still there. We can always handle those jobs, and then switch back to our own car. This car is a shitbox. It has no pick up. If we need to drive fast, we'll be better off in our car, instead."

Steve agreed they should switch cars, but he had no intention of going into that building. It was a deathtrap and there was still a riot on the next block with shots being fired. That was more important.

"The Housing jobs can wait," he stated firmly. "We need to deal with that riot, before things get too out of control. Those gunshots are probably our guys."

Ricky wasn't too sure. He spent a few years in the military and could tell those shots were coming from Emergency Service Colt M4

Carbines, not 9mm handguns. He shared his opinion, "That sounds more like ESU. Those shots are not coming from handguns."

"All the more reason for us to get there and help out," Steve replied.

They stopped behind their original patrol car, got out of the other car, and prepared to switch vehicles.

Steve suggested, "Let's be quick about this. I can see, at least, three patrol cars down the hill from here and one looks like it crashed into the support beam of the el."

"Ouch," Ricky cringed. "That's not good." He quickly unlocked the doors to their original patrol car, and then looked downhill toward West 125th Street. "Yeah, I see them." Before he could sit inside the car, he heard someone calling them in Spanish. "Did you hear that?"

The yelling grew louder, "*POLICIA!*" It was a female's voice.

Steve turned to see where the yelling was coming from. Of course, it was 3170 Broadway. He noticed a woman banging on her fourth floor window. He told Ricky, "I see her. There's a woman on the fourth floor calling down to us."

Again, she called, "*POLICIA!*" She pounded desperately on her window and waved frantically when they both looked up at her. She shouted in broken English through a heavy Spanish accent, "JOO NEE TO COME, *RAPIDO!* THE MANG, HE'S OUTSIDE THE *PUERTA! POR FAVOR!*"

Steve and Ricky looked at each other and sighed. They couldn't just ignore her.

Just then, the dispatcher called over another job in the building, "In the 2-6, I'm getting another EDP at 3170 Broadway. Female caller states unknown male is on the fourth floor banging on doors and screaming in the hallway."

Steve spoke into his radio and said, "26 Eddie to Central. Show us 84 at 3170 Broadway. We'll see what we can do."

The Central Radio Dispatcher responded gratefully, "Thank you, Eddie. Can you also handle a 34 on the tenth floor, which is also coming over as an EDP? I'm also showing a possible jumper on the roof. Oh, dear. I'm now getting a job of disorderly males on the eighth floor hallway. I'm sorry, Eddie, but while you're there, can you also see if you can find Housing 92-20? I still have them at that location."

Ricky complained, "Whoa! Is she nuts??? We can't handle all of those jobs!"

Steve assured him, "Don't worry. We won't. I have a strong feeling they are all probably related to this infected mess. We'll just take the elevator to the fourth floor and deal with the one EDP. If he's infected, we'll shoot him and leave. No time to be subtle about it."

Ricky agreed, "That's fine by me."

They entered the lobby and came to a full stop when they noticed a dead body on the floor. It was definitely a step up from the blood trail they found earlier.

Ricky commented, "Okay, this wasn't here when we left the building."

Steve pulled out his gun and said, "Be ready for anything." He noticed Ricky already had his gun drawn. They both checked the rest of the lobby to make sure there were no surprises around any corners. It appeared empty.

Steve pressed the elevator's call button and they waited. When the elevator doors opened, they immediately retreated to the exit of the building, almost tripping over the dead body. Inside the elevator were five infected males. All of their faces had been eaten, along with parts of their bare arms. They stumbled clumsily out of the elevator and began walking slowly toward the officers. There was no other way to describe it. These guys looked like zombies.

Ricky's wrist ached and itched, as he held his gun up and aimed at the infected males. When Steve said to take them out, Ricky was already pulling the trigger. Together, they took out all five infected. The gunshots echoed loudly in the lobby, causing them to step back out of the building. As they did, the other elevator arrived. It was also full of infected! There were three that stepped out first, followed by another two that stood in the doorway of the elevator a little too long. The door began to close on them. One fell forward and the other stepped back inside. The doors closed with him in it.

The first three that had already exited lurked closer toward the exit, where Steve and Ricky stood with guns out. In addition, two that were shot began standing up, as another appeared in the stairwell.

"Shit," Ricky cursed. "Are you kidding me??? Did you aim for their heads when you shot these guys?"

Steve was agitated when he shot back, "I aimed for whatever I could hit! There are too many! There's no time for marksmanship! We need to get the hell out of here!"

Ricky didn't argue with that idea.

They turned and ran for their car.

Ricky looked up at the woman on the window and shouted, "Keep your door locked and stop yelling out of the damned window!" When he turned around a body splattered down beside him. "Holy shit! Did you see that? Are we wearing 'jumper' targets on our heads? That's the second person to land a few feet away from us!"

"Forget it! Let's get back to the car and find our people," Steve shouted.

The Hispanic woman watched in despair, as the police ran from her building without helping her. She began saying her prayers, but that was not going to save her or anyone in the building from the virus that spread quickly from floor to floor.

CONTAMINATION EFFECT

Chapter Nine

0325 HRS, 26TH PCT:

THE BODY OF Officer Robert Jenkins had been lying on the floor in the male officers' locker room restroom for about an hour. He had been covered with a blanket taken from the male officers' dormitory. Sergeant Ryan Taylor sat nearby outside of the restroom. Someone had to stay with the body, until it could be processed and removed. With the way things were going, there was no telling when that would be. It was a miracle they were able to get an EMT to pronounce the body dead.

Ryan wondered if it might have been wiser to have the EMTs transport the body to the hospital, while they were still here. Of course, it was too late now. Besides, they were needed on West 125th Street to help an injured Housing officer. It was a good thing they were nearby for that, he thought.

Since there weren't any spare officers around that could guard the body, the sergeant proudly volunteered.

He felt bad about Robert. He had only known him for a year, but it was enough time to know that he was a good guy and a hard worker. Most of the guys liked him. Therefore, his suicide was going to be a tough blow to take for the rest of the officers.

Ryan looked at the time on his watch. It was still early with about five hours to go before the end of tour. It was going to be a long night. He hoped no one else would die. One dead officer was already too many.

He became confused when he noticed a strange shadow appear over his watch. Was there someone else in the locker room with him? He turned to see if anyone was behind him. His eyes shot wide open when he saw Robert's imposing figure standing over him. Apparently, the shot that killed him did not destroy his brain. Before Ryan could react, the reanimated Robert grabbed him by the throat, lifted him up, and bit into his chin. He pulled back his teeth and ripped Ryan's bottom lip off, but his grip did not loosen. He was not done with his meal, yet. He took another chunk, this time from Ryan's left cheek.

Ryan cried and tried to scream, but he could not get a sound out with Robert's large hand clamped around his throat. He had trouble trying to breathe and began losing consciousness. Meanwhile, Robert took another bite out of Ryan's face and just chewed.

Lieutenant Andrews was seated behind the desk upstairs on the main floor. He was stressed out. This night was turning out to be one of the worse in his career. Several of his officers were infected with a strange virus, another committed suicide in his station house, and there was a full-blown riot a block away from the precinct. In all his eighteen years on the job, he never dealt with anything as bazaar as what was going on tonight. The stress was only making his bad knee act up. The pain was killing him. Oh, what he would give to be home with his legs up on the sofa, watching television.

And where the hell were those detectives from Night Watch? According to the powers that be at the borough base, they were tied up with some mess at Harlem Hospital. Surely, whatever was going on in the confines of the 32nd Precinct could not be as bad as what was happening in the 26th Precinct tonight? Well, perhaps on every other night of the year, but certainly not tonight! This was serious business.

Didn't they read the 49 that Charles emailed earlier? Surely, that report should have been enough for them to realize this was something out of the ordinary.

A short time later, David and Elizabeth entered the building using the handicap entrance ramp that led in from the driveway. David closed the doors behind him and helped his weary partner to the nearest seat. He then went in front of the desk to address the lieutenant.

"It's crazy out there, Lou," he started, as if the lieutenant was not already aware of the situation outside. "We lost the hospital. We're losing 125th Street. Cops are dying around us and now my partner is infected with this damned virus."

Lieutenant Andrews sat up and asked, "What? Wait! Back up a minute. What do you mean we lost the hospital and exactly which cops are you referring to that are dying around us?"

David updated the lieutenant and told him how badly things went at the hospital. He explained about how his partner was attacked, the newly deceased members of the service from that incident, and added his personal observations from the riot on West 125th Street, which he had to pass on the way to the station house. Things were really looking bad out there.

The lieutenant looked grim and tried to think of his next move. The situation had grown worse. He didn't believe it possible. How much worse would things get before they could finally start to get better? Was there no end to this madness?

No longer having the hospital as an option, it became necessary to find a safe place to keep Elizabeth, before it was too late. They cleaned up one of the precinct's holding cells and locked her inside for everyone's safety. Naturally, she did not like the idea, but she knew it was the best solution under the current circumstances. The lieutenant made certain she had a blanket and a pillow from the female officers' dormitory. David bought her some snacks and a bottle of water from the vending machines in the muster room, although she did not want any of it. She felt too sick to eat or drink and figured it would only make her feel nauseous, if she forced herself.

"I feel weak, Dave," she told her partner. "I think I'm burning up, too. It's funny, my arm hurts, but it also itches like crazy."

David stood just outside the cell and tried to comfort her, as best he could. He suggested, "You should try to drink some water. It may help with the fever. Do you want me to find you some Tylenol or Aspirin?"

"Yes, please. Thank you, Dave," she called out weakly.

David stepped back outside and checked his equipment bag, which was in the backseat of their patrol car. He knew he had some painkillers in there somewhere.

0330 HRS, LINCOLN FRIED CHICKEN:

Alissa could not believe her rotten luck. Of all the nights to come to Harlem, it figures it would be the end of the world.

She could still hear her best friends coaxing her, "Let's go to the city! We haven't hung out in years! It will be great! We'll go to the club, have a good time, and then have a sleep over just like the good old days."

Really? This was nothing like the good old days, as far as she could recall. First, they stood her up, which is the part that really pisses her off. Next, a damn car crashes into the freaking Dunkin Donuts, before she could have her Mocha Latte! And then to top it off, there's a riot on the streets with insane mutant cannibals running around trying to eat everyone.

Really???

She was lucky to find shelter in the fried chicken place near Broadway. She thought she was done for sure when she was running down the street with the girl that works at Dunkin Donuts. She looked over at her and realized she still didn't know her name.

"Hey, my name's Alissa. What's yours?" She held out her hand to shake the traumatized girl's hand. She looked terrified, as she kept staring out through the gate.

The girl looked at her and gave her a half smile. She took her hand and shook it flimsily and said, "Waleska."

Alissa wondered what kind of name was Waleska. The girl looked like she could be Hispanic like her, or maybe she was Indian? Of course, she could be from the West Indies? Alissa didn't bother to ask. Instead, she asked, "Why do you keep looking out there? They can't get us in here. The cops and firemen will keep us safe."

Waleska remained staring out the window when she responded, "My kids are home. I want to be with them. I live over that way." She pointed across the street up Old Broadway.

"Oh. Sorry," Alissa replied. Now, she understood. She looked over at the other girl, who was already in the restaurant when they first ran in about fifteen minutes ago. She seemed indifferent to what was going on outside, as she finished up her Snack Box of fried chicken.

Alissa asked, "What's your name?"

The girl looked at her, as she finished chewing her chicken. She was very attractive with fair skin and long dark curly hair. Alissa admired her cheekbones and how she wore her eyeliner. Alissa stared at her, waiting for an answer.

The girl wiped her mouth with a napkin and took a sip of her bottled water. She put the bottle down and said, "Elizabeth, but people either call me Liz or Beth. No one really calls me by my full name. I don't like it."

"Oh," Alissa replied coyly. "I'm Alissa. Hi, um, Liz."

Liz smirked, "So I heard. Hi, yourself."

Nearby, the firefighters distracted them both. The burly one had been looking through the gate silently for several minutes. He slammed his powerful hands against the glass door hard and cursed, "Damn it! I can't believe he got himself killed like that!"

Another younger and shorter firefighter grabbed him by the shoulder and said, "Take it easy, Gordon! We don't need you breaking that glass, brother. Yanko sacrificed himself to save us all. Don't damn him for it. He did what he thought was right. Any one of us would have done the same, if in his shoes."

The other two firefighters, John and Paul, agreed, "Absolutely. Definitely."

Charles wiped the sweat from his baldhead with a napkin and said, "Your buddy did a good thing for us. We won't let his sacrifice be in vain."

Grant added, "Yeah, he saved our lives."

Gordon glanced at the officers and moaned, "Yeah, I suppose you guys are right. It just pisses me off that we couldn't do anything to help. We just had to stand here and watch. At least, when those bastards pulled Richie out of the rig, we were able to fight back."

The shorter firefighter behind him said, "I know, pal. I'm angry, too. We all are, but make no mistake. We will get our chance to fight back, again, once we get the heck out of here."

Gordon looked at his young friend and grinned, "Now, you're talking, Sean. We need to think of a way out of this rat dive."

The manager behind the counter exclaimed, "Hey! My restaurant is good! Not a rat dive! Cops eat here! Tell him!" He pleaded his case to the officers.

Grant admitted, "Yeah, it's not bad. I've gotten food here a few times."

Winston nodded, "Yeah, me, too, once in a blue moon."

Gordon shrugged, "Fine. I'm sorry I insulted your fine establishment, kind sir. Thank you for allowing us to hide in here like rats in a goddamned cage. We are extremely grateful. Now, how do we leave?"

Sean told him, "Calm down, dude. There's a back door. I was here when we did the fire inspection last month."

Gordon looked at Sean and smiled, "Thank you, my friend. I feel better already."

Suddenly, they could hear a helicopter passing overhead. It seemed to hover directly over them, and then the police radios all came to life, "Aviation 213 to Central. Show us 84 at the Level 2 Mobilization in the 2-6. Can you advise the D.I. we are here and ask him what he needs us to do?" The loud sound of the rotors could be heard in the background of his transmission making it hard to hear what he said.

The dispatcher acknowledged, "10-4, Aviation. Duty Inspector, are you on the air? Aviation wants to know what you need them to do."

Deputy Inspector Ehrenberg sounded out of breath when he responded, "Aviation, I need to know the extent of this riot on West 1-2-5. How far does it reach?"

The Aviation Unit shined a bright searchlight over the street, which made the infected go wild outside. The searchlight moved up and down the street. After a quick scan, Aviation responded, "Looks bad, Inspector. It looks like it stretches from Broadway to Amsterdam on West 1-2-5, and then it goes north on Broadway to West 1-3-7, north on Amsterdam to West 1-3-5, and you also have some activity on West 1-2-6, between Amsterdam and Broadway."

The Deputy Inspector was quiet for a moment, but then he said, "Acknowledged. Just, uh, keep us informed. Thanks."

Aviation responded with more, "There are also two unusually large fires in the confines of the 3-2. One looks like it's in the area of Harlem Hospital. We show another mobilization in that command that came over City Wide radio."

Edward commented, "Jesus Christ. That's really bad. We're screwed, guys. This is so bad."

Grant nudged him and gestured to the civilians that were listening intently. He whispered, "Let's try not to look too out of control here."

Edward whispered back, "Grant, we are so damn out of control, it ain't funny."

Grant nodded, "Yeah, I know, but they don't need to know that. We don't want them panicking, especially while we are trapped in here with them."

Debbie looked out the window through the gate and got excited. "There's that EMT from the accident! He's one of them!"

Charles scoffed, "That's just great. Another confirmed loss."

Edward added, "That reminds me, so are those guys from 3-0 Frank, who found Debbie for us. I saw them myself. They had that crazy look in their eyes."

"No!" Debbie cried out. "Not them!"

Charles was startled when his cellphone began ringing. He answered it, "Hello?" It was the Deputy Inspector and he wanted to know how things were going over at Broadway. Needless to say, he was not too pleased to learn Charles and his officers were trapped in the Lincoln Fried Chicken. "I didn't have a choice," he explained. "It was either that or death. We were overrun and I didn't have the manpower to hold the intersection, but don't worry. ESU saved the day. They're holding it down outside. Well, if we all had carbine rifles, then it would be a different story. What? I didn't catch that last part. Hello? Inspector?"

It sounded as if his phone had fallen on the ground and there was yelling and screaming in the background.

"Shit," Charles muttered. "He's gone. They got the inspector."

Debbie began crying. Grant comforted her. Most of the officers there from the 26th Precinct had known the inspector for a long time. He was once their Commanding Officer. He was one of the best they ever had. Now, he was gone.

0335 HRS, 26TH PCT:

A yellow taxicab pulled up in front of the 26th Precinct and stopped blocking the street. The driver and his two intoxicated female passengers got out and entered through the main entrance. They walked into the building arguing loudly.

One female passenger yelled after him in a drunken slurred voice, "You *need* to take us to our... *densti-nation!* Come back here, you fat bitch! I'm speaking at you!" She barely spat out the words.

The taxi driver did not turn around, but answered back, "Go to hell, skank! I'm done with you both! Your ride ends here!"

Julie looked up from the cellphone game she was playing and rolled her eyes in annoyance. She put the phone away in the drawer of her desk and stated in a loud stern voice, "Hey! Do not bring that shit in here! You come in here like people. Otherwise, you can turn around and get out! We have enough problems tonight!"

Lieutenant Andrews looked over to the window at the three visitors, who just stormed into his station house on the worst night of his life. He was not happy, but Julie seemed to be handling it. The window in front of her separated the desk area from the main lobby. It was a safety precaution installed to protect department personnel. There was even a metal roll down gate, just in case.

The taxi driver apologized, "I'm sorry. The name's Gary and I'm on the job."

Julie stopped him and asked, "Wait. Which *job* are you talking about exactly?"

Gary responded timidly, "I'm a taxi driver. These..."

Julie shook her head and interrupted him, "No! First of all, you are not on 'the job' because if you were you'd be wearing a uniform like me. Are you a cop?"

He shook his head negatively.

She continued, "Therefore, you are not on 'the job,' so do *not* identify yourself to an officer by saying you are on 'the job.' Okay?"

He nodded silently, as she reprimanded him.

The two drunken passengers he entered with were both giggling uncontrollably behind him. It frustrated the hell out of him, but he remained calm and respectful.

Julie then asked, "Okay, so what can I do for you, sir?"

Gary explained, "You gotta help us. We can't drive around in that freakin' zoo out there. There's cops shootin' people and savages bitin' other people. I saw a car crashed into the Dunkin Donuts, for Christ's sake. Besides, I can't drive around no more with these drunks."

The girl, who was arguing with him before, shouted, "Screw you, fag!"

Gary turned to face her and responded, "What? Look who's talkin', you dike!"

The girl shot back, "Say that to my face, you fat prick! I'll kick your ass!"

Julie stood up and shouted, "Hey, hey! That's enough! You're in *my* house, now! I do the yelling! Not you!" She then added more calmly, "In fact, you guys can't be in here. I'm going to have to ask you to leave."

The girl protested, "Say what? Y'all need to be providing us with protection! We pay your damn salary."

Julie thought about what was going on outside and knew it would be wrong to kick them out. She swallowed her pride, took a deep breath, and said, "Fine. Whatever. You can stay, but there's no need to be nasty, if you are coming to us for help. Is that clear? It's uncalled for."

The girl nodded and replied, "You right. My bad. I'm sorry, boo. It's just crazy sick out there. We can't drive down a street without someone jumping on the car."

"Okay," Julie replied, "First of all, my name is Julie. Not boo. Now, I understand it's crazy out there. We are fully aware of what's going on and we are doing what we can to handle it. You can stay, for now. Just keep it down and sit in the complaint room on the right."

The girl looked confused and said, "That's the left."

Julie sighed, "My right, your left. Doesn't matter. That room there," she pointed.

The girl smiled and said, "Oh, that's cool. Yo, Julie. Y'all got a bathroom up in here? I gots to go!"

Julie pointed, "It's right down that hall on the left."

"My left or your left?"

Julie glared at her silently and pointed in the direction she needed to go.

The girl giggled and said, "Thanks. By the way, my name is Eva and this is Edie."

Julie said nothing.

Edie called after her friend, "Wait up! I think I need to go, too!"

Gary shook his head and mumbled to himself, "Freakin' dikes."

Julie became agitated and said firmly, "Sir, you can sit in *that* room. I don't need to hear your nasty comments."

"Oh, sorry, Officer Julie. Thank you," he said, as he stepped into the complaint room.

The two civilian employees in the complaint room looked up from their computers at Gary, who sat down and made himself comfortable.

Ms. Butler looked back down at her computer and tried to ignore Gary. However, Mr. Brown asked in his Georgian accent, "Can I help you, sir?"

Gary looked up at him and answered, "Huh? Oh! No, thank you. The cop that looks like a little boy told me I could wait in here."

Mr. Brown scoffed, looked him up and down, and commented disapprovingly, "Mmhmm."

Back at the desk area, Lieutenant Andrews sat and listened to the radio. He tried to keep apprised of what was going on outside. He had so many questions. The biggest one was probably, "Why?" He couldn't wait for Charles or the Deputy Inspector to return.

The lieutenant was so caught up on what was going on outside, he forgot to pay attention to what was going on inside. Robert's seemingly dead body stumbled slowly up the stairs from the locker room and bumped into the door. It opened slightly, and then closed. He moved forward, again, and pushed with his body opening the door. He stood there for a moment and looked around, but then heard the lieutenant's chair squeak. He had shifted because of the pain in his knee. Robert instinctively moved in the direction of the sound. He stepped into the desk area and approached the lieutenant from behind. He bent down and grabbed Lieutenant Andrews in a tight hug, before proceeding to bite him on the ear.

"ARGH!"

Julie turned around instantly and almost fell off her chair when she saw Robert chewing on the lieutenant's ear. She gasped in horror and froze up. A second later, David came running into the station house from the driveway. He saw what was happening and wasted no time. He ran behind the desk and pulled out his gun.

Robert turned to face him with his blank stare. He moved forward to attack, but David aimed his weapon and fired one shot straight to

Robert's head. Robert fell backward, knocking the lieutenant off his chair. Robert was dead, again.

"Sorry, pal," David whispered, under his breath.

Eva and Edie rushed out of the bathroom to see what was going on. Gary also stepped out of the complaint room with Mr. Brown and Ms. Butler behind him.

David looked toward the entrance past the window at all the faces, who were watching him. He swallowed and holstered his gun. He felt guilty for shooting his friend. He helped the lieutenant up and onto his seat.

"Are you okay, Lou?"

Lieutenant Andrews held his ear with one hand and shook his head, "Ow! Damn it! It hurts! Did he bite off my ear?"

David checked his ear and saw it was partially missing. He answered, "He took part of it. Sorry." He really didn't know what else to say. He pulled a pill bottle from his pocket and said, "I have painkillers, if you want."

The lieutenant grabbed the bottle and took three. He then handed the bottle back to David, who had a worried look on his face. The lieutenant already knew why. Of course, the night would have to end this way. This time, he was the one that was infected. He opened up the property room, which was behind his desk. He grabbed some fresh gauze from a white box and wrapped it around his head tightly. He took one look at David and Julie and swallowed nervously. He bowed his head and went into the holding cell area.

"Lock me in," he instructed.

David grabbed the cell key and did as the lieutenant requested. Deep down he knew it was the best decision. Still, he asked, "Are you sure about this, boss?"

Elizabeth was lying in the next cell watching what was going on. She felt too weak to say anything, but she was saddened by what she was seeing. She hoped no one else would be infected.

Lieutenant Andrews nodded and said, "Tell Charles and find Ryan. He should be downstairs, but be careful," he warned. "He could be infected, as well."

David nodded and took a deep breath. He left the bottle of painkillers within reach and asked the lieutenant, "Can you make sure she takes some?"

The lieutenant agreed, "I'll take care of it."

David left the cell area and stood in front of the door to the staircase that led down. He pulled out his weapon and went downstairs ever so cautiously with his gun out in front of him. Turning around at the middle landing made him nervous. He hoped there would be no surprises around the corner. There weren't. Once he reached the bottom, he opened the door to the locker room and stepped inside. He immediately saw Ryan's bloody corpse on the floor near the restroom at the far end of the locker room.

"Oh, damn."

He approached Ryan and stood over his corpse. It was a dreadful sight to behold with the way his face had been mauled. David stared down at him for what seemed like an hour, although it was only about thirty seconds. At first, it was shock, but then it was more like he was waiting.

Ryan did not move.

David exhaled, holstered his weapon, and moped out of the locker room. He went back upstairs with a heavy heart. Another good man had died.

CONTAMINATION EFFECT

Chapter Ten

0335 HRS, W. 125TH ST., BETWEEN AMSTERDAM AVE. AND BROADWAY:

WHEN RICKY REALIZED he could not enter West 125th Street through Broadway because of the fire truck and Emergency Service truck that blocked the road, he decided to go the wrong way on a one-way street. He turned right at West 126th Street, and then made another right at the next block, which was Old Broadway.

"Stop the car," Steve instructed, before they went down the next block to West 125th Street. "I'm going to give the sergeant a call. If he doesn't answer, we'll try someone else. If none of our guys answer, I don't see a reason for us to risk our lives."

"Good point," Ricky agreed.

Steve waited for Charles to answer. He answered after the second ring. "Oh, good. You're still alive," Steve said with relief. "Where are you guys? You're in Lincoln Fried Chicken? Ricky and I are directly across from you on 126th Street. Can you see us through Old Broadway? What do you need us to do?" He listened and replied, "Okay, we'll do that. You should know the hospital is lost to us. The infected have taken over the ER, which means it's a matter of time before they run out to the streets. Sector Adam didn't make it out. All of our guys there are either infected or dead. Well, Sector Frank got out, but Liz was bitten. Dave took her to the station house. I told him to lock her somewhere safe. I also have an ambulance on stand by for us on Claremont Avenue. One of the EMTs, who took Kahn to the hospital, is there waiting. By the way, I noticed a wrecked patrol car on Broadway. We have keys to Sector Adam's car. It's parked in front of 3170 Broadway. I'll bring them to you." Charles said something to him that made Steve reply, "Don't worry. We'll be fine. ESU can cover us. Okay. Be there in a minute." He hung up.

Ricky asked, "So what's the plan?"

"We'll drive straight to the entrance of Lincoln Fried Chicken. Considering that bus and car are in the way, just pull up next to them and point us toward Amsterdam. I'll get out and give them the keys. First, I'll ask ESU to provide cover fire. Keep the car running. Once I drop off the keys, I will haul ass back to my seat. He wants us to try and pick up any SRG survivors we can find and extract them to a safe location, such as the precinct or their vehicles."

Ricky eyed him apprehensively and asked, "Are you ready?"

Steve nodded, "Let's do it."

Ricky drove to West 125th Street and slowed down near the ESU truck. Steve rolled down his window and shouted up to Iliadis and O'Grady, who were still shooting infected from the top of their truck.

"Can you guys cover me? I need to take something to the guys in the chicken restaurant!"

Iliadis shouted down to him, "We got you covered!"

Ricky moved the car forward and stopped parallel to the restaurant. Steve jumped out and ran behind the parked bus and onto the sidewalk. O'Grady picked off one of the infected that were about to chase Steve. Iliadis took out another.

Charles opened the door to the restaurant. Steve stuck his fingers through the gate and passed him the keys to the car.

"Thanks," Charles said. "Now, get out of here and get somewhere safe."

Steve nodded, "Yeah, just make sure you do the same. Don't stay in that deathtrap too long. I'll see you around."

"You know it."

Steve took a quick peek into the window of the restaurant to see who else was with Charles. He smiled when he saw that Grant, Edward, Marc, Debbie, and Winston were alive and well. They waved and smiled back.

Edward called out to him, "Watch your ass, Steve! Get off the streets already!"

Steve chuckled and turned to go. Suddenly, he saw about five infected people running straight toward him, along the sidewalk. They were behind the bus, so the guys from ESU could not see them, yet. He ran for his patrol car and slammed the door shut, just in time. They almost rammed into the car, but Ricky sped away leaving clear shots for ESU. O'Grady and Iliadis took them all down.

"Holy shit, that was close," Steve exclaimed, as Ricky ran over two more infected, and then struck another one with the car.

"This is kind of fun," Ricky grinned.

"You are a sick man, Officer Colon."

"Screw these guys! They killed some of our friends," Ricky reminded him. "I should drive all around Manhattan and run them all over, and then things can go back to normal."

Steve pointed to a group of cops who were fighting off infected. They were pinned against the bus stop shelter near Amsterdam. "There," he said, "Let's help those guys."

Ricky skidded to a halt hitting two more infected with the front end of the car. He opened his window and shouted, "Get in the car!"

The three officers ran for the car. One ran around to the other side, since there was no way they could all get in on the same side. Officer Cliff Torres got in and moved to the center of the back seat, so the other two officers could get in on either side. Sergeant Gregg Kepster got in the car on the passenger side and shut the door. The third officer was trying to get inside behind Ricky when two infected people grabbed him and began yanking him.

"HELP!" He screamed, "THEY GOT ME!"

Cliff and Gregg grabbed his arm and tried to pull him in, but the infected were already biting into his arm. Ricky stepped on the gas and the car raced forward. The momentum made the rear door close onto the officer's left arm, but it knocked one of the infected off of him. The other infected male lost his grip on the officer's arm, but grabbed onto his leg, as he fell to the ground. The infected man wrapped his hands around the officer's ankle and bit through his pants into the calf of his leg. The officer let out a violent scream.

Ricky looked into his mirror and saw the infected man was being dragged, as he drove. He drove the car onto the sidewalk and sped north on Amsterdam. The streets were backed up with traffic and there were infected people attacking drivers and passengers, so the sidewalk was the best option. Ricky steered the car closer to the buildings and the infected was eventually knocked off.

However, it was too late. The officer had been bitten twice on his arm and once on his leg. He would soon become one of them.

"Oh, man! Those bastards got me good! They bit me about three times!"

Ricky glanced at Steve and gave him a look that said what he felt. They needed to get rid of that officer before the infection took hold of him. Ricky drove off the sidewalk and turned westbound onto West 126th Street. He had to screech to a halt when he noticed a yellow taxi was blocking the street.

"You've got to be kidding me! Even in a time like this these damned taxi drivers have to piss me off! He looked into his rearview mirror and warned his passengers. "Hold on," he said. "We're going backwards."

He went in reverse back to Amsterdam and stopped short before hitting a car that was blocking the intersection. He turned back onto the sidewalk and raced north on Amsterdam. He kept glancing to the road and commented, "This traffic is unbelievable. It wasn't like this before."

Steve reminded him, "We didn't have a bunch of vans blocking the intersection at 125th Street before. Forget about our precinct. Get us to the 3-0 Precinct."

When the car came off the sidewalk at West 133rd Street and Amsterdam, it became apparent that continuing north on Amsterdam was not going to be easy. Traffic was backed up a few more blocks and there was a mob in the streets only two blocks up on West 135th Street.

"Damn," Steve muttered. "This is worse than I thought. Those are infected up ahead."

Ricky turned the car left and headed toward Broadway, instead. He figured maybe the traffic would be lighter. The intersection looked clear at West 133rd Street. He stopped at Broadway and looked north toward West 135th Street. A mob was in the street there, as well, and more cars blocked the way.

"Screw this," he said. "We're going on the highway." Before Steve could offer up an opinion, Ricky was speeding downhill toward Twelfth Avenue. There were still infected people in the street near the nightclub. He drove right through them, as if they weren't even there. Bodies went flying in the air on both sides. The side view mirror broke off on the passenger side. He smirked, "I don't need that mirror."

Their patrol car turned onto the northbound entrance ramp of the Henry Hudson Parkway and Ricky raced up to the roadway.

Steve had been holding on tight. Finally, he said, "Take it easy! If we crash, it won't do us any good!"

"Then we won't crash," was Ricky's response, although he slowed down immediately when the car entered the parkway. There appeared to be heavy traffic ahead, as well as a traffic jam far behind them.

Steve glared at him and remarked, "Good job, Speed Racer. Now, we go nowhere."

The wounded officer groaned in pain behind them. Steve and Ricky both looked at each other worried and braced for what may come, if they could not get the officer out of the car in time.

Gregg was also worried. He asked the officer, "Stan, how are you feeling?"

Stan shook his head and replied, "Not so good, boss. I feel hot. Itchy. It really hurts, too."

Cliff, who was sitting in the middle and was therefore closer to Stan, became deeply concerned. The Deputy Inspector told them this virus was extremely contagious and stressed the importance of avoiding bites, at all costs.

Ricky whispered to Steve, "This isn't going to end well."

0345 HRS, 26TH PCT:

David was seated behind the desk of the precinct, in place of the desk officer. He watched the cells on the security monitors and could see the lieutenant and his partner, Elizabeth, each in holding cells, side by side. He felt miserable. It was no secret what would happen next and there didn't seem to be a way to stop it. All they could do was sit and wait for the inevitable.

The phone rang startling him and snapping him out of his misery, for the moment. He picked it up and answered, "2-6 Desk, Officer Castillo. How can I help you?"

It was Charles calling. He wanted to know how things were going at the station house. David filled him in on the bad news about Robert, Ryan, and told him that his partner and the lieutenant were now infected and locked safely in the holding cells. Charles let him know that they were biding there time in Lincoln Fried Chicken. He also told David about the inspector's demise.

"Stay put and we'll try to come to you," Charles told him, before hanging up.

"Right. Stay put," David repeated to himself. "Where does he think I'm gonna go?"

Julie, who was seated nearby, turned around and asked, "What did you say?"

"Nothing. Just talking to myself."

She looked as if she was going to say something else, but the telephone at her desk rang and she answered it, "Hello, 26th Precinct, how can I help you?" She listened to someone complaining about the noise coming from West 125th Street. "Ma'am. I guess you are not aware there is a riot going on at that location."

David snickered and turned back to the security monitors, ignoring the rest of the conversation. He watched his partner, who was lying still in her cell. She said she felt weak, so he figured she was resting. The lieutenant sat in his cell staring at the floor. The poor guy looked dumbfounded. In an instant, his future was stolen from him. Yet, there he is sitting in a holding cell bored out of his mind, as he waits for it to happen. That is torture, David thought.

He decided to check on them both figuring they might enjoy some human contact, even if for a moment. He stood up and began to walk away from the desk area when someone came running into the front door. David turned around and went back to the desk. He made a mental note to lock the front doors, after this guy left.

Julie finally hung up the phone and greeted the guy, "Hi, can I help you?"

The guy was looking around frantically, but said nothing. He tried to pull open a door that led up to where the detectives' office was located. The door was secured with a security keypad lock.

David became concerned. Who the hell was this guy and why wasn't he speaking? "Hey! What do you want?" He asked with authority.

The guy looked at him, and then looked at Julie. He looked terrified. He ran into the complaint room. Now, David was worried. Whoever this guy was, he needed to go. David walked fast toward the door, which led out to the lobby. Julie did not budge from her seat. Instead, she peeked out through the window to see what the man was doing.

David opened the door and the man grabbed it. He tried to force his way into the desk area. David had to punch him in the face to stop him. He then pushed the guy down to the floor. David stepped out and closed the door, so the man could not enter the secured area behind the desk.

The man remained on the floor and looked toward the main entrance. His eyes opened wide and he said, "They're coming!"

At that moment, there was a furious banging against the front doors, which were glass. David walked over to look and saw there were about six infected people pounding on the glass. Apparently, they were not good at pulling doors open or they would have already been inside.

Everyone stepped out of the complaint room to see what was going on. As they did, the man on the floor began rolling around and screaming in pain, while the infected pounded harder on the doors.

David knew all too well what was going on. He shouted to the others, "We need to get away from this guy before he changes! He's infected!"

"Just shoot him!" Gary the taxi driver shouted.

David thought about it and figured, why the hell not? He pulled out his weapon and tried to aim at the man's head. It was hard to get a clean shot with the way he kept squirming around on the floor and jerking back and forth abruptly. David stepped closer and stood over him, but the man kicked his leg upwards and caught David off guard. His gun flew out of his hand and slid across the floor down the hallway that led to the restroom and several offices.

"Shit!" David cursed, as he went to retrieve his weapon.

The sound of glass hitting the floor and shattering could be heard followed by incoherent yelling and screaming. They had broken through the first set of glass doors. David grabbed his gun quickly and leapt over the man, who was still twisting and turning wildly on the floor and screaming in pain. All of a sudden, he stopped screaming.

David froze. He turned to face the man and aimed his gun at the man's head. The man's eyes flared up and became wild with desperation and rage. His mouth dropped open in the ready position to bite the nearest piece of flesh. However, before he could stand up, a loud bang was heard, and he dropped back to the floor with a thud. He was dead.

The civilians all covered their ears instinctively when David fired the shot.

He pulled open a set of double doors that led to the muster room and told the civilians to get inside. The doors had to be pulled open, so they would be relatively safe inside once the second set of glass doors gave out. He hoped the infected that were pushing up against the doors and banging away on the glass probably wouldn't think to pull the door open, if they had not done so already with the other doors. The doors to the muster room were not made of glass, so they would not be broken easily. They all listened to David and ran through the doors. He told Julie to pull down the roll gate, so the window would be sealed, as well. She stood up and could not reach it.

David closed the door and ran around the desk and into the area behind the desk. He rushed to Julie's desk and grabbed the gate. He tugged at it, but it was stuck. It had been up so long from lack of use that he could barely budge it. He tried pulling from a different angle.

The glass on the front doors began to crack and Julie stepped back. She thought about running for the rear door, but David was in her way.

David shouted at her, "Don't just stand there! Help me!"

She hesitated and stretched her arms up as far as she could. Her fingertips were touching the bottom of the gate. David gave it a good hard yank and it came down enough, so that Julie could get a good grip on it. Together they pulled it down just as the glass busted out and fell to the floor. The infected fought their way around the metal frame of the door and slammed into the roll down gate at the window.

David and Julie looked at each other and let out deep breaths.

"We need to get the hell out of here," he told her. "I have my patrol car out by the gas pumps, but I can only fit four with me."

She replied, "Screw the taxi driver and those drunk bitches. They can get away in his taxi."

David shrugged. It sounded like a plan that might work. Staying in the precinct definitely would not work. He grabbed a fresh battery for his department radio, and then sent Charles a text message on his cellphone telling him not to return to the precinct. Next, he took one last look at his partner in her cell. She was either asleep or unconscious. However, the lieutenant was standing up against the door.

"What's going on out there?"

David answered somberly, "There are infected in the building. We need to leave. I'm… I'm sorry. You should both be safe in there."

The lieutenant looked horrified at the thought of being left in the cell unattended.

Suddenly, someone in the muster room screamed in terror.

0347 HRS, LINCOLN FRIED CHICKEN:

As the night went on, it became more apparent that they were fighting a losing battle. The 911 calls kept flooding the system. There were calls coming in from all over of disorderly people, violent emotionally disturbed individuals, assaults, vehicle accidents, and criminal mischief. The radio dispatcher tried calling sector cars to handle these jobs to no avail. There were sectors that had not been answering their radios for over an hour from both the 26th and 30th Precincts.

When the radio dispatcher tried calling the 30th Precinct to speak with a supervisor, there was no answer. The phones at the 26th Precinct were busy.

Charles had just hung up his cellphone, after speaking with David, who was at the 26th Precinct. He could not believe how the night kept getting worse by the hour. Ryan and the Deputy Inspector were both dead and now the lieutenant was infected. That left Charles in charge. A lot of good he was doing hiding out in a fried chicken fast food restaurant. He looked out the window and saw the two ESU officers still shooting infected from the top of their trucks. He needed to be outside with them.

He turned and looked at everyone in the crowded restaurant. It was far too small for them to stay there much longer. There were too many of them. It was up to him to come up with a plan. If he was in charge, he needed to play the role properly.

His cellphone rang and he answered it. It was Steve Blake. "What's going on, Steve? Did you manage to save anyone? Please, tell me you did."

Steve told him about the three SRG officers he and Ricky grabbed up and about how they had to head to the highway because there was nowhere else to go. He did not mention that one of the officers was infected, but he said they were still stuck in traffic. It was frustrating, but refreshingly normal.

Charles laughed and said, "I'd love to be stuck in traffic, right now, instead of where I am. You guys get somewhere safe. We will do the same. Keep me updated. Talk to you later," he said, as he ended the call.

Grant asked, "Traffic? What traffic?"

Charles told them all about his conversation with Steve.

Edward sounded hopeful and said, "That means this thing still hasn't spread uptown. We can get help from the 33rd and 34th Precincts!"

Marc perked up at the idea of hope.

Debbie had just bought some food. She leaned on the counter and started eating chicken. The other officers looked at her and she stated, "I'm hungry. Sue me. Who knows when I'll get to eat, again?"

Charles said, "Eat fast. We need to get out of here. That's our first priority. Those ESU guys can help us. They are doing a good job of keeping Broadway clear." He turned to the firefighters and asked Sean, "You mentioned a back door before. Where does it lead?"

"Broadway," Sean replied.

"Perfect," Charles said. He told the manager, "We are going to need to access the back door of your establishment." The manager complied right away and opened the door for them to go behind the counter. Charles gave him a nod and said, "Thank you." He turned to his officers and said, "Let's go. We are leaving."

Gordon stated, "We're leaving, too. If we can get back to our truck, we should be able to help out better than being trapped in this dive."

The other firefighters all agreed.

Waleska stood up and said, "I want to go with you. I need to get to my kids."

Charles and Gordon looked at her and before either of them could respond, Alissa also stood up and said, "I need to get the heck out of here, too. This place is a deathtrap. You guys know it. If we stay here too long, we won't ever be able to leave."

Liz agreed, although she remained in her seat. "I've been watching those people, since this thing started up," she said. "At first, I thought it was a passing thing, but the longer I sat here, I realized this was something big. I've seen those maniacs force their way into that bus out front and slaughter everyone inside. I've watched them run back and forth chasing after people and God help anyone they caught. I've seen them climb up onto your fire truck, but do you know what I haven't seen? Not one of them even thought to pull the door to this restaurant open. Whatever is wrong with them, it is obviously affecting their intelligence. They seem to be running on adrenaline and instinct. They are dangerous, but they can be stopped, if you are willing to do the job. People will die. It's part of war. Staying anywhere surrounded by them for too long is only going to end in death. If you are leaving, I am going with you."

Charles and Gordon looked at each other, and then looked back at her. Charles asked, "Who are you?"

Liz stood up and emptied her tray into the trash. She then replied, "I'm just a woman, who doesn't plan to sit here and wait to die. Now that you boys are finally on the same page as me, I think we've wasted enough time in this dump."

Gordon grinned and turned to the other guys. "I like this chick. If she wants to come along, I have no problem with it. I have a feeling she can handle herself."

She responded, "I have some military experience and lots of street experience."

They all took a moment to take in her appearance. She wore long, black, leather boots up to her knees, tight blue jeans, and a black t-shirt that read, "No Lives Matter."

Grant said, "She's got my vote. They all do. We can't leave them behind to die. She's right. It's only a matter of time, before this place is overrun. Even if it isn't, we can't expect anyone to stay here for however long this lasts. It could be days."

Winston turned to his fellow officers and asked, "How long do you expect this to last?"

Grant shrugged, "Who can really say? Based on how this night has been going since the start of our tour, it just keeps going downhill. I honestly don't see an end in sight, anytime soon. This may take some help from the National Guard."

Charles agreed, "I'm with Grant. I have someone I can call, who works at police headquarters. She can get the ball rolling."

Gordon smiled, "Excellent! Give her a call!"

Charles looked at him and reminded him, "It's about 4 am, so... no. She starts at 6:30. I'll give her a call when she gets to work."

Edward commented, "I hope she doesn't live upstate. It might be hard getting to work."

Charles shook his head, "Nope. Brooklyn. She takes the Brooklyn Bridge to work. She should be fine." At that moment, he got a message on his cellphone. It was from, David, one of his officers.

The message was short and it was all in caps signifying its urgency. It read, "DO NOT COME BACK TO THE 26!"

"Hmm. Castillo says we can't go back to the precinct. He didn't say why."

Edward assumed, "It must be overrun. It's only a block away from here. We are so screwed. I should have just become a fireman like my dad wanted."

Gordon placed his hand on Edward's shoulder and said, "A lot of good that would have done."

"Oh, yeah. Sorry, guys," he replied.

Charles considered their options and had an idea that may help. Before he could say anything about it, one of the firefighters, John, who kept looking out of the window said, "Guys, it looks like ESU is in trouble."

Charles rushed to his side and peered out of the window. He could see there were about twenty infected people surrounding the side of their truck that faced east toward Amsterdam. The force of them pushing up against the truck was causing it to rock. It became too unsteady for the officers on top, who were now having difficulty aiming their Colt M4 Carbines.

Suddenly, one of the officers fell off into the crowd below. Debbie gasped in horror, while Charles bowed his head in sadness. The infected swarmed around him. His younger partner immediately began firing down at them, but he knew it was too late. Detective Iliadis was gone.

Edward uttered, "No. Not another one." He frowned, "Oh, man. We're dropping like flies."

Just then Aviation came over the radio, "Aviation 213 to Central. Can you raise the supervisor in charge of the mobilization on West 1-2-5?"

Before the dispatcher could do so, Charles answered, "2-6 Sergeant is on the air. Go with your message, Aviation."

"Sarge, do you still need us? We'll need to refuel soon."

Charles took a moment to breathe and responded in a slightly shaken voice, "Yeah." He cleared his throat, "Ahem! Can you give me an update on the farthest reach of the riot?"

Aviation responded, "That's a four, Sarge. It looks a lot bigger. The crowd extends from Broadway to St. Nicholas, up to West 1-3-5 on Amsterdam and south on Amsterdam to West 1-2-2. At Morningside Avenue it also goes south toward the park. Traffic is backed up on Amsterdam and on the Henry Hudson Parkway both ways. Looks like you have accidents on both the north and southbound lanes. There appears to be people running around between the cars. West 135th Street is a mess, too, from Riverside to Amsterdam. There's also a situation at West 113th Street at the hospital."

The Central Radio Dispatcher added, "I'm getting several calls of a fire at the hospital. Aviation, can you verify that for me?"

"That's a four, Central. We do see smoke and FDNY is at the scene. It doesn't look good. Looks like the riot skips all the way from West 122nd to 113th Street, which doesn't make any sense, unless they cut through the park from Morningside. There are also three large fires burning in the confines of the 3-2. We're not sure if they are in relation to what's going on in the 2-6."

Grant groaned to the others, "Shit. It's spreading out of control."

Aviation transmitted another message, which sounded extremely grim, "We advise all units to... *bzzzt*... out from Infected Zone and regroup further north... *bzzzzzt*... borough. The north... *bzzt*... lost from our point of view." Unfortunately, their message was partially disrupted by static and was unclear.

Charles became worried about what he thought they said. He wanted them to repeat it, to make sure he heard them right. He went over the radio and stated, "10-5 that last message!"

"All units should pull out of the Infected Zone and regroup either further north or out of the borough. Manhattan North looks like it is lost to us. Central, show us returning to Floyd Bennett Field to refuel.

Good luck to you guys. God be with you." The sound of the helicopter could be heard overheard fading into the distance.

The Central Radio Dispatcher had already been frustrated, but now she was confused. Unable to wait any longer, her voice came over the radio seeking answers. "2-6 Sergeant, can you *please* 10-3 me? I don't know what's going on out there!" The frustration and impatience was evident in her voice, so the sergeant knew it was time to explain everything to her.

"10-4," he answered with reluctance. He pulled out his cellphone and called her up.

She was desperate to know the situation that was going on in the confines of the precinct. She was having trouble getting through to units in both the 26th and 30th Precincts. She told him she was holding several jobs in both precincts, but there were no available sector cars to assign them to. After what the Aviation Unit said, she couldn't wait anymore. She needed to know exactly how bad things were, especially since she lived in Harlem with her husband and two small children.

That last part was the real kicker.

Charles broke the bad news to her and gave her the entire rundown of what went on throughout the night explaining how he believed it was all related. She could not believe her ears, but it all finally began to make sense to her. He told her about the loss of the many officers, including the Deputy Inspector, and told her how they were losing ground fast.

She remained silent throughout his explanation and waited for him to mention her neighborhood. When he did not, she had to ask, "What about Hamilton Terrace?"

He told her it was free of infection, for the moment, and he hoped to keep it that way. However, he advised her to call her husband and have her family leave Manhattan, as soon as possible.

She thanked him for his frankness and hung up the phone.

About a second later, she went over the radio one last time, "All units... 10-6 for a voice change. Please, be safe. Goodnight." It was the last radio transmission they would hear from that dispatcher and from any other for quite sometime, which only strengthened the realization that they were on their own now.

CONTAMINATION EFFECT

Chapter Eleven

0355 HRS, 26TH PCT:

S OMEONE IN THE muster room had just screamed in terror, while David was in the holding cell area speaking with the lieutenant. It was a long hitch-pitched scream that made David's hair stand on end. He hurried out of the holding cell area and into the muster room, where the others were waiting. He stopped dead in his tracks when he saw Sergeant Ryan Taylor standing there with them over Julie's mutilated body. Ryan was using his hands to tear open her chest. He then dove his face into it and began dining on her innards.

One of the girls in the muster room fainted from the sight. It was the one named Edie. Eva bent down and tried desperately to wake her up. The movement caught Ryan's attention. He moved away from Julie and began walking toward the girls. In that instant, the other civilians fled the muster room and regrouped behind David, since he had the gun.

Eva yelled, "Shoot this monster already! I can't get my friend up!"

David aimed his gun at Ryan's head and fired one shot, but it only struck him in the neck. Ryan bobbed forward and stumbled for a second, before rotating and turning his attention on David. The sight of his half-eaten face made David sick to his stomach. He took aim and fired, again, this time killing him, or so he hoped. Ryan fell to the floor and did not move.

"Help us," Eva pleaded, again. She was still bent over her friend.

David rushed over and holstered his weapon. He asked, "Was she bitten?"

Eva shook her head and said, "No, she fainted."

Relieved David picked her up and carried her out of the muster room.

Eva commented admiringly, "Ooh, you're so strong."

David rolled his eyes and said, "Someone open that door for me. I have a car outside. We need to get out of here.

Mr. Brown complied and opened the door.

"Thank you, Mr. Brown."

David looked down the long hallway of the handicap entrance and realized the door at the end was also closed. He had closed it earlier. Of course, he could push it open easily enough. However, as long as he was carrying Edie, he'd be vulnerable to attack and he wasn't having it. He turned to Gary and said, "I need you to go open that door for me. I'll be right behind you."

Gary looked down the hallway and asked, "Why can't you just push it open yourself?"

David explained, "Because if there are infected out there, I won't be able to fight them off. We'll both be slaughtered."

Gary scoffed, "So put that drunk down and get your gun out. Wake her ass up. I can't believe you plan to carry her to the car. Are you gonna wipe her little ass for her, too?"

Eva leered at him and shouted, "Jerk!"

Gary ignored her.

David glared at him and asked, "Why do you have to be such a dick? Just open the damned door, so we can get out of here."

"No," Gary replied calmly. "I won't be your human shield. Send one of these other suckers."

David rolled his eyes, "I am *not* asking you to be a human shield. I *thought* you were strong enough to fight them off and hold them back for me. I guess I was wrong."

Eva stepped forward and said, "I'll do it."

David explained to her, "You're drunk. Your reflexes are going to be slowed down by the alcohol."

Eva felt insulted and growled back, "Screw you! I can do it!" She marched down the hallway and pushed the door wide open, ignoring David's commands to stop.

"Wait! Stop! Don't open it, yet! I'm not ready!"

As soon as the door was pushed open, two infected women attacked Eva. She screamed in agony, as they ate her face and neck. They tore open her blouse to get at her chest, and then she dropped to the floor. They swarmed over her.

David immediately stepped back out of the hallway and whispered to Mr. Brown to close the door, which he did. David placed Edie down on a nearby table and turned to Gary, who was standing there with a smug grin on his face.

Gary scoffed, "You see? Just like I predicted."

David punched him in the mouth and grabbed him by the shirt. He pushed him against the wall and said, "That's exactly what I was trying to avoid, you dumb ass."

David let him go and pulled out his gun. He turned to the others and stated, "Now, we'll need to do things the hard way."

Mr. Brown assumed, "That's right. Shoot his dumb ass already."

Gary pleaded, "No, please, don't! I'm sorry Officer..." He paused and tried to read David's nametag, but read it wrong. "Cas-till-lio."

David took a deep breath and rolled his eyes, "That's not what I meant and my name is *Castillo*. Idiot." He shook his head in annoyance and continued, "We need to fight our way out of here. We'll no longer have the door as cover, so we'll have to charge into them and hope they don't charge at us first. I'll shoot as many as I can, but I'm not perfect. I might miss and once I'm out of ammo, we're gonna have to do this the super hard way."

Mr. Brown, Ms. Butler, and Gary all looked worried. That first way already sounded like the super hard way to them.

"First," David added, "We'll need to wake her up." He gestured to Edie, who was still lying unconscious on the table.

0358 HRS, BROADWAY:

The firefighter named Sean led Charles and his officers, along with the rest of the firefighters and the civilians through the kitchen of Lincoln Fried Chicken to the back storage room. They stopped when they reached the back door. Sean turned to Charles, who was directly behind him, and suggested, "Maybe you should take the lead from here, considering you have a gun."

Charles switched places with Sean and pulled out his gun. Grant also pulled out his gun and stepped ahead of Sean, who did not complain. Edward, Marc, and Debbie all pulled out their guns and prepared for whatever might be waiting outside that door. Gordon held his axe ready, too.

Before opening the door, Charles said, "Okay, remember the plan. We'll head to the patrol cars and do our parts. Debbie will drop off the civilians. Ed and Marc will shadow her car. Winston, stay on Broadway and get the guy from ESU to come with us. If he cannot bring the truck for whatever reason, have him get into your car, but we could really use that truck. Grant and I will head over to Claremont Avenue and find that ambulance Steve told us about. Hopefully, it's still there. The medical supplies will come in handy. I'll get the driver to follow us to Riverside Drive, where we will meet up at West 116th Street. Everyone got all that?"

His officers all nodded in agreement.

Charles looked to the firefighters and asked, "Are you guys sure you don't want to come with us? It should be safer further downtown."

Gordon replied, "Thanks, Sarge, but we want to get our truck and see if we can hook up with some of the other Fire Houses in the area."

"Understood," Charles said. "Good luck."

Gordon nodded, "Same to you guys."

Charles pushed his hand against the door and said, "Here we go." They were surprised no one was behind the building. They were all able to sneak to Broadway undetected. Charles handed the extra car keys to Debbie and said, "You know what to do. The car is right there. Take the civilians in your car, so we can get them off the street."

She grabbed the keys and nodded. Liz, Alissa, and Waleska followed her. Winston also followed and went to his patrol car, which was parked near hers in front of 3170 Broadway.

Edward and Marc got back into their patrol car, which was about fifty feet north of those cars and closer to West 125th Street, while Charles and Grant ran across the street to their car, which was already facing south, the direction they needed to travel.

The firefighters moved stealthily toward West 125th Street, until they were behind their truck. They needed to get O'Grady's attention, so he would not shoot them first. However, they had to do it in a way that would not get the attention of any infected people on the other side of the truck.

Lucky for them Charles already had a plan for that, as he watched from across the street and waited for them to get close enough. He went over his radio and called O'Grady, "O'Grady from ESU Truck 2! You got FD coming up behind you! Cover them, so they can reach their truck!"

O'Grady barely heard the radio transmission over his gunshots. He reached for his radio and responded, "10-5 that last message?"

"This is the 2-6 Sergeant to ESU. I need you to provide cover for FDNY. They are on Broadway and want to get back to their truck."

O'Grady stepped to the side of his truck that faced Broadway and looked down at the street level. He saw the four firefighters sneaking toward their truck and gave them the thumbs up signal. "I got your back," he told them.

Gordon and Sean tried to climb up from the rear of the truck, while John and Paul headed for the front.

John stood on the driver's side of the fire truck and looked inside. The keys were still in the ignition. He became startled when someone, or something, grabbed his leg. It was the reanimated corpse of their friend and co-worker, Richie, who had been lying on the street beside the truck. Richie caught him by surprise and pulled him down to the ground, causing him to hit his face and bust his lip open. Richie then crawled on top of him and began biting him.

Paul grabbed Richie and tried to pull him away, but John was already screaming out in pain.

Several infected that were nearby turned their attention away from O'Grady and toward the fire truck. They may not have been intelligent, but they knew screaming meant food was close. They began squeezing through the tight gap between the fire truck and Emergency Service truck. A few others went around the rear of the fire truck, instead.

Gordon and Sean had to think fast. Rather than get stranded on top of the truck, they opted for running toward the bus that was parked on the bus stop. Paul was grabbed by an infected from behind, who had gotten through the gap between the trucks.

O'Grady waited for that particular infected person to get into the right position, so he could shoot down at him. He killed him and the infected person's body was now stuck between both trucks blocking the way, so no more could pass through the gap.

Paul was saved.

O'Grady shot at the infected people, who chased after Gordon and Sean, allowing them to get behind the bus. He could not see if they made it inside from his vantage point. However, he did see more infected coming around the bus from the front end. They were out of his view, so he could not get a clear shot.

Paul yelled behind him and O'Grady quickly turned his gun down on Broadway. Richie had a grip on his leg and was biting through the thick uniform pants. O'Grady took careful aim and fired one shot into Richie's head ending his existence, once and for all.

Just then, Winston pulled up in his patrol car and got out. He called up to O'Grady, "Come on! We need to get out of here! We're all pulling out! Bring the truck!"

O'Grady replied hopelessly, "I can't! I don't have the keys! My partner had them and he's surrounded by these sons of bitches! I keep shooting them, but more keep coming!"

Winston frowned and said, "Then forget the truck! Grab what you can and jump down! It's not safe to stay here anymore!"

O'Grady picked up a bag of ammo magazines that he and his partner were sharing and climbed down the truck on the Broadway side. He rushed over to Paul and John and said, "I know you're both hurt, but we need to go. You're going to have to leave the truck behind. There are too many on the other side. If you try to move it, they will all spill out to Broadway."

John was holding his face and uttered, "Thanks, but I can't go. I'm infected. It's too risky."

Paul pulled up his pants leg and checked his wound. He saw that there were teeth marks on his lower calf, although there was no blood. He wondered if that meant he was safe.

"I think I might be good to go. Richie didn't break any skin. Look, no blood.

O'Grady said, "That's good enough for me. Let's go. He got into the passenger seat of Winston's car and they waited for Paul.

Paul pulled down his pants leg and turned to his buddy, John. He asked, "Are you sure about this, pal? I don't want to leave you here like this. Let me patch your face up, at least."

John protested, "No. Just get out of here. Go with them. Get home to your family and tell mine that I love them."

Winston began getting impatient when Debbie's car passed by him, followed by Edward's car. Their cars went up Broadway and stopped at West 126th Street.

Waleska told Debbie, "Here. This is my building."

Debbie looked out from the car windows and saw that the area looked quiet enough. There were no signs of any infected. "Go straight home and keep your doors locked," she said. "Somehow, we will find a way to send help."

Waleska asked, "You promise?"

Debbie replied, "You have my word."

Waleska smiled and gave Alissa a hug. They were both seated in the back of the patrol car together. "Be safe," she said.

Alissa replied, "You, too. I hope your family is okay."

"Thanks, to all of you. Please, be careful out here." She said, as she exited the car and headed to the entrance of her building. She was careful and kept looking around her, as she went.

Once it looked like she was safely inside, Debbie asked Liz and Alissa, "What about you two?"

Liz responded, right away, "I'm sticking with you cops. I'm not crazy. You guys have the guns, which gives you the best chance for survival. I live in Yonkers, so that's not happening."

Alissa said, "I was supposed to be staying over my friends' house. They stood me up. I'm pretty much stranded in Manhattan. I also live in Westchester."

Debbie sighed, "Okay. I guess you will both have to stay with me. I hope the Sarge won't mind."

Liz told her, "I doubt he'd expect you to leave us on any random street corner, just to get rid of us, especially considering the circumstances. We already know the train is not an option either."

Debbie agreed and made a U-turn. She waved for Edward and Marc to follow.

Meanwhile, Winston was about ready to leave Paul behind. He was getting very antsy. He turned to O'Grady and whispered loudly, "We need to get away from here! There's nothing to stop them from going around the back of the trucks anymore with you in here."

O'Grady was about to bring that to Paul's attention, but time was up. A group of infected had already realized they could go around the trucks. They rushed Paul from behind, while he was bandaging his buddy's face. The infected focused their attack on Paul, who was not infected, yet. He was torn to pieces, while John tried to stop the attack unsuccessfully. The infected didn't even bother with him, which Winston and O'Grady found odd.

Winston wasted no more time and sped away. He whipped a fast U-turn and almost smashed into the support beam from the elevated train tracks, which made O'Grady feel more fearful for his life than when he was facing dozens of infected from atop his truck. They followed after the other two patrol cars to Tiemann Place, before heading west toward Claremont Avenue.

0400 HRS, CLAREMONT AVE:

A few minutes earlier, Grant and Charles turned toward Claremont Avenue from Broadway and immediately saw the ambulance parked up the hill from them. Grant drove closer and Charles warned him to take it slow, just in case of trouble. They could not take any chances.

Perez reached out his window and waved at them. They felt relieved to see he was still himself.

Grant pulled up the car to the driver's side of the ambulance, so they'd be close enough to speak without having to get out of their vehicles. They greeted each other almost as if all were normal.

"Hey, what's up?" Grant said. "Have you seen anything strange up here?"

Perez responded, "Hey, Grant. Nah, man. It's been quiet. I mean, I heard a lot of gunshots, but that's over on 125th Street. It's dead up here. No pun intended. One of your boys told me to wait here earlier, in case

I was needed. There's a lot of crap going down at the hospital making it unsafe. I even lost my partner tonight. I still can't believe she's gone."

"We heard. I'm very sorry to hear that."

"I've been dealing with it. There's been a lot of death tonight."

Grant nodded, "Unfortunately."

Charles joined the conversation, "Hey, Perez! You got a first name?"

"Aramis."

Charles raised an eyebrow and asked, "Aramis? What kind of name is Aramis?"

Aramis groaned, "Come on, man. It's not like I came out of my mom's womb and told my parents what to call me. Besides, I like it. It's different. Makes me feel unique."

Charles smirked, "Very true. My bad. Well, I'm going to think of you as our doctor, so I might call you 'Doc' every once in a while. I hope you won't mind. Besides, I probably won't remember your real name and you are basically going to be our doctor for the time being."

"That's cool, but I'm not a doctor."

"Yeah, but you're the closest thing we have to one," Charles told him. "Considering Mount Sinai St. Luke's and Harlem Hospitals are both lost to us, we need to improvise."

"Yeah, I know. This sucks ass. Hey, whatever you guys need," he responded.

Charles explained the situation to him, "We need to pull out and get far away from here. This area is lost to us. Every time we think we can take it back, there are more infected people than we can count. Some are fast as hell, while others move around like snails. I can't even tell you how many cops we lost tonight. I won't risk anymore. I'm calling in the big guns, but first we need to make an important stop. I want you to follow us."

"You got it. Where to?"

"244 Riverside Drive. It's past 110th Street, somewhere in the 90s."

"Okay. I'll follow you."

Charles replied, "Good. We just need to make one other stop along the way. We're meeting up with a few of our patrol cars at 116th Street."

"Lead the way."

It did not take long for them to reach West 116th Street. Claremont Avenue appeared empty of life. Most of the lights in the buildings were off. It made Charles realize, they could not give up, yet. There were still so many people who had no idea of the danger that faced them come morning when they awoke to start their days.

"We need to beat this, Grant. These people count on us to keep them safe."

"We can only do so much. We're only human. We were outnumbered back there. We did our best to convince the manager from the restaurant to come with us. We can't force him to come with us and the firefighters had their own plan to get away. You know they like to do things their way. If we had stayed any longer, we probably would have died. Even Aviation told us to pull out. I trust their point of view. I don't want to die fighting a losing battle. The best thing we could do is get out of there and call for help. Let the military handle this in the way only they can. This has grown far beyond our control. So, don't blame yourself. You did the best you could under the given circumstances."

"I think I could have done better. I should have. Too many cops had to die."

Grant stopped the car and said, "We're here." He turned to Charles and said, "We are alive because of your actions. So are they," he pointed toward the three patrol cars that approached. They were both relieved to see that the others had made it back, although it was disappointing to not see the ESU truck with them, or the fire truck, for that matter.

Charles shrugged, "I suppose. Let's not waste anymore time. Get us to this moron's building, so we can wake his ass up. I want to give him a piece of my mind."

CONTAMINATION EFFECT

Chapter Twelve

0401 HRS, 26TH PCT:

A T LONG LAST, Edie was awake. David needed to tell her the bad news about her friend, Eva, but did not have the luxury of time to be subtle about it.

He explained curtly, "I'm very sorry, but your friend is gone."

"Huh? What do you mean she's gone?"

"She went out the back door and was attacked. She's gone. They got her. I'm really sorry."

"No! That can't be true!"

David exhaled in frustration. He did not have time for this.

Mr. Brown offered his condolences, "I'm sorry, but your friend is gone. Now, you need to get your shit together or we *all* gonna be gone, too."

David grabbed her by the shoulders and explained, "We really do need to go. The longer we wait, the less chance we have of escaping. You need to be strong. I'm going to get us out of here, but you need to pull yourself together. Hold it in and mourn her, later, when we're safe. Can you please do that?"

She sucked up her tears and sniffled one last time. She wasn't really ready, but she knew she had to be. She wiped her cheeks dry and summoned up all the courage she could muster. This was a matter of life and death. These strangers she was with would sooner leave her behind than risk their lives for her. She had to be tough, at least, for now. She took a deep breath and nodded.

"Good," David smiled.

He had a friendly sincere smile, she thought. Maybe *he* wouldn't leave her behind.

David turned toward the back door and fought off his fear. He told himself he needed to be strong and prepared himself mentally. He knew these people were looking to him for guidance and safety. He could not let them down. He took a deep breath and pulled out his gun.

"Follow me and stay close," he said, as he opened the door and walked down the handicap ramp. The other door had closed, when Eva was attacked. David knew there would be infected people on the other side of it and they would likely attack, once he opened it. Here goes nothing, he thought.

He opened the door and kept his weapon ready. Eva's body was right at his feet. Three infected women were eating her flesh, as if it were a pie-eating contest. He pushed the door open wide and struck one of them from behind, knocking her over. He aimed his weapon and shot another one point blank in the head. She dropped on top of Eva and did not move, again. The third stood up and charged at him. There was no time to aim and shoot, so he swung his gun downward hard on her head and knocked her to the ground. He then shot her in the back of the head finishing her off. The door began to push against him, as the last one was up on her feet and ready to come at him. He used the door as a shield and shot her in the side of her head. She fell to the ground.

He turned to the civilians within the corridor and noticed they were all the way back inside. He wanted to yell at them to stay close, but they came running as soon as they saw he was done fighting the infected.

"Unbelievable," he muttered to himself. "Come on, let's go!" He turned and went to his patrol car. He quickly pulled out the keys and unlocked the doors. "Get in," he instructed. He thought about sending Gary to his taxi and telling him to follow, but with Julie and Eva dead, there was enough room in his car for everybody. Sending him away now would just be mean. Still, it was extremely tempting.

"I got shotgun!" Gary called out loudly.

David narrowed his eyes and said sternly, "Will you keep quiet, you moron. They'll hear you." Just as soon as he said the words, they heard screaming coming from the front of the building. David got into the car and closed his door. He fumbled with the keys and finally inserted the correct one into the ignition.

Edie and Mr. Brown scurried into the back seat. Ms. Butler tried to squeeze her way in, but it was too crowded. Gary opened his door, got into the front passenger seat, and closed his door, just in the nick of time. A mob of infected came running wildly around the parked cars on the driveway and rushed toward their car like a pack of hungry wolves.

Mr. Brown shouted, "Hurry up and get your ass inside, Butler! We about to die!"

"I can't fit," she cried.

David took a chance and stepped on the gas pedal. He could not wait any longer. He hoped Ms. Butler would make it inside in time.

The infected solved her problem for them, as they grabbed her and yanked her from the backseat. Edie tried to grab her hand, but it slipped away fast when David sped off. The door slammed shut by the sheer momentum.

Within seconds the precinct was a block behind them. David went south on Broadway and didn't bother looking back.

"Sorry, Ms. Butler," he said with sincerity.

Mr. Brown was still gasping in shock from seeing his longtime friend get yanked out of the vehicle. He hoped and prayed she did not suffer long. His eyes welled up and he wiped away a tear. He kept his face turned toward the window and remained silent.

As David drove away, his thoughts went back to Elizabeth and Lieutenant Andrews. They were still trapped in the holding cells. There would be no escape for them, only infection.

Back in the station house, the metal roll down gate on the window of the telephone switchboard operator's desk was starting to give. It was dented inward from so much pounding. Within minutes, it was forced in causing it to break and it crashed loudly to the desk and onto the floor. As it did several infected fought their way through the window and into the desk area.

In the back room, in one of the holding cells, Lieutenant Andrews stepped back away from the bars of the cell. A wall that was painted black separated his cell from Elizabeth, who was in the very next cell. He listened to the breaking of the metal gate and knew the infected would soon find them in their cells. While they would be safe from harm, the infected would most likely try to get at them with tenacity.

He whispered to Elizabeth, "I hope you've made peace with our Lord. They sound like they will be here any second."

From the next cell, a guttural growl could be heard. It grew into unrelenting screaming. Elizabeth pounded away at the thick wall and tried to reach the meal that was inches away, but completely out of reach. Her infection had reached the next phase.

Lieutenant Andrews sat down and closed his eyes. He tried to block out all the screams around him by thinking of happier times and reliving memories. His torment would only last another half hour, before he'd be joining in on the screaming.

The 26th Precinct was lost.

0405 HRS, 244 RIVERSIDE DRIVE:

It was silent in the dead of night when four police cars and an FDNY ambulance pulled up in front of 244 Riverside Drive. The infection had not reached this area of Manhattan, yet, so it reminded them that there was hope. There was still a chance this thing could be beaten.

The plan was to pay a visit to Edward's cousin, David Frino. He was a scientist, who worked at the Science Center on Broadway. He was there when this outbreak began and was privy to some important background information that could possibly lead to finding a cure. It was imperative they speak with him, as soon as possible.

Charles and Grant exited their patrol car. Charles only wanted Edward and Aramis to go upstairs with them. Edward had the keys to the building and apartment, while Aramis could provide any medical attention, if needed. Everyone else was asked to keep quiet and wait in the vehicles.

Debbie and Winston gave Charles a quick update on what took place back on Broadway, regarding the civilians and firefighters. He didn't seem to mind keeping the civilians with them, for now.

Nearby, Aramis walked to the back door of the ambulance to grab some medical equipment from inside when he heard a thumping sound come from within. He paused and listened to see if he'd hear it a second time. His partner's body was inside on the floor. There was no reason there should be any noise coming from within because she was supposed to be dead. He tried to look through the small window, but his view of the interior was limited.

Edward asked, "What's wrong?"

Aramis kept trying to peek into the small windows on the back doors and answered, "I don't know. I thought I heard something inside. My partner is still inside, but she's supposed to be dead."

"What?" Edward asked surprised. "You have your dead partner in there? Was she infected?"

"Oh, she was definitely infected. She was bitten by that infected officer we transported."

Edward called the sergeant over and explained the situation. He didn't look too pleased.

He responded, "Are you insane? You've been driving around with your infected partner this entire time? Why didn't you leave her at the hospital?"

"Whoa! Take it easy! I didn't have a choice. By the time she died in the back, the hospital was off limits. I wasn't going to just dump her on the sidewalk. Besides, she was already dead."

Charles replied, "Oh? She's dead, huh? Why don't you open the door and tell that to her?"

Suddenly, there was a persistent banging sound on the doors coming from within. Someone inside definitely wanted out. It was soon joined by the muffled sound of someone screaming.

Aramis stared at the doors in shock. How could that be possible, he thought. He turned to the others and explained, "I swear she was dead!"

Charles nodded, "And we believe you. However, what you need to understand about this virus is that it only makes you think the infected are dead. They really aren't. Somehow, the infection keeps the body alive no matter how badly the person is injured. One of our guys shot himself in the head, but he came back infected and attacked a sergeant. Both were good friends of mine."

Aramis frowned, "Yo, this is some serious shit we're dealing with here. We're out of our league."

"I agree," said Charles. "That's why we're here, to get to the bottom of things. The guy who lives here might have knowledge that we could use to combat this thing properly. Once I speak to him, I'm going to contact someone I know at police headquarters. She will get the ball rolling and make the call to the National Guard, the Center for Disease Control, and whoever else we'll need."

He looked back toward the ambulance and said, "We can't leave *her* like that. It's too risky. She needs to be dealt with, first."

Aramis nodded reluctantly and asked, "Okay. So, how do we do this?"

Charles instructed him to open the door and stay clear, keeping the door in front of him like a shield. He would take the shot, once she exited the ambulance. Afterwards, they could move her body back inside.

The loudness of the shot would no doubt wake half the neighborhood, but people would be relieved to see four police cars and an ambulance already on the scene. Charles told O'Grady and Winston to stand by with an explanation, in case a sector car from the 24th Precinct was sent to investigate.

They agreed and stood to the side, while Aramis carefully opened one of the rear doors. His partner stumbled out and fell to the ground, making it easy for Charles to put one in the back of her head before she could stand.

BLAM!

Her body was quickly placed back inside of the ambulance, and then Aramis was able to grab his medical equipment bag, so he could take it upstairs with him. The doors to the rear of the ambulance were closed, once again.

In one of the parked patrol cars, Liz asked Debbie, "Did they just shoot an EMT and put her in the back of the ambulance?"

"I believe so," Debbie replied, also confused by what she saw. "The Sarge wants us to wait in the cars, so that's what we're going to do."

Liz replied, "You got no argument from me. I just want to know why we're here. Is this area safe?"

Debbie looked around at the peaceful neighborhood with Riverside Park across the street and wasn't sure. Normally, she would say, yes, in an instant, but now, she felt wary about anything that seemed too quiet. "I don't know," she answered with a hint of fear.

0410 HRS, CONFINES OF THE 26TH PCT:

Officer David Castillo could not believe the night he was having. In a matter of hours, he lost his partner, his friends, and his area of employment. On top of that, he wasn't sure if Manhattan would also be lost before the night was over. It certainly started to look that way, as he drove east going the wrong way across West 123rd Street from Broadway past Amsterdam toward Morningside Avenue. On Amsterdam there were infected running and walking south from West 125th Street. When he reached Morningside Avenue, it was the same thing. Recently infected people were running south, as if they were fleeing from a fire. It was, by far, the craziest thing he had ever seen, since becoming a police officer ten years earlier.

Edie stared out the rear window and asked, "Are they all infected?"

David replied coldly, "Yep."

Gary fidgeted uncomfortably in the front seat. He kept looking around, as if he lost something. He opened the glove compartment and asked, "Don't you guys keep extra guns in here?"

"No," said David. "Do me a favor? Stop touching shit."

Gary closed the glove compartment and pouted silently.

Mr. Brown did not say anything. His mind was still at the precinct, where he saw his friend being yanked out of the car. It was an image he would never forget. He dreaded the terrifying experience that must have followed for her. He had a feeling he was going to have nightmares for years.

Gary turned to David and inquired, "Where are we going? Every place seems to be just as bad. Do you even have a plan?"

David wanted to ignore him, but he knew his passengers in the backseat would have the same questions. For their sake, he answered,

"We'll check the 28th Precinct. It's a couple of blocks away from here. Maybe they can help, if it isn't already too late."

When their patrol car reached the next street, St. Nicholas Avenue, they were disturbed to see more of the same. Infected people were already attacking people at the Popeye's restaurant on West 125th Street. Cars were swerving to avoid infected in the street and crashing into each other. Drivers were then being attacked, as they exited their vehicles. People were running for their lives in every direction. It was total mayhem.

"Damn," David sighed. "We may already be too late."

He parked in a parking spot behind the 28th Precinct and said, "Stay in the car. I'll be right back." He turned off the car and took the keys with him when he left.

"Oh, real nice," Gary commented nastily.

David stuck up his middle finger, as he walked away and into the building. There was a smile on his face for the first time in hours.

Gary cursed and stepped out of the car, "Screw that fag. Who the hell does he think he is anyway? I need to smoke a cigarette." He lit up a cigarette and leaned on the hood of the car, while he puffed away.

Edie glared at him from the backseat. She wished she could hit the door lock button, but the car was equipped with a caged partition separating the front from the rear. The rear was mainly used for the transportation of prisoners. In fact, the child safety locks were usually kept on for the back doors, so she and Mr. Brown were actually locked in. Someone would have to open their doors from the outside, in order for them to exit the vehicle, which essentially meant Gary had power over them, for the moment.

He turned abruptly when he heard the back door of the precinct slam against the wall.

David came running out and shouted, "Get the hell back in the car!"

Gary dropped his cigarette and opened the front passenger door. He was grabbed from behind and pulled down to the street by three infected people, who began biting into his face with ferocity. He never even had time to scream.

David opened the driver's side door and got inside, just as one infected slid over the hood in an attempt to grab him. The car started up and shot backwards out of the parking spot. The infected person on the hood slid off the car and rolled onto the street. David changed gears and went forward when he noticed the other infected had left Gary and were chasing the car. More infected were running out of the rear door of the station house, after them.

Edie and Mr. Brown huddled together in the backseat in fear.

"Hang on!" David warned.

The car sped forward toward West 125th Street, knocking over about two people along the way. David wasn't sure if they were infected or not. He didn't care. If they were in the way, they were going down. He looked back using his rear view mirror for just a second. When he faced forward, again, he had enough time to see a city bus heading straight for them from the corner of his eye.

In the back seat, Mr. Brown shouted, "OH SHIT!"

An instant later, the bus slammed into the driver's side rear of the car pushing it into a spin. It came to a stop a few feet north of West 125th Street facing east toward a building.

0412 HRS, 244 RIVERSIDE DRIVE:

Charles, Grant, and Aramis followed Edward up to the third floor, where his cousin's apartment was located. He unlocked the door and tried to open it, but there was something blocking the way. They all pushed together and forced the door open. The sofa had been blocking the door.

Edward figured his cousin was being paranoid. No one would come to attack him up on the fifth floor.

He looked around the apartment and noticed the light in the living room was on, but most of the other lights were off. The only other light crept through from under the bedroom door, which was closed.

They entered the apartment and Grant closed the door behind them. He pushed the sofa against the wall to move it out of the way. Aramis stayed safely behind Charles and remained alert.

Edward knocked on the bedroom door and called out, "Hey, Dave! It's me, Ed. Are you okay in there?" There was a shuffling sound coming from within the room. An empty bottle was knocked over onto the floor in the bedroom. It did not break, but it rolled around the floor. Ed inserted the key and unlocked the door.

Charles pulled out his weapon and whispered, "Be careful. He could be infected."

Edward smirked, "I doubt it. He would have told me so when we spoke earlier. Probably just drunk. Poor bastard had a rough night, like us." He opened the door and was immediately pulled into the room by his cousin.

Charles and the others only had a chance to see David's hands reaching out of the room briefly, and then pulling Edward into the bedroom. Charles ran toward the entrance of the room with Grant close behind him. Edward was trying to scream, but his cousin was tearing the skin around his mouth off with his teeth, while his hands were digging into Edward's throat. Edward's hand fumbled blindly for his gun in its holster with little luck.

BANG!

Charles winced as he fired a shot into the back of David's head, which blasted out through his face and hit Edward in the head, as well. Both fell still, as death claimed them. The slide on Charles' gun was locked back, indicating that the weapon was empty. He closed his eyes at the painful realization that he just had to kill a friend.

"Shit," Grant frowned, while looking on sorrowfully. "Poor Eddie."

Charles nodded silently. Just then, he noticed a black and white composition notebook on the bed with a pen. Curiously, he reached over and picked up the book. He looked around the room to see if there was anything else that stood out. It all looked relatively normal, aside from the empty vodka bottle on the floor. He checked the notebook and saw that it was a journal. Apparently, David had been keeping a journal for the past two years, since he began working at the Science Center. The last poorly scribbled entries were made only minutes earlier. There were several very long entries made on the last day. Everything seemed to be documented in detail. Charles skimmed through the pages and read about the ten homeless males that were injected with Dr. Fox's experimental serum and about the secret underground laboratory under the Science Center. He realized that had to be ground zero for this contagion. The one thing that stood out the most was the word "anti-virus." David wrote about a syringe on the floor of a dorm room in the lab. That was the key to stopping this nightmare!

Charles' eyes lit up with a new hope.

Grant was watching and waiting, while Charles looked through the notebook. When it looked like he had come to an epiphany, Grant asked, "Well, what does it say?"

"You're not going to believe this, but there is a cure!"

Aramis replied excitedly, "That's awesome!"

Grant asked, "What is it?"

Charles grimaced, "There is a catch. It's down in an underground lab underneath the Science Center on Broadway, which would mean going back into the heart of the Infected Zone. Plus, according to this, there are more infected locked in the lab."

Grant sighed, "Oh, great. Why can't anything ever be easy?"

Charles asked Aramis, "Did you bring rubber gloves?"

"Yes, I have a box in my bag. What's the plan?"

"Let's put some gloves on and go through this whole apartment. Make sure there is nothing that looks like it might be contagious, like a toothbrush or comb. We'll lock anything that could potentially be carrying the virus in the bedroom with them."

Aramis handed them both rubber gloves and they began searching the apartment. As instructed, they placed any potential contaminants into the bedroom. Once they were done, Charles looked over the bedroom one last time, including down at Edward. He checked in the drawers and in the closet. Everything looked copasetic, so he closed and locked the door. He removed the keys and placed it in his pocket.

"Rest in peace, Ed." He turned to Grant and told him, "Call Nugent or Calderon and have them bring everyone upstairs. We're going to make this our temporary command center. There's a bathroom, if we need it and two large sofas. It will give everyone a chance to clean up and rest." He picked up the remote control and turned on the television. He searched for a news channel and found one. "And we can see how much the media knows about this mess."

"You got it," Grant replied. He dialed Marc's phone number using his cellphone and relayed the information.

CONTAMINATION EFFECT

Chapter Thirteen

0420 HRS, ST. NICHOLAS AVE:

DAVID CASTILLO OPENED his eyes and was startled by a husky man with a thick black mustache, who was pulling him out of the car. At first, he thought this was it. He was about to die, but then he realized the man was speaking to him. He appeared to be a city bus driver.

"Take it easy," said the bus driver. "We need to get you out of here. The streets are not safe. Give me a hand with him," he said to a tall tan-skinned man with short, wavy, dark hair that stood nearby. "He's awake."

The tall man approached and grabbed him by his other arm. Together, they pulled him away from the smashed patrol car and sat him down behind a parked van. Other people were already hiding there, as well. They huddled together as closely as they could.

David asked, "What happened?"

"You drove right out in front of my bus. I couldn't stop in time. I thought I killed you, too," the bus driver explained grimly. "It's good to see someone survived."

"Too?" David asked.

"Yeah, sorry, but the guy in the back seat did not make it. I think he died instantly."

David frowned and groaned wearily, "What about the girl?"

"I'm right here, Officer Castillo," Edie said. "I'm fine. I'm just a bit shaken up. How are you feeling?"

"Like if I were hit by a bus."

The tall man smirked, "Really? That's a hell of a coincidence."

The bus driver said, "We can't stay here. It's not safe. These crazy bastards are everywhere. They're attacking anything with a pulse."

David asked, "What about the bus?"

"Wrecked it. After I hit your car, I lost control and went into the window of Popeye's. We barely made it out of there alive. Lost two passengers in the process."

David replied, "Sorry to hear. Help me up. I want to take a look."

The bus driver and the tall man helped him to his feet. He was in pain, but he felt like he would be able to walk. He wasn't sure, if he could run, though. His left side was still aching from the accident. He peeked around the van and could see the entire intersection was overrun. There was a fire, too, which he thought might be useful for providing cover for their escape.

He looked toward the subway station. They were close enough to go downstairs unnoticed. Maybe they could use it to reach the next station and exit to safety. Of course, that all depended on whether or not there were any infected people down in the station. He searched the area for another option, but any other idea would mean they'd risk being spotted and attacked and he was in no condition to run or fight. That made his decision easier to make.

"We can try the subway. We'll take the tracks to the next station. It should be much safer there," he said.

The bus driver looked skeptical. He asked, "Are you sure that's a good idea? That's a long walk and you're hurt. I can't carry you that far."

David nodded, "I can make it on my own, as long as we don't have to run. First, we'll need someone fast to check it out and make sure it's not a deathtrap down there. They can give us a signal to enter, if it's safe."

Edie volunteered, "I'm fast. I used to run track in high school."

David looked at her with uncertainty and asked, "Are you sure you want to do this?"

"I can do it," she responded nervously. "You need someone fast and I bet I'm faster than everyone here."

The bus driver commented, "We'd better make this fast. I don't feel safe here. There are too many of us to stay hiding here for long."

David agreed. He faced Edie and told her, "Go. And be careful."

She peeked out from behind the van and saw that no one was looking her way. She swiftly ran to the subway steps and went down. A few seconds later, she emerged and waved them toward her.

The bus driver said, "It's clear. Are you ready?"

David nodded.

The bus driver and the tall man helped him to the staircase. The others followed quietly and they descended into the subway station. When they reached the bottom, they noticed several people appeared to be hiding in the station. David told everyone to wait at the gate near the turnstiles, including the other people in the station. He then limped over to the Transit worker in the booth with the bus driver's assistance to explain what was going on.

The Transit worker, a middle-aged African-American man, was looking at them strangely. He asked, "What the heck is going on up there? It sounds like World War III!"

David explained, "There was a viral outbreak. An infectious disease is spreading throughout the area. It's very contagious and extremely deadly. I suggest you come with us. We're heading to the next station using the subway tunnel. Either that or stay here and wait to die. The choice is yours."

The Transit worker in the booth stared at them both momentarily and unlocked the gate. He said, "I'll unlock the gate, but before I go anywhere, I need to call my supervisor."

"There's no time," David said. "The streets are overrun with infected people going all the way to the Hudson River. We already lost a few police precincts. The city is not going to send in any more cops. The next step is the military and I doubt they will stop to ask questions. They're just going to come and shoot anything that moves. You're supervisor can't help you, but we can, if you come with us now."

"Fine," he said grudgingly, as he grabbed his bag and stepped out of the booth to join them.

An African-American woman, who was hiding in the station, complained, "There ain't no way I am going into no subway tunnels!"

David replied, "Shhh. Don't let them hear you or none of us are going anywhere. We're lucky they haven't come down here, yet. If you stay here, you'll probably die."

She responded sarcastically, "*Probably* ain't the same as *definitely*. I'll take my chances and wait for help to come. I don't expect no police to help me anyway. Y'all go down there and be ready to deal with rats, cockroaches the size of rats, and crazy homeless people."

A young female, who had been a passenger of the bus, asked, "Rats and cockroaches?"

The tall man said, "The rats won't bother you. They run away from danger. Roaches could be a problem, but it's not as if they're gonna attack and eat us. That's exactly what's happening up there and if you stay here, it's gonna happen to you, too."

David agreed, "He's right. You guys can either come with us and live or stay and wait to die. We are done debating about it. Let's go downstairs. We need to take the downtown side. No more trains will be coming into this area from uptown, so it's our safest option."

The Transit worker replied, "I was informed about an indefinite delay in train service. My supervisor said it was due to police activity. Is this what he meant?"

David nodded, "Yeah, probably."

The bus driver said, "It's safe to say there won't be anymore buses either."

Regardless, the African-American woman chose not to follow them downstairs to the platform. A few other people also stayed behind and took their chances, which made the Transit worker uncomfortable.

He said, "I don't know if I should be leaving the booth with those people staying at the station. What's to stop them from breaking in and stealing?"

David answered, "They can steal whatever they want. None of them are going to live past the morning, if they stay behind. It's only a matter of time before the infected people on the street find their way down here and feast on their dumb asses."

The bus driver and the tall man helped David down the stairs to the downtown platform. The others followed closely. They walked to the far end, where another staircase led down to the tracks and into the tunnel.

There was one other person on the platform. He eyed them suspiciously and shouted, "Hey! Where are you guys going with that cop? He looks hurt. Officer, are you okay?"

"I'm fine. Thank you, sir," David responded. "Come with us. The train isn't coming. We need to get the hell away from here as fast as we can."

"What's going on?" The man asked. "I've been waiting a while."

A blond haired man, who had been on the bus answered, "There's a damn riot up there. People are attacking each other, looting, and acting like maniacs."

David explained, again, "No. There was a severe viral outbreak. The virus makes you behave violently and gives you the urge to attack and bite people. We tried to contain it, but we lost control of the situation. The safest thing to do is to get far away. There's a police facility in the subway station at 145th Street. I was planning to head there. It's safer to travel underground."

The man followed and said, "It all sounds unbelievable, but considering you are all willing to walk in the train tunnels for twenty blocks, I am inclined to think there might be some truth to it. Count me in."

"Wait a minute," the young female said. "Did you say twenty blocks? I don't know if I can walk through here for twenty blocks, especially with cockroaches and rats running around in the dark. Isn't there someplace we can just hide, until it's safe?"

David promised, "We'll take the tracks to the next station, which is 135th Street. At that point, you will each have the option to leave the tracks and take your chances on the streets, if that's what you decide. As for myself, I'm sticking to the tracks, until the station after that. I think it will be safer there, as long as we all steer clear of the third rail."

The Transit worker asked, "You heading to Transit District 3?"

"Yes," David nodded. "That's exactly where I want to go."

The man who was on the platform asked, "Isn't there a police station at 135th Street?"

David replied, "Yes, but they're dealing with the same problem thanks to several infected patients that were taken to Harlem Hospital earlier in the evening. The virus has been spreading fast. The best option is to leave Manhattan, if we can."

The tall man grabbed David and helped him to walk faster. "We'll have a better chance, if I help you walk," he said kindly.

David was grateful. He smiled and said, "Thank you, um..."

"Kirk."

"Thanks, Kirk."

"No problem. I have a buddy, who was a cop. He's retired now, but he's a good guy. I like to think there are other cops out there who are good, too."

"I'll try my best to live up to your expectations," David moaned, while limping along the dark subway tunnel.

The bus driver and Edie stayed close behind them, followed by the Transit worker, the blond male passenger from the bus, the young female, and the man from the platform.

As they walked deeper into the tunnels toward a curve, they heard the faint sounds of screams echoing behind them. They paused and knew it meant the infected had discovered the people hiding in the subway station at West 125th Street. They could only hope the infected would not be curious enough to explore the tracks.

The young female gasped, "Oh, my God."

Kirk shook his head and said, "They should have come with us."

David whispered, "No more talking, until we reach the next station. Let's pick up the pace."

They all agreed and moved along hastily keeping any protests they had about walking through the dark and dirty tunnels to themselves.

0430 HRS, 244 RIVERSIDE DRIVE:

Everyone gathered in the living room of the apartment, which was surprisingly larger than the typical apartment. There was plenty of space for all of them to be seated comfortably on the two sofas, while they watched the news on the large flat screen 3D television.

Alissa couldn't help herself when she commented abruptly, "Damn! This room is bigger than my whole apartment!"

The other officers were saddened when they learned of Edward's death. Charles felt guilty about it when he explained how he had no choice. Edward had already been infected. It was too late to save him. It was easier to shoot him and his cousin, at the same time.

Afterwards, the officers sat around with miserable expressions on their faces. They had seen so much death in one night. This would be a night they'd surely never forget. If things did not make a turn for the positive soon, it would also be the night they lost Manhattan to a virus.

On the television, newscasters could only speculate about what was going on because they did not have any reporters on the scene, who could comment. A few had been sent in, but they all went missing. A large portion of Harlem was being referred to as the "Infected Zone." It was basically the area from West 110th Street to West 145th Street, between The Harlem River and Hudson River. The ironic thing was that the infection had not even spread to the Harlem River, yet. That area was already being included probably because it was easier to block off from river to river.

One reporter on television said, "An experimental virus has infected hundreds, who have taken siege of Upper Manhattan. Police have tried tirelessly to contain the situation, which has grown out of their control. Authorities are warning that if you reside within the Infected Zone to stay in your homes and lock the doors. Do not attempt to go outside for any reason whatsoever. All forms of entry into the Infected Zone are banned, until further notice. People attempting to exit the Infected Zone will be stopped, detained, and thoroughly examined.

At the moment, it is understood the virus can only be spread through the passing of bodily fluids. It does not appear to be airborne. Authorities are still looking into what caused this viral outbreak, which began in the Manhattanville Section.

For further information, please call the number at the bottom of your screen."

While the others looked at the news or dozed off and took quick naps, Charles spent a few minutes looking through the journal for any answers to the many questions he had. He certainly found enough information to know that the journal was invaluable. Edward's cousin, David, documented everything in tremendous detail almost every day.

Charles looked at the time. It was still too early to contact his friend, who worked at police headquarters. However, she could be awake soon. No, he'd wait until she got to work.

He went into the kitchen and helped himself to a bottle of water from the refrigerator. It was refreshingly cold.

He wondered how his other officers were doing out there. He knew Steve and Ricky had taken to the Henry Hudson Parkway heading northbound. David told him not to return to the precinct, but he never explained why. Charles tried to call him, but there was no answer. The phone went straight to voicemail. That wasn't a good sign.

Grant approached him and asked, "How long are we going to stay here? Some of the others are getting restless. They think we should continue away from the Infected Zone and put some serious distance between it and us. The only problem is that we all live up north. No one wants to be trapped on an island. Not Manhattan and not Long Island."

Liz called out to everyone in the room "Hey, everyone listen to this report." She raised the volume on the television and they listened.

"This is Eric Colton reporting for Long Island News 12. I am standing outside of LaGuardia Airport in Queens, where an actual quarantine has been put into effect, regarding a viral outbreak of some kind. It is believed this has stemmed from a similar incident that is taking place in Manhattan, which has been dubbed the 'Manhattanville Incident.' Currently, planes are not being permitted to land or take off from the airport. The main terminal has been placed on lockdown, until further notice, pending word from the CDC. All in-bound flights are being diverted to JFK or Newark Airports."

Aramis exclaimed, "Damn! This is getting worse by the minute."

Grant's jaw dropped open. He had almost forgotten about the incident Taz from the 4 to 12 shift joked about. A man was bitten on the way to the airport. Of course, it was related! The infection had managed to spread into Queens. Who knew where else it had reached, considering the many hours that have passed?

He told the others about the person that was bitten on the way to the airport, just to confirm what they were already suspecting. Both incidents were indeed related.

Alissa gasped, "Jesus Christ! I can't believe this is happening! It's crazy!"

O'Grady said, "That settles it. We need to get the hell out of this city before we can't. They are already blocking off streets, if they are referring to the Infected Zone as someplace separate.

Winston disagreed. He suggested, "I think we should go to 1 Police Plaza. They will make sure police headquarters stays protected. We should be fine there. Downtown will be the best bet. They are not going to let this thing reach City Hall."

Marc replied, "Screw that! I want off of this island. Let's head to the boat basin at Riverside Park and take a boat to Jersey. We are already near it. It won't take long to reach. I guarantee we won't get stuck in traffic."

Alissa agreed with enthusiasm, "I think that sounds like a great idea."

Charles reminded them, "There's only one problem with that plan. We do not have a boat."

O'Grady said without a second thought, "We can commandeer one. I can pilot a boat. My dad has one."

Marc asked, "Where is his boat?"

"Montauk."

Aramis groaned, "Of course, it is. Why would we expect it to be close to us?"

"Oh," Marc frowned. "Well, we can still commandeer a boat, like he said. Let's get the heck out of here and do that. I don't like the idea of being here with those two locked in that room." He referred to the corpses of Edward and his cousin.

Charles said, "They're dead."

Marc replied, "Dead my ass. No disrespect, boss, but we're dealing with zombies." He pointed to Aramis. "His partner was dead, too, when he left her in the ambulance. Remember? That didn't stop her from getting shot."

Grant added, "That EMT at Debbie's accident scene was pretty much dead, too. Not to mention the girl who was lying on the street with half her face missing. Both stood up and began walking toward us. It might sound crazy, but we've been dealing with crazy all night. I think Marc is right. We are dealing with zombies. The faster we accept it, the easier we can deal with it."

Charles sighed, "You know any other day I would love to believe zombies are real, but not when I have to actually deal with a city full of them. It's more real than I'd like it to be."

Grant replied, "Okay, forget about what to call them. Let's decide what to do. We can vote. Who wants to leave Manhattan? Raise your hand."

Everyone in the room raised his or her hand, even Winston.

"That settles it, Sarge," he said. "We need to find a way off this island, while we still can."

Charles scoffed, "Well, they aren't going to let us just drive out. If they are calling this the Infected Zone, we are pretty much doomed to stay in it."

"Yeah, but you know where the cure is located," Grant reminded him.

"That might get me out, not all of you."

O'Grady said, "Let's just head to the boat basin. It's still dark enough outside that they may not notice us. Once daylight comes, I doubt we'd be able to get away with it. We need to make a decision soon or we are going to have less options available to us."

Marc stated, "I'm with him. Who else says we head for the river?"

Alissa, Debbie, and Aramis raised their hands. Liz didn't seem to care, as long as a decision was made that got them away from Manhattan.

However, Winston muttered pathetically, "I can't swim."

O'Grady assured him, "Don't worry. You won't have to, pal. Not with me at the helm. We'll be across the river in no time."

Grant shrugged, "What the hell? Let's give it a shot. What do you say, Sarge?"

Charles' eyes went from face to face. They each waited eagerly for him to make a decision. He decided to make the majority happy. "Use the bathroom, while you can. Once we leave here, we won't be coming back. Who knows when you will get the chance to use such a clean bathroom, again?"

The group was relieved to finally move on.

CONTAMINATION EFFECT

Chapter Fourteen

0435 HRS, HENRY HUDSON PARKWAY:

R ICKY TOOK THE next exit off the parkway at West 158th Street to escape the crawling northbound traffic. At the request of Sergeant Gregg Kepster, he drove straight to Columbia Presbyterian Medical Center. The plan was to drop off the infected officer named Stan, who was getting sicker.

By this time, Ricky was feeling feverish and a little nauseous himself. He wanted to take a break from driving, so he could check his wound. It had been feeling extremely itchy for quite sometime and was becoming numb. He took a quick whiff of it and could smell the pus coming out. At first, he had hoped he wasn't infected. After being stuck in traffic on the parkway for a few minutes he had time to reflect. Now, he was wondering how much time he had left, before he turned into a screaming maniac.

Gregg kept talking about the mess on West 125th Street. He couldn't believe things went so wrong back there. So many good cops died right in front of him and he felt helpless to stop it. The unfortunate part was that some of the people they were fighting weren't even infected! They just used the opportunity to fight the police. It made him so frustrated, he asked, "What the hell is wrong with these people?"

Ricky answered sarcastically, "That's just it. Don't you get it, Sarge? They're not people anymore. They're freaking zombies! Just like in the movies."

Steve refused to accept the silliness he was hearing and chimed in with his opinion. "Don't be stupid. First of all, zombies are allegedly slaves under the control of Voodoo and even that is a ridiculous notion. Second, the kind of '*zombies*' you are referring to do not exist in real life. You shouldn't believe everything that you see on TV or especially on the Internet. Seeing is not always believing anymore."

Ricky cried out, "Tell that to them! I don't care if you want to call them zombies or living dead..."

Steve interrupted him, "Now, *that* is an ambiguity. They cannot be living and dead, at the same time."

"I don't believe we are having this conversation," Ricky groaned, as he rolled his eyes.

"Actually, it is more like a debate," stated Steve without missing a beat.

"Damn it, Steve! Cut it out! This is serious!"

Gregg smirked, "Actually, I was referring to the so-called normal people in this city. When we were on 125th Street, we were fighting infected people and uninfected people. That's the only reason we could not maintain the wedge formation. We had two types of opponents, who fought entirely different battles. It was chaotic."

Cliff chimed in, "Tell me about it. We need to cut our losses and get the hell out of here. Harlem is done. We should drop Stan off at the hospital and go down to police headquarters."

Steve scoffed, "What are they going to do? Add more fuel to the fire? Here are some more cops for the virus, in case it hasn't already claimed enough! Ha! What a joke!"

Gregg suggested, "After we drop Stan off, I think we should check in with other precincts in the area to see what they are doing about this situation. We are close to the 3-3 and 3-4. This thing hasn't spread everywhere, yet. We can still contain it."

Steve could not believe what he was hearing. He looked over his shoulder and turned to Gregg. He asked, "With all due respect, Sarge. Have we been driving along the same streets together? This virus has spread too far to contain it. It's too late for that. They need to quarantine all of Manhattan North, at this point, before this spreads into the surrounding boroughs."

Gregg moaned, "Yeah, you're probably right. They were having a similar situation in the 3-2 earlier. They called for a mobilization around the same time you guys did because of that mess at Harlem Hospital."

Curious, Steve asked, "What mess?"

Gregg replied, "Some EDP that was brought in by the 3-0 earlier in the tour."

Steve rolled his eyes, "I am pretty damn sure that was related to our mess, which means there are infected all over Manhattan North already. We need to leave the borough, before they make it so we can't. I'm not dying in Manhattan."

Ricky asked eagerly, "Where would you like to die? I mean, where do you want to go?"

Steve scoffed, "Funny guy." He thought about it and answered, "Let's do as the Sarge suggested. I'm curious. Take us to the 34th Precinct, after we drop off Stan. I need to give Charles a call."

A few minutes later, their patrol car pulled up beside the Emergency Room entrance to Columbia Presbyterian Medical Center.

Gregg and Cliff both got out of the car and helped Stan inside, while Ricky and Steve waited in the car.

Steve turned to Ricky and began complaining, "Dropping this guy off here is a huge mistake. It's going to be the start of another outbreak. Before, when I spoke to Charles, he said they were watching the news. Our precinct is now considered part of the Infected Zone. There was even an outbreak at LaGuardia Airport. This thing is already in two boroughs, as far as we know. The safest place is away from New York City. We should ditch these guys and head out of the city. We can leave this place far behind and never look back."

Ricky laughed.

Steve said, "I was being serious."

Gregg left the hospital and got back into the car. He said, "Let's go, boys. I am leaving Officer Torres with him. I had them set up a quiet separate area for Stan. So, to the 3-4?"

Ricky looked at Steve, who nodded his approval in a subtle way that only they noticed. Ricky made a U-turn and headed north on Broadway toward the 34th Precinct.

0450 HRS, W. 135TH ST. AND ST. NICHOLAS AVE:

After about a half hour of walking, Officer David Castillo and his group emerged from the subway tunnel at the West 135th Street station. Walking through the tunnel was cooler than they thought it would be, considering it was a hot night outside, but it was still dark and filthy. They only saw one rat the entire time and it was on the center track away from them. There were three sets of tracks going through that area. They walked along the downtown side, which was to the far left.

They walked up the steps onto the platform and David sat down on the nearest bench. "I need to rest my leg," he said. It was aching a lot.

The tall man named Kirk stood beside him and waited patiently. He had helped David all the way through the tunnel without breaking a sweat. He was quite strong.

The bus driver also sat down. He was out of breath. "It's been a long time, since I walked that much. Been driving around too much." He turned to David and asked, "How are you feeling, Officer Castillo?"

"I'll be fine. I don't think my leg is broken or sprained. Probably just bruised. My whole left side aches. By the way, call me David," he said.

"I'm Wally."

David said, "Pleased to meet you, Wally. Thanks for saving my ass back there."

Wally replied, "Well, considering I smashed into your car, I thought it was the least I could do."

David chuckled a little, but it hurt too much to laugh.

Edie stared at him admiringly. When he noticed, she quickly looked away.

Kirk asked, "Are we going up here or do you still want to move on to the next station?"

David replied, "I want to go to the next station. The rest of you can decide what you are going to do. It should be safer upstairs than it was at the last stop. I just need to rest for a couple of minutes."

The man who they met on the platform of the last station said, "I'll head up and take a look around. I'll come back and let you guys know what I see." He walked off and went through the turnstile.

Edie said, "Maybe now would be a good time to introduce ourselves to each other. My name is Edie. Hello, everyone." She waved in a friendly manner and flicked her platinum blonde bangs out of the way, so people could see her face better. She had a friendly smile and a very pretty face.

Kirk responded, "Hey, Edie. Good to meet you. I'm Kirk, one of the last of my breed on this great continent. Native American with a mixture of Cherokee Creek and Chickasaw."

David looked up at him and replied, "I'm proud to know you, Kirk. You're a good man. Thank you for practically carrying me along through the tunnel. I couldn't have made it without your help. I really appreciate it."

Kirk blushed and said, "My pleasure, Officer."

"Please, call me David."

"Okay, David."

The young woman said, "My name is Millie Delgado. I was going to my older sister's house. She must be so worried."

The blond hair man stared at her disapprovingly and commented, "It's kind of late for a family visit, huh?"

Millie answered defensively, "I had an argument with my father. I was going to stay with her for the night." She was obviously upset by having to explain her reason for being out so late to a complete stranger. However, she understood the point of what they were doing was so they would not feel like they were with complete strangers.

The blond hair man replied, "It sounds to me like your father might be more worried than your sister. You should probably give them both a call."

"I can't. I forgot to bring my stupid cellphone with me when I left my house. I was so upset, I left in a hurry."

"Well, here," he said, as he extended his cellphone. "You can use mine."

Millie began crying and said, "No. I don't know my sister's number. It was saved on my phone. I never had to actually dial it and I am *not* calling my father." She paused and stared at the cellphone in his hand, and then added, "Thank you, though."

He put his phone away and sighed, "It's such a shame. So many people today rely on their cellphones. No one remembers phone numbers anymore."

The Transit worker agreed, "My daughters are the same. They spend every waking moment on their cellphones. They don't ever look at me when we speak. They just look down at their phones when they talk. I doubt they even know how I look!"

The blond hair man scoffed, "I know exactly what you mean."

Edie asked, "So, what are your names?"

The Transit worker responded reluctantly, "Wilkins. Just call me Wilkins."

The blond hair man from the bus said, "And I'm Mr. Hayes."

Edie frowned at both men for being so formal.

The man who went upstairs to check on things had just returned. Everyone turned his or her attention to him, as he began, "Would you believe that dumb ass in the booth expected me to pay to come back into the station, even after I explained what was going on to him? He didn't want to hear it. Good thing I had my ID with me. The guy's a jerk. Anyway, it doesn't look good up there. I could see straight across to the 32nd Precinct. It's on fire. It looks like that whole block is in flames. Plus, traffic is building up on St. Nicholas Avenue going toward 145th Street. There are a lot of police vehicles over there with their turret lights on. I'm going to have to agree with the officer. I say we keep going to the next station."

"Call me David. We were all just introducing ourselves."

"Oh, okay. I'm Kevin. I'm with Port Authority PD. I turn out at LaGuardia Airport. I was on my way home, after working a double shift of overtime. You know? Something big was going down at the airport, but I was busy all day with traffic duty, so I never found out the whole story. I have to wonder if it's related to what's happening here in Manhattan. I think we're at war. Either that or there was a terrorist attack."

David smirked, "Kevin, if that's all it was, I hate to say it, but I would be relieved. It's a lot worse. Do you have your gun with you?"

"Of course."

"Good. We may need it and I could use the backup. I guess I might as well let you all know what I know." David explained the entire situation to them and did not hold anything back. He told them about the infection, the chaos at the hospital, and the loss of the 26th and 28th Precincts.

Kevin looked very worried when he responded, "You're right, a terrorist attack would have been better to deal with than this nightmare. I don't know what to say. I'm speechless."

Mr. Hayes remarked, "You seem to be doing just fine. I think it's safe to say we all feel the same. This is hard to believe, but we know it's happening because we've seen it with our own eyes. The question is what can we do about it?"

David stood up and answered, "Well, the first thing we need to do is get to the next station. We can rest at Transit District 3. We should be safe there. They'll also have restrooms we can use. Are you guys ready to head back into the tunnel? It should be a straight shot this time. No turns. If you look, you can even see the light of the next station from here."

Millie hesitated going back into the tunnels because of her fear of rats and cockroaches, but she knew it was the only way to safety. Part of her wished she had stayed home. The other part of her was angry that she didn't take a cab to her sister's building, instead. It would have been costly traveling from Riverdale to First Avenue, but it would have been worth it.

Everyone else began walking toward the stairs to the tunnel without delay. Edie turned back to her and waved her on, "Come on, Millie. It'll be fine. We can walk together."

Millie took a deep breath and eventually followed. It was either that or she'd have to deal with the craziness on the streets alone.

0500 HRS, RIVERSIDE DRIVE:

"I hope this works out," Charles said to Grant.

He and the others had just left the apartment on Riverside Drive. They were back in their cars and driving into Riverside Park. This time it was only three patrol cars. They decided to leave one patrol car behind, as well as the ambulance containing the body of Aramis' partner. Aramis sat in the back of the sergeant's car. Liz and Alissa stayed with Debbie in her patrol car. Marc got into the car with Winston and O'Grady.

"We shall soon find out," Grant replied, as he turned the car onto the main path that went straight through the park that paralleled the Hudson River.

All three patrol cars traveled south silently through the park, until reaching the boat basin at West 72nd Street. They stopped the cars along the road beside the pier and got out. Most of them were anxious to leave Manhattan. Considering how early it was, there was no one else around. However, the sun was already rising in the east casting the first signs of daylight overhead.

There was a locked gate that prevented them from going out onto the pier, where about a dozen boats were docked. Grant grabbed the crowbar from the trunk of the car and went to work on the lock. It did not take long to pop it open.

He pulled open the gate and said to O'Grady, "Take your pick, *El Capitan.*"

O'Grady stepped out onto the pier and scanned the boats around him. They were generally the same. All were white with a main deck and lower deck. That's all they really needed for the speedy trip across the river. Comfort and style did not matter, as much as speed.

He settled on a sleek yacht that looked just right for their needs. "This one looks about right," he pointed to one on the left.

Liz moved closer and grinned, "Nice choice." She read the name on the side of the bow, "The Emancipator."

Debbie moved closer for a look and also agreed, "Yes, I like it, too." Being part African-American, she could truly appreciate the name, which signified being freed from slavery.

Charles was indifferent. He said, "Good, all aboard. Let's get out of here."

O'Grady slung his Colt M4 Carbine over his shoulder and held out his hand to help the others aboard. Debbie was the closest, so she went first. Once aboard, she stepped behind O'Grady. He pulled off his ammo bag and passed it to her, so she could hold it for him temporarily.

Debbie asked, "Don't you want me to hold the rifle for you?"

O'Grady shook his head and replied with a wink of his eye, "No one holds my rifle, but me."

Liz was next. CRACK! When O'Grady took her hand, a loud crack was heard in the distance, which distracted them momentarily. They paused and looked around.

Charles flinched and inquired, "What was that?"

As if in answer to his question, O'Grady's head blew open on one side and his body tilted toward the water seemingly in slow motion. His Colt M4 Carbine slid down his arm and its strap looped onto Liz's hand. In the next motion, his body fell into the river. O'Grady was dead.

Debbie screamed at the sight of O'Grady's death and another crack was heard coming from the same direction. It appeared to be from across the river.

Charles shouted, "SNIPER! Everyone get down!"

Before Debbie could react, she was hit next in the head, as well. Her body dropped down on the boat and lay still.

Charles cried out, "DEBBIE!"

Grant couldn't believe his eyes. First, O'Grady and now Debbie were dead in a matter of seconds. He saw Liz was still standing there and reacted fast. She held O'Grady's carbine in her hand and was in complete shock. She stared down at O'Grady's body floating in the river. The water around his head was turning red. All of a sudden, Grant grabbed her and pulled her down to the ground and she screamed.

He held her down and warned her. "Stay down! If they see you with the rifle, you're going to be the next target!"

Aramis raced back up the pier and ducked behind one of the patrol cars. Winston had not even stepped onto the pier, so he was already hiding behind his car when Aramis joined him.

Aramis called out, "Yo! Who the hell is shooting at us?"

Charles replied from the pier, "I have no idea! Everyone, stay down! Don't give that son of a bitch another clear shot!" Charles' heart was beating fast. He was furious. This wasn't what he wanted and now two more officers were dead. He wanted to pound his fists on the floor and scream at the top of his lungs, but what would that accomplish? Instead, he lay still fuming in his anger.

Marc and Alissa lay not far behind him.

Alissa was crying, "I don't want to die!"

Charles told her, "Do not stand up! Do not even move!"

Grant called back to Charles, "We can't lie on the pier all day. Pretty soon, the sun will be up and we'll be easier targets. What's the plan, Sarge?"

"I don't have a plan! Just stay alive! We'll think of something!"

Liz turned to Grant, who was lying beside her and said, "I have a plan."

"What is it?"

She showed him the Colt M4 Carbine in her hand and said, "I can shoot the boats at the far end, until they explode. The flames and smoke will provide us with some good cover."

Grant grinned, "Great plan!"

Charles agreed, "Do it! Listen up! When those boats explode, head back for the cars! We'll need to get out of here fast!"

Winston opened his door and waited. As he did another crack was heard in the distance. One of the tires on his car exploded and went flat. He groaned, "Aw, come on!"

Charles said, "Take the shot before he destroys our cars!"

Liz was already aiming for the farthest boat at the pier. She flipped off the safety switch with her thumb and pulled the trigger firing a single shot into the stern of the boat, where the engine and fuel tank were located. It exploded instantly into a brilliant merger of flame and black smoke. She aimed for the next boat and fired a second shot. Nothing happened. She fired a third shot, and then that boat also exploded pumping more black smoke into the air.

Charles stood up and shouted, "Let's move out! Back to the cars!"

Marc and Alissa stood up and rushed back up to the cars. Charles was right behind them. Grant was about to run to his car, but he paused when Liz jumped onto the boat, where Debbie's body lay. She bent over and picked up the ammo bag and the keys to her car, before jumping back to the pier.

Grant nodded his approval and the two ran for the cars. He and Charles got into their car, while Aramis and Winston got in the back seat.

Liz got into the passenger side of Debbie's car and unlocked the doors for Alissa, who got into the back. She then handed the keys to Marc and said, "You should drive."

He took the keys and got into the driver's side and replied, "And you should hand over that rifle. You're not authorized to use it."

She replied, "I may not be authorized, but I bet I can shoot it better than any of you. I had military training. I can shoot this weapon with precision."

"Fine, whatever," he said. He didn't have time to argue, as he started up the car and followed the sergeant's car.

Both patrol cars raced along the pier and another shot was fired at them. Luckily, it missed the cars and hit a streetlamp, shattering the bulb to pieces. Charles noticed where the shots were coming from. There was a boat in the river. It looked military to him.

He turned to Grant and said, "Get us away from the river and back on the road. Someone doesn't want us crossing the river."

Grant led them away from the boat basin and back up to Riverside Drive, where they stopped near a war memorial to catch their breath and formulate a new plan.

CONTAMINATION EFFECT

Chapter Fifteen

0502 HRS, 34TH Pct:

A S RICKY, STEVE, and Gregg drove north on Broadway through the confines of the 34th Precinct, they noticed something was going on. They expected things to look more normal, but there was no one out on the streets. It was unusually quiet out, although it was around five in the morning. There was a lack of vehicles on the road, too. They did not see one city bus or taxi on the road. However, a helicopter did pass overhead flying rather low.

Ricky pulled into an empty parking spot in front of the precinct. Steve and Gregg stepped out and began walking toward the entrance.

Ricky took a peek at his wound, before getting out of the car. It was swollen and the blackness had begun to spread. He was going to need a clean band-aid. Luckily, he had a few in his pocket. When he went into the station house, he went straight into the bathroom and washed his wound. He dried it with a paper towel and placed two new band-aids.

Gregg approached the desk and spoke to the desk officer. According to his nametag, it was a Hispanic lieutenant named Lt. Reymundo. Gregg began, "Sir, may I speak to you? It's regarding the situation in the 2-6." His words definitely caught the lieutenant's attention.

He noticed Gregg was a sergeant from SRG and replied, "You're not one of the guys that were here earlier."

"No, sir. We just drove up from 125th Street."

The lieutenant's eyes opened wide and he looked at Steve, who was wearing collar brass from the 26th Precinct. He became enraged and shouted, "What the hell are you doing here in my station house? Did you bring that Godforsaken infection up here with you?"

Ricky had just come out of the bathroom in time to hear the lieutenant yelling at them. He decided to hang back and waited out of sight.

Gregg tried to explain, "No, sir! Absolutely not! We are not infected. You can check us, if you don't believe me." He figured it might be wise to not mention the infected officer they dropped off at the nearest hospital. He hoped Steve would keep quiet about it, too.

Steve was indeed quiet. He had a feeling this was one of those times when you let the supervisors talk amongst themselves. He looked around for Ricky and noticed him by the door. Ricky motioned to him that he was going out to the car. Steve gave him a quick nod and looked back toward the lieutenant, who was not any less pleased with Gregg.

"If you are not infected, then why aren't you down there holding the line? You guys really screwed the pooch on this one! I'm down to two sectors because my guys are all sitting in cars blocking intersections across 155th Street! To make matters worse, I just got a call from the borough telling me that all bridges entering or leaving Manhattan are closed, until further notice! Therefore, the officers coming in for the day tour will not be allowed into Manhattan, which means we will be doing a double and maybe even a triple tour!" His face was turning red from yelling. "I gotta tell you, if I need to stay here four shifts in a row, I am not going to be pleased! I'm supposed to be starting my vacation pick today! Today was my last day! I have tickets to Hawaii and they were very expensive! What the hell happened, and don't give me that silly media sci-fi version? I want the truth, Sergeant Kepster!"

Gregg replied, "We are not sure how it started, but there was an outbreak in the 2-6. As a result, an experimental virus has been spreading and infecting almost everyone it comes in contact with, including cops. It spreads through bodily fluids, mainly through bites. I've seen a lot of good cops die in front of my face, including D.I. Ehrenberg. We tried our best to contain it, but the people began rioting out of fear or plain stupidity. Despite our best efforts, we were overrun and had to pull back. Even Aviation advised us, it was a losing battle. Throughout the night, several infected civilians and officers were transported to the local hospitals, which unfortunately led to another outbreak in the 3-2. This virus is spreading too fast and I'm not sure if we can stop it. We were barely able to get away in one piece."

Lt. Reymundo stood there thinking of what to do with Gregg and Steve. They waited awkwardly for his decision, while Ricky was outside sitting in the car. He started it up and waited. After about a minute, the lieutenant stated, "I want you guys back out on the street. My guys need help out there. I have one of my sergeants sitting in a damn unmarked car blocking Riverside Drive at West 1-5-5. Go there and relieve him and don't even think about asking me for a meal break!"

Gregg could not believe they were being sent out to block traffic. He hesitated and was about to protest, but the lieutenant cut him off.

"Get out there now, sergeant!"

Gregg and Steve turned and quietly walked out the door. They got back into the car, where Ricky was waiting, and closed the doors. Ricky had been listening to the news on the radio, but he turned it off when they got in.

He asked jokingly, "So, did he rip you guys a new ass or what?"

Gregg replied shamefully, "You can say that. He wants us to head over to Riverside, so we can block traffic.

Ricky responded in shock, "Block traffic??? The city is going down the toilet and he wants us to block traffic? Yeah, I don't think so. That's not happening."

Steve looked over at him curiously.

Gregg responded, "Do you really plan on disobeying a direct order from a lieutenant in a time of crisis? You could lose your job, officer."

Ricky turned back to face Gregg, who was seated in the backseat, and spoke candidly, "Here's the deal, Sarge. Tonight we lost more cops than I care to count. My precinct has been overrun and it's probably lost forever. The city has been divided into Infected Zones and Safe Zones with borders that keep changing for the worse. It's possible all of Manhattan could end up under quarantine and you think I plan on standing around like an idiot blocking traffic?"

Gregg asked, "Do you have a better idea that won't end with us being suspended or fired?"

"Yeah! As a matter of fact, I do! We can drive the hell out of this city, while we still can and stay alive! Screw that lieutenant and screw being suspended or fired! I'll get another job! One that doesn't turn me into a human target for every criminal with a grudge against the law because he got his stupid ass arrested for breaking the law and now hates cops!"

Steve smiled proudly and agreed, "I'm with him. We're leaving this city. You can either come with us or we can drop you off at Riverside Drive."

Gregg sighed heavily. He couldn't believe he was actually considering going AWOL with two guys that he hardly knew. What was he thinking? He loved his job. He wanted to be a cop in the NYPD, since he was in kindergarten. Now, he was being tempted to run away from it to save his own ass. He couldn't help, but feel guilty about abandoning his brothers and sisters in blue. He knew it was wrong.

However, there was also a part of him that knew Ricky was right. The city was being overrun, one block at a time, and there was nothing a few roadblocks were going to do to stop it. He had to face reality. Manhattan was in grave danger of being lost to a deadly virus.

Ricky pulled away from the precinct and began heading north on Broadway. Without taking his eyes off the road, he said to Gregg, "I take it you made up your mind."

Gregg hesitated, but then answered, "So what's the plan?"

0516 HRS, W. 145TH ST. AND ST. NICHOLAS AVE:

David's group had finally reached the light at the end of the tunnel. They stepped up out of the tracks and onto the platform at West 145th Street and St. Nicholas Avenue. Once everyone was off the tracks, they stopped to rest.

Millie griped, "I hope I never have to do that, again."

Edie commented, "You did fine. I'm proud of you." It was hard for her to be so positive knowing that her best friend had been killed about an hour earlier. However, being there to help someone else through a trying time was a good distraction. Still, she knew she'd have to take the time to mourn Eva's death sooner or later. She wondered, when that time came, who would be there for her?

Kevin spoke, "Head's up. Someone's coming."

A young Transit officer named Kalmanowicz approached them curiously. He noticed the black track dust on their clothing and asked, "Were you guys walking on the tracks?"

David exhaled and replied wearily, "Yes. We had to get away from 125th Street. The subway tunnel seemed like the best bet. Don't worry. No one here is infected." He took another breath and added, "I need to speak with a boss."

Officer Kalmanowicz escorted the group to Transit District 3, which was located within the subway station. David approached the desk and noticed that he knew the lieutenant. Her name was Lieutenant Luke and her husband used to work at the 26th Precinct, until he was promoted.

She looked at him and it was obvious he was a bit worse for wear. She asked, "Officer Castillo, what happened to you? Were you down at 125th Street?"

"Yes, ma'am," he nodded. "We lost control. Deputy Inspector Ehrenberg is dead. Lieutenant Andrews and my partner were infected. I had to lock them in holding cells and leave them for dead. The station house is probably swarming with infected, by now. The last time I spoke to Sergeant Foster, he was trapped at Lincoln Fried Chicken. I tried to go to the 2-8 for help, but everyone was either infected or dead. I drove away and the next thing I knew I was in an accident with a city bus. These people saved me and pulled me out of the car," he pointed to Wally and Kirk.

Kirk shot her a quick salute.

Lieutenant Luke gave him a half smile and looked back at David. She was staggered by what he told her. It was a lot to take in. She knew things were bad, but she had no idea the actual extent of it. At last, she responded, "You can stop running now. All of you are welcome to rest here and wait it out. We're at the edge of the Infected Zone, so you should be safe."

Kirk said, "Thank you, ma'am."

Edie and Millie were so relieved that they hugged one another.

A moment later, the desk phone rang and the lieutenant answered it.

Mr. Wilkins, the Transit worker, said, "Oh, that reminds me, I need to call my supervisor. Is there a phone I could use?"

Wally responded, "Yeah, so do I."

Officer Kalmanowicz escorted both men to a nearby telephone, so they could make their necessary calls.

Mr. Hayes turned to Kevin and said, "Do you really think we're safe here? I doubt it. I would feel better, if we were in the Bronx, out of Manhattan."

Kevin replied, "I don't think they will let us go, now that we're here. We should be relatively safe here, if this is the edge of the Infected Zone. I can't believe I just said that."

Kirk said, "I know. This is insane. Hey, Kevin, you mentioned there was something going down at the airport. I wonder, could it be possible that someone who was infected left on a flight and is spreading the virus somewhere new?"

"That would be really bad, if it were true," Kevin replied.

When Lieutenant Luke hung up the phone, she looked as though someone had just notified her regarding a death in her immediate family.

David noticed and asked, "What's wrong?"

She looked up at him and frowned, "We are now all in the extended Infected Zone. All the bridges have been closed. No one leaves Manhattan and no one enters."

Mr. Hayes rolled his eyes and stated, "I knew it. We're all going to die here."

Despair washed over Millie's face.

Even Edie was in shock. After all they went through to escape the Infected Zone, they were right back in it.

David asked, "What? Where does it end?"

Lieutenant Luke replied, "They pushed it up to 155th Street and included the Polo Grounds."

"Why?" He asked.

"Because the infected have broken past 145th Street and there's a riot at the Polo Grounds," she answered glumly.

The Polo Grounds was a Housing complex located just north of the Macomb's Dam Bridge at West 155th Street. While it was technically outside of the new border for the Infected Zone, it was secluded in a valley below the bridge, thus placing it below the regular street level at West 155th Street. In addition, the northbound entrance to the Harlem River Drive served as a fairly decent border conveniently separating it from the Safe Zone.

0530 HRS, UPPER WEST SIDE:

Grant had parked the patrol car in the shadow of the Soldier's and Sailor's Monument at West 89th Street and Riverside Drive. Marc parked his car beside him along the passenger side, so they could talk from within the vehicles without having to get out. This way, if it became necessary, they could leave in a hurry.

Marc looked across to Charles and said, "Who do you think was shooting at us back there, Sarge?"

"The military. They don't want us leaving. It's too risky. If the infection reaches New Jersey, it becomes a national crisis. Right now, it's only a New York City problem. I need to call someone. Give me a minute," he said, as he pulled out his phone and dialed one of his contacts. The person did not answer the phone, so he left a message, "Carmen. It's Charles Foster. Listen, I'm sorry to bother you so early in the morning, but I really need to talk to you. Can you call me before you go to work?"

Grant said, "Not for nothing, but I'm starving. Anyone else hungry?"

Marc answered, "Shit yeah!"

"Me, too," Alissa responded.

Winston asked, "What do you have in mind? The city is dying around us and you think someone is going to open, so we can buy breakfast?"

Grant replied, "Think about it. Just because we had a long night, doesn't mean everyone else went through the same thing. I am pretty damn certain there are a lot of restaurant and deli owners, who are not aware of what happened last night. They are going to open up today like they do every Saturday morning. We just need to make sure to choose a place below 86th Street, to be on the safe side. We'll go in, pick up some food, and make a subtle suggestion to listen to the news, as we leave. We can drive into Central Park and eat in the cars."

Alissa commented, "Ooh, I like that idea."

Aramis agreed, "Hell yeah! I could use some food, right about now. I'm low in energy."

Charles perked up, "Fine. Let's do it. I can't sit here and wait for her to call me. It could take an hour. I need to keep busy and besides, I'm hungry, too."

It was settled. They drove to Broadway and found a place, where they could buy breakfast. For a brief moment, it almost felt like a normal Saturday morning. They walked in together and placed their orders.

The employees seemed clueless as to what took place during the night. If they lived in the area, there is no reason they would know. Not everyone listens to the news, before going to work. Some only live a few blocks away from their places of employment, so the traffic reports are irrelevant. Plus, it was a Saturday morning, so traffic was usually light anyway. And the weather was great, since it was July.

Once they made their purchases, Charles said to the manager, "You may want to close up early today. It's a good day to stay home. Something big is going down uptown. I suggest you turn on the news and check it out."

"Yeah? Thanks, I'll take a look," he said. The manager turned on the television and the news came on. A report came on live from Washington Heights. There was mention about the expanded Infected Zone, which now included West 96th Street to West 155th Street, from river to river.

Charles got a phone call from Steve, as he was getting back into the car. Apparently, Steve, Ricky, and the sergeant from SRG were intending to leave Manhattan. Steve informed him about everything the lieutenant from the 34th Precinct said regarding the street closures at West 155th Street and also about how the day tour cops from outside of Manhattan would not be coming in to work today. Charles already expected that, since there would be nowhere for them to go anyway. He told Steve about the precinct being a lost cause and also about how they were shot at by a sniper when they tried to cross the river. He told them to be careful with whatever they were planning and to stay in touch.

By the time Charles hung up the phone, they were already entering Central Park. They parked along one of paths that was situated away from the main roads and enjoyed their breakfast in peace. Of course, they were perfectly aware it would be a temporary peace.

It came to an end fast when Marc decided to turn on the radio and listen to the news. There was something on about the airport, which caught their interests.

"... FAA is currently tracking flights that took off from LaGuardia and traveled to cities in Ohio and Florida last night. Port Authority believes it is possible someone carrying the virus could have traveled to one of these locations. As of 4 am, all flights going to or out of New York City have been cancelled. Police have yet to confirm if the incidents at LaGuardia and in Manhattan are related. However, the President has declared New York City a disaster area.

Again, if you have not heard, bridges and tunnels going into Manhattan are closed, pending the outcome of what has been dubbed the Manhattanville Incident. The National Guard has been placed at all bridge entrances to enforce the closures, only as a safety precaution. In addition, all transit services going into or leaving Manhattan are suspended, until further notice.

If you live in Manhattan, you are strongly advised to remain in your homes and lock your doors and windows. Police are saying it is extremely unsafe to be outside."

Marc turned off the radio and scoffed, "They might want to mention that if you try to cross the rivers, they will shoot you with deadly force!"

Charles' cellphone rang, again. This time it was his friend, Carmen, who worked at police headquarters. He quickly swallowed the last of his bacon, egg, and cheese sandwich and answered the phone call.

"Hello? Carmen! Have you seen the news? We had a major incident last night, one that could change the future of New York City forever. There was a viral outbreak in the confines of the 2-6." He went on for several minutes telling her what happened and explained there could be a cure, but was cut short. While she wanted to hear more, she was running late for work and had to hang up. She promised to call him back, as soon as she reached the office.

It was time for another waiting game. At least, this time, they had the peaceful serenity of Central Park on a Saturday morning to relax them.

0540 HRS, HENRY HUDSON PARKWAY:

Ricky stopped the car along the Henry Hudson Parkway near the exit for the Cloisters.

Gregg asked, "Why are we stopping here? I thought we were heading across the bridge."

Ricky turned to them both and said, "We are, but we need to be ready. There may be guards at the bridge, who will turn us away. If that happens, I need to know where you guys stand. Will you want to turn away and think of another plan, or will you be willing to take a chance and charge through any barricades that might be blocking the road? It's not a decision I should make alone, so I thought we should discuss it, first."

Steve commented, "Good idea. We should discuss this and what it will mean, depending on what we decide. Like the Sarge said, if we try to leave Manhattan, we will be considered AWOL."

Ricky rolled his eyes, "I already told you I don't care about that. I was in the military. I know all about real AWOL. This job is a joke. It won't be AWOL. It will be survival. When I was in the Army, I was trained to survive, not to wait to die. Make no mistake. I am leaving this city one way or another."

Steve looked to Gregg and said, "That just leaves us. What do you want to do? Honestly, I want to leave the city. I would rather be upstate with my family. I can't stay here too long and take the chance that I will become infected."

Ricky wanted to tell them about his wound, but he was afraid they would vote to leave him behind. If he was going to die, he preferred to go out making a difference. He knew he could find a way to get them across to the Bronx, even if it meant losing his life in the process. He had to try.

Steve continued, "On the other hand, my sister, Camille, lives in Queens with my nephew. That boy is like a son to me. He's my godson. I can't leave this city knowing they are at risk."

Gregg said, "Before we make a move, let's make a few personal calls. I'd also like to call my wife to let her know I am okay."

Steve agreed, "Let's get to it then." He took his cellphone out of his pocket and called his sister. He knew she was going to give him hell for calling so early on a Saturday. "Hey, good morning. I'm very sorry to be calling you this early, but it's extremely important you do exactly as I say. Something terrible has happened in the city. It's really bad. Apocalypse bad. There's no time to explain, but I need you to wake up the little man, get in the car, and head up into Westchester County. Just get the hell out of New York City, as soon as possible. Turn on the news and you'll see what I'm talking about. Just do it fast."

Meanwhile, Gregg also spoke to his wife and explained the situation to her. He said he would try and get to her, as soon as he could. They lived in Orange County, so he wasn't sure when he'd be home.

Ricky called his wife in Queens. He told her to head out to Long Island to stay with his parents. He also explained the whole story to her, as simply as he could without going into too many details. The main thing he wanted to do was to hear her voice, in case it would be the last time he ever did.

"I don't know when I will be home," he said. "I really can't say. We're going to try going to the Bronx to see how that works out. If we can get there without a problem, I will call you, again. In the meantime, just know that I love you very much."

They each spent about five minutes speaking with their loved ones. Once they were done with their calls, it was time to get back to planning their escape.

Steve decided, "Let me give Charles a call, too. I should let him know what we are planning to do. I also want to find out how he and the others are doing. The conversation lasted about five minutes. It was enough for them to update each other on what had happened.

"Let's take this slow, Ricky. Charles said they tried to take a boat from the boat basin earlier. As soon as they climbed aboard, one of the ESU guys was shot and killed by a sniper, who was on a military boat. The sniper got Debbie, too. She's gone."

"Are you kidding me? Oh, man. They're using snipers to keep us from crossing the river? That is dirty. We need to plan this just right or we'll never make it halfway across the bridge."

Gregg suggested, "Maybe we should go back to Riverside Drive and forget this idea. I don't want to get killed crossing a damn bridge."

Ricky protested, "I am *not* blocking traffic. We'll think of something. Give me time to come up with a good plan. Let's just stay here, for a moment. It's nice and quiet. I can think better this way."

Steve was surprised by Ricky's actions. He seemed very determined to leave Manhattan, no matter what the cost. Now, that he had spoken to his sister, he also wanted to leave. He hoped she could make it to the Bronx without incident. Getting to Westchester from there should be easy enough. All he would have to do after is find a way to meet up with her, so they could head upstate to his home.

For the first time, he found himself hoping he'd be able to see his family, again.

0545 HRS, W. 145TH ST. AND ST. NICHOLAS AVE:

Officers were running around frantic in Transit District 3. They found themselves in the Infected Zone and were told to remain within the station. Some officers and supervisors wanted to take their chances by heading north to get out of the Infected Zone. Lieutenant Luke had her hands full, as she tried to maintain order in her station house.

David used the opportunity to grab a set of van keys from the desk. He went over to where the others he arrived with were sitting and said, "This place is on lockdown, but I have a feeling it's not going to last. The lieutenant is losing control of her people. They don't like the idea of being trapped here. I don't blame them. I grabbed keys to one of the vans. We need to get the hell out of here, while we can. Who's with me?"

Kirk and Wally both stood up immediately, followed by Kevin, Edie, and then Millie. Mr. Hayes hesitated, but he didn't like the idea of being trapped either, so he stood up. The only one that remained seated was the Transit worker.

David looked at Mr. Wilkins and asked, "What about you?"

"I'm staying put. It's safer in here, than it is out there."

David replied, "It won't be for long."

"I'll take my chances," said Mr. Wilkins.

David couldn't force him to come. Nor did he want to. The van would be full enough with everyone else. He turned to the others and said, "Follow me and stay close. They might try to stop us from leaving. If they do, ignore them and keep going. It will be too much effort to stop us all from leaving, so they'll probably let us go. They have enough problems going on in here, as it is to be worried about babysitting us."

David grabbed a fresh battery for his portable radio and walked toward the exit. The others followed him. Around them officers were shouting and arguing about how they should proceed. No one even noticed them slipping out the door. They moved quickly through the station and up the staircase to the street. David looked at the keys and told them they needed to find van number 8150.

While remaining within close proximity to each other, they began looking around at the van numbers. There were several police vans angle-parked along St. Nicholas Avenue.

It was total mayhem on the street level. People were running in different directions. Abandoned police cars and metal police barriers were stretched out across the intersection blocking vehicular traffic from going north on St. Nicholas Avenue. Car horns were honking and traffic was backed up across West 145th Street going east toward the Bronx. It was difficult to tell if cars were being allowed to cross over the Macomb's Dam Bridge. This was something David was willing to find out.

"We need to find that van. I want to try and cross the bridge into the Bronx."

Wally looked confused and said, "I thought the bridges were closed."

"It's a chance I'm willing to take," replied David.

Millie ran up to David and claimed, "I found it! The van is right down here." She walked at a fast pace heading south on St. Nicholas Avenue, as the others followed closely. David struggled to keep up with the group. Kirk came up beside him and helped him walk. Luckily, the van was only about one hundred feet away.

"Thanks," said David. He unlocked the driver's side door and unlocked the other doors automatically, as he hit a button on the door. "Everyone get in," he instructed.

Kirk got into the front passenger seat, after helping David into the van. His legs were too long to sit comfortably in the back. The girls both scurried to the back row, while Mr. Hayes sat in the middle row. Wally and Kevin sat in the first row, directly behind David and Kirk.

David started the van and was relieved it had a full tank of gas. He adjusted the mirrors hastily and moved forward out of the parking spot. He was glad it had been backed into the spot. He saw a small opening in the roadblock on West 145th Street and drove through it. However, the traffic on that street was practically at a standstill because the bridge was blocked off going into the Bronx by a police barrier truck that had been left behind in the middle of the road.

He turned on the turret lights and hit the siren. It commanded some respect on the road. There was a small gap between two cars, which he forced the van in through. The cars moved out of the way, as best they could. David could see the annoyance in the faces of the drivers, as he passed in front of them.

"Deal with it," he muttered half to himself. "We're coming through."

It was a good thing there wasn't as much traffic on the westbound side, as there was on the eastbound lanes. There were a few cars, which had been turned away from the bridge at West 145th Street, but none that were in the way, as they drove through the intersection. It was still quite early in the morning on a Saturday and traffic was generally light at that time.

The van raced north on St. Nicholas Avenue for three blocks, before reaching a fork in the road. David veered right onto Donnellon Square and continued toward West 155th Street.

He noticed a police car from the 33rd Precinct blocking the road ahead. The car was parked between two wooden police barriers and its turret lights were lit. The officer on the post was standing outside of his vehicle and appeared to be pacing back and forth, stretching his legs.

The officer saw the Transit police van rushing toward his blockade and tried frantically to wave it down, so it could stop, but it did not. Instead, the van crashed through one of the wooden barriers sending it flying toward Edgecombe Avenue on the right. The cop leapt out of the way and took cover behind his patrol car, which was untouched. The van then made a hard right turn and smashed through another set of wooden barriers, as it continued going east on West 155th Street toward the entrance of the Macomb's Dam Bridge.

A line of interlocked metal police barriers was being used to block the entrance of the bridge. David braced himself and crashed right through them. Several barriers were knocked to the left and right, creating an opening for the van. As soon as he did, gunshots fired from the Bronx side of the bridge, where an armored vehicle waited. A soldier standing behind a concrete barricade on that side of the bridge took aim and shot a hole through the driver's side mirror. David slammed on the breaks instinctively. Another soldier fired a round into the windshield that shot straight through the van and came out of the rear window between the girls.

Both girls screamed and ducked down in the back row, while David exclaimed, "Holy shit! They're actually shooting at us!"

Kirk cried out, "No shit, pal! I thought you were the *po*-lice!"

Wally also ducked and shouted, "Hurry! Turn right down that ramp and head south to Seventh Avenue, before one of those bullets hits somebody!"

David did just that and made a sharp right turn away from the bridge crashing through another set of metal barriers in the process. The van ran over one, which caused it to swerve slightly out of control. David gripped the wheel tightly and straightened out the van. It fishtailed, as it went downhill onto Seventh Avenue and out of view from the gunners.

Mr. Hayes looked back and said, "I don't think they're following us."

Kevin assumed, "They're not going to cross that bridge into the Infected Zone. We should be safe here."

David continued driving, as he replied, "Yeah, except that we are way too close to the Polo Grounds, where people are rioting. We need to get somewhere safer. I've had my fill of riots for one day."

Kirk looked back and asked, "Everybody okay?"

Mr. Hayes looked behind him at the girls, who were still cowering down in their seats. They appeared unharmed. He faced forward, again, and responded, "We're a bit shaken back here, but no one is hurt."

"Yeah, Wally and I are good, too," said Kevin from behind Kirk.

"Great," Kirk replied. He turned to David and asked, "Where to now, *kemo sabe?*"

David exhaled and shrugged, "I wish I knew. Right now, I'm just trying to keep us alive." The van continued south along Seventh Avenue for about another block, before turning left down a quiet side street. It came to a stop on West 147th Street in front of a statue of Dr. Martin Luther King, Jr. David did not want to drive into the traffic at West 145th Street. He exhaled and buried his face into his hands. That was a close call, he thought. He almost got them killed with his desperation. It was a reckless decision. He would not make another. They were counting on him.

CONTAMINATION EFFECT

Chapter Sixteen

0558 HRS, UPPER WEST SIDE:

AT LAST, CHARLES received the call he had been waiting for all morning. His friend, Carmen, who was a sergeant at police headquarters, called him as soon as she arrived at work.

"Carmen, we've been trying to outrun this thing all night. I already lost half the cops on my tour because of it. I know how it started. I also know where there might be a cure. Here's the catch. It's five levels underground in a secret laboratory underneath the Greene Science Building on Broadway. Some fool scientist dropped a syringe containing a possible anti-virus under a bed in a dorm." There was a brief pause. "Never mind how I know. Just believe it's the truth," he said to her. "Okay, fine. I'll tell you. I spoke to someone, who worked there, right before he died. He confessed the whole thing to me," he lied. Charles was not about to mention the journal. He knew if anyone knew about it, they'd try to get their hands on it. He wasn't quite done with it, yet. He had plans to read it all.

Grant listened in on the conversation, as best he could from the driver's seat. Meanwhile, Marc and the girls talked amongst themselves in the next car. They were still parked in Central Park. Aramis and Winston were getting restless in the cramped back seat of the sergeant's car.

When Charles hung up, a few minutes later, he filled them all in on what was said.

"I have bad news and more bad news," he started. "They're talking about evacuating 1 Police Plaza," where police headquarters was located. "There's a good chance Manhattan will be placed under quarantine soon. She confirmed that the National Guard has been called in. They are using armored vehicles to guard every bridge and tunnel in and out of Manhattan, while military boats patrol the rivers to keep the infected from leaving. As we already learned, they have no problem firing upon the uninfected."

Aramis commented, "Damn! This keeps going from bad to worse by the hour. We are in serious shit."

Charles replied, "And we need to get out of it, before we lose our window of opportunity."

Winston frowned, "It sounds to me like we already did."

Grant perked up and said, "Maybe not. I have an idea that might work, but it's going to require getting wet and dirty."

Marc bowed his head and groaned, "Please, don't tell me you want to walk through the sewers."

Grant smirked, "Actually, no. I'm pretty sure most of them spill out into the rivers, at some point. Besides, we'd probably get lost. It was a good guess, though. I was thinking more along the lines of the Old Croton Aqueduct tunnels."

Marc turned to Grant and asked, "The what???"

"It was a 42-mile long tunnel that went from the Croton Dam upstate down the west side of Westchester County into the Bronx, across High Bridge, and into Manhattan. At one time, it went all the way down to Fifth Avenue, where the New York Public Library is located. In fact, the receiving reservoir was on the same spot as the Great Lawn, right here in Central Park. Eventually, a new aqueduct was built to replace it and the old tunnel was abandoned. Most of the tunnel below 135th Street has been removed, but the tunnel still exists north of there. We can take the tunnel straight up under Amsterdam Avenue, across High Bridge, and into the Bronx. The best part is no one will be the wiser," explained Grant.

Charles smiled, "You know what? That sounds so crazy it could actually work. How do we get in?"

Grant replied with a smile, "I just happen to know a way."

Charles asked, "What the heck are we waiting for?"

A news helicopter hovered overhead and filmed the destruction left behind from the previous night, as the two police cars exited Central Park and drove north along Central Park West. There were no other cars on the road. They drove around the traffic circle at West 110th Street and continued north on Morningside Avenue. The helicopter seemed to follow for a while.

At West 123rd Street the cars had to swerve around and avoid infected people, who were charging into their vehicles. It was hard to avoid hitting a few with the cars, but Marc ran over a couple on purpose. Alissa ducked down low in the backseat and kept her eyes closed. She kept thinking one would smash through the back window and grab her.

During the drive Charles sent text messages to both Steve and David to update them on what his friend had told him. He was glad when both responded back. It meant they were still alive. It was such a relief. It made him smile.

As the cars crossed West 125th Street, they had to go around a few crashed cars. One was on fire, although the fire was already burning out. Infected people were chasing after normal people, who had just woken up and stepped outside to go to work, totally unaware of the madness from the night before. It was terrible to watch without helping, but stopping would have only endangered their safety. There were too many infected running around. Some looked as if they were dead already, but still they stumbled around like heroine addicts. Those ones did not move as fast as the newly infected, who were actually capable of running like a perfectly healthy person. They were the scary ones to worry about. All it took was one bite to ruin your day.

Grant watched the slower infected, as he drove by, and thought they really did look like zombies. It was hard to believe, but he was seeing it with his own eyes. How else could people stand around or walk about with half their faces eaten off, yet, they do not act as if they are in pain? They only seemed to respond to one instinct. Hunger.

There was so much disaster on West 125th Street stretching from Broadway all the way to Lenox Avenue that the helicopter forgot about the two police cars and filmed the disaster footage. There were numerous fires burning out of control that were starting to spread from one building to another. People fleeing from the fires were running straight into mobs of infected, who ravaged them on sight.

Aramis saw an ambulance at the far end of the block on West 127th Street closer to St. Nicholas Avenue, as they passed that street. It made him think about his partner. He still had not come to terms with her death or with leaving her body behind in the ambulance on Riverside Drive.

He wondered to himself, why? Why did this have to happen? So many innocent lives have already been lost and there were still so many more to go. It was difficult knowing there were still people, who were home asleep, that had no idea what terrors awaited them when they finally started their days. It was a tragedy.

The cars finally came to a stop when they reached West 135th Street and Convent Avenue, where they saw a pretty young woman with long strawberry blonde hair standing in the middle of the street.

Aramis leaned forward to get a better look and asked, "Who the hell is that and why is she so damned hot?"

0601 HRS, UPPER MANHATTAN:

Ricky had driven out of the Cloisters and was taking Broadway straight up toward the bridge that crossed into the Bronx at 225th Street. It was Gregg's idea.

He sounded grateful, as he said, "Thanks for giving this a try, guys. I think it's worth a shot. Who knows? Maybe they will let us through. We have nothing to lose by trying."

Steve was skeptical about the plan. He didn't think they'd be allowed to cross over into the Bronx so easily. Otherwise, more people would be trying to leave. There were so many cars lined up to cross the bridge, but none of them were moving. Drivers were honking their horns with little effect.

Ricky was driving the wrong way on the southbound side to avoid traffic. There were only a few cars heading south. It was the ones that had given up on trying to cross and had made U-turns. They were simple enough to go around, although Gregg and Steve were on the edge of their seat every time Ricky came face to face with another car heading south.

Steve closed his eyes, unable to watch anymore, and groaned, "Did I mention that I really do not like this idea?" He flinched when he felt the car jerk to one side and heard Ricky say, "That was a close one!"

Ricky slowed down, as they got closer to the Broadway Bridge. He pulled up along the curb and stopped at the entrance. He then turned back to Gregg and suggested, "Maybe walking over with a white flag in hand might be wiser, than driving across."

Gregg chuckled and stepped out of the car. He stopped Ricky from getting out and said, "You guys wait here. I will go across and speak to them. I'll explain our case and see what they say."

Ricky hesitated, but closed his door and remained in the car.

As Gregg walked away toward the Bronx side, Steve uttered angrily, "If he leaves us here, I'm going to make sure I get to the other side, just so I can kill him."

Before Gregg got halfway across, two shots were fired at his feet. He immediately turned and ran back to the car. He climbed back into the back seat and was breathing heavily. No other shots were fired, aside from the two warning shots. Gregg was not hit.

Ricky turned back to Gregg and asked, "So, how did it go? What did they say?"

Gregg finally caught his breath and exclaimed, "Those bastards shot at me! I'm an NYPD sergeant in uniform and they shot at me!"

Steve replied sarcastically, "Well, did you tell them that? Maybe they didn't know."

Gregg glared at him, and then said, "That is not funny. I can't believe they shot at me. This is serious, you guys. If they aren't going to let us cross over into the Bronx, it doesn't leave us with many choices. We may as well head back to Riverside Drive, where the sergeant from the 3-4 is waiting."

Ricky shifted the car into reverse and drove backwards fast to the next intersection, as he stated, "I already told you. That is not an option for me."

"Then what the hell do you guys want to do? I give up! You be the bosses! I'll just sit back here and play passenger." Gregg crossed his arms and pouted.

Ricky grinned, "Finally." He turned the car onto West 218th Street and drove across to Inwood Hills Park near the river at Spuyten Duyvil. They were able to see the Henry Hudson Bridge from there. Far below it and closer to the Hudson River were the tracks to the Amtrak train, where a swing bridge was located. It was locked in the open position.

"Damn," he said. "I was hoping the railroad swing bridge would be straight, so we could cross over on foot. These bastards thought of everything."

Steve noted, "It's not that far to the other side. Too bad it's too dangerous to swim across. This is the roughest part of the rivers surrounding Manhattan. The early Dutch settlers didn't call it Spuyten Duyvil for nothing. We'd drown for sure in those waters."

Ricky groaned, "Yeah, I know."

Steve suddenly got a text message on his phone from Charles. He read the message, which was pretty long, and then said, "It's from the Sarge. He said the National Guard are watching all river crossings and will shoot to kill, if necessary. It's likely police headquarters will be evacuated and Manhattan will be placed under quarantine. Charles and the others are going to try escaping through some old abandoned underground tunnel."

Ricky replied, "Abandoned tunnel? Screw that! I'll take my chances above ground."

He played it off like he had no intention of going into any tunnels, but the truth was he didn't dare take the chance that his infection would kick in, while they were trapped with him underground. It was too much of a chance to take.

His eyes became watery and were burning. He looked into the mirror and saw they were bloodshot. He played it off by saying, "Damn, I did not sleep good yesterday. I am beat."

Gregg became concerned and asked, "Are you okay to drive?"

"Yes!" Ricky quickly answered, "It keeps me awake. Otherwise, I will be out cold for sure and this is not the time for sleeping."

Steve agreed, "Yeah, definitely not. Trust me. I'd love to close my eyes and sleep for a few hours, but I'm afraid if I did, I'd never wake up."

Gregg sighed, "I hear you. I'm tired, too. Hey, I still don't even know your names. Forget the sergeant crap. Call me Gregg from now on."

"I'm Steve. He's Ricky."

"Is that short for Ricardo or Richard?"

Ricky answered, "None of the above. It's just plain Ricky. My parents had a sense of humor."

The three of them laughed briefly. A moment later, they fell silent and stared across the water to the Bronx. It was so close, but so far out of reach. Time was running out.

0610 HRS, ESPLANADE GARDENS PLAZA:

David found a quiet place to park the Transit police van. There was a parking lot behind a large apartment building at the end of Esplanade Gardens Plaza. It would be easy enough to drive out in a hurry, if it became necessary. In the meantime, they could rest, for a few minutes.

David was going back and forth between the channels on his portable police radio. It was a good thing he grabbed a fresh battery, while at Transit District 3. When he listened to the radio division that his precinct and the 30th Precinct used, there was an eerie dead silence, as if no one was left to speak on the radio. It was too disturbing, so he switched over to the channel used by the neighboring 28th and 32nd Precincts. There was an occasional keying of the radio, but not much talking. It sounded like someone was trying to say something, but all that could be heard was heavy breathing. David wondered if someone was hurt and unable to speak.

He spoke into the radio and asked, "Is there a unit trying to call for help? What's your location, so I can help you?"

He waited for an answer, but there was none.

He switched channels, again, to hear what was going on over the citywide frequency. It was usually used for big incidents, such as what was currently going on. Aviation was describing what they were looking down on, as they flew over Harlem.

"There are several fires burning out of control. It looks like there are more infected than before. They're attacking anyone they see that isn't infected. Cars are trying to drive away, but there's nowhere for them to go. National Guard is maintaining control of the river crossings, for now. Might not last long."

Kirk asked, "I wonder what he meant by that. Maybe they're pulling back?"

David shook his head, "I doubt it. He probably meant the National Guard are going to run out of ammo, if they have to keep shooting every infected person or driver that try to cross into the Bronx. At some point, they are going to be overrun. That's not good."

Mr. Hayes commented, "I have a feeling this is going to spread into the Bronx, sooner or later. They may as well let us cross over. We can't stay hiding here forever. What happens when we run out of gas? What do we do when we get hungry? We need to come up with a plan to get out of here, before there is no Bronx to escape into."

Wally agreed, "He's right. I don't plan on staying trapped in Manhattan too much longer. Maybe if we split up into smaller groups, we'll have a better chance of escaping. I'm pretty sure I can get away on my own."

David disagreed, "No. We need to stay together. There's safety in numbers. If you have a plan, let's hear it. I'm open to ideas."

"I don't, but I'm thinking. There has to be a way. I wish my brother were with me. He'd probably think of something. He's nuts," Wally laughed. "Damn. I don't want to die here."

Millie spoke up from the back row of the van, "Neither do I! How long are we planning to stay here?"

David shrugged, "As long as it takes for us to come up with a good plan. I'm not going to risk driving around out there, where we could be attacked and killed. I also don't want to waste our gas, unless we have a destination in mind. So, everyone start thinking. Otherwise, this is where we will stay. It's safe and quiet."

Kirk agreed, "He's right. It doesn't pay to waste our gas driving around blindly. We could drive down the wrong street and trap ourselves. This spot is good, for now. Let's try to come up with a plan that won't get us killed."

Kevin added, "Yeah, there are enough of us to come up with something good."

Millie hesitated before saying, "What about the subway tunnels into the Bronx."

Wally said excitedly, "That's right! There are a few trains that use tunnels to reach the Bronx before coming out onto elevated tracks. There are also some that remain underground the whole way. That means we'll have a few options available."

Before David could respond, he received a text message from his sergeant. He looked at the phone cheerfully and said, "Holy shit! Charles is alive?"

Kirk asked, "Who?"

"It's my sergeant, guys. He just sent me a text message. Hold on." He quickly read the message and replied with his own message.

When he put the phone down, Kevin asked, "What did he say?"

"It's not good. One thing we already know. The National Guard is protecting all river crossings and tunnels in and out of the city, including the subways, which means that idea is a no go."

Wally cursed, "Shit!"

Millie acted upset, although she was relieved she would not have to go back into the subway tunnels. She really did not wish to do so. She got lucky before that there were not too many rats or roaches. She had a feeling she might not be so lucky the second time around. She knew it was better not to push her luck.

David continued, "There's more bad news. The city is abandoning us. They're evacuating police headquarters and plan on placing Manhattan under quarantine. That means we may never be able to leave."

Edie began crying and saying a silent prayer. She was losing hope. Millie held her hand and tried to comfort her. It was her turn to be the strong one. Edie stopped praying and smiled at her gratefully. No thanks were needed. The look and smile said it all.

Meanwhile, Kirk stated angrily, "Wanna bet? I'll find a way off this island, one way or another. I promise you that, my friend. They have not made an island that can hold me, yet."

David wondered what he meant by that, but decided it was best not to ask. In the meantime, they had some serious planning to do.

CONTAMINATION EFFECT

Chapter Seventeen

0625 HRS, CONVENT AVE:

"MY NAME IS Julia. I'm not one of them. I came close, though.

Last night my roommate, Nicole, came home at around 3:30 in the morning. Our other roommate, Angie, was already asleep, by that time. I was just about to get into bed myself. I had spent the last hour and a half posting photos from this past week on Instagram.

When Nicole came into our dorm room she was totally freaking out. She looked like she'd been in a fight. Her clothes were a mess. There were scratches on her arm and someone had actually bitten her on the leg. I mean, what the hell? Right?

Angie woke up, right away.

We both tried to calm Nicole down. Naturally, we thought the worst, based on her appearance.

She had gone out on a date with a new guy that she met in the neighborhood. Angie and I disapproved, but she insisted she'd be okay. He picked her up at 9 o'clock and took her to some club, where they danced for a few hours. Afterwards, they stopped at 125th Street for fish and chips. It must have been around two in the morning when they got there.

At least, that's what she thinks.

Thought.

Anyway, she said they were eating and messing around. He rubbed against her behind and tried to kiss her, which was a big turn off to her, considering he had fish breath. She tried to hint at him to chew some gum, which she had with her, but he was clueless. He told her he didn't want to ruin the flavor of the meal he just ate.

What an idiot.

They were hanging out with a few of his friends, so they took their time eating. People usually hung out inside or in front of that restaurant. It's pretty popular, especially to people just leaving the clubs on the weekends. It gets crowded fast.

At around 2:45 something happened that literally scared the living daylights out of everyone. Some crazy man was chasing after a kid. They came running out of the projects and crossed the street straight toward the crowd in front of the restaurant. The kid was smart. He ran into the crowd and disappeared. The man that was chasing after him didn't seem to care much about him anymore. A few tough guys stepped up and waited to beat his ass, but the cars passing by distracted him. One car swerved to avoid him and crashed into the Dunkin Donuts on the corner.

It was crazy.

There were cops across the street near that weird tower they use. One cop got out of his car and grabbed the man. Two more cops came running out of the projects and called out to their friend. That's when the crazy man attacked him and started eating his face. The other two cops pulled him off and arrested him. The cop up in the tower came down and helped his hurt partner.

The other two cops held down the crazy man, until an ambulance and a police car showed up. They put the hurt cop in the ambulance, and then another police car drove up on the scene.

A few guys were trying to find that kid that the crazy man was chasing. No one knew where he went. He was gone.

Someone spotted a large crowd coming from Broadway. Nicole said it looked almost like a wave of people were running toward them. There had to have been about a hundred.

Nicole's date ran for his car, so she followed. They still had time to get away. He opened the door, got in, made a U-turn, and drove off toward Morningside Avenue without her. She watched his car turn north, and then disappear from sight. That jerk left her there!

The crowd swarmed the entire block from Broadway to Amsterdam and attacked everybody in its path. A fire truck turned the corner from Broadway and was surrounded within seconds. The firemen had to fight for their lives. The crowd bit and scratched anyone they came into contact with, but mostly they grabbed and ate people. It was like a scene from a horror movie. People were running for their lives in every direction. It was every man and woman for himself or herself. No one helped anyone. About a minute later, there was no safe direction to go because those monsters were everywhere.

Nicole tried to run in her high heels, but she fell. Typical. I was so angry with her for not taking them off before running. She said someone grabbed her by the leg, while she was on the ground, and *bit* into her flesh! I was like *really?* She screamed and kicked him off, as he dug his fingernails into her leg.

Suddenly, there were gunshots. Someone shot him and he let her go. She didn't bother to see if he was dead. The gunshots continued and she ran. She thinks it was the police shooting at the crazies in the crowd. She kept running and didn't look back.

A few minutes later, she was at our City College dorm on St. Nicholas Terrace. The security guard at the desk in the lobby asked what was wrong, but she didn't want to explain that crazy story to him. He'd never believe it. She made up some lie about getting into a fight with a drunken girl at the club.

When Nicole came into the room and told Angie and I this crazy story, of course, we didn't believe it. Why would we? It sounded to us more like she was high on drugs and making up elaborate lies, so that we wouldn't jump to conclusions and assume she was raped. That's *exactly* what we thought.

Angie wanted to call security and report it, but Nicole begged her not to do it. She kept insisting she wasn't raped. We asked her to tell us the truth about what happened. She was sticking to her guns. She said everything she had told us was the God's honest truth.

I suggested we take photos of how she looked, including her injuries and damage to her clothing. That way, if she changed her mind and wanted to tell police in the morning, we'd have some kind of proof to show them. Nicole still insisted she was not raped, but allowed us to take photos of her clothes and injuries.

I still have them on my camera. Not that it matters anymore.

She took a long shower, against our advice. While she was in the shower, Angie and I discussed what we thought happened to her. We both firmly believed she had been raped. Angie said she would snatch up Nicole's underwear and put it into a bag to preserve any evidence that could later be used in court. I thought it was a good idea.

When Nicole came back from the bathroom, she lay on her bed and began crying. Angie and I tried to comfort her. Angie volunteered to sleep in the bed with her, so she could hold her. Nicole cried herself to sleep in Angie's arms like a scared little girl.

I eventually fell asleep. It must have been around five.

About an hour later, I woke up to the sound of screaming. I think I almost had a heart attack. By the time I came to my senses, I figured Nicole was probably having a nightmare. I turned on the light and my jaw dropped open. Nicole was straddling Angie on the bed and biting into her throat. Blood was squirting everywhere.

I jumped out of the bed and Nicole looked at me. I looked around quick for something that could be used as a weapon. Nicole leapt at me like a cheetah, but I grabbed the lamp and smashed it into her face. She fell back and rolled over the bed. I ran into my closet and closed the door. There was no time to make it to the exit. I figured she might think I went out and go after me. She definitely didn't see me duck into the closet, so I thought I'd be safe there.

One of our neighbors must have heard the screaming and called security because they came and busted our dorm room door open. Nicole attacked one of them knocking him back. He fell to the floor out in the hallway. She went for his jugular.

I opened the closet just a crack and could see her on top of him. There were two guards, though. The other one tried to get her off of his buddy. She got off him all right, and then she jumped on him. She bit into his face and ripped his nose off. I've never heard anyone scream the way that poor man screamed, in that moment.

Someone must have come out of their room to see what was going on because she looked up and ran after them. I heard screaming that eventually faded away.

I came out of the closet and quickly threw on my clothes and sneakers. I grabbed my bag and ran out of the room. I had no intention of going back. I took the stairs down to the ground floor. There was no one in the lobby.

I left the building and ran toward the stairs of St. Nicholas Park. I was going to take the train uptown to the Bronx. I have a friend, who lives there. I figured I could crash with her for a few days.

As I was about to run down toward St. Nicholas Avenue, I froze in my tracks. I looked beyond the park and saw several fires, including the police station at 135th Street. Plumes of black smoke were rising from different areas into the early morning sky and that's when I noticed the helicopters. There were about two. They were just hovering and watching what looked like the end of the world. I saw people running north on St. Nicholas Avenue. One grabbed another and began biting him. No, I am pretty sure he was eating him.

It suddenly hit me. Nicole had been telling the truth all along. I knew it had to be some kind of virus. She was infected when she got bitten and became one of them.

I knew, right away, I didn't want to go down to St. Nicholas Avenue. Instead, I decided to go to Amsterdam or Broadway, where I could catch a cab to the Bronx. I had to get far away, as fast as I could. If what Nicole said was true, it had been about two or three hours, since she'd left that crazy scene on 125th Street. There was a very good chance that virus was spreading. I couldn't afford to waste time.

That is, until I saw you guys. Well, that's my story and I'm sticking to it."

0645 HRS, W. 135TH ST. AND CONVENT AVE:

Charles looked at the young woman from City College and knew without doubt there was truth to her tale. He, Grant, and Marc were some of the cops that responded to the scene she described. If her friend, Nicole, carried the virus to the City College dorms, who knew how many others did the same to other locations? It was likely the virus could have been spread into other boroughs, not counting what was already going on at LaGuardia Airport.

"I'm sorry about your friends. You're welcome to come with us, if you want," he offered. "We are about to try something crazy, but it just may get us away from Manhattan."

"Thanks," said Julia. She stepped closer and thought about his offer. She was intrigued by what he said about trying something crazy. She asked, "What do you have in mind?"

Grant stepped around to the rear of the patrol car and said, "Think of it as an underground adventure." He opened the trunk and began taking out any necessary equipment he thought they might need. He removed useless items from his patrol bag and filled it with flares, medical equipment, rope, and an emergency blanket. He also grabbed the crowbar. They were definitely going to need it.

Charles asked him, "Are you bringing that bag?"

"Damn right."

"Good," Charles replied. He handed Grant the journal he recovered from the apartment on Riverside Drive and asked him to keep it safe in the bag. "We may need it," he said.

The others stood on the sidewalk at the southeast corner of West 135th Street and Convent Avenue. They waited nervously for Grant to lead them into the old aqueduct tunnel. They kept looking around over their shoulders making sure none of the infected surprised them.

Julia noticed Grant holding a crowbar, as he closed the trunk of the car. She realized they were standing next to an old gatehouse for the Croton Aqueduct System. These days it served as the Harlem Stage for City College, but she was well aware of what it used to be. She asked excitedly, "Wait! Are we going into the Old Croton Aqueduct Tunnel?"

Grant responded, "That's the plan. We want to try and take it all the way into the Bronx. With the bridges and regularly used tunnels being closely guarded, this could be our only option."

Julia moved closer to Grant. She said, "I thought they filled in the tunnel access during the 1980s. At least, that's what I read."

"They did, but, for some reason, they deliberately left one way in. There is a certain manhole with a ladder that leads down. I learned about it from one of the workers that worked on this place during the early 2000s when they were renovating it. You just need to know which manhole to open. It's not marked as being part of the Croton Aqueduct anymore. Luckily, I happen to know, which one to open."

He stepped over one of the many manholes surrounding the castle-like former gatehouse. He bent over and pried it open with the crowbar. Charles and Julia stepped close and looked down. It was dark, so Grant pulled out his flashlight and shined it down into the hole. They saw water at the bottom.

Julia's eyes widened with excitement, as she said, "This is incredible! I've always wanted to explore these old tunnels!"

Charles looked less enthusiastic when he asked, "How deep do you think that water is down there?"

Winston's face paled when he heard the word "deep." He did not know how to swim and didn't think there would be much water in an abandoned tunnel. Now, he was imagining a sewer tunnel with rushing water that could potentially bring about his demise. It did not help his confidence level. The thought of entering the tunnel was starting to look more and more like a bad idea.

After thinking about it for a moment, Grant responded, "I believe it's about waist deep in this area, which should be as high as it will get.

Winston sighed with relief and asked, "Are you sure about that? I can't swim."

"Relax, Winston. You'll be fine down there. It might be a bit cold, but it's not that deep. I promise, buddy."

Julia looked at Grant and asked, "Have you ever been in there?"

"Ask me, again, in about sixty seconds," he said, as he passed his patrol bag to Charles and began climbing down the ladder. The ladder's iron steps were rusted, but they felt sturdy enough to hold their weight. When he reached the bottom he called up, "Drop the bag. I'll catch it."

Charles fit the bag into the manhole and let it go. It fell right into Grant's arms. He then flung it over his left shoulder and asked, "Who's next? We don't have all day."

Julia volunteered without delay, "Me!" She hesitated when she noticed everyone else was looking at her. She was the new girl, after all. She asked timidly, "I mean, if that's okay with you guys?"

Charles nodded, "Go ahead. Like the man said, we don't have all day. Doc, make sure you bring that medical bag of yours."

Aramis held it up in his hand and replied, "I got it here, boss."

When Julia reached the bottom she looked around and admired the architecture. "Wow. This place is bigger than I thought," she stated. She loved the brick walls and arched ceilings. The gate chamber where they stood was one of the largest in the system. On the west side was a long dark tunnel that curved to the right, as it continued northbound to their destination. She stepped in part of the way and stared down as far as she could and was soon joined by Liz, who had just come down the ladder.

Liz noticed Julia was fixated on the long tunnel and said, "I guess this is where we need to go, huh?"

Julia nodded happily, "Uh huh." It seemed she had forgotten all about her dead roommates.

Alissa was next to climb down the rusted ladder. She looked down shakily and uttered, "Oh, my god. It's so dark in there. How deep did you say that water was?"

Grant called up, "It's about waist deep at this end! Don't worry! The water will recede further north, as we go!"

Alissa groaned, "Well, I suppose that's not so bad." She continued descending into the hole and complained some more, "Damn, this is tight. I hope my big ass doesn't get stuck."

Marc chuckled and said, "You can do it. I'll go down, right after you."

"Yeah, but you're a lot thinner than me! I like my snacks!"

He laughed, again, "You're not that big. Quit stalling and speed it up."

Alissa paused and closed her eyes, "Holy crap! Why does it have to be so high?"

Marc told her, "Open your eyes and look up at me. Don't focus on what's below you. Take your steps slowly, one at a time. Keep your eyes up here on me."

She did as he suggested and focused on his face. She found herself smiling at his handsome face. He smiled back reassuringly. Before she knew it, she was at the bottom.

"OOH! This water is cold!" She called up to him, "Thank you, Marc!"

"Don't mention it," he winked down at her. "I'll see you in a minute." He descended down the ladder and stepped into the water beside her. He immediately shivered and cried out, "Shit, you ain't kidding! This water is cold! I'm freezing my nuts!"

Alissa laughed. She welcomed the opportunity for some lighthearted humor in the dark times they were experiencing. It almost made her forget her current predicament. Almost.

Winston was next down the ladder. He went down slowly and stepped nervously into the cold water. He shivered briefly, but did not complain. He didn't dare walk around unnecessarily, in case he might fall into a hole. If there were one, he would be the one to find it. He knew that much.

Charles told Aramis to go down next. Aramis squeezed through the manhole with his medical bag and went down the ladder faster than most of the others.

Charles was the last one to join them.

Before he descended, Grant called up to him, "Sarge, use the crowbar to close the manhole! We don't want anyone following us down here! And we are probably going to need the crowbar to get out of here, so whatever you do, don't drop it! If it falls in the water, we may never find it!"

Charles looked down as he stepped onto the ladder and replied, "No pressure, though, right?"

"You got this, Sarge," Grant replied.

Charles hooked the crowbar into one of the holes on the manhole cover and dragged it in place over him, as he went down. Once the cover fell into place, it grew darker. He carefully unhooked the crowbar and climbed down into the large gate chamber with the others. As his body touched the water, he cringed. The water was about waist deep, just as Grant said it would be and it was cold.

"Whoa. Okay," Charles uttered. "I wish I were wearing thicker pants. I guess we're all going to be wet, for a while. Try to refrain from peeing in the water, if you are walking in front of me."

A few of the others chuckled.

Grant stepped near him and said, "Hand me the crowbar. I'll put it in my patrol bag."

Charles handed him the crowbar and said, "I think we can forget the 'Sarge' nonsense from here on. You know my name."

"If you say so, Chuck," he grinned, as Charles winced. He knew Charles hated being called Chuck. Grant turned and began walking into the curved tunnel. He called back to the others, "Stay close to me, guys. I have a pretty good flashlight. We should be able to find our way without a problem. It's a straight run to the 160s. It will curve a little to the right when we get closer to High Bridge."

Julia and Liz began following without a second thought, but Alissa froze in her steps and asked, "High Bridge? Please, tell me you don't mean the 160s, as in 160th Street."

"Okay, I won't tell you."

Alissa gasped, "Oh, my God! That's kind of far to go on foot, while wading through water! Isn't it?"

Marc also complained, "Jeez! Are you shitting me? You really expect us to walk through some sewer tunnel for thirty something blocks?"

Grant turned back and replied, "Of course not. This is an *aqueduct* tunnel, not a sewer, and we will be walking through it all the way to the Bronx, in case you guys have forgotten. That was always the plan. Nothing's changed. If you want to go back up there, be my guest, but you are not taking the crowbar."

Marc groaned, "Shit on me. Cold wet balls for more than thirty blocks. This is really going to suck major ass."

Charles looked back at him and said sternly, "Quit complaining and man up. We have civilians to protect."

"Yes, sir," Marc grumbled.

Aramis got a chuckle out of Marc's complaints, but then a realization struck him and he became worried. He asked, trying hard not to sound overly concerned, which he was, "So, what do we do when the batteries on your flashlight die? Just wondering. There's no way they can last, until we reach the Bronx."

Charles commented, "I have a flashlight, too, and I charged it fully, before going to work."

Winston also commented, "I got mine, as well, but it probably won't last long. I only charge it once a week."

Marc sighed, "Mine should last about a half hour, before it dies."

Aramis felt better knowing there were plenty of flashlights to keep the darkness at bay for their long walk.

Marc added, "We'll be able to see with no problem. Us guys are just gonna have numb nuts is all."

Aramis and Alissa laughed.

Grant ignored the complaints and said, "You guys with the flashlights, try to keep them off, until we absolutely need them. I charged mine fully yesterday morning. We should be okay for a while.

When mine dies, we'll switch to one of yours. Let's hope we can make it to the Bronx, before all our flashlights die. Our best option is to move fast and not stop more than we need to. It's a long ass walk."

One by one, they went into the tunnel and followed the curve heading north. Once they passed the curve, there was no doubt it was going to be a very long walk.

The former aqueduct gatehouse at West 135 Street.

The Old Croton Aqueduct Tunnel facing northbound.

CONTAMINATION EFFECT

Chapter Eighteen

0720 HRS, OLD CROTON AQUEDUCT TUNNEL:

T HE GROUP WALKED through dark tunnel, one at a time, with Grant in the lead. His bright flashlight beam lit the way for them. Tree roots clung to the brick walls on either side throughout the tunnel. At some points, the air appeared misty with fog. Occasionally, there was a rumble echoing from the streets above. And every once in a while, they went past a rusted ladder that led up to a manhole above.

Julia was in all her glory because she always dreamed of exploring the old aqueduct. Never in her wildest imagination did she think she'd be doing it with the NYPD as her escorts. She looked around taking in the scenery and memorizing each moment. The occasional stalactites on the ceiling made her feel like she was exploring a cave, instead. She wished there were time to take photos with her phone, but they were in a hurry to reach someplace safe. This was not a typical tunnel expedition.

Liz was not the type of person to complain. She just rolled with the punches. Walking through the tunnel did not bother her, especially not if their walk ended with them being safely in the Bronx. Her long boots kept her legs dryer than the others and she was enjoying carrying the Colt M4 Carbine too much. She made sure the ammo bag she wore over her shoulder did not get wet.

Aramis followed close behind with one goal on his mind and that was getting far away from Manhattan. He tried not to think about the past few hours, although it was hard. There was nothing to do, but think, as they walked along quietly. All he could do was think about his partner.

Charles walked behind him, also distracted by the events of the past night. He hoped this plan would work and they could finally be free of this nightmare. Of course, he knew reaching the Bronx would not be the end of it. At least, it would be the end of any immediate threats.

Marc sloshed along the water complaining silently with each step. He was grateful that it was gradually receding, as they proceeded north.

Alissa stayed close behind him. She hated being in the tunnel, but hated being eaten alive even more. It was her main motivation for following along. Still, she felt absolutely grossed out with each wet step she took.

Winston was dead last. He kept thinking the water would rise, at some point, or there would be a steep drop into a large pool of water. His fears were getting the better of him, as he dragged his legs along the water-filled tunnel. At last, he moaned, "I don't like this one bit."

Alissa agreed, "Neither do I. I really wanted to be home today. I have tickets to see a band in Poughkeepsie. I'll probably miss the show for sure, if it doesn't get cancelled."

Aramis called back, "What's the band?" His voice echoed throughout the tunnel.

"Retrofeelya. They're a great band! I really love their music."

Marc smirked, "Well, I'd worry more about us being able to make it all the way to the Bronx through this freaking sewer."

Liz corrected him, "Aqueduct."

"Whatever!" He scowled.

Alissa continued to complain. "It's my friends' fault. They're the ones, who asked me to come down to the city last night. Would you believe they stood me up? I could have been at my home in Poughkeepsie getting ready to go to sleep, after a good long night of video games. This blows!"

Grant said, "Don't think about it. I know a way to make this walk go by fast for you. Pretend we are on a tour and I'm your tour guide. Okay? So, after a devastating fire in New York City, it became apparent the city needed a new water system. The wells could not provide the pressure needed to fight fires. The bucket brigade was pretty much the most effective technique they had, at the time.

In the 1930s, they decided to begin construction on a new aqueduct that would bring water from the Croton River to New York City. The Croton Dam was built and so were over 40 miles of underground tunnels leading down to Fifth Avenue, as I mentioned earlier. The main reservoir was located pretty much on the spot, where they later built the New York Public Library. The receiving reservoir was several blocks to the north of that on the future sight of the Great Lawn in Central Park."

Marc griped, "You already told us that before."

"Julia wasn't around for that part," Grant explained. "When this aqueduct was built in the 1840s, a lot of people did not trust the new system. There were rumors that the workers hired to build the aqueduct, who were mostly immigrants, used to 'relieve' themselves into the water just to screw over the wealthier people, who would likely benefit the most from the new water system."

Alissa gagged, "Ew! Gross!"

Aramis laughed, "Ha, ha! I'm sorry, but that's hilarious!"

Grant added, "There were also complaints of tadpoles being found in the water. Plus, cockroaches were able to spread throughout the city fast through these dark, damp tunnels."

Liz commented, "Great. I was afraid you'd mention those. Now, I'm freaking out. Roaches are about the only thing I can't stand the sight of."

Grant reassured her, "Relax. I haven't seen one, yet. There's no food for them in here."

Julia's stomach grumbled at the thought of food. She chuckled, "There's no food for us either. I'm starving."

Aramis told her, "Oh, too bad. We ate breakfast before we met up with you."

"Damn, lucky you. Oh, um, sorry," she said to Grant. "Please, continue with the tour."

Grant smiled and continued, "In time, the people of the city began to trust the new aqueduct and used less water from the city's wells. A few public bathhouses were built throughout the city and some of the newer homes were being built with their own bathrooms. It was the start of a new era. Afterwards, there was little need for outhouses. Times were changing for the better, but there were some negative results. The well water table gradually rose from lack of use and many old basements began to flood. This led to the construction of the New York City sewer system in the 1850s."

Liz was amazed, as she asked, "How in the world do you know all of this?"

Grant replied, "I am a bit of a history buff and for good reason. Do you guys know who Alexander Hamilton was?"

Alissa replied, "As in the Broadway show?"

Marc scoffed, "I think he means more like as in one of the founding fathers of our nation."

Grant smirked, "Correct. He was also a personal aide to George Washington. Believe it or not, I am one of his descendents. It's one of the reasons I was so happy to be assigned to the 26th Precinct. The Hamilton Grange House is located in the confines of our precinct in St. Nicholas Park."

Marc responded, "Oh, that old house in the park that looks so out of place?"

"Right," Grant replied. "It was once his home. He named it after his grandfather's estate in Scotland. The house was actually moved twice from its original location, but I think it fits well in the park. It's almost how it used to be."

Winston asked, "Wasn't Alexander Hamilton killed in a duel against Aaron Burr?"

"Yes," Grant answered, "And then he was buried at the foot of Trinity Church. Anyway, getting back to the aqueduct. I've always been fascinated by these tunnels. The area where we entered was a gate chamber for the old and new Croton Aqueduct tunnels. Both were abandoned when a new aqueduct replaced them. The gates used to lead down to what was known as the Manhattan Valley. Today, we call that area 125th Street. The gates have been closed for decades. That's why the chamber had so much water in it.

Early on, a sewer was built underneath the area of 125th Street, which led out to the Hudson River. That old sewer still exists today. During the Prohibition Era tunnels were dug from the basements of buildings connecting to that sewer. Small boats would enter from the opening at the Hudson in the wee hours of the day. They'd travel through the sewer and deliver illegal alcohol directly to the basement tunnels of speakeasies and restaurants."

Charles finally commented, "Those bootleggers went above and beyond to get their drink on."

Alissa scoffed, "I don't blame them!"

Grant continued, "If you were to stand out on the Harlem Pier and look back toward the land, you can see the entrance to that old sewer. It's just before the southbound entrance to the parkway.

After 125th Street, the aqueduct tunnel traveled through another series of gates on the way up to Asylum Hill. The hill got its name because of the Bloomingdale Lunatic Asylum, which stood on the site of Columbia University. The tunnel connected to the old gatehouses on Amsterdam at West 119th Street and down to West 113th Street. The latter was converted into a nursing home sometime around the 1990s."

Aramis commented, "That's actually pretty interesting. I've always wondered about that old stone building at 119th Street. I pass it all the time on the way to the hospital. And I never would have guessed that nursing home across from the hospital was once part of the aqueduct system."

Charles commented, "You learn something new every day."

Marc griped, "Who cares? My balls are wet! The city is going to shit and you guys are yapping about this crap, as if we don't have a worry in the world. We better get paid some serious overtime for this. I know we won't be finishing up on time."

Charles said to him, "You're in the process of going AWOL and you think the city's going to pay you overtime? The same city that you just mentioned is going to shit? I wouldn't bet on it and don't be such a downer. Some of us could use the distraction." He gestured back to Alissa and Winston.

"Oh," Marc responded when he realized the distraction had been helping Alissa and Winston to forget about their situation, as well as Aramis, who almost forgot how depressed he was feeling.

Julia decided to get the conversation back on track. "So, Officer Hamilton," she said. "Considering your extensive knowledge of these tunnels, I take it you've been in them before?"

"Actually, no, I have not. By the way, you can call me Grant. It has always been one of my obsessions. I've read numerous books about it. Before I became a cop, I spent a good deal of my teenage years doing urban exploration, mainly on Long Island. It was a great way to put my mind in another place, usually in the distant past."

Marc asked, "Urban what?"

"Urban exploration," Julia repeated for him. She explained, "It's when people explore modern day ruins. I do it all the time."

Grant responded, "I used to run around with a bunch of friends, who I met, while visiting my cousin on Long Island. We were part of a group called Lost In Time. Our friend, Ray, was our leader. We explored abandoned hospitals, underground tunnels, Camp Hero at Montauk Point, and we even climbed to the tops of bridges. All so we could take photos and say we did it. It was so much fun.

Being a history buff, I used to enjoy looking up the history of these abandoned locations, just so I'd know where I was exploring. It helped me to connect better, if I knew the history. Of course, once I joined the NYPD, I put those days behind me."

Alissa asked, "Why? Is it because that sort of thing is illegal?"

"Not always. Some places are open to the public. Others are in public places making them publicly accessible. Then there are those that are closed to mostly everyone. It depends on the location. I saw myself more as a sort of archaeologist, kind of like Indiana Jones. I never forced my way into any place. I always went into openings that were already there."

Marc scoffed, "Eh, it still sounds illegal to me. I mean, come on! Climbing bridges??? That's insane, dude!"

Alissa commented, "I could never do that! I hate heights!"

Grant laughed, "Yeah, well, I suppose that was illegal and heights don't really bother me. It's falling from heights that you need to avoid. Besides, it was a long time ago. Now, I do things the right way... on job time."

Marc's curiosity was peeked, so he asked, "Really? Like where?"

Grant replied, "One time, I went to drop something off at the police lab in Queens. On the way back, I stopped at Roosevelt Island. It was a slow night, so I figured there was no rush to return to the precinct. I checked out the abandoned small pox hospital at the southern tip of the island. Another time, I got a buddy of mine from Harbor to take me to Hart Island, where there's an abandoned hospital, an old prison facility, and a Potter's Field cemetery."

Marc smirked at him, "Hmm. You sly dog! You senior guys have all the fun."

Julia commented, "Not to change the subject, but how do we even know where we are down here? Everything looks the same. Is there a way to know when we are close?"

Grant nodded, "Sure. The tunnel is starting to bend toward the right, which means we should be at around 150th Street. The water will gradually recede to about a foot deep by the time we reach 155th Street. The water gates are located at 172nd Street, under High Bridge Park. Trust me, you'll know when we get there. Afterwards, we'll cross under High Bridge into the Bronx."

Aramis said, "You mean cross *over* High Bridge."

Grant shook his head, "Negative, *under*. The tunnel takes us under the pedestrian walkway. That part will be perfectly straight. There are more water gates on the Bronx side. The tunnel will basically follow University Avenue going north, after crossing into the Bronx. We can look forward to more stagnant water, roots on the walls, and stalactites on the ceilings."

Marc rolled his eyes. "That sounds like so much fun! I can hardly wait," he said sarcastically.

Alissa said with her fingers crossed, "I am just glad we haven't seen any cockroaches."

Marc replied, "Shhh! They'll hear you!"

She chuckled.

They soon reached another tunnel, which crossed the old aqueduct, at which point Julia exclaimed, "Oh, great! Which way do we go?"

Grant took a moment to get his bearings and answered, "We continue straight. This should be the new Croton Aqueduct tunnel. It's not what we want."

As they continued forward, the water had finally begun to recede, just as Grant said it would. It was now down to their knees. However, having wet clothes that were exposed to the damp foggy air, only made them feel colder. It was a good thing it was summertime or their experience could have been a lot worse. It was already about as bad as it could get.

"We should be near 155th Street," Grant noted.

Marc replied, "Awesome, but my balls are already wet."

Grant rolled his eyes and responded, "Get over it already. You're not the only one. You need to cheer up, Marc. You'll see. When we're sitting in the Bronx somewhere nice and dry, you're going to thank me for this educational adventure."

Charles said, "I'm thanking you, now. We haven't had to deal with any infected people, which is a nice change."

Aramis agreed, "Amen, brother. Life up there," he pointed in the direction of the streets above them, "was getting too stressful for me. Believe me, I am grateful for this change of pace."

Winston added, "Yeah, I guess it's not as bad as I expected. The water is getting lower, which is very comforting. You did good, Grant."

"Thanks, buddy."

Liz stated, "Yeah, this was definitely a great idea."

The group continued walking north through the tunnel, unaware that every second wasted counted against their survival. It was imperative they reach their destination as soon as possible. Something big was coming and it was a game changer.

0730 HRS, ESPLANADE GARDENS PLAZA:

David yawned. He was exhausted. He turned to Kirk, who sat beside him in the front passenger side seat of the van. He was out cold. It seemed mostly everyone else in the van had fallen asleep. They had been parked in the parking lot for nearly an hour. Only he and Kevin were up.

Kevin asked in a low voice, "What's the matter? Can't sleep either? You should get some rest. We will probably have a long day ahead of us."

"I know. I can't. I left my partner locked in a holding cell. She's probably like the others, by now, but I can't stop thinking about her. She was a really good person. She didn't deserve this. A lot of good people have gone down because of this damned plague, or whatever it is."

Kevin patted him on the shoulder and said in a reassuring manner, "You seem to have a good head on your shoulders, Dave. I'm sure you did what you could, under the circumstances. You shouldn't beat yourself up over it. What happened here is beyond our control. We are lucky to be alive. Our job, now, is to keep everyone in this van alive. You and I have a responsibility as officers. It doesn't matter that I'm off duty or that we are from different departments. We are their protectors. You are not alone. I got your back, no matter what you think you need to do. If you need me to drive, say the word. I will make sure one of us is always looking out."

David considered Kevin's words and said, "Thanks, man. I appreciate it. I've been thinking. We really should go somewhere safer. Maybe go somewhere indoors, but keep the van close. We should find a spot with a garage that we can close. It should be a place with, at least, two exits on opposite sides. Any ideas?"

"How about a firehouse? Do you know if there are any in the neighborhood?"

David shook his head, "We are out of the confines of my precinct. I'm not too familiar with the places around here. I can tell you the ones in my precinct are in bad locations. Those animals already surrounded them making them out of the question.

Kevin frowned, but then glanced at Wally's uniform and suggested, "What about a bus depot?"

"No way. They have too many openings and are way too big to protect. Hospitals are out, too. There aren't any more left around here that are safe."

Kevin perked up, as he asked, "What about a church?"

David thought about the suggestion. The doors at most churches were certainly strong. Not many had garages, though. Riverside Church and St. John the Divine both did, but they were also too large to protect and there were too many doors to worry about. Finally, he responded, "Nah. That won't work either. Too many variables."

Kirk stretched out his arms and opened his eyes. He looked at David and Kevin and said, "I have an idea. How about we try another police station further uptown or further downtown?"

David shook his head and said, "No way. That's not even an option."

He wasn't crazy about the idea. He knew once he stepped into that kind of environment, again, the options would be limited. He'd no longer have the freedom or control to make any important decisions. He'd be just another pawn to be used on the chessboard by the white shirt bosses, who would likely be making their decisions from a safe distant location and passing them along down the totem pole. It was just how his job worked.

One of the girls stirred in the backseat. It was Millie. She sat up and fixed her hair as best she could without looking into a mirror. She looked at the guys up front and said, "I need to use the bathroom and I'm hungry. Can't we go somewhere else?"

David replied, "We're trying to think of someplace we can go, where we could be indoors."

She suggested, "How about we go further downtown? My sister's apartment is on First Avenue. It's where I was going when I was on the bus. Her apartment is high up on the twenty-eighth floor. I think it should be safe."

David asked, "Does her building have a parking garage?"

"I think so. It might be underneath."

Kevin said, "That could work, at least, temporarily."

David started up the van and asked, "What street does your sister live on?"

"Her building is at East 103rd Street."

The van pulled out of the parking lot and everyone else woke up. David tried to avoid the avenues and main streets, as he drove onto the FDR Drive heading south. Taking the drive would be the best way there. There weren't many cars on the road. The ones that were there had been abandoned. He had to drive carefully to traverse around all the abandoned vehicles. Some of them had blood-covered windows, so he made sure not to linger too long in any one spot.

For a brief moment, the obstacles reminded him of being back at the driver's training course for the NYPD. Those were simpler times, he thought, although he didn't think so, at the time. His days in the Police Academy seemed like so long ago. He'd trade anything to be back there in the past, rather than to deal with what was going on in the present. It was so unreal.

CONTAMINATION EFFECT

Chapter Nineteen

0735 HRS, OLD CROTON AQUEDUCT TUNNEL:

A S GRANT AND the others approached the next gate chamber at West 172nd Street, they passed a small tunnel that went off to the side. It was a short shaft that led into a flooded room. Its purpose was unknown to them, but above the room was a manhole that led out to High Bridge Park.

"No," Grant thought, as he disregarded it and continued into the gate chamber. He looked around with his flashlight, which was starting to dim. He could make out an ornate iron staircase that went around two smaller old water conduits. The staircase went up about two levels high and stopped at a door, which was probably sealed. Right away, he knew it had to be the High Bridge Tower.

On any other day, he would have gone up the ladder and stairs to check exactly where they led and to see if the door was locked, but today there was no time for exploring. He needed to get the group across the bridge to the Bronx. He still wasn't entirely sure, if that would be possible. He had been keeping his fingers crossed the whole way, hoping they would be able to find a way out, once they reached the Bronx.

Of course, he kept his doubts to himself.

Julia interrupted his thoughts when she commented, "That is so awesome! Do those stairs go up into the old water tower?"

"Yes," he replied.

Liz stepped into the chamber next with O'Grady's Colt M4 Carbine slung over her shoulder. The bag of ammo hung from a strap on her other shoulder.

Grant had forgotten she was carrying the weapon and ammo bag. He turned to her and asked, "Are you okay carrying that?"

"Shit yeah," she said without a second thought. "Why?"

He grinned at her and said, "Just checking." His flashlight dimmed slightly and he tapped it twice. It flickered and he frowned, "My flashlight is dying. It's much dimmer than before. It'll shut off soon. Hey, Winston, pass me your flashlight. It's already weak, so we may as well kill it off, before using one of the other flashlights."

"Okay, here you go."

"Thanks, pal. By the way, there's no water on the bridge, so this will probably be your favorite part of our journey."

Winston gave him a half smile.

Charles looked at Grant and asked, "Are you ready? The faster we do this, the better."

Grant acknowledged, "You're right. Let's get going. This part will be easy. Once we get to the other side, things will change. More importantly, we will be in the Bronx."

Aramis cheered, "Woo hoo! That's what I'm talking about!"

Charles turned to him and said, "It's probably best if we don't make our presence known down here. Someone might be able to hear us, if they are directly over the tunnel or near a manhole. We don't want that."

Aramis apologized, "You're right, Sarge. My bad. I just can't wait to be free from this tunnel and free from this nightmare."

Alissa agreed, "Me, too!"

The group proceeded across the length of the bridge traveling within the seven-foot diameter iron pipe. The interior of the pipe was covered in rust from top to bottom and there must have been about two or three small animal skeletons in there.

Each step pounded and echoed within, giving the impression the pipe was not securely grounded in place. The sensation did not feel safe and brought fear into the minds of some crossers.

Alissa tried to step lightly. She was half afraid her foot would push right through the rusted pipe and she'd end up falling all the way down into the river. The idea of being so high frightened her. Her heart began pounding fast and she walked slower and more carefully with each step.

Winston was also afraid of the same thing happening. The thought of falling into the river below was giving him a panic attack. He was grateful he could not see how high they were from within the pipe.

Grant walked fast and kept his steps light. Julia followed and did the same.

Liz also tried her best to walk carefully with her long leather boots, which had small heels. She was relieved she didn't wear boots with longer heels.

Aramis did not even consider the weakness of the pipe, as he walked. His mind was already on the other side of the bridge. He was hoping there would not be any blockages that would prevent them from entering the Bronx, especially after how much walking they did. Going back was not an option, he told himself. They had to get off Manhattan Island.

Charles and Marc bridged the gap between the ones in front and the two, who were dragging at the rear. Charles looked back and told them to keep up.

Marc asked the one question no one really wanted the answer to consider. "Hey, Grant. What's under this pipe? It feels kind of light. What I mean is it has that hollow feeling to it. I'm not too crazy about how it's vibrating with each step. Can it hold our weight?"

Grant hesitated answering the question. He knew if he did, it might start a panic. He lied and said, "It should be fine. We're almost at the other side."

Outside of the large pipe, where they walked, were metal catwalks on either side that traveled the length of the steel arched structure, which was added in later years to compensate for larger ships that passed under the bridge. There were gaps that separated the catwalks from the pipe and from the walls revealing a far drop to the river down below.

There were a few shafts along the way leading down into the hollow stone piers that supported the bridge, which dropped straight down and exited through small holes into the Harlem River to drain water overflow. The stone piers had been constructed to be hollow, so they would be light enough to be supported by wooden pylons buried in the river.

Several steel supports bracers held up the large water pipe, which they passed through, across the span of the bridge. Below that was nothing, but the drop to the river. Of course, at each of the far ends the pipe was much safer, as it was over the floor of the solid brick tunnel. It was only the part that passed through the steel arched bridge that was different. Fortunately, for those with a fear for heights within the pipe, they could not see that.

0740 HRS, E. 109TH ST. AND FIRST AVE:

When van number 8150 arrived at the East 106th Street exit, David made a right turn. He made another right at First Avenue, which was the next block over. There were practically no other vehicles on the roads, although there were a few. Most were not stopping for the traffic lights, until they noticed the Transit Police van approaching.

David wondered where they were going. He had not even considered the possibility that there were still people on Manhattan, who were unaware of what took place the night before. He hoped they were heading somewhere safe.

When they reached the building, where Millie's older sister lived, he was pleased to see there was indeed an underground parking garage. It was part of a three-building complex. A tollgate controlled from a nearby guard booth blocked the driveway leading down into the garage, but the booth was empty.

David stopped short of hitting the bar of the tollgate.

Kevin said, "Hold on. I'll go into the booth and open it. We shouldn't force it. It might damage the van to the point, where we can't use it anymore. I'd hate to be stranded without a vehicle."

"Good point," agreed David.

Kevin opened the side door of the van and walked around the front to the guard booth. It wasn't locked, so he was able to get inside without any difficulty. A moment later, the tollgate rose up out of the way. David drove the van through and Kevin closed the gate. Once he was back in the van, they continued into the garage. David parked near the elevator to the central building.

"Wait in the van," he said, which they did.

He then stepped out and looked around to make sure it was safe for them to be there. Kevin also got out and pulled out his weapon. He kept it in a holster that was clipped onto his pants and tucked inside under his shirt close to his belly.

Kevin observed, "It looks clear. I'll call down the elevator." He walked over and pressed the button. He kept his gun ready, just in case. When the elevator arrived and the doors opened, he aimed his gun inside. There was no one in the elevator. "It's clear," he stated.

Everyone got out of the van and David locked the doors. They squeezed into the elevator and Millie pressed the button for the twenty-eighth floor.

David said, "Be ready for anything. Kevin and I will get out first. Which way is the apartment, to the left or to the right?"

Millie answered with uncertainty, "Um, to the left. I think. Yes, it's on the left. Sorry, I haven't been here in a while."

Kirk replied, "No problem, kid. We'll find it. You girls stay close behind me."

The doors opened, a moment later, onto the twenty-eighth floor. No one moved. It seemed quiet enough. David and Kevin stepped out first and checked both to the right and left. The hallway was clear. They moved to the left and Kirk followed. The girls followed him closely, while Mr. Hayes and Wally took up the rear.

Millie pointed to an apartment door and whispered, "It's here. This is it."

David told her to knock and stand clear. She did as he said. He held his gun ready to fire, if an infected person emerged. The sound of shuffling feet could be heard coming from within. The locks on the door began to unlock and David put his gun down. He knew someone who was infected would not be able to unlock a door so easily.

When the door opened, Millie's sister jumped back and let out a short scream, "Oh!"

Millie stepped forward and said, "Michelle, it's cool! It's only me! These guys are with me. Can we please come in?"

Her sister was so excited to see her. She called out, "Millie! Where have you been? Oh, my God! I was worried sick!" She reached out and embraced her younger sister. David figured Michelle looked to be about thirty-five years old, while Millie was about twenty.

"I'm sorry!" Millie explained, "You won't believe the craziness I've been through!"

Michelle pulled away and said, "Well, actually, I was watching the news, until around four in the morning. I kept thinking you would end up in the background somewhere. I had to shut the TV off because it was freaking me out. Were you stuck in the riots?"

Millie nodded, "You could say that. I was on his bus." She pointed to Wally. "We drove right through the riot and t-boned his police car." She pointed to David. "After that, we had to make it on foot. We went down into the subway tunnels and walked to 145th Street. There was a police station in the train station. We thought we'd be safe there, but then we found out they expanded the Infected Zone and we were still in it! We took one of the police vans and David got us out of there. We tried crossing into the Bronx, but then soldiers started shooting at us! It was so crazy! One of the bullets went right past my head. I was so scared. I kept thinking we were going to die and that I'd never see you, again."

Michelle hugged her younger sister, again, and said in a soothing voice, "You're safe now, baby. I'm here. You can stay with me." She looked up over her sister's shoulder and said, "Oh, my goodness. I'm sorry." She stepped inside the apartment and pulled her sister in with her. "Everyone, please, come inside and close the door. You are all welcome in my home."

Kirk bowed his head and said, "Much obliged, ma'am."

They stepped into the small apartment and crowded around the living room. There really wasn't much room for all of them to fit comfortably. It was a one-bedroom apartment with a bathroom, living room, and kitchen. Technically, the kitchen and living room were the same room divided by a counter.

As David entered he said, "Thank you, Miss."

Wally sat on the sofa seat near the window. Mr. Hayes and Edie sat on the longer sofa. There was room for one more, but the guys were saving that spot for Millie. Kirk stood in the corner by the window that led out to the terrace, while Kevin leaned against the counter. David was still standing by the door, after closing and locking it.

Michelle looked at everyone and realized they were probably tired and hungry. They were certainly filthy from walking through the subway tunnels. Her white rug was already a disaster of black footprints. She tried not to think about it and asked, "Would you guys like some breakfast and coffee?"

David replied instantly, "You don't have to go through the trouble for us."

"It's no trouble," she said and immediately got to work on making whatever she could.

Millie eventually settled into the open seat on the sofa between Edie and Mr. Hayes.

David remained by the door, as if he were standing guard. He turned to Michelle and said, "You have no idea how much we appreciate your help."

She didn't even turn to face him when she replied, "Oh, please. After the hell you guys have been through, it's the least I can do. You kept my sister safe and brought her home to me. I should be thanking you."

David felt honored. She was right. They made it safely to her apartment. It wasn't much, but it was somewhere they could rest their heads for a while. He decided to send Charles a text message to let him know he was still okay. He waited a while, but there was no response.

Michelle said, "Don't be shy. Come on in. I'll get more chairs. I have some folding chairs out on the terrace."

Kirk stopped her and said, "Allow me, ma'am."

"Thank you," she smiled. She looked at her sister and said, "You lucked out, Millie. You found a great group of protectors. Such handsome well-mannered men, too."

0745 HRS, OLD CROTON AQUEDUCT TUNNEL AT HIGH BRIDGE:

Grant and the others finally reached the Bronx side of High Bridge, much to their relief. Now, there was a new dilemma to face. There was an arched doorway that looked like it had been bricked up long ago, which blocked their path. However, there was an opening at the very bottom large enough for someone to crawl through. It was a tight squeeze.

It would be especially tough for Alissa's larger frame and she knew it. Beads of sweat began to form on her brow, as she grew worried.

Grant bent down and looked through the hole using the flashlight.

Julia and Liz stood over him, while Aramis and Charles stood nearby. Marc stood back a distance away with Alissa and Winston, while they waited. Winston was looking back the way they had come. He could not believe the night they were having.

Marc spoke privately to Alissa making sure to keep his voice low, as he complained, "Great, it looks like our little expedition just literally hit a brick wall. If he says that we have to go back across the bridge, I am going to be pissed."

"That hole looks too small for me to fit. I don't want to go back the way we came," she replied, sounding worried.

Marc tried to cheer her up, "Hey, let them think about it, for now. You mentioned video games earlier. Which ones do you like playing?"

Alissa perked up and listed her favorite games. The two continued talking about video games and soon forgot about the small hole.

Meanwhile, Grant pulled out his crowbar and began loosening more bricks at the bottom to widen the hole. He was careful not to cause the entire wall to collapse and block their path completely. It did not take long before he felt satisfied with the size of the opening. He handed his patrol bag to Julia, got down on his belly, and crawled through. A moment later, he asked her to hand him his bag.

Afterwards, he told her to come through, which she did. She was able to go through easily because of her petite size. Of course, she had to take off her backpack, first. She pulled it through after.

Liz went into the hole next and also made it through rather quickly.

Charles told Aramis to go after her and called Marc, Alissa, and Winston over. "Let's go, people. The hole should be wide enough for all of us to fit.

While Charles bent down and crawled through the opening, Grant was checking out the next area. It was a curved tunnel with another tunnel that branched off to the side. He peeked into the smaller tunnel. It was dark. He pointed the flashlight at the ground and moved into the opening. There was a steep drop that fell into darkness.

Julia stood in the curved tunnel behind him and asked, "What do you see?"

"Trouble," he answered, as he backed out of the small tunnel. "We definitely aren't going that way. There's a drop and it looks far."

Lucky for them, he had chosen the correct path to the next gate chamber. Had they taken the other path, they would have fallen several hundred feet down a siphon into a small dark pit filled with sharp metal and debris. The pit itself is barely four feet in height and becomes narrower, as you go. There are no exits, other than the drop going down. While it is possible to climb back out, it would be extremely difficult even with a rope.

Grant looked around the larger curved tunnel. The walls and ceiling were made of brick, which looked as if they were bleached white in some areas. The ceiling was arched. The ground was partially flooded with water just above their ankles and it was filled with broken stones and other debris. Around the bend there was an incline that went up about one level.

"This must be the Bronx gate chamber," he presumed. "It looks like it might be tricky to climb to the next level, especially with our muddy feet, but after this it's smooth sailing. It's a good thing, we have a rope."

He pulled out the rope and waited for the others to come through the opening. Only Alissa and Winston remained on the other side of the brick wall.

Alissa turned to Winston and suggested, "You should probably go first. It I get stuck, at least you will be on the other side already."

He replied, "If I stay behind you, I could always push you through."

"That could work. Thanks, Winston."

He nodded and smiled.

Alissa bent down and began to crawl through the opening. It was still slightly snug for her larger frame. Marc tried to help her through from the other side.

What happened next surprised everyone.

KA-BOOM!!!

Marc cried out, "Jesus Christ! What the shit was that?"

An explosion rocked the tunnel causing debris to rain down upon them. Grant used his patrol bag and held it up over his head shielding Julia, Liz, and himself, as they huddled close together. A thunderous rumbling noise was heard followed by someone yelling in the distance.

Suddenly, Alissa slipped backwards out of the hole. Marc immediately grabbed her arm with both hands and pulled with all his might, but she was too heavy.

She screamed, "HELP!"

CONTAMINATION EFFECT

Chapter Twenty

0800 HRS, UPPER MANHATTAN:

IT HAD BEEN a long crazy night for the officers of the 26th Precinct. At long last, daylight had arrived. Unfortunately, the craziness in the city would not end with the rising of the sun. For some, it was still the same day, as they had not slept, yet.

Officer Steven Blake managed to close his eyes, for a few minutes. He just wanted to rest them, he told himself. The next thing he knew, he was napping and dreaming about being in Hawaii.

Next to him, in the driver's seat was his partner for the night, Officer Ricky Colon. Ricky was not in as peaceful a state of mind as his friend, Steve. No, not peaceful, at all. For he had been infected with a deadly contagious virus. It had finally overcome his body and was now urging him to feed. He noticed his partner asleep beside him and his mouth salivated. He longed to rip into his flesh. It was an urge unlike any he'd ever known. The desire to dine on flesh and blood excited him to the point of orgasm. He could hold back no longer.

Ricky leapt onto his partner and began tearing into his uniform to reveal the flesh beneath it. Steve awoke with a start and screamed for his life. Ricky did not care. He dug in deep with his hands, until he pulled out Steve's insides. They dripped with blood and slime that oozed through his fingers.

He placed a large chunk into his mouth and began eating. Oh, how delightful the taste, he thought. Why did he resist for so long? He ate another piece and kept wanting more.

All of a sudden, a series of explosions shook the patrol car and woke Ricky from his morbid nightmare. He opened his eyes in shock and asked, "Huh? What the hell was that?"

Next to him, Steve was staring straight ahead through the windshield toward the Hudson River Bridge. "Look," was all he said in response.

Ricky faced forward and watched, while the bridge collapsed into the Spuyten Duyvil below. The railroad crossing in the distance had also exploded sending splintered wooden ties and bent iron rails into the air. Both river crossings were destroyed.

Gregg commented from behind them, "I had a feeling they'd do this. They blew the bridges. It's easier than placing armored vehicles and armed guards at each one."

Ricky replied, "Blew the bridges? That means they had to pull back, first." He stared at the new gap between both sides, where the bridge once extended and mumbled to himself, "I can make that."

Steve turned to him confused and asked, "You can make what?"

Ricky ignored him, as he put the car into gear and drove them out of Inwood Hill Park. He took Seaman Avenue south and got onto the Henry Hudson Parkway going north.

Steve asked, "What are you doing, Ricky? You do realize this road is going to end at the destroyed bridge, right?"

Ricky did not respond. He felt nauseous, but fought the feeling. There was a certain determination in his eyes. He continued driving toward the entrance of the destroyed bridge.

Gregg began to worry, "Please, let me out, if you're planning to get us all killed. I'd prefer to take my chances on foot."

Steve put on his seatbelt and shouted, "Ricky! Slow down!"

Gregg also put on his seatbelt and began praying silently.

However, Ricky did slow down and gradually came to a stop shortly before reaching the edge of the newly created chasm. He opened his door and calmly stated, "I just want to have a look." He then stepped out of the car and walked toward the edge.

Both Steve and Gregg sighed with relief.

Ricky scanned the other side and noticed there were no guards waiting to shoot them. What was the point now? No one in his right mind would try to cross that way, after the bridge was destroyed.

Of course, Ricky was not in his right state of mind. He was infected and it was only a matter of time before he started freaking out and screaming in pain from the changes his body would undergo. The urge to vomit became overpowering. He keeled over and threw up. When he thought he was done, he coughed and more came out. He spit out the taste and pulled out a napkin from his pants pocket. He wiped his mouth and breathed heavily for a few seconds. It appeared his situation was growing worse. Soon, he'd be screaming and trying to attack Steve and Gregg. He thought about the nightmare he had. There was no time to waste. Jumping was their best option.

When he returned to the car and got inside, Steve asked, "Would you mind telling us what that was about?"

Ricky turned to them and admitted, "I'm infected."

Steve looked at him in disbelief and said, "That's not something to joke about."

"I'm not joking. Do you remember when Louie was under the ambulance earlier and I tried to help him out?"

Steve nodded, and then Ricky explained, "Well, he scratched my wrist with his bloody fingernail." Steve bowed his head in misery, as Ricky continued, "At first, I didn't think anything of it, but as the hours went by, it began to itch. I kept scratching it, until I noticed it was black and blue. It began hurting, but not on the surface. It hurt on the inside. My joints and muscles were aching. I still hoped it was nothing serious. I put a band-aid over it and tried to ignore it. It feels like its getting worse. On top of that, I have a fever and I feel weak all over." He paused, and then added, "I don't think I have much time left, so here's what I propose. We jump to the other side."

Gregg groaned, "Oh, my God. I knew you were going to say that. There are still guards on the other side, who will probably shoot us on sight."

Ricky replied, "I just looked and I don't see anyone. They probably pulled away, before blowing up the bridge. That gives us a small window of opportunity to make it across unnoticed, but we need to do this now. We can't afford to waste time."

Steve protested, "Are you crazy? We'll never make it across. Even if, by some miracle, we did, you just told us you're infected. Why would we want to spread the infection to the other side?"

Ricky hesitated before answering, "You're right. I'm not sure we can make it across in one piece, but I think it is possible. If we do, I don't expect to last much longer. You guys go and leave me behind in the car. Get to your families."

Steve asked, "And what about you?"

"Kill me," he replied glumly. "It's okay. I've had a lot of time to think about it."

Steve and Gregg sat silently in the car, as they considered his proposition. It was a crazy idea for certain. Would it even work? They each had doubts. Still, they wanted to escape Manhattan and their chances of doing so were decreasing with each passing moment. Staying in Manhattan for too long would only mean being surrounded by the infected.

Ricky waited impatiently, but he knew this was something huge to think about. His wrist was already numb. He could barely feel it. As a result, he had limited movement on that hand. Soon, his driving would become impaired. Time was wasting.

Steve thought about his wife and dog. At least, they were far from the city in Rockland County. He then thought about his sister and nephew. Did they manage to get away, as he instructed? He turned to Ricky and said, "Hold on a sec. I just need to make one call. It's very important."

He dialed his sister's number and asked, "Hey, Camille. Did you do as I asked? Are you and the little Don away from the city? Connecticut? That's great. Stay there. I'll be in touch, as soon as I can. I'm fine. Talk to you soon. Give my boy my best." Afterwards, he hung up.

Ricky inquired, "Are you guys ready? This is your last chance to get out of the car. I am not going to die in Manhattan."

Gregg frowned and reminded him, "Not for nothing, but that side still counts as Manhattan for a few blocks."

Ricky rolled his eyes and corrected himself, "I am not going to die on Manhattan Island."

Steve took a deep breath and said, "Let's do this, before I change my mind."

They made a U-turn and drove south going the wrong way in the northbound lanes. It was a good thing there were no cars on that portion of the parkway. Traffic had been blocked off by the 34th Precinct. Ricky swung another U-turn near the Dyckman Street exit and stopped the car facing north.

He turned to Steve and Gregg and told them to buckle up, but they had already done so earlier. He revved up the engine and focused his mind. He stared straight ahead and gripped the steering wheel tightly. This was it. There was no turning back, he told himself.

However, Gregg fidgeted in the backseat and considered getting out of the car, but he so desperately wanted to leave Manhattan that he was willing to go along with this foolish idea.

Ricky held the emergency brake down and stepped on the gas pedal, until he was literally burning rubber. He took a deep breath and released the emergency brake. The car screeched into gear and jerked forward. It sped up the parkway toward the chasm, and then there was a moment of weightlessness.

At the same time, they all shouted, "HOLY SHIT!!!"

The car jumped across the gap from the upper level of the bridge and slanted downward toward the lower level. The turret lights on top of the car struck the ceiling of the lower level and were torn clean off the top. The car smashed onto the lower level and actually bounced, before skidding out of control into the wall on the west side and spinning out into the wall on the opposite side, where it came to a halt.

The windshield was broken and covered in blood. All of the other windows had shattered with exception to the rear window. The front end of the car looked like an accordion. Steam leaked out of the engine through the bent hood smelling of burnt oil and anti-freeze. Three out of four tires were flattened. Broken glass was everywhere both inside and outside of the car. The front airbags had deployed, as well.

Inside the car, all was still. No one moved.

0800 HRS, E. 109TH ST. AND FIRST AVE:

Kirk opened the glass sliding door to the terrace and stepped outside. David and Kevin followed and stepped out with him. They had just heard a loud explosion that rattled the windows. It sounded like it came from the river. When the three men looked, they saw that the bridges crossing over into Manhattan had been blown up.

Kirk's eyes opened wide, as he commented, "I don't believe my eyes. They really went there. They blew up the bridges. We're officially stranded, folks."

Kevin held his head in despair, as some of the hope he had started slipping away.

David stepped back inside and told the others what they saw, "It looks like the bridges crossing into Manhattan have been blown up. At least, the ones on this side are gone."

Mr. Hayes commented, "You've got to be kidding."

Edie asked, "What are we going to do now?"

David replied, "I think I should go up to the roof and get a better look around. I want to make sure all the bridges are gone. I also want to know what's going on around us." He turned to Michelle and asked, "Is there an alarm up there?"

She shrugged and answered, "I'm not sure. I never went up there."

David walked to the door and unlocked it. He said, "I'll come back as fast as I can. Lock the door behind me."

Kirk asked, "Do you need a hand or are you able to walk on your own?"

"I should be fine. Michelle gave me some painkillers. They seem to be doing the job. Thanks, though."

"You're welcome," Kirk said with a smile.

Edie stood up from the sofa and asked, "Can I come with you? I want to see."

David hesitated and nodded, "Okay, come on, but stay close to me. We need to avoid trouble. If I have to run, I don't think I'll be able to. My side still aches a little."

"I will. Thank you," she replied. She followed him out of the apartment and they took the staircase to the roof. When they reached the roof landing a motion sensor alarm began ringing loudly. They covered their ears and pushed the door open. It was already being held open by a paint can.

David told Edie, "Make sure that can stays in place. I don't want to get locked up here."

"Okay," she replied. She carefully stepped around the can and closed the door slowly, until it rested against the can, again.

The building was quite tall, giving them an outstanding view of the city. They looked around them and could see multiple plumes of black and gray smoke in every direction. David went from one side of the roof to the other and no matter which way he looked, there was fire and smoke. Every single bridge had been destroyed. There were also fires burning out of control to the north. There were helicopters flying around at the edge of the city. Some were news copters, some belonged to the NYPD, and there also appeared to be military helicopters patrolling the borders of the city.

David wondered if he could get a police helicopter to land on the roof to pick him and the others up. It was certainly worth a try. He turned up the volume on his portable radio and switched it to the citywide channel.

"Are there any Aviation units on the air?" His question was met with silence, as Edie wandered off to the edge of the roof. He kept his eyes on her and tried, again, "2-6 portable to Aviation. Can you hear me?"

The radio came to life with a fast burst of static, and then a voice was heard, "Aviation 213 on the air. I thought all you 2-6 guys were gone."

David grinned and responded, "Not all. A few of us are still around. We're just spread out. I don't suppose I can trouble you for an EVAC from a rooftop."

"Uh, sorry. That's a negative. You have my deepest apologies, but we are no longer authorized to land in Manhattan. The best I can do is drop down a care package. What's your location?"

David frowned and told them the building's address. Within seconds a police helicopter zoomed in and hovered overhead. The wind from the rotors was powerful, so Edie moved as far away, as she could. The helicopter lowered down to about fifty feet over them and a package was dropped near David. He looked up and waved his thanks. The two officers within gave him a salute, before lifting up higher and flying away toward Randall's Island.

He bent over and winced from the pain. Bending over agitated his injuries from the car accident. He quickly pulled a knife from his gun belt and cut open the package. He looked inside and saw there were some water bottles, food rations, ammo clips, an extra radio battery, and some basic medicines. He closed it up and noticed Edie standing at the far edge of the roof. He went over to her to check on her.

Edie stared out toward Upper Manhattan. Her shoulders trembled and she sniffled. It was obvious she was crying.

He put his hand on her shoulder and spoke softly when he broke the bad news, "They can't pick us up."

She continued crying, but managed to utter, "I can't believe this is happening. My best friend is dead. *Zombies are real???* The whole city is going to burn and we're going to die!" She broke down and David held her. She sobbed uncontrollably for several seconds.

He tried to comfort her and said, "I won't let that happen. We'll get out of here. I promise."

They stayed there momentarily in each other's arms not saying anything. Finally, she sniffled and he pulled away and asked, "Are you ready to go back downstairs?"

She wiped her tears and regained her composure. When she was ready, she nodded quietly.

David struggled to pick up the box of supplies and wished he had let Kirk come along, instead of Edie. She obviously still needed time to mourn her friend, which he understood. He felt terrible about his partner, Elizabeth, but he knew he had to be strong. There would be time to mourn later, after they were safe.

He led her back into the building and they went downstairs back to the twenty-eighth floor. He cautiously opened the door and looked into the hallway. It was empty.

"Come on," he said and she followed. "Do me a favor and knock on the door."

"Okay." She knocked and said, "It's us, Edie and David."

Michelle opened the door and let them back in. She asked, "Well, what did you guys see?"

David entered carrying the box and shook his head. He said, "The bridges are gone... *all* of them. There are several fires burning to the north. The south looks okay, for now, but it won't be long before the infection reaches down there. Manhattan is a lost cause. We need to escape, more than ever. However, a friendly eye in the sky was able to drop us some supplies." He placed the box down on the coffee table in the living room and winced from the pain.

Kirk noticed and said, "I knew I should have gone with you. What's in the box?"

He, Kevin, and Wally gathered around the box.

Wally asked, "Was that on the roof?"

"You could say that," David moaned, as he took another painkiller and drank some water from the kitchen sink. "It's water, food, ammo, medicine, and a spare battery for my radio."

Mr. Hayes asked, "Where'd you get that from?"

"NYPD Aviation Unit," David responded. "And no, they can't rescue us. I already asked. This was the best they could do for me. I'm grateful they did this much, considering I didn't ask for it."

"So, does that mean we're safe here?" Mr. Hayes inquired.

"Well, yeah, but we'll have to leave, at some point."

Kevin asked, "Where do you suggest we go? Anyplace else is as good as here. I say we stay here, until we figure out a way off the island."

Wally agreed, "Yeah, I don't think we'll be safe driving around blindly."

David replied, "We can stay here for a while, but I don't want to be trapped here. I was thinking we should head as far south as we can. See what happens. Maybe we can find a more secure place to hide out."

Kirk asked, "And then what? We wait to die? Hiding out is fine, while supplies last, but we barely have enough. We'll need lots more food and water. Medical supplies, too."

David replied, "I won't argue with that. We stay here, for now, and gather supplies to fill the van."

Wally said, "The van barely has room for all of us. We should wait, until we find a safe place, and then start gathering supplies. We can go out in small groups. It will be safer."

Kevin suggested, "So, let's start thinking of places that would make good safe houses. There are a lot in Manhattan, especially further south. It's only a matter of getting there and securing the location for ourselves, if someone else has not already beaten us to it."

Kirk agreed, "In that case, David is right. We shouldn't waste too much time here. We need to think fast and make some moves, while we still can."

Mr. Hayes nodded, "I agree."

Michelle said, "I don't want to stay here, if it's not safe. My sister and I need to stay together. Take us with you."

David assured her, "Don't worry. We weren't going to leave you behind. We are a group and we need to stick together. We'll all survive this thing, as long as we do it as a team."

An aerial view of the Manhattan fires, shortly after 8 am.

Looking across High Bridge toward Manhattan.

0800 HRS, HIGH BRIDGE TUNNEL ON THE BRONX SIDE:

The sound of crunching metal and crumbling stone practically drowned out Alissa's cries for help, which echoed in the tunnels. She felt herself gradually slipping away and hung on for dear life. Marc tried desperately to pull her through the small opening at the bottom of the wall. He simply was not strong enough and the hole was still too tight for her to fit through.

Charles and Aramis rushed over to help, since they were the closest.

Marc grunted, "Ugh! I can't pull her through." Sweat poured down his forehead, as he struggled to hold her slippery arm. He pulled as hard as he could.

"Ow! My arm," she cried. "You're breaking it!"

"I'm trying to help you!"

She looked at him with desperation. Only her head and arm were still on the Bronx side of the opening. She responded with fear, "I know! Please, don't let go! I'm falling!"

Charles was confused. He had no idea what was going on, but he grabbed hold of her arm, too. It was so slippery from the sweat that it was difficult to get a good grip.

Her head began slipping out through the hole to the other side, but Marc refused to let go. He was slowly being pulled through the hole with her.

Charles shouted to Aramis, "Grab him by the waist and don't let go! I have her hand!" He then called out to Alissa, "Alissa! Give me your other hand! Hurry!"

"I'll fall!" She cried from the other side of the wall.

"You're falling now!" He cried out. Charles leaned into the wall, but then backed away from it when he noticed it had become unstable. It was vibrating and the bricks began shifting, as if it were on the verge of collapse. Metal and stone was still crashing down from the other side and Alissa screamed even louder.

"I'M SLIPPING!"

Marc explained desperately, "No! We'll pull you up, but you need to give us your other hand! Hurry! This arm is slipping! I can't hold it much longer!"

Grant rushed over with the rope. He had managed to tie one end around his waist. He tried to pass the other end to Alissa and said, "Grab the rope, Alissa!"

She cried, "I'm scared! I don't want to fall!"

Marc reassured her calmly, "Trust me. We'll be able to pull you up together..." His voice trailed off and he fell silent. He closed his eyes and bowed his head in shame.

On the other side of the wall, they heard Alissa's voice echo in the distance, as she fell, "AAARRRGGGHHH!!!"

Charles cried out, "NO!!! Damn it!" He instinctively punched the wall and it gave out. He jumped back, as the bricks all crumbled down. Luckily, Aramis was paying attention and yanked Marc back in time by his waist, before he was buried under the rubble.

Aramis gasped, "Shit! That was close!" He looked down at Marc and asked, "Hey, man. Are you okay?"

Marc looked up at him from the floor and was breathing heavily with tears in his eyes. Somehow, he managed to mutter through the lump that had formed in his throat, "Yeah. Thanks." He was all choked up, although he tried to hold it back.

Aramis felt bad for him. He didn't know what to say, so he just stood there.

Charles stood nearby in complete shock. The concept of what just took place still had not fully occurred to him. Somehow, Alissa had mysteriously fallen to her death and through his own carelessness he could have killed or seriously injured Marc. However, even that was not as disturbing as the astounding sight before his eyes. The entire bridge was gone. It had collapsed and fallen into the river below. Now, they could see straight across to the Manhattan side, where the High Bridge Tower loomed on its hill.

And then, there was poor Winston. He must have fallen to his death with no one to try and save him. It all happened so fast, but why? How?

Liz gasped, "Oh my God!" She held her hands over her mouth and asked, "Is she?"

"Yes," Charles replied grimly. "So is Winston. The entire bridge is gone."

Julia asked, "How is that even possible? Did it collapse?"

Charles replied soberly, "I have no idea."

Marc was distraught and still on the floor when he cried, "Why didn't she just give me her other hand? We could have saved her!"

Aramis helped him up and consoled him, "It's not your fault. You did what you could."

Grant looked up at the ceiling, which was still raining dust down around them, and fumed, "Damn it! Those bastards must have blown the bridge! If we had been a few minutes later, we would have all fallen into the river."

Julia frowned, "Jesus Christ! I suppose we should be grateful."

Charles breathed heavily and replied, "Why don't I feel grateful?" He stood at the precipice staring down hopelessly at the wreckage and debris that was scattered across tracks and expressway below. A long portion of the bridge on the Bronx side passed over the Metro-North railroad tracks and the Major Deegan Expressway, before touching ground at the Bronx side of High Bridge Park. The large water pipe and steel portions of the bridge must have fallen into the Harlem River because he did not see a lot of metal in the debris. It was mostly stone.

He pointlessly wiped away the dust from his uniform and suggested, "Let's keep moving, before more of the tunnel collapses."

No one said anything. They stepped over the debris and walked around the bend of the curved gate chamber. It was already time for them to face another challenge, reaching the elevated portion of the next tunnel. They took a moment to catch their breath.

About a minute later, Grant passed the other end of the rope to Aramis and instructed, "Hold onto the rope and pass it back to the others. Everyone, be sure to grab this rope. Leave me some slack, so you don't pull me back down. I'll climb up, first. When I say the word, each of you will follow me, one at a time. Use the rope to steady yourself. Take it slow and don't wrap the rope around your wrists," he warned. "It will burn through your skin. Grab it as best you can and be careful. Our feet are muddy, so it will be very easy to slip and break our necks."

He carefully scaled up the inclined portion of the tunnel, but kept slipping down. He had been wearing gloves for most of the night, so his grip wasn't in question. It was his feet that could not find a decent hold. His boots were caked in mud, so they had no traction. He kicked off the mud against the walls and tried, again. Finally, after several frustrating attempts he made it to the higher level.

"Shit, that was not easy," he complained. He found a good place to stand and planted his feet firmly. When he was ready, he called down, "Okay, Aramis. You come up next."

Aramis held the rope tight and climbed up, while Grant pulled at the rope. The rope was nice and steady, since it was being pulled from both ends. Charles held it tightly at the bottom. Once Aramis reached the top, Grant pulled him up by hand the rest of the way.

"Thanks, Grant!"

Liz was next. Climbing up the incline was a bit tricky for her, since her long leather boots had small heels. Fortunately, she was able to use the heels to her advantage and lock her feet into place, as she climbed. Holding on to the rope definitely made the climb easier.

After she reached the top, it was Julia's turn. She was petite and therefore very light, which made it easy to pull her up.

Grant turned to Aramis and said, "I'm going to need your help to pull Charles and Marc up. They are a bit heavier, especially with the added weight of their bullet proof vests and gun belts."

"You got it, man," he answered. He moved into place in front of Grant and grabbed the rope firmly. He was also wearing gloves and had been since they first met with him. Together, they pulled Charles up, and then Marc.

Afterwards, Grant shook off his hands. They were hurting. He untied the rope and handed it to Aramis. He asked, "Can you please wrap up the rope and pass it back to me when you're done? I need to rest my hands a minute."

"No problem."

Grant carefully pulled off his gloves and there were rope burn marks around his hands. It wasn't too bad. At least, the marks would go away in time. There was nothing that could be done about Winston and Alissa. They were gone forever. Two more victims of the virus, although not directly.

The beam on Winston's flashlight died out, almost like it died with him. Without a word, Charles passed Grant his flashlight. Once that died, they would have to resort to using cellphone lights. Grant hoped to be out, by then.

There was barely enough time to shed any tears for the dead. The group continued vigilantly through the Croton Aqueduct tunnel. The plan had worked, for the most part. They made it into the Bronx. Now, they had to find a way out of the tunnel. It had to be far enough away from High Bridge that they could emerge unnoticed.

CONTAMINATION EFFECT

Chapter Twenty-One

0845 HRS, E. 109TH ST. AND FIRST AVE:

DAVID AND THE others had finally come to a decision. They wanted to head somewhere safe, but it had to be someplace further south from their location. Suddenly, it occurred to David. There was a place that no one would be able to reach them, where they could find a great deal of safety... The Intrepid! It was an old United States aircraft carrier that had been converted into a museum back in the early 1980s. It was docked at Pier 86 on West 46th Street.

"That's where we can go," he told the others. "It's armored and high above the ground. We can easily control who comes aboard. There's plenty of room for supplies and it has a helicopter deck, in case they ever decide it's okay to send in rescue teams. It's perfect."

Kirk grinned, "I like it! Let's do it!"

Wally and Kevin nodded.

Mr. Hayes was a little more skeptical. He asked, "What if someone already beat us to it?"

Kirk replied with a smile, "We'll convince them that sharing is caring."

Mr. Hayes shrugged, "Uh, okay. If you say so."

David turned to Michelle and suggested, "Pack anything you think we can use. Think long term stays. We'll need soap, toothpaste, toilet paper, pain medication, whatever you have."

Michelle grabbed a bag from the hall closet and began filling it with supplies. Millie and Edie helped her. Michelle also gave the girls clean clothing to wear, which they appreciated.

Kevin went into the kitchen and said, "We should pack as much food as we can carry, especially canned goods and drinks." Michelle passed him another bag that he could use. He began filling it up with food from the refrigerator and pantry.

Kirk said, "Don't grab too many things that need to be refrigerated. We don't need to lug around spoiled food."

"I know. I'm grabbing drinks," replied Kevin.

"Oh," Kirk responded. "I'll help."

Wally asked, "What about blankets and towels?"

David nodded, "Good idea. We'll need that, too."

Mr. Hayes stepped out onto the terrace and looked down at Randall's Island. He did not notice any activity on the island. He wondered if it were occupied or empty. He wondered what other islands might be good for them to hide out on. He came back inside and asked, "What about leaving Manhattan with the ship? Maybe we could head out to Long Island?"

Wally asked, "Do you know how to operate an aircraft carrier? I sure don't, but I would imagine it takes a fairly large crew."

Mr. Hayes frowned, "I didn't think of that. Well, how about we go to Roosevelt Island, instead?"

David turned to him and stated, "If we are spotted trying to leave Manhattan Island, we will be shot. That's a chance I won't take, again. It's too risky. Besides, that island might be heavily guarded. We stick to the plan. We're going to The Intrepid."

Mr. Hayes nodded and sat back down on the sofa. He rummaged through the box of supplies that David brought down from the roof. There sure were a lot of rations. He wasn't too keen on the idea of eating rations. He stood up and went into the kitchen to see what Kevin was packing. The food from the pantry didn't seem much more appetizing. They were definitely going to have to go on a food run, once they got settled at The Intrepid or maybe even before they got there.

"We should make, at least, one more stop for supplies, before we go to The Intrepid," he suggested. "Perhaps, at a pharmacy, where they sell food and medicine."

Kevin stated, "That may not be a bad idea. What's around here, Michelle?"

"Well, there's a pharmacy over on Second Avenue. It's only a block away."

"Perfect," Kevin responded. "Let's go there, and then we can take Second Avenue straight down to 47th and cut across to the West Side."

David agreed, "Sounds good. Are we ready to go?"

Michelle answered, "Just about." She jammed one last item into a suitcase and said, "Okay. Done."

Everyone was done packing. They crammed supplies into two suitcases and a duffle bag. Now, they had to carry it all down to the parking garage. At least, they didn't have to use the stairs.

David and Kevin stepped out in the hallway, first. It was clear. They waved everyone else out.

Kirk insisted on carrying both suitcases, since they were heavy. Wally carried the box of supplies and Mr. Hayes had the duffle bag filled with food and toiletries. Michelle locked up the apartment, while Edie pressed the button for the elevator. Millie carried a handheld crank radio that Michelle kept in her kitchen, in case of an emergency. This certainly qualified.

There was absolutely no way they could all fit in the elevator with the bags, so they had to make two trips down. Once everyone was in the garage, they loaded up the van and got in. They drove out of the garage and Kevin went into the booth to open and close the tollgate for them.

Two minutes later, they pulled up to the pharmacy on Second Avenue. Strangely, it appeared to be open for business. David went inside with Kirk, while the others waited in the van. Mr. Hayes soon joined them.

David and Kirk looked at him and wondered why he followed them in, so he explained, "Hey, it was my idea. I have a few necessities

I wanted to get. If it makes you feel better, we can use my credit card to pay for everything."

David shrugged, "Fine by me." He began looking around for things they could use.

Kirk grabbed a basket and walked around the small shop filling it with necessities.

Kevin stocked up on protein bars, health snacks, and vitamins.

When they were done, they approached the counter with a small mountain of merchandise. The store clerk rang them up and bagged their items. He then said, "That will be $231.71."

Kirk laughed and walked away from the counter, before he lost his temper. He knew, right away, the clerk was taking advantage of the emergency and overcharging them.

Mr. Hayes' eyes were about as wide open, as his mouth.

David thought he heard wrong and asked, "How much did you say?"

"$231.71, please."

David narrowed his eyes and leaned in close, as he said in a low voice, "If you are seriously planning to overcharge us, then I'm afraid I'm going to have to beat your ass. I know both things are wrong, but maybe two wrongs will make a right, since two rights don't make a wrong."

The clerk swallowed nervously and cleared his throat, "Ahem! I'm sorry, I almost forgot to add the discount for city workers." He recalculated the prices and corrected himself. "That brings your total to $115.85. Please."

David looked at Mr. Hayes and said, "Pay the man."

Mr. Hayes handed his credit card to the clerk.

Just then, the manager stepped out from the back and saw David in his uniform. He immediately snatched the credit card from the clerk and placed it on the counter. He slid it toward David and said, "Please, excuse my employee, officer. He's new around here. Police do not need to pay in my shop during a time of extreme emergency. Take what you need and be safe out there."

David pushed the credit card back and insisted, "Thank you, but we can pay for what we need. With the way the city is going to hell, you will need every dollar you can get to recover from what's going on."

"Exactly what is going on, officer?"

"The end of days. I suggest you close up shop and head home, as long as you don't live anywhere above 110th Street."

A grim expression came over the manager's face, as he charged the card and handed it back. "Thank you," he said. "I guess I will be staying open."

Kirk said, "We'd invite you to come with us, but the van's full. Find a hotel far downtown. You don't want to stay open too long. Trust me. It won't end well."

They left the pharmacy and got back in the van. The van headed south on Second Avenue hopeful that their plan to hide at The Intrepid would work out.

0855 HRS, OLD CROTON AQUEDUCT TUNNEL:

The tunnels in the Bronx took on a slightly different appearance than those under Manhattan. While they also had tree roots spreading along the walls, there were much more. They almost resembled veins, which gave them an eerie appearance. A slippery gray layer of mud covered the floors in some areas, where there was a low amount of water. The ceilings were lined with stalactites, which served as home to numerous bats that slept peacefully, unaware of the intruders lurking through the tunnel below.

As the group walked further into the Bronx, the water level began to rise. After a few minutes, they were wading through nearly three feet of stagnant water. They were sick and tired of having wet feet. Finding an exit became a priority. They no longer wanted to be underground. The aqueduct tunnel had served its purpose. It had also seen the death of two from their group. Enough was enough.

After almost an hour of trudging through flooded tunnels, they reached a staircase that led up to a sealed rusted door. A crack at the opening revealed sunlight. At long last, they found a way out!

Aramis asked, "Do you think we can get out through here?"

Grant put his gloves back on and pulled out the crowbar from his bag. He then replied, "We are sure as shit going to give it our best try." He jammed the flat end into the crack and began prying at the door, but it was tough. It refused to budge and the rust made it harder to move. He turned to Aramis, who stood behind him and said, "Give me a hand with this."

"Sure thing. Let's do this."

Together, they used muscle and leverage to force open the door, causing it to burst open. Rust crumbled down around them and the heavy iron door creaked loudly, as it swung outward to the left. The sunlight hit them hard and temporarily blinded them when they stepped out of the doorway and into a small walled-in area on the south side of the street. An old black iron gate was the only thing separating them from Burnside Avenue.

Grant pushed it open and they stepped out onto the sidewalk. They were free, at last.

Aramis cheered, "Yes! We did it!"

Julia stepped out and looked around. Once her vision cleared, she asked, "Where are we? I'm not familiar with the Bronx."

Aramis looked across at the next street over and read the sign. He answered, "Well, that's University Avenue up there on the next block."

Grant put away his crowbar and said, "We're on Burnside Avenue. I remember this area. I came here a long time ago. It's kind of funny. This door here was the way I considered entering the tunnels back when I was a teenager. I never would have imagined coming out this way, after traveling all the way through the tunnels from Manhattan."

Marc stood by the gate and leaned against the wall it was connected to. He wasn't in the mood to celebrate. All he could think about was Alissa's hand slipping through his and the look on her face when she realized she was about to die. He closed his eyes and tried to erase the image. It didn't work.

Charles took out his phone and noticed a missed text message from David. He also had a missed call from his friend, Carmen. There was no signal, while they were down in the tunnels, but now, there were a few notifications appearing on his phone. He decided to call Carmen, first, to get an update on the situation.

She filled him in on everything she knew, in regards to what was going on. She and the top brass had been relocated to Metro Tech Center, the NYPD communications center in Brooklyn. She confirmed that the military planted explosives at all river crossings and exploded them simultaneously at 8 am sharp. Manhattan was now officially under quarantine. The airspace over Manhattan had just been declared a no-fly zone with exception to military aircraft. The NYPD helicopters were grounded indefinitely at Floyd Bennett Field, as of 9 am. A pilot and his co-pilot had gotten into trouble for dropping packages to people in the Infected Zone.

Carmen asked how Charles and his officers were doing. He hesitated and considered not telling her the truth, but she insisted she was passing him confidential information and implied she would get into big trouble, if anyone knew she was talking to him. She only wanted to help him any way she could. He decided to tell her some of the truth, without being too specific.

"We're in the Bronx. We found a way out, before the bridges were blown," he confided. When she asked which bridge he used, he did not say. He only told her, they were safe and had no plans of making official contact with the NYPD. He was going AWOL, along with his officers.

She understood his position and told him she'd be in touch when she learned anything else. She advised him to remove the collar brass from his uniform that indicated he was from the 26th Precinct. He did so and told his other officers, Grant and Marc, to do the same. Considering how filthy and wet they were, they already intended on getting rid of their uniforms the first chance they got. There was no point in advertising they were cops anymore.

Next, Charles called David. He had no problem telling him exactly how they got out of Manhattan and explained that option was no longer a possibility with the bridges out. He made sure to mention the quarantine, which David did not take too well. They agreed to stay in touch, for as long as possible.

Charles had one more phone call to make. He called Steve. The phone rang several times, and then it went to voicemail. He hung up and tried, again. Still, there was no answer. He put the phone away and sighed.

"Rest in peace," he said.

Grant looked at him and asked, "Who?"

"Steve isn't answering his phone anymore."

"Oh," Grant responded. That was another friend lost because of the virus. He wondered when it would end, if ever. He had a feeling there would be a lot more deaths to follow in the near future.

Liz turned to him and Charles with her hands on her hips and asked, "So, where do we go from here? Do we stay together or should we go our separate ways?"

Grant turned to her and replied, "I think we should stay together. This isn't over, yet. Not by a long shot. We need somewhere where we can regroup and prepare for the next phase. The Kingsbridge Armory is not too far away from here. We should be able to lay low for a while, if we can get inside."

"I agree," Charles said. "We should stay together, at least, until we figure this out. If you know how to get there, lead the way."

Liz responded, "Wait. What do you mean by the next phase?"

Julia and Aramis looked on curiously and wondered the same thing.

Grant explained, "This virus has managed to spread over most of Manhattan in less than twelve hours at a time when there was only a night time weekend crowd. It's Saturday morning. Not a lot of people are aware of the events from last night. They are going to wake up to a city that's already under quarantine. People are going to be pissed off and that also means people outside of Manhattan, who have family there. We already know the infection has spread to the airport. Who knows if it managed to slip past us to somewhere else and we just don't know it, yet? This nightmare isn't over. It's just beginning."

Everyone looked at Grant and realized he was right. This was only the beginning.

An Old Croton Aqueduct exit on Burnside Avenue in the Bronx.

0930 HRS, 47TH STREET:

David turned the van onto East 47th Street and headed west. Before he reached the West Side, his cellphone began ringing. He pulled over to the curb and pulled it out of his shirt pocket. He could not believe it. It was Charles.

"I need to take this call," he said. He answered the phone, "Charles! I can't believe it! I thought you were done. Where are you? What??? You made it to the Bronx?"

Everyone in the van suddenly became very interested in the phone call. They paid close attention to whatever David said.

"Man, I can't believe you made it out! I guess we're stuck here for a while. We're heading down to The Intrepid. Hopefully, we can stay there, until we can get rescued. Say what? Quarantine? I knew it."

The others in the van were disturbed by the word "quarantine." It made their situation feel more hopeless.

David continued with his conversation on the phone, "Yeah, we'll watch out for snipers. Thanks. Hey, let's stay in touch. I'll try to keep my phone charged. I was able to buy a new charger at a pharmacy. Yep. These people don't get it. They'll learn soon enough. Take care."

Kevin asked, "How did he get out?"

"They took an old aqueduct tunnel that crossed a bridge into the Bronx. Of course, we won't be able to get out the same way, since all the bridges were blown up. The island is now under quarantine. We're on our own."

Kirk responded, "No worries, pal. We were already on our own. Let's get to The Intrepid and wait this thing out. We should be able to get along just fine. We're doing okay, so far. It's not as if we have any other choices."

David sighed, "You're right." He continued driving toward the West Side.

There were a few cars on the road. David wondered where they were going. Nowhere, he realized. No one was going anywhere, as long as they were trapped on Manhattan. The island was under quarantine. That quarantine would never be lifted. The city was lost. He already knew that much.

Soon, they arrived at the West Side. They stopped at the corner and looked toward the Intrepid. The van remained stopped there for about a minute, as David studied the scene. There appeared to be a few cars parked near the entrance to Pier 86. It was difficult to see if anyone was on the Upper Deck of the ship, although there were plenty of historic planes.

Mr. Hayes became impatient and asked, "What are we waiting for?"

David answered, "I just wanted to make sure there was no trouble waiting for us. Everyone, be ready for anything." He drove forward and approached the entrance. He drove past the main museum building and a few old army tanks that were on display as part of the museum exhibits. He continued onto the pier and came to a stop between the first two staircase towers that were used to board the ship.

"Let's leave the supplies in the van temporarily," he said. "I want to scout the area and make sure it's safe, before we start unpacking and making ourselves comfortable. Kirk, you, and Wally come with me. If I run into trouble, I want my muscle with me. That's definitely you guys. Kevin, stay with the van, since you have the only other gun."

Kirk interrupted, "Ahem! Well, that's not entirely true, my friend. I am carrying, as well."

"I'm not even going to ask," David commented with a slightly amused look on his face. "Just keep it in check."

"Oh, don't worry. I don't need it. I prefer to rely on my fists to get the job done," Kirk responded, while cracking his knuckles.

David smirked, "And that's why I want you to come with me."

They grinned at each other and the three got out of the van. They approached the first tower with caution. It was a complete surprise when someone opened the door from within the main museum building. David was about to aim his gun, until he noticed it was an elderly man in a security uniform.

"Whoa! There's no need for that, officer. Welcome to The Intrepid," he said. "Please, put your weapons away. Will you be joining us aboard the ship? She's well protected."

David, Kirk, and Wally looked at each other and felt confused. They didn't know what to say. Was this guy for real? Exactly how many other people were inside?

The elderly guard said, "I suppose you didn't expect to find anyone here. Well, I worked here for fifteen years, before the renovation in 2006, and then I came back to work here, again, after it reopened, two years later. There are ten of us in total. The others are onboard. Is it just the three of you then?"

David shook his head and replied, "We have others. They're in the van."

"Well, bring them aboard. You're all welcome to stay with us. You'll be safe here. We were getting ready to close down the gates of the main building and head up to the ship."

"Okay." David and the others agreed.

The elderly guard, whose name was Vanvooren, seemed harmless enough. The others exited the van, while he closed the gate to the museum's main building. Together, they brought in the supplies up the staircase of the first tower and into the ship's main entrance. As he escorted them inside, he introduced the group to the rest of the people on board.

David was pleased. At last, it looked like they would be safe for a while. Still, he couldn't help wonder how long their luck would last.

THE MANHATTANVILLE INCIDENT:
PART THREE

"Brundlefly"

BRUNDLEFLY

Chapter One

*T*HE FOLLOWING ACCOUNT, *which occurred several hours earlier, was taken from the journal of David Frino:*

<u>July</u>

Friday, 11:43 pm:

Okay, I just wrote down the events from earlier tonight and needed to take a break. My arm is tired. I've been writing like a madman for the past hour. I must say it was not easy to write the words, let alone think them. At least, not while my Kat is still out there.

I keep thinking about her. I keep seeing her face and that wild look in her eyes. I think she really wanted to kill me. There was so much anger and hate. She was full of aggression. I can't blame her. Why did I leave her alone in the locker room? What was I thinking?

What happened to her is totally my fault. I fully accept that. I should have found a way to get to her. Had we escaped the lab together, she'd still be with me. I messed up. I allowed fear to take over and I left her there.

I hope she can be cured. Nothing else in the world matters more to me than that. I wish she could have been contained in the lab. At least, then it would be easier. Who knows where she is now? She could be anywhere? It's driving me crazy thinking about it.

God, I love her so much.

I need to focus on something else or I will most certainly go out of my mind. This whole thing has given me a splitting headache.

Well, here's something I should mention. I just spoke to my buddy, Marc. He took long enough to call. I sent him a text message over an hour ago. When I started to tell him about the homeless men, I could tell he did not believe me. My cousin, Ed, was with him. He said he'd call me soon. In fact, I think my phone is ringing.

Saturday, 12:15 am:

I just had a long talk with Ed. I am so glad he called me back. I tried calling him about an hour ago, but he said he was standing rollcall and could not answer. I keep forgetting he can't talk on the phone during that time. My mind is such a mess.

Anyway, I told him everything that took place tonight. Well, I didn't mention the fact that Dr. Fox looked like a freaking zombie. He would have thought I was pulling his leg. I told him everything else, though. I think he believed me, for the most part. I sure hope so. Everything counts on it. This virus has to be stopped, before it spreads.

While I was speaking to him, I heard a job come over his walkie-talkie about some guys running and screaming on Broadway. If that's what I think it is, then they are going to have their hands full tonight.

Ed said he would speak to his supervisor. He might call me later tonight.

My head is killing me, probably from all the excitement. I'll take some aspirin. That should help. Afterwards, I will wait for Ed's call.

Saturday, 12:35 am:

While I was in the bathroom, I noticed the scratch on my right arm is swollen. It stings and it feels so itchy. I want to scratch it badly, but I don't want to make it bleed. I rubbed alcohol over it and put on a band-aid. Of course, it probably stings because of the alcohol. I also changed the dressing on my right hand.

I can't believe I cut it with a broken light bulb when I was in the lab. That was stupid and careless of me. At least, it doesn't itch!

Saturday, 12:50 am:

The scratch on my arm really hurts a lot. It still itches like crazy, too. I have been trying to ignore it, but I can't. I don't know how much more of this I can take.

Saturday, 1:10 am:

I tried calling Kat. Her phone rang a few times, and then went to voicemail. I don't know why I thought she might answer. I guess I'm fooling myself. I will not accept that she is lost to me. There is a cure. Dr. Fox made one. She will be found and she will be cured. I have to believe that.

Saturday, 1:15 am:

Damn! My phone rang and I automatically assumed it was Kat. It was only my cousin. I got so angry that I threw my phone. I think I broke it. The screen cracked and it came apart. I put it back together and turned it on. I am waiting for it to load up. I am such an idiot. Why did I throw the phone?

Just as I thought, it doesn't seem to be working right. I damaged it. I can't make any calls on it. I hope Ed calls back. I wonder if he found Kat. I am so glad they had a chance to meet. If he sees her, he will know her. Hopefully, he can detain her long enough, so she can be cured.

A terrible thought just occurred to me. What if the anti-virus doesn't even work? Did Dr. Fox even have a chance to test it? No, I doubt it. Otherwise, things would have worked out differently.

That damned egotistical prick single-handedly ruined both Kat's and my life with one phone call. I never should have answered when he called. I was so tempted to ignore it. Kat and I were having such a perfect evening. It was beautiful.

Oh, Kat. I wish you were here.

Saturday, 1:50 am:

I tried watching television. It only reminded me of Kat. I can't get her out of my mind. Normally, that would be great, but not now. The same images keep coming back to me. I see her wild expression, as she tried to attack me. I see her tackling Ivan and tearing into him. His screams are echoing in my mind. Why didn't the moron run when I told him to?

Why is it that people never listen when someone is trying to warn them? Why must people learn the hard way?

I wish I had ratted Dr. Fox out when I had the chance. I knew he was up to no good. I felt it in my gut. The only reason I held back is because of Kat. She wanted me to give him the benefit of the doubt. How could I not listen to her? How could I not want to please her?

I wanted to marry her. I still do. Will that ever happen? I honestly do not know the answer to that question.

Saturday, 2:20 am:

I felt so frustrated I went to bed. I couldn't sleep. I kept tossing and turning. It's hard to find a comfortable position. My arm is aching and the area, where I was scratched, is still very itchy. I just peeled off the band-aid to take a look. It's starting to swell up. It's turning black and blue, too. Come to think of it, my right hand is starting to itch, too. It figures.

I wonder. Maybe I caught an infection. I'll rub on some more alcohol. It will be uncomfortable, but that should kill any germs. I might even have something else in the medicine cabinet that will help ease the itching.

Saturday, 2:45 am:

I am really trying to get past the itching and the pain, so I can try to get some sleep, but I can't for so many reasons. Number one is that I keep seeing Kat's face. I feel like I let her down. I know I did. She's my girlfriend and I left her there to get attacked. Even Dr. Fox took a piece out of her! I can't believe he bit her face. That bastard! I should have killed him, right then and there.

Kat, I am so sorry. I hope you will be able to forgive me when this is all over. Please, understand I only did what I had to do in order to survive. I promise, we will be together, again, soon. I will not let you down a second time. You are my world. I will make sure you are cured, if it's the last thing I do.

My right arm and hand are starting to feel numb from all the itching, unless it's because of all the alcohol I put on. I may have over done it.

Just great. I'm starting to feel sick. I think I have a fever. My head feels very warm. I still have a headache, too. I think I feel nauseous.

Saturday, 2:56 am:

I just puked my guts out. I barely made it to the bathroom in time. Luckily, I got it all in the toilet. I really hate vomiting. The smell of it makes me want to vomit more and when I look at it, it's the same. It's so disgusting. I feel disgusting.

While I was in the bathroom, I took a look at myself in the mirror. My eyes are bloodshot. I look terrible. If someone saw how I look, they'd think I was high on drugs.

Maybe, I just need some sleep.

BRUNDLEFLY

Chapter Two

Saturday, 3:07 am:

I WAS LYING in bed, and then I had a disturbing thought. I don't know why I didn't think about it before. Maybe I was in denial or something. It would make sense, though. I remember Kat was feeling the same way, after she was bitten. She kept complaining about itching. What if I'm infected with the virus? She scratched me pretty deep on my arm. She could have passed it on to me.

Oh, that would be so fitting. Here I am blaming myself for what happened to her and she already got revenge on me for it by passing it along to me. What am I saying? I'm being silly. I know she didn't infect me on purpose. She loved me... *LOVES* me, as much as I love her.

If I am infected, why haven't I changed, yet? It's been several hours, since I was scratched, unless it goes by the rate of infection. Hmm. I was scratched and she was bitten several times.

So, if I am infected, that means I probably don't have much time. I'd better take some precautions, just to be on the safe side. God, I hope I am wrong.

Saturday, 3:16 am:

Okay, here's the deal. The same virus that infected Dr. Fox and my beautiful Katherine might be flowing through my veins. I seriously hope not, but if that is the case, I owe it to the world to document how I feel throughout the process. Yeah, maybe it's a bit morbid, but I am a scientist and a hematologist. It's my duty.

I don't want to run around infecting other people, so I've barricaded the front door with the sofa. I wish I had a deadbolt, but I don't. I also locked myself in my bedroom. If I should happen to change, at least, I won't be able to hurt anyone from in here.

I'd like to state for the record, I am scared shitless. I don't want to be infected and I surely do not wish to die anytime soon. I need to live simply for one reason. I have to make sure Kat is cured. Well, I suppose I need to cure myself, too, if I am to cure her.

This is insane.

Saturday, 3:22 am:

I'm sorry. I thought about no longer writing in my journal, but I know this is something I have to do. If I should die, before I can be cured, this journal might help save lives.

If there are any doubts, as to a cure. I've already mentioned it previously. Dr. Fox said he had an anti-virus in a syringe. The idiot dropped it under one of the cots in the dorm of our underground lab at the Greene Science Center. You will need a special key for the elevator to access the fifth level. I have placed my key on the dresser in my bedroom.

There are about two infected homeless men still in the lab, so be cautious. You will also have to contend with Dr. Fox and whatever he has become in the dorm. If I didn't know any better, I'd say he was a zombie for the simple reason that I thought he was dead, but then he seemingly came back to life and tried to eat my girlfriend. If that doesn't make him a zombie, I don't know what does!

Try to disregard whatever you believe to be real or not and keep an open mind. When you see him, you will know what I mean.

As for me, I feel feverish and nauseous, again. I hope I don't throw up a second time. I really hate vomiting. My right arm has been itching a lot and aching, but now it is starting to feel numb. I can barely move my right hand. It's a good thing I am left-handed or I would not be able to document any of these sensations or experiences.

I believe I was infected when my girlfriend, Katherine, scratched me on the arm. It was deep enough to break through my skin and cause me to bleed. Come to think of it, there were also several instances when I came into contact with her blood, after she became infected. At the time, I had an open wound on my right hand. It was wrapped, but not thoroughly. Damn.

Hold on.

Saturday, 3:27 am:

Oh, man. I just threw up, again. I had to unlock the bedroom door fast. I made it to the bathroom, though. Still, it was pretty gross. Twice in one night is bad. This time, I believe there was blood in it. It was definitely mostly liquid. Okay, that's as much as I want to talk about vomit.

Of course, I locked myself back in my bedroom. I wish I felt brave enough to return to the lab. I'd find that anti-serum myself and finish off Dr. Fox for what he did. I'm not even sure if I have enough time. I will probably lose control of my faculties soon. I can't take any unnecessary chances.

While I was in the bathroom, I thought about when Kat threw up. It was only once and she changed very soon afterward. She became extremely aggressive and almost animalistic. It was as if she reverted to a savage state with only one instinct... to attack the uninfected. She chased me up the stairs and out onto the sidewalk, but was completely distracted when we passed Ivan. She attacked him and forgot all about me.

I wonder. That could be it. The bacteria in the virus are probably searching for new hosts to carry them, so they can feed on "fresh meat." I already know the bacteria had an insatiable hunger. We learned that much from the experiments at the lab. I fear this virus will continue to spread, as long as there are carriers out there.

My time might be running out faster than I thought.

Ugh! I just noticed the scratch on my arm smells putrid! Pus is starting to secrete through the open wound. My hand is black and blue, but there's no pus oozing from it.

I just had an amusing thought. I know it's not a time for amusement, but this is coincidental. I'm almost like Jeff Goldblum's character, Seth Brundle, in *The Fly* when he was changing into "Brundlefly" at the climax of the film.

Here's a fun fact for you. Flies are necrophageous. That means they feed on the flesh of the dead. Yes, just like zombies. Actually, many insects are necrophageous. Will I become necrophageous?

I won't lie. It's a pretty cool word. Necrophageous.

Honestly, I'm starting to feel hungry. The last thing I ate was that delicious pie at Kat's apartment. I miss her. Maybe I should have a snack. No, it's too late to eat.

That's funny. I'm trying to think healthy and here I am infected with a potentially deadly virus, which is oozing pus from my arm. A late night snack is the least of my worries.

I really miss Kat.

Saturday, 3:40 am:

I'm really hungry. I could go for a nice big steak, right about now.

I'd get up from the bed and go to the kitchen, but I don't think I can. I'm aching all over. I feel so weak and tired. To make matters worse, the entire right side of my body is feeling itchy. Why does this damn thing itch so much?

Saturday, 3:51 am:

I keep thinking about Kat. I keep seeing her face. I want to see her. I need to see her. I love her more than anything else in the world.

I'm so sorry, Kat. I failed you.

Food. I want food. Steak. Burgers. Roast beef. Chicken. I can taste it all! I want meat! I'm so hungry!

Can't feel my right arm. My right side hurts... and itches. I got a headache. Burning up with fever, too. My eyesight's getting blurry.

It's so quiet and peaceful here. Good place to die.

No, need to live. Need to cure Kat. Need to cure me.

Saturday, 4:02 am:

I am here. I am not.

Hungry!!!

My scalp feels itchy. My arm stinks. It's black. Rotten.

I feel so tired.
Have to stop writing... soon.
Must eat.
Ne-cro-pha-ge-ous.
Ha, ha!
KAT.
Here I comes!

Saturday, 4:08 am:
Hungry.
Hey, Jeff... I Brundlefly, too!
Kat... it hurts!
Who at door?

That was the final entry from the journal of David Frino.

THE MANHATTANVILLE INCIDENT:
PART FOUR

"Metropolis Of The Undead"

METROPOLIS OF THE UNDEAD

Chapter One

I T'S EARLY SATURDAY morning on the first morning of the Zombie Apocalypse. Less than twelve hours ago, a deadly virus was unleashed on the streets of Manhattan. Anyone, who becomes infected, changes into something violently different controlled by the instinct to feed and pass along the virus. As far as it is known, the virus can only be transmitted through bodily fluids. It takes full control of the body and eats away from the inside. When the body dies, it becomes reanimated turning the person into a zombie.

That might sound like the plot of a b-rated horror movie, but it is all too real. Although, some people still have not accepted that truth, while others have no idea the terror that awaits them. The future of mankind is at stake, as the virus continues to spread like wildfire.

In a futile attempt to contain it, the city government has placed the island of Manhattan under full quarantine. All bridges and tunnel crossings have been destroyed. The National Guard has been brought in and now patrols the rivers. The airspace over the city has been turned into a no-fly zone. It seems all hope is lost.

Or is it?

Not long ago, a police car from the 26th Precinct jumped from Manhattan over the newly created chasm of the Henry Hudson Bridge, landing across the river on the lower level of the southbound side. When the car landed, it crashed and came to a stop. At that moment, it appeared all occupants were dead. However, they were not.

Sergeant Gregg Kepster woke up in the backseat from an intense pain in his legs. Both had been crushed against the lower part of the cage behind the front seats of the patrol car.

"Oh, man... Jesus Christ! What the hell is wrong with you, Ricky?" He winced and cried out, "Holy shit! My legs! You crushed my legs!" He stared down at his legs, which felt wet and warm. He knew it had to be blood, but he could not see under his pants. "Oh, man, oh, man, oh, man," he whimpered from the pain. "Guys! Wake the hell up! You need to get me out of here! Jesus! My legs!"

Gregg began to worry that he would die, before Ricky and Steve awoke. He became frustrated and wondered why he ever went along with Ricky's foolhardy plan to jump over the chasm. He could have found another way to escape Manhattan. Either that or he could have just swallowed his pride and reported to the location he was ordered to go to by the 34th Precinct lieutenant. It was too late to think about that now. Regrets would only slow him down.

He cried from the pain, which was becoming unbearable. He almost would have preferred to be paralyzed. At least, then he wouldn't feel as though a tank were driving over his legs. It was a burning pulsating pain. He could feel the bones jabbing through his skin. If he could will himself to die, he'd do it, just to no longer feel the pain.

After several minutes, Ricky began to stir in the seat in front of him. He moaned quietly and moved his head off the steering wheel and away from the deflated airbag. He leaned his head back against his chair's headrest and grunted.

Gregg called out, "Ricky! You gotta get me out of here! My legs are crushed!"

Ricky turned back instantly and made eye contact with Gregg, except his eyes were different. They were filled with pus and seemed empty. Ricky's mouth opened and he made biting motions, as he tried to move toward the cage that divided the front and rear seats. He wanted to bite Gregg, but there was no way he'd be able to reach him.

"Oh, no," Gregg uttered in horror.

Suddenly, Steve began to move in the front passenger seat. Gregg couldn't help wonder, was he going to be like Ricky? He fought the urge to call out to him. He didn't need both of them staring at him hungrily. Instead, he waited and watched.

Steve groaned and shifted in his seat.

Ricky immediately turned to him. He opened his mouth and tried to lean in Steve's direction. His seatbelt and proximity to the steering wheel, which had been pushed inward against his chest, prevented him from moving his body to the right toward Steve.

Gregg wasn't sure if Steve was infected, but if he wasn't, he was in serious danger. He began yelling, "Steve! Wake up! Snap out of it! Ricky is trying to bite you!"

Steve groaned, again, and began moving his head around. He opened his eyes and turned to his left. His eyes shot wide open when he saw Ricky reaching for him. He moved as far to the right as he could, pressing up against his door. His eyes filled with tears, as he watched his friend's empty expression.

"No, Ricky. Oh, no," he mumbled, as a tear rolled down his cheek. This was not the first friend of his he lost because of that damned virus. It was too much death for one day. No more, he thought. Please, no more.

"Steve!" Gregg called out from behind.

Ricky turned his attention back to Gregg, but since the cage separated them, he turned back to Steve and tried to stretch, as far as he could to the right.

Steve responded, "Yeah, yeah. I hear you. I'm sort of busy. Give me a minute." He knew he had to get the hell out of the car. When he tried to open his door, it would not budge. He looked to his right and noticed it was jammed against the wall. He sighed, "Oh, you've got to be kidding."

He would not be getting out that way.

Gregg suggested, "Go through the windshield! It's your only chance! And please, hurry! My legs are killing me!"

Steve examined the windshield and knew Gregg was right. That was his only way out. He reached over and unhooked his seatbelt. As soon as he did, he felt a sharp pain stab him in his side. He cried out,

"Ow! Shit! I think I broke a rib. I hope it's only one." He grimaced from the pain and tried to move more carefully.

Gregg complained from behind, "If you only broke a rib, you're freaking lucky! My legs are both crushed back here!"

Steve froze and thought about what Gregg said. Even if he got out and was able to get Gregg out, how the hell was he supposed to carry him around with a messed up rib? He breathed deeply and tried not to think about it. Now was not the time. Instead, he focused on the windshield... one problem at a time, he told himself. He kept an eye on Ricky, as he tried to push out the windshield and tried to stay out of his reach.

After several weak attempts, he finally managed to push out the windshield. It fell flat on the hood of the car. Now, came the hard part, climbing out without agitating his broken rib. He took a deep breath and focused his mind, which was not easy to do with Ricky trying to bite his left arm every few seconds.

"Ugh! Damn it!" He fell back in his seat and tried to fight the pain. It was no use. He needed more space to move. He looked at Ricky, who was leaning toward him and making biting motions. There was a certain amount of desperation in his eyes that Steve did not notice before.

Gregg moaned in the backseat, "Please, Steve... hurry up. My legs..." He broke off into tears. The agony was torturing him.

Steve knew what he had to do, although he did not wish to do it. He unsnapped his holster and pulled out his 9mm handgun. He aimed it at Ricky's head from a safe distance and said, "I'm sorry, kid. Rest in peace."

BANG!

Gregg cried out, "Jesus Christ! Give me a warning, next time! That shit was loud!"

Steve ignored him. He stared at Ricky's lifeless body and watched as the blood gushed out of his head and down his face. He forced himself to turn away and climbed out of his seat and through the front window. The pain in his side poked at him, but he ignored that, too. The pain he was feeling in his heart was much stronger. He crawled over the windshield and was grateful that he was still wearing his gloves.

When he got off the hood of the car, he stood up and leaned against the car momentarily. The pain in his side was hard to deal with, but it couldn't be worse than what Gregg was feeling.

He walked over and tried to open the back door. It was stuck. Of course, it was, he thought. Why would any of this be easy for him? He could see Gregg growing weaker by the minute. For a moment, he considered leaving him.

Gregg looked at him from within and pulled out his own weapon. He pressed it against the glass, as if he were going to shoot it. Steve quickly moved out of the way. Once he did, Gregg pulled his arm back and slammed against the window with his gun shattering it.

"Get-me-the-hell-out-of-this-damned-car!"

Steve approached the door and looked inside at Gregg's legs. It did not look good. There was no way Gregg would be able to walk and he could not carry him with a broken rib. He tried to think of what he could do, but he did not know. He felt helpless.

"Damn it, Steve! What are you waiting for?"

Steve shook his head and took a step back, as he replied grimly, "I'm sorry. I can't do it. Even if I can get you out, you can't walk and there's no way I can carry you. What do you expect to do... crawl behind me? Let me go for help. I'll come back for you."

Gregg was angry, at first. He glared at Steve, but then he realized he was right. He had not thought about what would happen, after he got out of the car. He just wanted the pain to stop. It was more than he could bear. He wasn't sure if he could wait for Steve to return. Besides, who was going to help two people that just escaped the Infected Zone and carried the virus over into the Safe Zone?

No one. They would be lucky if they were not shot on sight.

"No, Steve," he finally said. "You get out of here. Go to your family and get to safety." He winced from the pain and ordered, "Leave me here. Just go, before someone finds us."

Steve looked confused. He asked, "What about you? I can't just leave you..."

Gregg interrupted him and stated firmly, "Get away from here, before someone finds you. That's a direct order. I will take care of me."

Steve was about to say something else, but then he realized what Gregg meant. He also knew Gregg was right. He could not linger around too much longer. If someone saw the car jumping, they'd come soon. If they saw him, he'd be shot for sure and these sacrifices would have been for nothing.

"Go!" Gregg ordered, again.

Steve nodded and turned his back on Gregg. He began walking north along the parkway and paused only when he heard the sound of the gunshot behind him. A moment later, he passed out.

When Steve awoke, he felt the sun beating down on him. He covered his face with his hands and rubbed his eyes. He looked around him and realized he was lying on the Henry Hudson Parkway. He felt weak, tired, and hungry. He wondered how long he had been unconscious. Based on the position of the sun, he figured it had to be around noon. He stood up slowly and felt dizzy. His uniform stunk, too. Once he pulled himself together, he began walking north. It hurt to walk because of his rib, but he pushed on.

Eventually, he walked off the parkway and made his way through deserted streets. He had finally made it to the Bronx, but at what cost? Ricky and Gregg were both dead and he was alone, or was he?

He pulled out his cellphone, which only had about twenty-five percent charge on it. He noticed he had several missed calls from his supervisor, Charles, his wife, and his sister. He didn't know what to say to his wife or sister, yet. He figured calling Charles would provide him with an update on the situation going on around him, so he decided that was the most important call to make, if he had to choose. Besides, he did not have enough power to call his family. They would definitely keep him on the line, until his phone died and he really needed to know what he should do next. He felt so lost. The last he heard, Charles and his group were going to attempt leaving Manhattan through some old abandoned tunnel. If that crazy plan worked, then surely they'd be in the Bronx, by now.

The phone rang and Charles answered, "Steve?"

"Hey, Sarge," he said wearily, as he walked. "Where are you guys?"

"Sweet Christmas! I can't believe it! I thought you were dead! It's great to hear from you! We made it out! The tunnel led us right into the Bronx!" Suddenly, his tone changed and he sounded morose when he added, "Unfortunately, they blew up the bridge and we lost a few in the fall, but yeah, we made it."

Steve replied unenthusiastically, "That's great. We, uh, tried something crazy, too. Ricky jumped the gap left behind when the Henry

Hudson Bridge was blown up. It didn't work out too well, although we did make it across." He hesitated, and then continued, "He's dead. It's just me."

Charles was quiet, for a moment. He exhaled and said, "I'm sorry to hear that. He was a brave man to try that jump."

"Yeah, brave and crazy as shit. He was also infected."

"What? You're kidding?"

"No. Louie scratched him when he was trapped under the ambulance. Louie's hands were covered in blood, so I guess some of the blood got into Ricky's skin. He was hiding it from me all night. He only came clean before we made the jump."

"Wow," Charles exclaimed in disbelief. "That is something. All night? He took a big chance keeping that information from you. Hey, wait a minute. Whatever happened to the SRG guys you picked up on 125th Street?"

Steve explained, "One was infected, so we dropped him off at Columbia Presbyterian Medical Center. Sergeant Kepster wanted to leave his other guy behind to guard him. That was the last time we saw those guys. The sergeant, Gregg, made the jump with us. He... didn't make it either." Steve decided to leave out the part about how he shot himself.

"That's a shame," Charles said.

They both remained silent, until Steve said, "Well, my cellphone is going to die soon, so I guess I'd better hang up. For what it's worth, I'm glad you guys made it out, too."

Charles said, "Steve, why don't you meet up with us? We are somewhere safe and probably not far from you."

"Yeah? Where?"

"The Kingsbridge Armory near Jerome Avenue. It's pretty secure. There's a bunch of us here. We're staying here, until we can figure out our next move. You're more than welcome to join us. You shouldn't be out there alone."

"What about the job?" Steve asked.

Charles scoffed, "Screw the job! They abandoned us! As far as I'm concerned, we're on our own, from now on."

Steve replied with a smile, "I like the sound of that. Count me in. I'm at..." He looked up at the nearest street sign, "Kappock Street."

Charles responded, "Kappock? Hold on a sec." He spoke to someone at the other end, where he was at and returned, "Okay, I'm going to put someone on the phone that can give you directions from there. I'll see you soon."

Steve spoke to someone named Frank, who gave him directions on how to get to the armory on foot. It didn't sound too difficult, but that was before Steve realized the mayhem that was just beginning in the Bronx.

By the next morning, the incident that began in Manhattan was all over the news. People were in an uproar about Manhattan being placed under quarantine. The destruction of the river crossings pushed the already agitated people over the edge. Many had families in Manhattan. Some had homes there and were now cut off from it indefinitely. The rash actions led to protests, which were spawning riots in several areas. The police were severely undermanned and were having a difficult time dealing with it. The National Guard had to assist, wherever possible. They focused on the area of the river crossings, since they were already posted there, before the destruction of the bridges.

To make matters worse, there were reports of potential infection outbreaks in approximately three different areas of the Bronx. Was it possible that some people, who were infected, managed to get out of the city prior to the closing of the river crossings?

Absolutely.

When Steve reached West 230th Street he continued straight toward Broadway. There were no cars driving on the road, which he found odd. As he grew closer to Broadway, he began to hear what sounded like a large crowd. He slowed down and approached with caution. He was way too tired to deal with a crowd and hoped it was nothing he would have to worry about. The closer he got to Broadway, the more careful he became. He used parked cars to conceal himself, so no one would notice him. He didn't know what to expect, but he was ready for the worst-case scenario.

From Broadway, he could see there was a mob at West 225th Street, right at the entrance to where the bridge into Manhattan used to be. Large shipping containers were brought in to block the road that led up to the bridge, which had been destroyed and turned into a pile of bent steel rubble.

Steve froze stiff at the sight of the crowd. Immediately, he assumed they were infected and got flashbacks of West 125th Street. He pictured people running and falling, twisting in pain, and getting shot by police. He saw his friend, Kahn's face, as he was forced to put a bullet into his head, after Kahn had become infected at the scene of that riot.

He closed his eyes and shook away the bad memories. When he opened them, he studied the scene at West 225th Street and Broadway more carefully. Those were not infected people. They were shouting something at the police and National Guard, who blocked the former bridge. It sounded like, "Manhattan is not a prison! Let our people go!" The chant was being repeated over and over.

Steve thought it was best for him to avoid the crowd. He moved quickly across Broadway, which brought great pain to his broken rib. He had to stop briefly for a rest. When he was ready, he moved on. West 230th Street became Exterior Street on the east side of Broadway. Steve walked slowly along that street, which eventually met up with West 225th Street, just west of the Major Deegan Expressway.

The northbound lanes of the expressway were backed up with traffic. It seemed people were trying to put some distance between them and the city.

After the expressway, West 225th Street became Kingsbridge Avenue. Steve noticed a few cars that were on fire along Bailey Avenue, which crossed Kingsbridge going both north and south. He wondered if the protestors caused the fires.

"Freaking savages," he grumbled under his breath.

It wasn't too much further, until he reached the armory. All he had to do was hike up the hill several blocks. Piece of cake, he thought, under normal circumstances.

What he really wanted to do was change out of his smelly uniform already. His t-shirt under his bulletproof vest was soaked in sweat and sticking to his chest like a second skin. Besides, he did not want anyone to know he was a cop, especially not while the people were protesting. He stayed on the north side of Kingsbridge, as he walked east, ducking behind parked cars along the way. There were a few people running downhill on the south side, which he tried to avoid. He wasn't sure why they were running, but he wanted no part of it. He was done playing cop for a city that did not appreciate its police force.

The walk uphill was hard, but Steve made it. As he approached University Avenue, he noticed there were more people outside. They were not protesting, but they were breaking into shops and looting. That was even worse, he thought. He really had to ditch his uniform and fast.

One grocery store owner ran up to him and begged, "Please, officer! Do something! They're taking everything from my business!"

Steve felt bad. He wanted to help, but he knew if he did, he'd be completely on his own. There would be no backup. He also needed to keep in mind that he was limited in ammunition. He had already shot most of the rounds in his gun's magazine during the earlier riot on West 125th Street and in the Housing projects. He still had two full clips on his belt, but whatever was in his gun would run out very fast. There had to be about one or two rounds left, at the most.

The grocery store owner pleaded, once more, "Please, officer! Don't just stand there! Do your job!"

Fine.

Steve went into the shop and saw two looters inside. They were teenagers. He shouted, "Hey, get the hell out of here!"

They stopped and watched him nervously, expecting him to arrest them. When they realized he was alone, they figured he was no threat and continued putting items into duffle bags, which hung from their shoulders.

He was afraid that would happen. He pulled out his weapon and fired one shot across the room shattering a glass refrigerator door.

The teenagers stopped at the sound of the gunshot. A bottle of soda spilled onto the floor beside their feet. They looked at Steve, again, who was still pointing his weapon in their direction.

He warned, "The next shot goes into your damned head. Don't test me."

They turned to leave the store, but he stood in the way of the entrance and instructed, "Drop. The. Bags!" His gun was pointed at one teenager's head.

The bags fell to the floor and the teenagers put their hands up.

Steve stepped aside and said, "Get the hell out of here."

They looked at each other and ran out the door without saying a word. The grocery store owner came back into the store and saw the bags on the floor. He looked so relieved and said, "Thank you so much, officer! Please, stay, if you can."

Steve responded, "Sorry, I need to be somewhere." He thought, for a second, and suggested, "You should come with me. I'm heading to the armory."

The grocery store owner replied, "The armory is locked up tight. No one is getting in there. I'm locking up, closing the gate, and going home."

Before leaving, Steve asked, "Hey, I don't suppose you have a jacket I can use?"

"I may have one in the back. Let me check." He went into a back door and returned carrying a white butcher's coat. He held it up and said, "This is all I have, but you can have it. Take anything you need. I owe you."

Steve grabbed the jacket and stared at it. It would have to do. He put it on and said, "Thank you. I don't want to take advantage of you, but I could use some painkillers and a bottle of water. I might have a broken rib."

The grocery store owner handed him a bag filled with several types of painkillers and offered, "Take it. Please. The water is over there in the fridge." He pointed toward the refrigerators lined up against the wall.

Steve grabbed a bottle of water and said, "Sorry about your refrigerator door."

The grocery store owner replied, "It's a small price to pay to make up for what they tried taking from me. Thanks, again. Are you sure you don't want anything else?"

Steve was really hungry, but what he wanted would take way too long to make. He opted for a pack of Hostess coconut-flavored donuts. "I'll just take this. Thank you."

"No, thank you! Be careful out there!"

"I will."

Steve waited for him to close up his shop and pull down the gate, before continuing toward the armory. While he waited, he took two pills and washed them down with a sip of water. He then gulped down the donuts, as if he hadn't eaten in days. He drank some more water and placed the bottle into his coat pocket. He'd save the rest for later. It was only two more blocks to the armory.

When Steve finally saw the armory, he noticed there was a chain link fence that appeared to go all the way around it. It was about ten feet tall. He wondered how he was supposed to get inside without breaking his neck. He pulled out his cellphone and called Charles. He asked which way he should enter. Charles told him to climb over the fence and he'd open up the main entrance doors on the Kingsbridge side of the building between the two towers.

"Climb over the fence? Oh, boy," he complained. That's what he was afraid he'd say. He knew that was going to be a challenge with his broken rib. Who was he kidding? It would be a challenge without a broken rib. He was no spring chicken. Climbing over fences was something he had not done in a very long time.

He crossed the street and walked toward the brick armory building. It was huge and took up an entire city block. The two towers had cone-shaped pointed roofs and were roughly nine stories in height. They were positioned close together on either side of the main entrance, which faced Kingsbridge Avenue on the south side of the castle-like building.

Steve noticed the pipe holding the fence up was bent near one of the gates at the west side in front of the large hangar-like portion of the building. That would be the easiest spot for him to climb, he thought. He went over the fence and lost his footing. He fell to the other side and rolled on the floor in pain, as he held his ribs.

"Shit! Just what I needed," he cried out. He remained lying there for a while, until he was ready to stand. He got up slowly and picked up his bottle of water, which had fallen out of his pocket and rolled toward the fence.

People hurried up and down Kingsbridge Avenue in a hurry to get somewhere. Every once in a while, a car would race by. Hardly any of them bothered to stop for the red lights. No one seemed to care that he was walking on the inside of the fence at the closed armory. Either that or no one noticed.

When he reached the large black iron doors between the towers, he walked up the steps and shook them hard causing them to rattle. Charles appeared from within with a young Puerto Rican man dressed in a security uniform.

Charles greeted him, "Welcome to our castle, Steve. This is Frank. He works here. You spoke on the phone earlier."

Steve nodded at Frank, who did the same back at him.

One of the heavy iron doors was opened wide and Steve entered. Frank immediately closed the door, once he was inside.

The iron doors of the Kingsbridge Armory.

METROPOLIS OF THE UNDEAD

Chapter Two

C HARLES WELCOMED STEVE into the Kingsbridge Armory. He led him past the multi-arched entrance lobby, through a set of half-wood, half-glass, double doors, and into an empty hangar, the size of a football field. The vast rectangular room was only lit by the natural lighting that came in from the many windows at the far ends and over the second floor mezzanine, which looked down on the first level.

The others were waiting in this larger room and watching him, as he entered.

A group of teenage girls sat in a circle at the center of the room near four other people, who were asleep on the floor over a large tarp that had been stretched out across the center of the room like a rug. The four that slept were lying on blankets. Not far away, Steve saw an attractive young woman dressed with a black t-shirt, blue jeans, and long black leather boots. She was holding a Colt M4 Carbine, the same type the

Emergency Service Unit carried. On the other side of the hangar was Grant, Charles' driver.

He was walking toward Steve with a smile on his face. He immediately noticed Steve's attire and asked, "What's with the smock, Steve? You look like a dentist or a veterinarian."

Steve replied dryly, "Butcher, actually. Wait. Why not a doctor?"

Grant shrugged at him and scoffed.

Steve sneered, "Dick."

Grant chuckled, reached over, and patted him on the back warmly. He said, "It's damn good to have you with us. I'm really glad you made it out. For a while, we thought you were dead. You didn't answer when Charles called you yesterday morning."

Steve forced a smile and said, "Thanks. I thought I was dead, too..." His voice trailed off abruptly and he stared at Grant in confusion, as he asked, "Wait! Did you say *yesterday?*"

"Yeah. Today is Sunday. Charles called you yesterday morning, after we got out of the aqueduct tunnels, but you didn't answer."

"Holy shit," Steve exclaimed in shock. "I lost a whole day. I thought today was still Saturday."

Grant didn't know what to say. He asked, "Were you unconscious or something?"

Steve nodded, "Yeah. Twice. Once after the crash, and then, again, when I got out of the car."

Grant frowned, "You may have a concussion. You should let Aramis check you out. I'll wake him up. He's asleep over there on the floor. Hey, Steve?"

"Yeah?"

"For what it's worth, I'm really sorry about Ricky, and Pat. They were good guys. Shit," he shook his head. "We've lost so many good people," he frowned. "Debbie was shot right in front of our faces. Those motherfu..." He stopped himself. "They blew up the bridge, while we were crossing it! Winston Fong and a civilian girl were killed. They were so close to escaping."

Nearby, Marc Nugent woke up feeling exhausted from his short rest. He was wondering whom Grant was talking to about the bridge. He didn't want to be reminded of it. When he saw Steve standing there, he sat up fast. He could not believe his eyes.

Steve frowned at Grant and stated, "Yep. It sucks. I can't believe they were shooting at us, while we are in uniform. Actually, I do believe it. God, I hate this job."

"We're done with it. We're not going back."

Steve shook his head and responded, "Neither am I. Ricky and I... we decided we were leaving the moment they shot at us. Well, it might have been a bit before that."

Grant walked over to Aramis and nudged him. "Hey, Aramis, wake up, pal. We need your medical expertise."

"Huh? What?" He turned and looked up at Grant through half-closed eyes. "Oh, yeah. Sure thing. Give me a minute," he said. Grant felt bad waking him up because he had one of the later guard shifts and had not slept enough, yet.

"Steven!" Marc shouted, as he stood up and approached Steve. "Wow! As I live and breathe. I can't believe you're standing here!"

Steve was surprised to see Marc. He looked at him and scowled, "What on Earth are you still doing around? You're more resilient than a cockroach."

Marc smiled proudly, "Yeah, well..."

Charles walked over to them and said, "Grant, did you tell Steve about Dave?"

"No, not yet."

Steve asked, "Do you mean Castillo? What about him? Is he…?"

Charles grinned, "He's at The Intrepid. He's got a whole group with him."

Steve scoffed, "The Intrepid? Is he planning to ride that thing out on the river?"

Charles shrugged, "Who knows? He's been playing it by ear. We've been staying in touch. Grant has one of those universal cellphone chargers in his bag, so some of us have been able to charge up our phones in here. The power is on, but we are keeping the main lights off at night. We don't want to be noticed by anyone outside. We only use the lights in the restrooms. No windows."

Steve turned to Grant and asked hesitantly, "I don't suppose that charger of yours will charge up an iphone?"

Grant shook his head, "Sorry, we already tried. Roberto over there on the floor has one." He pointed to a sleeping male in his twenties. "He's still asleep. Don't worry. You can use my phone, if you need to.

Just add your important contacts into my phone, so you will have the numbers you need. Here."

He handed Steve his cellphone and Steve took it.

"Thanks."

"No problem, pal. Let me know when you're done. I'll introduce you to everyone."

Aramis walked over and immediately recognized Steve. He said, "Hey! You made it out! Good shit! It's just you?" He asked, while looking around.

"Yeah, just me. The others didn't make it."

"Dude, that really blows. I'm so sorry, man. Hey, let me check you out. So, what's wrong?"

Steve explained his injuries to Aramis and gave him the bag of painkillers the grocery store owner gave him. Aramis took the bag and did the best he could with the equipment he had available. He wrapped up Steve's chest with gauze and told him to make sure to get a lot of rest.

Marc stood nearby and stared at Steve in disbelief. He was glad to see someone else made it out. He liked Steve as a person. Despite how much grief they gave each other. It was good to see him alive and well. Seeing him actually allowed him to temporarily forget his grief.

Meanwhile, Frank spoke to Charles nearby. He asked, "Sarge, how long do you think we'll be safe down here? We don't have enough provisions for everyone. We're going to need food and water soon."

Charles agreed, "Yeah, I've been thinking about that. I might be making a supply run today. I'm going to talk to everyone, once everyone is up. We'll decide on a plan of action together as a group." A moment later, his phone rang and he said, "Excuse me. I've got to take this call." It was his friend, Carmen, at MetroTech Center.

Frank nodded and walked away toward the entrance lobby. He preferred to keep an eye on it and he wanted to keep an ear out, in case anyone from the outside tried to get in. What he did not realize is that someone else was already in the building with them. Within the shadows, an unknown figure lingered close by.

Sometime later, after everyone was awake, Charles called a group meeting at the camp, which was situated at the center of the hangar.

Everyone gathered around him curiously and waited to hear what he had to say.

"Okay, thank you for your attention. For those that haven't already noticed, one of my officers from Manhattan was able to escape and has now joined our group. His name is Steve Blake. We can go through introductions in a minute. I think it will be good for us to do it together, so we can learn a little about each other. If we are going to stick together, we shouldn't be strangers.

First, I need to update everyone on what's going on. A few of you were awake last night, while I read from the journal that we recovered at 244 Riverside Drive. Based on David Frino's accounts of what happened at the lab on Friday, we learned there is a possible cure for this virus. Well, I just spoke to my contact in Brooklyn and she was very curious about the details of that information. I have a feeling the government is planning to send someone to retrieve that anti-serum. If they are successful, this nightmare could come to an end, so I gave her whatever details could be useful."

A few people in the room began mumbling amongst themselves.

Charles continued, "However, until that day comes, we are knee deep in shit, so to speak. It seems Manhattan is not the only place the virus has affected. LaGuardia Airport has been in lockdown, since yesterday. It has been confirmed that one person carrying the virus took a flight to Ohio and a similar outbreak has occurred there. At the moment, they believe it is contained to one region, but that's what we thought the other night on 125th Street."

Roberto groaned, "Oh, man! That's crazy! This thing already spread to Ohio?"

Charles nodded, "That's what I've been told and that's not all. Here's the real kicker. There have been three incidents right here in the Bronx, which they believe might be related. The details are still sketchy."

Marc commented, "Oh, no way! Give me a freaking break!"

Grant asked, "Did she say where in the Bronx?"

Charles said, "She didn't know enough, yet. She's going to call me back when she learns more. I didn't tell her where we are, for our own safety. I don't want *anyone* knowing we are here, which brings me to my next issue. We can probably hide out here for a few days, but we are going to need supplies. Before we risk our asses trying to get some, there's something I need to know. Do we want to stay here?"

Grant nodded, "I think it's a good spot. At least, until we figure out our next move like we originally planned when we first came here."

Roberto said, "This place is safe enough for us to stay here for weeks. There's an underground bunker. Right, Frank? Tell them."

Frank nodded, "Yeah, it's fairly safe. The whole place is fenced up. All doors are locked. Nobody is going to come in here, unless I open the door. The bunker down below can hold us comfortably for quite some time. Like the Sarge said, we're just gonna need some supplies."

Liz asked, "What about our families? Can we contact them and let them know where we are? My cellphone died last night and I have not spoken to my parents since Friday. They live in Yonkers."

Steve said, "I really need to call my wife and sister, too. They must be worried about me."

Charles responded, "Call your families and let them know you are safe, but please, do not tell them where we are hiding. If they let it slip out to the wrong person, we could have unwanted problems. Keep in mind that we are trespassing and a few of us are AWOL in a time of extreme emergency, not to mention most of us are not even supposed to be in the Bronx. We were under quarantine. If the wrong person learns we are here, this little survival camp is going to come to a fast end."

Grant said, "I think we are all in agreement that staying here is in our best interests, for now. If you guys need to charge your phones, you can try my charger or use my phone." He specifically looked at Steve and Liz when he said that.

Steve nodded at him.

Liz moved close to him and whispered, "Thank you."

Roberto's sister, Nikki, asked, "So, if we are staying here, does that mean we are limited to this floor or can we explore the rest of the building?"

Charles answered, "Let's stick to this room and the restrooms, until those of us with guns have had a chance to fully search the building. I don't want anyone getting hurt or running into trouble. We didn't really check this building yesterday the way I wanted to do. I'd like to do that this afternoon, and then go out for supplies later. First, let's take care of the introductions."

They were completely unaware of someone, who was secretly watching from the upper level mezzanine. As far as they knew, they were the only ones in the armory. So, exactly who was this mysterious person spying on them?

The group was gathered in the armory's hangar. Since there was a new addition to the group, Charles thought it would be a good time for them to introduce themselves. Besides, his initial group from Manhattan had not been properly introduced to the people that were already hiding out in the armory when they arrived the day before and he wanted to know who was sharing his shelter with him.

He began, "We'll keep this brief and to the point. I'll start off. My name is Charles Foster. I was born and raised in Brooklyn. I'm not married. I don't have any kids. I am... *was* a sergeant for the NYPD. Some of you call me 'Sarge' out of habit or respect, but I no longer want to acknowledge that title. Maybe you still look to me as a leader because I wear these stripes. Well, we are in a whole new reality than the one we knew yesterday. I'm only taking this one step at a time. I don't really have a long-term plan anymore. The job that I dedicated myself to for eighteen years abandoned us and left us to die. My main goal now is our survival. The way I see it, we are on our own. Our best option is to stick together. I can promise you this much. If you stick with me, I will do whatever I can to keep you alive. I have ten years of military experience to back up my promise. Any questions?"

Roberto spoke up, "Yeah, just one. If you don't want us to call you Sarge, does that mean we can call you Charles?"

"Yes, please do," Charles nodded. "So, who wants to go next?"

The room fell silent, so Grant answered, "I guess I will. My name is Grant Hamilton. I grew up in the Bronx, but spent a lot of time on Long Island and in Westchester County. I've been a cop for the past seventeen years. I enjoy history, urban exploring, and photography. I am also unmarried with no children. I live in Yonkers, but I also have a family home out on the island near Riverhead."

Liz asked, "Aren't you going to mention your historical family ties?"

"Most of you already knew. It didn't seem worth mentioning, again, but I guess now that you called me out, I should."

She smirked, "Sorry."

"It's fine," he smiled at her. "I'm descended from Alexander Hamilton, one of the founding fathers of the country."

Roberto replied, "No shit? That's pretty cool, bro. You should be proud of that. I'd be telling everyone, if it were me." He chuckled.

Grant smiled bashfully, "You'd think differently if you grew up with it. My teachers in school loved me for it. My friends thought I was lucky. A few kids made fun of me, but it was nothing that really bothered me. As I got older, I came to realize how ignorant people in this country could be. It amazed me how many people had no idea who Alexander Hamilton was, or who the founding fathers were. One person even accused me of lying because he believed Alexander Hamilton was a made up character from that Broadway show."

Roberto shook his head in disbelief and responded, "There are way too many ignorant people in this country that don't know their history. It's a shame. I love American history."

Julia said, "I think it's awesome that your family has significant ties to the birth of our country."

"Thanks, guys. I appreciate it," he smiled. "Well, I'm done, if anyone is ready to go next."

Roberto said, "What the hell? I'll go next. My name is Roberto Christopher Medina. I was born here, in the Bronx, and I've lived here all my life. I love my family, love my city, and love my country. This is my younger sister, Nicole," he pointed to a pretty teenage girl, who sat next to him. "And that's my cousin, Giselle," he pointed to the girl on the other side of his sister. "That's pretty much all there is to tell."

"Hi, uh, you guys can call me Nikki," his sister corrected. "I'm seventeen years old. I... I just want everything to go back to normal soon. My mother is still out there and I'm very worried about her."

Roberto put his arm around her and said to her in a comforting voice, "She's a tough woman. I'm sure she's fine. She's probably home worrying about us."

Giselle spoke next, "I guess that means it's my turn, *if* we are going clockwise?"

Charles replied, "The floor is yours."

"As my cousin said, my name is Giselle... uh, Gonzalez. Some people call me GG. I'm eighteen. I was visiting my cousins and my aunt for the weekend. I hope this nightmare ends soon, too, because I need to get back to my grandmother."

Another teenage girl sat to the left of Giselle. She was a pretty African-American girl with long straight hair. She looked at Giselle, who appeared to be finished, and then she began, "Hi, guys. I'm Zonnie. These are my friends," she gestured to Giselle, Nikki, and Roberto. "I'm seventeen, as well. I was actually thinking about becoming a police officer. Right now, I just want to go home." She began crying, but still spoke. "When Frank let us in here yesterday morning, I didn't realize it was going to be an over night stay. I figured we would only be here a few hours... and the police would settle the situation outside. I've been checking the Internet and things don't seem to be getting any better. My parents have been blowing up my phone because they are worried sick! Now, my battery is dead and I'm starting to realize the severity of our situation. I'm sick of wearing the same clothes! I mean, come on! How long do we need to be here?" She bowed her head and wiped her cheeks dry.

Charles answered, "That remains to be seen, Zonnie. I wish I had something reassuring to tell you, but I don't. It's not safe out there. People are rioting and looting. There's no telling what could happen to you, if you went out there. We need to play this safe. Believe me, I'd like nothing more than to tell you things will be back to normal soon. The sad fact is, I don't think things will ever go back to how they were, at least, not for a long time. The virus is spreading fast and it's already in the Bronx. We know that much. It probably won't be long before those rioters and looters outside are replaced with infected people. When that happens, it's only going to get worse. Either way, it's dangerous out there.

As I stated earlier, I plan to go out soon for supplies. When I do, I will try to find cellphone chargers, especially for an iphone. I know some of you need that kind. If your phone is an android, Grant does have one in his bag. Just let him know and he will let you use it."

She nodded sorrowfully with a look of worry on her face.

Julia sat next to her, so she spoke next. "Hello. My name is Julia Duncan," she said. "I was a student at City College majoring in computer science, before this crazy weekend changed that. I like painting and reading comic books. My parents think I spend too much time on social media, but my biggest passion is urban exploring."

She glanced at Grant, who shared the same passion, and they both smiled at each other.

Liz was next. She adjusted the Colt M4 Carbine on her shoulder and began, "My name is Liz, but I will also respond to Beth. Please, do *not* call me Elizabeth. I like dancing. I'm pretty good at it. Not that it matters much anymore. I live in Yonkers with my parents. I didn't go to college, but I served two years in the United States Marines Corps. I can shoot an apple off your head with this carbine from fifty yards away."

Grant smiled in admiration and commented, "Sweet."

"That's hot!" Aramis chuckled. He introduced himself next, "My name is Aramis Perez. I was also in the military. Marines, like you," he gestured to Liz. "Served four years."

"Semper Fi," she nodded at him.

"Semper Fi," he replied with a proud grin. "I've been working as an EMT for FDNY for about four years. On my days off, I play bass guitar in a heavy metal band called The Terror. I love watching wrestling. I wanted to be a wrestler, while growing up. Obviously, that didn't work out. I worked and lived in Manhattan for the past few years, so now I'm pretty much screwed." He grinned, but then his grin faded away and he continued, "My partner... she was killed by an infected police officer that we transported to the hospital. I still haven't really come to terms with that. She was a great person. It doesn't seem real to me." He paused to wipe his eyes, which were starting to fill with tears. He sighed and continued, "About an hour later, she... she came back to life," he half-chuckled and shook his head. "It's so crazy, man. The sergeant, Charles, had to put her down. We left her in the back of my ambulance. I can't help thinking that maybe she, somehow, came back to life, again. I'm sorry, guys. This is harder than I thought."

He stood up and walked away.

Grant called after him, "Take all the time you need, brother."

Frank stepped closer and said, "That might be a hard act to follow, but I'll try. I'm Frank. I work security here. I was here when this craziness began on Friday night. I listened to the news all night. When the bridges were blown up the next morning, that's when the shit really hit the fan here in the Bronx. The explosions shattered windows and created a panic. People demanded to know what was going on in Manhattan. They knew the news was holding back information. Either that or they didn't have the whole story. I knew things were going to go from bad to worse, so I told my buddy, Rob, he should come by for a while. You know? Just to play it safe. He only lived a couple of blocks away. I never thought we'd be spending the whole weekend here, although it seemed like the smartest idea, at the time."

Charles looked at Roberto and asked, "So, you guys know each other?"

Both nodded and replied, "Yes," at the same time.

Marc spoke up next, "Well, my name is Police Officer Marc Nugent. Oh, I guess you can forget the officer part, since I am now *jobless*. I live in Nassau County, *but* I probably won't be able to get home anytime soon." As he spoke, his tone was very sarcastic. "I hate my new former job. I hate this stupid city. I hate infectious diseases. I hate pretending there's not a world of terror surrounding us. *We are wasting time playing Romper Room!* People are dying around us! We need to get the hell out of this place, before we end up trapped here!" He laid back down on the blanket in frustration.

Charles commented, "Marc makes a good point. Are we really wasting our time here? Should we move further away and keep running every time the virus gets too close? How far can we run, before there's no place safe left for us to go? These are relevant questions. If anyone has a suggestion, I'd love to hear it."

Steve, the newcomer to the group, was the only one that had not been properly introduced, yet.

Therefore, he decided he should be the one to answer. He said, "Obviously, everyone is upset. No one *wants* to be here and with very good reason. We all have families we'd rather be with in this time of crisis, but trust me when I tell you, we are safer in here, than out there. I just came from out there," he pointed toward the doors." It's complete madness! There are cars on fire, shops being looted by teenagers, people rioting and protesting over something they have no control over. And these are people that haven't even had to deal with the infected, yet! They're destroying their neighborhoods like savages, instead of preparing for the hell that's about to hit them like a tsunami! Mark my words, when the infection reaches this area, they are all going to be infected within the first hour because they are not prepared to defend themselves. They are too busy being stupid!"

He took a deep breath to compose himself and added, "So, do I think we should stay here? Hell no, but it is better than what's waiting out there. Unless we have a really good plan to get past the animals, then we need to keep our behinds here, where it's safe. This place is an armory! It's like a fortress! I'd rather be here, than out there."

The room was silent, as his words sunk in. At last, Charles applauded, "Thank you, Steve. I guess we'll remain here, until further notice."

Everyone in the room knew it was the right decision, so there was no need to discuss it further. For a moment, the person, who watched them from the upper level, was tempted to reveal himself. He had a feeling these were good people, after listening to their introductions. He felt like he would be safe with them, but he was afraid they might not feel the same about him.

METROPOLIS OF THE UNDEAD

Chapter Three

C HARLES GRABBED A few volunteers and conducted a search of the building. Frank led the way, since he knew the building well. Also with them were Grant, Marc, Liz, and Roberto. They began their search with the ground floor. Frank showed them all of the entrances around the building and they made certain each was secure. As they passed the different rooms and restrooms, he showed those to them, as well. The paint on the walls was chipped in most places. At times, it seemed there was more chipped paint on the floors, than on the walls. They managed to find a few leftover tools from the renovation crew that had been working on the building, which was a great find.

Grant grabbed a few of the more useful tools, so he could later add them to his patrol bag, which was back at their camp in the hangar. Charles, Roberto, Frank, and Marc helped him carry the tools, in the meantime. Roberto was the first to volunteer. He intended to utilize the tools as weapons, if it became necessary. He figured it was better to be safe, than sorry. Frank did the same, since he was unarmed.

Some areas of the building had mesh gates blocking the way, but Frank had the keys and unlocked them. They agreed the gates should be relocked, after they were done searching those areas. It was good added protection, in case someone found a way inside.

Once they were done searching the ground floor, they dropped off most of the tools and proceeded to the upper mezzanine, which was easily accessible from the ground floor of the hangar via staircases at either side. Roberto kept an iron wrecking bar with him to use as a weapon, which was part hammer and part crowbar, while Frank grabbed a hammer. Grant retained a flashlight to replace his, which needed to be recharged. In his patrol bag, he also had a spare flashlight that originally belonged to his friend, Winston, who fell to his death when the bridges connecting to Manhattan were blown up a day ago. However, that flashlight also needed to be recharged. For the moment, he lacked the means to charge both flashlights.

The group stuck together and checked both mezzanine balconies that overlooked the hangar, one at a time. There were rows of old-fashioned wooden seats that folded up. The seats were lined up on tiers going the length of the hangar on both the north and south sides. The walls were made of brick. Every few feet there were arched windows that looked out to the front and rear of the building.

Charles did not like how vulnerable the mezzanine made him feel. He examined the area and suggested, "We need to have someone standing watch up here. It's a good place to keep an eye on the entire camp. Maybe even two people, so there can be someone on either side."

Grant offered, "If you want, I can stay up here, once we're done. First, I need to explore this building. I've been wanting to come in here for too long to limit myself."

"Sounds like a plan. Thanks, Grant. We'll take turns," Charles said.

Liz volunteered, "I'll stand watch up here, too. I like having this kind of vantage point."

Grant replied, "Cool. Thanks, Liz. We can watch each other's back." She nodded.

For the time being, they resumed searching the upper levels as a team. They continued all the way to the top floors, searching every single hallway and room. There were some very large rooms, a few smaller rooms, and even rooms with fireplaces, but as far as they could tell, there was no one else in the building. All of the wooden doors had been left wide open and every room was empty, for the most part.

It was time to search the basement and any other levels below. Surprisingly, there were quite a few rooms on the lower levels. Frank turned on the lights, as they went from room to room. The lights did not work everywhere, so they resorted to flashlights. Only Grant and Frank had flashlights that worked, except for the one attached to Liz's Colt M4 Carbine. She took point for the long dark corridors. A lot of the brick walls were covered in graffiti. Columns supported the ceiling in some areas. One area looked more like a subway station.

Charles asked Frank, "How far down does this place go?"

"It goes down about six levels."

"Six? Sweet Christmas," Charles gasped. "This place is way too big for my taste. I don't feel comfortable knowing there are so many dark rooms below us, where someone could be hiding. We need to stock up on supplies and think of a better plan for the near future, as soon as we can."

As they reached one of the final rooms, they heard a noise coming from the shadows. Liz held up her hand indicating for them to stop and they did. Everyone listened carefully. It was too quiet.

Finally, she whispered, "I heard something. I'm going to check it out."

Charles, Grant, and Marc pulled out their 9mm weapons and prepared themselves for a fight.

Liz stepped close to the doorway with her carbine pointed forward. She shined the flashlight over the barrel into the room and slowly moved across the doorway, scanning the room, as she sidestepped. Suddenly, the light stopped on someone, who was crouched down in the corner hiding in the dark.

His hands were held up, as he said, "Don't kill me! I work here!"

Liz demanded, "Who the hell are you?"

The officers moved close to her rear, so they could see who was inside and provide cover fire for her, if necessary.

"My name is Daniel Rivera! I work for Ventucci!"

When Frank heard the name, he stepped closer to the doorway to see who was speaking.

Liz instructed, "Step out of the room slowly. Keep your hands up and come out here, where we can see you better."

Daniel complied.

Charles asked Frank, "Do you know this guy, Frank?"

Frank studied him, for a moment. Daniel was tall and lean, but muscular. He appeared to be in his fifties. He was dressed in casual attire, although his pants were dirty. Finally, Frank nodded, "Yeah, he definitely looks familiar."

Daniel repeated, "Yeah, I told you! I work for Ventucci! I do construction and electrical work for him and sometimes masonry. Whatever he needs. Just don't shoot me."

Charles lowered his weapon and said, "Put your hands down. Who's Ventucci?"

Liz, Grant, and Marc still kept their weapons trained on Daniel, as he dropped his arms to his sides and breathed a sigh of relief.

Frank explained, "Ventucci's in charge of the renovation crew that have been working on the armory. This guy's legit."

Charles turned to Daniel and asked, "What are you doing here and why are you hiding down here in the dark?"

Daniel explained, "I didn't have anyplace to stay on Friday night, so I figured no one would notice, if I came here. Ventucci let me have a key, so I could check up on our tools." Roberto looked down at the wrecking bar in his hand and suddenly felt guilty. Daniel continued, "When I saw the guard, I panicked and hid. I stayed out of sight because I didn't want to get arrested. I thought I could sneak out in the morning and no one would be any wiser, but then he let in a bunch of kids. After that you guys came in and I knew I had to hide. I saw your uniforms and thought you were here to find me. Eventually, I realized you were here to hide and I wondered why, so I listened to you read from that notebook. I couldn't believe what I was hearing. I got scared. I didn't know if I should stay or leave."

Liz responded angrily, "You've been spying on us, since we got here???"

Daniel turned to her and put his hands up, as he explained, "No! I mean, yes, but it wasn't on purpose. I told you I was scared. I wanted to join your group and make my presence known, but I was afraid someone would shoot me, if I surprised them."

Marc sneered, "You're probably right about that."

"You see?" Daniel responded excitedly. "*That's* why I stayed hiding. Honest. I'm no spy. You gotta believe me. I did my time in the United States Army when you were still in diapers."

Charles sighed and said, "Okay, fine. From now on, there's no more lurking in the shadows. You stay with us. Got it?"

"Absolutely! I got it! Thanks, Sarge! Er, I mean, Charles. It is Charles, right?"

Charles shook his head and scoffed, "You sure you aren't a spy?"

"Honest! I told you! I served in the Army! Well, it was a long time ago, but I served."

"Okay, whatever, let's get back upstairs," Charles said. "I think we found what we were supposed to find. I need to plan my supply run."

They walked back upstairs to the ground floor, but Liz and Marc both kept an eye on Daniel. They did not trust him one bit. He kept talking nervously and explaining his reasons for hiding during the walk upstairs.

"I was just scared. You understand, right? I didn't mean to spy on you. Honest."

Roberto smirked, "Yeah, yeah. We get it. Hey, tell Ventucci that I'm going to borrow this thing, for a while," he held up the wrecking bar and chuckled.

Daniel replied, "Huh? Oh, the wrecking bar? Yeah, sure, no problem."

"Wrecking bar, eh? I like the sound of that," Roberto grinned.

Frank commented, "I bet you do. Just don't wreck this place."

"Never! I have too much respect for this building and its military ties. However, if anyone out there tries to get stupid with me, my sister, or my cousin, it's lights out forever with this thing."

Sometime later, at the camp, Charles hung up his cellphone. He had just finished speaking to his friend, Carmen, at MetroTech Center. She provided him with the latest update, but could not talk long. It was more bad news, which he passed along to the others. She advised him that looting and rioting in the Bronx was keeping the Bronx precincts busy. A similar situation was developing in Brooklyn and parts of Queens. People were upset about the way the mayor and governor handled the situation in Manhattan. They felt they were too hasty and didn't try harder to contain the virus. It was his idea to pull the police top brass out and blow the bridges, while collapsing the subway tunnels. He also made the order to place the entire island under quarantine without any plan to evacuate uninfected people.

Of course, he was making these decisions from a relatively safe distance away on Long Island.

Marc grumbled, "What a dick! He could have evacuated people and didn't even bother??? Unbelievable!"

Steve scoffed, "Why should he start caring about the city now? He didn't care before. It's exactly what I'd expect from a douche bag like him."

Aramis shook his head, unable to believe his ears. "Wow," he said. "A few bad decisions and this city and its people are suffering the consequences."

All three teenage girls looked at each other and held hands. Nikki kept thinking about her mother, while Giselle's mind was on her grandmother. Zonnie became even more worried, as she thought about her parents. Liz was also thinking about her parents. She still had not spoken to them.

Charles said, "It looks like we may have to get that supply run done sooner, rather than later. It's just as I thought. Things are going to get much worse out there and there's no relief in sight. Leaving the city might be our best bet, before the entire city is placed under quarantine."

Marc asked, "So, what are we waiting for? Let's hit the bricks!"

Charles replied, "Not until I've heard back from David Castillo. He's still in Manhattan. I'm going to fill him in on what's going on and give him a chance to meet up with us. Afterwards, we will see about getting out of here and heading north."

Marc scoffed, "They might be trapped on that island indefinitely! Are we really going to risk our asses waiting for them?"

"Yes!" Charles growled.

Grant turned to Marc and whispered, "Patience, young Padawan. At this rate, you'll never become a Jedi Knight."

Marc rolled his eyes and pouted, while Roberto chuckled.

Liz approached Grant and asked if she could borrow his phone. He handed it to her and she said she'd be upstairs on the mezzanine speaking to her parents.

Meanwhile, Charles had already begun preparing to leave the armory for a supply run. He only wanted two people to come along with him, at the most. He didn't want to go out in a large group. He figured a smaller team would be more efficient.

Grant asked, "Do you want me to go with you?"

"No, I need you to stay here and secure the place. I want to make sure someone capable that I know and trust will be here to let me back in later."

Grant nodded, "No problem. You should use my patrol bag to carry anything you find. I'll empty it out, and then I'll head upstairs with Liz. We'll cover you, as you leave, just in case you need eyes up high."

Charles agreed, "Yeah, that sounds like a good idea. Thanks."

Grant emptied the contents of his patrol bag onto the tarp at their camp. Aramis, Roberto, and Daniel stood nearby watching to see what he was carrying in there. Grant handed the empty duffle bag to Charles, who took it and placed the strap over his shoulder.

"Thanks," he said. "This should be good enough. I'll see if I can find another bag, too. We're going to need more like this."

Grant nodded and asked, "Who are you taking with you?"

Charles looked around and saw Roberto standing nearby. He said, "I was hoping one of these local gentlemen would be willing to come along. I would feel better having someone with me, who knows the area."

Roberto answered without a second thought, "I'll go with you. I grew up around here, so I know these streets like the back of my hand. I only have one condition."

"What's that?"

"I want to check on my mother," Roberto said, sounding worried.

"Deal."

"Thanks. I appreciate it."

"Not a problem."

Charles walked over to Marc, who was sitting near Steve a few feet away. Both Marc and Steve looked up at him.

Steve asked, "What's up, Charles?"

"I'm going on a supply run. Marc, I need you to come with me. I want someone who's armed to watch my back. Are you up for it?"

Marc shrugged, stood up, and replied, "Sure thing, boss, er, Charles. I'm anxious to see what's going on out there anyway. This place is making me stir crazy. By the way, sorry about before."

"Good man. Get ready. We're leaving soon." Charles turned to Aramis and said, "I plan to search for medical supplies. Is there anything specific you need for your bag?"

Aramis replied, "I have a full supply in my bag, but anything you can find will be helpful. We don't know how long we are going to be on our own. Supplies can run out when you least expect it. I think I noticed a Duane Reade across the street when we arrived."

Roberto said, "Yeah, there's one on the next corner. We can hit that up first, if you want."

Charles nodded, "Yes. We'll go there, first. Are you guys about ready to move out?"

After a quick bathroom break, Roberto and Marc were both ready. They met up with Charles in the main lobby, who was speaking with Grant and Frank.

Charles faced Grant and issued some instructions. He said, "Keep a close eye on the new guy and make sure Steve gets plenty of rest. We need him to recover, as fast as possible. I gave Dave the heads up and told him to contact you, since I will be busy for the next hour or so."

"10-4. Aramis is going to stay alert and keep an eye on both Steve and Daniel. Liz is already upstairs in the east tower. She'll watch over you guys, until you are no longer in her view. I'm going up to join her, once you leave. Frank can help keep an eye on Daniel, right?" He turned to Frank, who nodded.

"Definitely," Frank responded, before unlocking the iron doors.

As Charles and the others stepped out, Grant said, "Be careful out there."

"Will do," said Charles. "I'll text you when we are on our way back."

It was about 3 pm when Charles, Marc, and Roberto left the armory. Frank closed the door behind them and Grant headed up to the tower to watch them from the second floor window. Liz already had them in her sights. She watched them climb over the fence and run toward the next corner. Once they passed under the elevated train on Jerome Avenue, she lost sight of them.

When Charles, Marc, and Roberto reached the Duane Reade, they realized the gate was down. The owner had locked up before leaving.

"Damn," Charles said.

Roberto asked, "Should we leave it?"

Charles thought about it. It was possible they could find another place that was open. He looked around and saw that there was no one else around them. Most of the businesses in the area were either closed or wide open. There really was no need to break into someplace, yet.

"Let's get back to it, later, if we need to. It looks like there's another drug store that's open on the next block. We'll check that out, first. Come on."

They walked to the next block past Morris Avenue. The other drug store was indeed open. It had already been ransacked, too. It sold various items that could be useful. Most of the merchandise on display in front were scattered across the sidewalk and street. Open bottles of liquid cleansers had been spilled creating a slippery mess in front. Crushed cardboard boxes that once held items blocked their path leading into the store. They entered cautiously and noticed a mess inside, as well, but there did not seem to be anyone inside.

Charles warned, "Be careful. Let's see if we can find anything useful. For now, let's focus on the necessities. We need food, bottled water, painkillers, bandages, and it would be great, if we can find a cellphone charger or two. Oh, and see if you find duffle bags, so we can carry more stuff."

"Right," said Marc. He walked off and began searching the drug store. Right away, he found a few bags they could use. He called out, "I found some duffle bags!" He gave two to Roberto and kept two for himself.

They filled the bags with whatever they could find, and then moved on to a nearby grocery store, where they loaded their bags with food, water, and snacks. As they did, Charles felt terrible. He hated resorting to looting, especially while he was still in uniform. He wished there were another way.

Once most of the bags were full, Charles turned to Roberto and said, "Okay, this will do. Let's go find your mom."

Roberto nodded and they left the store.

As soon as they stepped outside, a police car from the 52nd Precinct pulled up. Roberto mumbled, "Ah, shit. The jig is up."

The officer in the passenger side saw that Marc and Charles were both in uniform, and then he noticed the chevrons on the sleeves of Charles' shirt. He immediately shouted, "Sarge! Are we glad to see you! It's a freakin' madhouse out here! We're losing control! All of our supervisors are out at the hospital or station house with line of duty injuries!"

Charles responded sincerely, "I'm really sorry to hear that. Tell me, has the infection from Manhattan reached anywhere around here, yet?"

The officer replied, "Not that I know of, but we're having trouble keeping the protestors, rioters, and looters at bay. Our hands are pretty much full, boss. According to the citywide frequency, there are similar incidents in Queens and Brooklyn, too. It's the same all over. Outbreak or no outbreak, we're being overrun by crazies. What do we do?"

Charles sighed, "Damn. I was afraid of that. I'm sorry to say this, but the city is lost. Go home to your families, while you still can. They need you, now, more than ever."

The officer that was seated in the driver's seat asked, "What about the job? I mean, won't we get in trouble for going AWOL, especially now?"

Charles shrugged and stated, "Look around you, gentlemen. The top brass have evacuated Police Headquarters and abandoned everyone in Manhattan. Even with the bridges blown up, every borough is losing control. The job is done. All that matters is getting to safety. If you have families, go to them, before you lose them. Leave the city and don't look back. It's the safest bet."

The driver responded skeptically, "Uh, sure thing, boss." He noticed the numerous duffle bags they were carrying and asked, "Um, do you... *need* anything from us?"

Charles shook his head calmly and said, "Nope. We'll be fine. We have Roberto." He gestured to Roberto, who grinned at the officers in the car.

Both officers looked at each other, momentarily, and then looked back at Charles, who was smiling back at them.

The officer in the passenger seat raised an eyebrow, before shrugging indifferently and stating, "I don't even want to know. Good luck, Sarge."

"Thanks. You, too." He waved at them.

The officers drove away slowly and made a u-turn. They went eastbound back in the same direction from where they came, leaving the area. They had no intention of ever returning.

Marc looked at Charles and Roberto with relief. "Well, that was interesting," he said.

Charles smirked, as his smile faded, "Yeah. I was almost worried we were going to have a problem. Well, let's not push our luck. Lead the way, Roberto."

Roberto nodded and led them back under the elevated train along Kingsbridge Avenue heading westbound. They passed a large market on the way, so they went inside and stocked up on more food. They made sure not to take anything that had to be refrigerated.

When they exited the market someone threw a bottle in their direction that shattered on the sidewalk in front of Charles. The three of them ducked and ran back into the market. A small group of about five men came running from the next block. They each held bottles in their hands, which they began throwing toward the entrance of the market. The men shouted profanities and cop slurs, as they made a stand outside of the market.

Charles and Marc pulled out their weapons and prepared to fire upon the men, but then they heard a shot coming from across the street, followed by a bottle breaking nearby and a man screaming. Another shot was fired and another bottle was destroyed. The men began running for their lives and dropped the rest of the bottles on the sidewalk, breaking them. The men disappeared around the corner on Davidson Avenue and did not look back, as they fled.

Charles peeked out and saw Liz's rifle sticking out from the tower's second floor window. She was still watching their backs. He smiled and led the others back outside. They moved quickly toward University Avenue and turned left going downhill for one block. Roberto's building was on the next block, which inclined uphill, again.

As they moved south, they saw a police car racing north on University Avenue, followed closely by a police van. Both vehicles had their turret lights on and sirens blaring. They screeched, as they skidded into a left turn going west onto Kingsbridge Avenue, and then disappeared from sight. Charles wondered where they were heading.

At this rate, it would not be long before the Bronx shared the same fate as Manhattan.

When they reached Roberto's building, they hurried into the courtyard and Roberto opened the front door, which was locked. They went up the three flights of stairs to his apartment and he unlocked the apartment door.

He burst inside excitedly and shouted, "Ma! Are you home?"

There was no answer. He went from room to room, but no one was home. Charles and Marc waited at the door, out of breath from their journey.

Roberto cursed and punched the wall, making a hole in it, "Damn it! She's not here! I thought she'd be here!"

A moment later, he walked into his bedroom and plugged his cellphone into the charger, which was on his nightstand. He changed into all black clothing and put on his boots, instead of his sneakers. He then proceeded to fill a black knapsack with spare clothing. He placed a tactical M48 sabotage fighting-knife into his boot and packed some toiletries into his knapsack, before wearing it on his back. The only thing he didn't need was a hairbrush, since he kept his hair very short.

When he stepped out of his room, he noticed how worn out the officers looked standing at his doorway. They had both been wearing filthy uniforms for the past two days, so he figured they might want to take the opportunity to change to avoid any further unnecessary trouble.

"Since I'm not sure when I'll be back here, if you guys want to change into some of my spare clothes, you are more than welcome. My closet and dresser are in here." He pointed to his bedroom.

Charles looked up and answered with a smile, "Shit yeah, my brother. Thank you!"

"Amen to that," responded Marc.

They went into his room and went through his clothing, until they found something to their liking. Both men were elated to finally change their socks, but they kept their boots. Roberto had a different shoe size than them, so they had no choice. Charles settled for some camouflage cargo pants and a black t-shirt, although he kept his bulletproof vest and gun belt. Marc opted to also keep his gun belt and bulletproof vest, while putting on a pair of dark blue denim jeans and a gray t-shirt.

While they got dressed, Roberto grabbed another bag for Nikki and packed some essentials for her and Giselle. He was going to have his hands full carrying bags, but the girls would be upset, if he did not bring something for them.

He checked his phone and saw there were three missed calls and several messages from his mother. He became excited and shouted, "Mom!" Without reading the messages, he immediately called her back. There was no answer. It went straight to voicemail. He tried calling, again, but it was the same. He checked the messages and his heart sank.

The first one read, "Where are you guys? I called the house looking for you. Go home and lock the door. I'll be home soon."

The second message read, "Things are crazy out here! I hope you're home. Be there as soon as I can. There's something big going down."

The last message read, "I love you. Take care of your sister. Not sure when I'll be home."

Each message was sent within a two-hour time frame on the night before, which meant she should have been home, by now. She was not. Roberto wondered where she could be. He hated not knowing. He wrote a note and left it on the floor in the hallway, so she could not miss it. It told her they were safe at the armory and instructed her to call either of them, right away.

There was nothing else they could do. He made them some ham and cheese sandwiches, which they devoured. They drank up all the juice in the refrigerator, used the bathroom, and left. Roberto locked the door and hoped his mother would return and find his note. All he could do was hope.

METROPOLIS OF
THE UNDEAD

Chapter Four

L IZ RETURNED TO the mezzanine overlooking the lower level of the hangar. There was no point waiting in the tower. Charles, Marc, and Roberto were too far out of view. She looked across from her. Grant stood on the opposite mezzanine and saw her looking his way, so he waved. She waved back casually. It seemed like the appropriate response, despite the circumstances.

She looked down at the others. They looked distraught, which also seemed appropriate. It was still hard for her to believe what was happening. One moment she was eating fried chicken and the next there was a full-blown riot on the street. The rest was like a crazy roller coaster ride from hell.

The last thing she expected was for it to be related to a deadly contagion or that she would end up walking miles through underground aqueduct tunnels all the way to the Bronx. And then, there were the many deaths she witnessed. It was more than anyone should ever have to witness. Now, here she was standing guard in an abandoned armory holding a police issued Colt M4 Carbine.

Nobody would ever believe her, if she told the tale. It was sort of funny, in a way.

Holding the weapon made her feel as if she were back in the military. That was also amusing. She only joined as a means of escape from her mundane life. Suddenly, it didn't seem so mundane.

Outside, she heard the sound of police sirens in the near distance, which temporarily distracted her from her memories. She estimated it had to be coming from a few blocks away. It sounded like a fleet of vehicles to her, but she could be wrong.

She'd certainly been wrong many times in the past. She was wrong about the military changing her life for the better. When she got out she decided to stay with her parents, until she could get back on her feet. That was a year ago. She was still living with her parents and she had a dead end job. It was taking a lot longer to get back on her feet than she expected.

She wondered if things would ever go back to normal, not that her life was so great. Even her social life sucked. She had not been on a date in over three years. Of course, she spent the past year being anti-social, which did not help and the two years before that was spent in the military.

Perhaps, this series of events was her chance to redeem herself and prove that she had worth. She could pull what she learned during her military experience and use that to benefit the group. After all, the police trusted in her enough to allow her to keep O'Grady's weapon. These guys treated her with respect and trusted in her to watch their backs. That was something to be appreciated.

Her thoughts drifted back to the passing sirens. Grant didn't seem to notice them. Did he even hear it?

Liz decided to speak with him. She went down the stairs to the main level of the hangar, so she could head across to his mezzanine. He sure noticed that because he was looking right at her. She waved him down to meet her on the ground floor. He went down the stairs on his side and they met halfway.

"What's up?" He asked.

"Did you hear those sirens a moment ago?"

"I thought I heard sirens, but then I didn't. I wasn't sure if I imagined it."

"They were real, all right," she assured him. "Does your police radio still work? Maybe we can hear what's going on outside."

He shook his head, "No can do. Battery died last night. Steve's radio is dead, too. I already checked earlier."

"Well, that sucks. Hopefully, the guys are okay out there."

"I can easily text Charles and find out." Grant did just that. He sent a brief text message to Charles and asked if everything was okay. Charles responded almost instantly and told him they were at Roberto's apartment. Grant passed along the information to Liz. "They're fine. They are at Roberto's home."

She felt relieved and sighed, "That's good, I guess."

In the next moment, she found herself staring at the weapon that hung from her shoulder. It felt strange, yet familiar. She never thought she would hold one, again.

Grant eyed her with concern and asked, "Okay, what's on your mind? You seem to be a million miles away."

She scoffed and asked, "What isn't on my mind? When we were on the move, I was distracted by us getting to our next destination. Now, that we have been here over a day, my mind keeps wandering. I've been thinking about the people we saw die. Those officers shot right in front of me, and then Alissa's face when she knew she was about to die. I can't believe things went downhill so fast."

Grant frowned, "Tell me about it. Watching someone die is never easy. I've been trying not to think about it. It's crazy." He paused and sounded agitated when he stated, "I figured between one of the world's largest police departments and the help of the National Guard, this would have been contained and resolved, by now."

"I guess everyone has his or her limits," she noted with disappointment.

Grant smirked, "You said a mouthful." He decided to change the subject. He still did not feel ready to deal with the deaths of his friends, so he asked, "Hey, what do you think you'd be doing, right now, if this had been a normal weekend?"

She seemed to appreciate the change of conversation and smiled. She answered, "That's an easy one. I'd be sitting at Barnes and Noble on Central Park Avenue, while rummaging through bargain books, listening to music on my earbuds, and probably sipping on a tasty

Caramel Frappuccino. I always use to forget about the rest of the world whenever I did that. I would love to forget about the world, now."

Grant's eyes lit up and he replied, "Oh, that's right! You live in Yonkers, too. Have you ever been to Untermyer Park?"

"Yes, I love that park and the contrast of the seasons," she smiled." It's so beautiful during the warmer months and sort of spooky during the cold months."

"So very true indeed," he agreed. "One of my favorite pastimes is walking through Untermyer Park on a warm summer day with my camera when the flowers in the walled garden are in full bloom and the water in the moats are running with dozens of coy swimming around."

"Yes! And there's that simple, but perfect, waterfall that flows down from the old iron gazebo!"

Grant replied, "You mean the Temple of Love at the Eagle's Nest."

"Huh?"

He explained, "That's what that area is called."

Steve commented, "Well, what do you know, Grant? You guys could have dated, if things had turned out differently."

Grant and Liz turned to Steve and both began to blush. They had not realized anyone was listening to their conversation. Grant wondered how long Steve had been listening. He smirked at the idea of him and Liz dating, but then he found himself thinking about how attractive she looked, even after the ordeal they'd gone through. She was gorgeous. He secretly began fantasizing about the idea and it made him smile.

Liz was embarrassed, so she figured it was time to make her leave. She said, "I guess I'd better get back up to the mezzanine. Signal me when Charles texts that he's on his way and I will head over to the tower."

"Okay," Grant replied.

"See you later," she smiled and walked away.

He watched her as she walked toward the stairs, and then caught himself. He turned around and walked toward the other stairs to his mezzanine.

Before he reached the stairs, Nikki and Giselle intercepted him. Nikki asked, "Hey, Grant! I couldn't help notice you were texting on your phone a little while ago. Have you heard from Charles? I'm really worried about my brother."

"As a matter of fact, I was texting Charles. They are over at your place."

"They're at my place???" She asked sounding surprised. "Did they find my mother?"

"I'm sorry. I don't know. He didn't say, but I will ask him for you. Hold on a sec." Grant sent a message to Charles and waited for a response.

Nikki clasped her hands together, as if in prayer, and said, "Oh, thank you so much!"

Giselle uttered glumly, "I hope titi was home when they got there."

Grant's phone hummed with a new message, which he read. It was brief and to the point. He looked up at Nikki and Giselle and said, "She wasn't home. Sorry."

Nikki looked as if she wanted to cry. Giselle put her arm around her to console her.

Grant felt bad, so he said, "Try to think positive. She might be safe somewhere else. Her cellphone battery could be dead or maybe she lost her phone, so she cannot get in touch with you guys. She could be waiting for this thing to blow over, for all we know. I know it isn't easy, but try to be patient. This hell on earth is unlike anything that's ever taken place. Who knows when it will end, or if it ever will? We might all be in for a lot of pain in the near future, so we need to be strong and we need to stick together. There's no telling how bad things will get."

Nikki frowned.

Giselle asked, "You don't think they'll find a way to stop it?"

"They who?" He asked. "Look around. You're with the police and we couldn't do jack shit to stop it. We saw it firsthand. The world is going to shit on a silver platter. At this rate, we'll be lucky if we can survive the week."

Nikki groaned, "This has got to be the worst pep talk I ever had."

Giselle wanted to laugh, but held it in. It wasn't the time.

Grant apologized, "Hmm. Sorry about that. I suppose it is pretty bad."

Nikki managed to chuckle briefly, and then Giselle did, as well. She felt like maybe she didn't need to hold back, after all.

Grant grinned and said, "Hey, but, at least, I got you girls to laugh."

Nikki nodded, "True that." She then asked, "I guess as a cop, you've dealt with death a lot, huh?"

He stopped grinning, breathed deeply, and replied more seriously, "More times than I would have preferred."

Giselle inquired, "When was the worst time?" As soon as she asked the question, she regretted it. Did she really want to hear this, now? It was too late to think about it.

Grant replied, "Honestly, they were all bad. I had a friend who committed suicide very recently. That was definitely the worst. There were also very young victims of terrible crimes, elderly victims of crimes, cops that I knew, who died saving people at the World Trade Center. Would you believe some of the guys, who didn't die that day, died years later from cancer, as a direct result of that day? Oh, and about a year ago, another cop I used to work with was killed in the line of duty. For the record, I am not even counting all of the deaths caused by this damned virus and there were quite a few.

I suppose the hardest part is reserved for the family and friends, who are left behind. Their lives are turned upside down and inside out. They know death is always a danger with my job, but they put it out of their minds and hope it will never happen to the person they care about. I'm guilty of doing the same. However, when it does, you feel like you are empty and lost inside. All those plans you made for the future mean nothing. Life becomes like death. It's the hardest thing in the world.

The huge cop funerals with the uniforms and American flags only pound the reality of the loss in deeper. You see all those cops lined up coming to pay their respects and you feel proud for a moment, but then the pain hits you like a sledgehammer. You ask why, but there is never a good enough reason.

Afterwards, families have to pull themselves together and try to move on, but it is never easy. Every time a police car passes by or whenever they hear a siren, the pain just comes back. It never ends. The pain is always with you. Maybe *that* is the worst part.

As police officers, we're ready to put our lives on the line to save the lives of others. We may joke and kid around with each other, sometimes, but when the shit hits the fan, it's time to rock and roll. You don't think about dying. The adrenaline takes over and you react. Seldom do you have time to think about what you are doing. Instead, you think about staying alive, at all costs, even if it means breaking the rules. Deep down, you know you need to survive, just to avoid putting your family and friends through that hell."

Giselle asked, "Do you have a wife and kids?"

"Me? No. I never got the chance. I probably never will with the way things are going. I guess it's for the best. Otherwise, I'd be going crazy trying to get to them."

"Yeah, I suppose," she agreed.

Nikki commented, "I think you're better off being single with no kids in a situation like this. It makes it easier for you to deal with your own issues without having to worry about someone else's."

Grant responded, "Ah, that's the catch. Being a police officer, you tend to worry about other people, before you worry about yourself."

Giselle smiled at him, "You guys have really been great with us."

"Yes, definitely," Nikki nodded. "Thank you for everything. You know? I think this conversation actually helped me a little."

"Really?" Grant was surprised "That's awesome."

Giselle giggled, "You're a funny guy. Thanks for taking the time to talk to us."

"No problem, ladies. Now, if you will excuse me, I need to get back up to the mezzanine." He walked off to the stairs and went back up to the second level.

Just as he reached the top of the stairs, he got a message from Charles. They were on their way back. He looked across to Liz and waved his arms to get her attention. When she saw him, he pointed in the direction of the towers to let her know they were on their way. She understood, right away, and headed for the west tower.

When she got there, she positioned herself on the window facing University Avenue, and then she waited.

Back on the ground floor, Zonnie approached Frank and asked him to walk her to the bathroom because she felt nervous going alone, after they found Daniel hiding in the lower levels.

Logically, he agreed.

As they walked to the main lobby, they talked quietly amongst themselves.

Zonnie whispered, "I want to go home already. How much longer do you think we'll need to stay here?"

He shrugged casually, "It depends. According to the cops, whatever is going on outside is nothing I want any part of. It's much safer in here."

She responded, "I understand that, but don't you think it would be better if we were with our families? What if they are evacuated to somewhere safe, while we are stuck in here?"

"That would suck."

"So, don't you think we should, at least, try to get home?" She tried to sound convincing, believing she could manipulate him into thinking her way.

He shrugged, again, before answering, "Well, I live alone, so it doesn't really matter to me. My apartment is only a block away on Davidson. Maybe you guys may want to consider it, though. Just remember. It could be dangerous. Not everyone lives close by. Do you think the cops will want to escort everyone home?"

"I don't need an escort. I am perfectly capable of finding my own way home. Thank you."

"Well, they probably won't let you go."

"You see? That's what I'm worried about," she said. "I don't plan on being a prisoner here. I want to be with my family, where I know I'll feel safer. I've got nothing against these guys, but they are not my family." Her eyes began to fill with tears, as she continued, "If this is the end of the world, I'd rather be with them. Don't you understand, Frank?"

"Yeah, of course, I do," he said.

They had already reached the restroom, by this time. Zonnie began to sob uncontrollably. Frank stood there feeling awkward. He didn't know what to do. He'd never been in this kind of situation. How should he react without coming off like a pervert? She was just a kid. She helped him out by moving into his arms. He patted her on the back and tried to comfort her in a fatherly way.

"There, there," he said. "Don't cry. Try not to think the worst."

She sniffled and said, "I'm trying, but I'm so scared."

"I know."

She gradually pulled away from him, while keeping her arms around him. She stared him in the eyes a little too long for his comfort and smiled. She was very pretty with smooth features and beautiful big brown eyes, but she was still a minor and he was twenty-four years old.

"Thank you for walking me here, Frank, and making me feel better. You're a good man. You don't have to wait for me. I think I might be a while. I need some time alone, so I can pull myself together. Okay?"

He nodded, as she went inside. He decided to use the men's room, since he was already near it. When he was done, he washed his hands and face with cold water. What he really needed was a cold shower.

Once he left the restroom, he walked toward the entrance to the hangar. That's when he realized the front door was open. Instinctively, he reached into his pocket and noticed the keys were not there.

"Zonnie…"

Charles, Marc, and Roberto hurried along University Avenue each lost in his own thoughts. Their hands were full, since each man was carrying about two to three duffle bags filled with supplies. Therefore, they knew they had to reach the armory, as soon as possible. If they had to fight, they'd risk losing some of their supplies.

Charles tried to think of how much longer they should remain at the armory without risking their chances of escape. They couldn't stay too long, but he, at least, wanted to speak to David and his friend, Carmen, before making the decision to move on.

As for Marc, he was just glad to be out of his uniform. After wearing the same clothes for two days and walking through the aqueduct tunnels, he was dying to change into something clean and dry. He was glad Roberto was able to give them clean clothing to wear.

Of course, Roberto's mind was on his mother. He hoped, wherever she was, that she was safe. He couldn't bear to think that something terrible could have happened to her. No, he told himself. She was fine. She'd contact them, as soon as she was able. He had to believe that.

As the trio turned right onto Kingsbridge Avenue, they heard what sounded like the roar of a crowd. It seemed to be getting louder.

Roberto asked, "What the hell is that?"

Marc commented, "Whatever it is I don't like the sound of it."

Charles didn't plan on sticking around to find out. His gut instinct was telling him to run. He said, "We need to get back to the armory, ASAP! Move!"

They ran east along Kingsbridge Avenue and crossed the street to the armory. Charles leapt over the fence like a gazelle impressing himself, and he even did so while carrying two duffle bags filled with supplies. Robert tossed over his bags and Marc did the same. Both began climbing over and flinched at the sound of gunfire. It took a moment before they realized it was only Liz shooting from the tower above, providing them with cover fire.

Charles looked past the fence to see what she was shooting at and his eyes and mouth gaped open wide. He shouted, "Hurry up! Get over the fence!"

Dozens of infected people came running through the street toward them.

Roberto glanced over his shoulder and saw how close the mob of infected were getting. He shouted, "Holy shit! They're right on our asses!" He immediately pulled himself over the fence and jumped down to the other side landing on his feet.

However, Marc lost his footing and slipped back down. His boots were still caked in mud from the previous morning. He got up quickly and began climbing, again.

As Charles and Roberto screamed for him to hurry, Liz kept firing more and more rounds into the crowd. There were too many infected for her to make a difference and they were moving too fast for her to get clear shots.

When Marc reached the top, someone grabbed his left foot and tried pulling him back down. Charles pulled out his gun and shot that infected person in the face. The person went limp and dropped to the sidewalk, but another infected person had latched onto Marc's other leg. Roberto climbed the fence and grabbed Marc by the arm in an attempt to pull him over.

"I got you, bro! Get your leg over the top!"

Marc was able to get his left leg up, but he felt a gripping pain in his other leg. Someone was biting into his right ankle.

"Argh! Get the hell off!" He kicked hard and the infected man fell back. In that moment, Roberto was able to pull him over. They both fell to the ground within the fenced area.

Charles felt a sick feeling in his stomach. He knew Marc was infected. He also knew it was unwise to bring him back into the armory because it put everyone else at risk. At the same time, he did not have it in his heart to abandon Marc and leave him outside.

"Charles!" Roberto was calling him. He and Marc were already inside the armory. The door was open. Frank stood inside waiting to close it.

"I'm coming," he said. He picked up his two bags and hurried inside.

More and more infected ran against the fence and pushed into it with all their might. They were determined to reach their potential victims that got away. The fence was starting to give out and was leaning in toward the armory. It would only be a matter of time, before they forced it down and the perimeter around the armory would be compromised. Those within would be trapped.

Frank slammed the door shut and locked it. Before Charles could say anything, Frank confessed, "Zonnie is gone."

Charles turned to him and demanded, "What do you mean she's gone?"

"She tricked me by playing up the tears and swiped the keys from my pocket. She let herself out about ten minutes ago. She was determined to get home to her parents. Luckily, she had the brains to leave the keys in the door, so we could lock it, again."

"Damn! That girl's going to get herself killed!" He exhaled and tried to remain focused. "There's no way we can go after her," he frowned. "I hope she makes it home because she's on her own. We have another problem to think about." He gestured toward Marc and said, "Marc is infected."

Frank, Charles, and Roberto were each looking at Marc, who was still breathing heavily from his ordeal. He closed his eyes and wanted to cry, as the reality of his situation set in.

"Shit on me," he groaned.

Just then, a loud crashing was heard outside, followed by metal rattling against the ground. Within seconds fists began pounding on the iron doors of the main entrance. The infected had broken down the fence.

METROPOLIS OF THE UNDEAD

Chapter Five

IT WAS EARLY in the evening on Sunday in Manhattan. The sun was low in the western sky over New Jersey casting its beautiful orange glow on the horizon. Soon, it would be dark and with the arrival of nightfall would come the third night of the Zombie Apocalypse.

On the Hudson River floated a massive aircraft carrier by the name of The Intrepid. In 1982, The Intrepid opened in New York City as a sea, air, and space museum. Four years later, it was declared a National Historic Landmark.

Commissioned in 1943, it participated in numerous campaigns during World War II. It was one of twenty-four Essex-Class aircraft carriers built during the war. Once known as "The Fighting 'I,'" she was the fourth U.S. naval vessel to bear the name, The Intrepid.

Today, it is moored snuggly in its berth, surrounded by an unusually eerie silence. There are no cars driving on the roads nearby. No people walking around in the area. The air is still, yet, danger stirs in the distance making its way further downtown, deeper into the heart of the city.

It is a plague of unprecedented proportions. Anyone, who is unfortunate enough to become infected by its deadly parasites, is transformed into a mindless carrier with an inane desire to feed and spread the virus to other potential hosts. Even death is no escape.

Only a few have managed to elude the virus and remain in Manhattan, which has been placed under quarantine. One group of survivors has taken refuge aboard The Intrepid, although for safety reasons, they must remain below the Flight Deck and out of sight, at all times. They have resorted to turning off the deck lights, as not to attract any unwanted attention to their position. If the military boats that patrol the waters spot them, they risk being shot. However, if they are seen by any infected, it could mean a relentless siege upon their temporary shelter. Instead, they remain hidden and have done so, since Saturday morning.

Police Officer David Castillo led his group here on that first morning, after it began. His group consisted of a young woman named Edie, another woman named Michelle, an off duty Port Authority cop named Kevin, a bus driver named Wally, and several of his passengers, which included Kirk, Mr. Hayes, and Michelle's younger sister, Millie. They joined up with another group of survivors that already found shelter aboard the large vessel. Together, they have been coexisting, but as their patience begins to wear thin, people are looking to David for answers.

Bobby McDonald was one of those people and it was starting to get on David's last nerve. Bobby was always good at pushing people's buttons. In fact, he got off on it. His attitude got him into plenty of fights, while growing up. It taught him to be tough. He liked to be called "Big Bad Bobby," although no one ever really called him that, but himself.

He spent the past three years working for the New York City Department of Sanitation and turned out at the District 7 garage on West 57th Street, which covered the Upper West Side. Prior to that, he worked for the Department of Environmental Protection for five years.

Bobby paced back and forth along the stage in the Allison and Howard Lutnick Theater, which was located on the Hangar Deck near the main entrance of the museum. He was frustrated from being cooped up in the museum for so long. He was beginning to regret his decision to seek shelter there and wondered if his chances would have been better had he tried to escape, before the bridges connected to Manhattan were destroyed.

"There has to be another way than this," he complained. "Hey, Dave, what about the sewers? You tried them, yet?"

"No, but we walked through subway tunnels for about an hour."

"Yeah, but the subways are definitely going to be blocked off. I'm talking about the sewers, man." He pointed downward excitedly with his forefinger. "People tend to forget about them. It's a friggin' maze! Even DEP guys get lost down there!"

Millie grumbled from a cushioned seat in the second row of the theater, "Oh, God. I seriously do not want to go through the sewers. The subway was bad enough."

Bobby looked at her and responded sarcastically, "Hey, sweetheart. You can always stay here and get eaten by friggin' zombies. I'm looking for a way out of this deathtrap."

Millie scoffed, "Ugh." She really did not like Bobby, nor did she like being called "sweetheart" by the likes of him. She found it disrespectful and grossly inappropriate.

Claude, Bobby's fellow sanitation worker, said, "Take it easy, Bobby. These people are scared."

"Yeah, who isn't, Slick? It's *Dawn of the Friggin' Dead* out there *28 'hours' Later!*"

Michelle sat beside her younger sister and leaned in close. She whispered, "Ignore him, Mil. He's a sanitation guy. Don't expect much respect from a guy, who deals with garbage all day."

Edie, who sat on the opposite side of Millie, chuckled.

Kirk was seated in the front row next to David, Kevin, Wally, and Claude, who sat a couple of seats away from the other three. Kirk thought Bobby might actually be onto something. He nodded his head in agreement, leaned forward in his seat, and commented, "You know? The sewers just may work. It could be a long shot, but if they haven't been collapsed or flooded, we could easily cross over to the Bronx."

Mr. Hayes scoffed from his third row seat.

Kirk glared back at him and Mr. Hayes looked away.

David wasn't quite convinced either. He smirked and said, "I don't know, Kirk. You heard what Bobby said. Even the workers get lost down there. How are we going to do any better? We could end up spending hours roaming around blindly and come up somewhere else in Manhattan."

Bobby faced David and replied, "That's very true, Dave, except for one small detail. I know the sewers pretty well."

Mr. Hayes smacked his lips together in annoyance and rolled his eyes. He was starting to think Bobby was full of more crap than the sewers he was going on about.

However, David was intrigued, so he asked, "Really? How is that?"

"I worked there for five years, man," Bobby replied with a sly grin on his face.

Claude stated, "I can vouch for that."

"That's interesting," David replied.

Mr. Hayes raised an eyebrow and glanced suspiciously at Bobby.

At last, someone had an idea that sounded doable. A smile began to form on David's face. It must have been contagious because Kirk, and then Kevin were also smiling. Wally and Mr. Hayes were both skeptical, which was understandable. It was a crazy plan, but it sure beat waiting to die.

Jerry, one of the employees of The Intrepid Sea, Air, and Space Museum was checking the Flight Deck to make sure it was clear. It was the uppermost deck of the ship and, therefore, the most vulnerable to intruders. Jerry was in his forties and had been working at the museum for about seven years. This was the first time he did not want anyone to come aboard. As far as he was concerned, there were already too many people on board. Still, he felt safer having a police officer around.

It was starting to get dark. The sun was almost completely set. He adjusted his orange baseball cap, so it would not interfere with his vision. He figured taking a quick walk across the Flight Deck couldn't hurt. He only wanted to make sure no one else was trying to get into the museum entrance from the pier. He used the planes and helicopters on the deck as cover, while moving to the far edge of the port side.

The pier appeared to be clear, although he thought he saw movement on the street below. He moved toward the bow of the ship and looked down to the street, while standing in the shadows under the Lockheed

SR-71 Blackbird. The large black jet plane hid him from sight. About five people were walking along the street heading south. They looked disoriented, as they crossed from one side of the street to the other, and then back, again, for apparently no reason.

Jerry wondered if they were lost, searching for a possible shelter, or infected. Either way, he did not want them to see him, so he remained in the shadow of the plane and did not dare move. Once they were about two blocks away, he returned to the interior of the ship.

All of a sudden, he heard a thunderous roar approaching at top speed, followed by the shrieking sound of wind passing overhead. It sounded like a jet plane. He stayed inside and closed the door. He hurried down to the Hangar Deck, where mostly everyone else was hanging around.

He stopped at the Information Desk, where Tracy and Deirdre, two other museum employees sat, and asked, "Where's that cop? What's his name? David?"

Deirdre replied in a high-pitched voice, "I think he's still in the theater with the rest of his group."

Tracy confirmed with a hint of attitude, "Yep, they're in there, all right." She wasn't too happy that the security guard, Mr. Vanvooren, kept allowing strangers into the museum, as if it were a public fallout shelter.

Deirdre asked, as she adjusted her glasses on her nose, "Why? What's wrong?"

"I'm pretty sure a jet plane just flew over us and it sounded like it was flying low."

"Oh, my! Are you sure, Jerry?"

"I remember how they sounded, after 9-11. It was the same."

Tracy looked worried, as she responded, "That could be very bad."

Jerry nodded, "I agree. That's why I plan to tell the cop." He turned away and walked into the theater. He walked toward the stage and stopped near Bobby. Everyone in the theater watched and waited to hear what he had to say.

"Excuse me," He began. "I was making my rounds and heard something that might be of interest to you."

Bobby asked rather rudely, "Yeah? What's that?"

Jerry turned to face him and said, "A jet plane passed over the ship a few minutes ago." He then looked at the others in the theater. "It sounded very low, as if it were checking the Flight Deck."

David asked, "Were you on the upper deck, at any time, in the last few hours?"

Jerry hesitated a moment and answered, "Yes, but I was careful not to be seen. I stuck to the shadows of the planes and was only out there for a minute."

Claude commented, "They could have been using night vision or thermal heat signatures to spot you. There's no hiding from the military." He shook his head.

Kevin sighed, "Oh boy."

David became upset and asked, "Why would you go up there for any reason?"

"Well, to make sure no one else was trying to sneak aboard, for one thing. Might I remind you that you are not in charge here?" Jerry sounded defensive. He did not feel like he had to explain his actions to any of the newcomers. "Besides, I saw some people in the street. I believe they were infected."

Wally replied, "Just what we needed." He buried his face in his hands.

Edie became worried, too, and wondered if the ship truly kept them safe from the infected. She recalled how she once believed she'd be safe at the 26th Precinct, until it was overrun. She tried to keep her fears to herself. She did not wish to worry Millie or Michelle.

Meanwhile, Kirk explained to Jerry, "It's not about who's in charge, buddy. It's a safety issue. If the military see someone on this ship, they will assume we are trying to use it to escape Manhattan. You could put the group in danger, if you were spotted. Not smart and not cool."

Jerry explained, "The military knows this ship isn't going anywhere. As long as we are choosing to use this place as a shelter, I feel it is our obligation to keep it safe from trespassers. Did you consider that someone else may try to sneak aboard and steal this ship, so they could escape?"

Mr. Hayes said, "He's got a point. We can't expect that no one else will want to use this ship. It's very possible."

David sighed, "Fine. Never mind that. Are you sure it was a military jet?"

"Positive," replied Jerry.

"In that case, we need to get out of here by morning. It's not safe here anymore. If they know we are here, snipers might start watching our every move waiting for a clear shot to take us out."

Bobby asked, "Then why wait 'til morning, when we're easier to spot?"

"Because it's too dangerous out there," David answered. "You heard the man. If the infected are out on the street, they could be anywhere. If we are going to escape through the sewers, I would, at least, like to make sure nothing is lurking in the shadows around me. Besides, we need time to pack up and prepare."

Bobby grumbled, "If, if, blah, blah! Okay, whatever, Dave. If you want to wait until morning, that's fine by me. I'll give you that, but know this… come morning, I'm out of here with or without you guys."

Declan, another employee of The Intrepid Sea, Air, and Space Museum and Deirdre's nephew, had been showing some of the exhibits from the Exploreum to Damian, Josh, and Pablo. For the past two years, Declan had been a member of museum's staff. It was a job he took a lot of pride in. Even with the city in disarray, he didn't mind taking the time to take a few people on a tour.

Besides, it was a good way to keep occupied and not think about what was going on outside. That's how Damian, Josh, and Pablo felt, as well.

Damian and Josh are best friends, who were originally planning to take a long drive up to the Finger Lakes. They were supposed to meet up with a few other friends, once they reached their destination. Yesterday their plans were changed thanks to the Fox Serum Virus. Instead, they are trapped in Manhattan with little hope of escape.

Pablo showed up to work at the Circle Line ferry super early on Saturday morning. No one else ever made it in. When he learned of the viral outbreak, he headed for The Intrepid. He knew it was a safe place to wait it out, until things cooled down. The last thing he expected was for the city to fall under siege to a virus. A day later, he is still hiding out at The Intrepid.

When David's group arrived yesterday morning, somehow, it increased the threat level of the virus for everyone that was already aboard the ship. Knowing that even a police officer was trapped with them made them realize how bad things had actually gotten.

It seemed like a good idea when Declan offered to take them on a tour of the exhibits. None of them had ever been aboard, so everything was new to them.

Jerry found them and said, "Declan! Actually, all of you, we need you to come to the theater near the bow. We are having an important meeting. Please, hurry and meet us there."

He left before Declan could ask any questions.

"Hey, um, okay. Be right there, I guess," he muttered to himself.

Pablo turned to him and asked in a heavy Spanish accent, "What joo think dat waz abou?"

"No idea," Declan said pitifully, as he began walking toward the exit of the Exploreum with his long arms at his sides. "Come on," he said, while beckoning them. "I guess the tour is over." He was a tall, muscular, young man, so when he spoke, people tended to listen. The others followed him curiously from the Exploreum to the theater. It wasn't too far from their location.

Once they entered the theater, they noticed everyone else was already there waiting. Jerry was standing on the stage, along with David and Bobby. The others were scattered and seated in different rows.

Jerry addressed Declan and his tour group and asked them to be seated. Afterwards, he stated, "It has come to our attention that our safety here is no longer guaranteed. We believe our time might be very limited. Bobby, here, has come up with a risky solution and a possible way out of Manhattan. David's group will likely be going with him. What we want to decide is if it is the best option for the rest of us. Whatever we decide, we cannot stay here anymore."

Declan looked disappointed and asked, "Aw, why not? What's wrong with staying here? There aren't too many places in Manhattan stronger than a military aircraft carrier."

David answered for Jerry, "I completely agree that this is a good shelter, but that only depends on absolutely no one knowing we are here. It is very possible the military are aware of our presence here. If that is the case, then we are no longer safe here. Mark my words, they will try to shoot us and possibly even sink us, if they think we are trying to use this ship to leave Manhattan."

"Oh, my goodness!" Deirdre cried out. She asked, "What are our other options?"

David shrugged, "Go home, go somewhere else, take your chances staying here, or come with us. There really aren't any other choices."

Mr. Vanvooren asked, "When do you plan to leave, Officer Castillo?"

David noticed he said *you* and not *we*. He replied, "Those of us, who choose to leave for the sewers, will be leaving tomorrow morning. The rest of you have until then to decide what you will do. In my opinion, this sewer trip might be our only final chance to leave Manhattan, so I am *not* passing it up. I know it will be difficult, but if we do this together, we can make it. I'm not at one hundred percent myself. My leg still hurts from a car accident, but I am willing to give this a try. I highly recommend you all do the same."

There was a lot of whispering and murmuring in the auditorium of the theater. It was indeed a tough choice to make. Not everyone was convinced it was a good idea.

The Intrepid Sea, Air, and Space Museum docked at Pier 86.

METROPOLIS OF
THE UNDEAD

Chapter Six

T HE TIME IS 2345 hours on
Sunday night. A black Special
Ops rubber raft carrying an elite six-man team drifts silently into the
Harlem Pier at West 125th Street under cover of darkness. Each member
of the team is dressed in a black uniform from head to toe, while wearing
black camouflage face paint to eliminate any possibility of facial shine
from the lights. Their ages range from 22 to 35 years old.

One medium build Hispanic male named Martinez quietly rowed
the raft past the pier to a low point of the shoreline near the southbound
entrance ramp of the Henry Hudson Parkway to avoid the bright lights
of Harlem Pier Park. He is the youngest member of the team and a
sniper, by expertise.

Once the raft ran aground, each team member secured his or her
gear and departed the raft. They moved into the shadows underneath
the elevated parkway to a position of cover.

A tall muscular Hispanic male, Lieutenant Hernandez, was team leader. He adjusted his black-framed glasses and checked his portable GPS indicator. "It's not far," he said. "It's approximately two blocks due east. Stick close and watch for infected. Attach suppressors to your weapons. We're going silent. I'll take point. Move on my mark. Go," he ordered and moved swiftly across Twelfth Avenue.

The other team members followed closely. None made a sound, as they moved stealthily from the south side of West 125th Street to the north side, and then continued onto the university grounds at that location. They stopped only when they reached the west entrance to the Science Center. The glass doors were locked.

Corporal Williams, the team's demolitions expert, suggested, "Should we break the glass?" He was African-American, as well as being the oldest and more experienced team member.

Hernandez replied, "Negative. According to our Intel, there is an open entrance. Let's go around to the other side from the right. Move on me." He led the way.

They walked along West 129th Street and saw that the entrance was locked there, as well. Next, they continued to Broadway, where they turned left and headed north. Several windows were broken on that side at the ground level. There was dried blood smeared across the floor of the darkened lobby.

"Bingo," said Sergeant Santiago. A lean muscular Hispanic male, he served as the team's computer technician, electrician, radio specialist, and resident hacker.

Hernandez turned to another team member and instructed, "O'Connell, you take point from here. Martinez, take up the rear. Everyone else stay on me, single file."

O'Connell stepped up and led the way with his MK 48 machine gun. He was a good-humored Irishman with broad-shoulders and a thick blond mustache. He used the flashlight attached to his heavy weapon to light the way, as they entered, one at a time.

He noticed what appeared to be a dead body on the floor in the south hallway. It smelled ripe, so there was no need to check on it. There were way too many flies hovering over it anyway. Chances are they were now carriers of the virus. Whoever it was on the floor had been dead for quite a while.

The team's medic and biologist, an Italian female named Soriano, commented, "Well, that's just great. It was nice of them to leave us a stinker."

Williams whispered, "It's just ripe enough for me to lose my mood for food."

O'Connell pointed out to the others, "Elevator bank ahead."

Hernandez stepped forward and looked at each elevator, until only one set caught his interest. "These two here should take us down to the fifth level," he indicated. He pressed the elevator call button and turned to his team and said, "Santiago, you'll have to hack the security mechanism. A special key is required and we did not have time to fetch it from Riverside Drive."

"No biggie," Santiago replied. "Step aside. I got this."

The elevator arrived seconds later. When the doors opened they were hit with a horrid stench, and then a reanimated corpse lunged forward from within. He latched his teeth onto the lieutenant's wrist.

Santiago shouted, "Holy shit!!"

Hernandez did not scream out in pain, but he did say, "What the...?" He instinctively punched the zombie in the face knocking its jaw loose. He then pushed the zombie away and back into the elevator. Next, he pulled out a large hunting dagger from its sheath on his left leg and shoved it into the zombie's head from the chin upwards to its brain. It squirmed momentarily, and then stopped moving. When he yanked his dagger out, the corpse dropped to the floor. The lingering odor of rotten flesh filled the air.

Williams stepped closer for a better look and commented, "Hot damn! He stinks! Infected my ass! I don't care what anyone says! *That* is a damned zombie!"

Santiago covered his nose and exclaimed, "Jeez! Are you okay, Lou?"

"No, it broke skin, which means I'm probably infected," the lieutenant replied with a grim expression on his face." Damn," he frowned almost emotionlessly.

Soriano moved closer and said, "Let me check your wound." She pulled out a flashlight and pulled up his sleeve. The skin was definitely broken, although it was not deep. "Maybe not," she said feeling hopeful. "I think we can catch it in time." She went through her first aid pack to find what she needed to tend to his wound.

"It doesn't matter," he said trying to sound indifferent, although he really wanted to scream and yell obscenities. Instead, he kept his cool. "We have a mission to do. That's our priority."

Martinez asked, "What the hell was he doing in the elevator?"

Hernandez replied, "I didn't ask." He then barked out a few orders, "Williams, help me drag this thing out of the elevator. Santiago, get in there and get us to the fifth level. Martinez, hold the doors open for him. Soriano, can you please get me some alcohol for this wound? Thanks." He winked at her.

They held their breath and dragged the corpse out of the elevator, leaving it on the floor near the elevator bank. While they did so, the others carried out his orders. Within seconds, Soriano was wiping his wounded wrist with alcohol and antibacterial ointment, before covering the wound with dressing. By this time, they were all standing in the elevator, so Martinez was able to let go of the doors. They closed automatically, but the elevator remained on the ground floor.

Santiago slung his M27 infantry automatic rifle over his shoulder and worked as fast as he could on the key mechanism using several tools from his personal toolkit. He almost gagged twice from the smell, but was eventually able to turn the switch. The elevator began to descend.

The wound on their lieutenant's wrist began to itch slightly.

The doors of the elevator opened onto the fifth underground level. They quickly stepped out into a dark corridor, lit only by a light near the elevator bank. Across from them were the sealed double doors into the main laboratory. There were large windows on either side of the door. The one on the right was covered in blood from the inside. Only a few lights were on within the laboratory. The rest were broken. One kept blinking on and off creating an eerie strobe effect. The dim lighting and blood on the window made it difficult to see anything else. Behind them, the elevator doors closed.

Hernandez stated, "Stand by," and then moved closer to the window on the left side. He could see several lab tables, some knocked over chairs and animal cages, closed doors to the left and straight ahead on the far side of the room, and one broken door. Otherwise, the laboratory appeared to be empty. He turned to Williams and said, "Blow this window open. We'll enter through here."

Williams stepped forward and acknowledged, "You got it, sir." He pulled out some C4 from his pack and began setting it around the edge of the large window. He told the others, "You might want to go to the end of the hall and cover your ears. It's about to get loud down here."

The team moved to the far end of the long corridor near the exit to the stairwell. Martinez checked the door and noticed it was unlocked.

"In here," he said. "We can hold it, so it doesn't close all the way. It should muffle the sound a little."

They stepped into the stairwell and waited for Williams to join them. Seconds later, he came running. They let him in and Martinez held the door closed just enough to block the sound of the blast.

KA-BOOM!

A loud explosion filled the corridor, followed by the sound of heavy broken glass slamming into the walls and hitting the floor.

They waited a few seconds and listened for yelling or moaning, but it was quiet. They felt safe enough to re-enter the corridor. As they approached the broken window, they heard screaming. It was loud and inhuman. Suddenly, a wild chimpanzee covered in blood leapt out of the window and rushed toward them hooting and screaming.

O'Connell opened fire with his MK 48 machine gun and sent it flying back in a hail of bullets. It fell to the floor with a heavy thud and no longer moved.

Martinez joked, "Ooh! Nice job, O.C. You sure showed that little chimp who the boss is around here."

Without missing a beat, O'Connell replied, "Maybe I should have let him bite your little brown ass? Nah, on second thought, you're probably too spicy for him."

Martinez replied with a smile, "You would know, O.C."

Santiago and Williams both chuckled, although Soriano was not too pleased about the dead ape. She hated to see animals killed unnecessarily. However, the chimp did look seriously disturbed and he was attacking, which she found strange. She wondered if it was infected. Could the virus infect animals, too? It was a scary thought.

Hernandez warned, "Be careful. There could be more inside. I saw a bunch of cages on the floor in there near the south wall."

O'Connell reached the broken window, first. He pointed his machine gun into the window and scanned the room. Again, it appeared to be empty and it also stunk like days old death. He did not like how the one light kept flickering on and off at the center of the large room. It was creating too many shadows from the tables. He cleared away broken glass and climbed in through the window, while looking around. Boxes of files were scattered across the floor. There were a couple of dead apes in their mangled cages. A few bloody white sheets lay sprawled beside them. The rotting corpse of a man lay beaten to death beyond the cages. These dead bodies certainly explained the intense odor.

O'Connell watched them for about thirty seconds to make sure they did not move. When he felt satisfied they were dead, he continued checking the immediate area. Near the window was a desk. He made sure no one or nothing was under it, dead or alive, before giving the signal for the others to enter.

Hernandez entered next, followed by Martinez. They helped Soriano through, and then Santiago and Williams followed. There was a closed door directly to the left of them past the desk, which led into the preparation room for the biohazard lab.

O'Connell asked, "Should I check it?"

Hernandez shook his head and replied, "Negative. We have no business in there. We need to get to the dorm, which should be one of those two doors on the other side of the lab," he pointed using his wounded hand and felt a stinging pain in his wrist. He tried to ignore it.

They fanned out and moved cautiously through the main laboratory with weapons ready. When they reached the two doors, they turned their attention on the broken one. A light was on inside. The battered door was lying on the floor of the main laboratory, as if it had been broken from the inside out. It was a pretty good indication that whatever was inside had already come out.

O'Connell stood in front of the open doorway and noticed another dead body was lying on the floor in that spot. Apparently, someone had bashed its head in. When it appeared to be safe, he prepared to step inside.

All of a sudden, Soriano began screaming at the top of her lungs. O'Connell pivoted and faced her direction. He saw that something had her by the ankles. Whatever it was managed to pull her down to the floor violently and knocked her weapon from her hand. It was another zombie! He had been crawling along the floor and now was biting into her right leg through her thick uniform pants.

Hernandez moved in for the kill. He tried to aim his HK MP7A1 submachine gun at its head, but he didn't want to risk shooting Soriano in her leg. He moved closer and knelt on the floor, so he could get a clear shot. As soon as he fired a round into the head of the zombie, two ragged-looking chimpanzees came rushing out of the open doorway behind O'Connell.

The chimpanzees appeared to be rabid. They jumped onto O'Connell knocking him back to the floor and began biting and beating him mercilessly, while screaming. Williams shot one with his MK 18 Mod 0, but then it leapt toward him. Next, Martinez aimed his M107 light fifty-caliber sniper rifle and shot it a second time, while it was in the air. It dropped to the floor and died. Santiago shot the other chimp twice and killed it, as well.

Another chimpanzee came swinging down from the lights and landed on Hernandez's back. It bit into his neck, before he flipped it off of him. When it hit the floor, it turned to them and screamed. He shot it in the mouth and killed it.

Williams shouted, "What the hell is this? The attack of the *Planet of the Apes?*"

As if in answer to his question, another chimpanzee came out of a storage closet located at the north end of the room, to the far right of the open doorway. This one looked very different from the other four. It wasn't behaving aggressively. Instead, it showed signs of intelligence. It was capable of turning doorknobs because it seemed to be hiding in the closet. Somehow, it knew it was safe to come out, now. It appeared to be injured because it limped and whimpered pathetically, as it approached them.

A silent shot was fired into its head and it dropped to the floor. Martinez scanned the rest of the room using the night vision scope of his M107 sniper rifle. It looked like they were alone, but he wasn't going to fall for that, again. He remained vigilant.

Santiago said, "Martinez, I think you just killed the only normal ape in the room."

"Screw that, Sarge! I'm not taking any chances!"

Hernandez felt dizzy, but he found the strength to stand. He leaned against a long lab table for support, took off his helmet, and looked around at his team. Soriano was lying on the floor crying from the pain in her leg. Her helmet was also off. She was infected like him. O'Connell was also lying nearby, except he was completely still. He was either unconscious or dead. Meanwhile, Santiago, Williams, and Martinez had their rifles ready for anything.

Hernandez gritted his teeth and said, "Check the other room and be careful. We can't risk anyone else getting attacked. When you open the door, shoot *anything* that moves. The mission objective should be in there. It's in a syringe on the floor, underneath one of the cots."

Santiago replied, "Yes, sir." He looked at the other two and said, "On me." They both flanked him on either side. He faced the door and said, "On the count of three. Ready?" Both men nodded and he counted, "One… two… three!" He pulled the door open and they stepped back simultaneously with weapons aimed into the doorway.

The stench of death hit them first, followed by the rotting mangled corpse of Dr. Herbert Fox stumbling forward. They gasped at the ghastly sight of him and tried not to breathe in the overpowering smell. His innards were exposed and began falling out of his open stomach, while he staggered toward them. Pieces were splattering onto the floor in front of him. He stepped on his own intestines making a squishing sound.

Santiago gagged and fought the urge to vomit.

Before Dr. Fox's shuffling feet could cross the threshold, several rounds were fired into his upper body. He fell backwards from the force of the shots, but he did not die, for how can you kill what is already dead? He tried to stand up, so the three men shot him a few more times. Still, he moved, much to their surprise. This time, Martinez aimed for the head. One shot stopped him permanently. At long last, Dr. Fox was truly dead.

Williams exhaled and wiped the sweat from his brow. He took off his helmet and groaned, "This is some crazy shit straight out of a Romero film."

Santiago peeked into the room and saw that it was empty. The light was on. It was a small square room. Inside were four cots, ten chairs, and a trolley cart. The cart and most of the chairs were knocked over. There were nearly a dozen syringes on the floor and a lot of blood.

He became confused. How were they supposed to know which syringe contained the anti-serum? Then he remembered what his lieutenant said. It was supposed to be underneath one of the cots. He bent down and made sure not to touch any of the blood on the floor. He spotted a syringe under the first cot on the right side of the room. It also happened to be the one cot that was drenched in blood.

He turned back to Martinez and said, "Do me a favor? Get me one of those white sheets on the floor near those monkey cages. Make sure it doesn't have any blood on it."

Martinez went and retrieved the cleanest sheet he could find. He rolled it up, brought it back, and handed it to Santiago.

"Thanks," he said, as he took the sheet and laid it out across the floor from the entrance to the cot, covering the blood. Most of it was already dry, but some still seeped through the sheet because there was so much. He carefully entered the room and pushed the cot away with his boot, revealing a single syringe with a white plastic cap. He bent over and picked it up. He noticed it was different from the others. It had to be the right one. He felt it in his gut.

When he came out of the dormitory, he proudly held up the syringe containing the anti-serum. He then placed it carefully into his toolkit.

Hernandez commented weakly, "Good man. Our mission is almost accomplished. All you need to do is get topside and head to the extraction point for an EVAC with the package intact. Go to the baseball field in Morningside Park. It should be at around West 112th Street. Pop some green smoke and the chopper should come for you guys."

Santiago eyed him curiously and asked, "*Should?* Wait. What about you?"

"We're infected. They won't pick us up," he explained. "You'll need to do this without us."

Soriano looked at him and responded in surprise, "*Say what?*"

Santiago shook his head and said, "I don't like that plan. I don't want to leave you guys down here. It's not right. I'm a marine and we never leave a man behind."

Williams protested, "Uh, uh! No way! We came here together, boss! We leave together! Like he said, no man gets left behind!"

"You have your orders, Corporal," Hernandez stated firmly. "O'Connell is in no condition to move. Soriano can't walk and I'm bitten in two places. Take that anti-serum and get it somewhere safe. Don't worry about us. I'll deal with it. Keep in mind, that anti-serum is the key to getting off this island. Without it, there will be no pick up. They will need verification that you have it."

Soriano demanded, "Wait! What do you mean you'll *deal with it?* What the hell are you planning to do?"

"My job," he stated coldly, as he pointed his sidearm at her head and pulled the trigger one time. Next, he turned the gun on himself and did the same, before the others could react.

Santiago shouted, "NO!" It was too little, too late. He took off his helmet, revealing his sweat-covered baldhead, and threw it across the room, as he cursed, "SHIT!"

Williams stated, "*Daammnn!* That's some cold ass shit, right there." He turned away from the scene and shook his head in disbelief.

Martinez removed his helmet and bowed his head in silence. He said a prayer for his fallen teammates.

It looked like they were on their own, whether they liked it or not.

O'Connell began to stir on the floor of the main laboratory. He moaned subtly, causing his remaining three teammates to look in his direction. Santiago, Williams, and Martinez could not believe their eyes, as he began to stand up and fumbled over toward them falling back to the floor. He extended one arm, as he tried to reach for them, while pulling his body over the floor and crawling toward them with the other arm. O'Connell had an empty look in his eyes, as if his life and soul had been sucked away from him. It was the same look the man in the elevator had and the same one Dr. Fox had, only moments ago.

There was little doubt O'Connell was dead. Now, he was one of the infected, a zombie. His reanimated body continued on, driven only by an insatiable hunger.

Williams became distraught and took a step back. O'Connell was one of his best friends. Seeing him like this was heartbreaking. His eyes became watery and uttered, "Oh, no. Not you, man. Why did we come here? This place is Hell!" He threw his helmet down at the floor in a fit of rage.

While he yelled, Martinez wasted no time. He took aim and fired a single round from his sniper rifle into O'Connell's forehead. O'Connell stopped moving immediately. Martinez lowered his rifle and apologized, "Sorry, my brother. Go with God and rest in peace."

Santiago became even more flustered than he already was before and cried out, "We need to get the hell out of here, already! This is bullshit!" He turned to leave, but then stopped in his tracks.

"No, wait. First, there's one more thing I want to check. That room," he pointed toward the preparation room. He noticed it was connected to another lab, which could be seen through a large window over the fallen cages. "That looks like where this thing all started. We should destroy it to make sure no one can ever find it. In fact, let's blow this whole place! Williams, set some charges around the lab. I'll get that door open. Martinez, cover me."

Williams set some explosive charges with timers in key places that would do the most significant damage, while Santiago and Martinez approached the door to the preparation room.

Santiago gripped the doorknob and glanced over his shoulder at Martinez, who was aiming his rifle at the doorway. He turned back toward the door, pulled it open, and then jumped back out of the way.

Inside was another zombie. He began shuffling forward and Martinez shot him once in the head. He went down like a bag of rocks.

Santiago commented, "Jeez! How many of these things are down here?" He stepped into the room and turned on the light. He scanned the rest of the room with the barrel of his M27. There were no more infected within, but there was another door for the smaller laboratory. It required a keycard to access it. Santiago grinned. It was time to work his magic. He took out his toolkit and began fiddling with the keycard slot.

Soon, Williams joined them in the preparation room. He said, "This place is set to go."

Santiago responded, "Not yet. We need to destroy this lab, too. I don't even want the slightest particle of dust to survive. Let me get this door open and you can place more explosives in here."

Martinez looked back toward the main laboratory and asked, "Guys, should I grab their dog tags? I feel like we owe them, at least, that much."

Santiago got the door open and said, "There! It's open!" He turned toward Martinez and replied, "Yeah, maybe we should."

Williams disagreed and stated, "Negative! Think, man! Those guys are infected! If you so much as get a drop of their blood on you, it could mean curtains for you, too. Leave those tags, where they are, soldier. They need to be purged with everything else down here."

Santiago had to agree, "He's right. Let's finish up here and get the hell out, ASAP. How much time are you giving us?"

"I set them for twenty minutes. Should be plenty of time for us to get out and get far enough away."

"Good. Do this room, too."

They could easily see through the glass door that no one was inside the biohazard lab. Williams set more explosives, and then they passed back through the preparation room to the main laboratory and climbed out through the broken window to the main hallway.

Martinez pressed the button for the elevator.

Williams ran past him and said, "Skip the elevator, man! If something goes wrong, we're dead. Take the stairs."

The other two followed him to the emergency stairwell and they ran all the way up five flights to the ground floor. A door led them to the loading dock area. They ran up the ramp and onto the street. It only took a moment to get their bearings. Broadway was hard to miss with the elevated train tracks over it. They ran in that direction and continued south toward West 125th Street.

As soon as they turned the corner, the ground shook under their feet and every single window of the Science Center shattered. Glass came crashing down to the streets like a monsoon from every floor of the building. It almost felt like there was a five second earthquake, but they knew it was the underground explosion. A few car alarms went off from cars that were parked along Broadway.

Williams turned back and saw the Science Center was still standing. He was almost positive there would be a partial collapse. He was impressed with the integrity of the structure. The building was a lot stronger than he thought. The sound of the car alarms worried him, though. It might attract unwanted attention.

He turned and faced forward, but did not see Santiago or Martinez. Uh oh, he thought. Where did they go? His heart began to beat faster. He stepped forward and groaned, "Shit."

In that instant, someone grabbed him from behind and yanked him back.

METROPOLIS OF THE UNDEAD

Chapter Seven

S ERGEANT SANTIAGO HAD pulled Corporal Williams back and into the doorway of a closed restaurant. He pressed his finger to his lips and said, "Shhh! Look," he pointed. "There are infected across the street."

Williams looked and could see several of the reanimated infected wandering aimlessly along West 125th Street, or were they? They seemed to have no purpose. Yet, something was driving them forward. It was as if the vibration from the explosion was calling them.

Williams still could not believe there were "zombies" in New York City. Had he not seen them with his own eyes, he would have denied it. He wondered how many had been created by the virus, since day one. A whole weekend had passed in a city of millions. It was very possible there could be hundreds or thousands, by now. It was a terrifying thought.

Martinez raised his M107 and suggested, "I could probably take these 'zebras' out, before they even cross the street."

Santiago shook his head, "Negative. Stand down and conserve your ammo. It's a few blocks to Morningside Park from here. Wait for them to pass. They're moving west. When they pass that police truck at the intersection, we'll use it as cover and move east."

Martinez frowned and lowered his sniper rifle.

Williams said, "Not that I'm complaining or anything, but I thought our briefing said the infected could run after you. So far, all we've seen are a bunch of drunks." He was referring to how they walked, which resembled a drunken person.

Santiago replied, "Would you prefer runners? Be grateful for small gifts. Let's go. Stay behind the cars." He hurried east and the others stayed close behind.

The smell of smoke lingered in the air, indicating something had burned. There was also a hint of barbecue meat combined with rotten meat. As they got closer to Amsterdam Avenue, they knew where the smell was coming from. At some point, during the weekend, there was a huge fire that took out a number of structures all the way to the corner. Most were burnt to the ground and with them many people. Charred bodies were laid out on the street. It was likely not all were infected. There were also corpses in the street that had been riddled with bullets. Hundreds of flies had accumulated over the mass of dead bodies.

Martinez said a silent prayer for the fallen, and then they crossed Amsterdam Avenue. Two lanes of heavy traffic extended north on Amsterdam, as far as the eye could see. Most vehicles appeared to be empty. There were police cars and vans were blocking the intersection at West 125th Street. There were also bloody handprints on two of the white police vehicles. Dozens of spent shell casings were piled on the floor near the cars.

Williams commented, "I guess this was where they made their last stand during the riots."

Martinez pointed to a car stuck in the permanent traffic jam. "Hey," he said, "There's someone in that car and they're moving!" He used the scope from his sniper rifle to get a better look, and then he frowned, "Forget it. It's another zebra." He checked another car and said, "And there's another one."

Santiago looked around at the police vehicles and said, "Wait a minute. We don't have to walk. Check these cars. One of them may have the keys in it."

They went through every single police vehicle with no luck. The only one that had keys also had a dead battery.

Williams stated, "It looks like we're shit out of luck. Battery is dead on this van." He looked around the street and saw plenty of corpses, but none were cops. "Where are the dead police?"

Santiago answered, "Don't forget our initial Intel came from cops, who escaped this area. They probably took the car keys with them, not realizing they would not return." He shrugged and said, "The hell with it. We walk. It's only a few more blocks."

They continued east along West 125th Street, until they reached Morningside Avenue. They could see a crowd further east on the next avenue over. It was difficult to tell if they were infected or not. A city bus was blocking part of the intersection. The front end had crashed into a fast food restaurant on the northeast corner. There were burning fires in the distance.

Santiago whispered, "Let's not be seen. Quick! Follow me and stay close." He led them south along Morningside Avenue crossing the intersection at West 125th Street.

Someone screamed loudly in the distance. It wasn't a normal scream. There was something creepy about it. The scream came from St. Nicholas Avenue, where the crowd was gathered. It was followed by what sounded like a stampede.

Martinez stated, "That doesn't sound good."

"No shit," replied Williams. "I think they spotted us."

Santiago shouted, "Run!"

Zombies walking across West 123 Street.

As the three soldiers ran south on Morningside Avenue, a vicious hungry crowd turned the corner from West 125th Street. If Williams was still wondering about the runners, the only thing he had to do was turn around. There had to be about thirty of them chasing after what was left of their special ops unit.

The important thing was that they had the anti-serum. All they needed to do was reach the landing zone and wait for pick up. Of course, they could not expect to be picked up, if they were being chased by a screaming infected mob. Somehow, they had to lose the crowd, before reaching the park.

Santiago led them into the nearby Housing Development. His guys were close behind, as were the infected. He leapt over a fence and ran along the grass. The others did the same. It was not as easy for the infected to jump over the fence. A few stumbled over and some were pushed over by those behind them.

He stopped and said to Williams and Martinez, between heavy breaths, "Shoot these screaming bastards... We can't lead them... into the park!"

They took up their firing stances from the Housing parking lot and used the parked cars to conceal themselves. Round after round was fired at the infected taking them down, one at a time. Only a couple managed to get close. One jumped over the fence and onto Santiago. The other chased Martinez around a car, until Williams could get a clean shot. The one that was on Santiago had him pinned to the ground. It salivated over him and drool went onto Santiago's face.

"Ugh! Gross!" He spit to the side and shouted, "Guys! Get this disgusting bloody meat sack off of me!"

Martinez took it out with his sniper rifle, but blood splattered onto Santiago's face. To make matters worse, the infected corpse dropped onto him. By the time Williams and Martinez tried to help him up, infected blood had poured over his uniform and face. As soon as they saw the blood, neither of them wanted to touch him. They immediately backed away.

Martinez gasped, "Oh, man!"

Santiago looked up at him and groaned, "I have blood on my face, don't I?"

Williams nodded, "Yeah, man. Sorry."

"It's my fault, Sarge," Martinez confessed. "I am so sorry."

"No, he drooled into my mouth, before you shot him." He then vomited, almost on cue. After spitting a few times, he explained, "I was already infected the minute that happened. Don't blame yourself, kid. It's on me. Literally."

What they did not realize was that the fight was not over, yet. The muzzle flashes from their weapons and gunshots, even though they were silenced, alerted more infected to their presence. It did not help that the previous group of infected had been screaming at the top of their lungs during their desperate attempts to reach their potential victims. Soon, more infected began running toward the parking lot from every side.

Santiago shouted, "Run! There's too many!"

They ran through a path that went around a school and exited onto West 123rd Street, where more zombies were approaching from Amsterdam Avenue. Luckily, the park was in sight. Santiago had one last plan. Perhaps, they could lose them in the park and maybe hide, until the mob passed. The three exhausted soldiers ran into the park with a new mob of infected chasing close behind them.

Williams pulled out a grenade that had been hanging from a clip on his shoulder. He pulled the pin and tossed it into the mob. Unfortunately, by the time it exploded, some of the infected had already moved out of position. The blast only took out two infected, who were blown to pieces.

On the park path, they ran into three of the slower reanimated infected, or zombies. They each looked as if they had been dead for, at least, two days. Martinez struck one with his rifle and knocked it back into some bushes. Williams ran smack into one and knocked it down. He had not even seen it because the path was so dark and he was still focused on the grenade he threw. They were able to avoid the third zombie easily by running around it.

The soldiers found a park house and decided to make a stand there. They turned back and began shooting their pursuers. However, once again, their gunshots brought more into the park on their right side. They began running deeper into the park. Santiago tripped over a dead person and scraped his hand on the ground. He hurried to get up. Martinez offered him a helping hand, but Santiago waved him away.

"No, don't touch me! Keep going! The baseball field isn't much further! Find a place to hide and start shooting these pricks!"

"I'm on it!" He replied, as he ran ahead.

Williams waited for Santiago to get up and they ran together. All the while, infected chased them through the poorly lit main path of the park. The baseball field was already in sight. There was no way they could mark the landing zone without drawing more infected toward them.

Suddenly, shots were fired and infected began to fall one by one. It was Martinez. He had climbed to the top of the fence that covered home plate and the batters' box. He was lying on the top of the fence and firing at the infected from a safe position high out of reach. It gave Santiago and Williams a fighting chance. They shot as many infected, as they could, while staying mobile. The field gave them a lot of space to maneuver. However, they were getting tired of running, while the infected were relentless.

Santiago began to feel nauseous and dizzy. The exhaustion was getting to him. He was pushing himself beyond his limits and his body was slowly dying on the inside. His stomach cramped up and he fell. Surprisingly, the infected ignored him and chased after Williams. Perhaps, in some strange way, they realized he would soon be one of them.

A few other infected were trying unsuccessfully to reach Martinez. Meanwhile, Santiago lay virtually still on the field.

Martinez focused his energy on shooting down the infected that were chasing Williams. He needed to make every shot count. He was starting to run low in ammo. When there were only a few infected left, Williams was able to shoot some himself. All that remained were the group trying to reach Martinez. Williams took them out with one swoop of his gun set to automatic mode. He kept shooting, until his weapon clicked, indicating it was empty. By then, all of the infected that chased them were dead.

"Thanks, Corporal," said Martinez.

"No. Thank *you*. They would have surely caught up to my tired ass, if not for you and your excellent shooting."

"So, we're even then."

"Yeah, sure thing, kid," Williams replied. It was then that he realized Santiago was down. He walked closer for a better look and saw that he was not moving. He cried out, "Santiago! Are you still with us?"

There was no answer. Suddenly, he began to convulse on the grass. His eyes opened wide and he began screaming in pain. He twisted and turned on the ground kicking his legs outward. He was changing.

Martinez aimed his rifle at him and waited, while Williams backed away.

"Shit," Williams muttered. He also aimed his weapon at Santiago, except he did not wait. He fired two shots and Santiago's head practically exploded.

Afterwards, Martinez climbed down from the fence and walked over to Williams. They both looked down on Santiago's nearly headless body. It was a shame, they thought. He was so close to making it out, only to get infected and killed in the final hour. Both shared a moment of silence for their friend and sergeant.

And then it was back to reality. Time was of the essence. They needed to grab the syringe and release a canister of green smoke for the helicopter.

Williams stated, "Mark the LZ. I'll grab the syringe. I want to get far away from this damn island of the dead, ASAP." While Martinez released the green smoke into the air, Williams carefully searched Santiago's belt for his toolkit, but could not find it. He began to worry and said, "Shit. Tell me he did not drop it somewhere."

"What? The syringe? Nah, man! Check his toolkit."

"I am! I can't find it! It's not here!"

Martinez bent down and helped check. The toolkit was indeed gone. There was only one possible explanation. It must have fallen off, at some point, but when? Was it somewhere in the park, near the Housing Projects, or could it have fallen off on West 125th Street? They had each climbed into several police vehicles, they ran, they jumped, and even fell. It could have fallen off anywhere.

They searched the field desperately hoping it fell off, while Santiago was there. In the distance, a military helicopter could be heard approaching.

"Shit!" Williams cried out, "We need to find it or they won't pick us up! Hurry up! Keep looking!"

"I am! Bro, that thing could be anywhere!" Martinez had a thought, "Hey, maybe we could explain that we retrieved it, but it fell. We'll back track, until we find it."

"Yeah, they'll listen to that," Williams replied sarcastically. "Wake up, kid. If we don't find that syringe in the next two minutes, they will never come back for us, even if we did, somehow, manage to find it. That helicopter was waiting nearby. Once it leaves, it ain't ever coming back."

A few seconds later, a black UH-60 Blackhawk helicopter was hovering a few hundred feet over the baseball field. A spotlight was turned on to where they stood frozen in place.

A voice called down from a PA system, "Do you have the package?"

Martinez looked at Williams, who really wanted to cry. He shook his head regretfully and without another word, the helicopter rose up and flew west disappearing out of sight. As the sound of its rotor faded away, it was replaced by screaming coming from outside of the park.

It was time to run, again.

Williams and Martinez knew all too well what that screaming meant. More infected must have seen the helicopter and, now, they were coming. Both men ran out of the park and exited onto West 110th Street. They needed to put some serious distance between themselves and those screams. They opted for heading east toward Central Park, since they could see it from their position.

When they reached Central Park West, they stopped short. There were zombies standing around them, who were looking at them, as if they were dinner. They were slower than the other infected, but still dangerous, especially in large numbers. There had to be about a dozen of them. There was no time to aim and shoot each one and running around them would be difficult with the line of empty police cars that were blocking the street. It was the only option they had.

Martinez asked, "Should we check these cars for keys?'

"Screw that! It will take too long! Keep moving east!"

Martinez rolled his eyes and frowned. He really wanted to drive a police car, or any car. He was getting tired of running. He can't exactly shoot a sniper rifle, while running, and he needs to be perfectly calm just to make a good shot with one. Carrying the rifle wasn't helping. It was cumbersome and starting to feel like a burden, even though M107s were generally light models, compared to other sniper rifles.

When they reached Seventh Avenue, there was another entrance leading into the park. As they were about to enter, they saw more zombies coming toward them from within the park. Plus, recently infected people were running toward them from Seventh Avenue, followed by a fire truck!

Williams could not believe they actually had a fire truck! They were driving! He stared in shock, but then noticed something was different. The guys on the truck weren't infected. The front passenger was hitting infected with an axe and the driver was running them over. These guys were alive!

"Look at that fire truck! Those firefighters are alive and they're killing the infected! If we work together, we can take them out. You take out the slow ones in the park and I'll help these guys take down the runners."

Martinez nodded and began aiming at the slower zombies. He had time to shoot them all, before any could get too close. However, he was running dangerously low in ammo. Soon, his fancy sniper rifle would be no better than an iron pipe.

"I got the zebras on this side," He said, and then he pulled out his side arm and helped take out the runners.

The fire truck came to a stop over two infected men and both firefighters jumped out with axes in hand, ready for battle. They were both geared up with their helmets, breathing masks, thick gloves, and long raincoats to prevent blood from getting on their skin. The apocalyptic firefighters chopped away mercilessly at the infected, until none were left.

Martinez applauded, "Nice! These guys are bad ass! Rescued by New York's Bravest! What an honor. Thanks, guys!"

The driver was the strong hefty type. He rested his bloody axe over his shoulder, pulled off his mask and helmet, before saying, "No problem, G.I. Joe. It's all in a day's work. This is how we roll, these days. Hey, let me ask you something. Did that fancy helicopter just drop you guys off into this putrid shit hole?"

Williams shook his head and answered, "Actually, it just stranded us here. We were supposed to recover a possible anti-serum for the virus, but our sergeant lost it, before he was killed. Without the anti-serum, we didn't stand a chance of getting picked up. Now, we're just as stuck as you."

"Aw, you're breaking my heart. So, let's go find that damned anti-serum and call the freaking helicopter back... simple solution!"

"Not so simple," Williams explained, "It won't be coming back and we can't call it. No radios. It wasn't part of the deal."

"You're shitting me," said the burly firefighter.

The other firefighter, who was shorter and younger, turned to him and asked, "Hey, Gordo. Do you think we should let them ride with us? They could prove to be useful with those rifles. You're driving, so I'll leave it up to you."

"Sure. Why not? You guys need a lift somewhere?" The driver asked, while glancing at their rifles and trying not to be obvious about it.

Martinez replied like an excited schoolboy, "Hell yes! I would love to ride on a fire truck! I don't care where we go!"

Williams sighed, "Please, excuse my young friend's enthusiasm. We would be very grateful, if you could give us a ride. We've been running for nearly an hour. I'm Williams. He's Martinez."

The driver replied, "Pleased to meet you. Technically, it's a fire *engine*, Engine 37, to be exact. I'm Gordon and this is *my* young friend, Sean. So, where can we take you?"

"You can take us to The Intrepid Sea, Air, and Space Museum, if you don't mind. I hear they have a submarine. Maybe I can get us out of here," Williams grinned.

Gordon smiled, "I like the sound of that. Hop on, brother."

Williams and Martinez got into the rear seat of the cab, behind Gordon and Sean. The truck's engine purred like a mountain lion and they headed south into the park down the West Drive toward West 59th Street.

METROPOLIS OF THE UNDEAD

Chapter Eight

IT WAS ALMOST dawn as Fire Engine 37 traversed its way down the West Drive of Central Park. There were a few random infected in the park and slow zombie or two, but none that were an immediate threat. They did have to run over two that were in the road, though.

Gordon commented, "That's the second one that got in the way. This baby is going to need a thorough washing and waxing when this is all over."

Williams spoke from the seat behind him, "That's an interesting thing to say. Do you really think this will be over someday and things will go back to normal?"

"I really wasn't thinking about it when I said that," Gordon frowned." It just came out. I guess I'm still getting used to this apocalyptic crap. Part of me doesn't want to accept it. Sean and I lost a few good buddies the other night when this began. A lot of people were killed during the riots."

Williams asked, "Why didn't you try to leave that first night? I would have been out!"

"Honestly, it never crossed my mind. We were on duty. We had jobs to do. When all hell breaks loose, we are the ones who run into the fires of hell, not away from it. It wasn't until the cops told us that we were trapped in what was being called the 'Infection Zone,' or whatever, that we realized the situation was beyond our control. We tried to make a break for it, but we needed our baby. We couldn't leave her stranded in the middle of the riots."

Williams asked curiously, "What baby?"

"This one," Gordon tapped the steering wheel with pride. "Shoot! It took two hours of waiting and hiding before we could get the keys from our dead friend and reclaim what was rightfully ours. We tried to get back to our station, but couldn't because it was blocked by infected runners. We checked on a few other stations, but they were all out on runs, never to return. The next option was trying to leave the city. By then, it was too late, so we decided to go to war."

Martinez commented, "I'm impressed. That's very heroic." He pointed ahead, "There's another zebra on the road."

Sean asked, "Zebra? Why call them zebras?'

"Huh?" The question caught Martinez off guard, but then he realized how his terminology could be confusing to others, so he explained, "Well, because of our alphabet. X-ray, Yankee, Zebra."

"Oh, I get it," Sean replied.

Gordon drove straight for him, but then saw something that made him hesitate. He squinted for a better look and swerved around to avoid the person on the road, but did not stop. He exhaled with relief and kept going south.

Martinez groaned, "You missed it on purpose?"

Sean was confused and asked, "Why did you go around him?"

"I wasn't so sure he was infected. He looked at the rig in that last moment and I thought I saw fear in his eyes. Those things don't show fear. Maybe it was just some homeless guy. I don't know. I didn't want to take a chance and kill someone normal."

Williams stated, "Good call and excellent reflexes. You drive this thing like a pro, but I was thinking. Maybe we don't have to run over every person on the road. Let's get to that sub in one piece."

"Agreed," Gordon replied.

Sean remembered there was a zoo in the park and thought out loud, "I wonder how the virus affects animals. I've hardly seen any stray dogs or cats, since this hell started. There's a zoo in this park. Do you think the animals will be safe?"

Williams responded, "I'd worry more about anyone that got too close to them. They're going to be very hungry having no one around to feed them during feeding time. Hopefully, they won't come in contact with any of the infected. We encountered a few apes in a lab that may have been infected. It affected them differently. They were still aggressive and violent, but they didn't reanimate, after being killed. They stayed dead. It was more like they had rabies or something similar."

Sean joked, "So, no mutated zombie animals like in *Resident Evil?*"

Martinez replied, "I sure hope not!"

The truck reached the southern end of the park and exited at West 59th Street. It turned right and drove westbound. The city had an eerie abandoned feeling to it. There were cars on the roads, which created a few random obstacles to avoid, but they were unoccupied. People had given up trying to escape and, for some reason, left their vehicles in a hurry, probably due to infected attackers.

Williams wondered how far down the virus had reached. Where were the survivors hiding? How many were left? Could most of the city's residents have already succumbed to the virus? If so, then why weren't there more infected on the streets? Were they asleep? Did infected people sleep?

He sure had a lot of questions, but no one who could truly answer them. Gordon and Sean had a limited knowledge of the virus. They probably had no idea, where it originated. For the moment, they did not have a need to know. That information was now classified. Williams felt glad he was able to blow up the lab and hopefully any research that led to the creation of the virus.

His only regret was losing that anti-serum, but it was much too dangerous to go searching for it, especially in the dark. It could have fallen anywhere. It was extremely unlikely the infected would allow a proper search. Of course, it was nearly daylight, now, but on the other hand, they were already almost on the West Side.

Getting on that submarine was all that mattered.

Gordon parked the fire truck facing northbound in a way that blocked access onto the pier. He did not want anyone to notice there was activity on the pier. He decided to stay with the truck, while the others checked on the submarine. Sean promised to get him, before the submarine moved an inch. Since his driver's side window was positioned facing west out to the pier, it became necessary for him to keep checking his side mirrors to make sure they were not disturbed.

He glanced at the others, who were walking toward the submarine. The sun was just starting to come up. A quick peek at his watch told him it was 5:57 am. He ran his fingers through his hair and wished he had a cold beer. The thought made him smile. He missed his guitar, too.

He turned on the radio and found a station that was actually playing music. He was sick and tired of listening to the news. That's all Sean ever wanted to hear. Everyone had theories about how the outbreak began. None sounded right. Blame was being tossed at the police for letting it get so out of hand, while the mayor was hiding out on Long Island. The people were outraged. They were calling for resignations and justice. Callers trapped on Manhattan made their pleas to be rescued, claiming the city wasn't completely lost, yet. Riots had begun in the surrounding boroughs because they were separated from loved ones in Manhattan, who were still okay. There was even a candlelight vigil at Battery Park.

The latest news was the most disturbing. Yesterday several infected had managed to cross over into the Bronx at Broadway, using the wreckage of the bridge to climb up and infect a mob of protesters on West 225th Street. No one expected the infected to swim across or to climb, but they did and when they did there were hundreds of idiot protestors waiting to be infected. The virus went through that crowd faster than a California wildfire. Swarms of infected moved north on Broadway toward Yonkers or east along Kingsbridge Avenue, while some jumped down to the Major Deegan Expressway and attacked people in their cars, who were stuck in traffic. There were limited escape options for those people. Hundreds of cars were left abandoned on the expressway, as a traffic helicopter reported seeing the mob of infected heading along the expressway in both directions, infecting anyone they could find.

It was disturbing and depressing. Right now, Gordon just wanted to sit back and enjoy the song playing on the radio. It was one of his favorites, *Hey, You* by Pink Floyd. He sang along quietly, while checking his mirrors constantly.

He glanced up briefly and something ahead caught his eye. It looked like a plane in the sky, but it was moving so fast. He lowered the music and heard what sounded like a rocket thundering across the sky. It was a military jet doing a flyby. It tilted slightly and Gordon could see it had a full payload of missiles under it.

"That's not good." He called out his window to warn the others, "Hey, Sean! Heads up, brother! I think you guys should get the hell back here, forthwith!"

Sean looked up and didn't see anything, but he could hear it coming back for another pass. Before he could say anything, there was a whistle and a whoosh, followed by a huge explosion.

BA-DA-BOOM!

Gordon cried out, "HOLY SHIT! SEAN!"

The missile did not hit the pier, nor did it hit the submarine. Instead, it struck the Flight Deck of The Intrepid creating a blast so large that it knocked a helicopter off the deck. The helicopter crashed down onto a parked police van between towers one and two, which was where Sean stood.

Gordon leapt out of the truck and ran toward the wreckage, but the helicopter exploded throwing him back against the fire truck and knocking the wind out of him.

Williams and Martinez climbed out of the submarine and leapt onto the pier. They wanted to help Sean. They could see his legs, but he was burning. It was too late. They went back into the submarine and headed to the bridge. Williams could not get it started.

Martinez asked frantically, "What the hell happened out there?"

"The military happened. That loud roar was a jet passing over. They're bombing the aircraft carrier. This sub might be next, if we don't get it moving." There was another explosion outside. This one shook the submarine violently. "Too late," he cried out. "Let's get the hell out of here, before she sinks with us on it!"

They climbed out and jumped to the pier in the nick of time. The submarine began to heel toward the port side moving the exit further away from the pier. Flames blocked the pier, forcing them to go further out, near the Concord jet exhibit. They noticed a few other towers that led up to The Intrepid, as well as a ramp that went straight to the third deck, although there was no telling if the door would be locked or not and it wasn't wise to board a sinking ship. For the moment, it seemed they were trapped.

A few minutes earlier, inside The Intrepid, Declan awoke to use the restroom. It was very early in the morning. The others were still asleep. He hated waking up so early just to use the bathroom. It was always hard to fall asleep, again, afterward. He put on his glasses, so he wouldn't bump into anything and make any unnecessary noise. He sighed. Today will be everyone's last day on the ship, but him. He had no intension of leaving its safety. In the time he'd been working on the ship, it had become his second home. He loved The Intrepid with every fiber of his being and knew all there was to know about it. He believed leaving it would be a huge mistake. Had he been a sailor, he would have wanted to go down with it, if it came down to it.

In the next instant, there was a huge explosion on the Flight Deck and everyone else aboard awoke to a frightening scene. When David led his group here, he thought they would be safe. He never dreamed they'd wake up to flames and explosions. For the first time in nearly seventy-five years, The Intrepid was under attack.

"Everyone, wake up," he shouted, "We need to abandon ship!"

Kirk and Kevin had been sleeping on seats at the rear of the theater next to him, so they were up when he got up. Mostly everyone had been using the theater seats to sleep in. When they awoke abruptly, they were confused and disoriented.

David knew exactly what was going on. He knew it would happen, after Jerry said he saw a jet. It was the main reason they were planning to leave this morning. He thought they had more time, but it was painfully obvious he was wrong.

Everyone rushed to get out of the theater. Jerry and Mr. Vanvooren tried their best to help them exit in an orderly fashion. It was a good thing their essentials were packed the night before. They barely had time to grab their bags of supplies, while leaving.

David ordered in an amazingly calm voice, "We need to get off the ship fast, so let's not waste any time arguing or asking questions. Just get to the pier."

The ship was rocked by another hit. This time, it was hit below decks by the sound. The ship started to lean downward at the stern. They rushed down the first tower to the pier and saw the fire burning from the destroyed helicopter, which they realized was on top of their van. The heat was intense.

David gasped, "What the hell? I don't believe this! This has to be some kind of cruel joke!" He turned to the others and stated, "The van is destroyed!"

Kirk replied, "Oh, damn. I knew we should have parked somewhere else. What now?"

Damian stepped forward and stated quietly, "Well, my car is parked out front on the street. Josh and I have room for three more. We'll take you two and one other."

Deirdre overheard him and cried out, "What? That's terrible!" Suddenly, she looked around and shouted, "Oh, my God! Wait! Where's Declan? Is he still on the ship? We can't leave him!"

Jerry looked around, too, and didn't see him. He exclaimed, "I don't see him!"

David glared at Damian in disgust and responded angrily, "What about everyone else? There are eighteen of us!"

Damian shrugged, "Sounds more like there might be seventeen. Just saying!"

David scowled, "What a dick."

Claude interrupted, "Hey, guys. Our garbage truck is not far from here. Someone could fit in there with us. It's not very comfortable, but it's a ride."

There was a loud rumbling noise, followed by screeching tires on the Flight Deck. A smashing sound was heard, as something crashed into something else. They could not see what was happening, but it definitely sounded bad. It was high time to exit the pier. They hurried down the steps and ran past the main building. Suddenly, the large Lockheed SR-71 Blackbird slid off the deck and crashed in through the roof of the building. It was so heavy it caved in the structure and fell straight to the ground floor.

A cloud of dust and debris filled the building, as it continued to crumble. Outside, the remaining planes also slid off the deck in one chaotic instant. They each smashed into the main tower of the ship or right into the space shuttle exhibit, which was mostly underwater, by this time. One plane exploded when it hit the space shuttle, which was knocked into the Hudson River. The first staircase tower also collapsed.

Gordon rushed onto the pier and began pulling people from the wreckage. A few escaped unscathed, such as Kirk, Millie, and Edie, mainly because they ran fast. Kevin had already gone past the building, so he helped Gordon. Kirk also helped with rescuing the others. Together, they each pulled out, who ever they could. Kirk found David, right away, and carried him over his shoulder off the pier.

David coughed and spit out dust from his mouth. Kirk placed him down on the street and asked if he was okay, "How are you feeling, buddy?"

"Like I need a vacation," David groaned. "I don't think I have any new injuries, but I have a killer headache."

Kirk replied, "Well, that's probably because you're bleeding."

David felt his head and felt the wet warmth of his blood in his hair. He hoped he didn't need stitches. He was distracted when he saw Gordon helping Kevin pulling the others from the debris. What threw him off was that Gordon was wearing his firefighter's uniform.

"Are we saved?" He asked deliriously.

Kirk looked at him confused, and then looked in the same direction and realized what he might have been thinking. He explained, "Sorry, pal. That guy's flying solo. There is no rescue team. I'd better go help out. Will you be okay here?"

David nodded, "Maybe one new injury," and then he passed out.

When David began to come to, he still felt groggy. His vision was blurry and he could barely hear what was going on around him. The light was very bright and everything was moving too fast. Voices were unclear. His head was pounding. No, it was gunshots he was hearing. Someone was yelling out orders and someone else was just screaming incoherently. The pain was too much.

Must get more rest.

"I got you, pal," said a soothing voice. It sounded like Kirk. He can handle this. He'll keep everyone safe.

More rest.

Sometime later, David awoke with a start, "Huh? What?" He was drenched in sweat, as he looked around him. It looked like he was lying in the back seat of a car. "Where the hell am I?"

A female voice responded, "You're safe." It was a familiar voice.

"Edie, what happened?"

She looked over the front passenger seat at him. She smiled faintly and said in a soft voice, "We were waiting for you to wake up."

He stared up at her and she kept returning his gaze. Again, he asked, "What happened, Edie? Tell me."

"They sunk the ship. One of the big planes crashed into the museum building. It was pretty bad." She bit her bottom lip and hesitated, before saying, "A lot of people didn't make it."

"Who's dead?"

"Wait, there's more," she said. "Some of the guys pulled out the survivors. A few were hurt, like Wally. Tracy's back was hurt, too. She couldn't walk. The next thing we knew, those monsters attacked us! They were… everywhere!" She swallowed and her eyes got watery. She went on, "They killed Tracy, and then..." Her voice trailed off and she looked to the floor, as she tried to build up the strength to relive the awful memory. Unable to find the words, she spat out abruptly, "You don't understand! People were hurt and it was hard to protect them! We had to leave! We didn't have a choice! So many people died today," she sobbed.

He was becoming frustrated and sat up abruptly. The pain caused him to wince and lie back down. He took a deep breath and asked, "Edie, who is dead?"

"Michelle," she began crying.

He closed his eyes and understood this was going to be hard to listen to, let alone hard for her to tell him.

"Mr. Hayes was hurt, too, and then they ate him! It was horrible! He kept calling for us to help!"

"Jesus Christ." He felt terrible that he was unable to help. Still, he needed to know who was gone. He pushed on and asked, "Who else, Edie? What about that jerk, Damian?"

"No, we're in his car, but almost everyone who worked at the museum is gone, except for Jerry and he has two broken legs. Oh, Wally hurt his knee and that sanitation guy, Claude, has a broken arm, but they are okay. That's it."

"That was enough. Where are Kirk and Kevin?"

"They're outside. Do you want me to get them for you?"

He shook his head, "No, that's fine. Let them do what has to be done. One more question."

"Huh?"

"Where's Millie?"

Edie began to tear up, again. She cried, as she told him, "She tried to kill herself, after Michelle died. She wanted to let those things eat her. She didn't care. Kirk and Kevin dragged her away from her sister and had to put your handcuffs on her. She kept kicking and screaming. She's in the fire truck."

He instinctively looked down at his gun belt and noticed his handcuff case was unsnapped and his cuffs were missing, but then he looked up at her and asked, "What fire truck?"

"Gordon's fire truck," she answered simply.

"And who the hell is Gordon?" He demanded.

"He's a fire man. He helped us at the pier. He came with the soldiers."

"*Soldiers???*" At that point, David agitated some pain in his head and closed his eyes.

"Uh huh, there are two of them," she replied. "They are with us, now. Well, they're outside with the others." She looked at him and felt worried, so she asked, "Um, are you all right?"

"Yes… No." He shook his head. "Edie…"

"Yeah, Dave?"

He opened his eyes, took a deep breath, and said calmly, "I'm going to need you to do me a favor."

"You want me to get Kevin and Kirk?"

"That's my girl," he forced a little smile.

She smiled shyly and said, "K. Be right back." She wiped away her tears, got out of the car, and walked off somewhere nearby.

A few seconds later, Kirk and Kevin approached the car and opened the back door. They bent over to look inside and beamed at him.

Kevin said, "Man, am I glad you are awake! You had us worried, Dave!"

Kirk grinned, "I told you I'd keep you safe. How are you feeling?"

"I told you," he answered weakly, "Like I need a vacation."

"That's very consistent of you, my friend. Are you ready for some hard facts?" He asked, as the smile faded away from his face.

"Edie told me about the deaths and the infected attack. What I want to know, first, is where are we and how long have I been out?"

Kirk replied, "We're in a bus depot back uptown. We blocked the garage entrance with some buses. You've been out for two hours. Your buddy Charles called. I know that's the guy you've been staying in touch with, so I answered and gave him a head's up on our situation. I hope you don't mind. I normally don't answer other people's phones, but this isn't normal, what we're doing."

David sighed and winced from the pain. He said, "It's fine. What did he have to say?"

"He said they are waiting at the armory. If we can get to them today, we should because they can't keep waiting. Things have gotten really bad there. There are infected running in the streets. The virus has spread into the Bronx. The military pulled back to the Yonkers border and left the police to deal with it on their own."

"That means we might be able to cross to the Bronx," David responded excitedly.

"Easy, cowboy," Kirk said. "Don't forget all the bridges have been blown up and the tunnels have been collapsed."

"Yeah, but if the military pulled out, then there won't be snipers taking pot shots at us, if we try crossing the river on a boat."

Kevin said, "Except there are no boats left in Manhattan. The military bombed every single pier, not just Pier 86. They hit the boat basins, the Battery, South Street Sea Port, everything. We can try swimming across, but it won't be easy. You can't make it in your condition."

"Shit. Okay, we'll get back to that later. Next question, we have soldiers with us?"

Kevin nodded, "Two."

Kirk stated, "They were abandoned last night, after failing their mission. They're stuck like us. I thought about telling them to go to hell, but they have very useful skills. One is an explosives expert and the other is a sniper."

"*Sniper?*"

"Yeah, I asked if he spent any time playing 'Cop Hunt,' along the river, the other day, but he swore they were flown in yesterday, briefed, and sent out. He lost his rifle in the river. He said he was almost out of ammo anyway. These guys don't even have radios to communicate with anyone on the outside."

David sighed, "Okay, so, why are we back uptown?"

Kirk explained, "Gordon, a fireman, told us the infection is moving downtown, so there are more runners down there. It's mostly zombies above 110th Street. They're easier to avoid, or kill, if necessary."

"Sounds like not much has changed," he sighed. "So, is that what we're calling them? Zombies?"

"I see what you did there. That's funny," Kirk smirked. "You know? When you think about it, the word makes sense. You have those that run and you have slow reanimated corpses. *Zombies.*"

Kevin agreed, "Yeah, that's basically what we're dealing with and, to be honest, I'd much rather deal with the slow ones."

David shrugged, "Whatever. I really don't care what they're called. We need to think of the fastest way to get all of us to the Bronx *today.*"

Kirk asked, "Do you feel up to traveling?"

"I already told you twice. I need a vacation and I want to spend it beyond the Bronx away from this shit hole, but first I need to set up my travel plans and I am more than ready to do that."

"I hear you, pal. Let's do it. Oh, wait. That dude from the museum, Jerry? He's got two broken legs. He is definitely in no condition to travel."

David sighed, "Why don't we leave that decision up to him? If he thinks he can make it, then we will try with everything we got to help him. If he doesn't feel up to it, we can let him use this place as a shelter. Anyone else who is not willing to do what has to be done can stay here with him. I intend to leave this borough before dark, even if I have to crawl through sewers to do it."

Kirk tilted his head sideways and said, "Well, there is one more problem. We had to handcuff Millie and drag her with us because she became suicidal. That hot older sister of hers died when the plane fell through the roof. The poor kid was torn up. We couldn't just leave her."

"No, you guys did the right thing. It was for her own good. Her sister would have wanted her to live. I'll talk to her. Pass me a bottle of painkillers and help me out of here."

Tensions were high at the recently abandoned bus depot on East 126th Street and Second Avenue. Damian and Josh glared at Williams and Martinez, as if it were their fault that The Intrepid was sunk. Williams kept his hand on his MK 18 Mod 0 and was ready to shoot them both, if necessary. He maintained eye contact with both. They knew he meant business. Martinez was ready to pull out his sidearm, but tried not to look as obvious about it.

Jerry was sitting in a chair and complaining about the intense pain in his legs. Wally sat in a chair beside with a wounded knee. However, he preferred silence, so Jerry was getting on his last nerve. Gordon was kind enough to tend to their wounds, since he was a qualified Emergency Medical Technician, despite being broken up about the tragic death of his buddy, Sean. He knew keeping busy would take his mind off his pain. He had already wrapped Claude's broken arm for him.

Bobby stared at the fire engine, where Millie was resting. He wanted to keep an eye on her to make sure she didn't run away. Secretly, he was turned on about her being in handcuffs. All kinds of thoughts were going through his mind, but he kept them to himself.

Millie was in her own world of hurt. She didn't give a damn about what was going on around her. All she wanted was to die, now that her sister was gone. She loved her sister more than anyone else in the world. To see her die, tore her up inside. The image kept playing back in her mind over and over. If only they had more time. Why did she have to die?

Kirk and Kevin robbed her of her chance to be with Michelle. It made her angry.

Suddenly, the door opened and someone climbed in the back with her. It was David. He looked very sad and uncomfortable from the pain his injuries were causing. He said, "I'm really sorry about your sister. I didn't know her long, but I could tell she was a great person."

Millie sat up and moved over, so he would have space to sit, but she said nothing.

David continued, "I know it's hard for you to imagine life without her. I have a sister, too. For all I know, I may never see her, again. At least, you got that last chance to be with her and spend a couple of days together. I would give anything to see my sister, again. She's younger like you."

Millie looked at him with tears in her eyes and listened.

"Your sister helped us out when we had nowhere else to turn. I'll never forget that. She would be very upset with me or the other guys, if we let anything bad happen to you. Right now, we're the closest things we have to family, so we need to look out for each other. You stay close to us because we're going to protect you and keep you safe. We're going to get you out of Manhattan, today. You have my word."

"You promise?"

"Cross my heart and hope to die," he crossed his fingers over his heart. "Don't be angry with Kirk and Kevin. They were only keeping you safe. Be mad at me, if you have to be mad."

"I can't be angry at you."

"Why is that?"

"You're my guardian angel."

David scoffed, "I've been called a lot of things, Millie. I can honestly tell you that was never one of them."

"Well, it's true. Isn't it? I see it clearly, now. You came to me when I was more scared than ever and you have been guiding me, and the others, to safety ever since. When you are hurt, others are hurt and sometimes they die, but when you are awake, we are all safe."

"I wish that were true. The safe part, at least."

"I need it to be," she said sadly.

He nodded and exhaled. "Okay, so be it. Are we good? Are you going to try to hurt yourself?"

"No," she shook her head. "We're good."

"Give me your hands," which she did. He pulled out his handcuff key from his pocket and unhooked the handcuffs. He replaced them back on his belt and said, "Okay, your turn. *Please*, help me down from this truck."

She got out from the other side and came around to his side. He opened his door and she helped him down. He ached from the pain, which felt unbearable.

Kirk watched from nearby to make sure he didn't fall. He smiled in admiration at David for getting through to Millie. While Kirk did not know David well or for long, he knew he was a good man. There was no doubt in his mind about his character. He was a man with a lot of heart and that meant everything to him. David was the sort of man that he would follow into the very fires of Hell. The crazy thing was it almost felt like they were already there.

It was time to address the others. David called everyone's attention and explained how he was still planning on crossing into the Bronx despite his injuries. He wanted to know who was ready to do the same.

Williams asked, "Excuse me, but exactly what is your plan to cross into the Bronx? I was under the impression that the crossings were destroyed and are currently under heavy protection."

"They were destroyed, but the virus has moved into the Bronx, regardless. My source tells me the military has moved back, which means no more heavy protection. We should be able to cross the Harlem River without fear of being shot. The police have their hands full. There's no point in stopping anyone from going into the Bronx anymore."

Damian snarled at Williams, "Oh, please! Stop acting like you don't already know this shit! You G.I. Bros are probably behind this whole thing! We should kill these two, take their weapons, and be done with it!"

Josh agreed, "Shit yeah! I like the black guy's gun!"

Williams aimed his MK 18 Mod 0 at Josh and said, "You're welcome to try and take it, you yuppie bitch boys."

David raised his hands and shouted, "Whoa! Let's all calm the hell down! We are *not* going to war against each other in here!" He turned to Damian and Josh and explained, "First of all, the military did not start this virus. As far as I know, it was one demented scientist with his own agenda."

Martinez asked, "How do you even know that?"

"I have my sources. Second, you two idiots are not getting your hands on any firearms, while you are in this group. You're too unstable and I don't want to have to shoot you." He was still looking at Josh and Damian.

Next, he turned to Williams and asked, "Why did they send you into a Quarantined Zone?"

"It was a classified mission, but since we were left for dead, I don't mind telling. We were sent to retrieve a possible anti-virus from a secret lab."

David asked, "At the Science Center?"

Williams and Martinez looked surprised.

Williams stated, "You sure have a good source of information."

David shook his head and smirked, "I have a feeling our sources of information are both coming from the same place. Do you know Charles Foster?"

"No. I never heard of him. Why?"

"He's been in contact with a friend, who might be telling her superior officer, who is probably passing the information to the military. It doesn't matter. We're all in the same boat, which means we should be on the same team. No fighting amongst ourselves. There's no point. Let's learn to play nice, so we can get out of here, together. I don't have the patience to baby-sit you guys."

Wally said, "I have a bad knee, but I'll tough it out. I don't want to stay here another night."

Kirk assured him, "I'll be your crutch, Wally. Don't worry. I promise wherever I go, I'll bring you with me. At least, until we get off this island."

"Thanks, man."

Claude said confidently, "My arm is busted, but that never stopped me before. It won't stop me now. Let's do this."

Bobby chuckled, "That's my man! Slick Claude! No one can hold him back!"

Claude blushed with modesty.

Only Jerry had a problem. He said, "I'd much rather head back to my apartment on the Lower East Side, but you guys dragged me all the way uptown. How am I supposed to get home?"

David shrugged, "I really can't tell you. These guys saved you, but if you prefer it, you can stay here and make your way downtown when your legs heal."

"I'll starve to death! I can't walk!"

Bobby responded coldly, "If you can crawl, you'll be fine."

David glared at him and said, "Ignore the stupid comments. You'll need to make a decision, Jerry. We can help you, as long as you are coming with us. Maybe Damian and Josh can help carry you."

Damian turned to him and cried out, "The hell I will! Let the G.I. Bros do it!"

Williams rolled his eyes and muttered to Martinez, "This cat's pushing his luck."

David replied, "In that case, you two guys can stay with him and take care of him." He pointed at Damian and Josh. "If you're not willing to help out, then we don't need you with us."

"Ha!" Damian scoffed, "You wanna bet? I don' take orders from you! We civilians outnumber you! We pay your salary! Keep in mind you were lying in *my* car, pig!"

David rolled his eyes and held his tongue. He tried to control his temper. If he had not been injured, this conversation would be going much differently.

Kevin, Wally, Edie, and Millie were giving Damian dirty looks. They were beginning to think it would be best for him and Josh not to come along. Like David, they did not justify the insult with a response.

On the other hand, Kirk did not feel the need to be so civil. He narrowed his eyes, walked over to Damian, and glared down at him. He grabbed Damian by the shirt and lifted him off his seat and into the air, so they were eye level to each other. Considering Kirk was a foot taller, it made a huge difference. He then asked calmly, "Are you seriously giving my buddy, Dave, a hard time, in front of me, you prissy little pissant? Please, tell me you are, so I can crack your face in half." He clenched his big fists and you could hear his knuckles crack.

Damian swallowed nervously and stammered with a shaken voice, "N-No, man. It's, uh, cool. I was… only joking. Yeah. We'll carry him. N-No problem. R-Right, Josh?"

"Gladly," said Josh, while staring at Kirk's big fists. He always thought he was tall, but Kirk was a giant. His fists looked like sledgehammers ready to strike. Josh did not want to take a chance that Kirk would actually kick both their asses and they'd be left to die, while everyone else escaped. It was always wise to pick your battles and this was one they could not win. Not, yet, anyway.

Bobby chuckled and said, "Great! Now, that the crybaby whining bullshit is settled, let's load up on one of these buses and head for the sewers! The Park Avenue entrance is not far from here. It should take us under the Harlem River to around 138th Street in the Bronx."

Millie made a face of disgust. She was dreading going through the sewers. She thought having her sister by her side would make the experience slightly more tolerable. That would not be the case. However, a moment later, her guardian angel came through, again, and brightened up her mood.

David smirked, "Actually, there might be another easier way."

METROPOLIS OF THE UNDEAD

Chapter Nine

Y ESTERDAY…
Charles gestured toward Marc and said, "Marc is infected."

Frank, Charles, and Roberto gazed over at Marc, who was out of breath from running and trying to climb over the fence, while an infected person was chomping on his leg. Roberto was able to help him over, but it was too late. Marc could not believe he had been bitten. He wondered how he could have been so careless. They were going to kick him out for sure. He was as good as dead. He closed his eyes and wanted to cry, as the reality of the situation started to set in.

"Shit on me," he groaned and a tear forced its way out. He instantly wiped it away, so no one would see it. He pretended it was sweat he was wiping off his face. Be strong, he told himself. You need to be strong!

All of a sudden, a loud crash was heard outside. The perimeter fence had been torn down in front of the armory's main entrance. The disturbing sound of metal rattling against the ground immediately followed, as the infected began stepping over the fallen fence. Seconds later, they pounded against the iron doors, screaming savagely for the meals that had just escaped their grasp. The infected were literally outside their front doors. There would be no more supply runs indefinitely, so it was a good thing they just finished one.

Marc was brought into the main lobby, but no further. His blood was infected. Charles instructed him to hold his wound and try to control the bleeding.

He shouted, "Doc!"

Aramis rushed out to the lobby and replied, "Yo! I'm here! What's up, boss? Holy shit! What happened?"

Charles explained with desperation, "The wound in his leg needs to be wrapped, but be careful because he was bitten! Make sure you wear rubber gloves! I don't need you getting infected, too!"

"Infected??? Oh, man…"

Aramis and Marc locked eyes. In that moment, Aramis could feel his pain. He hurried back to the hangar room and returned with his medical bag. He carefully began tending to Marc's wound. It wasn't deep, but the skin had been broken. Aramis cleaned it, as best he could, patched it up, and dressed it. Not that it made any difference.

Still, Charles did not want Marc's infected blood everywhere. Everyone knew he had become the equivalent to a ticking time bomb. The only question was when?

It was decided Marc would be left in the former homeless shelter on the east side of the armory, where he could be locked up and separated from everyone else. No one wanted to take a chance that he might change and bite anyone. A few in the group had already been through that experience and were not in the mood to repeat it.

There was really no need to lock the door because Marc would not be capable of opening it, once the change took place. They figured he had about an hour before he would begin reacting violently. His wound was starting to itch him, which meant his time was already running out. It was a shame because he was a young guy with his whole life ahead of him, or so it seemed, until a few minutes ago.

There was time for everyone to say his or her goodbyes. Marc cried, as did the teenage girls. Steve wanted to, but he held it in quite well. No one could tell that he actually cared. Liz felt bad and gave him a hug. He had started to grow on her, during their time in the aqueduct tunnels.

The others, who did not really know him well, such as Frank, Nikki, Giselle, Julia, and Daniel felt bad, but kept their distance. Roberto felt guilty that he wasn't fast enough to help him, so he apologized. Marc did not blame him, though. He blamed himself.

In the meantime, Charles and the rest of the group discussed their options. What would they do, once the infection took a hold of him? Ultimately, Marc volunteered to end it himself. After all, he had his own weapon. He felt it should be his own doing, so no one would have to live with the guilt. The others thought he was brave to take on such a responsibility. Charles commended him for it.

That's when the door was finally locked.

They waited nervously for the gunshot. Fifteen minutes went by and it was silent, aside from the infected yelling outside. A half hour later, they were starting to wonder what was going on. After an hour, they figured maybe he was waiting for the last possible minute. That had to be it, some thought.

Finally, a gunshot echoed throughout the first floor.

Daniel cried out in surprise, "Oh, shit!"

Nikki and Giselle both gasped and began crying.

Grant and Charles looked at each other. Each of them sighed with regret. Another cop was dead. Another friend was gone.

Steve bowed his head and could no longer hold back his tears. He wiped them away, as they came. How many more friends would he have to lose because of this virus?

Liz also wiped away some tears, while Roberto slammed his fist on the floor, where he sat. If only he'd been faster, he thought.

Aramis closed his eyes and wondered how much longer they each had, before it was their turn to make that decision.

An awkward silence fell over the armory's interior, momentarily. The infected heard the gunshot and moved around to the east side of the building on Jerome Avenue, where the sound seemed to originate. They had to leave the fenced in area to get there, which left the Kingsbridge side empty, for a short time. Had the group been ready, this might have been a good time for them to flee, but they were not. In time, the infected would return to the front doors and resume their relentless pounding.

The Kingsbridge Armory during the evening.

This morning...

Steve was still in pain due to his injured rib. Otherwise, he felt a little better. The medication he received was helping. However, he barely slept at all, so he was exhausted. His eyes searched the hangar for Charles, but he did not see him. Grant was putting on his gun belt nearby. He had just woken up, as well.

Steve asked him, "Grant, did anyone ever check on Marc? I mean, that kid was an idiot. Someone should make sure he did the job right. We really don't need him waking up and breaking through that door."

"I'm not sure. I'll go check on him myself."

"You probably shouldn't go alone." He started to get up.

"I know, but you stay put. You need to recover," Grant said. "I'll take someone else with me." He looked around to see who else was awake. At that time, he also noticed Charles was not at their camp and neither was Liz. He instinctively looked up to one side of the mezzanine and did not see anyone. He walked to the other side of the room, so he could check the other mezzanine. Liz was sitting up there holding her rifle, which was pointed upright, while staring down at him. They locked eyes briefly.

He then walked out to the main lobby, where he saw Charles and Frank.

"Good morning, guys. What's going on with Marc?" He asked, right away.

Charles answered glumly, "I was just about to check."

"Good. Let's go together."

Charles nodded and turned to Frank, "Lead the way, Frank."

They followed Frank to the entrance of the old homeless shelter. Before unlocking the door, Frank listened. The three of them remained quiet and waited for any sign that Marc was still moving. There was none. Frank slowly unlocked the door and stepped aside. He had no intention of going in with them.

Charles and Grant drew their weapons and stood on either side of the doorway. Once they were ready, Charles cautiously opened the door. No one attacked. It was quiet.

They stepped inside and into the main corridor. They began checking each corner of every room, until Grant finally found him.

"He's in here," he called out.

Charles followed his voice and saw Grant standing over Marc. He had handcuffed himself to an old steam pipe to make sure he stayed put. His gun was still firmly in his hand. He gagged himself with his t-shirt, so he wouldn't scream, disturb anyone else, or bite. The only thing he did not do was to fulfill the promise he made. His reanimated body had already passed the first stages of infection. He was a zombie. His dead eyes followed Charles and Grant as they moved, motivated by hunger. He made biting motions, but his mouth was gagged well, so he was no danger to them.

Charles shook his head sorrowfully and uttered, "The poor bastard couldn't do it."

"No one else needs to know," Grant responded. "Let's give him some dignity. We can end it quietly for him. I don't think he would have wanted to go on this way."

"Right. Do you have a knife?"

"Yeah, here on my belt," Grant answered. "Watch out, give me some space."

Charles stepped aside and Grant moved closer with his knife in his hand. He put on his leather gloves and shoved the blade into the side of Marc's temple. He made sure to push it in deep, until Marc stopped moving. Grant pulled out the knife and the t-shirt from Marc's mouth. He found a dry part of the shirt and wiped the knife as clean as he could. He put it away and placed the shirt over Marc's face. He then carefully removed Marc's weapon from his hand, along with the two extra magazine clips from his gun belt.

He noticed Charles was watching him, so he said, "We're probably going to need a lot of weapons and ammo in the near future. There's no point leaving these here."

"I'm not arguing. Give the weapon to Doc. I trust him with it."

"Okay. What about Marc?"

"We'll lock this area up for good. This is now his crypt. Rest in peace, Marc Nugent," Charles stated sadly, as he turned to leave.

Grant looked down at Marc one last time, and then followed Charles. Frank locked the door when they stepped out. None of them said a word.

Now...

Later that same morning, Liz was aiming her Colt M4 Carbine out of a third floor window in the west tower facing the front of the Kingsbridge Armory. She scanned the area in front of the main entrance using the weapon's scope. In the past day, dozens of infected people forced their way into the perimeter of the fence that once kept them separated. Within the last few hours, mostly all of them had undergone an incredible transformation. Liz watched as their bodies died, fell still, and then reanimated. Moments later, the armory was surrounded by nearly a hundred zombies, who still tried desperately to gain access into the armory's heavy iron doors to no avail. There was no doubt they knew there was food inside.

"This is crazy, Grant. They literally died and came back to life, but they refuse to leave."

Grant moved toward her window and leaned over her shoulder to have a look. He had been silently observing the situation for about five minutes from a different window in the tower. "Came back to life? I don't know," he said. "Smells more like death to me."

"They are pretty gross." Her eyes moved up toward him. He was still close to her. She turned to him and said, "I'm sorry about your friend. I'm sorry about all of your friends. You've lost a lot this past weekend. It can't be easy. I don't think the others realize how hard this must be for you guys, you, Charles, Steve, and Aramis. You're good at hiding your pain."

He frowned and looked at her. "I suppose," he said. "Thanks for the sympathy. I appreciate it. We are trying to be strong for the benefit of the group. We can't afford to break down and cry for every friend we lose. Not while we still have a job to do. Once we get to safety, who knows how we'll react? I'm trying hard to push my feelings aside and focus on staying alive, but as you said, it's not easy."

"You know? If you want to take a break, I could watch on my own."

He looked away and said, "Thanks, but I've been in survival mode for three days already. I won't be ready to turn it off, until I can go home and be myself, again."

"So, this isn't the real you?" She asked, while still looking at him.

"Well, it is, but it's only part of me. I have a more relaxed side, too."

"Like when you walk through the park and take photos?"

He looked back at her and smiled, "Exactly."

She chuckled, "It sounds better than staring at *zombies* with a gun in your hand."

"Tell me about it," he scoffed.

They both turned back to looking out from the same window. A moment later, she asked, "Hey, can I please use your cellphone to call my parents, again? I keep thinking about them. I told them to go to my uncle's house, but they're so hardheaded. I want to make sure they listened to me."

"Of course, take it." He handed his cellphone to her and she stepped a few feet away to make her call. He watched her walk away, and then turned back to the window, so he could continue looking down at the zombies. Watching her was definitely much better, but the numerous zombies had him worried. He knew it would not be long before they spread around the perimeter and surrounded the entire building. If there was an escape plan to be made, it had better come soon, or the entire building might become a tomb for them.

Poor Marc, he thought. He was so young. His mind began drifting through the faces of his fallen friends, since the outbreak began. The emotions started to get to him. He wiped his eyes.

A few seconds later, Charles entered the third floor tower room, where they were. He walked past Liz, who was engaged in conversation, and over toward Grant. "Hey," he asked, "How's the view?" Before Grant responded, he glanced out of the window and saw the accumulation of zombies out front. "Damn," he breathed heavily. It was enough to make him worry, too. He sighed and commented, "It looks like there are a lot more than yesterday."

"Oh, yeah," Grant nodded. "Did you make your calls?"

"Mmhmm. Of course, there's more bad news. My friend at MetroTech Center told me several infected have crossed over into the Bronx not far from our location. Naturally, I told her we were fully aware of that fact. They've also lost control of the situation at LaGuardia Airport. A few infected were able to slip past the quarantine, leading to outbreaks in Astoria and East Elmhurst.

With more boroughs in danger, the National Guard has pulled back their forces and established stronger borders around the Bronx and in Queens, leaving the Harlem River unprotected. They started erecting electrified fences with barbed wire. In addition, they've brought in hundreds of shipping containers into Brooklyn by sea and into the Bronx via the Metro-North railroad to use as walls. Heavy naval patrols have been deployed in the Long Island Sound and along the Hudson River. They are not messing around.

However, we still have a chance. If we plan to head north, we need to do it by tonight. Tomorrow, we will have to fight our way out and we do not have the firepower to do that. I already told everyone downstairs to pack up what we can."

"Okay, what about Dave? I thought we were going to wait for him."

"We are waiting. That's the only reason we're not leaving right this minute. Now, that the National Guard is out of the way, he can easily cross the river from Manhattan to the Bronx. His group should be able to reach us today. There's only one problem. He got hurt this morning and is unconscious."

"What??? How did that happen?"

"Military jets sank The Intrepid and blew up the entire pier."

Grant gasped, "Holy shit! Are you kidding me? Those bastards have absolutely no regard for history! Why not just bomb the whole city and be done with it?"

"Let's be careful what we wish for, especially while we are still here. I'm sure the military is only following orders. David was hurt in a building collapse, which was part of the museum. A bunch of others were killed. Someone named Kirk, who has been with David since the first night, is keeping him safe. I told him what was going on and he said he would make sure to get David to us today. I already let him know, we will be gone by tonight."

"Okay, so, we are going to need a vehicle," Grant suggested. "Something big and someone with a CDL license to operate it without getting us killed."

"Agreed," Charles said, "I'll go back down and see if anyone qualifies. You should come down when you're ready, so you can pack up your gear. There's no point looking out anymore, at least, not until David gets close."

"Okay, I'll be down in a bit. I'm just waiting on Liz. She's calling her parents. They don't want to leave Yonkers. Too stubborn, I guess."

"Yeah, well, Yonkers is the next step for us and the virus. If they couldn't contain it on an island, there's no way they can keep it from leaving the Bronx. It's going to happen. I want to be back in Orange County when it does."

"That sounds good. Mind if I join you?"

"Sure, why not? I have plenty of room at my place," Charles said with pride. "Come to think of it, it would make a great compound."

Grant replied eagerly, "Let's do it then. We can stop by my place in Yonkers, grab my weapons, ammo, and survival gear, and then head to your place. Besides, I'd really like to get out of these clothes. They're sticking to my skin!"

Charles chuckled, "I feel your pain, my brother. It looks like we have ourselves the making of a solid escape plan. We only need a vehicle and a driver."

"I'll head up to the top level and see what I can see from the tower windows. We should be able to spot a potential ride from there. Maybe there's a bus nearby or a long van."

"Good idea," Charles agreed. "I'll see you downstairs." He then headed to the staircase and went back down to the ground floor.

Liz had gone out into the hallway to speak, but she had just returned. She handed Grant his cellphone and said, "Thank you."

"You're welcome. So, did they leave?"

"Yes! Finally! I got them to drive up to my uncle's house in Yorktown Heights. They should be safe there. I hope. They didn't want to leave without me! I had to tell them I was never going back home, so they could leave. They're so stubborn! Sometimes, it drives me crazy."

"They're probably just worried about you."

She smirked, "Yeah, I know. So, hey! What did Charles have to say?"

"We got ourselves an escape plan."

She raised her eyebrows in surprise and asked, "We finally have a plan?"

"Yes, indeed," he grinned at her.

He told her everything he and Charles discussed, and then the two went upstairs to the top floor of the tower, so they could search for an escape vehicle. Time was limited, so they needed to hurry.

Charles informed the others in the hangar of the plan. They began packing whatever they could because they would not be returning. Some of them were sipping coffee from Styrofoam cups. Roberto created a makeshift stove using a few bricks and some candles. He had grabbed the coffee pot and coffee from his apartment.

Nikki took a sip from her cup and turned to him with a look of worry. She asked, "What about mom? You said you left her a note to come here!"

"Well, I'll just have to leave her another note," he answered, before taking a sip from his cup. "She knows our cellphone numbers by heart. She can call us when she gets a chance."

"What if she doesn't have access to a phone?"

Roberto turned to her and grabbed her firmly by the shoulders. He explained, as calmly as he could, "Listen, Nik. I am just as worried about mom, as you, but she is not the one in here, surrounded by freaking zombies! *We* are! Right now, I need to stay focused on keeping you safe. You and GG are my top priority. It's bad enough Zonnie is out there and not answering her phone. I can't weigh myself down worrying about things I have no control over. Pack your stuff back in your bag. We're leaving with these officers. They can keep us safe."

Giselle scoffed, "You mean like what happened to Marc?"

"Hey! That was on me," Roberto replied angrily, and then he took a deep breath to calm down.

"*You?*" She asked surprised. Suddenly, she felt terrible. It hadn't occurred to her that he would blame himself for what happened to

Marc. She placed her hand on his shoulder and said softly, "I'm sorry, Rob. I didn't know. I thought…"

"That's just it. Stop thinking," he stated. "Forget what you think you know. That's over. You don't know what's going on out there. It's gotten so much worse than when we first came here. I'd much rather deal with rioters and looters. I can easily kick their asses, but that," he pointed toward the main entrance, where pounding could still be heard from outside. "I can't fight those… *things* out there! They need to be killed and I don't have a gun! Even if I did, it wouldn't matter. Marc had his gun and they got him. If they infect me, I'm done. End game."

Roberto walked away to finish his coffee in peace. He needed some space. Being confined to one room with everyone was starting to get to him. He was generally a private person.

Grant and Liz casually entered the hangar and everyone stopped what they were doing to face them. They were obviously all feeling a bit jumpy. The coffee probably didn't help, although some of them swore they needed it. Craved it was more like it.

Liz sniffed the air and asked, "Do I smell coffee?"

Aramis showed her the pot and said, "There's still some left, if you're interested. Rob made it. It's Café Bustelo. Very tasty and strong."

Liz walked over and happily grabbed a Styrofoam cup from a nearby bag. Aramis poured her some coffee and she breathed in the smell savoring it.

Grant, on the other hand, went straight to his patrol bag and began putting whatever he could into it. Coffee wasn't his thing. He hated the after taste. What he really wanted was to change his clothes, but it would have to wait a little longer.

Steve sat helplessly nearby using the butcher's coat he had as a cushion for his behind. He had nothing to pack, so he watched the others. He hated being injured. He felt so useless.

Grant noticed his expression and the fact that he wasn't being his usual chatty self. He knew the pain of the recent losses must have been affecting him deeply, as well. He decided to make conversation with him, in hopes of cheering him up a bit.

"Hey, Steve, how are you feeling? Are you up for traveling?"

Steve snapped out of his stupor and turned to Grant to answer, "If it gets me out of this city, I am up for mostly anything. Wait. Maybe I should rephrase that. I almost forgot I'm talking to your wise ass."

Grant chuckled and replied, "Relax. I'm taking it easy on you, until you get better. How does Yonkers sound for starters? We're going to stop by my place to grab some stuff, and then we'll heading across the bridge to Rockland. We can stop by your house on the way."

"That sounds great, except my wife already took my dog and went to her parents' house."

"Oh? Where do they live?"

"Ohio."

Grant's expression changed. He knew there had been an outbreak in Ohio. He could not recall if Charles had mentioned it to Steve. Grant definitely did not want to worry Steve. Plus, he was uncertain in which city the outbreak occurred. His silence had already spoken a thousand words.

Steve sounded worried when he said, "I tried calling her, but she hasn't answered. She left as soon, as she learned I was still alive. I haven't spoken to her since."

Grant sat down on the tarp next to him and said, "Okay, well, that was only yesterday. Maybe she's still driving and she's in a dead zone with no cell towers. She'll probably call you, as soon as she reaches her parents' house. Have faith in her."

Steve scoffed, "I appreciate what you're doing here, but it doesn't take that long to drive there. She should have been there yesterday. I don't know. Maybe she's upset that I left her waiting a day, before calling. I just hate not knowing."

"I understand," Grant nodded. "Why don't you send her a text message and let her know we are leaving the city? Tell her you hope to see her soon."

"You must be joking. She'd never believe it was me!"

Grant chuckled. "I forgot you're a regular romantic," he joked sarcastically. "Think positive, pal. We'll get you out of here in one piece, and then we can focus on getting to our families."

Steve thought about his sister and nephew. He was grateful he was able to get them to leave their home in Astoria. He knew she would definitely be a lot safer in Connecticut, although he really missed his nephew, most of all. That boy was like the son he didn't have. At least, he was safe. It was a small comfort.

At that moment, Charles got a call on his cellphone. He answered excitedly, "Hello! I'm glad to hear you're okay!" There was a pause.

"Yes, we're still here, but you really need to hurry. We have to get up to Westchester County tonight. By morning, it will be a whole new ballgame. Worst-case scenario, we can meet up in Yonkers." He paused, again, before saying, "Okay. Stay in touch and let me know how that works out. I hope to see you soon."

He hung up and turned to the others to say, "Good news. David is awake and he's got a plan for crossing into the Bronx. He will contact me in a couple of hours. In the meantime, we need to secure a vehicle. Does anyone have a CDL license?"

Aramis raised his hand.

METROPOLIS OF THE UNDEAD

Chapter Ten

D AVID HAD A plan of his own, although he only needed a few people to implement it. He recruited Gordon to drive the fire engine, which was essential for the plan to work. He brought Williams along, since he had a good rifle. Kirk was his muscle because he was going to need it. That was it. Everyone else was left to wait at the bus depot. Kevin was left in charge of things, since he was a cop with a gun.

The plan was simple. They'd drive to the 26th Precinct, where the Emergency Service Unit kept a rescue raft in the supervisors' garage. They could hook up the trailer that the raft rested upon to the fire engine. Afterwards, they would return to the garage and pick up the others. Together, they could use the raft to cross the river to the Bronx. Very simple, aside from the zombies and infected they had to get past.

Getting across town to the precinct was rather simple, although they had to make a couple of detours due to streets that were blocked off by abandoned vehicles or burnt out wrecks. Gordon explained how he came across numerous fires on that first night. Most of them burned out of control.

"It was madness," he said, as he drove the wrong way across West 126ᵗʰ Street from Broadway and eventually came to a stop at the precinct's apron, where the fuel pumps were located.

It was the only way to reach the precinct's garage. Cars were blocking access entering west from Amsterdam Avenue and a yellow taxi had been left in the middle of the street in front of the station house. David knew the taxi belonged to a taxi driver named Gary, who was killed by infected in front of him only a couple of days earlier. It was funny how it seemed like so long ago. The days were dragging.

The face of David's partner, Elizabeth Neal, came to mind. The last time he saw her, she was lying in the holding cell. Lieutenant Andrews was in the cell next to hers. Both were infected. It was very likely they would both still be in those cells as zombies. David dreaded seeing them, again, but how could he not check on them? He was the one that left them there. He owed it to them to show them mercy, if they were indeed still lingering within.

He turned to Gordon, who sat in the driver's seat waiting for him to make the next move. He said, "Before we do this, there is something I need to do. I'm going to need help. When I left here, the building was crawling with infected. They should be zombies, by now, so it won't be too hard to take them out."

Gordon asked, "Is it really that important for you to go in there and kill them?"

"It's not them. It's my partner. I owe it to her."

Gordon nodded, "Say no more. We got your back."

"Without a doubt," said Kirk from behind him.

Williams said, "It's your plan. We play it your way. Just keep in mind, the more we shoot, the faster we will be surrounded by them. They are attracted to the sound."

David nodded, "I'll keep that in mind. No shooting, unless we have to, guys."

They got out of the truck and the others followed David past the fuel pumps. There was a lot of blood on the ground in that area. David remembered it was where Ms. Butler was attacked. He was glad not to see a half-eaten corpse. Of course, it probably meant she became one of *them*. It was depressing to think about it because she was a kind person.

There was more dried blood outside the back door. Edie's friend, Eva, was killed in that spot. David hated reliving the memories of that first night, one step at a time. He wanted to be done with this nightmare already.

He opened the door and was relieved to see the hallway was empty, but the smell was horrendous. They cautiously walked into the building. It turned out there were more than a few zombies inside.

"Shit," he complained.

Every infected person that was there at the time when he left was there waiting as zombies. They had been trapped inside with no means of opening the doors. There were too many, which was going to make it difficult to fight them without shooting.

David opened the door and shouted, "Quick! Get behind the desk area! We can kill them from there!" He ran ahead and led the way. He made sure the door at the opposite end was still locked to make sure they were not surprised from behind. He grabbed the key from the desk and opened up the property room.

He had almost forgotten that Robert Jenkins' body was lying on the floor behind the desk. He tried not to think about it. He was dead and he would not be getting up, again. Still, Robert was his friend. He was a good man. It made David angry to leave the body on the floor, but what else could he do?

Kirk urged him to hurry, "They're getting closer, Dave! Should we start shooting?"

"No! Wait! Here, take this," David handed Kirk a fire hydrant wrench to use as a blunt instrument. Gordon already had his axe ready to swing. David gave Williams a broomstick and instructed, "You hold them back with the stick, while Gordon chops them. Kirk, you hit the ones lined up in front of the desk."

Kirk grinned, "Sounds like fun. I don't mind a game of Whack-a-Zombie." Kirk wasted no time and began bashing zombies on the head with the heavy wrench.

Meanwhile, Williams did what David suggested, while Gordon took out one zombie, after another. The plan was working out well. The number of zombies was dwindling.

David could see the mauled body of Julie on the floor of the muster room next to the body of Sergeant Ryan Taylor. David turned away and noticed the security cameras were still active. He could see two people in the holding cells. He knew exactly who they were.

He turned to look through the window and saw them both there staring hungrily at him. It was odd seeing familiar zombies in police uniforms. Their faces had begun to rot making them look different from their normal selves. Their eyes and cheeks were sunken in and darkened. It broke David's heart to see his partner. She was such a sweet and funny person. To see her looking like something he has come to hate was a shot to the heart. He stepped around behind Williams and into the holding cell area.

David stopped in front of Liz's cell and pulled out his knife. He stood closer, so she would press against the bars. He said, "I'm so sorry," and then plunged the blade into her forehead. She let out faint sound and died. When he pulled back the knife, her body dropped to the floor. He showed his lieutenant the same mercy. He then opened their cells and took their weapons and ammunition. He wanted to put their bodies on the benches, out of respect, but he was afraid of getting infected. The smell was bad enough. He locked the cell doors and closed the door to the room.

Kirk, Williams, and Gordon had been standing at the doorway waiting for him. The other zombies were dead.

Kirk asked, "That was your partner, huh?"

"Yeah, she was a great girl. I couldn't leave her like that."

Williams said, "Don't worry, man. We understand. Do what you need to do."

David looked toward the door to the locker room and said, "Actually, I would really love to change into my normal clothes, if that's all right with you guys?"

"I don't blame you," Gordon replied. "Change your clothes and get your personal stuff. I'm pretty sure we're never coming back here."

David agreed, "True indeed. Can one of you come downstairs with me to the locker room, in case there are more? I don't want to be caught with my pants down."

Kirk chuckled and said, "Literally. Yeah, I'll go with you."

David handed Kirk the 9mm Smith and Wesson that belonged to Lieutenant Andrews and said, "Here. Take it. It's yours now."

Kirk took it and admired it, as if it were a collector's item. "Thanks," he said with a smile.

David nodded. He kept his partner's Glock 19.

They went down to the locker room together, but there was no one there. There were no zombies downstairs. David was able to change into his civilian clothes peacefully. It felt so nice to be free of the added weight from his sweaty bulletproof vest and heavy gun belt. He didn't even bother to put his uniform into his locker. He left it scattered about on the bench and floor, as he removed it. He kept his extra weapon magazines, his knife, mace, handcuffs, and ASP expandable baton and put them into his pants pockets. He placed his 9mm Smith and Wesson handgun into a pancake-style holster and attached it to his belt. The Glock 19 was tucked into his back, under his shirt. He grabbed a new pair of leather gloves from his locker and put them on, which he had been saving for when his old ones ripped. Considering he had them with him the entire weekend, he was more than ready to replace them.

He had gone into the bathroom to wash up a bit, but when he saw the blood on the floor, he changed his mind. He knew it belonged to Robert Jenkins. The blood outside must have belonged to Sergeant Taylor. He didn't want to see any more reminders of dead friends.

After he was dressed, he said, "Let's head up to the garage."

David opened up the garage from within. He entered through a side door near the fuel pumps. Williams guided Gordon, as he backed in the fire engine. Kirk helped David clear off some junk from the raft. They kept a long rope that was on it. Williams noticed it was very similar to the rubber raft his team used when they arrived at Manhattan. He had forgotten about that raft. It would serve as a good back up.

"Hey, I just remembered something. When my team arrived, we used a raft just like that. We left it on the rocks near the Hudson River at the Harlem Pier. It should still be there."

David asked, "Did you hide it from view?"

"Not really. We weren't planning to use it, again. The motor had a limited fuel supply."

"In that case, chances are it's been deflated, shot, or blown to pieces."

"That could be true," Williams frowned. "Still, it's only a few blocks away."

Kirk commented, "It's too risky going there for a 'maybe.' This one should be good enough."

Williams reminded him, "Yeah, but there are a lot of us. We'll need to make about two or three trips. If we had two rafts, things could go much smoother. We could tie one to the other with the rope."

David sighed and said, "We'll go check. It can't hurt. Two rafts would be better than one."

Kirk nodded skeptically, "You're the boss."

Together, they were able to figure out how to hook the trailer to the rear of the fire engine. Now, all they had to do was check for the other raft, get back to the others in one piece, and then drive to the closest point where the Bronx could be easily reached by boat. Gordon already knew the best place to cross would be at the Spuyten Duyvil Creek from Inwood Hill Park.

It seemed risky to drive all over the place tugging the rafts on a trailer behind a fire engine, so David had an idea, but first they needed to check for the other raft and they were going to need the trailer.

They closed the garage and got into the fire engine. Gordon drove west toward Broadway, where he turned left. He made a right turn at West 125th Street and went toward Twelfth Avenue.

There were a few zombies on the road that approached the bright red "food truck." Gordon smashed into them and ran them over. He turned on the windshield wipers and tried to clean away the infected blood, but it only smeared across the glass.

"I guess it doesn't really matter," he said. "We'll be leaving this baby behind when we cross over into the Bronx."

"Damn straight," replied Williams.

They drove past the abandoned ambulance and accident scene from Friday night, before passing under the Henry Hudson Parkway. Williams told Gordon to turn left at the next street, which was Marginal Street. The fire engine came to a stop near the southbound entrance of the parkway.

Williams stepped out and walked toward the river's edge. He was surprised to see the raft was still there and in good condition. He let the others know, so they could help him carry it to the trailer. They tied it to the other raft, so that one was on top of the other.

Afterwards, they returned to the 26th Precinct. David told Gordon to back the fire engine into the garage. Once that was done, he shut the garage door.

He told Kirk, "You guys wait here with the truck and rafts. I'll take Williams back to the depot with me using my personal car. It will be much faster that way. We'll be back with everyone else on a bus, in no time. Wally can drive it. Will you guys be okay staying in here, until we get back?"

Gordon replied, "I don't have a problem with it. That sounds like a better idea than us driving around with this thing on our back."

Kirk agreed, "Yeah, no problem. We shouldn't risk damaging the rafts. Just hurry back. If you're not back in one hour, we're heading over."

David agreed, "Okay. That should be more than enough time." He and Williams left through the side door.

David led Williams to where his car was parked. It was a white BMW. First, they had to cross through a small park to the next block to reach it. At least, it would be facing the right direction, eastbound.

There was a zombie lurking in the darkened park. David used his ASP expandable baton to beat its head in. It took three hits to kill it. He wiped the baton clean using the zombie's t-shirt and they continued to West 129th Street, where his car was parked.

Williams commented, "That was pretty nasty."

David shrugged indifferently.

They got into his car and took off toward Amsterdam Avenue. Due to the extensive amount of abandoned cars that blocked the avenue, they had to go around. David drove north along the sidewalk and turned left into a path that went through the Manhattanville Houses. They came out on the other side and took Broadway south to LaSalle Street. David took that street going east back toward Amsterdam, and then he took West 123rd Street the wrong way to Morningside Avenue. He sped the whole way.

Suddenly, Williams shouted, "Wait!"

The car came to a screeching halt and David asked, "What's wrong?"

"I think this is where we lost the anti-serum."

"I thought that didn't matter anymore."

Williams looked at him with concern and stated, "It might not get me picked up, but it matters more than anything in the world, if we ever want this to end. Think about it. This could be a cure for the very thing that could cause our extinction."

David sighed and nodded. He knew Williams was right. "Let's try to be fast. What exactly are we looking for out here?"

"It's a small toolkit containing a syringe with a white cap. The toolkit is a black leather case about the size of a sandwich. It might be along this path on the left or in the parking lot at the other end. Worst-case scenario it's in the park, in which case it will be somewhere along the main path. Either way, I know I will deeply regret it for the rest of my life, if we don't, at least, try to find it."

David said, "I know the parking lot you're talking about. It's the housing lot for Grant Houses on 125th Street. You take the path and start backtracking your steps. I'll drive around to the other side and check there."

"Uh, okay," he hesitated getting out of the car. He wondered if David was planning to ditch him. Was that really a chance he was willing to take? He was not so sure.

David realized what he was thinking based upon the look on his face and reassured him. "I won't leave you out here, if that's what you think. That's not how I roll. I promise I'll wait for you at the lot. Just don't take too long."

Williams nodded, "Thanks. Check near the iron fence. We left a trail of bodies to guide the way."

"Okay, see you there."

David drove around through Morningside Avenue to West 125th Street avoiding two zombies that were standing in the middle of the street. He did not want to get their infected blood on his clean white BMW unnecessarily. He knew he was being silly, but he did not care. He had a feeling he would have to kill them later. He'd be ready.

He really hated this idea, but Williams was absolutely right. They needed this anti-virus. If they could find it, it could make all the difference in the world. They had to hurry, though. He wished Kirk and Gordon had cellphones. He didn't have anyone's number at the depot. This was such a rushed plan and Charles was waiting. David was getting anxiety.

He pulled into the parking lot and got out of his car when he found the first dead zombie. He bent down and checked under the nearby cars. He did not see a black toolkit.

Moments later, Williams approached from the path and pointed at another dead zombie on the ground. "That was the guy that jumped my buddy, Santiago. Check around him and under him."

David pushed the body over with his foot and gagged at the smell. There was nothing there. "I don't see it," he said, while holding his nose.

"Damn! I was sure it would be here," Williams frowned. "That means it has to be in the park. Santiago fell down, at some point. He tripped over a dead body. I bet that's when he dropped it. It has to be. We've got to check there, man. After that, we can go, but we need to see if it's there."

"Okay, fine." David was getting frustrated. He felt like they were wasting time. He didn't think they were ever going to find that toolkit. "Get in the car," he ordered.

They both got in and drove back to West 123rd Street. David entered the park with his car and drove along the path heading south. They went slowly, so Williams could try to recall the right spot.

"It was right before the path veered left near a playground," he remembered.

David smirked, "I know the spot you mean. I've driven through this park more times than I can remember. Keep an eye out on the ground, just in case. It would suck, if I ran it over."

They soon reached the curve and David stopped the car. Williams got out and walked toward the bushes. He searched desperately and could not believe his eyes. He bent over and shouted, "I found it!" He picked up the toolkit and looked inside, but then cried, "No!"

David got out of his car and walked over to him and asked, "Did it break?"

"Yes," he muttered. "Damn it! I really hate this place! I can't believe this crap!"

"Bring it anyway," David stated calmly. "It has samples of the anti-serum in there. Keep it closed and bring it along. Who knows? Maybe it can still be helpful to someone."

Williams nodded and placed it into his backpack, along with his explosives. He hoped David was right. Maybe a cure could be salvaged from the broken syringe.

They got back into the car and raced out of the park. David sped over to West 116th Street avoiding a small group of infected that tried to chase after the speeding car. When they reached First Avenue, David turned north and headed back toward the depot. They still had time, he thought, as he floored the gas pedal and drove around abandoned vehicles on the road. It was like a crazy obstacle course.

Williams turned to him and asked, "What's the real hurry, Officer Castillo?"

"Call me David, please. I'm not an officer anymore," he replied assuredly. "I have my reasons. Actually, several," he said. "I don't want Kirk and Gordon to drive those rafts across town, so we need to get back before that hour is up. Another reason is I have friends waiting in the Bronx and they can't wait forever. By tomorrow, *your people* will make it a lot harder for us to leave the Bronx."

"*My* people???"

"The military! I'll be damned if I am getting trapped in another borough of this city! Plus, there are those two assholes we left behind at the depot. I really don't trust them."

Williams smirked, "Ah, now we're on the same page. I'm with you on that one."

David stopped his car outside of the bus depot and they stepped out. They both pulled out their weapons and looked at each other. Hopefully, everything would be fine. They had to crawl underneath a bus to get back inside the depot. It was parked sideways to block the entrance. That was part of the plan. It was to keep the others inside safe from any passing zombies.

When David and Williams emerged into the garage on their bellies, their worst fears were realized. Damian was standing over them with a gun in his hand. He pointed it at them and grinned devilishly.

"Come on in, nice and slow," he instructed them, which they did. He allowed them to stand up, before he said, "Okay, toss your guns down in front of you. Nice clothes, officer. I like your style. It's too bad. I was kind of hoping you could die in uniform. Personally, it would have been a better privilege for me to waste a fully dressed pig."

David threw his Smith and Wesson to the floor in front of him. Williams dropped both his weapons, too, although he had left his bag of explosives in the front passenger seat of David's car.

Damian did not recall the bag, but he did notice they were missing two people. He asked, "Traveling kind of light, huh? Where's the fireman and mountain troll?"

"They're already waiting for us at the river," David lied. He studied his options carefully. Damian was only about five feet in front of him. Josh was a few more feet behind holding another gun and casually pointing it downward. Kevin was lying on the floor next to him, as if he had just been struck. Bobby was on his knees next to him. There were a few people lying in the background. David did not want to focus on that, yet. It would be too distracting. He had to do this fast. He had practiced this maneuver at the NYPD shooting range, in the past. He knew he could do it. He could not afford to miss. Otherwise, someone could die. He only had a brief window of opportunity to try his best.

He maintained eye contact with Damian and sneered, "I see your boy back there has plans of his own." It was just enough of a distraction for Damian to glance back over his shoulder at Josh and for Josh to let down his guard. David only had seconds to react. He reached behind him and pulled out the Glock 19, bringing it up, and pointing it at Damian. He fired one shot into Damian's side, and then two shots past him at Josh. Only one made its mark hitting Josh in the shoulder.

Williams saw his chance and dove to the ground grabbing his sidearm and pointing it at Josh in one fluid movement. He fired two shots from the ground hitting Josh in the pelvic region and upper thigh.

David took the opportunity to shoot Damian, again, this time in the neck. He walked closer and shot him one more time in the face. He then walked over to Josh and shot him in the head.

Williams stood up with the weapons in his hand and returned David's Smith and Wesson to him. He took it and re-holstered it. It was time to assess the damage.

Bobby stood up and exclaimed, "Hot *damn!* That was some friggin' crazy ass action hero shit! You guys saved the day!" He then looked over to the floor and bowed his head. He then shouted, "Those bastards killed my boy, Claude! They shot 'Slick' right before you arrived!" He fought back his tears.

David walked over to Kevin and helped him to his feet. He seemed relatively okay. Perhaps, a little winded. David asked, "What about you? Are you okay?"

"Yeah, thanks," he replied, while rubbing the back of his head. "Those jerks blindsided me. They grabbed my gun. They jumped the soldier and took his gun, too. Those animals tortured him, before killing him slowly. They cut the kid's ears off like in that Tarantino movie. Sick pricks!" He spit down at them.

Williams gasped. He had just noticed Martinez's body tied to a chair nearby. He had blood all over his face and his ears had indeed been brutally cut off. It was monstrous.

"Those damned sons of bitches! If they weren't already dead, I'd kill them!" He ran over and kicked Josh in the head hard with his steel-toed boot, and then he walked over to Damian's corpse and stomped on his head repeatedly, until he crushed it."

Kevin scowled in disgust.

Bobby stared angrily wishing he had done the same when it would have made a difference.

David did not see any point in stopping Williams. Those guys deserved far worse and he knew Williams needed to release his anger, somehow. David had a feeling he probably would have done the same thing, had it been Kirk or Kevin tied to that chair with no ears.

Just then, he thought about the girls and Wally. He asked Kevin, "Where are the others?" He hesitated before asking, "Who's on the floor over there?"

Kevin answered grimly, "That's Claude and Jerry. They're both dead. Wally is over there on his chair," he pointed to Wally, who was several few feet away. He was wearing a blindfold. "He's fine, but he was going to be their next victim. They wanted to kill off the wounded."

David replied, "Those sick bastards!"

In that moment, Kevin exclaimed, "Oh, man! We have to get the girls! They're both tied up in the trunk of that jerk's car!"

"They're what???" David rushed over to Damian's car, which was a BMW Z1, and reached into the driver's side window. He popped open the trunk and hurried to the rear of the car. He sighed in relief when he saw both Edie and Millie were alive and unharmed. He pulled the gags off their mouths and helped them both out, before untying them.

Edie was first. She hugged him and said, "Oh, thank you so much! I thought they were going to take us and do awful things!"

"They won't be hurting anyone ever, again," he said. "I'm sorry I left you with them. You're both safe. I'll make sure to keep you safe, from now on."

After Millie was untied, she said, "Thank you for saving me, again. You know? Somehow, I knew you would. I knew you'd come back in time. It's like I told you. You're my guardian angel." She smiled faintly.

He half smiled and replied, "I'm no angel, but I'll be your guardian. I promise I won't let anything happen to either of you. Not while I'm still breathing."

Edie and Millie held each other and let out a few tears, along with some smiles of relief. Edie was already thinking the worst. She had imagined all kinds of hellish scenarios that made getting eaten by the zombies sound like a pleasant alternative.

David walked over and looked down at the bodies of Jerry and Claude. He was too late to save them. He shook his head regretfully. He could not help wonder if it would have made a difference had they not stopped to look for the anti-serum. Bobby said they just killed Claude. Every second wasted might have saved a life. Still, the anti-serum was important. He just didn't know what good it would do any of them. They were not scientists. He was furious.

However, there was little time for mourning. Time was running out. They had to get back to the precinct fast.

"Guys, I hate to sound insensitive, especially considering what just happened, but we really have to leave here, *now*. We are extremely pressed for time, if we plan on escaping Manhattan and the Bronx, before nightfall. And make no mistake that is the plan."

They quickly gathered up what little supplies they were able to salvage from The Intrepid and loaded everything onto a bus. Wally climbed aboard with a little assistance from Kevin and got into the driver's seat. Bobby got on next, while Williams helped the girls aboard. He did not get on. Instead, he looked at David. His bag was still in David's car.

"Are we bringing your car for the ride?"

David hated leaving his BMW behind, so he figured he could escort the bus back and leave it at the precinct. He answered, "You know it. Come on."

Seconds later, the bus followed David's BMW across town back to the 26th Precinct.

METROPOLIS OF THE UNDEAD

Chapter Eleven

K IRK WAS GROWING extremely impatient. It had already passed an hour and he knew it without even needing to check a watch, although he did not have one. He noticed Gordon was wearing one on his wrist, so he asked, "Hey, what time is it? Has an hour gone by, yet? It feels like they're taking too long. They should have been here, by now."

"Actually, it's been an hour and ten minutes, since they left," Gordon responded, while examining his Rolex watch. It had been a gift from his ex-wife. It was the only useful thing she ever gave to him. "I knew it!" Kirk shouted. "Something's wrong. They ran into trouble. I can feel it in my gut," he stated, while pacing back and forth in the garage.

Gordon tried to reason with him, "Give them another five minutes or so. I mean, it is the Zombie Apocalypse out there and they had to go across town twice making detours, just like when we came here. Realistically, it'll probably take longer than an hour, especially when you take into account that they need to get the others, along with whatever supplies you guys have."

"You got a point," Kirk said, while rubbing the stubble on his chin. All of the guys had some form of stubble or facial hair, considering none of them had been able to shave, since Friday, and it was late Monday morning.

There was a faint sound in the distance. Gordon tapped him on the shoulder and said, "Hey, listen up. Do you hear that? Someone's coming."

They heard a vehicle approaching, and then coming to a stop outside. About a minute later, the side door opened and David entered looking rather grim.

"Sorry, we took so long," he said with a long face. "There was some trouble at the depot. Williams and I had to kill those two murdering assholes, Damian and Josh. They tortured and killed the other soldier, Martinez."

Gordon replied, "I had a bad feeling about those weasel dick pricks."

David continued, "They also executed Jerry and Claude and had the girls tied up in the trunk of their car. They were about to shoot Bobby and Wally when we arrived. Unfortunately, we arrived too late to save Claude. They had just shot him." The guilt and regret in his voice was obvious. It really bothered him that he and Williams arrived only minutes too late to save someone.

Kirk was pissed off. He hated that he was not there to help. He responded angrily, "Are you shitting me? Oh, man! I wish I could have been there! I would have ripped those punk bitches' heads off with my bare hands! Damn it!"

"Well, we handled it just fine," said David coldly. "They're dead and won't be a problem for anyone else. Let's not bring it up around the others. They're still upset by the experience, especially Williams. Are you guys ready to go?" He asked, changing the subject.

Gordon replied, "Yeah, ready when you are," and then he climbed in the fire engine.

Kirk exhaled angrily and climbed into the passenger side of the truck. He felt like he was robbed of an opportunity to mete out justice. He called out from the window, "Get that garage open and we'll follow you."

David pressed the button to open the garage door and stepped outside. He got back into his BMW and revved up the engine. The fire engine rolled forward slowly and emerged from the garage. David sped down the street toward Broadway, where the bus waited, and stopped. Wally pulled the bus out behind his car and Gordon fell in line behind the bus. David looked north on Broadway and did not like what he saw. It looked like the road was blocked, so he decided to lead them toward Riverside Drive. He hoped the road there would be clear.

The three-vehicle convoy turned south on Broadway and continued to West 122nd Street. David then turned right and headed west to Riverside Drive. Once there, they traveled north to Dyckman Street. There were a few vehicles that had been left on the road, which caused them to make a few minor maneuvers. Plus, there was debris from the George Washington Bridge. The road was otherwise empty.

The city was starting to resemble a ghost town. If you saw anyone out on the streets, chances are they were probably infected. The majority of fast infected had spread out to the south and north, which happened to be where they were heading. In between, it was mainly the slower zombies that ruled.

There were a few scattered zombies roaming the streets during their drive uptown. David went around them, while Wally smashed into every one of them on purpose. Gordon preferred not to do that anymore. His window was already difficult to see through.

They knew if they remained in the city for much longer, they would be stuck and eventually run out of food. Their only hope of survival was to leave the city and meet up with the others.

It was half past noon when their convoy finally reached Inwood Hill Park. They drove into the park and got as close as they could to the Spuyten Duyvil Creek. They were surprised to see the small pier had been destroyed along with the white boathouse that once stood beside it. David figured the military would have overlooked such a small insignificant pier.

There were two zombies walking about in the park that immediately took notice of them and began making their way toward the potential buffet.

Kirk casually stepped out of the fire engine and said, "I got this one on the right." He walked right up to the first zombie and bashed its head in with the fire hydrant wrench, which he was still carrying. He liked it and thought it was a good alternative to shooting one of the two guns he now had in his possession. He preferred to use his hands whenever possible, or perhaps a blunt instrument, as opposed to resorting to a gun. Guns simply were not his style.

Williams got out of David's car and walked over to the other zombie. He jabbed his Bowie hunting knife hard into the side of its head, although almost got scratched in the process when the zombie reached out to grab him. Lucky for him, he wore long sleeves on his black ops uniform. He reminded himself to be more careful in the future.

They looked around and saw the rest of the park was clear of any walking dead.

David got out of his car and went toward the bus. Wally opened the door and David said, "Keep everyone on the bus, until we get the rafts in the water. Let's not take any chances."

"Okay," Wally agreed, before closing the door.

David turned to Kirk and Williams and said, "I was hoping the pier would still be here, but we really don't need it. Let's get those rafts in the water."

They guided the fire engine closer, so Gordon could get the trailer as close as possible. Once it was in position, the four men removed the rafts from the flatbed trailer. Together they carried them along the grass and placed them down near the water. Williams secured the rope to both.

Gordon warned, "The water here is pretty rough. We might have a hard time getting across. It's too bad we don't have life vests."

David shrugged and answered, "Then we'd best be as careful, as possible, because I am not going to be discouraged by rough water when I am this close to finally leaving Manhattan." He held his forefinger and middle finger an inch apart from each other.

"Okay, this is your plan. We do it your way," Gordon replied. "Let's just play it safe. Make sure everyone holds onto the ropes."

"Absolutely," David agreed.

Williams looked across to the other side and saw trees. It looked like another park. He said, "I don't think we'll have a problem. These rafts can hold, at least, six at a time. There are only about ten of us. We'll cross over in no time. I can operate the first one myself, if you want. I have experience with these kinds of water crafts."

"Perfect," David replied. "That is a great idea. Thank you. It sounds like we're set. Let's get these rafts loaded, so we can head out."

Williams climbed into the first raft, along with Kirk, Gordon, Wally, and Bobby, since they were heavier. The first raft had the motor and would be pulling the second. David, Kevin, Edie, and Millie got into the second raft.

Kirk grinned back at those in the second raft and could tell the girls looked nervous. He said, "Relax, this will be a cake walk." He turned to Williams and said, "Take us to the other side."

Williams stated, "No one stand up and we should be fine. Hold on to each other and grab the rope. We don't have any life vests, so you don't want to fall in."

Gordon added, "Especially not here. The water here is crazy. I won't be jumping in to save you."

Williams commented nervously, "That's probably not an encouraging thing to say, right now."

"Duly noted," Gordon replied.

The ride across the creek was very bumpy, but the first raft had a motor, which worked well enough against the current. They reached the other side in a manner of minutes without incident. Everyone was a lot wetter. They found themselves near the Metro-North railroad tracks. There were trees beyond that and a fence that separated them from the baseball field of John F. Kennedy High School.

Bobby jumped off first with the rope in his hand. He pulled the first raft closer to the shore. Kirk stepped out next and helped Bobby pull the rafts in. Once everyone from the first raft was ashore, they helped the others from the second raft.

Kirk reached out to David and said, "Let me give you a hand, Dave."

"Thanks. My leg is killing me."

Kirk held out his hand and helped him onto the rocks, and then he helped both girls to the shore, followed by Kevin, Bobby held the rope tight.

David looked around to make sure there was no trouble awaiting them. It looked rather peaceful. He pulled out his cellphone and sent a text message to Charles. He kept it simple. He wrote, "Made it across the river. Contact you soon!" At last, they were free from Manhattan Island. He was so excited that he could barely contain his smile.

Edie nudged him and said, "Way to go. You did it. You actually got us out of there. I feel like I owe you my life." She stared at him admiringly.

"Huh?" He eyed her curiously, and then said, "Don't be silly. We did this together as a group. I can't believe we made it."

Kirk reminded them, "It's not over, yet, folks. We may need to fight our way to the Kingsbridge Armory, where your friends are waiting. That's not going to be easy, considering this side of the river is newly infected. It will be like that first night. Our best bet is to secure a vehicle from the start. I can drive mostly anything. Plus, we also have Wally and Gordon."

Millie gasped at the thought of more infected. "So, there are probably going to be more of those infected that can run here, right?"

"Yep," said Kevin, as he checked the ammo in his weapon. "Probably a lot, too."

Millie looked terrified.

Edie held her close and said, "Try not to think about it. These guys will do their best to keep us safe."

It was not very reassuring. Millie thought about how Mr. Hayes was killed by infected at The Intrepid. It happened so fast. No one had time to do anything, but watch.

The group followed a trail to Teunissen Place. Kirk helped Wally walk. His knee was still hurting badly. David was able to walk, but with a limp. His leg was hurting, though. He hoped they could find a vehicle soon.

They eventually made their way to West 228th Street and continued toward Broadway. They could see the elevated train tracks and several vehicle wrecks on the street below. They heard loud, incoherent, animalistic, screaming and knew what it meant. The infected were near.

Edie and Millie both froze up instinctively.

David urged them on. "Come on," he said. "Keep moving. We can't afford to linger anywhere with them nearby. We need to get across Broadway." He looked ahead and saw the grounds of a Housing Development. "We can cut through those Housing Projects."

Kevin was also looking at them. He agreed, "Good idea. The street on the other side should lead us to Kingsbridge Avenue."

"Perfect," replied David. "So, that's our plan."

Kirk looked at David and could see that he was in pain. He asked, "Dave, do you need a hand walking?"

"No, I'll manage. Keep helping Wally."

Bobby glanced over at Kirk and said, "Hey, take a break, big guy. I'll help him, for a while."

"Are you sure?"

"Yeah, I got him."

"Thanks," said Kirk.

The group moved across Broadway as quickly as they could with Kevin in the lead. He kept his gun out, just in case. Williams and Gordon took up the rear to fight off any infected that chased after them, while Kirk and David stayed closed to the girls. Bobby and Wally were behind them.

Just as they ran onto the Housing grounds, one infected person on Broadway spotted them. It only took that one to cause a ruckus. He screamed out hungrily and ran in their direction. About thirty other infected people followed!

Williams saw the mob and shouted, "Run! They're coming!"

As they stepped up the pace, some of them went into panic mode. Kevin was ready to shoot anything that got in his way, even though he already knew shooting would only bring more. He was not thinking straight. They had gone through too much to reach the Bronx, to fail now.

He spotted someone stepping in front of him on the trail. He did not even stop to think if it was an infected person or not. He stopped, took aim, and fired his gun. The person's head jerked back and the body went limp and fell.

David looked ahead at him and shouted, "No! Don't shoot!"

"Sorry!" Kevin shouted, as he began running, again.

Five more infected came running at them from within the Housing grounds' basketball court, which was off to their left. The infected charged at them flanking them from the side. One grabbed onto David's arm. He fell backward to the ground when he tried to pull away. Kirk came to the rescue and swung the fire hydrant wrench hitting the infected person in the head and knocking it down.

Another leapt toward him, which he spun and tossed to the side like a rag doll. Before it could get up, Bobby kicked it in the head and stomped on its face with his boot. He continued running, while helping Wally, although it was getting more difficult by the second. Wally was unable to run due to his knee injury. Bobby pulled him along, but the two were moving slow.

Williams was so tempted to turn and shoot into the mob of pursuers, but he would likely miss a lot of shots and expend ammunition unnecessarily, only to end up attracting more infected in the long run. He decided to keep running, instead.

Gordon turned to swing his axe at any that got too close. He chopped off the head of an infected using that technique. However, his actions were slowing him down. He realized he stood a better chance, if he just ran as fast as he could, so he stopped fighting and ran.

Up ahead, Kevin was the first to make it to the other side. He hopped over the waist-high chain link fence at the outer edge of the Housing parking lot on Exterior Avenue.

It turned out Millie was a fast runner. She made it next, so he helped her over the fence.

Edie was right behind her. She went over the fence quickly, but was followed by two of the infected. One grabbed the back of her blouse and she screamed instinctively. She turned and tried to pull away, but the infected person followed her over the fence. Millie picked up a bottle and broke it over the infected person's head, which caused it to let go of Edie's blouse and face her. Edie pushed the infected person with all her might and knocked it back toward a fire hydrant. It fell down and hit its head on the top of the fire hydrant, cracking its skull and damaging the brain. The infected was dead.

Nearby, Kevin was wrestling with the other infected and trying to prevent it from biting him. David soon caught up and helped pull it back toward the fence. Kirk then bashed it in the head with his wrench and killed it. He and David went around the fence, afterward.

David took a moment to catch his breath. He was so tired and his leg was hurting a lot. He knew he was pushing himself too hard. If they didn't stop to rest soon, he would only agitate his injury more. He just wanted to lie down on a comfortable bed.

Further back along the path, the infected were gaining on the others. Williams decided to draw some away by breaking off to the left and running through the playground and basketball court. Some of the infected took the bait and followed him, just as he hoped.

It gave Gordon a chance to turn and fight, again. He swung the axe hard with his muscular arms and chopped down more than a few infected. His long coat was cumbersome and was making him tired.

Bobby and Wally were still far behind. The bulk of the mob was right on their tails. Bobby noticed no one was watching them or near enough to help. Wally grunted in pain, as he struggled to hop along and keep up. Bobby glanced behind them and saw two infected were about to grab him by the back of his sanitation uniform.

"Oh, no you don't!"

Without thinking, he pushed Wally away and ran off toward the playground. He leapt over a small fence and dodged around the playground equipment. Several infected chased after him and were still close enough to pose a danger, but they were not as close as before. He had a brief chance to look back, so he did, but he could not see Wally. He wondered to himself. Did they get him? Guilt began to eat away at him.

Not far away, Gordon had just chopped off another head. He looked back and saw Wally on the ground trying to stand. He hurried toward him, but before he could get close enough the infected had begun swarming toward him making him difficult to reach. Wally punched a few away knocking them back, but there were too many. He could not possibly fight them all by hand. Still, he tried. He grabbed one by the neck and tossed it aside, and then punched another one.

Gordon tried desperately to get closer to him, so he could assist. He swung his axe wide and knocked back three infected, at once. He glanced around and wondered what happened to Bobby. He was supposed to be helping Wally. Was he dead?

Suddenly, he stopped short and froze. He felt his heart drop when he saw two infected tackle Wally and knock him to the ground. They tore into him violently, as another joined in, although Wally did not scream. He kept fighting with his dying breath. He fought valiantly for all the good it did. The arm, in which, Gordon was holding his axe went limp and he dropped his arm to his side. He was still holding the axe, but only barely.

It was such a horrible experience to helplessly watch someone die. Unfortunately, it wasn't the first time he had to do so. He was getting very tired of it. He turned around and moved forward. There was nothing he could do to help anymore.

Williams reached the parking lot and ran around the fence. A few infected were directly behind him. He simply could not shake them, so he did the only thing he could. He turned and shot them with his MK 18 Mod 0 using a parked car on the street as cover. He hated having to use his weapon, although it did have a suppressor attached to the barrel, which silenced his shots to a certain extent. He realized the noise was not so bad, considering the yelling and screaming that was going on around him. It was not the same as the night before when the infected were also being drawn to its muzzle flash. It was daylight, so that was not an issue.

He decided to take advantage and crouched down behind the car. He kept shooting more infected, as they reached the parking lot, making it easier for Gordon and Bobby to reach the others. Williams did not stop shooting, until his weapon was empty. Luckily, he still had a few spare magazines.

Gordon climbed over the fence to where the others waited. Bobby soon followed him causing Gordon to stare at him in disbelief.

Before he could say anything, David asked, "Bobby, where's Wally?"

Bobby frowned and lied, "I'm sorry, guys. He didn't make it. He tripped and before I could go back for him, they were all over us. I had to keep running or I'd be dead, too!"

Gordon eyed him angrily and responded, "Oh, really? Then why did I just watch Wally fight off a bunch of infected on his own, before they overpowered him? Oddly, you were nowhere to be seen. I tried to help, but I was too late. What's your excuse?"

David, Kevin, and Kirk looked at Bobby and waited for an answer.

"Hey, I'm not lying! We were surrounded! I tried to fight off some infected and we got split up," he explained. "They chased me and I lost Wally. I thought he was killed instantly."

Gordon responded, "I thought you said he tripped."

"He did! That's how we got surrounded and split up!"

Gordon did not believe him one bit. He thought Bobby was full of crap. As far as he knew, Bobby left Wally to save his own ass, although he could not prove it. He decided to keep quiet and let it go, for the time being. They were not out of the woods, yet.

Kirk became angry. He grabbed Bobby by the arm and said, "I better not find out you're lying!"

"Honest! He fell and we got split up! I'd never leave a guy to die!"

Gordon still wasn't buying it. Bobby had shifty eyes and he never trusted anyone with shifty eyes. Plus, Bobby was a jerk.

Kirk stared at Bobby, while breathing heavily, and then let him go. He looked back toward the path with regret in his eyes and groaned, "I should have been the one to help him. This is my fault. Damn it. Maybe he'd still be here."

David touched his shoulder and said, "You can't blame yourself."

"I promised him I'd help him!"

Williams reminded them, "Hey, you guys might want to save this for later. I killed a few, but there are still a lot more and they keep coming! Let's get the hell out of here, while we can! We need to move!"

David nodded, "He's right. Let's go!"

Kevin had already started running south. He only turned back to say, "Come on! This way!"

The others followed without haste.

As the group ran over the overpass of the Major Deegan Expressway, they could hear dozens of screams below and extending out to the north and south of their location. Edie looked over the side and saw that infected were attacking vehicle occupants. Some tried running, but were chased down and slaughtered.

"Oh, my God! This is horrible!"

David grabbed her arm and pulled her along. "Don't draw their attention up here to us. Keep moving."

Millie peeked down and gasped in horror. Traffic was congested in both directions due to the recent destruction of the bridges and the many abandoned cars, which left fewer options for those still trying desperately to flee the city and finding themselves unable to go anywhere. The vehicle occupants were easy pickings for the increasing number of infected on the roadway.

Eventually, David had to grab her, too. "Come on!"

Soon, they reached the intersection of Kingsbridge and Bailey Avenues. They faced east and looked uphill along Kingsbridge Avenue. It was such a long steep hill. It would only feel longer on foot, especially for David with his injured leg. He grimaced at the thought of climbing the hill.

Kevin noticed an abandoned city bus about half a block north on Bailey Avenue. He turned to the others and said, "Hey! We should check out that bus! I've had training in operating buses, so I might be able to drive it. It will be much easier getting to the armory in a vehicle."

David replied, "Great! Let's go check it out."

Kevin said, "I'll run ahead. Worst case scenario, maybe I can hotwire it."

David asked, "And you can do that?"

"Hell no! I can try, though."

Kirk stepped up and said, "I'll go with you. I can hotwire anything. Call it one of my many useful skills and let's leave it at that."

Kevin smirked, "You're a funny guy, Kirk. There's a trick to starting up a city bus, but come on. Let's give it a try."

The two of them ran ahead to the bus and climbed aboard. Fortunately, for them, the bus was still running and it still had three quarters of a tank of gas. Who knew how long it had been idling?

The others soon caught up and got on the bus. Most of them sat down close to the front, except for Bobby and Gordon, who sat closer to the rear.

Once everyone was seated, Kevin shut the door and shifted the gear into drive. He turned back to David, who sat nearby, and said, "I think it will be too risky to take Kingsbridge straight up. Call it a hunch. We can go this way about a block," he pointed north on Bailey, "and come back around to the rear of the armory. I know this neighborhood pretty well. My cousins lived around here. We used to hang out in these streets as teenagers."

"I'm from Queens," David replied. "Do what you gotta do. I'll give Charles a heads up and let him know to be ready for pick up. I have no idea how many are in his group, but we can probably all get away in this bus."

While David called Charles, Kevin turned right at Albany Crescent, and then made another right at Perot Street, which led them to the reservoir. He turned onto Reservoir Avenue and followed it around the reservoir toward the armory.

During their ride, they did not encounter any infected people, but there were a group of teens running across a nearby street. Kevin thought about going after them to offer them a ride, but then he had second thoughts. For all he knew, those teens were bad news. They might have been amongst the looters or rioters. Besides, they did not even look toward the bus, which should have caught their attention.

David asked, "Did you see those kids?"

"Yeah. Uh, why do you ask?"

"Just checking."

Kevin sighed in relief and kept driving. For a second, he was worried David was going to think like a cop and help them. He was grateful David did not mention it, again. Soon after, he drove past Walton High School, and a moment later, they had reached the rear of the Kingsbridge Armory at West 195th Street. He stopped the bus a safe distance away across the street from the northwest corner of the armory. It was too risky to get any closer. It was obvious the fence surrounding the armory was holding in about a dozen zombies and that was only around the west side of the building. Who knew how many others were near the front?

"Shit. How are your friends supposed to get past them?" Kevin asked.

Kirk stood up and looked over Kevin's shoulder. He shook his head and commented, "Wow. That looks pretty bad. Good thing they didn't notice us."

David leaned forward in his seat and studied the situation. He replied, "I have no idea." He decided it was time to call Charles, again.

Williams and the girls looked from their windows on the driver's side of the bus. It was hard to see anything from their angle.

Meanwhile, Bobby sat across from them, a few rows back, and stared out of the passenger side windows at the sidewalk. He was not paying attention to the others. Guilt was written all over his face. He could see it in his reflection. He kept reliving the moment when he pushed Wally away and left him for dead. He knew it was a lousy thing to do, but it was the only thing he could do to survive.

At least, that's what he kept telling himself. He was glad no one actually saw what he did. They believed what he told them, even that nosey fireman. How dare he accuse him in front of the others? Bobby convinced himself he did what was necessary and believed he could find a way to live with the guilt. His survival had to come, first, before he could even think to help anyone else. That's just how it had to be.

What he did not know was that Gordon was watching him like a hawk from across the bus.

METROPOLIS OF THE UNDEAD

Chapter Twelve

IN THE ARMORY, the others waited impatiently. They knew they were leaving today, but had no idea what time. Charles had them waiting for David and his group to escape Manhattan, so they could meet up. His plan was to get them all out of the Bronx by nightfall. According to his contact, Carmen, at MetroTech Center in Brooklyn, the military was going to establish new borders by morning, making it very difficult for anyone to leave the Bronx.

Charles and Grant already had plans to leave the Bronx, make a stop in Yonkers, and then travel beyond that to Orange County. Of course, anyone from their group that wanted to join them would be welcome to do so. As far as they were concerned, big changes were coming on the horizon. The virus was playing a huge role in that. They had to see the full picture. This was about their ultimate survival.

Charles had just gotten off the phone with David. He called everyone over to the main camp in the hangar for an update. "Hey, everyone come closer!"

Mostly everyone was already at the camp, aside from Frank and Liz. Frank stood at the doorway and stared across the lobby at the main entrance in fear. He hoped the doors would hold against the nonstop pounding of the undead. Liz had gone up to the tower to watch out for David's group, once they received word that the group had successfully crossed into the Bronx. She had just come back down, after seeing the bus pull up at the rear.

She said, "A bus just parked out back across the street. I believe it's them. They're just waiting in the bus."

"Yes," Charles replied. "I just spoke to David. This is it, people. It's the moment we've been waiting for. We're leaving the armory. Thanks to our friends at the front doors, we'll have to use the back exit. It's a good thing our ride is already waiting for us back there."

Frank stated, "Going out the back will be easier. I have the keys. We'll have to unlock the gate, too."

Liz commented, "It's not going to be that simple. There are infected trickling toward the rear of the building from Jerome Avenue and more within the fenced area outside of the hangar on the opposite end of the armory. The bus is parked across from the hangar on the other side of the street. They're facing south."

Nikki and Giselle looked at each other nervously and held hands. They were not so sure they were ready to leave the safety of the armory.

Frank said, "Unfortunately, there are roll down gates on the outside of every door back there with padlocks, which need to be unlocked from the outside. There's only one door that we can use to exit out to 195th Street. I'm sorry to say that's our only option. I can unlock the fence easily enough. It has barbed wire, so climbing over it will be a mistake."

Charles nodded in acknowledgment, "Okay, so this is going to be a battle. Not everyone will be able to do what has to be done out there. I won't sugarcoat it. We need to protect Nikki, Giselle, and Julia. Steve, do you feel ready for this?"

"I've been ready, since I got here."

"Good. Frank, your job is to deal with the door and gate. Can I count on you?"

"Yes," he nodded. "The keys I'll need are in my hand. I'll unlock the gate, as fast as you can clear it for me."

"Good. I also want you to lock it back up. We don't need whatever infected are left in the perimeter to follow us. Can you do that?"

"Yeah. Hopefully, that should not be a problem," he responded nervously.

Next, Charles turned to Daniel and said, "Daniel, this is your chance to pull your own weight. I need you to help Grant, Roberto, and Doc with carrying our supplies. The girls will also carry what they can, but not you Liz. Keep firing that weapon at anything that comes near our group. Steve and I will do the same. We'll clear the path and provide cover fire for our escape. That's the plan. Are there any questions?"

No one had any, which meant they were ready to move out.

As Frank led them to the exit, Charles sent David a text message to let him know they were about to leave the building. He told him to move the bus closer to Jerome Avenue across from their exit, but to remain on West 195th Street and to keep it pointed facing west. They'd probably be leaving in a hurry.

Frank unlocked one of the exits on West 195th Street and held the door. He took a deep breath and asked, "Ready?"

"Do it," Charles ordered.

The door opened and the bright sunlight hit them in the faces temporarily disorienting them. Some of the slow zombies nearby noticed the door open and began rushing toward them, as fast as they could. They did not run, but they were moving fast enough to be a threat.

Frank's eyes gaped wide open, but Charles pushed past him and began shooting. He took the time to carefully aim for the first few and hit each one dead on in the head. However, his gunfire had sounded the dinner bell. More infected rushed around the building from the front. Others from blocks around reacted to the gunshots and started heading in their direction.

He shouted, "Now, Frank! Get that gate open!"

Frank ran toward the gate and fumbled with the keys, even though he supposedly already had them ready. His nerves were getting to him.

He kept pushing the key in the wrong way. Finally, he got the lock opened and flung both gates open.

Charles was furious. It would be a lot harder to close both gates. They only needed one open. However, there was no time to argue. He stood by one gate and closed it himself. He remained there and continued shooting any zombies that got too close. Fortunately, he was only dealing with the slow ones, so it was not too bad. He prayed that would not change.

The bus had been moved to where Charles suggested. It rolled forward a few feet and was directly across from their exit.

Williams became nervous and complained, "Oh, man! They are shooting too much! They're gonna bring the whole neighborhood down on us!"

Kirk stood up and moved close to the front doors. He said, "Let me out, so I can help them." Kevin opened the doors and Kirk stepped out.

Gordon went out with him with his axe in his hand. "I'm going with you," he said.

Aramis hurried out of the gate with his hands full. He carried his medical bag and another duffle bag filled with food. Grant and Julia followed him closely. Each carried two bags filled with supplies. Kirk and Gordon met them halfway and cleared a path for them.

Afterwards, they hurried over toward the fence to help Charles.

Roberto had to practically push Nikki and Giselle out of the armory, so they could head toward the fence and out to the bus. They were too frightened to move.

Daniel and Steve were next out the door, while Liz was the last person to leave the armory. Once she got outside, she lifted her Colt M4 Carbine and began taking carefully aimed shots from in front of the doorway. Just then, Frank locked the door behind her, which distracted her. She realized they would not be able to retreat inside, if they were overrun. She began firing slower, so she could aim with more precision at the closer zombies.

Meanwhile, Frank was waiting impatiently near the fence, so he could lock it, as well.

Less than a minute later, about sixty of the faster infected people appeared at Jerome Avenue. They screamed hungrily and raced toward the group of people, who crossed the open street to the bus. Kirk and Gordon assumed the role of protectors and stood in the middle of the street, prepared for battle. Steve began aiming and shooting his gun at the infected.

Daniel saw the oncoming crowd and cried out, "Oh shit! The hell with this!" He began running and went past Roberto and the girls, heading straight for the bus.

Aramis had just boarded the bus ahead of him, followed by Grant and Julia.

When Grant saw David, the two friends hugged. He said, "It's great to see you, Dave! Thanks for the ride!" He looked back and said, "Hey, I think I know that firefighter that ran past us, a moment ago. Gordon, right?"

David nodded, "Yeah. That's him."

Grant was glad to see Gordon was still alive. It had been days, since they saw him last at West 125th Street.

Across the street, Charles shouted, "Liz, let's go, so we can lock this gate!"

She stopped shooting and ran out of the fenced area into the street. Charles and Frank immediately shut the gate. Frank threw the padlock back on and locked it, just in time. Zombies banged into it from the inside trying to get through, but they were trapped within the perimeter of the armory. Charles, Frank, and Liz raced across the street, while dodging infected. They had to run a very wide arc to avoid running into the rest of the incoming mob that just arrived.

Charles yelled, "This is *not* what I had in mind!"

The infected swarmed into the group like a tidal wave. Only Aramis, Grant, Julia, and Daniel made it safely onto the bus, before it was too late. Kirk swung his wrench like a madman smashing into head after head. Gordon had to move back because he was running out of space and time to swing his axe. Roberto dropped his bags and began swinging his wrecking bar wildly at the attacking infected. Charles, Steve, and Liz opened fire and shot as many as they could.

Nikki and Giselle were both knocked down by the wave of infected. Within seconds, they were completely surrounded. The girls screamed for help, but it was hard to hear them over the noise of the screaming and shooting. They held each other tight and cried, while a dozen infected took turns tearing into their warm flesh.

Roberto saw a crowd of infected swarming in one spot and knew whoever they were attacking had to be part of the group. He raced over to help and began smashing heads with speed and precision. A few infected turned their attention to him, but he did not let them get close enough to bite. He swung at their jaws and began knocking out their teeth, so they could not bite him or anyone. He began a pattern of striking them in the mouth, and then smashing in their heads. He moved like he was trained to fight them, taking out one after another. Any that got too close were kicked back. Finally, he was able to see who was on the ground. He became enraged when he saw that it was his sister and cousin.

"NIKKI! GG! NOOO!!!"

Suddenly, Roberto was like a beast unleashed. He swung the wrecking bar harder and more ferociously than before. He killed each infected with a single deadly blow. He pulled out his tactical M48 fighting knife. In a matter of seconds, there were more than a dozen bodies piled on the street around him.

Charles heard his primal scream and rushed forward to his aid. He began shooting the infected around Roberto. Liz kept her distance, but also continued shooting infected using carefully aimed shots. Roberto's yelling was heard from within the bus. Grant rushed to the front window and saw what was happening outside. He stepped toward the doors with his gun in his hand.

"Open the door," he shouted to Kevin. "They need help out there or they'll be killed! I can't just wait in here, while they fight for their lives out there!"

Aramis stepped forward and said, "I'm with you, brother! Let's get out there and make a difference or die trying!"

Kevin opened the door and out went Grant and Aramis, followed by David and Williams. The four of them began shooting the infected from behind parked cars. Williams tossed a grenade into a group of charging infected and they exploded into pieces.

Daniel sat in the bus breathing heavily and feeling anxious. The sound of the grenade shook him. He looked across at Bobby, who refused to make eye contact. Instead, he turned toward Edie and Millie, who had their faces and hands pressed against the windows, as they tried to see what was going on outside. He thought about helping and felt himself standing instinctively. He marched toward the front of the bus and said to Kevin, "Screw it! Let me out, too!" He held a hammer in his hand. "They said I need to earn my keep, so that's what I'm going to do, even if it means my ass!" He had the look of death in his eyes.

Kevin admired his bravado. He opened the door and said, "Good luck!" He would have liked to help, too, but he needed to stay put and be ready to drive away, once everyone was on board. It did not stop him from aiming his gun out the window and taking a few shots at passing infected.

Frank slammed his hands on the door of the bus and shouted, "Let me in!" Before Kevin could comply, two infected tackled him to the ground. Edie and Millie both screamed simultaneously.

Julia curled up in the backseat of the bus and closed her eyes. She covered her ears with her hands and prayed they would make it out of there alive, although she knew that possibility was slipping away the longer they stayed. It felt too much like this was the end, so she began crying.

Outside, Steve ran for cover and slid across the hood of a parked car, dropping down behind it. He found himself next to Grant and Aramis, who were both shooting the infected that chased after him.

"We got your back," Aramis told him.

Steve sighed in relief and nodded. He looked at his gun and noticed it was empty. The slide was locked to the rear. He took the opportunity to reload. His broken rib was stabbing into his side. The pain was torture, but he did not have time to think about it. He loaded a new magazine and continued shooting.

Nearby, David and Williams shot up as many infected, as they could, as did Charles and Liz from a safe position away. They had moved behind parked cars on the other side of the street.

Liz turned to Charles and said, "This is a never ending battle! We're going to run out of ammo! It's suicide! We need to make a run for the bus!"

He nodded and said, "Let's go!"

They both ran around the cars and raced across the street. As Charles ran past Kirk and Roberto, he shouted, "Get to the bus! We're leaving!" He bent down and picked up Roberto's bags on the way, since he was passing them.

David began moving for the bus, so Kevin could get the door open. He noticed the two infected that were eating Frank. He shot them in the back of the head, and then put another bullet in Frank's head. They did not need him reanimated and attacking.

"Open up, Kev!" He pounded on the doors.

Kevin opened and let him in. David stepped up into the bus and sat down near the front.

When Charles and Liz reached the safety of the other side of the street, Liz turned and began shooting, again. Charles ran straight into the bus with both bags. Aramis helped Steve inside, whose rib injury was aching a lot.

Daniel slammed his hammer into the head of an infected person and made his way over to where the dead girls lay. He stared down at them for a moment and felt sad. They were both so young and afraid. He bent over and grabbed their bags, and then ran back toward the bus.

Kirk looked around and saw Roberto kneeling on the floor with his head bowed. He looked like he was crying. A sea of dead infected surrounded him like a pile of sandbags in a machinegun nest. Kirk went over to him and asked, "Hey, man. Are you bit?"

Roberto shook his head, but said nothing.

Kirk said softly, "I'm sorry for your loss, but we need to go. Now!"

Roberto nodded, but did not move. Kirk moved closer and helped him up. He escorted him back toward the bus, but then froze in place when he saw Gordon's half eaten body on the street. His hand was still gripping the axe tightly and there were headless corpses on the ground around him.

Kirk gasped in shock, "Oh, no! No!" He uttered weakly, "Damn. Gordon… not you." In the past few hours, he had taken a liking to Gordon. He seemed like a stand up guy. He exhaled deeply and looked away. He took another breath and pressed on, leading Roberto into the bus.

As he climbed into the bus, he said grimly, "Gordon's gone." He then helped Roberto to the back of the bus. He noticed Bobby staring up at him with wide eyes from his seat. Kirk said to him with a hint of sarcasm, "Thanks for the assist, Bobby."

Bobby glared at him and answered snobbishly, "I don't have a weapon, man! I'm not going to risk my ass for people I don't even know!" He then mumbled, "My only friend is dead and gone."

"Well, I guess that's what makes you such a great likable guy, *Big Bad* Bobby," Kirk said, as he sat across from him. Now, it was Kirk, who was glaring at him. He waited for Bobby to say something else that pissed him off, so he could have an excuse to take out some anger on someone.

However, Bobby looked away toward the floor. He had nothing else to say. His shame already spoke volumes.

David looked out through the front window and saw Gordon's bloody corpse. He sighed heavily. He had hoped this pick up would go a lot more smoothly. Instead, so many people were killed. Why did so many people always have to die? This was, by far, the absolute worst weekend in his life.

Grant, Liz, and Williams finally ran into the bus. They were the last ones. Grant wasn't getting on, until he knew Liz was ready to go and Williams made sure he was the last one to get on.

Once he was in the bus, he shouted, "Get us the hell out of here, before they surround the bus!"

Kevin shifted the bus into drive and it began moving forward. Infected people ran up to the bus and tried to slam through the windshield with their hands. Kevin stepped on the gas pedal and ran them over like bowling pins. Everyone held on tight, since there were no seatbelts. He drove faster back toward Reservoir Avenue, where he made a right turn, leaving the armory behind, along with the dead bodies of Nikki, Giselle, Frank, and Gordon.

Kevin headed north along Goulden Avenue near Lehman College on his way toward Moshulu Parkway. Grant told him to take it to the Saw Mill Parkway, so they could reach Yonkers. When they reached Moshulu Parkway, they realized the road was blocked by garbage trucks. They'd have to go a different way.

Grant instructed him to take Broadway, instead. They traveled downhill heading westbound along Van Cortlandt Avenue and passed over the Major Deegan Expressway. The expressway was definitely not an option because there were miles of abandoned cars blocking each lane in both directions.

Once they reached Broadway, they had to dodge or run over infected. There were cars crashed into each other and into shops. Some cars were on fire, as were a few businesses. It looked like a war zone. People were running to escape infected. Mobs of infected chased people through Van Cortlandt Park, which was on their right. Kevin drove faster to avoid any trouble.

Daniel made comments, regarding what was going on in the park. "Oh, man! Did you see that? They came out of the trees! Holy shit! They caught him! This is crazy!"

No one responded. None of the girls wanted to look either. Neither did Bobby.

As they got closer to the Yonkers border, near the end of the park, they saw a large roadblock ahead. There were military vehicles and Yonkers police cars with their turret lights on. They were shooting at dozens of infected that charged the border. It was chaotic.

Kevin slowed down and stopped the bus, along the curb, beside the park. He looked over his shoulder at the others and asked, "What should I do? They're not going to let us through without a fight."

Charles looked through the front window and studied the scene. He considered their options, looked back at Grant, and asked, "Where is another street we can head up into Yonkers?"

Grant replied, "Take the next left. It should take us straight to Riverdale. We can head into Yonkers through there. Hopefully, it won't be as busy."

Kevin did as he said and made the left turn. He followed the street straight to Riverdale Avenue. At that point, he turned right and continued north. As it turned out, that street was also closed off and protected with a roadblock. At least, there were no infected to worry about.

Charles said, "Stop the bus at the corner. I'll walk over and talk to them."

Kevin pulled over and stopped.

Grant tapped Charles on the shoulder and reminded him, "Keep in mind, you're not in uniform anymore. They won't listen to a word you have to say."

Steve smirked, "No offense, Charles, but they'll probably shoot you just for being black."

David shook his head in astonishment. Steve had not lost his flair for words, he thought. Not even in a Zombie Apocalypse.

Charles wasn't offended, though. They were friends and often joked around. Instead, he chuckled and responded, "You may have a point there."

Grant suggested, "Maybe Steve and I should go with the soldier. We're wearing uniforms, so they might hear us out." He gestured toward Williams, who stood up and stepped forward willingly.

"I'm in," he said.

Charles nodded in agreement. He stated, "Okay, but be careful and make sure they understand that none of us are infected. If they insist, I'm sure we'd all be willing to submit to testing."

Kirk responded, "What kind of testing are we talking about here? I'm no lab rat."

David said, "Relax, Kirk. It'll be fine, once they realize we're not infected. Of course, that doesn't mean they are going to let us through. I have complete faith that the government will find another way to screw us over and keep us trapped in the Infected Zone."

Kirk scoffed, "I have a feeling you're going to be right."

Grant, Steve, and Williams stepped out of the bus and began walking toward the roadblock, where a combination of soldiers and police stood. Rather than shout instructions at them or fire a warning shot, they opened fire. Steve was shot twice in the chest knocking him back. Grant dived for the ground and pushed Steve down. Williams ran behind a parked car and returned fire using his MK 18 Mod 0.

Of course, perhaps it might not have been wise to exit the bus carrying it, he thought. It was too late to think about it.

Charles and David ducked behind seats, as shots burst into the windshield. Everyone else in the bus also ducked to avoid being shot.

Millie cried to Edie, "Not this, again!"

Kirk shouted, "Everyone stay down!"

David yelled out to the others, "Get back on the bus!"

Williams replied, while shooting, "I'm a little busy, at the moment!"

Grant shouted, "Steve is down! I can't get him to the bus on my own! I need help!"

Kirk stepped past David and Charles. He jumped out of the bus and ducked low. He grabbed Steve and lifted him up over his shoulder. He told Grant, "Cover me!"

Grant shot back in the direction of the roadblock and hit a few windows on the vehicles. The glass shattering provided enough of a distraction and gave them time to get on the bus. Kirk took Steve to the rear of the bus and placed him on the last row of seats. Aramis moved closer and tended to his wounds.

Williams jumped into the bus and yelled, "Close the damn door and get us out of here!"

For some reason, the bus did not move and the front door remained opened. David looked up at Kevin and noticed he had been shot in the head. His body was being held in place by his seatbelt.

"KEVIN!!!"

Kirk turned around and rushed toward the front of the bus. He knew there was no time to mourn his friend. He had to act fast, before the tires were shot up. He reached over and unfastened the seatbelt. He pulled Kevin out of the driver's seat and took his place. He shut the doors and warned the others, "Hang on! We're ramming right through these assholes!"

He shifted the bus into neutral and revved up the engine. Once he was ready, he shifted into drive and the bus jerked forward. He raced straight toward what looked like the weakest point of the roadblock and rammed through it at full speed.

At that moment, Williams dropped two grenades out of the window behind them. The explosions destroyed the other vehicles and caught the Yonkers police and soldiers off guard.

Kirk shouted, "Yes! That was awesome! That was for you, Kevin!"

Grant told him, "Get us off this road. Turn right over there, after that park, onto Vark Street. We need to make sure they don't know where we went." Kirk did as he suggested. Next, Grant had him turn onto South Broadway, and then onto Nepperhan Avenue. From there he led Kirk through a few side streets, until they reached a park.

Grant said, "We need to ditch this bus fast. There are three schools in the area. We should be able to find a school bus."

Charles asked, "Wait! How's Steve, Doc?"

Aramis turned to him and shook his head sorrowfully, "I'm really sorry, boss. He didn't make it. I tried my best, but it's not easy treating a GSW, while on the move and I'm limited with what I have." He abbreviated gunshot wound, out of habit, but Charles knew what he meant.

Grant and David frowned.

"Damn it!" Charles cursed. He slammed his hand against the window and took a deep breath. He said, "It's not your fault. You did your best, Doc. Grab his weapon. We can't afford to leave it."

Aramis grabbed both weapons. Steve had his Smith and Wesson in his gun belt, but he also had a Glock 19 tucked into his belt that he recovered from a dead Housing cop on the first night of the Zombie Apocalypse. Aramis placed both weapons in his medical bag, for now, along with any remaining ammo clips. Aramis already had Marc's gun, so he had no use for another. He figured he could give the spare guns and magazine clips to Charles later. It was best to let him decide whom to give them to. However, he had a feeling, at some point, it would be best for everyone to have his or her own protection, considering the way things were going.

David and Grant looked at each other, and then they looked toward the back of the bus at Steve's body. It sucked that he would have to die, just as they finally made it out of the city.

Next, David looked down at Kevin's body. He hated how many people had to die, so they could gain their freedom. What hurt most was that they did not even die at the hands of the infected. They were killed for no good reason. He clenched his fists out of anger.

He bent down and picked up Kevin's gun, along with his off duty clip-on holster. He mumbled under his breath, "I'm sorry, Kev." He began to feel overwhelmingly guilty for still being alive, while others continued to die around him.

Grant patted him softly on the shoulder to console him.

Charles stood tall and stated, "Grab whatever you can! We're getting off this bus. We can't stay here. They'll find us for sure. Let's try for a school bus, like Grant suggested." He asked Kirk, "Can you drive one?"

"Shit yeah. I can drive anything. I don't even need keys."

Charles looked like he was about to say something.

As David stepped off the bus, he shook his head and said, "Don't ask. That's my friend, Kirk."

Bobby was the last one to get off the bus. When his feet touched the pavement, David shoved Kevin's Glock into his hand and said, "Here! Now, you have a weapon. Next time, I'll expect you to help us."

METROPOLIS OF THE UNDEAD

Chapter Thirteen

THEY FOUND A small school bus van that Kirk was able to hotwire. Everyone got on and Kirk took the wheel. Grant guided him toward his home, where they could stop to wash up and gather more supplies and survival gear. Grant had a house near the northern end of Nepperhan Avenue.

The school bus pulled up in front of his house, which was a two-story home. He stepped to the door and said, "You should all come inside. Get cleaned up. We might be here a while. You can hang out in the living room and dining room. There are more than enough seats."

Everyone got off the bus and followed him to his front door. He pulled out his keys and unlocked the door. There was a pile of mail waiting on the floor, which made him chuckle. The last memories of normal life, he thought. He picked up his mail and tossed it into the garbage.

He pointed his twelve guests toward the living room and dining area and said, "You guys can hang out in there. I'm going up to shower and change. You're welcome to do the same, but I suggest we make it fast. I can provide you guys with clothing, so you can change out of your work uniforms." He looked at Aramis and Bobby. "There's a second bathroom down the hall near the kitchen. *Don't touch anything* in the kitchen. We'll be taking whatever's good, so I want to pack it up. I'll serve you guys something to eat, before we leave. I don't need anyone making a mess. This is still my home, so have some respect."

The others filed into the living room and dining area, where they found seats and made themselves comfortable. They began taking turns using the second bathroom.

Grant went upstairs to his bedroom and returned with clothing, shortly afterward. He handed a pile to Aramis and another to Bobby. They each looked up at him gratefully for the opportunity to change into civilian clothes. Aramis liked the t-shirt he was given because it had the image of the Grim Reaper on it. He liked the irony, since the Grim Reaper took lives, while he was a saver of lives. Grant left another pile of spare clothing on the dining room table for the other guys, if they wanted to change, as well.

"Take what you need," he told them. He went back upstairs to his bedroom and closed the door behind him. He removed his uniform shirt, bulletproof vest, and t-shirt. It felt so nice to be free of those filthy sweaty clothes. He unfastened his gun belt and dropped it to the floor. Just then, there was a knock at his door. Curious, he opened it, wondering who it could be. He was hoping to shower in peace.

He changed his attitude when he saw that it was Liz. She looked so pretty. "Oh. Hey, what's up, Liz?" He explained, "Sorry. You caught me, while I was changing."

She stared alluringly into his eyes and asked, "I don't suppose you have room for two in your shower? I'm feeling pretty dirty." She eyed him up and down, and then bit her bottom lip hungrily.

Without a word, he pulled her into the master bedroom and closed the door, making sure to lock it. He took her into his arms and they kissed deeply. She pulled off her t-shirt and he unhooked her bra. He had to help her pull her long boots off, and then they pulled down their pants. They gradually made their way toward the bathroom, which was in his bedroom, while still kissing and breathing heavily. Grant turned the shower on, and then they stepped into the tub and closed the sliding door.

Meanwhile, Charles stood downstairs in the living room and looked around at the hundreds of CDs and DVDs on Grant's shelves. He looked through the movies and chuckled to himself. He wondered if life would ever feel normal enough to watch movies, again. There was a nice selection to choose from.

Edie, Millie, and Julia had been taking turns using the guest bathroom, first. The guys knew they did not stand a chance, until the girls were done, so they waited patiently. Roberto sat quietly in a sofa chair and wished he were alone. His mind was on his family and friends, who were now dead. Kirk sat nearby on the longer sofa and felt saddened by the loss of everyone that died in the past twenty-four hours.

David sat at the dining room table with Williams and Aramis. They each had long faces, too.

Daniel and Bobby sat on the other sofa opposite from Kirk. Bobby did not wish to sit near Kirk, since they did not particularly like each other, but he wanted to sit on a sofa. He felt sad, too, but it was more for the loss of his dignity, than for his friend, Claude, who died earlier in the day. He felt immense guilt for causing Wally's death. It was a lucky turn of events for him that Gordon was killed outside of the armory. He was the only person, who blamed him for it. Of course, now he felt guilty about not helping at the armory, thanks to Kirk and David.

After the girls were done with the bathroom, the guys took turns going. Each had to go. By the time they were done, two hours had gone by. Grant and Liz were still upstairs in the master bedroom. Charles had a feeling he knew exactly what they were doing, so he decided it was a good time to speak to the others about the new plan to head upstate.

He stood up and began, "Once we leave here, our plans are to drive upstate across the Hudson to Orange County. Grant and I will be going to my place. It's a little bigger than this house. It can easily be converted into a stronghold, where we can ride this thing out. You are all welcome to come, or you can take this opportunity to go off on your own. Maybe you have families you want to be with? I don't know, but this is the time to make your decision. Are you with us for the duration, or is this the end of the line?"

Williams stated, "I have been abandoned by my government. As far as they're concerned, I'm already dead. The way I see it, they can keep thinking that. I'll go with you guys, if you wouldn't mind having a demolitions expert in your group."

"You, my brother, are more than welcome with those skills," Charles said with a smile.

David said, "I live in Queens. I know there's no chance of getting back home. I feel like we should stick together. I don't think this thing will be over anytime soon. Not by a long shot."

Kirk agreed, "I'm with him. Count me in."

Edie looked at David and Kirk, and said, "I'm with you guys 'til the end." She then looked at Millie and nudged her.

"I don't have anywhere else to turn," said Millie. "I won't go back to my parents. Besides, they are in the Bronx."

Julia said, "I'm sorry to hear that."

"Don't be. I really don't care," she replied coldly.

Aramis chuckled, "Shit, man. That's cold. I lived in Washington Heights. The freaking zombies probably have my home surrounded, if it hasn't been burned to the ground! My home is gone and my job is gone. I have nowhere left to turn, so I'm in this for the long haul."

Julia asked, "Don't you guys think the military can get this virus under control? I think the hard part is behind us."

Williams scoffed, "The military doesn't know jack shit about what's going on! My mission was a complete failure because we went in totally unprepared! They're going by limited Intel, which probably came from Charles, and they don't even have the slightest clue what we're really dealing with!"

Bobby rolled his eyes and asked, "Does that even matter? It has nothing to do with us. Is there really a point to staying together, now that we are out of the city?"

Kirk explained, "Wake up and smell the shit, folks. This is our reality, now. Things will not be going back to normal. We'll be lucky, if they don't get worse too soon. Who knows what tomorrow will bring? I think it's better to be safe than sorry, but if you want to go home, be my guest. No one is going to stop you."

Roberto surprised everyone by finally speaking, "You know? My mother is probably dead. My sister and cousin are definitely dead. My best friend is dead. If we don't wake the hell up and make a stand, it's only a matter of time before we're all dead. This is a war we're fighting and the dead are winning. If Charles can provide us with a safe haven to go, then I am going with him. I can't go back to my home. It's gone. You guys think you can survive out there on your own? What makes you think this shit won't come up here into Yonkers? It already started. They'll be lucky if they can hold it back as long as the Bronx did. There are no rivers dividing Yonkers from the Bronx. It's going to keep on spreading, until we're overrun. That's our future, plain and simple. Personally, I think we should go on a hunt and kill them all, but that's my opinion and everyone knows opinions are like assholes. Everyone has one and no one cares."

The room fell silent, as his words sunk in.

When Grant and Liz finally emerged from the bedroom, they were carrying two duffle bags filled with clothing, flashlights, emergency blankets, weapons, and ammunition. They also carried two sleeping bags. Both looked much happier and cleaner than they had over the past weekend.

Aramis teased, "Oh, nice of you guys to join us." He grinned.

Liz grinned back innocently.

David stared at the bags and asked, "You had all of that shit in your bedroom?"

"Yeah," Grant answered. "Where else am I supposed to keep it? In my living room?"

Charles stepped forward and admitted, "I know you said to stay out of the kitchen, but you were taking too long and we were starving. I took the liberty of cooking all the frozen food you had, since we won't need it and can't take it with us. I made sure no one else went into the kitchen. We've been sharing portions. There are still some left keeping warm in the oven."

"That's fine, Charles. Thanks. Sorry, we took so long. I had a lot to pack."

"I'm sure you did. I hope you packed it well," he smiled coyly.

Liz rolled her eyes and chuckled, while Grant blushed and said nothing. Grant and Liz went into the kitchen to eat something. There were some beef patties and pizza left. Afterwards, they went through the pantry and pulled out food that they could take with them, such as canned goods.

Charles came into the kitchen and said, "I spoke to the others. They're all coming with us to my place. Is it safe to assume you'll also be joining us, Liz?"

"Well, it's never good to assume, but yes, I will be going, too."

"Good. You've been a good asset to the group."

"Why thank you, Charles," she said with a smile.

He nodded and suddenly had an odd expression on his face. He reached into his pocket and pulled out his cellphone. "It's Carmen," he said. He answered it and listened, as she updated him.

Meanwhile, Julia sat on a sofa with Millie and Edie on either side of her. Kirk lost his spot when he went to the bathroom. She pulled out her laptop from her backpack and plugged it in to a nearby wall outlet. Once it loaded up, she tried to access the Internet, but required a password for the Wi-Fi. She called out from her seat, "Grant! What's your Wi-Fi password?"

The others sitting in the living room looked at her curiously and suddenly wanted to know the answer to her question.

Grant peeked out from the kitchen and said, "Alex with a capital 'A,' followed by 9-11-17-89. That's Alex9111789."

She raised an eyebrow in curiosity at his interesting choice for a password.

He explained, "It's Alexander Hamilton's birthday."

"Oh!" She grinned. "Pretty clever. Thanks!"

"No problem," he replied, as he ducked back into the kitchen.

Julia logged onto the Internet and began searching for recently uploaded videos that had anything to do with the viral outbreak. David and Aramis did the same using their cellphones.

David came across a report stating how several fugitives, who are considered to be armed and dangerous, escaped from the Infected Zone and broke through a roadblock using a city bus. Two soldiers and a Yonkers police officer were killed in the incident. He felt terrible. The report made them out to be monsters, although there was another untold side to the story, their side. It did not matter. Their side would probably never be told.

David didn't bother telling the others about it. He decided to keep the information to himself.

Julia noticed there were numerous videos that had been posted over the weekend. One in particular showed the scene below, as seen from the rooftop of a tall building in the Washington Heights area of Manhattan. She immediately called Aramis over, so he could see if it was his neighborhood. He put his cellphone back into his pocket and went over to check her computer.

They watched as the person recording the video showed the infected running after victims through the streets below. When he panned across the city, fires were visible in the distance. The video had been recorded during the daytime. There was also a helicopter hovering over the Hudson River. The guy recording the video speculated that the helicopter might be filming from a different angle, but the only helicopter footage that could be found was from a Westchester News 12 traffic helicopter over the Major Deegan Expressway, which showed infected pulling drivers from their cars or climbing in through the car windows. Edie and Millie recalled seeing more of the same earlier.

That particular footage was from Sunday afternoon. It was unclear when the first video was recorded, but it had to be either on Saturday or Sunday, shortly before dusk based on the angle of the sun, which was already starting to set in the west. The guy recording the video is apparently attacked near the end. Yet, someone saw fit to upload his video regardless.

Aramis commented, "Damn! Yo, that's crazy! Washington Heights is done! And those people in their cars were like sitting ducks! They had nowhere to run and nowhere to hide!"

Roberto responded, "That's why we need to make sure we are ready to fight, at all times, so that never happens to us."

Kirk nodded in agreement.

Bobby asked, "What do you expect us to do?"

Roberto sat up in his seat and answered, "We learn from each other. We all have useful skills. Some of those skills can be easily taught. Liz and the cops can shoot and are very tactical. Williams said he's an expert with explosives. Aramis has medical knowledge. Kirk can drive anything and knows how to hotwire cars. Julia said she's good with computers. Daniel knows construction. We can teach each other."

Daniel nodded, "Yeah, I can teach whatever you guys need to know. I have a degree in mechanics and engineering. I know construction, masonry, plumbing, and electrical wiring."

Bobby smirked at Roberto, "And what do you know? You're just some teenage kid."

"First of all, moron. You don't know me. So, don't act like you do. I may look young, but I am no kid. I'm twenty-five years old. In half that time, I've spent my life training to kick the ass of people like you. I'm a black belt in martial arts."

"Oh, uh, that's actually kind of cool," he responded. He felt foolish.

For about fifteen seconds, it was quiet, but then Aramis began laughing. Kirk and David both chuckled, as well. Eventually, the girls joined in.

Williams smiled at Roberto and said, "I like your style. What's your name, again?"

"Roberto, but you guys can call me Rob. Please, do *not* call me Bobby. It's such a childish name."

Aramis giggled like a little girl, which made Kirk laugh more. Only Bobby wasn't amused.

Charles, Grant, and Liz walked into the living room and noticed mostly everyone had the giggles, except for Bobby. The laughter stopped when the three entered and everyone wondered why they looked so serious.

David asked, "What's wrong?"

Grant and Liz looked at Charles, so he could explain.

He said, "I was just speaking to my contact, Carmen. She sounded desperate and kept asking if we were the ones, who broke through the blockade on Riverdale. I told her I had no idea what she was talking about. She said something big was going down, which could mean very big changes. She said she would contact me first thing in the morning, and then she worried me when she mentioned that she hoped I was with the group that broke through the blockade because if not, she wasn't sure if we would ever speak, again."

Williams looked worried and commented, "That's an odd thing for her to say. It sounds to me like she knows something that she's not ready to talk about, yet."

Charles nodded, "Yeah, that's what I think. Considering it's already dark, we're going to stay here for tonight, but I suggest we load up the bus with our supplies, before we get too comfortable. We may have to leave in a hurry come morning."

He walked over to Aramis and asked, "Do you still have Steve's weapons and ammo?"

"Yeah, in my bag. He had two guns on him. Do you want them?"

"Yes, please. I want to make sure anyone, who is capable of shooting is armed."

Aramis opened his bag and handed the weapons and ammo to Charles. He took them and walked over to Roberto. He handed him Steve's Smith and Wesson, along with the gun's extra magazine clips, and said, "Take this gun, Rob. I think you more than earned the right to use it."

Roberto looked up at him from the sofa seat and took the gun. He admired its smooth stainless steel finish and said, "Thanks, Charles. I appreciate it. I still plan to use my wrecking bar, but this will definitely come in handy."

"No problem." Charles walked away and approached Liz next. He gave her the extra 9mm that Steve had been carrying. He said, "Here you go. I don't expect you to shoot that Colt M4 at everything. Sometimes, subtlety is better."

She took the Glock 19 and replied, "Thanks for trusting me with these weapons."

He scoffed, "Please! You shoot better than most of the cops I know."

She chuckled and tucked the weapon into the jeans that Grant gave her to wear. They were an old pair he had in his closet from when he was younger. The jeans were a little baggy on her, so the gun helped to fill the extra space around her waist. She also had to wear a belt to keep them from falling.

David saw what Charles was doing and decided it was time to give away his partner's Glock. It helped him when he needed it, but it would serve someone who was unarmed much more than it would him. He already knew, who should have it.

"Edie. Can I talk to you in private?"

She nodded and followed him into the kitchen.

He pulled out the Glock from his pants and handed it to her. He said, "This belonged to my partner, Elizabeth Neal. It has sentimental value to me. I was going to keep it, but I thought you should have it. I want you to be able to protect yourself and Millie when I'm not around."

She felt so honored. Her mouth gaped open, as she took the gun from him.

"Please, be very careful with it," he warned. "Never point it at someone, unless you plan on using it on that person. It's simple. Just pull the trigger. There is no safety."

"Thank you so much, David. I promise I'll be very careful with it."

"You're welcome."

She hugged him and flashed him a warm smile, before going back into the living room to show Millie. He followed her and hoped he did not make a mistake by arming her. She had no weapon training, as far as he knew. She noticed him watching her and acted like a kid, who was caught doing something wrong. She tucked the weapon away into her pants, and then Millie waved at him. They both giggled.

David sighed and sat back down at the dining room table. He rested his head on his hands and stared out of the window.

Williams patted him on the back and grinned, "Women, huh?"

Grant had only one guest room. He offered it to the girls. Millie, Edie, and Julia agreed to share the room. They looked at Liz and wondered if she'd be joining them, but she had other plans.

Liz waved them on to go into the room without her and turned to Grant. She whispered into his ear, "I think your room has plenty of space for two. Don't you?"

He smiled when he felt her warm breath in his ear. It affected him like a drug. He turned to her and nodded dumbly, "Yeah, I believe so. I'll go ask Charles if he wants to join me."

She made the funniest face and he burst out laughing. It had been a while, since he actually wanted to laugh. Tension had been so high for days. It felt great to unwind and the look on her face was priceless.

"Oh, man! Thanks for that," he said. "I really needed a good laugh. It's been way too long. I was only joking, Liz." He became more serious, as he explained, "Of course, you are more than welcome to the space. I just didn't want to make any assumptions, especially in front of the others. It didn't seem proper."

She grinned and patted him on his cheek softly with gentle slaps, as she replied, "Smart move, wise guy. Thank you. I think I can trust you to behave like a gentleman."

"Gentleman?" He thought. He hesitated before answering, but then said, "I guess I can do that."

"Me, on the other hand?" She stated, while still grinning, "Watch your back, mister. Once I've had a taste, I tend to want more, especially if it's something good." She squeezed his cheeks together with her fingers forcing his lips to pucker up and gave him a quick kiss, before letting go of his face.

He swallowed nervously, but in a schoolboy crush kind of way. She was so beautiful. He had been admiring her beauty for the past few days, but it never seemed right to act on it. Somehow, things felt more normal being in his home. It was like the past few days were just a crazy nightmare that had finally ended, except it didn't. It was only on hold for a while, but it was long enough to act on his feelings. He wanted this woman badly. Everything about her was absolutely perfect!

She slipped into his bedroom and he had to force himself to walk past the door. He opened a linen closet in the hallway and pulled out extra blankets and pillows. He went downstairs, placed them on the living room sofa, and said, "This is the best I can offer, guys. It's clean and warm. No infected outside to worry about. If you get thirsty in the middle of the night, please, help yourself to some juice or iced tea in the fridge. Do not touch the bottled water because we will be taking those with us. There's only a limited supply. Okay, I'll see you guys in the morning." He started for the staircase.

Charles approached him and pulled him to the side. He got close and whispered, "Treat tonight like it's the last night of your life. I hope it's not, but hey, you never know."

Grant smirked and began walking upstairs.

Aramis called out to him, "Hey, Grant!"

Grant turned around and responded, "Yeah?"

He whispered, "You go get yours, brother!" He cheered him on silently.

Most of the other guys laughed, except for Bobby, who was too busy being a hater. He would have liked spending a little time with one of the girls himself. Instead, he had to settle for sleeping in a room with a bunch of guys. It was a total sausage fest, he thought.

Grant blushed and went upstairs. He entered his bedroom and closed the door. Once again, he locked it. He found it funny because he never locked his bedroom door before. Yet, this was the second time he did so in the same day.

Liz was lying on his bed waiting, only wearing one of his t-shirts. The light was off, but the lamp on the nightstand was on. She beckoned for him to come closer and he did. He crawled onto the bed from the bottom and worked his way up to her legs. His hands caressed the smoothness of her recently shaven legs. She moaned at his touch. He hovered over her and she pulled him closer. Their lips met, once more, and, somehow, it was even better than before.

In the guest room, Julia sat up with Edie looking at her laptop. They viewed different videos on the Internet, which had to do with the outbreak. Edie wanted to see other videos, but Julia kept coming back to the first one from earlier. It bothered her that the guy recording it was apparently killed at the end. She wondered who posted the video for him. She also wondered what the helicopter was doing in the background. It could have been helping people, but instead, it just watched. It made her angry.

Edie was excited about the gun David gave to her. She kept examining it, which was making Julia nervous. Eventually, Edie agreed to put it away, but her mind was still on David and the fact that he trusted her to have a weapon. She really liked him.

As for Millie, she had gone to bed early, or so they thought. Her eyes might have been closed, but she was awake and listening to everything. She heard the videos playing out their horror. She could hear the girls whispering about it. She even heard Aramis say something silly down in the living room. If she listened hard enough, she could hear Liz moaning in the next room. And every once in a while, she swore she could hear her sister, Michelle, telling her to be strong because the worst is yet to come. All she really wanted to do was sleep, but it seemed her awareness level was operating at peak efficiency, for some reason.

Meanwhile, some of the guys began to doze off in the living room. They slept in seated positions on the three sofas or on the living room rug. It was easy to fall asleep in a home, after sleeping on the cold hard floor of the armory or in a theater seat at The Intrepid.

Williams was the first to pass out. He had not slept in over twenty-four hours. Yet, now, he was sleeping like a baby at one end of the longest sofa. He snored loudly. Next to him was David, who only fell asleep out of pure exhaustion and pain. Kirk slept at the other end of the same sofa. He also did not have trouble falling asleep. He felt safe. That was all that mattered to him. At long last, they were safe.

Across from them on the other sofa was Bobby, who was still awake. He had a lot on his mind. The guilt was a large part of it, but there was another feeling he was having trouble resisting. It had been weeks, since he was laid. The past weekend was spent sleeping in the same room with several other girls, but he was not getting any action. He wished he could find a way to sneak into the room with the girls. He just wanted to watch them, as they slept. Watching them would be enough for him. Afterwards, he could go to the bathroom and finish himself off, just to release some tension.

Instead, he had to deal with Daniel, who was snoring loudly next to him, and Williams, who was also snoring. They slept in awkward positions, which made it difficult for them to breathe properly. If it were up to Bobby, he would end their breathing problems permanently. He covered his ears with a pillow and sighed in frustration.

On the other side of Daniel was Aramis, who also had trouble falling asleep. Knowing that Grant and Liz were in the bedroom together made him think about his dead partner. She was beautiful, too, with long dark curly hair. Aramis and her had only been friends, but there were many nights when he wished for something more. Seeing her die was heartbreaking for him. It was the reason why he kept her body close in the back of his ambulance. At the time, he was still hoping they would find a cure for the virus. Once he realized, she would never be the same and Charles shot her in the head, everything changed for him. He knew nothing would ever be the same from that moment on. He hoped he was wrong.

Tears came to his eyes, which he quietly wiped away. He told himself it was okay to cry, since no one could see him in the dark. However, it was only in the dark when he would see her face as clear as day. He missed her so much.

Roberto sat curled up in the sofa seat alone. He was also awake. His mind was on his sister and cousin. Seeing them dead was the hardest thing he ever had to face. His eyes were tearing up, just thinking about it. He wondered if his mother shared a similar fate. He wanted to think positive and hope that she was still alive out there somewhere, except he felt that if she were, then she would be terrified and worried sick, or maybe worse. In a way, he knew it would be better if she died a quick painless death. It would be easier for him because, otherwise, how else could he justify leaving the city without finding her, first?

He told himself she was gone, but it wasn't so bad because Nikki and Giselle were with her. They could finally be together and it was for the best. The world they left behind was never going to be the same. Life was going to get very difficult from here on. They would surely suffer, if they had to live through it. He knew he could handle it because he was stronger and colder. He was made for a world like this. They were not.

Charles was the only one, who chose to sleep on the floor. There really wasn't any room for him anywhere else. Besides, he wanted the others to be comfortable. It had been a long hard weekend for all of them. It didn't really bother him to sleep on the floor. In fact, Grant's rug was quite comfortable.

He was also awake, although he was getting sleepier, by the minute. He wondered what Carmen was hiding from him. Whatever it was, it scared him. He wanted to be up early, so they could eat breakfast and head out to his home in Orange County. The bus was already loaded and ready to go.

Only when he could finally walk through the door of his house would he feel truly at home, again. Tonight, it was Grant's turn. He certainly earned it. It was his plan that got them out of Manhattan, in the first place. It was a good plan. He smiled and fell asleep, soon after.

In the master bedroom, Grant and Liz were laying in each other's arms, after making love. After everything they had been through the past few days and all the selfless acts of bravery, it felt really nice to do something selfish. They had spent a lot of time together and during that time, there was a lot of sexual tension between them. It was a good feeling to be able to act upon it. It felt so normal.

Liz swirled her crimson-painted fingernail over his chest making small circles, while resting her head on his shoulder. She tried to pretend things were normal and imagined that they could have a regular courtship with dating, holding hands, walks through Untermyer Park, romantic candlelit dinners, movie dates, and trips to exotic locales. If only life could be that way, but it wasn't.

She found it sort of amusing. There was a time when she never would have thought to date a cop. She could not imagine how it would be having to worry every day or night and wonder if her boyfriend would get shot or killed in the line of duty. Yet, here she was lying in bed with one that she only knew for a weekend during the Zombie Apocalypse.

Of course, she had a new fear. Would he get infected or killed by zombies. In a way, that also seemed funny to her. It's something she never dreamed she'd have to worry about.

"What's on your mind?" He asked, while talking quietly. It was getting late and most of the others in the house were already asleep.

She answered, "I was just thinking."

"About what?"

"Stuff."

"Oh? Very interesting," he responded jokingly, "I think about stuff all the time."

She chuckled and said, "You have a nice house. I would have liked visiting you here, had things been different."

"I would have loved having you over. I'm sorry I didn't give you the grand tour. The backyard is pretty cozy. I have a swing back there and a fire pit."

"Oh, really? I like that. Those can be romantic," she replied. She found herself imagining them hanging out in the backyard having barbecues and sitting together on the swing. The idea made her smile, although she kept it to herself.

"It's nice when you want to read a book, too," he added. "I have so many that I haven't read, yet."

She perked up and responded, "I *love* reading books."

"Good, because I packed a whole bunch of books into the bus." He asked, "What kind do you like best?"

She smirked, "Horror books. Got any of those?"

"Lots," he answered. "I even have survival books, which are going to come in handy. We can look through the books when we get to Charles' house."

She nodded and rested her head back down on his shoulder. She stared at him a moment. He was so handsome, she thought. She smiled happily and said, "I have a feeling we're going to have a lot of time to read in the next few days or weeks." She thought about it and said, "Jesus. How long do you think things will go on like this?"

He shrugged, "Who can really say? Honestly, I don't really see an end in sight. Things have gotten so bad. If we want things to be normal, again, we'll have to leave New York and go somewhere far away. Otherwise, this is probably how our lives are going to be for a long time."

"Do you think there's a place we can go, where we can truly be safe?"

"I suppose. It would have to be really far away and isolated. It would help if we were the only people there, too. The more people, the worse it will be. We are our own worst enemy."

"Yeah, that's so true. People are so good at destroying natural environments. We leave a path of destruction everywhere we go. No place is safe, once we know about it. So many people are careless slobs with no respect for property, animals, or even other people. It's a shame." She sighed. "If we could go anywhere without other people being around, where would you like to go?"

He thought about it and responded, "I would be happy just about anywhere, as long as I can be surrounded by tall trees and maybe a lake or river with majestic mountains in the background. I always admired how they lived during the frontier times. You could find yourself a nice spot and build your dream home without worrying about paying rent or a mortgage. Simpler times. I think what's happening now could possibly lead to something like that happening, again. We're already experiencing a breakdown in government, as far as New York City goes. If more cities become infected elsewhere, who knows how things will turn out?"

"The idea scares me, but I see what you mean. Life would be simpler without paying bills and the common worries we have today, although I'm not so sure I like replacing them with the constant threat of zombies."

They both chuckled.

Grant kissed her on the forehead and said, "Whatever happens, I'm glad we met. You've made the past few days more bearable for me. Thank you."

She smiled and replied, "Yeah, same here. You're a pretty cool guy. I think my parents would like you."

He smiled.

They both closed their eyes and fell asleep in each other's arms. For one night, it was as if their lives were normal and for a few hours they could forget about the rest of the world.

METROPOLIS OF THE UNDEAD

Chapter Fourteen

CHARLES EVENTUALLY FELL asleep, but he was awoken by his cellphone, which vibrated in his pocket at around eight in the morning. He groaned and tried to ignore it, but then realized it could be Carmen. He popped up and tugged his phone out of his pocket, as he tiptoed into the kitchen. There was no point in waking the others, yet.

"Hello?"

It was indeed Carmen. What she had to tell him was more devastating than anything he had ever imagined. It was a quick phone call, but she made it very clear that it would likely be the last call he would be receiving from her, for a while. She wished him the best and hung up. For a few seconds, he stood there and processed what she told him. He could not believe his ears.

A few seconds later, after he snapped out of it, he rushed into the living room and shouted, "Everyone wake up! We need to get the hell out of Westchester County! They're going to nuke New York City!"

Mostly everyone in the living room jumped up at the sound of his voice. The words that came out of his mouth did not fully register with most of them. A few were still half asleep and wondering why he decided to appoint himself the position of human alarm clock. Unfortunately, there was no time for subtlety and no time for breakfast. Charles went upstairs and banged on the bedroom doors. He shouted, "Let's go, people! I have no idea how much time we have, so we need to move our asses, forthwith!"

Grant opened his bedroom door looking half asleep. He yawned and asked, "Hey, what's going on?"

Charles repeated, "They're going to drop a nuke on New York! Hurry up! We need to leave, right now!"

The words echoed in Grant's mind. He turned and woke Liz up, and then began getting dressed quickly. She jumped out of bed and ran into the bathroom to wash up, as best she could. She had hoped for a nice cozy morning shower, but that was no longer a possibility. Once Grant was dressed, he grabbed a bunch of necessities and dumped them into a backpack, which he flung over his shoulder.

"Let's go, Liz," he said. "Don't forget your rifle."

The other girls were hurrying to get ready, too. Julia was the first out of the room and out the door. One would think she was already completely dressed and ready to go when she woke up. She came back inside and complained, "No one is on the bus, yet?"

Kirk ran out and replied, "I'm coming! I'm coming!"

Everyone hurried to get outside. Some ran into the bathrooms, first, which was understandable. Grant ran into the kitchen and loaded up a large cooler with the bottles of water from the refrigerator. He dumped all the ice from his freezer into it and dragged the cooler out into the dining area. It was difficult, since he was also carrying the backpack, which was stuffed with items. He wished he had given the bag to Liz, so she could carry it. David noticed he was having a hard time and helped him out. Together they carried the cooler out to the bus.

"Thanks, Dave. This thing is freaking heavy!"

"Don't mention it." David pushed the cooler to the rear of the bus and shoved it under a seat.

Williams and Daniel ran into the bus behind him and sat in the rear row. The seats were set up with two seats side by side on both sides of the small bus. Julia sat alone in one of the back rows, where many of the packages had been stored. Charles and Bobby were next to board the bus. Charles sat beside David close to the front, while Bobby sat somewhere near the back row.

Roberto stumbled out of his seat and put his boots on. He thought he would get to enjoy a normal day and some morning coffee, but he was wrong. So much for that idea, he thought. When he saw Liz coming down the stairs holding her rifle and going outside, he went into the bathroom of the master bedroom to pee. He washed his hands, gargled some mouthwash, threw water on his face, and rushed out to the bus.

Grant had gone back inside to wait for everyone else to leave his house. He wanted to lock up, although he did not see the point in doing so. It was more out of habit. Still, it seemed right to wait for the others. He rushed them to speed it up.

The other girls were still using the upstairs bathroom, while Aramis was in the downstairs bathroom getting ready. Afterwards, he ran out to the bus and sat in a seat opposite from Roberto. The girls were still not ready.

"Hurry it up, girls," Grant called up the stairs. "The bomb won't wait!"

Millie came running down the stairs carrying her bag and hurried out to the bus. Edie finally came out of the bathroom and followed Millie outside. They sat beside each other and held hands.

Bobby watched them from where he sat. He touched himself and smiled wickedly. The filthy thoughts that went through his mind are not worth mentioning.

Grant locked the door and ran to the bus. He got on and sat next to Liz, who sat behind Kirk and across from Charles and David.

Kirk asked, "All aboard?"

Charles ordered, "Drive!"

Leaving Yonkers was much easier than leaving Manhattan or the Bronx. Things were still fairly normal in the suburban city, for the most part. A few citizens were going about their daily business. People were going to work, although schools were closed. The roadblocks were mainly set up to prevent anyone from entering Yonkers from New York

City. There were not many things set in place to stop anyone from leaving Yonkers and heading north into the rest of Westchester County.

Kirk drove the small bus north along the Saw Mill Parkway. It was early in the morning on a Tuesday, but the regular morning commute was not what it normally was anymore. Many businesses had closed down due to the emergency situation that went on in the city. People were strongly advised to remain in their homes, until the situation could be contained. That was a joke. Still, the roads were fairly clear of traffic, aside from those families that did not wish to take a chance by sticking around and waiting to see what happened next. Those were the smart ones.

They entered the Westchester County Expressway and headed west toward the bridge that would eventually take them across the Hudson River to Rockland County. Orange County would come afterward. It would finally put some serious distance between them and the virus, which was the plan.

While they drove, Julia was checking her laptop. She searched the Internet for updates on the viral outbreak. She checked the latest news feeds and tried to find anything that would hint about a possible nuclear solution. There was a lot of news, but nothing about using nukes.

She did notice that last night the power had gone out in Manhattan and parts of the Bronx, Queens, and Brooklyn. She found it interesting. It made her wonder why the power had even stayed on as long as it did in Manhattan. The mayor was quoted as saying, "I am sorry to say that Manhattan is officially lost to us. We fear the connecting boroughs may be next. Pray for us."

She chuckled and thought he was a pretentious buffoon. Manhattan had been lost for days. If he had not been hiding out on Long Island with his head up his ass, he'd know that.

Another article talked about how the Center for Disease Control and Prevention in Atlanta was trying to work on a cure for the *Fox Serum Virus*. That's what they were calling it. She instantly realized Williams was right. The government was definitely getting their Intel from Charles' conversations with his contact at MetroTech Center. There was no other possible way they could have known Dr. Fox's name or the fact that he created the virus.

She couldn't wait to tell the others about this article. She wondered how they could be working on a cure. It had to be a lie to ease the public. Williams failed in his mission. He said so himself. The CDC had nothing to go on, as far as she knew.

Kirk slowed down and said, "We have trouble ahead."

There was a vehicle checkpoint right at the entrance to the new bridge that replaced the Tappan Zee Bridge. They assumed the police had to be searching for the alleged fugitives, who rammed their way through a roadblock the day before.

Charles said, "Relax. Keep driving. Don't bring unnecessary attention to us. They can stop us and ask us questions, if they want. It won't prove anything. As far as they need to know, we are just campers traveling to the Finger Lakes."

Kirk replied, "That sounds well and good, except for two small details. The bus is stolen and I don't have a driver's license. This is really going to slow us down a lot. Is that really what we want, right now?"

"Shit," Charles replied. "I forgot about the bus being stolen. You not having a license can also present a problem and it's too late to change drivers. They're going to notice. Not that it really matters when they find out the bus is stolen."

"That kind of limits our options," Kirk replied. "Think fast or I will."

David asked, while still looking ahead, "Charles, was your friend absolutely sure about them nuking the city today?"

"Absolutely positively sure. She just didn't know what time it would happen. She believed it would be early in the day."

"Ram the cars and get us through," David suggested. "If they chase us, we'll deal with it. I'd rather be in trouble a safe distance away, than to die here for something stupid. A nuke is nothing to take lightly."

Williams explained, "You ain't kidding, my man. Not for nothing, guys, but a nuke will cause fires within a fifty-mile radius. We will need to be a lot further, if we plan to escape unscathed. So, if you plan on being chased, may I suggest not stopping, until we run out of gas? Hopefully, this bus can handle a high-speed pursuit."

"It will have to," said Charles. "Do it. Ram them. As we pass, shoot their tires. There are only two cars. If we slow them down, it might give us a chance to get away."

Liz responded without missing a beat, "I got the one on the left." She pulled up her Colt M4 Carbine and aimed it out of the window.

Williams said, "I'll take the one on the right." He positioned himself at the window and prepared to fire his MK 18 Mod 0.

Kirk stepped on the gas and floored the pedal. He raced around the cars in front of them and ran over the cones that diverted traffic to the checkpoint. Liz did not have a clear shot, yet, but Williams fired one shot and flattened the front tire of the state police car on the right. The police ran for cover when they realized they were being shot at. When they went past, Liz had to stick her weapon out of the window to take her shot. She hit the front tire and continued shooting across to the rear tire.

They made it through. As they crossed the bridge onto Interstate 87 going north, Liz had a moment when she could look straight down the Hudson River toward New York City. She could see the destroyed remnants of the George Washington Bridge and kept preparing for the flash and mushroom cloud, but it did not come. In a way, she was slightly disappointed. She knew it meant the state troopers would be hunting for their bus and it also meant the infection still had a chance to spread further.

Kirk raced past a parked New York State Trooper vehicle that was waiting just on the other side of the bridge. Williams did not have time to take out its tires.

He said, "We're in trouble. We just passed another state trooper. I'm pretty sure he will have no problem keeping up with us." They could already hear the siren behind them.

Charles stated, "Don't stop, no matter what." He looked into the side mirror and could see the state trooper right behind them. In the next instant, there was a bright flash, which almost blinded him. He had to close his eyes and look away.

Kirk noticed it, too, and asked, "What the hell was that? Was that it?"

Suddenly, an incredibly loud explosion was heard rumbling behind them. It sounded like someone dropped a mountain from the clouds. It was a deep reverberating that continued. Charles looked into the mirror, again, and saw the mushroom cloud rising in the distance.

"Sweet Christmas," he exclaimed. "They actually did it! They dropped a bomb on the city!"

Millie and Edie both gasped in horror.

Roberto sighed with a heavy heart, as he looked out of the window and tried to see behind them. He became certain of one thing. His mother was at peace. He sat back in his seat and closed his eyes, as a tear slid down his cheek.

Grant and Liz held hands and squeezed tightly.

It was hard to believe it had finally come down to the nuking of New York City. A virus had managed to bring about what decades of the Cold War and terrorist threats could not accomplish. The United States would never be the same. A major city had been destroyed. Millions were dead.

Kirk drove as fast as he could to get away from the effects of the blast. He was not sure how far it would reach and he did not want to find out. He swerved in and out of traffic around the other cars that headed north on the expressway. A few slowed down and pulled over to the side to see what had occurred. None of them expected a nuke to be dropped, so it took them by surprise. Even the state trooper slowed down and broke off his pursuit. It seemed like their school bus was the only vehicle driving at top speed. Everyone else had to stop and look. People pulled out cellphones and were taking photos or recording videos.

"Welcome to the new age," Kirk muttered, while looking into his mirror. He kept driving fast and continued to put miles between them and the explosion.

New York City was gone and with it so was a large part of the viral outbreak. Of course, so much time had passed that the infection had already spread beyond the city. Outbreaks had been occurring in New Jersey and Ohio, since the first night. It was contained well for the first day, but even in those places things had gotten too far out of control. Unfortunately, it was far too late to contain the virus. It was already nationwide.

The president had declared it a national crisis. He insisted steps were being implemented to contain the threat. Very few believed him.

The nuclear explosion was rapidly creating new problems, which would have to be dealt with by New York, New Jersey, and Connecticut. Nuclear fires were spreading outward in a fifty-mile radius, just as Williams said they would. They would continue to burn for the next few days, before ultimately burning out on their own weeks later. Radiation would be another problem to deal with from the nuclear fallout.

In the end, millions of people would die from this drastic decision, made by the president, in an attempt to erase a problem he could not handle.

Yet, the Fox Serum Virus was still out there claiming victims. It was far from over.

The survival group watched the following YouTube video, while they were in Yonkers:

A video entitled "Hell on Earth" uploaded by user Valen213 on the YouTube website shows what has become of the city. The video was recorded from a very high rooftop of a building in Manhattan's Washington Heights. In the video you can see various fires and multiple plumes of smoke rising from all around the city stretching as far as the eye can see. The view is facing south from West 178th Street.

"I'm recording from a rooftop in Washington Heights. The city is burning," says the male voice with a somber tone. "No one really knows how it began or who patient zero might have been, the poor bastard. All we know is that it started on Friday night."

He pans the video down toward the streets and you can see people running for their lives along Broadway and Wadsworth Avenue. Screams can be heard echoing up to the rooftop. The male recording the video is describing the mayhem in a deep, shocked, monotone voice, as if he cannot believe what he is seeing.

"People are running everywhere, but there's nowhere to escape. The infected people are chasing them down. They are relentless. It's as if they desperately want to spread their infection. (BANG! BANG!) Whoa! I heard gunshots!"

More gunshots are fired in the distance and he struggles to find the location, but cannot. The gunshots have stopped.

"It's over. I wonder if there are still any cops left down there. The 34th Precinct is not far from me, just a few blocks up from here." The camera slowly pans back toward the left and he says, "There goes a helicopter to the south, past the hospital."

The camera focuses on a helicopter flying over the Hudson River in the distance, but it is only hovering in place.

"Are they watching? I thought they were going to rescue someone, but it looks like they are just watching. Maybe they are recording what they see, too. I wonder. They have a pretty decent angle from up there. It's amazing how people in this world are so obsessed with voyeurism that they would sooner record someone dying, rather than to help them, just so they can post it online. Hmm. Is that what I'm doing?"

If there was another video recorded from the helicopter's angle, it remains unknown.

The camera zooms in closely on the helicopter, but the details are unclear. It's too far out. The male zooms back out and his camera is turned downward abruptly.

"What the…? Holy shit!"

The camera then spins and moves fast over the floor. The person breathes heavily, as he runs into a darkened doorway, where the footage ends.

The only caption, which is posted under the video, is "Looking down at Washington Heights from a rooftop during an actual zombie apocalypse. I never thought I'd see the day. Rest in peace, buddy."

The video has over 100,000 views, 10,457 likes, and 1,971 dislikes. There are well over 500 comments. Many are calling it a fake, but those that know the truth say otherwise.

THE MANHATTANVILLE INCIDENT:
PART FIVE

"Patient Zeros"

PATIENT ZEROS

Chapter One

IT IS A Friday afternoon during the first week of July, mere hours before the Zombie Apocalypse. It was a warm and sunny day. Dr. Herbert Fox, a brilliant scientist and researcher, decided it was a perfect day to spend his lunch break outside by the free mental health clinic. He normally took his lunch break earlier in the afternoon, but today he wanted to be near the clinic at a specific time.

Where else would he be able to find the willing volunteers he needed for his experiment? It had to be someone with little or nothing to lose and preferably someone who would not be missed, in case anything was to go wrong. It only seemed natural that the various homeless patients frequenting the free clinic were prime candidates. All of them had some form of mental illness. Therefore, convincing them would not be difficult for a genius like him. Of course, these volunteers would also have to be suffering from cancer. It did not matter if the cancer was in remission, so long as the cancer cells were present. The experiment counted on it.

This particular experiment was unsanctioned by Herbert's employers at Columbia, which meant it had to remain highly secretive. Not even his co-workers, David and Katherine, were aware of it. Although, it was directly related to the research they had been working on for the past year.

Herbert considered bringing them in on it, but David was too pretentiously honest for his own good and Katherine lacked the clearance to enter the biohazard laboratory. No, it was best for Herbert to work alone on this phase of the experimentation, especially considering he was breaking rules and violating laws. The less people, who knew about it, the better off he was.

Once he was able to prove he is correct, everyone would praise him and give him the respect he deserves. The whole world would know his name. He'd be famous!

Herbert strongly believed he was on the verge of finding a cure for cancer and quite possibly all diseases. He had already proven the possibility of success with primate trials. Despite his assistant's opinion, he was ready for human trials. He knew his Fox Serum would work better on a human test subject, due to a human's physiology. It was always intended for human use.

All he needed was a few volunteers and that was the main reason he was standing outside of the free clinic. He decided using homeless people would serve his needs best. He knew if he promised them a sum of money and a free meal, they'd do anything he asked. If he could get both male and female subjects, it would be perfect.

However, today there only happened to be males visiting the clinic. It was a disappointment, but it would have to suffice. He already had the laboratory prepared and his schedule was free for the weekend. There would be no interruptions.

He lit his cigarette and inhaled deeply. The smell of burning tobacco helped him to focus. It was a shame smoking was not allowed in the laboratory. He let out a breath of smoke and narrowed his eyes, when he spotted one of his potential test subjects leaving the clinic.

"Excuse me, sir," he began. "My name is Dr. Herbert Fox and I run one of the top research laboratories here at the Science Center. I don't suppose you have cancer?" It was the fourth time he made the introduction and asked the question in the past ten minutes. So far, he had been unable to find someone with cancer. It was getting frustrating.

The man, who was a middle-aged African-American, leered at him suspiciously and asked, "What's it to you? Why do you care?"

Herbert grinned and responded rather slyly, "I can cure you, if you are brave enough."

The man seemed skeptical when he replied, "Whatever, man. There ain't no cure for what I got. I done heard it all before."

Herbert insisted, "There is no doubt people have made false promises to you. However, I alone can deliver on what I am saying. The cure for cancer does not exist, yet, but I have created a serum that has successfully pushed cancer into remission. The next step is annihilating it completely from the body. All I need are some volunteers. There's no fee and no insurance is required. I have full authority to waive all fees and insurance requirements for this project. In fact, we pay you $100 for giving us a few hours of your time. Did I mention, there is also a free meal in it for you?"

The man looked intrigued. He raised an eyebrow and asked, "A free meal and $100? And I don't need no insurance?"

"That is correct, but this offer is only available to patients with cancer. It will only take about two to three hours of your time, if you qualify. Are you interested?"

The man nodded, "Yeah, sure, but I doubt you can help me. I have pancreatic cancer."

"It matters not what form of cancer you have. I assure you, my serum can and will cure you of your condition. You will walk away from here a new man, Mister...?"

"Jones. Larry Jones."

Herbert tossed his cigarette on the floor and stomped it out, before extending his hand to shake Larry's hand. Larry hesitated and looked at his hand cautiously, but shook it anyway. What Herbert was promising seemed too good to be true. In Larry's experience anything that seemed too good to be true was usually coated with lies and deceit. He wondered, what would this doctor have to gain from him? He had nothing to offer and frankly nothing to lose. He was dying. If this guy was promising a cure for his cancer, why not give it a try?

Larry said, "Okay, count me in, Doc."

"Excellent, Mr. Jones. You will not regret your decision. In fact, I will make you famous. How would you like to go down in history as the first person cured of pancreatic cancer by my Fox Serum?"

"Honestly, Doc. I just want to live beyond this year and I'll be happy. They told me I only have about two to three months to live."

Herbert assured him, "I give you my word. You will live beyond that time. Now, I am busy, until 6 pm. There is a place, where you can wait. I will provide you with the meal I promised and retrieve you promptly at 6:05 pm. Will that be okay with you?"

Larry shrugged, "I ain't got no place else to be. What time is it, now?"

Herbert looked at his watch and replied, "2:15 pm."

Larry asked, "You said I could eat something?"

"Absolutely," Herbert nodded. "What would you like?"

"Well, I haven't had a decent meal all week. Anything with meat would be fine with me."

"Very well. Come inside. Follow me. I will take you to the café. You can wait there for me." Herbert led Larry through the lobby and into the café. He bought him a meal, as promised, and thanked him. "Thank you very much for your time, Mr. Jones," he said. "I greatly appreciate it."

"Sure thing, Doc. That roasted chicken looks delicious! Thank you very much. I appreciate it. Oh, um, when do I get paid?"

"After, of course. The meal is on me. The food here is splendid. Enjoy it, Mr. Jones. The money, however, is delivered only upon completion. You will be pleased to know, it will be paid in cash."

Larry grinned happily, as he ate and nodded his approval.

Herbert left him to eat his meal, while he went back out to the free clinic to find a few more volunteers. It took him slightly longer than expected. He had to extend his lunch break by an extra half hour and he did not find the last volunteer, until the last five minutes. All ten men waited patiently for him in the café, while he completed his regular workday.

At 6:05 pm on the nose, Dr. Herbert Fox entered the café, where his ten volunteers waited. He collected them and escorted the men to the elevator. Once they were inside, he inserted his special key and took the elevator down five levels to his secret underground laboratory. There was almost something sinister about it.

They followed him out of the elevator and he used his keycard to unlock the main laboratory doors. The security camera in the hallway had been deliberately pointed away, so they could not be seen. When they entered the laboratory the doors closed automatically behind them.

He watched the other security camera in the corner, as he walked them toward the dormitory. It was stuck in one position facing the biohazard laboratory window, just as he adjusted it several minutes earlier. He did not wish anyone to notice his guests. He knew he would have to fix both cameras, before security noticed and contacted him.

So far, so good, he told himself.

The security guard, who was watching the monitors, was his good friend, Ivan. Herbert had a feeling Ivan was quite busy admiring the stack of nudie magazines he had given him, before going to the café to pick up his volunteers.

Once the men were out of view, Herbert re-adjusted both security cameras and returned to the dormitory, where the men waited. There were ten chairs in the room between the four cots. They were set in a semi-circle.

"Please, have a seat, gentlemen," he told them. Next, he handed them pens and forms attached to clipboards to fill out. He explained it was mandatory for him to document their pedigree information.

None of the men argued. They each answered the questions and wrote down their names, dates of birth, approximate weights and height. There was also a box to fill out what type of cancer they had. No other information was required for this experiment.

Herbert was amazed they were each capable of reading and writing. He always figured most homeless people to be mindless savages. Naturally, he usually kept that opinion to himself.

Once the forms were filled out, he collected them and read each to make sure they were filled out properly. He went over their names reading them aloud and expecting an acknowledgement of some kind. It was his way of making sure they answered to the name that was written.

"Larry Jones," he looked directly at Larry, who perked up at the sound of his name. "You will be Test Subject Number One." Larry nodded silently and Herbert continued, "Jose Figueroa, you are Test Subject Number Two. Lester Rowland, you are Test Subject Number Three. William Deeds?"

"Yes, sir."

"You are Test Subject Number Four. Anthony Laurie is Test Subject Number Five. Melvin Thompson, you are Test Subject Number Six. Jeffrey Haines. Test Subject Number Seven." He turned to face the last three men and stated, "Lyndsey Butler, you are Test Subject Number Eight. Wallace Weeks is Test Subject Number Nine and James Edwards? You will be Test Subject Number Ten."

"Number ten, got it," he responded with a gruff voice, and then rolled his eyes.

Herbert got the impression at least one of the men had grown impatient from waiting so long to begin. He decided to remind them of their main motivations for being there.

"I wish to thank each of you for participating in this greatly significant experiment. You are about to make history with me. When this is over, you will have all been cured of your cancerous cells. On top of that, you will be $100 dollars richer. Chances are television shows will be seeking you out to conduct interviews, as well. The world will want to know the first men cured of cancer."

A few of the men seemed skeptical, but there were also some who were already fantasizing about the possibility that Herbert was telling them the truth. How great it would be to beat cancer and live longer. The hundred dollars wasn't much, but it might make a good stepping-stone to a brighter future.

One of the men, Lester, was only doing this to get his hands on enough money, so he could score some drugs and end his life faster. He wasn't buying into the pipe dream that Herbert was selling.

Herbert excused himself, while he stepped out to prepare the syringes and injections for each volunteer. While he was gone, it gave the men a chance to speak amongst themselves.

James asked skeptically, "Do you guys believe this yahoo?"

Jose replied, "I don't know, man, but what do I got to lose? If he cures me, that's great. If he doesn't, I still get $100 to buy myself food for the next two weeks. Win, win, I say."

Lester responded, "If this fool is giving us free food and money, I really don't give a shit about my cancer. I'll still be homeless, the way I see it, so what's the point? I just want that loot, so I could smoke some rock, son!"

A few of the guys laughed, but Larry did not. He decided to share his opinion and said, "I hope he is telling the truth. If not, I only got three more months to live. Truth be told, I don't wanna die. I gots lots more living to do, before I go. I'm gonna make this money count for something. If I can beat this cancer, I don't plan on doing it as a homeless man. I want my life back and I plan to take it back."

Melvin clapped and said, "Right on, brother. That's what I'm talking about."

Anthony smiled, "Amen. Let's use this opportunity to take our lives back. I like that."

Larry smiled at them both. He tried to hide how nervous he felt. If this experimental serum worked it would change his whole life. That meant everything to him. He closed his eyes and prayed to himself.

Herbert sat at his computer, which was on the opposite end of the main laboratory from the dormitory. It was situated against the east wall between the main entrance and the entrance to the preparation room. He placed the ten clipboards on his desk beside him and began typing in each of his test subjects' information onto an already prepared document.

"Let's hope these test subjects do better than their predecessors," he mumbled to himself, referring to the apes he had been testing the various incarnations of his serum on for the past few months.

When he was done, he saved the specially encrypted file in a hidden folder on his personal miniature external hard drive, which he promptly removed and placed into his lab coat breast pocket. Considering he was breaking rules and several laws, he decided to retain the information somewhere off the record, for the time being.

He turned off his computer and entered the preparation room at the far end of the main laboratory, where he suited up for the biohazard laboratory. He kept his safety equipment in his personal storage locker. Whenever entering the high bio-safety level environment, he was required to dress appropriately, especially if he planned on working with deadly contagions. This time around, he was only getting his special serum, which he kept stored in the biohazard laboratory for safety reasons. He donned his thick rubber gloves and a respiratory mask, and then passed through the entrance corridor, a tiled hallway with thick safety glass doors on either end.

Once it was sealed completely, he entered the biohazard laboratory. He walked toward the storage cabinets and pulled out a sealed plastic beaker filled with his Fox Serum. He swirled it around gently. It was a thick fluid with a reddish tint that resembled blood. He grabbed a metal tray from a different cabinet and placed eleven empty syringes on it. He proceeded to fill ten of them with his blood-like serum, one by one. There was no need to rush, so he took his time and did it carefully.

When he was done, he placed the beaker back into the cabinet and closed the door. He grabbed another plastic beaker marked Anti-Serum. It was filled with a clear liquid, which was a special concoction he created to serve as a fix, in case his serum had any adverse side effects. He doubted he would need to use it, so he did not bother to prepare ten. One would suffice. He filled the last syringe and returned the beaker back to its place in the cabinet. He placed a white colored cap onto that particular syringe, so he would be able to tell it apart easier.

He picked up the tray and walked over toward the sink. He threw out his rubber gloves and washed his hands and face thoroughly. Afterwards, he dried his hands and put on a new pair of rubber gloves. He picked up the tray and left the biohazard laboratory, passing back through the entrance corridor and into the preparation room. He removed his mask and returned to the main laboratory.

He placed the metal tray containing the syringes onto one of the laboratory's plastic trolley carts and pushed it toward the entrance of the dormitory. He unlocked the door and pushed the cart inside, closing the door behind him.

The homeless men all turned to face him, as he selected one of the syringes and held it up. He asked, "Gentlemen, are you ready to proceed?" He then looked directly at Larry, or Test Subject Number One, and grinned.

Larry gulped.

Herbert explained, "The serum has to enter your bloodstream for it to be properly effective. I assure you, it will not hurt. It will only be a little prick. You will barely even notice it." He stuck the needle into Larry's left arm and injected the serum.

Larry winced and closed his eyes. He took a deep breath, as the other men watched nervously. They knew they were next. Whether or not the serum would work did not matter to them, at the moment. The injection they were each about to receive was quite real and the needle was slightly longer than they expected it to be.

Melvin gasped, "Oh, boy. Did I mention I really don't like needles?"

While Herbert injected the next man, he turned to Melvin and said, "You have a few seconds to get over it. I shall get to you shortly, Test Subject Number Six."

PATIENT ZEROS

Chapter Two

L ARRY JONES WAS born and raised in New Orleans, where he lived the good life for many years. Unfortunately, he did not realize it, at the time. Had he known what he knew now, he would definitely do things differently.

There was a time when he thought he might become a famous jazz musician. He began learning how to play the alto saxophone at the age of fourteen. By the time he was seventeen, he would stand on a street corner, usually on Royal Street, and play for the tourists. Sometimes, they tossed him a few bucks. On any given week, he could usually rake in about $200. It was more than enough to meet his needs for the next few years.

In time, he hooked up with a few other musicians and they started their own jazz band. They called themselves the Lonesome Boys. The name suited them fine, until they added a female singer to the group. Her name was Tammy Grey. Larry was the one who thought of the idea to call themselves Tammy and the Lonesome Boys. The others liked it, so they agreed.

Tammy and the Lonesome Boys spent the next seven years playing on Royal Street, at Jackson Square, and even at the Preservation Hall on St. Peter Street. They became a local sensation. Everyone loved them. They started pulling in between $500 and $1,000 for each gig.

Of course, Larry started to realize he loved Tammy more than the music. A romance began between them that would be the downfall of the band. The bass player also had a thing for Tammy. When Larry and her started dating, it caused a rift in the band. Jealously led to petty arguments, which led to fights, and ended with the bass player quitting. Tammy and the Lonesome Boys were finished.

Tammy decided to move to New York City because she had dreams of singing on Broadway. Larry followed her like a little puppy and spent all of his savings to get them set up somewhere nice in Greenwich Village. It did not take the couple long to realize living in New York was far more expensive than life in Louisiana.

Larry got a temporary job, but did not take it too seriously. He had high hopes of making it big as a musician in the big city. He figured with Tammy's voice, they could have a new band in no time. Unfortunately, life has a way of kicking you in the balls, so to speak. Tammy had no intention of being in another band with him. She had her own dreams she longed to fulfill. Once Larry's money was gone, she found someone else to help her achieve her goals and left Larry high and dry. It did not take too long before his high hopes died and were replaced by hopes of being high, as depression got the better of him.

Larry spent most of his free time getting drunk or smoking marijuana. He typically began his afternoons playing jazz music, until the memories of Tammy would drive him to drink. At night, he would smoke some marijuana to relax his nerves, and then spend the rest of the night drinking some more.

It was the same routine every weekend. Before he knew it, this became his daily ritual. As a result, he lost his job, could not pay his rent, got kicked out on the street, and became homeless. His life had truly taken a turn for the worse when he had to sell his saxophone, in order to eat.

After five years of living in New York City, Larry had completely ruined his life and hit rock bottom. He lost any aspirations of ever regaining what had become so far out of reach. Once hope was abandoned, he really did not have much else left.

Over the next ten years, he was in and out of jail for petty thefts. He began stealing as a means of survival, but later did it just to go back to jail. At least, while in prison, he was able to get free room and board. He learned to play the system and allow it to work for him.

It was during this time when he delved heavily into drug use. He hated using drugs, but it was the only way he could numb himself to the world he lived in. Crack cocaine became his drug of choice. It was the easiest and cheapest to come by.

He would usually go into the subway tunnels, where he could be alone. That's where he preferred to get high. There was no one around, but the rats and cockroaches, to see him at his all-time low. He was too embarrassed to be around people whenever he got high. At least, in the tunnels he could hide from the rest of the world.

Sometimes, he would have to hide from track workers or urban explorers. It amazed him how busy the subway tunnels could be with activity. He constantly asked himself why teenagers would want to lurk around those dark tunnels seeking adventure. What was the point? Personally, he hated being down there. Most tunnels were dark, damp, and dirty.

It turns out Larry was pretty good at hiding. He lived in the subway tunnels for nearly a decade without batting an eye. It seemed time flies when you aren't having fun.

During one of his arrests, he became sick and was taken to the hospital. It was then that he learned he had pancreatic cancer. Within the same hospital visit, he also became aware of the fact that he had less than four months to live.

Now, here he was in the dorm room of an underground lab, letting some wacko scientist inject him with what one of the other volunteers referred to as a pipe dream. Was it or was it something more?

When Jose Figueroa first arrived in New York, he was ten years old. His family left their home in Vega Alta, Puerto Rico, to start anew in New York City. His father got a job in construction. At the time, jobs were plentiful. His mother took a part-time job babysitting for the neighbor's kids.

They lived in the Bronx. Jose hated the move. He only spoke Spanish, so he was admitted into bilingual classes in school. He felt segregated from the general student population and began to hate school, as well. Sometimes, he would get into fights with Caucasian kids because he did not speak any English. This led to him skipping out on school. Instead, the streets became his school. He made a few not-so-good friends, who definitely had a bad influence over him. However, through them he finally began to learn the English language.

When his parents learned he was cutting classes, his father beat him. Jose felt so angry he ran away from home. It would not be the first time. He would run away two more times, before ending up in a juvenile facility. He spent a good three years going in and out of Spofford, back when it still went by that name.

Eventually, a family court judge decided he had behavior issues that could only be resolved at a mental health facility. That's when he spent his first month at Bellevue. He would return a few more times over the next fifteen years. He also spent time at a few state hospitals on Long Island, but mostly it was Bellevue that viewed him as a regular.

By the time Jose was in his twenties, he was living in Spanish Harlem on Manhattan's Upper East Side. He worked several odd jobs, in an attempt to pay rent, while supporting his drug habit. He found that by getting high, he could forget his worries. He had plenty. He was always behind in his rent, his mother was sick, and his father was an abusive drunk, who beat her.

Jose's first arrest came when he beat his father for beating his mother. The time he spent in jail turned him on to some new drugs. He began shooting up heroine for a while. It led to his second and third arrests. He got into a fight, while he was high, and another time he broke the window of a store because he got angry.

Anger management was always a weak character trait for him. It was why he got into so much trouble as a kid. He was always breaking things or getting into fights whenever he got angry. He simply did not know how to control his temper.

When Jose was in his thirties he tried to get control of his life. He quit the drugs and found himself a decent job as a dishwasher in a restaurant. This relatively peaceful period lasted about two years, before he began smoking marijuana. The marijuana soon led to smoking crack, and then he was shooting up with heroine all over, again. He lost his job, lost his home, and found himself living out on the streets.

One day he felt ready to give up on life. He overdosed on heroine and woke up a day later at the hospital, where he was diagnosed with cancer. Just perfect, he thought. The depression caused him to get transferred to the psych ward, where he spent about a week.

Soon, he was back out on the streets. He wandered around Manhattan aimlessly for what he thought was weeks. Instead, it was months. Months turned into years.

Just when Jose felt like he was ready to give up, again, someone told him about the free clinic on Broadway. He decided what the hell? He had nothing to lose by going.

It was there that he met Dr. Herbert Fox, the man with the big dream. Dr. Fox sold his dream like a car salesman selling a lemon. He managed to coax Jose and nine other men into giving him a try. Jose figured if he could, at least, get rid of his cancer, then just maybe he could get his life back in order. That was the plan.

Looking back on it, now, he was starting to have second thoughts, after being injected with Dr. Fox's experimental serum. Jose felt his will gradually slipping away. His mind became clouded. He felt his anger fighting to be released. He wanted to break something. The pain he began to feel in his arm was unbelievable. He shut his eyes tight and tried to resist the temptation to scream.

He wished he were back in Puerto Rico, where life was simpler for him. Ah, those were the good old days.

Lester spent his whole life stealing. It was the one thing he was good at, although, sometimes, he could not even do that right. As a young boy, he used to steal his friends' toys. In school, he would steal art supplies, so he could draw and color at home. His mother never bought him crayons. She never bought him toys either.

She spent a lot of her life working from home in her bedroom with one customer, after another. Weekends were the busiest days for her. Men would often line up in the living room waiting their turn. Lester was not allowed out of his room during business hours. He was told to lock the door and watch TV. He hated watching television.

Lester never knew his father. His mother had no idea, which of her "lovers" was the culprit. It was one in a long line of customers.

Whenever his mother was not lying on her back or down on her knees working, she would spend her money getting high. Surprisingly, the rent was always paid on time and they always had food in the fridge, so child services never had a need to pay them a visit. She would buy Lester his clothes at the end of August whenever the stores had those back to school sales. He would get nothing else for the rest of the year, except on his birthday and at Christmas time. She usually bought him either a cheap toy from the 99 Cent Store or a comic book from the Optimo Store on the corner. His gifts were never gift-wrapped.

If there was something else Lester wanted, he had to steal it. It was the only way he could ever have anything nice. He usually did not get caught. Whenever he did, he would run his ass off. Come to think of it, running was another thing he did well. He ran a lot during his teenage years. He ran from storeowners, gangsters, hoodlums, and from the police.

Lester's luck finally ran out when he was eighteen. He had just snatched a woman's purse, while she was getting off the bus on the Grand Concourse in the Bronx. He ran like a marathon runner, but a "Good Samaritan" knocked him on his ass and held him down, until the police showed up. Since it was only his first offense, the judge was lenient on him.

When Lester was back out on the streets, he decided to step up his game. He began stealing cars, instead. It was a better and faster way to get away. He would sell the cars to guys that ran chop shops on Hunt's Point or elsewhere in the South Bronx. In time, he became good at stealing cars. He did this for about two years and made some decent cash. He only stopped after getting arrested.

Three police cars chased him for several miles from Manhattan into the Bronx. He had no idea how they knew his car was stolen. He had just taken it from Morningside Avenue. There was not a soul around. He raced across West 125th Street and crossed over the Willis Avenue Bridge. He messed up when he veered left, instead of right. He could not make the turn at the speed he was driving and skidded into a wall near some Housing Projects. The cops boxed him in and yanked him from the car.

The judge was not so lenient, this time around, and he did about a year at Riker's Island. It was there where Lester found the Nation of Islam and drugs.

By the time, he was out of prison, he was craving crack. He would steal things to sell for money and spend the money on drugs. He usually "smoked up" in building lobbies or on rooftop landings, since he no longer had his own home. He lost that while he was locked up.

He lost touch with his mother more than a year earlier, after he left home. As far as he was concerned, he had no use for her anyway. Going to her for help was never an option.

Lester preferred to be homeless. It gave him a certain freedom. He no longer had to worry about paying bills, which was a huge load off his shoulders. He could easily steal when he was hungry and he had no problem sleeping wherever he laid his head.

Before he realized it, he had smoked away the next five years of his life. Nothing else mattered to him, but his next fix.

One day he began feeling pains in his abdomen. He ignored it, at first. The pains persisted over the next few weeks and he began seeing blood in his stool. He eventually found himself at the hospital. They told him it was colon cancer. He did not care. He went out and got high, again.

Lester was still unsure why he bothered going to the free clinic. Perhaps, he was looking to see what he could steal. It was one of the reasons he agreed to meet with Dr. Fox. He wondered what kind of expensive equipment he could steal from the laboratory. Another big motivator was definitely the $100, Dr. Fox was offering to any volunteers.

He closed his eyes and fought the pain he felt. He knew, right away, the pain was not from the cancer because it was happening to the other guys, as well. They had all been injected with an experimental serum minutes earlier, which was intended to kill their cancer cells. However, the intense pain made it feel more like it was going to kill them, instead.

Unable to contain himself any longer, Lester screamed out in agony.

Next to Lester sat William Deeds, and beside him was Anthony Laurie. Both men were African-Americans, who led parallel lives. They were both born and raised in Brooklyn. They each began smoking at early ages. William started the habit at a party when he was fifteen, while Anthony lit his first cigarette at the tender age of twelve. For over twenty years, these two men were habitual smokers ranging from several cigarettes a day to one pack a day.

Therefore, it should not have come as a surprise when they were diagnosed with lung cancer. As it happens, the news hit them both quite hard.

William became so distraught that he became hooked on anti-depressants. He tried desperately to stop smoking, but had trouble breaking the habit. He tried several tricks that his friends suggested and even tried going cold turkey, but he could not follow through. He always found himself holding a cigarette. This made him even more depressed.

After nearly a year of struggling with his vices, he decided to give up and go out on his own accord. He took an overdose of anti-depressants and ended up at the hospital in the psych ward, where he spent the next month.

By the time he was released, he lost his lease on his apartment. He was already behind in paying the rent. The super was not going to tolerate it any longer. William's things had been tossed out on the street and were taken away by sanitation. He had nothing left.

Afterwards, he moved around a bit and stayed with friends a few days here and there, but he felt like he was imposing and that made him uncomfortable. Eventually, he decided to live on the streets.

Anthony, on the other hand, was able to stop smoking. After learning he had lung cancer, he sought out treatment, but could not afford to keep up with it. He lacked medical insurance and went through his savings account too fast to keep up with the chemotherapy.

Soon, he did not have enough money to pay his credit card bills or his rent. He was forced to declare bankruptcy and found himself living in his car a month later. He did not have any family to turn to and was too proud to seek help from his friends. He thought it was just a bad string of luck and that he would be able to bounce back in no time.

He learned that finding a job was not easy without a legal address. He turned to selling his possessions on street corners, but the police stopped him from doing so because he did not have a vendor's permit. Next, he turned to panhandling, or begging for money. That did not last long. The police arrested him for "aggressive panhandling" and he was forced to spend the weekend in jail.

By the time, he got out and returned to where his car was parked, he realized it had been towed away. He could not afford to pay the tickets on his car, the towing fee, or the impound fee. His car, which had become his home, was lost to him.

This led to a nervous breakdown. He was taken to the hospital, where he spent a few days in the psych ward. It was through them that he learned of the free clinic. He always hoped God would provide him with salvation, someday. He believed that everything he went through was a test of his faith. When he met Dr. Fox he thought his prayers were answered.

Instead, William and Anthony sat next to each other screaming for help that would never come. At first, they both wondered if the cancer was finally claiming them, but then they realized the other men were also screaming in pain. Was it something in that injection the creepy doctor gave to them?

There was one thing both men agreed upon, although it was never spoken. Surely $100 was not worth this amount of pain.

As Melvin Thompson screamed, he saw his life flash before his eyes. He was disappointed it was not a good life. Nothing good ever seemed to happen to him. Ever since he was a young boy, he had bad luck. He was accident-prone and broke both legs by the time he was twelve from different incidents. He had chicken pox, measles, the mumps, pink eye, and every other sickness he could acquire, before he turned fifteen. Plus, he was held back from graduating and had to remain in middle school for an extra year.

Even his parents had bad luck. His father, a handsome and successful African-American, was killed when someone tried to rob him of his hard earned leather jacket. His mother, a beautiful Puerto Rican woman, was raped in front of his eyes, while coming home late from visiting relatives. He was just a child, at the time. It was enough to mess with his head for the rest of his life.

Melvin grew up filled with hatred, mostly for criminals. He got into lots of fights during his youth and, sometimes, had to spend time at juvenile facilities, which caused his mother unneeded stress. He often had to spend weeks apologizing and making it up to her, afterward. It was the reason he had to redo the ninth grade. He had missed too much school that year.

Once when someone tried to steal his sneakers, he beat the person within an inch of his life. That landed him in prison, where he spent the next few years surrounded by criminals. Needless to say, he got into dozens of fights, while in prison. He hated everyone around him and they did not care for him either. Most of his time was spent locked in the hole away from other prisoners. That suited him just fine.

When he finally got out of prison, Melvin was able to get a job working as a janitor. He did that for about five years. He did not mind it. No one bothered him and he went about his business. He always did his job well and usually went straight home.

Occasionally, he might visit his mother and bring her things that she needed. He tried to be a good son to her. She did not deserve to stress over him anymore. He took care of her and made sure she did not want for anything. In return, she would cook him his favorite meals. She was a great cook, too. As far as he was concerned, no one could cook steak or pork chops better than his mom.

When she died, it hit him hard. He became very depressed and ultimately turned to drugs and alcohol as his salvation. In reality, they became his downfall. He lost his job and was kicked out on the streets. He even spent a little time in the psych ward of Bellevue Hospital, after trying to kill himself.

He tried to jump in front of the subway train, but someone pulled him back in time. This was probably his lowest point.

After being released from the hospital, Melvin would sleep in shelters whenever possible. He could never stay long because he kept getting into fights with people he thought were shady. Eventually, there was not a shelter around that would allow him in because they already knew his reputation for fighting.

Melvin was forced to beg, in order to eat. He refused to steal. He would not become a criminal. He would sooner die of starvation, first. Sometimes, he would get lucky and someone would buy him a meal or give him handouts or leftovers. He had no shame, so he took it gladly. A man in his position could not afford to feel pride.

If he felt too depressed, he would call 911. An ambulance would take him to the hospital. There, he could get a free meal and sleep on a comfortable bed for, at least, one night. He even had access to a bathroom with toilet paper, which beat using an alleyway and newspapers.

During one of his more recent hospital stays, he learned about the cancer that had been eating away at his prostate. He wondered why he, sometimes, had difficulty while urinating. The hospital referred him to the free clinic, where he met Dr. Fox.

Now, he was wishing he had chosen to jump in front of a train, again, instead. The pain he was feeling was overwhelming. What made it even scarier for him was the fact that Dr. Fox, the one person, who could help him, was standing there with his thumbs in his ass, as if he had no idea what to do.

To the left of Melvin was Jeffrey Haines. He and the next two men, Lyndsey Butler and Wallace Weeks, had spent the past few years of their lives being homeless. Each of these men had some form of cancer eating away at them. They each volunteered to be injected with Dr. Fox's experimental serum, all for the measly sum of $100 and a free meal.

From their points of view, it seemed like a good idea. They were each going to die, sooner or later, and none of them was living a good life. What did they really have to lose? If anything, they stood more to gain, if the cure turned out to be legit. It would mean a new beginning for them.

What they did not know was that the serum had not yet passed the required approvals and trials. It had not even been properly tested. They would be the test subjects, the guinea pigs.

Now, they were paying the price for their foolishness.

Jeffrey was having difficulty seeing anything. His vision had become clouded and his heart raced. His breathing was becoming asthmatic and he began coughing and wheezing. Pain shot out from his arm to the rest of his body in a matter of minutes.

Lyndsey cried from the pain he felt. It was unlike anything he had ever experienced. The pain seemed to stab at him from the inside out. His organs felt like they were shutting down. Everything hurt and there was nothing he could do, but suck it up. He could not move from the seat, where he sat. It was too painful to move. The only thing he could do was scream.

Wallace Weeks struggled so much that he fell from his seat toppling it over with him. He wriggled around on the floor and twisted into weird contortioned shapes, as he screamed in pain. He wondered what was happening to him. Why was he feeling such great pain? Was it from his cancer? Did it finally come to claim him?

No, it couldn't be that. It had to be because of the injection he received no less than ten minutes ago. Whatever it was in that serum was eating away at him from the inside.

Herbert did not know how to react to what he was witnessing. It was definitely not the reactions he expected the men to have. The apes did not behave in this manner. They were not in any obvious pain when they were injected. Why were these men hurting so violently? What could have gone wrong?

He became terrified and filled with dread. What was he going to do?

He thought about injecting them with the anti-serum. That might help to ease the pain and reverse the effects of the serum. In that moment, he wished he prepared more than one syringe with the anti-serum. It would have to suffice. He grabbed the syringe with the colored white cap and removed said cap. He decided he would begin with Test Subject Number One, Mr. Jones. It seemed appropriate.

Before he could step forward, the syringe was snatched from his hand. When Herbert turned to face whoever had taken it from him, he found himself face to face with Test Subject Number Ten, James Edwards, a large angry man, who was fed up with what was going on.

It seemed James was still in control of his faculties, for the moment. He saw what was happening to the others and became furious. He knew it would affect him the same way in a matter of minutes, if not seconds. He glared at Dr. Fox and broke the syringe in half with his bare hands. He then grabbed him by the neck and squeezed tight.

Herbert immediately closed his eyes and, in that moment, thought he was about to die.

James Edwards had always been a very angry man and with good reason. When he was a child, his uncle sexually abused him on more than one occasion. When James told his father about it, he was beaten for lying. He spent the next week out of school to hide his injuries. The school took notice of the absences and sent over the school nurse to check on him. When she saw the condition he was in, she confronted his father. His father only beat her, too.

After his father was arrested, James was put into foster care. He did not have a mother. She had run out on his father long ago. His new foster home treated him okay, for the most part. It was an older Puerto Rican couple that could not have a child of their own. They tried to engage him in conversations, but he had no interest in what they had to say. He felt like an outsider and did not think he would ever fit in with them or their culture.

When his foster family could no longer care for him due to extreme financial difficulties, they took him back to the child services. They were sad to see him go, but he welcomed the chance for a change of pace.

He spent about a month without a foster family. By the time a new foster family accepted him into their home, he was fed up with the whole foster care system. He hated his new home and ran away within the first week, after punching out his foster brother for trying to touch him in an uncomfortable way.

When the police found him, he ended up spending time at a juvenile facility, before being returned to foster care. A week later, he ran away a second time and lived on the streets for about a year, before getting arrested for stealing. Afterwards, it was back to the juvenile facility, and then it was back into foster care.

He continued in this way, until he was sixteen. By that time, he was through being passed around. He ran away and made sure to stay away. He relocated from the Bronx to Manhattan, where he found a job. He could not read or write well, but he knew enough to get by. He slept in the park, on the subway trains, or with friends from work. He never had a home of his own.

James got into a fight at work and ended up beating his co-worker to death. He was arrested and spent the next fifteen years of his life in prison. He did a lot of working out and a lot of fighting during that time. He spent a good deal of time seeing the prison psychiatrist, too, who tried to help him cope with his anger issues.

By the time he was released from prison, he was in his mid-thirties. While in prison, he developed a heavy smoking habit. He started by smoking a pack a week, moved up to a pack a day, and upon his release he was ready for almost two packs a day. The only thing holding him back was the simple fact that he could not afford to buy cigarettes.

It was inevitable that he would end up with lung cancer.

He turned to petty theft to support his habit. He still did not have a home or a job and, frankly, he did not want one. He preferred living free, as he did. It was like living off the land, the way they did in the old days. That's how he saw it.

In reality, he was living off of his victims. He stole purses, broke into cars, robbed people that were coming out of the subway, and did a lot of shoplifting. He was like a human parasite, which was ironic considering what was going through his body this very moment.

He fought the pain as best he could and stood up from the chair. He reached out and snatched the syringe from Dr. Fox's hand and snapped it in two. He then grabbed the doctor firmly by his scrawny neck and snarled, "No. More. Injections!"

Just as he was about to punch the feeble doctor, he keeled over in pain and was forced to release him. The pain was too much to take.

PATIENT ZEROS

Chapter Three

HERBERT TOOK A step back and felt the air coming back to his lungs. He coughed and watched in horror, as his homeless test subjects screamed loudly and twisted from the pain. He was uncertain what was happening to them and it scared him. How could his serum create such pain in these test subjects? Why didn't it affect the apes in the same way? Sure, he tweaked the ingredients a little, but not that drastically. There had to be a logical explanation. Perhaps, it was something different in their physiology? Could it be something in the human mind that was being affected differently? If only he could find out.

He thought about going back to the biohazard lab to fill another syringe with anti-serum. He was uncertain if it would work to counter the effects the men were feeling, but what other options did he have? Then again, there was also the fact that Test Subject Number Ten almost strangled him for trying to use the other syringe he had. There was no surprise they would feel leery about being injected by anything else he had to offer, considering what they were currently experiencing.

Either way, he could not remain in the dormitory, in case anyone else felt violent urges toward him. He backed away slowly and opened the door. He slipped out quietly and closed the door. The screams were immediately silenced. At last, he was able to breathe, again.

It was incredible how silent it was in the main laboratory, compared to the madness he just escaped. He placed his ear against the door and listened, but he could not hear the screams. It never occurred to him that the door and walls were soundproofed. How utterly convenient, he thought.

He paced back and forth, as he tried to think of a solution to his dilemma. He could not very well leave ten homeless men in the dormitory. Something would have to be done tonight, although he had the entire weekend, before anyone else would come to the lab. No, it had to be tonight.

There was no other way around it. These men needed to be given the anti-serum. It was the best option available to him, but how could he inject them with the way they were behaving? If only he had someone to help him.

David.

Yes, of course! He could call his assistant, David, and have him help out. It would mean having to swallow his pride and explain everything that occurred today. David was surely going to be upset about it. He would not like the idea of breaking the rules or keeping secrets. This was certainly going to lead to other problems down the road.

It was either deal with that or deal with the ten men alone. The answer was simple.

He pulled out his cellphone and was about to call David when he remembered there was barely any signal in the underground laboratory. Still, there might have been enough to send out a text message. He took a chance and typed, "Call me." As it happened, the message went through. He figured the simpler the message, the better.

He sat down on a seat near one of the long lab tables and took a moment to catch his breath. How could he have been so foolish to try this experiment without taking better precautions? He should have made up a believable excuse about safety protocols and strapped them into the chairs. Of course, he did not possess any straps that would properly bind a human.

He looked at his watch and noticed it had been about five minutes, since he texted David. He sent another message and let David know it was a matter of urgency. He wrote, "David. I am at the lab. Please, call me on the landline."

Upon sending the message, his cellphone received a notification indicating that the message was not sent. He sent it a second time and got the same message back, "Message not sent. Try again?" The signal was too weak, despite the fact that the other message went through without a problem. He became frustrated. Why was his phone choosing now to act up? He restarted it and waited impatiently for it to load up. Once it did, he typed the message and sent it, again. This time, his phone sent the message.

"Oh, thank Goodness," he sighed and rested the phone on his lap.

Now, it was time to wait. He hoped David would call back soon. He did not wish to wait too long. Who knew what was going on in the dormitory? He stared at the door apprehensively. It occurred to him the door was not locked. He quickly stood up and heard a loud bang, which startled him.

Just then, one of the apes in the cages on the south side of the laboratory screamed loudly, stirring a few of the other apes from their sleep.

The combined sounds scared Herbert half to death. He had forgotten about the apes that were locked securely in their cages nearby. There were still seven left out of the original twelve.

When he looked down, he realized his cellphone had slid off his lap and fallen to the floor. He could tell instantly the screen was cracked. He cursed, "Damn it!" That must have been the loud noise!

He shoved his right hand into his pants pocket to pull out his keys and his eyes opened wide. They were not there. Where could they be?

A shiver went down his spine as he remembered he had taken them out to open the door earlier, while pushing the wheel cart into the room. His keys were still on that plastic trolley cart beside the metal tray with the used syringes. He needed those keys to access the preparation room, biohazard lab, and the elevator.

He wondered what might happen, if he returned to the dormitory. Would the men be angry with him for leaving them? Perhaps, if he entered with the first aid kit, they would be more likely to show him some appreciation. There was one nearby.

On the other hand, what was the point? Would anything in that kit really work on them? It would only give them false hope, making them angrier. There was only one thing that would truly work. He needed to prepare another syringe filled with anti-serum, but first he needed those keys!

Herbert slowly opened the door to the dormitory and peeked into the room. The ten men were rolling around on the floor and moaning, so they did not notice him. He quietly grabbed the keys and retreated back out the door. He locked it and breathed a sigh of relief.

With that, the dormitory was properly secured, he rushed over to the preparation room and stepped inside. He opened his locker and put on his respirator mask and a new pair of rubber gloves. Next, he went through the entrance corridor and into the biohazard lab.

Once inside, he walked over to the storage cabinet, where his anti-serum was kept and pulled out the plastic beaker. He grabbed an empty syringe from a box on the counter and realized there was only one left.

"Damn, I've used them all up," he uttered to himself.

There was no time to worry about using the same syringe on all ten men. He figured guys like them were used to sharing needles anyway, so what did it matter? The important thing was that he injected them with the anti-serum, before they died on the floor of the dormitory. Getting rid of ten dead bodies would be far more difficult than paying off ten failed test subjects to keep quiet about what took place.

It would be fine, so long as there was no permanent damage. Besides, they had cancer anyway.

He carefully filled the syringe with the anti-serum and covered it with a white plastic cap, before placing it safely into the lower front pocket of his lab coat. He put away the beaker containing the rest of his anti-serum, and then proceeded to the sink to wash up, as required. He tossed out the rubber gloves and turned on the water faucet.

The sink was located against the wall near the double thick window that looked out into the main laboratory. As he allowed the water to run over his hands, he stared through the window momentarily and hoped he could clean up this mess before morning.

After he was done washing up, he left the biohazard lab and walked through the separate entrance corridor. As soon as he was back in the preparation room, off came his mask. He never bothered putting on a fresh pair of rubber gloves.

He rushed out to the main laboratory and checked the landline phone on his desk. It was connected to a digital answering machine. There appeared to be no new messages, which disappointed him. He was hoping David called, while he was in the biohazard lab. Unfortunately, that was not the case.

"Come on, David. What are you waiting for? Call me back already," he complained.

He walked to the dormitory and pulled out his keys to unlock the door. "You can do this," he tried to coax himself. "You do not need David's help. Just go inside and inject those ingrates."

The key turned in his hand and the door was unlocked. He gripped the doorknob with his sweaty hand and turned it slowly. The door popped open and he gradually pulled it outward toward him. He took a deep breath and slipped into the room with the syringe in his hand.

Just then Test Subject Number One, aka Larry Jones, stood up. He seemed to be the most reasonable of the ten volunteers, thought Herbert.

He said in a calm soothing voice, "I can take away the pain, if you can trust me, once again, Mr. Jones. This syringe contains a..."

Before he could finish the sentence Larry screamed and lashed out at him, knocking the syringe from his hand and causing it to slide under one of the cots in the room.

"Wait! You don't understand," Herbert tried to explain, as the other men began to stand and glare at him with wild staring eyes. He swallowed nervously and stepped back out of the room, pulling the cart in front of the door. As he closed the door, Larry grabbed the cart and tossed it aside sending it crashing to the floor. Herbert quickly locked the door and moved away from it.

The apes began hooting and grunting in their cages, again.

"Oh, shut up already!"

Herbert was glad the cages were covered with white sheets. It was bad enough the noises were agitating them. He did not need them watching his every move, too.

He sat back down on the seat near the long lab table feeling defeated. He could not believe he lost another syringe containing the anti-serum. He could not afford to keep wasting his precious anti-serum. There was no way he was about to fill another syringe, especially since he was fresh out of empty ones. If he was going to inject the test subjects with the anti-serum, he was going to need the syringe that fell under the cot. How could he possibly reach it without being attacked by his enraged test subjects?

He began to realize the severity of the situation. If he could not clean up this mess by the end of the weekend, it could blow up in his face. His experiments would never reach completion. He could lose his job and years of work would have gone to waste. It was possible he could even face criminal charges. No, he could not let it come down to that. He had to resolve this matter tonight. His very future depended on it.

He knew he could not handle this alone. The best course of action was to try contacting David, again, as much as he did not wish to do so. Maybe he could make him understand. He would have to help him. After all, his future was at stake, too. Was it not?

There was no time to lose. He could not wait any longer. He walked back toward his desk, picked up the telephone, and dialed David's cellphone number.

Herbert felt a swell of relief wash over him when David finally answered his phone. "David! At last! Thank God! I've been trying to reach you all evening!"

"I was busy," David replied. "What's the problem, Doc?"

Herbert responded anxiously, "David, you were right! I messed up. Please, you must come to the lab! It's an emergency!"

David responded in an annoyed voice, "Are you nuts? I'm not going to the lab, now! I'm in Queens and I don't drive. Whatever it is will have to wait until Monday."

When Herbert heard him say he was in Queens, he knew instantly what it meant. David had to be at Katherine's apartment. There was no way he would keep this a secret from her, but would she be able to keep the secret?

Herbert hesitated, before finally replying, "I see. You are with Katherine. I am sorry, David, but I really need your help." The desperation in his voice was starting to become apparent, as he pleaded, "You do not understand. Something has gone terribly wrong! I... I cannot explain it over the phone. You need to come quickly!"

The apes in the room were becoming agitated due to his loud voice, so he had to talk over them.

David became suspicious and asked, "What the hell was that? Was that an ape? I'm not going there, until you tell me exactly what you did. What are we dealing with here? Who's there with you?"

This was Herbert's last chance. Either he comes clean or he makes up a lie and hangs up the phone. He knew he needed David's help. In a fit of frustration he shouted, "Okay, fine! I'm afraid I have done something I should not have done and, now, they are having a violent reaction. There are too many for me to control on my own. I... I need your help, David! Please!"

David demanded, "They? What do you mean *they?* Please, tell me you are referring to the chimps."

Herbert answered with regret in his voice, "Actually, no. I mean my human subjects."

"Human??? Are you kidding me???"

Katherine could be heard whispering on the other end of the phone, "What's going on, David? What did you hear? Is he...?"

She did not get a chance to finish her question because David interrupted her and asked, "How many humans, Doc?"

Herbert hesitated. He was ashamed to say that he had ten homeless men locked in the dormitory.

David demanded more loudly, "Damn it! How many???"

"Ten."

David responded in shock, "TEN??? Are you insane?"

Herbert explained, "You must believe me! They all volunteered! They're homeless! Bums with nothing to lose! They each had mental issues and some form of cancer. They were eager to be cured, in exchange for a few measly dollars. I was only trying to help them." He paused to catch his breath and added, "Besides, I figured, if anything went wrong, no one would miss them. They are already dead, as far as the rest of the world is concerned. Surely, you must understand. I did it in the name of science and medicine!"

One of the apes began hooting in the background, while another thumped on his cage.

David replied angrily, "No, I must not understand! That does not make it any better! They are people, for Christ's sake! What the hell is wrong with you, Doc? Damn it! Don't you realize you're going to get us all fired, or worse? I don't plan on going to jail for your screw ups!"

"Please, David! That's why I need your help! No one must ever know about this. Not even Katherine. You are the only one I can truly trust."

David snapped back, "Yeah, well! It's too late for that! Kat is right next to me! She already heard part of the conversation and I don't plan on keeping this a secret from her like you did to both of us! If you want my help, she is going to know everything that I find out or else you are on your own!"

Herbert was afraid of that. He just needed confirmation. He hesitated for a split second, and then agreed, "Fine, bring her with you, if you must. Please, understand, I was keeping this from you both for your own good." He paused briefly and added with sincerity, "I did not want to involve you."

David asked, "Then why the hell are you calling me, now?"

Herbert answered desperately, "Because, David. I am frightened. I don't know what else to do. I tried to administer the anti-serum, but they attacked me. They have become quite volatile. They keep screaming like mad men! I had to leave the room. Now, I don't know what to do. Please! Help me, David! You are my only hope!"

David thought about it, for a moment, before responding more calmly, "Okay. Relax. Take a deep breath. Now, tell me. Where are they, at this very moment?"

Herbert took a deep breath and answered, "They are in the dormitory."

"Damn it! I knew it! I knew you were up to something. Oh, man. I cannot believe this shit. Why didn't I just check the dorm when I had a chance?"

Herbert hated having to listen to his subordinate yell at him, but he had to take it, for now. He ignored the rhetorical question and pleaded his case, one more time.

"David, will you help me? I am begging you. Time is running out."

David let out a heavy sigh and answered reluctantly, "Yeah, sure. What did you do with the anti-serum? Is it still in the dorm with them?"

"Yes," Herbert responded shamefully. "It was in a syringe, but I accidentally dropped it. I believe it rolled under one of the cots on the right side of the room."

"Damn," David replied, before letting out another loud sigh. "Never mind that," he said. "We'll think of something, later. We'll be over, as soon as we can. It may take a while."

As soon as Herbert realized they were coming to help him, he tuned out everything else David said. He did not need to hear any other complaints. Together, they would resolve the issue. He felt grateful and sighed with relief, as he replied, "Oh, thank you, David! That is a fine idea. I am sorry I kept this from you. I was wrong to do so. You are a lifesaver. And thank Katherine for me, as well."

"Right. Whatever," David replied, as Herbert hung up the phone.

PATIENT ZEROS

Chapter Four

HERBERT LOOKED AT his watch and scoffed. Twenty minutes had passed, since he last spoke with David. He wondered what was taking them so long. He, at least, expected a phone call, by now. He figured there was no traffic, since it was way past rush hour. They had to be arriving any minute. Of course, he was not taking into consideration the weekend traffic from the bar and club crowds. After all, what did he know about such things? He rarely went anywhere, aside from his home and the laboratory.

The telephone rang at around 9:30 pm. Herbert rushed over to his desk and picked up the receiver. He answered with excitement, "Yes! David?"

"No, sorry, Dr. Fox. It's Ivan upstairs at security."

Herbert's face sagged with disappointment when he realized it wasn't David. He sounded slightly annoyed, as he replied, "Yes, Ivan. How can I help you?"

"I was just wondering if you are going to be staying over tonight."

"Yes, and I would prefer not to be disturbed, if you can manage that," he responded rather rudely. He caught himself and changed his tone, as he said, "Oh, wait. Actually, I am expecting David to arrive. He should be here, shortly. Be sure he is not delayed. I need to see him immediately."

"You got it, Dr. Fox," Ivan replied with indifference. "If you need me, you know where to find me. You have a goodnight."

"Of course. Goodnight," he said curtly, and then he hung up the phone abruptly and shook his head.

The call made him rethink things. If Ivan was calling down, then he was probably checking the cameras and noticed him walking around. It would not be good for him to see anything he should not be seeing. Herbert turned off the lights of the main laboratory, so Ivan would not show too much interest in what was going on. The cameras were infrared, but if the lights were off and someone who was authorized was down in the laboratory, Ivan would likely disregard those particular cameras and focus on the rest of the building.

He walked over to the door leading into the dormitory and stood in front of it for a while. It was a shame he could not hear what was going on inside. He was curious what his test subjects were doing. For all he knew, they could have dropped dead. They certainly seemed like they were in enough pain to do so. Surely, it could not hurt to take a peek inside.

He pulled the keys out from his pocket and inserted the proper key into the lock. He turned it slowly and unlocked the door. His hand wrapped around the doorknob and twisted. The door opened slightly. He did not hear any screaming, which made him think he might be correct. What if they were dead?

From within the room, James Edwards was the only man left with any awareness of what was going on. He figured that was probably because he was the last one to be injected with the serum. He knew he did not have much time. He felt his mind rapidly slipping away. The pain had coursed through most of his body and was currently attacking his brain. His head felt like it was on fire. The urge to vomit was becoming harder to resist.

The others around him were already different. Whatever effect the serum was having on them had taken hold of them. They were not themselves. It was evident in their expressions. Their bloodshot eyes were wild and crazy.

Suddenly, the door opened. That fool doctor was back. James thought he must have been a glutton for punishment. If he wanted in, that was fine, but he would not be sneaking out, again. James grabbed him and yanked him into the room. He grabbed the doorknob and pulled the door shut.

For a brief moment, Herbert found himself standing in the center of the room surrounded by ten angry-looking men. Test Subject Number Ten, the man named James, blocked his only escape route. A slight grin appeared on James' face, right before the other nine men attacked Herbert and began eating him alive. He screamed and cried, as they tore into his flesh. He felt himself falling backwards onto a cot. The men dug into his chest and ripped it open. The last thing he saw before his death was the expression on James' face, as it changed to something horribly scary.

Outside of the dormitory in the main laboratory everything was silent. The apes stirred in their cages for a while, but eventually fell back asleep.

When David and Katherine finally arrived, it was too late. Dr. Herbert Fox was dead. They would eventually find his reanimated corpse in the dormitory, along with the first men to be infected by the Fox Serum Virus. It would be David, who would open the door and inadvertently release these infected men upon the world. By that time, they were more than ready to leave the room, where they had been trapped for the past few hours.

The infected men rushed the door knocking David back with the force of the door and leaving him temporarily stunned, while they ran into the main laboratory. Initially, they did not even notice him, but they did notice the apes hooting and hollering in their cages on the other side of the large room.

Fortunately for Katherine, she hid in the locker room, where she was safe.

When David finally awoke he noticed the infected men had managed to rip open the cages and kill two of the apes, although the apes fought back and killed one of them in return. William Deeds was literally beaten to a bloody pulp and torn apart by the angry apes, although he did not feel any pain when he died. For him, the pain had already passed. All that remained was an insatiable hunger, and then there was nothing.

That was a side effect of the Fox Serum Virus. Once an infected person died, their body was later reanimated and the hunger would continue. This would not be the case for his battered body.

However, the virus in William Deeds had passed along to the apes. It would not affect them in the same way, as it did the humans. At first, they did not show any of the symptoms that the men displayed. It would not take hold of them for about another hour or two. By then, there was no one left in the lab, aside from a few remaining infected men on the verge of death and reanimation. The virus affected the apes in the same way rabies would infect a dog. They became aggressive and extremely violent, except when killed, they would not reanimate.

In a desperate attempt to clear the laboratory of infected, David managed to trick six of them by spraying a fire extinguisher into their faces. They charged blindly into the elevator, where they were sent upstairs to the second floor of the Science Center. He would not see them, again.

Sadly, Katherine had already been infected, after being attacked and bitten by Lester and Jose. David came to her rescue and permanently killed Jose Figueroa with a hard blow to the head. Once his brain was destroyed, the Fox Serum Virus could no longer control his body. He was dead and would not be reanimated.

While searching for Herbert, Katherine was bitten, again, this time, by Herbert. They did not realize it, at the time, but he had become the first official zombie of the apocalypse. David still believed there was a chance he could be cured, so he inadvertently locked Herbert in the dormitory, along with a syringe containing the anti-virus.

He knew Katherine required immediate medical attention and would have to be taken to a hospital. During his struggle to escape, he also locked two of the infected men in separate rooms. Larry Jones was locked in the preparation room of the biohazard lab, while Lester Rowland was locked in the locker room. Not long after, Lester was able to break free from the locker room, although he remained trapped in the main laboratory with the infected apes.

David helped Katherine out of the laboratory, but once her infection spread throughout her body, she changed drastically. She had become exactly like the infected homeless men. An uncontrollable need to feed and pass along her infection had become her sole priority. David became her prime target. She lashed out at him and dug her bloody fingernail into his skin, but he was already infected. As he was cleaning her wounds earlier, he came in contact with her infected blood, more than once. It was only a matter of hours, before he would change, too. She only sought to speed up the process.

Katherine chased him up the emergency stairwell and out onto the streets. In the process of making his escape, David unintentionally led her right into the security guard, Ivan, who she attacked and ravaged. After murdering Ivan, Katherine wandered off to Twelfth Avenue, where a passing vehicle would hit her and ultimately lead to the deaths of several EMTs, a police officer, and the driver of the car that hit her. All of whom would become reanimated as zombies.

As for the homeless men that were led into the elevators, five of them eventually found their way down to the ground floor and out onto the streets, where they wreaked havoc.

Anthony Laurie ran straight into the glass windows of the Science Center, smashing through them and making his exit to Broadway, where he turned south. He made his first attack on someone trying to get into a taxicab. When that person got away, he chased someone else up the stairs into the elevated train station at West 125th Street, where he successfully infected everyone on the platform and attacked people coming off the trains.

Melvin Thompson followed Anthony out of the building through the first floor windows onto Broadway. He also ran south, until he noticed a group of teens hanging out in front of the Grant Housing Development. He veered toward them and charged full speed into the crowd. He began biting into any piece of flesh that was not covered by clothing. When they ran from him, he chased them into the lobby and up the stairs. Over a period of about two and a half hours, he single-handedly infected over twenty residents of the building, before leaving through the rear door and running out onto West 125th Street and starting a riot. He was one of the first to be shot and killed by the police.

Anthony and the ones he infected at the train station later joined the riot.

Jeffrey Haines took slightly longer to exit the Science Center. Once he made it out of the building, he ran straight across Broadway and through the Manhattanville Housing Development. The police spotted him, but lost him in the darkness of the night. After attacking a drunken person seated on a bench, he found his way to Amsterdam Avenue, where he attacked several more victims. He continued his vicious assaults on West 135th Street attacking every person in sight and spreading the infection to nearly fifty other people, before his body began to die and he was reanimated as a zombie. Even then, he would continue to spread the virus over the weekend.

When Lyndsey Butler found his way out of the Science Center, he went in a different direction. He wandered toward West 132nd Street and followed the noises of the night. He made a left toward Twelfth Avenue, where he immediately spotted a large crowd a block away at the nightclub on West 133rd Street. His intense hunger drove him to sprint straight into the nightclub, where he joined the infected Katherine, who was already infecting the drunken crowd, by this time. Together, they were able to infect nearly one hundred victims, including two police officers from the 30th Precinct.

All it took was one bite and you were done.

Wallace Weeks was next to leave the Science Center. He was not too far behind Lyndsey, except he ran north on Broadway and kept going, until he reached West 135th Street. There was a bunch of people hanging out and enjoying the warm summer night in front of 3333 Broadway. Wallace began attacking as many as he could, before being apprehended by the police. He was transported to Harlem Hospital, where he broke free and went on a rampage through the emergency room attacking nearly a dozen victims.

Meanwhile, the earlier victims he attacked had begun changing, as well. Some had also gone to the hospital, while a few went home. Soon, the infection was spreading like fire through the hospital and at 3333 Broadway. No one was safe.

Only James Edwards did not find his way out of the Science Center. Instead, he lingered in the very same elevator, where David Frino trapped him. Unaware of how to open the doors on his own, he stood within the elevator and waited for them to be opened for him.

Ultimately, it would take a small military special ops team to finally take down James Edwards, Larry Jones, Lester Rowland, and rotted corpse of Dr. Herbert Fox, as well as the infected apes. Of course, these soldiers would pay a high price for these kills, as would the entire city.

Newly infected people continued swarming the streets at a rapid pace and infecting anyone in their path. In the beginning, people that were bitten escaped in their cars, only to carry the infection into the surrounding boroughs and New Jersey. Meanwhile, the reanimated zombies followed along at a much slower pace lurking in the shadows and finishing off anyone that managed to slip by, until the entire city had finally fallen and become a metropolis of the undead.

An infected homeless man on the steps of Riverside Park.

THE MANHATTANVILLE INCIDENT: PART SIX

"Man's End"

MAN'S END

Chapter One

WHAT YOU ARE about to read is a story about humanity's survival in the Zombie Apocalypse. It has been several weeks, since a nuclear warhead was dropped over New York City. It is mid-summer, but it is already beginning to feel like autumn. The days have been cooler and the nights have been darker.

The belief was that by dropping the bomb over Manhattan, it would take out the entire region affected by the Fox Serum Virus, an experimental vaccine gone horribly wrong. The belief was a foolish one built on lies and misinformation. The virus had already spread beyond the city further than expected, which essentially made dropping a nuke pointless.

On that first night of infection, there had been infected people that escaped the initial riots and managed to make their way back home. They were the ones to take the virus far and wide. First, the virus found its way to the outer boroughs, the Bronx and Queens, which connected to Westchester County and Long Island, and then it crossed over to the nearest state, New Jersey. One infected person took a flight to Ohio and single-handedly crippled that state contributing to the downfall of the east coast.

With outbreaks in New Jersey and Ohio, it was inevitable before the states in between felt the sinister touch of the virus. By the end of the first week, the first signs of infection had reached Pennsylvania and West Virginia. A week later, there were outbreaks in the neighboring states of Michigan, Indiana, Kentucky, and Delaware. It became a domino effect, as infected people took foolish risks, knowing full well they could spread the virus.

Meanwhile, the nuclear fires had spread as far as New Jersey, Connecticut, and Westchester, Nassau, and Suffolk Counties. They were allowed to burn themselves out. Some fires burned for weeks. Long Island had become a deathtrap, as the virus was able to spread across to Montauk Point unchecked. Those with boats escaped to the surrounding islands, isolating themselves indefinitely.

Radiation became an added threat to those in the tri-state area. Anyone who remained too close to the blast zone had to worry about radiation sickness or the long-term effects, such as cancer, which ironically was the reason for the creation of the experimental serum that became the virus. Nuclear fallout was also causing problems for certain types of electronic equipment and interfering with cellphone signals. Many cell towers had been destroyed, which also made accessing the Internet a problem for locals.

By the third week, it seemed like the civilized world was fighting a losing battle. There were riots, which led to anarchy. State militias had taken over, where the governments failed. The Union was facing its worst catastrophe, since the American Civil War. State officials were calling for the head of the president for failing his duty to his country.

The southern states were demanding a break from the Union for the second time in the history of the country. They wanted fences and walls put up to keep the virus in the north. Some were calling it karma for the American Civil War and for the removal of certain historic statues depicting Confederate heroes of the south. To make matters worse, states in the west also wished to secede from the Union.

This time, there was no army to stop these threats, only threads of bureaucracy.

The Center for Disease Control and Prevention made false promises that a cure would be found and things would be set right. They were pressured into rushing their research and things went wrong, as they often do when important things are rushed. A week later, the CDC had fallen.

Apparently, several test subjects that were secretly collected from New York on the night before the nuke went off had escaped. They caused havoc in the facility and escaped into Atlanta causing another viral outbreak, this time in the south. It spread quickly through Georgia and into the Carolinas.

This huge set back led to the involvement of the World Health Organization. Its main focus became keeping the virus confined to the eastern United States. However, there are always people who cannot comprehend the significant danger involved when they think selfishly. Of course, someone that was infected fled into Canada and within days there was a full-blown outbreak in Ontario.

The fifth week saw random gas leaks that remained unchecked leading to explosions. Fires burned out of control because there was no one to put them out. Arson became commonplace, as did looting and random acts of violence. Unchecked heavy rains led to floods. As a result, ghost towns have been popping up all over, while people flee to other states in hopes of finding salvation.

In the end, dropping a nuke caused more problems than it solved.

Small pockets of survivalist groups were the only ones, who really stood a chance in any of the Infected States of America, as they had become known. The governments had either abandoned these states or were overthrown by militia forces. People were forced to defend themselves.

Never before did the second amendment mean so much to the people of the United States. There were many well-regulated militias that became necessary for the security of every state, which meant the right of the people to keep and bear arms was detrimental for their survival and that right should not be infringed. Otherwise, the strong would surely overpower the weak.

In Monroe, a city of Orange County, NY, there existed a two-story home with a full-sized attic and basement on Cromwell Road that was modified into a fortress. Tall fences laced with barbed wire were erected around the property. A moat was dug along the outer perimeter of the fence, filled with water, and stocked with piranha. A gate had been added to the entrance road leading into the compound. A four-story lookout tower was erected, along with an addition to the house that extended outward into the backyard.

The new addition was a sixteen-foot by twenty-foot room that served as a common room for everyone, taking the place of the living room. The living room was converted into a dorm room for the males. Extra beds were brought in from neighboring houses, which had been abandoned.

The basement of the house was in the process of being converted into a large fallout shelter with a secret tunnel that would lead to the far edge of the property. It would serve as an emergency escape tunnel should the need to leave arose. There was still much work to be done. It was a lot of work for the small group that resided at the compound and it kept them quite busy during that first month. Every person had his or her own specific duties, but they helped each other, as well.

Daniel Rivera was sort of the chief engineer. He was in charge of all construction projects, since he had the experience and skills. There were plenty of strong young men to help out as part of his work crew, but Bobby McDonald was one of his hardest workers. He was especially good when it came to building the tunnel. It reminded him of his youthful days working with the Department of Environmental Protection. All of the guys did their part to help out. Even the girls helped, wherever they could.

Charles Foster oversaw security of the compound, since it had been his home. He knew all of the ins and outs of the property. Angelo Williams helped by setting deadly explosive booby traps around the borders of the compound or by taking turns with Liz Mayaguez volunteering to stand watch in the tower.

Charles also served as the unofficial leader of the group, considering he had supervisory experience. There was never a vote and no one really called him the leader, but everyone knew it and accepted it. They often looked to him for answers. It was just the way things were.

Julia Duncan was surprisingly helpful with setting up security cameras and monitors, which could be accessed from one central location in the basement of the house. That room became the security hub. She also kept the group apprised of any pertinent information she learned, while searching the Internet. The underground tunnel became a special interest for her, since she loved exploring tunnels.

Grant Hamilton became the weapons master, mainly because he came into the compound owning most of the weapons and boxes of ammunition. They were stored in a small room down in the basement. It fell to Grant to help the others with weapons anyway he could. He taught those, who did not know, how to shoot and clean their weapons, such as Roberto Medina, Kirk Kamassa, and Bobby. He showed them how to load their weapon magazines and taught them how to deal with malfunctions. He was no expert, but he had plenty of experience, thanks to his seventeen years in the NYPD.

An area near the far edge of the property served as a decent firing range. Rounds were shot out into the woods at the concrete frame of an old burned out house, if they missed their targets. Shooting was only done during the daytime, while someone stood watch in the tower.

While Grant trained the others how to shoot, Roberto was teaching them how to fight without using weapons. A gym had been established in the basement using exercise equipment and large mats that were recovered from the abandoned high school during a supply run. Roberto, Kirk, Daniel, and most of the girls spent a lot of their free time using the gym to keep in shape. They normally worked out in a co-ed atmosphere.

Millie Delgado mainly did the cooking, since she was so good at it. Occasionally, she had help from Aramis Perez, who cooked rather well. Cooking was not done every day. Sometimes, the group ate simple meals, such as sandwiches, soups, or frozen dinners. Things they could prepare for themselves.

It became necessary to build a hen house behind the tool shed, which was east of the house. They were able to find three live chickens, a rooster and two hens. It was not much, but it was a start. None of them had any farming experience, but David Castillo's grandmother had chickens when he was a kid. The idea was his, so he owned it. He tried to learn about what needed to be done by checking the Internet. Julia printed out an instructional manual that she typed up for him. She liked doing things like that.

Kirk got the idea to paint their stolen mini-school bus black and reinforced it with armor plating that would protect the tires and windows. Shooters in the bus would be able to open or close the armored window coverings. He also thought they could add a triangular pointed battering ram in the front, while adding a reinforced spiked bumper on the rear end. Daniel used his mechanical know-how to bring Kirk's vision to life. They also welded spikes onto the wheel rims, so they could easily flatten the tires of any passing vehicle, if necessary. The bus became like a tank.

Kirk decided to give it a name. He called it The Intrepid, in honor of the sunken aircraft carrier that provided them with shelter at the beginning of the apocalypse. He painted the name on both sides of the bus using yellow paint, so it could be seen easier.

The survival books that Grant brought with them from his home came in handy. They were stored on shelves in the common room and made available for all to use. There were two books about how to survive in the wilderness, a book that showed which plants were edible and which were poisonous, and a few books on hunting and fishing. There was even a book dedicated to survival in a Zombie Apocalypse, although, at the time it was written, it was intended as a joke. Now, it was irony.

Charles stood on the front porch with Grant. They stared out across the property and wondered how else it could be improved.

Liz looked down on them from the tower, which stood four-stories in height, so they could see over the house and past the tall trees that surrounded the property. Its base was wide enough to have a room at the bottom level. Stairs went up to the second level and a long ladder took you to the top lookout deck. There were binoculars mounted onto a rotating stand, which had been Williams' idea. Liz looked through the binoculars and scanned the entire perimeter of the compound. She spotted a deer in the woods and aimed her Colt M4 Carbine at it. From where she stood, she knew she'd be able to hit it.

Firing the weapon on the compound would not be an issue, since it was located off the beaten path in the middle of nowhere. All of the nearest houses had been abandoned during the past couple of weeks. They were the last holdouts in the neighborhood. Plus, her weapon had a suppressor to silence the sound.

She breathed slowly and gradually pulled the trigger back, until the rifle went off.

The deer dropped instantly. She called down to Grant and Charles, who were looking up at her, and said, "Anyone interested in having venison for dinner? There's a buck lying outside the fence in the woods"

Grant gave her the thumbs up signal. It had become a common communications gesture for the group, especially when words could not be used for whatever reason. He walked toward their fairly new blue pick-up truck, which they acquired in town a week earlier, after someone foolishly left it with the keys in the ignition. Along the way, he called out to Kirk and Roberto, who were nearby putting away tools into the tool shed. They gladly went with him to pick up the deer.

Williams opened and closed the gate when they left to save them time.

This was a common routine for the group, whenever they were blessed enough to actually hit a deer, rather than scaring it away. It looked like they would be eating well tonight.

Millie hated making venison, but it was the one meat they seemed to get, most of the time. There were always herds of deer running around Monroe, especially in the surrounding woods. Besides, she sure knew how to cook it well.

Williams, on the other hand, knew how to clean the deer and separate the meat, so they could make jerky, which had a conveniently long shelf life. He was also the only one in the group with any real hunting experience. He taught Kirk and Roberto how to clean their kills, but was still in the process of teaching Grant, Charles, and David, who were reluctant learners when it came to such things. It amused him.

Living off the land took a lot of getting used to for these city folk. They had to learn how to garden and grow their own crops. Of course, they were learning how to hunt and clean their prey, so it could be cut up and cooked. Smoking the meat was another necessary lesson to be learned.

Williams knew all about that sort of stuff. Being in the military had turned him into an excellent survivalist.

Aramis stepped outside and asked, "Was that a gunshot?"

Charles turned to him and replied, "Yep. Liz shot us a deer for dinner."

"Awesome! Meat! I'll go let Millie know. She'll love that." He laughed, knowing how much she hated cooking venison. He went back into the house, leaving Charles alone to stare out over the property.

Down in the basement, Daniel, Bobby, and David were working on the tunnel. They had gotten pretty far with it. Soon, it would be at the farthest desired point. Supporting the tunnel was the hard part. They worked hard to keep it from collapsing. Wooden beams and wooden planks were strategically placed throughout the tunnel's length. They were lucky enough to raid a lumberyard two weeks earlier. The haul provided them with plenty of wood for their projects.

Daniel studied their progress and said, "I think it's coming out good. We're just going to need a few more feet, before we can open it up at the ground level."

David griped, "Thank God! I'm getting tired of working underground. I feel like a damn mole."

Bobby grinned, "This is good stuff, Davy boy! We're getting down 'n' dirty! Why else do you think I worked in the sewers, and then in sanitation? I love this shit!"

Daniel chuckled, while David made a sour face.

Julia stood at the entrance to the tunnel and called out, "Hey, guys! Good news! Venison cutlets and mashed potatoes for dinner tonight!"

David smiled in relief, "Yes! At last, some good news!"

Bobby replied, "Yeah, that sounds friggin' delicious! I can taste it already!"

"All I taste is dirt," said David.

Daniel and Bobby laughed.

Julia looked around admiringly and studied their work. She commented, "It's coming out really nice, guys. Great job."

"Thanks," Daniel replied proudly. "Hopefully, we can be done, soon."

The guys finished up and exited the tunnel, so they could wash up, before dinner. Naturally, they would have to take turns showering in the guest bathroom on the first floor. The women were the only ones that used the main bathroom in the former master bedroom on the second floor, since the master bedroom had been converted into the women's dorm, similar to how things were at Grant's house.

He and Liz were allowed to use any bathroom together, since they were the only couple in the group. They were also the only ones that did not sleep in dorm rooms, aside from Charles. He slept in the attic, while the couple shared the guest bedroom on the second floor.

The set up seemed to work for everyone. At least, no one complained. It was how things had been for the past month, since they arrived at Charles' home. Presently, it was home to the entire group. No one knew how long things would be this way. They stopped asking, after the first three weeks. They all just accepted it.

Amazingly, there was still hot water. They wondered how long it would last, before they lost that luxury. As a back up, there was an old well on the land, located behind the tool shed. Cleaning it out would be another job for another day. Getting their hands on a solar water heater would also be helpful.

When it was dinnertime, the group sat at the dining room tables. There were two of them, which was more than enough to seat all thirteen of them. The dining room was a bit crowded, but they had knocked down a wall in the kitchen to make more room, after the new table was brought in two weeks earlier.

Charles always sat at the head of the old dining room table, since he was used to that seat. Grant and David sat at either side of him. Liz sat next to Grant, while Kirk sat next to David. Roberto liked to sit across from Charles. Williams sat at the head of the new table with Daniel and Bobby to one side, Aramis and Julia on his other side, and Edie and Millie both seated opposite from him.

That was the usual set up for group meals. They preferred to keep the same seats to give them some semblance of ownership and normalcy. It was important to them. They each had their spots and even sat in them whenever they ate alone.

They normally tried to have someone keep watch outside, but great meals like this were rare. It was a special occasion. Besides, Williams promised to eat fast and head right out, afterward.

Once dinner was cooked, everyone served his or her own portion. That was the rule. They had to serve themselves and wash any dishes they dirtied. Nobody wanted to pick up after someone else. They all did their own laundry, too. There was a washing machine and dryer in the garage.

Aramis was the first to say something about dinner, "Mmm! You outdid yourself, Millie. This is delicious!"

"Thank you. You don't think it's too salty?"

"Hell no! It's perfect!"

David raised his glass of water and turned to Millie, "Yes! My compliments to the chef!"

She smiled bashfully. Everyone always complimented her on her cooking, but she never got used to it. She was always embarrassed by it. She was also the only one to ever complain about the meals she prepared. She often thought her meals were too salty or not salty enough.

Aramis found it funny because each meal always tasted perfect to him. He especially loved when she made rice and beans with some sort of meat. They usually had venison chops. Those meals reminded him of the past when things were normal.

Grant looked at Liz and said, "And thank *you* for shooting us a nice-sized deer, my dear. It was a good clean shot."

She grinned and replied, "I couldn't let the opportunity pass me by. When I saw the deer, I knew it would make a great dinner for us. It was love at first sight." She chuckled.

He smiled at her warmly.

Charles happily agreed, "You said a mouthful. This beats frozen dinners and canned food any day." He took a mouthful, chewed it, and swallowed. "Mmm. Hey, Millie, did you add garlic to these mashed potatoes?"

"Yes. Why? Did I use too much?"

"Mm!" He took another spoonful. "No way! It's perfect! They taste excellent!" He said with his mouth full of food.

David made a foul face and laughed. He asked, "Didn't your mom ever teach you not to talk with your mouth full?"

Charles began laughing. He finished chewing and swallowed, before answering, "We have new rules for our society. Didn't you get the memo?"

David smirked and shook his head.

Most of the others laughed.

Julia said, "Hey, I can always type one up and print it out for you, if you want?"

"Good idea," Charles joked.

Aramis cried out, "Oh, no! That's all we need!" He then laughed.

Grant turned to her and said, "Don't you dare! You better not waste our paper and ink on that crap! Don't let this crazy man convince you to be wasteful. He loses his mind whenever he eats good food."

The others laughed.

Edie smiled at Millie and said, "I told you everyone would like it. You worry too much, Mil."

Millie enjoyed how everyone praised her cooking. It made her feel good. She had finally found her place in life. It only took a Zombie Apocalypse to accomplish that goal. Still, she wished her sister were still alive to partake in her happiness. At least, she had her new family.

Charles looked around at the group. He was glad things were working out for them. He liked what they created together. It was a wonderful new beginning. He hoped it could always be this good, but deep down he knew it was only a matter of time, before the serenity of their compound was challenged.

He was never the positive type. He preferred to be realistic. What they had was nice, but it was only temporary. He was not going to lie to himself. That's why it was so important for them to prepare for war, so they would be ready when the time came.

Grant, Roberto, and Kirk were the only other people, who truly understood that.

MAN'S END

Chapter Two

D AVID WALKED OUTSIDE at 11 am and began loading up the pick-up truck with a few tools. He was going out on a routine supply run. The weather was perfect for it.

Roberto came out to help. He asked, "How long are we planning to be out there?"

"Until we get everything we need. I'm still waiting for Aramis to bring me a list. I already have lists from Millie, Daniel, and Julia."

He scoffed, "Jesus Christ. This is going to take days. Isn't it?"

"Let's hope not," David smirked. "We're only taking enough bottles of water and food for three days tops. I'd like to be back tonight, if possible."

"Now, you're talking, bro. Let's try for that. Come to think of it, I need cigarettes anyway."

Kirk left the house and walked over to them. He had just taken a shower, after working down in the tunnel with Daniel and Bobby. He looked into the cargo area of the truck, saw the tools, and commented, "Looks like we're just about ready to go. What time are we leaving, Dave?"

"As soon as Aramis gives me his list."

Kirk joked, "You mean his list of demands?" He spoke with an Arabic accent and said, "I want a million dollars and a helicopter! Praise Allah!"

Roberto and David laughed.

Aramis came running out to them from the house with a piece of paper in his hand. When he stopped and caught his breath. "Sorry," he said, "I had a lot of long names to write down. Freaking meds can't have simple names. Are you sure you don't need me to go? It will be a lot easier for me to find this stuff. I know what most of it looks like."

David thought about it, but then said, "It's probably better for you to stay here. You're the only EMT we have, which makes you very valuable to the group. It's best if we don't take chances."

"Fine," Aramis sighed with disappointment. "So, basically, I'm a prisoner here."

"No, definitely not a prisoner, but you are grounded, young man. Now, get back to the house, before I take out my belt."

They all laughed.

Aramis joked, "Shit! I swear it feels that way, sometimes!"

Roberto patted him on the shoulder and said, "We need you, bro. Isn't it nice to be needed?"

"Yeah, I guess. Be careful out there, man. We've been lucky, so far. I keep thinking our luck is going to run out."

Roberto smirked, "Damn it, Doc. If you're not going to be positive, I might have to ban you from talking to me. This is not what I want to hear, before going out for supplies."

"True! My bad! I'm sorry. Seriously, though, you guys be careful."

"Thanks," said David. "We plan to be very careful. That's why I'm bringing these two guys with me. They're my bodyguards."

Kirk snarled and flexed his muscles, "Grrr! Don't worry, Aramis. We'll be back with your supplies, before you can say, '*Anowa chipisala'cho.*'"

"*Anowah chipsie salad cho-what?*" Aramis asked confused.

Kirk laughed and said, "I'll tell you when I return, my friend." He then climbed into the driver's seat and closed the door.

Roberto got inside next on the passenger side and shifted over to the middle to make room for David, who climbed up and closed the door.

He looked out of his window and asked Aramis, "Can you get the gate, please?"

Charles rushed over to see them off, as Aramis opened the gate for them. David told Kirk to wait, so he could see what Charles had to say.

"I'm glad I caught you, before you left. There's something you need to know. Julia was checking Internet feeds and she saw a report of infected in Rockland County from yesterday. That means it's coming closer. We think they came up through New Jersey."

Roberto rolled his eyes, "Great! Why doesn't that surprise me, just as we are about to go out on a supply run?" He looked at Aramis and said, "This is your fault, bro!"

David commented, "That's still a few miles south. We have time."

"Regardless, try to hurry back early," Charles warned. "You guys be very careful and avoid people, if possible. It's too bad we no longer have our police radios."

David replied, "They wouldn't work out here anyway. We've been doing fine without them. I'll see if I can find some two-way radios somewhere, if it makes you happy."

Charles nodded, "Yes, it would. Thank you."

Kirk gripped the steering wheel tight, looked over at him, and said, "Don't worry, Charles. I already have the map you made for us memorized. I'll bring them back in one piece."

"Good. See that you do. I'm counting on you." Charles pointed at him.

David smirked, "Don't wait up, dad. We might be a day or two."

Charles called after them, as they began to pull away, "Funny, smart guy! If things look bad, forget the supplies and come back! We'll figure something out!"

David waved his hand out of the passenger side window and they left the compound. They turned right onto Cromwell Road and disappeared from view behind the tall trees that lined the road.

Charles stepped back inside and said, "Let's lock it up, Doc."

He and Aramis closed the gates and locked them.

Williams watched from the tower and could see the pick-up truck for a little longer. He watched it reach the next road, where it turned left, and then went out of range. Once it was gone, he looked around the property making sure to scan every section. He thought about his buddy, Martinez, who was a sniper and would have loved standing in the tower with his M107 light fifty-caliber sniper rifle. Thinking about dead friends was depressing, so he quickly thought about something else.

He watched Liz on her patrol. She walked the grounds within the perimeter of the fence and checked it, from time to time, making sure there were no openings. He admired her grit. She was a good soldier. He wondered what she did, before the apocalypse. It was obvious she had military experience with the way she carried herself and her weapon. He wondered why she did not stick with it.

That Grant was a lucky guy, he thought.

"That damn Grant is a lucky bastard," said Bobby, as he watched Liz walking into the house. He and Daniel were sitting on outdoor chairs drinking bottles of water. They had just finished working down in the tunnel and were exhausted. Daniel had just taken a shower and it was Bobby's turn, but he was in no hurry. He didn't mind being dirty, especially when he was thinking dirty thoughts.

Next, he trained his eyes on Edie and Millie, who were walking toward the garden. Millie wore a short summer dress, while Edie had on shorts and a tight t-shirt.

"Oh, man. It should be illegal for a woman to walk around looking that sexy," he said.

Daniel turned to him and asked, "Huh? What's illegal? Are you talking about the girls?"

"I was saying it should be illegal for a woman to walk around with her ass hanging out of her shorts. Millie is too friggin' skinny for my taste, *although* she has pretty green eyes. I'll give her that. Now, Edie is just right for me. Oh, man, oh, man. I love those tight little shorts and that perfect juicy ass."

Daniel looked in the direction he was looking and noticed what he was speaking about. "Oh," he responded. "Yeah, that is *pret-ty* short."

Bobby scoffed, "I'll say it is. Dude, I love it when girls wear sexy clothes. Wakes me right up."

"Where did they get those clothes from?" Daniel asked.

Bobby rolled his eyes and explained, "Millie was running away from home the night it all began. She had a bunch of clothing with her. When she finally made it to her sister's house, they packed more clothing, as if they needed it. After her sister died, Millie kept everything of her sister's, even though her sister's clothes were too big. She gave most of them to Edie and Liz, who can fill them out better."

"Oh! Okay. I was wondering how they always had a nice change of clothes and we're all stuck wearing hand-me-down clothes from Grant and Charles." He chuckled.

Bobby said, "Tell me about it!" Bobby laughed, too. A short time later, he asked, "Hey, you wanna hear something crazy? I had the craziest dream last night."

"Oh, yeah? Well, lay it on me. It's not like I have any television to watch." He chuckled.

Bobby began telling his dream, "I was trapped on an island and there were only women left in the world, but they were all aliens from another planet." Daniel chuckled and Bobby continued, "Don't get me wrong, they were still hot! As a matter of fact, I was about to get down and dirty with one, until I realized her vagina was like a mouth. It had lips and teeth and it could speak to me in their language. They all had it like that! It was friggin' nuts! I kept thinking Vagina Dentata! Vagina Dentata! You know? Like the movie?" Daniel nodded, although he had no idea, which movie Bobby was referring to. Bobby added, "It was pretty scary, man. I thought it was going to bite my thing off and eat me."

At that point, Daniel began laughing hysterically. The thought of it was so silly that he had to laugh.

Edie and Millie wondered what he found so funny. They continued tending to the soil around the growing vegetables and watered each one accordingly. They were in the process of growing their own potatoes, tomatoes, onions, peppers, and garlic. It would take more time before most of the vegetables matured. In the meantime, they did have a few oregano plants they could forage and some sweet peppers to collect. Mille was carrying a basket with her to do just that.

Edie whispered to Millie jokingly, "I bet Bobby just told him his penis size."

Millie and her both giggled.

Bobby stared at them and wondered why they were giggling. He found it to be a turn on. He said, "It's a damn shame. I hate seeing sweet ass go to waste. They're definitely rug munchers. It's a major loss for us guys, especially during these trying times. Now, Liz, on the other hand.... the ass on that girl is special. I'd love to grab her by that long curly hair and..." He was interrupted, before he could finish.

"Don't forget she's already taken," Daniel reminded him.

Bobby scoffed, "Ha! I'm not worried about Grant. I can take him."

Daniel began to feel uncomfortable with their conversation. He didn't like that Bobby was being disrespectful. He shook his head and said, "I don't know, Bobby. It's never good to poke the sleeping bear. Maybe it's a good idea to keep your mind on your work. You're a hard worker, one of the best we've got. My old boss, Ventucci, would've loved having a guy like you in his crew. I'd hate to lose you."

Bobby turned to him and asked, "Lose me?? How? You think they can do anything to me? *Big Bad Bobby?* Please, Dan! Sleeping bear, my ass! That's friggin' rich!" He laughed. "They need me around here. I'm a hard worker, like you said."

Daniel felt Bobby was talking a little too loudly and he did not want to draw negative attention their way. He got up and said, "I'm beat. I'm going inside to see what kind of books we have around here. I think we're gonna need some engineering books. I'll see you later." He walked off slowly toward the house, as he enjoyed the warmth of the sun.

By then, Millie was done filling her basket. The girls left the garden and went into the house.

Bobby stared and watched them, as they walked. He shifted in his seat and replied, "Okay, Dan! Check you later!" He stood up and said to no one in particular, "I guess I should go inside, too. I could use a nice cold shower to bring down the swelling the girls left me with."

Grant was down in the basement armory. It was more like a walk-in closet, than a room. Charles had fitted it with doors long ago and used it for storage. Essentially, it was still being used for storage. Since the group's arrival, they had moved a storage locker and tool cabinet into the new armory. The long weapons and boxes of ammunition were kept in the storage locker, while the smaller weapons and gun cleaning equipment were kept in the tool cabinet. Grant also added some hooks on the wall for hanging things, such as hunting knives and daggers. He used the top of the tool cabinet to clean the guns and kept the door to the armory open for ventilation.

There were quite a few weapons that were stored in the armory. His old Glock 19 was one of them. He opted for carrying his Walther PPK, instead. Also in the armory were his Ruger GPNY .38 Special caliber stainless steel pistol and his Karr K9 9mm. Charles donated two of his military weapons to the armory. He had a Beretta M9 pistol and an MP5 submachine gun. He preferred to carry his Smith and Wesson, instead. He did not like dealing with the safety switch on the Beretta and ammo was limited for the MP5. It was only for emergencies. On the other hand, Grant maintained several boxes of ammunition for each of his guns, so there were plenty of rounds for those weapons. Williams had given up two of his eight grenades and all six sticks of dynamite he carried for the armory. There were also a few pocketknives, which Charles and Grant confiscated from would-be perpetrators over the years as cops. That was the extent of the weapons in the armory, but they hoped to improve their collection.

After creating an inventory, which Grant wrote on a piece of paper, he handed the list over to Julia. She was in the security hub, which was the next room over. She sat at her computer and said she would transcribe the list for their records. She enjoyed creating lists. It was one of her more useful skills.

"Thanks," he said to her. "I knew I could count on you."

"No problem, Grant. You can always count on me," she smiled at him.

He stood beside her, while she typed and asked, "Why do you like hanging out down here all the time? You don't get much time to socialize with the others."

"I've never really been into socializing. I'd rather be doing something I love and I love computers. I love it down here. It's like having my own private office."

"That's cool, I suppose."

"Yep," she nodded. "Besides, I get to socialize with you, Danny, Rob, and Kirk. Charles comes down to talk to me, too. Danny keeps me entertained. Boy, can he talk! Once you get him going..."

"Yeah, I noticed," Grant chuckled. "He likes reminiscing about his glory days."

"For real!" She nodded. She then turned around, looked up at him, and asked, "What about you? Are you happy with how your life is now? I mean, do you miss being a police officer?"

"Yes and no," he replied. "Yes, I am happy with how things are for me, personally," he pointed to himself. "My life is very different, but I have Liz, which makes up for a lot of things I lost. She's the best." Julia turned to face her computer and secretly rolled her eyes, while he went on, "As for being a cop, I don't miss it at all. It was a stressful thankless job. You go out of your way trying to be a good cop and treat people with respect, but all it takes is some stupid ass cop to mess up and your good efforts were for nothing. In the eyes of the public, you are just as much an asshole as him. Why? Because you are a cop. It's bullshit and I was tired of it."

"That sucks," she said, while she typed up his list. "I bet you were a great cop!"

"Eh, I was okay. Greater cops than me died because of that damn virus."

"Well, you're still *my* favorite police officer," she smiled brightly at him. "I bet not many others were into urban exploration like you."

He smiled back at her and replied, "Thanks. That is a rare interest for a police officer. A lot of cops might have been into it before they joined the Police Department, but once you are on the job, you tend to avoid things that are illegal. You tend to avoid a lot of things, including family members."

"Why didn't you stop exploring?"

"I don't know," he shrugged. "I guess I preferred to put my interests, before my job. I didn't let being a cop change who I was before. Urban exploring is fun, so why should I stop enjoying it?"

"You shouldn't!"

"I know, so I didn't. Being out there and seeing so much abandonment, only reminds me of it."

"That's what makes you awesome in my book. You are true to yourself." She hoped she was not laying it on too heavy. She did not want to be too obvious about her feelings for him.

He chuckled, "Thanks, Julia. You're pretty awesome, too."

She turned around and asked, "Do you really think so?"

"Of course," he said with a smile. "You're smart, pretty, cool, and you have a great laugh."

Her eyes lit up and her heart skipped a beat. She wondered did he like her, too? She thought maybe if she told him how she felt, he might admit his feelings. Who knows where that could lead… a forbidden kiss, perhaps?

Just then, Charles entered the room and she pouted. He walked over to them and said to her, "Ah, I knew I'd find you here."

"Where else am I going to be?" She beamed at him, although she was really upset that he interrupted her time alone with Grant. If only he had waited a few more minutes, then maybe she could have gotten Grant to kiss her.

Grant asked, "What's up, Chuck?"

"Must you call me that?"

Grant shrugged and grinned innocently at him.

"I have a proposition for our girl, Julia." Charles turned to her and asked, "How would you like to be the new quartermaster?"

She was intrigued and asked, "Exactly what would that entail?"

"Well, you would be in charge of our inventories and keeping complete lists on the computer. You wouldn't necessarily have to be the one taking the inventories. Instead, you can collect the inventory lists that are taken by others and catalogue them. Anytime we are low on supplies, you would be the one to provide a complete list to whoever is going on a supply run, rather than having them collect several lists from everyone on the compound. It can become ridiculous having them go out with several lists. One list would be more efficient. If anyone needs something, they let you know and you can add it to the list. Before each supply run, you will print a copy of the list for each person going, just in case. What do you think?"

She considered his idea and thought it was a good one. "Okay, I'll do it."

"Excellent. Thanks. I knew I could count on you."

She smirked at how reliable everyone seemed to think she was and joked, "Do I get a pay increase? Medical benefits? People to boss around?"

He chuckled, "You can have an extra half hour of sleep in the morning and you get all the paper you need. If you want to print money on the paper, that's entirely up to you. I, personally, won't arrest you for counterfeiting. I'm not sure about Grant or Dave."

Grant snickered, "I'd probably just shoot her, since we don't have a prison."

"That's just great! Thanks a lot, Grant," she replied sarcastically. "And here I thought we were friends."

"Hey, we are!"

Charles chuckled and said, "Thanks, again, Julia. I'll leave you alone with this traitor." He left the room and walked toward the stairs to go back up.

Grant looked hurt. "Me, a traitor? That's not cool." He called after him. "I'm just keeping order around here, Charlie!" He turned back to Julia, shook his head, and whispered, "I'd never shoot you." He winked his eye at her and walked away toward the unfinished tunnel to check on the progress.

Amused, she smiled and stared at him momentarily, and then went back to typing the list. She frowned and wished she had made a move on him, before Liz did. She really wanted to, but it never seemed like the right time. He spent too much time with *her* at the armory. It was the story of her life. She always waited too long to react and almost always lost out on great opportunities. She sighed.

A short while later, Aramis entered the room. "What's up, pretty lady?"

"Hey, Aramis," she smiled.

"I was just talking to Charles. He told me about putting you in charge of our inventories. I thought I could offer my assistance, if you need it. The long names on the different medicines can be difficult to remember and, sometimes, hard to spell. I figured I could help out with that."

"That's sweet, but totally unnecessary," she said. "Once I have everything listed on the computer, it will only be a matter of selecting what we need, copying and pasting it to the list, and printing it out. Easy as pie. Besides, I have a fairly high IQ. I'll manage."

"Oh, okay," he frowned. He looked disappointed. He hoped to find an excuse, so he could spend more time with her. He liked her and thought she was very pretty. She never seemed to notice him, though. She spent too much time in front of the computer.

She noticed his disappointment and asked, "Is there anything else?"

"Huh?"

"Is there another reason you came down here to see me?"

"Oh, uh, yeah. I guess. We don't really get to see much of you, since you are always down here. I thought maybe we could get to know each other and become friends."

"We are friends," she responded plainly.

"Yeah, I know. I meant, you know, maybe… *really close friends*."

"Oh, I see."

He decided to take a chance and said, "You're very beautiful. I thought so when I first saw you. It's a shame to hide that beauty down here, where no one can truly appreciate it."

She was touched. "Thank you, Aramis," she said. "Really, I am deeply flattered, but I'm afraid I'm not interested. I'm sorry."

He pouted.

She then added, "Don't get me wrong. You are a handsome man. You have a nice complexion and great hair. I also think the goatee looks good on you. *However*, I'm not too crazy about that whole *Fu Manchu* mustache you've got going on there." She waved her hand over his face. "That doesn't mean it doesn't look good. It's just me. I'm not into that sort of thing."

"I can shave it off or trim it," he suggested with a glimmer of hope in his eyes.

"No! Don't do that! It's what makes you… you." She began to feel awkward. She hated the idea of breaking his heart, but her heart already belonged to another in her mind. She confessed, "Honestly, it would not make a difference. The truth is… I'm… uh, I'm… a lesbian!" She almost wanted to grin because her excuse was so brilliant. Now, none of the guys would bother her, after he spread the word.

"Oh, I'm sorry," he said. "My bad. I didn't realize it. Hey, say no more. I won't bother you, again. We're still cool, though, right?"

She smiled, "Almost like besties. No worries."

"Good. I'm glad." He turned to leave, but then paused. "You know? If I can still help out with anything, just let me know," he offered.

"Well, you can start putting together a list of the most important medicines we need and the ones we already have. I'd like to get started on this inventory project, right away. I hate procrastinating."

"Okay. You got it! See you in about an hour." He went back upstairs in a good mood, despite being disappointed.

She thought about his visit and smiled. At least, she knew where she could find a back up, if she ever got tired of daydreaming about Grant. *As if!*

MAN'S END

Chapter Three

KIRK FELT QUITE comfortable in the driver's seat of the pick-up truck. It was a new model and still had that new car smell. He was surprised they found such a decent vehicle with the keys in it. He wondered if the owner had been somewhere nearby the day they took it. He hoped not. That would be a shame.

He was glad it was such a beautiful day. He kept his window open, so he could take in the fresh summer air. The abundance of trees along the roadside only added to the fine air quality. He enjoyed driving. It gave him a sense of freedom, especially since he no longer had to pay attention to the old traffic rules. He was never one to follow the rules. Driving was something he could not do before the apocalypse, considering a traffic court judge had revoked his driver's license a year earlier.

Alas, that was another story for another time.

Kirk followed Cromwell Hill Road east toward Route 17M, where there was an abandoned Shop Rite supermarket. That would be their first stop, providing there was still anything left to loot. They had already been there twice in the past month and during both instances they noticed others had also been looting it. This time around, they were going to need a lot of food. Millie wrote out the longest list from everybody. Food was their top priority, after all. Fresh supplies were becoming difficult to locate, especially with the power out. Frozen meat was no longer an option and neither were dairy products.

It was a quiet ride, as they drove. It was only about three miles away. Roberto decided to break the silence by asking, "Hey, Dave? What are you? Puerto Rican? Dominican?"

"I'm a mutt," David answered with a smug grin. "My family is a melting pot of all races. There are Puerto Ricans, Cubans, Dominicans, Italians, and blacks. I even have a Jewish uncle, who's a rabbi!"

Roberto chuckled, "No shit?"

Kirk grinned, "Maybe that's why I like you so much. You're so versatile."

David smiled and nodded, while staring out of his window. He watched the roadside for any signs of life. There were none, aside from a squirrel running up a tree.

Roberto said, "I'm just a plain old *Nuyorican*." He turned to Kirk and asked, "What about you, Kirk? You look like you might have some Hispanic in you."

"Actually, I don't. I'm one hundred percent Cherokee, part Creek and part Chickasaw."

"Really? What's your last name, if you don't mind me asking?"

"Kamassa. It sort of means elder," he explained.

Roberto seemed fascinated by that even more. He responded with a smile, "Now, that's cool. You are a true native of this country, a real American. I like that."

Kirk smirked, "Anyone from the neighborhood, where I grew up would disagree."

"The hell with those people!" Roberto replied angrily, "We appreciate you for who and what you are. From now on, we're your friends and family. Nobody else matters anymore, so forget about them. You can leave your past in the past, if that's what you prefer."

Kirk glanced at Roberto from the corner of his eyes and smiled. He responded, "For you to think of me that way means a lot, considering your real family is gone. I know how much they meant to you. I'm deeply honored that you feel that way about me. I've never really had a best friend growing up. It's funny how it took the Zombie Apocalypse for me to find true friends."

David added, "I agree with Rob. We'll stand by you through thick and thin. You were there for me in my time of need and I will never forget that. You saved my ass."

Kirk chuckled, "I'm glad I could help."

"Me, too!" David exclaimed.

Roberto began thinking about his family and fell silent. The nightmare of watching his sister and cousin die played over in his mind, as much as he tried to push it away. On top of that, it bothered him how he never got to find his mother. He had no idea what happened to her. He tried to tell himself it was quick and painless, so that she did not have to suffer. He shook off the bad memories and his mind drifted back to his new adopted family.

"We're living in a very different world," he said. "The rules have changed. The way I see it, we're just like a real family. We do for each other and I know that we'd die for each other, if it came down to it. Some already proved that point, allowing us to go on, as far as we have. They made the ultimate sacrifice and we need to make sure it wasn't done in vain. I hope and pray no one else will ever have to do the same, but we need to be realistic. Others will die, in time. I just hope not today!"

David replied, "Amen to that."

Roberto had a feeling the Grim Reaper was not done with them, by a long shot, but he kept the thought to himself. He wanted them to feel positive vibes.

The three were quiet for the rest of the ride, each deep in his thoughts. David thought about his former partner, friends in the NYPD, and family members he never got to say goodbye to. Roberto thought about his mother, his sister, and his cousin. Not to mention, there were other family members of his out there, who also paid the price when the bomb was dropped over New York City. He wondered, who would be next to go. As far as Kirk knew, his adoptive family was still alive and living in Harrison, New York. His blood relatives were safe from the virus in the mid-western states. He was not thinking about any of those relatives. Instead, his mind was focused on keeping his new family safe.

The entrance ramp leading into the parking lot of Shop Rite.

They drove up the entrance ramp, which led to a hill, where a large parking lot was located. There were several stores on the left and more on the right. They stopped in front of the Shop Rite, which was to their left. Kirk waited, before turning the ignition off. First, they looked around and made sure there was no one else around. It was better to be safe than sorry. They could not assume they were the only ones left in town, scavenging to survive. Just because they had not seen anyone in over a week did not mean there were not others out there, who were hiding. They scanned the rooftops and distant hills ahead, watching for anything that stood out.

David observed, "Well, nothing looks out of place, as far as I can recall. I don't think anyone's been here, since we last came. The shopping cart in front of the exit door is exactly how I left it."

Roberto replied, "Someone could have put it back the way they found it."

It was possible, but it did not really make sense to David. He responded, "I don't think anyone would waste their time doing that. There'd have no reason to."

Kirk said, "Unless they want to keep their existence secret from us because they are afraid of us."

David replied, "Well, if they are afraid of us, then they probably won't bother us, while we look around." He opened the door and stepped out of the pick-up truck. He pulled out his Smith and Wesson, while continuing to look around. If anything went down, he preferred to be ready.

Roberto stepped out next with the wrecking bar in his hand.

Kirk sighed and turned off the truck. He took the keys, got out, and closed the door.

The three of them walked slowly toward the supermarket entrance. The glass sliding door was stuck in the open position. David moved the shopping cart out of the way, so they could enter. It was lying upside down. Once they were inside, he put it back in the same position. They did a quick check of each aisle, until they were satisfied that the place was empty.

David grabbed another shopping cart and walked through the farthest aisle to the left. Kirk read off the items from the list and they grabbed what they needed, placing each item into the cart. They were also able to get a bunch of things from Aramis' list at the pharmacy and a couple of items from Julia's list in the stationary section. While they shopped, Roberto stood atop a counter and kept an eye on the entrance and staff areas to make sure no one surprised them. He held his gun, in case he had to shoot.

After they were done, they packed what they could into milk crates and plastic bags. Kirk grabbed a few tabloid magazines and threw them into the cart.

David eyed him curiously, so Kirk explained, "It's for the girls! They get bored when they're not busy cooking, tending to the garden, and looking pretty."

"*R-I-G-H-T,*" David said, not believing a word.

Roberto stepped down from the counter and grabbed a magazine from the cart. He looked at the headlines and chuckled, before tucking the magazine into his back pocket.

Kirk and David looked at each other and chuckled.

"What?"

"Oh, nothing," Kirk replied.

Roberto asked, "Did you grab my cigarettes?"

"I got you three cartons."

"Nice! Thanks, bro."

"You're very welcome," Kirk responded.

They walked toward the exit, moved the upside down cart from the doorway, and pushed their cart through. Once they were outside, David put the other cart back in place.

It only took a minute to load their items into the back of the pick-up truck. Afterwards, they covered everything with a tarp, which had already been left in the rear for just that reason.

It was time to move on to the next location, an auto repair shop on the other side of Airplane Park. That's where they hoped to find most of the tools on Daniel's list.

When they arrived at the repair shop, they noticed a white van parked next to it. They hesitated to get too close because they were uncertain, if the owner or driver was nearby. The van was not there on their last visit.

Kirk stared at the van and parked a safe distance away from it in a nearby parking lot. He asked without taking his eyes off of the van, "What do you think? Scavengers like us?"

"Could be," David responded. "Let's just wait and see what happens. We're making good timing with gathering the supplies, so we have time to kill."

Roberto looked around at the wooded area behind them, and then at the nearby rooftops. He scanned anywhere someone could hide. There were several houses in the area. He kept a special close eye on them. As it turned out, he did not notice any movement whatsoever, but he still was not quite convinced they were alone. He had a stinging feeling the driver of the van was not far.

"Maybe one of us should go out and look around," he said feeling uneasy. "I don't like staying here like sitting ducks."

David agreed, "Maybe you're right. Odds or evens?"

"Never mind that crap, bro," Roberto responded. "Let me out. I'm getting antsy sitting in here. I need to do something."

Kirk smirked, "Just don't die. I mean, be careful. You know?"

"Yeah, of course," Roberto responded confidently.

David opened his door and stepped aside, so Roberto could get out. He then got back into the truck and closed the door. Like Kirk, he also had his window open, so he could listen for any sounds.

"Good luck," he said.

"Thanks," Roberto replied, as he walked away. "I'll check the van out, first." He carried his wrecking bar, although also kept his gun within reach in his waistband. He cautiously approached the rear of the van and peeked into the rear windows. When he realized they were tinted, he moved on, since he could not see inside.

Kirk and David looked on anxiously. David took out his gun and held it in his hand, resting it on his lap. He was ready for a fight.

Roberto moved around to the passenger side of the van and slowly stepped toward the front. He pulled his gun up and aimed at the passenger side window. He tried to remember the tactics Grant showed him when approaching a car. He arced outward, as he moved forward, stepping away from the vehicle to maximize his point of view, while still aiming at the window. It looked like no one was in the front, so he cautiously moved closer. He looked into the window and saw that the front was indeed empty. There were no keys in the ignition, which was disappointing.

He waved Kirk and David over and waited for them to join him. They got out of the pick-up truck and walked toward him. When they got close enough, he said, "Let's check the back. Kirk, can you open the door, while Dave and I get ready for whatever comes?"

Kirk nodded in agreement and they took their positions. He silently counted down from three using his fingers. When he reached one, he yanked open the rear passenger side door.

Both Roberto and David aimed their weapons inside and prepared to shoot. They were relieved to learn the van was empty. However, it meant the driver was somewhere else and that worried them. It was very probable the driver was hiding in the very auto repair shop they came to visit.

Kirk looked toward the open garage door and said, "I guess we can't wait out here forever. We might as well get this over with already."

"I'm with you," said Roberto.

They carefully approached the open garage and stepped inside with guns drawn. They waited for an attack that did not come. After a few seconds, they continued walking deeper into the garage. They checked everywhere, but there was no one in sight. They quickly collected the tools Daniel wanted and headed back outside.

As they walked past the white van, Roberto said, "Maybe we should hotwire it and take it back with us. We could sure use a van like this for carrying big loads."

David asked, "Did you check if the keys were inside?"

"Yeah, they're not in the ignition."

David opened the driver's side door and checked the overhead visor. When he pulled it down, the keys fell to the seat. He looked at Roberto and said, "That's how you need to check for keys."

Roberto smirked, "Nice. Why didn't I think of that?"

"Next time you will." David asked, "Do you want to drive it back?'

"I would love to, except I don't know how to drive, so that probably wouldn't be the best idea. I wouldn't want to wreck it, as soon as we found it."

Kirk said, "Remind me to teach you one of these days."

"I'll do that. Thanks."

"It's easy once you get the hang of it," Kirk said.

"Hold this, please." David handed the tools he was carrying to Roberto and got into the van. "Let's make sure it starts," he said, as he turned the ignition. The van turned on. David grinned, but then he noticed the gas tank was almost empty. He frowned, "We'll have to stop for gas, before we go anywhere else. It's almost on 'E.'"

Kirk sighed, "Of course, it is. We can't expect this to be too easy."

Roberto chuckled.

David had a thought. Considering they had two vehicles, it might be a good idea to head back home. They were able to get most of the supplies on the lists, so there was no point staying out any longer. Soon, it would be dark.

Kirk and Roberto agreed. They were not too keen on staying out overnight anyway. They decided to put the tools in the back of the van. Kirk and Roberto went back to the pick-up truck and started it up. They would follow David to the gas station.

A little while later, they returned to Route 17M, where they made a pit stop at the Sunoco gas station, across from Airplane Park. As they approached the gas pumps, they found two red five-gallon gas cans sitting on the floor beside them. They wondered who could have left them behind. Apparently, whomever they belonged to left in a hurry.

Kirk eyed them curiously and commented, "Well, look at that. It appears someone was trying to gas up. I wonder why they changed their minds."

Roberto immediately looked around suspiciously, but he did not see anyone in the area. He remained on guard.

Kirk pointed the gas cans out to David, who was still seated in the driver's seat of the van. He was busy looking through their supply lists. "Hey, Dave. Check it out. Somebody left us a pair of gas cans. We may as well fill them up, too."

David folded the lists and got out of the van. He put them into his pants pocket and walked over to the gas cans. He lifted each to check if they were empty. They were. He shrugged and said, "Someone else's loss is our gain."

Roberto got out of the truck and told Kirk, "I'm going inside with him to check it out. I want to make sure no one else is around."

"Cool. I'll keep an eye on the vehicles and get the pumps ready."

Kirk also stepped out of the truck and waited by the gas pumps, while David and Roberto went into the A-Plus mini-mart to activate them. As soon as they stepped inside, they noticed the place had been completely ransacked. Nearly every shelf was empty or knocked over. There was food and broken glass bottles scattered on the floor, which was wet and sticky from the mixed drinks that had been spilled. Whoever looted the place was messy and wasteful about it. It almost looked more as if there were a brawl inside.

Roberto looked over the counter and didn't see anybody. A bunch of merchandise had been knocked over back there, as well. There were some cigarettes and lighters spread out on the counter. He grabbed them and shoved them into a bag from behind the counter.

"This will come in handy," he muttered to himself.

Next, he checked the restroom. It was empty, although it stunk like urine. The toilet looked like it had not been flushed in days. The toilet paper was completely unrolled and was all over the place. It looked like vandals had used the bathroom as a playground. He was disgusted when he noticed human feces had been spread across the wall into a message that read, "This place is full of shit." He quickly closed the door to avoid gagging.

"Damn animals."

He shook it off and rubbed his chin with one hand. He took in the scene of the mini-mart, one more time and wondered what could have happened. Someone destroyed the place on purpose, but why? It made no sense to him. It was extremely wasteful. It definitely meant other people were around. He still could not get over how mostly everyone in town just got up and left fearful that the virus would soon reach the area. It was like being in an episode of *The Twilight Zone*.

David finally figured out how to turn on the gas pumps. He grabbed a few bags from behind the counter and passed some to Roberto. There was no need for words. They filled the bags with whatever they could salvage from the floor. When they were done, they went back outside to the vehicles. David pumped gas into the van, while Kirk topped off the tank of the pick-up truck. Afterwards, he would fill the two gas cans.

Meanwhile, Roberto pulled out a pack of cigarettes from their recently acquired loot and held onto it for later. He walked around, while the others finished pumping gas. His eyes watched everything around them like a hawk. He gripped his gun and pulled it out. It was too quiet. He did not like it. It felt like they were being watched.

Kirk finished up first and loaded both gas cans into the rear of the van, before getting into the pick-up. He thought it was best to keep the gas cans and tools separate from their food.

Roberto wanted David to hurry, but he did not say so. Instead, he hovered over him like the secret service guarding the president. His eyes continued to dart in every direction, as he watched for any signs of trouble. His gun was ready.

David noticed his strange behavior and asked, "What's up, Rob? Something wrong? Did you hear something?"

"Not yet. I don't think we're alone. Let's get out of here, before something happens."

David placed the nozzle back on the pump and closed the gas cap. He looked around briefly and got into the van. He started it up, while Roberto walked over to the pick-up and climbed into the passenger side. Kirk had already started it up and was ready to go.

Roberto turned to him and said, "Keep an eye out, Kirk. I have a bad feeling about this place."

Kirk exhaled and replied, "You, too, huh? I noticed a bunch of flies outside, while I was waiting for you guys. Where there are flies, there is usually death, or shit. Both things are not good."

"Yeah, this place is definitely shitty," Roberto smirked. "I feel like someone is watching us. Maybe they are watching to see what we do or waiting for a moment to make their move. I hope I'm wrong. Whatever the case, I don't like it. I hate feeling vulnerable."

"I hear you. Do you think it could be the driver of the van?"

"Maybe. That's a damn good possibility, in which case that person is going to be pissed. The shop looked like it was hit by a tornado inside. Someone destroyed everything for no reason. We were barely able to salvage what we could. I think whoever did it is the same person that's out there watching and it could very well be the driver of the van, considering there were gas cans waiting to be filled."

"Mmm. Maybe we interrupted him? Let's head back, before it gets dark. I think we should take the long way to throw them off, just in case they are watching to see which way we go."

"Good idea, bro. Do you know the way?"

"It's like I told Charles earlier, I memorized his crazy map." They both chuckled, and then Kirk said, "Hold on. Let me tell Dave the plan." He called out from his window to David, who was on the opposite side of the gas pumps from them, "Let me lead, Dave. I'll explain later."

David replied from the driver's side of the van, "I was going to follow you anyway."

"Okay," Kirk said with a wave. He then pulled out onto Route 17M and began driving north.

What they did not notice was the dead body of the gas station clerk, who had been dragged behind the building and left in the bushes.

They continued along Route 17M and reached Museum Village Road, where they made a left. There were no other vehicles following, or on the road. The entire area was desolate. If anyone had been watching them before, they were far out of view, by now. About a minute later, they merged onto Bull Mill Road, and then eventually got to Cromwell Road.

When the two vehicles reached the gate to the compound, Kirk honked his horn once to let them know they were back. He stepped out of the truck to unlock the gate. They only had two keys for the master lock that was used to lock it. One copy was kept in the garage of the house. The other was usually with the driver of whatever vehicle left the compound, which happened to be him.

Williams approached them and waited, so he could lock the gate, after they entered. He noticed the van and grinned, "Nice. I see we got a new ride."

Kirk nodded happily, as he drove onto the property. David followed with the van. They parked the vehicles beside their armored school bus, The Intrepid. Those were the only vehicles they owned, but they hoped to acquire more in the near future. Of course, more vehicles meant they were going to need more gas, which would soon be harder to come by. Therefore, they needed to limit their driving to supply runs. No exploration missions.

Williams peeked down the road both ways to make sure they were not followed. He then closed and locked the gate.

Charles, Daniel, and Aramis came out of the house to greet them. Charles said, "Welcome back. You returned much earlier than I expected."

David replied, while still in the driver's seat of the van, "We're done. We got almost everything on the lists, including a bonus. Someone was kind enough to leave this van for us with the keys in it." He slapped the side of the door proudly.

They exited the vehicles and began unloading the food. Charles, Daniel, and Williams helped out. Kirk climbed up into the rear of the pick-up and passed down the milk crates and bags of food. Each took a milk crate or two bags of groceries and went into the house. The bags had been fully packed, so they were heavy. There were bags of rice, a variety of canned and boxed food, cooking oil, various condiments, snacks, and multiple bottles of drinks. There were two milk crates and eight bags in total.

Before Aramis would help, there was something he needed to know. He asked Kirk, "So, big guy. About that translation you owe me. What was it that you said earlier?"

Kirk handed him a milk crate filled with food and tossed in a special bag from the pharmacy. He then answered, *"Anowa chipisala'cho.*

It means 'until I see you, again.' That little bag contains some extra goodies for you that weren't on your list."

A smile stretched across Aramis' face, and then he took the crate of food into the house. Once inside he put the crate down on the kitchen counter and grabbed the bag. He checked inside and found multivitamins, supplements, probiotics, antacids, band-aids, ointments, and boxes of condoms, as well as the medications and medical supplies he requested.

Millie and Edie scrambled nearby to put away the groceries, while the other guys brought in the last of the food.

Grant came upstairs from the basement and went out to help. He had spent the better part of the day in the armory, where he organized everything to make it easier to find. When he reached the vehicles, he was surprised to see the van.

"Ooh, impressive. Tell me you also have the keys."

David held them up and jingled them in his hand.

"Awesome!"

The rear and side doors of the van were opened, so it would be easier to remove the tools and gas cans. The guys each grabbed something and carried the tools and gas cans to the garage. There was also a bag of tools that had been in the van when they found it, which was an added bonus.

Daniel was the most excited. He stood in the garage and rummaged through the tool bag from the van, before checking to see what they brought from his list. A few tools were duplicates, but that was fine. It never hurt to have extra tools.

"Oh, man! This is great! Good work, guys! I can't believe you found all of this stuff! You know? My old boss, Ventucci, had every one of these tools, too. That man had every tool in the book. If only he could see me, now. Thank you." He was so happy.

Roberto smiled and said, "No problem, Danny." He then walked over to Charles, pulled him to the side, and said, "We may have a problem. While we were in town, we had confirmation that someone else is out there. The van was parked near that auto repair shop. It wasn't there the last time we went. Someone also made a huge mess in the gas station shop. They even spread shit on the bathroom walls into a message that read the place was full of shit. Obviously, we are not talking about someone normal. I felt like we were being watched the whole time we were there."

Charles considered what Roberto told him and answered, "We'll have to play it safe, from now on. No more supply runs for, at least, a week. Maybe whoever is out there will move on. We knew the town wasn't empty, so it's not a surprise someone else is still lingering around."

"Yeah, but this person doesn't seem right in the head, writing messages with shit. They might also be pissed off, if it turned out we stole their van and gas cans."

"That would certainly make me angry."

"I doubt you'd write stupid messages using shit."

"Yeah, that will never happen," Charles chuckled. "Let's not tell *everyone* about what you saw in that bathroom. There's no reason to worry them. We'll let a few guys know, so we can beef up the defenses anyway we can. I don't want us getting caught with our pants down. Someone needs to know there might be a psychopath out there."

Roberto agreed, "Ain't that the truth."

A basic hand drawn map of Monroe, NY.

MAN'S END

Chapter Four

THE NEXT WEEK went by without incident. Charles made sure someone was always in the lookout tower, while someone else was always patrolling the inner perimeter. Those duties usually fell upon him, Grant, David, Roberto, Williams, Liz, Aramis, and Daniel. They were the ones, who could handle guns better. There were eight of them, so they took turns two at a time and worked in four-hour shifts to avoid boredom or fatigue. Grant let Daniel use his old Glock, since he did not have his own firearm.

While Kirk and Bobby were both very strong guys, they were better with their hands. Shooting was not their forte. For the moment, shooters are what were needed to secure the compound, especially from the tower. It took skill to shoot from that high up.

Meanwhile, Julia sat at her computer in the basement and watched the security monitors. It had become an obsession for her. She often spent hours sitting there watching what was going on. There were only four cameras, so it was not difficult to watch all four on a split screen monitor at once. She could even rotate the cameras and zoom in from where she sat.

"Little sister is always watching," became her catchphrase.

One camera was mounted at the top of the fence looking out toward the entrance road. The second camera was in the backyard of the house facing away toward the woods, where the fence marked the perimeter. Another camera had been mounted high up in the tower. It looked down over the northern part of compound with ease. The last camera had been set up in the basement behind her. It faced down the length of the long, dark, unfinished tunnel.

Every once in a while, when she was alone in the basement at night, that particular camera would give her the creeps. She found herself staring and expecting someone to appear. Every sound she heard would freak her out. She could not wait, until permanent lighting was installed.

Daniel and his work crew were making significant progress with the tunnel, but it still needed a few yards to go. It was already about three hundred feet long, which was a remarkable achievement, since they did the whole job using manual digging tools like miners of the past.

The tunnel currently led to a dead end. That would change once it was completed. There would be an opening on the ground near the perimeter fence, which would be locked from within. It was only meant to serve as an emergency exit.

Julia found herself staring into that very dark tunnel. In that moment, she was startled by the sound of someone opening the door upstairs and coming down into the basement. She hoped it was Grant, but was disappointed to see it was only Edie. She rolled her eyes and refocused her attention on the monitors.

Edie approached and sat down in the seat beside her. Julia made no reaction and did not say anything to her. Edie frowned and asked, "Is there something wrong? Are you mad at me?"

Julia replied shortly without looking at her, "No. I've been very busy."

"Yeah, I heard. Quartermaster. Is that all because it seems more like you've been avoiding me, since we arrived here a month ago. Is there a problem between us that I don't know about?"

"That's all in your mind," Julia answered amusingly.

"Is it? You come to our dorm room late at night and go straight to sleep. You're usually the first one awake, so you're gone, by the time Millie and I wake up. I have no idea how you can survive on such little sleep. During mealtimes you barely look my way. You can't even look at me, now. Can you?"

Julia replied coldly, "I told you. I'm busy. Besides, who can sleep with that damn rooster around?"

"Oh, please. Don't lie to me. Cut the crap. I know you're upset."

"Oh, that's rich! The biggest liar here is calling *me* a liar!"

"Ha! I knew it! You are upset with me!" All of a sudden, Edie lowered her voice and pleaded, "Julia, please. I know what this is about. Don't tell anyone. You promised."

"Well, it's been a month and I haven't said a word. Have I?"

Edie shook her head and realized she was right. "No. Thank you," she said.

Julia sighed and grabbed her head in frustration. She took a moment before saying, "It's not my place to tell anyone. It's *your* secret. I just don't like being made into a liar. By keeping your secret, it makes me a liar. So, I figured by staying away from you, I wouldn't be put into that position."

Edie nodded sadly, "I understand. I just thought we could be friends. We're all here together for who knows how long? Plus, we got along so well at Grant's house that night."

"Honestly, things would have been fine, if I never learned your secret."

"What does my secret have to do with us being friends? What difference does it make?"

"It makes a huge difference to me," Julia replied. "Look. No offense, Edie, but I'm a private person. I enjoy my alone time. Don't read too much into it. It's me, not you."

Edie scoffed, "Oh, okay. That line." She wiped a tear away from her face and said, "Well, I guess I'll leave you to your privacy!"

"Thank you. That would be appreciated."

Edie pushed the chair away with an attitude, knocking it over, as she stood up. She stomped away and went back upstairs.

Julia sighed and felt bad. She reached over and picked up the chair. She wondered if maybe she had been too hard on Edie. It was for the best, she told herself. The less people she felt close to, the better off she was in the end. She had never really been one for making close friends. They'd probably only die anyway.

David, Kirk, and Roberto were standing in the backyard discussing their recent supply run with Charles, Grant, Liz, Aramis, and Bobby. There were still a few items that were needed, which they failed to acquire. Soon, it would be time for another supply run.

Roberto asked, "Well, how long do you think we can go without these items?"

Charles explained, "It's not so much how long we can go, but what will we do when we can no longer find these items? We need to take one thing into consideration. If there are still others out there, it means we are competing for the same supplies. It's first come, first serve. The longer we hide out and wait, the less likely we will be to find the items we need. A supply run that might take one day could end up taking a week, instead."

Grant said, "He's got a point. The clock is ticking. We'll need to go back out sooner, rather than later. We should definitely get propane for the generators, more bottled water, lots of batteries, and we could use as much fuel as we can store. It won't hurt to find ammunition, too."

David asked, "How much propane do we have left?"

Charles wasn't sure, so he let Grant answer, which he did.

"Oh, we still have eight tanks, which is plenty. We need to think long term. Once those tanks are empty, we won't be able to go to the market or gas station to get more. That's why we need as many as possible. Our survival depends on it. The same goes for the water. We need to stock up on as many gallons or bottled water that we can find. If we can fill the van up, it will be fantastic. We need to stop thinking of this as a temporary solution. This is our future. I'll go out myself for the next supply run. I'll just need one person to come with me, as back up, since the van only seats two comfortably."

Before Liz could volunteer, Bobby spoke up, "I'll go with you!"

"Thanks, but we can decide that when the time comes. There's no need to do it here." That was Grant's subtle way of telling Bobby he would rather take someone else, but Bobby was insistent.

"It's not a problem," he said. "I wanna go. I haven't been out there, yet. It's time for me to go out and pull my weight for the team."

Grant replied, "Don't be ridiculous. You do plenty around here. I heard Daniel considers you his best worker."

Bobby had a smug grin on his face when he responded, "Well, that might be true, but I still need to do my share on the outside. It's only right. Count me in, buddy."

"Okay, cool. Uh, thanks."

It was obvious to Charles, David, and Liz that Grant did not want to take Bobby along. They were the ones who knew him best, so they could tell he was trying hard to be polite about it. Each of them had grins that they tried to hide.

Liz tried less to hide her amusement. She stared at Grant, saw his frustration, and chuckled. She knew she'd have fun teasing him about it later.

David chuckled briefly, too, and then looked at his watch. When he saw the time, he nudged Roberto. "Come on, Rob. It's about that time. Our turn for guard duty."

"Oh, shit!" Roberto exclaimed. "I almost forgot about that! Let me run to the bathroom real quick. I'll meet you out front." He went into the house.

David waved at the others and also went inside. "Goodnight," he said.

"Goodnight, Dave." Charles waved back, and then he turned to Grant and asked, "So, Grant? When do you and Bobby want to make that supply run?"

Liz tried hard to hold back her laughter. She had to turn away and fake a cough.

Aramis thought she sneezed because he said, "Bless you."

"Thank you," she snickered. "I was trying to cough. I mean I was coughing."

"Oh, okay," he replied, sounding confused.

Meanwhile, Bobby was looking at Grant and waiting eagerly for him to decide. He might have been a little too eager to go out there with him, which seemed odd, since the two hardly spoke to each other. In truth, Bobby knew it would be a prime opportunity for an unfortunate accident to happen. When Grant could not return due to an unforeseen death, Liz would be available for the taking. He thought it was a perfect plan. There would be no witnesses. Of course, he would have to work on his acting, so he could look convincing when he came back alone. He wanted to play it up good.

Grant glowered at Charles and responded, "Let me sleep on it. I'll get back to you tomorrow. Actually, I might need to take two people with me, after all. Three is safer than two."

Bobby frowned at the idea. His sudden change in expression went unnoticed by the others. Having another person could ruin his plans, depending on who else went with them. He would have to prepare for the possibility that two may have to die.

David stood on the front porch and waited for Roberto. As he waited, he thought he heard someone nearby. It sounded like it was coming from around the corner of the porch. He walked around to investigate and saw Edie. She was standing alone in the dark and appeared to be crying.

He approached her from behind and asked, "Edie? What's wrong? Why are you crying?"

She turned to face him and was startled to see him standing so close to her. She let out a small scream, "OH!"

"Hey, take it easy. It's only me. What's wrong?" He became worried.

She collapsed into his arms and he held her close. As she cried, he tenderly caressed her back and tried to calm her down.

"Shhh. Whatever happened, I'm here, now," he assured her. "Everything's going to be fine. Let it out. If you're not ready to talk about it, now, that's okay. I'm here for you, no matter what. I once told you I wouldn't let anything happen to you. I meant it."

She held him tighter and cried harder.

He held her and closed his eyes. It felt good to hold her in his arms. He never realized how nice it would feel. He was tempted to give her a gentle kiss on the forehead, but thought a move like that could give the wrong impression. It was a brotherly thing to do. He liked her and wanted her to know it. He didn't want her to think of him as a big brother. He already felt that way with Millie. Edie was different.

She slowly pulled away from him and as she did they made eye contact. She wet her lips and stared at his eagerly. She wanted to kiss him so desperately.

It was what David wanted, too. He sensed this was his chance to finally kiss her. He moved in close, but just as their lips almost touched, she pushed him away abruptly.

"No, I'm sorry! I'm not ready for this," she cried, and then she ran off into the house.

David called after her, "Edie! Wait! Come back! Edie!" He followed her back around to the front of the house, but she had already gone inside.

Roberto was standing on the front porch smoking a cigarette. He watched David and had seen Edie running inside. There was no need to ask what took place. It was none of his business and he knew it. The last thing he wanted to know about was personal drama. Still, he liked David and cared if he was not feeling happy. David was definitely not happy.

"You okay, bro? Maybe she just needs some time alone. Girls are funny that way."

David did not know what to say. He still had no idea what just happened. One minute they were about to kiss, and in the next minute it was not right, for some reason that was unknown to him. He rolled his eyes and realized that maybe it was too late. He was already in the friend zone with her. Kissing would only ruin their friendship. It made him so frustrated. Suddenly, he felt like smoking a cigarette, too, and he didn't even smoke!

Roberto could see his pain and frustration. He walked over and patted him on the back. He smirked, "The good news is you have the next four hours to think about it, my friend."

David looked at him and sighed.

Roberto suggested, "Maybe you should take the tower, as long as you are not feeling jumpy. Let me walk around. I'll be more alert. You can relax with your thoughts up there. Just don't relax too much. We need to keep an eye out for trouble."

"I'll be fine up there," David answered. "I could use the time alone. I'll see you later."

"You sure you're okay?"

"I'm peachy," he growled back, while walking away.

"That good, huh?" Roberto chuckled and walked over toward the fence to relieve Williams, who was coming around the bend.

David went into the tower and went up to the second level. He called up to Daniel, "I'm coming up, Dan!" He then climbed the metal ladder to the top.

Daniel was busy looking through the binoculars.

David asked, "What are you looking at?"

"Nothing. I think. I'm not really sure. I thought I saw a light in the distance. I thought maybe it was a car on that far road." He pointed in the direction of Bull Mill Road.

"Are you sure?"

"No," he shook his head. He chuckled, "For all I know, it might have been firefly. That's why I was checking with the binoculars. I don't see anything, at the moment."

David grabbed the binoculars from him and said, "Let me see."

Daniel stepped aside and tried to see with his own eyes. It all looked like darkness to him. It was already midnight, so everything looked dark beyond their fence.

David asked, "Was the light moving or standing still?"

"I think it just blinked on and off, unless it moved behind a tree. That's just it. I'm not sure. It happened so fast. I almost missed it. If I had blinked in that instant, I never would have noticed."

David sighed, "Okay. Well, I'll take over. Go get some sleep. I guess I have something to focus my attention on for the next four hours. Yay me."

Daniel chuckled, "Yeah, you definitely need something to keep you busy up here. It can be very boring. I almost fell asleep before. I was glad I thought I saw something because it gave me something to do for the past ten minutes or so. Maybe it was only in my mind."

"So, this was fairly recent?"

He responded excitedly, "Yeah, man! It just happened, before you came up! I was trying to see if I could see it, but there's nothing out there. It was probably just a firefly. There shouldn't be anyone else around. Whoever you guys thought was out there probably left days ago. Still, it can't hurt to be cautious."

"I agree. Hey, you should probably get going, so I can concentrate and see if there's anyone out there. No offense, but I can't really focus with you talking to me."

"Oh, okay. Well, don't forget. It was out in that direction," he pointed, again. "Let me know if you see anything. I'll talk to you tomorrow. I'm beat anyway. I could use some sleep. Goodnight, Dave."

"Goodnight, Dan."

Daniel almost lost his footing and griped, "Man, this ladder needs some more light. It's dark in here. Mark my words, someone is going to fall and break their ass, someday. You'll see! Watch it be me!" He laughed.

"Yep. Be careful on the way down." David said, while staring into the distance. He rolled his eyes and sighed amusingly. He liked Daniel, but the man sure loved to talk. He was always so enthusiastic about whatever he was talking about. It was kind of funny, in a way. Over the next few minutes, David stared and stared. He waited several minutes for something to happen. When he realized, nothing would, he relaxed his focus and allowed his thoughts to drift back to Edie.

What was her problem anyway? If only she had waited another second, they would have already been kissing. He thought about how good it felt to hold her in his arms. Her body felt great against his. However, then he remembered how rejected he felt when she pushed him away and it made him angry. Why did there always have to be drama when it came to relationships?

He never even found out why she was crying, which really bothered him a lot. That part could not have been because of him. Someone did something to her and upset her, but who? There was no way she would tell him, now. He'd be lucky if she didn't spend the next few days avoiding him.

"Ugh, God. Just shoot me," he mumbled to himself. "I miss when life was simpler."

Grant and Liz had gone up to the second floor together. They walked into their bedroom and closed the door. Liz locked it. They had a few hours to kill, before it was their turn for guard duty. None of them were tired enough to take a nap. However, there was one sure way to pass that time, so it would be pleasant for both of them.

They began kissing and moved onto the bed. Clothes came off, one thing led to another, and they had a fantastic time, as always. Their relationship seemed to be working out well. They got along great. Their attraction toward each other was intense. The past month had been a wonderful growing experience for them. Of course, there was still much growing to do, but it appeared they were on the right path.

After they were done, they began talking, while lying in bed. They enjoyed doing that. It felt normal.

Liz began, "So, why don't you want Bobby to go with you on that supply run? Were you hoping to take me, instead? I can't go with you every time."

"Yeah, I know," he said with disappointment. "That's one reason, but there's more to it than that. I don't really like the guy. He gives me bad vibes. The things he says when we're working in the tunnel are disturbing. The guy's demented and annoying."

"I'm sure he's not that bad. Don't be such a meanie. Give him a chance to feel useful. We can go on the next supply run together."

"I suppose. I still think I should take two guys with me, instead of one. I wouldn't feel safe, if he were the only one watching my back. I need someone who is reliable in the field." At that moment, he thought about Williams, the only special ops soldier in the group. Surely, he was reliable in the field. "I'll see if Williams wants to come."

"Oh, that's a good idea. He hasn't been out in a while. He's probably tired of playing security guard. That's all he does these days."

"Yeah. He definitely has better uses. His talents are wasted on guard duty."

"Absolutely," she agreed.

He looked at her and caressed her face. She closed her eyes and smiled warmly. He kissed her on the lips and asked, "Are you sure you don't want to come?"

Her eyes shot open. "Grant! You spend most of your day with me. Don't you think you should get to know the other people around here?"

"Hey! I spend plenty of time with Charles, Daniel, Roberto, and Julia."

"Charles is your best friend. Daniel and Julia practically live in the basement, which is the only place you go when you're not with me. You and Roberto are likeminded. You're both crazy as shit. Those people hardly count. What about Aramis? Do you sit and talk with him? He's really nice. You both have some common interests."

"I already know Aramis, Liz. We've known each other for about two years. We talk every once in a while. You just don't see it."

"Oh. Okay. I didn't realize that. Good."

"Yeah. We worked together on numerous occasions, before 'Day One of the Apocalypse' changed everything. I also know Dave pretty well. I talk with Kirk sometimes when he's in the gym. We get along great." He thought about it and said, "Okay, I can't really say I've had many conversations with Edie or Millie. Those two keep to themselves a lot. Bobby is the only other person I don't usually talk to. We have absolutely nothing in common. I find him to be... how can I say this nicely? Full of shit!"

Liz laughed and replied, "Yeah, I know what you mean. Still, he needs this, babe. Let him have it. You never know. He might do some good out there. He might even save your life."

He scoffed, "I won't hold my breath."

"But then you might drown," she pouted.

"As long as he doesn't give me mouth to mouth!"

They both laughed.

MAN'S END

Chapter Five

THE NIGHT DRAGGED on. Roberto and Williams patrolled the perimeter below, while David sat in the tower staring into the distance. He kept looking around, but found himself returning to the area, where Daniel thought he saw the light. He picked up his sniper rifle and looked through the infrared scope.

Something fast moved past his scope and startled him. He lowered the rifle and looked around, but he did not see anything out of the ordinary. He thought maybe it was a bird or a bat that flew past. His eyes glanced back toward the distance and he saw a light. He immediately looked through the scope, again. There was definitely movement. It looked like a car was driving east on the road, although it was moving slowly.

"Hmm. I wonder what's going on out there," he said to himself.

The light continued along Bull Mill Road, but then made a turn toward their compound. Whoever was in the mysterious vehicle, they were coming their way.

David called down to Roberto and Williams, "Heads up, guys! We might be having company!"

Roberto clasped his hands together and said, "At last! Some action! Let's get into place, bro!"

Williams nodded, and they both positioned themselves behind piles of sandbags that had been set up like a machinegun nest. Charles, Grant, Liz, and Aramis came out of the house and took up defensive positions on the porch.

David could hear the vehicle's engine coming closer. He aimed the sniper rifle at it and followed it. There were too many trees to get a clear shot. Plus, he was unsure if shooting would be necessary, yet. They might have nothing to worry about. Perhaps, it was just a couple of town residents passing through.

Just then, David heard the all too familiar primal screams in the distance. His finger tightened on the trigger and his heart began pounding in his chest. Not, again, he thought. He tried to maintain his breathing and focused on trigger control.

One thought kept coming to mind. The infected were coming!

The vehicle slowed down and made the turn onto their entrance road. It came to a stop and began honking the horn loudly. The screams grew louder, as the infected came near. They followed the sound of the honking horn. The vehicle revved up its engines and smashed through their front gate, knocking down a large portion of the fence along Cromwell Road.

"Holy shit!" Roberto shouted.

Williams began firing his weapon at the vehicle and shot out both headlights and the windshield. The horn stopped and the vehicle slowed to a crawl. As it turned out, Williams' gunshots took over, where the horn began. It drew the infected closer to their property.

David could already see them. There had to be hundreds of them! His heart leapt in his chest. He began firing down with the sniper rifle, but he wasn't nearly as good a shot as Liz or Williams, so his shots were not accurate and he only had a limited number of rounds with him in the tower.

Down below, Charles, Grant, Liz, and Aramis were shooting at the infected, which charged onto the property. They hit a lot of them, but there were too many. Williams was overrun and eaten alive. His screams of torment echoed across the darkened valley.

Roberto swung his wrecking bar and fought his way through the field of infected. He bashed heads left and right, while making his way toward the house to make his stand with the others. He then pulled out a gun and started shooting. Soon, Bobby and Daniel joined them and also started shooting infected. The infected were attacking the house on three sides. Those that could not shoot properly, shot wild shots that were ricocheting off of things in the background. One shot hit a propane tank in front of the garage, which caused an explosion that set off a chain reaction with the other tanks. There was a huge explosion.

Bright orange and yellow flames shot up into the nighttime sky shining like a beacon for other infected in the area. The garage was burning brightly, as the fire spread quickly to the house. The porch on the south side was already engulfed in flames. The second floor was starting to spark up.

Millie and Edie ran out into the backyard screaming, but there were zombies out there waiting for them. David could see them from the tower. He took aim with the sniper rifle and shot each zombie. He was able to kill all four of them. The girls looked up at the tower and saw him. They knew he had saved them, again.

He still felt helpless. His other friends were rapidly losing ground. They retreated into the house, despite the fire. It was their only option. He aimed down at the infected and shot as many as he could to cover their escape. He was running low in ammunition and would soon have to resort to his handgun.

The infected rammed into the door leading up to the tower. They easily broke it down and rushed inside. David had to be ready. He pulled out a grenade and waited. They charged up the stairs, but stopped short at the bottom of the ladder. They glowered at him and reached up pointlessly, while screaming like savages. David dropped his grenade down on them and moved back. It exploded and blew them to pieces, destroying the ladder and trapping him on the top level.

He focused back on the house. He shot off his last rounds with the sniper rifle at those infected that tried to force their way into the front door and windows. He pulled out his Smith and Wesson and decided to save those shots for the ones that would make a difference.

The girls had run out toward the wooded area. David remembered the underground tunnel. The others would be able to get down to the basement and use the tunnel to get to where the girls were. They might be able to escape this mess.

However, he was trapped. There would be no escape for him. He was too high up to jump down four stories. He'd only kill himself, if he tried.

He watched powerlessly as the house burned to the ground. The roof began to collapse. If anyone were still inside, they would not last long. He hoped they made it down to the tunnel. He used the scope on the sniper rifle to check the area, where the escape hatch was located. He saw Millie and Edie standing there, but they were kissing!

"What the hell?"

Infected swarmed around them and began eating them, but they held each other tight and died in each other's arms.

Right at that moment, the hatch popped open and Charles climbed out, followed by Grant, Liz, and Roberto. They did not even notice the infected standing around them in the dark. It was doubtful they even saw them coming when they attacked. More infected jumped down into the escape tunnel, but there was no escape. Everyone was dead.

Wait! He wondered, what happened to Kirk? Did he die in the fire?

David sat alone high in his tower, while the compound was overrun with infected. The house and garage were a burning pile of rubble. The fire had begun to spread to the tower. The flames rose higher from the lower level. Black smoke filled the upper section, where he sat. Soon, he'd burn with it.

He would not die that way. He pointed his gun under his chin aimed upward and closed his eyes. His finger slowly squeezed tightly on the trigger and the gun went off.

BANG!

In that last moment, he thought he heard Robert Jenkins saying, "No, Dave!"

It was too late to stop. And just like that, it was over.

David awoke from his nightmare in a cold sweat.

"Jesus Christ! Damn, Daniel. You and your stupid light." David breathed heavily. He was extremely relieved that it had only been a nightmare. It was already daylight.

He looked around the male dorm and realized he and Roberto were the only ones still there. It had been a long night for them. Roberto was still asleep. He normally slept later than the others, despite the daily crow of the rooster. Everyone else had already woken up long ago. David got out of bed and yawned.

He went out to the bathroom to wash up. Afterwards, he went into the kitchen to grab a bite to eat. He served himself a bowl of cereal, minus the milk, since there was none. He sat down in his seat at the dining room table and ate. He did not bother using a spoon. He picked with his fingers, eating one at a time.

Aramis was sitting at the next table reading one of those tabloid rags that Kirk brought back from the supermarket. He looked up with a smile and said, "There he is! Good morning, David! Did you sleep well?"

"Nope," he replied, before shoving a handful of cereal into his mouth.

"That's a shame. I slept great. I have a lot of energy today. I think I'm going to head down into the basement and help the guys with that tunnel. Dan is down there with Bobby, and your boy, Kirk."

"Good idea. Who's on guard duty?"

"Charles and Williams are out there," he replied, as he stood up. "I'll catch you later, homey." He patted David on the back and went down to the basement.

After David finished his breakfast, he washed his bowl and turned to go outside. He ran into Edie, who had been using the bathroom. For a brief moment, they stared at each other, but then she turned away. Before she could leave, he grabbed her by the arm. She faced him and looked uncomfortable.

He asked, "Can we please talk about last night?"

"No," she replied. "I'm sorry, David. It was a mistake. It never should have happened."

"Why not? I like you, Edie. I thought you liked me."

She sighed, "Please, don't. Trust me. It will never work out. You're really a nice guy. You're very sweet and so handsome, but we're wrong for each other." Her eyes became watery, but she did not change her mind. She said, "Please, just leave it at that. Don't make this any harder than it has to be."

A tear slid down her cheek. He wanted so badly to wipe it away and tell her she was wrong. He moved closer and she immediately backed away. He stopped and let go of her arm. She began to walk away, but kept looking back at him.

He kept staring at her. The pain in his eyes was evident. Her words hurt him, although he tried unsuccessfully not to show it. As she walked away, he asked, "Why were you crying last night? Can you, at least, tell me that?"

She stopped, but did not turn around. She answered coldly, "That's personal. I'd rather not talk about it. Please, don't ask me, again."

"Fine," he said.

Now, he was angry. She was making him crazy. He no longer wanted to deal with it, so he gave up and she walked outside.

After she left, he felt torn. He was hurt and angry. He wanted to stop her and find out what was bothering her. At the same time, he never wanted to see her face, again. That's when he realized he was falling in love with her. Only love could make someone feel so conflicted and confused.

He felt depressed and sat down at the dining room table. He grabbed the tabloid and skimmed through the pages. He hated tabloid magazines and celebrity gossip, but it was better than dealing with Edie's sudden crazy mood swings. He wondered if there were any celebrities, who had been affected by the viral outbreak, not that he really gave a damn.

He sighed and leaned back against the chair. He really was not in the mood to look at a silly magazine. He wanted to fix things with Edie. How did they go from being good friends to being whatever they were at the moment overnight? It boggled his mind and made him so angry.

"Women," he mumbled, as he put his head down on the table and rested his eyes.

Grant went outside to talk to Williams, who was standing near the fence at the northern end of the property. He was looking out through the fence and wondering whatever happened to the people that used to live on the other side. They were one of the last families to leave Cromwell Road. Where did they go?

"Hey, Williams!"

He turned to face Grant and said, "Good afternoon. What's up?"

"Good afternoon to you, too. I wanted to ask you something."

"Shoot."

"I'm going on a supply run in about a day or two. Bobby decided to volunteer himself to come with me. I wanted to know if maybe you'd like to join us. I could really use someone reliable out there to watch my back. What do you say? I know you haven't been out there in over two weeks. I was hoping you might want to come along."

Williams thought about it and answered, "Sure. Why not? I could use a change of scenery. Thanks for the invite."

"No problem. Thanks for saying yes. I appreciate it. We'll be using the new van, since it has a lot of room for storage. I want to collect as many propane tanks and water as we can carry. If we see anything else that's useful, along the way, so be it."

"Well, count me in. I'll be happy to help anyway I can."

Grant smiled, "That's great. Hey, can I ask you something a little more personal?"

"What?"

"What's your first name? We've been calling you Williams, since the day we met. It seems a little formal. I think we are past that nonsense, but if you prefer to be called Williams that's your call."

"My name is Angelo," he smirked. "No one ever asked me, so I didn't think anyone cared enough to know."

"Well, I do." Grant reached out his hand in the form of a handshake and said, "I'm proud to know you, Angelo."

He shook his hand and smiled, "Thanks, man. The feeling is mutual."

Grant asked, "So, *Angelo*. What are you looking at out here?"

He turned back to face the fence and answered, "I was wondering about the family that lived there on the other side. I was curious where they went. They could have joined with us, but they chose to leave their home."

"I don't know, but it's a good thing they left, considering we scavenged their house and took their furniture."

Angelo chuckled, "Well, yeah! That goes without saying!"

Grant asked, "Do you have any family out there that you would want to reach?"

He shook his head and said, "If they were still alive, by some small chance, they probably thought I died on my last mission, since I never returned. It's for the best either way."

"I'm sorry to hear that."

"Yeah. Thanks. Shit happens," Angelo responded, as he stared out into the distance.

"I'll leave you to your thoughts." Grant turned to leave. "Thanks, again. See you later." He walked back toward the house.

A day later, things were no different between David and Edie. They did not speak anymore and hardly looked at each other. David was so angry with her that he did not care. Edie also stayed away from Julia. She was angry with her. The only person she spoke to was Millie.

Grant began to notice how certain people were avoiding each other. He was uncertain why, but he decided to see what was going on with those particular people. He approached Edie and Millie, first, while they were standing in the kitchen talking.

"We need to talk," he began.

They both turned to face him. All of a sudden, he felt awkward. Whatever was going on was none of his business. Yet, he had to say something.

He asked, "When do you girls plan on learning how to shoot? You spend a lot of time busy doing nothing. You need to learn how to survive. I can teach you how to shoot, if you want, but not if I have to chase you around to find you."

Edie scoffed, "Doing nothing? We cook most of the meals here and we tend to the garden!"

Millie responded defensively, "Heck yeah! Cooking for thirteen people isn't easy!"

"Neither is surviving the Zombie Apocalypse with no survival training. I understand you cook, but that does *not* take all day and all night. Our garden hardly has anything growing, yet, so unless you are standing out there using the Force to convince the vegetables to grow faster, tending to it should not take too much of your time. A couple of shooting lessons in the week won't hurt you."

"I think we're pretty safe here," Millie replied. "You guys all know how to shoot well enough. Why should I learn?"

"Millie, you might be safe today, but there may come a time when many of us are gone. You will have to go out and gather supplies on your own. Do you think you can do that?"

She stood there quietly, staring at the floor.

Edie shot back, "I have a gun. David gave it to me."

"Do you know how to use it?"

"Yeah, I've seen plenty of movies," she answered confidently. "You point and shoot. There's no safety, so it should be fairly simple. I bet even a monkey can do it."

Grant shook his head and explained, "It's a lot more complicated than that, Edie. You need to know how to control your breathing and trigger control, in case you have to actually aim and hit something. How you hold the gun makes a huge difference. Plus, if you don't clean and maintain your gun, it might not even fire when you need to use it. What happens when your gun jams? What will you do then? Die?"

She did not have an answer.

He continued, "You should also know how to load it properly. It's not easy when you have delicate little fingers with long fingernails. However, you did make a valid point. I'm sure a monkey could do a better job than either of you."

Millie gasped, "That's just mean!"

Edie added, "Yeah, why are you being such a jerk to us? What's wrong with everyone around here? You're all such haters!"

At last, he was getting to the real problem, he thought. Someone was giving them a hard time, but who?

He explained more kindly, "Hey, I am only trying to emphasize the importance of your survival training. I'm sorry, if I'm being mean to you or if other people around here are giving you a hard time. All the more reason for you to understand how important it is for you to listen to what I have to say. You both spend too much time hiding upstairs in the dorm. I want you to be able to take care of yourselves without having to count on the rest of us.

What's happening out there is all too real. You both lost people that were important to you, so you must understand the seriousness of the situation we are in. Let me teach you how to shoot. One lesson will change your life. I promise. If you don't like how I teach, then I won't bother you about it, ever again."

Edie gave in and replied, "Fine. When?"

"What about right now? I have some free time."

Millie looked at Edie and shrugged.

Edie said, "Okay. We'll give you an hour."

Grant sneered at her and replied, "No. That's not how this works. I'll start teaching and when I feel you've actually learned something, we are done for the day. The teacher always makes the rules, not the students. Didn't you ever go to school? Come on. Let's go down to the basement, so Millie can choose a weapon. I have the perfect gun for you, Millie. It's small and lightweight." He turned to Edie and said, "You said you already have a gun, right?"

Edie nodded, "Yeah. It's up in the dorm. Should I get it?"

"Yes, meet us down in the armory."

"Okay," she said. She then went upstairs to the female dorm to fetch her Glock.

Grant and Millie went to the basement. He opened the door to the armory and turned on the light. Julia sat in the next room at her computer. She did not come out to say hello, although she was listening to the sound of Grant's voice, as if it were the most wonderful song she'd ever heard. Nearby, Daniel, Bobby, and Kirk were deep in the tunnel working.

Grant placed his old Karr K9 on the top of the cabinet, so Millie could see it. He said, "This is a Karr K9. It's a 9mm. It was from my collection. You can use it, while I teach you. If you continue with the lessons and take them seriously, you can keep it."

Her eyes lit up. "Really?"

"Yes. It's unloaded," he told her. He pulled the slide open, locked it in place, and showed her the inside of the gun, so she could see that it was empty. He then released the slide and placed the weapon in her hand.

She held the gun and instantly liked the feel of it. He was right. It was fairly light. She pointed it at the floor and pulled the trigger back. It clicked and she was startled. She almost expected it to go off."

"I told you it's empty."

"I know. It just scared me. Guns scare me."

"What about zombies?"

Her green eyes narrowed and she replied, "I hate them."

"Good. Don't they scare you?"

"They used to, but now I hate them so much."

"Why?"

She looked at him and answered, "Because! They took everything from me! This whole thing is their fault! They ate my sister!"

"I know. I'm sorry about that. It's not really their fault, though. Someone created them. He was deranged. *He* did this to us. He started it all and caused the pain that we've gone through. They were just test subjects to him. He didn't give a shit about them. He lured them in with false promises and started the whole ball rolling."

She looked at him curiously and asked. "How do you know that?"

"Charles has a journal that belonged to a scientist, who worked with the man that created the virus. It explains how it began in detail. Again, I'm really sorry about your sister."

"Thank you," she frowned.

"We all lost people that meant something to us. That's why it's very important that you learn how to protect yourself and others. Do you understand?"

"Yes," she nodded.

"Good."

"Thank you for taking the time to teach me," she said humbly.

"You're very welcome. Who knows? Maybe someday you might save my life."

She chuckled, "I doubt it. I'm no hero. You guys are the heroes."

He smiled at her and she turned away timidly.

Edie came down and walked past the security hub, where Julia sat with her back to the door. Edie felt her anger build up. She had a feeling shooting would be a nice way to release that negative energy. It might be just the thing for her.

"I'm ready," she said to Grant. She noticed Millie was admiring the Karr K9 and chuckled. She had never seen Millie hold a gun or show any interest in them before today. She thought it was kind of cute, a small gun for a small woman.

Grant was glad she wanted to learn. He took the girls out to the makeshift firing range that he and Charles set up at the far end of the property.

Millie immediately noticed the abandoned concrete structure beyond the fence and asked, "What's that place over there?" She pointed at it curiously.

"It was a house that burned down in the 1970s, according to Charles. That's what's left of it. We'll be shooting in that direction. I'll set up targets in a bit. First, you both need to learn a few things."

Over the next hour, he taught them how to take apart their weapons and how to load them. Next, he had them each take turns shooting at paper targets that he pinned to a wooden stanchion in front of the fence. They enjoyed that part. They also shot at a few empty bottles that Charles had stored away in a bag for recycling purposes, until the zombies changed his plans.

By the time their first firearms lesson was over, three hours had gone by. There was no doubt there would be a second lesson in the near future. They both had a lot of fun and actually learned something useful. Grant was proud of them.

MAN'S END

Chapter Six

T HE DAY HAD finally come for Grant and his team to go out on a supply run. It was a warm and sunny morning. Angelo and Bobby were both eager to head out, so they were ready early. They would be taking the van, as planned. Grant would drive, since that was one of his specialties. They were set to leave right after breakfast. This time, they would only have one list, which was prepared by Julia.

After finishing his breakfast, Grant went to the basement armory and grabbed extra boxes of ammunition. He did not wish to risk running out of ammunition, if they ran into trouble.

When Julia saw him go there she rushed over from the security hub and handed him the list she printed. She also took advantage of the opportunity to speak with him alone.

"Here you go, Grant. I prepared this list just for you. It has everything that we need. Please, be careful out there. I'm worried the infected are getting closer." She kept looking at him, as if she had more to say, but didn't know how to get the words out.

"Thanks, Julia. I will," he said.

She then hugged him, catching him by surprise. "Good luck!" She held him a bit too long, which made it awkward. She finally let go and hurried back to her computer, feeling embarrassed.

He watched her, as she walked away, and began to wonder if maybe she had feelings for him. He had his doubts. He figured he was probably reading too much into her actions. It was just a friendly hug. Nothing more.

He went upstairs and stepped out onto the front porch. Charles and Liz were waiting for him. Angelo and Bobby were already standing near the van, looking rather impatient.

Charles observed them briefly, before turning to Grant. He asked, "Are you set to go?"

"Yep. Julia just gave me the list of supplies and I have extra ammo, just in case," which he showed him. "Hopefully, this goes nice and smooth, even with Bobby."

Liz assured him, "You'll be fine, babe." She hugged him tightly and gave him a kiss on the lips. She whispered into his ear. "You better come back to me. Okay?"

He looked into her eyes and smirked confidently, "Of course, I will."

Charles patted him on the back and said, "I'm glad you're taking Williams. He needs a change of pace. You guys be careful out there and check out the Dollar General. The other guys never got to it the last time. I want to know if it's still a viable option for supplies."

"Sure. No problem." Grant gave him a hug, too, and said, "Don't worry, Chuck. I got this. By the way, Williams' name is Angelo."

"Oh? He never told me." He then rolled his eyes and added, "Why must you call me that?"

"You never asked him," Grant replied with a wink of his eye. He grinned teasingly, ignoring the other question and walked toward the van. He unlocked the doors, so the guys could get in.

Liz watched him and began to wish she were going with him. Next time, she told herself.

Like a child, Bobby immediately yelled out, "I got shotgun!" He then got into the front passenger seat and strapped on his seatbelt.

Angelo did not really care. He opened the side door and got into the back. He realized it was not a normal passenger van. The rear did not have any seats, since it was intended for cargo. He sat on the floor and hoped for the best. At least, there was a rug.

Grant walked to the gate and unlocked it. He opened it wide and returned to the van. Once he was in the driver's seat, he turned on the van, looked back, and asked, "Are you okay back there, Angelo?"

Bobby eyed him curiously and asked, "Who the hell is Angelo?"

Angelo responded, "I'm good."

Bobby looked back at Angelo and asked, "Williams? You actually got a first name? Ain't that some shit? I'm impressed!" He chuckled.

Angelo smirked. He was starting to realize why Grant wanted someone else to come along on the supply run. He had a feeling it was going to be a long day.

Bobby shouted, "Woo hoo! Let's do this!"

Grant turned to him and reprimanded him, "Do *not* do that, again. This isn't a road trip. We need to be cautious whenever we go into town. Believe me, we do not want to be noticed. Save that immature shit for when we get back. If you insist on coming, then you need to take this seriously. We stay close together. Do not fire your weapon, unless you have no choice. No unnecessary talking and absolutely no yelling, unless you are dying. Are we clear?"

Bobby glared at him annoyed and replied, "Yeah. Crystal."

Grant rolled his eyes and pulled on his leather gloves, which were in his back pocket. He shifted the van into gear and began driving forward. As he drove through the open gate, he was already having regrets. He really did not want Bobby to come with him. He was getting a bad feeling in his gut.

Angelo was already looking forward to returning. He hoped they did not run into any danger. He was unsure if Bobby would be able to deal with it.

They took the same route as the other guys when they went into town. After reaching Route 17M, they made a right and followed it south. They drove uphill into the parking lot, where the Shop Rite was located and came to a stop across from the entrance.

Grant noticed the upside down shopping cart was no longer blocking the entrance. He was absolutely certain David specifically said he left it in the same position. If that was the case, it had been moved in the last week, which meant someone was definitely around.

Bobby stared at him and asked, "What are we waiting for?"

"I'm watching."

"Watching what?"

"Everything. David and I agreed to leave an upside down shopping cart at the entrance, blocking the doorway, so that we'd know if someone else had been here."

Angelo leaned forward and looked through the window to see what Grant was talking about.

So did Bobby. He commented, "I don't see no friggin' shopping cart."

"Exactly," Grant replied.

Bobby asked, "So, why the hell did David move it, if you agreed to leave it there? That was a dumb move on his part."

Grant rolled his eyes and sighed in frustration.

Angelo explained for him, "You're missing the point, Bobby. David said he left the cart blocking the entrance, as per their agreement."

"Yeah? So, where is it?"

Grant leered at Bobby and responded, "That's what I'd like to know!" He calmed himself down and said, "Look, just keep an eye out to see if you see anybody around. Whoever moved the cart might still be inside."

They watched the area and turned their eyes on every shop in the shopping center. There were a few next to the Shop Rite and some behind them on the opposite side of the parking lot.

Bobby noticed a Rite Aid and asked, "Why don't we loot the Rite Aid, while we're here? There's gotta be some good stuff in there."

"We already took everything we could out of that place two weeks ago," Grant answered.

"Oh, okay. Hey! What about that liquor store? There's gotta be a few bottles we can grab!"

Grant shook his head. "Definitely not. We're not here for booze. We're here for necessities. It's best if we all remain sober, considering things are not how they used to be. It's not safe or smart."

"I can handle myself just fine," Bobby replied.

"Goody for you. We're still not going in there."

Bobby crossed his arms in frustration and exhaled exaggeratingly.

Angelo suggested, "I could go check the supermarket, if you want."

"No," Grant replied. "Let's do it together. You and I will go in and spread out. Bobby, stand outside the door. If anyone else comes out, grab them and don't let them escape. Beat their ass, if you have to. I'm sure you can handle that, right?"

"Oh, yeah. Not a problem," he nodded.

"Good. Let's move out," Grant ordered.

The three of them stepped out of the van and approached the exit door with caution. The glass sliding door was still locked in the open position. Grant and Williams both had their weapons drawn. When Bobby noticed, he pulled out his gun, too. Holding the gun in his hand helped him to realize the seriousness of their situation. Grant was right. This was not a game. He began to feel nervous.

Grant gave him a hand signal telling him to wait at the entrance. He then pointed to Angelo and signaled for them to go inside, which they did. Angelo moved out wide to the right, while Grant went straight down the first aisle on the left to the far end of the market. Together they swept the entire supermarket, only to learn that it was empty. Whoever had been there was gone.

Grant returned to the exit door, where Bobby waited. Bobby wanted to shoot him and pretend he thought it was someone else, except he hesitated too long, and then Angelo showed up. Instead, he put away his gun to remove the temptation he was feeling to shoot them both. He had a feeling that would not go so well for him, if he tried. They were obviously more experienced using weapons than him. It was best to wait for another opportunity.

"What now?" He asked.

Grant answered, "We each grab a cart and shop. We need lots of water. Everything you can find. Other drinks that don't expire can't hurt. The more we can get, the better off we'll be later on."

Bobby asked, "What about food? Isn't that a necessity?"

"David already gathered plenty of food for us. This portion of the supply run is about liquids. The more water we can collect, the longer we'll survive."

"Well, if I see a snack I like, I'm taking it. You guys don't have to eat it."

"Bobby, get with the program. We're not here for your personal gain. We have a job to do. Either do it or go wait in the van. Stop acting like a damn kid. This is serious."

Bobby clicked his tongue with an attitude and pushed a shopping cart, moving away from them.

Grant wanted to shoot him so badly, but, of course, that would be wrong.

Angelo put his hand on his shoulder and said, "Don't mind him. It's like you said, he's a big child. Forget about him. Let's get what we came for. Let him grab whatever he wants. But the next time he wants to go on a supply run, he's banned."

Grant looked at him and, sort of, agreed, "Yeah, if he survives this one."

Angelo shrugged sympathetically and walked away, while pushing a shopping cart of his own.

Grant pushed his cart straight to the aisle, where drinks were located. Angelo was already loading his cart with several gallons of water. He filled in the spaces between with other drinks, such as flavored sparkling water, iced tea, and wine coolers. Grant grabbed packs of bottled water and filled his cart with those. He also took plenty of coffee and various packs of tea. He wondered where Bobby had gone.

Bobby was walking through the other aisles, loading his cart with food. He grabbed a bunch of canned soup, tuna fish, multiple packs of cookies, bags of potato chips, cheese doodles, Doritos, and lots of gum. He searched for batteries, but could not find any. Instead, he grabbed multiple packs of bar soap, toothpaste, toilet paper, tissue, and hair products. He found a few packs of paper plates and plastic cups. He took as many as he could fit into the cart. He also grabbed a large box of plastic utensils. Basically, he filled his cart with things that were useful, while deliberately not taking any drinks, aside from beer.. He found what he was doing to be quite humorous, so he grinned the whole time.

When he found a set of steak knives on a shelf, he considered the possibility of sneaking up behind Grant and slicing his throat open. He could probably do the same to Angelo, if he had to. He was strong enough to do it. He held the pack of knives in his hand, but then tossed it in the cart.

He remembered how he inadvertently caused the death of Wally, after they escaped Manhattan and ran from infected through the Housing Projects. What he did that day was in order to survive, he told himself. It was unintentional. He still had a hard time dealing with the guilt. Soon afterwards, he pushed himself to work hard on the tunnel to keep his mind occupied, so he wouldn't dwell on it.

The idea of murdering someone in cold blood was a very different prospect. How would he live with that kind of guilt? Just to get a girl? Was she really worth it? Every time he'd kiss her, the guilt would eat away at him, or would it?

This was going to take some serious contemplating. He needed to make sure he could live with it, before making that kind of decision. If it were only Grant, it would be much easier to decide, but Angelo, too? He was a nice guy. No, not yet, he thought. There had to be a better way. He shook off the idea and kept pushing the shopping cart through the aisles.

Meanwhile, at the front of the market, Grant grabbed a few bags from the cashier counters and threw them into his cart. Angelo was already waiting near the exit. A moment later, Bobby showed up with his fully loaded cart. When Grant saw the things in his cart, he was furious. He glared at Bobby, who tried to look innocent, as if he did nothing wrong.

Bobby asked, "Are we ready to go, guys?"

Grant came very close to drawing his weapon and shooting him. He was just about fed up with his nonsense. He fought the urge and took a deep breath. It's not right, he told himself.

Bobby shrugged and asked, "What's the problem? You said we were going shopping for necessities. Come on! Are you gonna tell me we don't need soap or toothpaste? Hair gel? Shaving cream?"

Angelo shook his head disapprovingly and said, "You're a damn fool, Bobby."

Grant ignored Bobby and pushed his cart outside. He walked fast toward the van and was so distracted he forgot to look around and make sure they were alone. The other two followed closely without saying a word. None of them noticed the lurking zombie that appeared at the far west side of the parking lot.

They unloaded the carts, one at a time, and put everything into the back of the van, including the items Bobby collected. They threw most of that stuff into the empty bags from Grant's cart. Each of them kept their backs turned to the supermarket and the desperately hungry reanimated corpse that gradually approached from behind.

He was a rotten one that looked to be about four weeks into his infection stage. His clothing was ragged and covered in blood, some from his victims and some of his own. He continued onward driven by the parasites of the virus in search of fresh nutrients and another host to infect. He approached the three men without making a sound. There was no moaning or groaning and no screaming like with the newly infected who were in constant pain.

The unsuspecting men still made no notice of him, after they finished loading the groceries into the van. However, his smell was quickly becoming apparent.

Grant sniffed the air and noticed the smell of death, but it was too late. Before he could turn around, the zombie reached out silently with his rotten hand and grabbed the back of Bobby's t-shirt. It pulled him backward and opened its mouth wide.

Bobby immediately looked over his shoulder and saw Grant and Angelo standing to the other side of him. He became fearful, as he wondered who could be grabbing onto his shirt. When he turned and saw the open mouth of the zombie moving in closer to bite him, he screamed and fell backwards, pulling the zombie down on top of him.

"ARGH! GET THIS FRIGGIN' THING OFF OF ME!!!" He pushed the zombie upward, holding it away from him.

Grant reacted instantly and with brutality. He kicked the zombie in the neck with his boot and prevented it from biting down on Bobby's hand. Grant reached behind the zombie and grabbed its belt, hoping it was strapped on properly. He yanked it off of Bobby with all of his might and swung it away toward the ground. It fell hard, rolled over, and looked up at him expressionless. It reached up to grab him, but was too far out of reach. Grant pulled out his Walther PPK and shot it in the face killing it.

Angelo barely had time to retrieve his weapon from the van during the few seconds it took for Grant to pull the zombie away and kill it. He was impressed.

Bobby lay on the ground breathing fast. His heart was practically beating out of his chest. He looked up at Grant, who was glaring down at him with his eyes narrowed. He blamed Bobby for distracting him. For a split second, he wondered why he even bothered to save Bobby. The funny thing was that Bobby was wondering the same thing.

Angelo reached down and helped Bobby to his feet.

"Thanks," Bobby said with a shaken voice. "I owe you one, Grant." He was sincere about it, too. Grant saved his life, even though he did not deserve it. That had to count for something.

Grant thought about what just took place. He noticed Bobby had a significant change in attitude. Perhaps, a good scare was precisely what he needed to wake the hell up and get with the program.

"Wait here," he stated sternly. He pushed the carts into each other and pushed them back into the supermarket. He flipped one cart upside down and moved it into place at the exit door. There was still the matter of who moved the previous cart. There was no way it was the zombie or he would have been waiting for them inside. Someone was still out there, he thought.

He returned to the van and said, "Let's go. We need to get to the Dollar General. Let's hope we don't run into anymore of those walking pus bags."

The Dollar General near Route 17M in Monroe.

They drove to the Dollar General store, which was further south and west of Route 17M. They turned onto County Road 3 and pulled into the parking lot. Grant parked the van across from the entrance and waited. He looked around. This time Bobby did not ask any stupid questions because he was also looking around. Angelo had a limited view from the back of the van, so he had to trust in them.

Grant said, "It looks clear, but let's play it safe. There might be more infected in the area. We don't need another one sneaking up on us. We got lucky before. It might not happen that way, again. Keep in mind, we also might have someone else out there, who could be a threat. Let's keep it tight. Ready?"

Angelo answered, "You lead, I follow."

Grant looked at Bobby, who swallowed nervously and nodded. He turned off the van and stepped out. Bobby also stepped out on the passenger side. Angelo got out last using the side door. The three of them went toward the entrance, which was wide open. Looters had broken the doors open a few weeks earlier, so there were no doors.

David and Grant had used the same strategy here as with the Shop Rite. They left one of the yellow shopping carts turned upside down at the entrance, blocking the doorway. It was still there, but it had been moved slightly. Someone must have gone inside here, as well, but it could have been anytime in the past three weeks. David never had a chance to check during his recent supply run.

Grant made the same motions as earlier and indicated for Bobby to wait at the door, while he and Angelo looked around inside. The store was not large, so it was easy to see there was no one inside. Grant grabbed another shopping cart and pulled out the list Julia gave him. They were in need of propane tanks, batteries, candles, moist wipes, gardening tools, and other miscellaneous equipment. There was also more water, which they took. By the time they were done going through the store, two shopping carts were required to carry the items back to the van.

"One more stop," Grant said.

They got into the van and he drove them to the auto repair shop on the other side of Airplane Park, where the van was found. There were several specific large tools and equipment that Daniel requested, which would help with finishing the escape tunnel, such as a heavy-duty jack and some jack stands to support the wood that held up the dirt.

Grant parked the van in front of the garage with the rear doors facing in toward the garage entrance. He and Bobby stepped out, followed by Angelo. They walked into the garage, which was rather large. They began searching for the tools and equipment they needed.

A short time later, Bobby announced with excitement, "Here it is. This is exactly what we need to get the job done." He tapped it and grinned with satisfaction. He was glad he would be able to tell Daniel that he found it. Not Grant and not Williams, or Angelo. Whatever. He felt proud of himself.

"Good work," said Grant. "See if there is anything else we could use to help with construction or repair projects around the compound."

Bobby asked, "Shouldn't we bring this thing out to the van, first? It's what we came for. Why risk losing it?"

Angelo agreed, "He's got a point. This is not like the markets. These things will take time. We should get it done, as soon as possible, especially if we are expecting trouble."

"Yeah, you guys are right," Grant admitted, much to Bobby's surprise. "Let's bring this stuff out to the van. Wait. Better yet. Let me back the van into the garage. I'll be back." He went outside to get the van, while they waited.

Angelo walked deeper into the garage, since they had not done so, yet. He wanted to make sure they cleared the place properly, like they had done at the other two locations. Bobby waited near the jack and brought the jack stands closer together, so they would be easier to load into the van.

Grant slowly backed into the garage and stopped the van just before where Bobby stood waiting. Bobby opened the doors and realized they would have to shift things around to make space. That would take more time. He and Grant got to work, while Angelo checked the main office.

As soon as he peeked into the office, he was struck on the back of the head. He fell to the floor and was unconscious. The assailant picked up his MK 18 Mod 0 and stepped over his body. He did not have time to waste, so he began shooting at Grant and Bobby. Fortunately, he was a lousy shot.

Grant pushed Bobby into the van and used the open door as cover. He ran around to the other side and pulled out his gun. He then dropped to the floor and tried to aim for the guy's feet. Grant hoped he was not wearing thick boots.

The man kept moving back and forth, making himself a difficult target. He was shooting blindly, while shouting, "You assholes got a lot of nerve, stealing my van and taking my gas cans, and then you have the balls to come back and flaunt it in my face! I'll show you thieving bastards!"

At last, Grant had a clear shot. He fired his gun and hit the shooter in his ankle, right through his cheap boot.

"Ow! You son of a bitch! You shot my foot! That's not cool!"

Grant fired a second time and hit the man's other foot, at which point he fell. Grant shot one more time and hit him in the chest. He then stood up and walked closer.

The man was bleeding out on the floor, but he was still alive, although he barely moved. The chest wound looked serious. Grant knew he would die, soon enough.

Bobby exited the van and ran over to the man, while holding a jack stand in his hand. He was about to bash him in the head with it. Grant stopped him and said, "No! You might dent it."

Bobby scoffed and put it down. "You're right," he said. "Daniel wouldn't like that." He pulled out his gun and aimed it at the man. He wanted to shoot him for causing them to feel fear, although it still did not feel right and hesitated.

The man began to moan. He shifted slightly on the floor. Bobby's trigger finger was itching to move. The man's movement was enough for Grant. He did not hesitate. He shot the man clean in the head ending his life.

Bobby looked at Grant, who said coldly, "If you hesitate, it might get you killed. We no longer live by the same rules, as before. You do what you have to do to survive, even if it means killing someone else."

Bobby felt a realization come over him. Grant understood. He knew things were different and he was adapting to survive. It made Bobby wonder. By that rationale, would he also have pushed Wally away into a crowd of infected, so he could escape?

Grant bent down and checked the man's pockets. He pulled out his wallet, looked through it, and dropped it on top of him. Bobby wondered what he was looking for. Suddenly, Bobby was very interested in how Grant thought. Here was a former New York City police officer that was shooting people, looting stores, and checking wallets. Why??? He had to know.

"What were you looking for?" He asked, half afraid it was the wrong thing to say.

"I wanted to see if he lived around here. If he did, that might mean he's not alone. I don't want to have to worry about someone looking for revenge when they find him dead."

"Oh." Bobby asked, "Well, does he live around here?"

"No. He lived in Tuxedo Park. His name was Kocher. I'm not sure if I pronounced that right. Not that it matters." Grant walked into the back room and found Angelo on the ground. "Oh, no! Angelo!" He bent down and noticed the blood on the back of his head. "Angelo?"

Bobby blocked out Grant's cries and thought about everything he told him. If he hesitated, it might get him killed. He needs to do what he has to, in order to survive, even if it means killing someone else. The rules have changed. It's not the same as before. He aimed his gun at the back of Grant's head, but then he heard a woman scream somewhere behind him.

Damn.

MAN'S END

Chapter Seven

GRANT, BOBBY, AND Angelo had run into some trouble during their supply run. While at the auto repair shop, a man named Kocher surprised them and attacked from behind. Grant shot and killed him. While checking to see if Angelo was okay, he heard a woman screaming from somewhere outside.

He turned and saw that Bobby was already aiming his weapon in the direction of the screams. He was learning, Grant thought. He almost felt proud of him.

Angelo began to awaken. He winced from the pain and moaned, "Did anyone get the license plate of the truck that hit me?"

"Glad to see you're okay, pal. We were attacked, but I took care of him. However, it sounds like we might have another problem. Will you be okay, if I leave you here a moment?"

"I guess. What's going on?"

"A woman screamed. Be right back." Grant hurried over and stood beside Bobby. He asked, "Which way do you think it came from? Can you tell?"

"No. I don't know. It's hard to say. Maybe across the street from one of those houses out there," he suggested.

"Let's go check it out, but be careful. It could be a trap. She might be with Kocher over there," he gestured to the body lying on the floor behind them.

Bobby nodded his acknowledgment.

They walked slowly outside with their guns pointed forward. No one could be seen. They looked toward the homes across the street from the repair shop and wondered if someone could be waiting to attack them for killing Kocher.

Bobby gradually aimed his gun at Grant, but then stopped and pointed it away. He figured he might need him, if things go wrong. Instead, he asked, "Should we check the houses?"

"No. We won't hunt for her. If she's out there, then..." he stopped what he was saying and his mouth stayed open. "Ah, shit. Here we go, again." He sounded annoyed.

"What? What is it?" Bobby looked where Grant was looking and saw another zombie stumbling around. He did not see them, yet. "Oh, man. Not another one of these clowns. That's not good."

"No, it definitely isn't. We can't afford to shoot the guns, in case there are more nearby. At the same time, we can't afford to let it live. We need to kill it."

"Why? If he doesn't see us, we can wait until he leaves and head out. We got everything we came to get."

"If we let it live, it will infect and kill others. We don't need that. It's a risk to someone, regardless. This thing needs to die. They all need to die. Remember that. Wait here. I'll handle it."

Bobby watched, as Grant grabbed a crowbar from the van and walked over toward the zombie. He swung the crowbar and struck the zombie on the head. The hit did not kill it, though. It only turned it away. Grant shoved the pointed end of the crowbar straight through the zombie's ear and into the brain. When he pulled out the crowbar, it dropped to the floor and remained motionless.

He then searched the area to make sure the zombie had not already attacked a woman, since they heard a female scream. When he turned the corner, a woman came running out of one of the houses. Grant immediately drew his gun and prepared to shoot her. She realized it and froze in place.

"Please, don't shoot me!" She begged with her hands up.

He lowered his weapon only slightly and asked, "Are you okay?"

While keeping her hands up high, she replied, "Y-yes, I think so. Did you kill it? That horrid thing!"

"Yes," he said. He holstered his gun and said, "You can put your hands down."

"Oh. Thank you." She dropped her arms at her sides and said, "It almost bit me, but I managed to get away and hid in that house. I can't believe it was hunting me to finish the job!"

"So, you weren't bitten?"

"No, it only scratched me on the leg," she responded with relief, as she looked down at her leg.

She was wearing shorts, so Grant easily noticed the bloody scratch down her right leg. He figured she probably had no idea she was infected. He felt bad for her. He inquired, "Are you alone?"

She became nervous and hesitated, before answering, "Uh, y-yes. I mean, I was with the group hiding out at the Village Hall, but I couldn't stay there. Those people are crazy! They were talking about using me as a breeder to repopulate the human race! I was like, no way! I had to get away!"

Grant acted casual, as she spoke, so he would not reveal his true feelings. However, knowing that others were hiding out in town worried him, especially if they were bad enough to cause her to run away.

She stopped talking and studied him briefly. He was being too quiet and it worried her. She asked, "What about you? Are you alone?"

He shook his head, "No. I'm with two others. They're nearby."

"Oh? Were you the ones that were shooting before?"

He sighed and responded, "Yes and no. Someone was shooting at us, so I had to shoot back. He didn't leave me a choice." He wondered if it had been another person from the Village Hall.

She eyed him warily and still did not feel safe enough to approach, yet. It was obvious to him she was afraid, which was perfectly understandable. Of course, if she knew what he knew, she'd be terrified.

He lied to her and said, "You should be okay, now. There's no one else around besides us. Find yourself a car and get far away from here. We won't stop you."

"Wait. I thought... uh, can't I go with you? I won't be a bother."

Again, he shook his head, "No. Sorry. No room." Taking her with them was definitely not an option, as long as she was infected. He wanted her as far away as possible.

"I won't take up that much space! I could... uh, maybe sit on your lap?" She forced a smile. It seemed she was almost willing to do anything not to be alone anymore.

Grant did not care. He shook his head, "Nope. I'm sorry. You're better off on your own."

At this point, she became desperate and begged, "Please, don't leave me out here!"

Bobby had been trying to listen in on their conversation, but he could not hear everything that was being said. He also could not see around the house to where they stood. He decided to approach and see whom Grant was speaking to. The only thing he knew was that it was a woman, who sounded desperate and afraid. That was good enough for him. When he saw what she looked like, his eyes lit up and his mouth watered. She was absolutely gorgeous with long wavy light brown hair, alabaster skin, and legs to die for.

"Hey, there," he said, trying to sound cool. "Are you okay, Miss?"

"Oh!" Seeing another man startled her. She knew Grant mentioned he was with two others, but she hoped they were female, old, or very young. She responded hesitantly, "I'm not too bad. Thank you."

"You look hurt. Maybe you should come with us?"

She answered excitedly, "Really???"

"No, she can't," Grant insisted and she frowned.

Bobby was confused. Why wouldn't Grant want to save this hot girl, who is obviously harmless and scared to death? He demanded to know the answer. "Why can't she come?"

"She doesn't even fit in the van."

She repeated her idea, "I can sit on someone's lap! I promise I won't be a bother!"

"Oh, dude! Did you hear that? She can sit on my lap! Let her friggin' come, man!"

Grant sighed and walked over to Bobby to explain privately. When he got near, he said, "Let's talk in private. I know you're thinking with the wrong head and I honestly don't blame you. She's very pretty. However, she's also infected. The zombie scratched her on the leg. She told me so. She doesn't realize it, but she's going to turn. It probably won't happen for a few more hours, but it will happen."

Bobby looked so disappointed that he looked like he might cry. He groaned, "Are you kidding me? Look at that ripe piece of ass. She is sooo hot! What a damn waste." He sighed.

"Sorry, Bobby. She can't come. She's a danger to the group."

"Okay, fine. I have another request. Let me have her for ten minutes. That's all I need. I'll take her back into the house and do what I gotta do. When I'm finished, I'll waste her myself."

Grant looked at Bobby with disgust. Any little bit of respect he had begun to feel toward him was gone. Once more, he felt like shooting Bobby. This time, it was much harder to resist the temptation.

Bobby could feel the look he was giving him and did not like it one bit. He asked, "What? Are you going to judge me? Might I remind you that you murdered a guy back there? You ain't exactly innocent."

"That was different," Grant said through clenched teeth. "He was trying to kill us. It was self-defense. Besides, you could end up infected yourself. Have you even considered that?"

"Aw, come on, man! I'll wear a condom. Let me have this. You said it yourself. She's as good as dead. I just need to get my rocks off. Give me five minutes. I'll owe you forever."

Grant responded, as calmly and as humanly possible, "Bobby, if you ask me to let you rape her, again, I am going to shoot you in the dick and leave you here. Are we clear?"

Bobby could no longer hold in his anger. He shouted, "No! Screw that! You get to have sex with Liz all night long! Why can't you let me bang this chick? She'll probably let me do it anyway!"

The woman heard and became frightened. That certainly wasn't what she wanted. She noticed the van and ran toward it, hoping to steal it. She prayed the keys were inside, so she could get away from them. It seemed Grant and Bobby were both too distracted to notice her.

Grant replied to Bobby, "What the hell is wrong with you? You can't just have sex with a girl because you want to! She needs to make that choice, too! We're not savages!"

"No, we're just killers. Right?"

"Sometimes, we need to make hard choices to survive," Grant replied, as he narrowed his eyes and quickly pulled out his Walther PPK. He aimed it in Bobby's direction, causing him to piss his pants out of fear. All of his bravado instantly slipped away, as the gun went off. Bobby flinched and closed his eyes. In that instant, he saw his entire life flash before his eyes. It became painfully apparent to him that he deserved this fate. He was ready to die.

A few seconds later, he realized he was still standing. He opened his eyes and saw Grant standing in front of him. The man, who he began to think of as his judge, jury, and executioner, was none of those things. Still, Bobby felt fear in his heart. Whatever Grant was to him, he was no man to be trifled with or taken lightly. The new world was changing him and he was adapting quickly.

"Cut the shit and let's go, idiot. I wasn't aiming at you! I was aiming at her," Grant pointed past him.

Bobby turned around slowly like a frightened child and saw the woman lying on the ground in front of the van. She had been shot in the chest. He felt so relieved that he smiled, but then he asked, "Why?"

"I had to shoot her," Grant replied. "She was trying to steal the van. You really need to stop distracting me with your bullshit already or you're going to get us killed. She said there are other survivors hiding in the Village Hall."

"So what?"

"She said they were crazy and I'm inclined to believe her. Obviously, she preferred to take her chances out here on her own, rather than stay in there with them. We need to get back and warn the others. Help me get Angelo into the van. We don't need anyone coming around to see who did all that shooting. If I remember correctly, the Village Hall is not too far from here."

For once, Bobby did not argue. He went back into the garage with Grant and they lifted Angelo to his feet. They each grabbed one side and helped him walk back to the van.

Angelo sniffed and smelled urine. "Ugh! Damn!" He asked, "Why does it stink like piss, all of a sudden?"

Grant snickered, "Ask Bobby."

Bobby looked shamefully forward and said nothing.

Angelo wasn't sure he wanted to know anymore.

Grant instructed, "Let's put him in the front seat. I don't need you stinking up the only other seat in the van. As a matter of fact, you're not getting into the van with those pants on."

"What? Do you want me to take them off?"

"Yes, as a matter of fact, I do. No, not here, dipshit!"

Bobby had actually begun to unbuckle his belt and was unzipping his pants. They were actually the same pants that Grant had given him to wear back at his house a month earlier.

"Use your brain," Grant told him. "Go back into the garage and see if there's a mechanic's jumpsuit in the office. Either that or put on Mr. Kocher's pants."

"Dude, I ain't taking no pants from a dead guy!"

"Then you better hope you find a mechanic's jumpsuit that fits you. Otherwise, you're walking home and it's a long ass walk."

"Are you kidding me, right now?"

"Do I look like I'm kidding?" He did not wait for a response. He yelled, "Next time, don't piss your damn pants! Grow the hell up already!"

Bobby rolled his eyes and went into the garage. He was sick and tired of Grant. He wanted to hit him so badly, but he was afraid of getting killed. He started to think Grant was crazier than him! The guy had no compulsions about killing someone. It was bad enough Bobby felt resentful that Grant saved his life twice earlier. It meant he owed him his life and he hated owing someone that he despised, even if he did admire his train of thought.

It was no surprise that Grant was fed up with him, too. He wanted to shoot him and be rid of him, but then Bobby would be right. It would make him a murderer and that's not who he wanted to be. He had no problem killing someone, if that person was a threat, but he did not wish to kill anyone in cold blood. He had to maintain some type of self-control. Bobby might have been a perverted jerk, but he had his uses. He was very helpful to Daniel. They could not afford to lose a hard worker. Not yet, at least.

Considering the amount of hatred being felt between both men, it was a good thing none of them acted on their impulses.

Grant bent down and checked the girl's pockets. It surprised him to learn she was not dead, yet. She tried to swing at him, but failed to make contact. He grabbed her arm and held it down. He leaned in close and whispered, "I'm very sorry, it had to be this way. If it's any consolation, you were infected the moment that zombie scratched you. You would have been dead by tomorrow. Actually, you would have become one of *them*. Is that what you want? I did you a favor and saved you from that pain."

"Go to hell, asshole," she cried.

He replied regretfully, "I'm already there."

He knew he had to finish the job or she would still change eventually. Killing someone who seemed normal was not so easy. It felt too much like murder, but he told himself it was a necessary kill. She was infected. He held up the crowbar and she stared at him with fear and hate in her eyes. He looked away from her face and focused on the crowbar. He took a deep breath and drove it down into her skull, creating a crunching noise that made him flinch.

The deed was done. She was gone. For some reason, killing her reminded him of when he had to shove his knife into his friend, Marc Nugent's, temple at the Kingsbridge Armory, after he changed. That was something he tried to forget, but the memory was suddenly coming back to him more than a month later and it hurt just as much.

Bobby had just returned, at that moment, wearing a mechanic's jumpsuit. When he saw Grant stab the woman in the head with the crowbar, he cried out, "Jesus Christ, Grant! You can't leave well enough alone? You already shot her!"

Grant stood up and shot back angrily, "I already told you she was going to change! She'd end up crawling around waiting to bite someone! I had to finish the job!" He felt frustrated, but suddenly realized who he was speaking to and exclaimed, "Why the hell am I explaining myself to you? Get in the damn van, you creep!" He pointed the bloody crowbar at him, before wiping it clean with the woman's clothing.

Bobby was appalled. He got into the van and did not say another word. It amazed him how the man he originally set out to kill had subjugated him in a matter of hours. He thought he could handle Grant with ease, but he underestimated him. Now, he just wanted to go back home, after a humiliating day.

Liz was not worth the trouble.

Grant walked around to the driver's side and got in. He put the keys into the ignition and started the van. A moment later, he was driving toward Route 17M.

Angelo looked out of the window and down at the dead woman feeling utterly confused. He could tell he missed a lot. There was a tremendous amount of tension in the air. He glanced back at Bobby, who looked like a child who'd been punished by his wicked stepfather. Grant had a fury in his eyes that he had never seen. He wanted to ask them what happened, but he had a feeling none of them would give him a straight answer.

For now, he minded his business, kept quiet, and faced forward, just like his father would have told him to do. That man was truly wise, he mused.

The drive back home was a quiet one, but it went by fast. Nobody wanted to speak. There were a few more hours of daylight to go, by the time they returned to the compound. Grant hit the horn once to announce their presence, and then he got out to unlock the gate. He opened it, got back into the van, and drove inside. He then got back out to close the gate.

It was an annoying process, but it was the only system they had. Hopefully, Daniel could come up with something better, someday. An electronic gate would be nice, he thought.

Liz came running toward them and threw her arms around him. He held her tight. It was nice to be able to do so.

Bobby watched, as he got out of the van, and felt jealous.

She asked, "How did it go? We thought we heard a lot of gunshots earlier. It sounded more like fireworks. There were too many to be gunshots."

"I'm not going to lie. We ran into trouble," Grant confessed. "Those were gunshots."

"What?"

David approached with Kirk and Roberto at his sides. They were ready to help bring everything into the house or garage, depending on what it was that was brought back. Charles was up in the tower looking down at them. He wanted to go down, but he figured he could find out what happened later.

Grant explained, "I have bad news, more bad news, and some good news. The first bad news is the infection has finally reached Monroe. We ran into two zombies today, but we killed them both."

Bobby was surprised he did not brag about killing both on his own. He would have.

Roberto exclaimed, "Ah, shit! So much for our peace and quiet."

David immediately turned pale and swallowed nervously. He remembered the awful nightmare he had the other day and felt his skin go cold. He dreaded it coming true.

Liz felt her excitement from having Grant back home drain from her body. She was starting to like living at the compound. She did not want to leave. Where would they go?

"The other bad news is just as bad, if you ask me," Grant continued. "There is a group of survivors hiding in the Village Hall, who want to use women as breeders, so they could repopulate the human race."

Roberto commented, "Ah! Here we go! The crazies are out! That didn't take too long!"

David responded, "Great, so, now we'll have to be careful not to run into survivors or infected, from now on."

Roberto asked, "Isn't that what we've been doing anyway?"

Grant replied, "I suppose. Honestly, I'd rather deal with infected. They don't shoot back."

"And they can't open doors," added David.

Kirk stepped forward and asked, "What's the good news?"

"We ran into the person that was spying on you. According to him, you took his van and stole his gas cans. It was just as you suspected, Rob. He almost got the drop on us, too. I had to shoot him. He hit Angelo on the head and knocked him unconscious. Aramis should take a look at him, ASAP."

Roberto replied, "He's on guard duty, walking around here somewhere." He paused to think about it and asked, "So, *that's* the good news?"

"Well, he's no longer a threat. Can someone take over for Aramis, so he can help Angelo?"

Kirk said, "I'll do it," but then he asked, "Wait a minute. Who's Angelo?"

Grant explained, "That's Williams' first name." He did not realize no one else knew his first name, but him. He felt privileged.

"Oh, okay." Kirk nodded. "I had no idea."

"Me neither," Roberto commented. "I was wondering who you were talking about."

Kirk started to walk away and called back, "I'll go find Aramis."

"Thanks," Grant replied. He then looked at the others and stated, "There's more. We ran into a woman. Unfortunately, she was already infected. One of the zombies we took out scratched her leg."

David asked, "So, what happened to her? Did you...?" He hesitated.

"Yes. I had no choice. Besides, she tried to steal our van."

Liz commented, "That's a shame. It would have been nice to have another woman around here. I mean, nice for the rest of you guys."

Roberto knew what she meant and appreciated the thought, although he doubted he would ever want to fall in love with a woman in these times. He would never stop worrying about her. It would be too distracting for him. While he did envy the relationship Grant and Liz had, he was grateful he did not have to deal with those emotions. It was hard enough not thinking about the family members he lost.

Meanwhile, Bobby was listening nearby and waited for Grant to out him as a would-be rapist. He already hated him for it. He did not want to get banished from the compound, but he had a feeling that was exactly what would happen. There was no way they would want him around, after knowing that.

However, Grant did not mention it. Nor, did he mention how Bobby pissed his pants. He only told them about the potential dangers, and then about the supplies they acquired. He didn't even complain about how Bobby deliberately gathered food, instead of drinks. Grant kept it all to himself. Angelo had no idea what went down with the woman, so his secret was safe. No one would think any less of him.

He began to wonder why. It was the perfect opportunity to get rid of him. Why didn't Grant do it? Bobby started to think maybe he was not such a bad guy, after all.

Seconds later, Aramis came rushing over and checked Angelo's wound. He then helped him inside. As he did, the other guys and Liz began unloading the supplies and equipment from the van. There was a lot and much of it was heavy.

Daniel soon joined them and helped unload the van. He was extremely enthusiastic about the things they brought back for him. He could not stop talking about how happy he was and what he could accomplish with the new tools and equipment. He was very appreciative. It was therapeutic to see his reaction because everyone else began to feel optimistic.

For a brief moment, Grant and Bobby had forgotten about the trouble that went down in town. Truthfully, Bobby never wanted to think about it, again. He was too ashamed.

Not far away, Kirk had taken over patrolling the perimeter fence for Aramis. He did not mind. He was in the mood to take a walk anyway. Given the grim news that Grant told them, he had a few ideas he wanted to consider, in regards to upgrading their defenses. It was something they had to consider.

He chuckled to himself when he heard how excited Daniel became, after seeing the new tools and equipment. He liked Daniel. He seemed like a decent man.

Bobby, on the other hand, was a different kind of person than Kirk normally preferred hanging out with. Bobby rubbed him the wrong way. Kirk had a feeling there would come a time when he'd be pushed too far and might have to pummel Bobby. He hoped that day was far off.

If he knew what Grant knew, Bobby would be dead.

Kirk examined the fence at the far end of the property. It did not seem strong enough to repel an attack from zombies or other humans. The wheels in his mind began turning, while his stomach began growling. He was starving.

He wondered what they would do when food ran out. It was inevitable. He found himself thinking about cannibalism and almost gagged. No. Freaking. Way.

Soon, it would be dinnertime and with that would come the darkness. There was a certain fear and paranoia that usually came with the darkness. Those feelings would be amplified, from now on. Not only did they have infected to worry about, but also there were unstable people hiding nearby. They hoped there would be more time, before the infection reached Monroe. The infected would only make those survivors more desperate. That would make them dangerous. Time was running out.

The group would need to rethink their long-term plans for the future and it's something they would have to discuss, soon.

MAN'S END

Chapter Eight

T HE NEXT MORNING, most of the group sat around in the common room, after breakfast. Only Julia was absent. She watched over the compound using the surveillance cameras, so that most of them could be present for an emergency meeting, which had become necessary to discuss the latest revelations.

"Little sister is always watching," she said to herself.

Everyone sat around the room on sofas and sofa seats, which faced the center of the room. There were more than enough seats spread out around the room, so they did not have to crowd on top of each other. Still, some sat next to each other, such as Grant and Liz, David, Kirk, and Roberto, Daniel and Bobby, and Edie and Millie.

Charles, who sat alone on a sofa seat, began, "We have a big decision to make today. We need to decide if this place is safe enough for us to remain here. The infected have already reached this area and we all remember what it was like to hide from them in New York City. When they come, they bring death and destruction with them. There are also other people nearby, who could possibly become a danger to us. Personally, I thought this place was perfectly safe, before I became aware of these threats. I am not so sure anymore. What I want to know is what you guys think. Should we stay or should we go?"

Kirk answered, "We've already put so much hard work into this place. It would be a shame to leave."

Bobby added, "Especially when you take into account building the watchtower and digging the escape tunnel, which is almost finished!"

Daniel nodded, "Yeah, man. We are so close to finishing it. I'd hate to think all that trouble was for nothing. Isn't there something we can do to make this place safer?"

Charles asked, "So, you don't mind staying here and being surrounded by the undead, like we were at the armory in the Bronx?"

Millie cringed at the thought. She was glad she didn't have to go through that.

Daniel seemed uncertain, as he answered, "I don't know. It just seems like such a waste."

Kirk suggested, "I've been thinking about one thing we could do. Why don't we build a wall? I know it sounds crazy, but hear me out. We could start out by covering the fence with drapes, curtains, and blankets, so that no one could see inside. Little by little, we could start building a wall within the perimeter of the fence. That way, if they get past our moat, which will be frozen come wintertime, they will still have to go over the barbed wire fence, and then an even taller wall. This place will become a fortress."

"I like that idea," said Angelo with a smile.

Grant also liked the idea. He agreed, "So do I. It sounds like a lot of work, but we can do it. We can use cinderblocks and bricks and do it one side at a time."

Charles asked, "Where would we get that many cinderblocks and bricks? I doubt any of the nearby home improvement stores have enough to supply such a large project."

"We don't have to get fresh materials," Grant replied. "There are a lot of buildings in Monroe that are made with cinderblocks and bricks. We could always strip those buildings down and reuse the material for our wall. The van and pick-up can both carry a few hundred pounds."

"I don't know," Charles responded. "That sounds like twice the work."

"It's just an option," Grant stated. "The bottom line is building a wall could work. We could also improve the gate. Add armor plating like the guys did with the school bus. We need to make it so that nobody can see inside of here. We're too vulnerable."

Angelo said, "But they'd still be able to see the watchtower."

Kirk replied, "They might see our watchtower, but they don't have to necessarily see if anyone is in it. We can block up the openings with sheets of metal and leave small openings on each side to look or shoot through."

David thought about his nightmare and added, "We should also make an emergency exit for anyone in the watchtower. There should be a way out, if someone gets trapped up there, even if it's just a rope ladder. It's too high to jump down from."

Liz nodded, "I agree. Sometimes, I feel vulnerable when I'm up there. You become an easy target. I don't like it. I love the view, but I hate the paranoid feeling I get from being up there."

Kirk responded, "That should be simple enough. We have plenty of rope. I can easily thread together a rope ladder. I'm good at tying knots."

"Works for me," Liz replied.

Roberto said. "Okay, it definitely sounds like most of us want to stay here. My question is what do we do about the other people in town? Do we continue to avoid them, make friends with them, or eliminate them? Those seem to be our only three options, unless I'm forgetting one."

Millie stared at Roberto in surprise, and then looked around the room at everyone else. She could not believe eliminating a group of survivors was one of the options he suggested and no one disputed it. She wondered what they were becoming when murder was an option for their survival, although she did not say anything to make her opinion known.

Edie sensed something was wrong and whispered, "What's up, Mil?"

"Nothing," she lied. "I'm fine. I just wish things could go back to normal."

Charles heard them whispering and asked, "Is there something you ladies wish to add? Please, don't hold back. We are all in this together."

Edie looked at Millie, who stared down at the floor and shook her head. She was shy, so speaking to a large group was very intimidating for her.

David told her, "It's okay to speak your mind, Millie. We're all friends here." He glanced at Edie, after he said the words. In a way, he was talking to her, as well, and she knew it. Now, it was her who looked down with nothing to say.

Grant said, "If anyone has an opinion they'd like to share, this is the time to do it. Don't wait until it's too late and you end up feeling regret. Your opinion just might guide us in the right direction."

"Why do we have to kill anyone?" Millie asked, all of a sudden.

"Because if we don't, they probably won't hesitate to kill us," Grant answered, right away. "We are living in a different kind of society, now. The old rules no longer apply. The old laws are history. It's survival of the fittest out there. That's why I insisted on teaching you how to shoot. We will each need to know how to defend ourselves. Roberto is willing to teach everyone how to fight and block. I highly recommend you take him up on it. I've already had to kill one human, who wasn't infected."

Roberto added, "I'm sure there will be more incidents like that. I only wish there was more time in the day. I barely have time to teach anyone anything with us taking turns doing guard duty every day."

Charles had a suggestion that would help with that issue. He said. "I was thinking about that myself. If we extended the length of time for each shift, it will free the rest of us up for a longer period of time. I was thinking six-hour shifts, instead of four."

Grant said, "I don't have a problem with that."

David agreed, "Neither do I. It gives us more time to do other things in between shifts. I might actually be able to sleep better. I keep having nightmares about the infected attacking. Sometimes, I'm here. Other times, I'm back in New York City. I've been feeling drained."

Kirk said, "Longer shifts would definitely mean better sleep. I'd like to start helping out with that, too. I know my shooting sucks, but I could patrol on the ground. I already did it once."

Bobby added, feeling guilty, "Yeah, I suppose I could do the same."

Charles said, "Great! Thank you both. So, longer shifts are in? We all agree?"

Everyone that normally took part in the guard shifts agreed.

Edie finally spoke, "Uh, maybe I could help with that, too. I think with a few more lessons from Grant, I'd be ready to do some guard duty. I'd really like to do more around here, but I also think some of you guys should help with the gardening, or at least learn how to do it."

Grant nodded, "She makes a good point. I'll definitely teach anyone that wants to know how to shoot. At the same time, I will learn about gardening myself."

Liz said, "I'll learn, too. Maybe I could help with the cooking, as well."

Bobby offered, "I know how to make spaghetti and meatballs."

Aramis grinned, "Oh, man! I haven't eaten that in ages! Hey! I can make rice, beans, pork chops, steak, and beef stew. Man, I can do the works. We just need to find some real meat."

David replied, "It's getting harder and harder to find meat. The meat at the markets is gone. The rest spoiled. We had to throw some out back when the power went out in town. It was stinking up the aisles. It's a shame we only have a few chickens. If we eat them, no more eggs."

"Hey, I happen to like eggs in the morning," said Grant with a raised eyebrow.

Daniel chuckled, "Hell yeah! I'd rather have the option to eat a little bit of eggs, once a month, than to eat chicken for two days and have no more eggs or chicken, after. Screw that!"

Roberto agreed, "I'm with them, although I would love to eat some chicken, right about now."

Grant sneered, "Yeah. Let's not talk about food. It's depressing. I think everyone here should spend more time reading the survival books I brought. They can be very helpful to us."

Millie said, "I've been reading them."

"Really? That's great," Grant smiled at her.

She grinned proudly, and then went back to acting shy.

David said, "I have an idea that can help make this place a little less accessible. We can block off Cromwell Road at either end with cars. We'll just leave an opening on the sides large enough for one car to squeeze through. It might discourage any infected from walking through Cromwell and finding our place."

Charles stated, "That is an excellent idea and it's something we can get started on today."

Grant offered, "I'll definitely help out with that."

Kirk and Aramis also volunteered.

"I'll head to the watchtower, while you guys do that," Liz said.

Grant added, "It shouldn't take too long. We can use neighborhood cars and push or tow them into place using The Intrepid. There are still a few out there."

"Yeah," Kirk agreed proudly. He liked that Grant was using the name he had given to their mini-school bus.

"Good," Charles said, as he stood up from his seat. "Well, it sounds like we have a lot of work to do. Let's not waste anymore of the day sitting around talking. I think we made some progress here. We all seem to agree that staying here is in our best interests, which means we need to fortify our defenses better. Building a wall sounds like the best way to do that. Guard duty shifts will be extended to six hours. It will be very helpful that more people are willing to help guard. We are also going to start making use of the knowledge available to us, as well as the people, who are willing to teach their skills."

The others nodded in agreement.

He added, "I personally plan to start helping Julia downstairs because that girl is becoming a drone. All she does is sit in front of that computer. She even eats down there. It's unhealthy."

Aramis asked, "So, is the meeting over?"

"Yes," Charles replied. "I believe so. Thank you, everybody, for giving your input. It was appreciated."

They all stood up and dispersed to other locations. There was indeed much to be done.

Kirk started up The Intrepid. Grant, David, and Aramis were inside with him. Liz opened the gate for them. After they drove out, she locked the gate and went up to the watchtower. From her vantage point, she could see The Intrepid making the rounds in the neighborhood.

Their first stop was a house further north on Cromwell Road. There was an old car that had been left on the driveway. It was in need of repairs. They attached a chain to it, which they hooked to the rear end of The Intrepid. Kirk drove slowly and pulled the vehicle a few inches. The tires immediately began to screech, so Grant stopped him.

"Wait! We should be quiet about this. We don't need the whole town hearing what we're doing. We need to break into the car and put it into neutral. It won't matter if the windows are broken."

Aramis stood up and said, "Let me out. I got this."

Kirk opened the door and let him out. Aramis walked over to the car and looked around the ground. He picked up a rock and smashed the rear passenger side window. He reached in and opened the door, and then climbed in and unlocked the front driver's side door. He got out of the car and got back in through the driver's side door. Kirk found the whole thing amusing and chuckled.

David said, "I hope there's a method to his madness."

Grant and Kirk both laughed.

When Aramis returned, they were leering at him.

"What?"

Grant asked, "Why didn't you just break the driver's side window?"

"There's a reason for that, my friend. If I did that, there would be glass all over the driver's seat. I had a feeling I might have to sit on that seat, for a while, until I could shift it into neutral. I didn't want to sit on glass. I'd have glass in my ass!"

They laughed and seemed satisfied with his reasoning.

Kirk suggested, "Since you made sure the driver's seat was nice and clean, why don't you sit in that car and keep your foot ready to press the breaks when necessary, so the car doesn't ram into us, while we tow it?"

Aramis sighed and went back outside. He got into the car and waited.

They proceeded to pull the car from the driveway and onto Cromwell Road. They towed it to the intersection, where Cromwell Road met with Old Quaker Hill Road. The car was positioned sideways across the road. About fifteen minutes later, a second car was placed next to it. They made sure to leave an opening at the far end, so they could drive through, like David suggested.

Next, they did the same thing at the other end of Cromwell Road, where it intersected with Cromwell Hill Road. It took them about an hour to get that road blocked with about four cars, since it was a wider intersection.

When they were done, they returned to the compound.

It was time to work on the tunnel. It was close to completion, so the eagerness to get the job done was overpowering. Kirk, David, Grant, and Aramis went down to the basement and joined Daniel, Bobby, and Roberto, who were already working on the tunnel. Together, they were able to get a lot done. The new tools and equipment was a major help, as well. They were able to do twice as much as normal with less worry that it would collapse on them.

By the end of the week, the tunnel was finally complete. All that remained was to open it up at the ground level and connect it to the underground. Afterwards, would come the installation of a door. They planned to put camouflage over it to keep it hidden from plain view on the outside. They were able to find a roll of fake grass at the Dollar General that could be cut down to size.

Creating the opening for the door took another three days. Daniel took measurements and a door was built. That took another day of hard work because it had to be attached to hinges and insulated to prevent rain or melted snow from leaking into the tunnel. It would be another week before all additional work and finishing touches were completed on their new escape tunnel.

At last, it was ready. The tunnel was six feet in height, four feet wide, and four hundred feet long. The inside was finished with cement all around. A wooden ladder at the far end led up to the opening, which was ten feet up. The opening was two feet by two feet in size and covered by a thick wooden door that was three feet by three feet.

With each day that went by, the group took the time to cover the perimeter fence with blankets, rugs, curtains, and drapes. The materials were tucked under the barbed wire and draped over the fence to block the view from the outside. They found plenty of materials in the abandoned neighboring homes. The covered fence would serve well to hide their presence, until a proper wall could be erected.

From her basement hideaway, Julia moved the watchtower camera around the compound and could see most of the fence around the perimeter with only one blind spot due to the position of the camera. It did not have a view of the south side of the compound. That, to her, was their weakest point. She wanted to add more cameras to the grounds, but they did not have any spare cameras and finding more would not be easy. They also required more video cables.

She opened up the Internet browser on the computer and searched for places nearby that would have the necessary equipment in stock.

There was a Best Buy in the area of Woodbury Commons. It was not too far from their location.

She began preparing the next supply list with special instructions on where to find the items she needed. She added another computer monitor to the list, too, that way she could set up four more cameras on a split screen like the one they already had on the desk in front of her. Four cameras for each monitor would suffice. They definitely needed another camera on the other side of the watchtower. One had to be added over the escape hatch of the tunnel, as well. Adding one in the garage would also be wise, since it connected to the house.

Charles came downstairs and entered the security hub room, where she sat. He approached and stood over her, while looking at what she was doing on the computer. She paused to look up at him.

"Oh. I'm sorry. I didn't want to disturb you," he said apologetically. "I can wait, until you're done."

"It's okay. I'm just preparing the list for the next supply run," she explained casually.

"Already?" He asked warily. "The guys are a bit jumpy about going back out so soon. What do we need? Is it important?"

"Well, yes. You could say that. If the plan is to beef up our security, it is very important. We're going to need more cameras, cables, and another monitor for starters. An alarm system couldn't hurt, but that might be stretching it a bit. I suppose there's no hurry for these items, but we will need this stuff whenever reasonably possible."

"I see. I'll talk it over with the boys. Have you learned anything new on the Internet?"

She nodded, "I found a few more virus outbreak related videos. One from Ohio was pretty disturbing. It showed a family of four being pulled out of their car and eaten alive, while some sick bastard hid nearby and filmed the whole thing."

"That is sick. People are demented."

"Yeah, totally. I've seen a lot of footage like that. Some fool recording, while others are attacked. A few are pretty sad. Oh, I even found one from the first night of the outbreak. It was filmed on the 1 train on Broadway, as it left the station at West 125th Street. Wasn't that in the area you guys covered?"

"Yes, it was. Can I see it?"

"Sure, I saved it to my favorites. Hold on. Let me bring it up for you."

She opened the video and it played out. Charles could see someone recording from a cellphone, as an infected person ran onto the train from the platform at West 125th Street and attacked people at random. They screamed and ran around the car with nowhere to run. The doors had already closed and the train was moving on to the next station at West 137th Street. When it arrived at the station people fled from the train in terror, while being chased by the infected person. The video ends there.

Charles commented, "That is insane. It helps explain why the guys at the 30th Precinct were too busy to help us out with the riot on 125th Street. I will never forget that night."

"You and me both. I watched one roommate devour the other one about four feet from where I was sleeping! I was lucky to wake up! I would have been next on the menu!"

"Yes, indeed."

They remained quiet for a few seconds, while she returned to typing the supply list.

Suddenly, Charles spoke, "Hey, I just remembered. The reason I came down here is to give you a break. The others upstairs are celebrating the completion of the escape tunnel. They're sitting around in the backyard enjoying the sun. Why don't you go up and spend a little time socializing. They'd like for you to join them, for once."

"Ugh!" She flipped her hair back out of her eyes and exhaled. "Honestly, parties are not my thing. I prefer my solitude." She looked over at him and said, "I'm good. You should go back up and enjoy it yourself. You and the boys have been running around like madmen trying to make us safe and sound for weeks. You guys could use a little down time."

"True, but you've been working hard down here, too, and without a break. You should take one, even if it's a short one. Besides, I have a headache and there's actually something I would like to look up on the Internet." She looked unconvinced. He insisted, "Go on! At least, go up for thirty minutes. Quit hogging up the computer. You can grab a bite to eat, drink something, and use the bathroom, if you need to."

She sighed and gave in, "Fine. Thirty minutes and I'm back."

"Deal."

She stood up to go upstairs and he slid into her seat, so he could access the computer. It was the only computer in the house, aside from her laptop, which required Wi-Fi to access the Internet. His was connected to his cable network, which was still working, for the time being. He supposed there was no one around to shut it down.

He was not lying to her. There really was something he wanted to look up. They were going to need masonry supplies to build that wall they talked about. He wanted to check what locations in the area would have the supplies they required.

MAN'S END

Chapter Nine

WITH CROMWELL ROAD blocked off at both ends and the completion of the escape tunnel, it called for a celebration. Mostly everyone was in attendance. They hung out in the backyard of the house. There was no music, as to not attract attention from afar, much to the disappointment of many. In the end, they agreed it would be too risky to listen to music, especially while outdoors. After all, these were different times they lived in.

Julia stepped out to the yard and saw everyone sitting or standing around talking. There were a few sitting on outdoor seats around a cooler near a table with an umbrella over it. Edie and Millie were sitting together on an old sofa-sized swing chair. A few of the guys sat on lounge chairs or folding seats. Aramis stood up from his seat and applauded when he noticed Julia because she actually took the time to step away from the computer. He also admired how lovely she looked.

"All right! Look who decided to join us," he declared cheerfully.

Grant was standing near the doorway with Liz and David. He walked over and put his arm around her in a friendly way. "Welcome to the party, Miss Duncan. It's good of you to take the time away from your busy schedule to spend time with us peasants."

She snickered, "Ha, ha, very funny. Charles made me come up."

"Well, that makes more sense," he chuckled.

David commented, "Yep. That's Charles for you."

Julia really enjoyed having Grant's arm around her. She hoped the moment would last long and was already glad she decided to come up.

Much to her disappointment, he took his arm off of her and asked, more seriously, "Now that you're here, have you learned anything new about what's going on with the government?"

"What government? We don't have a government anymore," she said plainly. "The entire system has collapsed. To be honest, I'm surprised the Internet is still up and running. I thought it would have gone down, by now, but hey, as long as it is up, I will check it every day. Like the saying goes, knowledge is power."

Aramis said, "I still can't believe things have gone this far without any chance of getting better. I would have thought our government was more capable of handling any situation thrown their way. It fell apart so quickly."

Kirk responded, "Well, let's face it. It's been falling apart for years. This country has been on a downward spiral since the early 2000s, if you ask me. All it took was a little chaos, followed by some anarchy, to push it overboard."

Roberto disagreed. "I don't think it's been that bad. Well, maybe in the past few years, but not since the early 2000s. I think we were pretty strong in the early 2000s, especially after 9/11."

"True," Kirk agreed. "I'll give you that."

Grant nodded in agreement. "Yeah, that was a powerful time."

Julia looked at him and thought he looked especially handsome today. Unfortunately for her, Liz thought the same thing and grabbed his hand. They held hands and smiled at one another. Watching them made Julia feel jealous and disgusted, although she hid it well.

David took a drink from a bottle of water, and then commented, "All that shit doesn't matter, now. It's the past. We need to think about our future. This here, what we have, is our new government." He pointed around.

"Dave's right," Kirk said. "So, what does that mean? Do we start voting? Are we even a democracy?"

Roberto replied, "Bro, without a doubt, we are! Our meeting the other day was an example of that. We might not make our votes official, but we sat down together and decided on what we should do. That's a democracy."

"True," Kirk admitted.

Angelo grabbed a wine cooler from the cooler and said, "You guys are giving me a headache with all this talk about politics. I thought this was supposed to be a celebration. You see, man? This is why we need some music up in here!"

Liz agreed, "Yeah, I wish we could listen to music, too. I really miss it. I have songs going on in my head all the time. I used to listen to music every day."

"Same here!" Angelo stated. "I want to listen to some Motown oldies."

"Well, we can't," said Grant with regret. "Don't get me wrong. I love music, too, but it's too dangerous. If *anyone* hears that music, our location is compromised. Our safety would be at risk and nothing matters more than our safety. *Nothing.*"

Liz put her arm around him and said, "Lighten up, babe. We get it. I'm just saying it would be nice to listen to music. You know? I think you need a wine cooler, too."

Angelo pulled one out of the cooler and passed it to her. She opened it and gave it to Grant.

"Here you go, babe. Piña Colada. Isn't that one of your favorites?"

"Actually, it is! You remembered? Nice," he smiled at her and took the bottle. He then turned to Angelo and said, "Thanks, Angelo. Excellent selection, my friend." He took a sip and relished the flavor. "Damn, that's good! Nice and cold, too."

Julia's mouth was watering for more than a drink when she asked, "Can I have one, too?"

"Sure," Angelo replied. He looked into the cooler and pulled one out for her. He opened it and passed it over.

"Thank you," she smiled. She took a long swig from it. It really was refreshing.

Aramis looked around and smiled. He observed, "I guess this is our end of the summer party, huh? Too bad we can't make it a barbecue. I would love a burger, right about now."

Millie responded from the swing nearby, "We could make some, if you guys bring back meat on your supply runs. I always put it on the list."

David replied, "It's easier said, than done. There isn't any meat. There are no more dairy products either and no bread. We were lucky to find the chickens we have. All we ever find out there are canned foods, bottled drinks, and boxed food, providing the rats haven't gotten to it, yet."

Aramis replied, "Well, it's a good thing we have Mil! She can bake bread, churn butter, and she's a great cook! I mean, come on! How many twenty-year-old girls do you know that can bake bread and churn butter, let alone cook a meal as good as my grandmother?"

Millie blushed, "My mother taught me a lot. My father used to teach me a few tricks, too, from the old Delgado family recipes, before he became a jerk."

Thinking about her parents made her lose the urge to continue talking. On the first night of the apocalypse she had been angry with them. She ran away from home, after an argument with her father. There was a brief time when she had a chance to return home, after escaping from Manhattan, but she chose not to make any contact with them and remained with the group. She knew once the bomb was dropped on New York, her parents had to be dead. There was no question about it. It was something she still had not made peace with, yet. She only took time to mourn for her sister, Michelle, who she missed dearly. The death of her parents was suddenly weighing heavy on her mind.

Edie noticed her change in mood and put her arm around her. She said, "Cheer up, Mil. We're celebrating here. Your face looks like you should be at a funeral. What's wrong?"

"I might as well be. I was thinking about my parents."

"Oh. Sorry. Well, at least, they never had to become infected. They spent their last moments being normal. That should bring you some comfort."

"I don't really know that for sure. It's just what I assumed. Who knows what really happened in their last moments? I know one thing for sure. They were probably worried about me." She sighed.

Edie hugged her. "Aw. I'm so sorry. They are definitely at peace, now. I know that much."

Bobby was already finishing his second beer, by this time. He looked at them, turned to Daniel, and snickered a little too loudly, "This is my kind of celebration. We got beer, nice weather, and some rug munching lezbos! All that's missing is the music, like Lizzie said."

All of the women and some of the men glowered at him simultaneously.

David also overheard him and became infuriated. He charged over to hit him. Bobby put his arms up in defense to block, while holding his beer in his right hand. Daniel immediately stood up and got in the way. He held David back and said, "Whoa! Don't do it. This is supposed to be a nice time for us. Don't let him get to you. He's drinking and you know he has diarrhea of the mouth."

Roberto stepped in and grabbed David's arm, "Yeah, besides stupid childish comments like that are not worth fighting over, especially when they come out of the mouth of an *asshole*." He glared at Bobby, who looked away sheepishly.

David reluctantly agreed. He exhaled and turned away from Bobby. In that moment, he accidentally made eye contact with Edie, who looked at him with concern. When she realized he saw her staring at him, she swallowed nervously, and shifted away from Millie slightly. It was enough for him to notice. He wanted to go over and speak with her, but they had not spoken in over a week.

Grant watched Bobby with gritted teeth. He hoped Bobby would look his way, so he could throw him a threatening look, but Bobby was too busy looking down at the ground. He knew he messed up and looked ashamed that he was busted.

Angelo just sat back and watched, while sipping on his wine cooler. He figured, if there were to be a fight, it would be the closest thing to entertainment he'd have to enjoy. He had no doubt Bobby would lose a fight against David or Grant. He had seen those two in action and they were no pushovers. He liked that about them. They meant business, while Bobby seemed like he was all bark and no bite.

The afternoon was uneventful, although it seemed less like a celebration. Julia returned to the basement, while Charles took her place in the backyard. She told him about Bobby's comment and about how David almost kicked his ass. He did not waste any time going out to the yard.

"So, what did I miss?" He asked, pretending not to know.

Grant answered offhandedly, "Nothing we can't handle. Did you find anyplace nearby, where we could get some cinderblocks, cement, and bricks?"

Charles noticed David was standing nearby with his eyes on Edie and did not appear to be worried about Bobby. While Charles was slightly bothered by the diversion in conversation, he was not going to push the issue. If his former officers considered the situation handled, he felt he could let it go. He answered, "As a matter of fact, I did. There are a few places that need to be checked down by Woodbury Commons. It's further out, but everything we need should be in that area. There's a Home Depot, Home Goods, Best Buy, Target, BJ's Wholesale, Walmart, and even a BMW dealership. I figured we may as well get another car, since there will be so many for the taking with the keys and I've always wanted a Beemer."

"They're okay," David said. He then eyed him curiously, "Exactly, what do we need from Best Buy? We don't exactly watch DVDs anymore or listen to CDs like we used to and cellphones are useless."

"That might be true, but we still use computers and we need security cameras and cables. Julia made us a list. This will be a big mission. There is a lot to collect. We're taking the pick-up and the van. I'm going, too. We'll have two groups with two goals. Once we get to the shopping center, we will split up and meet back when we are done. We'll come home together."

Grant asked, "When?"

"That remains to be seen. It depends on when we're ready for another supply run."

Grant looked skeptical, "We need to keep in mind, there is a very good possibility there could be infected in that area. It could be extremely dangerous or super simple. There's no real way of knowing without actually going there to find out. By then, it's too late. Whoever goes should be prepared to fight or kill, if necessary."

"Agreed. Do you have any suggestions?"

"Does the rule still apply about not sending too many assets out together?"

"Unfortunately, yes. It's a chance we can't afford to take."

"Fine. If you're going, then I'm going and, this time, I want Liz with me to watch my back," Grant said. "I trust her marksmanship." He eyed her and she smiled. "We all should."

"You got it," Charles replied. "Who else would be good for this one?"

"Kirk and Roberto," Grant answered, "But you don't want me and Rob out on a run together, so maybe Angelo in his place."

"Right. I also don't want you, David, and me out at the same time. One of us must always stay here. Angelo can take Roberto's place. We can't leave this place defenseless, so having David, Roberto, Daniel, Bobby, and Doc around should be fine, until we get back. Right?" He waited to see if Grant disagreed with leaving David and Bobby behind together.

Grant considered it and answered, "I think it should be fine."

Charles nodded, "Good. So, that's our team then. Kirk and Angelo will take one vehicle. You, Liz, and I will be in the other. On the way back, I will be driving my Beemer." He grinned momentarily and continued, "We'll load the vehicles with whatever we can carry, and then take the interstate back to Museum Village Road at Exit 129. That way we can avoid the downtown area of Monroe."

"Sounds like a plan," Grant said. "Maybe we shouldn't wait too long. We can head out in two days, if you'd like. We'll brief everyone that's going later tonight. It can wait."

"Okay."

Liz commented, "I think waiting two days will be good. Some of these guys look like they might need to sleep late and get some well-needed rest tomorrow."

Charles glanced at Bobby, who was drinking his third beer. He wondered how many beers he had and thought it might be time to cut him off, before he went through their entire supply. He approached him and Daniel and asked, "You guys realize we only have a limited supply of beers, right?"

Daniel replied, "I haven't drank any. I don't drink beer. That was more my sister's thing. I let Bobby have my share."

"It doesn't quite work that way, Dan. Based on the number of empty bottles on the table, it appears he already had enough. Let's just say, no more and leave it at that. Okay?"

Bobby groaned, "Aw, come on, bossman! Let me enjoy this so-called celebration in the only way I know how. It's all I got! I ain't got no sweet piece of ass to keep me happy. I can't listen to any rock music. There's no TV. All I got is this." He held up his bottle of beer and kissed it. "Don't take this away from me. Be a sport! What do ya say?"

Charles was not changing his mind. "Enjoy that drink, Bobby. It's your last one for today. We all need to share them. You already had more than your share."

Bobby frowned and pouted, "It's okay. I get it. Give the black man some power and he has to get over on the white man."

"You know it's not like that," Charles replied angrily, "So, don't even go there."

Grant's trigger finger suddenly began feeling itchy.

Daniel quickly responded, "I think he just needs to sleep it off. I'll take him back to the dorm. I'm sorry about that, Charles. Don't mind him." He stood up and pulled Bobby from his seat. Bobby was a big guy, but Daniel was strong, considering his age. He had no problem getting Bobby on his feet. "Let's go, Bobby, before they banish you for good. I'm putting you on time out."

Bobby sucked his teeth and mumbled something inappropriate under his breath, as they left.

Charles called after him, "I didn't quite catch that, Bobby. Can you repeat it?"

Daniel answered, "He was just saying goodnight to everyone. Right, Bobby?"

Bobby looked at him and flashed him an ignorant grin.

Roberto watched as Daniel escorted Bobby into the house. He shook his head and said to Kirk, "That guy is going to piss off the wrong person and get himself killed."

Kirk chuckled, but he knew Roberto was absolutely right. Bobby was flirting with danger and making enemies of too many people with the means to shoot him.

David had been watching Edie throughout the afternoon. She knew it, too. She kept looking back at him. Deep down she wanted to look at him and maybe even speak to him, but was too afraid to confront him, after the way things had been going between them. She felt bad about hurting his feelings, but she was only doing what she thought was for the best.

He also wanted to speak to her, but was worried she would reject him and push him away, again. He knew that would make him angry and he was already bottling up enough anger for one day. He did not need to add to it.

Millie noticed how they kept looking at each other. It made her feel sad to see them that way. They had been going on like this for too long. She thought it was time for them to cut the crap. They were both adults. There was no reason they could not, at least, be friends, if nothing more. She felt it was her duty to make them realize that.

She turned to Edie and asked, in a low voice, "Why don't you talk to him? I know you like him. Let him know. The guy's been walking around looking miserable for days. He's such a good person. He doesn't deserve this. Talk to him. Tell him how you feel."

"Millie, you know it's not that easy. He doesn't know," Edie whispered.

"Well, tell him."

"It's not that simple. He wouldn't understand."

"How do you know? David's a good man. Look at the way he looks at you."

Edie sighed, "I know. I just can't. I'm scared he'll hate me and never look at me like that, again."

"How long are you going to keep your secret?"

"I haven't thought about it. I wish I could keep it forever."

Millie rolled her eyes. She said, "I think you should tell him. He might surprise you. For all we know, time is running out. We don't know how many days we have left. Don't you want your last months, or years, to be spent with a good man at your side?"

"There's nothing in the world that I want more," she responded dreamily.

"Then go talk to him," Millie urged. She pushed Edie off of the swing.

Edie turned back and leered at her. Millie grinned devilishly. Edie shook her head and chuckled. She built up the strength she needed and walked toward David. He perked up and gazed at her, waiting to hear what she had to say. At the last minute, she lost her courage and continued past him into the house. His eyes followed her and he felt confused. He then glanced at Millie, who was waving for him to go after her. He stood up and followed Edie into the house.

"Edie! Wait up. Can we talk in private? Maybe upstairs, where we can be alone."

Edie swallowed nervously and nodded, "Okay, um, sure."

He walked upstairs to the second floor hallway and she followed. It seemed private enough for a talk, so he turned to her and spoke his mind.

"Edie, we need to stop playing this game. There's no reason for it. Life is too short. I like you and I know you like me. So, what's the problem?"

She stared into his eyes and wanted to kiss him desperately, but she knew she couldn't. She looked away and did not know what to say or how to respond.

He grabbed her chin with his hand and gently lifted it up, so she was facing him, again. "Talk to me, Edie. Tell me what the problem is and we can fix it together. I can't keep walking by you and not saying anything to you. I can't keep looking at you without wanting to take you in my arms and kiss you." He moved closer and stopped within an inch of kissing her and said, "Tell me you don't feel the same way and I will leave you alone."

She could feel his breath on her lips and it made her wild with passion. It took everything she had to hold herself back. She began to tremble, but he placed his hands on her shoulders to steady her.

He demanded, "Say something, Edie. Say something or so help me God, I'm going to kiss you."

Her lips parted wanting him to do as he said, but then she closed them and began to cry. "No, please, don't. I-I can't," she hesitated. "I have to tell you something. It's really important. I just don't know how to say it."

"Just say it already! Whatever it is, it won't make a difference."

"Y-you can't say that," she cried. "You don't know. It will change everything."

"Tell me!"

"No!" She pulled away from him. "I'm not ready to lose this! I'm sorry for being selfish, but I know once I tell you the truth, this will be over and I don't want it to be! I want you to keep looking at me the way that you do! I want you to want me the way that you do!"

"What could be so bad that you think I won't like you anymore? Edie, I can't stop thinking about you. The way things have been the past week have made me miserable. I want us to be more than friends. I want us to be together. Take a chance. Trust me. I won't let you down."

"No, but I will let you down and I can't do that. I won't."

"That makes no sense! You are already letting me down, by doing this!"

"Maybe, but, at least, I know you still want me and that feels so good."

"You're right. You are being very selfish. How long do you think you can keep me on a leash, before I get tired of it? Don't wait, until it's too late. We can't afford to live in a life of regrets, not with the way things are now."

"Believe it or not, David. I feel the same way. That's why I can't tell you."

He became frustrated. The mood was gone for him. The moment was lost. He turned away from her and said, "Fine. Whatever. I'm not going to beg you, if that's what you want. You know? I was willing to give one hundred percent of myself to you, but if you'd rather play games, then it's your loss. Have a good night." He went downstairs.

She wanted to call him back, but what was the point? She still was not ready to tell him her secret. This kind of secret was a deal-breaker and she knew it.

She stormed into the female dorm and threw herself on her bed. She cried and cried, until she had nothing left. Afterwards, she forced herself to get up and changed into a long t-shirt, which is what she normally wore for bed. She lay back on her bed and stared at the ceiling with the lights off. The rooster crowed outside, breaking the silence. Not long after, she finally fell asleep.

Bobby had been lying in bed for over an hour, but he was too agitated to sleep. Regardless of what the others thought, he did not think he was intoxicated. In fact, he felt far from it. What he felt was horny. He had not been with a woman for far too long and it was driving him crazy.

He stepped out of the dorm and found his way up the stairs. He stepped slowly because they seemed to be rotating under his feet. "Whoa, maybe I am drunk," he chuckled. He rubbed his hand over his groin when he reached the second floor. He faced the female dorm and knew exactly what would ease the pressure that was building up in his pants. He was going to need a quick release, but first he wanted some inspiration. He figured the girls might not miss a pair of panties. He hoped to find a used pair, if possible. The smell would certainly help him reach his orgasm faster.

He turned the doorknob and casually opened the door. His eyes immediately focused on Edie, lying in her bed, and he froze. He waited for a few seconds to see if she'd move. He soon realized she was asleep. She did not have a blanket on, so her bare legs were showing, which made him feel harder and more willing to enter the room. He did not dare turn on the light, so he left the door open to allow a crack of light into the darkness with them.

He tiptoed stealthily to her bed, until he was standing over her. He stared down at her beautiful face and wanted to caress her. His hand reached out and hovered over her face, but did not make contact. It gradually moved down over her body toward her legs, but he still did not touch her.

Suddenly, his forefinger gently touched her knee. She did not react. He slid his finger slowly up her thigh and pulled her t-shirt up a few inches, revealing more of her smooth flesh. She remained asleep. He heard her breathing heavily and knew she was in a deep sleep.

He began to feel braver and more confident. He could do this, he told himself. She might not even wake up. He just had to be gentle about it. There was a slight chance if she woke up during the act, she might go along with it. Who knows? All he had to do was take a chance and see what happens.

He was tired of feeling miserable and sexually frustrated. This was what he really needed. She looked like she could use it, too, he told himself. He had a feeling it was going to be a good night.

He took his boots off and then undid his pants. He was not wearing a belt. He pulled his pants down and let them stay around his ankles, and then dropped his boxer shorts. The next part had to be done with finesse. He slowly climbed onto the bed and carefully pulled her legs apart. He moved closer and positioned himself over her. He was so ready for this. There was only one obstacle. She was still wearing her panties. They would have to come off. That would be the moment of truth.

Slowly he reached under her t-shirt and felt her belly, until he found the elastic band of her panties. He grabbed it and began to pull them off.

At that moment, Edie awoke and her eyes shot open. She was about to scream, but he placed his hand over her mouth. She struggled and tried to push him off, but he was too strong and he put his full weight on top of her. He leaned close and whispered, "Shhh! Don't fight it. It's okay, baby. I won't hurt you. I've been watching you and I think you got a sweet sexy ass. You make me so hard every time I look at you. I know you want this. You need it. I need it, too."

She kept trying to push him off, while attempting to move her arms and legs. She managed to push her legs closed, but he forced them back open and moved in closer, until he was pressing against her.

"Come on. Cut the crap and stop being a tease. This is the apocalypse. The old rules no longer apply. We can skip the bullshit foreplay and get right down to business. We're both adults here. Why waste our last days playing games?"

She tried to bite his hand and he slapped her hard across the face. He then placed his hand back over her mouth and moved close enough for his hot breath to heat up her eyes. His breath stunk of alcohol and his body odor was also strong. It disgusted her. She tried to knee him in the groin, but he was ready for that move. He blocked her and did not allow her legs to stop him from his goal.

He exhaled angrily and warned her. "I've been more than patient with you, baby, but you're starting to piss me off. I know what you need and I got it right here. Lay still and be a good bitch, while Big Bad Bobby lays down his pipe. Trust me, it's big enough to make you real happy. By the time I'm done, you're gonna forget all about your skinny little girlfriend."

She bit his hand and he yanked it away long enough for her to scream, "STOP IT! GET THE HELL OFF OF ME, BOBBY!"

He slapped her on the face, again, and pushed his hand down over her mouth hard. He said, "The more you struggle, the hornier I get. We need to get these tight panties off, so you can breathe right, but no more Mr. Nice Guy." He grabbed them by the elastic band and ripped them off. He then pushed himself into her, but stopped abruptly when he felt her penis.

"What the f...? Holy shit stain! You have a dick? How the... ARGH!"

Bobby screamed, as someone grabbed him by the hair and yanked him off of her, dragging him across the floor and out of the dorm room. Once he was in the hallway, he looked up to see Grant.

From within the room, he could hear Edie shouting, "DAMN YOU, BOBBY! I HATE YOU!"

Bobby looked up at Grant and held his arms over his face to protect himself from being punched. Grant only glared down at him. Bobby then tried to explain, while pulling his pants back up, "H-hey there, buddy! We were only messing around! It was a joke! You know? Come on! I can't rape her! I mean him!" He corrected himself. "She's one of those *trans-testicles!* Go look for yourself! It's sick, dude!"

Grant was not hearing him. His eyes filled with fury and he wanted to tear him apart. He reached down and grabbed Bobby by his neck. Bobby flinched and his eyes filled with fear. He quickly turned his face away, just as Grant punched him. He struck him hard on the ear and let him go.

Bobby held his ear and wanted to cry from the pain, but he did not. He whimpered, "Ow! My ear! Damn it, Grant! That really hurt! Shit! I can't hear anything, man! What did you do to my ear?"

Liz shook her head in disgust at Bobby. She turned on the light to the female dorm and rushed over to Edie's side. She was about to comfort her, when she noticed Edie's penis was exposed. Liz froze instinctively and did not move any closer. Once she processed what she had seen, she pulled the blanket over Edie, who was shaking and crying.

Liz tried to disregard the awkward feeling she was experiencing and asked, "Are you okay, Edie?"

Edie was sobbing into her hands and took a moment to answer. "I can explain," she cried.

"There's no need to," replied Liz. "It's your business."

David also heard the screaming and rushed upstairs. He knew Edie was on the second floor and hoped nothing happened to her. When he reached the second floor, he saw Grant standing over Bobby, whose left ear was bleeding, and demanded, "What's going on?"

Charles and Millie were not far behind him.

Grant did not respond. He merely stepped away from Bobby and went into his room. They watched him, feeling utterly confused.

As soon as he left, Bobby tried to explain, "We were only wrestling! It's no big deal! You guys can go back downstairs. There's nothing to see up here. The show's over." He chuckled weakly.

Bobby was hoping Grant would keep their secret, again. After all, there was no need to tell the others about what had just taken place. He got his hit in, so he should be satisfied. When Bobby tried to get up, he felt dizzy from the pain he felt and partly from his intoxication. He still could not hear out of his left ear. He then realized his boots were still in the female dorm and swallowed nervously. There was no way he could retrieve them, while David and Charles stood nearby watching.

Meanwhile, they thought he meant he had been wrestling with Grant. They looked toward his room and wondered why he went inside without saying a word to them. They had not noticed Liz and Edie in the female dorm, yet.

Bobby did not know what they were thinking. He looked at David and explained, "She pulled one over on us, Dave! She's been friggin' lying to us, since day one! She's not even a *she!* She's a *he* and she's got a dick!"

David's eyes opened wide and he began breathing faster. His heart felt as if it were beating a hundred beats per second. Was he talking about Edie? He felt his fists clench, as the anger built up. He better not mean his Edie.

Just then, Liz stepped into the hallway and shouted, "You're a real asshole, Bobby! You know that? You sick piece of shit! You're lucky I don't have my rifle with me or I'd shoot you in the dick!" She kicked him hard in his groin, causing him to cry out in pain.

Charles and David both turned to her in shock. They thought Bobby meant her and understood why Grant was standing over him. He must have hit Bobby. They gawked at Liz and could not believe she had been a man the whole time. She was so beautiful.

However, Millie was not fooled. She knew exactly whom he meant, considering she already knew Edie's secret and had known for a long time.

Grant returned to the hallway with his Walther PPK in his hand and stood over Bobby, who pled for mercy.

Bobby cried out with tears in his eyes, "NO! GRANT, PLEASE! I'M SORRY, MAN! BANISH ME! PLEASE, DON'T KILL ME! I'M BEGGING YOU!"

Charles could not believe his eyes and quickly called out, "Whoa! Grant! What are you doing? Put the gun down!"

Grant stated coldly, "I already warned this piece of shit once. We will not tolerate rapists in this group."

"BUT I DIDN'T RAPE HER! SHE'S A *MAN!* SHE'S GOT A DICK!!!"

Edie shouted from the dorm through tear filled eyes, "GO TO HELL, YOU PRICK! SHOOT HIM, GRANT!"

David looked toward the dorm room and became confused when he heard Edie's voice. He was afraid to look into the room, but forced himself to move toward the doorway. When he saw Edie curled up on the bed, his original fears were confirmed. It wasn't Liz. It was Edie and she was... *a man???*"

Edie looked up, in time, to make eye contact with David, who stared at her, hoping he was wrong about what he just heard. She burst out into tears and looked away from him. He tried to catch his breath. His heart felt like it stopped beating. He barely heard when Charles yelled.

"GRANT! STOP!"

BANG!

The loud sound of the 9mm in close quarters surprised them, even though they knew it was about to go off.

Millie was startled and let out a short scream.

Charles turned away, closed his eyes, and shook his head in frustration.

David flinched and turned back toward the hallway. He noticed Grant holding the smoking gun and looked down on the floor to see Bobby's face had been blown across the rug and onto the nearby wall. Suddenly, he felt cheated. It should have been him, who killed Bobby.

MAN'S END

Chapter Ten

ROBERTO, KIRK, ANGELO, Aramis, and Daniel came running upstairs when they heard the sound of the gunshot. Even Julia emerged from the basement to make sure everything was okay. When she saw the others running upstairs, she followed.

Bobby's corpse lay on the floor bleeding from a gunshot wound to the face. There was no doubt he was dead.

Liz explained how she and Grant had gone up to their room to be alone when they overheard Edie struggling with Bobby, who was on top of her with his pants down around his ankles. Everyone was in shock when they learned he tried to rape her. She did not tell the others that Edie was a transgender, but they had already overheard him shouting she was a man. It wasn't hard to put two and two together.

It was the secret she had been keeping, all along. It was the same secret Julia found out back at Grant's house in Yonkers and the reason Julia felt like she was being forced to lie to the others and, instead, chose to avoid Edie. It was the reason why Edie would not let David get too close. She knew once he learned the truth, there would be problems. Now, the secret was out. Everyone knew the truth.

Edie sat on her bed crying, while David stood at the doorway of the room. The others crowded in the hallway behind Grant, who was still holding his gun.

"Holy shit!" Aramis cried out. "Is that Bobby on the floor?"

Grant turned and noticed everyone had been staring at him. He stated, "Don't any of you dare feel bad for this piece of shit. I found him on top of Edie, trying to rape her. That kind of behavior will not be tolerated around here. These girls will not live in fear. Not while I'm around. If you have urges you need to tend to, you do that shit in the privacy of the bathroom with your damn hand."

Roberto replied, "You won't have to worry about that kind of shit from any of us, bro. That piece of shit was in a league of his own. He had it coming."

Angelo smirked. He knew that more than anyone. He had been waiting to see how long Bobby could last, before pushing someone over the edge. It did not take as long as he thought.

Julia stared at Grant admiringly and felt more attracted to him than ever. After seeing the lengths he was willing to go to keep her and the other girls safe, it was a major turn on for her. She had a feeling *she* would be going to the bathroom to be alone with her hand, although she wished it could be different. She envied Liz even more than before.

Charles was taken aback. He had not realized what Bobby had done, until it was too late. He wished Grant had reacted differently, but no one else seemed surprised.

David was heartbroken, surprised, angry, and confused, all at once. He hated that everyone was there with him, in this moment. He looked down at Bobby and wished he had fired the shot, instead. He resented Grant for stealing that moment from him. He hated Bobby for trying to rape Edie. However, more than anything, he was disappointed. Edie felt more out of reach than ever, as he glanced her way. She did not dare face him. She was too ashamed.

Millie pushed past the guys in the hallway and stood in front of David, who was still in the doorway of the female dorm. She looked at him and whispered, "So, now you know her secret."

David nodded silently.

"And?" She asked.

"Not now, Mil. I'm going to need time to process this. Stay with her," he looked back at Edie. "She's going to need you." He went downstairs. Roberto and Kirk went down with him.

Millie went into the dorm room and closed the door.

Angelo looked at Aramis and said, "I don't suppose he'll be needing your medical assistance."

"No," Aramis smirked. "I'm pretty damn sure he doesn't."

Grant grabbed the rug from the hallway and began wrapping Bobby's body. Liz helped him. Angelo and Aramis bent over and helped, too. It almost felt criminal. Together, they wrapped him in the rug, carried him downstairs, and out to the backyard. Julia went down with them.

Charles stood in the hallway, staring at the blood splattered on the wall.

Only Daniel remained with him. He, too, was in shock about Bobby's death. He was also the only one, who would mourn his passing. Bobby may have been a jerk, but he was his friend. They had spent mostly every day together, over the past month. It was going to be difficult no longer having him around to talk to or joke with. It made Daniel sad, although he knew what took place was justice. Bobby was a bad man and he had it coming, like Roberto said. That did not make his execution any easier to accept.

Daniel went downstairs to make sure the others, at least, gave Bobby a proper burial. He did not want them to desecrate his body. Despite his transgression, he was still a friend and part of the group.

Charles went up to his room in the attic. He wanted to be alone. For the first time, he found himself worrying about the fate of his group, as if the threat was within the group. Was this how punishments for crimes would be dished out, with a gunshot to the head? He understood there were no jails, trials, or judges, but he did not think it was good for one person to decide on such a drastic fate. It should have been discussed first. He expected better of Grant.

Later that night, Millie had asked Aramis to come into the dorm and take a look at Edie's face. It took a lot of convincing, before Edie would agree to it. Her face was bruised and she had a black eye from when Bobby struck her. Aramis gave her something for the pain and placed a cold pack on her face to ease the swelling. It was all he could do. Fortunately, there was no actual penetration. It was only an attempted rape, although that was bad enough. Aramis said a few comforting words and left her to rest.

The next morning was rough. Edie did not sleep a wink, so she was exhausted. Millie stayed up late with her and did not sleep well herself. Julia was afraid to go into the dorm because she did not wish to disturb Edie, so she slept on a sofa in the common room.

Charles also had trouble sleeping. He kept thinking about what happened and tried to think of solutions to make sure it did not happen, again. Was the alcohol to blame? Bobby was drunk, but that was no excuse for his actions. The alcohol only brought out his inner demons, which he had been keeping inside for too long. It would have happened regardless of the alcohol. The alcohol only made it easier for Bobby to act on his feelings. It gave him false courage, while taking away his reason.

What about Grant? Charles knew he would have to speak with him, sooner or later. He dreaded the thought. What would he tell him? Did he deserve to be punished for executing one of their own? He loved Grant like a brother. The last thing he wanted was for their friendship to change.

Grant blamed himself for what happened. He knew what Bobby was capable of doing and did not warn anyone. He kept what happened in Monroe to himself. How could he justify shooting Bobby, while they did not know what he wanted to do to that infected girl? He should have told them, and then they would have easily understood. He wondered if they thought he was psychotic.

He was also worried about Edie and how she was taking it. There was no Rape Counseling Unit for her to turn to. They did not have a psychiatrist to help her through her feelings. They barely had a doctor. How was she going to deal with this trauma?

At around 11 am, Daniel began digging a grave for Bobby behind the garage. Charles heard the sound from the attic and looked out of the rear window. He saw Daniel down below and decided to help him. There was no reason for him to dig the grave alone, so together they dug a grave about four feet deep. Next, Daniel gathered some leftover wood that had been lying around on the property and began building a coffin. He did not want to simply throw the body into the ground wrapped in a rug.

For now, the body was being stored in the basement tunnel because it was cooler down there. It was enough reason for Julia to keep out of the basement, for a while.

By noon, Edie was still curled up in bed. Millie sat by her side consoling her when Julia entered the room. Millie looked toward the door, but when she realized it was only Julia, she returned her attention to Edie.

Julia stepped forward and said, "I'm so sorry this happened to you, Edie. I can't even begin to understand what you are going through. I feel like shit for abandoning you as a friend. Maybe if I didn't, I would have been here last night. This could have been prevented."

Millie said, "It's not your fault. No one could have stopped this from happening, except Bobby. He would have found another way. Maybe he might have attacked you both. This was on him."

"I suppose. Still, I feel guilty and I'm sorry. Edie, I don't want us to be enemies. I want to be here for you. I want us to be friends." Edie did not respond, so Julia added, "You don't have to say anything to me, now, but if you ever want to talk to me, you can. I will listen."

Millie explained, "I really don't think she wants to talk. If you want to help, let her rest."

"Oh. Okay. Can I maybe bring up some food or water? Tea?"

"That would be nice," Millie responded. "I think tea should be fine."

"Right. Will do. Be back in a bit." Julia left the room and went downstairs to the kitchen. She noticed Roberto, Kirk, Angelo, and Aramis were sitting there, drinking black coffee. It was better than using the powdered milk they had in storage. "Is that coffee?" She asked.

"Yep," Aramis replied. "Rob made us a pot."

Roberto turned to her and asked, "Do you want a cup? There's more in the pot."

"Yeah, thanks. I don't mind if I do." She poured herself a cup and filled a second pot with water, which she set to boil. She then sat with them and began drinking her coffee.

Aramis asked, "How is she doing?"

"She won't speak to me. I'm bringing her some tea. She's still crying. Millie is with her."

Kirk shook his head. "It's a shame something like that could happen here in our home. You think you're safe here, but then that happens."

Angelo said, "That man was trouble from the start. Something was bound to happen. That day when I was knocked unconscious, I know something went down between him and Grant. I don't know what, but I know it was something big. Bobby was talking a lot of shit to him up to that point, even after Grant saved his life. But when I was knocked out, things changed. I woke up and noticed the dead infected girl on the ground. Bobby had pissed his pants and needed to change his clothes. Afterwards, he was almost afraid to open his mouth around Grant."

"Wait," Kirk interrupted, "He peed his pants?"

Roberto sneered, "Why didn't you tell us this when he was alive? I would have loved to break his balls about this. Now, I kind of feel bad."

"Damn! Yo, that's crazy," commented Aramis. "I wonder what happened to make him pee his pants. Grant must have put the fear of God into him."

Julia came to his defense and commented, "Whatever Grant did to Bobby to make him piss his pants, I am sure he was justified. Bobby was a jerk. I heard him say a lot of things, while he was working in the tunnel. He didn't know I could hear him, but I could. He badmouthed every one of you, at least once. The guy was a sick pervert. I didn't feel comfortable being down there alone with him. Daniel usually kept him in line, but when no one was around, he would say things that made me feel very uncomfortable."

Roberto asked, "Why didn't you tell someone? I would have gladly kicked his ass for you."

"There was no need to go that far," she said. "I know he was only talking crap. I'm pretty good at ignoring ignorant people. Besides, I always had my can of mace ready to spray him in the face. Lucky for me, I never had to use it."

"Too bad Edie wasn't so lucky," Aramis said.

Roberto asked Julia, "Did you know about Edie?"

She had been sipping from her cup and put it down to answer. "I found out that night we stayed at Grant's house in Yonkers. Millie knew since Manhattan."

Kirk raised his eyebrows. "That's some secret." He paused a moment to think about it, before saying, "I know what happened is terrible, but

I would have loved to see the look on Bobby's face when he realized he was trying to put a peg against another peg, rather than into a hole."

Roberto chuckled, "Yeah, that must have been priceless. Of course, had I seen him in that moment, I probably would have killed him myself."

Aramis held back his laughter, knowing it was an inappropriate time to laugh.

Angelo looked around at them and commented, "You guys are demented."

At that point, they all laughed.

Just then, Charles walked in. "Ahem!" Everyone stopped laughing and turned to him. He asked, "We need help to put Bobby's coffin into the grave, if you're not too busy."

All four men stood up and filed outside to help. Charles was glad he did not have to ask twice. He wasn't sure what they were laughing at, but had a feeling he did not want to know. As they stepped outside, Julia took two cups of tea, which were ready, upstairs to Millie and Edie.

Outside, the guys lifted the wooden coffin, which now contained Bobby's corpse, and placed it down over two ropes that were near the grave. Next, they grabbed the ropes and pulled them, until the coffin was lifted into the air. Slowly, they moved it over the grave and lowered it down. The ropes were pulled out and tossed to the side. Daniel and Charles picked up shovels and began to toss the dirt back into the grave. Kirk grabbed another shovel and helped. Angelo picked up the last shovel and also helped.

Roberto lit a cigarette and took a puff. He stepped close to the edge of the grave and looked down. "He wasn't the best of us," he began, "and he might not have been the worst of us, but he was one of us. Rest in peace, Bobby McDonald. The nightmare is over for you."

Aramis added, "Amen."

Daniel glanced at them and appreciated the gesture. He fought back the tears, as he buried his friend. He was glad to have other friends around to help, in his moment of grief.

Grant and Liz looked out of a second floor window and watched.

"Should we go down and help?" She asked him.

"Hell no," he replied. "They can handle it. I wouldn't spit on his grave, if it were on fire. He wanted me to let him rape that infected girl we ran into about a week back."

"Oh, my God. Why didn't you say something?"

"I wanted to forget it happened. I thought I scared some sense into him. His justification was that she was going to die anyway. I wanted to shoot him then and there, but I didn't. I should have."

"You would have looked like the bad guy had you killed him then without any witnesses. How could you know he'd do something like this to a friend?"

"Because of what he said. In his mind, raping a girl was acceptable. That was enough reason to kill him and not allow him to return to our group. It should have been enough for me. Instead, I let it slide and Edie paid the price. Never again, Liz."

She grabbed his arm and moved close to him. He put his arm around her and they continued to look out of the window for a few seconds more, before getting back to scrubbing Bobby's blood from the wall.

David sat alone up in the watchtower. He could not see what was going on behind the garage, but he knew what was happening. He wondered if Bobby truly deserved to be buried near the house. If it had been up to him, Bobby would have been left on the side of the highway.

Once the grave was covered, Daniel bent down and placed a flower on it. "Your work here is done and I am grateful for your help," he said. "Rest in peace."

Sometime later, Charles stood at the kitchen sink. He poured the rest of the alcoholic drinks down the drain, one at a time, until every can or bottle was empty. Never again, would someone be intoxicated at the compound.

It would be another two days, before Edie finally emerged from the female dorm room. It was already mid-day. She had just taken a shower, in which she spent most of the time crying. Out of respect for her privacy, Grant and Liz had been using the first floor bathroom, instead. It gave Edie plenty of time to be alone with her thoughts and her nightmares. Every time she fell asleep she had another and each was more intense and realistic than the last. She felt like she was drowning in her fears and needed a change of scenery, so she built up the strength and finally went downstairs.

The house was quiet. It sounded like some of the guys were down in the basement, probably working out in the gym, she thought. She stepped outside on the porch and wondered who was on guard duty. She looked up at the watchtower and could not tell, who it was because of the new metal coverings that were added to hide the person from view.

She went back inside and went past the common room. Daniel was reading a book and did not notice her. She kept walking and stepped out to the backyard. She saw Angelo and Aramis sitting outside. They were talking about something. She could not hear the conversation, nor did she want to.

She turned around and went into the kitchen to make something to eat. She checked the cupboard and looked into the refrigerator, but nothing looked appetizing. The urge to eat had passed.

Edie went in the garage, more out of curiosity, than anything else. She turned on the light and looked around at the tools. She touched a few and held them in her hand, but then put them back. There were shovels hanging on the wall, which still had fresh soil on them. She had a feeling she knew why and turned around to leave the garage. She flicked off the light and closed the door.

She leaned against the wall in the hallway and felt frustrated. She wanted to be somewhere else, far away from everyone. That would never happen, not if she wanted to survive. She asked herself how badly did she want to live in a world, where the main goal was to survive each day. That was no fun anymore. No more good times to be had. What was the point of surviving?

She considered leaving and wondered how long would it take before anyone noticed she was gone. She walked toward the front door and before she stepped back out to the porch, she came face to face with David.

"Edie? You're up." He was quite surprised to see her walking around, although it was nice to see her.

"David!" She was also surprised. She wanted to disappear and hide. It would have been easier than talking to him, of all people.

He studied her and asked, "Where are you going?"

Her heart pounded in her chest and she replied nervously, "I was just, uh, going for a walk. I wanted to stretch my legs." She did not dare make eye contact with him.

"Can we walk together? I'd really like to talk to you."

She thought about it and knew she was not going to get rid of him easily. He must have been waiting days to speak with her. Deep down, she knew she owed him an explanation. She could not deny him that chance. Not now. "Okay," she nodded reluctantly.

They walked out toward the perimeter fence at the northern end of the property and gradually followed it around the compound. It was a peaceful day out. The sun was up high, the birds were singing, and squirrels were gathering nuts for the coming winter.

David did not know what he could say without putting his foot in his mouth. There were questions he wanted to ask and apologies he wanted to make. He felt bad about what happened to her and only left her alone for the past few days because he thought that was what she wanted. Plus, it did not seem appropriate to hound her so soon, after the attack. Even now, it did not feel right, but he had to know. He had to hear it from her lips. He hoped he would not regret asking.

"Wow. So, um, you're really a man? That was the big secret you didn't want to tell me."

Edie swallowed and exhaled. She knew this conversation was inevitable. She replied unenthusiastically, "I *was* a man."

David seemed confused, as he asked, "*Was?* You're body says different. I mean, you still have your..."

She interrupted him. "*Yes!* I do, David. I'm transgender. I identify as a woman. That's what I am in my mind and in my heart. I've always felt more like a woman, even before I realized it."

"Oh, okay. I guess. When was that exactly?"

"A very long time ago." She rolled her eyes and stopped walking. "Now, do you understand why I didn't want to tell you? I'm sick and tired of people thinking I'm some kind of freak."

He felt awkward and did not dare interrupt her. He knew she needed to get this out, so he listened, as she went on.

"I thought I could start fresh with you guys. I hoped everyone could accept me as Edie McQueen without having ever known me as Eddie 'the Queer.' I guess I was wrong. It'll be back to the same old bullshit. Everyone will look at me differently, from now on. I'll be the subject of gossip, an entertaining joke for everyone to discuss, when I'm not around. As soon as I enter a room, it will become quiet. It might not even be because of me, but that's how it will feel to me. I've already been through this nonsense with my family and friends from before. I hated it. I don't want to go through it, again. I really don't. I'm so done with that part of my life." She turned away from him and wiped away the tears from her cheeks.

He reassured her, "I won't let anyone make fun of you or talk about you behind your back. That's not right. I won't allow it."

"Oh, that's great. Are you going to be my guardian angel, too, like with Millie? David, you can't be everyone's hero. You shouldn't have to be. People should just not be assholes to their friends or family and everyone would be a lot happier."

David replied, "That's not who I am. I'm not a hero and I don't try to be. Forget everyone else, for a moment. Let's talk about us. You should have told me, rather than leading me on."

"Get real, David! That's not exactly a conversation opener when meeting new people!"

"Yeah, but you knew how I felt about you. It wasn't fair to let me think we had a chance when there was none whatsoever."

"None whatsoever, huh?" She asked, sounding hurt and angry.

"Well, I'm sorry, but I'm not gay and I never will be," he replied plainly. "Whatever future I thought we could have is gone. It's like you're a totally different person from who I knew."

Edie shot back, "If you don't think we have any kind of future, then why are we even speaking? And another thing, I'm not a different person! I'm still me! If anything, *you're* the one, who will be different, from now on!" She wiped away more tears and began walking, again.

He called after her, "Edie..."

"Screw you, David," she responded angrily, as she kept walking away.

He caught up to her and walked beside her, but he said nothing because deep down he knew she was right. He said some stupid things, which could not be taken back. He knew that he would. Now, he felt bad, although he did not dare try to hold her to comfort her. She probably would not have let him anyway. Plus, he did not want to give her the wrong idea that he was okay with them still being a couple. He definitely was not anymore.

Somehow, he felt like the girl he liked had died and was replaced by her twin brother. He knew it was a silly and terrible way to think, but that is how he felt and it made him sad. It was difficult for him to understand how she might have felt, but he wanted to try for the sake of salvaging their friendship.

Edie felt similar feelings of regret, anger, hurt, and disappointment. She also felt isolated, rejected, and alone. These were the feelings she thought she left behind, before the apocalypse, but it turned out she was wrong. They had come back to haunt her and, this time, there was nowhere she could go to escape from them. There were no more bars or dance clubs, and no other civilized cities near enough for her to make a new start. It seemed she was stuck to deal with her pain and she hated it. She desperately wanted to run away. She wished she could crawl into a hole and die.

However, what would that accomplish? Nothing.

Instead, she cried. It was all that she could do.

After walking silently for a while, David said, "I'm sorry, Edie. I'm being a selfish jerk. I hope we can still be friends. I really do care about you. That won't change." She stopped walking and listened, as he gently put his hand on her shoulder and explained, "It's going to take time for me to adjust to this, so I hope you'll understand. I want you to know that I don't hate you and I don't blame you for keeping your secret. I get it. I'm sorry I can't be the man you need me to be."

She stared at him and continued to cry, but she was no longer walking away and that was a start, he thought.

He took a chance and stepped closer, so he could put his arm around her. He hoped she would not take it the wrong way. "It will be okay, in time," he told her. "I'm so sorry that asshole hurt you. They say time heals all wounds. It really does, although it might take a long time."

She leaned on him and felt a glimmer of hope that he could be right. She wanted to feel happy, again, someday. Although, she knew the dream was over. They would never be together in the way she hoped and that pain was going to take a very long time to get over.

MAN'S END

Chapter Eleven

A WEEK HAD gone by, since the attempted rape of Edie and Bobby's execution by Grant. The body had been stored overnight in the basement tunnel and was buried a day later, but his death still lingered strong on the compound. Daniel was angry with Grant, while Charles was disappointed in him. Julia felt uncomfortable sitting down in the basement alone for too long. Edie was still having nightmares about being attacked.

The incident also led to the revelation that Edie was transgender, which added more pressure on her. She was feeling stressed out. Fortunately for her, Grant was around to show her a good way to relieve that stress.

"Hold it firmly," he said. "Stay focused and pull it back slowly. When it goes off, it should not surprise you. Just let it happen, while keeping the sights on the target. Be sure to keep the front sights and rear sights aligned. Don't forget to breathe."

BANG!

The gun went off and she tried to see where the shot struck.

"Very good," he said. "You're getting better."

"Thanks," she smiled. Each time she fired her Glock, it felt fantastic. She kept picturing Bobby's image on the target. First, she imagined shooting him in the groin, and then in the head, although Grant urged her to aim for the center mass of the target. Either way, shooting felt exhilarating.

Grant turned to Millie and said, "Okay, it's your turn. Remember. Don't shoot them all, at once. There is no need to rush, while you're here. Out there, it will be different. For now, I want you to take your time. Finger on the trigger, aim at the target, align your front and rear sights, breathe, and shoot."

BANG!

She missed because she anticipated her shot and flinched.

"Try not to let the sound of the shot scare you," he instructed her. "You're flinching with each shot. Relax, Millie. You can do this. Pretend you are cooking and my instructions are the recipe."

"Okay." She confessed, "It's just that the shells scare me when they pop out. You said they're hot and I keep thinking I'm going to get burned."

She began to turn toward him with the gun in her hand pointed outward, but he grabbed her wrists and stopped her.

"Always keep your weapon pointed downrange or, at least, away from other people. Don't aim it at anyone, unless you intend to use it. That's very important. We absolutely cannot afford to have any accidental shootings."

"I'm sorry," she pouted. "I'm really messing up today."

"It's fine. You're still learning. Don't be so hard on yourself. Remember what I told you. Think of it as cooking. Keep your sights on your target. Maintain trigger control and breathe steady. Squeeze the trigger gradually. Do not anticipate the gunshot. Instead, focus on the sights being over the target." The gun went off and she hit her intended target dead on. "Excellent! You see? I knew you could do it!"

She was overjoyed and grinned. So was Edie, who gave her the thumbs up.

Liz came out to watch Grant teach the girls how to shoot. She sat down on a nearby folding chair and listened in.

When he noticed her there, he asked, "Hey, gorgeous. Would you like to shoot a few? I don't want you to get out of practice."

"If you say so," She smirked at him, before standing up and stepping forward. He was about to hand over his Walther PPK, but she waved it away. "No thanks," she said. She pulled out her Glock from the pancake style holster at her side, which he gave to her. "I have my Glock with me," she grinned. "I'm trying to get into the habit of carrying it whenever I leave the house."

"Good. That's my girl." He was proud of her. He decided to always carry his weapon, after the incident with Bobby. He never wanted to be unprepared, again. It made him happy to see his preparedness was rubbing off on his girlfriend.

She aimed at the target and fired five consecutive shots in a tight circle. She then fired one more at the very center, before holstering her gun.

Both Edie and Millie watched with gaping mouths. They were amazed at how well she shot.

Grant checked the target and was also astonished at her accuracy. "Damn, baby! That's great," he commented. "I guess you're done for today."

She chuckled, "I used to go shooting every month with my cousin, who was a retired cop, until he moved to Florida. That was before I joined the marines. By the time I graduated from my twelve weeks at boot camp, I was a marksman. Afterwards, my School of Infantry training at Camp Geiger only added to my skills. So, don't worry, babe. I always got your back."

Grant smiled proudly at her.

Edie and Millie were quite impressed. It was inspiring for them to see another woman shoot so well. They both wanted to feel as confident as she felt with a weapon in their hand. Grant saw how they reacted to her and knew how helpful it would be to have her there during their lessons, so he asked her to help out with their training. She gladly agreed much to his delight.

They continued shooting together for another hour or so. Edie and Millie were doing much better. David watched from the watchtower and was pleased that they were trying something different and enjoying it.

He had been upset with Grant for killing Bobby and stealing the opportunity from him. After seeing how Grant was teaching the girls how to shoot, he realized how silly he was behaving. Grant was one of the good guys. He was his friend and a fiercely loyal one, at that.

There was no one better to have watching his back, than friends like him. David felt fortunate to have several friends like that.

Julia came upstairs from the basement holding a list in her hand. She searched the house for Charles, who was up in the attic, reading survival guides. She knocked and entered.

"That's not how the act of knocking works, Julia. You're supposed to wait, until I let you in or tell you it's okay to enter."

"I know. I'm sorry. I skipped a step or two." She handed him the list and said, "We really need this stuff. How long are we going to wait for the next run? I thought we weren't going to wait this long. It's been more than two weeks, since the last one."

"I am aware of that. You do realize someone was almost raped last week and someone else was executed for it. Right?"

"Yeah, that's why I waited a week, before I printed the list. Regardless of the drama going on around here, we need to remember that there is an immediate danger out there. The longer we wait, the harder it will be to get these things."

He sighed, "You're right. I'll put together the team, first thing in the morning."

"Thank you," she said, as she left.

He had been stalling going out on the supply run, mainly because he did not wish to be around Grant. It worried him how Grant would behave, if they were to run into others. It was becoming too easy for him to turn to his weapon for a solution. He did not hesitate when it came to killing a human.

He stood up and went downstairs. If he was going to do this, he needed to have that talk, first. Otherwise, he was going to be too distracted during their supply run and he did not want that.

Grant was sitting at the dining room table eating with Liz. Millie and Edie were sitting at their table eating, as well. They had just finished cleaning their weapons.

Charles stood at the doorway and asked, "Grant? Can I have a word with you, when you're done? No rush. I'll be waiting out on the front porch."

"Sure. I'll be right there. Almost done."

Not long after, Grant stepped out onto the porch and asked, "What's up?"

"I've been wanting to talk to you about something. I don't want you to feel offended. It's about the way you handle certain situations. For example, the way you handled the incident with Bobby last week."

"I did what needed to be done. We don't have jails. There are no judges and juries anymore. I caught that bastard red-handed. He was guilty beyond a reasonable doubt. He was a threat. I ended the threat. I don't see the problem."

"You executed him in my house," Charles explained, obviously still in shock.

"*Our* home. Right?"

He sighed, "Yes, in our home. You didn't give him a chance to explain. You didn't even wait for the rest of us to learn what was going on."

"When we were cops, when did we ever have time to wait for everyone else to learn what was going on, before we reacted?"

"Never," Charles admitted. He knew Grant was right, but he still did not like it.

"Exactly. What's different? He committed a violent felony in my presence. I ended him. I couldn't afford to let him get away with it, a second time."

"Second time? What do you mean by that? When was the first?"

Grant exhaled and told him about how Bobby begged to let him rape the infected girl they ran into, since she was on death's bed anyway. He also mentioned how Bobby had given him a hard time during the supply run, more than once. The man was basically reckless and dangerous to keep around.

At last, Charles understood why Grant did what he did. It made him feel better to know the entire story. He wished Grant had not kept it from him, in the first place.

Confused, he asked, "Why didn't you tell anyone?"

"I knew if I told everyone, no one would want him around. He'd be banished. It seemed cruel to condemn someone, even him, to being out there alone, especially with potential dangers nearby. Not to mention, if we had kicked him out, he would be able to go to the other survivors at the Village Hall and lead them straight to our gates. He could have told them the ins and outs of this place leaving us completely vulnerable to attack. I thought it was best to keep it quiet and hope he learned from the experience," he explained. "I guess I put too much faith into a lost cause."

"No," Charles replied. "I think you handled it exactly how I would have handled it. I'm sorry I ever doubted you."

"No worries. I didn't even realize you did."

Charles patted him on the back and said, "You and I have been through a lot together, huh? You've been like my right arm. I don't know if I say it enough, but thank you. I am truly glad to have you by my side, watching my back."

"It's what we do. There's never been a question about it for me."

"Well, I'm glad you are so certain. I don't always feel so sure about what I'm doing. I doubt myself, from time to time. I try not to, but I'm afraid I will make the wrong decision and cause more deaths. I already caused enough, since that first night."

Grant asked, "What? Are you crazy? You did not cause anyone's death!"

"Yes, I did," he insisted. "This whole thing is partially my fault. I was the patrol supervisor that night. I failed to see the severity of what was going on and did not contain the situation when I still had time to do so. Before I knew it, we lost control, and then it was too late." He paused and added regretfully, "Thousands of people have died because I failed to do my job!"

"Hey, don't you dare think that way! Jesus Christ. Have you been blaming yourself for the Zombie Apocalypse, this entire time?"

Charles looked down shamefully at the porch and sighed.

Grant grabbed him by the shoulder and said, "Listen to me. You did not start this shit. Some bat shit crazy old fool in a lab did. You read it yourself. Read the damn journal, again, if you need to. You did the best that you could, considering the circumstances. If anything, you saved lives that night. All of us here are safe because of you. We are alive because of you. You got us away, before the bomb was dropped. Think about that. Shit. You're my hero, Charles. I look up to you, man. You're like a brother to me."

"Thanks. That really means a lot," Charles smiled and looked up at the sky, so Grant would not notice that his eyes were watery. "It looks like it's going to rain."

"Yeah, I guess."

"Oh, before I forget. If it's not raining in the morning, I'd like to head out on that supply run to the Walmart shopping center near Woodbury Commons. Julia is bugging me about getting those supplies and I know Kirk is eager to start his wall."

"Sounds good. I'll let Liz, Kirk, and Angelo know to get their gear ready. We leave after breakfast, right?"

Charles faced him and replied, "I'd like to leave early. Let's say around 10 am?"

"Will the stores even be open that early?"

"Yeah, I think..." he stopped himself and realized Grant was joking. "You got me."

Grant laughed. "Yep. You fell for that one, hook, line, and sinker."

They both laughed and enjoyed the late afternoon breeze. Summer was coming to an end. It was already September. Soon, it would be fall.

Charles skipped ahead in his mind and wondered what it would be like during the winter months. So far, they had been dealing with summer weather, which was easy. Winter during the Zombie Apocalypse would be a completely different experience for everyone. He also wondered how it would affect the infected. Could the virus survive in cold weather? That was certainly something to think about.

Droplets began to fall, as the sky grew darker and it drizzled. It looked like it was going to rain harder, before dark. Charles hoped it would clear up by morning. He wanted to get this supply run over with already. The sooner they began construction on that wall, the better off they would be.

The rain was coming down hard and heavy. Most of the guys sat around the common room and talked. Roberto spoke to Kirk and David. Grant looked through books with Liz and Millie. Aramis and Angelo discussed their time in the military.

Edie was down in the gym working out. She wanted to get herself back into shape. She felt like she had been slipping the past couple of weeks. It was time for her to toughen up. She did not ever want to be a victim, again. She wanted to be a fighter.

Julia kept an eye on the grounds using the cameras in the next room over, while Charles stood guard in the watchtower. Nobody was patrolling the grounds due to the inclement weather, but every once in a while, somebody would step out onto the porch to check on things.

Daniel had recently acquired an interest in the cameras and security system. He wanted to know how he could improve it, but first needed to know how it worked. Julia did not mind his company, as long as he was paying attention to her lessons in how to use the cameras.

However, whenever she stopped teaching, he began talking and telling stories.

"This system is not as complicated, as I thought," he said. "I'd be more worried about falling asleep watching the screen." He chuckled. "Don't you get bored?" Before she could reply, he said, "This would bore the hell out of me, if I did it all day long like you. I can't seem to sit still for too long, unless I'm relaxing. I could probably handle a few hours of this, at the most. After that, forget it. I prefer to keep busy with my hands. That's why I like to work. You know?" He did not wait for her to answer. "That's what I need to do. I need another project to work on. I'll feel more like myself, once we get started on that wall. It's going to be one hell of a job with the limited materials and equipment we have at our disposal, but we can do it. We have a lot of good workers." He paused. "Damn. It's a shame Bobby won't be around to help with that. He was my hardest worker."

"He was also a perverted jerk," she replied.

Daniel fell silent. It was obvious he did not want to hear any more insults about Bobby. As far as he was concerned, the man was dead and paid the ultimate price for his crime. Daniel thought he paid too high a price for an attempted rape, but he did not voice his opinion about that. He knew he was alone on that front.

He stood up and said, "I think I'm going to see what's going on upstairs. I have some books I need to finish reading. I'll see you around." He walked out of the security hub and went upstairs.

"Okay. Later." She waved without looking back.

Daniel entered the common room and saw that it was a full house. Even Grant was there, the one person he was not in the mood to be around. He looked through the books on the shelf and grabbed one about hunting. He was about to leave the room, when Grant approached him.

"Hey, Danny. Can we talk?"

Daniel faced him reluctantly and replied, "About what?"

"In private. Out on the porch."

He agreed and they went out to the porch.

Grant began, "Look, I know you were close to Bobby. I wanted to tell you that I'm really sorry about how things turned out. It was never my intention to shoot him, but when I saw him on top of Edie and heard her screaming, I freaked out and reacted."

Daniel listened silently, which was unlike him.

Grant knew he was upset. He had to tell him everything. "There's something only a few people know. I think I should tell you, so that you can understand why I did what I did. That day when we went into town and found that infected girl, Bobby showed me his true colors. He deliberately went against everything I asked him to do, just to piss me off. I don't know if he was testing me or not, but he was certainly distracting me. He almost got us killed by the first zombie we encountered. It almost ate him, but I saved his life, despite the fact that he had been giving me a hard time. I didn't want him to get killed, especially not on my watch. I felt responsible for him. Later, when we found the girl and realized she was infected, he wanted to have sex with her, no matter what she wanted. He even begged me if he could rape her, since she was going to die anyway. He volunteered to kill her himself, after he was done with her. I couldn't believe my ears."

Daniel seemed more interested in hearing what he had to say and was looking at him, while he listened.

Grant continued, "I gave him a chance by not telling anyone when we got back because I didn't want him to get kicked out. I hoped he would've been grateful enough to change his ways."

Daniel began to understand and felt less angry. He also took into consideration how many times he listened to Bobby talk dirty about the women in the group. He had no respect for women.

Grant frowned, "He really let me down when he attacked Edie. I thought there was hope for him, but I was wrong. He only proved to me that he could never be trusted. To leave him alive would have been putting every girl here at risk, including my girlfriend, and I was not going to do that. He had to go and banishment was too good for him and too risky for us, as a group. I'm really sorry because I know you were friends. I had to do what was best for the group."

Daniel looked at him and appeared unconvinced, so Grant explained further, "Had we kicked him out, he might have wanted to get revenge by going to that other group of survivors and helping them to infiltrate our defenses. He knew everything about this place, including our weaknesses. There's no way I could've taken a chance like that, so... I shot him." He sighed, "Yes, I appointed myself judge, jury, and executioner. Maybe that was wrong of me, but I reacted in the moment. Given a second chance, I'd do it, again. What I did was for everyone's safety." He faced Daniel. "Make no mistake, I would go to great lengths to keep this place safe, even if it means taking lives. This is our home and our only sanctuary. Right now, nothing is more important than keeping everyone here safe."

"I understand where you're coming from. I guess I can't really blame you. Bobby liked to push people's buttons to see how far he could go. I know he tried with you because he envied you. He messed up big time. In a way, I blame myself. I never should have let him get drunk. Maybe he'd still be around."

"Daniel, he was who he was. You can't be expected to baby-sit a grown man. He would have done it anyway, if he thought he could get away with it. Alcohol had nothing to do with it. It's like you said, he was pushing the envelope every chance he got with me, David, and even with Charles. He was reckless, impulsive, and he had a serious problem with authority. I admit he was impressive when it came to labor work, but his bad qualities outweighed his good ones. His fate was inevitable. When it comes down to it, a person like him is too dangerous to keep around in a time with little rules and no government."

"Yeah, I guess." Daniel still seemed uncertain. He felt bad that Bobby had to die, but, at least, he knew the reasoning behind Grant's actions. It gave him a sense of closure. At the same time, he wondered how long it would be before the guys in charge would begin to make their own rules and laws. When that time came, would they impose them at gunpoint? It did not seem like too far-fetched an idea to Daniel. He had seen enough movies, where situations like theirs changed people with good intentions into ugly versions of themselves. Maybe Bobby was only the first.

Over the next several minutes, the two of them stood quietly on the porch and watched the rainfall, while deep in thought. They listened to it, as it pitter-pattered on the roof of the porch and poured down like an open faucet at the corners into growing muddy puddles on the dirt.

Daniel became distracted by the puddles and began thinking of a solution to fix the minor issue, before it became a flooding problem.

Grant didn't let it bother him. He inhaled and took in the fresh, cool, rainy air. "Well, I'd better head inside," he said. "I have a big day tomorrow. Goodnight, Daniel." He turned to go inside. He wanted to get a good night's sleep for the day ahead. Hopefully, it would no longer be raining.

"Okay. Goodnight," Daniel replied instinctively. He remained outside a little longer. He still had a lot on his mind. The rain eventually helped to clear it and relaxed his mood. It always had a very calming effect on him. A moment later, he heard the rooster crowing. It reminded him of when he was a young boy in Puerto Rico. The memory made him smile. Those were happier and simpler times. He longed for them.

He wondered if he could ever experience that kind of serenity, again. Perhaps, it was possible and maybe, just maybe, there was hope for this group, he thought.

MAN'S END

Chapter Twelve

T HE GROUP SET out early the next day. It was Grant, Liz, and Charles leading in the pick-up truck with Kirk and Angelo following in the van, as planned. It had stopped raining sometime during the night. They were ready earlier than expected, so they left and hit the road by 9:30 am. They went north and took Museum Village Road across to Interstate 86, which they took heading southbound. The road was clear of any other vehicles, which was the norm these days. Occasionally, one would pass abandoned vehicles. In time, they seemed more like obstacles that did not merit any recognition or mention.

It did not take long for the two vehicles to reach Exit 131, which was the last exit before the old toll plaza entering the New York Thruway. They each found themselves looking around in fascination. The last time they had been this far south was the day they raced up from Yonkers. It was also the day the nuke was dropped on New York City. It was a time they preferred not to discuss or think about. On the Internet, it had become widely known as "The Day New York Died."

There were a few abandoned vehicles along the exit ramp, which they had to go around. The cars had been left in a zigzag formation, which seemed odd. It almost looked like it was done purposely.

The Woodbury Commons shopping outlet center was to the left. It looked inviting, but they needed to go to a different shopping center for what they wanted. They turned right and made another right, soon after, into the BMW dealership. That would be their first stop, since it was along the way.

Four cars had been left blocking the two-way road. It was a tight squeeze, but Grant did not have a problem getting by. Kirk barely scraped the side of the van against one of the BMWs, as he went past.

Angelo looked out of the window to assess the damage and said, "I hope you have insurance on this van."

Kirk smirked, "I don't even have a driver's license, in case you forgot."

"Well, it's a good thing this is the apocalypse then, huh?" Angelo grinned.

"Yeah, it's a good thing," Kirk scoffed at the irony of the statement.

Grant stopped the pick-up truck and Kirk parked beside him.

Charles stepped out of the pick-up and looked around at the cars that were available. There were not as many as he hoped. Most of the cars were gone. He wondered if the owner of the dealership had relocated most of them long ago. The thought had not crossed his mind earlier. It was disappointing.

Kirk called out through the open window from the driver's seat of the van, "Let me know which one you want and I'll hotwire it for you."

Charles replied, "Thanks, but I plan on finding keys in the office, first, and then see what comes of it. Maybe I'll get lucky."

Angelo got out of the van and said, "If you're going inside, I'm going with you."

"Thanks. I appreciate it. Liz, can you cover us from out here, while we look around?"

"You got it." She got out of the pick-up and climbed into the rear cargo compartment for a better vantage point. She had her Colt M4 Carbine in her hands. She found a comfortable position and scanned the area with her scope to make sure they were alone. Her hair was tied back to keep it out of her way.

Charles called out to Grant and Kirk, "Keep the vehicles running, guys, in case we need to leave in a hurry!" They both gave him the thumbs up signal.

Charles and Angelo went into the dealership's main showroom building. There did not seem to be anyone within, but they were not taking any chances. They kept their weapons out, as they searched the building. There were several sets of car keys hanging from the wall of an office. Charles grabbed them all and they both went back outside.

"Okay, let's see if any of these give me what I want," he said, as he began clicking on the unlock buttons of the keys, one by one. The first one yielded no results, but the second was answered by a high-pitched chirping sound nearby. The lights on one of the BMWs flashed on briefly. Charles grinned and said proudly, "Bingo! There's my Beemer!"

He walked toward the car, which was a BMW M550i sport vehicle. It was a royal blue four-door sedan. He definitely did not want a two-door car. Four doors would be more convenient. Next, he opened the driver's side door and checked out the beige interior. He smiled when that new car smell hit him and allowed a moment to appreciate it. He gently slid his hand over the smooth leather seat. He sat down and admired the interior. The seat was extremely comfortable. He was glad the car was an automatic because it would make driving it easier. It was very spacious inside, too.

"Perfect," he said to himself. "I'll take it." He smiled.

For a moment, he forgot Angelo was standing next to him. Angelo responded jokingly, "Sorry, sir, but you are too low in social status to own this vehicle."

"Ha! Funny," Charles laughed. "Now that you mention it, maybe I should take one in every color, in case I get bored with blue."

"Now, you're talking, my man!"

They both laughed.

Charles started it up and the engine quietly hummed to life. It barely sounded like it was on, but the lights on the dashboard told him otherwise. The fuel indicated the tank was full, which was a relief. It would be one less stop for them to make on the way back home.

It was time to move on to their next destination. They still had a lot of "shopping" to do.

As the three-vehicle caravan approached the first entrance of the shopping center, they noticed an abandoned delivery trailer was blocking it. They moved on to the next entrance and it was also blocked by two abandoned vans with flattened tires.

Liz turned to Grant and commented, "It looks like someone might have been hiding out here, unless they are still here. We should be ready for anything. Be careful, babe."

"Always," he said, as he pulled out his weapon and placed it on his lap.

He continued to drive cautiously forward as the lead vehicle with Charles following in the BMW and Kirk in the van with Angelo. He slowed to a stop when he realized the next entrance, which was one of the main entrances, was also blocked.

This time, there was a more strategic blockade. Two dumpsters were used to block the outbound lanes leaving the parking lot. A tractor-trailer truck was behind them and there were piles of sandbags or cement bags set up atop the trailer to serve as a gunner's nest. A garbage truck was blocking the entrance lanes, but there were also two cars at either side of the main entrance for extra blockage, or to use as cover.

He believed someone was definitely using this place as a fortification. His eyes began searching for possible gunners. He did not want them to get ambushed.

Charles got out of his car and walked forward to the driver's side of the pick-up. He examined the set up at the entrance from there and asked, "What do you think?"

"I think we need to tread carefully from here on," Grant responded.

Charles nodded in agreement, "Yep. Sure looks that way."

Liz leaned forward in her seat. She had her eyes on the makeshift gunner's nest atop the truck and was waiting to see if she saw any movement. Her rifle was already in her hands.

Kirk and Angelo were still sitting in the van behind them. They watched and waited.

Angelo turned to Kirk and said, "Keep your eyes open, man. This doesn't look good."

"Yeah," Kirk agreed. "I don't like this one bit."

Suddenly, a shot was fired from the rooftop of a nearby Chili's restaurant at the ground near Charles' foot. The shot was immediately followed by a male voice that called out, "That was a warning! Don't make any sudden moves or the next shot will be a lot more painful! My gunner has a clear shot of, at least, four of you, so the choice is yours!"

Charles raised his hands in the air and turned around slowly toward the sound of the voice, although he could not see anyone, yet. He responded, "We come in peace! We're only looking to get supplies! We can barter, if we need to!"

The voice yelled back, "We already told you people to go to hell! We don't deal with crazies!"

Charles replied, "Whoever you're talking about is not us! We are a different group! This is our first time here in over a month! We just wanted to get supplies! We didn't know anyone was in control of this shopping center! We can leave and never come back, if that's what you want!"

"So, you're not from Monroe?" The voice asked.

Grant rolled his eyes when he realized they must have meant the group from the Village Hall.

"Well, yes," Charles explained, "but we are not with that group from the Village Hall! We know about them! We are definitely *not* with them!"

Someone appeared at the top of the tractor-trailer. It was a Caucasian man with a beard wearing army fatigues. He shouted, "How do we know we can trust you?"

Charles shrugged, "You don't, but you're the ones that have us at a disadvantage! As a show of trust, I will put my gun down, slowly!"

"Okay," said the man. "Do it. Slowly!"

Charles kept his left hand up, while he reached for his weapon and unholstered it ever so slowly. He then turned it around in his hand and bent down without breaking eye contact with the man. He placed his weapon on the ground and stood up slowly. He then raised both hands high and took two steps forward, so that his weapon would be behind him.

The man said, "You only! Step forward to the garbage truck! I'll come down and meet with you there, so we can talk! The rest of you stay in the vehicles or my buddy, Woody, opens fire! Got it?"

"Yeah, we got it," Charles replied. He looked at Grant and said, "Let's see how this plays out. Be ready, just in case."

Grant nodded.

Kirk turned to Angelo and commented, "*Woody???*"

Angelo shrugged subtly at him. He was holding a grenade in his hand. He hoped he would not have to use it.

In the vehicle ahead of them, Liz tried to keep her rifle low, so it could not be seen from the outside. The safety was off and it was ready to go. Her eyes were focused on Woody.

Charles walked forward and stopped near the garbage truck. The man in fatigues appeared in the driver's side window holding a handgun, which he pointed at Charles.

He said, "Don't try anything stupid."

"I promise. I won't. We are not here looking for trouble."

The man studied him a moment and smirked, "What do you want?"

"Supplies, like I said. We have a list. We were hoping to take what we needed, but we didn't think anyone would be here. We'd be willing to pay, somehow, if need be."

"You need the stuff that badly?"

"We are running very low. We are staying in an old house. There are others. Older people. They need medicine," he lied, hoping to gain some sympathy.

The man nodded and responded, "We can probably work something out. Of course, money means nothing these days. You mentioned earlier you could trade. What do you have to trade? Oh, and you can put your hands down." He lowered his gun out of view and seemed more relaxed.

Charles felt relieved and put his arms down. "We don't have much, but we are resourceful," he answered vaguely. It was his way of answering without giving away too much information. He asked, "What do your people need? Maybe we can come to an agreement that benefits both groups."

The man seemed to like the idea. He thought about it, for a moment, and replied, "Fuel. We need a lot of fuel. We've been here, since the start. Food supplies are running low for us, too, so we have plans to head out west. If you can bring us a few barrels of fuel, we can see about helping you out with your list."

Charles looked skeptical. He asked, "If you are running low, how do I know you can deliver what's on my list?"

"Well, what's on your list? Can I see it?"

"It's in my back pocket."

"Take it out slowly and hand it up to me."

Charles carefully reached into his back pocket to pull out the list, but Woody, who still had his sights on him, became nervous and shouted, "Alex! What's he doing?"

The man in the garbage truck, who's name was Alex, responded, "It's okay, Woody! He's only showing me a piece of paper!"

Charles was frozen still with his hand still in his back pocket. He put his other hand up, while he pulled out the list. He then held it up, so Woody could see it from his vantage point. Afterwards, he passed it up to Alex and put his arms back down.

Alex took the list and looked it over. "Hmm. This is a pretty extensive list for a group of people hiding out in a small old house."

"I never said it was small. Only old," Charles corrected him.

Alex looked at him and smirked, "That's right. My bad. I'll tell you what, um, what's your name, buddy?"

"Charles Foster."

"Charles, huh? I'm Alexander Hill. My gunner is Woodrow King, but we call him Woody. I think we can work out a deal."

"Thank you. I appreciate it."

Alex looked at the long list, again. "We can give you pretty much all of this stuff, in exchange for say... ten barrels of fuel."

"Ten?"

"Yep. Ten."

"That's a lot of fuel."

"Yeah, I said we needed a lot. Didn't I?"

Charles nodded, "That you did." He exhaled. "Well, we don't exactly have that much fuel lying around."

Alex glanced at the list one more time, before handing it back down to Charles. He said, "If you really want this stuff, I'm sure you can find it. After all, you are a resourceful group. That's what you said, right?"

"Yes, I did." Charles wanted to kick himself for saying the words. How in the world were they going to get ten barrels, let alone the fuel to fill them?

Alex said, "You look worried, Charles. I want you to know that I appreciate your gesture of good faith when you put down your weapon and came here to speak with me. In return, I would like to make a gesture of good faith, so you know that I'm not full of shit. I'll give you one item of my choosing from that list, now, as a gift. You will get the rest when we get our fuel. Sound fair to you?"

Charles perked up. "Yes! That sounds great. Thank you! Do you need to see the list, again?"

"No need. Hang tight." Alex raised his hand and was holding a two-way radio, which was on the list. He spoke into it and said, "Hey, Aaron. Come in. It's Alex."

A male voice spoke from the radio and answered, "Yeah, go for Aaron."

Alex said, "Do me a favor? I need a brand new heavy-duty tarp. The biggest that we have. Can you get one to me? I'm in the garbage truck at the Industrial Drive entrance."

"One industrial tarp coming up," Aaron's voice answered.

Alex looked down at Charles and said, "How's that for service?"

"It's good. Thank you very much," he said, while eyeing the two-way radio. He would have preferred a set of those, instead, but he would take what he could get, for now. Hopefully, Alex would come through and let them get their own radios, later, once they pulled off the nearly impossible feat of bringing back ten barrels of fuel. Piece of cake!

Alex asked, "How long do you plan on holding out in Monroe? Things are looking bad. The infected are coming, Charles. Take your people and get away, while you still can."

Charles looked up at him and answered, "I appreciate the advice, but we're tired of running. We've been running, since day one in Manhattan."

Alex looked genuinely surprised. "No shit? You were in Manhattan when it started?"

"Yes, sir," Charles nodded. "We were right in the thick of things. We were lucky to make it out in time, before they dropped the bomb. I lost a lot of friends that weekend."

"Me, too. I mean, I wasn't there, but I lost a lot of friends."

"Are you military?"

"Not really. I was in the Reserves. They mobilized us and had us conducting roadblocks on the thruway. Waste of time. Like some wastoid infected was going to come driving upstate! Idiots."

Charles smiled briefly.

Alex asked, "How did you get out, if you don't mind my asking? I heard the city was blocked off, before the next morning. They weren't letting anyone in or out."

"We used the old Croton Aqueduct tunnels. We crossed over into the Bronx, just before they blew up High Bridge. We lost two people.

After that, we hid in an old armory, and then made our way into Westchester County."

"Oh? That's pretty clever. I'm sorry to hear about your losses." He sounded sincere.

"Thanks, Alex."

They both remained silent for the next minute or two, until Aaron arrived with a brand new tarp, still in the bag. He knocked on the other side of the truck, and then opened up and tossed the tarp inside on the passenger seat.

"Here you go, Al. Need anything else?"

Alex turned to him and replied, "No. Thank you. That will be all." Aaron closed the door and Alex grabbed the tarp. He passed it down to Charles and said, "Good luck. I hope to see you, soon."

Charles took the tarp and asked, "Will Woody be waiting to shoot us, when we get back?"

Alex scoffed, "Good one. No. Since we have no idea when you'll have my delivery, here's what you can do. Did you notice the first two entrances you passed, before reaching this one?"

"Yes," Charles nodded.

Alex continued, "Well, when you reach the second one, where the two vans are blocking, honk the horn one time for three seconds, and then wait, until we wave you closer. You have to be the one, who comes back, Charles. I already feel comfortable speaking with you. I will not be happy, if it's someone else. Is it a deal?"

Charles held up the tarp. "You already started on your part, so I have to fulfill my end. I'll try to get that fuel to you within the week. I can leave the list, if you want to start getting my stuff ready."

"No offense, Charles, but we'll cross that path when we get to it. Once you have something to actually negotiate with, I will gladly allow you and your people to enter the lot. I'll have my people get what you need then. It won't be a bother. We even have a forklift to unload the fuel from your vehicles."

"We are not giving up the fuel, until we see what we want. In fact, we are not entering the lot, until your people get what I need from my list. No offense, Alex."

"None taken, Charles," he grinned. "I like your style. If this trade works out, maybe we can trade, again, in the future. I think it will be beneficial to both parties."

"I thought you were planning on leaving and heading out west."

"I am. That's the plan anyway. Unfortunately, not everyone is on board with that plan. We're still working out the kinks. The fuel will go a long way into helping us make a final decision. Who knows? If we all end up leaving, this place can be yours. Think about that, while you're gathering our fuel."

"Okay. Thanks. I guess I'll be going then."

"God speed, Charles."

Charles looked back and waved, "Thank you."

He turned and walked back toward Grant and Liz.

Just then, Alex called after him, "Oh, Charles!"

Charles stopped in his tracks. He had a really bad feeling things were about to go south fast. He exhaled and turned slowly.

"Don't forget to pick up your weapon," he said. "You may need it."

Charles looked down at his gun and bent over slowly. He kept waiting for the sound of gunfire. When his hand touched his gun, he swallowed nervously and expected Woody to shoot him. He did not. Charles slowly stood up and holstered his gun. He looked at Alex, who was chuckling.

"Relax, Charles! We're good! We have a deal! Remember?"

Charles nodded half-heartedly and said, "Thanks. See you around." He turned and walked to the driver's side of the pick-up.

Grant commented, "That was interesting. So, we have a deal? What's the deal?"

Liz listened eagerly.

"Yes, we made a deal," he explained. Charles went into detail and told them the deal.

Grant asked, "Are we really going to get ten barrels of fuel?"

"We can surely try. It will have to be from another gas station away from Monroe. I don't want to use up our fuel supply. We'll head further north toward Chester and Goshen. Get what we can and hope it will be enough."

Grant nodded, "We'll definitely get it, if that's what you want us to do. We can do two runs simultaneously."

"I don't know if I like that idea," Charles responded.

"One at a time works, too, but it will take twice as long. Have faith in us, Charles. Dave and I can get this done. Two groups. One will go to Chester and the other can continue up to Goshen. Maybe we can be done in less than a week. If we're lucky, we might even find a few items from the list."

Charles sighed and gave in. It sounded like a solid plan. "Okay. Fine. Two groups. Let's head back home and plan this out properly. We're going to need fuel drums to store everything. Finding those will be the hard part." He frowned.

Liz asked, "Can we even trust these people to come through? What if they try to steal the fuel and give us nothing?"

Grant replied, before Charles could say anything, "They will be very sorry, if that happens. I have no problem setting up a back up plan, just in case, things go wrong."

Charles nodded reluctantly, "Agreed. We should have a back up plan. However, I think Alex seems sincere. That's not to say someone else in his group won't betray the deal. I got the impression they are not all on the same page. We'll play it safe, when the time comes. In the meantime, let's get out of here. We can take this road back to Monroe. Do you know the way from here?"

"Not really," Grant admitted. "This area wasn't on the map you drew."

"In that case, I'll lead. You guys follow. Keep an eye out for Woody and his rifle, as we go by. It would help to know exactly where he's perched."

Liz responded, "I already have eyes on his spot. Next time we come, I'll be watching for him. They won't catch us by surprise, again."

"Good." He looked at Liz and Grant. "You know? You two were made for each other."

They smiled at him and held hands.

Charles shook his head, walked back to the van, and gave Kirk and Angelo the brief version of the story. Afterwards, he got into the BMW and led his group back north using the local roads.

MAN'S END

Chapter Thirteen

B Y THE NEXT day, two groups of three set out from the compound in search of fuel and supplies. Both vehicles stayed together for part of the way, since they were going the same direction. They traveled north on Interstate 86 to different destinations. The first group consisted of Grant, Liz, and Angelo in the pick-up. Their search would begin when they reached Exit 123, which would take them through Goshen and New Hampton. The second group was David, Kirk, and Roberto in the van. They would be exiting earlier at Exit 126 and begin their search in Chester, as they made their way west through Florida and toward Warwick. Both groups were prepared to stay out overnight, if necessary, or until they found what they were looking for. Charles hated the idea of sending out two separate groups, especially people that were crucial to the overall survival of the group, but he knew their search would be more efficient this way.

Liz sat between Grant and Angelo during the ride. She turned on the car radio and searched the stations, but all she found was static and dead air. She opened the glove compartment and pulled out a CD, which she popped in for some driving music.

Angelo smiled and pretended he was with friends on a road trip. It was easier than believing the truth. He wished things could be normal. He missed his old life. Still, this new existence was exciting and filled with adventure and those were the reasons he joined the military. He managed to make some pretty decent friends, too. True friends, who he knew had his back. That made all the difference in the world.

Meanwhile, David drove the van, while Kirk sat in the passenger seat. Roberto relaxed on the rug in the back. He had a sleeping bag with him, which he used as a mattress. Kirk and Roberto had a debate about what they thought were the best and worst horror movies of the 1980s, while David kept his mind focused on the road and got off at his exit. He watched the pick-up continue north along the interstate and hoped their plan to split up worked out for the best.

Roberto felt the vehicle slow down and asked jokingly, "Are we there, yet?"

Kirk chuckled at the silly question and the way Roberto asked it.

David replied, "If you guys keep it up, I'm going to leave you both here."

They made a right turn and headed for the first gas station they found. As luck would have it, there was a fuel tanker tractor-trailer truck parked near the pumps. The driver's side door was wide open.

"Well, well. Check it out, boys. We hit the jackpot on our first try."

Kirk replied, "I can hotwire that bad boy and we can end our search today."

"No," David said. "The deal was for ten barrels of fuel. The truck is ours. We're keeping that *bad boy* for ourselves."

"Hell yeah, we are," agreed Roberto.

Kirk grinned, "Works for me."

They pulled into the gas station and stopped. The area seemed clear of infected and void of people, as well.

Kirk stepped out and walked toward the truck. He paused when he reached the driver's side. David and Roberto wondered why he delayed and prepared to go out and fight whatever he saw. Kirk hesitated, before reaching into the truck's cab and pulling out the corpse of the driver. The decayed body dropped to the ground and splattered exploding into an incredible odorous pile of blood and maggots. He then shook his head and came back to the van in a hurry.

A moment later, he stood beside the driver's side door and groaned, "Ugh! No freaking way! Don't make me do it, Dave. I swear I will vomit on you. That was the single most disgusting thing I ever had to do in my entire life."

Roberto laughed hysterically and David had to chuckle, too.

David stopped laughing when he realized someone was lying dead on the ground. That was not funny. He stated, "I'm sorry. It's really not funny. We'll figure something out."

Roberto also stopped laughing and, suddenly, felt guilty for it. Still, he asked, "What's the matter, Kirk? I thought you liked horror movies? Just pretend you are in one."

"I am in one, in case you haven't noticed!"

Roberto opened the side door and said, "Step aside. I'll clean it up, but you're gonna owe me one, and I mean big time, bro."

Kirk responded, "If you clean that up, I'll do your laundry for a week."

"I don't mind doing my own laundry. I was thinking more about you taking a few of my guard duty shifts."

"Done! Whatever, man! Just get that pile of maggots away from that truck, so I can get to work."

David shook his head and stepped out of the van. "Hold on," he said.

Roberto turned to face him and waited to hear what he had to say.

David stepped toward him and said, "That was probably a human being. Not some random infected person. He deserves a moment of silence out of respect."

Roberto nodded in agreement.

The three of them bowed their heads and said silent prayers for the dead truck driver. After they were done, David said, "Okay, do your thing, Rob."

Roberto was not the squeamish type. After seeing the deaths he'd seen, he had no problem dealing with the stinking bloated corpse of a stranger, or its maggots. First, he went into the gas station's mini-mart. He returned with cleaning materials and a broom. He dragged the body away from the truck by the boots, and then began sweeping away the innards that fell out when the stomach exploded. Afterwards, he wiped down the driver's seat and began spraying the area with disinfectants. The stench of death did not go away, but the truck was not as bad as before.

Roberto walked back toward them and lit a cigarette. He put it in his mouth and took a puff. He looked back toward the body on the ground, as he blew out the smoke and asked, "How do you think he died?"

David shrugged, "Beats me. Could be suicide or a heart attack. Maybe murder, although it doesn't make sense to kill him and leave him in his truck. To be honest, it's not my business to care anymore. We need the fuel. That's what matters, now."

"That's something Grant would say," Roberto commented. "What does the cop in you think?"

David smirked, "The cop in me died in Manhattan. The guy's dead. I feel bad for him, but there's nothing we can do about it. We have our own problems."

"Fair enough." Roberto seemed satisfied with his answer and continued smoking his cigarette. "Truck's all yours, bro," he looked at Kirk.

Kirk gagged from the smell and tried to keep his mind focused. He moved closer to the truck and climbed into the driver's seat. He was very pleased to see the keys were in the ignition, but when he turned them, it would not start. The battery was dead. Of course, it was nothing a set of jumper cables could not solve. Fortunately, they just happen to have some in the back of the van.

A few miles away, Grant and his group reached their exit and pulled off the interstate. They made a left going under the interstate into New Hampton and reached their first stop, which was the Orange County Department of Public Works. It was the perfect place to search for fuel drums. Hopefully, some would even be filled. Judging by how high the grass in front had grown, it was probably abandoned.

It was a lucky break for them when Julia found the site, using Google maps on her computer. She immediately informed Grant about it to help him with his search. Naturally, he was grateful. The look on his face was thanks enough for her. She enjoyed making him happy anyway she could.

He still had no idea how she felt about him. Why would he notice, considering he already had Liz? She was everything he needed in a companion. It was like Charles said. They were made for each other.

"Here we are," he said to her, as he drove onto the driveway and stopped at the closed gate. "Let's see if we can find what we need with one trip. I'd like to get this over with, as fast as possible."

Angelo asked teasingly, "Don't you like our company?"

"It's not the company. It's the distance from home. I don't like being this far from safety. Would you care to do the honors?"

Angelo grabbed his bag, which was filled with explosives and a few random tools. He got out and walked over to the fence.

It was about six to ten feet tall and barbed wire lined the top of the gate and fence. They could have probably crashed through it, but that might have damaged the pick-up. There was an easier way.

Angelo placed a stick of dynamite into the chain that held the gate closed. He then lit it and ran back to the pick-up and climbed inside.

"Fire in the hole! Back away!"

Grant hit the gas pedal and they drove backwards returning to the main road. He continued back a few yards at a fast pace. Just as he got far enough, the gate exploded from its hinges and flew across the roadway.

"KABOOM!"

"Okay. Door's open," Angelo grinned.

"So it is," Grant replied. "Thanks, pal."

They drove onto the entrance road slowly and entered the main parking lot. It was filled with white government vehicles. A few large orange trucks were parked against a large brick warehouse. The building had it's own fuel pumps, which included diesel fuel. There was even a short fuel tanker truck.

"Wow! We really hit the jackpot," said Grant with excitement. "We need to come back here with the others. This place can provide us with all the fuel we need. We'll fill the fuel truck and take one of those flatbed trucks to use for gathering building materials for our wall."

Angelo asked, "You want to do that, now? I can drive a truck, but can she?"

Liz responded, "I can't even drive a car and you want me to drive a truck?"

"No," Grant said. "That's why I said we need to come back with the others. We'll take one truck back with us today and come back for the rest tomorrow. Let's drive around the warehouse and see if there is anything else we can use."

He shifted the pick-up into gear and drove around the warehouse. There were more trucks parked along the side and a few at the rear. They drove further west into the next parking lot, past another building and found about two-dozen different construction vehicles, along with large pipes and building materials.

Angelo looked around at everything and commented, "You ain't kidding, man! We hit the mother lode here. Hey, I say we check the buildings, too. There might be more goodies inside."

"I agree," said Grant. "However, we can do that when we return with more people. It'll be safer that way. I want to be ready for any surprises. Let's just grab the fuel truck and head back, before it gets dark. Hopefully, the keys are in it."

"This is your show," said Angelo. "We play it your way."

He drove back into the first parking lot and went past the rows of white government vehicles, until he stopped near the fuel pumps. The fuel truck was parked a few feet away, near the building's u-shaped loading dock area.

Angelo said, "I'll go check it out. You guys can wait here. I'll be fine."

"Be careful," Liz warned.

"Thanks. I will. If anything, I have my handy MK 18 Mod 0. This baby always has my back."

Grant turned to Liz and said, "Regardless, keep an eye on that warehouse. Watch the windows." He looked out of his window and noticed another brick building on his side of the lot. It looked like the main office building. His mind began to work fast. He knew there had to be a lot of very useful maps inside. It would behoove them to acquire those maps. "Damn it," he grumbled.

"What is it?" Liz asked.

"I was looking at this office building over here on my side. I would *really* like to search it. We could probably find a lot of useful area maps of the county, along with sewer maps and anything else that could help us get an edge over other survivor groups."

"Cool! Do you want to check it, before we leave? I'm okay with that idea. We have all day. There's plenty of time to do a building search, especially if it can benefit our group. Right?"

"Yeah, let's do it. Hey, what's going on with Angelo?"

"He's good. I've been watching him. The warehouse looks clear from out here. I don't think he has the truck keys, though. He hasn't gotten inside, yet. He keeps walking around it."

"Damn. No problem. Let's check the warehouse, too. We're going to need those keys. I'd rather go through the warehouse, while it's still bright outside. I'd hate to waste my flashlight's battery power too soon. The offices can wait a little. It's got lots of windows to light the way."

They both grabbed their gear and Angelo's explosive bag and exited the vehicle. They walked over to the fuel truck, where Angelo was standing perplexed. He could not figure out how to get the door open without damaging the window.

Grant said, "Change of plans, pal. I guess we're going into the warehouse to find the keys. We'll do a quick walkthrough of the building. Afterwards, we want to hit up the office building across the way. I have a feeling we can acquire some very detailed maps of the county, which will hopefully include sewage and waterlines. Useful things to have."

Angelo nodded, "You lead. I'll follow. Thanks for bringing my bag." He took his bag from Liz and pulled it over his shoulder.

"You're welcome," she said.

Grant walked around the truck and said, "Let's head inside through here. There's an open door ahead."

Liz and Angelo followed him, as he stepped up the loading dock and entered the building.

The interior of the building looked like the typical industrial warehouse. There were large rooms with high ceilings filled with stacked construction materials, a forklift, offices, and storage rooms. There were no people and no infected within, which was their main concern. However, there was a foul odor, which worried them. It was hard to tell what it was or where it came from.

"Ew! What is that terrible smell?" Liz asked. She searched for the source and found several fuel drums grouped together against a wall.

"Hey, look what I found," she pointed at them. "We can use the forklift and put those into one of the flatbed trucks outside, if we can find the keys. At least, it gives us another option."

"Nice. Good idea," Grant replied. "Let's check in this office for the keys." He pointed to a room.

Liz and Angelo gathered behind him, as he opened the door and scanned the room with his flashlight. It appeared to be safe, so he entered. Liz stood at the doorway and watched over him, while Angelo watched their backs. He tried hard to hold his breath, but the smell was pretty bad.

"Please, hurry in there. This place smells worse than a zombie's ass." Liz chuckled.

"Bingo!" Grant found a bunch of keys hanging from the wall on hooks. He grabbed every one of them. There were twenty sets of keys in total.

Suddenly, a noise was heard coming from behind a pile of cardboard boxes. Angelo and Liz both pointed their weapons in that direction and waited. Nothing happened.

Liz turned to Angelo and whispered, "You heard that, right?"

"Yeah."

From within the office, Grant asked quietly, "What's going on?"

Liz turned to him and silently put her forefinger to her lips. "Shhh!" She used her rifle to point in the direction of where they heard the noise.

There didn't seem to be anything else of interest in the office, so Grant tiptoed to the doorway and peered out to see what she was pointed at. He noticed the pile of boxes and wished he did not have his hands full with so many keys.

Angelo and Liz cautiously moved forward and each went around the boxes on opposite sides to trap whatever was hiding behind them by flanking it. Their weapons were held high and were ready to fire. Grant stayed back and did not dare move for fear that the sound of jingling keys would distract them even for a second.

As soon as they reached the other side of the boxes they came upon a small family of raccoons. The mother raccoon snarled and screamed loudly at them. They realize she was only protecting her young and backed away quickly. Both felt a tremendous amount of relief.

Angelo wiped the sweat from his brow and grinned at her.

Liz turned to Grant and said, "Raccoons."

He sneered, "Well, at least, you guys didn't shoot the poor things."

Angelo scoffed, "It would have served them right for stinking up this place and scaring the bejesus out of me!"

The trio chuckled and decided to go back outside. Grant handed them each six sets of keys, so they could check the trucks that were parked in the loading dock area. There were three, two flatbed trucks and the fuel truck.

Liz walked to one of the flatbeds and inserted a few keys in a row. After only four tries, she had succeeded. She shouted with excitement, "I got one open!"

"Excellent," Grant responded encouragingly.

About a minute later, Angelo declared with disappointment, "None of these work on the fuel truck."

Grant didn't have any luck either with the second flatbed. He and Angelo switched places. Grant couldn't get the fuel truck open either, but Angelo was able to open the other flatbed truck with one of the keys he had. Liz decided to see if she had the keys to the fuel truck, so she walked over to it. It turned out she did.

With all three trucks unlocked, they knew they could take them back to the compound at any time, after returning with more qualified drivers. In the meantime, they would only take the fuel truck back, since it was the main priority, but not yet.

There was something Grant wanted to check out, first. He stared across at the office building and suggested, "Let's check out that office building, and then we'll take the fuel truck home. We'll come back tomorrow for the fuel drums and both flatbed trucks. They will definitely come in handy."

Liz asked, "Shouldn't we bring back the fuel drums, first, since that's what we're trading, and come back for the other stuff tomorrow?"

"I've thought about that, but I think having a truck we can keep refilling would be better to have. We could always fill empty barrels, if we need to. Having the truck gives us more options. If it comes down to it, we could always give them the fuel truck. I doubt we'll have to do that. Don't worry. We'll eventually take everything we need from here."

"If you say so, babe."

Angelo asked, "So, we're really going in there today?" He gestured toward the office building with his weapon.

Grant looked at the building and considered it one more time, before saying, "Yes, we are really going in there today."

It was a fairly big building for them to check going room to room. It would take a lot of time. If they encountered any threats inside, there would be limited space to fight. Angelo was getting flashbacks of infiltrating the Science Center building that housed the underground lab, where the Fox Serum Virus was created. He lost a few highly trained friends in there, after infected apes and zombies attacked. In the end, he had to blow the whole place up, along with any real chance of finding a cure.

He dreaded a repeat of that fateful night.

Of course, he and David did manage to recover the broken syringe containing the last remnants of the anti-virus. That had to count for something. He kept the syringe in his bag, in hopes that someday he could, somehow, complete his original mission. Since that time, he rarely let his knapsack out of his sight.

Thinking about the residue of a rare anti-virus possibly being used to save the day, now, seemed like a cruel joke. Who was left to save it and who was left to save?

Moments later, Grant, Liz, and a very hesitant Angelo approached the rectangular office building with caution. They did not think it was occupied, but it was best not to assume such things. They entered with guns out, ready to fire. It was so quiet in the building, you could hear a pin drop. Once they cleared the lobby, they moved through the main corridor of the ground floor, checking each room they passed.

Grant whispered, "Let's take the stairs down to the basement. There's probably an archive room or storage room, where we can find maps."

The other two nodded silently.

Unlike the ground floor, the basement was not brightly lit by sunlight, coming in through the windows. Instead, it was quite dark. The building's lack of power forced them to use their flashlights.

Liz and Angelo both had flashlights mounted to the front ends of their rifles, which kept their hands free to operate the weapons. Liz looked around them, scanning the area, while they moved forward.

It was hard for her to shake the eerie feeling she felt, as they walked through the darkness, in search of maps. There were so many random places, where someone, or something, could hide and pop out and surprise them. This time, she was ready, in case there was another raccoon. Of course, the darkened basement was much scarier than the warehouse. In a way, she felt like she was playing a video game in the first-person mode, except if she died, there would be no reset button to press.

Angelo whispered from behind her, "Remind me why we are down here, again? I mean, I thought he wanted to do this building, after we returned with more people."

"Maps," she responded shortly. "He likes maps."

"He likes maps? Okay. So, maps it is. Well, I just want it to be noted that the black guy always dies in horror movies, so please watch my back and my front."

She chuckled, "Of course."

"Thanks. Much appreciated."

Finally, Grant stopped and exclaimed in a loud whisper, "I think we found something! These long cylinder containers look about the right size for storing blueprints or maps." There were a bunch of them stacked on shelves in a storage area. He opened one up and placed the flashlight down. Carefully, he pulled out a rolled up parchment from the cardboard container and unrolled it. It was an old map of the entire county dated in the late 1900s. "Oh, yeah. This will do nicely," he grinned, and then rolled up the map and placed it back into the container.

It took a while to go through each container. Grant did not want to waste time and energy carrying them all back to the truck. They would only take the useful ones. He specifically wanted maps of Orange County, its towns and villages, roads, water pipelines, and underground tunnels. There were over fifty containers, so it took longer than expected. Grant and Angelo searched together, while Liz kept an eye on the dark basement. They searched diligently for the blueprint of the Village Hall, but could not find it. They disregarded any blueprints of buildings that were not located in Monroe or were not of any interest.

About an hour and a half later, they were finally ready to leave the basement and the building. Grant found a sack that could be used to carry the containers. They took the staircase back up to the ground floor and went out the way they came in.

When they got back to the pick-up truck, Angelo asked, "So, should we head to our next location or do you want to bring the fuel truck back?"

Grant replied, "Honestly, I'd love to go to the next spot, since it's not far." There were several medical facilities nearby that they wanted to check out. Julia had also found those on the map at the time when she noticed the public works. However, he thought about it and knew it would have to wait. He said, "Come to think of it, I don't think we should take a chance with this truck. It will be very helpful to have it. We shouldn't risk losing it, although I have an idea that might work. It's still early. I'm not against taking the truck home and coming back out here with another driver to pick up the fuel drums and both flatbed trucks. We have plenty of time, before nightfall."

Angelo asked, "Who else can drive a truck?"

"Aramis can do it," Grant replied.

"Great. Let's go for it," Angelo agreed.

Grant and Liz got into the pick-up, while Angelo walked toward the fuel truck and climbed inside. He started it up and followed them out of the complex to Interstate 86. They drove south back toward their exit and took Museum Village Road back to the compound. It was the safest most isolated route.

The ride home was fast and uneventful.

When they arrived at the compound gate, Grant got out to open it. He got back into the pick-up and drove inside followed by Angelo in the fuel truck. Aramis looked down from the watchtower and felt excited when he saw the bright orange fuel truck. He knew how much having it would help them. He wished he could be down on the ground to see it up close.

Once the gate was closed and locked, Grant went looking for Aramis, not realizing that he was up in the watchtower the whole time. He went into the house followed closely by Liz, who took a moment for a bathroom break.

Millie was sitting alone in the kitchen, reading a book, as he walked in and asked, "Hey, do you know where Aramis is at?"

"Wow! You're back fast!" She looked up at him with a look of surprise on her face.

"Yeah, we found a fuel truck, but we need to go back out to pick up some fuel drums. And we need another truck driver. So, where's Aramis?"

"He should be up in the watchtower. I know Edie is patrolling the grounds and she said she had guard duty with him."

"Is she? Awesome. That's good. I'm proud of her. Thanks."

Millie smiled and nodded at him.

Charles came upstairs from the basement and ran into Grant, before he went back outside to find Aramis.

"You're back already? Did something go wrong? Is everyone all right?"

"Oh, hey! We're fine. We did it, Charles! We found an ass load of fuel!" Charles' eyes lit up, as Grant spoke. "I need to go back out there with Aramis, so he can drive a flatbed truck back. We have the keys with us. Come outside and have a look at what we found."

When they stepped outside, Charles was ecstatic to see the fuel truck. Angelo leaned against it proudly with his arms crossed and wearing a huge grin on his face because the look on Charles' face was priceless.

"That's amazing! You found a gas truck?"

Grant nodded. "That's not all," he said. "We also found the ten barrels of fuel for Alex and his people, as well as two flatbed trucks for us. Plus, there are fuel pumps at the site and we managed to acquire about a dozen county maps."

"No way! That's fantastic!"

"We're going back to pick up the flatbed trucks and fuel drums. We just need Aramis to drive one of the trucks. I don't suppose you can relieve him in the watchtower and have him come down?"

"Yeah, sure! I wish I could go myself!"

"You'll get your chance because we definitely need to return for the building materials. There are stacks of metal, cinder blocks, bricks, and pipes. More trucks, too, if you want to use them as tanks."

"Hmm. That's an interesting thought."

Once Charles had time to get over his excitement, he went up to the watchtower and sent Aramis down. Aramis was just as excited to finally go on a supply run. He hated being the only person with medical knowledge. It made him too valuable to risk losing, which basically made him a prisoner of the compound. Thanks to one of his other skills, at last, he could go out!

"When are we leaving?" He asked eagerly.

Grant answered, "As soon as you're ready. Grab your gear."

"Gear? What gear? My medical equipment?"

"No, your weapon and holster. Bring a few band-aids and alcohol wipes, if it makes you feel better. We won't need that stuff. We're going to pick up some trucks, fuel, and then we're searching for fresh medical supplies. I estimate we should be home before dark."

"That sounds awesome, man! I'll be right back!"

While he ran off to get ready, Grant carried the sack containing the cylindrical containers and brought them into the house. He took them to the basement and left them in the security hub with Julia.

She asked, "What are those?"

"Maps and blueprints. Check them out. See if you can find a place to store them in here, while you're at it. I've got to go back out. We found the fuel we need."

"That's great! I knew you could do it!"

"Thanks for the vote of confidence. I'll see you later."

She smiled, as she watched him leave.

He went back upstairs and met up with Liz, who returned from her bathroom break. She followed him into the garage, where he switched keys. This time, they would be taking the new BMW, since it seated four people comfortably.

He grabbed the brand new tarp and they got into the car. They took a moment to appreciate the new car smell.

"Ah, this is sweet," he said.

"And comfy," she added, from the front passenger seat.

He backed the car out of the garage and turned it to face the gate.

Angelo got into the backseat and grinned. "At last, I get to ride in the Beemer. Damn, it smells good in here," he said, as he strapped on his seatbelt and dropped his knapsack on the floor between his legs. He rested his rifle on his lap.

Moments later, Aramis joined them. He got into the car and stated, "Okay. I'm ready. Yo, this car is freaking awesome!"

The other three laughed.

Once more, they went out with the intention of returning to the Orange County Department of Public Works to bring back new work vehicles and the fuel drums they required to trade with Alex's group. Grant hoped David's group was having as much luck as them.

Charles felt saddened, as he watched the BMW leave the compound, from the watchtower. He hoped no harm would come to it, or to his friends, of course. He felt some comfort knowing that Grant was a good driver. He knew he could trust him with his new Beemer.

Either way, it quickly became apparent to him that they were going to require another vehicle, which could be used for supply runs that seated about four people comfortably.

MAN'S END

Chapter Fourteen

DAVID, ROBERTO, AND Kirk had a good start to their day. They were fortunate enough to find a fuel tanker truck, as soon as they exited the interstate. Of course, it took a little bit of cleaning up, before it could be started, but they finally moved on.

Their next stop was a nearby pharmacy, where they found plenty of medicine and other supplies. It was a fairly quick stop that only took several minutes. They were supposed to check on a Lowe's Home Improvement store on the opposite side of the interstate, but it was agreed that could wait for the next supply run. Much like Grant's group, they decided not to push their luck by driving around for too long with the fuel truck. It was too valuable.

While on the interstate heading south, David could not believe his eyes. He slowed down and pulled over to the side of the road. Kirk was following in the fuel truck. He stopped behind the van curious as to why David pulled over.

Roberto was also curious. He turned to David and wondered what was wrong, so he asked, "What's up, bro? Why are we stopping? Pee break?"

"Look," David said simply, while facing the field to the right.

Roberto turned to see what he was looking at and his eyes filled with excitement. "Holy shit! Is that a cow? Wait, should I have said 'holy cow,' instead?"

"Yep," David chuckled. "You know what that means?"

"Hell yeah! Real milk for my coffee! No more of that powdered crap!"

"Exactly. All we have to do is get it."

Roberto screwed up his face and asked, "How the hell are we supposed to pull that off?"

"I have no idea."

Kirk had gotten out of the truck and walked over to the driver's side. He knocked on David's window. When David opened it, Kirk said, "Hey, check it out. There's a cow out there."

"We know! That's why we stopped, dummy."

They stared at the cow and thought about how they could go about getting it into the back of the van. That alone would be an incredible feat. Trying to get the cow to go along without any rope or experience in wrangling steer was another thing entirely. The one thing that motivated them was the fact that they had not had any real milk in over a month.

Roberto got out of the van and said, "The longer we wait, the more likely she's bound to get too far out of reach."

"Wait!" David called after him. "We need to be careful not to scare it."

"Her," Roberto corrected him. "She's a her."

Kirk scoffed, "At least, we hope it's a her. So, what's the plan on getting ole Betsy? Do we go over and ask nicely if she wants to come with us, so we can squeeze her boobs for milk, once a week?"

David smirked, "Yeah, something like that."

Roberto shook his head and got out of the van, feeling amused. David got out, too, and the three of them stepped over the guardrail. They walked slowly toward the cow, which was about twenty yards into the field and grazing on grass without a care in the world.

David realized how much space she had to move, if she chose to run. "Spread out, boys. Maybe we can lure her back toward the van."

Kirk asked, "Uh, exactly how are we going to get her to step over the guardrail?"

David stopped. He hadn't thought about that. There was a road ahead, though. He had an idea. "Don't scare her," he said. "I'm going to get the van to that road over there." He pointed. "We can lead her to it, but not until I get the van in place."

"What about the fuel truck?" Kirk asked.

"That can wait, until we have her in the van."

Roberto said, "No, both of you go and drive to the road. I'll keep an eye on her."

David asked, "Are you sure?"

"Yes. Trust me. It's better if you stay together. I got this. My sister had a lot of pets, while growing up. I know how to deal with animals."

Kirk scoffed and asked, while holding back his laughter, "Did she ever have a freaking cow?"

"No, just dogs, but same shit. They both have four legs and know fear. It's all in how you talk to them that matters. She needs to know I'm not a threat."

Kirk shook his head and chuckled, "Okay, but if she runs away, it's on you."

David hesitated. "I don't know about this. We can't lose that cow."

"Don't worry, bro. We won't." Roberto urged him, "Just hurry."

David and Kirk rushed back to the vehicles and made u-turns on the interstate. There was no time to go all the way to the next exit, so they could take the northbound side. Besides, with no traffic on the road, it really did not matter. They got back to Florida and stopped at Route 94 on the overpass.

David got out of the van and looked over the interstate, facing south. He was able to see pretty far to the south, but he could not see a road along the right side that would take them to the field.

Kirk waited in the driver's seat of the fuel truck and reminded him, "Don't forget there's another overpass, further out, before that field. Maybe the road crosses over the interstate, from one side to the other, and then goes past the field."

"That's right! I forgot about that!" David got back into the van and sped off going east with Kirk not far behind. They turned right at Brookside Avenue, which was also Route 17M. David remembered that 17M crossed Museum Village Road on the other side of the interstate in Monroe. That had to be the road on the other side of the field. They would be able to take that road back home, after getting the cow.

He was right. They soon crossed over the interstate on the overpass. Route 17M then veered left and ran parallel to the interstate. It was also in that area, where Roberto and the cow were waiting.

David and Kirk were both in awe, when they saw Roberto gently rubbing his hand down the cow's face. The cow did not seem to mind. In fact, she liked it. She was even eating grass from his hands.

"You've got to be kidding me," Kirk smirked to himself. He then began chuckling.

Roberto yanked a handful of grass from the ground and gradually led the cow toward the van. David got out and opened the rear doors, and then waited patiently with a grin on his face. Roberto was able to coerce the cow into following him toward the van. Getting it to go into the van was going to be trickier, since the cow could not physically step up into the rear.

He immediately noticed the problem and said, "We're going to need a ramp for Betsy. I don't think she can climb up that high. Either that or she doesn't want to."

David looked down at the height of the van's rear and groaned, "Shit. I didn't think of that." He looked around for a quick and easy solution. There was a farm just down the road. It was probably where she came from, he thought. He hoped there would be some heavy flat pieces of wood that could be used as a ramp. He turned to them and said, "I'll be right back." He then ran over to the farm to search, while the other guys watched over the cow and both vehicles.

Kirk casually exited the truck and tried not to startle the cow. He walked closer to Roberto and expressed his amazement. "I don't know how you did it, but I'm truly impressed."

Roberto gave Betsy some more grass and said, "Feeding her is one thing. She might not like me so much when we yank on her tits for milk."

"That won't bother her. She's a farm girl. They like that sort of thing."

Both men laughed softly, as not to scare the cow.

Sometime later, David returned lugging a large plank of plywood. He also had a rope in his hands. Kirk went over to help him and they carried the plywood to the van together.

Roberto looked at it and noticed how thin it was. Feeling concerned, he asked, "Will that hold her weight?"

"It better!" David cried out. He tossed the rope to Roberto and said, "Since you two are buddies, why don't you wrap that around her neck? It will be easier to pull her and guide her into the van." He then placed the plywood on the ground and rested it against the rear of the van.

Roberto stared at the rope dumbfounded and tried to figure out how to tie it into a lasso. It was harder than he thought.

Kirk offered him a helping hand and said, "Give it to me. I can tie it into an adjustable noose for her." It only took him a minute, before he was finished and handed the rope back to Roberto. "It's all yours, Rob. Do your thing."

"Thanks, bro. Nice work." Roberto gently placed the rope around Betsy's neck and tightened it just enough, so that it wouldn't slip off her head. "Easy girl. That wasn't so bad, huh? That's a good girl." He rubbed her neck softly, as he spoke to her, to keep her relaxed.

David said, "Let's try to get her inside, so we can head back."

Roberto grabbed some more grass and tugged on the rope gently to goad her into moving forward. He pulled the rope toward the rear of the van and stepped inside.

Betsy followed, but stopped at the ramp. She looked upward and mooed.

Kirk positioned himself a little to her rear, while also being off to the side. He figured he could give her a little shove, while Roberto pulled her forward.

"Yah!" Kirk slapped her on the behind and prodded her gently.

Roberto pulled on the rope and she stepped forward up the makeshift ramp and into the van. Just as she stepped off the plywood, it cracked.

David pushed it off and closed the rear doors. "It served its purpose. Let's go," he told Kirk, who nodded and got into the fuel truck.

Roberto sat in the front passenger side seat and held onto the rope. Betsy shifted around nervously in the back of the van, but she had nowhere to go.

David sat in the driver's seat and they traveled south along Route 17M. He drove slowly, so Betsy would not react badly to the movement. She already seemed quite nervous. He did not want to agitate her any further.

Several minutes later, they arrived at the compound. David unlocked the gate and drove inside. Once the fuel truck was in, he closed the gate. It was a tight fit maneuvering the long tractor-trailer truck into the driveway from the small road, but Kirk managed it. He only knocked over one tree. Needless to say, they were taken aback when they saw the orange industrial fuel truck parked next to The Intrepid.

Kirk parked next to it, stepped out, and commented, "Do you believe that?"

Roberto laughed heartily and replied, "Hey, we can never have too much fuel! At least, now we can give a truck to those other people, instead of hunting for barrels to fill."

Edie approached and said, "Welcome back, boys. It looks like this is our lucky day."

David asked, "Did Grant's group come back with this truck?"

"Yep, right before they went back out to pick up a couple of flatbed trucks and the barrels of fuel for that other group."

"What? They went back out for more?"

She nodded, "Yep. They hit the jackpot at some public works facility. Grant said they found building materials, too, for the wall."

Kirk smiled and responded, "That's great news. Things are looking up."

While David and Kirk spoke to Edie, Roberto went to the shed and returned with a cinderblock. He placed it in front of the side doors of the van and went to get another two. He set them up one by one like steps outside of the van to help Betsy out. Once the blocks were in place, he opened the door and led her out by the rope. She hesitated to step down and mooed. He tugged on her rope, while Kirk honked the horn of the van. At that point, she eagerly stepped down and moved away from the van.

Edie exclaimed, "Holy crap! Is that a cow? How the heck did you find a cow?"

David smiled and explained, "It was grazing on a field beside the highway. Rob was able to get it into the van. It looks like milk is back on the menu."

Edie was so excited she clapped. "That is awesome! Wait until I tell Millie!"

Roberto felt a moment of pride, as he escorted Betsy to the side of the house. He tied her rope to the porch and stated, "She's going to need a barn."

Kirk replied, "Daniel will like the idea of having a new project. I'll let him know. He'll appreciate the distraction. We can also put the chickens in there."

David commented, "We're going to need a lot more wood to build a barn."

"Yes, indeed," Kirk agreed. "I guess we'll make the barn, before we get started on the wall. The wall will take a lot longer to complete."

Roberto responded, "I think we can work on both at the same time. One will be cement blocks and the other will be made from wood and since we're low in both, it depends on whatever we have available, at the time. As we find building supplies, we can work on whichever is easier."

Charles called down from the watchtower, "Hey, how in the world did you manage to get a cow in the van?"

David pointed to Roberto, "It was him. The man's a pro."

"That's fantastic! Nice job!"

Just then, the BMW pulled up to the gate with two large orange flatbed trucks behind it. Both trucks were filled with supplies. One had fifteen fuel drums, while the second had large pieces of metal, several buckets of cement, and a bunch of cinderblocks hidden away under a sturdy industrial tarp, which was the same one Alex gave them.

David opened the gate for them and they entered. It was getting pretty crowded with all the large trucks. They were going to have to clear some grass and establish a parking area. One more project to keep them busy.

When Grant saw the other larger fuel truck, he said, "I see today was a good day for supplies. We got the fuel for that other group and two fuel trucks for us. We're going to be set with gas for a long time."

David replied, "It sure looks that way. So, what's under the tarp? A Lamborghini?"

"I wish. It's just a few bags of cement, about three dozen cinderblocks, several metal pipes, and some heavy duty sheet metal to use around the compound."

"Oh, that's all? We found a cow," he bragged ever so casually.

Everyone in Grant's group turned to David in surprise. As if on cue, Betsy let out a moo. They all looked in her direction.

Liz smiled in amazement. She knew having a cow meant they could go back to drinking real milk, again. The thought pleased her greatly. She was also a coffee lover and liked milk with her coffee.

Kirk said, "I think today calls for a celebration."

Grant tilted his head and responded, "Or we could unload these trucks and go back out for another load. There's an entire warehouse full of supplies, ripe for the picking."

Kirk shrugged indifferently, "I can't argue with that. We're going to need a lot of building materials."

David suggested, "We never got a chance to go to Lowe's either. We could hit up both spots and fill up both flatbeds." He looked at his watch. "It's only 3:45 pm. If we hurry, we can be back in time for dinner."

"Let's do this," Grant said. "All right, guys! Help us unload these flatbeds. We're going back out on one more run. The faster we can unload, the faster we can get there, load up, and come home."

Liz said, "I'll go find Daniel, so he can help. He's going to love all of this new stuff."

Kirk replied, "Oh, good. Thanks. I really want him to see this."

David noticed Aramis was rather quiet, considering he had just gone on his first supply run. It seemed odd, considering how much he had been bugging them to let him join them, at least one time. He approached him and asked, "What's wrong, Aramis?"

Aramis shook his head and replied, "I feel depressed. I was so eager to go out there and help out that I never stopped to think about what I'd see. It's like a ghost town. The people are all gone. Nature is starting to take over because everything's abandoned. It's depressing to think that so many people had to give up their homes and businesses because of this damned virus, which hasn't even reached that area, yet. It's such a waste."

"Welcome to the new world, pal," David patted him on the back.

Over the next half hour, they all pitched in and unloaded one of the flatbed trucks. Daniel was indeed excited to see everything they brought back. It was a great haul collectively. They decided to leave the fuel drums on the second flatbed, so they would be ready for delivery on the next day.

While they worked, Kirk commented, "This would be a lot easier with a forklift."

Grant replied, "Well, then. You can do the honors and drive one back from where we're going because there just so happens to be one there."

Kirk grinned, "It will be my pleasure."

Later that day, they went back out as one group, using the van and the flatbed to retrieve more building supplies. This time, Aramis opted to remain at the compound. So, did Liz. Instead, Grant, David, Kirk, Roberto, Angelo, and Charles went back out to the Orange County Department of Public Works, and then to the Lowes Home Improvement Store. It was the only time Charles, Grant, David, and Roberto left the compound at the same time. Together, they loaded up the flatbed and filled it with enough supplies to keep them busy for days. They wouldn't even need to unload it, right away, since the second truck would be empty, once they delivered the fuel and it could be used for the next supply run. The best part was they no longer needed everything on the list and they had a forklift! They also had enough lumber to build a barn for their growing family of livestock.

Sometime after dinner, Grant and Liz went outside for their shift of guard duty. Grant did ground patrol, while Liz went up to the watchtower. Charles, Daniel, and Kirk went down to the basement to go over future construction plans with Julia. Millie sat in the common room reading a book about farming and Edie sat nearby pretending to read a horror novel.

However, she was really thinking about David and wishing she still had her secret, so that he would show an interest in her like he did before learning the truth about her. These days, he seemed distant. He was still cordial with her, but she missed how he used to look at her.

Millie asked without turning away from her book, "What's on your mind, Edie? I know you're not reading that book. You've been on the same page for a half an hour."

"Huh? Oh. Uh, I was just thinking."

"About David?"

"Yes," she admitted. "I really hate that any chance I had with him has been blown. I regret not going for it when I had a chance."

"He would have eventually found out anyway, and then he would have been mad at you for lying to him."

"It wouldn't have been lying really. I just wasn't going to tell him."

"Did you really think he wouldn't find out??"

"I figured I'd deal with it when it happened. I was hoping that, by then, he'd be so in love with me that he wouldn't care. This is not the same world we lived in before. Things are different. I hoped he would think differently. I hoped our love would be so strong that he would be willing to overlook it. No one else would have known what I was, so it would be okay. That perverted prick, Bobby, ruined everything!" She closed the book and slammed it down beside her."

Millie reminded her, "You had plenty of chances to kiss David, before that happened. You are the one that stopped it from happening. What Bobby did was terrible, but you turned your back on David long before that night."

Edie sighed, "You're right. I had my reasons, though. I didn't want to lead him on. I wanted to be honest with him, but how do you tell a straight guy that you used to be a man? It's not the best conversation starter, before beginning a romance."

Millie felt sympathetic toward her plight. She had no idea what to say to make Edie feel better. The only thing she could do was hope she would get over David, in due time. Deep down, she really hoped things would work out for them, but she knew David was turned off by the whole idea, once he learned the truth. He could not look past what was below Edie's waist. In a way, she couldn't really blame him. It was not what he wanted. She exhaled sadly and continued reading.

Edie sat in her seat quietly contemplating the failed relationship she almost had with him.

Meanwhile, David, Roberto, Kirk, Angelo, and Aramis sat outside in the backyard. They formed a circle around the fire pit. They were very careful to only use the fire pit when it was very dark outside, and it was, considering winter was just around the corner.

Kirk chuckled to himself and said, "I still can't believe we found a cow. How cool is that?"

Roberto answered, while smoking a cigarette, "It's a beautiful thing, bro. I'm looking forward to having some real coffee tomorrow morning. I'd even be willing to wake up early and get the milk myself, as long as Betsy doesn't mind."

David was surprised. "Wow. You're willing to wake up early? That is something."

The other guys laughed quietly. They all knew perfectly well that Roberto was always the last person to wake up each day. He always stayed up late and woke up late.

"It's for a good cause," he said with a crooked smile. "Of course, I'll probably have to set my 'rooster alarm clock' a bit later than what he's used to. That damned bird wakes up too early for my sake. I usually use him to let me know when it's time for bed!"

Everyone laughed.

Aramis commented, "Man, I'm really looking forward to a good cup of coffee. It'll be nice to have something that reminds me of how normal life felt."

David studied him and could tell he was still bothered by how desolate the towns and villages around them have become. It was something David had learned to appreciate. He did not like having to worry about running into someone that he might have to shoot in self-defense. Grant might not have a problem shooting people, but David preferred not having to resort to that sort of thing. The last uninfected people he killed deserved to die for murdering their friends. He probably would have killed Bobby, too, if given the chance, but to go out and have to worry about possibly killing someone every time they went out for supplies disturbed him.

Angelo warmed his hands by the fire and said, "It's going to be a rough winter. It'll be our first winter during the apocalypse. When the snow comes, we're going to suffer, especially being upstate like this. We're lucky to have heaters for the dorms, but it will still be bad."

Roberto responded, "We'll be ready, by then. We can reinforce this whole compound and gather enough supplies so that we won't have to go back out, until the snow melts."

Aramis asked, "Instead of preparing for the winter, wouldn't it be better to go south and set up someplace warmer? We could go far away from the infection."

David answered, "The warmer it is, the more likely we are to run into other survivors. That would be a mistake. The idea is to be isolated from everyone and everything. We're much safer that way."

"I guess that makes sense," Aramis frowned.

Roberto said, "Bro, keep in mind, there are some sick people out there. It's total anarchy. We might not see it, but homes are being looted, people are being murdered, and women are getting raped. No one is out there to stop these things from happening. The cops are in here with us. We're safe, at least, for now. Enjoy it, while you can." He took a long puff of his cigarette.

"That's a really good point," Aramis replied soberly. "Damn. I thought I was depressed before."

Kirk turned to Roberto and commented, "That's interesting what you said, Rob. It doesn't sound to me like you think we can stay safe in here. Remember, we're turning this place into a fortress. We even have armored trucks, now. Once that wall is up, I promise, no one will be able to get in here. If they do, they'll be very sorry."

Roberto agreed, "You said it, brother."

They gave each other a high five. Afterwards, everyone sat quietly and stared into the fire, each with his doubts and fears, but all with the confidence that together they could survive anything.

MAN'S END

Chapter Fifteen

I T WAS AROUND 3:30 am when David woke up in a cold sweat. It was that same nightmare, again. Zombies were overrunning the compound. Everyone was dead and he was trapped up in the watchtower with no way to escape from the hordes of living dead that were trying to reach him from below. This was the third time he had the same nightmare, at least, as far as he could remember. For all he knew, he was having it every night. He had not been sleeping too well.

He closed his eyes and tried to go back to sleep. Someone in the dorm was snoring. It sounded like it might have been Angelo. It was coming from his side of the room. David missed the days when he could sleep alone in a room. Would he ever be able to sleep a normal night's sleep, again? He had no idea. It had been so long, since he slept a good night's sleep.

There was so much on his mind lately. His heart was still a mess because of Edie. He felt betrayed because of the secret she kept from him. Originally, he had been under the impression she was going to tell him she was pregnant. He would have been okay with that. However, when he learned she was once a man, it turned his already insane world upside down. He wasn't gay! There was no way he was going to kiss another man, even if she was calling herself a woman, these days. She still had a penis for Christ's sake! How could he possibly overlook a thing like that? How did she expect him to? It was unfair for her to lead him on and make him think they had a chance. It made him angry, just thinking about it.

On the other hand, he tried to see it from her point of view. She really feels like she is now a woman. She seems to believe it with her heart and soul. Maybe she did not plan to fall for him. He certainly had no intention of falling in love with anyone, while there was a full-blown Zombie Apocalypse underway. As it turned out, he did have feelings for her, in the beginning.

He considered his options briefly and decided. No. Out of the question. He could never do it. *She still has a penis!* That is absolutely unacceptable. No way!

He sighed and turned on his side. He hated whenever his mind raced with thoughts in the middle of the night. All he wanted to do was sleep, but too many thoughts were entering his mind and it was making it difficult to fall asleep, again.

He considered getting out of bed, but that would only leave him feeling drained for the rest of the day. He needed more sleep. Yes, more sleep, he told himself. Sleep. SLEEP!

Okay. That wasn't working. He had to use the bathroom, so he got up and tiptoed out of the dorm. He walked down the hall and went into the bathroom. After he finished his business, he washed his hands and looked into the mirror.

"What are you doing, David?" He asked himself.

What was the real answer? Was he just surviving, day to day? He might have been surviving, but he really wasn't living anymore. He used to have happy moments, whenever he was not working. He asked himself, when was the last truly happy moment in his life? He could not recall.

Well, he was happy, after he escaped Manhattan and when they found the cow.

He went to the common room and sat down on a sofa. He lit a candle and grabbed a random book from the shelf. It was a book about ghosts in New Orleans. He put it back, uninterested.

"Freaking Grant and his weird ass books."

David put his head back and closed his eyes. It was nice and quiet. This was what he needed to sleep, peace and quiet in a room with no one else around. It felt so serene. A moment later, he began to feel drowsy.

All of a sudden, he heard what sounded like an explosion in the distance. His eyes shot open and he popped right up. He wondered where it came from and how far away it could have been. Was it the other group from the Village Hall? What were those idiots doing? Maybe it was something else. He needed to know.

He rushed outside and went straight to the watchtower. He had no idea, who was on guard duty, so he announced himself, "It's David! I'm coming up!"

When he reached the top of the ladder, he was surprised to see Edie in the watchtower.

"David! You scared me," she said. "What are you doing awake? Are you here to relieve me?"

He stammered, "Edie… I uh, I didn't expect you to be up here. I um…" He quickly pulled himself together and said, "I heard something. It sounded like an explosion. Did you hear it?"

"Yes! I did!" She pointed toward downtown Monroe. "It came from that way. I saw a quick flash, too."

"I wonder what it was. It's gotta be that other group hiding out in the Village Hall."

"Hmm. Do you think they could be fighting infected?" She asked.

"Maybe. Have you heard any gunshots?"

"No."

"Then it's probably something else. Who knows what those idiots are up to? We haven't been to town, ever since we found out they were there. We've been going further out for our supplies, mostly to the north. We agreed it was best to avoid them." He noticed the binoculars. "Hey. Pass me those binoculars."

She handed them to him and he looked toward downtown Monroe. There was a faint glow and he could make out smoke. Something was definitely burning.

"Something is on fire," he told her.

"Is it a building?"

"Maybe. It could be a car, too. It's hard to say. There are too many tall trees in the way."

She asked, "What do we do?"

"Nothing," he replied. "There's really nothing we can do, except for hope it doesn't affect us in any way."

He handed the binoculars back to her and suddenly felt awkward. Here they were alone in the watchtower. He never thought that would happen. There was a time when he would have liked the idea of being up there alone with her. Now, it terrified him. He did not want her to get the wrong idea and try to kiss him, so he decided it was time to make his exit.

"I, uh, better head back down," he said.

"Oh, okay," she responded, sounding disappointed.

"Goodnight."

She replied sadly, "Goodnight, David."

He climbed down the ladder and went down the stairs, and then walked back toward the house.

MOO!

He was startled at the sound because he had forgotten there was a cow tied to the front porch. He turned to Betsy and groaned, "Oh, shut up and stop taking sides."

She tried to pull herself free from the rope that held her in place. It was agreed not to allow her to roam free, until they collected their first batch of milk in the morning. David wondered if Roberto would follow through on his promise to milk her early in the morning. He would pay to see that, although he had his doubts. Roberto was definitely not a morning person.

Edie looked down and watched him walk into the house. There was so much she wanted to say to him, but what was the point? She no longer stood a snowball's chance in hell of being with him. It made her depressed. She suddenly felt so alone.

"Stop it, Edie," she told herself. "You're better than this. No man is worth your tears."

She turned around and picked up the binoculars. She looked toward downtown Monroe and decided to see if there were any new developments. She wished she knew what was going on over there. Perhaps, it was time for her to start going on supply runs. She felt ready, or was it just curiosity?

Whatever the case, she managed to get David off her mind, for a while.

David had already gone back into the house. He figured he would try his bed in the dorm, again, although he had no idea how he was going to sleep, after what just happened. He wanted to tell someone about it, but what would that accomplish? Everyone would begin to worry. No, it was going to have to wait until morning. It was for the best. There did not appear to be an immediate threat.

As if spending time alone with Edie wasn't already enough to distract his mind, the explosion and fire were quickly moving to the top of the list. What had exploded? What was burning? He honestly hoped it was the Village Hall. It would be easier than having to deal with that group in the long run.

The next morning, after breakfast, a meeting was called in the common room. Most of the group was in attendance with exception to Aramis and Angelo, who both had guard duty. Even Julia was at the meeting.

David spoke and informed them of the explosion. "It looked like it came from downtown Monroe. It didn't look too large, but there was something burning."

Roberto asked, "What do you think it could have been?"

"I was hoping it was the Village Hall, but I doubt it. I have a feeling those people had some action last night. It could mean there are more infected in town, although I did not hear any gunshots."

Grant reminded him, "Gunshots only attract more infected. They probably realize that, too. Maybe they were using blades and blunt instruments."

"True. I didn't think of that."

Charles stated, "Whatever happened, we need to consider how it might affect us. If it was a battle against infected, we need to be ready for them to come this way. If it was the end of the Village Hall, then any survivors from that group will be searching for a new place to live. Either scenario could be a potential threat to our location. They probably know we are around and might try to find us."

Grant responded, "We've been very careful to avoid going through the downtown area. We only use Museum Village Road, when we go out on supply runs."

"Yes," Charles said, "But whenever you train someone with the firearms, you are firing rounds into the woods. They can probably hear the shots."

Grant nodded, "That's probably true, but it has been a few days, since we've done any firearms training."

Edie said, "We don't need to train anymore. We have the basics down. I think we might even be good enough to handle a gun out there, if given the chance."

Charles replied, "It takes a lot more time than what you've had to know what you're doing. Guns are dangerous, especially when used by someone with inexperience."

"Well, Grant can keep teaching us the safety aspects, but we don't need to actually shoot. We've been hitting our targets dead on. Right, Millie?"

"Yep!"

"I can still train them without shooting and focus on weapons safety," Grant agreed. "It will suck, but they have gotten very good at shooting. In time, they might even be ready to go on supply runs."

Millie responded, "Oh, no. That's okay. I don't want to do that. I'd much rather stay here, where it's safe. Besides, someone has to feed our livestock."

However, Edie felt differently. "I would like to go out and help. I think I'm ready."

Charles asked, "Are you sure you'd want to go out there?"

"I can't hide in here forever. I survived Manhattan during the worst days of the outbreak. Going through an abandoned town in upstate New York can't possibly be worst."

Kirk smirked, "She's got a point there, Charles. I say we don't underestimate her. Give her a shot. She may surprise us, assuming she's actually ready."

Roberto suggested, "I can make sure she's ready, if you're willing to do some combat training?" He looked at her.

"Yes, I am," she replied. "Absolutely! I wanna learn how to fight. Please, teach me."

"Okay, you got it. We can begin today, if you want."

"Awesome!"

Roberto looked at Julia and suggested, "You might want to take us up on some of the training we are offering, Julia. There's gonna come a day, when you won't have that cozy computer to sit behind."

She perked up, as if she had just woken up and realized she was somewhere different than where she fell asleep. "Huh? What's that?"

Roberto chuckled.

Charles said, "Julia, it might be a good idea, if you took a more active role in this meeting. You are our eyes and ears of what's happening behind the scenes. Have you learned anything new over the Internet?"

"Oh, uh, no. Not really, at least, not as far as the virus goes. However, there was an earthquake on the West Coast yesterday, an 8.0. It hit San Francisco, causing major damage. It's estimated that hundreds of people died. The state militia had their hands full with rescue operations. Last week, there was a tsunami that tore through southern Japan killing hundreds. Oh, and an American freighter ship was found adrift at sea, off the coast of southern England. Supposedly, there were numerous virus survivors found on board."

"That's interesting. Nothing about the virus in New York?" He asked.

"Only the usual BS about how they are trying to contain it and keep it limited to the East Coast. Some fool talked about building a wall beyond the Rocky Mountains, which is essentially already a wall. I think they've given up on this half of the country."

"Screw them," Roberto said.

Charles frowned and shook his head.

"I'll keep checking," Julia stated, trying to sound reassuring. "As long as the Internet is up, there's always hope." Her eyes met with Grant's and she looked away timidly.

David changed the subject and asked, "Charles, when are we delivering the fuel to that group? I take it we won't be going today?"

"No," Charles replied. "That will happen tomorrow and I'd prefer to take the same group that they already met. I don't want them to know what our numbers are. I also think it would be best for them to see familiar faces when we arrive."

"Good idea," Liz said. "It makes sense. Plus, we already know what to look for when we get there. We saw where they were hiding, so we won't be surprised when they appear. Someone new might react differently and sudden moves can get someone killed."

"Absolutely," Charles nodded.

Daniel asked, "Will you be delivering the ten barrels they asked for or are you giving them one of our two fuel trucks?"

"Only what they asked for," said Charles. "The trucks belong to us."

Roberto asked, "I'm still thinking about the group in town. What are we going to do about them? Should we go see what's going on or are we planning to ignore them and pretend they don't exist, until they come knocking on our door?"

Kirk looked to Charles to see what he'd say. The subject was still bothering him, as well.

While Charles tried to think of an answer, Grant stated, "The other group we met doesn't even want to deal with them. They called them crazy. The girl I ran into said they wanted to turn her into a breeder. Even we've been avoiding them. As far as I'm concerned, they are a danger to our group. We should take them out, before they come after us, like Rob said."

Charles replied, "We can't just attack them and take them out. Remember, they're people."

Grant sighed and responded, "They're dangerous people, Charles, who are way too close to home."

Roberto and Kirk both agreed.

Charles began to feel outnumbered and tried to explain. "Guys, come on. Going after them could bring danger right to our doorstep. It's too risky. I don't like it one bit. We have the advantage, only because they don't know where we are. We can't risk them following us back here. Leaving them alone is our best option. Maybe it's like David said. If they were overrun by infected last night, they could be gone."

"Could be," David responded. "It was only a guess."

Roberto said, "All I'm saying is someone should go check. No cars. Just one person on foot, namely me."

Charles shook his head, "Absolutely not. This is where I have to put my foot down. No one-man missions. This isn't the movies! You're too valuable to the group to risk sending out alone. *Nobody* goes out without back up."

"Then come with me," Roberto replied.

Charles hesitated. He still did not think it was a good idea.

Grant stepped up and said, "Send me with him. We'll go out this evening. We can stick to the trees. We'll dress in black. No one will even know we're there. I have a lot of experience sneaking around in the dark. I used to do it all the time when I was a teenager going through abandoned hospitals. We will not get caught."

Roberto agreed, "Yeah, we'll be back before bedtime. The two of us can move easier on foot in the dark and you know we can take care of ourselves just fine."

Charles hated sending Grant and Roberto out on supply runs at the same time, but this was no supply run and he knew if anyone could scout the town at night unseen, it would be them. Reluctantly, he agreed. It was set. They would leave after dinner.

In the hours that followed, Angelo gave Grant and Roberto a quick lesson on disarming explosives and spotting booby traps, just in case the other group had set up tripwires. Kirk took Roberto's guard shift for him, as they agreed the previous day, which gave him more time to focus on preparing for their night mission.

Aramis decided to make dinner for everyone tonight. He prepared some ziti with tomato sauce. Unfortunately, he had to do without the ground beef or cheese, since they did not have any. While he worked on dinner, Grant decided to step outside for some fresh air.

Kirk was sitting at the edge of the front porch fiddling with a pile of rope.

Out of curiosity, Grant asked, "What's with all the rope? Tying nooses?"

Kirk snickered, "While it may appear I am up to something sinister, Mr. Hamilton, I assure you, it's quite the opposite. I'm finishing up the rope ladder for the watchtower. Dave has been bugging me to get it done. The guy cracks me up. He had a nightmare that he was trapped up there and, ever since, he's been restless about not having an escape ladder. Yet, he keeps volunteering to go up there! It's pretty funny, if you ask me." He chuckled.

"Maybe he's facing his fears or something. It is a good idea to have an escape ladder. A rope ladder seems like the best option. Thanks for taking the time to make one."

"Eh, don't mention it. You know I like to keep busy working. This is how I have my fun," he grinned.

"You are definitely a pretty handy guy to have around. We're lucky to have you with us. Is there anything you can't do?"

"Oh, plenty! For example, I'm terrible when it comes to dancing ballet." He chuckled. "Can you imagine me in a tutu?"

Grant scoffed, "That would be something to see!"

They both laughed.

Kirk became more serious and said, "You guys make sure to be careful out there tonight. I'd love to join you, but I suppose two would be smarter than three. Not to mention, I've never really been good at being the sneaky type."

"Thanks. We got this. Trust me. It'll be a cakewalk for us. We should have no problem sneaking around without anyone seeing us, infected included. I'm bringing the crowbar and Rob is bringing his trusty wrecking bar. He loves that thing."

"Well, it is an awesomely destructive tool."

"Yes, it is. I have no doubt that if anyone, or anything, gets in our way, we'll make short work of them."

"I am inclined to agree. I think from everyone here, you guys seem to be the most capable when it comes to surviving in the apocalypse. You both have a certain ballsy quality about you, which I admire."

Grant chuckled, "I guess so, if that's how you want to put it. I like to think that we have no qualms about doing what has to be done. We won't hesitate to kill someone and we both have a lot of patience, so we can hide and wait for as long as we need to, if it comes down to it. Hopefully, we can be back in time for my beauty sleep." He smiled jokingly.

"See? That's what I mean," Kirk smirked. "Not many here will talk about actually killing people, and then make a joke in the same sentence. I find it funny because you were a cop. You were trained to help people."

"Actually, that was a different sentence," Grant corrected him.

Kirk was amused.

Grant continued, "On a serious note, I did help a lot of people. I believe I was a good cop. I never abused my authority and never had a civilian complaint filed against me.

As a cop you learn to cope with crazy situations. After a while, you build up shields and become numb to the insanity. It's easier for us to shut it down and ignore it, so we can focus on the job we need to get done. The idea of shooting a person is something we are taught as part of our survival. Early on, we know there may or may not come a time, when we have to take police action and fire our weapon. For some, it is the absolute last thing they ever want to do."

He paused and added, "And then there is the small minority like me, who grew up with a different mentality. It's all about survival. Either they kill me or I kill them and I am *not* about to let anyone kill me. I have no problem taking a life, if it means my survival. Before, I had to follow the rules of society, which I had no problem doing, but those days are over. I accepted that fact on the first weekend, after I saw so many of my friends and co-workers die. I won't ever hesitate. Hesitation gets you killed. There's no saving those walking pus bags, so that's not even an issue. As for other survivors, if they are still trying to follow our old ways to a certain extent, like we are, then I say live and let live. However, if they are taking advantage of the weak and forcing people to do things they don't want to do, I say to hell with them. I'd sooner shoot them dead, than risk letting someone becoming a victim."

"I hear you, my friend."

"Good, I hate to think I was talking to myself all this time."

Kirk scoffed and shook his head. "It's good that you've managed to maintain a sense of humor, after everything you've been through. I have a hard time getting Daniel to laugh."

"I learned at a young age that it's important not to go through life with a stick up your ass. Not that he has one. Don't get me wrong. I like Daniel. I'm just saying it's not healthy or wise for anyone to always brood about life's woes."

"Oh, I agree wholeheartedly."

Grant went on, "Life will always try to piss in your cereal, but I never let it get me down for too long. Death is a part of life. It happens. It's sad when it happens to friends and family, but you know it will happen to them, someday. It shouldn't be a surprise to us. We can't break down and lose ourselves every time we're faced with death. The idea is to live life to the fullest, as if it will end soon. Make the best of each moment. Don't waste too much time dwelling on the bullshit. Life is too short."

"Sad, but so true," Kirk agreed, again.

Liz interrupted their conversation, when she stepped out of the house and called them. "Dinner is ready, guys," she said.

Grant looked at her and responded, "Thanks, my dear. We'll be right in."

"Okay, babe," she replied, before going back inside.

Kirk stood up and dangled the rope ladder down in front of him. He said, "I finished it, just in time. What do you think?"

"It looks good. I hope it will be sturdy enough to hold us, if we ever need to use it."

"Yeah, me, too," Kirk replied with uncertainty.

"Hey. Thanks for listening to me ramble on. Sorry about that. Sometimes, I get started on a topic and I really get going."

Kirk chuckled, "It's all good. I enjoyed this talk. It gave me some interesting insight on you. Now, let's get some grub."

He put his arm around Grant and they went inside. The group enjoyed a fine meal. When they were done eating, Grant and Roberto went outside and slipped through the front gate. Grant took a copy of the gate key with him, in case they arrived late. Besides, they were not really expecting anyone to wait around all night by the gate, until they returned.

Of course, Liz was not planning on going to sleep, until that time. She took to the watchtower, as soon as they left, so she could watch over them, during their walk toward Cromwell Hill Road. She used the scope on her rifle to keep an eye on them. Due to their dark attire and the tall trees that blocked part of the view, she lost sight of them almost instantly, much to her dismay.

They were on their own.

MAN'S END

Chapter Sixteen

THE TIME WAS approximately 8 pm, as Grant and Roberto moved swiftly through Cromwell Hill Road heading east. They mostly stuck to the trees whenever possible. The area was largely residential and there were no streetlights, so the darkness hid them well. They were also dressed in black, which helped. None of them said a word. Silence was paramount.

Several minutes later, they reached the point, where their road meets with Quaker Hill Road. It took them a lot longer than they expected. They still had to reach Route 17M, which took them another ten minutes. Walking these roads was tiresome, but they moved fast and remained alert.

They went across Lake Road, past the Dollar General store. After passing the park, the road changed to Lake Street. Milltown Parkway took them south along the Monroe Ponds and placed them in a parking lot behind the Village Hall and former Monroe Town Office building. The parking lot had a few scattered cars in it, so crossing it seemed like a bad idea. Someone could be waiting to strike.

Grant pulled out the hand drawn map Charles made, which had been tucked away in his rear pants pocket. He examined it carefully, before folding it and placing it back in his pocket.

Roberto whispered, "Do we cross this parking lot?"

"Too risky. There's too much open space for my taste. The map is not very specific for this area, but the Village Hall should be on that next street, which means we are behind it. We should go around to the next corner south from here, where the movie theater is located, and take that street across."

Roberto nodded and they moved out. They continued south past the Monroe Free Library to Smith Field Court, which was a small one-block street. They made a left and stopped, after they reached Stage Road. A line of cars was being used as a wall to block the street going north. Luckily, it provided them with sufficient cover to get a better look. They stepped out onto the street and moved stealthily behind the cars.

Grant became quite interested when he noticed a police station up the street from them. He wondered if they might find weapons and ammunition inside. Of course, there was a huge possibility that the group hiding out in the Village Hall already raided the building and was still utilizing it.

Roberto pointed out, "Look at that two-story building with the columns in the middle of the block on the right. I think I saw movement in the second floor window at the corner."

Grant realized he was referring to the police station. He became convinced the group at the Village Hall was definitely using the police station for their own needs. It certainly would make sense. Suddenly, he began to wonder if there were any other buildings they could be using around them. As far as he knew, they might have been in the heart of the group's survival zone. He became a little worried and realized they needed to tread more carefully.

"I suddenly feel like a roach in a roach motel. We need better cover than this."

He moved west off the street and hid behind some bushes near a small shop at the northwest corner of Smith Field Court and Stage Road. Roberto moved quietly with him. Together, they peeked up the street from the corner and tried to assess the situation.

"It's a safe bet they're using multiple structures on this block," Grant whispered.

"Agreed. We know there's no way they're not using that police station. That would have been the first place I went, if I were on this street. They might be using these houses, too, for all we know." He pointed to the houses across the street. "They have good vantage points for gunners."

"We might be in over our head here," Grant replied. "Who knows how many people could be in their group? It could be a lot more than ours. Definitely more than the two of us."

"What about the explosion from last night? Where do you think it took place? I haven't seen anything that looks like it exploded and nothing that has been burned."

Grant agreed, "Yeah, everything seems fine, as far as buildings and vehicles go. I wonder what could have exploded. Whatever it was should have some fire damage on it and it should still smell like smoke. I haven't smelled any smoke, which means we are not even close."

"Me neither." Roberto sniffed, again, to make sure.

"We need to get a higher vantage point, so we could see this street better." He looked up and noticed the roof eave of the shop, where they were hiding was just above them by a few feet. "I think we can reach this. Give me a boost up to this roof. I want to take a quick look from up there."

Roberto studied his body frame briefly and said, "I think you might be heavier than me. Maybe you should give me a boost and I'll check. Besides, I'm younger and more agile."

"Okay, fine. Rub it in, why don't you?"

Roberto chuckled, as Grant gave him a boost and pushed him up to the small roof's ledge. Roberto pulled himself onto it and crawled toward the edge. He studied each building on the street, as far as he could see. To his left, he noticed a room with a light on the top floor of the Village Hall, which faced Stage Road. The light kept flickering, as if it were candlelight. He watched the window for a few minutes, but did not see anyone moving within. There was no visible activity in the other buildings.

Finally, he climbed back down.

Grant commented, "You sure took your time up there. Did you see anything interesting?"

"As a matter of fact, I did. There's a candlelit room on the top floor of the Village Hall. I waited to see if someone would appear in the window, but there was no one."

"You didn't need to see anyone. The fact that a room is being lit by candlelight is enough for us to know there are still other people here. Let's start heading back. We can resume checking for burned out structures on the way home."

Sometime later, they were walking westbound on Lake Street, which cut right through Crane Park. Everything was dark around them and the road was only lit by the moonlight.

Roberto tapped Grant on his shoulder. "Hold up. I heard something coming from the park."

They both looked around them into the shadows and could hear footsteps on the grass approaching from the north side of the road. Their eyes moved in that direction and they noticed a dark figure stumbling clumsily toward them.

"Shit," Roberto exclaimed. "It looks like a zombie. Either that or a drunk crippled mute."

"Probably a zombie. We can't leave it around. Let's take it out."

Roberto nodded in agreement and held out his wrecking bar.

The zombie continued moving toward them, staggering drunkenly, and as it grew closer, so did its horrendous stench. Its legs dragged over the ground slowly, held down by the added weight of undigested food, which had forcibly seeped through its overstuffed stomach.

Grant got a good whiff and complained, "Damn. He's a ripe one. Let's go take him out on the grass or we'll be here waiting all night."

"Tell me about it."

They walked toward the zombie flanking it on two sides. It reached out for Grant, since he was slightly closer and better lit by the moonlight.

Roberto approached it from behind and swung his wrecking bar, hitting it in the back of the head with full force. The zombie flew forward and dropped to the ground. It convulsed for a few seconds, before remaining still.

"It's a homerun," joked Grant, "and the crowd goes wild!"

Roberto chuckled, and then noticed another body on the ground, not far from them. "Hey, look over there," he pointed. "Someone's lying on the grass near the flagpole."

They walked toward the body and noticed it was another dead one. It also smelled pretty odorous. They figured the other group must have killed it.

"Whew!" Grant covered his nose and mouth with his gloved hand. "He smells worse than his buddy."

Roberto frowned, sounding worried, "This is two more than I've ever seen in this town. Plus, there were the two you killed when you were with Angelo and Bobby. More are gonna come. I feel it. I don't like it. It's too close to home. This is really bad."

"Yeah. Let's go home, before we run into another one."

They looked around them, as they walked back toward Cromwell Hill Road. It was a long walk. They kept thinking they'd run into another zombie or maybe one of the faster infected ones. With every turn they made and every shadowy area they passed, they were on edge. They found themselves walking faster.

As soon as they turned onto Quaker Hill Road, they heard something coming through the wooded area behind them on High Street, which intersected with Quaker Hill Road. They both turned around to see what it was and were relieved to see a deer peering across at them.

Roberto cursed it for startling them. "Damn stupid deer almost gave me a heart attack."

Grant replied angrily, "I'm kind of tempted to shoot his sneaky ass, but that would be too noisy."

Roberto said, "I'll be glad when we get back to the house. I think I'll make myself a nice cup of black coffee. Interested? Oh, never mind. I forgot. You don't like coffee."

"No, I do not. Thanks, though."

"You don't know what you're missing, bro. It's good stuff. It'll put hair on your ass," Roberto chuckled.

Grant scoffed, "I can do without that. Thank you. Let's not get complacent. Pay attention to our surroundings. We're not home, yet."

Roberto sighed, "You're right. My stomach was getting ahead of me."

They reached Cromwell Hill Road a few minutes later and had to turn right.

"This is it," Grant called after Roberto, who kept walking straight.

"Shit. I was ready to go right past it. How can you even tell in the dark?"

"I have a photographic memory and I'm pretty damn good with directions. I only need to go somewhere once and I will always remember how to get back there."

"That's a useful skill to have when you're sneaking around in the dark," Roberto said.

"Yes, indeed. I spent a lot of my teenage years sneaking around in the dark, back when I used to explore abandoned psychiatric centers on Long Island."

"Now, that sounds like fun. I would've loved to explore abandoned hospitals as a teenager."

"Oh, it was. It was very educational, too. You'd be surprised what you learn going through those old buildings. We used to go to the Kings Park Psychiatric Center, Pilgrim Psychiatric Center, Central Islip, Creedmoor, and another hospital in Nassau County. Sometimes, my friends and I would find patient files, old medical books, and even old clothing hanging on hangers in closets."

"No shit? That's crazy, bro. Hey, did you ever run into a former patient?"

"Never," Grant shook his head. "We mainly ran into other urban explorers, security on unlucky days, and a strange assortment of animals and insects."

"Did you ever get busted?"

"Nope. I was always good at avoiding trouble. Plus, I was a fast runner."

"Were you the type of cop, who used to chase down robbers and shit?"

"In the beginning, I used to love the idea of running after the bad guys, but then I got wise, after I fell and hurt myself. Afterwards, I used to chase down perps in my patrol car, instead, and wait for them to get tired. Why should I overexert myself unnecessarily? Whenever possible, I liked to box them in and hit them with the door to knock them down."

Roberto laughed, "I would have paid to see that."

Grant grinned proudly, "I only got to do it once or twice, but it was funny."

They continued walking silently for the rest of the way, until they finally reached the gate of their compound.

When Liz heard someone at the front gate, she pointed her rifle downward and used the scope to see who was there. She was extremely glad to see it was only Grant and Roberto. They were back, at last. They both appeared to be safe and unharmed.

Charles had been sitting on an outdoor chair on the porch waiting for them to return. When he saw the gate open, he stood up and waited to greet them. He felt incredibly relieved to have them home. He was also eager to hear what they learned.

Grant and Roberto walked toward the house, once the gate was locked. They looked exhausted from their long walk.

Charles asked, "Well, what did you learn? Did you find the source of the explosion?"

Grant shook his head and replied, "We didn't see or smell anything with fire damage, but we learned the group at the Village Hall may be larger than we think. At least, they are spread out over the whole block. It looks like they are also using the police station, which could mean they have cops, too. A wall of cars is blocking off Stage Road on both sides of the block."

"We also found two zombies in the park," Roberto added. "One had already been taken out. The other was trying to stalk us, but I bashed its head in."

"*Its?*"

Grant replied, "Those things aren't people, Charles. We prefer not to think of them as 'him' or 'her' because it makes it a lot easier to kill them."

"All right. I can see your point. So, two more of them, huh? That's bad." He rubbed his chin.

Roberto nodded, "Yep." He lit up a cigarette and began smoking. He stepped away from them, so the smoke would not bother them or Betsy, who was tied nearby.

Grant asked Charles, "Do we still plan on heading south to meet with that other group in the morning?"

Charles nodded, "We really need those other supplies. I don't want to wait too long. I'd like to get this trade done, so we can move past it already. There's a lot of work to be done around here. Plus, I'm eager to see if these guys can become allies. It will be good to have allies in a time like this. It looks like they have a lot to offer us. I just hope they don't try to screw us over."

"They'd better not. What time should we be ready, so I can let Liz know?"

"It doesn't have to be too early. Wake up whenever you want. You should get some rest, after tonight's operation. I know you did a lot of walking. We'll go sometime after breakfast, once everyone is ready. The truck is already loaded and ready to go. Kirk will drive that. Angelo and I will ride with him. You and Liz can follow us in the BMW. I want us to have something fast that we can all fit into, just in case things go sour, as well as something big that can smash into things."

"10-4."

Charles was bothered that they could not locate the source of the explosion. He thought about it and wondered what could have blown up. Maybe they were looking in the wrong place. Before Grant turned to go inside, he asked him, "Hey, did you check the gas station on 17M? Is it still standing?"

"I thought about that, too. I caught a glimpse of it, as we walked along Lake Street, on our way back from the Village Hall. It looked fine, so I didn't see any point in going for a closer look. There was no smell of smoke anywhere along our route. The smell should still be very strong in the air, if there was a fire last night. I figured maybe it was further out, beyond Monroe. One of those other groups probably ran into trouble, while out on a supply run."

"True indeed. I never thought about that."

"All Rob and I smelled was death. Those two zombies were funky. Hopefully, we don't see more, anytime soon."

"Yeah," Charles replied nonchalantly, as if he were not really paying attention anymore. He seemed to be deep in thought. "Hmm. I wonder," he muttered half to himself.

"What's up?" Grant asked.

"What if the fire was much further south, past Monroe, like you said?"

Grant eyed him curiously. "Do you think it came from the shopping center, where Alex's group lives?"

"It's possible. They're really not that far away from us. I think if they had an explosion, we'd be able to see it at night and possibly hear it. What if they had trouble last night? We could be heading into danger."

"I don't know, guys," Roberto said, while still smoking his cigarette. "For David to hear an explosion, while in the house, coming from all the way down there would have to mean it was pretty damned big. Isn't that shopping center a few miles south from here."

Charles considered it and said, "Yes, it is."

Roberto disagreed, "I think the explosion occurred somewhere closer. Grant and I just weren't looking in the right place."

Charles replied, "Hmm. I guess we'll find out in the morning."

"Yeah, I guess so," Grant responded, sounding worried.

MAN'S END

Chapter Seventeen

KIRK ENTERED INTERSTATE 86, heading south shortly after noon. He drove the flatbed truck at a steady speed of about 30 miles per hour. There was no need to go faster, especially while hauling ten fuel drums. Angelo sat quietly beside him with his bag of explosives at his feet and his MK 18 Mod 0 on his lap. Charles was riding shotgun. His eyes darted in every direction, as he searched for any signs of danger.

Grant and Liz followed at a safe distance in the BMW. Grant did not want to get too close, in case the truck had to stop short. Plus, he wanted a wider range of vision ahead of him. Liz kept her Colt M4 Carbine ready.

It was not long before they came to an unscheduled stop. Someone had deliberately left a line of burnt cars across the roadway on both the south and northbound sides, just past the overpass for Bakertown Road, which was only about a mile before their exit. In addition, the police station on the northbound side had been burned to the ground. The smell of smoke was still prevalent in the air. It appeared they had discovered the location of the mysterious explosion.

Kirk commented, "This was definitely done on purpose. Do you think it's their way of telling us not to bother coming back?"

Angelo looked to Charles for an answer.

Charles had not considered that option. He responded, "I hope not. If they didn't want us to return, all they had to do was say so. It wouldn't have been a problem. I think this might have been the group from the Village Hall. They already made enemies with Alex's group. This could be a way of preventing his group from utilizing the interstate or interacting with us."

"That's what I think," said Angelo. "I believe this is their way of stopping us from forming an alliance with them."

"Could be," Kirk agreed.

Behind them, Grant and Liz waited impatiently. They were on their guard, once they noticed the line of burned cars blocking the road. They immediately expected an ambush. Liz aimed her rifle at the overpass, which they still had not gone under.

Without taking his eyes off the road, Grant asked her, "Do you see anyone up there or anything else out of the ordinary?"

"No," she replied. "It looks clear. Maybe they got tired of waiting, if they were ever waiting, at all."

"Check the road ahead. See if you can spot anything beyond the burned cars."

She nodded and pointed her rifle straight ahead. She looked through the scope and scanned the road, gradually moving from left to right. She paused when she thought she saw someone moving.

"Anything?"

"Maybe," she replied. "I thought I saw something move."

Meanwhile, in the truck ahead, Kirk was looking at the burned cars in front of him. He turned to Charles and said, "I can easily push our way through with this truck. Just say the word."

Charles nodded, "Do it."

As soon as Kirk used the truck to push an opening between two of the burned cars, Angelo spotted a figure walking along the road beyond the cars.

"Look! We've got company," he said. "It looks like one of the slow reanimated ones."

Kirk noticed it was only one and suggested, "I can run him down, too, if you want."

"No," Charles said. "The blood is contagious. We don't need it splattered across the front of this truck. Just go around it."

"Around it? Are you sure? Shouldn't we kill it?"

"It's an unnecessary risk. What if one of us gets bitten? What if there are more nearby? Let's just get where we're going."

Kirk raised his eyebrows disapprovingly and replied, "Okay. If you say so." He drove the truck around the zombie, who turned instinctively to follow them.

When the BMW reached him, there was no question about what needed to be done. Grant stopped the car and Liz said, "I got this." Before she could aim her rifle, Grant stopped her.

"No! No gunshots. I'll use the crowbar." He got out of the car and grabbed the crowbar from the trunk. He walked over to the zombie, which was now moving toward him. He drove the sharp end of the crowbar into its face and yanked it out slowly. The zombie fell to the ground.

Before returning to the car, Grant wiped the crowbar clean on the zombie's clothing.

In a matter of seconds, they were moving, again.

Kirk noticed what they were doing in his side view mirror, so he slowed down and waited for them. Charles also noticed and rolled his eyes in frustration. He was hoping Grant wouldn't stop to kill the zombie, but he should have known better. Kirk smiled, as he looked in the mirror, because it was what he would have done, too.

The group reached the shopping center, shortly afterward. What they saw shocked them. There were small fires all around. Black smoke had already long since turned white, as the fires were starting to burn out. Dozens of zombies roamed around aimlessly. The shopping center had fallen to the dead.

Kirk uttered, "Holy shit. They were overrun."

"Damn," exclaimed Angelo. "That is a bitch. It looks pretty bad. Not to mention, having this many so close to home is definitely not good for us."

Kirk replied, "Oh, I agree. We need to kill as many as possible. We can't leave these meat sacks roaming around to cause havoc up our way. They've got to go."

Charles did not disagree. He was too busy wondering if they were too late to save lives. His eyes searched desperately for any sign of survivors, and then he saw someone waving at them. It was Woody with his rifle and he was back on the roof of the Chili's restaurant.

"There! It's that guy Woody!"

Kirk and Angelo looked ahead and saw him waving frantically. Kirk waved back, so that he knew they spotted him. It worked. Woody sat back down and waited.

"Should I drive closer and pick him up? We can probably drive right under, so he can jump down onto the truck."

Charles responded, "We'd have to get past their barricade, first. That might not be so easy. We can drive as close as possible. He'll have to come down and get to us on foot. Go get him. Angelo and I will get out here. We have a lot of killing to do and we'll have to use our knives. If we shoot any of them, we'll risk bringing them all down upon us."

Kirk and Angelo nodded. Charles and Angelo jumped out of the truck, while Kirk drove forward to pick up Woody.

Grant pulled up next to Charles with his window down and commented, "This is some crazy shit, huh? What now?"

"We do it your way. We kill them all, but no shooting."

"Hell no," Grant agreed. He turned to Liz and suggested, "Why don't you see if you can get on top of the tractor-trailer, where Alex was that day. Keep an eye on the car and watch our backs. I'm going with them. If you need to shoot to save us, then don't hesitate. Otherwise, don't shoot anything."

She nodded and he opened his door to get out of the car.

"Wait!" She reached over and kissed him on the lips. "Please, be careful, Grant."

He looked into her eyes and said, "Thanks. I will. I promise. You be careful, too."

"Okay. Promise."

They both got out of the car and followed Charles and Angelo through the garbage truck and into the shopping center parking lot.

Liz climbed onto the hood of the garbage truck and was able to reach the ladder on the rear door of the tractor-trailer. She watched

Grant and the others move through the parking lot. For a moment, she felt sick to her stomach, but wasn't sure why. Her nerves were bothering her like never before. She'd provided cover fire for them in the past, but this felt different. It was going to be hard to hold back from shooting, but there was more to it that bothered her. She tried to ignore her feelings and climbed up to the roof of the truck. She got down low on her stomach, so she would not be noticed and pointed her rifle into the large parking lot below. Her eyes immediately locked onto Grant. Her palms became sweaty and she was overcome with fear. She bit her lip in frustration. What if something happened to him?

She realized that's what felt so different. Now that they were a couple, she was worried about his safety. She dreaded the thought of him getting infected or dying. It had only been about two months, since they became a couple, but it made dealing with this reality so much easier. He even made her laugh, but it was more than that. She genuinely cared about him. He had become her whole world. She wished she had told him how she felt, before he left. She realized she loved him. She wondered if he would have said it back or would he joke about it? She hoped she would get a second chance to find out.

Charles, Grant, and Angelo tried to stick together, as they fought their way through the crowd of undead. At first, it wasn't so bad. They were killing one after another. However, there was far more than they could handle. It began to look like they were in over their heads.

Liz hesitated with her finger on the trigger. She knew Grant would not want her to hesitate. He thought hesitation could get someone killed. She could not hesitate, especially not when it came to saving his life. Before she knew it, she fired her rifle. A zombie went down behind Grant. He looked toward her and waved his thanks. She smiled and fired, again. Another one went down next to Charles.

Someone else fired a rifle and took down another zombie.

Liz looked around and noticed Woody was still perched on his rooftop nearby. He waved at her and she looked back into the lot. For a second, her heart skipped a beat. She did not see Grant! Where was he? She became frantic and started shooting zombies that looked like they were focused on moving toward his general direction.

Several zombies took notice of her and moved toward the truck. In time, a small crowd of hungry zombies gathered below her. They reached up pointlessly for someone they could not reach. She paid them no mind. As long as they could not get to her, they were not a problem to worry about.

Grant had gotten separated from Charles and Angelo. He searched for them, but there were too many zombies in the way and they were coming for him. He turned and ran, heading for the nearest shelter, which was the Walmart Supercenter. The doors had been partially barricaded, but they were forced open. The glass was broken on a few doors and blood was smeared across the floor inside. He promptly realized this was not the best place to run into, but it was too late to turn around. The zombies were following him inside!

Outside, Charles and Angelo ran through the parking lot in search of Grant. Somehow, they had been separated in the chaos.

Charles called out, "Grant!" Several zombies, whose attentions were now focused on making him their next meal, answered his call. "Shit." He tried to dodge them, stabbing them in the head, whenever possible.

Angelo shoved his dagger into their heads, as well. He tried to stay close to Charles. He knew it was best for them to stick together. They stood little chance of surviving on their own. His thoughts drifted to Grant. He hoped he was okay.

Grant was busy running through the aisles of Walmart. He dodged and weaved around zombies, while trying to find a good vantage point, where he could make a stand and hopefully take out enough to make his escape. He shot any that got too close, which probably was not his best idea. The zombies were able to hone in on his location easier with every shot he fired. The fact that he kept moving is the only thing that saved him from being trapped and mauled.

The zombies almost got him once, but he climbed over some display shelves and threw large heavy items down upon his relentless pursuers. Unfortunately, his aggressive actions did not dissuade them from going after him. There were too many, so he had to keep moving.

Grant found himself in an aisle stocked with tires. There were many sizes. He grabbed one of the biggest tires he could lift and rolled it across the aisle at the nearest zombie, who was knocked over by it like a bowling pin. He grabbed another tire and rolled it in the same direction, since there were more zombies coming from that side. The tire went into the same zombie, before rolling around and finally falling flat. A different zombie walked right into it, tripped, and fell. Grant kept rolling out tires at them, until he had a mess of tires on either side. He only shot at the easy targets. He could not afford to miss.

The zombies were having a hard time getting past the tires. It gave Grant the opportunity he needed to make his move. He stepped closer and began taking them out with his crowbar, one by one.

Meanwhile, Charles and Angelo were still running around the parking lot. Dozens of zombies chased them around, as fast as their rotting legs would permit. It was not fast enough to be an immediate danger, so long as Charles and Angelo did not allow themselves to become surrounded.

Woody and Liz were still providing cover fire for them. Both had crowds of zombies around their locations, which made it difficult for Kirk to reach Woody with the truck. He had to park it and start killing as many as he could. He used his fire hydrant wrench and swung hard. He killed many, but it seemed with every one he killed, two more came. He soon realized he needed to retreat and ran back to the truck.

He got inside and moved it away from the area. He tried to draw away some of the zombies in the process by honking his horn, which was pretty loud. It attracted a lot more of the undead than planned.

From within the Chili's restaurant, a group of faster recently infected people came charging toward the flatbed truck. They had been the real reason why Woody was trapped on the roof. It was members of his former group, and now, they were after Kirk.

He drove the truck around the shopping center, luring a large horde of infected and zombies away from the Walmart and Chili's. They followed the sound of his honking horn and moved toward Best Buy at the far northern end, which gave Charles and Angelo time to catch their breath.

Liz began shooting the zombies around the Chili's restaurant, while Woody shot at the ones at the foot of the tractor-trailer, where she was perched. There were about fifty in total. By using teamwork, they were able to take them all out. However, Woody was now out of ammo.

He lay back on the roof of Chili's and took a moment to rest.

Liz turned her attention back to the parking lot and searched through her scope for Grant. He was nowhere in sight. Her heart was pounding through her chest, as she began to think the worst.

"Grant, where are you, babe? Please, God, don't be dead."

Inside Walmart, Grant stopped to catch his breath, as well. After several minutes of killing hungry zombies, he was able to rest for a few seconds against an empty tire shelf. He wiped his brow and sighed in relief. His arms were aching from lifting the heavy tires, throwing them, and swinging his crowbar. He was absolutely exhausted.

While he rested, he made sure to remain alert and listened for any noises around him. The last thing he needed was to get caught off guard. However, the store was silent. He noticed he did not hear any gunshots outside either and that worried him. He began to wonder about the safety of his friends.

Just outside of the department store, Charles and Angelo walked past a parked car in the parking lot and stopped when they heard someone banging from within the trunk. They both looked at each other in surprise and wondered if it could be Grant or another survivor from Alex's group. Of course, they were prepared to kill, if it turned out to be another zombie, instead.

Charles checked the car door and it was unlocked. He popped open the trunk, while Angelo aimed his weapon, ready to fire at a moment's notice.

When the trunk flew open, a Caucasian man in his early thirties with red hair held up his hands and yelled, "WHOA! DON'T SHOOT ME! I'M STILL ALIVE!"

Charles immediately inquired, "Are you infected? Did you get bitten or scratched?"

"No," the man shook his head. "They didn't touch me." He looked around and noticed countless dead bodies scattered across the parking lot. "Christ! Did you guys kill them all?"

Charles shook his head, "No, but luckily we killed enough to hear you. Otherwise, you'd be stuck in there."

"Thanks. It was the only option I had," he said, while climbing out of the trunk. "They had me surrounded. They attacked us at night and caught us by surprise. My name is Devin. Devin Ross."

"I'm Charles Foster and this is Angelo Williams. Where's Alex?"

Devin shrugged and responded with regret. "I have no idea. I know his brother, Aaron, was attacked by those monsters." A spark of realization appeared on his face and he asked, "Are you the guys that wanted to trade with us?"

"Yes. I'm sorry to say, we arrived too late to help."

"Charles! Angelo! Nice of you guys to watch my back!"

When Charles turned and saw Grant exiting the Walmart, a rush of relieve washed over him. He was ecstatic to see his old friend alive and well. "Grant! Sweet Christmas! We thought you were a goner!"

"Well, I almost was," he replied, while walking toward them. "I was chased down like a boy band at an all girls junior high school!"

Angelo laughed heartily and patted Grant on the back. "It's good to see you alive," he said with a smile.

Grant noticed Devin and asked, "Who's this guy? The last survivor?"

"Apparently," Charles frowned.

"I'm Devin," he responded.

Grant stepped forward. "Hello, Devin. Grant Hamilton, at your service." He bowed. "I'll kill zombies and clear out your local Walmart, but I do not do windows."

Devin smirked.

Angelo shook his head in amusement.

Grant realized there were no zombies standing in the vicinity. He couldn't believe it. He turned to Charles and asked, "Did you guys kill all of the zombies out here?"

"No," Charles answered. "Kirk led most of them away with the truck. Your girl and Woody did their part, too."

He looked toward the truck blocking the entrance of the shopping center and saw Liz looking back at him. He waved. Liz was so happy to see him, she was crying, as she waved back. Of course, he could not tell from where he was standing, which was fine by her.

Kirk managed to drive completely around the shopping center and had finally returned to where Liz and Woody waited atop their perched positions. He left the horde of infected and rotten zombies somewhere on Bailey Farm Road behind a Target department store. He figured he and his pals would be long gone, by the time they realized how to get back to the front section of the shopping center.

He called up to the tractor-trailer from the driver's seat, "Liz! What's the situation?"

She looked down at him and gave him the thumbs up signal.

He exhaled with relief and drove forward to check on Woody. He saw Woody sitting at the edge of the roof rubbing his shaggy brown beard.

"Hey, buddy. Need a ride?"

Woody grinned and said, "I'd love one. Gimme a moment to get downstairs." He stood up and walked off toward the rear of the roof, so he could get back into the building. A few minutes later, Woody emerged at the main entrance of Chili's with a bloody rifle.

Kirk did not recall him holding a bloody knife, when he saw him on the roof. Feeling worried, he asked, "Did you run into trouble in there?"

"Yeah, but nothing I couldn't handle," Woody answered proudly. He began limping toward the truck and explained, "There was still one inside waiting for me. He almost got me, too, but when he tried to bite me, his teeth fell out! Ha, ha! He never broke my skin, but I broke his head with my rifle!"

Kirk swallowed nervously and asked, "Did he bite you on the leg?"

"Nope. He tried to bite me. His teeth was so rotten, they fell right out."

Kirk stepped out of the truck and held his hand up stopping Woody from coming any closer. He stated, "This is very important. Answer honestly because if I find out you're lying to me, I swear I will twist your head off with my bare hands and shove it up your ass."

The threatening remark caught Woody off guard and he froze in place, unsure what to do.

"Did his saliva make contact with your bare skin, at any time, when he tried to bite you?"

Woody explained desperately, "No! I told you his teeth fell out!"

"Forget about his damned teeth!" Kirk shouted angrily. "I'm talking about his saliva! Did he slobber all over you? Where exactly did he try to bite you?"

Woody pointed to his shoulder and shouted, "Here! He tried to bite me here! What the heck is the big deal about his spit being on me? People spit at me before and it never killed me!"

"The infection is passed through bodily fluids, not only bites," Kirk explained more calmly.

A look of terror came over Woody, as his eyes and mouth gaped open. He became frantic and shouted, "Oh, shit! Oh, shit! Oh, shit!" He dropped his rifle and tore off his shirt. When he noticed more blood on his pants, he pulled them off, too. He stood there hopping around in his underwear and socks.

Liz was watching and could not help, but laugh. However, she stopped when she noticed Woody had a prosthetic left leg from the knee down.

Kirk also felt the urge to laugh, but refrained, especially when he noticed the prosthetic leg. He tried not to stare and figured he would not even mention it, unless Woody brought it up, first. He watched him hop around awkwardly and understood the fear of being infected. He did not wish it on anyone. He had heard enough stories from David, who saw too many friends go through the transformation.

"Don't worry," he said. "I think you'll be fine. Hey, I'm sorry I threatened to twist your head off. I was caught up in the moment. We'll get you some clothes, before we go."

Woody looked at him pathetically and stopped hopping around. He realized how silly he must have looked and said, "Thank you, mister." He then explained, "I didn't know their spit could infect me. We always thought it was the bites that was dangerous. That explains how it spread so fast the other night. My people was infecting themselves without even knowing it."

"That sucks. Ignorance is usually part of the problem. I wish I had some clothing I could give to you."

"I'm not ignorant," he mumbled. "And I don't care about being part *nekkid*. Back when I was in college, I used to streak across the campus one time every semester."

Kirk chuckled and responded, "Well, if it's all the same to you, I'd prefer it if you refrained from getting nude and streaking."

"Okay. I won't. That won't be a problem," he shook his head negatively. "It was only when I was in college, one time every semester." He repeated. He then reached down and tried to wipe the blood from his rifle, using his discarded clothing, as best as he could. Afterwards, he wandered off toward the parking lot in his underwear, as if he did not have a worry in the world.

Kirk was curious where he was going and wanted to follow, but did not want to leave the truck alone. Instead, he got back inside and kept an eye out for the horde. Woody baffled him.

Liz also watched Woody curiously, as he strolled carefree through the parking lot barely clothed. He walked to a nearby car and opened it. He reached inside and pulled out a duffle bag. Inside were spare clothes, which he proceeded to put on. He pulled his pants over his sneakers and struggled to pull them up. He then put on a plain white t-shirt and a flannel shirt over it. The last thing was his Yankees baseball cap.

Charles, Grant, Angelo, and Devin walked toward him, just as he was done getting dressed.

"Devin!" Woody called out with a huge grin on his face. "You're alive!"

Devin shook his hand and said, "Thanks to you. You did a phenomenal job of killing those things the other night. It's great to see you made it, too."

Woody chuckled, "Phenomenal?" He then looked around and asked, "Are we the last ones?"

"Yeah, I think so," Devin stated grimly.

Charles asked Woody, "Did you see what happened to Alex?"

"He was torn apart. His body is in Chili's and in the parking lot next to it. He's also a little on the grass and..."

Devin stopped him. "We get the point, Woody. Details are not necessary."

"Oh, sorry. I liked Alex. He was always good to me. That's why I liked him."

"We all liked him," said Devin. "He was a good person."

Charles glanced at Grant, who was looking back at him. They were both thinking the same thing. There was something up with Woody. Angelo was also eyeing him curiously. He showed signs of autism.

Liz called down to them, "If we're going to collect our supplies, we might want to hurry it up! I can see some zombies in the next parking lot over, past the Walmart! We don't have much time, before they realize where we are and come back!"

Grant called back, "Stay down and make sure they don't spot you! Stay up there and act as our eyes, while we load the truck!" He turned to Devin and said, "We might need another vehicle to carry the supplies. You're coming with us, right?"

He had not thought about it, until now. He realized there was nothing left for him there, so he answered, "Yes. Woody and I will both go with you, if you don't mind taking us in."

Charles responded, "We will be glad to have you on the team, but we are still going to need the supplies we came for and if there is another car we can bring, it will be a huge help to us."

Devin answered, "My car, where I was hiding, has no fuel. Woody's car has no fuel either. He can't drive anyway because he doesn't know how. There might be something around here we can take. Let's check later, after we get your supplies. We kept most of our supplies in the Home Depot, since it was basically a warehouse anyway. We should go there, first, and grab as much as we can. There's food, weapons, and ammo. We'll try to get as much of your supplies as possible. Exactly what do you need?"

Charles pulled out his list and handed it to Devin.

"Oh, boy. That's a lot. Well, we have some of this stuff in our own supply cache. Either way, this is going to take time, which is something we don't have much of. We'd better get started."

Devin was able to move one of the cars aside, so Kirk could bring the flatbed truck into the lot. They climbed aboard and he drove the truck to the Home Depot, where they began loading it up.

While the guys loaded up the truck, Woody was distracted. He noticed a familiar black Ford Explorer, which was parked nearby in the lot with the driver's side door wide open. He walked over and noticed the vehicle was still running. There was someone lying on the ground near the driver's side. Woody saw that it was one of his friends, who must have been attacked, while trying to escape.

"Max?"

There was no answer. Woody leaned down and turned the young man over. His eyes were open, but he was clearly dead. His neck and chest had been torn open. He had also been shot between the eyes. Woody figured he must have been infected and was killed.

"Rest in peace, kiddo."

Woody grabbed the keys from the ignition and brought them over to Charles. He explained about the Ford Explorer and told him it belonged to his dead friend.

"I'm very sorry about your friends, all of them. What happened here, today, is a tragic loss," he said with sincerity.

Woody frowned and asked, "We'll go home with you, right?"

"Yes, if that's what you want."

"I will like that very much. I don't like it here anymore. Alex is gone. He was my pal. I liked him. Almost all of my pals are dead and gone, except for Devin. He's still alive."

Devin placed a reassuring hand upon his shoulder and said, "They'll live on in our memories because we'll never forget them."

"Never," Woody repeated. "We'll never forget them."

It took about a half hour, before the truck and Ford Explorer were fully loaded with supplies. The men worked hard and fast to get the job done. Woody helped keep watch, while they worked. They took everything they could carry. There was too much to let go to waste.

Afterwards, Charles drove the Ford Explorer with Devin in the front passenger seat. Grant hitched a ride and jumped into the backseat, until they reached the BMW. Woody got into the truck with Kirk and Angelo.

Liz was already climbing down from the truck when they reached her.

"It's about time," she complained. "That horde was minutes away from making its way to your location. I was getting nervous."

Grant looked at Charles, who remained in his seat, and said, "You know that I hate the idea of leaving them out there. What if they eventually find their way to our compound? We should take out as many as we can, while we have the chance."

"How do you expect us to do that? There's too many of them. They almost overran us before. We might be able to kill a few, before they get too close, but then what?"

Angelo called out from the window of the truck and suggested, "I have my explosives. Maybe we can lead them into a trap."

Grant smiled. "That could work. We can set it between Home Depot and those shops to the right of Walmart. We have enough fuel to sacrifice at least two fuel drums. That can ensure a decent explosion that can hopefully take out a good number of them."

Charles agreed, "Fine. Let's get it done."

Grant walked over to the BMW, where Liz waited. She grabbed him and threw her arms around him. She squeezed him tight. Her actions caught him by surprise, but he hugged her back.

"I thought you were dead," she whispered into his ear. "Back when you were in Walmart."

"So did I, for a moment. It's nice to feel appreciated."

"I love you," she said. She didn't care if he felt the same. She wanted to say the words to him. She needed him to know how she felt.

He pulled away slowly and caressed her cheek. "I love you, too, Elizabeth."

She cringed at the sound of her name, which he knew she hated. However, hearing him say he loved her made it somewhat better. She pouted and said, "I hate that name."

"I know," he smiled and kissed her on the nose. "You and Chuck make it too easy for me."

Kirk called out, "I hate to break up this tender moment, really, but we need to move our behinds and set this trap!"

Grant chuckled and got into the BMW. Liz got into the passenger side and took her place beside him. They were ready to follow.

They headed back to Home Depot and carefully unloaded two of the fuel drums. They turned one onto its side and opened it slightly, allowing fuel to gradually leak out. Next, they pushed a few vehicles into place to add to the explosion. Once they were in place, Angelo set up some of his C4 near the fuel drums and vehicles. For extra effect, he left a couple of sticks of dynamite in places where they were sure to light up and explode, as after effects to the initial explosion, which he would set off using a remote detonator.

"We're all set," he said. "We just need to bring them down from up there," he pointed at the hill, where the other parking lot was located, behind the Home Depot.

Kirk said, "That's the easy part. Just do what I do and get ready to bolt."

Everyone got back into the vehicles, and then Kirk began honking his horn in an annoying fashion. Charles and Grant both followed suit and honked the horns of their cars, too.

The zombie horde began to emerge at the top of the hill, led by the recently infected. There were only a few of them, but they were practically racing to the sound of the car horns with their much slower counterparts in tow. There were way too many of them.

Kirk began to back away from the trap. Charles turned the Ford Explorer around and prepared to drive away, although he continued to honk his horn. Grant positioned his car a safe distance away and pointed it in the direction of the exit, while he honked his horn.

Liz shot the fast infected, before they got too close, since there weren't too many of them to worry about. Once the bulk of the horde was crammed between the buildings, Angelo hit the switch on his detonator.

KA-BOOM!

The first explosion took most of the horde and scattered it into pieces, leaving behind a flaming mess. A few seconds later, there were two additional explosions from the dynamite, which had been placed near the fuel tanks of two vehicles. Shrapnel flew high into the air and a flaming tire went bouncing away from the scene. The trap was a success! Most of the zombies were dead or in pieces. All of them were burning.

It was a shame to blow up so many useful department stores, but they had no intention of returning to the area. They already took what they needed and anything else they could carry. As they drove away, the shopping center was left to burn itself down. All future supply runs would be done further upstate, as they had been doing the past couple of days.

Charles led the way home in the black Ford Explorer with the new guy, Devin, riding shotgun.

Devin looked back at what had been his home for the past few weeks. He could not believe it was gone, along with mostly everyone that was there with him. So many decent people had been slaughtered or transformed into monsters. It saddened him greatly. Was there no hope for mankind, he thought?

Kirk followed them in the flatbed truck with Angelo and Devin's only remaining friend, Woody, riding in the cab, while Grant and Liz took up the rear in the BMW. None of them said a word during the drive home, making it a rather peaceful journey.

Rather than take Interstate 86 and deal with the blocked roadway, Charles led them back through the same route they took the last time they were in the area. He knew the back roads well, since he lived in the area for years. They were able to get back home without having to go anywhere near the interstate or the Village Hall.

MAN'S END

Chapter Eighteen

IT HAD BEEN nearly two weeks since the dreadful incident at the shopping center. The others in the group had welcomed both Devin and Woody into the fold with open arms. It was agreed that any help would be more than welcomed and the guys were willing to do their part to contribute. There were now two others, who could help with guard duty and construction chores, which was convenient since construction had finally begun on a twenty-foot wall that would eventually surround the entire compound. The wall was being erected within the perimeter of the existing chain link fence, leaving a three-foot gap in between to take the place of the moat outside of the fence, which would surely be frozen by winter.

A foundation along Cromwell Road was already being laid down, extending outward from the entrance gate. The same thing was being done on the other side of the entrance gate, extending to the south side of the compound. Those portions were significant sections to complete, while the portions that would later go around the rest of the compound could wait, since wooded areas surrounded those sides.

Daniel supervised the wall construction project, but mostly everyone pitched in and helped out. Millie lacked the physical strength to lift cinderblocks and sacks of cement, so she made herself useful by bringing water and iced tea to the workers. It was her idea to do so and it was greatly appreciated.

Whenever Daniel was not working on the wall, he was setting up lines for the new security cameras that were installed. The cameras only took a day to set up. The wiring was another two days because Daniel was busy with the wall. One of the new cameras was placed atop a temporary wooden pole overlooking the entrance. Once the wall was completed, the camera would be mounted there. A second camera was finally added to the blind spot of the watchtower, which faced south. They added a camera at the rear of the house on the second floor to watch over the backyard and the shooting range. The last camera was installed in the basement, near the staircase to keep an eye on the armory and security hub.

Julia tested each camera, which had been set up along with the previous four cameras on a new wide screen high-definition monitor. The screen was split into eight windows, one for each camera. The monitor was connected to a new improved computer with a faster Internet connection speed, more memory, and a dual graphics card to connect two monitors simultaneously. The old monitor was used for routine computer tasks, such as researching the Internet, updating and maintaining their inventory files, and typing up new supply lists. Each camera seemed to work fine and they even had infrared night vision capabilities, which was mandatory.

Once the cameras were ready to use, Julia was quite pleased. She felt as if she had new toys to play with. She kept rotating them and adjusting the zoom on a few, as she watched the others work on the wall. The increased number of security cameras meant they no longer required two people to conduct guard duty, at all times. They only needed one person to watch the cameras, while someone else either patrolled the grounds or sat up in the watchtower.

Woody, in particular, took to the watchtower almost immediately. He loved high places and was an excellent shot. He had actually won awards for competitive shooting during his youthful years. After his first day of watchtower duty, he complained when his shift was over and requested another one during the same day. At first, Charles hesitated, but he eventually gave in. It helped knowing that Woody was a marksman. He pretty much always carried his Black Hawk Axiom R/F Ruger 10/22 rifle with him.

Charles liked having new guys that were willing to do their part. He hoped it would inspire some of the others to learn new skills and increase their worth to the group. For instance, he thought it would be a good idea for others to learn how to work the cameras. So far, only he, Julia, and Daniel knew how to operate the security system. It required being familiar with the computer and monitor, while knowing how to control the cameras using the keyboard. Most importantly, one had to be alert and committed to the job. They would need to watch several screens at once. Boredom would be a crucial factor to overcome. It was not as exciting as patrolling the grounds, or even sitting in the watchtower and enjoying the view.

Millie enjoyed the idea of doing something different that did not consist of reverting herself to the dark ages, where women only slaved over hot stoves, tended the garden, did laundry, cleaned the house, and fed the animals. She was eager to help in other ways, so she was the first to volunteer. She was excited to learn a new skill and liked the idea of spending more time with Julia, who she believed spent far too much time alone.

Aramis also expressed an interest in learning how to use the security cameras. He figured if he could not go out on supply runs, then why not help out with monitoring the cameras? It was better than being limited to cooking, guard duty, and waiting around for someone to be sick or injured.

Charles thought Millie was truly inspired because she also wanted to learn a few basic medical skills. Her true reason for wanting to learn was so that Aramis would not have to be a prisoner of the compound any longer. She could see how disappointed he was about not being allowed on supply runs and wanted to help him. It was very selfless act on her behalf, which she kept to herself. Whenever they were not learning how to use the security system, Aramis taught her basic first aid skills.

Charles hoped others would step up and want to learn new skills, too.

Edie had already expressed an interest in going on supply runs, but she still was not ready. She knew it. Grant and Roberto had both offered her private lessons to teach her how to fight, while learning tactics and weapon safety. They encouraged her to learn as many skills as she could, so she asked Aramis to teach her first aid, as well. The guys believed she'd be ready for her first supply run fairly soon.

One thing that was certainly going to make supply runs easier, from now on, was having two-way radios. Their new Motorola MU350R weatherproof two-way radios were, without a doubt, among the most necessary additions to their inventory. They had already come in handy, while installing the additional security cameras. Daniel and Julia were able to communicate with each other during the process, which made the installation go more smoothly. The two-way radios would most certainly be a welcomed addition to future supply runs. They had twelve in total from two six-pack sets. The radios had a 35-mile range and each had batteries, which could last approximately twenty-four hours using rechargeable AA batteries.

It was a good thing they also stocked up on batteries of all types.

On September 11, Charles awoke feeling the need to pay special tribute to the NYPD, as a whole. He was one of the few, who still maintained a calendar and kept track of the dates. Today was a special day, he thought. As far as they knew, there were not many former cops left from the once 37,000-40,000 strong police department. In their group, there were only three former members. Sadly, the rest had been killed in that first weekend of the outbreak.

It was no excuse to disregard the anniversary. "Never forget" was the motto and he would never ever forget.

During breakfast, he brought up the subject with the others because he wanted to do something special to honor the memory of those they lost and this seemed like a good occasion for it.

"So, I was thinking," he began. "Do you guys realize what today's date is?"

Daniel scoffed, "Date? Who checks the dates anymore? I don't even know what month it is!"

A few of them laughed.

Grant finished chewing his eggs and responded, "It's September 11th, right?"

A realization came over everyone at the same time. They all knew the significance of the date, especially to those that were there at the World Trade Center during the terrorist attack in 2001.

Charles nodded, "That is correct. I'd like to do something special today. I found my old military flag in the attic. I was hoping we could raise it up on a pole to half-mast."

Aramis was confused and asked, "Um, do you even have a flagpole? I don't remember seeing one, unless I missed it?"

"No, I do not. However, I was hoping Daniel here could change that."

Daniel nodded, "I can definitely do that. It would be nice to see the flag, again. I'll see what I can find outside for Old Glory."

Grant commented, "We have some long metal pipes that we brought back from the public works facility. One of those might work."

"Yeah, I know," replied Daniel. "I was using some of them to protect the cables for the security camera system. They were perfect for electrical wiring."

"Good!" Charles smiled. "It's settled. I'd also like us to hold a brief memorial service, after we raise the flag. I'd like for all of us to be present. I hope that won't be a problem for any of you."

Aramis looked around at the group and answered for them. "I don't think anyone here will have a problem paying tribute to fallen heroes. I lost some friends on that day. I bet we all did."

There were a few murmurs and a lot of nodding.

"Thanks," said Charles. "I really appreciate it."

Just then, David scoffed, "Oh, man! I just thought of something!" Everyone looked at him and he said, "Labor Day came and went and I didn't stress over going to the West Indian Day Parade in Brooklyn! This is the first time, since I became a cop that I didn't even think about it."

Roberto asked, "What's so special about that parade?"

Grant answered, "It is a nightmare for cops to work. People always get shot the night before and there are also shootings during the parade. It's not so much the parade that's the problem. It's the criminal element that goes to the parade to cause trouble and ruin the day for everyone. Otherwise, there's a lot of good food and beautiful women dancing with big booties shaking."

Liz shot him a stern look.

"I'm just saying!" He said defensively.

Everyone laughed.

Charles agreed, "He's right. I hate to say it, but it was a terrible day for a cop to work, even on overtime. We usually referred to that kind of OT as 'Blood Money.' It wasn't worth the trouble, unless you had a nice cushy assignment somewhere behind the scenes. I always took that week as my vacation pick, whenever possible. It's a shame, too. It really could have been a nice day, if not for the morons that screw it up. The food is definitely good and the women... well, Grant said it best."

Kirk replied, "I wouldn't know. I hate parades and try to steer far from them. Too many people in one place usually mean I need to beat someone's ass."

They laughed, again.

Devin asked, "How many of you guys were on the job?"

Charles replied, "Three of us were NYPD. It was Grant, David, and myself. Doc was an EMT for FDNY."

"Doc?"

Aramis replied, "Yeah, that's what he calls me. He claims he does it because he has trouble remembering my first name, but I know he just does it to bother me. It doesn't work because I really don't mind."

Charles chuckled and Aramis pointed at him. "I'm on to you, man!" He laughed.

They finished up their breakfast and went outside together. Charles brought the flag out with him. As Millie and Edie fed the livestock, work began on creating a flagpole and setting it into place. Roberto and Kirk dug out a deep hole near the tool shed for the pipe, while Aramis tied a new rope to it, along with an old plastic pulley from the tool shed. Daniel used a drill to attack the pulley to the pipe. Afterwards, Kirk and David raised the pipe and shoved it deep into the ground. Roberto put the dirt back in place around it and patted it down. Afterwards, Charles proudly affixed the flag to the rope and, in under an hour, they had their very own adjustable flagpole.

Once it was completed, they marveled at their handy work.

Charles stated, "I'd like to thank everyone here. We would not be where we are today, if everyone did not do his or her part to contribute.

Together, we've survived insurmountable odds. We escaped a city of the living dead. We escaped a nuclear blast! We've managed to build this compound up, making it our home, a safe haven.

It's heartbreaking that so many other millions of people had to die. Do they get a memorial? No. Instead, one of the greatest countries in the world falls apart and disintegrates leaving countless others to fend for themselves.

It only makes me realize how insignificant our lives can be to others. That has to change, if the human race is going to survive this experience. We need to make our lives matter. We need to teach what we've learned and pass on our knowledge to others, so that our lives would have made a difference to someone. The human race is being exterminated in this country. Every moment we exist needs to matter. It has to mean something."

Angelo clapped, "Amen, brother. Preach on!"

Charles chuckled and continued, "Those men and women, who lost their lives all those years ago on this day, have certainly left their mark. We remember them. We 'never forget' them. That's what I want for those who died in July of this year. The government failed us in New York City. We needed help and they turned their backs on us and trapped us on an island, so that we could die with the virus, only it didn't turn out that way. We got out and so did the virus, while they sat and did nothing. As they loosened the noose, the virus spread even further. Now, the country is fighting a losing battle. Shit. We're not even a country anymore."

Roberto commented, "That's a damn shame because I really loved this country. It used to mean everything to me to call myself an American. Now, I feel ashamed. We're not really Americans anymore because the country has dissolved. We're just survivors, living from day to day."

Woody asked curiously, "What will happen now that the United States is no more?"

Charles shrugged and replied, "I wish I could tell you, Woody. The truth is I really don't know. It's like every state has become an individual nation. There's no more unity. The union is dead. So many people are dead. Soon, the entire country will be full of the living dead. What's to stop them from going to Canada and Mexico and infecting the rest of the continent?"

"Trump's walls?" Grant joked. "Oh, never mind. They were never built."

Kirk snickered, "Maybe they should have been built! At least, it would have helped stop the infection from spreading further."

Roberto commented, "You laugh, but it's true."

Charles responded, "I don't think anything will be able to stop the infection from spreading, at this point. It's too far gone. Our days are numbered. That's why we need to make the best of them, while we can."

Grant replied, "That's what I try to do, but you keep hindering me, Chuck."

He cringed at the nickname he despised and asked, "How so?"

"Let me kill all the infected that I see without always second guessing me. I know when I can handle a certain situation and I know when I can't. The more we kill, the less we will have to worry about later. If everyone kills every zombie they see, before we know it, there won't be anymore. We humans still have them outnumbered, but we need to fight to keep it that way. This is a war and we are the soldiers."

Roberto cheered, "Yeah, brother! You said it!"

Kirk agreed, "I'm down to declare war on Zs."

Devin agreed, "I think that's a good idea. It's just not always possible."

Charles stated, "That's my argument. We just don't have the numbers or the ammo to fight a war against the undead. I know you're very confident, but sometimes you can be too confident. It worries me. I don't want you to get in over your head. You're like family to me. I can't lose you, too."

Grant smiled, "I love you, too, buddy." He went over and gave Charles a hug.

A few of the others smiled, as they looked on.

Roberto said, "You know? That's pretty much how I feel. I lost most of my real family when that nuke took out New York City. This here, what we have, is the new definition of family, as far as I'm concerned. We've been through some crazy shit together and we've survived it all. Why? It's because we look out for one another. We stick together and watch each other's backs. We are *all* family and I will kill or die to protect you. This is war and we're fighting to win. The enemy is not taking prisoners. Neither should we. Let's kill them all."

Kirk put his arm around him and said, "I'm with Rob, but I'm not going to let him die for anyone. In fact, I won't allow any of you to die, if I can help it. You guys have been more like family to me, than my real family ever was. You have no idea how much that means to me. Thank you for that from the bottom of my heart."

Millie was touched by the moment and wiped a tear from her eyes. Edie noticed and hugged her.

Millie then said, "I'm so glad to have a family like you guys. You've kept me safe from those monsters and from myself. You don't judge me or criticize me. You don't yell at me and belittle me. Instead, you make me feel needed and treat me with respect. Believe it or not, I actually like being here better than I liked being at my old home, despite what's going on out there."

Edie smiled, "Yeah, I love all of you guys. Thanks for always being so good to me, too." She looked at David, in particular. "I don't know where I would be, if I didn't have you guys in my life. You're the best."

David made eye contact with her, but quickly looked away, after feeling awkward.

MOO!

It seemed Betsy wanted to say her piece, too. Everyone laughed.

Over the next two weeks, the compound was quite bustling with activity. Construction continued on the wall. Everyone helped out in shifts. They worked each day from around eight or nine in the morning, until sundown. There were no days off and no holidays. It was a huge project, so every day counted. By the middle of the month, they managed to complete the entire section facing Cromwell Road, which was a major accomplishment. However, with the constant work that was going on, they were going to need more cinderblocks and cement, at some point.

While the guys lifted the heavy blocks to place them, Liz and Edie applied cement. They also added water and mixed the cement to keep it from hardening. Through teamwork, they were able to move fast. The most amazing thing was that no one complained about not having enough breaks or about how hard they were working. They were not even getting paid for their time. It was a labor of love. They wanted to do the job because, ultimately, they knew it meant their protection.

Occasionally, Daniel thought about Bobby. He wished Bobby had not gotten himself killed. He knew he would have been the hardest worker on the line.

Sometimes, he'd take a step back to admire their work. It was coming out good. The wall on both sides of the main gate was just about finished. Once that portion was done, they planned on installing an improved reinforced entrance gate. They already had the materials needed for the job. Daniel designed the new gate himself using a welding torch.

During a break, everyone sat around feeling exhausted. Millie brought out some iced tea and bottles of water for them. She then went back inside.

"Ah!" Daniel enjoyed a cold sip of iced tea. "I wonder how long we'll be able to enjoy cold drinks."

Charles replied, "We have plenty of propane tanks to keep the generator going for years. If that breaks down, we have four more generators to take its place. I think we'll be okay for a good long time."

Aramis added, "From your lips to God's ears!"

Roberto scoffed, "If there were a God, he abandoned this world long ago."

Charles replied, "I don't know about that. We were saved from death, more than once. I think God's been watching over us the whole time. It was time for a big change, but he has plans for us."

"Eh, maybe," Roberto shrugged.

Grant was not religious, so he chose to stay out of this conversation. Instead, he turned to Liz and admired her beauty. Her hair was tied behind her head, but a few curls had escaped and were hanging down the sides of her face. She had bits of cement around her cheeks, forehead, and nose. Yet, somehow, she still looked absolutely gorgeous.

She noticed him staring at her and asked, "What? Do I have something on my face?"

He scoffed, "Oh, yeah! Some hair, bits of cement, and a lot of beauty." He winked and smiled at her.

She blushed and wiped her face with a rag. She leaned over toward him and they kissed.

A while later, Millie came out of the house, again, and asked, "Does anyone else need something to drink?"

Charles looked around and no one said anything. He answered for everyone, "No, thank you. I think we're all good, for now. Stop spoiling us."

She smiled, "Okay. I'm going to check on our garden and the livestock." She went into the garden area, which was not really enclosed by much. A small fence about a foot high was used to keep rodents out. The garden was on the north side of the house fairly close to where Betsy was kept.

She looked at Betsy and shook her head. She figured poor Betsy must have hated being tied to the porch. She was running out of grass to eat, while there was a whole field nearby. The guys still had not gotten around to finishing her barn, although they did start it. For the moment, only a wooden frame stood in the field nearby. They worked on it, whenever time permitted. The wall facing the road had been their main priority. Betsy would have to wait a little bit longer.

Millie petted her neck and said, "Sorry, Betsy. No house for you, yet. Hopefully, it won't get too cold before they finish your barn. Now, if you'll excuse me, I need to check on our veggies."

MOO!

"I know, I know. You wanna devour them. I can't blame you. It's such a tease for them to be this close within your view, but you can't reach them. Lucky for us and not so lucky for you, huh?" She frowned and Betsy looked away from her.

MOO!

"Don't be mad, Betsy. It'll all work out."

Millie turned her attention to the vegetables and she became excited. "Oh, wow!" It seemed many of them were finally starting to grow. She shouted, "We finally have new vegetables!" She began picking them and placing them into her basket. There was a sufficient amount of green onions, sweet peppers, and tomatoes, as well as plenty of oregano. The potatoes were almost ripe, but still needed a few more weeks. Unfortunately, the carrots, garlic, and white bulb onions still needed more than a month's time, before they would be ready.

The others cheered when they heard Millie's announcement. It was truly something to celebrate. It meant new meals could be put on the menu, at long last.

She then went to the small hen house, behind the tool shed. The rooster crowed loudly when he saw her. She threw some grains of rice into the three cages. It was the only meal available to feed them. She wished they had a cornfield, but that would require corn, which they did not have.

"Don't worry," she said to them. "We won't eat you ladies, unless things get really bad. Just keep giving us eight to ten eggs every week and you can each get a new chick, once a month. We can't afford to let you have more. There's not enough food to go around."

There were already four little chicks in the cages with the two fully grown hens. She knew once they were old enough, the rooster would have to do his thing. She hated the idea, since it would be incest. On the other hand, it would give them more opportunities for eggs and maybe even a chicken to eat, once every few months. However, that also bothered her. They already felt too much like pets, although she tried hard not to grow attached to them. The fact that it was mainly her, who fed them, did not help.

One thing she remained adamant about is that she did not dare name them.

MAN'S END

Chapter Nineteen

HALLOWEEN HAD ARRIVED with barely a notice. Only a few missed the holiday and reminisced about old days of trick or treating, eating tons of candy, dressing up in costumes, going to masquerade parties, watching horror movies, telling scary stories, and playing scary pranks on people. It made them miserable that these were things they could no longer enjoy, aside from telling scary stories and playing pranks.

It did not seem appropriate to play pranks on people, while everyone was on edge about potentially being eaten by zombies. That also limited the whole scary story experience, but a good imagination could go a long way. At least, that's what Grant believed.

It was early in the evening when he sat outside with Liz, Angelo, Roberto, Kirk, Daniel, Devin, Woody, Aramis, Edie, Millie, and Julia around the fire pit in the backyard. Charles was in the basement watching the cameras, while David was up in the watchtower. The moon was practically full and shined like a white spotlight in the nighttime sky.

Grant decided to tell a story. The others were eager to listen. They knew he had a love for history, so they figured the story would take place somewhere in the past. They were absolutely correct.

"I'm going to tell you the tale of the Devil of Devil's Den."

Devin grinned because he had once been to Devil's Den in Gettysburg. He had a feeling he was going to enjoy this story.

Grant continued, "For those of you, who are unaware, Devil's Den is a rocky boulder-filled region surrounded by hills in the southern end of Gettysburg, Pennsylvania. Imagine that you are there, except the date is July 2, 1863. It is the second day of the Battle of Gettysburg during the American Civil War. The afternoon air is hot and humid, as the temperature rises into the high nineties. Mosquitoes and flies barely give the men a break, always in their faces, as if the heat wasn't bad enough. Dead bodies from both sides litter the area creating an undeniable odor, which cannot be ignored.

General Lee's forces seem to have the Union Army on the run. It looks bad for the north, but they are not ready to give up, yet. No matter how many times Lee's men attack, the Union Army fights back.

By mid-day, the Union Army was being overrun at Little Round Top, which is a hill in southern Gettysburg that overlooks Devil's Den. The Union troops from Maine fought hard to defend their position, despite the fact that they were running dangerously low in ammunition. It got to the point, where they had to use bayonets to drive back the Confederate troops. It was a ploy that worked.

Meanwhile, below in the rocky valley known as Devil's Den, the battle raged on. Confederate sharpshooters hid behind large boulders and fired relentlessly upon the Union troops in the hills, known as Little Round Top and Big Round Top. It seemed like they were getting it from all sides.

One particular Union soldier named Pete from the New York regiment was hiding behind a large rock near the top of the hill. Whenever he tried to move to the right, he was shot at, so he tried the left side. More musket rounds peppered the hillside near his rock. He was trapped. Someone down at Devil's Den was determined to blow his head off. Poor Pete begged God to let him live through this war.

His pleading wasn't based on a selfish need to survive. It was quite the contrary. His family needed him and the money he was sending home. His young wife, Trudy, was five months pregnant with their first child. He didn't want to leave her in her greatest time of need. He needed to get back home to her. He needed to survive, not only this epic battle, but also the war, which seemed to have no end in sight.

What Pete didn't know was that he was descended from a woman named Sarah, who was accused of witchcraft and hung during the Salem Witch Trials, nearly two hundred years earlier in 1692. Pete was not descended directly through her, but her family blood flowed heavily through his veins.

Before Sarah died, she made a vow to take revenge on her accusers and killers. When she was hung, no one wasted another thought on her idle threats. The rope from the hanging tree gripped tightly around her throat and squeezed, until her neck snapped. She died instantly.

For many years, her angry spirit lingered, as she waited and bided her time. She caused mischief here and there, but she wanted her act of vengeance to count for something. There really was no hurry for her to act, since she literally had eternity to make her move. As far as she was concerned, she could spread out her vengeance over decades or even centuries, if she chose to do so, as long as she was sticking it to the families of those who wronged her.

Of course, her accusers and those responsible for her death eventually died. Who knows if she had a hand in any of those deaths? It was highly probable. Her ghost had become quite devious, so if she did cause a death, she always made it look like it was 'natural causes' or 'accidental.'

Still, her revenge would wait for something bigger. It had to matter more to her.

It just so happened that one of those descendants of her accusers was hiding behind a boulder at Devil's Den taking pot shots with his musket at Union troops in the nearby hills. Johnny Reb was having a grand old time messing with one particular soldier, who was hiding behind a rock.

Sarah did not like the idea that it was someone from her bloodline he was shooting at. She became angry and saw this as her opportunity to have some fun, while doing some good for her bloodline. Maybe she would even finally have her revenge. She mustered up all of her energy and pushed Johnny forward. He struck his head hard on the rock in front of him and missed his shot completely. He became angered by this and furiously searched the area around him. He wondered who dared to push him and where they could have ran off to so fast. He was ready to knock someone out, but there was no one there. After a while, he shrugged it off and figured it was the heat getting to him.

He took aim and saw a clear shot that he couldn't possibly miss. He steadied his breathing and fired, but his weapon was yanked sideways and his shot hit another Confederate in the back.

Again, Johnny looked around in confusion. He could not believe he missed that perfectly easy shot. More importantly, he was livid for having accidentally shot one of his own men. He hoped no one noticed. The last thing he needed was to be marked as a traitor.

Johnny decided to change his position and moved to a different location that was slightly higher on the rocks. This new location actually provided him with a better vantage point, which delighted him.

Across the valley, Pete still wasn't in the clear. He knew he could not remain in that spot any longer. The insects were crawling all over him and biting into his skin. They were eating him alive and he couldn't take anymore. To top it off, the sun was beating down mercilessly on his face. Sweat was pouring down his body and soaking his already filthy uniform. He couldn't even fire back, since he was out of ammo. He decided it was time to make a break for the tree line behind him. He prayed to God that he would make it for the sake of his family.

'For the sake of his family.'

Sarah's ghost could certainly appreciate that. She stood behind Johnny, as he took aim at Pete, who was running uphill toward the trees. Pete dodged and weaved, but Johnny was pretty sure he'd hit his mark, this time. Just then, Johnny felt someone push him so hard that he fell over the rock he was hiding behind. He tumbled forward down the large boulders, until he hit the rocky ground several feet below and snapped his neck. He died instantly.

Rumor has it, there was a photograph taken of his body, as it lay dead on the rocks.

One of Johnny's fellow Confederates watched in horror, when he fell. Not only did he see Johnny get pushed, he saw who pushed him. His hair immediately streaked white from fear. What Sarah did not know was that nearly two centuries of festered anger changed her ghostly appearance into something unspeakably horrifying. The Confederate soldier screamed in terror at the sight of the dark ghostly demon and ran for his life. Some believe the others followed in retreat, at that moment, fleeing from Devil's Den and helping the Union Army with a victory.

Later, when the Confederate soldier told people what he'd seen at Devil's Den, they thought he was crazy. For years, he insisted there was a devil at Devil's Den. However, sometime after the war, he had to stop telling his story, just to avoid being sent to the lunatic asylum.

As for Pete, he survived the war and eventually returned home to his wife, Trudy. When their daughter was born, for some reason, Pete really liked the name Sarah."

When Roberto realized Grant was done with his story, he commented, "Nice. I like it. A story of revenge and justice!"

Liz smiled at Grant and said, "I liked it, too. Thanks, babe."

Julia's smile faded when Liz gave Grant a kiss. She was angry with herself for still believing there was a chance that he would like her in the same way. She knew it was pathetic. Still, there was a dark part of her that secretly hoped Liz would get killed during a supply run, so she could be there to console him. Just thinking that way made her feel terrible, but she could not help herself. The heart wants what the heart wants, she thought, hoping it would justify her feelings.

Kirk said, "That was an interesting story, Grant. I admit, I was expecting you to tell us something much more scarier with zombies and lots of gore and death."

Grant replied, "Don't you think we see enough of that from day to day? I wanted to make you guys think about something else and forget about this reality, at least for one night."

Aramis said, "Well, you did a good job, my friend, because I completely forgot we were living in the Zombie Apocalypse, until you guys just mentioned it. I suddenly feel depressed."

Millie said, "I liked it very much. I was pretending I was watching a movie. Thanks, Grant."

Edie agreed, "Yeah, thank you for that. I enjoyed it, too, even though I'm not crazy about Civil War stories. I do like a nice witch tale, though."

"I liked it!" Woody shouted. "It was cool, really cool! I liked it!"

Devin tapped him on the shoulder and said, "Hey, take it down a notch, Woody. We don't want anyone out there to hear us."

"Oh, sorry. I forgot. It was cool. I liked it."

"We know. It's okay. Just try to remember, from now on." Devin then turned to Grant and said, "That was a pretty wicked story. Thanks. I see you're pretty knowledgeable of the Civil War. I love anything that has to do with that war."

"Thanks," Grant replied. "Yeah, I love that stuff, too. I love history. Wait until I tell you who I'm related to…"

"That was a great story, Grant!" Julia interrupted loudly. She had been longing to compliment him, for quite sometime, without arousing any awkward feelings and this was her chance. "I absolutely loved it! You missed your calling. You should have been a novelist. I would have been your biggest fan." She smiled.

He laughed, "If I had become a novelist, I'd probably be dead, right now!"

Angelo sneered, "For real, man."

Devin was staring at Julia, as if she were crazy. He thought there was no need for her rude outburst. He also found it disgusting how she was obviously kissing up to Grant, while his girlfriend sat nearby. At that moment, Devin decided he did not like Julia.

She scowled when her compliment failed. She felt stupid, which made her angry. It only upset her more when she noticed how Devin was leering at her. She turned and went into the house without saying goodnight to anyone. Ironically, Devin was the only one that noticed her departure. He did not care one bit.

Daniel stood up and made an announcement, "Thank you, Grant, and everyone else. I'm really glad I decided to sit out here with you guys tonight. I didn't think it was possible, but this was a good birthday for me. I feel lucky to be a part of this family."

Millie looked shocked, as she exclaimed, "Oh, my God! Today's your birthday? Why didn't you tell us earlier?"

"It's okay, Mil! Don't worry about it. I wasn't planning to tell anyone, but I had such a nice time talking with you guys that I wanted to thank you for making my birthday better than I thought it could be."

Millie was still in shock. She frowned, "I wish we had known. I would have made you a special meal or something. Maybe I could have tried to make a cake. I think we have everything we need to bake one, even fresh eggs. I know! I'll make you one tomorrow."

"No! Don't go through the trouble! Please! Save it for Thanksgiving. I'd much rather eat a cake on that day, if we still can. Who knows if we'll even be around that long? Then again, I think this place is pretty strong. Once we get the wall up, it'll be a fortress. I guarantee nothing will be able to get in here. You'll see!"

Grant walked over to Daniel and shook his hand, which distracted him from saying anything else. "Happy birthday, Danny. I'm glad I could help make your birthday special. You have been an amazing and invaluable member of this group. I look forward to spending your birthday with you next year."

"Thank you," he smiled. "That would be great." They hugged each other.

At that point, everyone else got up and lined up to wish Daniel a happy birthday. They surrounded him and patted him on the back or on the shoulders. He felt so happy to have so many people that cared enough to wish him happiness. It really was a happy birthday for him.

By early November, the barn to house their livestock was finished. They took apart the old hen house to reuse the wood. The rooster and hens would have a better set up within the new two-story barn. A partition inside would separate them from Betsy, who had room to roam. The chickens really did not need much space, so Betsy had the run of the ground floor. The barn was built without an actual floor, so she could eat all the grass she pleased. The frames of the walls were buried partially into the ground to keep them anchored. The second floor was used for storage and could be accessed through a wood staircase or a ladder. The exterior of the barn was painted red.

It was Grant, who had the idea to paint it red, because it reminded him of the old red barn at the Sherwood House Museum in Yonkers. It was an old Colonial farmhouse from the mid-1700s. He had gone there a few times, back when he was able. He always enjoyed the flea markets and the Annual Candlelight Tour at Christmas time. It felt satisfying to have something that reminded him of when things were normal.

While the livestock got settled into their new home, Millie and Edie were picking potatoes and carrots from the garden. The potatoes and carrots were finally ready. Millie planned to save some potatoes for their Thanksgiving dinner.

From out of the blue, Woody called down from the watchtower and shouted, "Deer! There are deer on the other side of the fence!"

Kirk called up to him, "Not for long, if you keep yelling, buddy! Can you shoot one with your rifle, before they get away? If you can hit one, I'll go get it personally!"

Woody did not reply. Instead, he pointed his Black Hawk Axiom R/F Ruger 10/22 rifle at the deer, while they grazed beyond the fence on the neighbor's property to the north. The grass had grown quite high, so they were having a feast. Woody fired one shot, which echoed across the compound.

CRACK!

The loud gunshot made everyone below cringe. They had forgotten that his rifle did not have a suppressor on it to muffle the sound like Liz's rifle.

"I got one!" Woody shouted excitedly. "I got one!"

Charles rushed over to the foot of the tower and called up to Woody, "That's great, but don't shout so loud, Woody! Remember, we need to be quiet!"

Woody gave him the thumbs up signal like he was taught.

Charles made a mental note to make sure there was always a working two-way radio in the watchtower. In fact, he decided anyone on guard duty should carry one, from now on. Julia, or whoever was watching the monitors, could play the role of the radio operator.

Kirk looked at Charles, who was deep in thought, and said, "I'm sorry, man. I didn't think his rifle would be so freaking loud. I'd better get out there with the pick-up and grab that deer, before something else beats us to it. You wanna come along?"

"Sure. Let's make this fast. Daniel, can you do me a favor and open the gate for us, so we can get out of here quick?"

"Yeah, sure. Go ahead. I got it."

"Thanks. Be ready to open it when we get back. We won't be long."

"Okay."

Kirk and Charles drove out and went onto the neighbor's abandoned property to retrieve the deer. They were able to locate it fast. It was still breathing. They watched it, for a short time, and felt a moment of guilt. It died shortly afterward.

"Load it up," Charles instructed.

They lifted it and placed it into the rear cargo area of the pick-up. Kirk drove them back to the compound and Daniel closed the gate behind them.

When Kirk got out of the pick-up, he said, "Hey, Mil! It looks like meat is back on the menu!"

She called back, "We also have potatoes and carrots! Maybe I'll make us some venison stew tonight."

Kirk and Charles looked at each other happily. Their mouths were watering at the thought of a real meal. They knew they were going to eat well tonight.

MAN'S END

Chapter Twenty

B Y MID-NOVEMBER, THE cinderblock wall was only partially completed along the south side of the compound. A few feet extended across, but then stopped short, before reaching the garage. However, the side facing Cromwell Road was finished. The front security camera had been remounted atop the new twenty-foot tall wall at the entrance overlooking the entrance road. A small mesh metallic platform was added on the east side of the entrance gate at the inside of the wall next to the camera, so guards can look out over the entrance wall and defend it, if necessary. A ladder led up to the platform. A new improved and taller reinforced gate was installed next to it and attached to the wall. It was locked using a heavy deadbolt and the old chain that was used on the former gate with a padlock to secure it.

The new gate had been recovered from someone's home in the neighborhood, but Daniel made several improvements to it using a welding torch and lots of spare metal, making it quite sturdy.

On the week prior to Thanksgiving, it became apparent they were in need of more cinderblocks, cement, a snowplow, salt, more water, and lots of food for the coming winter. A large group headed out initially, against Charles's better judgment. The group would eventually split up, once they loaded up the cinderblocks. One group would return with the building materials, salt, and snowplow, while the other group would stay out and search for food.

Grant and David would lead both groups. This would be the first time they used their two-way radios on a supply run. They brought enough so that each vehicle would have one, which meant there was an extra for the snowplow driver, if they found a snowplow. Charles was monitoring a radio, back at home. Angelo drove one of the flatbed trucks with Grant riding shotgun. Liz stayed home because she was not feeling well. Devin went along to take her place and rode with them. It would be his first supply run, as part of the group. David drove the Ford Explorer, which served as the lead vehicle. Kirk rode shotgun with him. Roberto and Edie sat in the backseat. It would also be Edie's first supply run.

Naturally, she was both excited and nervous to be on a supply run. She looked out of the window, as they drove north on Interstate 86. Every once in a while, she caught David glimpsing into the rearview mirror at her. She smiled at him and he smiled back, which made her very happy.

Kirk and Roberto were talking and comparing ultimate fighting with boxing, but she was not paying much attention to their conversation. She was too focused on the view and on David.

"Where are we going, David?" She asked, while trying to sound innocent and naive.

David answered, "First, we're going to Exit 126. There's a Lowe's in Chester, where we can load up on building materials. After that, we need to make a stop at the Orange County Department of Public Works. It's a little further north, but not far. Once we get there, we'll grab some more building materials and a snowplow, which Kirk will be driving back. That's why he has a radio, too. He'll follow the other guys home, and then the three of us will go find some food and water."

"Cool," she grinned. "So, it's a full day. I like it."

Roberto turned to her and said, "Don't worry. This should be an easy run. We'll keep you safe."

"Oh, I'm not worried. This is great! I like being back out on the road. It's been so long, since I've ridden in a car, without running for my life. I've always liked road trips. That's what this feels like to me. It's fun."

Kirk smiled and was amused at her innocence. "Yeah, you could say that," he said.

David stated, "It's good to have you with us, Edie. I hope that you'll feel comfortable enough to go on other supply runs with us." He eyed her in the rearview mirror and smiled, while he spoke, which made her day.

She smiled back at him. She felt deliriously happy and was high on life. This day was going great for her. David had already smiled at her a few times, since they left. His smile was so warm and friendly. She was on top of the world. As they drove, she found herself staring into the mirror at him a lot. She really loved his eyes and thought they were dreamy. She thought the day could not be anymore perfect.

Behind them, Devin and Grant spoke about the American Revolutionary War. It was a great interest to Devin, who also loved history. He could not believe that Grant was descended from Alexander Hamilton. He found it amazing and was grilling Grant about his upbringing and family history.

Angelo tried to focus on driving, but he listened, as well. Every once in a while, he'd offer his two cents into their conversation. They didn't mind.

When they reached their first destination, they parked near the loading dock. It would be easier to load up the flatbed that way.

Grant picked up his radio to let Charles know they had reached the first destination, as per their agreement. "Breaker, breaker, Baby Bear to Papa Bear. Come in. We've reached the first branch. We're gonna grab some honey. Will let you know when we're ready to move on to the next branch. Over."

Angelo and Devin both looked at him with confused expressions on their faces and he laughed. They stepped out of the truck and walked up to the loading dock.

While they walked, Angelo snickered, "You *is* a crazy fool, my man."

Charles finally responded over the radio, rather awkwardly, "Uh, Papa Bear to Baby Bear. Seek mental help, while you're out there. Over."

This time, Angelo and Devin laughed.

"Laugh it up, boys," Grant said. "One day, you're going to be happy I'm this deranged."

David turned to Grant and asked, "How in the world did you ever pass the NYPD psychological exam?"

"There was a psychological exam?" Grant eyed him curiously.

David smirked, "You've got issues."

Roberto chuckled, "It takes crazy to deal with the bullshit the apocalypse throws your way."

Kirk asked, "Is that what the ridiculous radio chatter was about?"

Grant looked at Kirk and responded, "Hey, it's not my fault Papa Bear needs to get laid. Believe me, he'd be a much happier man."

"I can relate to that. I'd be a lot happier, too, if I got laid," Roberto replied.

The other guys laughed, except David.

"You guys are idiots," He said, and then he reminded them, "Remember, we have a lady present today. Let's try and pretend we are respectful and dignified, at least, for appearances sake."

Grant looked at the other guys and scoffed, "In other words, he wants us to act like we're from another planet."

The other guys laughed and Edie was cracking up along with them.

She snickered, "You boys don't have to put on an act for me. Be yourselves. I'm having a great time. Keep in mind we've been living under the same roof for almost five months. Nothing you guys say will surprise me, unless you tell me that one of you used to be a woman."

Her joke caught them off guard. They were uncertain, if it was safe to laugh, or if she were being sarcastic. The dead silence bothered her more than any stupid remark they might have made.

"Jesus Christ, boys! Lighten up! I was joking! I thought we were having fun!"

They all began laughing. It was still very awkward, but kind of funny.

Once they finished up at Lowe's, they headed up to their next location. Kirk started up the snowplow without having to hotwire it, since Grant still had all the keys to every government truck on the grounds. It was actually a large dump truck with a heavy plow attached to the front. The rear was already loaded with salt, so they did not have to go through the trouble of loading it themselves. Devin got into the snowplow with Kirk, who followed Angelo and Grant in the flatbed. It was time for the group to split up.

Roberto got into the front passenger seat of the Ford Explorer. He offered the seat to Edie, but she preferred to stay in the back, so she could keep watching David through the mirror. It was far more subtle than staring across at him. Of course, that was not the excuse she gave him. She claimed it was more comfortable in the back. Roberto knew better, once he noticed how she stayed behind David, as he drove.

They headed back to Exit 126 and turned right onto Route 94. David drove west toward the towns of Florida and Warwick. They had not gone there for food, yet. He wanted to try someplace new. Route 94 was a long and winding road with not much to see. There were some abandoned homes and lots of farms, but no businesses. They made sure to stop and check for corn. They were able to salvage some.

By the time they reached Florida, Route 94 veered to the left and joined with North Main Street. There were plenty of businesses in the area. They stopped across the way at a small shopping center and decided to check out the restaurant and gas station mini-mart.

The mini-mart was easier to check, since it wasn't closed with a roll down gate. The three of them exited the Ford Explorer and approached the entrance. David led the way. Edie walked closely behind him and Roberto stayed in the rear to watch their backs.

Roberto looked to Edie and warned, "Keep on your toes, Edie. There are a lot of dangers we need to be aware of, while we're out here. There are lots of hungry stray animals, a potential for infected, and then there are other humans, which can be the most deadly of all."

"Okay," she said, as she kept her 9mm pointed downward in front of her like Grant showed her.

David added without looking over his shoulder, "And be very careful not to aim your weapon at any of us."

"Oops! Gotcha." She turned the gun away from his ankles.

After checking the shop, they were disappointed. It had already been stripped clean of mostly everything, so they did not waste too much time in there. They drove closer to the Copper Bottom Restaurant and stopped in front.

Roberto told them, "I'll look inside through the window. Hopefully, this isn't a dead end, too." He got out of the vehicle and peered into the darkened windows. It was hard to tell if there was anything inside worth salvaging.

Suddenly, David called him back to the vehicle. "Rob, get back inside! Hurry up!"

Roberto rushed back and climbed inside. He was ready for a fight. "What happened? Infected?"

"No, I mean, I don't know. I don't think so. I saw someone crossing over down the street," he explained, while backing up into the street and shifting gears. He sped forward heading south on North Main Street in the direction of where he thought he saw someone. "He went this way. At least, I think it was a he." He slowed down to a crawl and instructed, "Keep your eyes peeled. He had short dark hair and was wearing a green camouflage hoody and blue jeans. He looked young."

Roberto and Edie searched out of their windows and studied every building and house they passed. David drove extremely slowly, which gave them time to pay attention to details.

Roberto asked, "Dave, why are we looking for this guy? I thought the plan was to stay away from other people."

"Yeah, I know, but this guy looked like a kid. My conscious won't allow me to leave a kid out here to fend for himself, not with the way things are, now. Soon, it will be winter. If we can help this kid, I'd like to try."

"Okay. I just hope we don't regret it."

David glanced over at him, and then focused on the road. He hoped the same thing.

"There!" Edie pointed. "He's next to that pizza shop! FraNico's!"

David hit the brakes instinctively and Roberto jumped out to run after the kid, who bolted down the side street. Roberto was able to grab him by the hood and yanked him back. The kid fell down. Roberto stood over him, exhaled, and said, "Don't even think about kicking me or I'll break your legs."

The kid lay still on the ground, out of breath. He looked to be in his mid-teens. He seemed healthy, but did not look too happy that he was caught.

David and Edie ran over and also stood over him, but kept a few feet back.

David instructed, "Don't scare him, more than he already is. Kid, we're not here to hurt you. We only want to help. I'm a cop. I mean I used to be. Are you alone out here?"

The kid looked up at David and asked, "Can I stand up?"

"Not, yet," David replied, while holding his hand out. "Answer my questions, first."

The kid propped himself up on his elbows, so his head wouldn't be on the street and he began talking. "I can take care of myself. I don't need your stinking help. Just let me go and pretend you never saw me."

Robert looked down at him and looked over at David. "I like this kid. He's tough."

"That might only get him into more trouble, being out here on his own." David looked back at the kid and said, "What's your name, kid?"

"Stop calling me kid. I'm not a *kid*. A kid is a young goat," he replied with an attitude. "My name is Sam. I'm sixteen years old."

Edie crossed her arms and said, "Not for nothing, Sam, but for your information, a 'kid' is also a young person. It depends on how you use the word."

Sam leered up at her and shot back, "Well, not for nothing, but nobody likes a know-it-all."

Roberto chuckled and held his hand out to help Sam up. "Come on. Get up. You've spent enough time on the ground."

Sam took his hand and Roberto pulled him up. Once he was on his feet, he wiped off his jeans and the back of his hoody.

David said, "We have a place, where you can stay. There's food, water, power, and safety. We even have books, if you like reading, and animals."

Edie commented, "I doubt it. Most kids, these days, can't look up from their cellphones long enough to know what a book looks like. Either that or they're too busy playing video games."

Sam eyed her and replied, "Maybe you haven't noticed, miss, but there hasn't been any power for months. I threw my cellphone away a long time ago and I haven't played a video game, since July. Do you always have a stick up your ass or are you also capable of being nice?"

Roberto tried hard not to laugh, but it was showing.

David smirked, "Okay, let's play nice. This is not helpful. She's very nice, once you get to know her. My name is David, that's Roberto, and she's Edie. We'd like to help you, Sam. It's not safe for you to be out here alone, especially with winter coming."

"Who says I'm alone?" As soon as he said the words, he regretted it. He did not want anyone to know he had family nearby. "I mean, I am alone, but I can take care of myself."

The others weren't fooled.

David asked, "Do you have someone that you're taking care of? Is it an elderly person, a baby? Sam, we have food. We can help you. We can take you in and keep you safe. I know it's hard to believe a stranger, but I really wish you would trust me. We're not going to hurt you. We're good people."

Sam eyed them skeptically. He really wanted to believe them, but he was scared. He had his family to think about. The decision he made could affect them in a positive way or it could be incredibly negative, if they turned out to be bad people.

"How do I know you're good people? You could be lying to me."

Roberto explained, "If we wanted to hurt you, we would have done it a long time ago. When I caught you, I didn't hit you. Did I? I was only trying to stop you from running away. We can't help you, if we can't find you. Like David said, he used to be a cop in New York City. There are more former cops, where we live. We also have an EMT, so if you are protecting someone who is hurt or sick, he can help."

Sam began to let his guard down and no longer felt the urge to runaway. His gut instinct was telling him they were good. He wanted to listen. More importantly, he needed an EMT.

"I'm not alone. My mother is taking care of my little sister. We don't have any more food and we ran out of clean water, so I filled up some water bottles with water from the stream. I think my mom and sister got sick drinking it. I was trying to find food and clean water, but there's nothing left out here."

David said, "Take us to them. We can help. We have water with us in the car."

Edie added, "And I know some first aid. I've been learning."

Sam nodded. He walked back toward North Main Street and they followed. He faced south and said, "They're down this road. It's a long walk."

"We're not walking," Roberto replied. "Get in the backseat."

Sam told David which way to go, as they drove south on North Main Street. They turned right into Country Club Drive, which led them to a private residential area called Cedar Crest. Sam told them to turn left. They started around the complex along the small road, which was littered with speed bumps, so David had to drive slowly. There were two-story houses on both sides of the road. The road was practically shaped like a bean, as it encircled the homes at its central region. Behind them, at the very center was a park, complete with playgrounds, tennis courts, a gazebo, and a swimming pool. At one time, the residents maintained the area nicely, but these days the grass was overgrown, the road was covered in leaves, and stray dogs roamed around in packs, hunting for food.

"It's this house over here on the right." Sam pointed to an off-white colored house that stood, just past a patch of tall grass that engulfed a path, which led to the park behind it.

David stopped in front of the house, although its driveway was empty. Most of the driveways they passed were empty. It appeared the residents had packed up and left for greener pastures that were not in danger of imminent infection.

They exited the vehicle and followed Sam along the path to the rear entrance. There was a short flimsy wooden gate that stood between them and the backyard. Sam opened it and they went into the yard. Next, he pulled the sliding door open and stepped inside. They followed him into the house and found themselves in what looked like the dining room. The table had been turned on its side and was partially blocking the way. Sam shoved it aside and led them down a step into the living room.

"You guys can wait here. I'll go up and let my mom know we have company." Sam went up the stairs to the second floor.

The living room was void of personal effects. There were no paintings or photo frames hanging from the wall. There was an empty space on a table, where a television must have sat. There were only two sofas, a glass coffee table, another table against the wall, and an old piano near the foot of the staircase.

Roberto whispered to David and Edie, "Be ready for anything. I wouldn't put it past this kid to try and trap us." After saying that, Roberto walked over and checked the nearby closet, kitchen, and bathroom. There was a door in the kitchen, which led to the laundry area and garage, beyond that. There was no car within. Instead, it was loaded with boxes. Things were scattered across the floor, as if the owners made a mess trying to find things they would take with them.

When Sam came back downstairs, he was helping his mother walk. She looked very thin and weak, but otherwise attractive. Sam helped her to the sofa, where she sat down.

"Who are you people?" She tried to sound tough, but it was obvious she lacked the strength to do anything, but sit and talk.

"We're here to help," answered David. "I guess you can call us the rescue team."

Edie handed her a bottle of water. "Here. We brought water."

Sam's mother immediately reached for the bottle of water and opened it. She drank a few gulps and forced herself to stop. "Oh, my God! Thank you so much!" She handed the bottle to Sam and said, "Give some to your sister."

He took the bottle and ran upstairs.

His mother eyed their guests curiously and asked, "Why are you really here?"

David replied, "We told you. We're here to help. We can take you someplace safer, where there's more food and water."

Edie added, "We also have showers and medicine."

"Shut up! Are you for real?" She asked.

"Yes," David nodded. "I was a cop with the NYPD. We have a small compound to the south. There are others with us. We have power generators, running water, and we're building a wall. We already have a fence around the property. You and your children will be safe with us. If you need medical attention, we can provide it."

She began crying. She could not believe it. Her prayers had been answered. Someone had come to rescue her family, after weeks of starvation and hiding from hungry dogs. She wiped her tears and looked up at David. "Thank you. You're very kind and so handsome."

Edie wasn't too crazy about that remark, although she knew it was true.

David smiled awkwardly and introduced himself, "My name is David." He introduced the others, as well. "This is Edie and Roberto."

"My name is Joy," she said. "You've already met my son, Sam. My daughter, Glenda, is upstairs. She's very hungry. Do you have any food with you?"

Edie replied, "I brought some protein bars. Here, take one." Joy took it and began unwrapping it. Edie asked, "Is it okay for me to go upstairs, so I can check on Glenda? I have another bar for her."

Joy nodded, "Yes. Thank you." She spoke with her mouth full. "I'm sorry. I'm so hungry."

Roberto waited for her to chew and swallow, before asking, "Is this your home?"

Joy hesitated, and then shook her head guiltily. "We didn't break in. The back door was unlocked. Honest."

"Relax," he said. "You're not in trouble. I was just curious. How long have you guys been staying here?"

She tried to recall. "About two months. I think. I was planning to drive us away, after they issued the order to evacuate, but my car broke down nearby. Sam tried to fix it. He's very handy, but we needed a new part that we couldn't find. We were stranded. We moved from place to place, until Sam found this house. The dogs chased us here! We were lucky it was unlocked. We've been here ever since. For a while, we were okay, but it was scary at night. The dogs howled a lot. They eventually moved on.

We've been sleeping together in the same room. There's a big bed upstairs. The food started to run out about three weeks ago. Sam's been finding whatever he could, but it goes so fast. We got sick, after we drank the water from the stream. It made us vomit a lot. I lost my strength. Glenda's still sick, too. Sam is the only one strong enough to find what we need. He's pretty tough."

"He's a good kid," Roberto replied. "I like him already."

Joy smiled, "He really is. He's been taking care of us."

David said, "Well, now, we're going to take care of the three of you. You're going to be back to your normal self in no time."

Edie and Sam came down with Glenda, who was strong enough to walk downstairs on her own. Edie was holding her hand. She looked frail and appeared to be about five years old. Sam was carrying a duffle bag, which contained all of their worldly belongings.

Edie looked at David and said, "She's sick, but I think she'll be fine, once she gets some real food into her."

David frowned because they still had not found any food and that was the purpose of why they were even in Florida. He did not think it would be wise to move on to Warwick to continue the search. He wanted to get these people home. The supply run could always wait, until tomorrow.

A short while later, they were all in the Ford Explorer and heading back to Interstate 86. It was agreed the food and water would wait for another time. Joy and Glenda needed to be tended to by Aramis.

They took the usual exit for Museum Village Road. David slowed down, as he reached the top of the exit ramp. Suddenly, there was a loud popping sound that came from outside. At once, they heard a hissing noise.

"What the hell was that?" Roberto asked.

David sighed. He already knew what it was and could not believe his luck. He wondered why a simple food and water run could not just go right. He opened his window and looked down. His suspicions were confirmed when he saw the tire. He groaned, "We have a flat tire."

Roberto chuckled, "Oh! Is that all? It sounded like we ran over a giant balloon and popped it." He stepped out of the vehicle and said, "It's nothing we can't fix, bro."

Sam said, "I know how to change a flat."

David replied, "Thanks, Sam, but we got this."

"Shit," Roberto cursed. "I think we have a problem, Dave. One of the tires on my side is flat, too. The rear tire and there are jacks on the ground. This was done on purpose."

"What? Are you kidding me?"

Suddenly, Edie called out from the backseat, "Look! There's a car coming!"

David and Roberto turned around and saw a black and white police vehicle approaching. It was an SUV similar to theirs.

Roberto's face contorted in confusion, as he asked, "What the hell?"

At that moment, Sam shouted something and Roberto was struck on the head from behind, knocking him unconscious. David turned around and saw a man dressed in blue denim, from top to bottom, standing there with a pipe in his hand. He stood over Roberto ready to hit him, again, if he moved.

David reached for his gun, but a gruff voice from behind shouted, "I wouldn't do that, if I were you!" He froze and the voice instructed, "Turn around nice and slow, cowboy." David let go of his gun and did as he was told, but he did not put his hands up, since he was not told to do so.

A middle-aged heavyset man in a police uniform sat in the police SUV, aiming a revolver at him.

David explained, "I'm on the job! NYPD!"

The cop laughed and replied, "There ain't no more *N-Y-P-D*, boy. The only thing you are is at the end of your road." He fired his gun and hit David in the chest knocking him back to the ground.

Edie screamed in terror, "DAVID! NO!" She did not hesitate. She pulled out her gun, reached out the window, and aimed it at the cop. Before he realized, who had shouted, he was dead. Her shot hit him square in the forehead and he died, while sitting in the driver's seat.

Joy and Sam ducked down to protect Glenda.

The man in denim swung his pipe and knocked the gun out of her hand, while also breaking one of her fingers. She screamed in pain, as he opened the car door and yanked her out. He picked up her gun and aimed it at the others.

"Get out! Now!"

Joy, Sam, and Glenda complied and climbed out of the vehicle.

Joy pleaded, "Please, don't hurt my children!"

Edie was waiting for the right moment, so she could try and wrestle the gun from his hand. She tried to remember some moves that Roberto and Grant taught her. She had to be careful, though. Otherwise, she could get Joy and her children killed.

The man in denim aimed the gun at her face and said, "Turn around and start walking to the police truck, Annie Oakley. You're lucky nobody really liked that asshole or I'd kill you myself. Hey!" He yelled at Joy, who jumped because he startled her. "I want *you* to take your little girl and follow, Blondie."

"What? No! Please, don't hurt my children!"

"Shut the hell up or I'll smack you, bitch!"

Sam shouted, "Don't call my mother a bitch, you jackass!"

The man in denim backslapped Sam in the face and knocked him back against the Ford Explorer. Joy shouted and screamed, until the man pointed the gun at Glenda.

"I thought that would shut you up," he said. "Move!" He followed them toward the police truck. He placed handcuffs on Joy and sat her down on the road. He then aimed the gun at Edie. "Turn around and put your hands out or, so help me, I'll shoot this skinny bitch *and* her stupid kid."

Edie did as she was told and a set of handcuffs was placed on her wrists, as well. The man opened the back door of the police vehicle and pushed her inside. He then lifted up Joy and helped her inside. The backseat was caged and meant for prisoners, so they would not be able to reach the driver's seat.

Before he could put Glenda inside, she had disappeared. "What the f...? Where's that stupid kid?"

Just then, Sam fired a shot at him using David's gun and barely missed the man. The driver's side window of the police vehicle shattered into hundreds of pieces around the dead cop, spilling out onto the pavement, since the door was open. The man in denim immediately ducked and shouted, "Holy shit!" He fired back blindly and shoved the dead cop over to the passenger side. He then climbed into the police vehicle and closed the door. The engine was still running, so he shifted it into gear, turned the wheel, and raced away with tires screeching. The vehicle fishtailed and headed south on Route 17M.

Sam's eyes shot open wide and he raced to where the car was only moments earlier, when he realized his little sister had been hiding underneath it all along. Dreadful images of her lying dead on the ground raced through his mind. Please, be all right, he thought. Please, be all right! His voice broke, as he shouted, "GLENDA!" His heart pounded through his chest and his feet skidded, as he slid down to the ground beside her.

She looked up at him with a terrified look in her eyes and asked, "Is the bad man gone, Sammy?" Remarkably, she did not have a scratch on her.

He took her in his arms and answered, "Yes, he's gone!" He held her tight and did not want to let go. Tears rolled down his cheeks because his mother and Edie were also gone.

Roberto moaned, as he tried to stand up.

Sam swallowed nervously and walked Glenda back to the Ford Explorer. He took her around to the driver's side, so that she would not see David lying on the ground in a pool of blood. He sat her in the backseat and said, "Sit here and don't move. Okay?"

She nodded.

He then walked around the rear and stepped on a jack. He yelled, "Ouch! Damn it!" He lifted his foot and checked the bottom of his sneaker. The jack was stuck on the sole of his sneaker. He plucked it out and hurried around to the other side of the vehicle, so he could help Roberto to his feet.

"What the hell hit me?"

"A future dead man," Sam answered coldly. "He has my mom and your friend. He also shot David. They drove off in a police truck."

"He did what???" Roberto tried to shake it off. He looked into the Ford Explorer and only saw Glenda looking back at him. "Oh, no, no, no!" When he looked down on the pavement, he noticed David on the ground with a gunshot wound to his chest. The blood was pouring out of him. Roberto's eyes filled with tears and a swell of rage began to build up within. He squeezed his fists tightly and tried to hold it in. He wanted to scream.

Sam pointed south on Route 17M. "They went that way! We can still get them, if we hurry!"

The sound of Sam's voice seemed distant and unimportant. Roberto already knew who it was that ambushed them and he knew where to find them. There was no need to try and pursue them alone. It would not end well. He looked down at David and dropped to his knees, as Sam stood by impatiently.

Sam understood, though, so he did not complain. He may have been young, but he was not stupid. He had already seen death with his own eyes when his father shot himself. It broke him. This was different, but the pain was the same. Roberto and David were friends. Naturally, David's death was probably hitting Roberto hard. Sam bit his lip and gave him time to say goodbye, as much as it pained him to do so.

"Dave. I'm so sorry, brother. I let you down."

Roberto bowed his head in silence, as he knelt down beside David. Sam stood over him silently and waited eagerly to go after the man, who abducted his mother and Edie.

MAN'S END

Chapter Twenty-One

D AVID'S BODY WAS bleeding out, as he lay on the ground at the top of the exit ramp at Museum Village Road near Interstate 86. Sam stood nearby and narrowed his eyes, as he glared down the road, where the police vehicle fled with his mother and Edie as prisoners of a man dressed in denim clothing. Roberto knelt down over his friend's body and prepared his mind for the killing spree that would soon follow in the name of sweet vengeance.

Suddenly, David coughed and began to move. Roberto and Sam were both surprised. He was still alive!

Roberto shouted, "David! Can you hear me, bro?"

"Ugh," he moaned weakly. "Stop bleeding... apply... pressure..."

"Holy shit! I'm sorry, bro!" Roberto placed his hands over the wound and looked around frantically. "We need to get him back to Aramis! Sam! Help me put him in the car! Sam!"

"Yeah, I'm right here!"

"Grab his legs! We gotta get him back, before he bleeds to death!"

"What about my mom and Edie?"

"I already know who has them! We'll get them back! First, we need to get David to Aramis, so he can save him!"

"Where's Aramis?'

"Not where, who! He's our medic!"

Once David was in the rear cargo area of the vehicle, Roberto opened the driver's door and realized he did not know how to drive. He could damn well try, but it would be a huge chance to take with David bleeding to death in the back, a little kid riding with them, and two flat tires!

"What's wrong?" Sam asked.

"I don't know how to drive, but I'll do my best," he warned.

"Wait! Let me drive! I was taking driving lessons earlier this year, before... before everything! I can do it! Just tell me which way to go!"

Roberto looked at Sam, who looked very eager and confident to prove himself. "Fine, you drive, but no speeding. Take it easy and do it carefully. I'll put pressure on David's wound. Start by making a left here." Roberto put Glenda's seatbelt on and reached over the backseat to apply pressure on David's wound. He was in an awkward position, which made it difficult. At the same time, he had to pay attention to Sam's driving and guide him back to the compound. He had forgotten all about using the two-way radio.

It was an extremely bumpy ride. The flat tires made it very difficult for Sam to control the vehicle. Somehow, they managed to make it back in one piece. The rims of the Ford Explorer were already creating sparks by the time they reached Cromwell Road.

As they turned onto the entrance road, Roberto finally remembered about the two-way radio. He grabbed it from the glove compartment and gave Charles a heads up. "Charles, it's Rob! We got a problem! I need Aramis to meet us at the entrance gate, now! David's been shot!"

Charles' voice came over the radio and replied anxiously, "What? Shit! Okay! Uh, over!"

Roberto dropped the radio, which was now covered in blood, and held both hands down on David's chest. "Don't you die on me, bro! Don't you dare! Edie is counting on us!"

"And so is my mom," Sam added, sounding frustrated.

David moaned weakly, but said nothing.

The gates were opened and Sam forced the Ford Explorer inside. He slammed on the brakes a little too hard and apologized, "Oops! Sorry about that!" He looked back at Roberto and asked, "Is he...?"

"Not, yet. Don't even think it," he responded firmly.

Glenda looked back and forth at Roberto and her brother. She was scared and nervous. She wanted her mother back more than anything. She looked at Sam and said, "I'm scared, Sammy."

"Don't be. No one here is going to hurt you. I promise."

"I want mommy back."

"So do I, Glenda. Don't worry. These nice people are going to help us get mommy back. Don't be afraid. Okay?"

She nodded nervously, "Okay."

Kirk practically ripped open the rear door and froze temporarily, when he saw all the blood on David's chest. He made eye contact with Roberto and barely spat out the words, "Is David...?"

Roberto cried out, "He's still alive! We need to get him to Aramis!"

"Yo! I'm right here!" Aramis came and pushed his way past Kirk. He had his medical bag with him.

Kirk asked, "Do you want me to carry him out of the back?"

"No! He's already lost too much blood! I need to stop the bleeding and stabilize that wound, before we move him anywhere! I need some light in here!"

Roberto pulled out his flashlight and shined it down on David. The light made it appear worse than before. He began to feel sick. The stress was getting to him. Still, he held the light and did not falter.

Aramis worked feverishly on David. Kirk and Roberto helped out anyway they could. Charles stood by and stared in shock. He prayed for David to recover and survive this experience.

Grant and Liz came running over, but there was not much they could do. So, they waited.

Sam took Glenda and walked her away from the car. He did not want her to be there, if David died. He was not really sure where to go. The place was foreign to him. Nobody knew him or his sister. Everybody seemed too busy worrying about David to even notice them.

Millie was looking around and wondering what happened. She was about to ask someone, when she noticed Sam and Glenda walking toward the house. Curious, she approached them and said, "Hi. Who are you two? My name is Mildred, but you can call me Millie."

Glenda looked at her curiously, and then looked away timidly. She chose not to say anything to Millie. Instead, she moved behind Sam and stared down at the dirt.

Sam spoke, "I'm Sam. This is my six-year-old sister, Glenda. She's very shy and very scared. The people that shot David took my mother and Edie. We need to get them back."

Millie felt her heart stop at the sound of Sam's words. "David was shot??? Someone took Edie? Who? How was David?" Her eyes shifted to the Ford Explorer and all the activity that was going on behind it. "Oh, no! No!" Tears filled her eyes. "David..."

Sam realized that she did not know. He quickly explained, "Hey, he's still alive. That guy with the weird name is working on him. The fat cop shot him, but Edie killed him. That's when the man with the blue clothes and ponytail forced her and my mom into the police car and took them away. That jerk almost ran over my sister! I saw which way they went, but Robert said he already knows where they were going."

Millie could not believe her ears. David shot and Edie kidnapped. It was a lot to process. She wondered about the fat cop and police car. Who did he mean? Who could have taken Edie? Just then, she realized if Roberto knew, then it had to be the group from the Village Hall. She felt overwhelmed with worry and rushed over to check on David, forgetting about Sam and Glenda.

Sam rolled his eyes and took Glenda to the porch, where they sat down. He sighed and waited for the chaos to die down, so that someone would pay attention to him and his sister. He just hoped it was not too late to save his mother.

It was decided to strike at nightfall. It was time to put The Intrepid into action. Kirk would drive. He insisted. Charles, Grant, Liz, Roberto, Angelo, and Devin were going along for the ride.

Charles told Devin he did not have to come and that he actually preferred it if he stayed and watched over the compound, since they were leaving it vulnerable. However, Devin had an old bone to pick with the people from the Village Hall.

"Those guys stole supplies from me and flattened the tires on my ride, leaving me stranded. I had to walk all the way home. I owe those bastards. Besides, I like Dave and Edie. This is for them."

"Okay, I understand. Thank you," Charles replied.

Of course, Sam also wanted to go, but everyone thought he was too young.

He insisted, "I'm old enough to fire a gun and drive a car!"

Charles put his foot down. "No! We are not taking a minor into battle and that's final! Wait here and keep an eye on your sister. I promise, we will get your mother back. You have my word."

Sam frowned and pouted for all the good it did him. When he realized what vehicle they were taking, he kept an eye on it and waited for an opportunity. While the others were loading up The Intrepid with weapons, he snuck in through a rear window and ducked down under the farthest backseat.

As The Intrepid rode out into battle, Kirk gripped the wheel tightly. His thoughts were on David, but his heart would be in the battle. He had intentions to do some pretty nasty things tonight. His only regret was that Charles might think less of him, after it was all said and done. Having his respect meant a lot to Kirk. He thought of Charles as a mentor.

Daniel opened and closed the gate to save them time and they were off.

Woody agreed to remain up in the watchtower, while Daniel patrolled the grounds to make sure they were not attacked. Julia watched the cameras, while Aramis looked over David in the common room. He was still in critical condition. Aramis was able to remove the bullet fragment and was doing what he could to keep him stabilized, but it was touch and go, for a while. It did not look good.

Millie agreed to watch over Sam and Glenda, while the others were away. She had Glenda beside her, but could not locate Sam anywhere. She took Glenda by the hand and went down to the basement. They entered the security hub, where Julie sat in front of the computer.

"Hey, Julia. Can you do me a favor?"

"Oh, hi, Mil. Sure, what's up?"

"Can you look around with the cameras and find this little girl's brother. I thought he was in the bathroom, but he's not. I'm supposed to be watching them."

"Uh, okay, but isn't he like sixteen?"

"Yes," Millie replied.

"So, why would you need to baby-sit him? Maybe he's just looking around the grounds or talking to Daniel."

"I'd rather not guess. Can you just find him with the camera?"

"Sure thing. You know, for a twenty-year-old, sometimes you act more like your fifty."

"Oh, be quiet and find Sam." Millie was becoming upset. She was already worried about Sam sneaking off and doing something he shouldn't do. The last thing she needed was to hear smack from someone who hid behind a computer everyday.

They checked all eight cameras and rotated each to their limits. Sam was nowhere to be found. Of course, the cameras could not see within the house, garage, barn, or shed. Millie figured she could check those on her own.

"There you have it," Julia said. "A perfectly good waste of my time."

"Waste of *your* time? Oh, I'm sorry," said Millie with a touch of sarcasm. "Did you have a hot date with your finger and fantasies of Grant, again? I'll just leave you to it, so I can find this kid, before he gets himself killed. Thanks for your help."

Julia turned around in her seat and demanded, "What? How did you?" She scowled, "You got a lot of nerve talking to me like that! Who the hell do you think you are? I should slap you for that!" She then mumbled under her breath, "Skinny bitch."

Millie moved closer and said, "You can try, but you best be sure this 'skinny bitch' will knock you on your geeky little ass! Maybe next time, you might want to be more quiet when you masturbate!"

Julia's confidence faded quickly. Millie was bolder than she gave her credit for. Her expression changed drastically and she turned back around to face the computer screen. "I-I don't have time for this," she uttered. Her voice shook nervously, while she spoke. She really did not wish to fight, especially since Millie and Edie had spent a lot of time training with Grant and Roberto. The odds were not in her favor.

Glenda looked up excitedly at Millie and asked, as innocently as can be, "Are you really going to knock her on her geeky little ass?" She giggled at the thought of it.

Julia turned around and was appalled. By that time, Millie was already escorting Glenda back upstairs.

"No, honey," she replied. "That was only a figure of speech. Julia and I were playing a game called Chicken. You shouldn't repeat everything that you hear. Sometimes, there are bad words you shouldn't say. Let's go find your brother." They went upstairs, leaving Julia alone with her anger.

The Intrepid took the same route Grant and Roberto had taken during their night recon mission. The Intrepid would only serve as an escape vehicle. The assault would be on foot and it would be a two-pronged attack. One team would get to the rooftops, behind the Village Hall, while the second team would approach from the south side of Stage Road and sneak around through the backyards, until they reached the rear of the police station. Once they were in position, the first team would make their attack to take away the attention from the second team, who would try to locate and extract the prisoners.

The first team consisted of Grant, Liz, and Devin. They exited The Intrepid at Lake Street and ran for the fire escape of a white three-story building. They planned to climb to the third floor and reach the rooftop to strike from a higher vantage point. Their attack was meant to be a distraction, but if they could do some damage, so be it. Angelo gave Grant two of his grenades and told him to use them sparingly.

Charles, Kirk, Roberto, and Angelo made up the second team. They parked The Intrepid on Smith Field Court near the library, across from the movie theater, and moved toward Stage Road, but they would be splitting up, before reaching it. Angelo had a different path to follow.

Charles turned to him and said, "The former Town Office is the one-story brick building near the center of the block. If you pass through these backyards, you should reach it without being seen. The Village Hall is the white three-story building just past it. Well, technically it's two-stories with an attic. Those are your first two targets. Afterwards, you know what to do."

"Got it," he nodded confidently.

"There could be a shooter on the top floor of the Village Hall, so be sure to stay out of their line of sight. Liz should be able to give you the distraction you need. Let us know when you're in position and we can start. Once it looks clear and they're nice and distracted, you can make your way to the police station across the street. It will be the white building with the columns in front. We'll be hitting it from behind to draw away the heat from the front entrance. Got all that?"

Angelo nodded, "Brick building is the old Town Office. Village Hall is the taller white building, past it. Wait for Liz to make my move. Once they're distracted, head over to the police station."

"Good. Be careful. Remember, let us know when you're in position."

"No problem," Angelo replied. "Wish me luck." He ran northbound into the nearest backyard, splitting up from his team to set up explosives at key locations. He tried to stay out of sight, as he moved. He climbed over a guardrail and got into position. When the time was right, he would set off the explosives and create a world of chaos for the other group, setting up his group's escape. He kept a radio with him, so he could stay in touch with the others. However, he had to keep it off, once the explosives were live or he would risk setting them off. That was the real catch.

Charles, Kirk, and Roberto had continued past the wall of cars on Stage Road and snuck over to the other side of the street. They moved stealthily behind the homes, until they climbed down a mound to the parking lot, behind the police station. They hid behind a police SUV and waited.

"The Angel of Death is in position. Over," Angelo said into his radio.

Grant responded from his position atop a roof, overlooking the rear of the Village Hall. "10-4. Team 1 is in position and waiting to strike. Over."

Charles acknowledged using his radio, "10-4. Team 2 is also in position." He took a deep breath. There would be no turning back, once he added the next part. "Make it rain. Over."

Grant replied into his radio, "10-4. Prepare for the storm. Over."

That was the signal for Liz to begin her attack. She was perched atop a brick dance school, which made her the farthest one out. She aimed at her target, which was the rear of the former Town Office building. There were lights on in the rear windows. She fired one shot into a window to get their attention, and then waited thirty seconds to see if there was a reaction. One person foolishly peeked out of the broken window holding a handgun. She aimed for his head and fired a second shot. He went down.

Now, they knew she meant business. Next, she fired a random shot into one of the northern side windows to make it seem like there were people attacking from different angles. Her fourth shot was fired into a rear window on the ground floor of the Village Hall. Again, she waited thirty seconds.

Someone from the second floor went to the window and looked down into the parking lot. At that point, she fired and hit him directly in his face, before he spotted Angelo.

Angelo had begun setting explosives, behind the former Town Office. He figured the people inside would be stupid to look out of the windows with Liz shooting at them. When he was done, he moved over to the rear of the Village Hall, where he began setting more explosives.

At that point, it was Devin's turn to fire from his position atop one of the closer rooftops. He was armed with a Smith and Wesson M and P 15-22 Sport Rimfire rifle. It was one of several hunting rifles that were acquired from his former group's supply cache. He was no marksman, but he was not a bad shot either. He aimed his rifle into one of the ground floor windows of the Village Hall on the north side of the building, steadied his breathing, and fired.

The purpose of his shot was to provide a distraction, so Angelo could set his explosives without detection. As it turned out, it was too late for that. Someone had discovered him.

It seems there was a person, who was sitting out of view, in the backyard of one of the houses. When he noticed Angelo sneaking by, he followed him. As soon as he realized Angelo was up to no good, he wanted to do something about it. However, the fact that there was someone on a rooftop firing a rifle made him hesitate and keep his distance. At the same time, he could not sit idly by, while Angelo set up explosives, behind the buildings. He knew he had to act, before it was too late.

From a hidden position, behind some bushes, he raised his double barrel shotgun and aimed at Angelo. He hoped he would not be spotted by whoever was firing the rifle. It was dark, so he still wasn't sure if the shooter was in a building or on the rooftops. Therefore, he had to be careful not to be seen.

Before he could shoot, he was shot in the back. He screamed out in pain and fell to the ground, dropping his shotgun on the grass. His assailant fired a second shot and he was dead. Sam stepped into the moonlight and stood over the body with David's Smith and Wesson in his hand.

Angelo turned quickly fearful that he was about to be shot, until he noticed Sam, who picked up the shotgun and held it up, so he could see it.

Grant immediately spoke over the radio at the sound of the gunshot. "Someone find the source of that shot!" He scanned the parking lot with his binoculars.

Liz was already searching with her scope, as well. She instantly spotted Sam holding a shotgun.

Angelo quickly responded, "Disregard that. The Angel of Death has a guardian angel. We're still good. Over." He waved for Sam to hurry toward him.

Sam ducked as he ran toward Angelo and hid with him, behind the Village Hall. They tried to remain low, beneath the first floor windows.

Grant watched them from his position on the rooftop of the white building, which was adjacent to the brick building, where Liz was perched. He used his binoculars to see who was next to Angelo and was not pleased, when he saw that it was Sam. He exhaled angrily. This was certainly no place for an emotional teenager. Unfortunately, he was already in the thick of it and he was not going to leave willingly. They had to accept it and deal with it. Hopefully, the kid would not get in the way and live long enough to hear about it later. Grant turned to the windows of the Village Hall and checked to make sure they were clear. He frowned when he spotted someone in the top far right window. He let Liz know using the radio.

"Queen, take out pawn at the top right of the hall. Over."

"Check," she answered. She was itching to shoot someone, after that little scare with Angelo and Sam. She aimed her rifle at the top right window and saw the person Grant was talking about. She fired once and he went down. She also noticed someone else, who was trying to be bold on the ground floor window of the former Town Office. He was about to aim a gun at Sam and Angelo, but she fired at him and took him down, too.

"Another one for the Queen," she said to herself with a smile. She liked the codename Grant had assigned to her. It was fitting, considering her name. It did not really bother her that she was shooting living people. She spent time as a soldier and had a similar mindset to Grant.

She felt it was best to eliminate their enemies, before their enemies eliminated them. When the group from the Village Hall ambushed their friends, shot David, and kidnapped Edie and Sam's mother, they became the enemy.

Grant spoke into the radio, again, "We have runners crossing the street. Take them out. Over."

Liz responded, "I'm on it. Over." She spotted four people fleeing from the Village Hall and crossing the street to the police station. Before they could reach the entrance, she was able to shoot two of them. The other two ducked behind a short brick wall, hiding them from her view. "I only hit two. Over."

"Copy that. The Angel is on them. Over," replied Angelo into his radio. He was ready to move to the other side of Stage Road, so he gave the thumbs up signal and Devin fired a shot into a random window on the north side of the Village Hall to keep anyone inside from looking out long enough for Angelo and Sam to run across the north parking lot and onto Stage Road. There was another wall of cars at that end of the street, which could be used as cover.

However, as they ran, someone shot at them with a machine gun from one of the second floor front windows of the Village Hall that faced Stage Road. The bullets ricocheted across the sidewalk and followed them to the wall of cars, where they ran for cover. A few bullets riddled the cars and shattered a few windows, sending glass fragments raining over their heads. They barely made it and had to cover their heads, while staying low, until the shooting stopped.

It seemed there were still people inside of the Village Hall, who were a threat. The window was out of view from Grant's team of snipers, so Angelo and Sam would have to tread carefully.

Angelo exhaled and exclaimed, "Whoa! That was too close! Are you okay, kid?"

Sam was breathing heavily and responded, "Yeah, and my name is Sam, not kid!"

"Whatever, man! By the way, thanks for before. Sorry, I didn't say it sooner. I was a bit preoccupied. What are you doing here? This is a damned war zone! You're going to get yourself killed!"

"I already told you guys earlier, I want to help rescue my mom. I'm not afraid of these jerks."

"How old are you?"

"Sixteen," Sam answered.

"Well, if you want to live to see seventeen, stay close to me and do as I say. I'm not going to get myself killed, chasing you around. We'll have to wait here, for now, until Charles and the others do their part. Do you think you can sit still and wait?"

"Yeah, sure, whatever. I'm not in a hurry to get shot. I just don't like being treated like a little kid. I'm young, not stupid."

"Fair enough. As long as you act responsibly, you'll be treated that way. For the record, you being here… that was not acting responsibly. On that note, I'm not your father, so you won't hear anymore about it from me. Stand aside and let me do my thing."

Sam nodded and tried to peek through a car window. A bullet shot through the window on the other side and Angelo yanked him back down.

"And do me a favor? Keep your head down. Huh?"

Sam gulped nervously, "Uh, yeah! Sorry. I will definitely keep my head down."

Grant spoke into his radio, "Team 1 to Angel of Death. Are you guys good? Over."

"Just a little shaken. Over," Angelo responded.

Grant looked over the former Town Office building and could see the police station from his rooftop position. He was expecting someone to come out of the front entrance. If this group had ex-cops with them, they were probably using the police station as some sort of stronghold, he thought. And if they had a machine gunner in the Village Hall, there might be more in the police station.

Liz also watched and waited for the other two people that were hiding behind the short brick wall to show their heads. "Come on. Just pop up one time," she said to herself.

Meanwhile, Angelo crawled to the farthest car, which was closer to the east side of the street, where the police station was located. He aimed his rifle from just in front of the tire. He could see the two men that were hiding behind the short brick wall in front of the police station. He opened fire and shot one in the leg, causing him to yell. The next shot killed him.

The other guy made a break for it and ran through an alleyway to the rear of the police station. Liz shot at him, but missed. Angelo also tried to shoot him, but it was difficult from his position on the ground.

"Heads up, Team 2, you got a runner going your way!" Angelo warned into his radio.

"10-4," Charles responded over his radio.

Angelo stayed watching the front of the police station from his position on the ground, while Sam ducked behind him, near the wall of cars. That's where they would wait, until Charles and his team made their move.

Charles waited from his position behind a police SUV. He aimed his MP5 at the man, as he came around the corner of the small alleyway, between Stage Road and the rear of the police station. The man was running too fast for him to get a clear shot.

Kirk and Roberto stood at either side of the rear entrance of the police station near the garage, in case someone decided it was better to go out the back. The garage entrance was set inward underneath the ground floor of the police station. That's where Kirk and Roberto were waiting, when the man came around the rear and ran right into Kirk's fist.

The man fell back and lay unconscious. He was a puny man in his forties. Kirk bent over him, grabbed him in a chokehold, and snapped his neck.

"Sorry, little guy, but you're on the wrong side," he whispered.

Kirk and Roberto retook their positions on either side of the door, leaving the body on the ground of the driveway. Someone opened the door from within and froze, when they saw the body on the ground. It was a pause that he would regret. Kirk yanked him out and covered his mouth, so he could not alert the others inside. He then broke his neck, as well.

Charles moved in close and spoke into this radio, "We got him. Team 2 is going in. Over."

"10-4," said Grant. "It's time for a checkmate, Queen. Over."

Liz did not respond. Instead, she began firing into the police station glass entrance doors using full auto mode on her carbine. She only used short burst shots to get their attention drawn toward the front of the building, giving Charles and his team the distraction they needed to sneak into the rear undetected.

It did not take long before the occupants of the police station noticed their intrusion. The interior of the police station erupted into a battleground. Charles, Kirk, and Roberto found themselves in a firefight against two ex-cops from Monroe, who still wore their uniforms and bulletproof vests. As they pushed deeper into the police station, they could see that the jail cells were full of women.

Roberto ducked into a nearby corridor to avoid being shot and ran into another person, who was unprepared for a fight. He wasted no time and swung his wrecking bar, striking the person on the head and knocking him out cold. When he turned around, he came face to face with a really tall muscular man, who did not look too happy.

"You're gonna regret doing that to George," he said threateningly.

"Hello, there," Roberto replied in a friendly voice, before swinging the wrecking bar upward and hitting the man with an uppercut in the chin using the hammer side. His head jerked upward, but then he regained his composure and stared Roberto in the eyes. He then growled at Roberto, who grinned back. He had a feeling this was not going to be an easy fight. Judging by the way the man cracked his knuckles and neck, he was probably right.

Out in the other room, Edie became excited, as soon as she noticed Charles and Kirk fighting their way to reach her. She called out from the prison cell, "Charles! Kirk! It's Edie! I'm in here!"

Charles heard her and called into his radio, "Team 2 has eyes on the package! Bring the storm and get in here! We could use a hand, if you're not too busy out there! Over!"

That was the signal Angelo was waiting to hear.

"Copy that," Angelo replied into his radio. "Prepare for the storm! Over." He grinned and turned to Sam. "Cover your ears, Sam. Things are about to get really loud."

As soon as he did so, Angelo hit a switch and the rear of the Village Hall and former Town Office building exploded sending bricks, glass, and wood flying out across the rear parking lot.

BA-DA-BOOM!!

Grant, Liz, and Devin all ducked and covered their heads, in case any fragments of debris flew their way. Both buildings went up in flames. Moments later, the Village Hall collapsed from the damage and screams could be heard from within. One person ran out covered in fire. Devin fired two shots and put him out of his misery.

Sam kept his ears covered, not wanting to hear the screams. He began to realize he was in over his head. These people were not messing around. This really was a war zone and he was smack in the middle of it.

Angelo turned to him and said, "Hey!" When Sam looked at him, Angelo instructed, "Wait here! Don't argue! Just do what I say!" Sam nodded reluctantly, and Angelo stood up. He then proceeded toward the entrance of the police station, where he quickly set up some explosions at the base of the two columns. Afterwards, he smashed through the broken glass doors, entering the building, and fired his rifle killing two people inside.

In the staircase, Roberto smashed a chair over the muscular man's head. It only made him angry. Roberto ran upstairs and searched for a good place to make his stand. The man followed and charged into him pushing him into a wall and creating a dent in the sheetrock. Roberto recovered quickly and struck his opponent repeatedly in the back using the wrecking bar, but it did no good.

The man grabbed him in a vice grip and was squeezing the air out of him. He tried to reach for his gun, but first he would have to get past the man's strong grip. That was not happening. Not wanting to drop his wrecking bar, he jammed it down the rear of the man's pants with the pointed end facing downward, for a lack of a better place to put it. He then lifted his legs, bent his knees, and pushed forward against the man's chest, until he slipped out of his grasp and fell to the floor.

He instantly rolled backwards into a flip, but kicked forward, at the last minute, hitting the man in the face with both boots, as he charged forward. With the man temporarily stunned, Roberto leapt back to his feet and clapped both his hands over the man's ears as hard as he could, cupping them and popping his eardrums.

Roberto backed away to give himself room to move, while the man held his bleeding ears and shook off the pain. Roberto let loose with a round house kick to the man's face and followed that up with another kick into his chest that sent the man crashing through a door and into the next room.

He then pulled out his tactical M48 sabotage fighting-knife from his boot, stepped into the room and said, "You have my wrecking bar. I'm going to need it back."

The man reached out to grab him, but Roberto did the unexpected and charged at him with the knife. He intended to finish the job he started, but the man was not quite ready to go down, yet.

MAN'S END

Chapter Twenty-Two

WHILE LIZ AND Grant were both distracted by the explosion, they did not notice someone climbing up onto the roof, where Liz was perched. At the same time, that someone did not notice Grant on the next roof over. The man stalked Liz, slowly moving closer to her each second, while she looked through her scope oblivious to his presence. He pointed his gun at her back and was tempted to shoot and kill her, but then he realized she was a woman. His eyes moved to her rear end and he smiled mischievously.

"Stand up slowly and don't make *any* sudden moves or I will blow a hole into the back of your pretty skull," he said.

She felt a chill at the sound of his threatening voice and turned slowly. He was standing over her with his gun aimed at her face. He was a dirty looking man, wearing blue denim clothing. His face was unshaven and his brown greasy hair was slicked back and tied into a ponytail.

"Okay," she said. "Take it easy with that thing. I'll stand up."

"Oh, I *know* you will. Don't forget to let go of that rifle in your hand. I wouldn't want to have to shoot you by mistake because I thought you were going to try and shoot me. That would be a *damned* shame," he shook his head. He looked her up and down and smiled. "Mm mm! You look tasty."

She glared at him with disgust, as she placed her rifle on the ground and stood up slowly. "Okay, you got me," She said loud enough, so that Grant could hear over the gunshots coming from the police station on the next block.

Grant turned around curious whom Liz was speaking to and his eyes opened wide with shock, when he realized someone had her at gunpoint, only a few feet away. He cursed himself for not noticing someone was on the rooftops with them. He was so caught up with what was going on down below that he failed to watch their backs. However, he still had a slight advantage because the man in denim did not notice him. He hopped over to the next roof, where they were, since the roofs were practically connected, and then tried to sneak up on the man.

The man, totally unaware of Grant's presence, grabbed Liz by the neck and said, "You're coming with me, baby. We're gonna have some fun, while we still can. There's a nice comfy bed waiting for us downstairs." He pushed her forward and was about to bend over to pick up her rifle, when he noticed Grant approaching. "Where in the blue blazes did he come from?" He immediately grabbed Liz and pulled her in front of him, as a human shield.

Realizing he lost the advantage of surprise, Grant stated, "Let her go, if you know what's good for you." He was furious that he did not try to take a shot sooner.

The man held Liz in front of him at gunpoint and responded, "Uh uh! I don't think so! Who do you think you are, some kind of superhero, appearing out of nowhere like that? Drop the gun or she gets it!"

Grant shook his head and replied, "You got the wrong guy, asshole. This isn't a movie. Let her go or I'll kill you. Consider that your first warning." He continued to aim his gun undeterred.

"You are a funny guy! *However,* I think I have the upper hand here."

"Then you're in for a rude awakening, dickhead. Let her go or you die. It's that simple. I promise you. If you even harm a hair on her head, you're dead. *However,* if you let her go, I just may let you walk away from this. Keep in mind I'm not the one in immediate danger. I can't say the same about you. Do you really think I won't shoot you?"

The man looked into Grant's eyes and recognized the eyes of a killer, since he had the same kind of eyes. He glanced around, as he considered his options. He was standing at the edge of the roof with a gun aimed at him. Sure, he had a hostage, but he wasn't sure if the guy he was dealing with gave a damn about her. Was that a chance he really wanted to take? He could jump down to the fire escape, but he probably would not get far, before being shot at by two people. If he killed the girl, he was surely a dead man. The odds were not looking good.

"Okay, fine," he gave in. "You win, tough guy." He let her go and said, "She's all yours. Let's talk parley."

BANG!

"We just did," Grant said coldly. "We're done."

Liz scowled at him, "Jesus Christ, Grant! Thanks for putting my life on the line! Sometimes, you take too many chances!" She picked up her rifle and kicked the dead man's body so hard that it rolled off the roof. His body landed on the very fire escape he had been eyeing for his possible escape.

Grant stepped forward and explained calmly, "Baby, please, give me more credit than that. I had my sights between his eyes the entire time. I knew I could hit him at this range. I just wanted to try for a cleaner shot, first. It works better, if you're not in danger, so I did some negotiating."

"How did you know he'd go for it and let me go?"

Grant smirked, "It really didn't matter. I told you. I had a shot already. I knew I wouldn't miss. Not at this range. He was dumb enough not to use you to block his face, since he wanted to talk to me so badly."

She glared at him, momentarily, and shook her head. "You are so lucky I love you and that I believe you, but I'm still mad at you," she growled.

"I can live with that. Better that you're mad at me, than being raped or killed by that piece of shit. He's probably the same guy, who shot David. He fits the description Sam and Rob gave us. I *really* hate rapists. He's lucky I killed him fast. He deserved worse."

She did not respond, although she was relieved Grant was there to save her. Who knows what would have happened to her had he been further away on a different rooftop?

"Come on," he said. "It's time to join the others at the police station." He picked up his radio and spoke into it, "Red Devil, rendezvous with Team 2. Over."

Devin responded into his radio, "10-4."

Grant and Liz jumped down to the fire escape, where the dead man in denim lay. From there, it was only a short run down a flight of metallic stairs, before they reached the parking lot behind the Village Hall. They ran across the lot toward the rear of the destroyed burning buildings.

Devin had also used a fire escape to go down to the same parking lot from a three-story beige building, where he was situated.

The three met up and hurried past the burning debris to the wall of cars on the north side of Stage Road, where Sam waited. They ducked next to him and he eyed them with fear and uncertainty in his eyes. He still held the double barrel shotgun firmly in his hands.

Grant realized, then and there, that a lecture could wait for later. Sam obviously had enough going through his mind already. Grant extended his hand and said, "Give me the shotgun." Sam complied and Grant turned to Devin. He said, "Stay with Sam. If you see *anybody* that isn't part of our group exit the police station, shoot them down, unless it's a female. It could be a prisoner. Liz and I are going in. Listen to the radio for instructions."

Devin gave him the thumbs up signal and hunkered down beside Sam.

Grant and Liz ran along Stage Road and cautiously entered the destroyed front door of the police station. Angelo was pinned down behind a desk, which he turned on its side. Three men were hiding behind the larger main desk and shooting at him from across the lobby. Grant took cover behind a wall and began shooting at them with the shotgun. Liz did the same returning fire on full auto mode with her carbine. They immediately hit one, who did not notice when they entered the building.

Liz took a moment to reload, while Grant shot a light out over the other two men. Shards of glass rained down on their heads and Grant pulled the pin on one of the grenades Angelo had given to him earlier. He tossed it behind the main desk, where the men hid and ducked.

"Fire in the hole!" He shouted, just as it exploded, killing both men and destroying half the room in the process. Grant then rushed over to Angelo and noticed Angelo was wounded. "They shot you?"

"Eh, just a flesh wound… or two," Angelo groaned.

"I can't leave you alone for a minute. Huh?"

Angelo chuckled and recoiled from the pain. "Please, don't make me laugh. It hurts. Hey. I thought I told you to save the grenades for an emergency."

"Saving your ass seemed like an emergency to me. Where are Charles and the others?"

Angelo shook his head and responded, "I still haven't even seen them, yet. I heard shooting, which sounded like it was coming from downstairs and there was also some kind of ruckus upstairs."

"Ruckus? Can you describe the ruckus?"

"Sounded like a wrestling match."

Just then, there was the shattering sound of breaking glass. Outside, Devin and Sam aimed their weapons, as they saw Roberto and a huge behemoth of a man crashing through the second floor window and land on the sidewalk below. Roberto was on top of the man and used him to cushion the landing. When they hit the ground, Roberto yanked out his knife from his neck, rolled off of him, and lay still.

Sam cried out, "Holy crap! Did you see that?"

Devin nodded, "Yeah, these guys are crazy. I freaking love it. Help me get Rob to safety."

They both rushed over and dragged Roberto away from the sidewalk and back behind the wall of cars.

Devin asked, "Rob, are you okay?"

"Where's that big bastard? I still have another punch for him! I owe him one for hitting me in the gonads!"

"Lie still, buddy," Devin replied. "You just flew out of a window, for Christ's sake! I think he's had it. Take five. You've earned it."

Roberto rested his head on the ground and said, "Fine. Just make sure someone gets my wrecking bar."

"Where is it?" Sam asked. "I'll get it for you."

"Up that guy's ass," Roberto coughed out, as he tried to catch his breath.

"Oh," replied Sam with a confused look of disgust on his face. "Um. Why is it there?"

"Long story. It was a crazy fight, bro. You know what? I think I'll just get it myself."

As Devin and Sam tried to stop him, they noticed a group of people fleeing toward Stage Road through an alleyway from around the rear of the police station. It was the women! When Sam saw his mother, he called to her.

"Mom! Over here! Behind the cars!"

"Sam? Sam!" She was so weak, but extremely glad to see her son.

Edie helped her and led the group of women behind the cars, where they ducked down and hid together. Aside from Edie and Joy, there were seven other women. They were each extremely tired and weak from hunger.

Joy asked, "Glenda? Where's Glenda?"

"Don't worry, mom. She's safe," Sam replied.

Joy smiled and they embraced.

Devin had forgotten about trying to stop Roberto and spoke into his radio. "Red Devil has the package outside! Over!"

"10-4," someone answered. Devin wasn't sure, who it was, but it sounded like one of the guys. There was too much shooting going on in the background to tell.

Not long after, Kirk ran out of the back door of the police station and climbed the mound into the backyard to the south. He raced through the backyards and ran past the wall of cars at the south end of Stage Road. He continued west across Smith Field Court, until he reached The Intrepid.

Meanwhile, back at Stage Road, an unknown shooter began shooting at the group. Devin, Sam, and the women all hit the ground. They soon realized no one was shooting at them. Someone was shooting at Roberto from a house that was across the street from the police station. Roberto had gone to retrieve his wrecking bar. He was now taking cover behind the short brick wall in front of the police station.

Devin aimed his rifle and fired at the house, where the shooter was hiding, but missed the person. The person had stopped firing, probably to reload his or her weapon. Devin turned to the others and said, "I need to get to a better spot, so I can get a clear shot. Sam, stay with the girls. I'll be back in no time."

Before Sam could respond, Devin was on the move. He ran into a nearby alleyway that took him behind the police station. He planned to go around to the backyards beyond it, so he could break into one of the neighboring houses and get to a second floor window. He hoped, by doing so, it would provide him with a better vantage point that placed him on the same level with the shooter.

However, when he reached the rear of the police station, he spotted three men running for police cars. Only one of them was wearing a police uniform. They did not see him, which gave him the advantage. He reacted instantly and aimed his rifle at one of the men in civilian clothing. He fired a shot and hit the man directly in the back. The man fell to the ground and did not move. Devin then took cover behind another short brick wall, which extended along the length of the alleyway back to Stage Road.

The other two men immediately returned fire, as he expected they would.

Fortunately, Devin was able to aim from his position without being shot. He fired another round and hit one of the two men in his chest. The man fell back and hit the ground in pain. He was no longer a threat, so Devin focused his attention on the last man, who wore the police uniform. He hated the idea of shooting at a cop, but this was not the old world and that cop was now the enemy.

The cop returned fire, but then stopped. When Devin peeked out to shoot, the cop shot him in the left shoulder. He then jumped into a police car and started it up. Devin was down, but he was far from out. He aimed his rifle at the police car and shot out two of the tires.

The cop cursed and tried for another police car, but Devin blasted the windows to pieces in front of him, causing the cop to jump back and cover his face with his arms. In that moment, Devin fired three more shots and hit the cop in the side and in his left leg. The cop keeled over and dropped to the ground.

"I got you, you son of a bitch!"

Devin struggled to his feet and ignored his wound. He walked down to the parking lot behind the police station and finished off his three opponents using his knife to make sure they were dead. Next, he grabbed a first aid kit from the trunk of a police car and patched up his wound, as best as he could.

Afterwards, he pressed on and climbed the mound into the next backyard. He shot the lock on the rear door and kicked the door open. He hoped the house was empty. He was not ready to fight anyone up close and personal. Fortunately, the house appeared to be empty. He ran upstairs and headed for the front windows that overlooked Stage Road. He opened one window just enough to point the tip of his rifle out, aimed at the window across the street, and waited for the shooter to show himself. As soon as he appeared in the window, Devin shot and killed him instantly.

He sighed in relief and went into the bathroom to properly tend to his wound. Before he could do so, a crashing explosion of metal and glass startled him, causing him to jump. It came from outside. He rushed back to the front window and saw The Intrepid had burst through the wall of cars at the south end of Stage Road and stopped in front of the police station.

"That's my ride," he muttered to himself, as he hurried downstairs and out the front door.

Kirk honked the horn, which was very loud and distinguishable. Sam and the girls ran for The Intrepid. He helped Roberto inside, as well. A few seconds later, Devin came rushing into the bus. Kirk noticed his wound and helped him aboard.

"Did you get shot?"

Devin replied, "You could say that. I'll be fine. Don't worry about me."

The others were taking too long to come out. Kirk was not going to just sit and wait. He hit the horn, again, and said, "I'm going in. If things go south, I want you guys to take The Intrepid back home. I'll leave it running, just in case." He then charged into the police station with his fire hydrant wrench in hand.

Moments later, someone came flying through a front window. Multiple shots could be heard coming from within. There was a loud explosion at the rear of the police station. Afterwards, there was no more shooting and it became eerily silent.

Devin got up from his seat and stepped toward the front of the bus. He thought about sitting in the driver's seat, but hesitated.

Edie asked, "What's going on? Why is it so quiet, all of a sudden?"

"I don't know," Devin responded nervously.

Sam no longer cared about the battle, now that he had his mother with him. She looked like someone had beaten her, which infuriated him. He held her close and tried to comfort her.

Roberto tried to stand, but passed out in his seat from exhaustion.

It was left to Devin to make a decision. Leave, wait, or go in and find out what happened. What to do? He swallowed nervously, as he decided to go inside.

Suddenly, Kirk emerged carrying Charles over his shoulder. Grant and Liz followed helping Angelo to walk.

Devin let out a sigh of relief and stepped outside to help them onto the bus.

Once they were all seated, Kirk sat down in the driver's seat and rolled the bus back in reverse several feet. He shifted gears and smashed through the next wall of cars. He made an immediate left turn at the next street, which was Lake Street. As they drove away, Angelo hit the switch on his next detonator, before passing out from his injuries.

Behind them, the police station columns exploded, along with the face of the building, causing the second floor to collapse onto the first. If anyone inside had survived the assault, they were certainly dead, after the explosion.

The drive home seemed bumpier than usual, especially for those with injuries. There was a lot of moaning and groaning on the ride back, too. Everyone was exhausted. It was nearly six in the morning. The fighting had gone on all night. It had been a rough night for everyone.

The women, who they rescued, were nervous and frightened. For all they knew, they were going from one prison to another. They did not know these people. They only went along because it seemed like the best choice, at the time, and they trusted Edie enough to follow her to safety.

The Intrepid stopped in front of the iron gates of their compound on Cromwell Road. Kirk got out and unlocked it, just as Daniel approached to do the same. Kirk was able to drive straight in, while Daniel locked up for him.

When Kirk got out of the bus, he called to Daniel, "We need Aramis! Wake him up! We have a few gunshot wounds!"

Daniel rushed into house to get Aramis, while Kirk helped everyone off the bus. Grant and Liz focused on getting the wounded off the bus. Roberto was not too bad, but he was in a lot of pain. His entire body was aching, after the brutal fight he had. Devin was also able to walk on his own, but his shoulder was bleeding. Charles and Angelo were in worse condition and both needed to be carried inside.

When Aramis arrived, he wished more than ever that they had a stretcher. He never imagined they would need one, until David had been shot. Now, he was convinced they had to get one.

Meanwhile, Edie led the women toward the house. There were seven in total. Sam followed with his mother, who was very weak from starvation. The women all seemed broken in some way, either mentally or physically. A few looked around apprehensively, as they were escorted into the house. The tall fence, partial wall, and watchtower were quite intimidating to some of them, who were still unsure what they were getting themselves into with this new obviously aggressive group.

Edie took them into the common room, where they could sit and wait. She knew they were hungry and thirsty, so she asked Sam to help her bring them food and drinks, which he did. That helped to win a few of them over, but about two or three were still feeling on edge.

One was a very attractive Asian woman in her twenties. Her name was Kim. Of all the women, she was the most fearful and untrusting. She had the most reason to feel that way. While she was a prisoner of the other group, the men had been using her as their sex doll for weeks and she was not the only one.

A beautiful young woman named Delilah also suffered the same fate of being raped repeatedly. She became numb to it, after the first couple of weeks. She went through the motions, but had, somehow, disconnected her mind from the reality of her situation. She walked around like a mindless zombie and said nothing to no one. She did not react and she did not show any expressions.

Yvonne was an African-American woman in her thirties. She was another person, who did not feel they were safe, yet. She did not trust the people, who were her so-called rescuers, especially not the men. The way she saw it, they had only been transferred to a new prison. Perhaps, there would be no threat of rape, but it was still a prison, nonetheless.

Most of the other women seemed grateful to their saviors. When Edie and Sam provided them with food and drinks, they were very thankful. They felt this would be a better place for them. Joy felt the same way, especially after knowing that Sam and Glenda were safe.

Edie seemed sincere enough. After all, she had been with them in the prison cells. She knew their plight, all too well.

Once she had a chance to sit down and rest, Edie began to cry.

Sam noticed and left his mother's side to see what was wrong. He sat next to Edie and asked, "Did those people hurt you?"

"Huh?" She turned and noticed him sitting beside her. She answered, "No. Well, I think my middle finger is broken, but that's not what's bothering me. I-I was thinking about David... I still can't believe that bastard shot him." Her eyes became teary. "I thought I cried enough tears, while I was in that prison cell, but there will never be enough tears for his loss." She broke down and sobbed.

Sam immediately wanted to tell her that David had survived, but he was not sure if that was the case. The last he saw, David was in critical condition. Still, he had to say something hopeful. He placed his hand on her shoulder and said, "I'm not so sure he's dead."

She immediately faced him and demanded, "Why would you say that?"

"That man didn't kill David. He was still alive. Roberto and I helped him back and your medic was working on him. He was still in critical condition, when we left here last night."

Edie leapt to her feet and raced into the male dormitory. If David were alive, that's where he'd be resting and he would likely be the only one in there, for the moment. She was right. She ran to his side and knelt down beside his bed.

"David! Oh, my God! You're alive!" She rested her head on his chest, as she cried and hugged him gently. He was still too heavily medicated to even know she was there, but she felt him breathing and that made her so happy.

Soon after, Aramis and Kirk brought Angelo into the room and placed him on his bed.

Kirk saw Edie with David and realized the last time she saw him, she probably thought he was dead. He patted her on the back and said, "Don't worry. He's going to be okay. Dave's a strong guy. No one can keep him down for long."

She looked up at Kirk and smiled, "I know. He's the best."

"Yeah, he is. He's going to be glad that you are back safe and sound, but right now, you should let him rest. He needs it."

"Oh, okay. I'm sorry. I was just so happy to see that he was alive. I wasn't thinking."

"It's okay. I get it. Come on." Kirk put his arm around her and walked her out of the dorm. He asked, "How are you feeling? Did those bastards hurt you?"

"They didn't really have time, thanks to you guys. When I heard the gunshots and explosions, I knew my people had come for me. It made me so happy." Her eyes became teary. "God, I love you guys!"

"We love you, too, Blondie. I'm glad you're okay. Go get some rest."

Grant and Liz placed Charles on one of the spare beds in the male dorm. Aramis needed quick access to him, so taking him up to his room in the attic was too far. Charles had been shot in chest, but the round went right through, which was a good thing. It did not seem to hit any vital organs either. Grant was able to stop the bleeding at the scene using a first aid kit from within the police station, after tossing his other grenade down into the basement, killing several of the other group members, who were trying to escape into the parking lot.

Millie went into the dorm to assist Aramis. She looked sleepy. She hardly got any sleep because she was waiting up late for them to return. She had only fallen asleep two hours earlier, so she was barely in any shape to be of use to Aramis. Still, she had to try. He was overwhelmed. Grant and Liz also helped out.

In the common room, one of the women stood up and approached Sam. She was a heavyset African-American woman in her mid-thirties. She asked in a sweet voice, "Excuse me, young man?"

"Yeah? What's up?"

"Those men, who got hurt trying to save us? I'd like to help, if I can. My name is Angela. I used to be a home attendant and I was taking nursing courses."

"Really? That's great!" Sam responded excitedly. "I'll let someone know. Wait here. Be right back!" He hurried out of the common room and returned shortly with Liz.

Liz approached Angela and introduced herself, "Hi. I'm Liz. Are you the nurse?"

"Hello. My name is Angela. I was attending nursing school, but I've been a home attendant for five years. I have some nursing experience."

"And you want to help out?"

"Yes, I'd really like to, if you'll let me."

"Absolutely! Thank you so much! Please, follow me!"

Liz led Angela to the male dormitory and showed her where the medical supplies were being kept temporarily. "If you need anything else, other than what's here, we have more stored in the basement. Most of these guys have gunshot wounds. Whatever you can do to help will be fantastic. Hey, Aramis! This is Angela. She used to be a home attendant and she was taking nursing classes. She'd like to help out."

"That's awesome! Angela, I love you already!"

She blushed, since he was a handsome man.

"Please, put on some rubber gloves and come over here. We could really use a hand in here."

She grabbed a set of rubber gloves and went to his side to help with Angelo's wounds. He had been shot twice, although both were minor wounds in his leg and arm. She started by cleaning them.

Kirk returned to the dorm and helped out by tending to Roberto and Devin. Their wounds were much easier to dress and wrap. Grant was already working on that. The hardest part was pulling the bullet out of Devin's shoulder. Aramis had to do that part, but he left the stitches to Millie. He had already taught her enough for her to play the role of his other nurse.

The important thing was that everyone had returned. No one was killed. That's what Aramis kept telling himself. He hoped it would stay that way. It was bad enough when David was shot. He had to create a makeshift device to give David a blood transfusion. He was just grateful there were a few people with the same blood type. Otherwise, David could have died. He was glad his new patients were not in as dire a need for blood. Their wounds seemed less life threatening, but it was going to be a long morning.

Police Station in Monroe, NY.

MAN'S END

Chapter Twenty-Three

B Y MID-AFTERNOON, THINGS had calmed down at the compound. The excitement of the night before and early morning was finally dying down. Aramis and his provisional nursing crew were able to patch up the wounds inflicted to Charles, Angelo, Devin, Edie, and Roberto. The injured were resting peacefully, as were Aramis and his assistants.

Grant gathered the new people in the common room, so he could address them and let them know what's what. Introductions were also made, at this time.

The eldest began first. "My name is Maxine. I used to work at the Village Hall. As luck would have it, I was the first woman to be imprisoned by my former so-called friends and co-workers," she scowled. It was obvious the betrayal she felt had no bounds. There was a lot of anger she needed to deal with, but she was very grateful to this new group, who saved her and the others. "I really want to thank you for getting us out of there. I was at the end of my rope. You basically saved my life. I will never forget it."

"We only did what was right," Grant responded with a friendly smile.

A young teenage redheaded girl named Taryn stayed close to Maxine and did not speak much. She was still traumatized by her experience. She had been living in a house on Stage Road. Her parents were both killed for not going along with the new program and she was imprisoned. She was threatened with rape, more than once, but had not had to endure the brutal act thanks to Maxine's constant protection. Maxine argued that she was still too young and even volunteered in her place once.

Angela had already made her case as a former home attendant and nursing student. However, she was also a fine cook and baker, which was a welcomed addition. She was more than willing to help Millie out in the kitchen and Aramis with the wounded and sick.

Angela's friend, Yvonne, was also an African-American woman in her thirties. She did not have much to say to her rescuers. She did not trust them one bit. She kept waiting for them to show their "true colors." Things seemed too good to be true and she did not like it. After being raped by several men of the previous group, it was understandable why she would feel that way.

Chrysandra was a young woman in her twenties dressed in Gothic style. Her clothing was all black and matched her long sharpened pointed fingernails. Her face and body were covered in piercings. She seemed pretty tough, too. The subject was never brought up, but the men in the other group were unable to make a rape victim out of her because every time someone tried, she caused a serious physical injury. She was definitely a fighter with a fierce spirit and strong will, which her new group would learn soon enough.

"Call me Chryssy. It's easier to remember," she stated plainly. "Once these pleasantries are over, if it's not too much trouble, I'd really like to learn how to fight properly and shoot a gun. I mean, I can fight dirty, but you guys look like you have training. I like that. I want some of the same. I don't ever plan on becoming a victim, again."

Grant nodded, "That will not be a problem at all, Chryssy. Rob and I can help you with that, once he recovers. We can begin tomorrow, if you feel ready."

"Believe me, mister. I'm more than ready."

"Excellent. Please, call me Grant. No need to be formal here. We're like a family. We try to be. I'm glad we were able to rescue you ladies. I can't imagine the crap you must have gone through."

Chryssy nodded and gave him a half smile. She hoped he was being sincere.

Maxine responded, "Thank you so much for everything you're group has done for us. We greatly appreciate the trouble you went through. I'd like to do my part around here to help out. Perhaps, I can take on laundry duties and keep the place clean. I'm a bit of a neat freak," she smiled bashfully.

"That would be very kind of you, Maxine," Grant smiled warmly.

The next two women were a little more reluctant to speak and introduce themselves. They needed a little coaxing.

Grant tried to prod them gently. He began with the attractive Asian woman, who appeared to be in her twenties. "What's your name, miss?"

She looked at him nervously and answered, "Kimberly? Uh, I mean, call me Kim. I, uh…"

"It's okay, Kim. I understand if you feel uncomfortable speaking to me. You've all been through a crazy ordeal. It can't be easy for you. You don't have to be afraid anymore. Please, believe me when I tell you that we are not going to hurt any of you in any way. We want to help you, if we can, and we need your help, too. There are many ways you can help us, when you feel ready. You are all welcome to remain with us for as long as you like. You will be very safe here. As you may have noticed, we're building a wall."

Yvonne asked suspiciously, "Why?"

Grant turned to her and replied, "There are infected out there. We see more every time we go out for supplies. We can't have them rip these fences down, not after everything we've been through. This place needs to be safe for us. Winter is coming and it's only going to get harder. We have to be ready. If any of you would like to help with the construction, it would be a tremendous help. The men, who are injured, are going to set us behind schedule. Any help would be greatly appreciated."

Chryssy replied, "Count me in. I want to help. You guys seem pretty cool."

"Thank you, Chryssy."

Grant looked at the next woman, who seemed young. She appeared to be in her early twenties. It was obvious she was the most traumatized from all of them. She did not dare make eye contact with him or anyone else. She had not said a word, since her rescue.

He bent down and squatted not far from her. He tried to level himself with her line of sight, so she would not have to look up at him. He wanted to make himself as less intimidating as possible. She kept her long dark hair covering her face to avoid being seen.

"Hello," he said softly. "Can you please tell me your name?"

Maxine answered for her. "That's Delilah. I doubt she's going to answer you. She doesn't speak to anyone anymore. That poor girl's had it pretty rough. Give her time to get used to this place. Once she realizes you are the good guys, maybe she'll come around."

Grant nodded at Maxine and looked back at Delilah. He felt bad for her. He shuddered at the thought of the torment she must have endured for her to behave in this way. It made him angry. Using the gentlest voice he could muster, he stated, "No one will ever hurt you, as long as you are here, Delilah. I promise you."

She trembled, but did not dare look him in the eyes.

He sighed and stood up. The last people left to address were Joy and her children. He walked over and sat next to them. "Your name is Joy, right?"

"Yes," she nodded.

"I am so sorry for what happened to you and Edie. Please, don't blame David, Rob, or even Edie for what happened. They had no idea that other group would dare to do such a thing. For weeks, we've been deliberately using that exit off the interstate to avoid running into that group. I want you to know that we will do whatever we can to make you and your family feel welcome amongst us."

He looked at Sam and grinned, before turning back to her and saying, "Your son is a brave young man. He was determined to rescue you. Despite our telling him he was too young to go along, he proved himself to us and even saved my friend's life. I won't underestimate him, again. He's earned my respect and his place with this group." Grant's gaze turned back to Sam. "Thanks for that, Sam," he added.

"You're welcome, sir," Sam responded with respect.

"Grant. Call me Grant." He turned back to Joy and asked, "I'd like to train him and make sure he is more capable in the future, if that's okay with you? He already has good survival instincts."

"Thank you." Surprisingly, she agreed. "I think that would be very helpful. In fact, I'd also like to learn, if it isn't too much trouble."

"That can definitely be arranged and it will be no trouble at all," he smiled at her. He looked at Glenda and winked at her, before standing up. "My lovely girlfriend, Liz, will show you ladies to the female dorm. It's upstairs. Sam can stay next door in the dorm with the men, since he's a man, now."

Sam smirked proudly.

"Well, let's get you ladies settled," Liz said. "Grant?"

"Yeah?"

"We're going to need more beds."

"Right. Forgot about that. We'll have to make do, for now. We can go out on a supply run tomorrow. I think everyone is tired enough to sleep wherever today."

"For sure," Liz agreed.

Before she left, he asked, "Hey, Liz?"

"What is it?"

"Are you still mad at me?"

She stared at him momentarily and walked closer to him. She wrapped her arms around him and gave him a quick kiss on the lips. While still hanging onto him, she said in a low voice, "Yes, but I'm coming around. You earned some good points for yourself in here with how you spoke to everyone. I'm impressed."

"Points? I never knew I could earn points," he responded.

"Yeah," she nodded. "I guess I should have told you. They're not easy to earn."

"I guess I'll have to try harder then," he smiled and moved closer to her.

She looked him in the eyes and stated, "Never stop trying and you'll do just fine." She winked and turned away. "I'll talk to you later, mister." She turned to the women and said, "Okay! Come on, ladies! I'll show you around the house." They followed her and began a short tour of the house.

A few days had passed, since the battle with the other group. Grant, Liz, and Kirk had gone out on a quick supply run up north for beds, a stretcher, and a wheelchair, at Aramis' request.

David, Charles, and Angelo were still bedridden, while they recovered. Roberto was sore, but feeling much better. He was able to walk around, again. Devin's left arm was in a sling to relieve pressure on his shoulder, so it could heal faster. Edie had to keep her right hand wrapped, so her broken middle finger would have a chance to heal itself. Aramis was able to create a cast for her fingers, since they had so many different medical supplies. Of course, he'd gone through a lot over the past few days. It was more than he'd ever thought they'd use in such a short time frame.

Some of the new women were enjoying their newfound freedom. Angela and Millie had been getting along great in the kitchen and while tending to the wounded. They were quickly becoming friends. They also enjoyed having little Glenda around. Both were suckers for her cuteness and she took advantage to get treats out of them. Millie even let her feed the animals with her.

Glenda was a smart little girl. She was sneaky, too, just like her brother. Her mother turned her back for a second and it took twenty minutes, before they realized she was down in the basement with Julia looking at the computer monitors. She liked the tunnel, too, and wanted to go in, but Julia did not let her. It was obvious they were going to have to keep a close eye on Glenda because it looked like she wanted to explore everyplace in the compound with no fear of the unknown. She especially enjoyed playing in a first floor closet. There was no doubt she liked her new home better than where she spent the past few months.

Sam also enjoyed being at the compound. He was already learning about guns from Grant, Kirk was teaching him about cars, and Roberto taught him some simple fighting techniques. Roberto was still not physically ready to show Sam any of the complex moves. Sam was having a blast. He could not wait to learn everything he could from his new teachers, especially Roberto. He kept talking about how cool it looked to see him crashing out of the second-story window of the police station with that virtual giant he was fighting. It was, by far, the coolest thing Sam had ever seen. Roberto had himself an admirer.

Joy really appreciated how her children were taking to their new home and how the group had welcomed them. Her children meant everything to her, so if they were happy, she was pleased. She was still getting used to eating regularly, which was a nice change for her. She felt much better than when she was found in that house in Florida. She was almost fully recovered from her illness, so she was eager to earn her keep. She offered to help with anything from cooking to cleaning to guard duty.

She told Grant, "I can fight, I can cook, and I can do labor work. Whatever it takes to earn my spot. I feel like I have to do extra to make up for my children."

"That won't be necessary. Don't feel like you need to do anything. However, if there is something you want to help with, then by all means, we will appreciate it. I like to think of us as a family. We look out for each other. It's just what we do. There should be no obligations."

"I like that," she said. "Once I'm back to my full potential, I plan to pitch in and do some work."

Maxine had certainly been making herself at home and was cleaning everything she could. Grant had to tell her to ease up because she was going through their moist wipes too fast. He reminded her that it was not so simple to get more and water was more precious, these days.

She felt terrible. She quickly apologized, "Oh, my! I'm so sorry! I keep forgetting that the world is not what it used to be."

"It's okay," he replied. "Thank you for cleaning up. Just try to limit yourself. Sweep up and clear away the dust, as much as you want. There are also plenty of books in the common room. If you just want to sit down and read, that would be fine, too. Try to relax more, Maxine. You've earned it."

"Thank you, Grant. I'll do that. You're a such a fine leader."

Grant scoffed, "Ha, ha! I'm not the leader around here. Charles is more like our leader. This was his house. I'm kind of like a general. I suppose."

"Oh, pardon me. I thought you were the leader. Well, you'd sure make a good leader. You're a fine young man. You have my vote." She winked and walked away.

He laughed and went down to the basement. He found Julia in her usual spot behind the computer and monitors. She watched each camera vigilantly and did not turn around when she said, "Hey, Grant. Glad to see you're in one piece. How have you been?"

"Better than most," he responded sadly.

"Yeah. I hope the guys get better soon. So, been breaking in the new peeps?"

"Yep. I'm surprised you noticed. You really should spend more time away from this room. It's not healthy to isolate yourself the way you do. We have new people. Go mingle. They're *your* roommates."

"You should know, by now, that I'm not the mingling type, Grant. I say 'good morning' and 'goodnight' to them, when I'm in the dorm. That's good enough for me. I really don't like being around too many people at once. It makes me uncomfortable."

"Yeah, I've noticed. Anyway, I was wondering if you wanted more help down here. Maybe I can see if any of the new people have an interest in computers. First, I wanted to run it by you."

"If you think it's a good idea, I'm okay with it," she said without turning around. "I trust your judgment."

"Okay, thanks, Julia. Don't worry. I'll find you an appropriate assistant."

"I'm sure you will."

He watched her a while and felt worried about her behavior. He wished she would come out of her shell and realize there was another world beyond the basement. He remembered how excited she used to be about urban exploring. Where was that girl? He shook his head disappointed and went back upstairs.

As soon as he left, she stopped what she was doing. She rested her head in her hands and sighed. Her feelings for him were torturing her. She wished she could think of him as a friend, but she wanted so much more. It was driving her crazy. She could not even look at him. The urge to jump up and kiss him was too overpowering. It frustrated her so much.

"Oh, what I would do for some nice pot, right about now," she said to herself. She found herself longing for her college days. She missed smoking marijuana with her roommates. Studying for exams was an easier existence than this, she thought.

Kim sat outside on the front porch of the house. She stared at the heavy iron gates that sealed the entrance road, keeping her trapped within the fence and walls of the compound with so many strangers.

She wanted out more and more with each passing day. She still felt like a prisoner.

She noticed she was not the only person, who did not wish to be in the strange house. Delilah stood near the fence at the edge of the unfinished wall, staring out to the neighboring property on the south side of the compound, behind the looming watchtower.

Kim wondered what she was thinking. Was it the same thing that went through her mind?

Freedom – freedom from this place and freedom from other people. That's what *she* wanted.

Delilah pressed her pale face against the chain link fence and stared at the long blades of grass, as if she could stand there all day, watching the grass grow out of control. She certainly did not have anything better to do with her life. Not anymore, at least.

There was a time, though. She once had her entire life mapped out before her. She always wanted to become a lawyer. It was her lifelong dream. What a lawyer she would have made, too. Ever since she was a little girl, she was good at arguing her case. She liked arguing because she usually knew she'd win. On one hand, it got her into a lot of trouble, but on the other hand, she made a lot of friends and her friendship was loyal to the end.

After two failed attempts, she finally passed her Bar Exam, and then the unthinkable happened. A nuclear bomb was dropped over New York City and the world changed in an instant. Suddenly, zombies were real!

Before she knew it, she was forced to evacuate her home in Poughkeepsie. On her way to Elmira, where her grandparents lived, her car broke down in Monroe. It was what she got for buying a lemon. It had been her neighbor's car and it only cost her $1,000. It was the single worst investment of her life. She went to the police station on Stage Road for help. At first, they were very nice to her. They towed her car and dropped her off at a local hotel.

The next thing she knew there was chaos all around. People were panicking. It began as an orderly evacuation of Monroe, but things turned ugly fast, when a self-proclaimed militia, consisting of locals, banded together and began coordinating things. They took control of everything, including the police station and Village Hall.

Suddenly, no one was allowed to leave. People were being executed. Their bodies were taken to a field off Forest Avenue, thrown into a huge pile, and burned. It was horrible.

Eventually, hope began to slip away.

Soon, hungry desperate eyes were upon her. Hands touched and probed, beyond permission. She argued because it was what she knew how to do and was beaten badly for it. She tried to fight and was imprisoned at the police station. She cried and was humiliated in front of everyone, when she was strip-searched. Next, the men took turns with her because she was the "pretty one."

There was a time when she enjoyed being known as the pretty one, but not anymore. Now, she wanted to hide how she looked. She used her long wavy hair to hide her bruised face, but she felt like the men knew what she was doing. It was only a matter of time, before they might cut her hair short.

It was her last line of defense. After she lost that, she would become vulnerable, once again. She could not have that. There had to be something she could do, someplace she could hide. She turned and her eyes moved upward to the watchtower.

There!

Kim gazed up at the watchtower, from where she sat. It was difficult to see inside from the ground with all the metal plating around it. Plus, it was too high. She wondered what the view looked like from up there. How far would she be able to see? Would she see a place, where she could go to be alone? That was what she really wanted… to be alone.

She hated being around men. After being raped over and over, the last thing she wanted was to be around more men. It disgusted her. She felt angry with them, even if they were not the ones, who hurt her. It did not matter to her. Men were men. They were all alike, as far as she was concerned. They were filthy perverted pigs. Her fists clenched tightly causing her fingernails to dig into her palms. She closed her eyes and tried to calm herself.

She fought back the tears that wanted so much to be released. No more tears, she told herself. She spent enough weeks crying. That time was over. She thought she had nothing left, but apparently there was an endless supply that waited to moisten her smooth cheeks.

The images of each man's face that rode her kept passing through her mind's eye like angry clouds passing across the sky. Each was warped and hazy. Just when things seemed clear, they were back. She wondered if the nightmarish images would ever go away. Probably not, she thought. They were hers to keep forever, whether she wanted them or not.

Again, her anger built up within. She wanted to kill someone, but did not have it in her do commit such an act. She had never been a violent person. All her life, she tried to be kind and helpful to others. She had a good education and a great job. All of it went to shit in a matter of hours because of some stupid virus that got too far out of control.

Why did she ever come to Monroe? She could not even remember. It was the absolute worst decision of her life. It changed everything for her. She would never be the same person, again. That Kim was dead and gone.

Delilah walked into the watchtower and walked up the stairs. It was very quiet inside. She liked it already. She reached a long metal ladder, which she climbed to the top level. She was surprised when she noticed there was someone up there.

She froze, unsure what to do.

Woody turned around and said, "Hello. Are you here to relieve me?"

She nodded silently with her hair still covering most of her face. Only one of her pretty hazel eyes could be seen.

Woody sighed, "Oh, good! I really have to use the restroom. Thank you!" Before climbing down the ladder he said, "Uh, you probably should have brought a rifle with you. Anyways, I'll be back fast. Hey! You know what? It's really great that you ladies are here with us. We could sure use more women around here! It's a sausage fest," he laughed. "You get it?"

She stared at him, void of emotion and humor. Somehow, she could sense that he was not very bright. It was the innocent look in his eyes that marked him as a simpleton.

"Uh, I guess I'll head down. I'll be back fast. I just have to use the bathroom." He began to feel awkward because she was not speaking or responding, so he left quickly.

She watched as he climbed down the ladder and down the steps. She looked out through the hole in the metal plating and saw him enter the house. She wondered how hard life had been for him and how people probably thought everything was so easy for him, while, in reality, it had to be ten times harder than it was for everyone else. She knew firsthand because her brother was mentally handicapped.

Thinking about her younger brother, Denny, made her terribly sad. He died so many years ago. He was only fifteen, at the time. Two years younger than her. Everyone thought it was accidental, but she knew the truth. He killed himself, when he jumped into the swimming pool, because he hated his life. He wanted to drown. He even threatened to drown himself, once before. She never forgot that moment. How could anyone forget when a ten-year-old threatens suicide? It was one of the saddest days of her life.

She told her parents, but they did not want to pay for therapy on top of everything else they were paying for to take care of him. He was more of a burden to them, than anything else. They were relieved when he killed himself and she hated them for it.

Now, she understood. The tables had turned. She hated her life, too.

When Kim noticed Woody leaving the watchtower and walking toward the house, she stood up from the porch and walked toward the entrance gates. The last thing she needed was for him to make small talk with her. She was not in the mood. As she got closer, she noticed an elevated platform on the left side of the gates and decided to check it out. She figured if someone said something to her, then maybe she might stop, but no one seemed to notice.

There was a ladder leading up to the metallic platform. She climbed up to the top and stood on its mesh floor. It was more like a catwalk. She noticed a security camera on the twenty-foot wall. It was facing out over the entrance road, which went south at an angle for several yards, before eventually merging with Cromwell Road.

She could almost taste the freedom that road represented to her. She looked down and saw the grass and bushes below. Would she break her legs, if she jumped? Would the camera spot her? Was it even a working camera?

She reminded herself there was no power in Monroe. However, the house had power. Generators.

Well, there was only one way to find out. She lifted her leg over the wall and sat up on the top, straddling it. One leg was in and the other was out. This was her last chance to decide. She turned and faced the house. It was nowhere she wanted to be.

She jumped down and landed between the wall and the bush, scraping her left side against the hard branches. It was not her best idea. She was hurting. There was no time to worry about it. She looked up at the camera and waved, as she ran out of the entrance road and headed south on Cromwell Road.

When Julia saw Kim wave at the camera and leave, she felt like someone had to know. She hurried upstairs and ran into Kirk in the hallway.

"Kirk, one of the new girls just climbed over the wall and jumped down to Cromwell Road! She ran south," she said, sounding flustered.

"What? Why would anyone want to do that?" As he headed for the door to go outside, he asked, "Did you see which one it was?"

"It was that Chinese girl!"

"Asian. We can't assume she was Chinese."

"Whatever! You know what I meant! Stop wasting time!"

Kirk rolled his eyes and hurried toward the platform to see if he could see Kim and maybe call her back and talk some sense into her. However, he stopped abruptly, when he heard Julia scream. He turned quickly and saw her hands covering her mouth. She was looking at something in horror. He followed her eyes up to the watchtower and gasped.

Delilah's limp body was hanging from the watchtower with the rope ladder he made tied around her neck like a noose.

Grant, Liz, Roberto, and Millie rushed outside to see why Julia screamed. A few others soon joined them. The sight of Delilah's hanging corpse was a horrible unexpected sight.

Joy covered Glenda's eyes and turned away to take her back inside. She also had to pull Sam in because he was staring at the body with too much fascination.

Woody went out onto the porch, curious about why everyone was in shock. When he saw Delilah's body hanging from the watchtower, he broke down in tears and started to freak out.

"Oh no! Oh no! No! No! No! It's all my fault!"

Grant patted him on the back and said, "No, Woody. This was something she was determined to do, so don't blame yourself. There's no way you could have known. That girl was hurting too much."

Regardless, Woody still cried and felt guilty. He blamed himself for her death. He knew if he had not left her alone in the watchtower, this never would have happened. He should have been more suspicious because of her behavior. She did not even have a rifle! How could he be so foolish to think she was there to relieve him? He should have known better!

One thing was certain. Kim got the distraction she needed to get far enough away, so no one would find her, if they felt inclined to search. For the moment, getting Delilah down from the watchtower was more of a priority, than chasing after someone who did not even want to be there.

MAN'S END

Chapter Twenty-Four

WHEN THANKSGIVING DAY came, it was only three days after Delilah's death. While there was much for the group to be thankful for, no one really felt like celebrating. The mood all around the compound was dark and somber. It did not feel like a holiday.

The lack of a turkey only made things worse. They considered cooking one of the two fully-grown hens, but that would mean fewer eggs for the next four months or so. It was not a good idea, considering there were additional mouths to feed. A hen can only lay one egg per day and about five per week. The four chicks were still too young to lay any eggs. It was not a sacrifice anyone was willing to make for an eight-pound chicken. It was hardly enough to feed twenty-one people.

Despite not having a turkey, Millie and Angela prepared a nice dinner with Edie and Joy's help. They baked a cake to serve as dessert. Joy appreciated the chance to contribute. It meant a lot for her that it feel like Thanksgiving for the sake of her children. She wanted so badly for them to enjoy the holiday, but she understood it was bad timing for the group.

David was still spending most of his time sleeping. It was all he could do to recover. He needed rest. Aramis kept him medicated, so he would not feel any pain.

Charles and Angelo were still confined to beds, but, at least, they were awake, alert, and able to have conversations. Grant filled them in on everything that was going on. He told them about Kim running away and Delilah's suicide and funeral. She was buried next to Bobby. Grant did not like the idea of putting her next to him, but it was the only cemetery they had.

A week later, Charles was able to walk around, again. He was still weak and unable to go on supply runs, but he did not have to sleep in the dorm anymore. He could return to his own room in the attic. Being back in his room helped to cheer him up. It was depressing him to see David in the condition he was in. He hoped David would pull through.

Charles spent most of the next few days alone in the attic. He wanted to hide from the world for a while. Life was becoming too overwhelming and he needed a break from reality. He let Grant and the others handle things. He only went downstairs to eat and to use the bathroom.

One of the new women, Yvonne, noticed how he would disappear for hours each day. That was the life she wanted for herself. She hated being around these people. She would often watch Charles, whenever he showed his face and made sure he knew she was watching him. Every once in a while, she flashed a flirtatious smile his way, but he was too into his own wallowing to notice.

Meanwhile, construction on the wall finally resumed. Joy, Chryssy, and Sam joined the work crew outside, while Angela and Maxine helped Millie deliver refreshments. Maxine also kept busy cleaning the floors, which kept getting covered in cement.

Devin wanted to work, but his arm was still in a sling. Instead, he helped by taking shifts up in the watchtower. Woody did not like it as much as he used to. He still felt guilty over what happened with Delilah, even though everyone kept telling him it was not his fault. It festered within him.

While working on the wall, Kirk pushed himself harder to make up for the loss of the extra bodies, such as David, Charles, Angelo, and Devin, who could not help. He was glad Roberto felt strong enough to help out. A moment after thinking that, he noticed Roberto was staring off into the distance.

"What's up, Rob? You look deep in thought. Are you still in pain? Why don't you take a rest?"

"No, I'm good. I was thinking about the past few weeks and everything that's happened, since we've been here in Monroe. It made me think of my mother, my sister, and the rest of my family."

"You miss them, huh?"

"Without a doubt, bro."

"I guess you wish they were here. That's understandable."

"Hell no! Are you crazy? I'm glad they're not here."

Kirk was confused and asked, "What??? Why would you say that?"

Roberto answered, "Do you think I want them to live in this mad world? Trust me. I'm grateful they didn't have to see how cruel this world could truly become. I wouldn't want to worry about some assholes trying to turn them into breeders. These women we saved must have gone through a hell that we can only imagine. Who knows how messed up they're going to be, after that experience? They'd be lucky if they didn't have nightmares for the rest of their lives. Let's not forget the one that killed herself."

"Yeah, I hear you, brother. It couldn't have been easy for them, but we need to look on the bright side. That nightmare is over. They're safe now."

"Tell that to Delilah! I know they're safe and you know it, but do *they* believe it? Apparently, those two girls didn't think so. One killed herself, while the other ran off into the wilderness out there."

"Good point. I guess everyone deals with pain in the only way they know how. We can only hope to help, if they allow us, but we can't force it. They have to want our help," Kirk said.

"That's the real trick then. With the way we fought that night, they're probably scared of us. How do we let them know we're not dangerous, when they've seen us in full battle mode?"

Chryssy overhead them and answered, "By making us feel like we're part of the group. Don't treat us like guests or victims. Treat us like everyone else around here. Like this here, what we are doing? It helps me personally. I feel like I'm contributing to something greater than myself."

Roberto smiled at her and replied, "So you feel like what we have here is great?"

"Totally," she responded. "It's got security and people, who seem to care. This could be a good community under the right circumstances. There's hope for something good. Hope is a powerful thing in a time like this."

Kirk nodded in agreement, "You said a mouthful, young lady."

Roberto and Chryssy made eye contact and both smiled. They continued to work close to each other and made small talk for the rest of the afternoon.

It was December. More crops were starting to come in, but the weather was getting colder. They were going to need more supplies. Soon, the first snowfall of the season would come. They had to get in some last minute supply runs, before that time.

Devin's arm was finally free of his sling. He got the idea to go fishing with Woody. They were both good at it. They had five fishing rods and plenty of fishing gear thanks to the haul they got from their Walmart supplies stored by their former group. Kirk and Roberto agreed to go along to watch their backs.

Chryssy also showed an interest and asked if she could tag along. "My dad used to take me fishing all the time," she explained. "Worms don't gross me out. I'm good at netting, trapping, angling, and fly-fishing. Give me a chance. Don't make me a prisoner of this place. Let me do my part."

"Okay, sure," Roberto gave in. "You can go, but stay close to us. Don't go wandering off on your own."

Kirk added, "Yeah. We don't want to go looking for you."

"Deal. I'll stick to you like glue," she smirked. "You might even get sick of me."

Roberto smirked, "We'll see about that."

It was an early Sunday morning, when they headed out. Sunrise was still a half hour away. They used the Ford Explorer, even though David's blood still stained the rear cargo area. Daniel had cleaned it as best he could. Maxine also gave it a try, but it was too late. The blood had left its permanent mark. Kirk threw a small tarp over it and, somehow, that made it okay.

He drove them down to Round Lake. It was only five minutes away by car. The lake was pretty big. There were plenty of small piers they could fish from, which made their options seem limitless. Devin, Woody, and Chryssy each grabbed a fishing pole and attached their bait and weights. Kirk and Roberto stood watch over them. The area was desolate, as far as the eye could see.

By sunrise, their lines were in the water. Devin, Woody, and Chryssy each sat facing different directions on the pier to maximize their chances, while not crossing their lines. Woody preferred to be in the middle, so they let him have his way. Devin and Chryssy did not mind where they sat.

Kirk glanced up at the sun and squinted his eyes. "Man, it's bright. This is the earliest I've been up in a long time. I'm even more surprised that you're up so early," he said to Roberto.

Roberto grinned at him and replied, "Up early? I haven't even gone to bed, yet."

"Dude, you are nuts. You're going to be so tired."

"Then I will have no problem sleeping later. I *could* use a cup of coffee, right about now. It's a good thing I have my thermos with me." He took a sip and smacked his lips together exaggeratingly, "Ah! Now, that's refreshing. This is how you do it, bro."

"You sure love that thermos. I don't think I can remember not seeing you with it in the morning, since you found it."

"Yep. It was one of my best finds. That Dollar General served me well."

"It's too bad Dave couldn't be here," Kirk said with regret. "I miss having him around."

"Yeah, me, too. He's a good guy. I like hanging out with him. He always acts like he hates his life. He makes me appreciate mine, that much more. It's kind of amusing."

Kirk scoffed, "Yeah! I noticed that about him, too. It's hilarious."

Devin turned around and said, "Guys, can you please keep it down? You're going to scare away the fish. It needs to be quiet, if we're going to catch anything."

Kirk replied, "Oh! Sorry, pal. My bad."

Roberto pushed him playfully and said, "Yeah, Kirk. Keep it down. Jeez Louise."

"Oh, shut up, before I throw you in the lake."

Roberto chuckled, "That will really scare the fish, but I bet I'll catch one, first."

They finished up at the first pier by 10 am. It was a good haul for the first half. Devin and Woody each caught four fish, while Chryssy proved her worth coming back with six huge fish. Considering how many of them there were in the group, that only meant dinner for one day.

Rather than head back home, they moved on to another pier at the other side of the lake. Roberto was starting to regret not sleeping. He was beginning to feel tired from standing around doing nothing. The heat from the morning sun was only making him sleepier.

Kirk told him, "Why don't you lie down and take a rest. I can stand guard on my own a while. If I see or hear anything, I'll wake you up."

"Are you sure, bro?"

"Yeah, go ahead. I got this, Rob. Just lie on the pier. It's big enough. I'll make sure you don't roll into the water or accidentally get kicked in by me." He chuckled.

"Thanks. I could use a little nap." Roberto lay flat on the pier for about thirty seconds, before standing up, again.

Kirk asked, "What's wrong? Too uncomfortable?"

"Shhh!" He said. "Look. There, past the trees." He pointed at what looked like a zombie walking through the woods near the lake. "I don't like this. They're getting closer to home."

"Shit, that's not good at all," Kirk replied. He cracked his knuckles and said, "I'll handle it. There's only one. Stay here and keep an eye on these guys."

"No way. I'm going with you. You can make the kill, but I'm watching your back. Devin, heads up. We have a roamer in the woods. We'll take it out. Just stay alert, in case there are more."

"Oh, boy. Say no more. Thanks."

Kirk and Roberto walked toward the apparently lone zombie and it immediately took notice of them. It began lumbering in their direction. Roberto waited to act as bait, while Kirk went around it, so he could hit it from behind with his fire hydrant wrench. It was still his favorite weapon to use, when it came to killing zombies. He was glad he brought it along. He swung hard and bashed its head in.

They checked the area to make sure it was alone, but did not see anymore.

Roberto shook his head and said, "I don't like being out here surrounded by so many trees. The grass has grown so high that it could easily hide more. What if there's a crawler somewhere around here inching toward our ankles?"

"Good point. Let's get away from this tall grass and back out on the pier."

When they were back on the pier with the others, Devin asked, "Did you get it?"

Kirk answered, "Yeah, it's dead for real, this time. If it's all the same with you, I think we should wrap it up. There could be more out there and we still have to hoof it back to our ride. It's a good ten-minute walk from here. I'd rather not take chances."

Devin agreed, "Are you kidding? You had me at 'there could be more.'" He was already reeling in his line. "We're done here, Woody," he said, in case Woody was not paying attention.

"Okie dokey! I just caught another bass."

"Great job. Pack it up," Devin replied shortly.

Chryssy started to reel in her fishing line, but she felt a tug. "Hold on. I think I got something," she said. "Whoa! It feels like a big one!"

"Reel it in and let's pull it out," Devin said.

Roberto pulled out his gun and stood ready. For some reason, he had a feeling it was not going to be a fish at the end of that line. When Kirk saw him with his gun out, he stood ready, too. He knew what Roberto was thinking and began to think the same thing.

"I almost got it." Chryssy groaned, as she struggled. She pulled her pole back and reeled in her line slowly. She did not want to snap it. She pulled it in and finally it burst from the water.

Roberto aimed his gun and stopped himself short of shooting her fish. It was only a large Brown Bullhead. He sighed with relief and lowered his gun.

"Hey! Were you about to shoot my fish? Jesus Christ, Rob. Take it down a notch."

"I thought it was going to be a zombie."

"A zombie?" She looked at it and replied sarcastically, "Yeah, I can see how you could make that mistake. Look at those dead eyes." She giggled. "This is a sexy fish."

Roberto smirked and turned away, feeling embarrassed.

Kirk stepped close to him and said in a low voice, "That girl's getting to you. Are you sweet on her?"

Roberto scoffed, "No, of course not."

"Right. Sure," Kirk smirked. "I got my eye on you, Rob. You can't fool me. It's okay. She's kind of cute and she's got spunk. I like that about her."

"Be quiet or she'll hear you."

Kirk laughed.

They packed up and headed back to the Ford Explorer. The first haul netted them fourteen fish, but the second was even better. They caught another twenty. It was a fine mixture of Brown Trout, Brown Bullhead, Rock Bass, Largemouth Bass, and a Bluegill. Now, they had enough fish for two nights. Maybe even three, if they spread it right. Chryssy knew how to smoke the fish, so it could last longer. Of course, the ride home might have been more bearable with a strong air freshener.

Over the next week, they focused on the construction of the wall. The south side was completed and they were now working on the north side. They were running low in cinderblocks, even after another run to Lowe's. They were going to need a new place to go for blocks, if they were going to extend the wall all the way around the property, as planned.

During dinner, Daniel brought up the subject. "We're going to need more blocks. I think we have enough to finish about forty percent of the north wall. After that, we're done. Cleaned out! We should get another supply, before it gets too cold. It's going to have to be a huge haul. I'm talking big!"

Grant replied, "Lowe's doesn't have anymore. We cleaned *them* out. I suppose we could try the Home Depot that we blew up down by Woodbury Commons."

Liz objected, "No, Grant. I thought we agreed to stay away from that place. There were too many zombies down that way. It could be worse, now. It's too risky."

"She's right," said Charles, as he swallowed a mouthful of food. "It's not safe. We need to expand our search. I think there might be another place, further north in Wallkill."

Yvonne watched him and smiled at him, occasionally. He was finally beginning to notice her smiles and smiled back at her.

"I can check Google maps," Julia said, not noticing the smiling between Charles and Yvonne, "but the Internet searches have been taking longer lately. There's more lag. We could be losing Internet access."

"That sucks," said Sam.

"Tell me about it," she replied. "It was the only reliable thing I could still count on."

Angelo made a suggestion. "I think I may have a solution," he groaned. He was still in pain from his injuries, so every movement caused him to ache. "Do any of you guys remember that hill, just past the far end of the parking lot at the Shop Rite on 17M? There's a retaining wall holding up the hill. There has to be about a hundred cement blocks and they're big. We could use them, but you guys will have to get them without me. I'm still grounded. Aramis will kill me, if he catches me trying to go on a supply run."

"You got that right!" Aramis exclaimed. "You need to stay your broken ass here, until you recover fully, Corporal Williams."

Joy spoke out, "Aramis! The language! Please! I have my daughter here."

"Oh, man! I'm sorry, Joy. I keep forgetting we have a little princess with us. Right, Glenda?"

She giggled and Joy smiled.

Millie smiled at Glenda and said, "She's so adorable. How can you possibly forget her? Look at that little face. *Que linda!*" She said, which meant "how pretty" in Spanish.

"Thank you, Mil!" Joy said with pride. "That's my little princess. She can be a pain in my butt, sometimes, but she's cute as can be."

Glenda giggled, "Ma, you said *butt!* You're talking about me, right?"

"You know it, baby! You're my little butt girl."

Glenda giggled, "I'm not a butt girl!"

Suddenly, David walked into the dining room, surprising everyone. "Butt girl? Hey, what's that great smell? That's messed up. You guys are enjoying *another* delicious meal without me?"

"David!" Edie called out. She was ecstatic to see him up and about.

Kirk immediately stood up and helped him over to his seat. "It's nice of you to join us, *kemo sabe*. We missed you. Sit. I'll bring you a plate."

"Thanks, Kirk. So, what's on the menu?"

Millie answered, right away, "Garlic mashed potatoes and carrots with sautéed fish. Plus, Angela made a special treat, warm homemade biscuits. She made them from scratch and they are delicious!"

Angela blushed, "Oh, stop it."

David closed his eyes and inhaled. "Mm. That all sounds magical to me. It smells even better. So, were you guys planning on eating it all or were you eventually going to bring me some?"

Millie answered, "Don't be silly. Of course, we were going to bring you some. You're plate is in the oven keeping warm. We were just waiting for you to wake up."

He saw that she was not lying. Kirk pulled a plate out of the oven and brought it over to him. It had all the fixings on it and it was nice and warm.

"Thanks!"

"Dig in, bro," Roberto said with a smile. "It's good to have you back at the table. Before you know it, we'll be going out on supply runs together, again."

"Whoa!" Aramis said. "Let's not rush him into healing. He still needs a lot of time, before he's good enough to go back out there. How are you feeling, Dave?"

"Like crap, but my appetite is definitely returning because this smells really good and I'm going to devour it, so if you'll excuse me. My mouth is about to be full and I wouldn't want anyone to mistake me for Charles." He chuckled and began eating, relishing the flavors.

Charles smirked, "Real funny, Dave. Welcome back to our world."

Edie stared happily at David, while he ate. She was so happy, there were tears in her eyes.

It was nighttime in the female dorm room, a few days later. It was very crowded with all the new women around. They were severely filled to capacity and in need of a much larger room. There were four full-sized beds already, but it was not nearly enough. As it happened, that was all they could fit in the room, which once served as the master bedroom of the house. They each had to bunk together with a partner. Edie and Millie shared a bed, since they were close friends and did not mind. Maxine slept in the same bed with the teenage girl named Taryn because Taryn only felt comfortable with her. She was quite timid. Angela was a large woman and took up most of her bed, although she still had to share it with her friend, Yvonne. Julia felt forced to share her bed with Joy and Glenda, which silently annoyed her, so she tended to spend more time in the basement at night. As for Chryssy, she preferred to sleep in a sleeping bag on the floor. It was not as if she had much of a choice.

Using the bathroom in peace had become a rare treat. It seemed like someone always had to go at the same time as someone else and it was always a long wait. Much longer than before! It was a good thing they did not have to share their bathroom with the men or they would really be in trouble. Grant stopped using the female bathroom and had to use the male bathroom on the first floor, instead. There would be no more showers with Liz, out of respect for the other women and Glenda.

On this particular night, Joy waited until the late night hours, so she could pluck her eyebrows, figuring most of the girls were heading to bed. For some reason, only Glenda, Maxine, and Yvonne had gone to bed. Everyone else was still awake.

Millie was lying in bed, reading a book. Angela was lying in her bed, staring at the ceiling and wishing they had a television to watch. Julia was down in the basement sitting in front of the computer, as always. Taryn sat quietly near the window and gazed up at the stars. She liked it when the rooster crowed. It was a new experience for her. Chryssy was sitting alone outside in the backyard, doing the same thing. Edie could not sleep. She was too curious about what Joy was doing in the bathroom.

The bathroom door was wide open, since what Joy was doing did not require any privacy. She also did not wish to seem rude. If anyone had to use the bathroom, she would gladly get out, so they could do so. She tried to be considerate, which was appreciated by the other women.

Edie stood at the doorway and asked, "Why are you bothering with that?"

Joy replied, while staring into the mirror, "Girl, just because it's the apocalypse doesn't mean we have to stop caring about how we look. I know when you found me in that house in Florida I must have looked pretty damn ragged. Trust me, it was pretty embarrassing for me to have cute guys like David and Roberto seeing me like that. Never, again, Edie." She shook her head.

Edie felt a little threatened, when she heard Joy refer to David as cute. The last thing she wanted was for one of the new women to sweep him off his feet, especially one as beautiful as Joy. He was still the man of her dreams, whether or not he realized it. She was not giving up hope that he would get over the knowledge of her past and accept her for who she was today.

She asked, "Can you do my eyebrows for me?"

"Of course! You saved my ass that day. I would have starved to death. I'm almost done with mine. Get that sexy butt in here, girl. Have a seat." She gestured to the toilet. "Welcome to Joy Rahas' Salon and Tranquility Spa."

Edie chuckled, while Taryn now looked toward the bathroom, feeling left out. She walked to the doorway and asked in soft voice, "I don't suppose you cut hair at your salon?"

"Why the hell not?" Joy smiled. "If you can find me a pair of scissors, I'll give you a trim. I used to do this all the time for my little cousins."

Taryn grinned, "Awesome! Thank you." She then pouted, when she realized she did not have the slightest idea where to find scissors. They all knew this had been Charles' house and he was bald. Why in the world would he have scissors in his house?

Millie called out from her bed, "Edie and I have a pair. You can use it. It's in the bottom drawer under the sink."

Edie scoffed, "Duh! I forgot all about those scissors. It's been about two months, since we used them. I used to keep my hair short, but I've been growing it out and Millie likes her hair long."

Joy said, "Your hair looks great, Edie. I love that platinum blonde color. How often do you dye it?"

"About once a month! I'm a natural blonde, but not this light."

"Me, too, but I prefer to dye it blood red," she grinned and tossed her long red hair around briefly. She had lovely hair and a friendly smile. "I think I'm down to my last bottle of dye. Sammy found me a few bottles back in Florida."

Taryn asked, "You're from Florida?"

"The village, not the state."

"Oh."

Joy replied, "Yeah, I know. Not as interesting."

Edie and Taryn chuckled. It seemed Joy's bright personality was helping Taryn to finally come out of her shell. She was also rapidly winning Edie over. It was pleasant to have someone so cheerful around.

Chryssy entered the dorm and was curious why Taryn was staring into the bathroom. She was not shy, so she walked over and peeked over her shoulder. "Anything interesting going on in here?"

Edie chuckled, "Just us bitches being girls."

Joy cracked up laughing, which made Taryn laugh, too.

Chryssy shook her head and smirked, "Why in the world are you plucking your eyebrows?"

Joy explained, "Because we always need to look good."

"I think I look just fine with my brows intact," she responded.

Joy looked at her and said, "Shit. If my eyebrows were as perfect as yours, I'd probably feel the same. I thought for sure you plucked your eyebrows."

"Nope," Chryssy shook her head.

Joy commented, "And the hair? You dye it jet-black, right?"

"Sometimes. My hair is already black, but I like it to look shiny."

"What about your fingernails? Why do you paint them black?"

"I like them black," Chryssy looked down at them. "It's not for anyone else. It's for me. They're my weapons of choice. That's why I sharpen them."

Joy eyed her with caution and smirked, "Girl, you are a bad ass."

They laughed. In the minutes that followed, they continued talking about painting their fingernails and wondered if Edie or Millie had any nail polish lying around.

Angela had a feeling it was going to be a long night. She kept her eyes closed, as she listened to their conversation, since she did not have a television to watch. It almost felt as if she were at the salon, where she and Yvonne used to enjoy going. It felt nice, so she let her imagination take over and, soon, fell fast asleep.

MAN'S END

Chapter Twenty-Five

TARYN HAD BEEN doing well with the computer and security monitors. Julia was grateful that Grant found a knowledgeable assistant for her. It took some convincing on Maxine's part, before Taryn would even listen to Grant. She was still very standoffish due to the murder of her parents and being held prisoner with the looming threat of rape constantly over her head.

It was a nice change to be with this new group. It just took time for her to become comfortable enough to be away from Maxine. Once she finally did, she proved to be a natural with computers. She did not take nearly as long to teach, as it took Daniel to get acquainted with the computer. He was intelligent when it came to engineering and mechanics, but his computer skills all came from Julia's lessons. Taryn, on the other hand, was already a computer geek and although she was very shy, at first, once she was in front of the computer, she opened right up.

"You're getting very good at this," Julia complimented her. "Are you sure you'd have no problem watching so many screens, at once, without getting bored to death?"

"I think I can handle it. This is kind of fun," she said with a slight smile. "Thank you for being so kind to me, Julia."

"Thank you for letting me!"

"Spending time with you is easy," Taryn admitted. "You're kind of close to my age and we both like computers. I guess I feel like I can relate to you."

"Well, I'm glad," said Julia. "How old are you anyway?"

"Fifteen."

Julia frowned. She thought about Taryn's time in captivity and wondered what kind of suffering she endured. All she knew was that Taryn had to watch her parents get killed in front of her. She learned that much from Maxine. She felt so bad for Taryn. She was so young.

Taryn asked, "Why are you being so quiet, Julia? Did I do something wrong?"

"No. I was, uh, thinking about you. I'm really sorry about your parents. Maxine told me."

Taryn stopped using the computer and looked down at the keyboard. She was trying to forget about all that. She wanted to put it behind her. Thinking about it hurt too much.

Julia realized what she had done and apologized, "Oh, man! I'm so sorry I even brought it up. Please, forgive me. I just feel so bad for you."

"Thank you, but I really don't want to talk about it."

"I understand totally. I'm such an ass. I should've kept my mouth shut." Her mind raced for something to talk about that would help Taryn to forget about it, again. "Hey, do you want to hear something crazy? I was in Manhattan the day the outbreak began. I woke up and found my roommate eating my other roommate."

Taryn turned to her and commented, "Oh, my God! Really? That is so gross!"

"Yeah, it was. I grabbed my shit and ran out of there so fast. That's when I ran into Grant and the others. They were about to escape the city, using an old aqueduct tunnel. I went with them. It was so cool, at first. We waded through stagnant water and walked miles through an underground tunnel. We crossed a bridge and it literally exploded, taking two of us with it. It was insane."

"No way! That must have been so scary!"

"Absolutely! It was only the beginning. We finally got out of the tunnels in the Bronx, where we walked several blocks. We managed to hide out in an old abandoned armory that looked like a brick castle and went several levels underground."

"That literally sounds awesome," Taryn said.

"It was, but it was scary. After a while, the zombies had us surrounded. We had to escape through a back door. That's when I met David, Kirk, Edie, Millie, and Angelo. They saved us and took us into Yonkers, where we stayed at Grant's house. He had such a nice house."

Taryn asked, "You like him. Don't you?"

Now, it was Julia, who had been caught off guard. She asked, "Why would you think that?"

"I don't know. I guess it's the way your eyes light up, whenever you say his name or when he's around. It's okay. I won't tell his girlfriend. Your secret is safe with me."

Julia thought about it and decided to confide in Taryn. She needed someone she could talk to about it or she might go crazy. It helped to have a sympathetic ear. "Okay, I admit it. I like him. I never intended to like him. It just happened the moment I first saw him. He's everything I want in a man."

"That's sad," Taryn replied. She felt sympathy for Julia and wondered if the real reason Julia was depressed was because she could not have Grant and probably spent too much time alone in the basement. At least, that's how it seemed from her point of view. She asked, "So, you never stood a chance?"

"Well, actually, I did. I just didn't realize it, until it was too late. I thought Liz was already his girlfriend, but she wasn't. They didn't hook up, until we went to his house, which means I had about two days to make a move and I messed up. I took too long and Liz stole him, right out from under my nose. It took me a long time to accept it. I still get hives when I see them together. I keep thinking that could have been me with him. We would have been so perfect together. We both like exploring abandoned locations. Maybe I would have gone out on supply runs with him, instead of her. Who knows?"

"Well, it's too late to wish for what could have been. There are other cute guys here. Why don't you show Grant what he's missing. Go after one of those other guys."

"It's not like playing a game, Taryn. My feelings are for him. My heart already wants him. I can't just transfer that to someone else because he's unavailable. I've been biding my time. I keep thinking maybe something will happen to her out there and he will become available, again. I know it's a terrible way to think. I hate that I feel that way. I can't help it, though."

Taryn did agree it sounded a bit warped, but she was not going to tell Julia. She wanted to be supportive and tried to offer some reasonable advice. "Did you ever think about swearing off men and trying women?"

Julia looked at Taryn and said, "You're a bit young for me, but I have considered it."

"No! Not me! I would never!"

"You should never say never. You don't know what you'd do, until you are in the position to do it. Trust me. Life can be funny that way."

"I guess. It just seems gross to me. That's not how it was meant to be."

"That's your parents talking." She caught herself, again, when she saw Taryn's expression change, at the mention of her parents. "Shit. I'm such an ass. Sorry."

"It's okay," Taryn lied.

"Never mind me. What about you? That boy, Sam, is close to your age. He's a handsome boy. What do you think of him?"

Taryn shrugged, "I don't know. I haven't really thought about it."

"Well, don't wait until it's too late like I did. Snatch him up, while you still can. That other girl, Chryssy, is young, too. She could be your competition. You just don't know it, yet. After Sam, all you're left with are guys that are too old for you. Trust me. Sam is your best bet at a normal relationship. You're young. Live a little. Life is too short to waste being alone. Take it from me. I hate being lonely. I wish I had someone to hold me in his arms. I wish someone would look at me like I was the most beautiful thing he'd ever seen."

Taryn began to feel sorry for Julia. She thought about what she said and did not want to feel the same way and end up like her. It seemed like Julia was miserable. Sam wasn't bad looking. Maybe Julia was right. Life is too short. It was something to consider.

Later that afternoon, Charles came downstairs from the attic. He was getting tired of hiding up there alone and felt ready to be around others. He walked out to the backyard to see if anyone was out there, since it was a nice day. Mostly everyone was working on the wall, so Yvonne was the only person sitting out there and she looked bored out of her mind.

"You know? We do have books," he said. "It beats sitting out here doing nothing."

She turned to him and smiled, "Hello, stranger. I'm not the reading type and I do *not* do hard labor. Why don't you sit out here and join me? It's a nice afternoon."

"Thanks. I don't mind if I do." He sat down in a seat beside hers and asked, "So, how are you liking our home, so far?"

"It's definitely better than sitting in a damn jail cell. I'll give you that," she replied. "The guys here don't seem to be flocking over me either, which is a nice change. Everyone around here always seems to be too busy for socializing, not that I'm complaining. I enjoy the solitude. I wish I had my own room like you. You're lucky."

"Well, it was my house."

"And you let everyone stay here? That's very generous of you. I don't know if I would have done the same."

"We went through a lot together as a group, before coming here," he explained. "It seemed like the right thing to do, at the time. I don't regret it. These are good people."

"Yeah. Well, I'll have to take your word for it. I really haven't taken the time to notice. I'm not sure I want to stay here. I've been considering my options."

Charles looked disappointed and asked, "Why don't you want to stay here with us? This place is safe. We help each other out. It works. You should give it a chance. You may like it."

"Well, I do like certain things about it." She stared at him momentarily, and then added, "I just don't know if I want to be around so many people that I don't really know or trust. There's no privacy. I need my space. If I had my own room like you, I might change my mind. I just don't see myself staying here too much longer and there's nothing to really keep me here."

"That's too bad," he responded.

She looked at him and grinned, "Why do you want me to stay so badly?"

"I didn't say anything like that. I just said you should stay here because it's safe. Isn't it better for you to be safe? It's dangerous out there. You should know that, by now."

"Mmhmm. So, then you don't really care if I stay or not?"

"Yeah, I care. I don't want you to go out there and get captured by more sickos. I won't be feeling up to another rescue anytime soon. You'd be on your own. Why be on your own when you can be part of a family?"

Curious, she asked, "So, you think of these people as family?"

He nodded, "Yeah, why not? It's basically what we've become."

"That's interesting," she replied. "I see something different, from my point of view."

"Really? What do you see?"

She answered, "I see a group of white people, biding their time in your crib and running things, while you hide away up in the attic 'cause you feel like you've maybe lost control of something you once had a handle on."

"Really??? That's deep," he responded mockingly. "Maybe you might be onto something, but it's not how you put it. Yeah, I was hiding away in the attic, but it's only because I was feeling overwhelmed by the responsibility of leading this group and keeping everyone alive and happy. I needed a break. My injury seemed like a good time for me to rest. I saw that everything seemed to be under control with exception to that suicide. That girl had a lot of issues, though, which she brought with her, when she came. There was no changing that. It was inevitable. She was only waiting for the right chance to do what she probably wanted to do for weeks.

Another thing, I don't see myself as being *overrun* or *oppressed* by 'white people.' We have a nice mixture here. There are African-Americans, Hispanics, and Caucasians. We don't mention race here. We are all equal, under God. That racial crap is over. It's an ugly part of humanity that is best left in the past. Don't bring it here because we don't need it." He seemed almost angry with her.

"Wow. Okay. Sorry. I didn't realize I touched a nerve," she said, feeling awkward. She realized it was not in her best interest to get on his bad side, so she said, "Let's forget about everyone else, for a minute. I'm really more interested in you. Tell me about yourself. What did you do, before it all went bad?"

Charles relaxed and answered, "I was a cop in the NYPD. Actually, I was a sergeant."

"You worked for the man? I see. That explains everything."

"What's that supposed to mean?" He sounded angry, again.

"I didn't mean to offend you. I just meant that I see why you feel the need to help others by taking them into your home and why you think of these guys as your family. I take it some of these guys were cops with you? You were their supervisor, right?"

He crossed his arms, "Yes. What's your point?" He became defensive.

"No point. I could just tell. That's how you cops are. You look out for the blue family. I've heard of the 'Thin Blue Line.' You guys do anything for each other, even cover up for one another."

Charles exhaled and responded, "If you're trying to give me a reason to back your earlier decision to leave, it's working. I'm thinking more and more that you should explore your other options, if you'd rather not be around a bunch of former cops."

Her smug expression changed quickly. She stated, "That's not what I want or what I'm trying to do. I'm really sorry. I just have so much anger stored inside me." She opted for a new route, since her conversation was failing miserably. It was time to get on his sympathetic side. "Some of those bastards were cops. They did terrible things to us." Tears began to fill her eyes. "I was forced to do disgusting things that still make me nauseous, just thinking about it." She cried and wiped away her tears.

Charles sighed and said, "It's fine. I understand. You're going to be okay, now. If you stay here, nothing like that will happen to you. You will be safe. You have my word."

"Are *you* going to protect me?"

"Yes, if it comes down to it. I can *and* will protect you, but so will everyone else here. It's not just me. We are *all* here to keep you safe. This is bigger than any one person."

"How gallant of you." She wiped away her tears.

"You're a hard woman to please, huh?"

She looked at him and stared at his body. Her eyes then moved back to his and they locked. She said, "There's really only one way to please me. It takes a certain kind of man."

"*O-kay*," he responded awkwardly.

She shifted closer in her seat and asked, "Why don't you show me your room? I still haven't seen it." She half smiled at him. "I'd really like to see it. Can you show it to me?"

"Um, yeah. I guess I can do that. Come on. Follow me," he said. He stood up and led the way.

She followed him up the stairs to the attic. Once they got inside, she closed the door. When he turned to say something, she grabbed him and practically shoved her tongue into his mouth. They kissed passionately, and then she pulled off his robe. Her hands caressed his bare chest and he pulled her closer.

"Take it easy on me," he said. "I'm still hurting in places."

"Don't worry, baby. I'll be gentle, this time," she grinned.

They kissed, again, and eventually moved toward the bed, where they spent the rest of the day and night. It seemed she finally found a place, where she could have that privacy she craved and she intended to make the most of it.

The next morning, after breakfast, Roberto went down to the gym. He was getting himself back into shape. He needed to make his body strong, again. He began by stretching on the mats. He stretched his arms, legs, back, and neck. Next, he did a few basic exercises, such as push-ups and sit-ups. He did fifty of each.

When he was done warming up, he stood up and shook it off. It was time to hit the weights. He began with some twenty-five pound weights. He had one in each hand and did fifty reps with both. He then switched to a large barbell, which had fifty pounds on each side. He lifted it up to his chest, and then up over his head. He continued, until completing twenty-five reps.

Once he was done, he grabbed a jump rope and did some jumping for about five minutes to cool off. He followed that up with about fifty jumping jacks. At last, he was feeling like his old self, again.

He didn't notice Chryssy standing at the doorway of the gym. She watched, looking impressed, as he worked out and finally said, "Damn, Rob! You're a beast!"

"Huh?" He turned around surprised. He did not expect anyone to be standing there watching him. "Are you stalking me?" He joked.

"No, silly. Just observing a master of his body at work. That's sexy. I didn't realize anyone really used this gym."

"Why have it, if we aren't going to use it?"

She placed her hands at her hips and replied, "I asked myself the same question every time I saw some useless piece of junk that my parents owned. They saved everything! You'd think they never heard of the garbage or making donations to the poor."

He chuckled, "I know what you mean. So, are you here to get that body into shape or to distract me from getting mine into shape?"

"I want to get toned like you. I'm not looking for big muscles, but I want to be stronger. I want to increase my endurance and stamina. Basically, I want to be a lean, mean, sexy ass machine."

"Well, you're almost there. You got the lean and mean down pact. I think with a few years of hard work and surgery we can get you the sexy ass machine part. No promises, though."

"Jerk. That's not even funny. I know you think I'm sexy because I've seen you watching me," she said with a smug grin on her face.

"Oh, you have? How do you know what I was thinking, while I was watching you?"

"That's easy. You're tongue was hanging way down on the floor. It was a dead giveaway."

"I see you came with jokes. Let's see if I can't work some of that humor off of you. Come here and get nice and close," he beckoned with his forefinger.

She walked over to him and stood directly in front of him about one foot away. "Here?"

He stared into her eyes and smirked, "Yeah, that looks about right." He bent down really close to her lower region. "I have something for you," he said.

"Do you?"

"Stretch out your hands," he said, as he came back up slowly.

She did as she was told and he placed the ten-pound weights into her hands.

"I'll start you off light, so you don't break. I'm going to need fifty reps with each hand. You can alternate, if it helps. That might be easier."

"Gee. Thanks. You really know how to treat a girl."

"Girl? I don't see a girl in front of me. I see a lean, mean, sexy ass machine! Am I right?"

"Damn skippy!"

He backed away and began counting, "Let's go! One, two, three!"

An hour later, they were done with their workout. It was time to hit the showers. They each went to their own bathrooms, although after the sexual tension they felt in the gym, it was obvious they would have both preferred to shower together. Perhaps, had they been alone in the house, things might have played out differently. While showering, they were both thinking about each other.

Afterwards, they met up in the kitchen. Roberto needed a drink of water, so he grabbed a bottle from the refrigerator. He smiled when he saw her come into the kitchen for the same reason.

"That's exactly what I needed."

He passed her the bottle and grabbed another one for himself. He opened it and took a sip of water. "Ah! Nice and cold," he said. He turned to her and looked at her admiringly. "Look at you, looking all nice and clean," he said with a smile. "That was a good workout, huh? We got nice and sweaty!"

She chuckled and replied, "Yeah. Thanks. So, how many days a week can we do that?"

He answered, "We can start out with three times a week. Keep it up for about a month and you will get where you want to be. You're not too far off. Honestly, you're really in good shape already."

She stepped closer and batted her eyes at him playfully, before saying, "I'm glad you think so." She then turned away and said, "It's warm in here. I'm going out for some fresh air. Are you coming?"

She strutted out onto the porch, making sure to shake her firm behind, while she walked. She was wearing tight black jeans and a tight white t-shirt, which emphasized the shape of her body well. Her movements were hypnotizing for him.

He gulped down his bottle of water and replied, "Yeah, I could use some fresh air, right about now." He quickly followed her outside and stood beside her on the porch. He was very taken by her. He found it sexy how her wet black hair draped partially over her face. For once, she was not wearing dark lipstick or eyeliner. He could see her face clearly and it was absolutely beautiful.

She looked around the grounds from where she stood and her eyes turned up to the watchtower. A wicked smile appeared on her face. She turned to him and asked, "How much privacy can a person have up there in that tower?"

"A lot. One person usually goes up at a time. It's kind of small up there."

"Do you think two people fit comfortably?"

He shook his head, "No. That's no place to mess around. If you go up there, you need to take it seriously. The person in that watchtower becomes our eyes and ears, while they are up there. They're also the only alarm system we have. If danger comes near, we need to know about it. So, I would say, it is not the best place for two people, especially two people, who might be thinking naughty thoughts."

She pouted, "Party pooper."

"However, that van over there," he pointed. "It's perfect for two people, who might want to be alone. The black school bus next to it is even better because it has cushioned seats and a nice long back row seat. I just thought I'd throw that out there, since you're asking."

She smirked, "I think I'm ready for my next workout. Wanna join me in the school bus?"

He grinned, "We actually call it The Intrepid."

"The what?"

"Intrepid. Never mind. It's not important. I'd love to join you. Let me get the keys, first. They're in the garage. We keep all the vehicles locked, when they're not being used."

"Ooh. The garage, huh?"

"No way!" He said sharply. "There are cameras around here. Julia might see us going in there together. Hey, why don't you go wait for me by The Intrepid and I'll meet you there in a few? It will be less obvious that way."

"Cameras," she responded. "Right." She then smiled, "That's kinky. Maybe another time."

He scoffed, as she walked away shaking her behind for him, again. Feeling excited, he went into the garage to get the keys for The Intrepid and hoped Kirk would never find out about this. He walked to The Intrepid, where she waited looking as eager as he felt.

"Well," she said, "Are you just going to stand there and leave me waiting?"

"I just want to make sure we're not the movie of the week."

He looked around and up at the watchtower to make sure no one was looking, before he opened the door. She quickly stepped inside and he followed. They walked to the rear of the bus and sat down in the back row. She climbed onto his lap and wrapped her arms around his neck. They stared into each other's eyes, and then he pulled her closer. She leaned in to kiss him. It was awkward, at first, because they were both nervous.

Despite Chryssy's confidence, this was her first time kissing someone in over two years. She spent much of her time, before the apocalypse being a loner. For some reason, there was something about Roberto that attracted her like a magnet. She wasn't sure if it was pure lust and she really didn't care. All she cared about was being with someone of her choosing, someone who seemed to get her and she believed it was him.

It had been so long since Roberto thought about a girl in the way he was thinking about her, in this moment. Ever since he first laid eyes on her, he felt there was something different about her. She was both exciting and gorgeous, at the same time. He looked forward to exploring everything he could about her.

Their lips locked in a fit of passion, while their hands explored freely. It seemed they both found what they were looking for because they did not come out of the bus, until dinnertime.

MAN'S END

Chapter Twenty-Six

IT WAS THE week before Christmas and all through the compound, there was not a spare cinderblock to be used for the wall. It was time for another supply run.

Daniel pleaded his case to Grant, "I'm telling you there is not one spare block we can use. It's all gone. We still have more than half the north wall to go and we haven't even started on the wall bordering the woods. We're gonna need another supply run and this one has to be big. Take both flatbeds, if you need to. Find whatever you can and bring back anything that isn't tied down. I want to get this wall done, before it gets too cold to work."

"Okay. Relax, Danny. I'll take out a crew myself. We'll bring back everything we can find. We'll try the south, again, since the north is tapped out. I'm going to need to take a lot of muscle with me."

"Fine. We can't do any work anyway. Take all the muscle. I'll even go, if you need me to."

"If we take two flatbeds, I'm actually going to need you to come. I won't risk taking Aramis and David is out of the question. Angelo still isn't ready to go back out either. I guess Kirk can drive one and you can take the other. Can you drive a flatbed?"

"Yeah, sure. So, when do we leave? I'm ready today."

"Tomorrow morning will be fine. I need time to get the crew together and they need time to prepare. This is a big job. I'll go talk to Charles, too. He needs to know."

Daniel scoffed.

Grant asked, "What is it?"

"Why do you even pretend that you're not the one, who's really in charge around here? Don't ask Charles. Just tell him."

"It's not like that, Dan. Charles is in charge. Oh, jeez. I can't believe I just said the name of a TV show. Regardless, he is our leader."

"You could have fooled me." Daniel walked away with his hands in the air.

Grant was bothered by his words. It was not the first time someone mistook him for leading the group. Sometimes, he felt like he was in charge, too. He wondered would it be so bad if he were? He had some good leadership qualities and the guys seemed to respect him.

No. What was he thinking? Charles was the leader of the group. He was the sergeant. This was his home. It's just how it was meant to be.

Grant went up to the attic and knocked on the door. "Charles, it's Grant. I need to talk to you about a run. We need supplies."

Charles called out from behind the door. "Go ahead! Get what you need! Let me know when you get back and don't forget to take a radio!"

"I'm leaving tomorrow."

"That's fine! I'm kind of busy, at the moment!"

Busy? Grant put his hear to the door and heard laughing. There was a woman's voice, too. He immediately understood. He went down to the common room and found Liz reading a horror novel.

"Hey, babe," she said without barely taking her eyes off the book. "This is such a great book! I am so glad you brought these books. We really need more."

"What are you reading?"

"*The Shining.*"

"Ah, the master of horror himself. Yeah, it was definitely one of his best. We can try to find some more books when we get a chance." He paused and asked, "Hey, Liz?"

"Yeah, babe?"

"Did you know Charles was messing around with one of the women?"

"Yep. Yvonne."

"Oh. Her? She's so… anti-social."

"Yep, but she's also very pretty and Charles has probably been feeling lonely. Leave him be. Let him enjoy some fun for a change."

"Yeah, of course. I just didn't know. I'm surprised he didn't mention it to me. We used to talk about everything. Wait a minute. How did you know?"

She looked around the book at him, as if to say, are you really asking me that?

"Never mind. I forgot," he rolled his eyes. "Women's intuition is a powerful all-seeing skill. Blah, blah, blah. Right?"

"Almost. You're learning, but I do *not* say blah, blah, blah," she said in a mocking Count Dracula voice imitating the animated film, *Hotel Transylvania*.

He sighed, "Right, and neither do vampires. Anyway, I'm going on a supply run tomorrow. We need building blocks for freaking *Pink Floyd's* wall. Do you want to come?"

"Can't," she shook her head. "Not today and not tomorrow."

"Is it that time of month already?"

"Yep. Feeling crampy. The blood fest should begin tomorrow, hence the vampire mockery." She turned a page in the book and continued reading. She suggested, "Take Kirk with you."

"I am. I need to take Daniel, too. It won't be enough. It's going to be a big haul. We're taking both flatbeds for this trip. I'm going to need at least two other people."

"What about Rob?"

"Liz, you know Charles gets his panties in a bunch whenever I suggest taking Rob with me on a supply run. He doesn't like having the two of us out there at the same time. We're the combat trainers."

"That's just silly. You and Rob make a great team. You almost think alike. You're both nuts. Hey, what about Devin? His shoulder is healed."

"Take me where?" Devin asked, as he entered the room, holding a book. He was coming in to change it for another one.

Grant turned around to face him and said, "I need some guys for a supply run tomorrow morning. How's your shoulder feeling? We'll have to do a lot of heavy lifting."

"I'm good. Count me in. I've been easing the strength back to my arm by lifting some of the lighter weights. Call it my own physical therapy."

"Great. Thanks," Grant replied. "We're leaving, after breakfast, as usual."

"Sounds good to me. Now, if you'll excuse me, I need to grab another book to read. Not working has given me a lot of free time to catch up on some good books."

"I'm glad you like them. I plan to get some more soon. Most of those came from my house."

"Awesome! You have some interesting taste in books, but I like it. Ah, this one looks good. Jack Vance. *Planet of Adventure*."

"That is a great book," Grant said. "I read it years ago. Enjoy. I'll see you in the morning."

He left the room in search of the other guys.

Grant entered the male dorm room, where he found Kirk and Aramis speaking with David, who was lying in bed.

"Hello, boys."

"Hey, Grant," Aramis said.

"What's up?" Kirk asked.

David just waved.

Grant said, "Kirk, I am in need of your expertise. Well, one of them. We're heading out on a big supply run tomorrow morning, after breakfast, and I need you to drive a flatbed. We're taking both trucks. Daniel will drive the other one."

Kirk asked, sounding surprised, "Daniel? Wow. He's actually going with us on a supply run? That's a first. The chief engineer himself."

"It's either that or I take Aramis and I think that would be a mistake, considering David is still not well. Sorry, Aramis."

He smirked, "Man, I'm used to it already. I'm like the Prisoner of Charleskaban in here. God forbid, if I should go out on a supply run with you guys. The world would come to an end. Oh, wait. It already did. Didn't it? My bad."

Grant chuckled, but he felt bad for Aramis. He was right. He had virtually become a prisoner the moment he arrived at the compound.

Aside from one supply run to pick up the trucks, he had not left at all. Grant walked over to him and placed his hand on his shoulder, "If David wasn't lying here wounded then I would definitely bring you along. We really do need you here, though. Now, more than ever."

"Yeah, I know. Thanks, Grant." Aramis frowned.

Grant went out to the front porch to find Roberto. He figured he'd probably be out there smoking a cigarette like he often did. When he didn't find him, he tried the backyard. Joy was sitting out there with Sam and Glenda. Glenda was running around playing. For a moment, he considered asking Sam, if he wanted to go, but he regained his senses and went back inside the house.

Next, he went down to the basement, where he checked the gym. Roberto was in there training Chryssy, Edie, and Millie.

"Rob, can I speak to you a moment?"

"Sure. Be right out."

"Okay, thanks." Grant waited in the hallway near the entrance. When Roberto walked out, he said, "I'm going on a supply run tomorrow morning, after breakfast. I was wondering if you wanted to go. I'm going to need some muscle and you're one of the strongest guys in the group."

"You need me to kick someone's ass for you, bro? Just say the word."

"Funny. No. We're out of cinderblocks. We need to find a shit load. We're going to try taking them from that retaining wall near Shop Rite. We'll be taking both flatbed trucks."

"I don't have a problem with it, but won't Charles complain if we both go out together?"

"He probably would, but I have a feeling he won't even know we're gone. He's been spending a lot of time up in the attic. He's even got himself a girlfriend to keep him company."

"Really?" Roberto asked surprised. "That dirty devil! Which one?"

"Yvonne."

"*Her?* She's so… I don't know. What's the word I'm looking for? Rude? Mean? Ungrateful? Bitchy?" He shrugged, "Oh, well. At least, she's got a pretty face and a nice ass. Good for him."

"Yeah. Whatever. So, are you in?"

"Grant, do you really have to ask? You and I alone are pretty damn tough, but together? We're unstoppable! I only have one condition."

"What?"

"I want to bring Chryssy along. She's in training. This will be good for her."

"That young Goth girl? What is she like seventeen years old?"

"Bro! She's twenty-one. I think she can handle it. She's impressed me lately and you know that's not easy to do. I think a day of lifting blocks will do her some good."

"If you think she's ready and can handle it, then I don't have a problem with it."

"There's one more thing, but don't spread it around too much. She and I, we're kind of a thing."

Grant looked at him in surprise and responded, "No shit? Cupid's been on a roll, shooting arrows at people around here."

"Come on! You didn't think you and Liz would be the only couple all the time. Did you?"

"Actually, I did. Nah, I'm kidding. I'm happy for you, Rob. You deserve some happiness. I hope you and her last a long time. Just know, it gets harder when you have someone like that to care about, someone to worry about. It can become a bit of a distraction. Keep her safe because if something happens to her, it will drive you mad."

"Bro, you think I haven't thought about that? I watched my sister die. I didn't think I'd ever let myself be close to anyone else, again, but I was wrong. You guys became my new family. I realized I couldn't live without truly living. You know what I'm saying?"

"Totally. You need sex."

Roberto laughed, "Ah, man. I like you, Grant. You speak the truth. Let me ask you this. Do you love Liz? I mean, are you in love with her?"

"Absolutely. She's the light in my day."

"Do you think she feels the same about you?"

"I know it. She told me so."

"Good. That's great, bro. I'm really happy for you both. Well, that's what I want and I think I might have found it with Chryssy."

"I hope so, brother. You deserve it. Bring her along. I'll make sure to help you keep her safe."

"Thanks. Maybe it can be almost like a double date."

Grant shook his head, "Liz won't be coming. She's got that pesky monthly visitor."

"Ah, that sucks, bro. No fun for you this week."

"It's fine. We have plenty of fun doing other things, too. Oh, man. I just thought of something. Do you know where we keep the condoms?"

"Condoms? We have condoms?"

"Shit yeah! We do! Grab a box from the top drawer of the white storage bin in the garage. The last thing you want to do is get this girl pregnant. This is no place for a baby. Not, yet. Maybe when the walls are finished. You need to be careful, Rob. We can't bring a baby into this world, until we've created a safe environment for one. Don't screw up. I wouldn't want you to have any regrets."

"Thanks, bro. I'll go get a box and keep it in my bag. Wow. I didn't realize we had condoms," he scratched his head.

Grant shook his head and chuckled, as he went upstairs, while Roberto walked back into the gym to resume his training class with the girls.

Unbeknownst to both men, Julia had been listening to their conversation from within the security hub. She stood at the doorway and wiped away her tears. Hearing how much Grant loved Liz made her both angry and sad. She began to feel anger toward Grant for not seeing the opportunity he could have had with her months ago.

She sat down feeling frustrated.

Taryn came into the room, not long after, and sat down beside her. She seemed happier than usual. "Hi, Julia," she said with a smile.

"Hey," was Julia's dull response.

Taryn realized she was upset and asked, "What's wrong?"

"I think I hate Grant."

"Oh." Taryn noticed the anger and hatred in Julia's face. It scared her a little. She thought about leaving and coming back later, but she was afraid it would offend Julia, so she stayed. She sat quietly next to her and watched the computer monitors.

Julia was too busy staring straight ahead.

Later that night in the female dormitory, the women were preparing for bed in their overcrowded room. A single candle lit the darkened room. Not long after most of the women went to sleep, Julia climbed out of bed and snuck out of the room to go downstairs.

Taryn was still awake and wondered what she was up to, so she followed her. When she stepped out to the hallway, Julia was nowhere to be found. Taryn figured she probably went down to the basement to sit by the computer, even though Charles had already agreed to sit down there for the night. Yvonne even agreed to keep him company. Therefore, it was doubtful Julia would want to go down there and be a third wheel, unless her plan was to send them away, so she could stay down there alone.

Taryn hoped that was the case because if not, she was worried about why else Julia might have snuck out of bed in the middle of the night, especially in light of her recent confession.

The door to Grant and Liz's room was closed and there was no light coming from under the door. She had a feeling they were probably sound asleep. Grant had plans to head out early the next day, so he needed his rest.

She went downstairs to the first floor and noticed candlelight coming from the kitchen, so she went there. Sure enough, Julia was in the kitchen, standing in front of the sink.

"Hey, Julia," Taryn whispered. "What's wrong? Can't sleep?"

Julia immediately turned around because Taryn startled her. However, Taryn instantly became startled at the sight of Julia, holding a large kitchen knife in her hand. She gasped in horror.

Julia scowled at her, "You scared the hell out of me! What are you doing down here? Are you following me?"

"Uh, no. Well, sort of. I was only concerned," Taryn answered nervously. "Why are you holding that knife?"

"It's none of your business, Taryn. Go back to bed."

"No," she shook her head. "Not until you tell me what you're up to," she responded defiantly, although she was trembling with fear.

Julia walked toward her, while still holding the knife, and stopped right in front of her. She said through clenched teeth, "I like you, Taryn, so I'm going to ask you, again, real nice. Go back upstairs and mind your business."

Taryn swallowed nervously and shook her head. Again, she said, "No, Julia. Please, put the knife away and come upstairs with me. Don't do anything that you'll regret."

Julia breathed heavily and turned around. She stomped back over to the sink and slammed her hands down on the sink. "Ow! Damn it!" She cried out. "Look what you made me do! I cut my hand!"

"Let me help you. I'll clean it up." Taryn approached her nervously and stopped at her side. She looked at Julia and pleaded, "Please, put the knife down, Julia, and let me help you. I'm your friend. Remember?" She slowly reached for the knife to take it away, but Julia glared at her and she froze. She immediately withdrew her hand.

After the longest minute of Taryn's life, Julia dropped the knife into the sink. She turned away slowly and sat down at the dining room table. Taryn grabbed a bunch of paper towels and wrapped Julia's hand. She also cleaned the blood from the sink and floor, where it dripped. Taryn found a first aid kit in the kitchen pantry and began tending to Julia's open cut. She cleaned it and applied a large band-aid.

"You should probably ask Aramis to give you stitches tomorrow."

"No, I'm fine. Quit fussing over me."

"I'm only trying to help," Taryn explained.

Julia sighed and dropped her head onto the table over her arms, which were folded, as if it were naptime in kindergarten. She began sobbing uncontrollably, making Taryn feel even more awkward. As Julia cried into her arms, she mumbled, "I hate my life! Why can't things ever go my way, for once? I only wanted to be happy, but no. I can't have that luxury." It was difficult for Taryn to understand half the things she was saying, since she was speaking into her arms, but she got the gist of it.

Taryn put her arm around Julia and said, "Your time for happiness will come, but not if you do destructive things like this. You need to be patient. You'll find the right man for you and when you do, you're going to forget all about Grant. You'll see. It's going to be okay. Just be patient. Okay?"

Julia looked up at Taryn and touched her face, which made Taryn tremble, again. "I'm so sorry," Julia said. "I didn't mean to scare you. I know you're my friend. Please, forgive me."

"Of course, I forgive you, Julia. I totally understand. Don't worry. It's water under the bridge. Let's just pretend that never happened and never speak about it. Okay?"

Julia nodded and sniffled.

"What's going on? Is everything all right?" Roberto asked, as he stood in the doorway.

Both girls jumped. They had not expected anyone else to be up. It was so late. Julia wiped away her tears and Taryn stammered to give him an excuse for why they were sitting in the dining room so late at night with Julia crying.

"Uh, w-we were just, um, t-talking. Julia wasn't feeling well and we, uh, didn't want to wake the other girls. That's all."

"Ah, I see," he responded, unconvinced. "Well, as long as everything is all right, I'll leave you to it." He walked out to the porch to smoke a cigarette, shaking his head. He knew something was up, but was not too sure he wanted to know what it was, considering the parts that he overheard.

Taryn escorted Julia back upstairs to the dorm room and they went to bed. A short while later, Roberto went back into the dining room and noticed a drop of blood on the table. He touched it and it was still wet. He walked into the kitchen and saw the bloody knife in the sink. He cleaned it and put it back where it belonged, and then washed his hands.

"Hmm," he thought, as he stared at the stairs, leading up. "That's an interesting turn of events."

MAN'S END

Chapter Twenty-Seven

THE NEXT MORNING, both flatbed trucks drove out through the gate and left the compound. Aramis locked up for them, so they wouldn't have to stop and waste time. He climbed up to the platform and watched, as they headed south on Cromwell Road. Liz watched from the watchtower with her rifle in her hand.

Kirk drove the lead truck. Riding with him were Roberto, Chryssy, and Grant crammed into the cab of the truck. Daniel drove the second truck and followed closely. He was unfamiliar with the roads and did not want to get separated. Next to him were Woody and Devin.

Both trucks reached Route 17M and turned left to go toward Shop Rite. As they drove, they noticed the town was not as abandoned as they left it. There were several zombies roaming around the grassy fields of the park, who were now following the trucks as fast as their rotted legs would take them.

Grant closed his eyes and sighed. "Shit. There are a lot more of them than I ever hoped to see up this way. Stop the truck, Kirk. We need to take them out."

Kirk stopped and Daniel stopped behind him, feeling confused. He would have expected them to drive faster, not stop and wait for the zombies to catch up.

Chryssy turned to Grant and asked, "Dude, why can't we just drive away from them?"

"Because they'll catch up to us. We're not going far. We can't afford to leave them around. If they reach our compound, it will be harder to deal with them because of the wall."

Roberto also explained, "Lesson one for today... never leave alive, what you can kill today. You don't want to be the poor sap that gets surrounded by these flesh-eating freaks. We need to kill all of them, if we can and we can't use guns. Stay in the truck. Let us handle this, but watch us and learn."

She nodded, "Okay. Be careful."

Grant rammed his knife into the head of the closest one. Kirk swung his fire hydrant wrench and knocked another one down. He then finished him off with another hit to the head. Roberto joined them and swung his wrecking bar so hard that the rotted zombie's head was knocked off.

"Holy shit," he said. "Did you guys see that?"

Kirk chuckled, "Homerun, buddy. Just watch it with that zombie juice. We don't want to get any on us. That would not be good."

"No, sir," Roberto agreed. "It would not."

Daniel watched in utter confusion. He asked, "Why are they wasting time killing them?"

While getting out of the truck, Devin replied, "Because they are too close to home, would be my guess. We can't leave them roaming around. They might find the compound. I'm going to help."

Daniel sighed, "Okay, but this is definitely going to burn up some of the energy we need to load up these two trucks, but what the hell?"

Daniel was not going to let his younger friends handle the zombies on their own. He grabbed a metal shovel from behind the seat and climbed out of the truck. He walked toward a lumbering zombie and used the shovel to slice off its head with one swing. Next, he pushed another one back with the shovel and knocked it to the ground, before slamming the shovel into its neck, pushing it down with his foot, and chopping its head off, as well.

Woody closed his eyes and began praying. He already knew shooting was unwise, unless all other options had been expended. He did not bring any other weapon, other than his rifle. He was not very good at close quarters combat either, so he knew waiting in the truck was his best option. He hoped no one would get bitten or upset with him. He prayed for his friends to walk away from this fight safely.

Chryssy watched, as Roberto smashed a zombie's head in with a single blow, coming down hard from the top with the hammer end of his wrecking bar. She also observed the other guys make their kills. There were about ten zombies in the park, so they each killed more than one.

When they were done, they got back into the trucks and continued up 17M and into the parking lot for Shop Rite. There were a few zombies in the parking lot, as well. Kirk used the truck to run them down. Daniel followed suit and did the same, running over the ones Kirk already hit and taking down a few more.

They stopped when they reached the hill at the far end, near the retaining wall.

Grant turned to Chryssy and said, "Keep your eyes open. Don't let anything sneak up on you or on us. The undead ones don't make much noise, so it's very easy for them to get close, unless they really stink badly, which is usually the case, fortunately for us. Of course, this strategy works best, if you don't have a stuffy nose."

"Which I don't. So, keep my nose open, too?"

"Exactly," Roberto said. "We'll make a warrior out of you, yet. Come on, it's time for today's workout." He pointed at the hill, after they stepped out of the truck. "We have to get all of those stones onto these trucks, but first, we'll need to remove them from the hill, which won't be easy. We have to be careful not to get buried by dirt."

She nodded, "Okay. That sounds insane, but doable."

Kirk smirked, "This will be fun, as long as we are not interrupted."

Some of them grabbed shovels. There were only four. Kirk would use a pickaxe, instead. Woody climbed onto the roof of one truck with his rifle and sat down. He would keep watch, while they dug out the large stone blocks. Chryssy also stood watch and made sure no zombies approached.

Woody observed a few zombies that they ran over were still crawling toward them at a snail's pace. "We have a few crawlers coming our way from the parking lot. Should I shoot them?"

"No," Grant responded. "Do you have a knife?"

"I'm sorry, I don't," he shook his head with regret.

Chryssy stepped forward and said, "I do. Should I go stab them in the head?"

Grant turned to Roberto and let him answer that question.

Roberto asked, "Do you think you can do it without hesitating?"

"Yes," she replied. "They're super slow and I have my work gloves on."

Grant asked, "Have you ever killed one?"

She shook her head, "No, but I'm not afraid to kill one."

Grant looked at Roberto and said, "She shouldn't go alone for her first kill. Go with her and show her how to do it. Make sure she doesn't get any blood on her. Not a drop."

Roberto nodded and took Chryssy to the parking lot to teach her how to kill crawling zombies. He demonstrated on the first one and walked her through the next one, which she did. She did not hesitate. In fact, she almost seemed to enjoy it. He let her kill the next one on her own. She did well.

The others had been completely crushed by the heavy tires of the trucks, so they were dead.

She asked, "How did I do?"

"Good, but don't allow yourself to become overconfident. Overconfidence can get you killed. Always be very careful and think of each kill as if it can kill you because, in most cases, it probably can. The infection is passed along through their bodily fluids. If their blood or saliva gets on you and penetrates your skin, you will change within the hour. It will be a very painful process, too, because you will feel your body dying from the inside out. Please, don't ever underestimate these things."

"Things? Aren't they still people?"

He shook his head, "No. They aren't. Not anymore. It will be best if you remember that. Once someone is infected that person is as good as dead. After their bodies die, they become something else entirely, something very dangerous. They become ruthless hunters."

She swallowed nervously. "Thanks for the lesson. I'll definitely be careful."

"You better," he winked at her and she smiled.

Over the next several hours, they worked hard to remove the large stones and load them onto the truck. There were over two hundred stones. Once the first truck was full, it was time to move the second truck closer.

However, it would not start. Daniel tried, again, but the truck stalled out on them.

Grant asked, "What's wrong?"

Daniel replied, "I think it's the starter."

Kirk agreed, "Yeah, that's what I was thinking, too. That sucks."

Grant rolled his eyes in frustration and asked, "Do you think you guys can fix it?"

Daniel scoffed, "Yeah, I know I can, but it's going to take a few hours and parts that we don't have with us. We don't even have them back in the garage. The best bet is to leave this truck behind. Finish loading the other one, until there's no more room, and take the load back home."

Devin asked, "How are we going to all fit on one truck that's fully loaded?"

Daniel smirked, "That's a really good question."

They both looked to Grant for an answer. He sighed and answered, "When the truck is full, Daniel can drive it back. Whoever we can squeeze onto the truck goes back with him. The rest of us will have to wait for a pick up. Someone will have to come back for us using the Ford Explorer."

Roberto said, "I'll wait with you, bro."

Chryssy looked worried and stated, "It will be dark soon. Won't it be dangerous? What if more of those 'things' show up?"

"If they do, we'll have to kill them. Hopefully, that won't be the case."

Kirk said, "I think I should stay with you guys, too. I don't like the idea of leaving you out here."

Grant reminded him, "It won't be the first time Rob and I are out here without a ride. We'll manage. I would prefer if you went back and came to pick us up. You know the way in the dark."

Devin said, "Grant's right. I'll wait with them."

Kirk looked at Devin and asked, "Are you sure, pal? This place looks a lot less inviting at night."

"Yeah, I remember. As long as the group from the Village Hall is dead, we'll be fine. We have a radio, so we should be okay. If we have to hide, we'll let you know where to pick us up."

Grant added, "It might also be a good idea to bring a person to act as your gunner, so you can focus on driving, just in case, and don't forget to grab another radio, so we can be in touch. Okay. Not for nothing, we should finish loading this truck, before it gets dark. Time is wasting."

They all agreed and went to work. It took them another hour and a half, before the rear of the truck was fully loaded with the large cement stones. By then, the sun had gone down. There were still a few stones stuck into the side of the hill, which they could always return for another time.

Kirk got into the driver's seat and Daniel climbed in with him. Chryssy hugged Roberto and climbed into the truck next. Woody got in last and closed the door.

He said, "You guys be very careful. I don't want you to die."

"Thanks, Woody," Devin replied. "Believe me. We don't want to die either."

Kirk looked at Grant, Roberto, and Devin and felt apprehensive. He said, "I'll be back as fast as I can. Where are you going to be waiting?"

Grant replied simply, "We'll wait in this other truck, where it's safe."

Kirk nodded, "Good call. Just lie low, if you see more zombies. It's too dangerous to go around fighting them in the dark."

Devin checked the area and observed how dark the parking lot had gotten. The lack of streetlights made it almost pitch black. The only light was the moonlight above. He responded, "Did you say if we *see* more zombies? I doubt we will be able to see anything in about fifteen minutes. Hurry back."

Kirk nodded and waved, as he drove away.

Grant climbed into the driver's seat of the stalled truck. Devin got into the middle and Roberto got in last. He closed the door and they began their waiting game.

When Liz saw only one truck returning, she became worried. Her heart almost stopped when she did not see Grant exit from the truck. She raced down from the watchtower and ran over to Kirk, as he closed the gate.

"Where's Grant???" She demanded.

Kirk turned to face her and he responded, "Relax, Liz. Grant is fine. The other truck stalled out. We had to ditch it. Grant, Rob, and Devin volunteered to wait for me. I'm going back to get them. I just need to grab the keys to the Ford. I was going to take Woody with me to get them, but why don't you come along, instead? I know you're a great shot."

"You bet your ass I'm going with you. Let me just run to the bathroom real quick. Do NOT leave without me!"

"I wouldn't dream of it. Hey, Woody," He called out. "Do us a favor? Take the watchtower for a few, until we get back."

"Um. Okay," Woody replied reluctantly, before moping away to the watchtower.

Julia was watching through the security cameras and also noticed that Grant did not return. She began freaking out. Based on Liz's reaction and how she ran down from the tower, and then raced into the house, it did not look good. Julia wanted to go outside and find out what happened to Grant. She prayed he was okay and regretted ever saying that she hated him. It wasn't true. She did not hate him. She loved him! When she saw Liz running back out toward the gate and get into the Ford Explorer with Kirk, she became even more curious. Daniel opened the gate and they went back out. He then closed the gate. Why?

She needed to ask Daniel what happened. He would tell her. She hurried upstairs, abandoning her post and leaving the monitors unattended. She raced outside, grabbed onto Daniel's arm, and demanded to know what happened to Grant.

"Daniel! Where's Grant? Why didn't he come back with you guys? Where's the other truck?"

"That stupid truck broke down. Why are you acting so crazy?"

"Uh, it broke down? Oh, I thought… um, I mean, I'm glad everything is okay. I'll, uh, see you later. I need to get back downstairs." She turned and went back into the house, feeling like a complete fool. She cursed herself for making a scene. Only after heading back into the house did she realize that Chryssy was staring at her like if she were a crazy person.

She went into the bathroom and closed the door, until she felt calm. She splashed water on her face, and then went downstairs. As she sat down at the computer, her eyes focused on the monitors and she thought she saw something move through the trees. She zoomed in close and realized what she was looking at. There was a zombie at the fence facing the woods to the west!

Suddenly, Julia heard Grant talking over his radio. "Kirk, get your ass back here! There are too many of them! We're being overrun!" Next, there was yelling in the background, followed by several gunshots.

A moment later, Kirk's voice could be heard responding, "Hang on, buddy! We're coming! Grant? Grant!" There was silence on the radio.

Julia sat frozen in her seat and almost forgot about the zombie outside of the fence.

Kirk and Liz arrived behind the Shop Rite near the hill, where the truck was left. Grant, Roberto, and Devin were not inside.

"They were supposed to be waiting in the truck," Kirk said with a look of surprise on his face. "Why would they leave the truck?"

"You heard what he said," Liz replied. "They were being overrun." She got out of the truck and turned on the flashlight, which was attached to her Colt M4 Carbine. She pointed it around and checked the ground. There were several dead zombies around the truck. A chill went over her when she saw the two-way radio on the ground. She bent over and picked it up.

Kirk asked, "What is it? What did you find?"

She tried to speak, but could not muster up the strength. She turned and showed him the two-way radio. It was still turned on. She forced the breath out of her mouth and said, "Grant..."

"Oh, man." Kirk shuddered. "Liz, that doesn't mean anything." He was not so sure if he believed his own words. He stepped out of the truck and walked over to her. "Maybe they dropped it and couldn't get to it in time. They probably ran somewhere nearby to hide. Maybe they're in the Shop Rite?"

He turned on his flashlight and looked as far as he could see across the parking lot. There was something else on the ground in the direction of the exit ramp to Route 17M. He rushed over to see what it was. His legs almost buckled under him, once he saw what it was that was on the ground.

Liz called after him, "What is that, Kirk? Kirk!"

He picked it up and swallowed nervously. He turned around and was holding Roberto's wrecking bar, which was dripping with blood. He mumbled, "Rob would never leave this behind."

Liz noticed what it was and fear gripped her tightly. She gasped and her hand went over her mouth in shock. "Oh, my God. No," she whispered. Dreadful thoughts passed through her mind and her eyes became watery. She began breathing fast and heavy. She thought she was going to hyperventilate.

Kirk was still standing there a few feet away from her with the bloody wrecking bar in his hand. His voice broke as he asked, "What do we do, Liz?"

"We need to find them! Let's get back to the car and drive around!"

"Right," he responded, although he was not so sure if his legs could carry him back to the Ford Explorer. He felt so numb. He forced himself forward, until he got back into the driver's seat. Liz was already inside. He drove across the parking lot in the direction of where he found the wrecking bar. A thought occurred to him and he turned toward Shop Rite, instead. The shopping cart in the open doorway had been moved. A glimmer of hope came over him and he stopped.

"Grant would move that cart on purpose to let us know someone was inside. It's been moved. We should check inside."

"Okay," she responded weakly. Considering the wrecking bar was away from Shop Rite, she didn't think they would be inside, but she was willing to check everywhere to find them.

As they went into the Shop Rite, Kirk was still holding the wrecking bar. He had not even realized it was still in his hand. It was a good thing he had on gloves. The blood on it could very well be infected. He prayed it did not belong to any of the guys.

Liz pointed her rifle and light ahead of her, while going through each aisle. She came across a zombie, who turned to face her and walked in her direction. She aimed quickly and shot it in the head.

Kirk called from another aisle, "Liz! Are you okay over there?"

"We're not alone in here! Watch your back! There might be more!"

They met up a couple of minutes later near the cashiers. The zombie she shot was the only one in the supermarket. They hurried back out to the Ford Explorer and left the parking lot. When they reached Route 17M, they had to decide which way to turn, north or south?

Liz pointed across at Crane Park. There were zombies wandering around blindly over the grass in the park. There were more near Airplane Park on the other side of Millpond Parkway to the north, right before the parkway curves toward the south.

"Let's follow the zombies," she suggested. "We can kill some along the way."

Kirk nodded in agreement. At the same time, he hoped none of the zombies would be their friends. He was uncertain if he could kill one of them, if it came down to it, especially not Roberto. They had become such close friends over the past few months. Kirk loved him like a brother.

As Kirk and Liz drove south along Millpond Parkway, they began to see larger clusters of zombies. There were unquestionably a lot more than they expected to find. There had to be nearly a hundred.

Liz hesitated to shoot because she did not want them to swarm around the vehicle. Running them down would only result in getting body parts caught in the wheel wells, and then they would really be in trouble. She wished she thought to bring a knife with her.

Kirk stated, "There are too many, Liz. We can't go this way. We might not make it out alive. I'm sorry, but I'm turning around." He swung a fast u-turn, which only attracted more zombies. He drove forward a few feet and stopped. "I have an idea," he said. "If our boys went down that way, they are probably knee deep in zombies. I know a way that will get them to follow us, instead, and maybe give the guys a fighting chance."

"Then let's do it," she urged.

He honked the horn loudly and kept his hand on it for several seconds, until he had the attention of every zombie in the area. He turned to her and said, "Start shooting as many as you can. Focus on the ones that are too close to us. I'm going to get them to follow us. I'll take them back south. Maybe they'll return to where they came from."

He turned left onto Route 17M and sped south coming to a stop at Lake Road. He hit the horn, again.

"Hold on," Liz said. She got out and climbed into the backseat, so she could easily move from one side to the other. She then began shooting at the zombies in the park, firing one shot at a time and taking the time to aim, so no shot would be wasted. She killed about seven zombies, but the horde kept coming, so she kept shooting.

Kirk waited and let her shoot as many as she could. He honked the horn, so they'd keep coming. As long as they came spread out the way they were, it was easy for her to take them out, one by one. Kirk wished his shooting skills were better, but they were not. It was best to leave the shooting to the expert.

Liz began shooting faster and taking less time to aim. She was still hitting them, but not all were dying. There were just too many to get them all. She suggested, "Now might be a good time to drive away. I can't get them all and I'm running low in ammo."

"Say no more. Put on your seatbelt," he responded. He drove south on 17M, until it met up with Stage Road and turned south onto Stage Road. He honked the horn repeatedly to ensure that the horde of zombies was still following. He led them down, until he reached Orange Turnpike.

Liz asked, "Do you even know where we're going?"

"South," he said. "We'll worry about getting back home, once these bastards are far away from it. It can't be too hard to find our way back."

"Okay," she said. "I just hope this helps Grant and the others."

Kirk replied, "Either way, it will help us, if we lead them away from Monroe."

She nodded hopefully. Her mind was on Grant. She wanted to believe he was okay. He had to be hiding out somewhere. Leading the horde away would give him the chance he needs to get to safety. It was going to be too hard to find him, but she knew he and Roberto could always walk back home, once the area is cleared out. They've done it before. Devin just had to stick close to them and he'd be fine.

A short time later, she asked, "Where are we, now? Do you know?"

"Liz, I have no freaking idea. I told you. I'm just driving. I promise, we will find our way back. For now, I need to keep going south with as little turns as possible. I believe we're still on Orange Turnpike. I'll take this as far as I can go."

He drove slow enough to allow the zombies to keep up. He was grateful, there were no newly infected in the crowd. That alone, gave him hope that his friends were still okay, wherever they might be. He had to believe it.

They eventually reached Route 17 at Southfields. Kirk turned off the lights on the Ford Explorer and sped up. He made a fast left and began heading back north at a fast speed. He flicked the lights back on, so he would not crash. He suddenly felt a burst of confidence. He knew where he was, once he realized they were near Woodbury Commons. He got back onto Interstate 86 and headed up toward Exit 129 for Museum Village Road.

They were both glad to leave the horde in Woodbury. Kirk hoped the zombies would not find their way back north, again.

"I think we should head back home," he said, sounding defeated. "Hopefully, our long joy ride got most of the zombies to leave the area. I'll head back out, first thing in the morning, and search for the guys. Those guys are very resourceful. They were made for this world. They're probably hiding somewhere safe. If we try to look for them, it will only keep the zombies in town. We need to allow the stragglers time to follow the rest of the horde. It'll be a lot easier to search in daylight and with a lot less zombies." He kept his fingers crossed.

She frowned, but she knew he was right. "You can stop trying to sound convincing. I agree with you, but I'm going with you tomorrow morning," she insisted.

"That goes without saying," he responded.

Of course, Liz wanted to keep looking. It did not sit well with her to leave Grant and the others out overnight. Unfortunately, she was down to her last few rounds of ammunition and did not bring a back up weapon. Besides, Kirk was right. They needed to give the zombies time to follow each other out of town, as per the plan. In the morning, she'd be ready with lots more ammo and a knife.

She prayed the guys were somewhere safe. They had to be.

Roberto's bloody wrecking bar.

MAN'S END

Chapter Twenty-Eight

S OMETIME EARLIER... Grant stared out across the darkened parking lot near Shop Rite. His back was aching from all the heavy lifting he had done earlier. He could not wait for Kirk to come back and pick them up, so he could take a nice refreshing shower.

He wondered how long it would be before the water stopped coming through the pipes. They had been lucky so far. Things could change over the winter. Waterlines could become damaged and with no one left to repair them, clean water would become a memory. He dreaded that day.

Of course, they could always revert to the old ways and use the old well, which had been boarded up for decades. At least, they would not have to dig a new one. Acquiring a cistern would also be helpful.

Roberto also had a lot on his mind, but the disturbing incident from the previous night was at the forefront. He knew he had to tell Grant about it. He hoped he would get a chance to do it in private and without someone sitting between them. However, this seemed like a good enough time as any to mention it. He began, "Hey, Grant?"

"Yeah?" Grant turned to him.

"I want to talk to you about Julia. I know you two are friends, but do you know that she wants more than that?"

Devin looked at Grant.

Grant asked, "What makes you say that?

Devin turned to Roberto.

"Last night I found her in the kitchen with Taryn. She was crying. I only overheard part of the conversation, but I know it was about you. When I asked what was wrong, they gave me some excuse about Julia not feeling well, and then they went upstairs. I found a knife in the sink and there was blood on it. I also noticed a fresh drop of blood on the dining room table. She cut herself and I think it was because of you, bro."

Devin raised his eyebrows and looked straight ahead. He always knew she had issues, but this?

Grant sighed with concern and asked, "Did you hear them say anything specific?"

"Taryn told her not to do anything destructive and that she would find the right man. I figured you needed to know about this, considering we already had one suicide recently."

"Yeah, thanks. It is good to know. Maybe I'll have a talk with her."

Roberto nodded, "That would be a good idea."

Grant looked out of his window and stared across the parking lot. Suddenly, a large shadow figure in the distance caught his eye and distracted him from his thoughts. There was movement at the far end of the parking lot. It might have been a deer, but he was not quite sure. There were more of them daring to venture into town over the past few weeks. They no longer had to worry about people, so why not?

Three deer leapt out of the shadows, past the front of the truck, and fled up the hill.

Roberto cried out, "Whoa! What the hell was that?"

"Just a family of deer," Grant responded calmly.

"Why were they running so fast? They scared the shit out of me."

Grant exhaled and responded, "I hope we don't need to find out." He faced the direction where they came from and waited. Everything seemed still for about a minute. Suddenly, there was movement. Was it another deer? He hoped so. No, it was a person, most likely another zombie.

He sighed in annoyance, "Heads up, boys. It looks like someone invited himself to the party. I believe his ETA, at the rate he's walking, is about three minutes. That's just enough time to listen to a Beatles song, if the radio actually played music like it used to. Of course, there is the small fact that the truck won't start, so that's not an option, regardless."

Devin commented, "That's too bad. I wouldn't mind listening to *Hey Jude* or *Let it Be.*"

Grant turned to him and said, "You do realize that *Hey Jude* is about seven minutes long and I'm pretty sure *Let it Be* is longer than three minutes, too. I was thinking more along the lines of *A Hard Day's Night* or *Help*, which we can certainly relate to, considering our current predicament."

"Yeah, you're right," Devin nodded. "I guess I just prefer the later years."

Roberto interrupted them and said, "I like the Beatles, too, but now is not the time. We have another two coming on my side. I'm going out to take care of them."

Grant replied, "I'll get this guy on my side."

They both stepped out of the truck and walked toward the zombies. Roberto stabbed the closest one in the head with the pointed end of his wrecking bar and drop kicked the other one, so he could hit it, while it was down. Grant pulled up his gloves nice and tight, before jabbing his knife into the eye of the zombie in the parking lot. It tried to reach for him, but fell limp and died.

Grant noticed three more coming up onto the entrance ramp of the parking lot from Route 17M. "I have three more coming from 17M, but they're spread apart." He waited for them to get closer, so he could kill them, too.

Devin got out and stood beside him. He glanced over at Grant and said, "I thought you could use a little help from your friends."

Grant chuckled at the Beatles song reference and replied, "Thanks. I get by with a little help from my friends."

Roberto said, "Guys, while we wait for those pus bags to get here, would you mind leaving the songs alone and helping me with these two? They're coming kind of fast, compared to the last two."

Devin turned and said, "I got this, Grant. Let me know when our other friends get closer."

Roberto and Devin took out the two zombies and looked around to see if more were coming. It was so dark that it made it difficult to see anything that was more than a few feet away. It was a good thing their eyes were starting to adjust to the darkness.

"They're getting closer," Grant said.

They each picked a target and went for it. Each zombie was killed brutally and efficiently. However, there were still more to follow. Two more approached from 17M.

Grant groaned, "What the hell? Which one of you guys has the zombie cologne? They keep coming!"

"Those damn deer led them right to us," Roberto complained.

Five more zombies came up the ramp from Route 17M, after the other two. Now, they had seven to contend with or so they thought. Another three were right behind the last five. To make matters worse, there were two more coming from the back road on Roberto's side, and then another one behind them.

He suggested, "Let's take these three out, first. They're closer."

Grant was beginning to think waiting in the parking lot was no longer a good idea. "We should relocate. Shit. I just thought of something. If we let these zombies continue in this direction, they will eventually reach home. Let's lead them away in the opposite direction."

Roberto asked, "What about killing them?"

"There are too many," Grant replied. "We can kill any in our way, as we go. Let me grab the radio from the truck."

Roberto told Devin, "Let's kill these three, while he does that."

"Right."

They both picked a zombie and killed it, while Grant grabbed the two-way radio from the truck.

"Hurry up, Grant," Devin urged.

Roberto said, "Shit! Four more coming from this back road!"

Grant considered their options and said, "We'll head east. This parking lot is big. We'll have room to maneuver around them. Come on!"

The next two zombies were nearby, so he stabbed one. As soon as he did, he saw three more zombies coming from the north end of the parking lot. "Oh, you've got to be kidding me!"

He lifted up the two-way radio and shouted into it. "Kirk, get your ass back here! There are too many of them! We're being overrun!"

Nearby, Roberto swung his wrecking bar at a zombie and it slipped out of his hand. He shouted, "Shit! Stupid! Stupid! Stupid!" He pulled out his gun and began shooting at the next five that approached from

THE MANHATTANVILLE INCIDENT

the east. He looked around, but could not see his wrecking bar. It was too dark to see anything.

As more zombies approached, Devin shouted, "Forget it, Rob! You can get it later!"

Roberto scowled and pulled his knife from his boot. Shooting was not the smartest idea.

Grant shouted, "Let's get the hell out of here, guys!" He began to run, but tripped over something and dropped the radio. When he looked to see what he tripped over, he noticed it was a zombie that had been crawling along the darkness. He kicked it away and stood up. He was about to go for the radio, but the other three zombies were too close.

Devin shouted, "Leave it! We'll come back for that later, too! There's no time!"

They fought their way past the approaching zombies and did not hear when Kirk responded through the radio, "Hang on, buddy! We're coming! Grant? Grant!"

The three men ran for their lives and headed east through the parking lot. They dodged and weaved or killed whenever possible. More zombies kept coming, making it difficult to make a stand. The gunshots drew in every zombie in the area and there had been quite a few following the family of deer.

Once Julia came to her senses, she ran upstairs to the first floor and shouted to anyone who would listen, "There's a zombie in the woods at the west fence!"

Aramis came rushing out of the male dorm and asked, "Did you just say there was a zombie at the west fence?"

"Yes!" She nodded frantically. She pointed toward the backyard, "He's in the woods, but he's looking into the fence! He knows we're in here! He's not going away and soon we'll have more! They'll push the whole fence down!"

"Relax, I'll take care of it," he responded. He ran outside and picked up one of the long thin pipes that were stacked near the east wall facing Cromwell Road. He ran around the house to the fence at the far west end of the compound. He stopped and searched for the zombie. It was hard to find in the dark.

"Ah, there you are," he said to himself. He walked closer and saw that the zombie was standing knee-deep in the moat just outside of the fence, which placed the zombie's head at waist height. Aramis watched it for a few seconds and wondered why the piranhas had not begun eating it. He remembered it was December. The first day of winter had come and gone. The piranhas probably died when the water began getting colder.

He shrugged indifferently and aimed the pipe through the fence at the zombie's head. He pushed it through with all his might, but only succeeded in knocking the zombie over into the moat. The pipe was not sharp enough to penetrate the skull.

He pulled the pipe back inside, feeling disappointed.

Angelo came up from behind him and said, "You might want to use something more effective, when killing these things." He aimed his MK 18 Mod 0 at the zombie's head and fired one shot killing it. His weapon had a suppressor attached to the barrel, which muffled the sound. Attracting more zombies would not be an issue.

Aramis shrugged and commented, "Hey, it's not my fault. I lack experience in the field. I haven't killed many Zs, since this thing started. No one gives me the chance."

"Trust me. You're lucky," Angelo said. "It's not fun fighting these things. They can easily overrun you, especially in large groups. The less you see, the better off you are and the longer you'll live."

Aramis sighed, "Yeah, I know you're right. I just wish I had more experience. There's gonna come a day, when I'm going to need it."

"That's probably true. If you want my opinion, I think you should insist on going out on some supply runs, at least when we need medical supplies. Keep on teaching others first aid, so that when someone gets hurt, you're not always the go-to-man."

"They're still going to come to me. I'm the only one, who's actually certified. Nobody wants to take a chance with an amateur in a life and death situation."

Angelo stated, "That's fine and good, but I meant when someone has a minor injury. Let one of your 'nurses' handle it. Give them their experience, while you supervise. I'm sure you'll agree that experience makes all the difference in the world. Once they get experience, you will eventually get your chance to have yours."

"Thanks," Aramis said. "I think I'll take your advice. Oh, and thanks for handling this character for me." He gestured to the dead zombie floating in the moat.

Angelo looked down at it and griped, "Aw, man! Someone's going to have to remove that from there in the morning, otherwise it's going to stink up the area. Why do I have a feeling it's going to fall on me to do it?"

"Hey, it's your kill," Aramis smirked.

Angelo grumbled.

After escaping the parking lot, Grant, Roberto, and Devin ran eastbound across Route 17M and into Crane Park. They knew they would have the same advantage of movement, as they did in the open parking lot. The last thing they wanted to do was get trapped on a dead end street or in an abandoned house or building.

The zombies from the parking lot followed them down to Route 17M. When the guys looked to the south, they realized why the zombies kept coming. There must have been about one hundred zombies marching up the road like an invading army.

Roberto's jaw dropped open. "Holy shit! Look at all of those bastards!"

Devin commented, "I wonder if they're part of the horde that attacked my old group. They came from the south up through New Jersey, I bet. We heard there were outbreaks in New Jersey earlier in the summer. Things got pretty bad, after New York City was nuked."

Grant stated, "Speculate later. Run now. Remember, we want them to follow us, so don't run too fast. Let's try to keep about a block's distance between us and them."

Roberto and Devin agreed.

Grant led them outside of the park to Millpond Parkway, where they headed south. They rested, while waiting for the horde to cross the park.

Once the zombies caught up, he said, "Okay, let's move."

Next, they ran toward where Lake Road becomes Lake Street on the east side of Crane Park and waited, again. It was a good thing none of the zombies were newly infected or they might have really had a problem. It was not so bad running from the slow moving zombies, as long as they maintained their one-block head start.

Roberto asked, "Where exactly are we taking them? Do you have a plan?"

"Yes," Grant responded. "South and away from here. We don't go south anymore. Once they're all headed south, we can hide somewhere and wait for them to pass us. In the meantime, I figured we could head up to the same rooftops on Lake Street, where we hid during our fight against the other group. That way we can watch the zombies from a safe vantage point, while staying out of sight."

"Good plan," said Devin, as he nodded in agreement.

"Thanks. Let's get moving. We'll head up the same way Liz and I did that day. There's a fire escape ladder on Lake Street that will get us into a third floor window. Afterwards, we can climb out a back window onto the roof and cross over to the roof of the dance school. Follow me."

He led them to Lake Street, where they jumped up to the fire escape ladder of a white building. They hurried up to an open third floor window and ducked inside, before they could be seen.

"Okay, come on," he led them through the apartment. "There's another window we can climb out through to get onto the roof. We can walk to the next roof and watch over them, while we wait it out."

They followed him out through a window onto the roof and over to the next roof, just as he said. From there, they had a good view of the rear parking lot and the dark streets below. There was just enough moonlight shining down on the lake in the park to create a reflection of light that allowed them to see the zombie horde walking south along Millpond Parkway and through the park.

The zombies wandered around in search of their elusive food with no luck. They had no idea to look up to the rooftops. Most continued walking south, while a number of them turned onto Lake Street and walked east. There were also a few that stood in the park and went nowhere.

Grant, Roberto, and Devin were crouched at the edge of the rooftop and looking down at the horde of zombies. It was disappointing to see that the horde was not leaving the area, as expected, but at least they were no longer heading west toward the compound. Still, too many zombies were lingering in the area.

Grant complained, "Well, this sucks. It looks like we might be spending more time up here than expected. Hey. What have we here? It's about time. Here comes our ride." He pointed at the Ford Explorer.

Roberto shook his head and said, "Ain't that a bitch? Our ride is here and we're stuck all the way up here without a radio to let them know where we are. You know something, bro? It's almost kind of funny, when you think about it. Hmm. I wonder if I can see my wrecking bar from here."

Grant grinned, "Don't worry, Rob. We'll get it back, even if we have to make it into a supply run. We'll need that radio, too. I'm sure the zombies won't steal our stuff."

"How can you always be so sure? I don't trust these bastards one bit."

Devin shook his head and chuckled in amusement. He was glad to be with two people, who could keep their head and still joke in a time like this. The guys from his old group were nothing like these guys. This group was insane! It almost seemed like they were having fun.

"Hey!" Grant complained, "Where is Kirk going? He made a u-turn!"

Suddenly, they heard Kirk blasting the horn of the Ford Explorer.

Devin said, "It looks like he's trying to draw them away from us. Sweet."

Grant replied, "I doubt it, since he has no idea where we are, right now. However, it does look like he's trying to get them all to follow him."

"Eh, same difference," Devin shrugged.

They watched as Kirk turned south onto Route 17M, and then came to a stop on the other side of Lake Road. He began honking the horn, again. Suddenly, they noticed Liz get out from the passenger side and jump into the backseat.

"Liz?" Grant looked worried. He did not expect Kirk to bring her along, but then he remembered his last radio transmission. She might have overheard and insisted on coming, which meant she was probably worried sick.

"It looks like she came to get her man," Roberto smiled, while patting Grant on the back.

Grant did not pay attention. He was too busy thinking of a way to signal her without letting the zombies know where he and the other guys were hiding. He watched her shoot down about a dozen zombies in the park, before more entered the park and crossed over to go after them.

Devin watched in amazement and commented, "She's pretty good. Was she military?"

"Yeah," Grant answered. He sighed. He could not think of anyway to get her attention, especially not while she was shooting. He wanted to wave at her, but he knew she was going to be too focused on aiming to look up at the rooftops, past the park. Kirk continued honking the horn, while Liz kept shooting zombies. She began shooting at a faster rate, as the bulk of the horde drew near.

"Get out of there," Grant said, knowing they could not hear. "What are you waiting for, Kirk?"

As if on cue, Kirk began driving south. Grant got up and hurried to the south side of the roof, so he could see. When they reached the next intersection, Kirk honked the horn, again. When the zombie horde got close, they continued south. Grant watched, until they were out of view. Amazingly, most of the zombies followed them south, until there were only a few stragglers in the area.

Roberto looked down and said, "We can navigate through these slowpokes. I say we head back for the radio and my wrecking bar, and then contact Kirk for a pick up somewhere safe."

Grant walked to the southeast corner of the roof and looked down at the rear fire escape. The parking lot below was empty of zombies. He turned to Roberto and said, "I like the way you think. Let's head down this way. It's much faster than the way we came up."

He jumped down to the fire escape below and went down the metallic steps to the parking lot, just as he did on the night they fought the other group. Roberto jumped down next, followed by Devin.

When they reached the parking lot, Grant suggested, "We might need some extra ammo and I know where we can find some."

Roberto asked, "What do you have in mind?"

Grant gestured east toward the rubble of the destroyed Village Hall and former Town Office building. Just beyond those ruins were the remains of the police station.

Devin grinned, "Good thinking. There has to be more than a few guns lying around."

They walked over and searched the rubble of the destroyed buildings. The smell of death was pretty strong, so they had to either hold their breath or pull their shirts over their mouths and noses, as they searched. Animals, or zombies, had devoured most of the corpses from the other group, but there was still enough rotten meat to create a funky odor, including one zombie that was trapped in the rubble.

Several minutes later, it was agreed they had more than enough extra weapons and ammo to carry. They made sure to kill the trapped zombie, too. It was time to acquire a ride. There were still a few police vehicles parked behind the police station. Devin knew the dead bodies in the lot had keys to some vehicles. He had shot out the tires and windows of two vehicles, but there was still another SUV that was intact. As luck would have it, the body next to that particular vehicle had the keys in his skeletal hands.

"Gross," Devin scowled in disgust.

Grant did not care. He bent over and grabbed the keys from the corpse. He unlocked the door and got into the driver's seat, before he inserted the key into the ignition. Once he turned it, the police SUV started right up without a problem. He grinned. They would not be walking back, after all.

Roberto called out, "Shot gun," and then got into the front passenger side, while Devin got into the backseat.

Grant drove the police SUV out of the parking lot and headed toward Lake Street. He continued along Lake Road to the west side of the park. On the way, they ran over two zombies that had not followed the others. Grant turned right at Route 17M and headed north. He turned up into the parking lot of the Shop Rite and hit the high beams. He turned the vehicle slowly, so that the lights would light up the parking lot. Oddly enough, the wrecking bar and radio were nowhere to be found.

"I knew it!" Roberto griped. "I told you those bastards couldn't be trusted! They stole my wrecking bar and even took the radio!"

Devin smirked, "Actually, I think Kirk and Liz might have found them and picked them up. This is where they would have come to find us, since it's where Kirk left us."

Roberto turned and looked through the partition to the backseat. He eyed Devin, and then spoke calmly. "You know? You could be right, bro." He then grinned playfully.

Devin scoffed and looked out of the window at the bodies they left in their wake.

Grant shook his head and chuckled. He almost believed Roberto was serious about thinking the zombies were thieves. He thought about their next move and suggested, "I guess we should go home. I'll get another radio and contact Kirk and Liz, so they can head back."

Roberto shrugged, "Works for me, bro. I could use a nice cup of coffee, after this crappy day."

Devin scoffed, "Coffee? Screw that! I'm going to take a hot shower, and then I'm going to bed! After a long day of heavy lifting, running for my life, and climbing, I'm completely drained!"

"Me, too," said Grant. "This was one hell of a workout."

Roberto grinned, "Actually, I had fun today. We should do this, again, sometime."

Devin knew what they said should not have surprised him, but it did. If any group was going to outlast a Zombie Apocalypse, it was this group, he thought. He counted himself lucky to be a part of it.

As Grant drove out of the parking lot and turned to go home, he said, "Uh oh." Suddenly, they hit a large bump. He had run over a zombie. "Damn! I don't remember any speed bumps on this road," he said.

Roberto laughed and Devin just shook his head in amusement.

Meanwhile, back at the compound, Kirk and Liz were pulling into the open gates. Kirk got out to close the gates, when Woody called down to him from the watchtower.

"Kirk, there's a car coming from the south!"

Liz jumped out of the Ford Explorer and stood next to Kirk with her rifle in her hand. They saw the police SUV approaching at a casual speed. For a brief second, she thought it could be survivors from the Village Hall group, so she aimed her rifle and looked through the scope. It was hard to see with the headlight beams shining brightly in her face.

Grant slowed down and tapped the horn once, which was their old custom when entering the compound, back before they realized there was another group in Monroe. He wanted them to know they were friendly.

Roberto stuck his head out of the window and shouted, "Put that rifle down, before you shoot someone, and keep that gate open! We're coming home!"

A huge grin stretched across Kirk's face and Liz practically jumped for joy, once they saw Grant and Roberto in the front seat of the police SUV. Grant pulled up next to the Ford Explorer and stopped. Liz ran to the driver's side and he stepped out to greet her. They embraced. Roberto and Devin also got out. Kirk went over to them and hugged them both.

Kirk stated with a smile, "I'm glad you guys made it back okay. Oh, I have something for you, Rob." He went to the Ford Explorer and pulled out the wrecking bar.

Roberto smiled and took it from him. "You saved my baby! Thanks, bro! I was looking for this. I thought the zombies took it."

Kirk looked at him oddly and chuckled.

They closed the gate and parked both vehicles. Afterwards, they went inside and did as they planned. After washing up, Devin went straight to sleep. Roberto prepared a pot of coffee for him, Liz, and Kirk, while Grant took a shower. Later, they sat in the dining room, drank the coffee, and laughed about how the night played out. Liz held Grant's hand and felt so happy he was safe.

Despite the craziness of the past few hours, it had been a very productive day. Not only did they gather up a truckload of stones for the wall, but also they managed to steer a very large zombie horde far away from the compound. In the process, they were able to acquire extra guns, ammunition, and a new vehicle.

Of course, they would have to return the next day for the rest of the stone blocks at the retaining wall. They were definitely going to need those blocks to finish their wall. Building up the wall was now a top priority, after that lone zombie found its way to the western fence from the nearby woods. Having a wall would prevent any passing zombies or other survivors from looking into the compound, since part of the fence was still uncovered near the woods at their firing range.

MAN'S END

Chapter Twenty-Nine

IT WAS THE morning before Christmas Eve. There was a light layer of snow on the trees and grass from an overnight snowfall. The warm morning sun had melted away any snow on the roads. It was not too cold out. The temperature for the day would rise into the mid-forties.

Grant and Liz had big plans for today, as they prepared the van to go out on a special supply run. For the most part, they kept their supply run secret. People knew they were going out, but they did not know the main focus of the run. They did not even take a list from Julia.

Before leaving, Liz said, "This is kind of exciting. I'm glad we're doing this. It will be a nice surprise for everyone. I just hope we don't run into trouble!"

"Don't jinx us," Grant replied. "Jesus Christ, we really need to sort out these vehicles. It's getting way too crowded out here." He stared annoyingly at the other vehicles that blocked the van in.

"Should we take one of the other vehicles, instead?"

"No, it has to be the van. Give me a moment to move those others out of the way."

"Okay, I need to use the bathroom anyway, before we go. I'll be right back!" She hurried into the house.

Grant grabbed all the keys from the garage and moved most of the vehicles from where they were parked. He decided to park them in a different way, placing their rears against the wall and the front ends pointed outward, so it would be easier to access each one. He laughed to himself when he realized it was the same way he learned to park police vehicles for the NYPD. They referred to it as combat parking. He had to admit, it was more efficient. Fortunately, Kirk had been teaching him to drive the bus and the trucks. He was already an excellent driver and a fast learner, so he picked it up easily.

He could not believe how many vehicles they had accumulated over the past few months. Aside from the white van, there was the black Ford Explorer, the blue pick-up truck, a royal blue BMW M550i, the Monroe Police Department SUV, and a black mini-school bus, which they named The Intrepid. Plus, there were several trucks parked on the grass along the south wall, which included a full-sized white fuel tanker tractor-trailer truck and several official Orange County trucks. There was a short fuel truck, the flatbed, a forklift, and a dump truck with a snowplow attached to its front. All were orange in color.

Once Grant was done, he pulled the van out and stopped in front of the gates. Liz had already come out of the house and was waiting. She got into the front passenger side and was carrying her rifle.

As soon as Grant began to unlock the gates, Sam came rushing over to him with his double barrel shotgun in his hand. It was the same one he acquired during the battle against the other group. Grant let him keep it, since he earned it, as long as he agreed to take lessons in how to operate and maintain it.

"Grant! Wait!" He called out. "Please, take me with you!"

Grant turned to him and was already shaking his head.

Sam tried his best to plead his case in hopes of persuading him. "You guys are going out on a supply run, right? I really need to go with you. Please!"

"Why?"

"Tomorrow's Christmas Day!" He announced, as if Grant might have forgotten. "I was hoping to find something for my little sister and my mom. Please, I promise not to get in the way. I promise I'll do whatever you say and I won't be a problem. Please," he begged. "This is very important to me!"

Grant sighed and gave in. He said, "Okay, but let your mother know that you are coming with us. If anything should happen, I want to make sure she knows that you're with me."

"Aw, do I have to?"

"You're not coming, if she doesn't know," Grant said defiantly. "And I'll find out, if you lie because I will talk to her later."

Sam frowned, "Fine. I'll go ask her."

"We'll wait for you here."

About five minutes later, Sam finally returned looking like he'd just come from getting his teeth pulled at the dentist. He stated, "She said I could go, but only if she could come, too. It took me a while to get her to realize I wanted to find her a Christmas gift. I was hoping to keep it a surprise. She ruined it."

"So, are you both coming?"

"No, just me."

"Okay, then why the long face?"

"She ruined my surprise," he said with disappointment.

Grant put his arm around him and explained, "It's not so much the surprise or what you get for her, it's the thought that counts. She will be happy because it's from you. I think she probably just wanted to come along, so she could get something for you, too, and to keep a close eye on you, of course."

Sam smirked, "Of course. Thanks, Grant." He smiled.

"Get in the back and hold onto something. There are no seats back there, but there is a nice rug to sit on. Make sure to keep your weapon pointed away from us at all times. In fact, put it down and leave it down, until we get out."

"Yes, sir!"

A short time later, they began their journey. They reached their first destination in no time, which was the Dollar General. They grabbed a few basic items from there, such as candles, permanent markers, tape, scissors, and three cartons of cigarettes. Sam found a toy for his sister, too.

Grant and Liz were both pleased to see that there were still no zombies roaming around. Diverting the zombies to the south had been a great idea. They wondered how long their luck would hold out.

Next, they took the interstate going north to Wallkill. They had not visited this area, yet, but Grant was checking Google maps on the computer, while Daniel was watching the monitors. He wanted to find specific stores that could be used for future supply runs, since they could no longer travel to the south. As it turned out, there was a Home Depot, Lowe's, and a Walmart Superstore all near each other in Wallkill. There was also a Christmas Tree Shop, which would be one of his priority stops today.

They exited and turned left, which put them westbound on Route 211. Grant wanted to check the Walmart, first. He knew he could find most of what he wanted there, so it was best to get it out of the way.

They pulled into the parking lot and walked toward the entrance. The glass doors were broken, so they stepped inside cautiously.

Grant had already told Sam to stay close to him, before getting out of the van. Sam did not argue. He knew he would be safer, if he did as Grant said. He respected Grant's experience.

Once inside, Grant gave Liz a boost onto one of the many empty shelves. She stood up high and was able to look around the entire store. It looked to her like they were alone. She carefully climbed back down and turned to him.

"I think it's empty," she said.

"Let's hope so," he replied. "Well, let's each grab a cart and start from the left. We can work our way across together. No splitting up."

"That's fine by me," she said with a smile. "I just *LOVE* shopping for free."

Sam beamed with excitement, "This is going to be fun, huh?"

Grant smiled and said, "Just stay close to us and listen up for any sounds. We don't want to be surprised. You hear or see anything that even makes you slightly suspicious, you let us know."

"No problem."

They began going through the aisles together, starting with the ones on the left. Over the next hour and a half, they worked their way across the entire store filling their shopping carts, as they went. By the time they were done, all three carts were jam-packed with merchandise. It was the ultimate shopping spree.

The plan was to collect supplies and Christmas gifts that would benefit everyone as a whole. The gifts were generally for them to share, although some were more for specific people. They grabbed winter clothing, workout clothes, regular clothes, underclothing, sleepwear, socks, gloves, work gloves, hard kneepads, night vision goggles, two drones, three laptop computers with carrying cases, batteries, an axe, toolsets, toolboxes, boxes of ammunition, two compound-bows with lots of arrows, a rubber raft, four life vests, a beanbag chair to keep in the van, large storage containers, boxes of condoms, nail polish, hair products, toiletries, about three dozen toothbrushes, hairbrushes, combs, towels, blankets, pillows, quilts, drinks, food, candy, coffee, a food processor, an acoustic guitar, music CDs to keep in the vehicles, jigsaw puzzles, board games, various books, coloring books, magazines, crayons, and plenty of toys for Glenda. Liz even helped Sam pick out some sweet smelling perfume for his mother.

It took several minutes to load everything into the back of the van, while trying to leave space for the next stop. It was a large haul. Any small items were placed neatly into the large storage containers, so that things would not slide or roll around, while the van was in motion.

Sam made himself comfortable on the beanbag chair and they were ready to move on to the next location, which was on the other side of the interstate. This time, they took Route 211 heading east, passing under the interstate, and made a right turn into the parking lot of the Christmas Tree Shop.

Sam gleamed with enthusiasm and asked, "Are we going to get a Christmas tree???"

Liz answered, "Yep. That was part of the plan, Sammy. The holidays just haven't felt like the holidays lately, which has been depressing. We hoped to change that by making it feel more like Christmas for everyone. We're going to wrap all of these gifts, before we go home."

"Can I help?"

Grant chuckled, "Why do you think we brought you with us? We can't wrap all of this on our own! We'll do it here in the parking lot, after we get the tree and other decorations."

"Awesome," Sam said.

Liz looked around the empty parking lot. There was not another soul in sight, which is exactly what they were hoping to find.

Grant turned to her and said, "Are you ready?"

"Let's go," she answered.

The three of them went into the Christmas Tree Shop. Naturally, the glass windows of the entrance doors were broken, as with most businesses lately. Back when things started going bad, looters were breaking into stores and grabbing whatever they could. It left many empty shelves in their wake, but there were always some useful things that were left behind. It's nearly impossible to carry everything in one visit and people were mainly taking what they needed, at the time.

Grant grabbed a shopping cart and said, "One should be enough for this place."

They went through the store and loaded the cart with Christmas ornaments, lights, and a few other decorations for the Christmas tree and the house. Sam grabbed a pretty plastic wreath that looked real enough. They also grabbed several rolls of wrapping paper and placed them into the cart. The last thing they went for was a Christmas tree. Grant decided to let Sam choose one.

"Which one do you like best, Sam?"

Sam walked past each one and examined them carefully. He liked two in particular. One was white and the other was tall and full. He asked, "I can pick anyone I want?"

"The choice is yours," Grant replied.

Sam smiled and said, "Cool. Thanks. Hmm. I kind of like this white one, but the tall one here is pretty awesome, too."

Liz thought about it and suggested, "Maybe we can even fit two in the van. What do you think, Grant?"

"It will be a little crowded for Sam, especially with all the gifts. Maybe we tie them both to the roof, if there's enough rope. There should be some rope in the van.

Sam nodded, "There is. I saw it, but I don't know if there's enough."

Grant replied, "Well, then. Let's see if we can find some. There has to be rope somewhere in this store."

They searched the store and were able to find the rope they needed to tie both Christmas trees to the roof of the van. Grant and Sam made two trips to carry each tree outside, while Liz pushed the shopping cart out to the van and began opening the first roll of holiday wrapping paper. Afterwards, they began to wrap mostly everything with the colorfully designed paper. They used the tape and scissors they grabbed from the Dollar General store and marked some of the gifts with the permanent markers, so they would have a hint of what was inside. They used code words that only they knew and it became like a game.

The only thing they did not wrap was the food, drinks, and toiletries. Those were priority items that needed to be stored into the pantries upon their return.

Sometime around dusk, they were back on the road, heading home with a fully loaded van and two Christmas trees tied to the roof. Liz gazed out of the window of the van and sighed sadly.

Grant glanced at her and asked, "What's wrong? Tired?"

"No. I was just thinking about last New Year's Eve. I was hanging out with my friends from work, and then I went home to spend time with my mother and father. We toasted with champagne to a better year. I hope my parents are safe. It's been so long, since I spoke to them. I miss them."

Grant became saddened. There was not much he could say or do to make her feel better about not knowing how her parents were doing. He often thought about his family, as well. He hoped they were okay. It was torture not knowing. He sent out emails a few times, but never got any responses.

He suggested, "Hey, do you want to pick up some bottles of champagne, before we head back? Maybe we should have our own New Year's party. There's a liquor store next to Shop Rite."

"As much as I would love to have champagne or a nice bottle of wine on New Year's Eve, Charles doesn't want us to have alcohol at the compound. We should respect his decision. Let's not forget what happened with Bobby," she said with a hint of hesitation, not really wanting to bring it up in front of Sam.

"Yeah, you're right. We don't need champagne to celebrate the New Year, but being alive this long is definitely something we should all celebrate together. It has been a good year for us, despite our pains and sorrows. We survived against impossible odds."

She looked at him and said, "Let's see how they take to celebrating Christmas, before we plan the next holiday. Some of them may not be in the mood to celebrate anything. We've seen so much death over the past few months. This will be the first Christmas without those people and without our loved ones. Think about Rob, who had to watch his family die in front of him. Do you think he will want to sit around and sing Christmas carols?"

"Sing? That was never part of the deal," Grant sneered.

Sam asked, "Are we really going to sing Christmas carols?"

"Probably not," Liz scoffed.

Without taking his eyes off the road, Grant said, "I figured once we decorate the house and they see the gift-wrapped items under the trees, they might temporarily forget that we're living through a nightmare. Of course, there will be those, who will feel depressed, no matter what. It can't be helped. I was hoping that by doing this little surprise, it will make the holiday season a little easier to deal with because maybe it will help to bring out the Christmas spirit in them. It would be great if everyone could see that we are a family and we still have each other."

Sam stated, "The Christmas spirit *always* wins out in the movies and cartoons. I think they're going to be happy, when they see what we've brought back. We need to think positive."

"They won't be seeing any of this stuff, until tomorrow morning," Grant responded. "Well, except for the stuff we didn't gift wrap. That stuff was our reason for going out, as far as they need to know. We're going to leave the rest of this stuff in the van, until late tonight. In fact, we will also have to leave the trees somewhere along Cromwell Road, before we get back. We'll bring them in tonight, after everyone goes to sleep, and then set everything up. I want them to be surprised, when they wake up."

Sam looked excited, as he said, "That's a great idea! I can help you bring the trees in tonight, if you want."

"I'll take you up on that offer. We can bring the trees in at around midnight. Mostly everyone will be in bed, by then. Liz is taking the watchtower duty tonight, so no one else will see us."

Sam asked, "Won't Julia see us on the cameras?"

"Yeah, but I can handle her. I'll get her to keep quiet about it. She'll listen to me," Grant said with confidence. "Tomorrow is going to be a great day."

Sam replied, "Today was already a great day. Thanks for letting me come along with you guys. I had a lot of fun. It almost felt like it used to, before everything changed."

Liz said, "We're glad you came with us, Sam. Remember. Keep this a secret."

"For sure!"

When they reached Cromwell Road, they untied the two Christmas trees and dropped them off near the wall. They drove into the compound and unloaded the storage container that contained the food, drinks, and toiletries, but left everything else in the van.

That night Angela and Millie hummed Christmas carols, while they cooked. Everyone enjoyed a fine dinner in the dining room. It was crowded, but it was nothing they were not already used to. As they ate, they spoke about things that had nothing to do with the Zombie Apocalypse, such as past Christmases. They reminisced and shared favorite holiday memories. There were no decorations and no actual singing of Christmas carols, but the feeling of Christmas was definitely in the air.

Grant, Liz, and Sam kept giving each other looks and smiling.

At around midnight, Liz stood up in the watchtower and looked down below, as Grant and Sam opened the gate and went out to get the Christmas trees. They hurried back inside, as they carried each tree in. Afterwards, the gates were locked and it was time to set everything up.

Roberto stepped out onto the porch and wondered what they were up to, so he walked over to the van and asked, "What's with the trees? Hey. Are those Christmas trees?"

Grant exhaled and answered, "Yeah, since you're here, how about giving us a hand carrying them into the common room?"

"Yeah! Sure!"

He grabbed the front end of the larger tree and together with Grant they carried it into the house. They stood it up in the common room and went out to get the second tree, while Sam brought in the storage container filled with decorations and lights.

Roberto looked into the container and at the trees and commented, "Wow. I can't believe you got all of this stuff. I didn't think I would ever see anything that would make me feel like it was Christmas, again. It's too bad we won't have gifts, but the trees will be a nice touch."

"Actually…" Grant started.

"No! You got gifts?" He looked so excited.

Grant and Sam looked at each other, and then back at him and smiled.

Grant said, "Help us decorate these trees. We can talk gifts later. Here's what we want to do…"

He explained how they also wanted to decorate the house. They hung the lights and ornaments on both trees with care, and then strung colored lights on windows, over doorways, and near the stairs. Sam was the one, who hung the wreath on the front door. Later, a red welcome mat was placed on the floor.

Liz looked down from the watchtower and smiled with joy, as colorful lights lit up the windows. She could not wait to see how the trees looked. She wanted to help, but someone had to man the tower.

After the decorations were in place, the guys went out to the van and brought the gifts inside. Roberto could not believe his eyes, when he saw the van was full of gift-wrapped items.

"Holy shit! You guys went through a lot of trouble to do this. Bro, I am impressed." He shook Grant's hand and said, "You are a good man and I'm proud to know you."

"Same here, brother. By the way, there are a few things in here that *you* are going to love. I grabbed them with you in mind."

"Really? Oh, man! I can't wait to see them."

"In the morning, my friend. In the morning," Grant grinned.

They placed the gifts underneath both trees spreading them out and stacking them neatly. It was picture perfect. For a good long while, they stood there staring at their handy work.

"I wish I could take a picture with my cellphone," Sam moaned sadly.

Grant perked up and said, "Hold that thought. I'll be right back." He went upstairs to his bedroom and returned holding a black camera bag. "I almost forgot I had this," he said. "I brought it from my house. Hopefully, the battery hasn't drained from lack of use."

Sam's eyes lit up with excitement. Even Roberto was surprised.

Grant pulled out his Nikon camera from the bag and told them, "Okay, guys. Stand in front, between both trees."

Roberto and Sam posed, while Grant snapped a photo of them. He then took another one of the trees and gifts alone. Afterwards, he handed the camera to Sam and said, "Go ahead and take photos of whatever you want to remember. We could always print them on the printer."

"Awesome! Thank you, Grant! Wow! I can't believe you still have a camera!" He walked around and began taking photos of all the decorations.

Roberto made some coffee and sat beside the Christmas trees, as he drank it. He turned to Grant and said, "You know, Grant? I think we should wake everyone, now. This is so much prettier with the lights on at night. It won't look the same in the daytime."

Grant thought about it and agreed, "It sounds crazy, but I believe you're right. Sam, can you, please, tell Liz to come inside, and then go down and get Julia? Rob, why don't you go into the dorm and wake the guys? I'll go up and tell the girls to come down. Of course, I can't forget about my man, Chuck, and his woman."

"Yeah, bro! Let's do this!" Roberto rubbed his hands together excitedly.

Grant, Roberto, and Sam went around and gathered everyone in the compound. They lied and said there was to be an emergency meeting in the common room. Everyone kept asking what it was about, but they were not telling. First, Liz came in from the watchtower, and then Julia came up from the basement. The men filed into the common room, followed by the women. They all gasped in awe at the amazing sight, before their eyes. Sam took photos of them, as they entered, little by little.

Grant and Liz put their arms around each other. Liz kissed him on the cheek and complimented him and his crew on the wonderful job they did with decorating.

Once everyone was gathered, they shouted, "Merry Christmas!"

Glenda's eyes lit up like headlamps. She ran toward the Christmas trees and shouted, "Santa Claus was here! Mommy, look! Santa Claus left us all these presents! I told you he wouldn't forget!"

Sam smiled lovingly and took several photos of his little sister. He was so happy for her. She was definitely the most excited from everyone, but she was not the only one feeling the Christmas spirit.

Joy began crying because she was so happy. She was worried that Glenda would not ever be able to experience Christmas, again. It made her so happy to see that she was wrong. She looked at Sam, who took a photo of her, and she pointed at him accusingly. "You knew about this! Didn't you?"

"Yeah, mom. That's why we went out earlier today. We did this all today. Rob helped us decorate. I even got you something, except it's buried somewhere in there!" He pointed to the large gift piles under both trees.

"I'm sure it will turn up, soon enough! Come here you!" She hugged him tightly and wiped her tears away. She never thought she would feel this happy, again. She turned to Grant and Liz and said, "Thank you so much. I can never repay you for what you've done. This means so much to me. You guys are really awesome."

Liz smiled and replied, "Don't thank us. It was Santa Claus. Right, Glenda?"

Glenda was still jumping for joy at the sight of all the large gifts. When she heard what Liz said, she looked up at her and asked, "Did you get to see Santa Claus?"

"Yes, I did. He told me there was more than one gift in here for you."

"Really???"

"Yep. Let me see if I can find one." She walked over to the tree and easily found one of the gift-wrapped toys.

Sam had written Glenda's name on every toy, which he personally gift-wrapped for her. She would also be getting the coloring books and crayons, which Liz wrapped for her, as well as some much needed winter clothes.

Glenda wasted little time in tearing open the first gift. It was a doll that Sam picked out for her. She beamed happily and ripped open the box. Afterwards, she held the doll and admired it, before hugging it gently. Sam took another photo to capture the tender moment.

The rest of the stuff was for everyone else to share. Everybody knew Glenda needed her own gifts. She was only a child, after all. In some ways, this was more for her, than for the adults, although it was having a similar affect on them. Everyone looked amazed and happy. Even Yvonne, who had not smiled once, since moving into the house, was smiling.

Kirk looked at Grant and Liz from across the room and gave them the thumbs up signal. He was proud of them for doing such an elaborate selfless gesture. It was just what the group needed, he thought. He stood next to David, who was feeling much better, and patted him on the back.

"Merry Christmas, pal," he said.

David turned to him and said, "Merry Christmas, Kirk."

They hugged.

Millie and Edie watched them and smiled. They were so thankful that David was alive and getting better with each passing day. It was great to see him walking around and smiling.

Julia looked at Grant and scolded him playfully, "I was wondering what you were doing carrying trees through the gates! I saw you! That was very sneaky, but very nice. Good job."

"Merry Christmas, Julia," he winked at her and smiled, which pretty much made her night.

Charles walked over to Grant and Liz. He grinned and stated, "You two outdid yourself with this one. It was a great idea. So, who gets to open the other gifts?"

Grant said, "We can do it together. These other items are for everyone. They're mostly things that we all need. There are some things that might be more for specific people, but I think there's something for everyone. Here," he grabbed a small rectangular box and tossed it to Roberto. "Why don't you open that one, Rob? You will probably enjoy it more than the rest of us, but feel free to share."

Roberto caught the gift and grinned heartily. "Thanks!" He tore into the wrapping paper and chuckled, when he saw what was inside. It was a carton of cigarettes. "You know me well, bro. This is my brand!"

"It's definitely not my thing, but I know that you feel you need it, from time to time, so enjoy, brother."

Sam grabbed one of the larger boxes and carried it over to Grant. He asked, "I know what's in here already, but would it be okay if I opened it? I'd like to open one, too."

"Of course, Sam!"

Sam grinned and ripped the paper off the box. It was one of the two drones they acquired. He read the details on the box and said, "I cannot wait to test this baby out tomorrow morning!"

Grant said, "I'll tell you what. Why don't you read up on the instructions because I'm going to need you to teach me?"

"You bet!"

Next, Grant handed a large gift to Aramis and said, "This gift is mainly for you, but I'm sure you will find a way to share it with us."

"*This* is for me?" Aramis wrinkled his face curiously and grabbed the long rectangular gift. He started to open it and his jaw dropped open. "Oh, man! I love you, Grant!" He tore off the rest of the paper with the excitement of a child, revealing a black and red acoustic guitar. Grant recalled hearing him talk about how he used to be in a band. Plus, he knew how bored Aramis got because he could never go out on supply runs. This would occupy his time in a way that would benefit them all. Aramis hugged Grant and said, "This is so awesome, man! I love it!"

"I figured you might appreciate that more than anyone else here."

"Oh, you know it! This is great!" He looked so happy.

Grant smiled warmly at him.

He and Liz continued to pass the other gifts out to specific people, so everyone would have a chance to open something. Everyone waited patiently for his or her turn. Each gift was specifically marked, so they would know who the best person was for that gift.

Glenda absolutely loved her coloring books and crayons, as well as the many toys her brother picked out for her. She was even excited when she saw the jigsaw puzzles and board games, although those were meant for everyone's enjoyment.

Julia particularly loved the idea of having drones and laptop computers. She thought the drones could be used for monitoring the immediate area and also on supply runs, while the laptops were good for whenever someone was away from the main computer in the security hub. They could also help anyone on a supply run with regard to checking maps and her lists.

She was even happier, when Grant handed her a gift. It was only ink for the printer, but because it came from him, it became the most wonderful gift she ever received.

"Oh, thank you, Grant! That is so sweet of you to think of me." She hugged him.

Liz noticed the exaggerated response and was about to say the gift was from her, too, but then she decided to let it slide. Why ruin a perfect night with silly jealousy? She knew Julia was harmless.

A moment later, Liz was distracted by Chryssy's reaction to Kirk's gift, which Liz had just handed to him. Chryssy seemed more excited than him. It was one of the two compound-bows.

"Whoa! Look at that beauty! That's sexy!" She exclaimed, "I love archery!"

Kirk asked, "Do you know how to use one of these?"

"Hell, yeah! My dad paid for lessons, when I was a kid. He had no choice, after making me watch all those *Hunger Games* movies. I don't want to brag, but I'm kind of good with a compound-bow." She smiled proudly.

"Good," Kirk replied, "Then you can teach me!"

"No problem," she agreed. "On one condition. I'd love to borrow it, every once in a while. I promise I will take very good care of it."

"You got a deal."

They shook hands.

As soon as Grant noticed her reaction, he desperately searched the pile of gifts. Once he found what he was looking for, he handed a similarly sized box to Chryssy.

She looked at it innocently and asked, "Is this for me?"

He nodded, "It's in your hands. Open it."

She smiled and opened it. It was the second compound-bow. This one was all black, while Kirk's was a green camouflage color. She became so happy that she cried, although she tried to hide it.

Grant said, "Merry Christmas, Chryssy."

"Oh, my God! Thank you so much!" She beamed with excitement, as she examined it in detail. "My dad gave me one of these years ago. I never thought I would hold one, again." She fought back her tears.

Roberto nudged Grant and teased, "Hey, bro. How am I supposed to out do a gift like that? You set the bar too high for me. Thanks a lot. I thought we were pals."

"Strive to do better for the ones that you love."

Roberto smiled admiringly at Grant and replied, "I like that." He patted Grant on the back. "Real smooth."

Grant grinned at him.

Daniel was also quite pleased with his gifts. He loved the new toolset and toolbox. Grant and Liz knew he could use some new tools to replace the battered ones. Plus, he was always misplacing the tools and forgetting where they were, so having extras was extremely beneficial.

"Oh, man! This is great! Thanks, guys!"

Grant nodded with a smile. "We figured it would help to have a new set."

"Yeah! Definitely!"

Liz said, "Merry Christmas, Danny."

"Thank you! Merry Christmas! I wish I had something for you two," he said regretfully.

Grant shook his head, "No need. You've given us so much of yourself already. Your tireless efforts on fortifying this compound are more than enough."

Angelo chuckled when he opened a gift and found a box of ammunition. It was all he needed. Ammunition was worth more to him than any material item.

Of course, there was plenty of new ammunition for everyone's weapons. Woody was more than pleased to get a box of ammo for his Black Hawk Axiom R/F Ruger 10/22 rifle. He was surprised Grant knew exactly which rounds to get.

Devin got a gift containing two books about the American Revolution and the American Civil War. He was already planning to read one tomorrow.

Most of the guys were fussing over who would get to test out the night vision goggles, first. Even Charles was eyeing them with interest. However, Grant had given them to Liz. She had no idea he even grabbed them from the store. There were so many gifts in the shopping carts that it was hard to keep track of them all. He made sure to wrap it, while she was wrapping Glenda's gifts, so they were a complete surprise to her.

"Ooh! These are so cool! Thank you, baby! I can't wait to test them out!" She embraced him, as the other guys stared longingly at the night vision goggles in her hand. It was a funny scene. Sam had to capture the moment with the camera.

A lot of the clothing gifts went over well, too. Roberto and Chryssy loved the hard kneepads. Edie, Millie, Joy, and Chryssy were each pleased to have new workout clothes. It turned out they really needed them. Roberto was working them too hard in the gym. Remarkably, Yvonne was happy to have gloves and a coat because she was in need of exactly that. Of course, everyone was happy to have new underclothes and socks.

Joy was especially overjoyed that her kids had new winter clothes. Of course, she also loved her perfume and hugged Sam for getting it for her. Grant took a photo of them together.

Sam also picked out a nice pair of earrings for Taryn with Liz's help. It seemed he had a little crush on her, which Liz found cute. Of course, Liz had to coax him to hand her the gift.

Both Millie and Angela loved the new food processor. They could not wait to use it for Christmas dinner. They were already planning what to cook.

As a joke, Grant gave Charles and Roberto each a box of condoms and David received a bottle of painkillers, since he was always getting injured. They were amused. David also got some hair gel, while hair dyes were given to Edie, Joy, and Chryssy. All of the women got nail polish, whether they used it or not.

Maxine had the funniest reaction, when she saw the new toothbrushes, hairbrushes, and combs. You'd think Grant and Liz brought back a load of ancient buried treasure with the way she went on.

By the time they were finished opening gifts, it was nearly four in the morning. Everyone was tired, but glad they had stayed up late to enjoy a night of holiday cheer. Naturally, Joy had some trouble getting Glenda to go to sleep, but it was not as if she had to go to school the next day.

When morning came, everybody woke up in a good mood. They went outside, eager to see the drones in action. Well, one of them anyway. Sam had already memorized the directions, which instantly made him the resident expert. He flew one of the drones over the compound and explored the area, while taking photos. Later, they checked them on the computer. The photo quality was excellent, which was no surprise, since they picked the most expensive drone models available.

Meanwhile, in the kitchen, Millie and Angela worked hard to make a fantastic breakfast for everyone. Angela began baking bread, as soon as she woke up, and they also baked a cake. Millie had help from Glenda collecting eggs and milk from the barn.

By noon, Glenda was coloring in one of her new coloring books. She was still incredibly excited that Santa Claus was able to find her. She thought he would not know, where to look, since she was no longer at her old house. She kept talking about how he probably used drones to find her. It made the others laugh. Her innocence was cute and had become a rare commodity in these harsh times.

It might have been the Zombie Apocalypse elsewhere in the country, but for the group at the compound, it was Christmas time and nothing else mattered today.

MAN'S END

Chapter Thirty

NEW YEAR'S EVE came and went virtually unnoticed by most of the group. The real part of winter had arrived. It grew colder, as temperatures dropped down to thirty degrees Fahrenheit, and with the cold came the first of the big snowfalls. It snowed all day on New Year's Day leaving about eight inches of snow on the ground, which would last for weeks. The roads were virtually impassible.

The snow on the ground posed a danger to the group's existence because if they were to leave the compound for any reason, they would have to use the plow or leave tracks behind. The last thing they wanted was for anyone to follow those tracks or cleaned roads directly back to the compound. Fortunately, there would be no need to go on any supply runs for a long time.

They had a sufficient supply of food and water to last more than two months. The snow was actually helpful in regards to stocking their water supplies because they could collect it and allow it to melt into clean buckets, so it could later be boiled and used. Unfortunately, the colder weather meant they would have to ration their food supplies better than before, so it could last longer.

Charles used his snow blower to clear paths from the house to the watchtower, barn, and around the house, while Kirk used the dump truck with the snowplow to clear snow away from the vehicles and make a path to the gates, just in case of an emergency.

In reality no one had any intention of going outside, other than to go up to the watchtower, which was very cold making it a far less favorable post than it had been during the warmer weather. Daniel hung two of the spare tarps inside to block out the wind, but whoever was inside had to lift up the tarps in order to see anything, which defeated the purpose. A sleeping bag was also added, so it could be used to keep warm. In addition, to make the post more bearable, the guard shifts within were decreased back to three hours for the remainder of the winter.

The snow also put a delay on the construction of the wall. The cold weather made it difficult to mix cement, since it was done by hand. It seemed work on the wall would have to take a backseat, until it warmed up. So far, the wall was only completed on the east and south sides. It was only nearly completed along the north side, while the west wall still had not been started. They were also running low on building materials, again, which would mean a trip to the Home Depot and Lowe's in Wallkill, once the snow was gone, regardless of cold weather. They did not wish to take a chance that those materials would be lost to them.

In the meantime, there were other things for them to do. Mornings were reserved for breakfast, reading books, and chatting. Someone would also go out to the barn to get milk from the cow and eggs from the hens. They took turns with those chores. Mostly everyone knew what to do, by now. During the early afternoon hours Roberto coached Chryssy, Edie, Millie, Joy, and Sam with getting into shape, while also teaching them hand to hand combat maneuvers. Sometimes, Grant, David, Kirk, and Aramis observed and took part in the lessons. Afterwards, people would shower and prepare for dinnertime. After dinner, Grant taught Sam, Joy, Edie, Chryssy, and Millie about gun maintenance. Julia was still training Taryn in how to monitor the security cameras, so they spent a good part of the day together in the security hub.

When it came to winding down, later in the day, they had ten jigsaw puzzles to do and five board games to choose from. There were plenty of books to read, as well. Sometimes, Aramis strummed on his guitar. He knew how to play well, so he was able to play full songs for everyone.

Spending more time in the house together also gave everyone the opportunity to get to know each other better. There were still certain people, who kept themselves busy and isolated themselves from others, such as Julia, Taryn, and Woody. They limited themselves to a very small circle of friends because they felt uncomfortable making new friends.

Of course, the couples took the time to build on their relationships. Charles and Yvonne spent hours together in the attic, which was really her choice. She wanted to have him all to herself and did not really like socializing with the other people in the group, mainly because she was prejudiced. Charles knew her reasons, but indulged her because he was enjoying the constant sex. He had gone too long without it.

Yvonne liked to tease Charles by doing sexy dances for him. It was one of her best weapons for keeping him to herself.

"It drives me crazy when you do that," he'd say.

She would smile and stare at him seductively, before performing some kind of sexual act with him. She felt very aroused by his masculinity. She loved rubbing his smooth baldhead. It turned her on, for some reason.

She felt a little guilty that she had originally been using him, so she could sleep in the privacy of the attic. As it turned out, the more time she spent with him, the more she liked him, although she was not in love.

Her beauty, on the other hand, blinded Charles. Yvonne was able to keep him wrapped around her little finger with really good sex as her most powerful weapon.

Below the attic, Grant and Liz spent about two days in their bedroom working on a 1000-piece jigsaw puzzle of a colorful landscape of the American mid-west. The pieces were laid out across the floor, as they focused on the edges, first.

They also did a lot of talking about their past, which turned out to be quite interesting. Grant learned things that he almost wished he did not know. One example was when he asked her what she did for a living, before the apocalypse. The last thing he ever expected her to say was that she was an exotic dancer at a bar in Yonkers called City Lights. His mouth gaped open in shock.

"Hey, relax," she sneered. "I was a *dancer*. Not a hooker. There is a difference."

"Um, yeah! I know! It's just, I never imagined you doing... something like *that*."

"Why not? Because it's degrading?"

He did not answer, but she could tell he was thinking it. She sighed and explained, "I'll have you know that I used to pull in about a thousand a week doing that."

"Okay, so it had its benefits," he admitted. "Still, I kind of imagined you doing... something else."

"Yeah? Like what?"

He shrugged, "I don't know. Executioner. Mercenary. Assassin for hire? I guess I really didn't think about it."

She scoffed, "You're an idiot, Grant. Lucky for you, I still love you or I'd have to punch you in the nose."

"Lucky for me then," he chuckled. "I had to fall for the one bad ass girl in the group, who could probably kick my ass. Why didn't you just stay in the military? You're obviously very good at what you do."

"Ugh! Please! I wanted to live my life without having to follow orders and fight other people's battles, especially on some foreign land, where we don't even belong. I prefer to choose my own battles. I only joined, so I would know how to fight those battles."

"That you do, my dear. I always feel safe when we're out there together. I know you'll watch my back and kill without a second thought."

"Well," she smirked. "I have to look out for my investment."

"Oh, really?" He laughed and pushed her over. He then climbed on top of her and they began kissing.

Roberto and Chryssy also enjoyed some couples' time. Unfortunately, they did not have a place in the house, where they could go to be alone, so they would usually grab car keys and sit in a vehicle together. They preferred The Intrepid, although they tried out other vehicles, too. The BMW had comfortable heated seats and the back was quite spacious. However, the heating feature usually made the seats too warm for Roberto's taste. The rear of the van was not too bad, especially with the beanbag seat, but it smelled greasy and they were out of air fresheners.

Chryssy fantasized about them having their own room. "If we had our own room, we could make love all day long on an actual bed. Wouldn't that be nice?" She asked.

"It sounds great," he responded, "But I don't need a room or a bed for that to happen. As long as I'm with you, anywhere will be fine by me."

"You nasty boy!"

Not every person had the good fortune of being part of a couple. Sadly, some only yearned for those they could not have.

Edie stared at David whenever he was around. She tried not to be obvious. She did not want to make him uncomfortable. Their friendship was in a good place, again, and she did not wish to ruin it. She knew there was no chance of being with him. It was not what he wanted anymore. The thought hurt her deeply, but she understood and did not expect anything from him. She settled for daydreaming about him and was grateful that he had not pursued a romance with anyone else. In her mind, he belonged to her.

Julia was another person, who was living in a dream world, when it came to romance. She still had strong feelings for Grant. She was grateful to have the computer and security monitors to suck up her free time because it made her life more manageable. Whenever she was not sitting at the computer, she was miserable. Her thoughts would drift to Grant and Liz being together and it would make her angry.

Taryn tried to talk her out of liking Grant, but it was like talking to a wall. Besides, she had her own heart to think about. Sam was spending more time downstairs in the armory with Grant, while learning gun safety. Sometimes, she would watch him from afar. They were close to the same age, but Sam seemed like he had too much on his mind to think about romance, even though he gave her those earrings. It was fine with her. She was not in a hurry. She was still unsure if he was right for her. She did not really know him well, but she wanted to. She just hoped she did not end up like the pathetic mess Julia had become.

She felt bad thinking that way about her. They were friends. She cared about her, but sometimes, Julia scared her. Sometimes, she scared her a lot.

It was about two weeks before the snow began melting away. Some areas were clear enough to walk on without being too noticeable, depending on where one walked. Going into town was not an option and driving was definitely not a good idea, yet. The roads were too icy and a car would leave a deeper impression on the snow than a person on foot. Keeping their location hidden was paramount.

Liz and Woody both reported seeing a family of deer roaming around the wooded areas that surround the compound. Deer was pretty much the only meat they were able to eat, so it was rare that they would want to pass up a chance to hunt one. One deer could feed the entire house for nearly two weeks.

Ultimately, a hunting trip was planned. Grant and Liz went north on Cromwell Road, while Devin and Woody went south. They gradually moved westward into the woods, after clearing the east wall of the compound. Each group carried a two-way radio to communicate with each other and with Kirk, who waited in the pick-up truck, which was already parked in front of the gate and ready to leave whenever it became time to pick up a deer.

Taryn watched the monitors, while Julia monitored the radio. If the hunting parties ran into trouble, they would contact her and she'd let the response group know. The response group consisted of David, Roberto, Chryssy, and Angelo, who sat in the common room discussing how they would respond.

David suggested, "I think the police SUV would be the best vehicle, except it reminds me of the day I got shot and that only pisses me off."

Roberto shook his head and responded, "Bro, I don't ever want to think about that day, again. I thought we lost you. I still can't believe you survived that gunshot, but here you are looking much better."

"Thanks for saving me that day. I owe my life to you, Sam, and Aramis. Shit, come to think of it, I also owe it to Kirk. I really need to stop getting hurt or I'm going to keep on owing people. Before I know it, someone is going to collect!"

Roberto chuckled, but then he noticed Chryssy was looking disappointed. He tapped her on the leg and asked, "What's wrong, sexy? You look like someone shit on your toothbrush."

"Oh, gross! Rob!"

He laughed, as did the others.

"I was just thinking about something," she said. "Why can't you and I go out and hunt the deer, too? It would finally give me a chance to use my new bow. It was made for things like this."

"I don't know. You should have said something earlier. I don't think it would have been a problem. It's too late, now. We're the back up team, so we need to stay put and listen to the radio."

"Which has been completely dead for a half hour!" She complained.

David said, "While it might seem like a bad thing, sometimes, that is the best thing in the world. Most of the time when you hear someone saying something over the radio, it means there's trouble. I've had my fill of trouble to last a lifetime. I like the quiet." He crossed his arms behind his head and relaxed in his seat, while the radio rested on his lap.

"I suppose," she said. "I wonder what's going on out there."

Angelo responded, "Probably a whole lot of nothing."

Not far from the compound, a few yards southwest of the south wall, Woody and Devin sat up in large trees with thick outstretched branches. They waited silently for deer to appear. It was a waiting game they had played together numerous times in the past. This was no different. After sitting in the trees for several minutes, they were rewarded. It had been a long wait, but they finally spotted one walking alone through the woods, unaware that Woody's rifle was bearing down on it.

CRACK!

The shot echoed for about a mile around.

Grant and Liz stopped and hoped the gunshot meant they were eating meat for dinner. Grant asked over the radio, "Hunter 1 to Hunter 2. Was that a confirmed kill I just heard? Over."

Devin responded over his radio, "That's a big 10-4. Over. We're going to need a pick up under the power lines. Do you copy, Chief? Over."

Kirk smirked and picked up his radio. He answered, "I told you. Call me Big Chief!" He laughed. "I'll be right there in a few."

He opened the gate and drove out. He then locked the gate and headed to Cromwell Road, where he went south. There were a few roads he had to take, before he could reach a path that led to another path, which followed the power lines. It took longer than he liked, but it was easier than driving through the woods in the snow. It was bad enough he had to worry about leaving tire tracks that would lead back to the compound, afterwards. However, carrying a deer back on foot was not happening.

While Woody and Devin waited near the dead deer, they decided to have a conversation. Woody wanted to reminisce about their old group and the days when they used to go hunting with them. Those were good memories for them both. They got so caught up talking and laughing that they failed to notice something crawling over the snow toward them. It was a zombie.

The crawling zombie grabbed hold of Woody's leg and began biting into his ankle. Woody barely even noticed, until Devin shouted.

"Woody! Watch out!" Devin began to aim his rifle at the zombie, but was afraid of hitting Woody by accident.

Woody panicked, until he realized the zombie was biting into his prosthetic leg. Once he noticed, he kicked the zombie off and aimed his rifle down at its head. He fired one shot and killed it.

CRACK!

Right away, Grant contacted them on the radio, "Hunter 1 to Hunter 2, was that you guys, again? Is everything okay? Over."

Devin answered, "Yeah. We had to take out a crawler. We're good. Over."

Woody still looked a little shaken up about almost being infected, as he gasped, "Holy smokes! Whew! That was a close call, huh, Devin?"

"Yeah, too close. We need to pay more attention, when we're out here. No more yapping. Stay alert."

Kirk was glad when he finally found Devin and Woody standing next to their kills. He saw the zombie on the ground and commented, "I see someone was trying to steal our dinner."

Woody bragged, "It's nothing we couldn't handle."

Devin leered at him and chuckled.

Kirk wondered how the zombie managed to get so close to the deer, before it was killed. He saw a long trail in the snow behind it, from where it crawled over. He had a feeling there was an interesting story there, waiting to be told, but figured it could wait for another time. He helped them load the deer onto the rear cargo compartment of the pick-up, and then they got inside the front.

Kirk spoke into his radio to let Grant know he had them. "Big Chief to Hunter 1. I have Hunter 2 and the package. Going home. Over."

Grant acknowledged, and then Kirk made a u-turn and headed back the same way he had come.

Woody stated proudly, "I'm the one that shot him, Kirk. I shot them both. The deer never knew I had him in my sights, but I got him good. I got the zombie good, too."

"That's very good, Woody," Kirk responded. "You're a good shot, buddy."

"Thanks."

"No, thank you. Because of your excellent skills, we will be eating well for the next week or so," Kirk smiled.

"You're welcome," Woody said, before looking down bashfully.

He was afraid to tell Kirk that the zombie bit his prosthetic leg. He thought Kirk would become angry. He remembered vividly the first time they met and Kirk yelled at him. He threatened to twist his head off and shove it up his ass. Woody did not want him to yell at him, again, nor did he want him to follow through with his threat. He prayed Devin would not say anything either. He did not.

Kirk and Devin both exchanged amused looks, glanced at Woody, and smiled. When Kirk faced forward, again, he almost hit a girl, who was standing in the middle of the road. He had to skid and veer away from her. The road was slippery, so he almost lost control. Luckily, he was able to come to a full stop before going off road and slamming into a tree.

Kirk turned to Woody and Devin and asked, "Are you guys okay?"

"Yeah," Devin replied. "Was that a zombie?"

"I don't know," Kirk responded. "It surprised me. I think it was a female." He looked into his side mirror and saw whoever it was that had been crossing the road was now lying on the snow. "I didn't hit her. Did I?"

Woody shook his head and insisted, "No, we didn't hit anything! Nothing at all!"

Kirk grabbed his fire hydrant wrench and stepped out of the pick-up. "I need to make sure," he said. "Keep an eye out for more, in case it was a zombie." He walked back to where the girl lay on the road. He used his foot to nudge her once and waited to bash her head open, if she attacked.

She moaned and tried to look up at him, but her long wild hair was covering most of her face. It was hard to tell if she were alive or infected.

He asked, "Are you okay? Can you understand me?"

She nodded and tried to speak, but her voice was very weak. She muttered softly, *"Please... help me... so hungry."*

He thought about it for a minute, and then decided to pick her up. He carried her over to the truck and wanted to put her in the back, but she was obviously very cold. She was only wearing a thin jacket and was shivering. He walked over to the passenger side and Devin opened the door.

He asked, "What are you doing? Is she dead?"

"No, man, but she's going to be, if we don't get her back home. Scoot over, so I can put her in there with you guys."

Devin said, "Wait. Let me get out, first. Obviously, she won't be able to open the door."

After he stepped out, Kirk placed the girl inside. Devin got back in and closed the door. Kirk went around and got into the driver's side.

Devin glanced at the side view mirror on the passenger side and noticed someone else on the road behind them. He said, "Hold on. There's someone else on the road back there." He turned around to get a better look and gagged. It was a rotted zombie. "Jeez! It practically looks like a skeleton."

Kirk went out with his wrench and whacked the skeletal zombie across the head. The blow broke the weakened head clean off the body. "Holy shit!" He cried out. "Did you guys see that?" He stared at the body, which lingered on its feet momentarily, before dropping to the ground.

He rushed back to the driver's seat and closed the door behind him. "That was wicked," he said. He then shifted the truck into gear and hurried back home.

Grant and Liz were already inside the compound when the pick-up truck arrived. Grant opened and closed the gates, so Kirk could drive straight in without having to get out.

Kirk rolled down his window and said, "Grant, we're going to need Aramis and the stretcher. We found a girl on Cromwell Hill Road. I think she's dying of hunger and possibly frostbite. There was a zombie that might have been after her, so it might be wise to check her for bite marks, too."

Liz commented, "Oh, boy. I'll get Aramis!" She ran into the house.

Grant looked at the girl closely, after Devin got out of the pick-up truck. He asked, "Devin, doesn't she look familiar to you?"

Devin looked at her, again, and then he recognized her. It was Kim, the pretty Asian girl, who had jumped over the wall and ran away from the compound back in November. He exclaimed, "Oh! Yes! I didn't recognize her with the hair covering her face!"

When Aramis came out with the stretcher, they placed her on it and carried her to the common room. It was the best place, where he could tend to her. Meanwhile, Kirk and Woody remained outside and took care of unloading the deer. They could not leave it out on the truck for too long. The smell could attract a bear and bears were becoming bolder and more territorial with fewer humans around.

Maxine was standing in the kitchen, as they walked by carrying the stretcher. She rushed over to help when she saw that it was Kim. She gasped, "Oh, my lord! Is that Kim? Dear God! The poor girl!"

Once they entered the common room, Aramis instructed Grant and Devin, "Let's put her down on the sofa. I need to check her for bites, before I do anything else."

"Definitely," Grant agreed.

Maxine rushed into the common room and said, "I'm heating up water and making some tea for her. She's probably freezing to death."

Aramis stated, "That's nice, but she might be too weak to drink anything. We definitely need to warm her up, but first, I need to get her undressed, so I can check her for bites."

"*Undressed?*" Maxine asked. "Oh, dear! Wait! Maybe I can do that for you," she suggested. "We must consider her privacy."

Aramis said, "Right now, I care more about our safety than her privacy, Maxine."

Maxine stood in his way. "Please, you don't understand! Let me undress her… in private. If I see *any* marks on her, I swear, I will let you know, straight away. Let the poor girl have whatever dignity remains, for Christ's sake." She leaned close and whispered, "Please, Aramis. Those men that held us captive assaulted her repeatedly. She was their favorite because she's so pretty. The girl was traumatized."

At last, he understood and sighed. He backed away and said, "Fine. You can check her, but make sure you also check for scratches."

"I will." She relaxed. "So, may we, please, have some privacy?" David, Angelo, Roberto, and Chryssy were still sitting in the room. They stood up and followed Aramis out. She then closed the door.

Devin went outside to help Kirk and Woody with the deer. David, Roberto, and Chryssy went into the dining room to sit down, while Grant, Liz, and Angelo waited impatiently in the hallway with Aramis.

After sitting down, Chryssy turned to Roberto and said, "Wow! I can't believe Kim is still alive, after all this time! I thought, for sure, she had been killed by that horde that passed through town."

Roberto turned to her and responded, "Yeah, me, too. I wonder where she's been living. She had to be inside of a house in the area or she would have died long ago."

David surmised, "If she was in a house, then the question we should really be asking is why did she leave? Did something chase her out?"

Roberto shook his head and said, "I don't know. I just hope those things haven't found their way back up here. It's the last thing we need with this cold ass weather. It will be harder to draw them away with the roads still icy."

Liz walked into the dining room, after overhearing their conversation. She sat down in her seat and suggested, "Maybe she realized she couldn't hack it on her own out there and wanted to come back here. She probably ran out of food."

All of a sudden, they heard a shrill scream of agony coming from the common room. It was hard to tell which woman had screamed. The sound scared the hell out of them.

Aramis rushed into the common room with Angelo and Grant behind him. They saw Kim had torn into and eaten from Maxine's chest. Maxine's bloody corpse was on the floor. They froze just long enough for Kim to charge at Aramis. Angelo reacted and pushed him out of the way, knocking Aramis to the floor, but then Kim went for him, instead. Her teeth clamped down tightly onto his left forearm.

"Ow! Get off me, you bitch!" He punched her in the face with his right hand and pulled his left arm free. The punch turned her around and positioned her facing the window, where she saw Kirk, Woody, and Devin walking by outside, struggling with the deer. She immediately leapt through the window, just as Grant fired a shot at her from the doorway.

"Shit! I missed! You were blocking my shot!" When he noticed Angelo was holding his wrist and Aramis was still lying on the floor, he became worried. He asked, "Are you guys okay?"

Aramis replied, while trying to stand up, "Yeah, I'm good!" He turned to Angelo and looked at the blood on his arm. A feeling of dread and guilt came over him. He realized Angelo saved him from being bitten.

Angelo avoided Grant's question and yelled, "Go get that bitch, before she bites someone else!"

For a moment, they forgot about Maxine's mauled corpse on the floor. Grant nodded, turned away, and raced out the front door to find Kim.

Joy and Millie came downstairs wondering what was going on.

As soon as they asked, Grant yelled, "Go back upstairs and lock the door! Now!"

They listened without questioning his order. Millie figured if Grant was acting paranoid, there had to be a very good reason for it. That was good enough for her.

Outside, Kim tackled Woody and began tearing into his flesh with her long fingernails. He screamed in agony and dropped his end of the deer on the ground. She then bit him on his bottom lip and ripped it from his face. His newly infected blood splattered all over the deer.

Kirk dropped his end of the deer and rushed over to Woody's side to pull her off, while Devin fell back and tried to pull out his gun. Kirk cautiously tried to grab Kim, while avoiding infection. It was not easy because she was covered in blood. He was not sure how much of that blood was infected. He cursed himself for not having his fire hydrant wrench with him. It was still in the pick-up truck.

Kim turned her attention toward Kirk and tried to latch onto him, so she could bite and infect him. Devin could not get a clear shot, since he was still on the ground. Kirk pushed her away, turned, and ran from her. He did not have time to pull out his gun and needed to put some space between them.

It gave Devin time to stand up and aim. He fired his gun once. The round struck her in the chest and pushed her back slightly, giving Kirk time to get away. However, Kim then charged after Devin. He fired a panic shot and missed, before turning to run for his life.

This time, Kirk chased after her and tried to shoot at her, but he was not very good at shooting, especially not a fast moving target. He had to be careful not to hit Devin by mistake.

Edie was up in the watchtower. She did not have a rifle and did not think she could hit Kim with her handgun, especially while she was moving, from her distance without accidentally shooting Kirk or Devin. It was a risk she could not take. She was nowhere near as good a shot as Liz or Woody.

Grant finally caught up with them and aimed his Walther PPK at Kim. He followed her with his weapon, as she drew closer to Devin, who was getting tired. He closed his right eye and slowly squeezed the trigger, until the gun went off and she went down. He sighed with relief.

By the time Devin and Kirk finally stopped running, they were both exhausted.

Edie called down from the watchtower, "Grant! What's going on down there?"

Grant turned and looked up at her. He shouted, "She was infected! She attacked a few people inside!"

Her eyes opened wide and her heart began beating fast, when she heard Grant mention that a few people had been attacked. One thought flashed through her mind. Who else was infected??? Were David and Millie okay?

Meanwhile, inside the house, Angela peeked from the kitchen and walked over to see what had occurred in the common room. When she saw Maxine's partially devoured body on the floor, she screamed and fainted. Her overweight body hit the floor hard.

Angelo looked at Aramis, who was now standing beside him, and commented, "Uh, uh. There is no way I am carrying that woman to a sofa. She stays there."

"Yeah, no shit," Aramis nodded in agreement. He turned and looked down at Maxine. Seeing her that way upset him. "It's a damn shame," he said. "I never should have left them alone."

"You can't save everyone, Doc," Angelo said. "Step aside." He crouched down and jammed his knife into her head. "She's going to come back as one of them, if we don't destroy her brain." He pulled out his knife and cleaned it on her blouse. "Sorry, Maxine. Rest in peace."

Daniel came up from the basement and stood in the doorway. He saw Maxine and asked, "What the hell happened up here? Was that girl they brought back infected?"

"Yeah, man, and now, so am I, thanks to her," Angelo confessed. He held up his bleeding arm to show Daniel.

Aramis felt overwhelmed by guilt and dread. He wished there were something he could do or say that would help. All he could think to say was, "Thank you. You took that bite for me."

"Forget it," Angelo replied soberly. "It's on me. I did what needed to be done. I'm a soldier at heart. Sometimes, I act before I think."

"I feel like shit. I wish there were something I could do for you."

"Well, actually, there is." He pulled off his backpack and handed it to Aramis. Give the explosives to my man, Grant. He'll know what to do with them." He reached into the bag and pulled out a small sealed plastic baggy. Inside was a broken syringe. "Take this. It's what's left of the anti-serum for the virus. There just might be enough to make a difference, someday."

Aramis took the bag and stared at it in shock. Finally, he asked, "How long have you had this?"

"Since Manhattan. Keep it safe. Who knows? It just may save the human race," he smirked. "At least, it was a nice dream to hold on to, while it lasted. It's all yours, Doc."

Aramis was speechless. This was big. Important. "Thanks," he said.

"Don't mention it," Angelo scoffed. "It might not even work, for all we know."

Just then, someone pounded desperately on the back door. Daniel hurried over to open it. As soon as he did, Woody burst inside, screaming maniacally. He attacked Daniel, knocking him backwards to the floor. The virus had taken over his body, turning him into a ravaging killer. He bit into Daniel's neck and ripped out a chunk of flesh, before crawling past Daniel on his hands and knees to where Angela still lay, after having fainted. He dug his face into her cleavage, which was bulging out of her nightgown, and began biting into her flesh. She awoke and began screaming in terror.

At that moment, the sound of a muffled rifle shot was heard.

Liz had rushed over from the dining room and shot Woody in the head with her rifle. She then fired another shot into Angela's head silencing her screams. She fired one more shot into Daniel's head and ended his misery. He had been squirming on the floor quietly, since his vocal cord had been torn from his throat. Afterwards, three infected bloody bodies lay in the hallway of the house.

Grant, Kirk, and Devin came in through the front door and stopped behind Liz.

"This was definitely not the kind of hunting I wanted to do today," she said.

A moment later, Angelo walked out of the common room. He looked down at the bloody mess of corpses in the hallway at his feet. He shook his head and sighed with disappointment. Too many were dead, he thought. Why did it always have to end the same way?

Aramis stood behind him and patted him on the back gently.

Charles finally came downstairs with Yvonne trailing behind him. At first, he thought they were training outside, but then he became suspicious, when he heard loud screams in the house, followed by multiple gunshots from a muffled rifle. He quickly got dressed and hurried downstairs to see what was going on. He immediately noticed the bodies on the floor in the hallway and gasped.

"Daniel! Is that Woody next to him and Angela??? Sweet Christmas! What the hell happened down here?" He looked at Angelo, whose arm was bleeding, and then at Grant and Liz, who were still holding their weapons in their hands.

Angelo looked up at him and answered, "I got bit." He held up his arm, for all to see.

Charles closed his eyes and didn't want to believe it. Liz got choked up and began to cry. Behind her David, Roberto, and Chryssy filled the rest of the hallway and were all in shock, as soon as they heard the bad news. There was going to be one more death, in addition to those, who were already gone.

Charles stepped off the bottom step and walked toward Angelo. He looked him in the eye and almost felt his pain. His eyes became teary, as the realization hit him. He mustered up the strength and inquired, "How? Who did this?" His voice came out, sounding weak and broken.

For a split second, Angelo was at a loss for words.

No one else seemed to want to speak either.

Kirk looked down at the floor and felt ashamed for bringing Kim back into the compound without checking her for bites, first. He felt like this whole mess was his fault. Because of him, several people were dead. How could he have been so careless? He could not believe Daniel was gone and soon Angelo would have to die, too. They were his family! And poor Woody and Angela. He did not even know about Maxine, yet. He became angry with himself and wanted to punch a hole in the wall, but how would that help?

He stepped forward and admitted, "It's all my fault, Charles. I brought that girl, Kim, back here. Do you remember the one, who ran away?" He did not wait for an answer. "I didn't realize she had been bitten, although I suspected it. Still, I couldn't just leave her out there to freeze to death. At least, that's what I thought, at the time. Maybe I should have. I messed up big time. I'm so sorry."

Angelo turned to him and said, "Don't blame yourself, big guy. What you did was out of the kindness of your heart. Don't ever second-guess those instincts. You're a good man, Kirk. I was damned lucky to have known you. Hell, all of you guys!" He looked around at them and Liz turned her face into Grant's shoulder to cry. Angelo noticed and was deeply touched to see that they cared so much about him. Somehow, knowing that gave him the strength he needed to face his destiny. He continued, "The past few months have been hard on us, but I am glad I was able to spend them with you people. It made all the difference in the world. I don't regret a single moment.

I have a final request. Don't let my death be in vain. Think of tonight as a wake-up call and learn from it. Even here, behind these twenty-foot walls, we are *not* safe. There's danger everywhere and if it is meant to find you, it will. You need to be more alert and take better precautions in the future." He glanced at Yvonne and said, "Learn to work together for the good of the group. I don't want any of you to have to deal with what I must deal with, now. I care about you guys. It's like Grant and Rob are always saying… we're a family. Thank you for being my family. Thank you for everything."

Grant said with tears in his eyes, "I'm going to miss you, brother."

"Well, the Angel of Death will always watch over you and keep you safe, my friend. Never forget that, you crazy bastard. I love you, man. All of you." He gave Grant the thumbs up signal and winked at him, one last time. He looked around at everyone one last time and noticed that Joy, Millie, Taryn, and Sam were peeking down from the top of the staircase. Millie had tears in her eyes and even Sam looked heartbroken. Good, he thought. Everyone he cared about was present for his final farewell.

He faced Charles and asked, "Are you still interested in taking notes about the virus? I remember you were doing that for a while, back in the beginning."

Charles was caught off guard. He hesitated and answered, "Uh, sure. Why do you ask?"

"The moment I was bitten, my arm began to itch. It itches so much that it burns. I think my flesh is dying. It kind of feels like when your leg falls asleep, and then you suddenly move it. You know that weird tingling sensation? Well, sort of like that, only different. Just thought you may want to know."

"Thanks. I'll, uh, make a note of that," he swallowed. In reality, taking notes was the furthest thing from Charles' mind. Still, he supposed it was good to know.

Angelo walked toward the back door to leave.

Charles called after him, "Wait. What are you going to do? Where are you going?"

"This is my endgame, Charles," he said. He tugged lightly at his salt and pepper goatee and frowned. He had already accepted his fate. "So, I'm going to end it, on my own terms... with this." He held up his MK 18 Mod 0 rifle. "By the way, Grant, I leave her to you. I know you'll take good care of her."

Grant nodded quietly, as they made eye contact. "Of course," he forced out the words and swallowed.

Angelo smiled at him. "I guess you can put me next to Bobby and that girl, Delilah," he shrugged indifferently. "I apologize for the mess I'll leave, in advance. Goodbye, everybody."

David said, "It's been an honor knowing you, Corporal Williams."

Angelo nodded at him, "Thanks. Same here, buddy."

Roberto wanted to say something, too, but he could not find the strength or the words, so he just stared proudly at Angelo for being so brave, while struggling to keep his tears inside.

There were tears in mostly everyone's eyes, but especially those who got the chance to know Angelo Williams. He had been an integral part of their family. Losing him, Daniel, Woody, Maxine, and Angela in the same day was a rough blow for them.

"Goodbye, Corporal Angelo Williams." Charles saluted. "We will never forget you."

Angelo returned the salute and went out into the backyard alone. He closed the door behind him. Julia watched him from the basement on the security camera, which loomed overhead near a second floor window. She watched him walk toward Bobby's grave. Everyone in the house stood still and stared at the back door. They were all waiting. Not long after, there was a muffled gunshot. Kirk turned away, as the tears came down and Julia gasped in horror in front of the computer monitor. For one more person, this nightmare was over.

Corporal Angelo Williams was dead.

MAN'S END

Chapter Thirty-One

IT WAS A cold, but sunny February morning on a Sunday. The birds were singing from their perches in the surrounding trees. The wind blew cold air gently over the dried ground. The most recent snowfall had finally melted completely away, but it was a sure bet there would be more snow, before the winter was over.

Grant and Charles stood quietly and watched over a small field of graves that formed the cemetery at the compound. It was hard for them to believe there were already eight people buried there. Wooden crosses marked each grave. It was the best they could do.

Charles glanced over at his old friend, who was deep in thought. He wondered what was going through his mind. There was a time when he would have just asked, but things had changed between them. Charles felt like there was a rift between them and he knew it was his fault. He had been spending so much time in the attic living in a fantasy world with Yvonne. For a short time, he almost forgot about how bad the world had gotten. In the process, he lost touch with reality and his friends, who had been counting on his guidance to lead them. Grant had taken up much of the burden and it was taking its toll on him.

So many people had died. Charles wondered was it because of Grant's leadership or because of his own failure to be there for his group? Should they both take the blame or was it none of their faults? These were the thoughts going through his mind. Still, he wondered what Grant was thinking.

Finally, he commented, "I guess we failed them, huh?" When Grant did not respond, he continued, "It doesn't even feel like a month has passed, since they died. It's like it was only yesterday. Do you think we could have done anything different to prevent their deaths?"

While still staring down at the graves, Grant responded, "If death has his eye on you, you can't run from it forever. They were going to die, regardless. I try not to dwell on what could have been or what should have been. I'd much rather think about how we can avoid something like this from happening, again. Most of these deaths were tragedies. I like to hope we can prevent future tragedies, but we need to be realistic." He turned to face Charles. "More people will die. It's unavoidable. Death is a part of life. We need to try and make the most of the time we have left together. It's like Angelo said. We need to work together for the good of the group. That means *all* of us."

Charles looked away and felt ashamed. He knew he was talking about him and Yvonne.

Grant moved closer and said, "There was a time, when I had the utmost respect for you, Charles. I'd follow you into certain death because I knew you were a good leader and would, somehow, find a way to get us out alive. I know you probably don't want to hear this, but ever since Yvonne came into your life, you've changed. I don't even know who you are anymore. That leader I followed and respected… he's gone. I'm my own leader, now. I do what I can to keep this group alive. I do what is best for the group, as a whole. I won't ever abandon these people. I know some of them look to me for guidance, so I need to make myself available. If you want to continue living in private, I can't stop you. This is still your house, but don't try to play leader, now. It's too late for that."

Grant walked away and went back into the house, leaving Charles alone at the cemetery. Moments later, he was down in the basement. He walked toward the armory and was about to unlock the door, but he hesitated. He slammed his fist into the door out of anger and closed his eyes. He felt bad with how he spoke to Charles, but he wanted to say those things for quite sometime and had to let it out.

Julia stepped out into the hallway and asked, "What's wrong, Grant?" She walked over to him and placed a hand on his shoulder. "Is everything all right?"

He turned to face her and it was obvious he was upset. He answered, "I just feel a little frustrated. I was talking to Charles out by the cemetery." He scoffed, "Shit. I can't believe we even have a cemetery." He sighed, "Anyway, I may have said some hurtful things to him, but he needed to hear it. He really let me down with the way he's been hiding in the attic all winter. I feel like the burden of leadership was thrust upon me, before I was ready and so many people paid the price."

"That doesn't make it your fault. You're a good leader. You're very smart and you always seem so sure of yourself. Your confidence makes it easy for others to follow you. You shouldn't blame yourself for the deaths of those people. It was Kim's fault for not telling Kirk she was bitten. That selfish bitch was more worried about her own ass than everybody here. Screw her!"

"I suppose you're right," he sighed.

"You know I am. Make no mistake. *You're* the one, who keeps us alive. You got us out of Manhattan. You guided us into Yonkers. If not for you, we wouldn't even be here. We'd be dead."

"I don't know about that. You're making my role seem bigger than it actually was."

"Stop being so modest. Grant, you are an amazing person." Her tone changed and she sounded more caring. "We are so lucky to have you here. I know *I* feel much safer with you around."

He looked at her and she smiled at him.

She took advantage of the moment and moved closer. His back pressed against the door. She whispered, "If you want, I could show you how appreciated you are around here. Her hand moved over his crotch and she leaned in to kiss him."

He grabbed her hand and slid out of her way. He asked, "Julia, what are you doing?"

"Kiss me, Grant. I promise you won't regret it. We can do it, right down here. No one even has to know." She held his hand and moved closer, again. "I want you inside me, so bad."

"Whoa!" He backed away and pulled his hand free. He explained, "I'm very sorry, but this *cannot* happen, Julia. You know I'm already with Liz and we are *very* happy together."

"Yes, and I don't need to be reminded of that." She scowled. "What I'm offering you is a chance to have more. If you still want to be with *her*, I'd be willing to share you. I've thought long and hard about it. A good man like you is too hard to come by."

"Thanks, but I *really* don't think Liz will feel the same."

She sighed and responded coldly, "Liz won't always be around. Someday, you're going to come running to me, once you realize what you're missing."

"No offense, but I seriously doubt that. Julia, listen to me. You are a very pretty girl. Don't limit yourself by going for someone you can't have. There are plenty of great guys around here that would be very good to you."

"Well, I don't want them!" She calmed herself and stated, "I want you. I love you, Grant. I always have, since the day we first met. It was love at first sight. Doesn't that mean anything to you?"

"I'm very flattered. Honestly. I just don't feel the same way. I'm sorry."

She grimaced at him and her nostrils flared. She allowed the hatred to take over and build up. She did not take her eyes off of him, as she tried to associate his appearance with her feelings of hatred. If she could not love him, then she would hate him.

He began to worry about her with the way she was looking at him. She was in worse shape than he thought. He knew he should have spoken to her much sooner, but he was desperately trying to avoid this conversation. He had a feeling it would become awkward, but he never knew it would be this bad.

"Why don't I leave you alone? I'll give you the time you need to think this through rationally. I'm sure you'll realize this is for the best. After all, why would you want to be with someone, who is not in love with you? Again, I'm really sorry, Julia. I hope we can still be friends." He backed away toward the stairs and went back upstairs.

Julia stood there wallowing in her anger for a while, but then the pain forced its way through. She screamed, and then dropped to her knees. She began to cry. She cried and cried, until there were no more tears. She wanted to get them all out because she never wanted to cry for Grant, again.

Sam sat alone in the common room and felt absolutely bored. He wished he could go outside and fly the drone, but it was too cold and windy for that. Instead, he was stuck in the house with nothing to do. From where he was seated on the sofa, he looked around the large square-shaped room. He gazed curiously at the books on the shelf and considered reading something, but he was not in the mood. He noticed the board games that he helped choose with Grant and Liz and smiled. That was a good memory for him. It was good to have memories like that to think back on. It helped fight off the terrible ones.

His eyes moved reluctantly to the window, which had been broken when Kim jumped through it a month earlier. He volunteered to help Kirk and Roberto fix it. They let him. Next, he glanced down at the floor and remembered how it was not that long ago when Maxine's dead body lay there covered in blood. It took a long time to get her infected blood out. He helped scrub it away. Ironically, she would have been proud of the good job he did. He was grateful his sister did not witness the horrors of that evening. Joy kept her locked away upstairs in the female dorm. Thank goodness for small favors, he thought.

He heard someone coming down the stairs and saw that it was his mother and sister. They stood in the doorway of the common room and both looked eagerly at him. His sister waved at him playfully and giggled. It made him smile.

Joy said, "Oh, good! There you are! Sammy, can you, please, do me a really big favor and watch your sister for a few hours? I promised Millie I would help her with dinner today."

He exhaled and blew his shaggy brown hair upwards away from his forehead. "Yeah, sure. It's not like I've got anything better to do."

"Thank you so much, baby! I really appreciate it! If I let her, she'd play in the closet all day!"

"No problem, mom."

She bent down and turned to Glenda. "Mommy has to go help with dinner in the kitchen. Go hang out with your brother for a while and do as he says, and stay out of the closet. Okay?"

"Okay, mommy." Glenda then went into the common room and sat on the sofa beside her big brother, who put his arm around her and held her close.

Joy smiled, and then walked off toward the kitchen.

Sam asked, "Do you want to play a board game?"

She answered excitedly, "Yes!"

He stood up and took her by the hand. "Come on. Let's pick one out together." He led her to the shelf, where the board games were kept and asked, "What about this one? Parcheesi?"

She shook her head, "Uh, uh."

"Okay. Ooh, what about this one!" He showed her the Monopoly box. "You can be the doggy, if you want."

"Yes! I wanna be the doggy!"

He placed the box on the floor and they both knelt down beside it. He opened it up and pulled out the folded blue and gray board, unfolding it as he did. He placed it on the floor in front of them, and then noticed Taryn was standing at the doorway watching.

"Oh, sorry," she said. "I was just on my way to the basement."

"Wait," he called out to her and she turned to face him. He asked, "Would you like to play with us? We're about to play Monopoly. It would be nice to have another adult. Please?"

She raised her eyebrows and asked, "Isn't that a very long game?"

He nodded, "That's the idea. I was hoping to keep her busy, until dinnertime."

Glenda eyed him suspiciously and said, "I know you're talking 'bout me, Sammy."

Taryn chuckled.

"Come on, Taryn. We never spend any time together. Please?" He shrugged helplessly at her.

She smiled slightly and nodded, "Okay. Sure." She figured why not? It beat hanging out in front of the computer with Julia and listening to her go on about a man she could never have. It was definitely the right decision. After Julia's recent failure with Grant, it would have been a dreary experience for her.

Taryn knelt down on the floor next to Sam and Glenda. She examined the game pieces and asked, "How do you play this game anyway?"

Sam and Glenda both looked at her in surprise. Sam asked, "You've never played this game?"

She shook her head in silence.

Sam said, "You're in for a real treat. This is a pretty fun game, as long as you're playing with a good group and not a bunch of *sore losers*." He leered at his sister.

"I am *not* a sore loser!"

"You better not be," he warned.

"I'm gonna beat you anyway," she giggled sneakily.

"No cheating either," he said.

"Aw, man!" She frowned.

Taryn chuckled, again. She could tell this was going to be an entertaining experience.

Sam showed her the game pieces and explained, "You'll need to pick one of these silver tokens. That will represent you in the game. I like the car," he said, as he snatched it up quickly.

Glenda announced, "I have the little doggy! Arf! Arf! Arf!" She played with the dog and pretended to pet it.

Taryn smiled and looked at the tokens. She picked one up and asked, "Is this an old boot?"

"Yeah," Sam said.

"It looks funny. I like it. Can I use it?"

"Yeah," he told her. "You can use whichever one you want, as long as someone else didn't already pick it. The boot is all yours."

He explained the basic instructions of the game, while passing out the money to each player. They rolled the dice to decide who would go first and the game began. Glenda went first, followed by Sam, and then Taryn. They moved their tokens around the board once, before buying any of the available properties. Sam was the first to make a purchase.

Glenda was upset, after she picked up a "Chance" card on her next turn that sent her token directly to jail. "Aw, come on! That's not fair!"

"Sure it is," her brother told her. "It can happen to either one of us. You just happen to be the first." He chuckled wickedly.

She frowned and pouted. "I don't think I like playing Moneyopoly. This game sucks," she griped and folded her arms in frustration.

Sam scolded her and said, "Hey. Don't start that. You said you were not a sore loser. Remember?"

She nodded sadly.

He said more kindly, "Don't worry. You won't stay in jail forever. Look at Taryn. She's not complaining and she just landed on my property. He grinned. And another thing, it's called MONOPOLY, not Moneyopoly." He shook his head and turned to Taryn. He held out his hand and waited. "Pay up!"

Taryn frowned, as she handed him the money she owed for landing on his property. She looked at Glenda and agreed, "I think you might be right. This game sucks!"

Glenda's frown faded away and she giggled. Taryn laughed, too.

About an hour into the game, Taryn realized she was enjoying herself very much. She was not the only one. Glenda looked very entertained. They were having a lot of fun together. Taryn also noticed Sam kept sneaking looks at her and she liked it. She liked him, too.

Later, after dinner, everyone sat at the dining room tables and talked, except Julia, who went downstairs to the basement, as soon as she was done eating. Charles excused himself and went up to the watchtower, soon after.

Grant looked at Millie and said, "Thank you for another delicious dinner, Millie. I don't know how you do it with the little resources we have available."

"Joy helped me." She smiled, but then asked, "Do you think it needed more salt?"

"It was perfect," he replied. He looked at Joy and said, "Thanks for helping her with dinner. I feel bad that she usually gets stuck cooking for so many people all the time, especially now that Angela's gone. She was very helpful in the kitchen."

Millie frowned, "I don't mind cooking. I miss Angela, though. She was sweet. I'm glad she taught me a few of her recipes. She was a great cook."

Edie said, "Yeah, she was awesome in the kitchen. I miss her, too."

Yvonne missed her, as well. They had been friends, before the apocalypse. She usually did not say much to anyone, but, this time, she felt the need to say something. "I really miss her, too."

Everyone turned to her and were surprised that she was still there, even though Charles had already excused himself. The fact that she was speaking to them was even more of a surprise. She went on without noticing their expressions. Either that or she just did not care. "Angela would have been so happy to know that you guys appreciated her. When we were in college together, she used to think no one appreciated her because of her weight. You guys took her in and treated her like one of the family, right from the start, without even knowing her. I just wanted to say thank you."

Unexpectedly, it was Millie who responded, "You're welcome, Yvonne. You know? You don't have to hide in the attic all the time. I'm usually pretty shy myself, so I know how it feels, when you'd rather not be around other people. It's awkward. Well, you shouldn't feel that way with us. We want to be your friends, if you'll let us. You can come down and hang out with us girls in the female dorm, anytime you get tired of the same four walls. It can't be that great up there."

"Oh, believe me! It's not!" She scoffed. She looked at Millie and said, "Thanks for the invitation. Maybe I'll take you up on that offer." She did not dare tell them the real reason she preferred to be alone.

"Good," Millie smiled. "It will be nice to get to know you."

Grant, on the other hand, had nothing to say to Yvonne. He stood up and cleared away his and Liz's plates and went into the kitchen. Liz watched him go. She knew he felt resentment toward Yvonne for the way she had been keeping Charles to herself in the attic.

Liz turned to Yvonne and asked, "Why do you spend so much time in the attic, if you don't like it up there? I know you're not shy."

Yvonne shrugged, "It's my room, so I figured I may as well stay out of everyone's way."

Liz did not find that answer to be truthful. Not one bit. She pushed the issue and said, "Actually, it's Charles' room. You just ended up sleeping there, one day, and never left. The girls were saving your sleeping space in the dorm, in case you ever returned for it. Isn't that right, Edie?"

"Yes, that is correct. No one has slept on that bed, since Angela's death."

Yvonne responded, "Oh? Well, don't wait for me to return. By all means, use the bed. I'm very happy, where I am. I have no plans to sleep in the dorm."

Edie replied, "Thank you. We will. Maybe Joy and Glenda can use it. They've been sleeping with Julia, who is probably not the best bunkmate."

Taryn looked down at her plate.

Joy said, "Ain't that the truth? It would be great to finally have a bed to ourselves! Honestly, I feel terrible sleeping on Julia's bed. It's like we've been a tremendous inconvenience to her. It makes me feel guilty.

I know that girl doesn't like me. She probably feels like I'm moving in on her space. I can tell she resents me for it."

Edie scoffed, "Oh, please. Don't pay Julia any mind. She hardly even goes into the dorm. She would be happier, if we moved a bed down to the basement for her. That girl is so anti-social, it's not even funny."

Millie added, "Yeah, I used to want to help out downstairs and learn how to watch over the security cameras, but something about Julia rubs me the wrong way. I can't deal with her high and mighty attitude. It makes me want to punch her."

Joy commented, "Damn, girl! I thought you were the sweet quiet one around here!"

Millie and Edie chuckled.

Right away, Yvonne felt uncomfortable. She wondered if that's how they thought and spoke about her behind her back. It made her feel depressed thinking about it. She wanted to change. She hated feeling like an outsider.

Taryn also began to feel uncomfortable, as she sat and listened to them talk about Julia. That was her friend. She felt the need to defend her. However, she felt too shy speaking to large groups, so she did not say anything.

Sam noticed she looked upset because he had been staring at her throughout dinner. Unlike her, he was not shy. Fortunately for her, he was good at being inconspicuous. He leaned in close and whispered, "What's wrong, Taryn? You look upset."

She looked at him and whispered back, "I feel bad that Julia is not here to defend herself. She's not a bad person. She's just misunderstood. She's going through a hard time and just feels better being alone. Is there anything wrong with wanting to be alone?"

"No," he shook his head. "Not at all. I wish we were alone, right now." He stared into her eyes and smiled.

She felt awkward and turned away bashfully, but she was smiling.

Sam suggested, "Would you like to go for a walk?"

She shrugged and responded, "Okay, I guess."

"Good. Come on. Let's take our plates to the kitchen, so we don't draw too much attention." He stood up and picked up his plate.

She did the same.

They took their plates into the kitchen and cleaned them together. Afterwards, they went outside to the backyard.

"It's kind of chilly," she said, while shivering.

"Yeah, we should put on our coats."

They went inside, grabbed their coats, and went back out to the backyard.

"Come on," he said.

She followed him to the barn, where they went inside and closed the door. Betsy was eating hay, peacefully, with a warm blanket over her back.

Sam and Taryn went upstairs to the upper level and sat down on a pile of hay.

"Ouch! This stuff hurts," she said.

"Yeah, it's better not to let it touch your bare skin. Try lying down on it. It's kind of comfy, as long as you are dressed with a thick layer of clothing like me."

They both lay back on the hay and looked up at the ceiling. It was incredibly serene in the barn. It didn't really smell too great, but it was not that bad.

Sam rolled on his side and propped his head up with his arm. He looked at Taryn and said, "This place can be really cool, if you take advantage of the great things that are around. Sometimes, I like to lie up here on my own. It's a good place to think."

"Yeah, it seems like it would be," she responded without really looking at him.

He knew she was very shy, so he did not rush her or try to make her feel uncomfortable. He tried to keep the conversation simple, hoping to make her feel more comfortable speaking to him. "Have you ever been to a farm?"

"No," she answered.

"Me neither. I bet this place is much cooler than a farm. Instead of a silo, we have a watchtower. Hey. Did you know there's an old well nearby, behind the tool shed?"

"Really?" She seemed interested in what he was saying because she rolled onto her side and also propped her head up with her arm, while facing him. Her long red hair got into her face, so she pushed it to the side behind her ear.

"Yeah, it's covered up, though," he said. Right away, he noticed she was wearing the earrings he picked out for her on Christmas. They had small little diamond-like stones, so they were not cumbersome for her. He said admiringly, "Those earrings look good on you."

"Thank you. You guys gave them to me on Christmas," she smiled.

"I know." He paused and added, "I picked them out for you."

"You did? That's awesome. Thank you. I really like them."

"I'm glad." He wanted to tell her how pretty he found her to be, but was worried it might be too forward. Instead, he opted for talking about something casual. "You know? I think I've learned a lot more being here, than I would have from going to school. I like to think of this place as the University of Life. Uh, not the barn, but the whole compound."

She commented, "That's a curious thing to say. What do you mean?"

"Well, think about it. I wake up in the morning and can exercise my body in the gym, at least during a few days a week. Roberto teaches those of us, who are willing to learn, how to fight and handle ourselves with and without a weapon. He shows us useful skills that will help save our lives out there. I also learn how to clean and shoot guns from Grant. He even let me keep the double barrel shotgun that I recovered the night we rescued you girls. Recently, he gave me Angelo's Bowie hunting knife because I saved Angelo's life that night. Roberto has been teaching me how to fight with it. That's not all. I also learn how to be a farmer. David taught me how to milk Betsy and Millie showed me how to collect eggs from the hens. She also taught me about the vegetables we're growing. Did you know carrots grow better during the winter months?"

"No," she shook her head. Listening to him speak fascinated her. He seemed so eager to learn more and she admired that about him. He sounded like he was learning so much.

He continued, "Kirk has been teaching me about cars, too. I helped him change the oil on the pick-up truck. He said once the weather warms up, he'll teach me how to drive. I already have a rough idea. I was taking lessons, before the virus ruined everything."

She looked saddened, after he mentioned the virus. He felt bad for bringing it up. It was because of the virus that people started going crazy. He figured it must have been difficult for her, considering the lunatics that held her prisoner also killed her parents.

"Do you miss your parents?"

"Every day," she answered sadly.

"I'm really sorry about what happened to them. I wish we could have saved them, too."

She looked at him and said, "I'm glad you guys saved us. I kept thinking every day that my turn would come soon. Those men took turns with Kim and Delilah. They even abused Yvonne. I think that might be why she doesn't like being around others."

"Man, that really sucks. I'm glad they never got to you. What stopped them?"

"Maxine. She was like a mother to me. I feel so bad that she was killed. She was so nice. I miss her. We used to bunk together, after we got here. Now, I sleep with Chryssy."

"What's her story? She's a bit weird. Don't you think?"

"No, she's really cool. Weird isn't a bad thing, Sam. I'm kind of weird. We all are in our own way."

"I guess."

"Do you know all of those piercings she wears and have you seen the way she sharpens her fingernails?"

"Yeah," he scoffed.

"Well, she used to fight those men off and cut them open. After a while, they gave up trying to rape her. She was too tough for them. I admired her for it."

"Wow. That is pretty awesome. No wonder Rob likes her."

"I'm telling you. She's cool. Give her a chance."

"I think you're pretty cool," he said with a smile.

She shied away and blushed.

"I really like you, Taryn." He hesitated, and added, "I think you like me, too. At least, I hope so. I was thinking. If you do, maybe you could be my..." He swallowed nervously. "Maybe you could be my girlfriend. You can think about it, if you want. I won't rush you. I can be very patient."

She looked at him and responded, "I like you, too, Sam. I would love to be your girlfriend." She tried very hard to return his gaze.

"Really?" He sounded surprised.

She shrugged, "Yeah, why not?"

"Awesome," he grinned happily.

She giggled and they lay back down on the hay. Their hands touched briefly. Sam took her hand and held it. She did not protest. They laid together holding hands, without saying a word.

MAN'S END

Chapter Thirty-Two

AFTER A COLD and hard winter, springtime was finally near. It was mid-March and the weather was starting to warm up. There were still cold days, but soon they would become a memory. The group had made it through their first winter in the apocalypse. It was unfortunate that not everyone made it. For those who did, they knew it was a blessing that could not be taken for granted.

Kirk decided to take charge of completing the wall, since it was originally his idea anyway. He felt he owed it to Daniel to complete it and made it his top priority. It had been too cold to work on it, until now. It was high time to get back to work. This time, everyone helped out.

Yvonne was tired of being the outsider. She put on a pair of work gloves and got dirty with the rest of the group. Charles was happy to see her mingling with the others. He hoped she would continue to interact positively with the rest of the group.

Even Julia helped with mixing the cement. She took turns with Taryn and Charles watching the security cameras, while someone with gun training always stood guard in the watchtower. Grant usually liked to be up in the watchtower, whenever Julia was mixing cement. He thought it best if he avoided being near her. The shifts in the tower had been extended to five-hour shifts, which suited him just fine. There was no way Julia could keep away from the computer that long.

Meanwhile, Joy had Glenda playing the role of assistant in the kitchen. Sometimes, she would help carry out bottles of water to the workers. She enjoyed helping the adults. It made her feel grown up.

By early April, the northern wall was nearly completed, going from east to west. However, they had finally run out of building materials. It was time for the first supply run of the year. There was no question about where they would go for supplies. Going south was out of the question. They would return to Wallkill to raid the Home Depot and Lowe's along Route 211.

David, Roberto, and Kirk jumped into the flatbed truck and headed up Interstate 86 to Wallkill. Grant stayed in touch with them over the two-way radio. He sat up in his bedroom with the door closed, so he would not be disturbed. He kept a book with him, so he could read, while he waited to hear from them.

Liz took a shift in the watchtower to keep busy, while he monitored the radio. Sam sat up there with her and watched over the team using a drone, until they reached the interstate. He was not sure how far he could push the drone, before losing control, so he did not take any chances. Being in the watchtower allowed him to have a better line of sight of it. Liz kept a radio with her, just in case Sam spotted any potential dangers to the team through the drone's camera, which he monitored using one of the laptops.

The group worked together like a well-oiled machine, each doing his or her part to make sure things went off without a hitch. Teamwork became a key factor in surviving the apocalypse.

Kirk drove, while David rode shotgun and Roberto sat between them. As the truck entered the interstate, Kirk joked, "I hope we don't run into traffic."

Roberto and David chuckled.

Back in the watchtower, Sam saw the truck enter the interstate via the drone's camera and stated, "They're on the highway and out of range. I'm bringing the drone back home."

"Okay," Liz said. She picked up the radio and spoke into it. "Queen to base. The Eye in the Sky is coming home. Over."

Grant responded from their bedroom, "Base acknowledged. Over."

He knew it would be a long wait, from here on, so he picked up his book and began reading. He figured he probably had time to get through the first few chapters, before they returned with a full load.

Charles went down to the basement to see how things were going and noticed Julia did not have a two-way radio next to her. He became confused because it was usually customary for whoever was sitting near the computer to have a radio, especially whenever there was a team out on a supply run. The reason was so that the person at the computer could check the Internet and maps for reference, as needed.

"Why aren't you listening to the radio? There's a team out there."

She turned to him and said, "Oh, hey there. I have one, but it's off. We don't necessarily do things that way anymore. Grant changed the system. He has a laptop and a radio, so he can keep in touch with the team. He also has a drone watching over them, until they're out of range. Now, I can focus on watching the monitors without being distracted. Well, until you came in. If you have a problem, you can talk to him. He's upstairs hiding in his room, so he doesn't have to be bothered by me."

"Thanks. That won't be necessary," he said. Charles took in everything she said and shrugged. He had no idea what was going on with her, but he really did not wish to get into it. It was none of his business. He turned to go and said, "I was only curious."

"Curiosity killed the cat, Charles. Just remember, little sister is always watching."

"Right. I'll be sure to remember that. See you later," he waved. He walked back upstairs, feeling bewildered. And people thought he had been acting strange lately!

He went up to the second floor and noticed Grant's bedroom door was closed. He stood in front of it and thought about knocking, but he hesitated.

Suddenly, Grant shouted, "Come in! The door is open!"

How did he know? Charles opened the door and peeked into the room. "Hey," he said.

"What's up, Chuck? I saw the shadow of your feet under the door. Plus, I heard you walking up the stairs. So, how can I help you?" He put the book down beside him and sat up on the bed.

"I was wondering how the mission is going."

"All good, so far. The guys are on their way to Wallkill, as we speak. They're going to hit up the Home Depot and Lowe's. If all goes well, we're planning another supply run tomorrow for food and drinks. Our cache is running low, after this long ass winter. David said he'd go back out with Rob. They'll be taking Edie and Chryssy with them. At least, that's the plan."

"Oh, okay. I guess you have everything under control."

"Someone's got to hold things down around here."

Charles stepped into the room and closed the door. He did not like the comment or how it came out. He demanded, "Why are you still breaking my balls about that? I thought we were friends. You wanted to play leader, so I gave you the chance to step up. What's the problem?"

Grant sighed and replied, "Fine. I'm sorry. The truth is I'm jealous. I miss hanging out with you. I feel like you spend all of your time with Yvonne. We used to spend hours talking about movies and comic books and all kinds of other crap."

"Yeah, before the Zombie Apocalypse. Come on, Grant. We haven't had a talk like that since July. Ever since this thing went down, we haven't been the same. You have Liz and I have Yvonne. Why can't we still find a way to get along, despite that?"

"You're absolutely right," Grant sighed. He gestured to the bed. "Sit down. Let's talk. I mean really talk."

Charles sat at the foot of the bed.

"How are things with Yvonne? Does she make you happy?"

"Yeah, she does, for the most part," replied Charles.

Grant raised an eyebrow and asked, "What do you mean by *for the most part?*"

Charles sighed, "She's a bit prejudiced, which really bothers me. I know it has a lot to do with how she was treated by the group that held her prisoner, so I don't push the subject. She has a lot of anger locked away inside and I really don't blame her."

"Without a doubt," Grant agreed. "Maybe she hasn't realized that we don't see race here."

"I told her that, but there's more. She is very anti-social. She doesn't like being around people at all, regardless of their race. It took a lot of effort for her to go outside and help with the wall. I was so proud of her for doing that. I think she even had a good time. She's finally starting to realize that the people here are good. I've been trying to convince her for months."

"Don't you think you'd be more convincing if she saw you spend time down here with us, every once in a while?"

"Yeah, probably," Charles nodded. "That's on me."

Grant asked, "Just out of curiosity, where do you see yourself a year from now?"

The question threw Charles off, but he tried to think of an honest answer. He said, "Here, in this house with everyone. I hope. Why? Where do you see yourself?"

"Surviving. Anywhere I have to be. Whether or not it's here, I can't really say. I would like to think so, but Angelo said something on the day he died that made me think. Maybe you'll remember. He said no place is truly safe. I hate to say it, but I agree. It got me thinking. We might feel safe here, now, but there are so many ways things can go wrong. All it takes is one mistake. You and I could be as careful as possible, but we are not alone here. I can't honestly say that I trust everyone else to be as careful as I might be. That presents me with a dilemma. Do I limit our supply runs to the same few capable people all the time, leaving the others with no experience in the field or do I give others a chance to prove that they can become as capable with the right amount of training and experience?"

"That is an interesting dilemma. Personally, I'd take my chances by sending the same capable people every time. I know it's not fair to the others, but it's the safer bet."

"And what happens when your most capable people are out there knee deep in trouble and you need to send a back up team to rescue them? You will be sending a team that is less experienced and not as capable, which means they will likely fail. All people could be lost because the rescue team had very little experience in the field and could not last long enough out there to save the team that was capable."

"You make a good point, Grant. That's why I felt it was okay to leave you in charge. You're smart enough to think like that. You can make these decisions. You call it a dilemma, while talking to me and trying to get my opinion, but I can tell you've already made your decision and I must admit, it sounds like the right one. I was wrong. You're already becoming a better leader than me. What do you need me around for?"

"Because you're my friend and until we just spoke about it, I wasn't really sure what course of action would be the best decision. Talking to you helped me to see things more clearly. Thanks."

"You could have spoken to Liz and came up with the same decision," Charles said.

"Maybe, but I guess we'll never know," Grant smiled. "The decision is made."

The supply team returned a few hours later with a fully loaded truck. They hoped it would be enough to complete the wall. To make the job easier, Kirk parked the flatbed closer to the northwest corner of the compound between the unfinished north wall and fence on the west side of the property. Unloading the truck could wait for tomorrow, since it was almost dinnertime and he was starving.

Early the next day, after breakfast, Kirk took a crew outside to unload the truck. He had Aramis, Devin, Joy, and Sam with him. They volunteered.

At around the same time, David was set to go back out using the Ford Explorer. As planned, he took Roberto, Chryssy, and Edie with him. Grant monitored the two-way radio, again, but this time from the watchtower with Liz. He also used the drone. Sam showed him how, although he was not as good at controlling it. He decided to just keep it close to home and sent it up, as high as it would go. He was still able to see the Ford Explorer, as it reached Interstate 86 and headed northbound.

Roberto popped in a random CD with rock music on it. In the backseat, Chryssy and Edie both began bopping and dancing. Roberto tapped his thighs, as if playing the drums. He looked at David, who was trying too hard to focus on driving, and chuckled.

"What's wrong, bro? You don't like this song?"

David replied, "Not really a fan of rock."

Roberto looked at him, as if he had two heads and shook his head. "I thought you were cool! This song kicks ass, right girls?"

Chryssy shouted, "Shit yeah!"

Edie was shaking her head wildly to the beat of the music and her platinum blonde hair, which was now down to her shoulders, was slapping back and forth. David noticed her in the rearview mirror and laughed. She paused, winked at him, and continued dancing to the song.

When they reached their exit, David took them into the parking lot of the Walmart. That's where they would search for the food and drinks they required.

"We're here," David announced.

Roberto turned back and said, "You heard the man. Fun time is over. It's time to put on your game faces, ladies. Grab your weapons and, remember, stay close to us. You two do not split up from us. You can stay with David or you can stay near me, but make sure you stay with one of us, if not both. Got it?"

"Yes," they said simultaneously.

They got out of the car and walked toward the Walmart. After checking out the store, they were satisfied no one was there. It was time to shop. They each grabbed shopping carts and played follow the leader through the store. David led the way with Edie right behind him. Chryssy was next and Roberto took the rear. They walked through each aisle and had a good time filling up the four carts.

When they were done, they pushed the carts outside to the Ford Explorer. Edie looked at all the merchandise and asked, "Is all of this going to fit?"

Roberto replied, "Don't worry. We'll make it fit, as best we can. We need to fill every single space and stack it high. Grant's really good at this part, but Dave and I picked up some pointers from him. Right, bro?"

"Yep."

Roberto suggested, "You ladies can stand watch, while we load the stuff. Make sure no one, or nothing, sneaks up on us."

"You got it, dude," Chryssy replied. She loaded an arrow into her compound-bow and was ready for action. She searched all around, but did not see anything out of the ordinary. She gently relaxed the tension on her bow, but remained alert.

When they were almost done, Edie asked, "Can I ride shotgun on the way back home?"

Roberto looked at David, who shrugged indifferently. He then answered, "Yeah, I don't have a problem with that. It will give me a chance to sit next to this sexy ass woman."

Chryssy chuckled and said, "Maybe I'll let you touch my butt, if you behave."

"Ooh!" Roberto grinned. "This could be an interesting ride back home!" He pushed the four carts into each other, so he could push them out of the way in one shot.

"Good grief." David rolled his eyes at them and got into the driver's seat. He started up the vehicle and Edie sat down beside him.

Roberto said, "Shit. Dave, give me a minute. I gotta drain the lizard."

"So, do I," said Chryssy. "Well, sort of. Can we use the restrooms inside? Is it safe?"

"Yeah, sure," he replied. "We'll be back, guys. Keep it running, bro. This won't take long."

David nodded. He turned to Edie and asked, "What about you? You don't have to go, too? I thought women always went to the bathroom together."

She smirked, "I can wait, until we get home. It's a short ride. Besides, I don't want to leave you out here alone. You might get lonely."

"It's fine. Really. I don't mind being alone."

Edie frowned, "Would you rather I go, so you can be alone?"

"Only if you need to go. If you can wait, then wait."

She sighed and asked, "David? Can I ask you something?"

He turned to her and said, "You just did, but if you have another question, don't let me stop you from asking it."

"David! I'd expect that from Grant, not you. Are all cops wise asses?"

"Yep. Was that your question?"

"No, silly. Be serious. If I were a real one hundred percent woman, do you think we'd be together as a couple?"

He sighed. He really did not want their friendship to go back to the awkward place it used to be. It was hard enough to get to this point. He answered, "Yes. I think we probably would've been a couple."

"Okay. That's all I wanted to know. Thanks," She smiled satisfied.

That was a lot less painful than he expected it to be. He relaxed in his seat. He casually glanced into his side view mirror and cried out,

"Holy shit! We gotta move!" He shifted the Ford Explorer into gear and screeched off toward the exit of the parking lot.

Edie was confused and asked, "What are you doing, David? What about Rob and Chryssy?"

"No time to wait!"

Suddenly, she saw and heard the two-dozen motorcycles that were pulling into the parking lot from Route 211. They immediately veered back onto the roadway and followed them.

"Shit! They're following us! We need to lose these clowns, so we can come back for the others," David said. "Call it in! Tell Grant what's going on!" They heard gunshots and the rear window exploded into pieces. "Keep your head down! They're shooting at us!"

Roberto and Chryssy reached the doorway of Walmart, just in time to see David and Edie driving away, while being chased by a motorcycle gang. Some of the gang members were shooting guns at their fleeing vehicle.

"Oh, shit!" He cursed. "That's a lot of motorcycles!"

Chryssy turned to him and asked, "What do we do? Do you think they'll get away?"

"I'm more worried about the six motorcycles that just turned into this parking lot. They're coming this way and Dave has my wrecking bar! Quick! Get inside! We need to find a place to defend ourselves!"

Six rowdy bikers dressed in denim jeans, obnoxious t-shirts, and black leather jackets kicked their way into the Walmart, believing that if they burst in like they owned the place, whoever was hiding within would cower in fear. It worked every time. No one dared cross the Road Demons. When they saw two people duck into Walmart, they figured it was time to crack some skulls.

They have never been more wrong.

Right away, one of them took an arrow to the eye. He shrieked a high pitch scream and fell to the floor, sobbing in pain. "Help me! Oh, God! It hurts! It hurts! Get the son of a bitch that did this to me!"

The other five ducked down and tried to find cover, so they would not end up with an arrow in them, as well, but it was already too late. The next arrow hit one directly in the heart. He died instantly.

Their leader, who was next to him, shouted to the others, "Shit! They got Tommy! Get down and stay down! They got freaking Injuns in here shooting arrows at us! Don't let 'em scalp you!"

One of them was holding an Uzi submachine gun. He stepped forward bravely and stated, "I got this, boss!" He pointed his weapon outward and sprayed a burst of rounds in a semi-circular motion ahead of them, shooting everything in sight, until he emptied his clip. As soon as his gun was empty, an arrow hit him in the neck. He gagged and choked on his own blood.

"Whoa!" The leader shouted, "Parley! We want to parley! Stop shooting the freaking arrows already!"

Roberto did not respond, so neither did Chryssy. They were not near each other, so she was following his lead. He told her to keep shooting, as long as she had shots, so she pulled back the cord and prepared to launch another arrow. She tried to get a clear shot at the three that were hiding, but could not. The one with the arrow in his eye was still whimpering on the floor near the doorway.

Suddenly, a shopping cart came rolling forward toward the other three. It looked like there was someone hiding under a blanket inside. The three remaining gang members aimed their handguns at the cart and began shooting, destroying a mannequin. From out of the left, a knife came flying through the air and hit one of them directly in his chest. He dropped to the floor clutching the knife in pain. Another arrow shot across the store and hit one of the other two in the ear, killing him. He fell to the floor with a thud.

The last man standing, who was the leader of the biker gang, ran behind one of the tall shelves. He ducked low and shouted, "When I catch you, I'm going to shove those arrows up your ass! The rest of my boys will be back soon! You're going to catch hell for this! You wait and see!" He snickered maliciously, although he was actually very nervous.

Near the entrance of the store, Roberto emerged from behind a large display shelf. He crept across the floor quietly and yanked his knife out of the dead man's chest. He had been listening to the gang leader yelling and already knew which direction to go, so he began stalking his next prey.

The gang leader moved forward cautiously, as he shouted his threats. He stopped, when he caught a glimpse of Chryssy atop a large shelf. She was lying down flat and holding her compound-bow sideways, pointed outward in his general direction. She had an arrow aimed near where he was, which told him she was not exactly aware of his position. That gave him the advantage.

Chryssy searched vigilantly for her target, as she tried not to become one herself. She was wearing all black with hard kneepads and fingerless gloves. Her straight jet-black hair was flung to one side. She was lying as low as she could, as she hunted for her target. She was hidden well, but not well enough.

The gang leader had a clear shot. He carefully aimed his handgun at her, but for a moment, he hesitated. It was as if she looked right at him, but how could that be? There was no way she could see him, behind the tall display shelves.

Just then, he was punched in the side of his head hard. The punch sent him reeling into the very display shelf he was hiding behind. He turned to face his attacker and pointed the gun at him, but he was not fast enough. Roberto grabbed his wrist and twisted it. The next thing he knew, the gun was out of his hand. Roberto then elbowed him in the face and grabbed him. He flipped him over onto the floor. The gang leader scurried to his feet, but was kicked in the groin. He keeled over and was kicked so hard against the display shelves that they fell over, making a loud ruckus, with him on top of them. He tumbled over to the other side and clumsily tried to stand, but he felt too dizzy. Roberto then hit him with a flying kick to the face that knocked him back to the floor.

At that moment, the gang leader was done. The fight was taken out of him. He raised his arms in the air and pleaded, "Okay! Stop! That's enough! I give up! You got me, man! No more!" He breathed heavily and stared up at Roberto, who stood over him menacingly. Roberto was also wearing all black with the hard kneepads and hard knuckled gloves. The man eyed him warily, as he struggled to his feet and asked, "What are you guys, anyway, some kind of Special Ops Unit? You got all that tactical fag gear."

Roberto did not answer, but he did sneer at him and narrow his eyes.

The gang leader cried out, "Hey! You can't kill me, Van Damme! You wanna know why? By now, my boys got your friends dead to rights. You're gonna need me to negotiate." He chuckled. "In fact, let's parley for their lives, right now. Maybe you and Pocahontas can walk away with your lives."

Roberto practically moved like lightning and ended up behind him. He grabbed the gang leader from behind and pressed his blade against his throat. He leaned in close and asked calmly, "Is that what you think? Well, I have bad news for you. I don't negotiate with pieces of shit like you." He then slit his throat open and pushed the man forward. His body crashed down onto the fallen shelves.

Roberto looked down at the name on the back of the gang leader's leather jacket and scoffed, "Road Demons, my ass." He spit on the jacket and walked away.

Afterwards, he went around and checked to see if the other bikers were dead. If they were not, then he made certain to finish the job. The one, who had been shot in the eye with an arrow, was crawling toward the exit doors. Roberto stood over him and plunged his knife into the man's head. It made a sound like watermelon being punctured. Next, he collected the arrows that were shot and wiped them clean using a bandana that one gang member was wearing on his head.

A short time later, he walked to the doorway and looked outside. The parking lot was empty, aside from the six Harley Davidson motorcycles out front. He listened and could hear the other motorcycles were still in the area somewhere in the distance. It sounded like they were somewhere to the east. They were still shooting, too, which meant David and Edie were still alive and on the run. They were also in grave danger because they were severely outnumbered.

Roberto turned back and yelled, "Chryssy! Come on! It's time to go!"

Edie yelled into the two-way radio, "Grant! We need back up! A motorcycle gang is chasing us through the mall parking lots and they're shooting at us! Please help us!"

Grant, Liz, and Kirk grabbed weapons and jumped into the police SUV. They raced out of the compound and hurried toward Interstate 86. Sam closed the gates behind them, while Devin went up to take over the position in the watchtower. Sam then hurried to the basement, grabbed a radio, and raced back outside to get a drone in the air.

Meanwhile, David was keeping the motorcycle gang busy by having them go in circles. He would enter one parking lot and exit from the other side, cross Route 211 and enter another parking lot, before doing the same. He did this two or three times, before they were onto his delaying tactic. They split up and waited for him at the parking lot exits, but he still had a few tricks up his sleeve.

He charged right at two bikers that were blocking the parking lot exit with their motorcycles. Apparently, they must have forgotten that a Ford Explorer is a lot bigger than two motorcycles. David smashed right into them sending metal, leather, and blood flying into the air.

David raced back across Route 211 westbound. One motorcyclist got really close to the passenger side of the vehicle and began shooting, but could not shoot straight, while riding his bike at top speed to keep up with David. Edie wanted to shoot back at him, but she was getting carsick from David's driving.

When David noticed the biker in the side view mirror, he swerved to the right really hard and hit the brakes. The motorcycle skidded and smashed into the side of the vehicle, sending its rider flying over the hood. He rolled to a stop on the pavement ahead. David stepped on the gas and ran him over.

Three more motorcycles raced up behind him, so he made the next left turn at high speed. Two bikers skidded and went down to avoid smashing into him. David lost control on the turn and flipped over. The Ford Explorer rolled three times and skidded to a halt, just before entering the interstate going south.

One motorcyclist that was behind him slowed down and waited for his boys to catch up. Eight more motorcycles soon approached and all nine rode out toward the overturned Ford Explorer. Suddenly, an arrow knocked one of the riders from his bike, as another bike came racing by behind them on Route 211. The rider, who was dressed in black, stopped and began shooting at them with an Uzi submachine gun. Five of them went down, before the ammo clip went empty. The rider in black flung the weapon over his shoulder, since it was attached to a strap. He then rode off, heading east on Route 211.

Two of the remaining motorcycles gave chase and went after the lone rider.

Roberto felt fear for the first time in months, but it was not fear for his safety. It was because he thought David and Edie might be dead. He had just enough time to notice the Ford Explorer lying on its side, before he opened fire with the Uzi at the biker gang members. It was a good thing that biker had an extra clip of ammo in his vest pocket. Too bad he did not have any more.

Roberto knew he needed to lose these guys fast, as he sped eastbound on the "borrowed" Harley Davidson. He only had two pursuers, which meant he could probably take them on and beat them, if he stopped. Of course, if they chose to shoot, first, that would pose a problem. He got an idea and led them into Lowe's. He already knew the lay out of that store, which gave him the advantage.

He charged through an open door on his motorcycle and sped down the nearest aisle toward the back of the store. He then got off the motorcycle and hid. Sure enough, the two bikers rode into the store on their motorcycles, just as Roberto hoped they would. He pushed a large pile of PVC pipes onto the floor making it impossible for them to continue on their bikes.

While they struggled to get off their bikes without falling, he shot the closest one in the back with his 9mm, and then picked up a ten-foot long PVC pipe and swung it at the other one knocking him off balance and down to the floor. Roberto then threw his knife into the biker's chest and leapt on top of him to push it in deeper.

Meanwhile, not far away, David opened his eyes. He tried to see straight, but everything was blurry. A warm wetness covered his face. He knew it was blood. There was pain all over his body, as his seatbelt tugged at him and secured him to his seat. He realized he was suspended in the air. The Ford Explorer must have rolled over, he thought, because it was lying on its passenger side.

He tried to unhook himself from his seatbelt, but immediately had a feeling that was a really bad idea. It did not help that he could barely see around the airbag that was in his face. The driver's side airbag was pressed tightly against him, which was making it difficult for him to breathe. Feeling frustrated, he reached for his knife, pulled it from its holder on his waist, and stabbed the airbag, deflating it.

He let out a gasp for air and turned to see if Edie was okay. His eyes gaped open, once he looked down and realized she was not even in her seat.

He cried out, "Edie? Edie!" He struggled to loosen his seatbelt and noticed the vehicle was rocking. The sound of boots could be heard walking on metal above him. Someone had climbed on top of the overturned vehicle. Maybe they were coming to rescue him, he thought.

"Well, well, looky here!" An unfamiliar male voice called down to him.

Nope. No rescue. Shit.

When David looked up, he saw a biker standing on top of the Ford Explorer's driver's side door. The biker glared at him and spit down on his face. David turned away in disgust, and then looked back up at the biker. He had greasy reddish hair, full sideburns, a thick mustache, and a goatee.

"I should piss on you, you filthy spick," the biker said. "You got my gang killed, so you deserve this." He pulled down his zipper and took out his penis.

David cringed and turned his face away, but before the first drop came out, there was an arrow sticking through the biker's waist.

"OW!" He fell off the vehicle and onto the pavement of the entrance ramp, where he began urinating all over himself, while contorting in pain. He cried out, "SHIT! DAMN IT!"

Chryssy ran closer and slowed down, as she reached the vehicle. She walked around to the side, where the biker lay. She jumped back, when she noticed the gun in his hand. He fired at her and missed. She dived over the guardrail onto the grass and rolled down the hill away from the entrance ramp.

David tried to release his seatbelt, but it was stuck.

The biker stood up and stumbled forward toward the vehicle. He moved toward the front and kicked in the windshield, which was already badly damaged and barely hanging in place. Once the windshield was out of his way, he stepped closer and looked at David.

"You and your damned *Hunger Games* friend suck ass! I'm going to shoot you in the face for making me piss on myself!"

Suddenly, a police siren could be heard in the distance, roaring loudly closer and coming from the south. The biker looked utterly confused.

"What the hell is that? I thought all them damned *pigs* were dead and gone!" When he turned to look at the oncoming police SUV on the opposite side of the road, he could not believe his eyes. It came to a halt and he wondered, if he was actually about to be arrested. "No way! This can't be happen…"

He never finished the sentence because Liz fired her rifle and sent a round straight into his face. It burst out of the back of his head, spraying blood and brain matter about seven feet behind him. His body trembled a second, before falling limply to the ground.

Roberto approached the scene of the Ford Explorer crash on the highway entrance ramp using the motorcycle he took. He still had the empty Uzi flung over his shoulder. He hoped Grant would have ammunition that could be used for it.

Chryssy climbed over the guardrail and ran over to him. They embraced and she said, "I wasn't sure if I would ever see you, again."

"I'm fine," he said shortly. "Hold on. I need to check on David and Edie." He pushed her aside gently and hurried around to the front of the vehicle. When he saw David was hanging in his seat, but was still conscious, he felt a rush of relief. "You really need to stop getting hurt, Dave," he stated.

David looked at him and forced a tiny smile.

Kirk, Liz, and Grant jumped over the divider and ran over to the crash site. They rushed to the front of the vehicle, where Roberto stood. He and Kirk cut David free from his seatbelt and helped him out through the opening, where the windshield should be. Amazingly, he did not seem as badly injured, as they expected him to be. The seatbelt and airbag saved him.

Kirk shook his head in amazement, as he looked at David. He smirked, "Unbelievable! I can't leave you alone, for a moment, without you getting into trouble. Never, again, *kemo sabe!* From now on, you and me are sticking together like glue."

David groaned his unclear vulgar reply.

Liz walked over to Chryssy and asked, "Are you okay, sweetie?"

"Yeah, I'm good. I think we got them all."

Grant asked, "What happened?"

She explained, as best she could, "I don't really know how it started. Rob and I came out of the Walmart, after using the restroom, and saw David and Edie driving away! They were being chased and shot at by a gang of bikers. Six of them came into the store after us. We had to kill them. It was either that or they kill us."

Grant told her, "Don't worry. You did the right thing. It's kill or be killed out here."

"Rob says the same thing. He killed their leader, and then took one of their bikes, so he could help David and Edie. That's when we saw them crash and roll over. I thought they were goners. I ran right over, as fast as I could, and shot that jerk that Liz killed. He was trying to piss on David!"

Liz scowled, "That sick prick! I should shoot him, again!"

Grant grimaced at the thought of being pissed on.

As soon as David was out of the vehicle, he asked, "Where's Edie?"

"I'm sorry, but I don't know," Chryssy answered regretfully. "I haven't seen her. I hope she's okay."

Grant immediately began searching the area around them along the road. He peered down the entrance ramp and realized she must have been thrown from the vehicle.

David pushed Kirk and Roberto away and walked over to the guardrail. He looked down along the grassy hill, but he could not see her. He slowly walked back toward Route 211, while checking over the guardrail to his left. Kirk and Roberto walked close behind him, in case he fell, but he did not. He was going on pure adrenaline and ignored any pain that he felt, as he continued back down the entrance ramp.

After walking nearly fifty feet, he finally spotted her lying in a thicket of tall grass and bushes. She was not moving.

"EDIE!!!" He climbed over the guardrail and slid down the grassy hill to her location. He knelt down beside her and shouted, "Edie! Can you hear me?"

She opened her eyes and smiled weakly, as soon as she saw his face over hers. She struggled to speak through the pain and said, "I'm sorry, David... stupid me.... wasn't wearing... my seatbelt."

"Don't worry. We're going to get you back home," he tried to reassure her. "Aramis will fix you up in no time. Just hang in there, okay?"

She moaned and whispered, "I-I can't... feel my legs. Are... are they still there?" She gasped from the effort it took to say the words.

"Yeah, you're still in one piece. Nothing is missing. It's going to be okay. You're just numb. It'll pass. Trust me, feeling the pain is not any better."

"David..." She stared into his eyes.

He asked, "Yeah? What is it?"

"I... I love you." She smiled weakly, and then closed her eyes and stopped breathing.

"Edie??? EDIE!!! Edie…" David broke down and cried, as he held her in his arms.

Kirk and Roberto kept their distance, for a while, and gave him time to mourn, before helping him and carrying Edie's body back up to the road. Grant went to get the police SUV and drove it around to the southbound side of the road. He parked behind the wreckage of the Ford Explorer.

The supplies that had been collected earlier were scattered all over the place. Some were damaged and rendered useless, but not all.

Liz gasped when she realized Edie was gone. "Oh, my God!"

They put Edie's body with David in the backseat of the police SUV, and then began loading whatever they could salvage into the rear cargo compartment. They were too low on food to leave the stash behind. It took several minutes, before they were done. Roberto was also able to find his wrecking bar, which he had left in the backseat.

Afterwards, Kirk got into the SUV and sat next to David in the backseat. He tried to comfort David, but he was inconsolable. Grant and Liz got into the front seats, while Roberto climbed back onto the motorcycle and shifted the Uzi to his side. Chryssy got on behind him and held onto his waist. She tucked her arm through her bow and rested it on her shoulder.

The two vehicles headed back home, sticking close together.

When they arrived at the compound, Sam already had the gates open with Aramis standing by. He had observed the vehicles, as soon as they drove up Cromwell Road, through the drone's live-streaming camera. Aramis and Grant removed Edie's body from the vehicle and carried her into the house on the stretcher. Liz and Chryssy followed, both in tears, while Roberto sulked angrily outside. He was angry with himself for not reaching David and Edie in time. In a way, he also blamed himself for what happened. Had they not stopped to use the bathroom, things would have turned out differently.

Grant and Aramis placed Edie's body in the common room temporarily, until a coffin could be built and a grave could be dug for her. Millie was devastated, when she saw Edie on the stretcher and realized she was dead. She collapsed on the floor in tears and crawled over to her.

"NOOOOO!!! EDIE!!!"

Grant and Joy had to help her up, but they could not get her to leave the room. They eventually gave up trying and let her cry. Joy held her and did her best to comfort her.

They eventually had to move Edie's body to the garage, where they covered her.

David still had not gotten out of the vehicle. Kirk tried to help him inside, but he refused and insisted on sitting in the Ford Explorer. He was not ready to deal with the reality of the situation. He remained in the vehicle for nearly an hour. Kirk stayed with him the whole time.

It was another somber day for the group. Sadly, it was way too soon, after the previous deaths to have to deal with another death. Edie was well loved by her friends, which only made it more difficult.

The next morning, they held a funeral for Edie McQueen. She was buried in the cemetery behind the garage. A wooden cross was added, shortly afterward.

MAN'S END

Chapter Thirty-Three

IT WAS A breezy afternoon in April. Leaves blew gently over the graves at the cemetery on the compound. Millie knelt down over Edie's one-week old gravesite and replanted some flowers that she picked along the tall grass near the west gate.

A voice from behind her spoke gentle words of comfort, "She didn't die in pain, if it helps to know it." It was David. "She said she couldn't feel anything."

"Is that all she said?" Millie asked without turning to face him.

"No." He hesitated, but then admitted, "She told me that she loved me."

Millie turned and looked up at him. She asked, "What did you say?"

"I… I didn't get to say anything. That was when she…" His tears came down.

"Oh. I'm sorry." She also began to cry.

They both stared at each other, and then David knelt down beside her. The pain they shared bonded their friendship, stronger than before. They hugged and held each other, as they cried.

Millie asked, "Did you love her?"

He pulled away and responded defensively, "Yeah, of course, I did."

"No, I mean, were you in love with her?"

He looked down at the grave. All of a sudden, he could not face her. He knew what she wanted him to say, but he could not lie to her. She would know it. He felt ashamed. Finally, he answered, "I cared about her very deeply, but I can never be in love with someone, who is a man, regardless of how they identify themselves. It's not who I am. I'm sorry, if that's not what you want to hear me say."

"I just want to hear the truth. If you say you were not in love with her, then you weren't. I would think if you were, then you wouldn't have wasted so much time. She loved you with all of her heart."

"Millie, if we're going to be honest here. She really wasn't a she."

"Well, in her heart she was and no one would have known any different, if not for that jerk, Bobby."

"That's not necessarily true. I would have found out, eventually. I almost kissed her."

Millie nodded, "Yeah, I know. She told me about that. It was very hard for her to turn away from you, but she didn't want you to do something without knowing fully what you were getting into. She was going to tell you the truth. She never got the chance. Before she knew it, her secret was public knowledge. It was a very difficult time for her. It was bad enough she was attacked, but for everyone to suddenly learn her biggest most personal secret was terrible. Did you know she thought about committing suicide?"

He shook his head, "No, she never told me."

"I talked sense into her. I also pushed her to become friends with you, again. She didn't want to because she felt hurt and angry that you would not accept her as a woman. Even now, you still don't."

He looked down and felt ashamed, but there was nothing he could do about how he felt. He did not want to be sorry for feeling what was in his heart. He faced her and said, "I would have loved her, if she were really a woman. I told her so on that last day we were together."

"Really? That's good. She must have been so happy to hear that."

"I think she was. You know? That was the last thing we were talking about, before that motorcycle gang showed up," he recalled.

"I'm glad you are feeling better," she said, changing the subject. "You spent enough time being bedridden."

He smirked, "Tell me about it! Actually, I was never really that injured. I had the seatbelt and airbag to protect me. She wasn't wearing her seatbelt. I thought she had it on. If I had known, I would have said something to her. I would have made her put it on and maybe she'd be here, now."

"Don't do that, David. Don't blame yourself. She was an adult. She knew how important it was to wear her seatbelt. It's not your fault. She would not want you to blame yourself for her mistakes. She would want you to be happy."

He scoffed, "It will be a long time, before I ever feel happy, again. I honestly do not remember the last time I felt happy."

"That's so sad," she said.

"Yeah, well. That's me. I'm generally not a happy guy. Blame it on my job. It made me so damn miserable that I think I forgot what real happiness feels like. It's hard to be happy, when everyone hates you."

"I don't hate you. No one here hates you."

He sighed, "Yeah. I know. I meant when I was still a cop. It's just how it was everyday. No one appreciated the good things I did, but if I made one mistake, I was a screw up. If some other cop messed up big time, then I was also to blame, somehow. One cop's stupid mistake affected every other cop in the city, no matter how good you might have been. The people didn't care. All cops are the same, in the eyes of the public. As far as the majority of the public was concerned, we were all abusive prejudiced pigs. Tell me, how can I be happy, when that's how most of the world sees me?"

"I'm so sorry things were like that for you guys. I always liked the police. Hey, at least, you don't have to deal with that anymore."

"Yeah, but it took a Zombie Apocalypse for that to happen and I'm still not any happier."

She pouted, "Life sucks."

"No, it doesn't. People suck. Life is a beautiful thing. The only thing that sucks about life is that it leads to death."

They both looked down at Edie's grave and quietly remembered her in their own way. The leaves blew around them in the breeze and tossed Millie's long dark hair to the side, as well. Light rain droplets began to fall down around them. Millie moved the hair away from her green eyes and glanced toward David, her guardian angel, as she once called him. In reality, he was more like her wiser older brother, she thought. When she noticed more tears rolling down his cheeks, she began to cry, again. They remained at Edie's grave for several minutes, before going back into the house to get out of the rain.

Work on the wall had continued over the next few weeks, whenever it was not raining too hard. The weather was warming up enough for them to spend full shifts outside. Cinderblock, after cinderblock they erected the northern wall, until it was finally finished.

By the end of April, they had finally begun erecting the west wall, which was the last wall they needed to build. The west side posed the biggest issues for them. The ground was lower and covered in tall grass, which made getting to the fence a pain in the neck. They had to hack a path clear through the grass, before they could even place the first cinderblock. Building up the west wall would also have an effect on their firearms training. They could no longer shoot at the abandoned concrete structure beyond their fence because the wall would be blocking it. It was a sacrifice they were willing to make.

One good thing came from working on the wall, together as a group. It united them and created stronger bonds of friendship. No one was exempt from helping. They all wanted to help out and do their part. The safety of the compound might have been the original motivation behind erecting a wall, but over the past few months so much had happened that the main motivation had changed. They did it in memory of those they lost, especially Daniel, who put so many hours into working on the wall, the new entrance gates, the watchtower, the underground tunnel, the barn, and the common room addition.

Working side by side with each other also had other benefits. The couples were able to work together. Grant and Liz, Charles and Yvonne, Roberto and Chryssy, and even Sam and Taryn all put in their time. It also seemed like a new couple might emerge, as Aramis and Joy were spending more and more time working next to each other. They became good friends and would often talk or joke with one another. Sometimes, they would flirt, although it never seemed to go any further than that.

Aramis watched Joy with admiration, as she lifted cinderblocks and put them into place. She was not the average "girly girl," he thought. He smiled at her and said, "You are incredible. Do you know that? Not many women I knew, back in the old world, could do what you're doing. There were a few, but those women usually looked kind of manly. You, my friend, are all woman."

"Aw! Thanks, sweetie," she smiled flirtatiously at him and even batted her eyelashes. "I work hard to be how I am. Exercise and eating right is the key."

"Yeah, well, it works. You look great, considering you have two kids. That tends to warp a woman's shape a little. I've seen it way too many times."

"No, baby. Too much rice and beans warps a woman's body. A baby destroys it! Try pulling a watermelon through your belly button. You'll see what I mean! Shoot! I had to work my ass off to get my shape back. When you guys found me, I was practically starving to death, but my body was still kind of flabby in places. I had to spend hours down in the gym getting toned, again. I am so glad you guys have a gym in the basement. Roberto has also been very helpful with training some of us."

He chuckled, "It's funny. You tend to refer to 'us guys' a lot. You seem to forget that you are part of us, now. You can say 'we,' if you want. No one will mind."

"I'm sorry! I didn't even notice that I do that. I just need to get used to the idea. Sometimes, I still feel like we're only guests here. You guys were here for so much longer. I'm still a newbie," she said.

"Nah! You people are part of the family. You more than earned your places here. Believe that."

"Thank you, Aramis. You're so sweet."

They smiled at each other and got back to work.

Not far from them, Sam and Taryn worked with the cement. Sam poured the heavy bags of cement into a wheelbarrow, and then added water, while she mixed it with a wooden stick. Once the cement was ready, they added thin layers to act as mortar over the cinderblocks. More cinderblocks would be placed over the cement and the cycle would resume.

Sam was very pleased that Taryn felt more comfortable being around other people. She was gradually overcoming her shyness with his help. She still had a long way to go, but she was nowhere near as bad when she first arrived.

Every once in a while, they made eye contact and grinned happily.

One night in May, after a hard day's work, a few of the group decided to wind down by sitting around the fire pit in the backyard. It was mainly the couples, but Kirk, Aramis, Joy, and Devin also sat outside. Aramis strummed his guitar, occasionally, adding mellow background music to the evening.

David was taking his turn up in the watchtower, which was fine by him, and Julia was down in the basement, as usual.

Grant turned to Charles, who was holding hands with Yvonne, and said, "I'm glad to see you both out here with us. It's been a long time, since we sat out here together. Huh, Chuck?"

Charles sneered, "Now, you know I don't like that name. Why do you always insist on calling me by it?"

"That's easy. Because I know you don't like it," Grant smiled.

Everyone laughed.

Yvonne squeezed Charles' hand and said, "I never knew you didn't like being called Chuck. Why? What's wrong with it?"

"Nothing really. I just don't like how it sounds."

"You're such a big baby, Chucky," she snickered.

Charles immediately turned to Grant. "Do you see what you've done? I'm screwed! She's going to call me that forever. Thanks a lot, pal."

"You're very welcome, my friend," Grant replied with a smile.

Liz said, "Don't let him get to you, Charles. You know he has an immature side. Just ignore it."

Grant poked her and asked, "Hey, whose side are you on, Elizabeth?"

"Ooh! Now, you're asking for it!" She punched him playfully on the arm.

"Ouch! That hurt, you freaking Amazon!"

She replied, "Good! You know I don't like it, when people call me that."

Yvonne scoffed, "Oh, come on! You, too? What's wrong with your name? It's beautiful!"

Liz shrugged. "I just don't like it. You can call me Liz or you can even call me Beth, but I never liked my full name."

Charles looked confused and asked, "Exactly what is your full name? I have only ever known you by Liz. I know it's short for Elizabeth, but what's your last name? After almost a year of knowing you, I still have no idea."

She rolled her eyes and sighed. Using a Spanish accent, she pronounced her full name for them. "My name is Elizabeth Claudia Mayaguez."

Joy asked, "Oh, like the city in Puerto Rico?"

"Yep."

"I have family from there," Joy said.

Liz thought about it and replied, "I'm pretty sure I do, too."

Charles commented, "That's not a bad name. Not like *Chuck*. I have no idea how Chuck ever became a nickname for Charles."

Grant responded, "At least your name isn't Richard. Otherwise, I'd be calling you Dick." He laughed.

Charles scoffed, "We'd be enemies, my friend. Where do these stupid nicknames even come from? Why can't names just be what they are? Why do we need nicknames?"

Grant chuckled, "Normal names have their downfall, too. Keep in mind I was named after a famous historical figure. Back when I was in school and I got into an argument with another kid, sometimes, they'd challenge me to a duel, since my ancestor died that way. I can't even remember how many times that happened. Maybe that's why I learned to shoot so well."

Liz turned to him and smirked, "I can imagine it must have been quite a lot, knowing you."

Aramis chuckled, "I don't know about that, Liz. Grant has such a warm personality."

They laughed.

Grant looked around at them and said, "Hey! I'm a nice guy. I might like to shoot assholes and kill zombies, but does that make be so bad?"

Roberto responded, "That makes you a hero in my book, bro."

Chryssy agreed, "Right on! You rock, dude!"

"Thank you very much," Grant said, while giving them both a high five. He then turned to Liz with a raised eyebrow. "Stop trying to make me look bad, woman."

She grabbed his lips with one hand and squeezed them together. She then moved in for a kiss, which made him smile.

"Aw," Joy teased. "How sweet. That's what I need. Someone who can make me feel happy like that." She glanced over at Aramis in a not so subtle kind of way.

He smiled at her and said, "You never know. The right person for you could be right under your nose."

"Could be," she agreed.

Sam responded, "Mom, could you be any more obvious?"

"Be quiet, Sam. Mom's working here," she said.

Everyone laughed.

Glenda stood at the doorway of the house and stared out to the backyard. She called out to her mother, "Mommy. I'm hungry."

Joy turned to her and said, "Okay, baby. Come here and give me a hug, first." She did and Joy sighed. "That's my girl. I love you, sweetie."

"I love you, too, mommy." Glenda faced the fire pit and asked, "Is that a dangerous fire?"

"No, sweetie. That's called a fire pit. It's a safe way for people to keep warm, when they are outdoors. It's almost like an outdoor fireplace."

"Oh. It's warm."

"Yes, it is. So, what would you like to eat?"

Aramis replied, "Roasted marshmallows would be great, right about now." He strummed his guitar strings gently.

Sam agreed, "Yeah, or s'mores!" He licked his lips and rubbed his hands together.

Glenda smiled excitedly, "That's what I want, too!"

Joy glared at Aramis and Sam and said, "Thanks a lot, guys."

"Oops!" Aramis cowered away, as he grabbed his guitar and stood up. "Well, I guess I'll be heading inside."

Roberto laughed and teased him. "Don't let her scare you, bro! You're not even in there, yet!"

Everyone laughed and Aramis pointed at Roberto. "Don't be an instigator!" He then made his exit with a smile on his face. "Goodnight, everybody!"

Roberto frowned, "There goes the music."

Charles stood up, looked at Yvonne, and said, "We should probably head inside, too. Goodnight, everyone. We'll see you at breakfast time."

She stood up and followed, but also said, "Goodnight."

The others wished them a goodnight and began going inside, little by little. Grant and Liz also went up to their room, while Sam and Taryn went down to the basement to sit by the computer with Julia. Only Roberto and Chryssy planned to remain outside because they wanted to be alone. Besides, it was not as if they had a shared room they could retire to.

Joy began walking inside and called Glenda to follow, "Come on inside, baby. Let's get you some food."

"Okay, mommy! I'm coming!" Glenda was very curious about the fire pit. She felt safe knowing it was not dangerous, so when no one else was looking, she grabbed a small stick that was burning lightly at one end and took it into the house with her. She placed it in the first floor closet, so she could play with it later. She did not want her mother to see it. Afterwards, she went into the kitchen with her mother.

The embers from the stick flickered and gradually spread in the closet, as a small fire began to burn, unbeknownst to everyone in the house.

MAN'S END

Chapter Thirty-Four

AFTER GIVING GLENDA a snack, Joy took her upstairs to bed. It was nearly midnight. Little did she know, there was a fire in the first floor closet and it was growing larger with each passing minute. The flames had already reached the coats hanging above it. The closet door was hot to the touch.

When they got upstairs to the dorm room, Joy went into the bathroom to trim her eyebrows.

Glenda figured this was her opportunity to get her glowing stick, so she snuck out of the room and went back downstairs.

Mostly everyone in the house was preparing for bed. Millie was already asleep. Many of the guys were in the male dorm goofing off, while most of the women were in the female dorm on the floor above. Only a few people intended to stay up longer.

David stood watch in the watchtower and stared out into the darkness, barely able to see anything beyond the walls of the compound. He could see the fire pit was still lit in the backyard of the house. Only the glow was noticeable from his point of view. It was the only light in the neighborhood.

In the backyard, Roberto and Chryssy held each other close, while kissing. The warm light of the fire pit made for a nice romantic evening, now that they were alone, at last. Of course, they did not notice the smell of the fire building up inside the house, since they were so close to the fire pit. Fire was burning through the closet door and embers were starting to fall onto the floor of the hallway.

In the male dorm, the other guys were now lying on their beds. Kirk and Aramis were discussing the possibility of paving some land to park the trucks on, rather than leaving them on the grass against the south wall. Devin was keeping busy reading a horror novel. He was the first to notice the smell.

"Kirk, did you guys leave the fire pit burning?" He asked, while sniffing the air.

"Yeah. When I came in there were still people out there."

"Oh, okay. It smells a lot stronger now, than earlier," Devin noticed.

Aramis smirked, "Ah, that's probably because they just put it out. When you put it out the smoke gets all over the place. It's a mess."

"Ah, that explains it," Devin replied, seemingly satisfied. He then resumed reading his book.

Glenda stared at the closet door in shock because it was up in flames. She thought she might be able to remove the burning stick and resolve the situation she created. She reached for the doorknob, but hesitated out of fear. She did not wish to get burned. At the same time, she did not wish to get into trouble. She slowly reached for the doorknob. When she felt how hot it was she instantly yanked her hand back and cried out, "Ouch!"

After burning herself, she hurried into the first floor bathroom, which was just down the hall. She closed the door and ran cold water over her aching hand, which had quickly turned red. The cold water helped to sooth it and made it feel a little bit better, but it still stung from the pain.

Meanwhile, outside in the backyard, Chryssy stopped kissing Roberto and smiled at him. She said, "I'm going to need a pee break, if we're going to stay out here a while."

Roberto agreed and said, "Yeah, me, too."

They both went into the house and found themselves face to face with the flames.

Chryssy cried out, "Oh, no!"

Roberto wasted no time and reacted. He ran past the edge of the flames and threw open the door to the male dorm room. He shouted, "Get your asses out of bed! The hallway is on fire!" He went into the room and grabbed his gear, stuffed it into his bag, flung it over his shoulder, and raced to the kitchen. He began filling pots with water, but already had a feeling it would be a waste of time.

Chryssy had followed him around the fire, except she went upstairs to warn the others. She also wanted to get her compound bow and other personal belongings. There really was not much for her to grab, so it did not take too long. As she reached the second floor landing, she yelled out a warning, "Everyone wake up! There's a fire on the first floor!!!"

Grant and Liz were sitting on their bed talking, when they heard the screams. They grabbed their weapons and raced out to the hallway of the second floor expecting the worse. Grant immediately smelled smoke and told Liz to pack their things. He saw Chryssy running into the female dorm and asked, "How bad is the fire?"

"It's pretty bad! The downstairs hallway is on fire!"

"Shit!" He called up the stairs to Charles and shouted, "Charles, there's a fire! We've got to get out of here!"

Charles heard Grant, jumped out of bed, and ran to the door. When he opened it the smell of smoke hit him. The smoke was starting to rise up the stairs and was filling the second floor hallway. He coughed and turned to Yvonne. "Get dressed! Hurry!"

Grant and Liz ran downstairs to see if they could put out the fire. It was already blazing out of control. The entire back doorway was ablaze. Grant kicked open the door to the male dorm and shouted, "Get the hell out of the house! There's a fire!" He then realized the room was already empty, unaware that Roberto had already warned the guys.

Next, he ran down into the basement to make sure Julia knew about the fire. Liz saw him run downstairs and followed him. They ran into Sam and Taryn, who were on their way up.

Grant said, "Get the hell out of the house, both of you!"

Sam asked, "Where's my mother and sister?"

Liz replied, "They're on their way down from upstairs! Don't go up there! There's smoke everywhere!" She then followed Grant to the basement and called after him, "We should try to save the weapons, ammo, and radios!"

"Right! Grab the radios and I'll pack the ammo! We can use the tunnel to get out! Make sure Julia gets her ass out, too!"

Liz ran into the security hub, where Julia was snoozing behind the computer. She nudged her hard, "Julia! Wake up, damn it! The house is on fire! We need to get out of here!"

Julia awoke with a start and gazed wearily at the computer monitors. She could see the fire at the rear of the house. Her eyes opened wide and she jumped up from her seat. She packed her laptop and placed it into her bag, which she kept with her, at all times. When she saw Liz put her rifle down for a second to pack the two-way radios, she seized the opportunity. She picked up the rifle and pointed it at her.

"I'm sorry, but you won't be coming with us, Liz."

Liz turned to face her and did not move, when she saw her own rifle pointed at her. She asked, "What the hell are you doing? We don't have time for this bullshit!"

"I'm sick and tired of *you* and *your* bullshit! You stole Grant from me!"

"*What???* Are you insane? You're really going to do this, now?"

"This is my one chance to finally be rid of you. I just wanted you to know that I will take very good care of him in *every* way. Don't worry. I'll tell him you died trying to save me, if that helps. I'll be sure to comfort him by giving myself to him body and soul. Goodbye, Elizabeth."

"Wait! Julia!"

BLAM!

David smelled the smoke getting stronger and noticed the flames flickering at the rear of the house from his vantage point up in the watchtower. He knew it was not the fire pit. The house was on fire. The yelling only confirmed his suspicions. He got flashbacks of his reoccurring nightmare and freaked out. He raced down the ladder and staircase, and then hurried toward the front porch.

A second later, Devin came running out carrying some food. "We need to salvage whatever we can," he said to David, who nodded. Devin dropped the food and ran back inside for more.

David followed and ran into the house, as well. He headed straight into the kitchen. Roberto was already in there packing what he could into milk crates and bags. Together with Devin, they carried a bunch of food and drinks out of the house. A short while later, Chryssy came out carrying her compound bow over her shoulder, while helping Millie out. Both were coughing. Roberto and David rushed to their side to get them away from the house.

After failing to put out the fire using wet blankets, Aramis turned to Kirk and said, "We need to make sure there's no one else upstairs! Charles hasn't come down, yet!"

Sam asked, "Where's my mom and sister?"

Aramis shouted for him to leave. "Get out of here! We'll find them!"

Sam replied, "I'm not going anywhere without my mother and sister!"

Kirk looked at him and stated, "Wanna bet?" He picked up Sam and carried him out of the house. He put him down next to Taryn and Roberto. "Do not let him go back in! I need to go help Aramis!" Kirk then ran back into the house.

Aramis reached the second floor and ducked down, while covering his mouth. He rushed into the female dorm and looked around. Joy was on the floor near her bed, but Glenda was nowhere in sight. He shouted, "Joy! We need to get out of here! Are you hurt? Where's Glenda?"

She glanced up at him and coughed. She was checking under the bed to see if Glenda had hid from the fire. The smoke was starting to get to her. She kept coughing.

Aramis noticed what she was doing and flipped over the bed with both hands. They saw that there was no one under the bed. He coughed and pulled Joy up from the floor. He then pulled her out of the room and to the hallway. She went along reluctantly, as she did not want to leave without her daughter. Finally, Aramis shouted, "Come on! We need to go! She's not in here!"

She turned and had a feeling he was probably right. She wondered if maybe Millie might have already helped Glenda out. Joy followed Aramis down the stairs. However, by this time, the bottom of the staircase had become engulfed in flames. They instantly realized they would not be able to escape that way. Aramis pulled her back upstairs and back into the dorm room.

Charles and Yvonne ran down from the attic and noticed Aramis and Joy going into the female dorm room.

Aramis shouted at them, "We need to get out through the windows! Come on! Follow us and close that door!" They did as he said and he led them to the nearest window, which faced the front of the house. He lifted it open and shouted to Joy, "Go! Hurry!"

She nodded and stepped out onto the eave that covered the front porch. She carefully stepped aside and Yvonne climbed out next. After her, Charles went out, followed by Aramis. The four of them climbed down to the edge and dropped down to the ground below. Sam rushed over to his mother and they hugged.

"Where's Glenda?" She asked frantically.

He shrugged, "I thought she was with you!"

Joy looked around and did not see her outside with the others. She turned to run back into the house, but Aramis grabbed her and held her back.

"No! It's too dangerous!"

Roberto stated, "Kirk is still inside. He's looking for her, but I still haven't seen Grant or Liz!"

Sam responded, "Me and Taryn saw them going down to the basement! Julia's still down there, too!"

"Shit!" Roberto cried out. He desperately wanted to go back inside, but knew it was unsafe.

Chryssy grabbed his hand and squeezed it to hold him. She had a strong feeling he might try to run in. If he did, she was going to do her best to stop him.

David felt his heart skip a beat.

Everyone gazed dumbfounded at the burning house, which was beginning to collapse. There was no way any of them could go back inside. It did not look good for anyone, who was still trapped inside.

Joy screamed, "GLENDA!!!" She dropped to the floor, as Aramis held her.

Devin tried to think of what could be done to help their continued survival and stated, "The garage is not burning, yet. Maybe we can salvage some of the tools and equipment."

Charles turned to him and said, "You and me. No one else goes in! Come on, let's hurry!"

They ran into the garage and began bringing out as many tools as they could. Roberto went to the entrance to help them. As they carried things out, he moved them away from the structure. They eventually had to cease their efforts when the garage caught fire. Only moments later, the ceiling collapsed onto the BMW, which had been parked in the garage.

Charles shook his head in disappointment, but then focused on the house, again. Some of his dearest friends were still inside. He prayed they made it out the back door and were standing on the opposite side of the house from them.

The fire continued to burn hopelessly out of control, while everyone looked on in horror. Joy sobbed relentlessly, as Aramis held her, because her daughter was still inside the house. Sam stared at the rising flames in shock. He could not believe his sister was still trapped within, along with Grant, Liz, Kirk, and Julia. For several minutes, no one spoke. There were only tears and feelings of sorrow, fear, anger, and regret.

Soon, similar thoughts began to go through their minds. Were their friends still alive? If so, would they be burned alive? Where will they live now that their home was destroyed? How did the fire start and what could have been done to prevent it? Was it accidental?

In the distance, two figures appeared to be walking through the smoke near the barn, just north of the blazing inferno that gradually destroyed their home. Sam was the first to notice them.

"Look!" He pointed. "It looks like someone else made it!"

David reached for his gun and pulled it out of his holster when he noticed the two figures moving toward them through the smoke. He hoped he was overreacting, but he had to be ready, in case he was right to be worried. His nightmare came flooding back to him. Did the zombies find a way inside? The fire must have drawn them to the compound!

"It's Grant!" Roberto said. "I know that walk!"

Charles smiled. He felt a swell of relief, knowing that his best friend was still alive.

David relaxed his guard and holstered his weapon.

It appeared Grant was carrying two duffle bags over his shoulders. The lower part of his face was covered, so he would not breath in the smoke. Who was with him? It looked like a female, but they still could not tell, since she was behind him. Her face was also partially covered and she was also carrying duffle bags. As she grew near, they realized it was Liz. Of course, it was. Who else would it be?

Charles called out, "Grant! Are you guys, okay? Do you need a hand with those bags?"

"We're good," he answered. "Thanks." He stopped walking and dropped the bags, when he reached them. "We saved the drones, laptops, radios, weapons, and ammo." He took a moment to catch his breath and added, "Oh, I also have Julia's laptop."

"That's great," Charles replied, and then he asked, "What about Julia?"

Liz dropped her bags next to Grant's and looked at him, waiting for him to answer.

He responded soberly, "She didn't make it."

What they did not say was why she didn't make it. Grant did not feel like explaining how he had to shoot her in the back of the head, after he saw her aiming Liz's rifle at her. Liz felt like explaining it even less.

Charles frowned, "That's a shame. Did you guys come out through the escape tunnel?"

Grant nodded, "Of course. There was no way we could get back up through the staircase. That was a deathtrap. The escape tunnel was our only option. It turns out all that digging wasn't a waste of time, after all. Bless Daniel and his great ideas."

Roberto walked over to Grant and Liz to hug them both. "I'm glad you guys made it," he said. "Kirk is still inside and so is Glenda. He was trying to save her."

"What???" Grant turned to face the fire. He felt a rush of dread, when he saw the remains of the house slowly collapsing. There was no way anyone could survive being in there. He shouted, "Kirk!"

There was no reply.

David felt tears forming in his eyes. He hated thinking it, but he had a strong feeling Kirk was already gone, along with Glenda. How could they survive such a terrible fire? The house was literally burning to the ground. In time, there would be nothing left but charred wood and debris surrounded by ashes.

Aramis was heartbroken about Julia, but did his best to comfort Joy. She was down on her knees, staring helplessly at the burning house. Sam tried to be strong, but he was also crying. Taryn hugged him and he dug his face into her shoulder to hide his tears. She also cried.

Suddenly, Kirk emerged from the smoke almost in the same way Grant and Liz had moments earlier. He was not approaching from the same angle, though. It looked like he had walked around the house from the rear. He seemed to be carrying something in his arms and was coughing from the smoke he inhaled.

Millie noticed him, first, although she did not like what she was seeing. She prayed that she was wrong about what he was carrying. She pointed, "It's Kirk! He's alive!"

Everyone looked up and saw him walking around the house with something in his arms.

Joy immediately stood up and ran toward him. It was not because she was so happy to see him. It was because she wanted to see what he was carrying. She prayed her daughter was alive and well.

"Is that my baby? Is she okay?" She demanded to know. As she got closer, she slowed down and stopped. He was indeed carrying her daughter. Joy began to have trouble breathing. Her legs could no longer carry her forward and she felt numb all over.

Kirk stared into her eyes, as he approached. He stopped right in front of her and looked down at the limp partially burned body in his arms. He wanted so badly to tell her that he rescued her baby girl, but that was not the case. He was too late. She had minor burns on several parts of her body, but it was the smoke that got to her in the end. Kirk also had burns on his arms, but he did not care about that. He did not have time to think about himself. Not yet.

Millie gasped in horror and covered her eyes. She did not want to see what was already burned into her memory. How does one un-see something so absolutely horrible?

Chryssy turned her face away and rushed into Roberto's arms. She also did not wish to see the small burned body.

Sam's eyes filled with tears.

Taryn turned to him and took his hand.

Kirk explained, "I'm so sorry, Joy. I tried to save her. I really did."

Joy broke down and grabbed her daughter from his arms. She dropped down to the floor and held Glenda's body. Sam pulled free from Taryn and ran to his mother's side and knelt down beside her. He wrapped his arms around her, while Kirk stood over them, feeling like the Grim Reaper. Aramis and Taryn wanted to go over and comfort them, but both felt like they needed to keep their distance, this time.

There was nothing they could do or say that would make Joy and Sam feel any less devastated.

Behind them, the fire continued to burn brightly. Kirk stood tall over the weeping family and was silhouetted by the flames. For a split second, he almost appeared ominous, but if anyone could see his soot-covered guilt-ridden face, then they would see the pitiful saddened expression he actually wore.

No one seemed to move from where they stood or sat, as the house continued to burn. The flames finally seemed to be dying down, after about three hours of going strong. The smoke rose high and faded from view into the twilight sky. Soon, it would be daylight.

Roberto knew someone had to say what he was thinking because they were probably all thinking it, so he asked, "What are we going to do, now? Our home is gone."

Charles had been thinking the same thing all night, but he did not want to say it aloud because he felt saying the words would make them more real. This just seemed like another terrible nightmare that maybe they could wake from.

He suggested, "Maybe we could rebuild?"

Yvonne pulled away from him and repeated, "Rebuild? Are you crazy? As long as it took to find cinderblocks to make the damned wall and you want to build a house, too? Uh, uh! No freaking way! I'm done building things! We need to leave this Godforsaken place already!"

"Where will we go?" He asked.

"Anywhere! Look around out there! There is an abandoned town! Pick a damned house!"

"Yvonne, why don't you calm down? There's no reason to be yelling," he said calmly.

"Are you kidding me? Someone just burned down our home and you expect me to be calm? You think this house just burned by spontaneous combustion? Pull your heads out of your asses, people! Believe you me! Someone in this group started the fire! Whether it was by accident or not, remains to be seen!"

Devin responded, "What's the point of thinking like that? It won't change anything. What's done is done. We need to focus on our next step. Either we rebuild like Charles said or we leave and find a new home. I'm okay with either choice."

"I don't care about the damned house! I want to bury my child!" Joy cried out.

Everyone turned to her and kept quiet.

Kirk knelt down and said, "The fire destroyed all of the crosses we made, but if you wish to bury her, I will dig a grave."

"Yes, please," she responded, as she wiped the tears from her eyes, although they were still coming down.

Roberto grabbed two of the shovels that were saved from the garage, before it burned and handed one to Kirk. "I'll help you," he said.

"Thanks."

They both went over to where the graves of their cemetery were located and began digging in a fresh spot.

Charles looked at Grant and asked, "What do you think we should do, Grant?"

"We went through a lot of trouble to build this wall, so we can hide from the world out there. If we leave, we will have to consider being open to unwanted encounters, again. I seriously doubt anyone is going to want to build a new wall from scratch. If we stay and rebuild, it won't be easy. It's like Yvonne said, we pretty much depleted the building resources for miles around. This decision might have to require a vote."

Charles voiced his opinion, "I say we try to rebuild. We could set up tents using our tarps, for now, or move into the barn. The weather is warming up, so it won't be too bad, as long as we have some kind of structure by the time it gets cold, again."

Yvonne complained, "That's crazy. There is no way I am going to live in a tent, while we are surrounded by empty homes. You guys do what you want. I think it's time for me to move on."

Charles stared at her with surprise and asked, "What are you talking about? What's wrong with you? Why are you being so unreasonable?"

She answered, "Because I'm tired of playing this game! Look, what we had was fun, for a while. I admit it. You rocked my world, baby. I won't lie, but I was only looking for a decent place to lay my head. There ain't no way I'm sleeping in a damned barn! You crazy! I'm leaving. It's that simple. I'll go to one of the nearby houses. If you want to join me, that's fine, otherwise it's been nice knowing y'all."

Charles was hurt by her words. He cared about her and thought she cared about him, too. He did not know what to say or how to respond.

Grant glared at her angrily. He certainly had a few things he wanted to say, but he held back out of respect for Charles' feelings for her.

Yvonne walked toward the gates and demanded, "Can someone please open this damned prison gate and let me out of here? I am not wasting another moment in here!"

Devin bent down and grabbed the key from a pile of keys they removed from the garage. He gladly walked over to the gates and unlocked them for her. "Goodbye," he said coldly.

She stared at him and said, "Really? Unbelievable!" She opened the gate, since he merely unlocked it. She expected him to open it for her and was furious that he did not. She left it open, as she stepped through and walked along the driveway to Cromwell Road. As she walked away, she mumbled under her breath, "White Devil."

"It's Red Devil. Ignorant bitch." Devin shook his head in annoyance, closed the gate, and locked it. Good riddance, he thought to himself. He turned around and walked away from the gates.

Charles was in shock. He could not believe she left him so easily. She did not even give him a second glance, after all the time they spent together. He was devastated, as his heart broke.

Only moments later, there was a shrill scream that came from Cromwell Road, a little to the south. It had to be her. They all knew it instantly.

Chryssy ran to the ladder and climbed up the platform to check. She put an arrow in her bow and prepared to fire, if need be. Charles was right behind her with his gun in his hand. They both tried to look past the trees, but the early morning shadows made it difficult to see anything. The sun still had not fully risen, so it was partially dark, which made it hard to see anything beyond the compound.

The silhouette of someone could be seen approaching from the south on Cromwell Road. It did not look like Yvonne. The shape was completely wrong. For some reason, its legs were bloated and baggy, as if it had over eaten, bursting its stomach and all of its ingested food had fallen down to its legs. Chryssy pulled back the arrow and waited to release it. She wanted whatever it was to get closer, first.

As soon as they realized it was a zombie, she shot the arrow and sent it whistling across the air, until it plunged through its head. His body bent backwards from the force of the arrow. He dropped to his knees, and then fell forward making a squishy sound. Afterwards, he ceased moving.

Chryssy cried out in disgust, "Ew! Gross!"

Charles swallowed nervously and became increasingly worried about Yvonne. Had the zombie attacked her or did it merely frighten her away? He wanted to call out her name, but hesitated, in case there was another one nearby. He did not want to call it to the compound.

It did not matter because, seconds later, they saw two more figures approaching. They knew it had to be more zombies. Chryssy prepared another arrow and shot it at the closest one. This one did not look as bloated as the previous one. Instead, it had skeletal features. The arrow shot into its open mouth, but the creepy rotted corpse was undeterred. Chryssy sighed and pulled out another arrow from the arrow pack on her back. She reloaded her bow and fired the next shot. This time, it went into the zombie's eye. It stopped walking, lingered for a moment, and fell to the ground. Chryssy prepared to fire at the last zombie. She waited until it was on the entrance road and killed it easily.

She shook her head and sighed. "That's three too many for my sake. I vote we leave this area," she said, as she turned to Charles.

He said nothing. Instead, he kept hoping to see a sign that Yvonne was still alive. He was angry with her, but that did not change the fact that he cared about her. He did not want her to die. He was not the type to wish death on anyone.

They both waited a couple of minutes. When no other zombies approached, Chryssy climbed down from the platform and walked toward the watchtower. She decided to go up and see if she could get a better look around the compound.

Charles remained on the platform. Hope kept him from turning his back and leaving. He needed to know Yvonne was okay. Again, he thought about calling out her name, even though he knew it was a bad idea. He figured the zombies probably saw the fire or smoke and followed it. Hopefully, there were no more in the area.

Just as Charles was about to call out her name, he heard her screaming, again. It must have meant that she was still alive!

"Yvonne! Come back, if you can make it! I'll cover you!" He aimed his gun outward, pointing it to the south.

A moment later, she came running for the gate and he realized it was locked. He rushed down the platform and grabbed the keys from Devin. He went to unlock the gate, but then Grant pulled his arm back and stopped him.

"Wait! Do *not* open that gate!"

Charles pleaded, "But she needs my help!"

Just then, she slammed into the gate on the other side from where they were standing. They could not see her due to the metal plating Daniel installed on the gates, but it was pretty obvious she was no longer herself. She slammed into the gate, again, and started pounding relentlessly. She screamed savagely and continued to pound on the gate.

At that moment, Charles realized his worst fear. She was infected. He closed his eyes and felt an overwhelming pain in his broken heart. He mustered up the strength to do what had to be done. Realizing this, Grant let go of his arm. Charles climbed up the ladder to the platform and gazed down to the other side of the gate. He could see her quite clearly from there. In fact, he saw her more clearly than he ever saw her. He saw her desperately hungry face. It was how she had always been. The fresh blood from the gaping wound in her neck seeped down her cleavage and soaked the front of her blouse. She beat the iron gates with her bare hands to the point that they were starting to bleed.

She did not notice him, looking down on her. He was grateful for that. It would be much harder, if he had to look into her eyes. He aimed his weapon at her head and took a deep breath. Without further hesitation, he pulled the trigger and killed her.

MAN'S END

Chapter Thirty-Five

GRAVES WERE DUG for both Glenda and Yvonne. Grant convinced the others it would be too much trouble to search for Julia's body under the rubble. Besides, they all agreed she would have preferred to be buried in the basement with the computer and monitors, where she spent most of her time. The truth was Grant did not want anyone else to see that she had been shot in the back of the head. While, he may have had a good reason to do it, he did not believe painting her as a bad person to everyone else was going to accomplish anything. In the end, it was best for him and Liz to keep that secret between them. She agreed.

The next few hours were extremely difficult for everyone. While part of the group mourned for the dead, the rest worked hard to load up some of the vehicles. It was decided by majority vote that leaving the compound would be the best idea for their long-term survival. The walls alone would not be good enough to keep them protected. They required a shelter that could house them comfortably and building one was out of the question. As Yvonne stated, there were so many abandoned locations out there that it made no sense to spend so much time and energy building a new house, especially since none of them knew much about constructing an entire house from scratch.

The remaining fuel from the tractor-trailer fuel tanker was used to fill the generators and vehicles they would take with them on their search for a new home. Each vehicle would carry a few generators, wherever there were places to store them. Kirk said he would drive the smaller fuel tanker truck. The spare fuel drums were loaded onto the vehicles that could carry their weight, such as the van and pick-up truck. Charles thought it would be wise to keep the van, since it could be used for storing equipment. David agreed and argued that the pick-up was good for the same reason. Grant wanted to bring the police SUV because it handled well on rough terrain and harsh weather. It was also capable of carrying over five people. Roberto wanted to keep the motorcycle he had stolen from the biker gang. Everybody agreed The Intrepid would be the best vehicle to carry any remaining passengers. Plus, it was the only vehicle that was heavily armored.

The other vehicles would be left behind. A decision had not been made on where they would go, yet. The plan was to travel in a northwesterly direction, until they were far enough away to never worry about the infection, again. There were still places where it had not reached.

At the same time, they did not wish to reach normal civilization, again. Staying away from people was the general consensus, for the moment.

Unfortunately, bringing the cow and eleven chickens along would not be prudent for a long journey, especially not with the vehicles they had. That meant it was time to cook what they could, so it would not go to waste. They killed one of their hens and cooked it over the fire pit, since it was undamaged by the fire. The meal would serve as breakfast, lunch, and dinner for everyone. It would be necessary to ration out the food they had left, if they wanted it to last.

It was not the first time they resorted to eating one of the hens. At one time, they had thirteen chickens, but it had been a long hard winter.

David figured they could place the cages into the rear of the pick-up and take the remaining chickens with them. It was either that or set them free.

The barn would serve as their home, until it was time to leave. There was no point in putting off their journey, so it was decided they would leave the next morning. They planned on cooking another hen for breakfast. Before leaving, they would release Betsy the cow.

There was not much talking done throughout that last full day, after the tragic fire. Nobody was really in the mood to talk. Everyone was exhausted from lack of sleep, crying, and loading the vehicles. They sat around on the hay up in the second floor of the barn. It was the only shelter they had left, aside from the old walk-in tool shed, the watchtower, and tarps that could be used to pitch tents.

Joy cried herself to sleep, while Aramis watched over her and tried to comfort her with little luck. He was worried her withdrawn behavior could lead to suicidal tendencies. Sam sat quietly a few feet away in the corner with Taryn. She held him close and gently caressed his soft brown hair.

Charles stared blankly at the ceiling, as he lay down. The events of the past twenty hours replayed in his head over and over. Yvonne's words left a stinging mark that probably would not go away, for quite some time.

Kirk sat next to David with his arms bandaged up. They wanted to talk about what happened, but not in front of everyone else, so they remained silent. David was grateful Kirk was alive, although Kirk was feeling guilty over not being able to save Glenda in time.

Millie lay close to them curled up in a ball. She could not believe how quickly things had gotten so bad. It was like one nightmare after another. They seemed to have no peace of mind.

Grant and Liz held each other close and did not speak, but both of them were thinking about what Julia tried to do. Liz felt hurt, angry, and betrayed. She thought Julia was their friend. She never imagined Julia harbored such jealousy and resentment toward her. Grant was surprised. He had no idea Julia would go to such lengths to claim him. He almost felt pity for her. Almost.

Roberto and Chryssy sat together on the platform near the wall. At first, they stood watch and waited to kill more zombies because the rising white smoke could be seen for miles. They managed to kill about six more, before dinnertime. Afterwards, it seemed no more would come, so they sat down.

During that time, Roberto smoked about three cigarettes. He felt stressed and needed to relieve that stress. Chryssy wished he would not smoke so much. She hated the smell.

Devin chose to sit alone up in the watchtower, since he could not sleep. Plus, he felt it was necessary for someone with a rifle to watch over the compound, considering so many infected managed to get so close, over the course of the day. He remained vigilant all night.

The night dragged out without further incident. However, only a handful of people were able to get the sleep they needed. The rest were too distracted by their thoughts.

When the rooster crowed at dawn, everyone awoke startled. It sounded a lot louder in the barn, than it ever did when they slept in the house.

Grant had almost forgotten where he was, as he mumbled, "What the f...?"

Suddenly, reality set in and he realized they no longer had a bathroom. It was a reality that disappointed everyone else, as well, as they tried to make themselves presentable.

Once everyone was ready, they had another hen for breakfast, as planned, with some eggs. They ate full servings and were able to pack some chicken for the road. David and Roberto loaded the rooster and the other eight hens into their cages and placed them on the rear of the pick-up truck.

Betsy the cow gave up her last milk to the group, and then she was untied. The barn door was left open for her. She would be free to move about on her own throughout the compound, which would remain locked to keep her safe. There was plenty of grass for her to eat, as the property was several acres in size. A clean bucket was left nearby to catch rainwater for her to drink.

The group finished packing what they needed from the items they were able to salvage. At last, they were ready to leave. Some were more than ready to start fresh elsewhere. It was a bittersweet farewell because so much time and work had gone into making the compound their home. When they finally left, it would be for very the last time.

They drove out and headed north on Cromwell Road. The caravan of vehicles took Bull Mill Road east to Museum Village Road and got onto Interstate 86 going north. They had to go the wrong way on the northbound exit ramp, since there was not a northbound entrance, at that location.

Grant led the group in the police SUV, since he had a better idea of the roads heading north. He used to spend more time than the others looking through the maps and he also drove north a few times in the past, before the apocalypse. Naturally, Liz rode shotgun with him.

Behind them were David and Millie in the pick-up truck with nine chickens. Four fuel drums had also been loaded into the rear cargo compartment, along with generators and whatever else they could carry. One of the tarps was tied loosely over the load to protect it from rain.

Charles and Devin followed them in the van. Roberto's motorcycle was stored in the rear, along with two more fuel drums and a few other supplies. Devin closed his eyes, as soon as they reached the interstate, since he had been up all night. He claimed he only wanted to rest his eyes for a while.

Aramis was next in The Intrepid. Joy sat in the second row of seats on the passenger side, while Sam and Taryn sat in the back row together. This vehicle was the quietest of the caravan. Joy and Sam were totally devastated and with good reason. Taryn did what she could to console Sam, but Aramis had to settle for looking back at Joy, whenever it was safe to do so, since he had to drive.

He thought about how badly he wanted to go out on supply runs, but very rarely got the chance to do so. Now, here he was on the road to nowhere in particular and all he wanted to do was go back to the compound, where he felt safe. The irony was almost funny. He'd laugh, if not for the grieving family in his presence.

Kirk drove the small fuel tanker. Roberto and Chryssy rode with him to keep him company. They took up the rear of the caravan.

Roberto shook his head and said, "I can't believe the night we had. One minute all was fine and dandy, and then everything went to hell. That poor kid must have been so scared. She was too young to die. It breaks my heart. I feel bad for Joy and Sam."

Kirk's guilt kept him from commenting.

Chryssy, who sat in between the two, asked, "How do you think that fire started? It couldn't have been the fire pit. We were out there and it was under control. By the time we went into the house to use the bathroom that fire was already burning. Plus, the fire pit was undamaged!"

"Yeah," Roberto agreed. "It looked like it was coming from the closet in the hallway."

Chryssy nodded, "That's what I thought, too, but the only thing in there were coats."

Kirk finally said something. "I found her in the bathroom. She was already on the floor passed out from smoke inhalation. The fire was just starting to reach her. I wish I had thought of looking in there sooner. I wasted too much time checking the other rooms."

Roberto turned to him and responded, "There's no way you could have known, bro. You did the best you could. Your actions made it possible for that woman to bury her child and have closure."

"I suppose."

"Bro, don't you dare ever doubt your worth to this group. You are an invaluable friend and even a hero to some of us. We would be lost without you. Never forget that."

"Thanks, Rob. That really means a lot to me. I want you to know I appreciate your friendship. It's been a very good thing for me. It's crazy how much better my life has been, since the apocalypse. For most people, it's the opposite, but not for me. For the first time, I feel like I am part of something bigger."

Roberto nodded, "You are! We all are! This is it, bro. This is our life, now."

Kirk managed to force a smile and began to feel better. He was glad to have Roberto in the same vehicle with him. He always felt better, after speaking with him.

Chryssy sighed, "I feel terrible about what happened last night, but I am glad we did not lose too many people in the fire. It could have been so much worse. Almost everyone was already in bed. We need to be grateful. I'm glad we were able to let everyone know in time."

"So am I," agreed Roberto. "Could you imagine if more people had died? It's hard enough dealing with the couple of deaths we had and what about that Yvonne? What a bitch!"

"Oh, man!" Kirk exclaimed, "Don't even get me started on that woman. I can't believe she played Charles like that. He's such a great guy. That was so wrong. She got what she deserved."

"Amen," Roberto said.

Over the next couple of hours, as the caravan continued heading north on Interstate 86, it became apparent how abandoned much of New York State had become. They had no idea how far spread the mass exodus had reached. It was like the end of the world. The greenery was starting to grow through cracks in the pavement on the roadways. Most of the roads were completely void of other vehicles. Small herds of deer were roaming freely along the roadsides and grazing on the tall grass. The group of vehicles had to drive around various old roadblocks that had been set in place, several months earlier and later abandoned. Occasionally, they might pass an abandoned vehicle, which had been stripped clean by scavengers. However, one thing that remained consistent was the lack of people. There did not seem to be a soul in sight.

By the time they reached Binghamton, several hours later, they decided to stop and refuel, while taking a bathroom break. Each driver had a two-way radio, so they could communicate with one another. They pulled off the interstate and into a gas station, out of habit. The vehicles were parked side by side. Kirk handled the refueling process, while Grant checked a roadmap of New York State. Roberto and Chryssy went into the Manley's Mighty Mart to check if it was safe. There was no one inside, but at least there was a semi-clean restroom they could use. As luck would have it, there was also random food and drinks within the mart that they were able to salvage.

A few minutes later, after Charles came out of the restroom, he walked toward Grant, who was still studying the map. He was using the hood of the police SUV as a table. Liz sat atop the fuel tanker and kept watch with her rifle.

Charles asked, "Where exactly are we heading? Do you have a plan?"

Grant answered without looking away from the map, "Kind of. I was thinking we could probably head up Interstate 81 to Syracuse. At least, from there we'd have a choice to stay in that area, head east to Albany, or go west toward Buffalo and possibly continue up into Canada. What do you think?"

"That sounds good to me. I think the further away we can get, the better off we will be. I would love it, if we could leave this damn virus behind for good."

"I hear you, pal." Grant looked up at him and said, "Hey, for what it's worth, I'm really sorry about what happened with Yvonne."

Charles rolled his eyes and replied, "If it's all the same, I'd rather not talk about her. She was a tremendous disappointment. She really pulled one over on me. I would much rather forget about it."

"I understand. Consider her forgotten."

Charles changed the subject and asked, "Were we able to save any of the books from the common room?"

"No, it was across from the closet and not worth the risk," Grant responded. "Anything in there was lost."

"That's a damn shame. Those books were great assets, especially the survival books."

"Yeah, I know."

David walked over to them and asked, "What's the plan, boys? Do we even have one?"

"We'll take Interstate 81 and head up to Syracuse. It's a straight run. If that fails, we can take Interstate 90 east or west from there. That will take us to Albany, Buffalo, or Canada."

"Canada?" David asked. "I think we should just head straight there. It's time to leave this country behind, once and for all. There's nothing left, but bad memories and anarchy."

"Very true," Grant agreed. "We should, at least, check Syracuse. It might be a good place to refuel or stock up on supplies."

David turned to him. "I thought we were trying to avoid large populated areas?"

"At some point, we'll have to pass a major city, unless we stick to the back roads. Getting supplies will be harder that way."

David said, "We can get supplies, after we've settled somewhere. I don't like the idea of going near any of those large cities. Think about all the trouble we had in one small town. It will be ten times worse in a city the size of Buffalo or Syracuse. I'm all for taking the back roads to avoid them. I don't care how long it takes. I've got nowhere else to be. Let's think safe, guys."

Grant and Charles looked at each other and nodded in agreement.

Charles said, "He's right. We shouldn't take unnecessary chances."

"Okay," Grant replied. "I'll check the best roads for us and mark them off with a highlighter. I have one in my vest pocket." He was wearing a black hunting and fishing vest with multiple pockets. There were even pockets, where he could fit extra ammunition clips.

Once everyone had used the restroom, they were back on the road. They left Binghamton and stayed on Interstate 86 heading westbound, instead of going north on Interstate 81.

The next time the caravan pulled off the interstate, it was at a small town called Kanona. They stopped at another gas station, so they could decide if they wanted to continue west or go north on Interstate 390 toward Rochester.

Grant, Charles, and David stood around the map, again, as before to discuss their options.

David asked, "Where would we end up if we stay on 86?"

Grant pointed to the map and explained, "It meets up with Interstate 90, right here before reaching Erie. Interstate 390 will also intersect with 90, before reaching Buffalo." He followed the road on the map with his finger to show them. "If we continue past Erie, we'll eventually reach Cleveland, Ohio. There were outbreaks in Ohio, so I don't plan on going anywhere near there. Who knows how bad things are there? I say we do as David suggested earlier. We go past Buffalo and cross over into Canada."

Charles nodded, "I think I'm ready to be a Canadian, eh?"

Grant chuckled.

David agreed, "Good. Canada it is. Let's get going."

"Hold on," Charles replied. "First, I'm going to need a bathroom break." He walked away and headed toward the restroom.

Grant and David had already gone, before studying the map, so they returned to their vehicles.

Once Grant sat down in the police SUV, he told Liz the plan. "Well, it looks like we'll be going to Canada."

"Oh, good," she replied. "I think that's our best option. As much as I love New York, I think it's time to move on."

Grant noticed something odd and looked past her. The van was leaving the gas station, which made no sense. He wondered where Charles was going, but then became suspicious when the van picked up speed, as it hit the road. He grabbed the two-way radio and asked, "Charles, where are you going?"

At that moment, Devin came running over to the police SUV and cried out, "Someone just stole the van!"

"Get in!" Grant ordered. "Where's Charles?"

"There," Liz pointed. "He just came out of the bathroom!"

Grant honked the horn to get everyone's attention, as he pulled up in front of Charles. "Charles, hurry up and get in! Someone just stole your van!"

"What???" He looked and saw that the van was gone.

"Get in!" Grant repeated.

This time, Charles did not delay. He ran around and got into the backseat on the passenger side, since Devin was already seated behind Grant.

As soon as he was in, Grant screeched the tires and raced out of the gas station. He turned right and headed west, after the van. While driving, he called into the radio, "We gotta go, people! Someone stole the van! I'm in pursuit! I have Charles and Devin with me! Make sure everyone is accounted for, before you follow! Over!"

The Intrepid immediately pulled out of the gas station and sped after Grant, joining the pursuit. "All aboard on The Intrepid, Grant," said Aramis. "We're right behind you, brother! Over."

David replied about a second later, "David here. I don't know if I want to go too fast with the load I'm carrying. Get that bastard and we'll catch up. Over."

Kirk responded, "Big Chief here in the tanker. I got all my peeps. It's probably not best if I drive this thing too fast, so we'll hang back and keep close to Dave. Over."

Roberto complained, "That son of a bitch took my motorcycle! It's in the van! I went through a lot of trouble to steal that bike! It's a Harley Davidson!"

"Don't worry, pal," said Kirk. "We'll get it back. You know damn well Grant's going to catch up to that weasel and when he does, it's not going to be pretty."

Roberto felt better knowing that, but he was still upset.

Ahead of them, Grant still had sight of the van. It was going south on Route 415. He floored the gas pedal and flicked on the turret lights and siren, out of habit, before he realized he was no longer a cop. He decided to leave them on anyway, hoping it would serve as an intimidating factor to instill fear into the thief. It would also make it easier for the others to follow them. He only hoped the lights and siren would not attract the wrong kind of attention, since they were racing past open fields.

Liz opened her window and stuck her rifle out. She aimed and tried to get a clean shot, but the driver of the van must have noticed because he or she began weaving back and forth.

"Careful, Liz," Charles warned her. "We have fuel drums in the back!"

"Damn, I forgot about those," she frowned and pulled the rifle back inside.

It quickly became apparent the thief was not alone. There was someone in the front passenger seat of the van. The passenger decided to take a cue from Liz and pointed a gun back at them, except he did not hesitate. He fired three random shots at them. Grant dodged and weaved to avoid the gunshots, slowing down slightly. At that point, The Intrepid went past them and took the lead.

Aramis wasn't worried about the gunfire, since the front of the bus had been fitted with armor plating.

Joy snapped out of her grief-stricken state, as soon as she heard the gunshots. Her eyes opened wide, when she noticed Aramis was directly behind the stolen van. She gripped her seat firmly and shouted, "Aramis! You're going to get us killed!"

"Relax, Joy. We'll be fine," he replied.

She glared at him.

Just then, the passenger fired a round at The Intrepid and hit the front armor, causing the round to ricochet off to the side. Joy ducked down behind the seat in front of her and Aramis swallowed nervously. He suddenly remembered the windows were not bulletproof. He hoped he had not spoken too soon.

The gunman stopped firing when the van reached a slight curve in the road. The driver of the van almost lost control, but regained it quickly. It gave Aramis the edge he needed to get right up behind the van. He bumped the rear of the van with the front end of The Intrepid hard and lifted it up slightly.

Grant followed closely and called into his radio, "Careful, Doc! Remember that the van's carrying fuel!"

Aramis tapped the van, again, just as Grant issued his warning. The van swerved to the left, and then to the right, before losing control and flipping over on its right side. It skidded over the road toward the supports of the overpass for Interstate 86 and slammed into them. Less than a second later, it exploded.

BOOM!

"Oops," Aramis muttered under his breath, as he came to a stop.

Grant also slowed to a halt, before reaching the overpass.

They both looked on from the safety of their vehicles, as bright flames and thick black smoke gradually swallowed up the van and hid it from view.

Joy peeked over her seat and adjusted her long red hair, which was a mess. She decided to tie it behind her head into a ponytail, while glowering at Aramis for putting her family in danger. "Nice going," she grumbled angrily with a not so subtle touch of sarcasm.

Aramis buried his face in his hands and sighed heavily. He knew he messed up. Anything that was in the van was lost, including the spare fuel drums and Roberto's motorcycle. He felt absolutely terrible about it. Plus, he certainly was not gaining points with Joy. It seemed his relationship with her might be over, before it even begins.

Moments later, David and Kirk caught up and stopped behind them. It was not too hard to find them. All they had to do was stay on the same road and follow the black plume of smoke that rose from the crash site.

When Roberto saw the van engulfed by flames, he slammed his hand on the dashboard. "Aw, come on! There goes my motorcycle," he groaned. He then sighed with disappointment, as Chryssy rubbed his leg caringly.

MAN'S END

Chapter Thirty-Six

THE GROUP EVENTUALLY continued north along Interstate 390. They were able to make the switch to Interstate 90 going west without going too far into Rochester, which was for the best. Someone had left a homemade banner hanging from an overpass on the interstate that read "ALL WHO ENTER ROCHESTER MUST SUBMIT TO NEW LAWS OR BE BANISHED!"

They pulled over one final time, before reaching Buffalo at Exit 48A, which led to the towns of Pembroke and Medina. Roberto got a kick out of the name Medina, since it was his surname. It was the first time he perked up, after the loss of his motorcycle.

"Hey, that's my last name! Medina!"

Chryssy replied, "That's awesome! We should totally stop there."

A few moments later, when they reached an overpass, Grant spoke over the radio and said, "Guys, we're making a pit stop at Exit 48A. It'll be dark soon. There's a hotel, where we might be able to rest for the night. I want us to be well rested, when we enter Buffalo during the daylight. Over."

Kirk turned to Chryssy and Roberto and said, "It looks like you're getting your wish."

Roberto smiled faintly. He was not too sure what they were going to encounter at this hotel or if the building was still standing. One thing was certain. They would need to check it thoroughly, if they were going to stay the night. There could be no surprises.

The four vehicles turned off the exit and went through the old toll plaza. They turned right onto Route 77 and pulled into the Econo Lodge Darien Lakes. The parking lot was empty and the main entrance was boarded up. Before stopping, Grant drove through the entire parking lot to make sure there was no one hiding, while the other vehicles waited near the entrance.

It seemed safe, so they parked their vehicles side by side near the entrance. This time, someone stayed with each vehicle. They were not about to let anyone steal another one out from under their noses. Devin patrolled the perimeter around the vehicles with his Smith and Wesson M and P 15-22 Sport Rimfire rifle and kept an eye on the road to watch for any other cars.

Grant, Charles, David, and Roberto stood in front of the main entrance of the hotel. Roberto used his wrecking bar to pry the wood off, so they could enter. Once it was off, they went inside and checked the desk area. The door was unlocked. They also checked the dining area and the gym. It looked as if the place had been abandoned for quite some time. There were cobwebs hanging everywhere. The room keys were kept behind the desk. There were two levels, so they decided to split up and check every single room.

Grant and Charles checked the ground floor rooms, while Roberto and David took the second level. It took them almost an hour to clear each room. Surprisingly, most of the rooms were in decent shape. It seemed staying the night would not be such a bad idea.

After checking the rooms, the guys met up on the ground floor in the lobby.

Roberto asked, "So, how are we going to do this? Are we supposed to just leave our vehicles unattended, while we sleep?"

David shook his head, "Hell no. That would be a bad idea. Someone has to keep an eye on them. We can do it in shifts like we did with the watchtower. It's only one night, so we can split it between two or three people."

Charles agreed, "That's what we'll do. All drivers should get some sleep. I'll take one shift. Devin can take another one, since he slept for half the ride. The rest of you get some sleep."

Grant said, "Why don't you and Devin take a nap, while we get settled? Some of us can keep an eye on the vehicles, until you guys wake up for your shifts. That way, you will get some rest, too."

"Sounds like a good plan to me."

Roberto suggested, "I think some of us should sleep on the second floor, while the rest sleep on the first floor that way we have eyes and ears on both levels. All drivers should be on the ground, so they're ready to go, at a moment's notice. Chryssy and I can take a second floor room. We'll stay up late and help with guarding the vehicles, too, at least for part of the night."

They all agreed and went back out to the vehicles to inform the others of the plan. Afterwards, they chose their rooms. No one would sleep alone for safety reasons. Everyone would have a roommate. Grant and Liz slept together in the room directly in front of the police SUV on the ground floor. Next to them were David and Kirk, who both decided to go to sleep early. Millie and Taryn took the room to the right of them. Joy, Sam, and Aramis were in the next room, although Aramis slept in his own bed. On the second floor were Roberto and Chryssy, and then Charles and Devin, in the room next to them.

Roberto and Chryssy spent the next few hours standing on the second floor fire escape, which faced north. There was a solid white wall they could hide behind, in case of danger. The fire escape did not wrap around the whole building, so they had a limited view of the parking lot and the road. However, they could also see the Subway restaurant in the connecting parking lot, the Denny's and gas station across the street, and the interstate in the distance, until it got too dark. There were no lights on anywhere, so they had to rely on moonlight, flashlights, and the night vision goggles. After a certain amount of time, everything looked dark, but their eyes gradually adjusted to the darkness and they could make out shapes.

Chryssy kept her bow in her hand with an arrow ready to launch, if need be. She scanned the area, using the night vision goggles, which she borrowed from Liz. There did not seem to be any potential targets around the trees or fields beyond the parking lot.

"What time are we going to bed?" She asked him. "I was hoping we would have a little time together."

He grinned, "Don't worry, we will. I just wanted to give the guys time to get a good rest that way they could both stand watch together. It's better when you have someone to keep you company. It makes the night go by faster."

"That's what I'm afraid of. I want to get some sleep, too," she pouted.

He put his arm around her and kissed her on the cheek. "We're going to sleep very good tonight because I'm going to wear you down, baby."

She leered at him and asked, "Oh, really? Well, I can't wait."

They kissed.

A short time later, Charles and Devin came out for their overnight shift. Roberto and Chryssy quickly disappeared into their room and locked the door.

Charles took a deep breath and said, "Smell that wonderful night air. It almost makes you forget all the crap we've gone through."

"Yeah, there has been a lot." Devin leaned on the waist high white wall and looked down to the ground below, while holding his rifle. His eyes moved all around the parking lots, as he checked for any movement, using the night vision goggles. There was none. "I don't know if we will ever find a place like the one we left behind," he said with a hint of regret. "It's crazy how desolate this state has become. And the only people we ever see turn out to be assholes."

"Tell me about it." Charles thought about how their van was stolen and felt angry. Next, he thought about his time with Yvonne and how she turned her back on him. He had to stop remembering the past because it was only making him upset. Instead, he tried to focus on the here and now. He looked up at the stars and wondered how many more days he had left to enjoy them. Finally, he said, "It's a beautiful night. We're lucky. It could have been raining."

Devin shrugged, "Yeah, I guess. That wouldn't bother me so much. I don't mind the rain. I'm pretty easy going, when it comes to weather. Now that I don't have to work anymore, it doesn't really matter to me."

Charles turned to him curiously and asked, "What did you do for a living? I don't believe we've ever spoken about it."

"I was a cop, too, in New Jersey."

"No kidding? That's funny. It actually makes a lot of sense. You carry yourself like a cop. I always assumed you worked for some small county doing some sort of law enforcement work."

"Yep, I did," he confirmed, while still looking out into the darkness. "Hey, I'm sorry about what happened with Yvonne. I know you liked her."

Charles sighed. "Yeah, I did."

They both fell silent and stared out into the night.

Liz lit a candle and placed it on the nightstand beside the bed. She leaned her rifle against the nightstand and got into bed. She pulled the blanket over her and felt relaxed. The bed was quite comfortable. Her eyes turned to Grant, who was sitting at the foot of the bed staring at the door.

"What's on your mind, babe?"

He answered without turning around, "I was thinking about yesterday." He shook his head. "I still can't believe how close I came to losing you. If I had been a minute later, you might not be here and I'm really not sure where my mind would be. What the hell could have possessed Julia to think that she could shoot you?"

"She was sick in the head. Whatever was going on with her had been going on for a while. We were just too blind to notice."

"Or maybe I was too blind," he muttered. He recalled when Roberto told him what he overheard that night in the dining room. Roberto believed Taryn was talking Julia out of doing something stupid. Roberto specifically said he heard them mention his name. By the time, Grant finally tried to speak to Julia, she tried to kiss him, and then all he wanted to do was avoid her. He began to think he should have taken a more active role in addressing the situation, before it got so out of hand. Would she still be alive today?

He felt guilty thinking that she was better off dead. Better for him or better for her? Was he just being selfish? He breathed in deeply and pondered how things could have gone wrong with Julia. They were supposed to be friends! Did he lead her on without realizing it? Was he too friendly with her?

He had so many questions and no chance of ever getting an answer from her, considering he shot her in the back of the head! He hated doing it, but he was not about to let her shoot Liz. No way!

Liz meant the world to him. Liz?

"Hello! Earth to Grant Hamilton!" She shouted.

"Huh?" He turned around. Suddenly, he realized he was still in the room with her. He gazed at her beautiful face and felt so lucky to have her in his life. Twice, her life had been threatened in his presence. What if he was not around the next time? Three strikes and you're out. He dreaded the thought.

She scoffed, "Baby, come to bed. You've been driving all day. You are so out of it."

"No," he shook his head. "There's something I should tell you."

He confessed everything about Julia. He told Liz about what Roberto overheard and about how Julia tried to kiss him that day in the basement.

Afterwards, Liz stared at him in surprise. "Why didn't you tell me all of this before? I had no idea that mental case was so obsessed with you. You put me at risk, by not keeping me in the loop."

"I realize that, now, and I'm sorry. It was never my intention. I never thought she would dare take it so far."

Liz stared at him in disbelief. "That skank tried to kiss you!"

"Yeah, but she didn't. I stopped her and I told her it was never going to happen. After that, I avoided her like the plague."

She replied, "I really think you should have told me about this sooner. This is important."

"Why? So you could have beaten her ass? There was no point in..."

"I would have liked to know! That's point enough for me! If someone in the group came on to me and tried to kiss me, wouldn't you like to know about it? Or would you rather I kept it a secret, so that you had no idea some guy, who *you* think is your friend, is obsessing about me, behind your back?"

He sighed. "You're right. I'm sorry. I should have told you."

"Yeah, I am right." She exhaled angrily and crossed her arms.

"Well, she's dead! I blew our friend's brains out! She'll never be a problem, again!"

He took off his boots, got undressed down to his underwear, and climbed into the bed beside her. He sighed, "It was wrong for me to keep secrets from you. I didn't want to give you anything to stress over. I thought I could handle it. She was supposed to be our friend. I guess I was wrong. I'm sorry."

She let out a sigh and brushed her hand through his hair. "I know it had to be hard shooting her because she was our friend, but she left you no choice. You saved my life... again. Think about it that way. I will. Thanks for always being my personal savior." She kissed him on the cheek.

"I'd do anything for you." Even kill a friend. He turned to face her. "I love you, Elizabeth."

She cringed at the sound of her name, but not as much as usual. Somehow, it did not sound so bad with the way he said it, she thought. She responded, "I know, babe. I love you, too. Are you ready to go to sleep?"

He shook his head, "I was kind of hoping for something else, before we started talking."

She chuckled and asked, "Candle on or candle off?"

"Definitely on."

They kissed and pulled each other close. Passions were high, so their lovemaking was intense. They spent part of the night wrapped in naked ecstasy, until the candle was eventually blown out.

The rest of the night went on peacefully. David and Kirk were first to wake up in the morning, so they gave Charles and Devin a break and let them take a much-needed nap, before the others awoke. They were able to get in a good two hours of sleep, which was greatly appreciated.

After scrounging up whatever food they could find from the nearby restaurants, they had breakfast in the dining area of the hotel. Unfortunately, the water was not running, so washing up and taking showers were not options. It was a good thing they still had moist wipes. Once they were ready, everyone got into the vehicles and they drove back to the interstate heading westbound. The next stop would be the City of Buffalo.

As they reached the former toll plaza entering the city, there were tall walls on either side of the interstate, so they still could not actually see the city. Overgrown weeds were forcing their way through the road and thick vines seemed to be swallowing up the wall, little by little.

Grant grew worried, as they drove past a "Welcome to Buffalo" sign. Someone had spray painted a warning over it with red paint that read, "INFECTED! TURN BACK NOW!"

Liz asked, "Do you think they were trying to tell the infected to turn back or are they trying to say there are infected, so we should turn back?"

He answered, "Considering they did not use a comma, after the word 'infected,' I'd say we might be in for some crazy shit."

"I was afraid you'd say that," she frowned.

He thought about it and said, "I'm kind of hoping that warning was written last year and things have calmed down, since then. It was a rough winter. It had to be worse up here."

Charles commented from the backseat, "It doesn't matter. Stick to the highway. We're just passing through."

Grant nodded, "Right. Let's hope so."

David called them over the radio and asked, "Did you guys see that sign? Over."

Grant answered, "10-4, Dave. Let's hope it was written last year. A lot might have changed, since July. It's almost been a whole year. Besides, we're only passing through. The interstate goes around the edge of the city. We should be fine. Over."

David did not respond, but Aramis did. "I don't like this one bit, guys. I just wanted to throw that out there. Over."

"I'm with Doc," Kirk replied into his radio. "Over."

Roberto turned to Chryssy and said, "Stay sharp. I might need you to shoot an arrow at someone. In fact, why don't we switch seats? You take the window."

She agreed and climbed over his lap, as he slid closer to Kirk.

They took the next exit for Interstate 290, which went north to Niagara Falls. The roadway was in terrible shape and there were numerous abandoned vehicles scattered along the road. They had to squeeze past some of them. Aramis and Kirk just pushed past them with The Intrepid and fuel tanker. After a while, Grant just told Aramis to take the lead. It would be easier for him to clear a path for the rest of the vehicles.

After going past an overpass, there was an overturned tractor-trailer truck that had apparently jackknifed. It looked like it had been there for months. There was a skeletal corpse on the ground nearby, which caused Millie to gasp, as they passed it.

The entire city looked dead. There were burnt out buildings, crashed cars, more skeletons on the roadway, and the smell of death was strong in the air. Large water puddles flooded certain lower sections of the road, probably from melted snow that had never been cleared.

As they drove across the overpass that went over Sheridan Drive, they could see several zombies walked through the street below.

Aramis glanced at Joy and said, "There is no way in hell I am stopping anywhere in this city!"

"You won't get an argument from me," she said, while looking down from the overpass, as they drove north.

A few minutes later, they merged into Interstate 190 and came to a stop, shortly before reaching a collapsed railroad overpass. It appeared to have been purposely blown up and now blocked the road.

Aramis sighed and called the others over the radio. "This might take a while, boys. There is *a lot* of iron on the road. Over."

Kirk drove past David and Grant and pulled up beside The Intrepid. He picked up his radio and said, "This is a job for the big boys! Let's move some iron, Doc!"

They both pushed debris out of the road, until they could clear a path large enough to squeeze through. Toward the end, they got out and did the rest by hand. Most of the guys helped with that part. Chryssy only had to shoot one zombie that got too close. She retrieved her arrow and waited for more. They never came. Once the guys were done, they got back into their vehicles and prepared to move on to the first bridge, which crossed the Niagara River and would ultimately take them to Canada.

Aramis started up The Intrepid and began to drive. He immediately noticed a loud thumping sound and stopped, again. He looked at the side view mirror and could see his rear tire was flat. "Damn it! We got a flat! It must have been from driving over all that debris. Crap."

Joy frowned and buried her face in her hands. This was just what they needed… to get a flat in freaking Zombie Land. All she wanted was to be someplace quiet, where she could grieve for her daughter in peace. She felt utterly overwhelmed by stress and began to cry.

Sam and Taryn noticed and tried to comfort her.

Aramis felt bad for her, but there was not much he could do to help her. He had his own problems, at the moment. This was not the best place to change a flat. He called the others on the radio and said, "We have a slight problem with The Intrepid. My rear tire went flat. Over."

Kirk already knew what that meant. They would not be changing the flat because there was no spare tire for The Intrepid, which meant they were going to have to ditch it. It broke his heart to even think it. He loved that bus. It saved their lives more than once.

"This really sucks," he sulked.

Roberto turned to him and said, "Relax, bro. We can change the flat fast. It's not a big deal. Chryssy and Liz can stand guard."

"It's not that simple, Rob. The Intrepid doesn't have a spare tire. It never did."

Roberto gaped at him in surprise. "Are you kidding me? So, what does that mean?"

"It means we are saying goodbye to The Intrepid today."

"Damn. That does suck." Now, he was sulking.

Chryssy asked, "What's the big deal? It's just a bus. We can find another one."

Roberto looked at her and explained, "Oh, baby! It's more than just a bus to us. That bus saved our asses and got us away from being nuked. It also saved your ass, in case you forgot. A lot of hard work went into making it an armored transport vehicle. We scrounged for those armored parts for weeks. Daniel welded them on."

She realized its importance. "Oh, so it has sentimental value to the group."

"Exactly!" He replied. "And now, we need to abandon it like we left our home."

Chryssy frowned, "When you put it that way, I can see why it might be upsetting. I know a lot of work went into the compound, since I was able to help with the wall."

After Kirk broke the news to the others, they took whatever supplies were on it and loaded them into the other vehicles. It appeared their road trip was about to get a lot more crowded and uncomfortable. Sam and Taryn squeezed into the police SUV with Grant, Liz, Charles, and Devin. Taryn had to sit on Sam's lap because the backseat only fit three comfortably. Aramis and Joy squeezed into the pick-up truck with David and Millie. It was a good thing Millie was slim. They were barely able to fit.

The group moved on, leaving The Intrepid behind. It was the third vehicle they lost during their long trek to Canada. They could not afford to lose another.

Grant took the lead, again, with the police SUV. David followed and Kirk took up the rear. When they reached the toll plaza, there were metal police barriers blocking the way. Charles and Devin stepped out to make an opening that they could drive through, and then squeezed back into the SUV. As the three vehicles drove across the South Grand Island Bridge, Grant began to slow down. The other vehicles also slowed down behind him.

David asked over the radio, "What's up, Grant? Why are you slowing down?"

"Something's not right," he responded. He stopped and stepped out onto the bridge. He walked forward a few feet and stopped when he realized there was no way they would be crossing the bridge. It was gone. It had been blown up just like in New York City. He stepped closer to the edge and looked down at the river. "Shit."

Charles, David, and Liz approached cautiously, when they realized the rest of the bridge was missing. It was difficult to notice from the toll plaza, since the bridge arced, as it went over the river. They had no idea that the bridge used to have a large steel structure, since it was now at the bottom of the river. None of them had ever crossed the bridge.

Liz gasped, "Wow! That's just great! What are we going to do, now?"

David crouched down and breathed deeply, as he stared ahead to the other side of the bridge. He wanted to be on that side so badly that he was wishing it and hoping it would just happen magically.

Charles looked at Grant and asked, "Is there another way we can cross?"

Grant shrugged, "Yeah, sure. I just have no idea how far we will have to drive to get to it and when we do, will it be worth the journey? What if they destroyed every bridge into Canada? It's a super long way to where the land connects out west. We're talking about hours, maybe even days of driving through more infected land." He exhaled and turned away from the view. There was no point in teasing himself anymore. He walked back to the SUV and pulled out the map from the glove compartment.

Sam asked, "What's wrong, Grant? Aren't we going to cross over?"

"Not unless we sprout wings from our backs. The bridge was destroyed. There's nothing to cross anymore."

"What??? How are we going to reach Canada?"

"That's what I need to check," he replied. He spread the map out on the hood and began searching for another way into Canada that was not more than three hundred miles away. There was another bridge they could check, which was not too far. Of course, it was likely that one was blown up, too. Still, they had to check.

They got back into their vehicles and headed back south on the interstate. They switched to the local roads going past the Village of Tonawanda. They made it to Niagara Street and headed west, until they reached the entrance to the Rainbow Bridge. When they saw that there were concrete barriers blocking the road, they did not feel hopeful.

Grant spoke into his radio and instructed the others to stand by. "I'll go check it out on foot," He added, before stepping out of the SUV. He turned to Charles and asked, "Charles, why don't you come with me, just in case there's a welcoming committee? I'd feel safer if someone was watching my back."

Charles nodded, "Sure."

Liz said, "Hey, I can go with you."

"No," Grant replied. "I need you to watch over us with your scope. You can do that from here. Be ready to shoot anything that tries to sneak up behind us."

"Okay. You got it, babe," she said.

Devin called out, "Hey, wait up! I'll go with you guys. I need to stretch my legs."

Grant and Charles waited for Devin to catch up.

The three of them walked toward the toll plaza. Each kept his weapon ready for anything. Grant also had the crowbar with him. He tended to keep it in the front seat for easy access.

There were two zombies lumbering around on the bridge. Grant approached the closest one and stabbed it in the face with the crowbar. Charles went past him and stepped forward to the farthest one. He kicked it in the chest and it tumbled backwards, falling off the destroyed bridge and into the river below.

Charles stood there and looked over the edge. There was a steep drop to the river. The roaring sound of Niagara Falls could be heard thundering to the south on his left. A moment later, Grant and Devin stood beside him. Together, they gazed at the magnificence of the falls briefly, for how can one not admire such immense beauty?

"Shit," Grant cursed, after a few seconds. "I knew it. This was a waste of time. Come on. Let's go."

They turned and walked back toward the SUV.

When Liz saw them return with disappointment on their faces, she asked, "No good, huh?"

Grant shook his head. He walked to her window and asked, "Can you please hand me the map?"

She pulled it out of the glove compartment and passed it out to him, and then he placed it on the hood, once more.

When David noticed he was checking the map, again, he rolled his eyes and sighed. It was starting to remind him of Manhattan all over, again. "Are you kidding me? We're never going to Canada," he said to Millie. "Maybe we should have taken a chance and headed west, instead of north. We might have been able to avoid the zombies in Ohio."

She felt the same frustration and began to worry. "Are we trapped, again?"

David answered, "No, don't listen to me. I'm only venting because I'm tired and hungry. We can probably still reach Canada, but it's going to be a very, very long drive. Otherwise, we might have to give up that plan and try for someplace else."

Aramis, who was still seated in the pick-up with them, suggested, "Why not try to cross the river by boat? It worked for you guys before. It might work for us, now."

David turned to him and responded, "Do you really want to give up our vehicles and continue on foot, once we reach the other side, knowing there are zombies around here? Besides, go take a look at that river. Those falls can create some pretty wild rapids. We'll never make it across."

"Nah, forget it. You're right. It was a stupid idea," Aramis frowned.

Millie let out a sigh of frustration and glanced into the passenger side view mirror. Suddenly, she panicked, when she noticed someone approaching from behind. She cried out, "Zombie!"

David jumped out of the pick-up with his gun in his hand and ran around the front end to shoot the zombie, while hiding behind the hood, in case it was a person with a gun.

"PLEASE, DON'T SHOOT ME! I'M NOT INFECTED!" The person shouted, while ducking down and covering her face with her hands.

Grant, Charles, and Devin each looked up from the map to see who had yelled. It sounded like a female.

David lowered his 9mm handgun and saw that it was indeed a young woman, who looked to be in her mid-twenties. She was very pretty, too. She had short dark hair, big brown eyes, and tanned skin. David did not care much about her appearance, though. He demanded, "What do you think you're doing, trying to sneak up on us? Are you trying to get yourself killed? I could have shot you!"

"I'm so sorry! Please, help me," she begged. "I'm alone. I've been alone for weeks. I'm tired of being alone. I just want... I want to be with normal people." Tears filled her eyes and she dropped to her knees. She wept and mumbled, "Please... help me."

MAN'S END

Chapter Thirty-Seven

G RANT STOOD READY to shoot the unknown young woman, while David hesitated to holster his weapon. She knelt on the ground and sobbed. Her clothes were dirty and torn. Her short dark hair was unkempt. She seemed sincere, but Grant was not going to take any chances.

"Were you bitten or scratched?" He asked, as he stepped around the hood of the police SUV with his Walther PPK still pointed at her.

"No," she answered weakly. "Please, don't shoot me. I've been through too much craziness to die like this. My name is Rachel. I've been trying to survive on my own for so long, but I can't do it anymore. I don't want to be alone anymore." She sounded utterly defeated. Even her movements and gestures were that of a broken woman, who was tired of everything.

"When did the outbreak hit Buffalo?"

She shrugged, "I don't remember. Last summer? Early fall? I used to be part of a bigger survival group."

"What happened to them?" Grant asked.

"I'm the last one. They're all dead."

"Are you absolutely sure you haven't been bitten *or* scratched by an infected person?"

She shook her head, "No. I've been hiding from them. It's so hard. I'm hungry and tired. I just want to leave this city already."

"Why haven't you already left?"

She shrugged, "I don't know how to drive. I've been waiting for someone to come, but no one has come, until you people. It's been weeks, since I've seen a normal person. Please. Will you help me?"

Grant looked at Charles, who seemed to be okay with the idea. He then turned back to Rachel and said, "I'm not sure. We really don't have room for another person."

"I can ride on the back of the truck. I don't mind." She stared at him with pleading eyes.

He sighed, "Okay, but you have to let our medic check you for bites and I need to frisk you first to make sure you won't stab or shoot him. Otherwise, no deal."

"Fine! Check me. I told you. I'm not infected. What do you need me to do?"

"Come closer, slowly. Keep your hands on your head." She did as he instructed. He then told Charles to cover him, while he searched her for weapons. Once he felt satisfied that she was clean, he called for Aramis. "Aramis! Can you check this woman for any signs of infection?"

He agreed and climbed out of the pick-up truck. He walked toward her and said, "Hello, ma'am. My name is Aramis Perez. I used to be a New York City Emergency Medical Technician for FDNY. I'm just going to check your body for scratches or bites. I promise I will not touch you in any way that is disrespectful. Why don't you come over to this police vehicle with me and you can sit inside, while I check you? Is that okay with you, Grant?"

"Absolutely."

Everyone else got out of the SUV, so they could have some privacy. He checked her thoroughly for any signs of infection. She did not seem to have any wounds at all.

Aramis stepped away from her and said, "She's good."

Grant walked next to him and looked into the SUV at her. She was seated in the backseat. He asked, "I don't suppose you know another way we can drive to Canada from here?"

She responded, "Um, I know where there's a marina that may still have a boat or two left, if any of you know how to operate a boat."

"No," he shook his head. "We do not. We really don't want to give up our vehicles. We have a full fuel tanker, which is a tremendous asset, and a lot of supplies to carry."

She responded, "Well, you're probably going to use it all up getting to Canada. I'm sorry to tell you this, but every bridge from the Great Lakes to Quebec was destroyed in September. So, unless you plan on driving all the way to Minnesota, there are no direct roads leading into Canada. On the other hand, if you don't mind going to New Brunswick, we can get there through Maine. No bridges to worry about."

"Maine???" Charles responded. "That's pretty damn far from here."

"Yes. I know," she nodded with regret. "That's why I suggested taking a boat."

Charles turned to Grant and said, "We need to think this through. How far are we willing to drive, just to reach Canada? Is it really worth it? Didn't Julia mention there was an outbreak in Ontario? I kind of remember her saying that once."

Grant asked, "You bring that up now that we are less than a mile away from it? We could have gone a different way from the start. We all agreed that Canada was the best route. I have no problem driving to Maine and into New Brunswick. We wanted to go as far north as possible. Didn't we?"

Aramis nodded, "He's got a point. That's what we agreed. I'm okay to keep driving, if we need to. I slept enough last night. It's not like I had anything else to do." He sighed, referring to his lack of luck with Joy, lately.

Devin said, "I sure didn't, but we could take turns driving. Give each other time to rest. Maybe pick up another vehicle on the way? I don't feel comfortable with the idea of ditching our rides. That's a really bad idea."

Charles agreed, "Yeah, honestly, neither do I. If you guys want to keep driving, I suppose we can do that. Let's talk to David and Kirk to see if they're okay with it."

They had a small meeting and discussed their options, while Liz kept her eye on Rachel. Sam and Taryn waited, before going back into the SUV with her. They stood outside and looked around to make sure no zombies got near.

The group's main concern was using up their fuel. They did not want to run out of gas.

Kirk stated, "We could drive all the way back across Interstate 90, but we're going use up a lot of our fuel reserves much sooner than we planned. It would also be in our best interest to acquire another vehicle, before we leave, so that we're not on top of each other for the long ride ahead. There has to be something around here with the keys in it. Of course, I could hotwire something."

"He's right," David said. "That is a really long way to drive through potentially hostile territory. Even if we took detours around major cities and stuck to the back roads, we're looking at a day's drive, if we want to take a chance driving at night."

Aramis asked, "Wouldn't driving at night be easier? Most people would be inside sleeping, so our chances of running into someone decreases."

Grant explained, "We'd be driving blind. They would see us coming miles away, while we'd be clueless to anyone around us, until it was too late. We could drive right into a trap."

"You make a good point," Aramis stated. "I didn't think about that."

Charles suggested, "Let's check the immediate area for a car we can use. It should have the keys in it *and* a spare tire."

Aramis agreed, "Absolutely!"

"Infected" spray-painted on the wall of an abandoned building.

They split into groups of three, as they searched the area for a vehicle they could take with them on their journey. Grant, Charles, and Devin checked the parking lots around them. There were quite a few. David, Kirk, and Aramis checked Niagara Street, First Street, and Main Street. Both groups took two-way radios with them.

The city looked like a war zone with torn clothing, rubble, and debris scattered on the ground. Bloody handprints were left on car doors. Everywhere they went, they saw the word "infected" spray-painted on walls and on cars. They had a pretty good idea the kind of hell that went on during the outbreak.

The others stayed with the parked vehicles. Roberto monitored the radio there. Chryssy climbed up to the top of the fuel tanker to have a bird's eye view around them. Sam sent a drone up to scout the area from above. He and Taryn sat on the back of the pick-up truck, where that drone was stored.

The drone flew overhead and Sam could see both groups walking further out in search of a vehicle. Next, he moved it further out near the river and stopped, as soon as the waterfalls came into view. Looking down at Niagara Falls from the drone was incredible. He and Taryn both enjoyed the view on the laptop and made sure to take a few screenshots, before Sam decided to bring the drone closer to them. He rotated the drone, so he could look over the nearby streets, and saw several zombies on a street, not too far from their position. He pushed it closer toward them and went a little lower to make sure what he was looking at were actually zombies and not people. There was no doubt in his mind.

"Uh, oh," he stated.

Taryn asked, "What's wrong?"

"Look at the screen. There are about six zombies only three blocks away to the east, near that really tall building. Oh, damn. I was afraid of that."

"Now what?"

"I think they can see the drone. They seem to be following it."

"So lead them away," she suggested.

"I can lead them away, for now, but they're just going to follow the drone, when I bring it back here, later."

She replied, "Well, then don't bring it back. We have another one. Send that drone away. Send it far away, until it's out of range."

"I guess I could do that. It would be a shame to lose a drone, though."

She said, "Either we lose a drone or we lead zombies to us. There might be more than the six you can see. Do you really want to take that chance, especially with the state your mom is in? She's really in no condition to fight."

"Okay, I'll sacrifice it. I knew I should have left it in the box. What a waste."

She put her arm around him and said, "You meant well. Don't beat yourself up over it. It's not really a waste. You're leading those zombies away from our friends."

"Hey, you're right. I am," he cheered up.

He lowered the drone to make sure the zombies could see it. They moved toward it and followed it wherever he moved it. He raised it higher and spun it around in the air. He then moved it slowly back and forth over Third Street, before landing it atop the Niagara Casino. All of the zombies converged on the casino building. There were about fifteen, now. He grinned feeling proud of himself.

Meanwhile, Grant, Charles, and Devin walked through the nearby parking lot of a shopping center on Rainbow Boulevard. There were quite a few vehicles parked in the lot. It was unlikely that any of them would have keys conveniently left in the ignition.

Devin noticed a zombie roaming through the parking lot. It saw him and began walking toward them. "Heads up, guys. We have an admirer. I got him." He pulled out his knife and stood between two cars, where he waited like bait.

As the zombie got close, he kicked it in the pelvic region and knocked it backwards to the ground. He then straddled it and plunged his knife into the zombie's eye socket. However, he did not hit the crucial part of the brain that would end its existence and it grabbed his arms. It reached up and tried to bite him.

"Shit! A little help here!"

Grant and Charles rushed over to help. They each grabbed one of the zombie's arms and it let go of Devin. He was able to pull out his knife and stab, again. This time, he stabbed it through the top of its skull and it stopped moving.

"Whew! That was a close call. Thanks, guys," he said.

Not far from them, near the entrance of the Rainbow Bridge, David, Kirk, and Aramis returned in a white ten-wheel tour bus with tinted windows that had a blue wavy design across the sides and the name "Lidia" written in script on white side panels on either side, near the front end. The bus stopped next to the other vehicles facing the opposite direction, since they could no longer go across the Rainbow Bridge. It was best to point it in the direction they would be leaving. Aramis was driving. He stopped and opened the front door to let David and Kirk out.

David spoke into his radio and called the other three back. There was no need to find another vehicle. The bus would serve their purpose well. The many seats within were quite comfortable.

With the group reunited, they sorted out who would ride where. The bus was tempting for the passengers of the other vehicles, but it was agreed no one would ride alone. Joy, Sam, Taryn, Millie, and Rachel got into the bus with Aramis. Charles took Millie's place in the pick-up truck and rode with David. Devin remained with Grant and Liz, since he enjoyed their company. Roberto and Chryssy remained with Kirk in the fuel tanker for the same reason.

They fueled up the vehicles and took the local streets on their way back to Interstate 290. They ran into a small horde of zombies on Roberto Moses Parkway and had to take a detour around it. They drove to Buffalo Avenue and took that down to River Road. Right before entering Interstate 290, they had to charge through several zombies that were in the street. Well, Grant rammed through the first couple and Kirk crushed three more. David was able to avoid getting the pick-up dirty and Aramis did not want blood on his new bus.

Within a few minutes, their caravan reached Interstate 90. They passed through the toll plaza area and left the Buffalo city limits. At last, everyone could relax. It was going to be a long ride heading east. The drivers were prepared to go the distance without stopping, until sundown. Everyone had a chance to use the restroom at the border center, where they were parked, so bathroom breaks could be delayed for a few hours. The tour bus had its own toilet. Unfortunately, it was clogged.

The long ride gave Millie time to learn a few things about their new friend. Normally, she was not one to initiate a conversation, but David asked her to find out what she could. She did not want to let him down.

"Are you originally from Buffalo?" She began.

"No, I moved here from Rochester, when I was ten," Rachel replied.

Millie asked, "How old are you now?"

"Twenty-two."

"Oh? I'm twenty, but I'll be twenty-one this month. I hope."

Rachel leered at her for making such a cryptic statement so casually.

It was quiet for a few minutes, but then Millie asked, "Where were you staying all this time?"

Rachel answered, "We were using the old armory on Main Street for a while, but we were overrun and had to leave. That's where most of my group died. Over the next few weeks, the rest of us went from building to building, until I was the last one left. To be frank, I was going to the Rainbow Bridge to throw myself into the river. When I saw you guys, it was like a gift from heaven."

"Wow. That is luck. You know? It's a funny coincidence, too. Some of our people were hiding out in an armory, back when this all began. Luckily, we rescued them before they got overrun. We barely made it. A lot of people died that day," she remembered. She sighed and added,

"So, it's a good thing *we* found each other, huh? Who knows how your day might have ended?" She chuckled.

"Uh, yes, I am very grateful. Oh, and thank you for this can of tuna fish. I was so hungry!"

Millie watched her clean out the can, and then she said, "You're welcome, Rachel." Afterwards, she turned to look out of her window.

The ride across the state was quite lonely without a soul in sight. There were occasional cars along the road, but not one person. As planned, they did not stop, at least, not yet. They drove around Syracuse and returned to Interstate 90. They also managed to get past Schenectady and Albany without drawing attention to themselves. Soon after, they crossed over the border into Massachusetts, where they drove through Auburn and Framingham, before finally switching to Interstate 95 going northbound.

By this time, a few of them were more than ready for a bathroom break, so they made plans to stop. They decided it would be a good idea to stop, before it got too dark. They needed time to find an appropriate location, so they could search it thoroughly and get settled for the night.

Many of the exits they passed looked too uninviting, so they kept going. They were hoping to find a place that was abandoned and isolated. Although, as far as they knew, everything appeared abandoned. Liz checked Google maps using one of the laptops and saw that Wakefield, Massachusetts, looked fairly isolated. That would be their destination.

At around 7 pm they reached Exit 39. They pulled into the parking lot of the Clarion Inn on North Avenue in Wakefield. There were two buildings shaped like the letter C. Their open ends faced each other with parking available at the center and around the buildings. The inn was situated beside a fairly large lake called Lake Quannapowitt, which was about three and a half miles long.

Right away, Chryssy knew they would be eating well, once she noticed the lake. She convinced Devin, Roberto, and Kirk to go fishing with her, so they could catch some fish for dinner. The lake had a nice variety of warm water species of fish. Together with Devin, eleven fish were caught in less than two hours. It would be more than enough to feed their group of fourteen.

While part of the group fished at the lake, Grant, Charles, David, Liz, and Aramis did a search of the buildings. They were empty. Later that night, everyone dined together, before heading to the rooms. As with the night before, it was no less than two people per room. Grant and Liz stayed together. Roberto and Chryssy shared a room. Charles bunked with Devin, again. David and Kirk stayed together. Millie stayed with Rachel and Taryn, although Taryn wanted to stay in the same room as Sam. His mother was not having it. Joy kept Sam with her. Aramis slept in the same room as them, but in a separate bed, again.

Once more, two volunteers were designated to watch over the vehicles. This time, Roberto and Chryssy agreed to take the job. It was only fair that someone else took guard duty, this time around. Besides, Roberto liked staying up late and Chryssy was eager to use the night vision goggles, again.

After a while, he turned to her and said. "I don't like this. It's too quiet. Why is it so deserted this far north? I expected to see more people, once we crossed into Massachusetts."

She replied, "Have you ever been to Massachusetts?"

"No."

"I have. I've been to Salem twice. This state isn't like New York. Some places always look this deserted, especially these small towns."

"Yeah, I get that, but this place doesn't look deserted. It is deserted. Why did they abandon this place, if the infection hasn't even reached up here?"

"We don't know that. Maybe it did. It's been almost a year," she reminded him. "Dude, we have no idea what's been going on in these other states. To tell you the truth, it scares me to find out."

He said, "You have no reason to be afraid, whenever you're with me. You and I make a great team. Remember how we took out those bikers at Walmart? Road Demons! Bunch of punks. That was some cool shit, right there! I was proud of you!"

She smiled modestly.

"Hm. Let's not talk too much," he said, sounding more serious. "I don't want anyone to sneak up on us. Keep those arrows ready, 'Katniss.'" He chuckled.

She laughed at the *Hunger Games* reference. It had always been one of her favorite films, as a young girl. She strived to be as good with her bow as Katniss Everdeen. When her father paid for her lessons, she thought it was the greatest thing ever. She never imagined the skills she acquired would ever truly save her life, but they did. If her father could only see her now, she thought.

She missed him dearly. She tried not to think about the day she lost him. It was a good thing her mother had a peaceful death. Dying in your sleep from a heart attack is much better than being torn apart by newly infected monsters.

Chryssy fought back the tears. She was glad to be wearing the night vision goggles. She focused on the here and now. She had to remain alert. She dreaded the thought of something happening to Roberto. He seemed to get her like no one else. She believed they were soul mates. She glanced at him and admired his rugged manliness. He always seemed so brave and confident, while still maintaining a sense of humor. There was no room for doubt in his mind. She thought that was so sexy. It made her smile.

He lit a cigarette and took a puff. It was his only fault, she thought. She tried smoking, after turning sixteen, but hated it. The smell smothered her clothing and would not go away. It was the same with him. It was a turn off. She wished he would stop.

"Have you ever considered quitting? You always try to stay in shape. Yet, you destroy your lungs every day with those cancer sticks. It's pretty gross."

"You don't like it?" He asked with indifference. "Eh, I'm almost out of them. I have about one pack left. I'll tell you what. When they're all gone, I'll quit. Just for you."

"No, Rob, do it for yourself," she insisted.

He smirked at her and nodded. Afterwards, he took a deep toke of his cigarette. If he was going to quit soon, he could at least enjoy his last few.

The next morning, after breakfast, they got back into their vehicles and traveled north on the interstate. It began to rain lightly, and then poured down for several minutes, before slowing and stopping. It was enough to wash some of the infected zombie blood from Buffalo off the vehicles.

As the small convoy made its way through town after town, thoughts began to lead to questions, which started a radio conversation. Perhaps, had they not been in such a hurry to get back on the road, they might have hashed out their thoughts earlier in the day.

That was not the case.

Roberto started the ball rolling by complaining about how empty everyplace had been. He had a hard time believing there were no people anywhere in New England. Rachel and the van thieves had been the only living souls they encountered, since leaving the compound two days earlier.

After several miles and nearly an hour of driving, Roberto kept putting ideas into Kirk's head. Kirk found himself questioning things that had not really occurred to him, until now. He suddenly had the urge to seek answers to the questions mulling around in his head, since there was nothing better to do. He picked up the two-way radio and asked, "Big Chief here. Rob and I have been talking. Where do you guys think all these people went? This state seems to be completely empty. Over."

Grant responded from the lead vehicle and explained, "Early on during the initial outbreak, Julia found reports on the Internet about government evacuation orders. Most people made mass exoduses from the East Coast and went out west. Some reports indicated there might have been people that went into Canada or across the Atlantic to Greenland and Europe, but that was nearly a year ago. Over."

David grabbed his radio and chimed in, "I find it hard to believe this entire state is empty. There has to be people somewhere. Why leave, if the infection hasn't reached the state? It makes no sense." There was a short pause, and then he added, "Oh, over."

Grant replied, "We shouldn't assume there wasn't an outbreak up here, just because we haven't run into zombies. We have no idea what's going on in port cities like Boston and Salem. The infection could have arrived by ship. We've been sticking to the interstate, keeping west of those cities, while pretty much avoiding every major city. It's hard to say what's been going on with the rest of the state. Over."

"True," David agreed. "I wasn't thinking about that. Over."

Aramis picked up his radio and asked, "Do you think it will be the same in New Hampshire? I mean, how far do we gotta go to get away from this nightmare? This is getting ridiculous already. I miss being part of a normal civilization. Over."

"We'll find out soon enough," Grant said. "According to the last sign we just passed, we're almost at the border. Let's hope soldiers with armored vehicles won't be blocking the road. Over."

Aramis swallowed nervously at the thought.

David sighed. He already got shot at, while trying to leave Manhattan. He did not wish to experience that a second time. One gunshot wound per lifetime was good enough for him.

Liz felt nervous, too, considering they were in the lead vehicle.

A few miles later, they crossed into New Hampshire. What they saw was more of the same. The roads and rest stops were empty with grass and weeds growing out of control. Abandoned cars littered the sides of the road. The vacant buildings that were visible from the interstate had vines growing up the sides. It was as if the entire world was empty, except for them.

"This really sucks," Aramis muttered to himself. He looked into his rearview mirror and saw that every one of his passengers was asleep. He let out a sigh of boredom.

They continued up Interstate 95 into Maine, which was a much larger state. The interstate became the Maine Turnpike. For hours, they drove north. It rained, again, and stopped. The radio conversations continued, as did the speculations. None of them really knew for sure why they did not encounter anyone. Maybe it was as Grant said. There was no Internet connection, so they could not verify the truth.

Sometime later, Taryn had woken up and decided to search the Internet using one of the laptops. She had a difficult time finding a Wi-Fi signal she could use, but kept trying. At last, she was able to get online. She searched for posts regarding evacuation notices for the entire East Coast. The most recent was from December. She learned there had indeed been outbreaks at several East Coast regions. Martha's Vineyard, Nantucket, Boston, and Cape Elizabeth all had multiple reports of infections by October.

She relayed the bad news to Aramis, who told the others over the radio.

Roberto turned to Kirk and commented, "That's crazy, bro! Here we are thinking we're out here alone and there are probably thousands of those things lurking around the coastal cities."

Kirk shook his head and responded, "I don't even want to think about it. Let's just keep going north and… wait a minute! I just got a great idea!" He grabbed his radio and said, "Grant, I was thinking. What are our chances of finding a place that has car ferries, where we can take our vehicles across into Canada? Over."

Grant responded, "That's not a bad idea. Let's pull off at the next rest stop, so we can check. Aramis, can you have Taryn check the Internet? Over."

"10-4, buddy. She's already on it," he said. "Over."

Taryn and Sam moved closer to the front of "Lidia." That's what they were calling the tour bus they found near the Rainbow Bridge in Buffalo. Taryn stated, "There are a few ferries that might work for us, but we'll need to head west. Our best bet is to cross into New Brunswick, first. Once we're in Canada, this interstate will meet up with a Canadian highway that we can take straight to one of the ferry terminals. It has a French name. Bear with me. It's called *Rivière-du-Loup* Terminal."

Aramis passed along the information to the others via the two-way radio.

Over the next few hours, they drove north along the painstakingly long turnpike, until they finally reached the Canadian border. They came to a stop in front of a chain link fence that was blocking the road.

While Grant considered a way to get past the fence without being noticed, Kirk stepped on the gas and drove straight into it with the fuel tanker, ripping the fence down and dragging it on the highway for nearly half a mile. The others quickly followed, before Canadian authorities noticed.

"YAHOO!" Kirk shouted. "We're officially Canadian!"

Roberto and Chryssy laughed and cheered.

Fortunately, there was no one around to see what they had done. That did not mean the border was not being patrolled. Near the fence, a trooper from the Royal Canadian Mounted Police rushed out of a portable toilet and gaped at the torn down fence. He looked at the highway and did not see any vehicles. He was too late. They were long gone. Even the fence was gone! Confused, he scratched his head.

Just before reaching the New Brunswick city of Woodstock, the group's caravan entered Trans Canada Highway 2, which went west. They were traveling quite fast toward their destination. Eventually, they slowed down to a steady speed, once they were far enough away from the border.

Rachel was confused by this new part of their journey. After hours of silence, she asked Aramis, "Didn't you guys say none of you knows how to operate a boat?"

"Yeah, what about it?"

"Well, how do you expect to operate a ferry? It's the same thing. And what makes you guys think there will even be a ferry waiting for us?"

He glanced back at her and responded, "Faith. You gotta keep the faith."

She sighed and looked out of her window. She watched the road and was surprised to see another vehicle going the opposite way on the eastbound lanes. "What the???"

Charles was also looking out of the window and daydreaming, when he noticed the passing car. "Sweet Christmas!"

Grant asked over his radio, "Did you guys just see what we saw? Over."

Aramis answered, "That's a big 10-4! Over."

Kirk replied into his radio, "It appears there is still life on Earth. Over."

They eventually caught up to another car on their side of the road, which they passed rather slowly. The driver of the vehicle stared at them strangely and seemed to want to keep his distance. Of course, that was probably because they were all gaping out of the windows at him.

Soon after, another car went past on the eastbound lanes, and then a truck. It was incredible! There were actually other people in Canada! There were cars driving on the roads! They went past a town and saw traffic on the roads. They could not believe their eyes. After almost a year, they finally found civilization.

Aramis felt so happy, he wanted to cry and he did. He happily wiped the tears of joy from his face, as he drove. He called back to his passengers, "Are you guys seeing this? We finally reached civilization! This is so awesome!"

Grant commented on the radio, "We may need to play things differently, from now on, people. That means keep the weapons hidden. We don't want to attract the wrong kind of attention. Let's hope the ferry is not too expensive. I don't suppose any of you still have money? Over."

Aramis answered over his radio, "Actually, I have $40 in my wallet. Over."

David scoffed. Using his radio, he asked, "Why in the world do you still have a wallet? I threw mine out months ago."

"I don't know, man! Force of habit?"

Kirk said over his radio, "I guess Doc is picking up the tab! Over."

Roberto laughed himself silly. He felt delirious. He and Chryssy were utterly amazed at the sight of other people and cars on the road. It was a beautiful thing, he thought. They made it. They finally made it to safety. He felt so happy that his smile would not go away. He put his arm around Chryssy and she rested her head on his shoulder and closed her eyes. It was a blissful moment.

At long last, they reached the ferry terminal. It was at the tip of a thin peninsula. They drove past homes and businesses, where people went about their daily routines. It was unreal. Other cars waited in line with them to enter the ferry. It was a relief to learn passage was free. Moments later, they drove onto the ferry and parked. They exited the vehicles and strolled to the bow of the ferry, where they casually leaned on the handrails and took in the ocean air. It was an amazing experience.

Liz leaned into Grant and he put his arm around her.

Sam and Taryn held hands and grinned, as they gazed out over the open water.

When the ferry pulled away from the terminal, there were seven other vehicles with theirs. The ferry rocked gently over the St. Lawrence River. It moved slowly toward the south and traveled around Hare Island, before heading west.

Charles said, "I never thought I would experience anything like this, again. I am in complete shock. I keep waiting for the bomb to drop and snap me out of this fantasy."

David chuckled, "Do you mean this isn't my dream? I was about to ask you to pinch me." Kirk pinched his arm and David yanked his arm away. "Ouch! Why did you do that?"

"You just said to."

Roberto and Charles chuckled.

Devin moved next to Grant and asked, "So, what's the plan for when we reach the other side? Any ideas, yet?"

"Let's keep the weapons hidden, until we know what's what. We'll drive around and get a feel for the place. I've never been to Quebec, so I don't mind exploring a little. We're going to have to make any money we have last. I might actually still have some money somewhere in my bag. I'll check later."

Devin scoffed, "I haven't had money on me, since October."

Liz chuckled, "My money burned in the fire. It wasn't much anyway."

Nearby, Millie and Rachel looked down into the river's water.

Rachel said, "I never dreamed this day would come. I'm so grateful to have this second chance at life." She turned to Millie and hugged her, which caught Millie off guard. "Thank you for being so nice to me," she said. "Talking to you has made this experience easier for me. I appreciate it."

"You're welcome, Rachel," she said. Millie thought about how scared she felt on that first night and how Edie was there to help her through it. Now, it was her turn to be the strong one. It felt weird.

They smiled at each other and looked out over the river. The breeze blew their hair around and onto their face, but it was a good feeling because it felt so normal.

Aramis watched them and grinned happily. He was glad they were becoming friends. He knew how hard it was for Millie, after Edie died. In fact, he hoped to become friends with Rachel, too. She seemed nice and she was very pretty. At first, he was not quite sure what to think of her, but after hearing everything she had to say during their long trek, he believed she was sincere.

He could not help wonder if things did not work out between him and Joy, maybe he might have a chance with Rachel, instead. Of course, he really wanted things to work out with Joy because he liked her a lot. He merely wanted to keep his options open.

That's when he realized Joy was nowhere to be seen. He could not believe she was not enjoying the fantastic view with them on the deck. He walked toward the bus and stepped inside. She was still in her seat sulking. He sat down beside her and said, "Hey, there, gorgeous. You should come and check out the view. It's refreshingly beautiful."

"I'm really not in the mood," she groaned.

He took her hand and said, "I'm really sorry about your daughter. I know it can't be easy, but you still have your son. Even he's out there. Come on. Come with me. The ocean air will be good for you."

"It's only a river, not the ocean. I really don't care to see it. I just want my baby back. I can't believe she's gone. I had her upstairs with me, and then I went to the bathroom and she was gone. Why did it have to be her? Why couldn't it be me, instead?"

"Don't think like that. Your life is just as precious. I, for one, am very glad you're still here."

"Stop. This isn't the time. My mind is on her. She was so young. She had her whole life ahead of her."

He frowned, "Yeah, I know. I'm sorry."

They sat together quietly for the rest of the ride, but he did not let go of her hand. He caressed it gently, and then just held it. She did not complain. Instead, she rested her head on his shoulder and cried. He sighed and kissed her on the forehead. He then leaned his head back against the seat and closed his eyes.

The ferry eventually docked at Traversier Saint Siméon.

MAN'S END

Chapter Thirty-Eight

U PON EXITING THE ferry, Grant noticed an oddly familiar sign with a dragon crest on it. For some reason, he followed the sign onto a road. Once more, he led the way in the police SUV, as the others followed. They drove west along Route 170, putting distance between them and the river.

For several miles, the road passed through the Jacques-Cartier National Park, a large wooded region. The road was small with only one lane in both directions. It took several minutes before they saw any structures. The first were a few houses on the north side of the road. Soon after, they came across more scattered homes on both sides of the road. There were also two more signs, depicting dragon's crests.

Eventually, Grant noticed two large pillars on the right that led to a long winding road. At either side of the pillars was a dragon crest on a shield with the letter C. He found it very intriguing and decided to check it out. He turned onto the road and the others followed.

David asked over his radio, "Do you know something we don't? Why are we taking this road?"

"Call it curiosity," Grant answered. "We passed several similar signs, since exiting the ferry. The dragon crest on the pillars reminds me of something from a book I read years ago. Over."

They soon reached a heavy iron gate and had to stop. The same crests were on both doors of the gate, which were connected to a wall that stretched around in both directions. The wall was about fifteen feet tall. It immediately reminded him of their compound in Monroe.

Devin leaned forward and said to Grant, "It looks like we've reached the end of the line."

Or the beginning, Grant pondered inquisitively, as he sighed, "Yeah, I guess so."

"So, what's with the crest?"

"It reminds me of the Pendragon crest of King Arthur," Grant recalled.

"Oh. Okay." Devin looked at it and said, "Yeah, I can see that."

Suddenly, the gate opened and they saw someone standing within. It was an average-sized man with blond hair and he was holding an M-16A rifle. He eyed the police SUV curiously and walked over to the driver's side, as he read the door. Grant rolled down his window.

The man asked in a Canadian accent, "Monroe Police Department, eh? So, what brings you here?"

"My name is Grant Hamilton. We've come a *very* long way. We're new to the country, so we were just… exploring. Sorry about trespassing. We meant no harm. I was following the dragon crests."

"I see," the man nodded. "It's the Pendragon crest, to be exact. So, where are you from?"

Grant chuckled, "I knew it! I love those stories about King Arthur and the Knights of Camelot. We're from New York."

"Hmm, escaping the infection, eh?"

"Yeah, you could say that. We just want to live normal lives, again. We're tired of running. We used to have a home like this with walls around it and a watchtower. We lasted there for almost a year, until it burned down a couple of days ago. We left and decided to head up to Canada. Seemed like a good idea."

"For sure. That's a shame *aboat* your home. How'd the fire start?"

"We're still uncertain. We believe it was accidental. It was tragic. Two dead. One of our people, a female, lost her daughter in the fire."

"*Soarry* to hear that." The man stared at him, for a moment, and sighed, "Well, then. Welcome to the Camelot Estate! We have plenty of room and could sure use some hard workers to help out with the farm and hunting game. There's just a small fee and one condition."

"Oh, yeah? What's that?" Grant asked.

"You'll have to wait *oat* here overnight, while I talk it over with the others. If, *and only if,* they agree, then we'll let you in tomorrow at say noontime. As for the fee, that fuel tanker there should cover all of your entry fees, if you have any fuel left in it. Fuel is very hard to come by. You know?"

Grant thought about it and looked at Liz and Devin. He turned back to the man, secretly keyed his radio, so the others could listen, and asked, "What are the basic rules around here that we should be aware of, *if* we agree to wait around all night, until you decide to let us in tomorrow?"

"Absolutely no *hosers* allowed. Everybody's got to pull his or her own weight. All our residents are provided with food, water, heat, a private room with a bed, and free run of the estate. Weapons are allowed, so long as you don't use them in here and *no* killing each other. That's a big no-no! Break those rules and you get *turfed oat* on your bum! Now, anyone who's got specific skills is especially welcome here. We need more hunters, fishermen, farmers, cooks, doctors, and drivers. It would also be great if you have any musicians and artists. Do you?"

Grant smiled, "My friend, you are in luck. We have all of that in our group. We also have firearms and hand-to-hand combat instructors, a sharpshooter, a paramedic, and a jack of all trades."

The man grinned and responded, "That's great. Oh, hey, I'm *soarry*. Where are my manners? My name is Terrance Philipse. By the way, you can park along the side there," he pointed to a clearing along the entrance path. "If you are all still here tomorrow *and* if my people agree, then we'll let you in at noon, like I said. You have my word there won't be any trouble from us throughout the night. I hope we can count on the same from you, eh?"

Grant nodded, "Of course. This should also give me time to discuss it with my group. We'll see you tomorrow. I hope."

"True. Perhaps, I shall see you tomorrow, eh?" Terrance waved, as the gates were shut.

Grant stared at him and flashed a quick friendly smile. As soon as Terrance was out of sight, his smile disappeared. Listening to Canadians speak was going to take some getting used to, he thought.

They parked the four vehicles side by side, so they could discuss their options without having to exit their vehicles. They merely had to keep their windows open. Kirk parked to the south closest to Route 170, so the fuel tanker could serve as an armored wall protecting them from any potential incoming threats. David parked beside him on his passenger side, while Grant parked next to David's passenger side. Aramis was inside at the far northern end, closer to the gate, so the bus would not block the entrance road.

Grant asked, "So, what do you guys think?"

"I don't trust these people," Roberto voiced his opinion. "If they have walls, why would they be so quick to let us in? They don't know crap about us. It might be a trick to steal our supplies."

Aramis said, "Maybe that guy was sincere about them needing help. For all we know, there could be five to ten people in there. I say we give them a chance and see what the deal is."

David was uncertain if he wanted to take a chance like that. Once they went inside, they could be trapped. He said, "I'm with Rob. These guys may have ulterior motives. They still haven't seen how many people we have. The bus could be filled, as far as they know. It's a big risk for them to let us in without even checking, so why do it, unless they have something devious planned? If it turns out they are sincere, it means they're idiots. They have very little safety protocols, which won't make me feel safe being in there."

Charles had to agree, "That's a very good point. This could be a deathtrap, one way or another. If not by them, then because of their negligence, somewhere down the road."

Grant replied, "That's all true, but if that's the case, we can teach them. Show them how to be more cautious. If they really do need people, we may very well outnumber them."

Kirk chuckled, "So, what? You want to take over their estate?"

"No, that's not what I meant. I was thinking about the safety of our group. If we outnumber them, chances are any decisions we make will be agreed upon, if we do it fairly and put it to a vote. The majority usually wins. We'll teach them to be safer. We never teach them everything we know, but we teach them enough to be smart. We're so far north they probably haven't even seen a zombie up here."

Liz looked at him and suggested, "We should ask them tomorrow, if there are infected nearby. Find out what kind of precautions they take against them, besides this wall."

Grant replied, "We will. Tomorrow."

Kirk asked, "Okay. What happens, if they don't let us in?"

Everyone turned to Grant for the answer to that question.

He surprised them by what he said. "We'll leave. We can't start off up here on a bad foot, if we want to sleep soundly. To force ourselves inside would mean we'd probably have to kill everyone inside. I have no problem with killing an asshole, who deserves it, but I will not become the asshole and kill innocent people, who are struggling to live peacefully."

Charles was relieved to hear him say that. He was worried Grant would say something totally different. Sometimes, it was good to be wrong.

Devin leaned forward from the backseat of the police SUV and commented, "I was hoping you'd say something like that. I want to believe that guy could be telling the truth, but it's become so hard to trust anyone these days."

Grant looked over his shoulder at him. "We don't have to trust him. It's going to take a long time, before he earns my trust. All we have to do is stay alert and see what he's offering. We might not even like it in there. We only got a glimpse inside. I did notice there seemed to be a lot of land, probably more than ten acres. I also saw what looked like a really long garage."

Liz added, "I saw some military-style barracks."

Devin nodded, "Yeah, so did I. I also noticed Terrance did not stink of sweat, which means they might have soap and deodorants. We lost a lot of that in the fire."

Chryssy asked, "Where do you think they hunt?"

Kirk looked around and said, "They probably don't have to go too far. There's got to be a lot of game in these woods."

She looked at the trees and replied, "I suppose you're right. I bet I can find a nice deer for us to eat for dinner."

Charles stated sternly, "No. Let's not hunt near their land, until we are accepted. They might see it as a sign of disrespect. They could be watching us with security cameras. They might even be using a listening device to hear our conversation, so be on your guard. For tonight, we can just eat whatever we have with us. We still have plenty of food. Hopefully, our options will increase tomorrow afternoon." He sighed. "I really hope they're good people."

Roberto replied, "They better be for their sake. I'll be waiting to strike at the first sign of betrayal. I will be ruthless, if I need to be. I don't like feeling trapped. It's like Grant said, they're going to have to earn my trust."

David turned to him and said, "And we are going to have to earn theirs."

Everyone turned to him and thought about what he said, knowing it was the truth.

The next few hours were very boring, as they sat in their vehicles and waited for the night to come, so they could go to sleep. In the meantime, they took turns dozing off and taking naps. There was always someone in each vehicle that kept watch. They locked their doors and closed most of their windows. Only a few were left open just a crack to let in some air.

Kirk stared out toward the main road. Next to him, Chryssy fell asleep on Roberto's arm. His eyes searched the trees diligently for cameras, but did not see any. David slept soundly, although uncomfortably in the driver's seat, while Charles kept watch. Grant and Liz were both awake. They whispered amongst themselves, while Devin snored in the backseat.

Aramis kept the windows of the bus closed and the doors locked. The windows were tinted, so nobody would be bothering them. He left the bus idling all night, to keep the air conditioner going on low. He turned back and noticed everyone on the bus was asleep, except for Millie. He walked toward her seat and sat down next to her.

"Hey, why are you still up?"

"I'm not tired," she answered. "I slept enough, while we were riding through Maine. I really miss those books we had back at the compound. I miss Edie, too."

He sighed, "I know what you mean. We've lost so many people to get where we are now. I hope this place is worth it. Look on the bright side. Maybe they have books inside."

"That would be nice. There's also something else on my mind, which is making it hard for me to sleep. What if things go wrong tomorrow? What if these people try to kill us or turn us into their slaves?"

"The guys are ready for something like that. You know they'll fight to the end."

"I know they're tough, but what if that's not enough tomorrow? What if there are too many of them in there and we're outnumbered? I really don't want to end up getting raped or killed."

"Believe me. Nobody does. Just stay close to me and I'll keep you safe. I won't let anyone hurt you. You guys are the only family I have left. My real family is gone, except for those that live in the Dominican Republic and I hardly know those people. They probably think I'm dead anyway."

"Well, now that we're in Canada, maybe you can take a plane to DR and see them. You can start fresh with them."

He whispered loudly, "Hell no! I would never want to live there. There's too much poverty over there. Even with the way we've been living the past few months, we were better off than most of my family on the island. I'm staying right here with you guys."

"What if we have to leave tomorrow?"

"Wherever we are will be home to us, whether it be bad or good. I'd be okay with it, as long as I have my family by my side. My *real* family."

She smiled and leaned her head back. "I think I'm getting tired, now."

"Good. Get some sleep. If you want to talk, you know where to find me." He got up and walked toward the front. As he walked past Joy, he noticed her eyes were open. He asked, "Mind if I join you?"

"Go ahead," Joy replied.

He sat down beside her and asked, "How are you feeling?"

"I feel like my daughter died three days ago. How do you think I feel?"

"Um, hostile? I'm only trying to be helpful, Joy," he explained.

She sighed, "I know. I'm sorry. You're very sweet. You've been kind to me and I want you to know I appreciate it. I just don't think I'm ready for normal human contact. I probably won't be for a while. Right now, I need my space and I need time to mourn. I hope you understand."

"Yeah," he nodded. His heart felt like it was shattering into a million pieces. "I understand," he said. He exhaled and stood up. He walked back to the driver's seat and sat down, feeling disappointed. He was heartbroken, but he was done wasting his time on her. No more.

Joy felt bad for him. She knew he liked her, but she did not wish to lead him on. He had been wasting his time, putting so much effort into trying to make her feel better, except she wanted to feel miserable. She felt like she did not deserve to be happy. Not anymore.

Millie overheard their conversation and became upset. Aramis spent so much time with Joy, over the past few weeks, for her to treat him that way. It wasn't fair. The poor guy could never get a break. If he was her type, she might go for him herself, but she did not think of him in that way. She really did not feel any attraction toward the guys in the group. They were more like big brothers to her. She wondered if she would possibly meet a nice guy at this new place. Maybe it was time for her to enjoy life's pleasures.

Grant and Liz seemed quite happy together. Roberto and Chryssy made a perfect match. Even Sam and Taryn were cute to watch, as their innocent romance blossomed.

She thought about David and Edie. It was a shame they never had a chance to be together. She was really hoping they would find happiness together. They were her two favorite people in the group. She felt the closest to them, for some reason. Maybe it was because David reminded her of her uncle, who was also named David. Edie had been like a sister to her from the first time they met. It did not matter that Edie was once Eddie. Millie always saw Edie for who she was on the inside, a beautiful caring woman with a love for adventure. She was also someone, who was missed dearly.

Millie wiped away a tear.

Perhaps, it was her turn for romance. Why not? Was there a Mr. Right waiting for her, beyond the wall, or would there be trouble? She frowned and became defiant. She felt ready to do what needed to be done, if things went wrong. Roberto and Grant showed her how to fight and shoot, but she would rather die, before becoming a prisoner to be raped. She kept the gun Grant gave to her hidden, just in case.

The next morning, they began waking up, one at a time. Kirk noticed Roberto had woken up and he said, "Good morning, my friend. Welcome to the land of the living. You were out like a light."

He responded, "I'd still be out, if not for the fact that this seat is hurting my ass."

Kirk and Chryssy chuckled.

Roberto then said, "Damn, I would kill for some coffee, right about now."

"Let's hope you won't have to," Kirk smirked.

In the next vehicle over, David opened his eyes and turned to see that Charles was already awake. He had been waiting impatiently for noon to arrive, so they could make a move, any move. The anticipation was getting to him. He was almost ready to leave, at this point.

Grant and Liz had been awake, for a while. Neither of them had slept well, so they were both tired. They watched the gate and waited for it to open. Both were wondering if they would have to fight, soon, or had they found a new home?

Devin awoke and sat up in the backseat. He looked around and realized they were still outside of the walls. He asked, "What time is it?"

Grant replied, "I haven't worn a watch in months, but the sun is pretty high in the sky. I'd say it's almost noon."

Liz gripped her rifle and adjusted her position in her seat. Her window was already open and she wanted to be ready to shoot, if she had to.

Aramis was out cold in the bus from staying up late. Sam had to wake him up.

"Hey, Aramis. Wake up. It's almost noon. Do you want a pop tart?"

"Huh? Oh, yeah. Thanks, Sammy." He took the pop tart and ripped open the foil wrapping. He ate slowly, as he watched the gates and waited for them to open. After he was done eating, he looked into the mirror and tried to fix his hair with his hands. He wanted to look presentable.

At exactly noontime, the gates opened. Terrance stood at the entrance and waved them inside. This time, he was not carrying his M-16A rifle.

Grant looked to his left and to his right. "Everyone be on your guard," he warned. "Let's not all get out, at once. Let's do this slowly and cautiously, the way we planned. Remember to park strategically. Devin and I will get out, first, to feel them out. Liz will cover us."

Kirk responded, "Rob, Chryssy, and I are ready. Just give the word."

David and Charles agreed. Aramis nodded, as well. He was nervous. They all were. This could very well be their last day on Earth, if things went terribly wrong.

They started up their vehicles. Aramis looked to his left and waited for Grant to enter the gates, first. Afterwards, David went in with the pick-up, and then Aramis followed. Kirk entered last with the fuel tanker, which was to be their admission fee. They wanted to keep the same line up, as the day before. They parked in diamond formation to leave a space between the vehicles, where they could hide and take cover, should they get into a gun battle with the people that lived on the estate.

Right away, they noticed about fifteen other people standing around watching. That alone, was already more people than they had in their group. So much for being in the majority, Grant thought.

The gates were locked behind them and Grant realized they had to show a sign of good faith, if this was going to work. He cautiously stepped out of the SUV, joined by Devin. Their weapons were holstered, although Liz waited in her seat with her rifle in her hand. She was ready to kill, if necessary.

Terrance approached them and reached out his hand to shake Grant's hand. They shook hands and Terrance smiled. "That's clever how your people parked. I get it. You still don't trust us, eh? Well, we are the sheep, who invited the wolves into our home. If anything, we should be the ones on guard, eh? That's jokes," he chuckled. "You'll soon see this place is quite safe. I assure you, you are not in danger here."

Grant replied with a smile, "If it's all the same, my friend here and I would like to look around, first, before the others exit the vehicles."

"True. By all means, Mr. Hamilton, allow me to give you a tour, eh?"

Grant and Devin looked at each other and nodded.

Roberto listened to what they were saying and turned to Kirk and Chryssy. He said, "This guy talks funny. He sounds like those people in that show, *Fargo*. You ever watch that?"

Kirk shook his head and replied, "I never liked watching television. It dumbs down the brain. Too much fake reality shows for my taste. It's a good moneymaker, though, I suppose."

Roberto looked back out of the window at the people, who stood around them. They seemed just as curious, but he did not get bad vibes from them. They looked pretty normal and non-threatening. Not one of them was holding a weapon, although some had weapons in holsters at their sides. There were men and women, but no children. There was even an elderly couple that was looking at him nervously.

About a half hour later, Grant and Devin returned with Terrance. They were both grinning from ear to ear.

Grant walked up to David and Charles and said, "This place is incredible! There are twenty people in total, including two children. We saw them. They were playing in a playground, behind the barracks. Some of these people are from New York. They fled here months ago. There's a food pantry, which looks more like a marketplace. They have a library, a recreation building with a gym and indoor swimming pool, a greenhouse, a medical research building with a real doctor, about ten acres of farmland, a barn filled with livestock, a working well, and the wall surrounds the entire estate. Plus, their garage is large enough to hold ten vehicles. Oh, and get this. They call garages '*parkades*,' like arcades?" He chuckled.

"Anyway, they only have a few cars in there, so ours will fit, except for the bus. It's way too long. I have a good feeling about this place. It could work. I think we found a decent spot to rest our heads."

Charles asked, "Who's in charge? Is it that guy, Terrance?"

Grant shook his head, "It's a democracy. They vote on everything. Terrance said the decision to let us in was unanimous. I don't know if that's true, but we are inside. He said they desperately need people with professional skills, which we have. Most of these people can do manual labor, but they lack the skills that we can bring to the table. Supposedly, some rich person managed to finagle his way into purchasing a portion of parkland, to build this estate, but then he died of a heart attack at the start of the outbreaks. He left this place to be used by a small survivalist group. There are only six of them left. The rest of these people were allowed in here, sometime later. The only catch is they have to do some kind of work. There are no free rides. Only the sick or injured are not required to work. Even the children do chores."

David shrugged, "That doesn't sound too bad. I don't mind working. We worked our asses off at our compound. What I want to know is do we get our own barracks?"

"Yes," Grant nodded. "We get two barracks to live in, however we please. Each has ten individual bedroom units the size of hotel rooms and every room has a full-size bed."

Roberto and Chryssy looked at each other and grinned, when they overheard that. At last, they could sleep together in the same room on a real bed. Working would not be a problem for them either. It was a small price to pay.

Kirk was also starting to get a good feeling about this place. If it had everything Grant mentioned, this was going to be close to perfect.

They all got out of the vehicles and gathered around Terrance, since he offered to take the entire group around for a thorough tour of the estate. The first place he showed them was the garage. Inside were two SUVs, a regular four-door sedan, and a military humvee. It even had a car lift, which Kirk loved. It made him think about Daniel. He would have really enjoyed the garage.

Next, Terrance pointed out several large solar panels, behind the garage, and explained, "We get our hydro from back here. The entire estate is operated by solar power."

Charles commented, "Impressive."

Grant turned to Terrance and asked, "So, Terrance. Why Camelot?"

He grinned, "That was my idea. I absolutely love European mythology and lore. I suggested it and the others liked the idea."

"Nice. I love that stuff, too," Grant admitted. "So does Devin. Right, pal?"

"Absolutely," Devin agreed. "The dragon crests outside were a nice touch."

"You betcha," smiled Terrance.

Kirk asked, "Has the infection reached this region of Canada?"

"No, not yet," Terrance replied, "But it has reached Ontario. Don't you worry, though, because even when it does reach this area, we should be safe in here from any pesky 'zeds.'" He chuckled. "The hunters will also do their part to clear them away."

Roberto and Chryssy glanced at each other. They already knew they wanted to be hunters.

As Terrance led the group toward the barracks, they passed a beautiful three-story brick mansion with porches and balconies, which was set back upon a hill. At the foot of the hill was a small cemetery with actual tombstones.

Grant asked, "What's with the cemetery? I recall you mentioning there was only six of your original survivalist group left out of ten. Is that where the rest ended up?"

Terrance stared toward the cemetery and hesitated. "Unfortunately, that is where some of our group were laid to rest," he confessed. "We had a rough winter, for sure. Frostbite became a serious issue, when the heaters broke down for two weeks. There were also two accidental deaths during the construction phase and one heart attack victim. Normally, there will be a funeral service in the parlor of the mansion, and then the doctor will prepare the body for burial."

Grant nodded, and then asked, "How many graves are filled?"

"Twelve," Terrance replied soberly.

Aramis whistled. It was a rough winter, indeed, he thought.

Charles asked, "Does anyone live in that mansion?"

Terrance answered, "Oh, no, sir. *Soarry.* We converted it into the medical and research facility. It also serves as our hospital. Dr. Jonathan Rhodes of your CDC in Atlanta has been working day and night to find a cure for the virus, ever since he arrived in September. He's a little obsessive. That man never books off work, so over time he's grown a huge bush of a beard." He chuckled.

Charles responded, "If that's the case, I have a certain journal he would be very interested to read. I've been keeping notes in it, too. I think he will find it very helpful."

"True," Terrance said. "I'll make an introduction, as soon as possible. For sure."

Aramis stepped forward and confessed, "I also have something he might want to take a look at. It's a broken syringe, which contains residue of a possible anti-virus. It was recovered from Manhattan on the first night of infection."

Terrance stopped in his tracks and turned around to face him. He asked, sounding surprised, "Really? However, did you come across an item like that?"

Charles and Grant also wanted to know, but David already knew it came from Angelo.

Aramis explained, "It came from a friend, an American soldier. He's passed on. We were in New York City during the first night of the outbreak. We were there that whole weekend."

Charles added, "We barely made it out, before they dropped the bomb."

Terrance gasped, "*Mon Dieu!* How in the blazes did you escape that *kerfuffle* with your lives?"

Grant explained, "That is a very long story, but if you'd like, I'd be happy to tell you over a nice warm breakfast. We're all very hungry." He chuckled.

"Ah, of course! I'm *soarry*. I should've realized you haven't eaten. Let's go into the mess hall and I'll have the cooks whip you up a small buffet feast and make sure it's all-dressed, for sure. How's that sound?"

Aramis thought it sounded a little confusing, but he got the gist of it. He smiled and replied, "That sounds like a great plan."

"Do you have coffee here?" Roberto asked.

"Oh, you betcha," Terrance replied. "Personally, I can't start my day without my morning *double-double*. Now, it won't be as good as Timmies, especially since we don't have any *Timbits* to go along with it, but it should please the palette."

Roberto smiled dumbly and nodded, "Good, good."

He had no idea what the hell Terrance just said, but he knew it meant there was some kind of coffee available. Terrance had been referring to a popular Canadian coffee shop named Tim Horton's, named after a hockey player. A double-double was basically coffee with a double shot of sugar and a double shot of cream or milk. Timbits were small bite-sized fried dough confectioneries, similar to American donut holes.

Rachel responded, "Ooh! That sounds delicious. I've had Timmies before. I love Timbits! Thank you so much for taking us in. I want you to know these are good people that I'm with. They helped me, even though they didn't even know me."

"Well, that's good to hear," Terrance replied. "I hope we shall also live up to your expectations. We are a humble group, but our doors are always open to people in need, so long as they're willing to help us *oat*, in return. Do you have a particular skill, Miss?"

"Rachel. My name is Rachel. I'm an artist. I like to paint."

"Oh, that's great," he grinned. "We don't have any paint, but we do have pencil crayons, if that helps?"

She looked at him confused, unfamiliar with the way Canadians refer to coloring pencils, and responded, "Yeah, I guess so."

"Excellent! I look forward to seeing your work!"

Seconds later, they were escorted into the mess hall. They sat down and enjoyed the best breakfast they had seen, since before the Zombie Apocalypse. There were scrambled eggs, fluffy pancakes covered with powdered sugar and maple syrup, back bacon, and fresh baked bread with churned butter on the side. Breakfast was served with a choice of coffee, orange juice, or apple juice.

Needless to say, everyone in the group devoured their meals. It had been too long, since they were able to eat so well.

After breakfast, the tour continued, and then they got settled into their new rooms. Terrance was ecstatic to learn they had several chickens with them. He was just as pleased to see Aramis' acoustic guitar. It seemed they had found their new home and it was a home free of infection. There was not a zombie around for miles. It was the ideal place to start fresh. Despite impossible odds, the family had actually grown, and for the moment, they were as safe as they were going to get.

Best of all, there was even a glimmer of hope that someday there could be a cure.

EPILOGUE

I T HAS BEEN an exact year since the first night of the Zombie Apocalypse. Over the past couple of months, the virus has spread further across the United States and Canada. Most of North America is dealing with new viral outbreaks, as hordes of zombies multiply and the infection reaches an all-time high. The entire Continental United States has been declared an Infection Zone by the United Nations. It has become a virtual No Man's Land and is considered unsafe to enter. Outbreaks have also been reported in South America and Europe bringing the infection to pandemic proportions. There seems to be no end in sight.

The world has essentially been divided into new groups. There are survivors, infected, zombies, and sleepers. The first category is self-explanatory. Infected refer to the newly infected, who can move as fast as the survivors. Zombies are reanimated corpses of the infected and move much slower because their bodies have died. The sleepers are people, who are in hiding within well-equipped underground bunkers, with the hope that a cure will eventually be found, and then they can emerge, once more, to find their place in the new world.

It seems more and more like the world is gradually coming to an end. There is still no known cure for the deadly virus that is sweeping across the globe. Nations are gripped by fear, as they continuously devise new strategies to stop the undead from taking over the world. Each plan has ended in abysmal failure. The people are quickly losing hope.

However, in the Canadian wilderness of Quebec, one group of survivors has come together with unique knowledge that just might make a difference. Dr. Jonathan Rhodes, formerly of the Centers for Disease Control and Prevention in Atlanta, Georgia, has been struggling for nearly a year to create a cure for the deadly virus that has already claimed the lives of millions. At long last, combined with the new research information he acquired from Charles Foster and Aramis Perez, he believes there is definite hope for a cure in the near future.

Meanwhile, the group from New York has more than settled into their new home. They have each become integral parts of the Camelot Estate. Grant Hamilton, Liz Mayaguez, Devin Ross, David Castillo, Roberto Medina, Chryssy Peters, and Joy Rahas have all become successful hunters, who help supply the estate with food, while patrolling for the potential threat of zombies. Kirk Kamassa took a job as head mechanic at the parkade, along with young Sam Rahas, as his apprentice. Millie Delgado now works in the kitchen with two other cooks and has quickly proven that she has the potential to become head chef. Rachel Zuckerman found work as an art teacher in a new school that was erected for the children. Taryn Bartell found work in the mansion, along with Charles and Aramis. Taryn and Charles help with research, while Aramis works at the hospital wing.

A few took on extra responsibilities, as well. David, Millie, and Sam help with farming. Most of the group assisted with building the new old-fashioned one-story schoolhouse. Millie serves as a nurse at the hospital wing, whenever she is not cooking or reading books. She also became the head librarian with Grant and Devin as her assistants, due to their love of books. Grant was put in charge of the armory and appointed as firearms instructor. Roberto kept his promise and quit smoking, so he could focus on his side job, as a personal trainer for those wanting to stay in shape. Charles helps organize an inventory of all the supplies. Joy helps out in the kitchen, as an assistant cook, while Sam is training to become a hunter. He has already been doing his part by using his drone to provide aerial reconnaissance.

While they strived professionally, they were also doing better personally. Grant and Liz had a wedding ceremony using the estate's ordained minister. Charles was the best man and Chryssy was the maid of honor. Sam was ring bearer and Taryn was the flower girl. Liz found it amusing that she was a traditional June bride. Rachel painted their portrait with newly acquired paints.

Roberto and Chryssy had an unexpected surprise, when they learned they would be having a baby. Grant playfully scolded Roberto for not using the box of condoms he was given for Christmas, and then congratulated them.

Sam and Taryn sometimes enjoy spending time with the other couples to learn how a strong lasting relationship should work. They find it to be helpful and educational, while also being quite entertaining. There have been many occasions to laugh with the other couples, since they enjoy having fun.

Every once in a while, the members of the group find themselves thinking back and remembering those they have lost over the past year. There have been too many names and faces to forget so easily. Kirk got the idea to erect a memorial made of plaster in their memory. Rachel helped to design it. She secretly used a combination of Grant and Liz, along with Roberto and Chryssy, as her models.

It turned out she had exceptional skills as a sculptor. The memorial was erected near the cemetery. It depicted a male and female couple standing tall, back-to-back, with weapons in their right hands and tools in their left hands, while a dead zombie lay at their feet. At the bottom was an inscription that read, "Survival lies in our ability to fight and rebuild."

The quote came from Grant. He thought it was fitting for their group. Everyone agreed.

Dr. Rhodes worked with Charles and Grant to create a real zombie survival guide that listed every known fact about the virus that they learned. When it was completed, Taryn uploaded it to the Internet. Their goal was to help others to survive, as they had done. Within days it was already being used as a guide by countries across the globe.

Whenever he was alone, Dr. Rhodes went to his private research laboratory in the basement of the mansion. No one else was allowed down there. He alone had access to this secured area. It was there that he experimented on trying to create a cure for the virus, using the residue of the original anti-virus given to him by Aramis.

Within this private laboratory were the reanimated dead bodies of those, who were supposedly buried in the cemetery. Dr. Rhodes secretly kept each corpse and injected them with samples of the virus that he acquired from a top-secret special military task force that infiltrated Manhattan, before it was nuked, unknown even to Angelo Williams and his Special Ops team.

This particular team had one mission. They were sent in to acquire live samples of the infection for the CDC. A command helicopter watched over them from the Hudson River, as they completed their mission and waited for their eventual extraction, which occurred under cover of darkness. It was those live samples that would ultimately bring about the downfall of the CDC. However, before the CDC went down, Dr. Rhodes was able to escape with blood samples from those infected that were captured.

In his lab, he secretly studied his batch of infected, who are strapped firmly to tables. Each is securely muzzled to prevent biting. The doctor has been working hard and testing new versions of the anti-virus.

As it happened, the doctor became too comfortable with his zombie specimens and accidentally got a little too close to one that was trying unsuccessfully to reach out for him. Of course, the doctor was not bitten or scratched. No, he was far too careful for that. Unfortunately, he was completely unaware of the small droplet of infected saliva that found its way onto the sleeve of his lab coat.

Sometime later, he wiped the sweat from his brow and that same droplet blended with the sweat on his forehead and made its way down into his eye. It was very subtle. Several minutes later, his eye began to itch.

"Life is real again, and the useless and cumbersome and mischievous have to die." - H.G. Wells, *The War of the Worlds*

FACTS ABOUT THE FSV

Origin of the Fox Serum Virus:

1. Professor Herbert Fox, MD, an obsessive biologist and apothecarist, secretly created what he called the **Fox Serum** in a newly built, state of the art, high-tech, experimental laboratory located on property owned by Columbia University, in hopes of creating a cure for cancer. This potentially noble, albeit, unsanctioned experimental serum was intended to be the ultimate cancer that could kill cancer.

2. The **Fox Serum** was secretly tested on homeless volunteers, who each suffered from some form of cancer. These individuals were sought out by the professor and paid for their time. With nothing to lose and everything to gain, they agreed. However, the serum had an adverse effect on the subjects and transformed into what has become known as the **Fox Serum Virus**. The unfortunate volunteers became extremely violent and incoherent. They attacked the professor and escaped the laboratory.

3. These "patient zeros" fled onto the streets of Manhattan unleashing the deadliest pandemic ever to occur in the history of mankind.

How the Fox Serum Virus is Spread:

1. The **Fox Serum Virus** is spread by aggressive mutated parasitic bacteria that eat away at live blood cells and take their place moving throughout the entire body and allowing normal bodily movement, thus causing the continued animation of a person, after they have died.

2. The infection can spread to living humans by biting, scratching, sexual contact, or through bodily fluids. It can also spread to animals, but they will not be affected in the same way. Instead, it will become more like a stronger aggressive strain of rabies. They will not die and turn into zombie beasts, as a result of the infection, and they can be killed through normal means. Make no mistake, they will still be dangerous and can spread the infection to others. The only exception would be primates, due to their extreme similarities to humans. They are affected in much the same way as humans, which means they will die and be reanimated into zombie apes.

3. The rate of infection varies from one person to another based on size and the amount of infection present in the bloodstream. At the time of the initial outbreak, the virus was more potent and so it was spread far more easily, as the rate of infection was much faster. One bite could change a person within minutes. Over time, it became diluted to a certain extent and would take a little longer to infect someone. A scratch from an infected person will bring about infection in 12-24 hours. If a person is bitten once, the incubation period could be anywhere up to one hour. Multiple bites will speed up the process significantly decreasing the time to mere minutes. A bite closer to the brain will increase the rate of infection, since the virus does not have to travel throughout the body to reach the brain.

4. Contact through bodily fluids could delay infection by several hours, but no longer than a day. It depends on the amount of bodily fluid. Therefore, if a person is bitten, but the skin is not broken, they will still become infected due to contact with saliva. If, for some reason, there is a blood transfusion or organ transplant from an infected individual, the change will begin instantaneously.

5. Generally, infected individuals will choose human prey over an animal because the bacteria living within the virus can sense which blood cells are a closer match to what it requires to thrive.

6. People, who were crippled while alive, will still be just as crippled if they become infected.

7. An infected pregnant mother will pass on the virus to her unborn child, although it is unlikely that child will ever be born. It would depend greatly on her rate of infection and the timing of the childbirth.

8. The bacteria within the **Fox Serum Virus** will live on, as long as its host continues to function in some way. It will reproduce at a fast rate and transfer into new hosts causing the infection to spread. For some reason, it has a need to grow and branch out into others. If all functions cease, the virus will become dormant, but the dead host will remain contagious.

Stages of the Fox Serum Virus:

1. There are four stages a person will go through when infected by the **Fox Serum Virus**. They are the **Infection Stage**, the **Rage Stage**, the **Death Stage**, and the **Zombie Stage**.

2. While a typical virus would take 1-2 days for infection to set in, this one works much faster for some unknown reason. During the initial **Infection Stage** the virus immediately attacks the victim's immune system, weakening the person and increasing the strength of the virus. It spreads through the bloodstream at an alarmingly fast rate, eventually causing multiple heart complications. Driven by hunger, the virus eats away at all unneeded interior components of the body, as it begins to spread. Its instinct is to continue spreading, so it immediately seeks out other hosts to infect. Early symptoms include itching around the infected area, high blood pressure, bloodshot eyes, fever, and skin discoloration.

3. Signs of extreme necrotising fasciitis become apparent, as the skin turns yellow due to the breaking down of red blood cells, similar in appearance to jaundice. This condition leads to gangrene, the death of cellular tissues, which directly affects the limbs, fingers, and toes, as well as internal organs, before spreading throughout the body. Much like with the bubonic

plague, or yersinia pestis, the body begins to decompose, while the victim is still living. This is what causes the itching sensation.

4. The muscles and nervous system are affected next. The infected person will begin to feel pain, followed by numbness. There will be stiffening in the muscles, as well. There are some characteristics of typhoid fever and rabies.

5. By this time, the infected person will also have bad breath, an increased amount of pus excreting from the eyes, a build up of wax in the ears. There will be feelings of nausea and extreme fatigue. There will likely be an urge to defecate or urinate, as the body tries to remove all unwanted waste, in a futile last ditch effort to remove the virus from the body.

6. If an infected person has time to sleep, they may experience nightmares about the attack or about changing.

7. The virus requires living blood cells to begin the process of reanimation, although live blood cells are only necessary for the earliest stage of infection. This need causes a hunger so great that the zombies will viciously hunt down living humans to eat the flesh and acquire the type of blood cells the bacterial organisms within crave.

8. Recognition might exist in an infected individual's earliest stage, which may delay its attack long enough to escape or kill it. However, once the rage of desperation kicks in, all bets are off. Run for your life or prepare to kill it!

9. The infection rate of each individual will depend on that person's health, strength, constitution, stamina, and resistance to disease, as well as how the infection was acquired. This can cause the infection to take anywhere from minutes to hours before it takes effect. However, no human is immune.

10. Depending on how the infection was acquired, it will likely hurt a lot. Swelling and bruising will begin within minutes. The infected area will turn red, before becoming blackened. The itching will be unbearable. The infection will spread throughout the body and becoming quite visible on the skin. The veins will appear darkened and prominent, while the eyes will appear bloodshot. This will occur in a timely fashion, in accordance with how the infection occurred and varies with each individual.

11. In the next stage, the infected individual eventually becomes anxious, agitated, and feverish, before becoming aggressively violent due to the intense pain of dying slowly. The infected person will cease to think rationally and transform into a raging lunatic, in need of food. However, it will be human flesh that the individual craves, not normal food. Throughout this stage, the infected individual will move as fast as he did prior to infection, which means he can still run, climb, swim, and chase down victims. This is the most dangerous stage of infection known as the **Rage Stage**. It is during this stage that the infection can spread to others the fastest.

12. During the **Rage Stage** the infected person is incapable of rational thought, which means thinking will not happen. The infected person relies solely on instinct. It cannot speak, open doors, nor utilize tools and weapons. There is only pain and hunger.

13. The **Rage Stage** can last anywhere between one to five hours, depending on the extent of the initial infection. Once the body succumbs to the infection and dies, the **Death Stage** begins.

14. In the **Death Stage** the body will die and rigor mortis will take place. Death will only be a new beginning, as the virus reanimates the infected individual's corpse transforming him into a zombie with the continued need to spread the virus.

15. During the **Zombie Stage** the cravings for human flesh will only grow, as the body begins to rot. Devouring flesh becomes more significant during this stage, so the body can replenish the dead organs with fresh blood and nutrients.

16. Once rigor mortis sets in, about three hours after death, a zombie will stiffen up temporarily, but the bacteria within the **Fox Serum Virus** can make continued movement possible. Normally, rigor mortis lasts about 36 hours, but not in the case of an infected person because the parasites speed up the process. They take over the muscle tissue and allow the body to become limber, once again. The body will become cold within 12 hours of death, a process known as algor mortis. The newly born zombie will move much slower than it did in the previous **Rage Stage**. The intake of fresh blood cells from victims will gradually eliminate rigor mortis and prevent it from returning.

17. Infected individuals might possibly urinate or defecate on themselves, at the time of death or while transforming into a zombie, adding to their wondrous aromas.

18. After infection occurs, the blood gradually becomes coagulated, since the heart is not pumping blood. The skin will become pale, or darkened in places where the blood has been allowed to pool. By that time, the virus no longer needs blood cells from its host to survive. The virus may also utilize the blood of its victims, as a back up, until blood is no longer needed. The parasites will jumpstart the heart and cause it to pump manually, as needed. This will keep the circulatory system going in a limited capacity, just enough to allow for continuous oxygen to flow to the brain.

19. The brain and central nervous system of an infected individual will remain working in a limited capacity. All actions are geared toward feeding and spreading the infection. After the infected body dies, the senses are still working in a limited capacity, although not as well, as before. Motor functions and coordination are also limited. The senses deteriorate over time, so a zombie that's been around for a year or more is essentially going gradually blind, deaf (due to wax build up), and can barely smell its own rot anymore, let alone a potential food source. The eyesight of a zombie is limited in the dark, so they must rely mostly on sound and smell. They are drawn to the smell of living uninfected flesh.

20. When infected individuals die and become zombies, they do not need to breathe because they are transformed into anaerobic organisms, which have metabolism without the necessity for oxygen. Therefore, they can still smell, much like other anaerobic organisms.

21. During the **Zombie Stage**, the pupils become dilated, but they will not lose their coloring, until the rotting becomes more apparent.

22. When a zombie eats beyond its stomach capacity it will eventually clog its digestive system. Forcing down more food will expand the stomach, until it explodes causing new foods to be dropped into the rest of the body, which will ultimately cause the zombie to have difficulty walking. After a significant

amount of time, a zombie can be too full to eat and will most likely vomit the unneeded food back out. As a way to counter this issue, the virus bacteria works desperately to break down whatever food it can and convert it into energy to keep its host moving.

23. The body of a zombie will begin rotting immediately, attracting flies that will lay eggs, leaving maggots behind. It will depend heavily on the weather, temperature, and environment. Rotting will take longer in the winter than during the summer. In addition, a zombie that feeds regularly will take longer to decompose, than one that has not fed as frequently. However, mostly all of them will stink horrendously.

24. Zombies that are fresh move faster than those that are old and rotted, and they maintain survival instincts such as eating, walking, limited climbing, and even swimming to a certain extent. Those are all natural instincts that most animals possess. Of course, zombies that remain in the water for too long will decompose at a faster rate. A zombie that has been rotting for a long time will barely walk and sometimes have to crawl, instead, because their bodies are too rotted to function properly.

25. The average zombie lifespan is based on his or her rate of rotting and how often sustenance is consumed. Consistent amounts of sustenance will keep them going for a long time, significantly slowing down the rotting process. Of course, the environment is also a factor, since the heat of summer will advance the rotting process, while the cold of winter can delay it. Once a zombie becomes weakened, it can never recover and get stronger.

Quelling Rumors About the Fox Serum Virus:

1. There is NO cure!
2. The virus is NOT airborne.
3. The virus was NOT created by the military.
4. If someone who is NOT infected dies, he will NOT become a zombie. Only those, who died as a result of the viral infection, will become zombies when their bodies succumb to death.
5. Infected individuals and zombies do NOT crave brains. They will eat any part of the human body, as long as it bleeds and has nutritional value. Usually, once they have passed along

the infection, they will move on to someone else, unless they require more sustenance.

6. Zombies are NOT your friends. They do NOT maintain any memories of their past life, aside from the natural survival instincts. The part of the brain, where memories are stored becomes badly corroded, after infection sets in. By that rationale, a zombie cannot be taught or trained.

7. Zombies do NOT have super human strength. They are just as strong as they should be based on their muscle mass and normal strength. They will, in fact, be weaker, once the rotting begins. However, newly infected individuals could very likely experience adrenaline rushes that give them the impression of having more strength and speed, making them more dangerous than the zombies.

8. Zombies do NOT run, but newly infected can and will chase after you.

9. Random body parts belonging to a zombie that have been removed from the body will NOT be reanimated. They will simply stop moving. However, the virus in the severed limb will remain contagious.

10. All previously dead people will remain dead, even if they somehow managed to come in contact with the infection. The infection will not pass on to a dead host.

11. A zombie's hair and nails will NOT continue to grow after death. Both require glucose and oxygen.

12. Zombies do NOT feel fear or anger. They are motivated by the hunger of the virus bacteria. However, the newly infected that have not died, yet, will indeed feel a great desperation, which could create feelings of extreme rage brought about by their intense hunger.

13. Zombies do NOT speak, but they moan, groan, growl, hiss, and scream only when something gets their attention. They do not walk around moaning for no reason. The newly infected also do not speak because they have no need for socializing or communication anymore, although they are fully capable of speech. Instead, they choose to yell and scream, probably out of frustration and pain, as they can feel their bodies dying.

14. Zombies do NOT sleep or get tired, but when they are extremely weakened by a lack of sustenance they might kneel, sit, fall down, or lay in a dormant state, until something stirs them, usually the smell of food. While in the dormant state, the bacteria fights to preserve its host, so that it can still react. They will still lack the energy to actively pursue such a meal, unless it is right in front of them or within reach.

15. Zombies do NOT fart because they do not have gas.

16. You cannot destroy an infected individual or zombie by burning or drowning. They can only be killed by blunt trauma to the brain or by removing their heads. Therefore, destroying the brain stem will kill them. A precise shot to the motor cortex region of the brain, located on top, will kill them. However, the head of a decapitated zombie can still bite and look around, but cannot make a sound, as it has no vocal chords. Once the brain is destroyed, it will cease to move.

17. You cannot pretend to be a zombie and hide or move amongst them. The virus will not be fooled and can sense fresh food nearby. Plus, zombies do not blink their eyes, so that will be a dead giveaway.

ABOUT THE AUTHOR

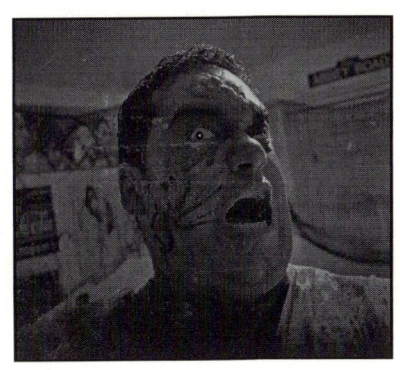

Jason was born in April of 1971and raised in the Bronx, New York. He lived with his parents on the second floor of a three family house surrounded by family both upstairs and downstairs from him. Ever since he was a small child Jason always had an interest in telling stories. He wrote his very first comic book-style story at the age of five in his parents' bedroom, while he watched television. It was the first of an ongoing science fiction story based on short hairy fictional creatures from another world. They were caught up in an intergalactic war against humans from Earth and another race of beings. Jason went on to do over ten comic stories based on these characters, drawing the pictures to go along with the story. He even won first prize in a book-making contest, while in the third grade.